WELCOME TO FAIRYLAND

THE JOY OF

FAIRY
TALES

LITTLE
RED
RIDING
HOOD

THE JOY OF FAIRY TALES

THE WORLD'S GREATEST FAIRY TALES
FROM COUNTRIES FAR AND WIDE

COMPILED BY GILL DAVIES

WORTH PRESS

This edition first published in 2011
by Worth Press Ltd, Cambridge, United Kingdom.
Selection, compilation, design © Worth Press Ltd.

Illustrations on pages 26, 78, 102, 103, 123,
138, 146, 147, 215, 219, 290, 331, 379 and 598
by Barbara Frith © Worth Press Ltd.

ISBN
978-1-84931-048-2

Design and typesetting Playne Books Limited
Trefin Pembrokeshire United Kingdom

Cover design Arati Devasher,
www.aratidevasher.com

Australian cover design
John Button, Bookcraft Limited
Stroud Gloucestershire United Kingdom
enquiries@bookcraft.co.uk

Printed in China by Waiman.
Hong Kong

List of contents

Introduction

Welcome to a magical world, peopled by kings and queens, princes and princesses, witches and goblins, ogres and giants, dragons and dwarfs. Welcome to a place of enchantment where elves dance in the moonlight and fairy wings glimmer in dappled forests, where toadstools flaunt their crimson spotted heads and the moss is soft as gossamer.

Whatever your age, whatever the demands of your busy day, magic offers an escape from reality, an opportunity to explore imaginative worlds and – however temporary the illusion – to believe in the stuff of dreams.

Settle down in a comfortable seat; find a child to sit upon your knee if you feel you need an excuse to turn back the years, for here awaiting you is a collection of wonderful tales from all around the world. Countless stories will unfold as you turn the pages, illustrated sometimes by the original artists and sometimes by totally different images, many from the works of world-renowned artists. The combination of exciting stories and inspiring art will soon whirl you away to a place where 'Once upon a time' begins a magical journey.

As well as the multitude of stories themselves, the book also reveals how ancient folk tales and legends developed, changed and spread in their retelling to become the familiar stories that people our childhood today. This journey through the fairy world is a fascinating story in its own right – a veritable fairground carousel of magic and adventure that has enriched our lives since story-making began, since families and tribes first gathered around a flickering fire to tell and retell legends and tales, handed down from one generation to another.

Generally, the classic fairy tale is a traditional story with supernatural elements that derived originally from these local folk tales. The magical creatures featured encompass a wide range of fantastical beings from talking trees to royal frogs and writhing sea serpents. Many traditional tales and characters have altered and grown through the centuries, gradually filtering through to a broad spectrum of nations – while some have remained rooted in their localities like Irish leprechauns and Scandinavian trolls.

Countless collections gather together the most famous stories but this volume is rather special. Of course, it does include many of the old much-loved favourites . . . but adds to these a plethora of tales discovered from many nations and some of the lesser-known stories chanced upon by renowned collectors and authors.

As well as the tales themselves, there are many fascinating facts about the stories, plus a wealth of background information. Many of the original tales were rigorous in their deliverance of punishment and just deserts so 'happily ever after' may well be accompanied by beheadings or unmerciful revenge. We make no apologies for this. These are the original tales and reflect the attitudes and morals of their age.

Whether we are dipping into *Aesop's Fables*, the *Arabian Nights*, excerpts from Shakespeare or classic full-length tales like *Alice in Wonderland*, we discover that most fairy tales, in fact, proffer no fairies at all. There may be talking animals, dwarfs, royal personages, enchantment, spells, wicked stepmothers, epic journeys and trials but no actual fairies! So a fairy tale does not need a fairy – it does need adventure and excitement, heroes and heroines, love – and a generous helping of magic or fantasy!

Such stories have existed for thousands of years but the name fairy tale was used first by Madame d'Aulnoy in the late 1600s. Many of today's fairy tales have evolved from centuries-old stories that have appeared, with variations, in cultures all around the world, with the earliest certainly intended for an audience of adults rather than children (with some of the original *Arabian Nights* tales including decidedly sensual elements) but, over the centuries, the stories have gradually become accepted as works to be enjoyed by the youngest amongst us – to be shared with their elders, of course, as bedtime tales which, one hopes – despite the lure of television and computers – remain an integral part of shared family entertainment, creating bonds and special time together, memories that remain a lifelong inspiration.

So now I shall let the enchantment lead you forward, to ride on magic carpets, to run through forest glades, to dance at the palace ball, to run rings round giants and fight a dragon or two. Do enjoy the banquet – a veritable royal feast of fairy tales awaits you.

Do fairies dream?

Do fairies dream? I think they must

As they float on clouds of golden dust

Or curl in gentle petal beds

And rest their little spellbound heads.

Do they dream of fairy tales . . .

Of Pinocchio in giant whales,

Of Aladdin with his magic lamp

And Rumpelstiltskin, apt to stamp?

Do they dream of flying high

With Peter Pan in star-filled skies?

Do they dream that witches stream

On broomsticks down a gold moonbeam?

Do they watch the beanstalk rise

To where the giant's castle lies?

Do they help Tom Thumb make friends?

And leprechauns find rainbow ends?

If I could catch a fairy dream

I'd wash it in a silver stream

And keep it by my pillowcase

In a little sachet trimmed with lace.

Then when I closed my eyes, I'd see

Which fairy dream might visit me.

I pray the ogres stay away

And gentle fairies come to play.

We hope that you continue – far beyond childhood – to enjoy the joy of dreaming, enjoy the joy of magical places – enjoy *The Joy of Fairy Tales*.

Gill Davies June 2011

The Story of Ali Baba and the Forty Thieves

This is just the start of a fairly long story – with some quite blood-thirsty moments. It has formed the basis for many a stage pantomime.

This Ali Baba tale may have been added to *One Thousand and One Nights* in the 1700s by a European translator, Antoine Galland, who possibly gleaned it from a Middle Eastern story-teller from Aleppo in Syria. However, Richard F Burton (the famous explorer, spy, poet and linguist) believed it be part of the original collection. The tales were gathered over many centuries from the Middle East, Central Asia and North Africa, with their origins in ancient and medieval folklore from Arabia, Persia, India, Turkey, Egypt and Mesopotamia. The oldest Arabic manuscript dates from the 1300s but its roots dig back deeply to the 9th century.

The collection is also called *The Arabian Nights*. The story goes that a king was told these tales by his wife, Scheherazade, to keep his continued interest in her; he had executed each of his former 1,000 wives after just one night of wedded bliss!

This original version includes the command "Open, Simsim!" which is usually "Open, Sesame!" in more recent versions.

In former days there lived in a town of Persia two brothers, one named Kasim, and the other Ali Baba. Their father divided a small inheritance equally between them. Kasim married a rich wife, and became a wealthy merchant. Ali Baba married a woman as poor as himself, and lived by cutting wood and bringing it upon three asses into the town to sell.

One day, when Ali Baba was in the forest, and had just cut wood enough to load his asses, he saw at a distance a great cloud of dust approaching him. He observed it with attention, and distinguished soon after a body of horsemen, whom he suspected to be robbers. He determined to leave his asses in order to save himself; so climbed up a large tree, planted on a high rock, the branches of which were thick enough to conceal him, and yet enabled him to see all that passed without being discovered.

The troop, to the number of forty, well mounted and armed, came to the foot of the rock on which the tree stood, and there dismounted. Every man unbridled his horse, tied him to some shrub, and hung about his neck a bag of corn which they carried behind them. Then each took off his saddle-bag, which from its weight seemed to Ali Baba to be full of gold and silver. One, whom he took to be their captain, came under the tree in which he was concealed, and making his

The robbers' cave was full of stolen treasure

way through some shrubs, pronounced the words: "Open, Simsim! [Sesame]" A door opened in the rock; and after he had made all his troop enter before him, he followed them, when the door shut again of itself.

The robbers stayed some time within the rock, during which Ali Baba, fearful of being caught, remained in the tree.

At last the door opened again, and as the captain went in last, so he came out first, and stood to see them all pass by him; when Ali Baba heard him make the door close by pronouncing the words: "Shut, Simsim! [Sesame]" Every man at once went and bridled his horse, fastened his wallet, and mounted again; and when the captain saw them all ready, he put himself at their head, and returned the way they had come.

Ali Baba followed them with his eyes as far as he could see them, and afterward waited a long time before he descended. Remembering the words the captain of the robbers used to cause the door to open and shut, he wished to try if his pronouncing them would have the same effect. Accordingly he went among the shrubs, and, receiving the door concealed behind them, stood before it, and said, "Open, Simsim! [Sesame]" Whereupon the door instantly flew wide open.

Now Ali Baba expected a dark, dismal cavern, but was surprised to see a well-lighted and spacious chamber, lighted from an opening at the top of the rock, and filled with all sorts of provisions, rich bales of silk, embroideries, and valuable tissues, piled upon one another, gold and silver ingots in great heaps, and money in bags. The sight of all these riches made him suppose that this cave must have been occupied for ages by robbers, who had succeeded one another.

Ali Baba went boldly into the cave, and collected as much of the gold coin, which was in bags, as his three asses could carry. When he had loaded them with the bags, he laid wood over them so that they could not be seen. Then he stood before the door, and pronouncing the words, "Shut, Simsim! [Sesame]" the door closed of itself; and he made the best of his way to the town.

When he got home, he drove his asses into a little yard, shut the gates carefully, threw off the wood that covered the panniers, carried the bags into his house, and ranged them in order before his wife. He then emptied the bags, which raised such a heap of gold as dazzled his wife's eyes, and then he told her the whole adventure from beginning to end, and, above all, recommended her to keep it secret.

Aladdin and the Wonderful Lamp

Aladdin is a Middle-Eastern story and is set in China but this China appears to be an Islamic country, where both people and ruler are Muslims, with Arabic names, and there is no sign of a Chinese emperor. Its exotic setting adds to the allure of the tale – one of the 1001 told by Scheherazade to her new husband, a king who has executed each of his other wives after just one night of wedded bliss. Anxious to hear the ends of the stories, he repeatedly postpones her execution and finally spares her life.

There once lived a poor tailor, who had a son called Aladdin, a careless, idle boy who would do nothing but play all day long in the streets with little idle boys like himself. This so grieved the father that he died; yet, in spite of his mother's tears and prayers, Aladdin did not mend his ways. One day, when he was playing in the streets as usual, a stranger asked him his age, and if he were not the son of Mustapha the tailor.

"I am, sir," replied Aladdin; "but he died a long while ago."

On this the stranger, who was a famous African magician, fell on his neck and kissed him, saying: "I am your uncle, and knew you from your likeness to my brother. Go to your mother and tell her I am coming."

Aladdin ran home, and told his mother of his newly found uncle.

"Indeed, child," she said, "your father had a brother, but I always thought he was dead."

However, she prepared supper, and bade Aladdin seek his uncle, who came laden with wine and fruit. He presently fell down and kissed the place where Mustapha used to sit, bidding Aladdin's mother not to be surprised at not having seen him before, as he had been forty years out of the country. He then turned to Aladdin, and asked him his trade, at which the boy hung his head, while his mother burst into tears. On learning that Aladdin was idle and would learn no trade, he offered to take a shop for him and stock it with merchandise. Next day he bought Aladdin a fine suit of clothes, and took him all over the city, showing him the sights, and brought him home at nightfall to his mother, who was overjoyed to see her son so fine.

Next day the magician led Aladdin into some beautiful gardens a long way outside the city gates. They sat down by a fountain, and the magician pulled a cake from his girdle, which he divided between them. They then journeyed onwards till they almost reached the mountains. Aladdin was so tired that he begged to go back, but the magician beguiled him with pleasant stories, and led him on in spite of himself.

At last they came to two mountains divided by a narrow valley.

"We will go no farther," said the false uncle. "I will show you something wonderful; only do you gather up sticks while I kindle a fire."

When it was lit the magician threw on it a powder he had about him, at the same time saying some magical words. The earth trembled a little and opened in front of them, disclosing a square flat stone with a brass ring in the middle to raise it by. Aladdin tried to run away, but the magician caught him and gave him a blow that knocked him down.

"What have I done, uncle?" he said piteously; whereupon the magician said more kindly: "Fear nothing, but obey me. Beneath this stone lies a treasure which is to be yours, and no one else may touch it, so you must do exactly as I tell you."

Aladdin discovers the magical lamp

At the word treasure, Aladdin forgot his fears, and grasped the ring as he was told, saying the names of his father and grandfather. The stone came up quite easily and some steps appeared.

"Go down," said the magician; "at the foot of those steps you will find an open door leading into three large halls. Tuck up your gown and go through them without touching anything, or you will die instantly. These halls lead into a garden of fine fruit trees. Walk on till you come to a niche in a terrace where stands a lighted lamp. Pour out the oil it contains and bring it to me."

He drew a ring from his finger and gave it to Aladdin, bidding him prosper.

Aladdin found everything as the magician had said, gathered some fruit off the trees, and, having got the lamp, arrived at the mouth of the cave. The magician cried out in a great hurry:

"Make haste and give me the lamp." This Aladdin refused to do until he was out of the cave. The magician flew into a terrible passion, and throwing some more powder on the fire, he said something, and the stone rolled back into its place.

The magician left Persia for ever, which plainly showed that he was no uncle of Aladdin's, but a cunning magician who had read in his magic books of a wonderful lamp, which would make him the most powerful man in the world. Though he alone knew where to find it, he could only receive it from the hand of another. He had picked out the foolish Aladdin for this purpose, intending to get the lamp and kill him afterwards.

For two days Aladdin remained in the dark, crying and lamenting. At last he clasped his hands in prayer, and in so doing rubbed the ring, which the magician had forgotten to take from him. Immediately an enormous and frightful genie rose out of the earth, saying:

"What wouldst thou with me? I am the Slave of the Ring, and will obey thee in all things."

Aladdin fearlessly replied: "Deliver me from this place!" whereupon the earth opened, and he found himself outside. As soon as his eyes could bear the light he went home, but fainted on the threshold. When he came to himself he told his mother what had passed, and showed her the lamp and the fruits he had gathered in the garden, which were in reality precious stones. He then asked for some food.

"Alas! child," she said, "I have nothing in the house, but I have spun a little cotton and will go and sell it."

Aladdin bade her keep her cotton, for he would sell the lamp instead. As it was very dirty she began to rub it, that it might fetch a higher price. Instantly a hideous genie appeared, and asked what she would have. She fainted away, but Aladdin, snatching the lamp, said boldly:

"Fetch me something to eat!"

The genie returned with a silver bowl, twelve silver plates containing rich meats, two silver cups, and two bottles of wine. Aladdin's mother, when she came to herself, said:

"Whence comes this splendid feast?"

"Ask not, but eat," replied Aladdin.

So they sat at breakfast till it was dinner-time, and Aladdin told his mother about the lamp. She begged him to sell it, and have nothing to do with devils.

"No," said Aladdin, "since chance has made us aware of its virtues, we will use it and the ring likewise, which I shall always wear on my finger." When they had eaten all the genie had brought, Aladdin sold one of the silver plates, and so on till none were left. He then had recourse to the genie, who gave him another set of plates, and thus they lived for many years.

One day Aladdin heard an order from the Sultan proclaimed while the princess, his daughter, went to and from the bath. Aladdin was seized by a desire to see her face, which was very difficult, as she always went veiled. He hid himself behind the door of the bath, and peeped through a chink. The princess lifted her veil as she went in, and looked so beautiful that Aladdin fell in love with her at first sight. He went home so changed that his mother was frightened. He told her he loved the princess so deeply that he could not live without her, and meant to ask her in marriage of her father. His mother, on hearing this, burst out laughing, but Aladdin at last prevailed upon her to go before the Sultan and carry his request.

Aladdin woos the beautiful princess

He was thunder struck, and turning to the vizir said: "What sayest thou? Ought I not to bestow the princess on one who values her at such a price?"

The vizir, who wanted her for his own son, begged the Sultan to withhold her for three months, in the course of which he hoped his son would contrive to make him a richer present. The Sultan granted this, and told Aladdin's mother that, though he consented to the marriage, she must not appear before him again for three months.

Aladdin waited patiently for nearly three months, but after two had elapsed his mother, going into the city to buy oil, found everyone rejoicing, and asked what was going on.

"Do you not know," was the answer, "that the son of the grand-vizir is to marry the Sultan's daughter to-night?"

She fetched a napkin and laid in it the magic fruits from the enchanted garden, which sparkled and shone like the most beautiful jewels. She took these with her to please the Sultan, and set out, trusting in the lamp. The grand-vizir and the lords of council had just gone in as she entered the hall and placed herself in front of the Sultan. He, however, took no notice of her. She went every day for a week, and stood in the same place.

When the council broke up on the sixth day the Sultan said to his vizir: "I see a certain woman in the audience-chamber every day carrying something in a napkin. Call her next time, that I may find out what she wants."

Next day, at a sign from the vizir, she went up to the foot of the throne, and remained kneeling till the Sultan said to her: "Rise, good woman, and tell me what you want."

She hesitated, so the Sultan sent away all but the vizir, and bade her speak freely, promising to forgive her beforehand for anything she might say. She then told him of her son's violent love for the princess.

"I prayed him to forget her," she said, "but in vain; he threatened to do some desperate deed if I refused to go and ask your Majesty for the hand of the princess. Now I pray you to forgive not me alone, but my son Aladdin."

The Sultan asked her kindly what she had in the napkin, whereupon she unfolded the jewels and presented them.

Breathless, she ran and told Aladdin, who was overwhelmed at first, but presently bethought him of the lamp. He rubbed it, and the genie appeared, saying: "What is thy will?"

Aladdin replied: "The Sultan, as thou knowest, has broken his promise to me, and the vizir's son is to have the princess. My command is that to-night you bring hither the bride and bridegroom."

"Master, I obey," said the genie.

Aladdin then went to his chamber, where, sure enough at midnight the genie transported the bed containing the vizir's son and the princess.

"Take this new-married man," he said, "and put him outside in the cold, and return at daybreak."

Whereupon the genie took the vizir's son out of bed, leaving Aladdin with the princess.

"Fear nothing," Aladdin said to her; "you are my wife, promised to me by your unjust father, and no harm shall come to you."

The princess was too frightened to speak, and passed the most miserable night of her life, while Aladdin lay down beside her and slept soundly. At the appointed hour the genie fetched in the shivering bridegroom, laid him in his place, and transported the bed back to the palace.

Presently the Sultan came to wish his daughter good-morning. The unhappy vizir's son jumped up and hid himself, while the princess would not say a word, and was very sorrowful.

The Sultan sent her mother to her, who said: "How comes it, child, that you will not speak to your father? What has happened?"

The princess sighed deeply, and at last told her mother how, during the night, the bed had been carried into some strange house, and what had passed there. Her mother did not believe her in the least, but bade her rise and consider it an idle dream.

The following night exactly the same thing happened, and next morning, on the princess's refusing to speak, the Sultan threatened to cut off her head. She then confessed all, bidding him ask the vizir's son if it were not so. The Sultan told the vizir to ask his son, who owned the truth, adding that, dearly as he loved the princess, he had rather die than go through another such fearful night, and wished to be separated from her. His wish was granted, and there was an end of feasting and rejoicing.

When the three months were over, Aladdin sent his mother to remind the Sultan of his promise. She stood in the same place as before, and the Sultan, who had forgotten Aladdin, at once remembered him, and sent for her. On seeing her poverty the Sultan felt less inclined than ever to keep his word, and asked the vizir's advice, who counselled him to set so high a value on the princess that no man living could come up to it.

The Sultan then turned to Aladdin's mother, saying: "Good woman, a Sultan must remember his promises, and I will remember mine, but your son must first send me forty basins of gold brimful of jewels, carried by forty black slaves, led by as many white ones, splendidly dressed. Tell him that I await his answer." The mother of Aladdin bowed low and went home, thinking all was lost.

She gave Aladdin the message, adding: "He may wait long enough for your answer!"

"Not so long, mother, as you think," her son replied "I would do a great deal more than that for the princess."

He summoned the genie, and in a few moments the eighty slaves arrived, and filled up the small house and garden.

Aladdin made them set out to the palace, two and two, followed by his mother. They were so richly dressed, with such splendid jewels in their girdles, that everyone crowded to see them and the basins of gold they carried on their heads.

They entered the palace, and, after kneeling before the Sultan, stood in a half-circle round the throne with their arms crossed, while Aladdin's mother presented them to the Sultan.

He hesitated no longer, but said: "Good woman, return and tell your son that I wait for him with open arms."

She lost no time in telling Aladdin, bidding him make haste. But Aladdin first called the genie.

"I want a scented bath," he said, "a richly embroidered habit, a horse surpassing the Sultan's, and twenty slaves to attend me. Besides this, six slaves, beautifully dressed, to wait on my mother; and lastly, ten thousand pieces of gold in ten purses."

No sooner said than done. Aladdin mounted his horse and passed through the streets, the slaves strewing gold as they went. Those who had played with him in his childhood knew him not, he had grown so handsome.

When the Sultan saw him he came down from his throne, embraced him, and led him into a hall where a feast was spread, intending to marry him to the princess that very day.

But Aladdin refused, saying, "I must build a palace fit for her," and took his leave.

Once home he said to the genie: "Build me a palace of the finest marble, set with jasper, agate, and other precious stones. In the middle you shall build me a large hall with a dome, its four walls of gold and silver, each side having six windows, whose lattices, all except one, which is to be left unfinished, must be set with diamonds and rubies. There must be stables and horses and grooms and slaves; go and see about it!"

The palace was finished by the next day, and the genie carried him there and showed him all his orders faithfully carried out, even to the laying of a velvet carpet from Aladdin's palace to the Sultan's. Aladdin's mother then dressed herself carefully, and walked to the palace with her slaves, while he followed her on horseback. The Sultan sent musicians with trumpets and cymbals to meet them, so that the air resounded with music and cheers. She was taken to the princess, who saluted her and treated her with great honour. At night the princess said good-bye to her father, and set out on the carpet for Aladdin's palace, with his mother at her side, and followed by the hundred slaves. She was charmed at the sight of Aladdin, who ran to receive her.

"Princess," he said, "blame your beauty for my boldness if I have displeased you."

She told him that, having seen him, she willingly obeyed her father in this matter. After the wedding had taken place Aladdin led her into the hall, where a feast was spread, and she supped with him, after which they danced till midnight.

Next day Aladdin invited the Sultan to see the palace. On entering the hall with the four-and-twenty windows, with their rubies, diamonds, and emeralds, he cried:

"It is a world's wonder! There is only one thing that surprises me. Was it by accident that one window was left unfinished?"

"No, sir, by design," returned Aladdin. "I wished your Majesty to have the glory of finishing this palace."

The Sultan was pleased, and sent for the best jewellers in the city. He showed them the unfinished window, and bade them fit it up like the others.

"Sir," replied their spokesman, "we cannot find jewels enough."

The Sultan had his own fetched, which they soon used, but to no purpose, for in a month's time the work was not half done. Aladdin, knowing that their task was vain, bade them undo their work and carry the jewels back, and the genie finished the window at his command. The Sultan was surprised to receive his jewels again and visited Aladdin, who showed him the window finished. The Sultan embraced him, the envious vizir meanwhile hinting that it was the work of enchantment.

Aladdin had won the hearts of the people by his gentle bearing. He was made captain of the Sultan's armies, and won several battles for him, but remained modest and courteous as before, and lived thus in peace and content for several years.

But far away in Africa the magician remembered Aladdin, and by his magic arts discovered that Aladdin, instead of perishing miserably in the cave, had escaped, and had married a princess, with whom he was living in great honour and wealth. He knew that the poor tailor's son could only have accomplished this by means of the lamp, and travelled night and day till he reached the capital of China, bent on Aladdin's ruin. As he passed through the town he heard people talking everywhere about a marvellous palace.

"Forgive my ignorance," he asked, "what is this palace you speak of?"

"Have you not heard of Prince Aladdin's palace," was the reply, "the greatest wonder of the world? I will direct you if you have a mind to see it."

The magician thanked him who spoke, and having seen the palace knew that it had been raised by the genie of the lamp, and became half mad with rage. He determined to get hold of the lamp, and again plunge Aladdin into the deepest poverty.

Unluckily, Aladdin had gone a-hunting for eight days, which gave the magician plenty of time. He bought a dozen copper lamps, put them into a basket, and went to the palace, crying: "New lamps for old!" followed by a jeering crowd.

The princess, sitting in the hall of four-and-twenty windows, sent a slave to find out what the noise was about, who came back laughing, so that the princess scolded her.

"Madam," replied the slave, "who can help laughing to see an old fool offering to exchange fine new lamps for old ones?"

Another slave, hearing this, said: "There is an old one on the cornice there which he can have."

Now this was the magic lamp, which Aladdin had left there, as he could not take it out hunting with him. The princess, not knowing its value, laughingly bade the slave take it and make the exchange.

She went and said to the magician: "Give me a new lamp for this."

He snatched it and bade the slave take her choice, amid the jeers of the crowd. Little he cared, but left off crying his lamps, and went out of the city gates to a lonely place, where he remained till nightfall, when he pulled out the lamp and rubbed it. The genie appeared, and at the magician's command carried him, together with the palace and the princess in it, to a lonely place in Africa.

Next morning the Sultan looked out of the window towards Aladdin's palace and rubbed his eyes, for it was gone. He sent for the vizir, and asked what had become of the palace. The vizir looked out too, and was lost in astonishment. He again put it down to enchantment, and this time the Sultan believed him, and sent thirty men on horseback to fetch Aladdin in chains. They met him riding home, bound him, and forced him to go with them on foot. The people, however, who loved him, followed, armed, to see that he came to no harm. He was carried before the Sultan, who ordered the executioner to cut off his head. The executioner made Aladdin kneel down, bandaged his eyes, and raised his scimitar to strike.

At that instant the vizir, who saw that the crowd had forced their way into the courtyard and were scaling the walls to rescue Aladdin, called to the executioner to stay his hand. The people, indeed, looked so threatening that the Sultan gave way and ordered Aladdin to be unbound, and pardoned him in the sight of the crowd.

Aladdin now begged to know what he had done.

"False wretch!" said the Sultan, "come hither," and showed him from the window the place where his palace had stood.

Aladdin was so amazed that he could not say a word.

"Where is my palace and my daughter?" demanded the Sultan. "For the first I am not so deeply concerned, but my daughter I must have, and you must find her or lose your head."

Aladdin begged for forty days in which to find her, promising if he failed to return and suffer death at the Sultan's pleasure. His prayer was granted, and he went forth sadly from the Sultan's presence. For three days he wandered about like a madman, asking everyone what had become of his palace, but they only laughed and pitied him. He came to the banks of a river, and knelt down to say his prayers before throwing himself in. In so doing he rubbed the magic ring he still wore.

The genie he had seen in the cave appeared, and asked his will.

"Save my life, genie," said Aladdin, "and bring my palace back."

"That is not in my power," said the genie; "I am only the slave of the ring; you must ask the slave of the lamp."

"Even so," said Aladdin "but thou canst take me to the palace, and set me down under my dear wife's window." He at once found himself in Africa, under the window of the princess, and fell asleep out of sheer weariness.

He was awakened by the singing of the birds, and his heart was lighter. He saw plainly that all his misfortunes were owing to the loss of the lamp, and vainly wondered who had robbed him of it.

That morning the princess rose earlier than she had

done since she had been carried into Africa by the magician, whose company she was forced to endure once a day. She, however, treated him so harshly that he dared not live there altogether. As she was dressing, one of her women looked out and saw Aladdin. The princess ran and opened the window, and at the noise she made Aladdin looked up. She called to him to come to her, and great was the joy of these lovers at seeing each other again.

After he had kissed her Aladdin said: "I beg of you, Princess, in God's name, before we speak of anything else, for your own sake and mine, tell me what has become of an old lamp I left on the cornice in the hall of four-and-twenty windows, when I went a-hunting."

"Alas!" she said "I am the innocent cause of our sorrows," and told him of the exchange of the lamp.

"Now I know," cried Aladdin, "that we have to thank the African magician for this! Where is the lamp?"

"He carries it about with him," said the princess, "I know, for he pulled it out of his breast to show me. He wishes me to break my faith with you and marry him, saying that you were beheaded by my father's command. He is forever speaking ill of you, but I only reply by my tears. If I persist, I doubt not that he will use violence."

Aladdin comforted her, and left her for a while. He changed clothes with the first person he met in the town, and having bought a certain powder returned to the princess, who let him in by a little side door.

"Put on your most beautiful dress," he said to her, "and receive the magician with smiles, leading him to believe that you have forgotten me. Invite him to sup with you, and say you wish to taste the wine of his country. He will go for some, and while he is gone I will tell you what to do."

She listened carefully to Aladdin, and when he left her arrayed herself gaily for the first time since she left China. She put on a girdle and head-dress of diamonds, and seeing in a glass that she looked more beautiful than ever, received the magician, saying to his great amazement: "I have made up my mind that Aladdin is dead, and that all my tears will not bring him back to me, so I am resolved to mourn no more, and have therefore invited you to sup with me; but I am tired of the wines of China, and would fain taste those of Africa."

The magician flew to his cellar, and the princess put the

"New lamps for old! New lamps for old!"

powder Aladdin had given her in her cup. When he returned she asked him to drink her health in the wine of Africa, handing him her cup in exchange for his as a sign she was reconciled to him.

Before drinking the magician made her a speech in praise of her beauty, but the princess cut him short saying:

"Let me drink first, and you shall say what you will afterwards." She set her cup to her lips and kept it there, while the magician drained his to the dregs and fell back lifeless.

The princess then opened the door to Aladdin, and flung her arms round his neck, but Aladdin put her away, bidding her to leave him, as he had more to do. He then went to the dead magician, took the lamp out of his vest, and bade the genie carry the palace and all in it back to China. This was done, and the princess in her chamber only felt two little shocks, and little thought she was at home again.

The Sultan, who was sitting in his closet, mourning for his lost daughter, happened to look up, and rubbed his eyes, for there stood the palace as before! He hastened thither, and Aladdin received him in the hall of the four-and-twenty windows, with the princess at his side. Aladdin told him what had happened, and showed him the dead body of the magician, that he might believe. A ten days' feast was proclaimed, and it seemed as if Aladdin might now live the rest of his life in peace; but it was not to be.

The African magician had a younger brother, who was, if possible, more wicked and more cunning than himself. He travelled to China to avenge his brother's death, and went to visit a pious woman called Fatima, thinking she might be of use to him. He entered her cell and clapped a dagger to her breast, telling her to rise and do his bidding on pain of death. He changed clothes with her, coloured his face like hers, put on her veil and murdered her, that she might tell no tales. Then he went towards the palace of Aladdin, and all the people thinking he was the holy woman, gathered round him, kissing his hands and begging his blessing. When he got to the palace there was such a noise going on round him that the princess bade her slave look out of the window and ask what was the matter. The slave said it was the holy woman, curing people by her touch of their ailments, whereupon the princess, who had long desired to see Fatima, sent for her. On coming to the princess the magician offered up a prayer for her health and prosperity. When he had done the princess made him sit by her, and begged him to stay with her always. The false Fatima, who wished for nothing better, consented, but kept his veil down for fear of discovery. The princess showed him the hall, and asked him what he thought of it.

"It is truly beautiful," said the false Fatima. "In my mind it wants but one thing."

"And what is that?" said the princess.

"If only a roc's egg," replied he, "were hung up from the middle of this dome, it would be the wonder of the world."

After this the princess could think of nothing but a roc's egg, and when Aladdin returned from hunting he found her in a very ill humour. He begged to know what was amiss, and she told him that all her pleasure in the hall was spoilt for the want of a roc's egg hanging from the dome.

"If that is all," replied Aladdin, "you shall soon be happy."

He left her and rubbed the lamp, and when the genie appeared commanded him to bring a roc's egg. The genie gave such a loud and terrible shriek that the hall shook.

"Wretch!" he cried, "is it not enough that I have done everything for you, but you must command me to bring my master and hang him up in the midst of this dome? You and your wife and your palace deserve to be burnt to ashes; but this request does not come from you, but from the brother of the African magician whom you destroyed. He is now in your palace disguised as the holy woman – whom he murdered. He it was who put that wish into your wife's head. Take care of yourself, for he means to kill you." So saying the genie disappeared.

Aladdin went back to the princess, saying his head ached, and requesting that the holy Fatima should be fetched to lay her hands on it. But when the magician came near, Aladdin, seizing his dagger, pierced him to the heart.

"What have you done?" cried the princess. "You have killed the holy woman!"

"Not so," replied Aladdin, "but a wicked magician," and told her of how she had been deceived.

After this Aladdin and his wife lived in peace. He succeeded the Sultan when he died, and reigned for many years, leaving behind him a long line of kings.

A Midsummer Night's Dream

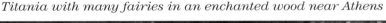

Titania with many fairies in an enchanted wood near Athens

These verse excerpts are from *A Midsummer Night's Dream* ACT 2: SCENES 1 and 2, set in a wood near Athens and penned by William Shakespeare – believed to have been written between 1590 to 1596. The text elements are from *Tales From Shakespeare* (For Children) by Charles Lamb and his sister Mary Anne Lamb. Mary Lamb wrote most of the comedies, and Charles the tragedies. Their book was illustrated by Arthur Ransome in 1899 and 1909.

Although this is Midsummer Night, which falls on 23 June, there are several references to May Day celebrations but such revels did sometimes take place further into the summer season.

Oberon the king, and Titania the queen of the fairies, with all their tiny train of followers, in this wood held their midnight revels.

Between this little king and queen of sprites there happened, at this time, a sad disagreement; they never met by moonlight in the shady walks of this pleasant wood, but they were quarrelling, till all their fairy elves would creep into acorn-cups and hide themselves for fear.

The cause of this unhappy disagreement was Titania's refusing to give Oberon a little changeling boy, whose mother had been Titania's friend; and upon her death the fairy queen stole the child from its nurse, and brought him up in the woods.

The night on which the lovers were to meet in this wood, as Titania was walking with some of her maids of honour,

Titania settles to sleep in a bower of flowers

she met Oberon attended by his train of fairy courtiers.

"Ill met by moonlight, proud Titania," said the fairy king.

The queen replied: "What, jealous Oberon, is it you? Fairies, skip hence; I have foresworn his company."

"Tarry, rash fairy," said Oberon; 'am not I thy lord? Why does Titania cross her Oberon? Give me your little changeling boy to be my page."

"Set your heart at rest," answered the queen; "your whole fairy kingdom buys not the boy of me." She then left her lord in great anger.

"Well, go your way," said Oberon: 'before the morning dawns I will torment you for this injury.'

Oberon then sent for Puck, his chief favourite and privy counsellor.

Puck (or as he was sometimes called, Robin Goodfellow) was a shrewd and knavish sprite, that used to play comical pranks in the neighbouring villages; sometimes getting into the dairies and skimming the milk, sometimes plunging his light and airy form into the butter-churn, and while

Titania sees Bottom as a handsome man despite his ass's head

he was dancing his fantastic shape in the churn, in vain the dairymaid would labour to change her cream into butter: nor had the village swains any better success; whenever Puck chose to play his freaks in the brewing copper, the ale was sure to be spoiled. When a few good neighbours were met to drink some comfortable ale together, Puck would jump into the bowl of ale in the likeness of a roasted crab, and when some old goody was going to drink he would bob against her lips, and spill the ale over her withered chin; and presently after, when the same old dame was gravely seating herself to tell her neighbours a sad and melancholy story, Puck would slip her threelegged stool from under her, and down toppled the poor old woman, and then the old gossips would hold their sides and laugh at her, and swear they never wasted a merrier hour.

"Come hither, Puck," said Oberon to this little merry wanderer of the night; "fetch me the flower which maids call Love in Idleness; the juice of that little purple flower laid on the eyelids of those who sleep, will make them, when they awake, dote on the first thing they see. Some of the juice of that flower I will drop on the eyelids of my Titania when she is asleep; and the first thing she looks upon when she opens her eyes she will fall in love with, even though it be a lion or a bear, a meddling monkey, or a busy ape; and before I will take this charm from off her sight, which I can do with another charm I know of, I will make her give me that boy to be my page."

Puck, who loved mischief to his heart, was highly diverted with this intended frolic of his master, and ran to seek the flower; and while Oberon was waiting the return of Puck, he observed Demetrius and Helena enter the wood: he overheard Demetrius reproaching Helena for following him, and after many unkind words on his part, and gentle expostulations from Helena, reminding him of his former love and professions of true faith to her, he left her (as he said) to the mercy of the wild beasts, and she ran after him as swiftly as she could.

The fairy king, who was always friendly to true lovers, felt great compassion for Helena; and perhaps, as Lysander said they used to walk by moonlight in this pleasant wood, Oberon might have seen Helena in those happy times when she was beloved by Demetrius. However, that might be, when Puck returned with the little purple flower, Oberon said to his favourite: "Take a part of this flower; there has been a sweet Athenian lady here, who is in love with a disdainful youth; if you find him sleeping, drop some of the love-juice in his eyes, but contrive to do it when she is near him, that

The fairies sing their queen to sleep with a pretty lullaby

the first thing he sees when he awakes may be this despised lady. You will know the man by the Athenian garments which he wears." Puck promised to manage this matter very dexterously: and then Oberon went, unperceived by Titania, to her bower, where she was preparing to go to rest. Her fairy bower was a bank, where grew wild thyme, cowslips, and sweet violets, under a canopy of wood-bine, musk-roses, and eglantine. There Titania always slept some part of the night; her coverlet the enamelled skin of a snake, which,

though a small mantle, was wide enough to wrap a fairy in.

He found Titania giving orders to her fairies, how they were to employ themselves while she slept. "Some of you," said her majesty, "must kill cankers in the muskrose buds, and some wage war with the bats for their leathern wings, to make my small elves coats; and some of you keep watch that the clamorous owl, that nightly hoots, come not near me: but first sing me to sleep." Then they began to sing this song:

"You spotted snakes with double tongue,
Thorny hedgehogs, be not seen;
Newts and blind-worms do no wrong,
Come not near our Fairy Queen.
Philomel, with melody,
Sing in our sweet lullaby,
Lulla, lulla, lullaby; lulla, lulla, lullaby;
Never harm, nor spell, nor charm,
Come our lovely lady nigh;
So good night with lullaby."

When the fairies had sung their queen asleep with this pretty lullaby, they left her to perform the important services she had enjoined them. Oberon then softly drew near his Titania, and dropped some of the love-juice on her eyelids, saying:

"What thou seest when thou dost wake,
Do it for thy true-love take."

. . . .Titania was still sleeping, and Oberon seeing a clown near her, who had lost his way in the wood, and was likewise asleep: "This fellow," said he, "shall be my Titania's true love"; and clapping an ass's head over the clown's, it seemed to fit him as well as if it had grown upon his own shoulders. Though Oberon fixed the ass's head on very gently, it awakened him, and rising up, unconscious of what Oberon had done to him, he went towards the bower where the fairy queen slept.

"Ah! what angel is that I see?" said Titania, opening her eyes, and the juice of the little purple flower beginning to take effect: "are you as wise as you are beautiful?"

"Why, mistress," said the foolish clown, "if I have wit enough to find the way out of this wood, I have enough to serve my turn."

"Out of the wood do not desire to go," said the enamoured queen. "I am a spirit of no common rate. I love you. Go with me, and I will give you fairies to attend upon you."

She then called four of her fairies: their names were Pease-blossom, Cobweb, Moth, and Mustard-seed.

"Attend," said the queen, "upon this sweet gentleman; hop in his walks, and gambol in his sight; feed him with grapes and apricots, and steal for him the honeybags from the bees. Come, sit with me," said she to the clown, "and let me play with your amiable hairy cheeks, my beautiful ass! and kiss your fair large ears, my gentle joy!"

The Pied Piper of Hamelin

The earliest mention of the story is on a 14th-century stained-glass window in Hamelin church (*c*.1300), believed to have been created in memory of a tragic historical event when all the children deserted the city – perhaps through plague as the Death figure was often depicted in motley dress. Others suggest that the children drowned in the river Weser, were killed in a landslide, sent on a crusade or dispatched to settle parts of Transylvania after the Mongol invasions. Both Goethe and Browning wrote poems based on the story.

Once upon a time . . . on the banks of a great river in the north of Germany lay a town called Hamelin. The citizens of Hamelin were honest folk who lived contentedly in their grey stone houses. The years went by, and the town grew very rich.

Then one day, an extraordinary thing happened to disturb the peace.

Hamelin had always had rats, and a lot too. But they had never been a danger, for the cats had always solved the rat problem in the usual way – by killing them. All at once, however, the rats began to multiply.

In the end, a black sea of rats swarmed over the whole town. First, they attacked the barns and storehouses, then, for lack of anything better, they gnawed the wood, cloth or anything at all. The one thing they didn't eat was metal. The terrified citizens flocked to plead with the town councilors to free them from the plague of rats. But the council had, for a long time, been sitting in the Mayor's room, trying to think of a plan.

"What we need is an army of cats!"

But all the cats were dead.

"We'll put down poisoned food then . . ."

But most of the food was already gone and even poison did not stop the rats.

"It just can't be done without help!" said the Mayor sadly.

Just then, while the citizens milled around outside, there was a loud knock at the door. "Who can that be?" the city fathers wondered uneasily, mindful of the angry crowds. They gingerly opened the door. And to their surprise, there stood a tall thin man dressed in brightly colored clothes, with a long feather in his hat, and waving a gold pipe at them.

"I've freed other towns of beetles and bats," the stranger announced, "and for a thousand florins, I'll rid you of your rats!"

"A thousand florins!" exclaimed the Mayor. "We'll give you fifty thousand if you succeed!" At once the stranger hurried away, saying:

"It's late now, but at dawn tomorrow, there won't be a rat left in Hamelin!"

The sun was still below the horizon, when the sound of a pipe wafted through the streets of Hamelin. The pied piper slowly made his way through the houses and behind him flocked the rats. Out they scampered from doors, windows and gutters, rats of every size, all after the piper. And as he played, the stranger marched down to the river and straight into the water, up to his middle. Behind him swarmed the rats and every one was drowned and swept away by the current.

By the time the sun was high in the sky, there was not a

Rats! They fought the dogs and killed the cats and bit the babies in the cradles

single rat in the town. There was even greater delight at the town hall, until the piper tried to claim his payment.

"Fifty thousand florins?" exclaimed the councilors, "Never . . ."

"A thousand florins at least!" cried the pied piper angrily. But the Mayor broke in. "The rats are all dead now and they can never come back. So be grateful for fifty florins, or you'll not get even that . . ."

His eyes flashing with rage, the pied piper pointed a threatening finger at the Mayor.

"You'll bitterly regret ever breaking your promise," he said, and vanished.

A shiver of fear ran through the councilors, but the Mayor shrugged and said excitedly: "We've saved fifty thousand florins!"

That night, freed from the nightmare of the rats, the citizens of Hamelin slept more soundly than ever. And

into the darkness, the door creaked shut.

A great landslide came down the mountain blocking the entrance to the cave forever. Only one little lame boy escaped this fate. It was he who told the anxious citizens, searching for their children, what had happened. And no matter what people did, the mountain never gave up its victims.

Many years were to pass before the merry voices of other children would ring through the streets of Hamelin but the memory of the harsh lesson lingered in everyone's heart and was passed down from father to son through the centuries.

Once more he stepped into the street and ere
he blew three notes sweet, out came the children,
running into the street

the strange sound of piping wafted through the streets at dawn, only the children heard it. Drawn as by magic, they hurried out of their homes. Again, the pied piper paced through the town, this time, it was children of all sizes that flocked at his heels to the sound of his strange piping.

The long procession soon left the town and made its way through the wood and across the forest till it reached the foot of a huge mountain. When the piper came to the dark rock, he played his pipe even louder still and a great door creaked open. Beyond lay a cave. In trooped the children behind the pied piper, and when the last child had gone

The Piper led them where waters gushed and fruit
trees grew, and flowers put forth a fairer hue

One lame boy was left behind;
his playmates had vanished for ever

Out came the children tripping and skipping as they ran merrily
after the wonderful music with shouting and laughter

31

The History of Whittington

This story was first recorded in 1605. It rapidly became a favourite, and was included in several other collections, including the fairytale collections of Joseph Jacobs. Richard Whittington was a real person, the son of a knight and himself a rich merchant in London. He served three terms as Lord mayor of London: 1397-99, 1406-07, and 1419-20. He died in 1423.

Dick Whittington was a very little boy when his father and mother died; so little, indeed, that he never knew them, nor the place where he was born. He strolled about the country as ragged as a colt, till he met with a wagoner who was going to London, and who gave him leave to walk all the way by the side of his wagon without paying anything for his passage. This pleased little Whittington very much, as he wanted to see London sadly, for he had heard that the streets were paved with gold, and he was willing to get a bushel of it; but how great was his disappointment, poor boy! when he saw the streets covered with dirt instead of gold, and found himself in a strange place, without a friend, without food, and without money.

Though the wagoner was so charitable as to let him walk up by the side of the wagon for nothing, he took care not to know him when he came to town, and the poor boy was, in a little time, so cold and hungry that he wished himself in a good kitchen and by a warm fire in the country.

In his distress he asked charity of several people, and one of them bid him, "Go to work for an idle rogue." "That I will," said Whittington, "with all my heart; I will work for you if you will let me."

The man, who thought this savored of wit and impertinence (though the poor lad intended only to show his readiness to work), gave him a blow with a stick which broke his head so that the blood ran down. In this situation, and fainting for want of food, he laid himself down at the door of one Mr. Fitzwarren, a merchant, where the cook saw him, and, being an ill-natured hussy, ordered him to go about his business or she would scald him. At this time Mr. Fitzwarren came from the Exchange, and began also to scold at the poor boy, bidding him to go to work.

Whittington answered that he should be glad to work if anybody would employ him, and that he should be able if he could get some victuals to eat, for he had had nothing for three days, and he was a poor country boy, and knew nobody, and nobody would employ him.

He then endeavoured to get up, but he was so very weak that he fell down again, which excited so much compassion in the merchant that he ordered the servants to take him in and give him some meat and drink, and let him help the cook to do any dirty work that she had to set him about. People are too apt to reproach those who beg with being idle, but give themselves no concern to put them in the way of getting business to do, or considering whether they are able to do it, which is not charity.

But we return to Whittington, who could have lived happy in this worthy family had he not been bumped about by the cross cook, who must be always roasting and basting, or when the spit was idle employed her hands upon poor Whittington! At last Miss Alice, his master's daughter, was informed of it, and then she took compassion on the poor boy, and made the servants treat him kindly.

Besides the crossness of the cook, Whittington had another difficulty to get over before he could be happy. He had, by order of his master, a flock-bed placed for him in a garret, where there was a number of rats and mice that often ran over the poor boy's nose and disturbed him in his sleep. After some time, however, a gentleman who came to his master's house gave Whittington a penny for brushing his shoes. This he put into his pocket, being determined to lay it out to the best advantage; and the next day, seeing a woman in the street with a cat under her arm, he ran up to know the price of it. The woman (as the cat was a good mouser) asked a deal of money for it, but on Whittington's telling her he had but a penny in the world, and that he wanted a cat sadly, she let him have it.

This cat Whittington concealed in the garret, for fear she should be beat about by his mortal enemy the cook, and here she soon killed or frightened away the rats and mice, so that the poor boy could now sleep as sound as a top.

Soon after this the merchant, who had a ship ready to sail, called for his servants, as his custom was, in order that each of them might venture something to try their luck; and whatever they sent was to pay neither freight nor custom, for he thought justly that God Almighty would bless him the more for his readiness to let the poor partake of his fortune.

All the servants appeared but poor Whittington, who, having neither money nor goods, could not think of sending anything to try his luck; but his good friend Miss Alice, thinking his poverty kept him away, ordered him to be called.

She then offered to lay down something for him, but the merchant told his daughter that would not do, it must be something of his own. Upon which poor Whittington said he had nothing but a cat which he bought for a penny that was given him. "Fetch thy cat, boy," said the merchant, "and send her." Whittington brought poor puss and delivered her to the captain, with tears in his eyes, for he said he should now be disturbed by the rats and mice as much as ever. All the company laughed at the adventure but Miss Alice, who pitied the poor boy, and gave him something to buy another cat.

While Puss was beating the billows at sea, poor Whittington was severely beaten at home by his tyrannical mistress the cook, who used him so cruelly, and made such game of him for sending his cat to sea, that at last the poor boy determined to run away from his place, and having packed up the few things he had, he set out very early in the morning on All-Hallows day. He travelled as far as Holloway, and there sat down on a stone to consider what course he should take; but while he was thus ruminating, Bow Bells, of which there were only six, began to ring; and he thought their sounds addressed him in this manner:

"Turn again, Whittington, Thrice Lord Mayor of London."

"Lord Mayor of London!" said he to himself, "what would not one endure to be Lord Mayor of London, and ride in such a fine coach? Well, I'll go back again, and bear all the pummelling and ill-usage of Cicely rather than miss the opportunity of being Lord Mayor!" So home he went, and happily got into the house and about his business before Mrs. Cicely made her appearance.

We must now follow Miss Puss to the coast of Africa. How perilous are voyages at sea, how uncertain the winds and the waves, and how many accidents attend a naval life!

The ship that had the cat on board was long beaten at sea, and at last, by contrary winds, driven on a part of the coast of Barbary which was inhabited by Moors unknown to the English. These people received our countrymen with civility, and therefore the captain, in order to trade with them, showed them the patterns of the goods he had on board, and sent some of them to the King of the country, who was so well pleased that he sent for the captain and the factor to come to his palace, which was about a mile from the sea. Here they were placed, according to the custom of the country, on rich carpets, flowered with gold and silver; and the King and Queen being seated at the upper end of the room, dinner was brought in, which consisted of many dishes; but no sooner were the dishes put down but an amazing number of rats and mice came from all quarters and devoured all the meat in an instant.

The factor, in surprise, turned round to the nobles and asked if these vermin were not offensive. "Oh! yes," said they, "very offensive; and the King would give half his treasure to be freed of them, for they not only destroy his dinner, as you see, but they assault him in his chamber, and even in bed, so that he is obliged to be watched while he is sleeping, for fear of them."

The factor jumped for joy; he remembered poor Whittington and his cat, and told the King he had a creature on board the ship that would despatch all these vermin immediately. The King's heart heaved so high at the joy which this news gave him that his turban dropped off his head. "Bring this creature to me," said he; "vermin are dreadful in a court, and if she will perform what you say I will load your ship with gold and jewels in exchange for her." The factor, who knew his business, took this opportunity to set forth the merits of Miss Puss. He told his Majesty that it would be inconvenient to part with her,

as, when she was gone, the rats and mice might destroy the goods in the ship – but to oblige his Majesty he would fetch her. "Run, run," said the Queen; "I am impatient to see the dear creature."

Away flew the factor, while another dinner was providing, and returned with the cat just as the rats and mice were devouring that also. He immediately put down Miss Puss, who killed a great number of them.

The King rejoiced greatly to see his old enemies destroyed by so small a creature, and the Queen was highly pleased, and desired the cat might be brought near that she might look at her. Upon which the factor called "Pussy, pussy, pussy!" and she came to him. He then presented her to the Queen, who started back, and was afraid to touch a creature who had made such havoc among the rats and mice; however, when the factor stroked the cat and called "Pussy, pussy!" the Queen also touched her and cried "Putty, putty!" for she had not learned English.

He then put her down on the Queen's lap, where she, purring, played with her Majesty's hand, and then sang herself to sleep.

The King, having seen the exploits of Miss Puss, and being informed that her kittens would stock the whole country, bargained with the captain and factor for the whole ship's cargo, and then gave them ten times as much for the cat as all the rest amounted to. On which, taking leave of their Majesties and other great personages at court, they sailed with a fair wind for England, whither we must now attend them.

The morn had scarcely dawned when Mr. Fitzwarren arose to count over the cash and settle the business for that day. He had just entered the counting-house, and seated himself at the desk, when somebody came, tap, tap, at the door. "Who's there?" said Mr. Fitzwarren. "A friend," answered the other. "What friend can come at this unseasonable time?" "A real friend is never unseasonable," answered the other. "I come to bring you good news of your ship Unicorn." The merchant bustled up in such a hurry that he forgot his gout; instantly opened the door, and who should be seen waiting but the captain and factor, with a cabinet of jewels, and a bill of lading, for which the merchant lifted up his eyes and thanked heaven for sending him such a prosperous voyage. Then they told him the adventures of the cat, and showed him the cabinet of jewels which they had brought for Mr. Whittington. Upon which he cried out with great earnestness, but not in the most poetical manner:

"Go, send him in, and tell him of his fame, And call him Mr. Whittington by name."

It is not our business to animadvert upon these lines; we are not critics, but historians. It is sufficient for us that they are the words of Mr. Fitzwarren; and though it is beside our purpose, and perhaps not in our power to prove him a good poet, we shall soon convince the reader that he was a good man, which was a much better character; for when some who were present told him that this treasure was too much for poor boy as Whittington, he said: "God forbid that I should deprive him of a penny; it is his own, and he shall have it to a farthing." He then ordered Mr. Whittington in, who was at this time cleaning the kitchen and would have excused himself from going into the counting-house, saying the room was swept and his shoes were dirty and full of hob-nails. The merchant, however, made him come in, and ordered a chair to be set for him. Upon which, thinking they intended to make sport of him, as had been too often the case in the kitchen, he besought his master not to mock a poor simple fellow, who intended them no harm, but let him go about his business. The merchant, taking him by the hand, said: "Indeed, Mr.

gentleman, and made him the offer of his house to live in till he could provide himself with a better.

Now it came to pass when Mr. Whittington's face was washed, his hair curled, and he dressed in a rich suit of clothes, that he turned out a genteel young fellow; and, as wealth contributes much to give a man confidence, he in a little time dropped that sheepish behavior which was principally occasioned by a depression of spirits, and soon grew a sprightly and good companion, insomuch that Miss Alice, who had formerly pitied him, now fell in love with him.

When her father perceived they had this good liking for each other he proposed a match between them, to which both parties cheerfully consented, and the Lord Mayor,

Dick Whittington's cat killed all the rats and mice in the King's palace

Whittington, I am in earnest with you, and sent for you to congratulate you on your great success. Your cat has procured you more money than I am worth in the world, and may you long enjoy it and be happy!"

At length, being shown the treasure, and convinced by them that all of it belonged to him, he fell upon his knees and thanked the Almighty for his providential care of such a poor and miserable creature. He then laid all the treasure at his master's feet, who refused to take any part of it, but told him he heartily rejoiced at his prosperity, and hoped the wealth he had acquired would be a comfort to him, and would make him happy. He then applied to his mistress, and to his good friend Miss Alice, who refused to take any part of the money, but told him she heartily rejoiced at his good success, and wished him all imaginable felicity. He then gratified the captain, factor, and the ship's crew for the care they had taken of his cargo. He likewise distributed presents to all the servants in the house, not forgetting even his old enemy the cook, though she little deserved it.

After this Mr. Fitzwarren advised Mr. Whittington to send for the necessary people and dress himself like a

Court of Aldermen, Sheriffs, the Company of Stationers, the Royal Academy of Arts, and a number of eminent merchants attended the ceremony, and were elegantly treated at an entertainment made for that purpose.

History further relates that they lived very happily, had several children, and died at a good old age. Mr. Whittington served as Sheriff of London and was three times Lord Mayor. In the last year of his mayoralty he entertained King Henry V and his Queen, after his conquest of France, upon which occasion the King, in consideration of Whittington's merit, said: "Never had prince such a subject"; which being told to Whittington at the table, he replied: "Never had subject such a king." His Majesty, out of respect to his good character, conferred the honour of knighthood on him soon after. Sir Richard many years before his death constantly fed a great number of poor citizens, built a church and a college to it, with a yearly allowance for poor scholars, and near it erected a hospital.
He also built Newgate for criminals, and gave liberally to St. Bartholomew's Hospital and other public charities.

Sleeping Beauty
(Little Briar Rose)

In the early 1600s, Italian Giambattista Basile published a collection of tales including one about a nobleman's daughter who, pricked by a poisonous thorn, falls asleep – only to be ravished by a rather ignoble prince who is already married. Charles Perrault, the French collector of folklore, published his version, *The Sleeping Beauty in the Wood* in 1697. In their rather later version in 1812, the Brothers Grimm modified the fairy tale as *Little Briar Rose* with a much happier-ever-after ending: the prince awakens Rose with a kiss and they marry soon afterwards. In Walt Disney's 1959 movie the good fairies called the princess Briar Rose to protect her but her real name remained Aurora – as used by Perrault in his more gruesome version.

In times past there lived a king and queen, who said to each other every day of their lives, "Would that we had a child!" and yet they had none. But it happened once that when the queen was bathing, there came a frog out of the water, and he squatted on the ground, and said to her, "Thy wish shall be fulfilled; before a year has gone by, thou shalt bring a daughter into the world."

And as the frog foretold, so it happened; and the queen bore a daughter so beautiful that the king could not contain himself for joy, and he ordained a great feast. Not only did he bid to it his relations, friends, and acquaintances, but also the wise women, that they might be kind and favourable to the child. There were thirteen of them in his kingdom, but as he had only provided twelve golden plates for them to eat from, one of them had to be left out.

However, the feast was celebrated with all splendour; and as it drew to an end, the wise women stood forward to present to the child their wonderful gifts: one bestowed virtue, one beauty, a third riches, and so on, whatever there is in the world to wish for. And when eleven of them had said their say, in came the uninvited thirteenth, burning to revenge herself, and without greeting or respect, she cried with a loud voice, "In the fifteenth year of her age the princess shall prick herself with a spindle and shall fall down dead." And without speaking one more word she turned away and left the hall. Everyone was terrified at her saying, when the twelfth came forward, for she had not yet bestowed her gift, and though she could not do away with the evil prophecy, yet she could soften it, so she said, "The princess shall not die, but fall into a deep sleep for a hundred years."

Now the king, being desirous of saving his child even from this misfortune, gave commandment that all the

She fell back upon the bed that stood there, and lay in a deep sleep

spindles in his kingdom should be burnt up. The maiden grew up, adorned with all the gifts of the wise women; and she was so lovely, modest, sweet, and kind and clever, that no one who saw her could help loving her. It happened one day, she being already fifteen years old, that the king and queen rode abroad, and the maiden was left behind alone in the castle. She wandered about into all the nooks and corners, and into all the chambers and parlours, as the fancy took her, till at last she came to an old tower. She climbed the narrow winding stair which led to a little door, with a rusty key sticking out of the lock; she turned the key, and the door opened, and there in the little room sat an old woman with a spindle, diligently spinning her flax.

"Good day, mother," said the princess, "what are you doing?" "I am spinning," answered the old woman, nodding her head. "What thing is that that twists round so briskly?" asked the maiden, and taking the spindle into her hand she began to spin; but no sooner had she touched it than the evil prophecy was fulfilled, and she pricked her finger with it. In that very moment she fell back upon the bed that stood there, and lay in a deep sleep.

And this sleep fell upon the whole castle; the king and queen, who had returned and were in the great hall, fell fast asleep, and with them the whole court. The horses in their stalls, the dogs in the yard, the pigeons on the roof, the flies on the wall, the very fire that flickered on the hearth, became still, and slept like the rest; and the meat on the spit ceased roasting, and the cook, who was going to pull the scullion's hair for some mistake he had made, let him go, and went to sleep. And the wind ceased, and not a leaf fell from the trees about the castle. Then round about that place there grew a hedge of thorns thicker every year, until at last the whole castle was hidden from view, and nothing of it could be seen but the vane on the roof.

And a rumour went abroad in all that country of the beautiful sleeping Rosamond, for so was the princess called; and from time to time many kings' sons came and tried to force their way through the hedge; but it was impossible for them to do so, for the thorns held fast together like strong hands, and the young men were caught by them, and not being able to get free, there died a lamentable death.

Many a long year afterwards there came a king's son into that country, and heard an old man tell how there should be a castle standing behind the hedge of thorns, and that there a beautiful enchanted princess named Rosamond had slept for a hundred years, and with her the king and queen, and the whole court. The old man had been told by his grandfather that many kings' sons had sought to pass the thorn-hedge, but had been caught and pierced by the thorns, and had died a miserable death. Then said the young man, "Nevertheless, I do not fear to try; I shall win through and see the lovely Rosamond." The good old man tried to dissuade him, but he would not listen to his words. For now the hundred years were at an end, and the day had come when Rosamond should be awakened. When the

prince drew near the hedge of thorns, it was changed into a hedge of beautiful large flowers, which parted and bent aside to let him pass, and then closed behind him in a thick hedge. When he reached the castle-yard, he saw the horses and brindled hunting-dogs lying asleep, and on the roof the pigeons were sitting with their heads under their wings. And when he came indoors, the flies on the wall were asleep, the cook in the kitchen had his hand uplifted to strike the scullion, and the kitchen-maid had the black fowl on her lap ready to pluck.

Then he mounted higher, and saw in the hall the whole court lying asleep, and above them, on their thrones, slept the king and the queen. And still he went farther, and all was so quiet that he could hear his own breathing; and at

When he reached the castle-yard, he saw the horses and brindled hunting-dogs lying asleep

last he came to the tower, and went up the winding stair, and opened the door of the little room where Rosamond lay. And when he saw her looking so lovely in her sleep, he could not turn away his eyes; and presently he stooped and kissed her.

And she awaked, and opened her eyes, and looked very kindly on him. And she rose, and they went forth together, and the king and the queen and whole court waked up, and gazed on each other with great eyes of wonderment. And the horses in the yard got up and shook themselves, the hounds sprang up and wagged their tails, the pigeons on the roof drew their heads from under their wings, looked round, and flew into the field, the flies on the wall crept on a little farther, the kitchen fire leapt up and blazed, and cooked the meat, the joint on the spit began to roast, the cook gave the scullion such a box on the ear that he roared out, and the maid went on plucking the fowl.

Then the wedding of the Prince and Rosamond was held with all splendour, and they lived very happily together until their lives' end.

Tom Thumb

From *"The Fairy Book"* by Miss Mulock
When in 1621, *The History of Tom Thumb* was published, it was the first real fairy tale to be printed in English. It would be another century before books aimed particularly at children began to be published as a matter of course and many of these were attributed to Tommy Thumb who became a regular part of the nursery library.

The ploughman's wife was thrilled to have a tiny son

In the days of King Arthur, Merlin, the most learned enchanter of his time, was on a journey; and being very weary, stopped one day at the cottage of an honest ploughman to ask for refreshment. The ploughman's wife, with great civility, immediately brought him some milk in a wooden bowl, and some brown bread on a wooden platter. Merlin could not help observing, that although everything within the cottage was particularly neat and clean, and in good order, the ploughman and his wife had the most sorrowful air imaginable: so he questioned them on the cause of their melancholy, and learned that they were very miserable because they had no children. The poor woman declared, with tears in her eyes, that she should be the happiest creature in the world, if she had a son, although he were no bigger than his father's thumb. Merlin was much amused with the notion of a boy no bigger than a man's thumb; and as soon as he returned home, he sent for the queen of the fairies (with whom he was very intimate), and related to her the desire of the ploughman and his wife to have a son the size of his father's thumb. She liked the plan exceedingly, and declared their wish should be speedily granted. Accordingly, the ploughman's wife had a son, who in a few minutes grew as tall as his father's thumb. The queen of the fairies came in at the window as the mother was sitting up in bed admiring the child. Her majesty kissed the infant, and, giving it the name of Tom Thumb, immediately summoned several fairies from Fairyland, to clothe her new little favourite:–

"An oak-leaf hat he had for his crown,
His shirt it was by spiders spun:
With doublet wove of thistledown,
His trousers up with points were done;
His stockings, of apple-rind, they tie
With eye-lash pluck'd from his mother's eye:
His shoes were made of a mouse's skin,
Nicely tann'd with hair within."

Tom was never any bigger than his father's thumb, which was not a large thumb neither; but as he grew older, he became very cunning, for which his mother did not sufficiently correct him: and by this ill quality he was often brought into difficulties. For instance, when he had learned to play with other boys for cherry-stones, and had lost all his own, he used to creep into the boys' bags, fill his pockets, and come out again to play. But one day as he was getting out of a bag of cherry-stones, the boy to whom it belonged chanced to see him.

"Ah, ha, my little Tom Thumb!" said he, "have I caught you at your bad tricks at last? Now I will reward you for thieving." Then drawing the string tight round his neck, and shaking the bag, the cherry-stones bruised Tom's legs, thighs, and body sadly; which made him beg to be let out, and promise never to be guilty of such things any more.

Shortly afterwards Tom's mother was making a batter-pudding, and that he might see how she mixed it, he climbed on the edge of the bowl; but his foot happening to slip, he fell over head and ears into the batter, and his mother, not observing him, stirred him into the pudding, and popped him into the pot to boil. The hot water made Tom kick and struggle; and his mother, seeing the pudding jump up and down in such a furious manner, thought it was bewitched; and a tinker coming by just at the time, she quickly gave him the pudding; he put it into his budget, and walked on.

As soon as Tom could get the batter out of his mouth, he began to cry aloud, which so frightened the poor tinker, that he flung the pudding over the hedge, and ran away from it as fast as he could. The pudding being broken to pieces by the fall, Tom was released, and walked home to his mother, who gave him a kiss and put him to bed.

Tom Thumb's mother once took him with her when she went to milk the cow; and it being a very windy day, she tied him with a needleful of thread to a thistle, that he might not be blown away. The cow, liking his oak-leaf hat, took him and the thistle up at one mouthful. While the cow chewed the thistle, Tom, terrified at her great teeth, which seemed ready to crush him to pieces, roared, "Mother, mother!" as loud as he could bawl.

"Where are you, Tommy, my dear Tommy?" said the mother.

"Here, mother, here in the red cow's mouth."

The mother began to cry and wring her hands; but the cow, surprised at such odd noises in her throat, opened her mouth and let him drop out. His mother clapped him into her apron, and ran home with him. Tom's father made him a whip of a barley straw to drive the cattle with, and being one day in the field he slipped into a deep furrow. A raven flying over picked him up with a grain of corn, and flew with him to the top of a giant's castle by the sea-side, where he left him; and old Grumbo, the giant, coming soon after to walk upon his terrace, swallowed Tom like a pill, clothes and all. Tom

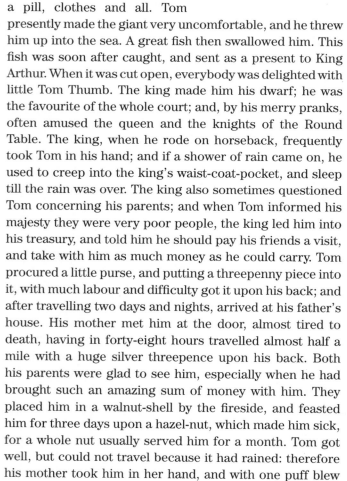

Tom's many adventures include meeting giants

presently made the giant very uncomfortable, and he threw him up into the sea. A great fish then swallowed him. This fish was soon after caught, and sent as a present to King Arthur. When it was cut open, everybody was delighted with little Tom Thumb. The king made him his dwarf; he was the favourite of the whole court; and, by his merry pranks, often amused the queen and the knights of the Round Table. The king, when he rode on horseback, frequently took Tom in his hand; and if a shower of rain came on, he used to creep into the king's waist-coat-pocket, and sleep till the rain was over. The king also sometimes questioned Tom concerning his parents; and when Tom informed his majesty they were very poor people, the king led him into his treasury, and told him he should pay his friends a visit, and take with him as much money as he could carry. Tom procured a little purse, and putting a threepenny piece into it, with much labour and difficulty got it upon his back; and after travelling two days and nights, arrived at his father's house. His mother met him at the door, almost tired to death, having in forty-eight hours travelled almost half a mile with a huge silver threepence upon his back. Both his parents were glad to see him, especially when he had brought such an amazing sum of money with him. They placed him in a walnut-shell by the fireside, and feasted him for three days upon a hazel-nut, which made him sick, for a whole nut usually served him for a month. Tom got well, but could not travel because it had rained: therefore his mother took him in her hand, and with one puff blew

him into King Arthur's court; where Tom entertained the king, queen, and nobility at tilts and tournaments, at which he exerted himself so much that he brought on a fit of sickness, and his life was despaired of. At this juncture the queen of the fairies came in a chariot, drawn by flying mice, placed Tom by her side, and drove through the air, without stopping till they arrived at her palace; when, after restoring him to health and permitting him to enjoy all the gay diversions of Fairyland, she commanded a fair wind, and, placing Tom before it, blew him straight to the court of King Arthur. But just as Tom should have alighted in the courtyard of the palace, the cook happened to pass along with the king's great bowl of furmenty (King Arthur loved furmenty), and poor Tom Thumb fell plump into the middle of it, and splashed the hot furmenty into the cook's eyes. Down went the bowl.

"Oh dear! oh dear!" cried Tom.

"Murder! murder!" bellowed the cook; and away poured the king's nice furmenty into the kennel.

The cook was a red-faced, cross fellow, and swore to the king that Tom had done it out of mere mischief; so he was taken up, tried, and sentenced to be beheaded. Tom hearing this dreadful sentence, and seeing a miller stand by with his mouth wide open, he took a good spring, and jumped down the miller's throat, unperceived by all, even by the miller himself.

Tom being lost, the court broke up, and away went the miller to his mill. But Tom did not leave him long at rest: he began to roll and tumble about, so that the miller thought himself bewitched, and sent for a doctor. When the doctor came, Tom began to dance and sing; the doctor was as much frightened as the miller, and sent in great haste for five more doctors and twenty learned men. While all these were debating upon the affair, the miller (for they were very tedious) happened to yawn, and Tom, taking the opportunity, made another jump, and alighted on his feet in the middle of the table. The miller, provoked to be thus tormented by such a little creature, fell into a great passion, caught hold of Tom, and threw him out of the window into the river. A large salmon swimming by snapped him up in a minute. The salmon was soon caught and sold in the market to a steward of a lord. The lord, thinking it an uncommon fine fish, made a present of it to the king, who ordered it to be dressed immediately. When the cook cut open the salmon, he found poor Tom, and ran with him directly to the king; but the king, being busy with state affairs, desired that he might be brought another day. The cook resolving to keep him safely this time, as he had so lately given him the slip, clapped him into a mouse-trap, and left him to amuse himself by peeping through the wires for a whole week; when the king sent for him, he forgave him for throwing down the furmenty, ordered him new clothes, and knighted him:

> "His shirt was made of butterflies' wings,
> His boots were made of chicken skins;
> His coat and breeches were made with pride:
> A tailor's needle hung by his side;
> A mouse for a horse he used to ride."

Thus dressed and mounted, he rode a-hunting with the king and nobility, who all laughed heartily at Tom and his fine prancing steed. As they rode by a farmhouse one day, a cat jumped from behind the door, seized the mouse and little Tom, and began to devour the mouse; however, Tom boldly drew his sword and attacked the cat, who then let him fall. The king and his nobles, seeing Tom falling, went to his assistance, and one of the lords caught him in his hat; but poor Tom was sadly scratched, and his clothes were torn by the claws of the cat. In this condition he was carried home, when a bed of down was made for him in a little ivory cabinet. The queen of the fairies came and took him again to Fairyland, where she kept him for some years; and then, dressing him in bright green, sent him flying once more through the air to the earth, in the days of King Thunstone. The people flocked far and near to look at him; and the king, before whom he was carried, asked him who he was, whence he came, and where he lived? Tom answered:

> "My name Is Tom Thumb,
> From the Fairies I come;
> When King Arthur shone,
> This court was my home.
> In me he delighted,
> By him I was knighted;
> Did you never hear of Sir Thomas Thumb?"

The king was so charmed with this address, that he ordered a little chair to be made, in order that Tom might sit on his table, and also a palace of gold a span high, with a door an inch wide, for little Tom to live in. He also gave him a coach drawn by six small mice, This made the queen angry, because she had not a new coach too: therefore, resolving to ruin Tom, she complained to the king that he had behaved very insolently to her. The king sent for him in a rage. Tom, to escape his fury, crept into an empty snail-shell, and there lay till he was almost starved; when, peeping out of the hole, he saw a fine butterfly settle on the ground: he now ventured out, and getting astride, the butterfly took wing, and mounted into the air with little Tom on his back. Away he flew from field to field, from tree to tree, till at last he flew to the king's court. The king, queen, and nobles, all strove to catch the butterfly, but could not. At length poor Tom, having neither bridle nor saddle, slipped from his seat, and fell into a watering-pot, where he was found almost drowned. The queen vowed he should be guillotined; but while the guillotine was getting ready, he was secured once more in a mouse-trap; when the cat, seeing something stir, and supposing it to be a mouse, patted the trap about till she broke it, and set Tom at liberty. Soon afterwards a spider, taking him for a fly, made at him. Tom drew his sword and fought valiantly, but the spider's poisonous breath overcame him:—

> "He fell dead on the ground where late he had stood, And the spider suck'd up the last drop of his blood."

King Thunstone and his whole court went into mourning for little Tom Thumb. They buried him under a rosebush, and raised a nice white marble monument over his grave, with the following epitaph:

> "Here lies Tom Thumb, King Arthur's knight,
> Who died by a spider's cruel bite.
> He was well known in Arthur's court,
> Where he afforded gallant sport;
> He rode at tilt and tournament,
> And on a mouse a-hunting went;
> Alive he fill'd the court with mirth,
> His death to sorrow soon gave birth.
> Wipe, wipe your eyes, and shake your head,
> And cry, 'Alas! Tom Thumb is dead.' "

Tom Thumb is so tiny that he can ride on a butterfly

The Story of Blue Beard

This story has Breton origins and may be based upon a medieval king there called Conomor the Cursed, a legendary cruel villain, locally said to be a werewolf; or perhaps Gilles de Rais, an aristocrat and prolific serial killer from the 1400s. It was published by Barbin in Paris in 1697. In this very bloodthirsty tale, the heroine wife – just like Lot in the Bible and Pandora who opened the box – succumbs to female curiosity and is lucky to escape a gruesome fate.

Many years ago there was a rich man who had a singular blue beard, which made him very ugly. Being left a widower, he wished to marry one of the two beautiful daughters of a neighboring lady, and at last the younger of these girls consented to be his wife.

About a month after the marriage, Blue Beard told his bride that he must leave her for a time, as he had some business to attend to at a distance. He gave her his keys, and told her to make free of everything and entertain her friends while he was absent, but ending by drawing one key from the bunch and saying:

"This small key belongs to the room at the end of the long gallery – and that, my dear, is the one room you must not enter, nor even put the key into the lock. Should you disobey, your punishment would be dreadful."

Blue Beard set out on his journey, and for a time his wife found pleasure in showing her friends all her magnificence; but again and again she wondered what could be the reason why she was not to visit the room at the end of the long gallery. At last her curiosity became such that she could not resist the temptation to take just one peep within the forbidden door. When she reached the door she stopped for a few moments to think of her husband's warning, that he would not fail to keep his word should she disobey him. But she was so very curious to know what was inside, that she determined to venture in spite of everything.

So, with a trembling hand, she put the key into the lock, and the door immediately opened. The window shutters being closed, she at first saw nothing; but in a short time she noticed that the floor was covered with clotted blood, on which the bodies of several dead women were lying. (These were all the wives whom Blue Beard had married, and murdered one after another!) She was ready to sink with fear, and the key of the door, which she held in her hand, fell on the floor. When she had somewhat recovered from her fright, she took it up, locked the door and hurried to her own room, terrified by what she had seen.

As she observed that the key had got stained with blood in falling on the floor, she wiped it two or three times to clean it; but the blood still remained; she next washed it; but the blood did not go; she then scoured it with brickdust, and afterwards with sand. But notwithstanding all she could do, the blood was still there, for the key was a fairy, who was Blue Beard's friend, so that as fast as she got the stain off one side it appeared again on the other. Early in the evening Blue Beard returned, saying he had not proceeded far before he was met by a messenger, who told him that the business was concluded without his presence being necessary. His wife said everything she could think of to make him believe that she was delighted at his unexpected return.

The next morning, he asked for the keys. She gave them, but, as she could not help showing her fright, Blue Beard easily guessed what had happened.

"How is it," said he, "that the key of the closet upon the ground floor is not here."

"Is it not?" said the wife. "I must have left it on my dressing table."

"Be sure you give it me by and by," replied Blue Beard.

After going several times backwards and forwards, pretending to look for the key, she was at last obliged to give it to Blue Beard. He looked at it attentively, and then said:

"How came this blood upon the key?"

"I am sure I do not know," replied the lady, turning as pale as death.

"You do not know?" said Blue Beard sternly. "But I know well enough. You have been in the closet on the ground floor. Very well, madam; since you are so mightily fond of this closet, you shall certainly take your place among the ladies you saw there."

His wife, almost dead with fear, fell upon her knees, asked his pardon a thousand times for her disobedience, and begged him to forgive her, looking all the time so sorrowful and lovely that she would have melted any heart that was not harder than a rock.

But Blue Beard answered:

"No, no, madam; you shall die this very minute."

"Alas," said the poor creature, "if I must die, allow me, at least, a little time to say my prayers!"

"I give you," replied the cruel Blue Beard, "half a quarter of an hour – not one moment longer."

When Bluebeard had left her to herself, she called her sister; and, after telling her that she had but half a quarter of an hour to live:

"Please," said she, "Sister Ann" (this was her sister's name), "run up to the tower, and see if my brothers are in sight; they promised to come and visit me to-day; and if you see them, make a sign for them to gallop on as fast as possible."

Her sister instantly did as she was desired, and the terrified lady every minute called out:

"Sister Ann, do you see anyone coming?"

And her sister answered:

"I see nothing but the sun, which makes a dust, and the grass, which looks green."

In the meanwhile, Blue Beard, with a great scimitar in his hand, bawled as loud as he could:

"Come down instantly, or I will fetch you."

"One moment longer, I beseech you," replied she, and again called softly to her sister:

"Sister Ann, do you see anyone coming?"

And just as Bluebeard's cruel blade was descending on her head,
In rushed the brothers with their swords,— they cut the murderer down,
And saved their sister's life, and gained much glory and renown;
And then they all with gold and plate and jewels rare made free,
And ever after lived content on Blue-beard's property.

Blue Beard's bride is rescued by her brothers

To which she answered:

"I see nothing but the sun, which makes a dust, and the grass, which looks green."

Blue Beard again bawled out:

"Come down, I say, this very moment, or I shall come and fetch you."

"I am coming; indeed I will come in one minute," sobbed his unhappy wife. Then she once more cried out:

"Sister Ann, do you see anyone coming?"

"I see," said her sister, "a cloud of dust a little to the left."

"Do you think it is my brothers?" continued the wife.

"Alas, no, dear sister," replied she, "it is only a flock of sheep!"

"Will you come down or not, madam?" said Blue Beard, in the greatest rage imaginable.

"Only one moment more," answered she. And then she called out for the last time:

"Sister Ann! Do you see no one coming?"

"I see," replied her sister, "two men on horseback coming to the house; but they are still at a great distance."

"God be praised!" cried she; "it is my brothers. Give them a sign to make what haste they can."

At the same moment Blue Beard cried out so loud for her to come down, that his voice shook the whole house. The poor lady, with her hair loose and her eyes swimming in tears, came down, and fell on her knees before Blue Beard, and was going to beg him to spare her life, but he interrupted her, saying: "All this is of no use, for you shall die;" then, seizing her with one hand by the hair, and raising the scimitar he held in the other, he was going with one blow to strike off her head.

The unfortunate woman, turning toward him, desired to have a single moment allowed her to compose herself.

"No, no," said Blue Beard; "I will give you no more time, I am determined. You have had too much already."

Again he raised his arm. Just at this instant a loud knocking was heard at the gates, which made Blue Beard wait for a moment to see who it was. The gates were opened, and two officers entered with their swords in their hands. Blue Beard, seeing they were his wife's brothers, endeavoured to escape, but they pursued and seized him before he had got twenty steps, and, plunging their swords into his body, laid him dead at their feet.

The poor wife, who was almost as dead as her husband, was unable at first to rise and embrace her brothers, but she soon recovered.

As Blue Beard had no heirs, she found herself the possessor of his great riches. She used part of her vast fortune in giving a marriage dowry to her sister Ann, who soon after was married. With another part she bought captains' commissions for her two brothers; and the rest she presented to a most worthy gentleman whom she married soon after, and whose kind treatment soon made her forget Blue Beard's cruelty.

A Voyage to Lilliput

A mural of Gulliver in Lilliput on the façade of a Bremen toy-shop

Never out of print since it was published in 1726, in *Gulliver's Travels* clergyman Jonathan Swift tells the story of a shipwrecked sea surgeon and captain who meets many unusual tribes including minute people in Lilliput and giants in Brobdingnag. The book is a satire that serves to depict the sorry state of European government and petty squabbles over religious differences.

Driven by a violent storm the ship in which Gulliver was sailing split upon a rock . . .

What became of my companions in the boat, or those who escaped on the rock or were left in the vessel, I cannot tell; but I conclude they were all lost. For my part, I swam as fortune directed me, and was pushed forward by wind and tide; but when I was able to struggle no longer I found myself within my depth. By this time the storm was much abated. I reached the shore at last, about eight o'clock in the evening, and advanced nearly half a mile inland, but could not discover any sign of inhabitants. I was extremely tired, and with the heat of the weather I found myself much inclined to

sleep. I lay down on the grass, which was very short and soft, and slept sounder than ever I did in my life for about nine hours. When I woke, it was just daylight. I attempted to rise, but could not; for as I happened to be lying on my back, I found my arms and legs were fastened on each side to the ground; and my hair, which was long and thick, tied down in the same manner. I could only look upward. The sun began to grow hot, and the light hurt my eyes. I heard a confused noise about me, but could see nothing except the sky. In a little time I felt something alive and moving on my left leg, which, advancing gently over my breast, came almost up to my chin, when, bending my eyes downward, I perceived it to be a human creature, not six inches high, with a bow and arrow in his hands, and a quiver at his back. In the meantime I felt at least forty more following the first. I was in the utmost astonishment, and roared so loud that they all ran back in a fright; and some of them were hurt with the falls they got by leaping from my sides upon the ground. However, they soon returned, and one of them, who ventured so far as to get a full sight of my face, lifted up his hands in admiration. I lay all this while in great uneasiness; but at length, struggling to get loose, I succeeded in breaking the strings that fastened my left arm to the ground; and at the same time, with a violent pull that gave me extreme pain, I a little loosened the strings that tied down my hair, so that I was just able to turn my head about two inches. But the creatures ran off a second time before I could seize them, whereupon there was a great shout, and in an instant I felt above a hundred arrows discharged on my left hand, which pricked me like so many needles. Moreover, they shot another flight into the air, of which some fell on my face, which I immediately covered with my left hand. When this shower of arrows was over I groaned with grief and pain, and then, striving again to get loose, they discharged another flight of arrows larger than the first, and some of them tried to stab me with their spears; but by good luck I had on a leather jacket, which they could not pierce. By this time I thought it most prudent to lie still till night, when, my left hand being already loose, I could easily free myself; and as for the inhabitants, I thought I might be a match for the greatest army they could bring against me if they were all of the same size as him I saw. When the people observed that I was quiet they discharged no more arrows, but by the noise I heard I knew that their number was increased; and about four yards from me, for more than an hour, there was a knocking, like people at work. Then, turning my head that way as well as the pegs and strings would let me, I saw a stage set up, about a foot and a half from the ground, with two or three ladders to mount it. From this, one of them, who seemed to be a person of quality, made me a long speech, of which I could not understand a word, though I could tell from his manner that he sometimes threatened me, and sometimes spoke with pity and kindness. I answered in few words, but in the most submissive manner; and, being almost famished with hunger, I could not help showing my impatience by putting my finger frequently to my mouth, to signify that I wanted food. He understood me very well, and, descending from the stage, commanded that several ladders should be set against my sides, on which more than a hundred of the inhabitants mounted, and walked toward my mouth with baskets full of food, which had been sent by the King's orders when he first received tidings of me. There were legs and shoulders like mutton but smaller than the wings of a lark. I ate them two or three at a mouthful, and took three loaves at a time. They supplied me as fast as they could, with a thousand marks of wonder at my appetite. I then made a sign that I wanted something to drink. They guessed that a small quantity would not suffice me, and, being a most ingenious people, they slung up one of their largest hogsheads, then rolled it toward my hand, and beat out the top. I drank it off at a draught, which I might well do, for it did not hold half a pint. They brought me a second hogshead, which I drank, and made signs for more; but they had none to give me. However, I could not wonder enough at the daring of these tiny mortals, who ventured to mount and walk upon my body, while one of my hands was free, without trembling at the very sight of so huge a creature as I must have seemed to them.

After some time there appeared before me a person of high rank from his Imperial Majesty. His Excellency, having mounted my right leg, advanced to my face, with about a dozen of his retinue, and spoke about ten minutes, often pointing forward, which, as I afterward found, was toward the capital city, about half a mile distant, whither it was commanded by his Majesty that I should be conveyed. I made a sign with my hand that was loose, putting it to the other (but over his Excellency's head, for fear of hurting him or his train), to show that I desired my liberty. He seemed to understand me well enough, for he shook his head, though he made other signs to let me know that I should have meat and drink enough, and very good treatment. Then I once more thought of attempting to escape; but when I felt the smart of their arrows on my face and hands, which were all in blisters and observed likewise that the number of my enemies increased, I gave tokens to let them know that they might do with me what they pleased. Then they daubed my face and hands with a sweet-smelling ointment, which in a few minutes removed all the smarts of the arrows. The relief from pain and hunger made me drowsy, and presently I fell asleep. I slept about eight hours, as I was told afterward; and it was no wonder, for the physicians, by the Emperor's orders, had mingled a sleeping draught in the hogsheads of wine.

It seems that, when I was discovered sleeping on the ground after my landing, the Emperor had early notice of it, and determined that I should be tied in the manner I have related (which was done in the night, while I slept), that plenty of meat and drink should be sent me, and a machine prepared to carry me to the capital city. Five hundred carpenters and engineers were immediately set to work to prepare the engine. It was a frame of wood, raised three inches from the ground, about seven feet long and four wide, moving upon twenty-two wheels. But the difficulty was to place me on it. Eighty poles were erected for this purpose, and very strong cords fastened to bandages which the workmen had tied round my neck, hands, body, and legs. Nine hundred of the strongest men were employed to draw up these cords by pulleys fastened on the poles, and in less than three hours I was raised and slung into the engine, and there tied fast. Fifteen hundred of the Emperor's largest horses, each about four inches and a half high, were then employed to draw me toward the capital. But while all this was done I still lay in a deep sleep, and I did not wake till four hours after we began our journey.

The Emperor and all his Court came out to meet us when we reached the capital; but his great officials would not suffer his Majesty to risk his person by mounting on my body. Where the carriage stopped there stood an ancient temple, supposed to be the largest in the whole kingdom, and here it was determined that I should lodge. Near the great gate, through which I could easily creep, they fixed ninety-one chains, like those which hang to a lady's watch, which were locked to my left leg with thirty-six padlocks;

and when the workmen found it was impossible for me to break loose, they cut all the strings that bound me. Then I rose up, feeling as melancholy as ever I did in my life. But the noise and astonishment of the people on seeing me rise and walk were inexpressible. The chains that held my left leg were about two yards long, and gave me not only freedom to walk backward and forward in a semicircle, but to creep in and lie at full length inside the temple. The Emperor, advancing toward me from among his courtiers, all most magnificently clad, surveyed me with great admiration, but kept beyond the length of my chain. He was taller by about the breadth of my nail than any of his Court, which alone was enough to strike awe into the beholders, and graceful and majestic. The better to behold him, I lay down on my side, so that my face was level with his, and he stood three yards off. However, I have had him since many times in my hand, and therefore cannot be deceived. His dress was very simple; but he wore a light helmet of gold, adorned with jewels and a plume. He held his sword drawn in his hand, to defend himself if I should break loose; it was almost three inches long, and the hilt was of gold, enriched with diamonds. His voice was shrill, but very clear. His Imperial Majesty spoke often to me, and I answered; but neither of us could understand a word.

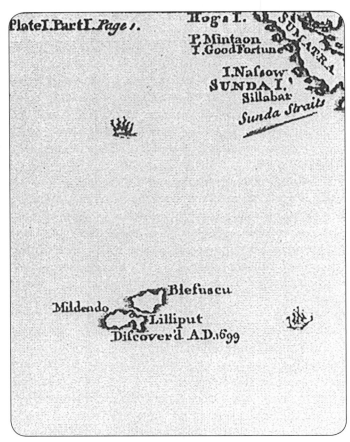

Gulliver's rough-drawn map

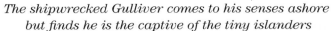

*The shipwrecked Gulliver comes to his senses ashore
but finds he is the captive of the tiny islanders*

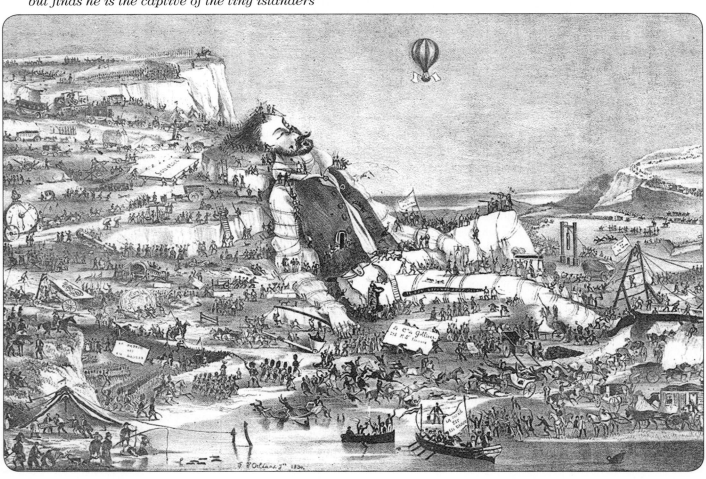

Beauty and the Beast

This story by Jeanne-Marie Le Prince de Beaumont was first published in 1756 in France as *La Belle et la Bête* with the earliest English translation appearing in 1757. The tale was intended for young ladies of quality (from five to thirteen) to be read to them by their governess, Mrs Affable. Although the basic plot of Beaumont's *Beauty and the Beast* comes from a widespread folktale, its most immediate source was a collection made by Gabrielle-Suzanne Barbot, Dame de Villeneuve, in whose 200-page-long version, the tale was said have been told at sea by a chambermaid to a young emigrant en route for the Americas.

There was once a very rich merchant, who had six children, three sons, and three daughters; being a man of sense, he spared no cost for their education, but gave them all kinds of masters. His daughters were extremely handsome, especially the youngest. When she was little everybody admired her, and called her "The little Beauty;" so that, as she grew up, she still went by the name of Beauty, which made her sisters very jealous.

The youngest, as she was handsomer, was also better than her sisters. The two eldest had a great deal of pride, because they were rich. They gave themselves ridiculous airs, and would not visit other merchants' daughters, nor keep company with any but persons of quality. They went out every day to parties of pleasure, balls, plays, concerts, and so forth, and they laughed at their youngest sister, because she spent the greatest part of her time in reading good books.

As it was known that they were great fortunes, several eminent merchants made their addresses to them; but the two eldest said, they would never marry, unless they could meet with a duke, or an earl at least. Beauty very civilly thanked them that courted her, and told them she was too young yet to marry, but chose to stay with her father a few years longer.

All at once the merchant lost his whole fortune, excepting a small country house at a great distance from town, and told his children with tears in his eyes, they must go there and work for their living. The two eldest answered, that they would not leave the town, for they had several lovers, who they were sure would be glad to have them, though they had no fortune; but the good ladies were mistaken, for their lovers slighted and forsook them in their poverty. As they were not beloved on account of their pride, everybody said; they do not deserve to be pitied, we are very glad to see their pride humbled, let them go and give themselves quality airs in milking the cows and minding their dairy. But, added they, we are extremely concerned for Beauty, she was such a charming, sweet-tempered creature, spoke so kindly to poor people, and was of such an affable, obliging behaviour. Nay, several gentlemen would have married her, though they knew she had not a penny; but she told them she could not think of leaving her poor father in his misfortunes, but was determined to go along with him into the country to comfort and attend him. Poor Beauty at first was sadly grieved at the loss of her fortune; "but," said she to herself, "were I to cry ever so much, that would not make things better, I must try to make myself happy without a fortune."

When they came to their country house, the merchant and his three sons applied themselves to husbandry and tillage; and Beauty rose at four in the morning, and made haste to have the house clean, and dinner ready for the family. In the beginning she found it very difficult, for she had not been used to work as a servant, but in less than two months she grew stronger and healthier than ever. After she had done her work, she read, played on the harpsichord, or else sung whilst she spun.

On the contrary, her two sisters did not know how to spend their time; they got up at ten, and did nothing but saunter about the whole day, lamenting the loss of their fine clothes and acquaintance. "Do but see our youngest sister," said they, one to the other, "what a poor, stupid, mean-spirited creature she is, to be contented with such an unhappy dismal situation."

The good merchant was of quite a different opinion; he knew very well that Beauty outshone her sisters, in her person as well as her mind, and admired her humility and industry, but above all her humility and patience; for her sisters not only left her all the work of the house to do, but insulted her every moment.

The family had lived about a year in this retirement, when the merchant received a letter with an account that a vessel, on board of which he had effects, was safely arrived. This news had liked to have turned the heads of the two eldest daughters, who immediately flattered themselves with the hopes of returning to town, for they were quite weary of a country life; and when they saw their father ready to set out, they begged of him to buy them new gowns, headdresses, ribbons, and all manner of trifles; but Beauty asked for nothing for she thought to herself, that all the money her father was going to receive, would scarce be sufficient to purchase everything her sisters wanted.

"What will you have, Beauty?" said her father.

"Since you have the goodness to think of me," answered she, "be so kind to bring me a rose, for as none grows hereabouts, they are a kind of rarity." Not that Beauty cared for a rose, but she asked for something, lest she should seem by her example to condemn her sisters' conduct, who would have said she did it only to look particular.

The good man went on his journey, but when he came there, they went to law with him about the merchandise, and after a great deal of trouble and pains to no purpose, he came back as poor as before.

He was within thirty miles of his own house, thinking on the pleasure he should have in seeing his children again, when going through a large forest he lost himself. It rained and snowed terribly; besides, the wind was so high, that it threw him twice off his horse, and night coming on, he began to apprehend being either starved to death with cold and hunger, or else devoured by the wolves, whom he heard howling all round him, when, on a sudden, looking through a long walk of trees, he saw a light at some distance, and going on a little farther perceived it came from a place illuminated from top to bottom. The merchant returned

"Beauty," said the monster, "will you give me leave to see you sup?"

God thanks for this happy discovery, and hastened to the place, but was greatly surprised at not meeting with any one in the outer courts. His horse followed him, and seeing a large stable open, went in, and finding both hay and oats, the poor beast, who was almost famished, fell to eating very heartily; the merchant tied him up to the manger, and walking towards the house, where he saw no one, but entering into a large hall, he found a good fire, and a table plentifully set out with but one cover laid. As he was wet quite through with the rain and snow, he drew near the fire to dry himself. "I hope," said he, "the master of the house, or his servants will excuse the liberty I take; I suppose it will not be long before some of them appear."

He waited a considerable time, until it struck eleven, and still nobody came. At last he was so hungry that he could stay no longer, but took a chicken, and ate it in two mouthfuls, trembling all the while. After this he drank a few glasses of wine, and growing more courageous he went out of the hall, and crossed through several grand apartments with magnificent furniture, until he came into a chamber, which had an exceeding good bed in it, and as he was very much fatigued, and it was past midnight, he concluded it was best to shut the door, and go to bed.

It was ten the next morning before the merchant waked, and as he was going to rise he was astonished to see a good suit of clothes in the room of his own, which were quite spoiled; certainly, said he, this palace belongs to some kind fairy, who has seen and pitied my distress. He looked through a window, but instead of snow saw the most delightful arbors, interwoven with the beautifullest flowers that were ever beheld. He then returned to the great hall, where he had supped the night before, and found some chocolate ready made on a little table. "Thank you, good Madam Fairy," said he aloud, "for being so careful, as to provide me a breakfast; I am extremely obliged to you for all your favours."

The good man drank his chocolate, and then went to look for his horse, but passing through an arbour of roses he remembered Beauty's request to him, and gathered a branch on which were several; immediately he heard a great noise, and saw such a frightful Beast coming towards him, that he was ready to faint away.

"You are very ungrateful," said the Beast to him, in a terrible voice; "I have saved your life by receiving you into my castle, and, in return, you steal my roses, which I value beyond any thing in the universe, but you shall die for it; I give you but a quarter of an hour to prepare yourself, and say your prayers."

The merchant fell on his knees, and lifted up both his hands, "My lord," said he, "I beseech you to forgive me, indeed I had no intention to offend in gathering a rose for one of my daughters, who desired me to bring her one."

"My name is not My Lord," replied the monster, "but Beast; I don't love compliments, not I. I like people to speak as they think; and so do not imagine, I am to be moved by any of your flattering speeches. But you say

you have got daughters. I will forgive you, on condition that one of them come willingly, and suffer for you. Let me have no words, but go about your business, and swear that if your daughter refuse to die in your stead, you will return within three months."

The merchant had no mind to sacrifice his daughters to the ugly monster, but he thought, in obtaining this respite, he should have the satisfaction of seeing them once more, so he promised, upon oath, he would return, and the Beast told him he might set out when he pleased, "but," added he, "you shall not depart empty handed; go back to the room where you lay, and you will see a great empty chest; fill it with whatever you like best, and I will send it to your home," and at the same time Beast withdrew.

"Well," said the good man to himself, "if I must die, I shall have the comfort, at least, of leaving something to my poor children." He returned to the bedchamber, and finding a great quantity of broad pieces of gold, he filled the great chest the Beast had mentioned, locked it, and afterwards took his horse out of the stable, leaving the palace with as much grief as he had entered it with joy. The horse, of his own accord, took one of the roads of the forest, and in a few hours the good man was at home.

His children came round him, but instead of receiving their embraces with pleasure, he looked on them, and holding up the branch he had in his hands, he burst into tears. "Here, Beauty," said he, "take these roses, but little do you think how dear they are like to cost your unhappy father," and then related his fatal adventure. Immediately the two eldest set up lamentable outcries, and said all manner of ill-natured things to Beauty, who did not cry at all.

"Do but see the pride of that little wretch," said they; "she would not ask for fine clothes, as we did; but no truly, Miss wanted to distinguish herself, so now she will be the death of our poor father, and yet she does not so much as shed a tear."

"Why should I," answered Beauty, "it would be very needless, for my father shall not suffer upon my account; since the monster will accept of one of his daughters, I will deliver myself up to all his fury, and I am very happy in thinking that my death will save my father's life, and be a proof of my tender love for him."

"No, sister," said her three brothers, "that shall not be, we will go find the monster, and either kill him, or perish in the attempt."

"Do not imagine any such thing, my sons," said the merchant, "Beast's power is so great, that I have no hopes of your overcoming him. I am charmed with Beauty's kind and generous offer, but I cannot yield to it. I am old, and have not long to live, so can only loose a few years, which I regret for your sakes alone, my dear children."

"Indeed father," said Beauty, "you shall not go to the palace without me, you cannot hinder me from following you." It was to no purpose all they could say. Beauty still insisted on setting out for the fine palace, and her sisters were delighted at it, for her virtue and amiable qualities made them envious and jealous.

The merchant was so afflicted at the thoughts of losing his daughter, that he had quite forgot the chest full of gold, but at night when he retired to rest, no sooner had he shut his chamber door, than, to his great astonishment, he found it by his bedside; he was determined, however, not to tell his children, that he was grown rich, because they would have wanted to return to town, and he was resolved not to leave the country; but he trusted Beauty with the secret, who informed him, that two gentlemen came in his absence, and courted her sisters; she begged her father to consent to their marriage, and give them fortunes, for she was so good, that she loved them and forgave heartily all their ill usage. These wicked creatures rubbed their eyes with an onion to force some tears when they parted with their sister, but her brothers were really concerned. Beauty was the only one who did not shed tears at parting, because she would not increase their uneasiness.

The horse took the direct road to the palace, and towards evening they perceived it illuminated as at first. The horse went of himself into the stable, and the good man and his daughter came into the great hall, where they found a table splendidly served up, and two covers. The merchant had no heart to eat, but Beauty, endeavouring to appear cheerful, sat down to table, and helped him. "Afterwards," thought she to herself, "Beast surely has a mind to fatten me before he eats me, since he provides such plentiful entertainment." When they had supped they heard a great noise, and the merchant, all in tears, bid his poor child, farewell, for he thought Beast was coming. Beauty was sadly terrified at his horrid form, but she took courage as well as she could, and the monster having asked her if she came willingly; "ye -- e -- es," said she, trembling.

The beast responded, "You are very good, and I am greatly obliged to you; honest man, go your ways tomorrow morning, but never think of coming here again."

"Farewell Beauty, farewell Beast," answered he, and immediately the monster withdrew. "Oh, daughter," said the merchant, embracing Beauty, "I am almost frightened to death, believe me, you had better go back, and let me stay here."

"No, father," said Beauty, in a resolute tone, "you shall set out tomorrow morning, and leave me to the care and protection of providence." They went to bed, and thought they should not close their eyes all night; but scarce were they laid down, than they fell fast asleep, and Beauty dreamed, a fine lady came, and said to her, "I am content, Beauty, with your good will, this good action of yours in giving up your own life to save your father's shall not go unrewarded." Beauty waked, and told her father her dream, and though it helped to comfort him a little, yet he could not help crying bitterly, when he took leave of his dear child.

As soon as he was gone, Beauty sat down in the great hall, and fell a crying likewise; but as she was mistress of a great deal of resolution, she recommended herself to God, and resolved not to be uneasy the little time she had to live; for she firmly believed Beast would eat her up that night.

However, she thought she might as well walk about until then, and view this fine castle, which she could not help admiring; it was a delightful pleasant place, and she was extremely surprised at seeing a door, over which was written, "Beauty's Apartment." She opened it hastily, and was quite dazzled with the magnificence that reigned throughout; but what chiefly took up her attention, was a large library, a harpsichord, and several music books. "Well," said she to herself, "I see they will not let my time hang heavy upon my hands for want of amusement." Then she reflected, "Were I but to stay here a day, there would not have been all these preparations." This consideration inspired her with fresh courage; and opening the library she took a book, and read these words, in letters of gold:

Welcome Beauty, banish fear,
You are queen and mistress here.
Speak your wishes, speak your will,
Swift obedience meets them still.

"Alas," said she, with a sigh, "there is nothing I desire so much as to see my poor father, and know what he is doing." She had no sooner said this, when casting her eyes on a great looking glass, to her great amazement, she saw her own home, where her father arrived with a very dejected countenance. Her sisters went to meet him, and notwithstanding their endeavours to appear sorrowful, their joy, felt for having got rid of their sister, was visible in every feature. A moment after, everything disappeared, and Beauty's apprehensions at this proof of Beast's complaisance.

At noon she found dinner ready, and while at table, was entertained with an excellent concert of music, though without seeing anybody. But at night, as she was going to sit down to supper, she heard the noise Beast made, and could not help being sadly terrified. "Beauty," said the monster, "will you give me leave to see you sup?"

"That is as you please," answered Beauty trembling.

"No," replied the Beast, "you alone are mistress here; you need only bid me gone, if my presence is troublesome, and I will immediately withdraw. But, tell me, do not you think me very ugly?"

"That is true," said Beauty, "for I cannot tell a lie, but I believe you are very good natured."

"So I am," said the monster, "but then, besides my ugliness, I have no sense; I know very well, that I am a poor, silly, stupid creature."

"'Tis no sign of folly to think so," replied Beauty, "for never did fool know this, or had so humble a conceit of his own understanding."

"Eat then, Beauty," said the monster, "and endeavour to amuse yourself in your palace, for everything here is yours, and I should be very uneasy, if you were not happy."

"You are very obliging," answered Beauty, "I own I am pleased with your kindness, and when I consider that, your deformity scarce appears."

"Yes, yes," said the Beast, "my heart is good, but still I am a monster."

"Among mankind," says Beauty, "there are many that deserve that name more than you, and I prefer you, just as you are, to those, who, under a human form, hide a treacherous, corrupt, and ungrateful heart."

"If I had sense enough," replied the Beast, "I would make a fine compliment to thank you, but I am so dull, that I can only say, I am greatly obliged to you."

Beauty ate a hearty supper, and had almost conquered her dread of the monster; but she had like to have fainted away, when he said to her, "Beauty, will you be my wife?"

She was some time before she dared answer, for she was afraid of making him angry, if she refused. At last, however, she said trembling, "no Beast." Immediately the poor monster went to sigh, and hissed so frightfully, that the whole palace echoed. But Beauty soon recovered her fright, for Beast having said, in a mournful voice, "then farewell, Beauty," left the room; and only turned back, now and then, to look at her as he went out.

When Beauty was alone, she felt a great deal of compassion for poor Beast. "Alas," said she, "'tis thousand pities, anything so good natured should be so ugly."

Beauty spent three months very contentedly in the palace. Every evening Beast paid her a visit, and talked to her, during supper, very rationally, with plain good common sense, but never with what the world calls wit; and Beauty daily discovered some valuable qualifications in the monster, and seeing him often had so accustomed her to his deformity, that, far from dreading the time of his visit, she would often look on her watch to see when it would be nine, for the Beast never missed coming at that hour. There was but one thing that gave Beauty any concern, which was, that every night, before she went to bed, the monster always asked her, if she would be his wife. One day she said to him, "Beast, you make me very uneasy, I wish I could consent to marry you, but I am too sincere to make you believe that will ever happen; I shall always esteem you as a friend, endeavor to be satisfied with this."

"I must," said the Beast, "for, alas! I know too well my own misfortune, but then I love you with the tenderest affection. However, I ought to think myself happy, that you will stay here; promise me never to leave me."

Beauty blushed at these words; she had seen in her glass, that her father had pined himself sick for the loss of her, and she longed to see him again. "I could," answered she, "indeed, promise never to leave you entirely, but I have so great a desire to see my father, that I shall fret to death, if you refuse me that satisfaction."

"I had rather die myself," said the monster, "than give you the least uneasiness. I will send you to your father, you shall remain with him, and poor Beast will die with grief."

"No," said Beauty, weeping, "I love you too well to be the cause of your death. I give you my promise to return in a week. You have shown me that my sisters are married, and my brothers gone to the army; only let me stay a week with my father, as he is alone."

"You shall be there tomorrow morning," said the Beast, "but remember your promise. You need only lay your ring on a table before you go to bed, when you have a mind to come back. Farewell Beauty." Beast sighed, as usual, bidding her good night, and Beauty went to bed very sad at seeing him so afflicted. When she waked the next morning, she found herself at her father's, and having rung a little bell, that was by her bedside, she saw the maid come, who, the moment she saw her, gave a loud shriek, at which the good man ran up stairs, and thought he should have died with joy to see his dear daughter again. He held her fast locked in his arms above a quarter of an hour. As soon as the first transports were over, Beauty began to think of rising, and was afraid she had no clothes to put on; but the maid told her, that she had just found, in the next room, a large trunk full of gowns, covered with gold and diamonds. Beauty thanked good Beast for his kind care, and taking one of the plainest of them, she intended to make a present of the others to her sisters. She scarce had said so when the trunk disappeared. Her father told her, that Beast insisted on her keeping them herself, and immediately both gowns and trunk came back again.

Beauty dressed herself, and in the meantime they sent to her sisters who hastened thither with their husbands. They were both of them very unhappy. The eldest had married a gentleman, extremely handsome indeed, but so fond of his own person, that he was full of nothing but his own dear self, and neglected his wife. The second had married a man of wit, but he only made use of it to plague and torment everybody, and his wife most of all. Beauty's sisters sickened with envy, when they saw her dressed like a princess, and more beautiful than ever, nor could all her obliging affectionate behavior stifle their jealousy, which was ready to burst when she told them how happy she was. They went down into the garden to vent it in tears; and said one to the other, in what way is this little creature better than us, that she should be so much happier? "Sister," said the oldest, "a thought just strikes my mind; let us endeavor to detain her above a week, and perhaps the silly monster will be so enraged at her for breaking her word, that he will devour her."

"Right, sister," answered the other, "therefore we must show her as much kindness as possible." After they had taken this resolution, they went up, and behaved so affectionately to their sister, that poor Beauty wept for joy. When the week was expired, they cried and tore their hair, and seemed so sorry to part with her, that she promised to stay a week longer.

In the meantime, Beauty could not help reflecting on herself, for the uneasiness she was likely to cause poor Beast, whom she sincerely loved, and really longed to see again. The tenth night she spent at her father's, she dreamed she was in the palace garden, and that she saw Beast extended on the grass plat, who seemed just expiring, and, in a dying voice, reproached her with her ingratitude. Beauty started out of her sleep, and bursting into tears. "Am I not very wicked," said she, "to act so unkindly to Beast, that has studied so much, to please me in everything? Is it his fault if he is so ugly, and has so little sense? He is kind and good, and that is sufficient. Why did I refuse to marry him? I should be happier with the monster than my sisters are with their husbands; it is neither wit, nor a fine person, in a husband, that makes a woman happy, but virtue, sweetness of temper, and complaisance, and Beast has all these valuable qualifications. It is true, I do not feel the tenderness of affection for him, but I find I have the highest gratitude, esteem, and friendship; I will not make him miserable, were I to be so ungrateful I should never forgive myself." Beauty having said this, rose, put her ring on the table, and then laid down again; scarce was she in bed before she fell asleep, and when she waked the next morning, she was overjoyed to find herself in the Beast's palace.

She put on one of her richest suits to please him, and waited for evening with the utmost impatience, at last the wished-for hour came, the clock struck nine, yet no Beast appeared. Beauty then feared she had been the cause of his death; she ran crying and wringing her hands all about the palace, like one in despair; after having sought for him everywhere, she recollected her dream, and flew to the canal in the garden, where she dreamed she saw him. There she found poor Beast stretched out, quite senseless, and, as she imagined, dead. She threw herself upon him without any dread, and finding his heart beat still, she fetched some water from the canal, and poured it on his head. Beast opened his eyes, and said to Beauty, "You forgot your promise, and I was so afflicted for having lost you, that I resolved to starve myself, but since I have the happiness of seeing you once more, I die satisfied."

"No, dear Beast," said Beauty, "you must not die. Live to be my husband; from this moment I give you my hand, and swear to be none but yours. Alas! I thought I had only a friendship for you, but the grief I now feel convinces me, that I cannot live without you." Beauty scarce had pronounced these words, when she saw the palace sparkle with light; and fireworks, instruments of music, everything seemed to give notice of some great event. But nothing could fix her attention; she turned to her dear Beast, for whom she trembled with fear; but how great was her surprise! Beast was disappeared, and she saw, at her feet, one of the loveliest princes that eye ever beheld; who returned her thanks for having put an end to the charm, under which he had so long resembled a Beast. Though this prince was worthy of all her attention, she could not forbear asking where Beast was.

"You see him at your feet, said the prince. A wicked fairy had condemned me to remain under that shape until a beautiful virgin should consent to marry me. The fairy

likewise enjoined me to conceal my understanding. There was only you in the world generous enough to be won by the goodness of my temper, and in offering you my crown I can't discharge the obligations I have to you."

Beauty, agreeably surprised, gave the charming prince her hand to rise; they went together into the castle, and Beauty was overjoyed to find, in the great hall, her father and his whole family, whom the beautiful lady, that appeared to her in her dream, had conveyed thither.

"Beauty," said this lady, "come and receive the reward of your judicious choice; you have preferred virtue before either wit or beauty, and deserve to find a person in whom all these qualifications are united. You are going to be a great queen. I hope the throne will not lessen your virtue, or make you forget yourself. As to you, ladies," said the fairy to Beauty's two sisters, "I know your hearts, and all the malice they contain. Become two statues, but, under this transformation, still retain your reason. You shall stand before your sister's palace gate, and be it your punishment to behold her happiness; and it will not be in your power to return to your former state, until

Beauty begged the Beast not to die

you own your faults, but I am very much afraid that you will always remain statues. Pride, anger, gluttony, and idleness are sometimes conquered, but the conversion of a malicious and envious mind is a kind of miracle."

Immediately the fairy gave a stroke with her wand, and in a moment all that were in the hall were transported into the prince's dominions. His subjects received him with joy. He married Beauty, and lived with her many years, and their happiness – as it was founded on virtue – was complete.

Peter and the Wolf

This story is from Sergei Prokofiev's introduction to his 25-minute-long musical piece written in 1936 as a new symphony to introduce music and the orchestra to children – a commission Prokofiev completed in just four days.

One morning, a young boy named Peter opened his gate and walked out into the big green meadow that was beyond it. On a branch of a big tree in the meadow sat a little bird that was Peter's friend. "All is quiet!" the bird chirped. A duck came waddling around. She was glad that Peter had not closed the gate and, seeing that it was open, decided to take a nice swim in the deep pond in the meadow. The little bird saw the duck and flew down upon on the grass. The bird settled next to her and shrugged his shoulders. "What kind of bird are you if you can't fly?" said the bird. The duck replied, "What kind of bird are you if you can't swim?" and dove into the pond. The bird and the duck kept arguing, and the duck swam around the pond while the little bird hopped along the edge of the pond. Suddenly, something caught Peter's attention. He looked around and noticed a sly cat crawling through the grass. The cat thought; "That little bird is busy arguing with the duck, I'll just grab him while he is busy!"

Very carefully, on her little velvet paws, she crept towards him. "Look out!" shouted Peter and the little bird flew up into the tree for safety, while the duck quacked as loud as he could at the cat, from the middle of the pond. The cat walked around the tree and thought, "Is it worth using up so much energy and climbing up so high into the tree? By the time I get there the bird will have flown away."

Just then, Peter's grandfather came out of their house. He was upset because Peter had gone in the meadow without his permission. "The meadow is a dangerous place! If a wolf should come out of the forest, then what would you do? You would be in great danger!" But Peter paid no attention to his grandfather's words.

Boys like him are not afraid of wolves. Grandfather took Peter by the hand, locked the gate and led him home.

No sooner had Peter gone back into his house, than a big gray wolf came out of the forest.

In a second, the cat climbed up the tree. The duck quacked, and leapt out of the pond. But no matter how hard the duck tried to run, she just couldn't outrun the wolf. He was getting closer and closer and catching up with her! Then, he grabbed her with his teeth and with one gulp, swallowed her. And now, this is how things stood: the cat was sitting on one branch, the bird on another, not too close to the cat. And the wolf walked around and around the tree, looking at the cat and the bird with very hungry eyes. In the meantime, Peter, without the slightest fear, stood behind the closed gate and watched everything that was happening. He ran home, got a strong rope, and climbed up the high stone wall that divided his yard from the meadow. One of the branches of the tree around which the wolf was walking stretched out way beyond the stone wall. Grabbing hold of the branch, Peter carefully and quietly climbed onto the tree. Peter said to the bird: "Fly down and circle over the wolf's head. Try to distract him! But, be careful that he doesn't catch you." The bird flew around the wolf and almost touched the wolf's head with his wings while the wolf snapped angrily at him with his jaws, from this side and that.

Oh, how the bird annoyed the wolf – how he wanted to catch him! But the bird was clever and very quick, and the wolf simply couldn't do anything about it. Meanwhile, Peter made a lasso with the rope and carefully let it down from the tree, catching the wolf by the tail.

Peter pulled on the rope with all his might! Feeling himself caught by the rope, the wolf began to jump wildly trying to get loose. But Peter tied the other end of rope to the strong tree, and the wolf's jumping only made the rope round his tail tighter. Just then, two hunters came out of the woods, following the wolf's trail and shooting their guns as they went. But Peter, sitting in the tree, said: "Don't shoot! Birdie and I have caught the wolf. Now help us take him to the zoo." Then came the triumphant procession. Peter was at the head. After him came the two hunters leading the wolf. And winding up the procession were Grandfather and the cat. Grandfather shook his head discontentedly. "Well, what would have happened if Peter hadn't caught the wolf? What then?" Above them flew Birdie chirping merrily. "My, what brave fellows we are, Peter and I! Look what we have caught! A giant wolf!" And perhaps, if you listen very carefully, you will hear the duck quacking inside the wolf, because the wolf, in his hurry to eat her, had swallowed her alive.

Each character and element of the story
is represented by a particular instrument
and musical theme . . .
Peter – string instruments
Bird – flute
Duck – oboe
Cat – clarinet
Grandfather – bassoon
Wolf – French horns
Hunters – woodwind
Gunshots – timpani and bass drum

The Tinder Box

This story was published in 1835. It is possibly one of the stories told to Hans Christian Andersen when he was a little boy by pauper women in an asylum where his grandmother worked. The place, its occupants and the tales the old ladies there told him often made the young Andersen afraid to go out in the dark!

A tinder box

There came a soldier marching down the high road: one, two! one, two! He had his knapsack on his back and his sword at his side as he came home from the wars. On the road he met a witch, an ugly old witch, a witch whose lower lip dangled right down on her chest.

"Good evening, soldier," she said. "What a fine sword you've got there, and what a big knapsack. Aren't you every inch a soldier! And now you shall have money, as much as you please."

"That's very kind, you old witch," said the soldier.

"See that big tree." The witch pointed to one near by them. "It's hollow to the roots. Climb to the top of the trunk and you'll find a hole through which you can let yourself down deep under the tree. I'll tie a rope around your middle, so that when you call me I can pull you up again."

"What would I do deep down under that tree?" the soldier wanted to know.

"Fetch money," the witch said. "Listen. When you touch bottom you'll find yourself in a great hall. It is very bright there, because more than a hundred lamps are burning. By their light you will see three doors. Each door has a key in it, so you can open them all.

"If you walk into the first room, you'll see a large chest in the middle of the floor. On it sits a dog, and his eyes are as big as saucers. But don't worry about that. I'll give you my blue checked apron to spread out on the floor. Snatch up that dog and set him on my apron. Then you can open the chest and take out as many pieces of money as you please. They are all copper."

"But if silver suits you better, then go into the next room. There sits a dog and his eyes are as big as mill wheels. But don't you care about that. Set the dog on my apron while you line your pockets with silver."

"Maybe you'd rather have gold. You can, you know. You can have all the gold you can carry if you go into the third room. The only hitch is that there on the money-chest sits a dog, and each of his eyes is as big as the Round Tower of Copenhagen. That's the sort of dog he is. But never you mind how fierce he looks. Just set him on my apron and he'll do you no harm as you help yourself from the chest to all the gold you want."

"That suits me," said the soldier. "But what do you get out of all this, you old witch? I suppose that you want your share."

"No indeed," said the witch. "I don't want a penny of it. All I ask is for you to fetch me an old tinder box that my grandmother forgot the last time she was down there."

"Good," said the soldier. "Tie the rope around me."

"Here it is," said the witch, "and here's my blue checked apron."

The soldier climbed up to the hole in the tree and let himself slide through it, feet foremost down into the great hall where the hundreds of lamps were burning, just as the witch had said. Now he threw open the first door he came to. Ugh! There sat a dog glaring at him with eyes as big as saucers.

"You're a nice fellow," the soldier said, as he shifted him to the witch's apron and took all the coppers that his pockets would hold. He shut up the chest, set the dog back on it, and made for the second room. Alas and alack! There sat the dog with eyes as big as mill wheels.

"Don't you look at me like that." The soldier set him on the witch's apron. "You're apt to strain your eyesight." When he saw the chest brimful of silver, he threw away all his coppers and filled both his pockets and knapsack with silver alone. Then he went into the third room. Oh, what a horrible sight to see! The dog in there really did have eyes as big as the Round Tower, and when he rolled them they spun like wheels.

"Good evening," the soldier said, and saluted, for such a dog he had never seen before. But on second glance he thought to himself, "This won't do." So he lifted the dog down to the floor, and threw open the chest. What a sight! Here was gold and to spare. He could buy out all Copenhagen with it. He could buy all the cake-woman's sugar pigs, and all the tin soldiers, whips, and rocking horses there are in the world. Yes, there was really money!

In short order the soldier got rid of all the silver coins he had stuffed in his pockets and knapsack, to put gold in their place. Yes sir, he crammed all his pockets, his knapsack, his cap, and his boots so full that he scarcely could walk. Now he was made of money. Putting the dog back on the chest he banged out the door and called up through the hollow tree:

"Pull me up now, you old witch."

"Have you got the tinder box?" asked the witch.

"Confound the tinder box," the soldier shouted. "I clean forgot it."

When he fetched it, the witch hauled him up. There he stood on the highroad again, with his pockets, boots, knapsack and cap full of gold.

"What do you want with the tinder box?" he asked the old witch.

"None of your business," she told him. "You've had your money, so hand over my tinder box."

"Nonsense," said the soldier. "I'll take out my sword and I'll cut your head off if you don't tell me at once what you want with it."

"I won't," the witch screamed at him.

So he cut her head off. There she lay! But he tied all his money in her apron, slung it over his shoulder, stuck the tinder box in his pocket, and struck out for town.

It was a splendid town. He took the best rooms at the best inn, and ordered all the good things he liked to eat, for he was a rich man now because he had so much money. The servant who cleaned his boots may have thought them remarkably well worn for a man of such means, but that was before he went shopping. Next morning he bought boots worthy of him, and the best clothes. Now that he had turned out to be such a fashionable gentleman, people told him all about the splendours of their town – all about their King, and what a pretty Princess he had for a daughter.

"Where can I see her?" the soldier inquired.

"You can't see her at all," everyone said. "She lives in a great copper castle inside all sorts of walls and towers. Only the King can come in or go out of it, for it's been foretold that the Princess will marry a common soldier. The King would much rather she didn't."

"I'd like to see her just the same," the soldier thought. But there was no way to manage it.

Now he lived a merry life. He went to the theatre, drove about in the King's garden, and gave away money to poor people. This was to his credit, for he remembered from the old days what it feels like to go without a penny in your pocket. Now that he was wealthy and well dressed, he had all too many who called him their friend and a genuine gentleman. That pleased him.

But he spent money every day without making any, and wound up with only two coppers to his name. He had to quit his fine quarters to live in a garret, clean his own boots, and mend them himself with a darning needle. None of his friends came to see him, because there were too many stairs to climb.

One evening when he sat in the dark without even enough money to buy a candle, he suddenly remembered there was a candle end in the tinder box that he had picked up when the witch sent him down the hollow tree. He got out the tinder box, and the moment he struck sparks from the flint of it his door burst open and there stood a dog from down under the tree. It was the one with eyes as big as saucers.

"What," said the dog, "is my lord's command?"

"What's this?" said the soldier. "Have I got the sort of tinder box that will get me whatever I want? Go get me some money," he ordered the dog. Zip! The dog was gone. Zip! He was back again, with a bag full of copper in his mouth.

Now the soldier knew what a remarkable tinder box he had. Strike it once and there was the dog from the chest of copper coins. Strike it twice and here came the dog who had the silver. Three times brought the dog who guarded gold.

Back went the soldier to his comfortable quarters. Out strode the soldier in fashionable clothes. Immediately his friends knew him again, because they liked him so much.

Then the thought occurred to him, "Isn't it odd that no one ever gets to see the Princess? They say she's very pretty, but what's the good of it as long as she stays locked up in that large copper castle with so many towers? Why can't I see her? Where's my tinder box?" He struck a light and, zip! came the dog with eyes as big as saucers.

"It certainly is late," said the soldier. "Practically midnight. But I do want a glimpse of the Princess, if only for a moment."

Out the door went the dog, and before the soldier could believe it, here came the dog with the Princess on his back. She was sound asleep, and so pretty that everyone could see she was a Princess. The soldier couldn't keep from kissing her, because he was every inch a soldier. Then the dog took the Princess home.

Next morning when the King and Queen were drinking their tea, the Princess told them about the strange dream she'd had – all about a dog and a soldier. She'd ridden on the dog's back, and the soldier had kissed her.

"Now that was a fine story," said the Queen. The next night one of the old ladies of the court was under orders to sit by the Princess's bed, and see whether this was a dream or something else altogether. The soldier was longing to see the pretty Princess again, so the dog came by night to take her up and away as fast as he could run. But the old lady pulled on her storm boots and ran right after them. When she saw them disappear into a large house she thought, "Now I know where it is," and drew a big cross on the door with a piece of chalk. Then she went home to bed, and before long the dog brought the Princess home too. But when the dog saw that cross marked on the soldier's front door, he got himself a piece of chalk and cross-marked every door in the town. This was a clever thing to do, because now the old lady couldn't tell the right door from all the wrong doors he had marked.

Early in the morning along came the King and the Queen, the old lady, and all the officers, to see where the Princess had been.

"Here it is," said the King when he saw the first cross mark.

"No, my dear. There it is," said the Queen who was looking next door.

The witch told the soldier to climb down the hollow tree where there was a dog with huge eyes

"Here's one, there's one, and yonder's another one!" said they all. Wherever they looked they saw chalk marks, so they gave up searching.

The Queen, though, was an uncommonly clever woman, who could do more than ride in a coach. She took her big gold scissors, cut out a piece of silk, and made a neat little bag. She filled it with fine buckwheat flour and tied it on to the Princess's back. Then she pricked a little hole in it so that the flour would sift out along the way, wherever the Princess might go.

Again the dog came in the night, took the Princess on his back, and ran with her to the soldier, who loved her so much that he would have been glad to be a Prince just so he could make his wife.

The dog didn't notice how the flour made a trail from the castle right up to the soldier's window, where he ran up the wall with the Princess. So in the morning it was all too plain to the King and Queen just where their daughter had been.

They took the soldier and they put him in prison. There he sat. It was dark, and it was dismal, and they told him, "Tomorrow is the day for you to hang." That didn't cheer him up any, and as for his tinder box he'd left it behind at the inn. In the morning he could see through his narrow little window how the people all hurried out of town to see him hanged. He heard the drums beat and he saw the soldiers march. In the crowd of running people he saw a shoemaker's boy in a leather apron and slippers. The boy galloped so fast that off flew one slipper, which hit the wall right where the soldier pressed his face to the iron bars.

"Hey there, you shoemaker's boy, there's no hurry," the soldier shouted. "Nothing can happen till I get there. But if you run to where I live and bring me my tinder box, I'll give you four coppers. Put your best foot foremost."

The shoemaker's boy could use four coppers, so he rushed the tinder box to the soldier, and – well, now we shall hear what happened!

Outside the town a high gallows had been built. Around it stood soldiers and many hundred thousand people. The King and Queen sat on a splendid throne, opposite the judge and the whole council. The soldier already stood upon the ladder, but just as they were about to put the rope around his neck he said the custom was to grant a poor criminal one last small favour. He wanted to smoke a pipe of tobacco – the last he'd be smoking in this world.

The King couldn't refuse him, so the soldier struck fire from his tinder box, once – twice – and a third time. Zip! There stood all the dogs, one with eyes as big as saucers, one with eyes as big as mill wheels, one with eyes as big as the Round Tower of Copenhagen.

"Help me. Save me from hanging!" said the soldier. Those dogs took the judges and all the council, some by the leg and some by the nose, and tossed them so high that they came down broken to bits.

"Don't!" cried the King, but the biggest dog took him and the Queen too, and tossed them up after the others. Then the soldiers trembled and the people shouted, "Soldier, be our King and marry the pretty Princess."

So they put the soldier in the King's carriage. All three of his dogs danced in front of it, and shouted "Hurrah!" The boys whistled through their fingers, and the soldiers saluted. The Princess came out of the copper castle to be Queen, and that suited her exactly. The wedding lasted all of a week, and the three dogs sat at the table, with their eyes opened wider than ever before.

The Three Billy-Goats Gruff

A Norwegian fairy tale
collected by Peter Christen Asbjørnsen and Jørgen Moe,
published between 1841 and 1844.
This English version appeared in 1859, adapted by Sir
George Webbe Dasent (1817–1896), a translator of folk
tales and a contributor to *The Times*.

The goats live in a wild mountain region

Once upon a time there were three billy-goats, who were to go up to the hill-side to make themselves fat, and the name of all three was "Gruff."

On the way up was a bridge over a burn they had to cross; and under the bridge lived a great ugly Troll, with eyes as big as saucers, and a nose as long as a poker.

So first of all came the youngest billy-goat Gruff to cross the bridge.

"Trip, trap! trip, trap!" went the bridge.

"WHO'S THAT tripping over my bridge?" roared the Troll.

"Oh, it is only I, the tiniest billy-goat Gruff; and I'm going up to the hill-side to make myself fat," said the billy-goat, with such a small voice.

"Now, I'm coming to gobble you up," said the Troll.

"Oh, no! pray don't take me. I'm too little, that I am," said the billy-goat; "wait a bit till the second billy-goat Gruff comes, he's much bigger."

"Well, be off with you;" said the Troll.

A little while after came the second billy-goat Gruff to cross the bridge.

"TRIP, TRAP! TRIP, TRAP! TRIP, TRAP!" went the bridge.

"WHO'S THAT tripping over my bridge?" roared the Troll.

"Oh, it's the second billy-goat Gruff, and I'm going up to the hill-side to make myself fat," said the billy-goat, who hadn't such a small voice.

"Now I'm coming to gobble you up," said the Troll.

"Oh, no! don't take me, wait a little till the big billy-goat Gruff comes, he's much bigger."

"Very well! be off with you," said the Troll.

But just then up came the big billy-goat Gruff.

"TRIP, TRAP! TRIP, TRAP! TRIP, TRAP!" went the bridge, for the billy-goat was so heavy that the bridge creaked and groaned under him.

"WHO'S THAT tramping over my bridge?" roared the Troll.

"IT'S I! THE BIG BILLY-GOAT GRUFF," said the billy-goat, who had an ugly hoarse voice of his own.

"Now I'm coming to gobble you up," roared the Troll.

"Well, come along! I've got two spears,
And I'll poke your eyeballs out at your ears;
I've got besides two curling-stones,
And I'll crush you to bits, body and bones."

The Troll guards the bridge

That was what the big billy-goat said; and so he flew at the Troll, and poked his eyes out with his horns, and crushed him to bits, body and bones, and tossed him out into the burn, and after that he went up to the hill-side. There the billy-goats got so fat they were scarce able to walk home again; and if the fat hasn't fallen off them, why, they're still fat; and so –

Snip, snap, snout

This tale's told out.

The Ugly Duckling

It was so beautiful out in the country, it was summer – the wheat fields were golden, the oats were green, and down among the green meadows the hay was stacked. There the stork minced about on his red legs, clacking away in Egyptian, which was the language his mother had taught him. Round about the field and meadow lands rose vast forests, in which deep lakes lay hidden. Yes, it was indeed lovely out there in the country.

In the midst of the sunshine there stood an old manor house that had a deep moat around it. From the walls of the manor right down to the water's edge great burdock leaves grew, and there were some so tall that little children could stand upright beneath the biggest of them. In this wilderness of leaves, which was as dense as the forests itself, a duck sat on her nest, hatching her ducklings. She was becoming somewhat weary, because sitting is such a dull business and scarcely anyone came to see her. The other ducks would much rather swim in the moat than waddle out and squat under the burdock leaf to gossip with her.

But at last the eggshells began to crack, one after another. "Peep, peep!" said the little things, as they came to life and poked out their heads.

"Quack, quack!" said the duck, and quick as quick can be they all waddled out to have a look at the green world under the leaves. Their mother let them look as much as they pleased, because green is good for the eyes.

"How wide the world is," said all the young ducks, for they certainly had much more room now than they had when they were in their eggshells.

"Do you think this is the whole world?" their mother asked. "Why it extends on and on, clear across to the other side of the garden and right on into the parson's field, though that is further than I have ever been. I do hope you are all hatched," she said as she got up. "No, not quite all. The biggest egg still lies here. How much longer is this going to take? I am really rather tired of it all," she said, but she settled back on her nest.

"Well, how goes it?" asked an old duck who came to pay her a call.

"It takes a long time with that one egg," said the duck on the nest. "It won't crack, but look at the others. They are the cutest little ducklings I've ever seen. They look exactly like their father, the wretch! He hasn't come to see me at all."

"Let's have a look at the egg that won't crack," the old duck said. "It's a turkey egg, and you can take my word for it. I was fooled like that once myself. What trouble and care I had with those turkey children, for I may as well tell you, they are afraid of the water. I simply could not get

them into it. I quacked and snapped at them, but it wasn't a bit of use. Let me see the egg. Certainly, it's a turkey egg. Let it lie, and go teach your other children to swim."

"Oh, I'll sit a little longer. I've been at it so long already that I may as well sit here half the summer."

"Suit yourself," said the old duck, and away she waddled.

At last the big egg did crack. "Peep," said the young one, and out he tumbled, but he was so big and ugly.

The duck took a look at him. "That's a frightfully big duckling," she said. "He doesn't look the least like the others. Can he really be a turkey baby? Well, well! I'll soon find out. Into the water he shall go, even if I have to shove him in myself."

Next day the weather was perfectly splendid, and the sun shone down on all the green burdock leaves. The mother duck led her whole family down to the moat. Splash! she took to the water. "Quack, quack," said she, and one duckling after another plunged in. The water went over their heads, but they came up in a flash, and floated to perfection. Their legs worked automatically, and they were all there in the water. Even the big, ugly grey one was swimming along.

"Why, that's no turkey," she said. "See how nicely he uses his legs, and how straight he holds himself. He's my very own son after all, and quite good-looking if you look at him properly. Quack, quack, come with me. I'll lead you out into the world and introduce you to the duck yard. But keep close to me so that you won't get stepped on, and watch out for the cat!"

Thus they sallied into the duck yard, where all was in an uproar because two families were fighting over the head of an eel. But the cat got it, after all.

"You see, that's the way of the world." The mother duck licked her bill because she wanted the eel's head for herself. "Stir your legs. Bustle about, and mind that you bend your necks to that old duck over there. She's the noblest of us all, and has Spanish blood in her. That's why she's so fat. See that red rag around her leg? That's a wonderful thing, and the highest distinction a duck can get. It shows that they don't want to lose her, and that she's to have special attention from man and beast. Shake yourselves! Don't turn your toes in. A well-bred duckling turns his toes way out, just as his father and mother do – this way. So then! Now duck your necks and say quack!"

They did as she told them, but the other ducks around them looked on and said right out loud, "See here! Must we have this brood too, just as if there weren't enough of us already? And – fie! what an ugly-looking fellow that duckling is! We won't stand for him." One duck charged up and bit his neck.

"Let him alone," his mother said. "He isn't doing any harm."

"Possibly not," said the duck who bit him, "but he's too big and strange, and therefore he needs a good whacking."

"What nice-looking children you have, Mother," said the old duck with the rag around her leg. "They are all pretty except that one. He didn't come out so well. It's a pity you can't hatch him again."

"That can't be managed, your ladyship," said the mother. "He isn't so handsome, but he's as good as can be, and he swims just as well as the rest, or, I should say, even a little better than they do. I hope his looks will improve with age, and after a while he won't seem so big. He took too long in the egg, and that's why his figure isn't all that it should be." She pinched his neck and preened his feathers. "Moreover, he's a drake, so it won't matter so much. I think he will be quite strong, and I'm sure he will amount to something."

"The other ducklings are pretty enough," said the old duck. "Now make yourselves right at home, and if you find an eel's head you may bring it to me."

So they felt quite at home. But the poor duckling who had been the last one out of his egg, and who looked so ugly, was pecked and pushed about and made fun of by the ducks, and the chickens as well. "He's too big," said they all. The turkey gobbler, who thought himself an emperor because he was born wearing spurs, puffed up like a ship under full sail and bore down upon him, gobbling and gobbling until he was red in the face. The poor duckling did not know where he dared stand or where he dared walk. He was so sad because he was so desperately ugly, and because he was the laughing stock of the whole barnyard.

So it went on the first day, and after that things went from bad to worse. The poor duckling was chased and buffeted about by everyone. Even his own brothers and sisters abused him. "Oh," they would always say, "how we wish the cat would catch you, you ugly thing." And his mother said, "How I do wish you were miles away." The ducks nipped him, and the hens pecked him, and the girl who fed them kicked him with her foot.

So he ran away; and he flew over the fence. The little birds in the bushes darted up in a fright. "That's because I'm so ugly," he thought, and closed his eyes, but he ran on just the same until he reached the great marsh where the wild ducks lived. There he lay all night long, weary and disheartened.

When morning came, the wild ducks flew up to have a look at their new companion. "What sort of creature are you?" they asked, as the duckling turned in all directions, bowing his best to them all. "You are terribly ugly," they told him, "but that's nothing to us so long as you don't marry into our family."

Poor duckling! Marriage certainly had never entered his mind. All he wanted was for them to let him lie among the reeds and drink a little water from the marsh.

There he stayed for two whole days. Then he met two wild geese, or rather wild ganders – for they were males. They had not been out of the shell very long, and that's what made them so sure of themselves.

"Say there, comrade," they said, "you're so ugly that we have taken a fancy to you. Come with us and be a bird of passage. In another marsh near-by, there are some fetching wild geese, all nice young ladies who know how to quack. You are so ugly that you'll completely turn their heads."

Bing! Bang! Shots rang in the air, and these two ganders fell dead among the reeds. The water was red with their blood. Bing! Bang! the shots rang, and as whole flocks of wild geese flew up from the reeds another volley crashed. A great hunt was in progress. The hunters lay under cover all around the marsh, and some even perched on branches of trees that overhung the reeds. Blue smoke rose like clouds from the shade of the trees, and drifted far out over the water.

The bird dogs came splash, splash! through the swamp, bending down the reeds and the rushes on every side. This gave the poor duckling such a fright that he twisted his head about to hide it under his wing. But at that very moment a fearfully big dog appeared right beside him. His tongue lolled out of his mouth and his wicked eyes glared horribly. He opened his wide jaws, flashed his sharp teeth, and – splash, splash – on he went without touching the duckling.

"Thank heavens," he sighed, "I'm so ugly that the dog won't even bother to bite me."

He lay perfectly still, while the bullets splattered through the reeds as shot after shot was fired. It was late in the day before things became quiet again, and even then the poor duckling didn't dare move. He waited several hours before he ventured to look about him, and then he scurried away from that marsh as fast as he could go. He ran across field and meadows. The wind was so strong that he had to struggle to keep his feet.

Late in the evening he came to a miserable little hovel, so ramshackle that it did not know which way to tumble, and that was the only reason it still stood. The wind struck the duckling so hard that the poor little fellow had to sit down on his tail to withstand it. The storm blew stronger and stronger, but the duckling noticed that one hinge had come loose and the door hung so crooked that he could squeeze through the crack into the room, and that's just what he did.

Here lived an old woman with her cat and her hen. The cat, whom she called "Sonny," could arch his back, purr, and even make sparks, though for that you had to stroke his fur the wrong way. The hen had short little legs, so she was called "Chickey Shortleg." She laid good eggs, and the old woman loved her as if she had been her own child.

In the morning they were quick to notice the strange duckling. The cat began to purr, and the hen began to cluck.

"What on earth!" The old woman looked around, but she was short-sighted, and she mistook the duckling for a fat duck that had lost its way. "That was a good catch," she said. "Now I shall have duck eggs – unless it's a drake. We must try it out." So the duckling was tried out for three weeks, but not one egg did he lay.

In this house the cat was master and the hen was mistress. They always said, "We and the world," for they thought themselves half of the world, and much the better half at

duckling, "so refreshing to feel it rise over your head as you dive to the bottom."

"Yes, it must be a great pleasure!" said the hen. "I think you must have gone crazy. Ask the cat, who's the wisest fellow I know, whether he likes to swim or dive down in

The other ducklings quacked, "What an ugly-looking fellow that duckling is!" as they set about pecking him

that. The duckling thought that there might be more than one way of thinking, but the hen would not hear of it.

"Can you lay eggs?" she asked

"No."

"Then be so good as to hold your tongue."

The cat asked, "Can you arch your back, purr, or make sparks?"

"No."

"Then keep your opinion to yourself when sensible people are talking."

The duckling sat in a corner, feeling most despondent. Then he remembered the fresh air and the sunlight. Such a desire to go swimming on the water possessed him that he could not help telling the hen about it.

"But it's so refreshing to float on the water," said the

the water. Of myself I say nothing.

But ask the old woman, our mistress. There's no one on earth wiser than she is. Do you imagine she wants to go swimming and feel the water rise over her head?"

"You don't understand me," said the duckling.

"Well, if we don't, who would? Surely you don't think you are cleverer than the cat and the old woman – to say nothing of myself. Don't be so conceited, child. Just thank your Maker for all the kindness we have shown you. Didn't you get into this snug room, and fall in with people who can tell you what's what? But you are such a numbskull that it's no pleasure to have you around. Believe me, I tell you this for your own good. I say unpleasant truths, but that's the only way you can know who are your friends. Be sure now that you lay some eggs. See to it that you learn to purr or to make sparks."

"I think I'd better go out into the wide world," said the duckling.

"Suit yourself," said the hen.

So off went the duckling. He swam on the water, and dived down in it, but still he was slighted by every living creature because of his ugliness.

Autumn came on. The leaves in the forest turned yellow and brown. The wind took them and whirled them about. The heavens looked cold as the low clouds hung heavy with snow and hail. Perched on the fence, the raven screamed, "Caw, caw!" and trembled with cold. It made one shiver to think of it. Pity the poor little duckling!

One evening, just as the sun was setting in splendour, a great flock of large, handsome birds appeared out of the reeds. The duckling had never seen birds so beautiful. They were dazzling white, with long graceful necks. They were swans. They uttered a very strange cry as they unfurled their magnificent wings to fly from this cold land, away to warmer countries and to open waters. They went up so high, so very high, that the ugly little duckling felt a strange uneasiness come over him as he watched them. He went around and round in the water, like a wheel. He craned his neck to follow their course, and gave a cry so shrill and strange that he frightened himself. Oh! He could not forget them – those splendid, happy birds. When he could no longer see them he dived to the very bottom. and when he came up again he was quite beside himself. He did not know what birds they were or whither they were bound, yet he loved them more than anything he had ever loved before. It was not that he envied them, for how could he ever dare dream of wanting their marvellous beauty for himself? He would have been grateful if only the ducks would have tolerated him – the poor ugly creature.

The winter grew cold – so bitterly cold that the duckling had to swim to and fro in the water to keep it from freezing over. But every night the hole in which he swam kept getting smaller and smaller. Then it froze so hard that the duckling had to paddle continuously to keep the crackling ice from closing in upon him. At last, too tired to move, he was frozen fast in the ice.

Early that morning a farmer came by, and when he saw how things were he went out on the pond, broke away the ice with his wooden shoe, and carried the duckling home to his wife. There the duckling revived, but when the children wished to play with him he thought they meant to hurt him. Terrified, he fluttered into the milk pail, splashing the whole room with milk. The woman shrieked and threw up her hands as he flew into the butter tub, and then in and out of the meal barrel. Imagine what he looked like now! The woman screamed and lashed out at him with the fire tongs. The children tumbled over each other as they tried to catch him, and they laughed and they shouted. Luckily the door was open, and the duckling escaped through it into the bushes, where he lay down, in the newly fallen snow, as if in a daze.

But it would be too sad to tell of all the hardships and wretchedness he had to endure during this cruel winter. When the warm sun shone once more, the duckling was still alive among the reeds of the marsh. The larks began to sing again. It was beautiful springtime.

Then, quite suddenly, he lifted his wings. They swept through the air much more strongly than before, and their powerful strokes carried him far. Before he quite knew what was happening, he found himself in a great garden where apple trees bloomed. The lilacs filled the air with sweet scent and hung in clusters from long, green branches that bent over a winding stream. Oh, but it was lovely here in the freshness of spring!

From the thicket before him came three lovely white swans. They ruffled their feathers and swam lightly in the stream. The duckling recognized these noble creatures, and a strange feeling of sadness came upon him.

"I shall fly near these royal birds, and they will peck me to bits because I, who am so very ugly, dare to go near them. But I don't care. Better be killed by them than to be nipped by the ducks, pecked by the hens, kicked about by the hen-yard girl, or suffer such misery in winter."

So he flew into the water and swam toward the splendid swans. They saw him, and swept down upon him with their rustling feathers raised. "Kill me!" said the poor creature, and he bowed his head down over the water to wait for death. But what did he see there, mirrored in the clear stream? He beheld his own image, and it was no longer the reflection of a clumsy, dirty, gray bird, ugly and offensive. He himself was a swan! Being born in a duck yard does not matter, if only you are hatched from a swan's egg.

He felt quite glad that he had come through so much trouble and misfortune, for now he had a fuller understanding of his own good fortune, and of beauty when he met with it. The great swans swam all around him and stroked him with their bills.

Several little children came into the garden to throw grain and bits of bread upon the water. The smallest child cried, "Here's a new one," and the others rejoiced, "yes, a new one has come." They clapped their hands, danced around, and ran to bring their father and mother.

And they threw bread and cake upon the water, while they all agreed, "The new one is the most handsome of all. He's so young and so good-looking." The old swans bowed in his honour.

Then he felt very bashful, and tucked his head under his wing. He did not know what this was all about. He felt so very happy, but he wasn't at all proud, for a good heart never grows proud. He thought about how he had been persecuted and scorned, and now he heard them all call him the most beautiful of all beautiful birds. The lilacs dipped their clusters into the stream before him, and the sun shone so warm and so heartening. He rustled his feathers and held his slender neck high, as he cried out with full heart: "I never dreamed there could be so much happiness, when I was the ugly duckling."

The story of the three bears

In this Andrew Lang version from his *Green Fairy Book* of 1892 there is no sign of a pretty little Goldilocks. Instead it is a curious old woman who tiptoes into the house while the bears are taking their morning constitutional. In one version the old lady is impaled upon St Paul's churchyard steeple for her sins. In yet another version it is a fox that steals the porridge. When Goldilocks does appear in the story she generally escapes by running into the forest but in some tales she promises to behave in future and then returns home.

The three bears had porridge for breakfast

Once upon a time there were Three Bears, who lived together in a house of their own in a wood. One of them was a Little, Small, Wee Bear; and one was a Middle-sized Bear, and the other was a Great, Huge Bear. They had each a pot for their porridge, a little pot for the Little, Small, Wee Bear; and a middle-sized pot for the Middle Bear; and a great pot for the Great, Huge Bear. And they had each a chair to sit in; a little chair for the Little, Small, Wee Bear; and a middle-sized chair for the Middle Bear; and a great chair for the Great, Huge Bear. And they had each a bed to sleep in; a little bed for the Little, Small, Wee Bear; and a middle-sized bed for the Middle Bear; and a great bed for the Great, Huge Bear.

One day, after they had made the porridge for their breakfast, and poured it into their porridge-pots, they walked out into the wood while the porridge was cooling, that they might not burn their mouths by beginning too soon to eat it. And while they were walking, a little old woman came to the house. She could not have been a good, honest old woman; for, first, she looked in at the window, and then she peeped in at the keyhole; and, seeing nobody in the house, she lifted the latch. The door was not fastened, because the bears were good bears, who did nobody any harm, and never suspected that anybody would harm them. So the little old woman opened the door and went in; and well pleased she was when she saw the porridge on the table. If she had been a good little old woman she would have waited till the bears came home, and then, perhaps, they would have asked her to breakfast; for they were good bears – a little rough or so, as the manner of bears is, but for all that very good-natured and hospitable. But she was an impudent, bad old woman, and set about helping herself.

So first she tasted the porridge of the Great, Huge Bear, and that was too hot for her; and she said a bad word about that. And then she tasted the porridge of the Middle Bear; and that was too cold for her; and she said a bad word about that too. And then she went to the porridge of the Little, Small, Wee Bear, and tasted that; and that was neither too hot nor too cold, but just right; and she liked it so well, that she ate it all up: but the naughty old woman said a bad word about the little porridge-pot, because it did not hold enough for her.

Then the little old woman sate down in the chair of the Great, Huge Bear, and that was too hard for her. And then she sate down in the chair of the Middle Bear, and that was too soft for her. And then she sate down in the chair of the Little, Small, Wee Bear, and that was neither too hard nor too soft, but just right. So she seated herself in it, and there she sate till the bottom of the chair came out, and down came she, plump upon the ground. And the naughty old woman said a wicked word about that too.

Then the little old woman went up stairs into the bed-chamber in which the three bears slept. And first she lay down upon the bed of the Great, Huge Bear; but that was too high at the head for her. And next she lay down upon the bed of the Middle Bear; and that was too high at the foot for her. And then she lay down upon the bed of the Little, Small, Wee Bear; and that was neither too high at the head, nor at the foot, but just right. So she covered herself up comfortably, and lay there till she fell fast asleep.

By this time the three bears thought their porridge would be cool enough; so they came home to breakfast. Now the little old woman had left the spoon of the Great, Huge Bear, standing in his porridge.

"Somebody has been at my porridge!" said the Great,

Huge Bear, in his great gruff voice. And when the Middle Bear looked at his, he saw that the spoon was standing in it too. They were wooden spoons; if they had been silver ones, the naughty old woman would have put them in her pocket.

"Somebody Has Been At My Porridge!"

said the Middle Bear, in his middle voice.

Then the Little, Small, Wee Bear looked at his, and there was the spoon in the porridge-pot, but the porridge was all gone.

"Somebody has been at my porridge, and has eaten it all up!" said the Little, Small Wee Bear, in his little, small wee voice.

"Somebody has been at my porridge!"

Upon this the three bears, seeing that some one had entered their house, and eaten up the Little, Small, Wee Bear's breakfast, began to look about them. Now the little old woman had not put the hard cushion straight when she rose from the chair of the Great, Huge Bear.

"Somebody has been sitting in my chair!" said the Great, Huge Bear, in his great, rough, gruff voice.

And the little old woman had squatted down the soft cushion of the Middle Bear.

"Somebody Has Been Sitting In My Chair!" said the Middle Bear, in his middle voice.

And you know what the little old woman had done to the third chair.

"Somebody has been sitting in my chair, and has sate the bottom of it out!" said the Little, Small, Wee Bear, in his little, small, wee voice.

Then the three bears thought it necessary that they should make farther search; so they went up stairs into their bed-chamber. Now the little old woman had pulled the pillow of the Great, Huge Bear out of its place.

"Somebody has been lying in my bed!" said the Great, Huge Bear, in his great, rough, gruff voice.

And the little old woman had pulled the bolster of the Middle Bear out of its place.

"Somebody Has Been Lying In My Bed!" said the Middle Bear in his middle voice.

And when the Little, Small, Wee Bear came to look at his bed, there was the bolster in its place, and the pillow in its place upon the bolster, and upon the pillow was the little old woman's ugly, dirty head, – which was not in its place, for she had no business there.

"Somebody has been lying in my bed, – and here she is!" said the Little, Small, Wee Bear, in his little, small, wee voice.

The little old woman had heard in her sleep the great, rough, gruff voice of the Great, Huge Bear; but she was so fast asleep that it was no more to her than the roaring of wind or the rumbling of thunder. And she had heard the middle voice of the Middle Bear, but it was only as if she had heard someone speaking in a dream. But when she heard the little, small, wee voice of the Little, Small, Wee Bear, it was so sharp, and so shrill, that it awakened her at once. Up she started; and when she saw the Three Bears on one side of the bed, she tumbled herself out at the other, and ran to the window. Now the window was open, because the bears, like good, tidy bears as they were, always opened their bedchamber window when they got up in the morning. Out the little old woman jumped; and whether she broke her neck in the fall, or ran into the wood and was lost there, or found her way out of the wood and was taken up by the constable and sent to the House of Correction for a vagrant as she was, I cannot tell. But the Three Bears never saw anything more of her.

Rumpelstiltskin

Goblins who made noises by rattling posts and rapping on planks were called *rumpelstilz* which in German means 'little rattle stilt'. There are many similar stories in other nations about mischievous household fairies – like the English Tom Tim Tot and boggart and Scottish bogie that can make dogs go lame, milk turn sour or cause things to disappear. The earliest known mention of *Rumpelstiltskin* was in Fischart's *Gargantua* of 1577 but it is Grimm's 1812 version that is probably most familiar.

O nce upon a time there was a miller who was poor, but who had a beautiful daughter. Now it happened that he got into a conversation with the king, and to make an impression on him he said, "I have a daughter who can spin straw into gold."

The king said to the miller, "That is an art that I really like. If your daughter is as skillful as you say, then bring her to my castle tomorrow, and I will put her to the test."

When the girl was brought to him he led her into a room that was entirely filled with straw. Giving her a spinning wheel and a reel, he said, "Get to work now. Spin all night, and if by morning you have not spun this straw into gold, then you will have to die." Then he himself locked the room, and she was there all alone.

The poor miller's daughter sat there, and for her life she did not know what to do. She had no idea how to spin straw into gold. She became more and more afraid, and finally began to cry.

Then suddenly the door opened. A little man stepped inside and said, "Good evening, Mistress Miller, why are you crying so?"

"Oh," answered the girl, "I am supposed to spin straw into gold, and I do not know how to do it."

The little man said, "What will you give me if I spin it for you?"

"My necklace," said the girl.

The little man took the necklace, sat down before the spinning wheel, and whir, whir, whir, three times pulled, and the spool was full. Then he put another one on, and whir, whir, whir, three times pulled, and the second one was full as well. So it went until morning, and then all the straw was spun, and all the spools were filled with gold.

At sunrise the king came, and when he saw the gold he was surprised and happy, but his heart became even more greedy for gold. He had the miller's daughter taken to another room filled with straw. It was even larger, and he ordered her to spin it in one night, if she valued her life.

The girl did not know what to do, and she cried. Once again the door opened, and the little man appeared. He said, "What will you give me if I spin the straw into gold for you?"

"The ring from my finger," answered the girl.

The little man took the ring, and began once again to whir with the spinning wheel. By morning he had spun all the straw into glistening gold. The king was happy beyond measure when he saw it, but he still did not have his fill of gold. He had the miller's daughter taken to a still larger room filled with straw, and said, "Tonight you must spin this too. If you succeed you shall become my wife." He thought, "Even if she is only a miller's daughter, I will not find a richer wife in all the world."

When the girl was alone the little man returned for a third time. He said, "What will you give me if I spin the straw this time?"

"I have nothing more that I could give you," answered the girl.

"Then promise me, after you are queen, your first child."

"Who knows what will happen," thought the miller's daughter, and not knowing what else to do, she promised the little man what he demanded. In return the little man once again spun the straw into gold.

When in the morning the king came and found everything just as he desired, he married her, and the beautiful miller's daughter became queen.

An altogether comical little man was jumping around the fire, hopping on one leg

Suddenly the door opened. A little man stepped inside and said, "Good evening, Mistress Miller; why are you crying so?"

One version of the story ends with Rumpelstiltskin driving his right foot so far into the ground that he creates a deep chasm into which he falls, never to be seen again. Another version has Rumpelstiltskin exploding, killing everyone within a mile; while the oral version originally collected by the Brothers Grimm ends with Rumpelstiltskin flying out of the window on a cooking ladle!

A year later she brought a beautiful child to the world. She thought no more about the little man, but suddenly he appeared in her room and said, "Now give me that which you promised."

The queen took fright and offered the little man all the wealth of the kingdom if he would let her keep the child, but the little man said, "No. Something living is dearer to me than all the treasures of the world."

Then the queen began lamenting and crying so much that the little man took pity on her and said, "I will give you three days' time. If by then you know my name, then you shall keep your child."

The queen spent the entire night thinking of all the names she had ever heard. Then she sent a messenger into the country to inquire far and wide what other names there were. When the little man returned the next day she began with Kaspar, Melchior, Balzer, and said in order all the names she knew. After each one the little man said, "That is not my name."

The second day she sent inquiries into the neighborhood as to what names people had. She recited the most unusual and most curious names to the little man: "Is your name perhaps Beastrib? Or Muttoncalf? Or Legstring?"

But he always answered, "That is not my name."

On the third day the messenger returned and said, "I have not been able to find a single new name, but when I was approaching a high mountain in the corner of the woods, there where the fox and the hare say good-night, I saw a little house. A fire was burning in front of the house, and an altogether comical little man was jumping around the fire, hopping on one leg and calling out:

"Today I'll bake; tomorrow I'll brew,
Then I'll fetch the queen's new child, too;
It is good that no one knows my game,
And that Rumpelstiltskin is my name."

You can imagine how happy the queen was when she heard that name. Soon afterward the little man came in and asked, "Now, Madame Queen, what is my name?"

She first asked, "Is your name Kunz?"

"No."

"Is your name Heinz?"

"No."

"Is your name perhaps Rumpelstiltskin?"

"The devil told you that! The devil told you that!" shouted the little man, and with anger he stomped his right foot so hard into the ground that he fell in up to his waist. Then with both hands he took hold of his left foot and ripped himself up the middle in two.

The Firebird
or Tsarevitch Ivan, the Fire Bird and the Gray Wolf

> The firebird is a huge, magical glowing bird that appears in Slavic (Russian) folklore in its dual roles as a blessing and a bringer of doom to its captor. Its superb elegant plumage glows like tossing flames; one feather can light a large room. The story inspired the 1862 Grimm story of *The Golden Bird* and Igor Stravinsky's famous 1910 ballet.

In a certain far-away Tsardom not in this Empire, there lived a Tsar named Vyslav, who had three sons: the first Tsarevitch Dimitri, the second Tsarevitch Vasilii and the third Tsarevitch Ivan.

The Tsar had a walled garden, so rich and beautiful that in no kingdom of the world was there a more splendid one. Many rare trees grew in it whose fruits were precious jewels, and the rarest of all was an apple tree whose apples were of pure gold, and this the Tsar loved best of all.

One day he saw that one of the golden apples was missing. He placed guards at all gates of the garden; but in spite of this, each morning on counting, he found one more apple gone. At length he set men on the wall to watch day and night, and these reported to him that every night there came flying into the garden a bird that shone like the moon, whose feathers were gold and its eyes like crystal, which perched on the apple tree, plucked a golden apple and flew away.

Tsar Vyslav was greatly angered, and calling to him his two eldest sons, said: "My dear children, I have for many days sought to decide which of you should inherit my Tsardom and reign after me. Now, therefore, to the one of you who will catch the Fire Bird, which is the thief of my golden apples, and will bring it to me alive, I will during my life give the half of the Tsardom, and he shall rule after me when I am dead."

The two sons, hearing, rejoiced, and shouted with one voice: "Gracious Sir! We shall not fail to bring you the Fire Bird alive!"

Tsarevitch Dimitri and Tsarevitch Vasilii cast lots to see who should have the first trial, and the lot fell to the eldest, Tsarevitch Dimitri, who at evening went into the garden to watch. He sat down under the apple tree and watched till midnight, but when midnight was passed he fell asleep.

In the morning the Tsar summoned him and said: "Well, my son, didst thou see the Fire Bird who steals my golden apples?" Being ashamed to confess that he had fallen asleep, however, Tsarevitch Dimitri answered: "No, gracious Sir; last night the bird did not visit thy garden."

The Tsar, however, went himself and counted the apples, and saw that one more had been stolen.

On the next evening Tsarevitch Vasilii went into the garden to watch, and he, too, fell asleep at midnight, and next morning when his father summoned him, he, like his brother, being ashamed to tell the truth, answered: "Gracious Sir, I watched throughout the night but the Fire Bird that steals the golden apples did not enter thy garden."

And again Tsar Vyslav went himself and counted and saw that another golden apple was missing.

On the third evening Tsarevitch Ivan asked permission to watch in the garden, but his father would not permit it. "Thou art but a lad," he said, "and mightest be frightened in the long, dark night." But Ivan continued to beseech him till at length the Tsar consented.

So Tsarevitch Ivan took his place in the garden, and sat down to watch under the apple tree that bore the golden apples. He watched an hour, he watched two hours, he watched three hours. When midnight drew near sleep al most overcame him, but he drew his dagger and pricked his thigh with its point till the pain aroused him. And suddenly, an hour after midnight, the garden became bright as if with the light of many fires, and the Fire Bird came flying on its golden wings to alight on the lowest bough of the apple tree.

Tsarevitch Ivan crept nearer, and as it was about to pluck a golden apple in its beak he sprang toward it and seized its tail. The bird, however, beating with its golden wings, tore itself loose and flew away, leaving in his hand a single long feather. He wrapped this in a handkerchief, lay down on the ground and went to sleep.

In the morning Tsar Vyslav summoned him to his presence, and said: "Well, my dear son, thou didst not, I suppose, see the Fire Bird?"

Then Tsarevitch Ivan unrolled the handkerchief, and the feather shone so that the whole place was bright with it. The Tsar could not sufficiently admire it, for when it was brought into a darkened room it gleamed as if a hundred candles had been lighted. He put it into his royal treasury as a thing which must be safely kept for ever, and set many watchmen about the garden hoping to snare the Fire Bird, but it came no more for the golden apples.

Then Tsar Vyslav, greatly desiring it, sent for his two eldest sons, and said: "Ye, my sons, failed even to see the thief of my apples, yet thy brother Ivan has at least brought me one of its feathers. Take horse now, with my blessing, and ride in search of it, and to the one of you who brings it to me alive I will give the half of my Tsardom." And the

Tsarevitches Dimitri and Vasilii, envious of their younger brother Ivan, rejoiced that their father did not bid him also go, and mounting their swift horses, rode away, gladly, both of them, in search of the Fire Bird.

They rode for three days – whether by a near or a far road, or on highland or lowland, the tale is soon told, but the journey is not done quickly – till they came to a green plain from whose center three roads started, and there a great stone was set with these words carved upon it:

Who rides straight forward shall know both hunger and cold. Who rides to the right shall live, though his steed be dead. Who rides to the left shall die, though his steed shall live.

They were uncertain what to do, since none of the three roads promised well, and turning aside into a pleasant wood, pitched their silken tents and gave themselves over to rest and idle enjoyment.

Now when days had passed and they did not return, Tsarevitch Ivan besought his father to give him also his blessing, with leave to ride forth to search for the Fire Bird, but Tsar Vyslav denied him, saying: "My dear son, the wolves will devour thee. Thou art still young and unused to far and difficult journeying. Enough that thy brothers have gone from me. I am already old in age, and walk under the eye of God; if He take away my life, and thou, too, art gone, who will remain to keep order in my Tsardom? Rebellion may arise and there will be no one to quell it, or an enemy may cross our borders and there will be no one to command our troops. Seek not, therefore, to leave me!"

In spite of all, however, Tsarevitch Ivan would not leave off his beseeching till at length his father consented, and he took Tsar Vyslav's blessing, chose a swift horse for his use and rode away he knew not whither.

Three days he rode, till he came to the green plain whence the three ways started, and read the words carved on the great stone that stood there. "I may not take the left road, lest I die," he thought, "nor the middle road, lest I know hunger and cold. Rather will I take the right-hand road, whereon, though my poor horse perish, I at least shall keep my life." So he reined to the right.

He rode one day, he rode two days, he rode three days, and on the morning of the fourth day, as he led his horse through a forest, a great Gray Wolf leaped from a thicket. "Thou art a brave lad, Tsarevitch Ivan," said the Wolf, "but didst thou not read what was written on the rock?" When the Wolf had spoken these words he seized the horse, and tearing it in pieces, devoured it and disappeared.

Tsarevitch Ivan wept bitterly over the loss of his horse. The whole day he walked, till his weariness could not be told in a tale. He was near to faint from weakness, when again he met the Gray Wolf. "Thou art a brave lad, Tsarevitch Ivan," said the Wolf, "and for this reason I feel pity for thee. I have eaten thy good horse, but I will serve thee a service in payment. Sit now on my back and say whither I shall bear thee and wherefore."

Tsarevitch Ivan seated himself on the back of the Wolf joyfully enough. "Take me, Gray Wolf," he said, "to the Fire Bird that stole my father's golden apples," and instantly the Wolf sped away, twenty times swifter than the swiftest horse. In the middle of the night he stopped at a stone wall.

"Get down from my back, Tsarevitch Ivan," said the Wolf, "and climb over this wall. On the other side is a garden, and in the garden is an iron railing, and behind the railing three cages are hung, one of copper, one of silver, and one of gold. In the copper cage is a crow, in the silver one is a jackdaw, and in the golden cage is the Fire Bird. Open the door of the golden cage, take out the Fire Bird, and wrap it in thy handkerchief. But on no account take the golden cage; if thou dost, great misfortune will follow."

Tsarevitch Ivan climbed the wall, entered the iron railing and found the three cages as the Gray Wolf had said. He took out the Fire Bird and wrapped it in his handkerchief, but he could not bear to leave behind him the beautiful golden cage.

The instant he stretched out his hand and took it, how ever, there sounded throughout all the garden a great noise of clanging bells and the twanging of musical instruments to which the golden cage was tied by many invisible cords, and fifty watchmen, waking, came running into the garden. They seized Tsarevitch Ivan, and in the morning they brought him before their Tsar, who was called Dolmat.

Tsar Dolmat was greatly angered, and shouted in a loud voice: "How now! This is a fine, bold handed Cossack to be caught in such a shameful theft! Who art thou, from what country comest thou? Of what father art thou son, and how art thou named?"

"I come from the Tsardom of Vyslav," answered Tsarevitch Ivan, "son of Tsar Vyslav, and I am called Ivan. Thy Fire Bird entered my father's garden by night and stole many golden apples from his favorite tree. Therefore the Tsar, my father, sent me to find and bring to him the thief."

"And how should I know that thou speakest truth?" answered Tsar Dolmat. "Hadst thou come to me first I would have given thee the Fire Bird with honor. How will it be with thee now when I send into all Tsardoms, declaring how thou hast acted shamefully in my borders? However, Tsarevitch Ivan, I will excuse thee this if thou wilt serve me a certain service. If thou wilt ride across three times nine countries to the thirtieth Tsardom of Tsar Afron, and wilt win for me from him the Horse with the Golden Mane, which his father promised me and which is mine by right, then will I give to thee with all joy the Fire Bird. But if thou dost not serve me this service, then will I declare throughout all Tsardoms that thou art a thief, unworthy to share thy father's honors."

Tsarevitch Ivan went out from Tsar Dolmat in great grief. He found the Gray Wolf and related to him the whole.

"Thou art a foolish youth Tsarevitch Ivan," said the Wolf. "Why didst thou not recall my words and leave the golden cage?"

"I am guilty before thee!" answered Ivan sorrowfully.

"Well," said the Gray Wolf, "I will help thee. Sit on my back, and say whither I shall bear thee and wherefore."

With the Firebird safely inside a cage, Prince Ivan flies home on a magic carpet

So Tsarevitch Ivan a second time mounted the Wolf's back. "Take me, Gray Wolf," he said, "across three times nine countries to the thirtieth Tsardom, to Tsar Afron's Horse with the Golden Mane." At once the Wolf began running, fifty times swifter than the swiftest horse. Whether it was a long way or a short way, in the middle of the night he came to the thirtieth Tsardom, to Tsar Afron's Palace, and stopped beside the royal stables, which were built all of white stone.

"Now, Tsarevitch Ivan," said the Wolf, "get down from my back and open the door. The stablemen are all fast asleep, and thou mayest win the Horse with the Golden Mane. Only take not the golden bridle that hangs beside it. If thou takest that, great ill will befall thee."

Tsarevitch Ivan opened the door of the stables and there he saw the Horse with the Golden Mane, whose brightness was such that the whole stall was lighted by it. But as he was leading it out he saw the golden bridle, and its beauty tempted him to take it also. Scarcely had he touched it, however, when there arose a great clanging and thundering, for the bridle was tied by many cords to instruments of brass. The noise awakened the stablemen, who came running, a hundred of them, and seized Tsarevitch Ivan, and in the morning led him before Tsar Afron.

The Tsar was much surprised to see so gallant a youth accused of such a theft. "What!" he said. "Thou art a goodly lad to be a robber of my horses. Tell me from what Tsardom dost thou come, son of what father art thou, and what is thy name?"

"I come from the Tsardom of Tsar Vyslav," replied Tsarevitch Ivan, "whose son I am, and my name is Ivan. Tsar Dolmat laid upon me this service, that I bring him the Horse with the Golden Mane, which thy father promised him and which is his by right."

"Hadst thou come with such a word from Tsar Dolmat," answered Tsar Afron, "I would have given thee the horse with honor, and thou needst not have taken it from me by stealth. How will it be with thee when I send my heralds into all Tsardoms declaring thee, a Tsar's son, to be a thief? However, Tsarevitch Ivan, I will excuse thee this if thou wilt serve me a certain service. Thou shalt ride over three times nine lands to the country of the Tsar whose daughter is known as Helen the Beautiful, and bring me the Tsarevna to be my wife. For I have loved her for long with my soul and my heart, and yet cannot win her. Do this and I will forgive thee this fault and with joy will give thee the Horse with the Golden Mane and the golden bridle also for Tsar Dolmat. But if thou dost not serve me this service, then will I name thee as a shameful thief in all Tsardoms."

Tsarevitch Ivan went out from the splendid Palace weeping many tears, and came to the Gray Wolf and told him all that had befallen.

"Thou hast again been a foolish youth," said the Wolf. "Why didst thou not remember my warning not to touch the golden bridle?"

"Gray Wolf," said Ivan, still weeping, "I am guilty before thee!"

"Well," said the Wolf, "be it so. I will help thee. Sit upon my back and say whither I shall bear thee and wherefore."

So Tsarevitch Ivan wiped away his tears and a third time mounted the Wolf's back. "Take me, Gray Wolf," he said, "across three times nine lands to the Tsarevna who is called Helen the Beautiful." And straightway the Wolf began running, a hundred times swifter than the swiftest horse, faster than one can tell in a tale, until he came to the country of the beautiful princess. At length he stopped at a golden railing surrounding a lovely garden.

"Get down now, Tsarevitch Ivan," said the Wolf; "go back along the road by which we came, and wait for me in the open field under the green oak tree." So Tsarevitch Ivan did as he was bidden. But as for the Gray Wolf, he waited there.

Toward evening, when the sun was very low and its rays were no longer hot, the Tsar's daughter, Helen the

Firebird depicted by
Ivan Yakovlevich Bilibin in 1903

Beautiful, went into the garden to walk with her nurse and the ladies-in-waiting of the Court. When she came near, suddenly the Gray Wolf leaped over the railing into the garden, seized her and ran off with her more swiftly than twenty horses. He ran to the open field, to the green oak tree where Tsarevitch Ivan was waiting, and set her down beside him. Helen the Beautiful had been greatly frightened, but dried her tears quickly when she saw the handsome youth.

"Mount my back, Tsarevitch Ivan," said the Wolf, "and take the Tsarevna in your arms."

Tsarevitch Ivan sat on the Gray Wolf's back and took Helen the Beautiful in his arms, and the Wolf began running more swiftly than fifty horses, across the three times nine countries, back to the Tsardom of Tsar Afron. The nurse and ladies-in-waiting of the Tsarevna hastened to the Palace, and the Tsar sent many troops to pursue them, but fast as they went they could not overtake the Gray Wolf.

Sitting on the Wolf's back, with the Tsar's beautiful daughter in his arms, Tsarevitch Ivan began to love her with his heart and soul, and Helen the Beautiful began also to love him, so that when the Gray Wolf came to the country of Tsar Afron, to whom she was to be given, Tsarevitch Ivan began to shed many tears.

"Why dost thou weep, Tsarevitch Ivan?" asked the Wolf, and Ivan answered: "Gray Wolf, my friend! Why should I not weep and be desolate? I myself have begun to love Helen the Beautiful, yet now I must give her up to Tsar Afron for the Horse with the Golden Mane. For if I do not, then Tsar Afron will dishonor my name in all countries."

"I have served thee in much, Tsarevitch Ivan," said the Gray Wolf, "but I will also do thee this service. Listen. When we come near to the Palace, I myself will take the shape of the Tsar's daughter, and thou shalt lead me to Tsar Afron, and shalt take in exchange the Horse with the Golden Mane. Thou shalt mount him and ride far away. Then I will ask leave of Tsar Afron to walk on the open steppe, and when I am on the steppe with the Court ladies-in-waiting, thou hast only to think of me, the Gray Wolf, and I shall come once more to thee."

As soon as the Wolf had uttered these words, he beat his paw against the damp ground and instantly he took the shape of the Tsar's beautiful daughter: so like to her that no one in the world could have told that he was not the Tsarevna herself. Then, bidding Helen the Beautiful wait for him outside the walls, Tsarevitch Ivan led the Gray Wolf into the Palace to Tsar Afron.

The Tsar, thinking at last he had won the treasure he had so long desired as his wife, was very joyful, and gave Tsarevitch Ivan, for Tsar Dolmat, the Horse with the Golden Mane and the golden bridle. And Tsarevitch Ivan, mounting, rode outside the walls to the real Helen the Beautiful, put her before him on the saddle and set out across the three times nine countries back to the Tsardom of Tsar Dolmat.

As to the Gray Wolf, he spent one day, he spent two

days, he spent three days in Tsar Afron's Palace, all the while having the shape of the beautiful Tsarevna, while the Tsar made preparations for a splendid bridal. On the fourth day he asked the Tsar's permission to go for a walk on the open steppe.

"Oh, my beautiful Tsar's daughter," said Tsar Afron, "I grant thee whatever thou mayst wish. Go then and walk where it pleaseth thee, and perchance it will soothe thy grief and sorrow at parting from thy father." So he ordered serving-women and all the ladies-in-waiting of the Court to walk with her.

But all at once, as they walked on the open steppe, Tsarevitch Ivan, far away, riding with the real Helen the Beautiful on the Horse with the Golden Mane, suddenly be thought himself and cried: "Gray Wolf, Gray Wolf, I am thinking of thee now. Where art thou?" At that very instant the false Princess, as she walked with the ladies-in-waiting of Tsar Afron's Court, turned into the Gray Wolf, which ran off more swiftly than seventy horses. The ladies-in waiting hastened to the Palace and Tsar Afron sent many soldiers in pursuit, but they could not catch the Gray Wolf and soon he overtook Tsarevitch Ivan.

"Mount on my back, Tsarevitch Ivan," said the Wolf, "and let Helen the Beautiful ride on the Horse with the Golden Mane."

Tsarevitch Ivan mounted the Gray Wolf, and the Tsarevna rode on the Horse with the Golden Mane, and so they went on together to the Tsardom of Tsar Dolmat, in whose garden hung the cage with the Fire Bird. Whether the way was a long one or a short one, at length they came near to Tsar Dolmat's Palace. Then Tsarevitch Ivan, getting down from the Wolf's back, said:

"Gray Wolf, my dear friend! Thou hast served me many services. Serve me also one more, the last and greatest. If thou canst take the shape of Helen the Beautiful, thou canst take also that of this Horse with the Golden Mane. Do this and let me deliver thee to Tsar Dolmat in exchange for the Fire Bird. Then, when I am far away on the road to my own Tsardom, thou canst again rejoin us."

"So be it," said the Wolf and beat his paw against the dry ground, and immediately he took the shape of the Horse with the Golden Mane, so like to that the Princess rode that no one could have told one from the other. Then Tsarevitch Ivan, leaving Helen the Beautiful on the green lawn with the real Horse with the Golden Mane, mounted and rode to the Palace gate.

When Tsar Dolmat saw Tsarevitch Ivan riding on the false Horse with the Golden Mane he rejoiced exceedingly. He came out, embraced Ivan in the wide courtyard and kissed him on the mouth, and taking his right hand, led him into his splendid rooms. He made a great festival, and they sat at oak tables covered with embroidered cloths and for two days ate, drank and made merry. On the third day the Tsar gave to Tsarevitch Ivan the Fire Bird in its golden cage. Ivan took it, went to the green lawn where he had left Helen the Beautiful, mounted the real Horse with the Golden Mane,

set the Tsarevna on the saddle before him, and together they rode away across the three times nine lands towards his native country, the Tsardom of Tsar Vyslav.

As to Tsar Dolmat, for two days he admired the false Horse with the Golden Mane, and on the third day he desired to ride him. He gave orders, therefore, to saddle him, and mounting, rode to the open steppe. But as he was riding, it chanced that Tsarevitch Ivan, far away with Helen the Beautiful, all at once remembered his promise and cried:

"Gray Wolf, Gray Wolf, I am thinking of thee!" And at that instant the horse Tsar Dolmat rode threw the Tsar from his back and turned into the Gray Wolf, which ran off more swiftly than a hundred horses.

Tsar Dolmat hastened to the Palace and sent many soldiers in pursuit, but they could not catch the Gray Wolf, who soon overtook the Horse with the Golden Mane that bore Tsarevitch Ivan and the Tsarevna.

"Get down, Tsarevitch Ivan," said the Wolf; "mount my back and let Helen the Beautiful ride on the Horse with the Golden Mane."

So Tsarevitch Ivan mounted the Gray Wolf and the Tsarevna rode on the Horse with the Golden Mane, and at length they came to the forest where the Wolf had devoured Tsarevitch Ivan's horse.

There the Gray Wolf stopped. "Well, Tsarevitch Ivan," he said, "I have paid for thy horse, and have served thee in faith and truth. Get down now; I am no longer thy servant."

Tsarevitch Ivan got down from the Wolf's back, weeping many tears that they should part, and the Gray Wolf leaped into a thicket and disappeared, leaving Tsarevitch Ivan, mounted on the Horse with the Golden Mane, with Helen the Beautiful in his arms who held in her hands the golden cage in which was the Fire Bird, to ride to the Palace of Tsar Vyslav.

They rode on three days, till they came to the green plain where the three ways met, and where stood the great stone, and being very tired, the Tsarevitch and the Tsarevna here dismounted and lay down to rest. He tied the Horse with the Golden Mane to the stone, and lying lovingly side by side on the soft grass, they went to sleep.

Now it happened that the two elder brothers of Ivan, Tsarevitch Dimitri and Tsarevitch Vasilii, having tired of their amusements in the wood and being minded to return to their father without the Fire Bird, came riding past the spot and found their brother lying asleep with Helen the Beautiful beside him. Seeing not only that he had found the Fire Bird, but a horse with a mane of gold and a lovely Princess, they were envious, and Tsarevitch Dimitri drew his sword, stabbed Tsarevitch Ivan to death, and cut his body into small pieces. They then awoke Helen the Beautiful and began to question her.

"Lovely Tsarevna," they asked, "from what Tsardom dost thou come, of what father art thou daughter, and how art thou named?"

Helen the Beautiful, being roughly awakened, and

seeing Tsarevitch Ivan dead, was greatly frightened and cried with bitter tears: "I am the Tsar's daughter, Helen the Beautiful, and I belong to Tsarevitch Ivan whom ye have put to a cruel death. If ye were brave knights, ye had ridden against him in the open field; then might ye have been victorious over him with honor; but instead of that ye have slain him when he was asleep. What praise will such an act receive?"

But Tsarevitch Vasilii set the point of his sword against her breast and said: "Listen, Helen the Beautiful! Thou art now in our hands. We shall bring thee to our little father, Tsar Vyslav, and thou shalt tell him that we, and not Tsarevitch Ivan, found the Fire Bird, and won the Horse with the Golden Mane and thine own lovely self. If thou dost not swear by all holy things to say this, then this instant will we put thee to death!" And the beautiful Tsar's daughter, frightened by their threats, swore that she would speak as they commanded.

Tsarevitch Dimitri and Tsarevitch Vasilii cast lots to see who should take Helen the Beautiful and who the Horse with the Golden Mane and the Fire Bird. The Princess fell to Tsarevitch Vasilii and the horse and the bird to Tsarevitch Dimitri, and Tsarevitch Vasilii took Helen the Beautiful on his horse and Tsarevitch Dimitri took the Fire Bird and the Horse with the Golden Mane and both rode swiftly to the Palace of their father, Tsar Vyslav.

The Tsar rejoiced greatly to see them. To Tsarevitch Dimitri, since he had brought him the Fire Bird, he gave the half of his Tsardom, and he made a festival which lasted a whole month, at the end of which time Tsarevitch Vasilii was to wed the Tsarevna, Helen the Beautiful.

As for Tsarevitch Ivan, dead and cut into pieces, he lay on the green plain for thirty days. And on the thirty- first day it chanced that the Gray Wolf passed that way. He knew at once by his keen scent that the body was that of Tsarevitch Ivan. While he sat grieving for his friend, there came flying an iron-beaked she-crow with two fledglings, who alighted on the ground and would have eaten of the flesh, but the Wolf leaped up and seized one of the young birds.

Then the mother crow, flying to a little distance, said to him: "O Gray Wolf, wolf's son! Do not devour my little child, since it has in no way harmed thee."

And the Gray Wolf answered: "Listen, Crow, crow's daughter! Serve me a certain service, and I will not harm thy fledgling. I have heard that across three times nine countries, in the thirtieth Tsardom, are two springs, so placed that none save a bird can come to them, which give forth, the one the water of death, and the other the water of life. Bring to me two bottles of these waters, and I will let thy fledgling go safe and sound.

But if thou dost not, then I will tear it to pieces and devour it."

"I will indeed do thee this service, Gray Wolf, wolf's son," said the crow, "only harm not my child," and immediately flew away as swiftly as an arrow.

The Gray Wolf waited one day, he waited two days, he waited three days, and on the fourth day the she-crow came flying with two little bottles of water in her beak.

The Gray Wolf tore the fledgling to pieces. He sprinkled the pieces with the water of death and they instantly grew together; he sprinkled the dead body with the water of life and the fledgling shook itself and flew away with the she-crow, safe and sound. The Gray Wolf then sprinkled the pieces of the body of Tsarevitch Ivan with the water of death and they grew together; he sprinkled the dead body with the water of life, and Tsarevitch Ivan stood up, stretched himself and said: "How long I must have slept!"

"Yes, Tsarevitch Ivan," the Gray Wolf said, "and thou wouldst have slept forever had it not been for me. For thy brothers cut thee to pieces and took away with them the beautiful Tsar's daughter, the Horse with the Golden Mane and the Fire Bird. Make haste now and mount on my back, for thy brother Tsarevitch Vasilii today is to wed thy Helen the Beautiful."

Tsarevitch Ivan made haste to mount, and the Gray Wolf began running, swifter than a hundred horses, toward the Palace of Tsar Vyslav.

Whether the way was long or short, he came soon to the city, and there at the gate the Gray Wolf stopped. "Get down now, Tsarevitch Ivan," he said. "I am no longer a servant of thine and thou shalt see me no more, but sometimes remember the journeys thou hast made on the back of the Gray Wolf."

Tsarevitch Ivan got down, and having bade the Wolf farewell with tears, entered the city and went at once to the Palace, where the Tsarevitch Vasilii was even then being wed to Helen the Beautiful.

He entered the splendid rooms and came where they sat at table, and as soon as Helen the Beautiful saw him, she sprang up from the table and kissed him on the mouth, crying:

"This is my beloved, Tsarevitch Ivan, who shall wed me, and not this wicked one, Tsarevitch Vasilii, who sits with me at table!"

Tsar Vyslav rose up in his place and questioned Helen the Beautiful and she related to him the whole: how Tsarevitch Ivan had won her, with the Horse with the Golden Mane and the Fire Bird, and how his two elder brothers had slain him as he lay asleep and had threatened her with death so that she should say what they bade.

Tsar Vyslav, hearing, was angered like a great river in a storm. He commanded that the Tsarevitches Dimitri and Vasilii be seized and thrown into prison, and Tsarevitch Ivan, that same day, was wed to the Princess Helen the Beautiful. The Tsar made a great feast and all the people drank wine and mead till it ran down their beards, and the festival lasted many days till there was no one hungry or thirsty in the whole Tsardom.

And when the rejoicing was ended, the two elder brothers were made, one a scullion and the other a cowherd, but Tsarevitch Ivan lived always with Helen the Beautiful in such harmony and love that neither of them could bear to be without the other even for a single moment.

The Frog Prince

This first tale in the Brothers Grimm
collection has inspired movies, songs,
operas and a 1971 Muppet Show version.
Throwing an enchanted creature against the
wall, along with kissing, was a well-known
way to undo 'shape-shifting' magic Since
this story found its way into so many media,
a popular encouragement to girls seeking
true love has been to advise them that they
have to kiss a lot of frogs before finding a
handsome prince!

In the olden time, when wishing was having, there lived a King, whose daughters were all beautiful; but the youngest was so exceedingly beautiful that the Sun himself, although he saw her very, very often, was delighted every time she came out into the sunshine.

Near the castle of this King was a large and gloomy forest, where in the midst stood an old lime-tree, beneath whose branches splashed a little fountain; so, whenever it was very hot, the King's youngest daughter ran off into this wood, and sat down by the side of the fountain; and, when she felt dull, would often divert herself by throwing a golden ball up into the air and catching it again. And this was her favorite amusement.

Now, one day it happened that this golden ball, when the King's daughter threw it into the air, did not fall down into her hand, but on to the grass; and then it rolled right into the fountain. The King's daughter followed the ball with her eyes, but it disappeared beneath the water, which was so deep that she could not see to the bottom. Then she began to lament, and to cry more

The Frog offers to find the golden ball

loudly and more loudly; and, as she cried, a voice called out, "Why weepest thou, O King's daughter? thy tears would melt even a stone to pity." She looked around to the spot whence the voice came, and saw a frog stretching his thick, ugly head out of the water. "Ah! you old water-paddler," said she, "was it you that spoke? I am weeping for my golden ball which bounced away from me into the water."

"Be quiet, and do not cry," replied the Frog; "I can give thee good assistance. But what wilt thou give me if I succeed in fetching thy plaything up again?"

"What would you like, dear Frog?" said she. "My dresses, my pearls and jewels, or the golden crown which I wear?"

The Frog replied, "Dresses, or jewels, or golden crowns, are not for me; but if thou wilt love me, and let me be thy companion and playmate, and sit at thy table, and eat from thy little golden plate, and drink out of thy cup, and sleep in thy little bed, – if thou wilt promise me all these things, then I will dive down and fetch up thy golden ball."

"Oh, I will promise you all," said she, "if you will only get me my golden ball." But she thought to herself, "What is the silly Frog chattering about? Let him stay in the water with his equals; he cannot enter into society." Then the Frog, as soon as he had received her promise, drew his head under the water and dived down. Presently he swam up again with the golden ball in his mouth, and threw it on to the grass. The King's daughter was full of joy when she again saw her beautiful plaything; and, taking it up, she ran off immediately. "Stop! stop!" cried the Frog; "take me with thee. I cannot run as thou canst."

But this croaking was of no avail; although it was loud enough, the King's daughter did not hear it, but, hastening home, soon forgot the poor Frog, who was obliged to leap back into the fountain.

The next day, when the King's daughter was sitting at table with her father and all his courtiers, and was eating from her own little golden plate, something was heard coming up the marble stairs, splish-splash, splish-splash; and when it arrived at the top, it knocked at the door, and a voice said –

"Open the door, thou youngest daughter of the King!"

So she arose and went to see who it was that called to her; but when she opened the door and caught sight of the Frog, she shut it again very quickly and with great passion, and sat down at the table, looking exceedingly pale.

The Frog enjoys his meal while the Princess weeps

But the King perceived that her heart was beating violently, and asked her whether it were a giant who had come to fetch her away who stood at the door. "Oh, no!" answered she; "it is no giant, but an ugly Frog."

"What does the Frog want with you?" said the King.

"Oh, dear father, yesterday when I was playing by the fountain, my golden ball fell into the water, and this Frog fetched it up again because I cried so much: but first, I must tell you, he pressed me so much, that I promised him he should be my companion. I never thought that he could come out of the water, but somehow he has managed to jump out, and now he wants to come in here."

At that moment there was another knock, and a voice said –

"King's daughter, youngest,
Open the door.
Hast thou forgotten
Thy promises made
At the fountain so clear
'Neath the lime-tree's shade?
King's daughter, youngest.
Open the door."

Then the King said, "What you have promised, that you must perform; go and let him in." So the King's daughter went and opened the door, and the Frog hopped in after her right up to her chair: and as soon as she was seated, he said, "Lift me up;" but she hesitated so long that the King had to order her to obey. And as soon as the Frog sat on the chair he jumped on to the table and said, "Now push thy plate near me, that we may eat together." And

she did so, but as every one noticed, very unwillingly. The Frog seemed to relish his dinner very much, but every bit that the King's daughter ate nearly choked her, till at last the Frog said, "I have satisfied my hunger, and feel very tired; wilt thou carry me upstairs now into thy chamber, and make thy bed ready that we may sleep together?" At this speech the King's daughter began to cry, for she was afraid of the cold Frog, and dared not touch him; and besides, he actually wanted to sleep in her own beautiful, clean bed!

But her tears only made the King very angry, and he said, "He who helped you in the time of your trouble must not now be despised!" So she took the Frog up with two fingers, and put him into a corner of her chamber. But as she lay in her bed, he crept up to it, and said, "I am so very tired that I shall sleep well; do take me up, or I will tell thy father." This speech put the King's daughter into a terrible passion, and catching the Frog up, she threw him with all her strength against the wall, saying "Now will you be quiet, you ugly Frog!"

But as he fell he was changed from a Frog into a handsome Prince with beautiful eyes, who after a little while became her dear companion and betrothed. One morning, Henry, trusted servant of the Prince, came for them with a carriage. When his master was changed into a frog, trusty Henry had grieved so much that he had bound three iron bands around his heart, for fear it should break with grief and sorrow. The faithful Henry (who was also the trusty Henry) helped in the bride and bridegroom, and placed himself in the seat behind, full of joy at his master's release. They had not proceeded far when the Prince heard a crack as if something had broken behind the carriage; so he put his head out of the window and asked trusty Henry what was broken, and faithful Henry answered, "It was not the carriage, my master, but an iron band which I bound around my heart when it was in such grief because you were changed into a frog."

Twice afterwards on the journey there was the same noise, and each time the Prince thought that it was some part of the carriage that had given way; but it was only the breaking of the bands which bound the heart of the trusty Henry (who was also the faithful Henry), and who was thenceforward free and happy.

The Happy Prince

This is one story from a collection of tales for children by Oscar Wilde that was published in 1888. It tells how a statue befriends a swallow and then, together, they bring happiness to others. Oscar Wilde's mother, Lady Jane Francesca Wilde, was a poet and journalist and his father was also a writer so he may have inherited his talents from either parent. His father was also an antiquarian and specialist in diseases of the eye and ear who founded a Dublin hospital one year before Oscar was born.

High above the city, on a tall column, stood the statue of the Happy Prince. He was gilded all over with thin leaves of fine gold, for eyes he had two bright sapphires, and a large red ruby glowed on his sword-hilt.

He was very much admired indeed. "He is as beautiful as a weathercock," remarked one of the Town Councillors who wished to gain a reputation for having artistic tastes; "only not quite so useful," he added, fearing lest people should think him unpractical, which he really was not.

"Why can't you be like the Happy Prince?" asked a sensible mother of her little boy who was crying for the moon. "The Happy Prince never dreams of crying for anything."

"I am glad there is some one in the world who is quite happy," muttered a disappointed man as he gazed at the wonderful statue.

"He looks just like an angel," said the Charity Children as they came out of the cathedral in their bright scarlet cloaks and their clean white pinafores.

"How do you know?" said the Mathematical Master, "you have never seen one."

"Ah! but we have, in our dreams," answered the children; and the Mathematical Master frowned and looked very severe, for he did not approve of children dreaming.

One night there flew over the city a little Swallow. His friends had gone away to Egypt six weeks before, but he had stayed behind, for he was in love with the most beautiful Reed. He had met her early in the spring as he was flying down the river after a big yellow moth, and had been so attracted by her slender waist that he had stopped to talk to her.

"Shall I love you?" said the Swallow, who liked to come to the point at once, and the Reed made him a low bow. So he flew round and round her, touching the water with his wings, and making silver ripples. This was his courtship, and it lasted all through the summer.

"It is a ridiculous attachment," twittered the other Swallows; "she has no money, and far too many relations"; and indeed the river was quite full of Reeds. Then, when the autumn came they all flew away.

After they had gone he felt lonely, and began to tire of his lady-love. "She has no conversation," he said, "and I am afraid that she is a coquette, for she is always flirting with the wind." And certainly, whenever the wind blew, the Reed made the most graceful curtseys. "I admit that she is domestic," he continued, "but I love travelling, and my wife, consequently, should love travelling also."

"Will you come away with me?" he said finally to her; but the Reed shook her head, she was so attached to her home.

"You have been trifling with me," he cried. "I am off to the Pyramids. Good-bye!" and he flew away.

All day long he flew, and at night-time he arrived at the city. "Where shall I put up?" he said; "I hope the town has made preparations."

Then he saw the statue on the tall column.

"I will put up there," he cried; "it is a fine position, with plenty of fresh air." So he alighted just between the feet of the Happy Prince.

"I have a golden bedroom," he said softly to himself as he looked round, and he prepared to go to sleep; but just as he was putting his head under his wing a large drop of water fell on him. "What a curious thing!" he cried; "there is not a single cloud in the sky, the stars are quite clear and bright, and yet it is raining. The climate in the north of Europe is really dreadful. The Reed used to like the rain, but that was merely her selfishness."

Then another drop fell.

"What is the use of a statue if it cannot keep the rain off?" he said; "I must look for a good chimney-pot," and he determined to fly away.

But before he had opened his wings, a third drop fell, and he looked up, and saw – Ah! what did he see?

The eyes of the Happy Prince were filled with tears, and tears were running down his golden cheeks. His face was so beautiful in the moonlight that the little Swallow was filled with pity.

"Who are you?" he said.

"I am the Happy Prince."

"Why are you weeping then?" asked the Swallow; "you

This story was first published in 1888

have quite drenched me."

"When I was alive and had a human heart," answered the statue, "I did not know what tears were, for I lived in the Palace of Sans-Souci, where sorrow is not allowed to enter. In the daytime I played with my companions in the garden, and in the evening I led the dance in the Great Hall. Round the garden ran a very lofty wall, but I never cared to ask what lay beyond it, everything about me was so beautiful. My courtiers called me the Happy Prince, and happy indeed I was, if pleasure be happiness. So I lived, and so I died. And now that I am dead they have set me up here so high that I can see all the ugliness and all the misery of my city, and though my heart is made of lead yet I cannot chose but weep."

"What! is he not solid gold?" said the Swallow to himself. He was too polite to make any personal remarks out loud.

"Far away," continued the statue in a low musical voice, "far away in a little street there is a poor house. One of the windows is open, and through it I can see a woman seated at a table. Her face is thin and worn, and she has coarse, red hands, all pricked by the needle, for she is a seamstress. She is embroidering passion-flowers on a satin gown for the loveliest of the Queen's maids-of-honour to wear at the next Court-ball. In a bed in the corner of the room her little boy is lying ill. He has a fever, and is asking for oranges. His mother has nothing to give him but river water, so he is crying. Swallow, Swallow, little Swallow, will you not bring her the ruby out of my sword-hilt? My feet are fastened to this pedestal and I cannot move."

"I am waited for in Egypt," said the Swallow. "My friends are flying up and down the Nile, and talking to the large lotus-flowers. Soon they will go to sleep in the tomb of the great King. The King is there himself in his painted coffin. He is wrapped in yellow linen, and embalmed with spices. Round his neck is a chain of pale green jade, and his hands are like withered leaves."

"Swallow, Swallow, little Swallow," said the Prince, "will you not stay with me for one night, and be my messenger? The boy is so thirsty, and the mother so sad."

"I don't think I like boys," answered the Swallow. "Last summer, when I was staying on the river, there were two rude boys, the miller's sons, who were always throwing stones at me. They never hit me, of course; we swallows fly far too well for that, and besides, I come of a family famous for its agility; but still, it was a mark of disrespect."

But the Happy Prince looked so sad that the little Swallow was sorry. "It is very cold here," he said; "but I will stay with you for one night, and be your messenger."

"Thank you, little Swallow," said the Prince.

So the Swallow picked out the great ruby from the Prince's sword, and flew away with it in his beak over the roofs of the town.

He passed by the cathedral tower, where the white marble angels were sculptured. He passed by the palace and heard the sound of dancing. A beautiful girl came out on the balcony with her lover. "How wonderful the stars are," he said to her, "and how wonderful is the power of love!"

"I hope my dress will be ready in time for the State-ball," she answered; "I have ordered passion-flowers to be embroidered on it; but the seamstresses are so lazy."

He passed over the river, and saw the lanterns hanging to the masts of the ships. He passed over the Ghetto, and saw the old Jews bargaining with each other, and weighing out money in copper scales. At last he came to the poor house and looked in. The boy was tossing feverishly on his bed, and the mother had fallen asleep, she was so tired. In he hopped, and laid the great ruby on the table beside the woman's thimble. Then he flew gently round the bed, fanning the boy's forehead with his wings. "How cool I feel," said the boy, "I must be getting better"; and he sank into a delicious slumber.

Then the Swallow flew back to the Happy Prince, and told him what he had done. "It is curious," he remarked, "but I feel quite warm now, although it is so cold."

"That is because you have done a good action," said the Prince. And the little Swallow began to think, and then he fell asleep. Thinking always made him sleepy.

When day broke he flew down to the river and had a bath. "What a remarkable phenomenon," said the Professor of Ornithology as he was passing over the bridge. "A swallow in winter!" And he wrote a long letter about it to the local newspaper. Every one quoted it, it was full of so many words that they could not understand.

"To-night I go to Egypt," said the Swallow, and he was in high spirits at the prospect. He visited all the public monuments, and sat a long time on top of the church steeple. Wherever he went the Sparrows chirruped, and said to each other, "What a distinguished stranger!" so he enjoyed himself very much.

When the moon rose he flew back to the Happy Prince. "Have you any commissions for Egypt?" he cried; "I am just starting."

"Swallow, Swallow, little Swallow," said the Prince, "will you not stay with me one night longer?"

"I am waited for in Egypt," answered the Swallow. "To-morrow my friends will fly up to the Second Cataract. The river-horse couches there among the bulrushes, and on a great granite throne sits the God Memnon. All night long he watches the stars, and when the morning star shines he utters one cry of joy, and then he is silent. At noon the yellow lions come down to the water's edge to drink. They have eyes like green beryls, and their roar is louder than the roar of the cataract."

"Swallow, Swallow, little Swallow," said the Prince, "far away across the city I see a young man in a garret. He is leaning over a desk covered with papers, and in a tumbler by his side there is a bunch of withered violets. His hair is brown and crisp, and his lips are red as a pomegranate, and he has large and dreamy eyes. He is trying to finish a play for the Director of the Theatre, but he is too cold to write any more. There is no fire in the grate, and hunger has made him faint."

"I will wait with you one night longer," said the Swallow, who really had a good heart. "Shall I take him another ruby?"

"Alas! I have no ruby now," said the Prince; "my eyes are all that I have left. They are made of rare sapphires, which were brought out of India a thousand years ago. Pluck out one of them and take it to him. He will sell it to the jeweller, and buy food and firewood, and finish his play."

"Dear Prince," said the Swallow, "I cannot do that"; and he began to weep.

"Swallow, Swallow, little Swallow," said the Prince, "do as I command you."

So the Swallow plucked out the Prince's eye, and flew away to the student's garret. It was easy enough to get in, as there was a hole in the roof. Through this he darted, and came into the room. The young man had his head buried in his hands, so he did not hear the flutter of the bird's wings, and when he looked up he found the beautiful sapphire lying on the withered violets.

"I am beginning to be appreciated," he cried; "this is from some great admirer. Now I can finish my play," and he looked quite happy.

The next day the Swallow flew down to the harbour. He sat on the mast of a large vessel and watched the sailors hauling big chests out of the hold with ropes. "Heave a-hoy!" they shouted as each chest came up. "I am going to Egypt"! cried the Swallow, but nobody minded, and when the moon rose he flew back to the Happy Prince.

"I am come to bid you good-bye," he cried.

"Swallow, Swallow, little Swallow," said the Prince, "will you not stay with me one night longer?"

"It is winter," answered the Swallow, "and the chill snow will soon be here. In Egypt the sun is warm on the green palm-trees, and the crocodiles lie in the mud and look lazily about them. My companions are building a nest in the Temple of Baalbec, and the pink and white doves are watching them, and cooing to each other. Dear Prince, I must leave you, but I will never forget you, and next spring I will bring you back two beautiful jewels in place of those you have given away. The ruby shall be redder than a red rose, and the sapphire shall be as blue as the great sea."

The gold statue

"In the square below," said the Happy Prince, "there stands a little match-girl. She has let her matches fall in the gutter, and they are all spoiled. Her father will beat her if she does not bring home some money, and she is crying. She has no shoes or stockings, and her little head is bare. Pluck out my other eye, and give it to her, and her father will not beat her."

"I will stay with you one night longer," said the Swallow, "but I cannot pluck out your eye. You would be quite blind then."

"Swallow, Swallow, little Swallow," said the Prince, "do as I command you."

So he plucked out the Prince's other eye, and darted down with it. He swooped past the match-girl, and slipped the jewel into the palm of her hand. "What a lovely bit of glass," cried the little girl; and she ran home, laughing.

Then the Swallow came back to the Prince. "You are blind now," he said, "so I will stay with you always."

"No, little Swallow," said the poor Prince, "you must go away to Egypt."

"I will stay with you always," said the Swallow, and he slept at the Prince's feet.

All the next day he sat on the Prince's shoulder, and told him stories of what he had seen in strange lands. He told him of the red ibises, who stand in long rows on the banks of the Nile, and catch gold-fish in their beaks; of the Sphinx, who is as old as the world itself, and lives in the desert, and knows everything; of the merchants, who walk slowly by the side of their camels, and carry amber beads in their hands; of the King of the Mountains of the Moon, who is as black as ebony, and worships a large crystal; of the great green snake that sleeps in a palm-tree, and has twenty priests to feed it with honey-cakes; and of the pygmies who sail over a big lake on large flat leaves, and are always at war with the butterflies.

"Dear little Swallow," said the Prince, "you tell me of marvellous things, but more marvellous than anything is the suffering of men and of women. There is no Mystery

Most of the swallows had flown away to Egypt

so great as Misery. Fly over my city, little Swallow, and tell me what you see there."

So the Swallow flew over the great city, and saw the rich making merry in their beautiful houses, while the beggars were sitting at the gates. He flew into dark lanes, and saw the white faces of starving children looking out listlessly at the black streets. Under the archway of a bridge two little boys were lying in one another's arms to try and keep themselves warm. "How hungry we are!" they said. "You must not lie here," shouted the Watchman, and they wandered out into the rain.

Then he flew back and told the Prince what he had seen.

"I am covered with fine gold," said the Prince, "you must take it off, leaf by leaf, and give it to my poor; the living always think that gold can make them happy."

Leaf after leaf of the fine gold the Swallow picked off, till the Happy Prince looked quite dull and grey. Leaf after leaf of the fine gold he brought to the poor, and the children's faces grew rosier, and they laughed and played games in the street. "We have bread now!" they cried.

Then the snow came, and after the snow came the frost. The streets looked as if they were made of silver, they were so bright and glistening; long icicles like crystal daggers hung down from the eaves of the houses, everybody went about in furs, and the little boys wore scarlet caps and skated on the ice.

The poor little Swallow grew colder and colder, but he would not leave the Prince, he loved him too well. He picked up crumbs outside the baker's door when the baker was not looking and tried to keep himself warm by flapping his wings.

But at last he knew that he was going to die. He had just strength to fly up to the Prince's shoulder once more. "Good-bye, dear Prince!" he murmured, "will you let me kiss your hand?"

"I am glad that you are going to Egypt at last, little Swallow," said the Prince, "you have stayed too long here; but you must kiss me on the lips, for I love you."

"It is not to Egypt that I am going," said the Swallow. "I am going to the House of Death. Death is the brother of Sleep, is he not?"

And he kissed the Happy Prince on the lips, and fell down dead at his feet.

At that moment a curious crack sounded inside the statue, as if something had broken. The fact is that the leaden heart had snapped right in two. It certainly was a dreadfully hard frost.

Early the next morning the Mayor was walking in the square below in company with the Town Councillors. As they passed the column he looked up at the statue: "Dear me! how shabby the Happy Prince looks!" he said.

"How shabby indeed!" cried the Town Councillors, who always agreed with the Mayor; and they went up to look at it.

"The ruby has fallen out of his sword, his eyes are gone, and he is golden no longer," said the Mayor in fact, "he is

The Prince used to lead the dances in the Great Hall

little better than a beggar!"

"Little better than a beggar," said the Town Councillors.

"And here is actually a dead bird at his feet!" continued the Mayor. "We must really issue a proclamation that birds are not to be allowed to die here." And the Town Clerk made a note of the suggestion.

So they pulled down the statue of the Happy Prince. "As he is no longer beautiful he is no longer useful," said the Art Professor at the University.

Then they melted the statue in a furnace, and the Mayor held a meeting of the Corporation to decide what was to be done with the metal. "We must have another statue, of course," he said, "and it shall be a statue of myself."

"Of myself," said each of the Town Councillors, and they quarrelled. When I last heard of them they were quarrelling still.

"What a strange thing!" said the overseer of the workmen at the foundry. "This broken lead heart will not melt in the furnace. We must throw it away." So they threw it on a dust-heap where the dead Swallow was also lying.

"Bring me the two most precious things in the city," said God to one of His Angels; and the Angel brought Him the leaden heart and the dead bird.

"You have rightly chosen," said God, "for in my garden of Paradise this little bird shall sing for evermore, and in my city of gold the Happy Prince shall praise me."

Five Children and It

First published in 1902, this delightful magical tale by Edith Nesbit has never been out of print since. This extract describes how the youngsters meet a Psammead – a sand fairy whose name a pun on the Greek word for sand and who is terrified of water and the 'nasty wet bubbling sea'. Their new acquaintance, who has eyes on long horns like a snail, is obliged to grant them one wish a day and so their adventures begin.

Grown-up people find it very difficult to believe really wonderful things, unless they have what they call proof. But children will believe almost anything, and grown-ups know this. That is why they tell you that the earth is round like an orange, when you can see perfectly well that it is flat and lumpy; and why they say that the earth goes round the sun, when you can see for yourself any day that the sun gets up in the morning and goes to bed at night like a good sun as it is, and the earth knows its place, and lies as still as a mouse.

Yet I daresay you believe all that about the earth and the sun, and if so you will find it quite easy to believe that before Anthea and Cyril and the others had been a week in the country they had found a fairy. At least they called it that, because that was what it called itself; and of course it knew best, but it was not at all like any fairy you ever saw or heard of or read about.

It was at the gravel-pits. Father had to go away suddenly on business, and mother had gone away to stay with Granny, who was not very well. They both went in a great hurry, and when they were gone the house seemed dreadfully quiet and empty, and the children wandered from one room to another and looked at the bits of paper and string on the floors left over from the packing, and not yet cleared up, and wished they had something to do. It was Cyril who said:

"I say, let's take our Margate spades and go and dig in the gravel-pits. We can pretend it's the seaside."

"Father said it was once," Anthea said; "he says there are shells there thousands of years old."

So they went. Of course they had been to the edge of the gravel-pit and looked over, but they had not gone down into it for fear father should say they mustn't play there, and the same with the chalk-quarry. The gravel-pit is not really dangerous if you don't try to climb down the edges, but go the slow safe way round by the road, as if you were a cart.

Each of the children carried its own spade, and took it in turns to carry the Lamb. He was the baby, and they called him that because "Baa" was the first thing he ever said. They called Anthea "Panther", which seems silly when you read it, but when you say it, it sounds a little like her name.

The gravel-pit is very large and wide, with grass growing round the edges at the top, and dry stringy wildflowers, purple and yellow. It is like a giant's wash-hand basin. And there are mounds of gravel, and holes in the sides of the basin where gravel has been taken out, and high up in the steep sides there are the little holes that are the little front doors of the little sand-martins' little houses.

The children built a castle, of course, but castle-building is rather poor fun when you have no hope of the swishing tide ever coming in to fill up the moat and wash away the drawbridge, and, at the happy last, to wet everybody up to the waist at least.

Cyril wanted to dig out a cave to play smugglers in, but the others thought it might bury them alive, so it ended in all spades going to work to dig a hole through the castle to Australia. These children, you see, believed that the world was round, and that on the other side the little Australian boys and girls were really walking wrong way up, like flies on the ceiling, with their heads hanging down into the air.

The children dug and they dug and they dug, and their hands got sandy and hot and red, and their faces got damp and shiny. The Lamb had tried to eat the sand, and had cried so hard when he found that it was not, as he had supposed, brown sugar, that he was now tired out, and was lying asleep in a warm fat bunch in the middle of the half-finished castle. This left his brothers and sisters free to work really hard, and the hole that was to come out in Australia soon grew so deep that Jane, who was called Pussy for short, begged the others to stop.

"Suppose the bottom of the hole gave way suddenly," she said, "and you tumbled out among the little Australians, all the sand would get in their eyes."

"Yes," said Robert; "and they would hate us, and throw stones at us, and not let us see the kangaroos, or opossums, or blue-gums, or Emu Brand birds, or anything."

Cyril and Anthea knew that Australia was not quite so near as all that, but they agreed to stop using the spades and go on with their hands. This was quite easy, because the sand at the bottom of the hole was very soft and fine and dry, like sea-sand. And there were little shells in it.

"Fancy it having been wet sea here once, all sloppy and shiny," said Jane, "with fishes and conger-eels and coral and mermaids."

"And masts of ships and wrecked Spanish treasure. I wish we could find a gold doubloon, or something," Cyril said.

"How did the sea get carried away?" Robert asked.

"Not in a pail, silly," said his brother. "Father says the earth got too hot underneath, like you do in bed sometimes, so it just hunched up its shoulders, and the sea had to slip off, like the blankets do off us, and the shoulder was left sticking out, and turned into dry land. Let's go and look for shells; I think that little cave looks likely, and I see something sticking out there like a bit of wrecked ship's anchor, and it's beastly hot in the Australian hole."

The others agreed, but Anthea went on digging. She always liked to finish a thing when she had once begun it. She felt it would be a disgrace to leave that hole without getting through to Australia.

The cave was disappointing, because there were no shells, and the wrecked ship's anchor turned out to be only the broken end of a pickaxe handle, and the cave party were just making up their minds that the sand makes you thirstier when it is not by the seaside, and someone had suggested going home for lemonade, when Anthea suddenly screamed:

"Cyril! Come here! Oh, come quick! It's alive! It'll get away! Quick!" They all hurried back.

"It's a rat, I shouldn't wonder," said Robert. "Father says they infest old places – and this must be pretty old if the sea was here thousands of years ago."

"Perhaps it is a snake," said Jane, shuddering.

"Let's look," said Cyril, jumping into the hole. "I'm not afraid of snakes. I like them. If it is a snake I'll tame it, and it will follow me everywhere, and I'll let it sleep round my neck at night."

"No, you won't," said Robert firmly. He shared Cyril's bedroom. "But you may if it's a rat."

"Oh, don't be silly!" said Anthea; "it's not a rat, it's MUCH bigger. And it's not a snake. It's got feet; I saw them; and fur! No – not the spade. You'll hurt it! Dig with your hands."

"And let IT hurt ME instead! That's so likely, isn't it?" said Cyril, seizing a spade.

"Oh, don't!" said Anthea. "Squirrel, DON'T. I – it sounds silly, but it said something. It really and truly did."

"What?"

"It said, 'You let me alone.' "

But Cyril merely observed that his sister must have gone off her nut, and he and Robert dug with spades while Anthea sat on the edge of the hole, jumping up and down with hotness and anxiety. They dug carefully, and presently everyone could see that there really was something moving in the bottom of the Australian hole.

Then Anthea cried out, "I'm not afraid. Let me dig," and fell on her knees and began to scratch like a dog does when he has suddenly remembered where it was that he buried his bone.

"Oh, I felt fur," she cried, half laughing and half crying. "I did indeed! I did!" when suddenly a dry husky voice in the sand made them all jump back, and their hearts jumped nearly as fast as they did.

"Let me alone," it said. And now everyone heard the voice and looked at the others to see if they had too.

"But we want to see you," said Robert bravely.

"I wish you'd come out," said Anthea, also taking courage.

"Oh, well - if that's your wish," the voice said, and the sand stirred and spun and scattered, and something brown and furry and fat came rolling out into the hole and the sand fell off it, and it sat there yawning and rubbing the ends of its eyes with its hands.

"I believe I must have dropped asleep," it said, stretching itself.

The children stood round the hole in a ring, looking at the creature they had found. It was worth looking at. Its eyes were on long horns like a snail's eyes, and it could move them in and out like telescopes; it had ears like a bat's ears, and its tubby body was shaped like a spider's and covered with thick soft fur; its legs and arms were furry too, and it had hands and feet like a monkey's.

"What on earth is it?" Jane said. "Shall we take it home?"

The thing turned its long eyes to look at her, and said: "Does she always talk nonsense, or is it only the rubbish on her head that makes her silly?"

It looked scornfully at Jane's hat as it spoke.

"She doesn't mean to be silly," Anthea said gently; we none of us do, whatever you may think! Don't be frightened; we don't want to hurt you, you know."

"Hurt ME!" it said. "ME frightened? Upon my word! Why, you talk as if I were nobody in particular." All its fur stood out like a cat's when it is going to fight.

"Well," said Anthea, still kindly, "perhaps if we knew who you are in particular we could think of something to say that wouldn't make you cross. Everything we've said so far seems to have. Who are you? And don't get angry! Because really we don't know."

"You don't know?" it said. "Well, I knew the world had

changed – but – well, really – do you mean to tell me seriously you don't know a Psammead when you see one?"

"A Sammyadd? That's Greek to me."

"So it is to everyone," said the creature sharply. "Well, in plain English, then, a SAND-FAIRY. Don't you know a Sand-fairy when you see one?"

It looked so grieved and hurt that Jane hastened to say, "Of course I see you are, now. It's quite plain now one comes to look at you."

"You came to look at me, several sentences ago," it said crossly, beginning to curl up again in the sand.

"Oh - don't go away again! Do talk some more," Robert cried. "I didn't know you were a Sand-fairy, but I knew directly I saw you that you were much the wonderfullest thing I'd ever seen."

The Sand-fairy seemed a shade less disagreeable after this.

"It isn't talking I mind," it said, "as long as you're reasonably civil. But I'm not going to make polite conversation for you. If you talk nicely to me, perhaps I'll answer you, and perhaps I won't. Now say something."

Of course no one could think of anything to say, but at last Robert thought of "How long have you lived here?" and he said it at once.

"Oh, ages – several thousand years," replied the Psammead.

"Tell us all about it. Do."

"It's all in books."

"You aren't!" Jane said. "Oh, tell us everything you can about yourself! We don't know anything about you, and you are so nice."

The Sand-fairy smoothed his long rat-like whiskers and smiled between them.

"Do please tell!" said the children all together.

It is wonderful how quickly you get used to things, even the most astonishing. Five minutes before, the children had had no more idea than you that there was such a thing as a sand-fairy in the world, and now they were talking to it as though they had known it all their lives. It drew its eyes in and said:

"How very sunny it is – quite like old times. Where do you get your Megatheriums from now?"

"What?" said the children all at once. It is very difficult always to remember that "what" is not polite, especially in moments of surprise or agitation.

"Are Pterodactyls plentiful now?" the Sand-fairy went on.

The children were unable to reply.

"What do you have for breakfast?" the Fairy said impatiently, "and who gives it you?"

"Eggs and bacon, and bread-and-milk, and porridge and things.

Mother gives it us. What are Mega-what's-its-names and Ptero-what-do-you-call-thems? And does anyone have them for breakfast?"

"Why, almost everyone had Pterodactyl for break-fast in my time! Pterodactyls were something like crocodiles and something like birds – I believe they were very good

"Don't you know a Sand-fairy when you see one?"

grilled. You see it was like this: of course there were heaps of sand-fairies then, and in the morning early you went out and hunted for them, and when you'd found one it gave you your wish. People used to send their little boys down to the seashore early in the morning before breakfast to get the day's wishes, and very often the eldest boy in the family would be told to wish for a Megatherium, ready jointed for cooking. It was as big as an elephant, you see, so there was a good deal of meat on it. And if they wanted fish, the Ichthyosaurus was asked for – he was twenty to forty feet long, so there was plenty of him. And for poultry there was the Plesiosaurus; there were nice pickings on that too. Then the other children could wish for other things. But when people had dinner-parties it was nearly always Megatheriums; and Ichthyosaurus, because his fins were a great delicacy and his tail made soup."

"There must have been heaps and heaps of cold meat left over," said Anthea, who meant to be a good housekeeper some day.

"Oh no," said the Psammead, "that would never have done. Why, of course at sunset what was left over turned into stone. You find the stone bones of the Megatherium and things all over the place even now, they tell me."

"Who tell you?" asked Cyril; but the Sand-fairy frowned and began to dig very fast with its furry hands.

"Oh, don't go!" they all cried; "tell us more about it when it was Megatheriums for breakfast! Was the world like this then?"

It stopped digging.

"Not a bit," it said; "it was nearly all sand where I lived, and coal grew on trees, and the periwinkles were as big as tea-trays – you find them now; they're turned into stone. We sand-fairies used to live on the seashore, and the children used to come with their little flint-spades and flint-pails and make castles for us to live in. That's thousands of years ago, but I hear that children still build castles on the sand. It's difficult to break yourself of a habit."

"But why did you stop living in the castles?" asked Robert.

"It's a sad story," said the Psammead gloomily. "It was because they WOULD build moats to the castles, and the nasty wet bubbling sea used to come in, and of course as soon as a sand-fairy got wet it caught cold, and generally died. And so there got to be fewer and fewer, and, whenever you found a fairy and had a wish, you used to wish for a Megatherium, and eat twice as much as you wanted, because it might be weeks before you got another wish."

"And did YOU get wet?" Robert inquired.

The Sand-fairy shuddered. "Only once," it said; "the end of the twelfth hair of my top left whisker – I feel the place still in damp weather. It was only once, but it was quite enough for me. I went away as soon as the sun had dried my poor dear whisker. I scurried away to the back of the beach, and dug myself a house deep in warm dry sand, and there I've been ever since. And the sea changed its lodgings afterwards. And now I'm not going to tell you another thing."

"Just one more, please," said the children. "Can you give wishes now?"

"Of course," said it; "didn't I give you yours a few minutes ago? You said, 'I wish you'd come out,' and I did."

"Oh, please, mayn't we have another?"

"Yes, but be quick about it. I'm tired of you."

I daresay you have often thought what you would do if you had three wishes given you, and have despised the old man and his wife in the black-pudding story, and felt certain that if you had the chance you could think of three really useful wishes without a moment's hesitation. These children had often talked this matter over, but, now the chance had suddenly come to them, they could not make up their minds.

"Quick," said the Sand-fairy crossly. No one could think of anything, only Anthea did manage to remember a private wish of her own and Jane's which they had never told the boys. She knew the boys would not care about it – but still it was better than nothing.

"I wish we were all as beautiful as the day," she said in a great hurry.

The children looked at each other, but each could see that the others were not any better-looking than usual. The Psammead pushed out its long eyes, and seemed to be holding its breath and swelling itself out till it was twice as fat and furry as before. Suddenly it let its breath go in a long sigh.

"I'm really afraid I can't manage it," it said apologetically; "I must be out of practice."

The children were horribly disappointed.

"Oh, DO try again!" they said.

"Well," said the Sand-fairy, "the fact is, I was keeping back a little strength to give the rest of you your wishes with. If you'll be contented with one wish a day amongst the lot of you I daresay I can screw myself up to it. Do you agree to that?"

"Yes, oh yes!" said Jane and Anthea. The boys nodded. They did not believe the Sand-fairy could do it. You can always make girls believe things much easier than you can boys.

It stretched out its eyes farther than ever, and swelled and swelled and swelled.

"I do hope it won't hurt itself," said Anthea.

"Or crack its skin," Robert said anxiously.

Everyone was very much relieved when the Sand-fairy, after getting so big that it almost filled up the hole in the sand, suddenly let out its breath and went back to its proper size.

"That's all right," it said, panting heavily. "It'll come easier to-morrow."

"Did it hurt much?" asked Anthea.

"Only my poor whisker, thank you," said he, "but you're a kind and thoughtful child. Good day."

It scratched suddenly and fiercely with its hands and feet, and disappeared in the sand. Then the children looked at each other, and each child suddenly found itself alone with three perfect strangers, all radiantly beautiful.

They stood for some moments in perfect silence. Each thought that its brothers and sisters had wandered off, and that these strange children had stolen up unnoticed while it was watching the swelling form of the Sand-fairy. Anthea spoke first –

"Excuse me," she said very politely to Jane, who now had enormous blue eyes and a cloud of russet hair, "but have you seen two little boys and a little girl anywhere about?"

"I was just going to ask you that," said Jane. And then Cyril cried:

"Why, it's YOU! I know the hole in your pinafore! You ARE Jane, aren't you? And you're the Panther; I can see your dirty handkerchief that you forgot to change after you'd cut your thumb! Crikey! The wish has come off, after all. I say, am I as handsome as you are?"

"If you're Cyril, I liked you much better as you were before," said Anthea decidedly. "You look like the picture of the young chorister, with your golden hair; you'll die young, I shouldn't wonder. And if that's Robert, he's like an Italian organ-grinder. His hair's all black."

"You two girls are like Christmas cards, then – that's all – silly Christmas cards," said Robert angrily. "And Jane's hair is simply carrots."

It was indeed of that Venetian tint so much admired by artists.

"Well, it's no use finding fault with each other," said Anthea; "let's get the Lamb and lug it home to dinner. The servants will admire us most awfully, you'll see."

The Selfish Giant

This is a moral tale by Oscar Wilde and tells how a mean giant learned to be kind and to share his beautiful garden and to relish every season of the year. It has been made into a Hungarian opera and a children's ballet in Australia.

Every afternoon, as they were coming from school, the children used to go and play in the Giant's garden.

It was a large lovely garden, with soft green grass. Here and there over the grass stood beautiful flowers like stars, and there were twelve peach-trees that in the spring-time broke out into delicate blossoms of pink and pearl, and in the autumn bore rich fruit. The birds sat on the trees and sang so sweetly that the children used to stop their games in order to listen to them. "How happy we are here!" they cried to each other.

One day the Giant came back. He had been to visit his friend the Cornish ogre, and had stayed with him for seven years. After the seven years were over he had said all that he had to say, for his conversation was limited, and he determined to return to his own castle. When he arrived he saw the children playing in the garden.

"What are you doing here?" he cried in a very gruff voice, and the children ran away.

"My own garden is my own garden," said the Giant; "any one can understand that, and I will allow nobody to play in it but myself." So he built a high wall all round it, and put up a notice-board.

Trespassers will be prosecuted

He was a very selfish Giant.

The poor children had now nowhere to play. They tried to play on the road, but the road was very dusty and full of hard stones, and they did not like it. They used to wander round the high wall when their lessons were over, and talk about the beautiful garden inside.

"How happy we were there," they said to each other.

Then the Spring came, and all over the country there were little blossoms and little birds. Only in the garden of the Selfish Giant it was still Winter. The birds did not care to sing in it as there were no children, and the trees forgot to blossom. Once a beautiful flower put its head out from the grass, but when it saw the notice-board it was so sorry for the children that it slipped back into the ground again, and went off to sleep. The only people who were pleased were the Snow and the Frost. "Spring has forgotten this garden," they cried, "so we will live here all the year round." The Snow covered up the grass with her great white cloak, and the Frost painted all the trees silver. Then they invited the North Wind to stay with them, and he came. He was wrapped in furs, and he roared all day about the garden, and blew the chimney-pots down. "This is a delightful spot," he said, "we must ask the Hail on a visit." So the Hail came. Every day for three hours he rattled on the roof of the castle till he broke most of the slates, and then he ran round and round the garden as fast as he could go. He was dressed in grey, and his breath was like ice.

"I cannot understand why the Spring is so late in coming," said the Selfish Giant, as he sat at the window and looked out at his cold white garden; "I hope there will be a change in the weather."

But the Spring never came, nor the Summer. The Autumn gave golden fruit to every garden, but to the Giant's garden she gave none. "He is too selfish," she said. So it was always Winter there, and the North Wind, and the Hail, and the Frost, and the Snow danced about through the trees.

One morning the Giant was lying awake in bed when he heard some lovely music. It sounded so sweet to his ears that he thought it must be the King's musicians passing by. It was really only a little linnet singing outside his window, but it was so long since he had heard a bird sing in his garden that it seemed to him to be the most beautiful music in the world. Then the Hail stopped dancing over his head, and the North Wind ceased roaring, and a delicious perfume came to him through the open casement. "I believe the Spring has come at last," said the Giant; and he jumped out of bed and looked out

What did he see?

He saw a most wonderful sight. Through a little hole in the wall the children had crept in, and they were sitting in the branches of the trees. In every tree that he could see there was a little child. And the trees were so glad to have the children back again that they had covered themselves with blossoms, and were waving their arms gently above the children's heads. The birds were flying about and twittering with delight, and the flowers were looking up through the green grass and laughing. It was a lovely scene, only in one corner it was still Winter. It was the farthest corner of the garden, and in it was standing a little boy. He was so small that he could not reach up to the branches of the tree, and he was wandering all round it, crying bitterly. The poor tree was still quite covered with frost and snow, and the North Wind was blowing and roaring above it. "Climb up! little boy," said the Tree, and it bent its branches down as low as it could; but the little boy was too tiny.

And the Giant's heart melted as he looked out. "How selfish I have been!" he said; "now I know why the Spring would not come here. I will put that poor little boy on the top of the tree, and then I will knock down the wall, and

The Selfish Giant would let no-one play in his garden

my garden shall be the children's playground for ever and ever." He was really very sorry for what he had done.

So he crept downstairs and opened the front door quite softly, and went out into the garden. But when the children saw him they were so frightened that they all ran away, and the garden became Winter again. Only the little boy did not run, for his eyes were so full of tears that he died not see the Giant coming. And the Giant stole up behind him and took him gently in his hand, and put him up into the tree. And the tree broke at once into blossom, and the birds came and sang on it, and the little boy stretched out his two arms and flung them round the Giant's neck, and kissed him. And the other children, when they saw that the Giant was not wicked any longer, came running back, and with them came the Spring. "It is your garden now, little children," said the Giant, and he took a great axe and knocked down the wall. And when the people were gong to market at twelve o'clock they found the Giant playing with the children in the most beautiful garden they had ever seen.

All day long they played, and in the evening they came to the Giant to bid him good-bye.

"But where is your little companion?" he said; "the boy I put into the tree." The Giant loved him the best because he had kissed him.

"We don't know," answered the children; "he has gone away."

"You must tell him to be sure and come here tomorrow," said the Giant. But the children said that they did not know where he lived, and had never seen him before; and the Giant felt very sad.

Every afternoon, when school was over, the children came and played with the Giant. But the little boy whom the Giant loved was never seen again. The Giant was very kind to all the children, yet he longed for his first little friend, and often spoke of him. "How I would like to see him!" he used to say.

Years went over, and the Giant grew very old and feeble. He could not play about any more, so he sat in a huge armchair, and watched the children at their games, and admired his garden. "I have many beautiful flowers," he said; "but the children are the most beautiful flowers of all."

One winter morning he looked out of his window as he was dressing. He did not hate the Winter now, for he knew that it was merely the Spring asleep, and that the flowers were resting.

Suddenly he rubbed his eyes in wonder, and looked and looked. It certainly was a marvellous sight. In the farthest corner of the garden was a tree quite covered with lovely white blossoms. Its branches were all golden, and silver fruit hung down from them, and underneath it stood the little boy he had loved.

Downstairs ran the Giant in great joy, and out into the garden. He hastened across the grass, and came near to the child. And when he came quite close his face grew red with anger, and he said, "Who hath dared to wound thee?" For on the palms of the child's hands were the prints of two nails, and the prints of two nails were on the little feet.

"Who hath dared to wound thee?" cried the Giant; "tell me, that I may take my big sword and slay him."

"Nay!" answered the child; "but these are the wounds of Love."

"Who art thou?" said the Giant, and a strange awe fell on him, and he knelt before the little child.

And the child smiled on the Giant, and said to him, "You let me play once in your garden, today you shall come with me to my garden, which is Paradise."

And when the children ran in that afternoon, they found the Giant lying dead under the tree, all covered with white blossoms.

The Giant's heart melted

Alice's Adventures in Wonderland

Lewis Carroll's Alice adventures are absolute nonsense of course – or are they? Her rabbit hole may have represented the stairs in the back of the main hall in Christ Church, Oxford, where Lewis Carroll was a mathematician (there are several references to mathematics and logic) and there is a griffon and rabbit carving in Ripon Catherdral where his father was canon.

Chapter VII
A Mad Tea-Party

There was a table set out under a tree in front of the house, and the March Hare and the Hatter were having tea at it: a Dormouse was sitting between them, fast asleep, and the other two were using it as a

cushion, resting their elbows on it, and talking over its head. "Very uncomfortable for the Dormouse," thought Alice; "only, as it's asleep, I suppose it doesn't mind."

The table was a large one, but the three were all crowded together at one corner of it: "No room! No room!" they cried out when they saw Alice coming. "There's plenty of room!" said Alice indignantly, and she sat down in a large arm-chair at one end of the table.

"Have some wine," the March Hare said in an encouraging tone.

Alice looked all round the table, but there was nothing on it but tea. "I don't see any wine," she remarked.

"There isn't any," said the March Hare.

"Then it wasn't very civil of you to offer it," said Alice angrily.

"It wasn't very civil of you to sit down without being invited," said the March Hare.

"I didn't know it was your table," said Alice; "it's laid for a great many more than three."

"Your hair wants cutting," said the Hatter. He had been looking at Alice for some time with great curiosity, and this was his first speech.

"You should learn not to make personal remarks," Alice said with some severity; "it's very rude."

The Hatter opened his eyes very wide on hearing this; but all he said was, "Why is a raven like a writing-desk?"

"Come, we shall have some fun now!" thought Alice. "I'm glad they've begun asking riddles – I believe I can guess that," she added aloud.

"Do you mean that you think you can find out the answer to it?" said the March Hare.

"Exactly so," said Alice.

"Then you should say what you mean," the March Hare went on.

"I do," Alice hastily replied; "at least – at least I mean what I say – that's the same thing, you know."

"Not the same thing a bit!" said the Hatter. "You might just as well say that 'I see what I eat' is the same thing as 'I eat what I see!'"

"You might just as well say," added the March Hare, 'that I like what I get' is the same thing as 'I get what I like!'"

"You might just as well say," added the Dormouse, who seemed to be talking in his sleep, "that 'I breathe when I sleep' is the same thing as 'I sleep when I breathe!'"

"It is the same thing with you," said the Hatter, and here the conversation dropped, and the party sat silent for a minute, while Alice thought over all she could remember about ravens and writing-desks, which wasn't much.

The Hatter was the first to break the silence. "What day of the month is it?" he said, turning to Alice: he had taken his watch out of his pocket, and was looking at it uneasily, shaking it every

now and then, and holding it to his ear.

Alice considered a little, and then said, "The fourth."

"Two days wrong!" sighed the Hatter. "I told you butter wouldn't suit the works!" he added looking angrily at the March Hare.

"It was the best butter," the March Hare meekly replied.

"Yes, but some crumbs must have got in as well," the Hatter grumbled; "you shouldn't have put it in with the bread-knife."

The March Hare took the watch and looked at it gloomily: then he dipped it into his cup of tea, and looked at it again: but he could think of nothing better to say than his first remark, "It was the best butter, you know."

Alice had been looking over his shoulder with some curiosity. "What a funny watch!" she remarked. "It tells the day of the month, and doesn't tell what o'clock it is!"

"Why should it?" muttered the Hatter. "Does your watch tell you what year it is?"

"Have some wine,"
the March Hare said in an encouraging tone

The book was published in 1865, three years after the Reverend Charles Lutwidge Dodgson (the author's real name) had rowed in a boat with the Reverend Duckworth, Vice-Chancellor of Oxford University and Dean of Christ Church, plus Duckworth's three young daughters – one of whom was called Alice.

"Of course not," Alice replied very readily; "but that's because it stays the same year for such a long time together."

"Which is just the case with mine," said the Hatter.

Alice felt dreadfully puzzled. The Hatter's remark seemed to have no sort of meaning in it, and yet it was certainly English. "I don't quite understand you," she said, as politely as she could.

"The Dormouse is asleep again," said the Hatter, and he poured a little hot tea upon its nose.

The Dormouse shook its head impatiently, and said, without opening its eyes, "Of course, of course; just what I was going to remark myself."

"Have you guessed the riddle yet?" the Hatter said, turning to Alice again.

"No, I give up," Alice replied; "what's the answer?"

"I haven't the slightest idea," said the Hatter.

"Nor I," said the March Hare.

Alice sighed wearily. "I think you might do something better with the time," she said, "than waste it in asking riddles that have no answers."

"If you knew Time as well as I do," said the Hatter, "you wouldn't talk about wasting it. It's him."

"I don't know what you mean," said Alice.

"Of course you don't!" the Hatter said, tossing his head contemptuously. "I dare say you never even spoke to Time!"

"Perhaps not," Alice cautiously replied: "but I know I have to beat time when I learn music."

"Ah! that accounts for it," said the Hatter. "He won't stand beating. Now, if you only kept on good terms with him, he'd do almost anything you liked with the clock. For instance, suppose it were nine o'clock in the morning, just

If you knew Time as well as I do," said the Hatter;
"you wouldn't talk about wasting it

time to begin lessons: you'd only have to whisper a hint to Time, and round goes the clock in a twinkling! Half-past one, time for dinner!"

("I only wish it was," the March Hare said to itself in a whisper.)

"That would be grand, certainly," said Alice thoughtfully; "but then – I shouldn't be hungry for it, you know."

"Not at first, perhaps," said the Hatter; "but you could keep it to half-past one as long as you liked."

"Is that the way you manage?" Alice asked.

The Hatter shook his head mournfully. "Not I!" he replied. "We quarrelled last March – just before he went mad, you know –" (pointing with his tea spoon at the March Hare) – "it was at the great concert given by the Queen of Hearts, and I had to sing:

Twinkle, twinkle, little bat!
How I wonder what you're at!

"You know the song, perhaps?"

"I've heard something like it," said Alice.

"It goes on, you know," the Hatter continued, "in this way:

Up above the world you fly,
Like a tea-tray in the sky.
Twinkle, twinkle..."

Here the Dormouse shook itself, and began singing in its sleep, "Twinkle, twinkle, twinkle, twinkle..." and went on so long that they had to pinch it to make it stop.

"Well, I'd hardly finished the first verse," said the Hatter, "when the Queen jumped up and bawled out, 'He's murdering the time! Off with his head!' "

"How dreadfully savage!" exclaimed Alice.

"And ever since that," the Hatter went on in a mournful tone, "he won't do a thing I ask! It's always six o'clock now."

A bright idea came into Alice's head. "Is that the reason so many tea-things are put out here?" she asked.

"Yes, that's it," said the Hatter with a sigh; "it's always tea-time, and we've no time to wash the things between whiles."

"Then you keep moving round, I suppose?" said Alice.

"Exactly so," said the Hatter; "as the things get used up."

"But what happens when you come to the beginning again?" Alice ventured to ask.

"Suppose we change the subject," the March Hare interrupted, yawning. "I'm getting tired of this. I vote the young lady tells us a story."

"I'm afraid I don't know one," said Alice, rather alarmed at the proposal.

"Then the Dormouse shall!" they both cried. "Wake up, Dormouse!" And they pinched it on both sides at once.

The Dormouse slowly opened his eyes. "I wasn't asleep," he said in a hoarse, feeble voice; "I heard every word you fellows were saying."

"Tell us a story!" said the March Hare.

"Yes, please do!" pleaded Alice.

"And be quick about it," added the Hatter, "or you'll be asleep again before it's done."

"Once upon a time there were three little sisters," the Dormouse began in a great hurry; "and their names were Elsie, Lacie, and Tillie; and they lived at the bottom of a well –"

"What did they live on?" said Alice, who always took a great interest in questions of eating and drinking.

"They lived on treacle," said the Dormouse, after thinking a minute or two.

"They couldn't have done that, you know," Alice gently remarked; "they'd have been ill."

"So they were," said the Dormouse; "very ill."

Alice tried to fancy to herself what such an extraordinary ways of living would be like, but it puzzled her too much, so she went on: "But why did they live at the bottom of a well?"

"Take some more tea," the March Hare said to Alice, very earnestly.

"I've had nothing yet," Alice replied in an offended tone, "so I can't take more."

"You mean you can't take less," said the Hatter; "it's very easy to take more than nothing."

"Nobody asked your opinion," said Alice.

"Who's making personal remarks now?" the Hatter asked triumphantly.

Alice did not quite know what to say to this: so she helped herself to some tea and bread-and-butter, and then turned to the Dormouse, and repeated her question. "Why did they live at the bottom of a well?"

The Dormouse again took a minute or two to think about it, and then said, "It was a treacle-well."

"There's no such thing!" Alice was beginning very angrily, but the Hatter and the March Hare went "Sh! sh!" and the Dormouse sulkily remarked, "If you can't be civil, you'd better finish the story for yourself."

"No, please go on!" Alice said very humbly; "I won't interrupt again. I dare say there may be one."

"One, indeed!" said the Dormouse indignantly. However, he consented to go on. "And so these three little sisters – they were learning to draw, you know –"

"What did they draw?" said Alice, quite forgetting her promise.

"Treacle," said the Dormouse, without considering at all this time.

"I want a clean cup," interrupted the Hatter; "let's all move one place on."

He moved on as he spoke, and the Dormouse followed him: the March Hare moved into the Dormouse's place, and Alice rather unwillingly took the place of the March Hare. The Hatter was the only one who got any advantage from the change: and Alice was a good deal worse off than before, as the March Hare had just upset the milk-jug into his plate.

Alice did not wish to offend the Dormouse again, so she began very cautiously: "But I don't understand. Where did they draw the treacle from?"

"You can draw water out of a water-well," said the Hatter; "so I should think you could draw treacle out of a treacle-well – eh, stupid?"

"But they were in the well," Alice said to the Dormouse, not choosing to notice this last remark.

"Of course they were", said the Dormouse; "– well in."

This answer so confused poor Alice, that she let the Dormouse go on for some time without interrupting it.

"They were learning to draw," the Dormouse went on, yawning and rubbing its eyes, for it was getting very sleepy; "and they drew all manner of things – everything that begins with an M –"

"Why with an M?" said Alice.

"Why not?" said the March Hare.

Alice was silent.

The Dormouse had closed its eyes by this time, and was going off into a doze; but, on being pinched by the Hatter, it woke up again with a little shriek, and went on: "– that begins with an M, such as mouse-traps, and the moon, and memory, and muchness – you know you say things are 'much of a muchness' – did you ever see such a thing as a drawing of a muchness?"

"Really, now you ask me," said Alice, very much confused, "I don't think –"

"Then you shouldn't talk," said the Hatter.

This piece of rudeness was more than Alice could bear: she got up in great disgust, and walked off; the Dormouse fell asleep instantly, and neither of the others took the least notice of her going, though she looked back once or twice, half hoping that they would call after her: the last time she saw them, they were trying to put the Dormouse into the teapot.

"At any rate I'll never go there again!" said Alice as she picked her way through the wood. "It's the stupidest tea-party I ever was at in all my life!"

"I'm late!" muttered the White Rabbit

The Dragon and the Prince

This Serbian tale was collected by
A. H. Wratislaw and published
in 1890 in his collection of *Sixty
folk-tales* from exclusively Slavonic
sources. The following version was
included in Andrew Lang's
Crimson Fairy Book.

There was an emperor who had three sons. One day the eldest son went out hunting, and when he got outside the town, up sprang a hare out of a bush, and he after it, and hither and thither, till the hare fled into a water-mill, and the prince after it. But it was not a hare, but a dragon, and it waited for the prince and devoured him. When several days had elapsed and the prince did not return home, people began to wonder why it was that he was not to be found. Then the middle son went hunting, and as he issued from the town, a hare sprang out of a bush, and the prince after it, and hither and thither, till the hare fled into the water-mill and the prince after it; but it was not a hare, but a dragon, which waited for and devoured him. When some days had elapsed and the princes did not return, either of them, the whole court was in sorrow. Then the third son went hunting, to see whether he could not find his brothers. When he issued from the town, again up sprang a hare out

A hare sprang out of a bush

of a bush, and the prince after it, and hither and thither, till the hare fled into the water-mill. But the prince did not choose to follow it, but went to find other game, saying to himself: "When I return I shall find you." After this he went for a long time up and down the hill, but found nothing, and then returned to the water-mill; but when he got there, there was only an old woman in the mill. The prince invoked God in addressing her: "God help you, old woman!" The old woman replied: "God help you, my son!" Then the prince asked her: "Where, old woman, is my hare?" She replied: "My son,

that was not a hare, but a dragon. It kills and throttles many people." Hearing this, the prince was somewhat disturbed, and said to the old woman: "What shall we do now? Doubtless my two brothers also have perished here." The old woman answered: "They have indeed; but there's no help for it. Go home, my son, lest you follow them." Then he said to her: "Dear old woman, do you know what? I know that you will be glad to liberate yourself from that pest." The old woman interrupted him: "How should I not? It captured me, too, in this way, but now I have no means of escape." Then he proceeded: "Listen well to what I am going to say to you. Ask it whither it goes and where its strength is; then kiss all that place where it tells you its strength is, as if from love, till you ascertain it, and afterwards tell me when I come." Then the prince went off to the palace, and the old woman remained in the water-mill. When the dragon came in, the old woman began to question it: Where in God's name have you been? Whither do you go so far? You will never tell me whither you go." The dragon replied: "Well, my dear old woman, I do go far." Then the old woman began to coax it: "And why do you go so far? Tell me where your strength is. If I knew where your strength is, I don't know what I should do for love; I would kiss all that place." Thereupon the dragon smiled and said to her: "Yonder is my strength, in that fireplace." Then the old woman began to fondle and kiss the fireplace, and the dragon on seeing it burst into a laugh, and said to her: "Silly old woman, my strength isn't there; my strength is in that tree-fungus in front of the house." Then the old woman began again to fondle and kiss the tree, and the dragon again laughed, and said to her: "Away, old woman! my strength isn't there." Then the old woman inquired: "Where is it?" The dragon began to give an account in detail: "My strength is a long way off, and you cannot go thither. Far in another empire under the emperor's city is a lake, in that lake is a dragon, and in the dragon a boar, and in the boar a pigeon, and in that is my strength." The next morning when the dragon went away from the mill, the prince came to the old woman, and the old woman told him all that she had heard from the dragon. Then he left his home, and disguised himself; he put shepherd's boots on his feet, took a shepherd's staff in his hand, and went into the world. As he went on thus from village to village, and from town to town, at last he came into another empire and into the imperial city, in a lake under which the dragon was. On going into the town, he began to inquire who wanted a shepherd. The citizens told him that the emperor did. Then he went straight to the emperor. After he announced himself, the emperor

The prince bravely fought the terrible dragon

admitted him into his presence, and asked him: Do you wish to keep sheep?" He replied: "I do, illustrious crown!" Then the emperor engaged him, and began to inform and instruct him: "There is here a lake, and alongside of the lake very beautiful pasture, and when you call the sheep out, they go thither at once, and spread themselves round the lake; but whatever shepherd goes off there, that shepherd returns back no more. Therefore, my son, I tell you, don't let the sheep have their own way and go where they will, but keep them where you will." The prince thanked the emperor, got himself ready, and called out the sheep, taking with him, moreover, two hounds that could catch a boar in the open country, and a falcon that could capture any bird, and carrying also a pair of bagpipes. When he called out the sheep he let them go at once to the lake, and when the sheep arrived at the lake, they immediately spread round it, and the prince placed the falcon on a stump, and the hounds and bagpipes under the stump, then tucked up his hose and sleeves, waded into the lake, and began to shout "Dragon! dragon! come out to single combat with me today that we may measure ourselves together, unless you're a woman." The dragon called out in reply, "I will do so now, prince – now!" Erelong, behold the dragon! it is large, it is terrible, it is disgusting! When the dragon came out, it seized him by the waist, and

they wrestled a summer day till afternoon. But when the heat of afternoon came on, the dragon said: "Let me go, prince, that I may moisten my parched head in the lake, and toss you to the sky." But the prince replied: "Come, dragon, don't talk nonsense; if I had the emperor's daughter to kiss me on the forehead, I would toss you still higher." Thereupon the dragon suddenly let go of him, and went off into the lake. On the approach of evening, he washed and got himself up nicely, placed the falcon on his arm, the hounds behind him, and the bagpipes under his arm, then drove the sheep and went into the town playing on the bagpipes. When he arrived at the town, the whole town assembled as to see a wondrous sight because he had come, whereas previously no shepherd had been able to come from the lake. The next day the prince got ready again, and went with his sheep straight to the lake. But the emperor sent two grooms after him to go stealthily and see what he did, and they placed themselves on a high hill whence they could have a good view. When the shepherd arrived, he put the hounds and bagpipes under the stump and the falcon upon it, then tucked up his hose and sleeves, waded into the lake and shouted: "Dragon, dragon! come out to single combat with me, that we may measure ourselves once more together, unless you are a woman!" The dragon replied: "I will do so, prince; now, now!"

The emperor had watched the fierce battle from a hilltop near by

Erelong, behold the dragon! it was large, it was terrible, it was disgusting! And it seized him by the waist and wrestled with him a summer's day till afternoon. But when the afternoon heat came on, the dragon said: "Let me go, prince, that I may moisten my parched head in the lake, and may toss you to the sky." The prince replied: "Come, dragon, don't talk nonsense; if I had the emperor's daughter to kiss me on the forehead, I would toss you still higher." Thereupon the dragon suddenly left hold of him, and went off into the lake. When night approached the prince drove the sheep as before, and went home playing the bagpipes. When he arrived at the town, the whole town was astir and began to wonder because the shepherd came home every evening, which no one had been able to do before. Those two grooms had already arrived at the palace before the prince, and related to the emperor in order everything that they had heard and seen. Now when the emperor saw that the shepherd returned home, he immediately summoned his daughter into his presence and told her all, what it was and how it was. "But," said he, "tomorrow you must go with the shepherd to the lake and kiss him on the forehead." When she heard this she burst into tears and began to entreat her father. "You have no one but me, and I am your only daughter, and you don't care about me if I perish." Then the emperor began to persuade and encourage her: "Don't fear, my daughter; you see, we have had so many changes of shepherds, and of all that went out to the lake not one has returned; but he has been contending with the dragon for two whole days and it has done him no hurt. I assure you, in God's name, that he is able to overcome the dragon, only go tomorrow with him to see whether he will free us from this mischief which has destroyed so many people."

When, on the morrow, the day dawned, the day dawned and the sun came forth, up rose the shepherd, up rose the maiden too, to begin to prepare for going to the lake. The shepherd was cheerful, more cheerful than ever, but the emperor's daughter was sad, and shed tears. The shepherd comforted her: "Lady sister, I pray you, do not weep, but do what I tell you. When it is time, run up and kiss me, and fear not." As he went and drove the sheep, the shepherd was thoroughly cheery, and played a merry tune on his bagpipes; but the damsel did nothing but weep as she went beside him, and he several times left off playing and turned towards her: "Weep not, golden one; fear nought." When they arrived at the lake, the sheep immediately spread round it, and the prince placed the falcon on the stump, and the hounds and bagpipes under it, then tucked up his hose and sleeves, waded into the water, and shouted: "Dragon! dragon! Come out to single combat with me; let us measure ourselves once more, unless you're a woman!" The dragon replied: "I will, prince; now, now!" Erelong, there was the dragon! it was huge, it was terrible, it was disgusting! When it came out, they seized each other by the middle, and wrestled a summer's day till afternoon. But when the afternoon heat came on, the dragon said:

"Let me go, prince, that I may moisten my parched head in the lake, and toss you to the skies." The prince replied "Come, dragon, don't talk nonsense; if I had the emperor's daughter to kiss me on the forehead, I would toss you much higher." When he said this, the emperor's daughter ran up and kissed him on the face, on the eye, and on the forehead. Then he swung the dragon, and tossed it high into the air, and when it fell to the ground it burst into pieces. But as it burst into pieces, out of it sprang a wild boar, and started to run away. But the prince shouted to his shepherd dogs: "Hold it! don't let it go!" and the dogs sprang up and after it, caught it, and soon tore it to pieces. But out of the boar flew a pigeon, and the prince loosed the falcon, and the falcon caught the pigeon and brought it into the prince's hands. The prince said to it: "Tell me now, where are my brothers?" The pigeon replied: "I will; only do me no harm. Immediately behind your father's town is a water-mill, and in the water-mill are three wands that have sprouted up. Cut these three wands up from below, and strike with them upon their root; an iron door will immediately open into a large vault. In that vault are many people, old and young, rich and poor, small and great, wives and maidens, so that you could settle a populous empire; there, too, are your brothers." When the pigeon had told him all this, the prince immediately wrung its neck.

The emperor had gone out in person, and posted himself on the hill from which the grooms had viewed the shepherd, and he, too, was a spectator of all that had taken place. After the shepherd had thus obtained the dragon's head, twilight began to approach. He washed himself nicely, took the falcon on his shoulder, the hounds behind him, and the bagpipes under his arm, played as he went, drove the sheep, and proceeded to the emperor's palace, with the damsel at his side still in terror. When they came to the town, all the town assembled as to see a wonder. The emperor, who had seen all his heroism from the hill, called him into his presence, and gave him his daughter, went immediately to church, had them married, and held a wedding festival for a week. After this the prince told him who and whence he was, and the emperor and the whole town rejoiced still more. Then, as the prince was urgent to go to his own home, the emperor gave him a large escort, and equipped him for the journey. When they were in the neighbourhood of the water-mill, the prince halted his attendants, went inside, cut up the three wands, and struck the root with them, and the iron door opened at once. In the vault was a vast multitude of people. The prince ordered them to come out one by one, and go whither each would, and stood himself at the door. They came out thus one after another, and lo! there were his brothers also, whom he embraced and kissed. When the whole multitude had come out, they thanked him for releasing and delivering them, and went each to his own home. But he went, to his father's house with his brothers and bride, and there lived and reigned to the end of his days.

Peter Pan

Peter could not understand why, but Wendy was just slightly disappointed when he admitted that he came to the nursery window not to see her but to listen to stories.

"You see, I don't know any stories. None of the lost boys knows any stories."

"How perfectly awful," Wendy said.

"Do you know," Peter asked, "why swallows build in the eaves of houses? It is to listen to the stories. O Wendy, your mother was telling you such a lovely story."

"Which story was it?"

"About the prince who couldn't find the lady who wore the glass slipper."

"Peter," said Wendy excitedly, "that was Cinderella, and he found her, and they lived happily ever after."

Peter was so glad that he rose from the floor, where they had been sitting, and hurried to the window.

"Where are you going?" she cried with misgiving.

A statue of Peter Pan blowing his pipes

From Chapter 3
***Come Away, Come Away!* 1634**
This mischievous boy who never grows up and who flies like a bird lives on the small island of Neverland with the Lost Boys, mermaids, Indians, pirates – including the ferocious Captain Hook – and a tick-tocking crocodile. Barrie's much-loved character first appeared in *The Little White Bird*, a 1902 novel for adults. The stage play was launched on 27 December 1904 and ever since then, its royalties have been donated to London's Great Ormond Street Hospital for Children.

"To tell the other boys."

"Don't go Peter," she entreated, "I know such lots of stories."

Those were her precise words, so there can be no denying that it was she who first tempted him.

He came back, and there was a greedy look in his eyes now which ought to have alarmed her, but did not.

"Oh, the stories I could tell to the boys!" she cried, and then Peter gripped her and began to draw her toward the window.

"Let me go!" she ordered him.

"Wendy, do come with me and tell the other boys."

Of course she was very pleased to be asked, but she said, "Oh dear, I can't. Think of mummy! Besides, I can't fly."

"I'll teach you."

"Oh, how lovely to fly."

"I'll teach you how to jump on the wind's back, and then away we go."

"Oo!" she exclaimed rapturously.

"Wendy, Wendy, when you are sleeping in your silly bed you might be flying about with me saying funny things to the stars."

"Oo!"

"And, Wendy, there are mermaids."

"Mermaids! With tails?"

"Such long tails."

"Oh," cried Wendy, "to see a mermaid!"

He had become frightfully cunning. "Wendy," he said, "how we should all respect you."

She was wriggling her body in distress. It was quite as if she were trying to remain on the nursery floor.

But he had no pity for her.

"Wendy," he said, the sly one, "you could tuck us in at night."

"Oo!"

"None of us has ever been tucked in at night."

"Oo," and her arms went out to him.

Wendy Darling, always a maternal character, is mending clothes for the Lost Boys in Neverland

"And you could darn our clothes, and make pockets for us. None of us has any pockets."

How could she resist. "Of course it's awfully fascinating!" she cried. "Peter, would you teach John and Michael to fly too?"

"If you like," he said indifferently, and she ran to John and Michael and shook them. "Wake up," she cried, "Peter Pan has come and he is to teach us to fly."

John rubbed his eyes. "Then I shall get up," he said. Of course he was on the floor already. "Hallo," he said, "I am up!"

Michael was up by this time also, looking as sharp as a knife with six blades and a saw, but Peter suddenly signed silence. Their faces assumed the awful craftiness of children listening for sounds from the grown-up world. All was as still as salt. Then everything was right. No, stop! Everything was wrong. Nana, who had been barking distressfully all the evening, was quiet now. It was her silence they had heard.

"Out with the light! Hide! Quick!" cried John, taking command for the only time throughout the whole adventure. And thus when Liza entered, holding Nana, the nursery seemed quite its old self, very dark, and you would have sworn you heard its three wicked inmates breathing angelically as they slept. They were really doing it artfully from behind the window curtains.

Liza was in a bad temper, for she was mixing the Christmas puddings in the kitchen, and had been drawn from them, with a raisin still on her cheek, by Nana's absurd suspicions. She thought the best way of getting a little quiet was to take Nana to the nursery for a moment, but in custody of course.

"There, you suspicious brute," she said, not sorry that Nana was in disgrace. "They are perfectly safe, aren't they? Every one of the little angels sound asleep in bed. Listen to their gentle breathing."

Here Michael, encouraged by his success, breathed so loudly that they were nearly detected. Nana knew that kind of breathing, and she tried to drag herself out of Liza's clutches.

But Liza was dense. "No more of it, Nana," she said sternly, pulling her out of the room. "I warn you if you bark again I shall go straight for master and missus and bring them home from the party, and then, oh, won't master whip you, just."

She tied the unhappy dog up again, but do you think Nana ceased to bark? Bring master and missus home from the party! Why, that was just what she wanted. Do you think she cared whether she was whipped so long as her charges were safe? Unfortunately Liza returned to her puddings, and Nana, seeing that no help would come from her, strained and strained at the chain until at last she broke it. In another moment she had burst into the dining-room of 27 and flung up her paws to heaven, her most expressive way of making a communication. Mr. and Mrs. Darling knew at once that something terrible was happening in their nursery, and without a good-bye to their hostess they rushed into the street.

But it was now ten minutes since three scoundrels had been breathing behind the curtains, and Peter Pan can do a great deal in ten minutes.

We now return to the nursery.

"It's all right," John announced, emerging from his hiding-place. "I say, Peter, can you really fly?"

Instead of troubling to answer him Peter flew around the room, taking the mantelpiece on the way.

"How topping!" said John and Michael.

"How sweet!" cried Wendy.

"Yes, I'm sweet, oh, I am sweet!" said Peter, forgetting his manners again.

It looked delightfully easy, and they tried it first from the floor and then from the beds, but they always went down instead of up.

"I say, how do you do it?" asked John, rubbing his knee. He was quite a practical boy.

"You just think lovely wonderful thoughts," Peter explained, "and they lift you up in the air."

He showed them again.

"You're so nippy at it," John said, "couldn't you do it very slowly once?"

Peter did it both slowly and quickly. "I've got it now, Wendy!" cried John, but soon he found he had not. Not one of them could fly an inch, though even Michael was in words of two syllables, and Peter did not know A from Z.

Of course Peter had been trifling with them, for no one can fly unless the fairy dust has been blown on him. Fortunately, as we have mentioned, one of his hands was messy with it, and he blew some on each of them, with the most superb results.

"Now just wiggle your shoulders this way," he said, "and let go."

They were all on their beds, and gallant Michael let go first. He did not quite mean to let go, but he did it, and immediately he was borne across the room.

"I flewed!" he screamed while still in mid-air.

John let go and met Wendy near the bathroom.

"Oh, lovely!"

"Oh, ripping!"

"Look at me!"

"Look at me!"

"Look at me!"

They were not nearly so elegant as Peter, they could not help kicking a little, but their heads were bobbing against the ceiling, and there is almost nothing so delicious as that. Peter gave Wendy a hand at first, but had to desist, Tink was so indignant.

Up and down they went, and round and round. Heavenly was Wendy's word.

"I say," cried John, "why shouldn't we all go out?"

Of course it was to this that Peter had been luring them.

Michael was ready: he wanted to see how long it took him to do a billion miles. But Wendy hesitated.

"Mermaids!" said Peter again.

"Oo!"

"And there are pirates."

"Pirates," cried John, seizing his Sunday hat, "let us go at once."

It was just at this moment that Mr. and Mrs. Darling hurried with Nana out of 27. They ran into the middle of the street to look up at the nursery window; and, yes, it was still shut, but the room was ablaze with light, and most heart-gripping sight of all, they could see in shadow on the curtain three little figures in night attire circling round and round, not on the floor but in the air.

Not three figures, four!

In a tremble they opened the street door. Mr. Darling would have rushed upstairs, but Mrs. Darling signed him to go softly. She even tried to make her heart go softly.

Will they reach the nursery in time? If so, how delightful for them, and we shall all breathe a sigh of relief, but there will be no story. On the other hand, if they are not in time, I solemnly promise that it will all come right in the end.

They would have reached the nursery in time had it not been that the little stars were watching them. Once again the stars blew the window open, and that smallest star of all called out:

"Cave, Peter!"

Then Peter knew that there was not a moment to lose. "Come," he cried imperiously, and soared out at once into the night, followed by John and Michael and Wendy.

Mr. and Mrs. Darling and Nana rushed into the nursery too late. The birds were flown.

Peter Pan and a pirate ship in Neverland

The Little Mermaid

Written in 1830, in the earliest version of the story Hans Christian Andersen originally ended the tale with the mermaid dissolving. He later added the 'daughters of air' sequence, showing how everlasting life can be achieved – even for a mermaid.

Far out in the ocean the water is as blue as the petals of the loveliest cornflower, and as clear as the purest glass. But it is very deep too. It goes down deeper than any anchor rope will go, and many, many steeples would have to be stacked one on top of another to reach from the bottom to the surface of the sea. It is down there that the sea folk live.

Now don't suppose that there are only bare white sands at the bottom of the sea. No indeed! The most marvelous trees and flowers grow down there, with such pliant stalks and leaves that the least stir in the water makes them move about as though they were alive. All sorts of fish, large and small, dart among the branches, just as birds flit through the trees up here. From the deepest spot in the ocean rises the palace of the sea king. Its walls are made of coral and its high pointed windows of the clearest amber, but the roof is made of mussel shells that open and shut with the tide. This is a wonderful sight to see, for every shell holds glistening pearls, any one of which would be the pride of a queen's crown.

The sea king down there had been a widower for years, and his old mother kept house for him. She was a clever woman, but very proud of her noble birth. Therefore she flaunted twelve oysters on her tail while the other ladies of the court were only allowed to wear six. Except for this she was an altogether praiseworthy person, particularly so because she was extremely fond of her granddaughters, the little sea princesses. They were six lovely girls, but the youngest was the most beautiful of them all. Her skin was as soft and tender as a rose petal, and her eyes were as blue as the deep sea, but like all the others she had no feet. Her body ended in a fish tail.

The whole day long they used to play in the palace, down in the great halls where live flowers grew on the walls. Whenever the high amber windows were thrown open the fish would swim in, just as swallows dart into our rooms when we open the windows. But these fish, now, would swim right up to the little princesses to eat out of their hands and let themselves be petted.

Outside the palace was a big garden, with flaming red and deep-blue trees. Their fruit glittered like gold, and their blossoms flamed like fire on their constantly waving stalks. The soil was very fine sand indeed, but as blue as burning brimstone. A strange blue veil lay over everything down there. You would have thought yourself aloft in the air with only the blue sky above and beneath you, rather than down at the bottom of the sea. When there was a dead calm, you could just see the sun, like a scarlet flower with light streaming from its calyx.

Each little princess had her own small garden plot, where she could dig and plant whatever she liked. One of them made her little flower bed in the shape of a whale, another thought it neater to shape hers like a little mermaid, but the youngest of them made hers as round as the sun, and there she grew only flowers which were as red as the sun itself. She was an unusual child, quiet and wistful, and when her sisters decorated their gardens with all kinds of odd things they had found in sunken ships, she would allow nothing in hers except flowers as red as the sun, and a pretty marble statue. This figure of a handsome boy, carved in pure white marble, had sunk down to the bottom of the sea from some ship that was wrecked. Beside the statue she planted a rose-colored weeping willow tree, which thrived so well that its graceful branches shaded the statue and hung down to the blue sand, where their shadows took on a violet tint, and swayed as the branches swayed. It looked as if the roots and the tips of the branches were kissing each other in play.

Nothing gave the youngest princess such pleasure as to hear about the world of human beings up above them. Her old grandmother had to tell her all she knew about ships and cities, and of people and animals. What seemed nicest of all to her was that up on land the flowers were fragrant, for those at the bottom of the sea had no scent. And she thought it was nice that the woods were green, and that the fish you saw among their branches could sing so loud and sweet that it was delightful to hear them. Her grandmother had to call the little birds "fish", or the princess would not have known what she was talking about, for she had never seen a bird.

"When you get to be fifteen," her grandmother said, "you will be allowed to rise up out of the ocean and sit on the rocks in the moonlight, to watch the great ships sailing by. You will see woods and towns, too."

Next year one of her sisters would be fifteen, but the others – well, since each was a whole year older than the next the youngest still had five long years to wait until she could rise up from the water and see what our world was like. But each sister promised to tell the others about all that she saw, and what she found most marvelous on her first day. Their grandmother had not told them half enough, and there were so many thing that they longed to know about.

The most eager of them all was the youngest, the very one who was so quiet and wistful. Many a night she stood by her open window and looked up through the dark blue water where the fish waved their fins and tails. She could just see the moon and stars. To be sure, their light was quite dim, but looked at through the water they seemed much bigger than they appear to us. Whenever a cloud-like shadow swept across them, she knew that it was either a whale swimming overhead, or a ship with many human beings aboard it. Little did they dream that a pretty young mermaid was down below, stretching her white arms up toward the keel of their ship.

The eldest princess had her fifteenth birthday, so now she received permission to rise up out of the water. When she got back she had a hundred things to tell her sisters about, but the most marvellous thing of all, she said, was to lie on a sand bar in the moonlight, when the sea was calm, and to gaze at the large city on the shore, where the lights twinkled like hundreds of stars; to listen to music; to hear the chatter and clamour of carriages and people; to see so many church towers and spires; and to hear the ringing bells. Because she could not enter the city, that was just what she most dearly longed to do.

Oh, how intently the youngest sister listened. After this, whenever she stood at her open window at night and looked up through the dark blue waters, she thought of that great city with all of its clatter and clamour, and even fancied that in these depths she could hear the church bells ring.

The next year, her second sister had permission to rise up to the surface and swim wherever she pleased. She came up just at sunset, and she said that this spectacle was the most marvellous sight she had ever seen. The heavens had a golden glow, and as for the clouds – she could not find words to describe their beauty. Splashed with red and tinted with violet, they sailed over her head. But much faster than the sailing clouds were wild swans in a flock. Like a long white veil trailing above the sea, they flew toward the setting sun. She too swam toward it, but down it went, and all the rose-coloured glow faded from the sea and sky.

The following year, her third sister ascended, and as she was the boldest of them all she swam up a broad river that flowed into the ocean. She saw gloriously green, vine-coloured hills. Palaces and manor houses could be glimpsed through the splendid woods. She heard all the birds sing, and the sun shone so brightly that often she had to dive under the water to cool her burning face. In a small cove she found a whole school of mortal children, paddling about in the water quite naked. She wanted to play with them, but they took fright and ran away. Then along came a little black animal – it was a dog, but she had never seen a dog before. It barked at her so ferociously

The Prince's ship was wrecked in a fierce storm

that she took fright herself, and fled to the open sea. But never could she forget the splendid woods, the green hills, and the nice children who could swim in the water although they didn't wear fish tails.

The fourth sister was not so venturesome. She stayed far out among the rough waves, which she said was a marvelous place. You could see all around you for miles and miles, and the heavens up above you were like a vast dome of glass. She had seen ships, but they were so far away that they looked like sea gulls. Playful dolphins had turned somersaults, and monstrous whales had spouted water through their nostrils so that it looked as if hundreds of fountains were playing all around them.

Now the fifth sister had her turn. Her birthday came in the wintertime, so she saw things that none of the others had seen. The sea was a deep green colour, and enormous icebergs drifted about. Each one glistened like a pearl, she said, but they were more lofty than any church steeple built by man. They assumed the most fantastic shapes, and sparkled like diamonds. She had seated herself on the largest one, and all the ships that came sailing by sped away as soon as the frightened sailors saw her there with her long hair blowing in the wind.

In the late evening clouds filled the sky. Thunder cracked and lightning darted across the heavens. Black waves lifted those great bergs of ice on high, where they flashed when the lightning struck.

On all the ships the sails were reefed and there was fear and trembling. But quietly she sat there, upon her drifting iceberg, and watched the blue forked lightning strike the sea.

Each of the sisters took delight in the lovely new sights when she first rose up to the surface of the sea. But when they became grown-up girls, who were allowed to go wherever they liked, they became indifferent to it. They would become homesick, and in a month they said that there was no place like the bottom of the sea, where they felt so completely at home.

On many an evening the older sisters would rise to the surface, arm in arm, all five in a row. They had beautiful voices, more charming than those of any mortal beings. When a storm was brewing, and they anticipated a shipwreck, they would swim before the ship and sing most seductively of how beautiful it was at the bottom of the ocean, trying to overcome the prejudice that the sailors had against coming down to them. But people could not understand their song, and mistook it for the voice of the storm. Nor was it for them to see the glories of the deep. When their ship went down they were drowned, and it was as dead men that they reached the sea king's palace.

On the evenings when the mermaids rose through the water like this, arm in arm, their youngest sister stayed behind all alone, looking after them and wanting to weep. But a mermaid has no tears, and therefore she suffers so much more.

"Oh, how I do wish I were fifteen!" she said. "I know I shall love that world up there and all the people who live in it."

And at last she too came to be fifteen.

"Now I'll have you off my hands," said her grandmother, the old queen dowager. "Come, let me adorn you like your sisters." In the little maid's hair she put a wreath of white lilies, each petal of which was formed from half of a pearl. And the old queen let eight big oysters fasten themselves to the princess's tail, as a sign of her high rank.

"But that hurts!" said the little mermaid.

"You must put up with a good deal to keep up appearances," her grandmother told her.

Oh, how gladly she would have shaken off all these decorations, and laid aside the cumbersome wreath! The red flowers in her garden were much more becoming to her, but she didn't dare to make any changes. "Good-bye," she said, and up she went through the water, as light and as sparkling as a bubble.

The sun had just gone down when her head rose above the surface, but the clouds still shone like gold and roses, and in the delicately tinted sky sparkled the clear gleam of the evening star. The air was mild and fresh and the sea unruffled. A great three-master lay in view with only one of all its sails set, for there was not even the whisper of a breeze, and the sailors idled about in the rigging and on the yards. There was music and singing on the ship, and as night came on they lit hundreds of such brightly coloured lanterns that one might have thought the flags of all nations were swinging in the air.

The little mermaid swam right up to the window of the main cabin, and each time she rose with the swell she could peep in through the clear glass panes at the crowd of brilliantly dressed people within. The handsomest of them all was a young Prince with big dark eyes. He could not be more than sixteen years old. It was his birthday and that was the reason for all the celebration. Up on deck the sailors were dancing, and when the Prince appeared among them a hundred or more rockets flew through the air, making it as bright as day. These startled the little mermaid so badly that she ducked under the water. But she soon peeped up again, and then it seemed as if all the stars in the sky were falling around her. Never had she seen such fireworks. Great suns spun around, splendid fire-fish floated through the blue air, and all these things were mirrored in the crystal clear sea. It was so brilliantly bright that you could see every little rope of the ship, and the people could be seen distinctly. Oh, how handsome the young Prince was! He laughed, and he smiled and shook people by the hand, while the music rang out in the perfect evening.

It got very late, but the little mermaid could not take her eyes off the ship and the handsome Prince. The brightly coloured lanterns were put out, no more rockets flew through the air, and no more cannon boomed. But there was a mutter and rumble deep down in the sea, and the swell kept bouncing her up so high that she could look into the cabin.

Now the ship began to sail. Canvas after canvas was spread in the wind, the waves rose high, great clouds gathered, and lightning flashed in the distance. Ah, they were in for a terrible storm, and the mariners made haste to reef the sails. The tall ship pitched and rolled as it sped through the angry sea. The waves rose up like towering black mountains, as if they would break over the masthead, but the swan-like ship plunged into the valleys between such waves, and emerged to ride their lofty heights. To the little mermaid this seemed good sport, but to the sailors it was nothing of the sort. The ship creaked and labored, thick timbers gave way under the heavy blows, waves broke over the ship, the mainmast snapped in two like a reed, the ship listed over on its side, and water burst into the hold.

Now the little mermaid saw that people were in peril, and that she herself must take care to avoid the beams and wreckage tossed about by the sea. One moment it would be black as pitch, and she couldn't see a thing. Next moment the lightning would flash so brightly that she could distinguish every soul on board. Everyone was looking out for himself as best he could. She watched closely for the young Prince, and when the ship split in two she saw him sink down in the sea. At first she was overjoyed that he would be with her, but then she recalled that human people could not live under the water, and he could only visit her father's palace as a dead man. No, he should not die! So she swam in among all the floating planks and beams, completely forgetting that they might crush her. She dived through the waves and rode their crests, until at length she reached the young Prince, who was no longer able to swim in that raging sea. His arms and legs were exhausted, his beautiful eyes were closing, and he would have died if the little mermaid had not come to help him. She held his head above water, and let the waves take them wherever the waves went.

At daybreak, when the storm was over, not a trace of the ship was in view. The sun rose out of the waters, red and bright, and its beams seemed to bring the glow of life back to the cheeks of the Prince, but his eyes remained closed. The mermaid kissed his high and shapely forehead. As she stroked his wet hair in place, it seemed to her that he looked like that marble statue in her little garden. She kissed him again and hoped that he would live.

She saw dry land rise before her in high blue mountains, topped with snow as glistening white as if a flock of swans were resting there. Down by the shore were splendid green woods, and in the foreground stood a church, or perhaps a convent; she didn't know which, but anyway it was a building. Orange and lemon trees grew in its garden, and tall palm trees grew beside the gateway. Here the sea formed a little harbour, quite calm and very deep. Fine white sand had been washed up below the cliffs. She swam there with the handsome Prince, and stretched him out on the sand, taking special care to pillow his head up high in the warm sunlight.

The bells began to ring in the great white building, and a

number of young girls came out into the garden. The little mermaid swam away behind some tall rocks that stuck out of the water. She covered her hair and her shoulders with foam so that no one could see her tiny face, and then she watched to see who would find the poor Prince.

In a little while one of the young girls came upon him. She seemed frightened, but only for a minute; then she called more people. The mermaid watched the Prince regain consciousness, and smile at everyone around him. But he did not smile at her, for he did not even know that she had saved him. She felt very unhappy, and when they led him away to the big building she dived sadly down into the water and returned to her father's palace.

She had always been quiet and wistful, and now she became much more so. Her sisters asked her what she had seen on her first visit up to the surface, but she would not tell them a thing.

Many evenings and many mornings she revisited the spot where she had left the Prince. She saw the fruit in the garden ripened and harvested, and she saw the snow on the high mountain melted away, but she did not see the Prince, so each time she came home sadder than she had left. It was her one consolation to sit in her little garden and throw her arms about the beautiful marble statue that looked so much like the Prince. But she took no care of her flowers now. They overgrew the paths until the place was a wilderness, and their long stalks and leaves became so entangled in the branches of the tree that it cast a gloomy shade.

Finally she couldn't bear it any longer. She told her secret to one of her sisters. Immediately all the other sisters heard about it. No one else knew, except a few more mermaids who told no one – except their most intimate friends. One of these friends knew who the Prince was. She too had seen the birthday celebration on the ship. She knew where he came from and where his kingdom was.

"Come, little sister!" said the other princesses. Arm in arm, they rose from the water in a long row, right in front of where they knew the Prince's palace stood. It was built of pale, glistening, golden stone with great marble staircases, one of which led down to the sea. Magnificent gilt domes rose above the roof, and between the pillars all around the building were marble statues that looked most lifelike. Through the clear glass of the lofty windows one could see into the splendid halls, with their costly silk hangings and tapestries, and walls covered with paintings that were delightful to behold. In the center of the main hall a large fountain played its columns of spray up to the glass-domed roof, through which the sun shone down on the water and upon the lovely plants that grew in the big basin.

Now that she knew where he lived, many an evening and many a night she spent there in the sea. She swam much closer to shore than any of her sisters would dare venture, and she even went far up a narrow stream, under the splendid marble balcony that cast its long shadow in the water. Here she used to sit and watch the young Prince when he thought himself quite alone in the bright moonlight.

On many evenings she saw him sail out in his fine boat, with music playing and flags a-flutter. She would peep out through the green rushes, and if the wind blew her long silver veil, anyone who saw it mistook it for a swan spreading its wings.

On many nights she saw the fishermen come out to sea with their torches, and heard them tell about how kind the young Prince was. This made her proud to think that it was she who had saved his life when he was buffeted about, half dead among the waves. And she thought of how softly his head had rested on her breast, and how tenderly she had kissed him, though he knew nothing of all this nor could he even dream of it.

Increasingly she grew to like human beings, and more and more she longed to live among them. Their world seemed so much wider than her own, for they could skim over the sea in ships, and mount up into the lofty peaks high over the clouds, and their lands stretched out in woods and fields farther than the eye could see. There was so much she wanted to know. Her sisters could not answer all her questions, so she asked her old grandmother, who knew about the "upper world," which was what she said was the right name for the countries above the sea.

"If men aren't drowned," the little mermaid asked, "do they live on forever? Don't they die, as we do down here in the sea?"

"Yes," the old lady said, "they too must die, and their lifetimes are even shorter than ours. We can live to be three hundred years old, but when we perish we turn into mere foam on the sea, and haven't even a grave down here among our dear ones. We have no immortal soul, no life hereafter. We are like the green seaweed – once cut down, it never grows again. Human beings, on the contrary, have a soul which lives forever, long after their bodies have turned to clay. It rises through thin air, up to the shining stars. Just as we rise through the water to see the lands on earth, so men rise up to beautiful places unknown, which we shall never see."

"Why weren't we given an immortal soul?" the little mermaid sadly asked. "I would gladly give up my three hundred years if I could be a human being only for a day, and later share in that heavenly realm."

"You must not think about that," said the old lady. "We fare much more happily and are much better off than the folk up there."

"Then I must also die and float as foam upon the sea, not hearing the music of the waves, and seeing neither the beautiful flowers nor the red sun! Can't I do anything at all to win an immortal soul?"

"No," her grandmother answered, "not unless a human being loved you so much that you meant more to him than his father and mother. If his every thought and his whole heart cleaved to you so that he would let a priest join his right hand to yours and would promise to be faithful here and throughout all eternity, then his soul would dwell in your body, and you would share in the happiness of mankind. He would give you a soul and yet keep his own. But that can never come to pass. The very thing that is your greatest beauty here in the sea – your fish tail – would be considered ugly on land. They have such poor taste that to be thought beautiful there you have to have two awkward props which they call legs."

The little mermaid sighed and looked unhappily at her fish tail.

"Come, let us be gay!" the old lady said. "Let us leap and bound throughout the three hundred years that we have to live. Surely that is time and to spare, and afterwards we shall be glad enough to rest in our graves. We are holding a court ball this evening."

This was a much more glorious affair than is ever to be seen on earth. The walls and the ceiling of the great ballroom were made of massive but transparent glass.

The little mermaid's heart was broken

Many hundreds of huge rose-red and grass-green shells stood on each side in rows, with the blue flames that burned in each shell illuminating the whole room and shining through the walls so clearly that it was quite bright in the sea outside. You could see the countless fish, great and small, swimming toward the glass walls. On some of them the scales gleamed purplish-red, while others were silver and gold. Across the floor of the hall ran a wide stream of water, and upon this the mermaids and mermen danced to their own entrancing songs. Such beautiful voices are not to be heard among the people who live on land. The little mermaid sang more sweetly than anyone else, and everyone applauded her. For a moment her heart

was happy, because she knew she had the loveliest voice of all, in the sea or on the land. But her thoughts soon strayed to the world up above. She could not forget the charming Prince, nor her sorrow that she did not have an immortal soul like his. Therefore she stole out of her father's palace and, while everything there was song and gladness, she sat sadly in her own little garden.

Then she heard a bugle call through the water, and she thought: "That must mean he is sailing up there, he whom I love more than my father or mother, he of whom I am always thinking, and in whose hands I would so willingly trust my lifelong happiness. I dare do anything to win him and to gain an immortal soul. While my sisters are dancing here, in my father's palace, I shall visit the sea witch of whom I have always been so afraid. Perhaps she will be able to advise me and help me."

The little mermaid set out from her garden toward the whirlpools that raged in front of the witch's dwelling. She had never gone that way before. No flowers grew there, nor any seaweed. Bare and gray, the sands extended to the whirlpools, where like roaring mill wheels the waters whirled and snatched everything within their reach down to the bottom of the sea. Between these tumultuous whirlpools she had to thread her way to reach the witch's waters, and then for a long stretch the only trail lay through a hot seething mire, which the witch called her peat marsh. Beyond it her house lay in the middle of a weird forest, where all the trees and shrubs were polyps, half animal and half plant. They looked like hundred-headed snakes growing out of the soil. All their branches were long, slimy arms, with fingers like wriggling worms. They squirmed, joint by joint, from their roots to their outermost tentacles, and whatever they could lay hold of they twined around and never let go. The little mermaid was terrified, and stopped at the edge of the forest. Her heart thumped with fear and she nearly turned back, but then she remembered the Prince and the souls that men have, and she summoned her courage. She bound her long flowing locks closely about her head so that the polyps could not catch hold of them, folded her arms across her breast, and darted through the water like a fish, in among the slimy polyps that stretched out their writhing arms and fingers to seize her. She saw that every one of them held something that it had caught with its hundreds of little tentacles, and to which it clung as with strong hoops of steel. The white bones of men who had perished at sea and sunk to these depths could be seen in the polyps' arms. Ships' rudders, and seamen's chests, and the skeletons of land animals had also fallen into their clutches, but the most ghastly sight of all was a little mermaid whom they had caught and strangled.

She reached a large muddy clearing in the forest, where

The little mermaids sisters sacrifice
their hair to save her

98

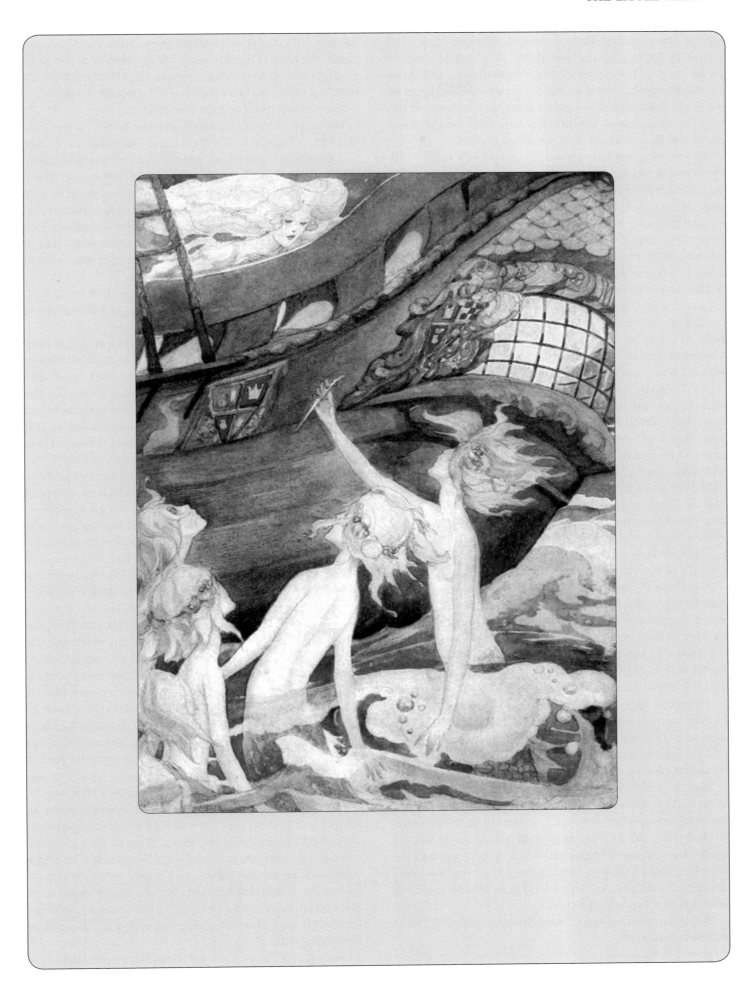

big fat water snakes slithered about, showing their foul yellowish bellies. In the middle of this clearing was a house built of the bones of shipwrecked men, and there sat the sea witch, letting a toad eat out of her mouth just as we might feed sugar to a little canary bird. She called the ugly fat water snakes her little chickabiddies, and let them crawl and sprawl about on her spongy bosom.

"I know exactly what you want," said the sea witch. "It is very foolish of you, but just the same you shall have your way, for it will bring you to grief, my proud princess. You want to get rid of your fish tail and have two props instead, so that you can walk about like a human creature, and have the young Prince fall in love with you, and win him and an immortal soul besides." At this, the witch gave such a loud cackling laugh that the toad and the snakes were shaken to the ground, where they lay writhing.

"You are just in time," said the witch. "After the sun comes up tomorrow, a whole year would have to go by before I could be of any help to you. I shall compound you a draught, and before sunrise you must swim to the shore with it, seat yourself on dry land, and drink the draught down. Then your tail will divide and shrink until it becomes what the people on earth call a pair of shapely legs. But it will hurt; it will feel as if a sharp sword slashed through you. Everyone who sees you will say that you are the most graceful human being they have ever laid eyes on, for you will keep your gliding movement and no dancer will be able to tread as lightly as you. But every step you take will feel as if you were treading upon knife blades so sharp that blood must flow. I am willing to help you, but are you willing to suffer all this?"

"Yes," the little mermaid said in a trembling voice, as she thought of the Prince and of gaining a human soul.

"Remember!" said the witch. "Once you have taken a human form, you can never be a mermaid again. You can never come back through the waters to your sisters, or to your father's palace. And if you do not win the love of the Prince so completely that for your sake he forgets his father and mother, cleaves to you with his every thought and his whole heart, and lets the priest join your hands in marriage, then you will win no immortal soul. If he marries someone else, your heart will break on the very next morning, and you will become foam of the sea."

"I shall take that risk," said the little mermaid, but she turned as pale as death.

"Also, you will have to pay me," said the witch, "and it is no trifling price that I'm asking. You have the sweetest voice of anyone down here at the bottom of the sea, and while I don't doubt that you would like to captivate the Prince with it, you must give this voice to me. I will take the very best thing that you have, in return for my sovereign draught. I must pour my own blood in it to make the drink as sharp as a two-edged sword."

"But if you take my voice," said the little mermaid, "what will be left to me?"

"Your lovely form," the witch told her, "your gliding movements, and your eloquent eyes. With these you can easily enchant a human heart. Well, have you lost your courage? Stick out your little tongue and I shall cut it off. I'll have my price, and you shall have the potent draught."

"Go ahead," said the little mermaid.

The witch hung her cauldron over the flames, to brew the draught. "Cleanliness is a good thing," she said, as she tied her snakes in a knot and scoured out the pot with them. Then she pricked herself in the chest and let her black blood splash into the cauldron. Steam swirled up from it, in such ghastly shapes that anyone would have been terrified by them. The witch constantly threw new ingredients into the cayldron, and it started to boil with a sound like that of a crocodile shedding tears. When the draught was ready at last, it looked as clear as the purest water.

"There's your draught," said the witch. And she cut off the tongue of the little mermaid, who now was dumb and could neither sing nor talk.

"If the polyps should pounce on you when you walk back through my wood," the witch said, "just spill a drop of this brew upon them and their tentacles will break in a thousand pieces." But there was no need of that, for the polyps curled up in terror as soon as they saw the bright draught. It glittered in the little mermaid's hand as if it were a shining star. So she soon traversed the forest, the marsh, and the place of raging whirlpools.

She could see her father's palace. The lights had been snuffed out in the great ballroom, and doubtless everyone in the palace was asleep, but she dared not go near them, now that she was stricken dumb and was leaving her home forever. Her heart felt as if it would break with grief. She tip-toed into the garden, took one flower from each of her sisters' little plots, blew a thousand kisses toward the palace, and then mounted up through the dark blue sea.

The sun had not yet risen when she saw the Prince's palace. As she climbed his splendid marble staircase, the moon was shining clear. The little mermaid swallowed the bitter, fiery draught, and it was as if a two-edged sword struck through her frail body. She swooned away, and lay there as if she were dead. When the sun rose over the sea she awoke and felt a flash of pain, but directly in front of her stood the handsome young Prince, gazing at her with his coal-black eyes. Lowering her gaze, she saw that her fish tail was gone, and that she had the loveliest pair of white legs any young maid could hope to have. But she was naked, so she clothed herself in her own long hair.

The Prince asked who she was, and how she came to be there. Her deep blue eyes looked at him tenderly but very sadly, for she could not speak. Then he took her hand and led her into his palace. Every footstep felt as if she were walking on the blades and points of sharp knives, just as the witch had foretold, but she gladly endured it. She moved as lightly as a bubble as she walked beside the Prince. He and all who saw her marvelled at the grace of her gliding walk.

Once clad in the rich silk and muslin garments that were

provided for her, she was the loveliest person in all the palace, though she was dumb and could neither sing nor speak. Beautiful slaves, attired in silk and cloth of gold, came to sing before the Prince and his royal parents. One of them sang more sweetly than all the others, and when the Prince smiled at her and clapped his hands, the little mermaid felt very unhappy, for she knew that she herself used to sing much more sweetly.

"Oh," she thought, "if he only knew that I parted with my voice forever so that I could be near him."

Graceful slaves now began to dance to the most wonderful music. Then the little mermaid lifted her shapely white arms, rose up on the tips of her toes, and skimmed over the floor. No one had ever danced so well. Each movement set off her beauty to better and better advantage, and her eyes spoke more directly to the heart than any of the singing slaves could do.

She charmed everyone, and especially the Prince, who called her his dear little foundling. She danced time and

The Little Mermaid is prepared to suffer greatly in order to have legs and be with the prince

again, though every time she touched the floor she felt as if she were treading on sharp-edged steel. The Prince said he would keep her with him always, and that she was to have a velvet pillow to sleep on outside his door.

He had a page's suit made for her, so that she could go with him on horseback. They would ride through the sweet scented woods, where the green boughs brushed her shoulders, and where the little birds sang among the fluttering leaves.

She climbed up high mountains with the Prince, and

though her tender feet bled so that all could see it, she only laughed and followed him on until they could see the clouds driving far below, like a flock of birds in flight to distant lands.

At home in the Prince's palace, while the others slept at night, she would go down the broad marble steps to cool her burning feet in the cold sea water, and then she would recall those who lived beneath the sea. One night her sisters came by, arm in arm, singing sadly as they breasted the waves. When she held out her hands toward them, they knew who she was, and told her how unhappy she had made them all. They came to see her every night after that, and once far, far out to sea, she saw her old grandmother, who had not been up to the surface this many a year. With her was the sea king, with his crown upon his head. They stretched out their hands to her, but they did not venture so near the land as her sisters had.

Day after day she became more dear to the Prince, who loved her as one would love a good little child, but he never thought of making her his Queen. Yet she had to be his wife or she would never have an immortal soul, and on the morning after his wedding she would turn into foam on the waves.

"Don't you love me best of all?" the little mermaid's eyes seemed to question him, when he took her in his arms and kissed her lovely forehead.

"Yes, you are most dear to me," said the Prince, "for you have the kindest heart. You love me more than anyone else does, and you look so much like a young girl I once saw but never shall find again. I was on a ship that was wrecked, and the waves cast me ashore near a holy temple, where many young girls performed the rituals. The youngest of them found me beside the sea and saved my life. Though I saw her no more than twice, she is the only person in all the world whom I could love. But you are so much like her that you almost replace the memory of her in my heart. She belongs to that holy temple, therefore it is my good fortune that I have you. We shall never part."

"Alas, he doesn't know it was I who saved his life," the little mermaid thought. "I carried him over the sea to the garden where the temple stands. I hid behind the foam and watched to see if anyone would come. I saw the pretty maid he loves better than me." A sigh was the only sign of her deep distress, for a mermaid cannot cry. "He says that the other maid belongs to the holy temple. She will never come out into the world, so they will never see each other again. It is I who will care for him, love him, and give all my life to him."

Now rumours arose that the Prince was to wed the beautiful daughter of a neighbouring King, and that it was for this reason he was having such a superb ship made ready to sail. The rumour ran that the Prince's real interest in visiting the neighbouring kingdom was to see the King's daughter, and that he was to travel with a lordly retinue. The little mermaid shook her head and smiled, for she knew the Prince's thoughts far better than anyone else did.

"I am forced to make this journey," he told her. "I must visit the beautiful Princess, for this is my parents' wish, but they would not have me bring her home as my bride against my own will, and I can never love her. She does not resemble the lovely maiden in the temple, as you do, and if I were to choose a bride, I would sooner choose you, my dear mute foundling with those telling eyes of yours." And he kissed her on the mouth, fingered her long hair, and laid his head against her heart so that she came to dream of mortal happiness and an immortal soul.

"I trust you aren't afraid of the sea, my silent child" he said, as they went on board the magnificent vessel that was to carry them to the land of the neighbouring King. And he told her stories of storms, of ships becalmed, of

The sea witch had taken away the mermaid's voice

strange deep-sea fish, and of the wonders that divers have seen. She smiled at such stories, for no one knew about the bottom of the sea as well as she did.

In the clear moonlight, when everyone except the man at the helm was asleep, she sat on the side of the ship gazing down through the transparent water, and fancied she could catch glimpses of her father's palace. On the topmost tower stood her old grandmother, wearing her silver crown and looking up at the keel of the ship through the rushing waves. Then her sisters rose to the surface, looked at her sadly, and wrung their white hands. She smiled and waved, trying to let them know that all went well and that she was happy. But along came the cabin boy, and her sisters dived out of sight so quickly that the boy supposed the flash of white he had seen was merely foam on the sea.

Next morning the ship came in to the harbour of the neighbouring King's glorious city. All the church bells chimed, and trumpets were sounded from all the high towers, while the soldiers lined up with flying banners and glittering bayonets. Every day had a new festivity, as one

ball or levee followed another, but the Princess was still to appear. They said she was being brought up in some far-away sacred temple, where she was learning every royal virtue. But she came at last.

The little mermaid was curious to see how beautiful this Princess was, and she had to grant that a more exquisite figure she had never seen. The Princess's skin was clear and fair, and behind the long, dark lashes her deep blue eyes were smiling and devoted.

"It was you!" the Prince cried. "You are the one who saved me when I lay like a dead man beside the sea." He clasped the blushing bride of his choice in his arms. "Oh, I am happier than a man should be!" he told his little mermaid. "My fondest dream – that which I never dared to hope – has come true. You will share in my great joy, for you love me more than anyone does."

The little mermaid kissed his hand and felt that her heart was beginning to break. For the morning after his wedding day would see her dead and turned to watery foam.

All the church bells rang out, and heralds rode through the streets to announce the wedding. Upon every altar sweet-scented oils were burned in costly silver lamps. The priests swung their censers, the bride and the bridegroom joined their hands, and the bishop blessed their marriage. The little mermaid, clothed in silk and cloth of gold, held the bride's train, but she was deaf to the wedding march and blind to the holy ritual. Her thoughts turned to her last night upon earth, and on all she had lost in this world.

That same evening, the bride and bridegroom went aboard the ship. Cannon thundered and banners waved. On the deck of the ship a royal pavilion of purple and gold was set up, and furnished with luxurious cushions. Here the wedded couple were to sleep on that calm, clear night. The sails swelled in the breeze, and the ship glided so lightly that it scarcely seemed to move over the quiet sea. At nightfall brightly coloured lanterns were lit, and the mariners merrily danced on the deck. The little mermaid could not forget that first time she rose from the depths of the sea and looked on at such pomp and happiness. Light as a swallow pursued by his enemies, she joined in the whirling dance. Everyone cheered her, for never had she danced so wonderfully. Her tender feet felt as if they were pierced by daggers, but she did not feel it. Her heart suffered far greater pain. She knew that this was the last evening that she ever would see him for whom she had forsaken her home and family, for whom she had sacrificed her lovely voice and suffered such constant torment, while he knew nothing of all these things. It was the last night that she would breathe the same air with him, or look upon deep waters or the star fields of the blue sky. A never-ending night, without thought and without dreams, awaited her who had no soul and could not get one. The merrymaking lasted long after midnight, yet she laughed and danced on despite the thought of death she carried in her heart. The Prince kissed his beautiful bride and she toyed with his coal-black hair. Hand in hand, they went to rest in the magnificent pavilion.

A hush came over the ship. Only the helmsman remained on deck as the little mermaid leaned her white arms on the bulwarks and looked to the east to see the first red hint of daybreak, for she knew that the first flash of the sun would strike her dead. Then she saw her sisters rise up among the waves. They were as pale as she, and there was no sign of their lovely long hair that the breezes used to blow. It had all been cut off.

"We have given our hair to the witch," they said, "so that she would send you help, and save you from death tonight. She gave us a knife. Here it is. See the sharp blade! Before the sun rises, you must strike it into the Prince's heart, and when his warm blood bathes your feet they will grow together and become a fish tail. Then you will be a mermaid again, able to come back to us in the sea, and live out your three hundred years before you die and turn into dead salt sea foam. Make haste! He or you must die before sunrise. Our old grandmother is so grief-stricken that her white hair is falling fast, just as ours did under the witch's scissors. Kill the Prince and come back to us. Hurry! Hurry! See that red glow in the heavens! In a few minutes the sun will rise and you must die." So saying, they gave a strange deep sigh and sank beneath the waves.

The little mermaid parted the purple curtains of the tent and saw the beautiful bride asleep with her head on the Prince's breast. The mermaid bent down and kissed his shapely forehead. She looked at the sky, fast reddening for the break of day. She looked at the sharp knife and again turned her eyes toward the Prince, who in his sleep murmured the name of his bride. His thoughts were all for her, and the knife blade trembled in the mermaid's hand. But then she flung it from her, far out over the waves. Where it fell the waves were red, as if bubbles of blood seethed in the water. With eyes already glazing she looked once more at the Prince, hurled herself over the bulwarks into the sea, and felt her body dissolve in foam.

The sun rose up from the waters. Its beams fell, warm and kindly, upon the chill sea foam, and the little mermaid did not feel the hand of death. In the bright sunlight overhead, she saw hundreds of fair ethereal beings. They were so transparent that through them she could see the ship's white sails and the red clouds in the sky. Their voices were sheer music, but so spirit-like that no human ear could detect the sound, just as no eye on earth could see their forms. Without wings, they floated as light as the air itself. The little mermaid discovered that she was shaped like them, and that she was gradually rising up out of the foam.

'Who are you, toward whom I rise?" she asked, and her voice sounded like those above her, so spiritual that no music on earth could match it.

"We are the daughters of the air," they answered. "A mermaid has no immortal soul, and can never get one unless she wins the love of a human being. Her eternal life must depend upon a power outside herself. The daughters of the air do not have an immortal soul either, but they can earn one by their good deeds. We fly to the south, where the hot poisonous air kills human beings unless we bring cool breezes. We carry the scent of flowers through the air, bringing freshness and healing balm wherever we go. When for three hundred years we have tried to do all the good that we can, we are given an immortal soul and a share in mankind's eternal bliss. You, poor little mermaid, have tried with your whole heart to do this too. Your suffering and your loyalty have raised you up into the realm of airy spirits, and now in the course of three hundred years you may earn by your good deeds a soul that will never die."

She had rescued the prince and loved him so much but now all that was at an end and she would join the daughters of the air

The little mermaid lifted her clear bright eyes toward God's sun, and for the first time her eyes were wet with tears.

On board the ship all was astir and lively again. She saw the Prince and his fair bride in search of her. Then they gazed sadly into the seething foam, as if they knew she had hurled herself into the waves. Unseen by them, she kissed the bride's forehead, smiled upon the Prince, and rose up with the other daughters of the air to the rose-red clouds that sailed on high.

"This is the way that we shall rise to the kingdom of God, after three hundred years have passed."

"We may get there even sooner," one spirit whispered. "Unseen, we fly into the homes of men, where there are children, and for every day on which we find a good child who pleases his parents and deserves their love, God shortens our days of trial. The child does not know when we float through his room, but when we smile at him in approval one year is taken from our three hundred. But if we see a naughty, mischievous child we must shed tears of sorrow, and each tear adds a day to the time of our trial."

Flowers and Fairy Rings

The magic of fairies and fairyland together with the beauties and secrets of the natural world have, for centuries, inspired many of the world's most famous authors including William Shakespeare, Robert Louis Stevenson and Walter de la Mare

The Flowers
Robert Louis Stevenson

All the names I know from nurse:
Gardener's garters, Shepherd's purse,
Bachelor's buttons, Lady's smock,
And the Lady Hollyhock.
Fairy places, fairy things,
Fairy woods where the wild bee wings,
Tiny trees for tiny dames....
These must all be fairy names!
Tiny woods below whose boughs
Shady fairies weave a house;
Tiny tree-tops, rose or thyme,
Where the braver fairies climb!
Fair are grown-up people's trees,
But the fairest woods are these;
Where, if I were not so tall,
I should live for good and all.

If You See A Faery Ring
William Shakespeare

If you see a faery ring
In a field of grass,
Very lightly step around,
Tip-toe as you pass,
Last night faeries frolicked there....
And they're sleeping somewhere near.
If you see a tiny faery,
Lying fast asleep
Shut your eyes
And run away,
Do not stay to peek!
Do not tell
Or you'll break a faery spell.

Some One
Walter de la Mare

Some one came a knocking
At my wee, small door;
Some one came knocking,
I'm sure...sure...sure;
I listened, I opened,
I looked left and right,
But naught there was a stirring
In the still dark night;
Only busy beetle
Tap-tapping in the wall,
Only from the forest
The screech-owl's call,
Only the cricket whistling
While the dewdrops fall
So I know not who came knocking,
At all, at all, at all.

The notion of fairy rings (sometimes called fairy circles, elf circles, or pixie rings) have been inspired by how clusters of mushrooms often grow in a ring or arc that can be over 10 metres (33 ft) in diameter and usually in forests or dark green grass. They have occupied a prominent place in European folklore as the location of gateways into elfin kingdoms – or places where elves gather and dance. Fairy rings are said to appear only when a fairy, pixie or elf is present and may disappear without trace in a few days

Brer Rabbit and the Tar-Baby

These fun stories about the folk hero originated from African trickster characters. Hares often feature in storytelling traditions in many parts of that continent although sometimes the tricksters are wily spiders, instead. It has also been suggested that the American Brer Rabbit represents the African slaves working in the cotton fields who so often relied on their wits for survival and perhaps for revenge. *Brer (sometimes spelt Br'er) is short for brother.*

One evening recently, the lady whom Uncle Remus calls "Miss Sally" missed her little seven-year-old. Making search for him through the house and through the yard, she heard the sound of voices in the old man's cabin, and looking through the window, saw the child sitting by Uncle Remus. His head rested against the old man's arm, and he was gazing with an expression of the most intense interest into the rough, weather-beaten face that beamed so kindly upon him. This is what "Miss Sally" heard:

"Bimeby, one day, after Brer Fox bin doin' all dat he could fer ter ketch Brer Rabbit, en Brer Rabbit bin doin' all he could fer ter keep 'im fum it, Brer Fox say to hisse'f dat he'd put up a game on Brer Rabbit, en he ain't mo'n got de wuds out'n his mouf twel Brer Rabbit come a-lopin' up de big road, lookin' des ez plump en ez fat en ez sassy ez a Moggin hoss in a barley-patch."

"'Hol' on dar, Brer Rabbit,' sez Brer Fox, sezee."

"'I ain't got time, Brer Fox,' sez Brer Rabbit, sezee, sorter mendin' his licks."

"'I wanter have some confab wid you, Brer Rabbit,' sez Brer Fox, sezee."

"'All right, Brer Fox, but you better holler fum whar you stan': I'm monstus full er fleas dis mawnin,' sez Brer Rabbit, sezee."

"'I seed Brer B'ar yistiddy,' sez Brer Fox, sezee, 'en he sorter raked me over de coals kaze you en me ain't make frens en live naberly, en I told him dat I'd see you.'"

"Den Brer Rabbit scratch one year wid his off hine-foot sorter jub'usly, en den he ups en sez, sezee:"

"'All a-settin', Brer Fox. S'posen you drap roun' ter-morrer en take dinner wid me. We ain't got no great doin's at our house, but I speck de ole 'oman en de chilluns kin sort o' scramble roun' en git up sump'n fer ter stay yo' stummuck.'"

"'I'm 'gree'ble, Brer Rabbit,' sez Brer Fox, sezee."

"'Den I'll 'pen on you,' says Brer Rabbit, sezee."

"Nex' day, Mr. Rabbit an' Miss Rabbit got up soon, 'fo day, en raided on a gyarden like Miss Sally's out dar, en got some cabbiges, en some roas'n-years, en some sparrer-grass, en dey fix up a smashin' dinner. Bimeby one er de little Rabbits, playin' out in de backyard, come runnin' in hollerin', 'Oh, ma! oh, ma! I seed Mr. Fox a-comin'!' En den Brer Rabbit he tuck de chilluns by der years en make um set down, and den him en Miss Rabbit sorter dally roun' waitin' for Brer Fox. En dey keep on waitin', but no Brer Fox ain't come. Atter while Brer Rabbit goes to de do', easy like, en peep out, en dar, stickin' out fum behime de cornder, wuz de tip-een' er Brer Fox's tail. Den Brer Rabbit shot de do' en sot down, en put his paws behime his years, en begin fer ter sing:"

"'De place wharbouts you spill de grease,
Right dar youer boun' ter slide,
An' whar you fine a bunch er ha'r,
You'll sholy fine de hide!'"

Br'er Rabbit begin fer ter sing

"Nex' day Brer Fox sont word by Mr. Mink en skuze hisse'f kaze he wuz too sick fer ter come, en he ax Brer Rabbit fer ter come en take dinner wid him, en Brer Rabbit say he wuz 'gree'ble."

"Bimeby, w'en de shadders wuz at der shortes', Brer Rabbit he sorter brush up en santer down ter Brer Fox's house, en w'en he got dar he yer somebody groanin', en he look in de do', en dar he see Brer Fox settin' up in a rockin'-cheer all wrop up wid flannil, en he look mighty weak. Brer Rabbit look all roun', he did, but he ain't see no dinner. De dish-pan wuz settin' on de table, en close by wuz a kyarvin-knife."

"'Look like you gwineter have chicken fer dinner, Brer Fox,' sez Brer Rabbit, sezee."

"'Yes, Brer Rabbit, deyer nice en fresh en tender,' sez Brer Fox, sezee."

"Den Brer Rabbit sorter pull his mustarsh, en say, 'You ain't got no' calamus-root, is you, Brer Fox? I done got so now dat I can't eat no' chicken 'ceppin' she's seasoned up wid calamus-root.' En wid dat Brer Rabbit lipt out er de do' and dodge 'mong de bushes, en sot dar watchin' fer Brer Fox; en he ain't watch long, nudder, kaze Brer Fox flung off de flannil en crope out er de house en got whar he could close in on Brer Rabbit, en bimeby Brer Rabbit holler out, 'Oh, Brer Fox! I'll des put yo' calamus-root out yer on dis yer stump. Better come git it while hit's fresh.' And wid dat Brer

Rabbit gallop off home. En Brer Fox ain't never kotch 'im yit, en w'at's mo', honey, he ain't gwineter."

"Didn't the fox never catch the rabbit, Uncle Remus?" asked the little boy the next evening.

"He come mighty nigh it, honey, sho's you bawn – Brer Fox did. One day arter Brer Rabbit fool 'im wid dat calamus-root, Brer Fox went ter wuk en got 'im some tar, en mix it wid some turken-time, en fix up a contrapshun what he call a Tar-Baby, en he tuck dish yer Tar-Baby en he sot 'er in de big road, en den he lay off in de bushes fer ter see wat de news wuz gwineter be. En he didn't hatter wait long, nudder, kaze bimeby here come Brer Rabbit pacin' down de road – lippity-clippity, clippity-lippity – des ez sassy ez a jay-bird. Brer Fox he lay low. Brer Rabbit come prancin' 'long twel he spy de Tar-Baby, en den he fotch up on his behime legs like he was 'stonished. De Tar-Baby she sot dar, she did, en Brer Fox he lay low.

"'Mawnin'!' sez Brer Rabbit, sezee; 'nice wedder dis mawnin',' sezee.

"Tar-Baby ain't sayin' nuthin' en Brer Fox he lay low.

Tar-Baby ain't sayin' nuthin'

"'How duz yo' sym'tums seem ter segashuate?' sez Brer Rabbit, sezee."

"Brer Fox he wink his eye slow, en lay low, en de Tar-Baby she ain't sayin' nuthin'."

"'How you come on, den? Is you deaf?' sez Brer Rabbit, sezee. 'Kaze if you is I kin holler louder,' sezee."

"Tar-Baby lay still, en Brer Fox he lay low."

"'Youer stuck up, dat's w'at you is,' says Brer Rabbit, sezee, 'en I'm gwineter kyore you, dat's w'at I'm a-gwineter do,' sezee."

"Brer Fox he sorter chuckle in his stummuck, he did, but Tar-Baby ain't sayin' 'nuthin'."

"'I'm gwineter larn you howter talk ter 'specttubble fokes ef hit's de las 'ack,' sez Brer Rabbit, sezee. 'Ef you don't take off dat hat en tell me howdy, I'm gwineter bus' you wide open,' sezee."

"Tar-Baby stay still, en Brer Fox he lay low."

"Brer Rabbit keep on axin' 'im, en de Tar-Baby she keep on sayin' nuthin', twel present'y Brer Rabbit draw back wid his fis', he did, en blip he tuck er side er de head. Right dar's whar he broke his merlasses-jug. His fis' stuck, en he can't pull loose. De tar hilt him. But Tar-Baby she stay still, en Brer Fox he lay low."

"'Ef you don't lemme loose, I'll knock you ag'in,' sez Brer Rabbit, sezee; en wid dat he fotch 'er a wipe wid te udder han', en dat stuck. Tar-Baby she ain't sayin' nuthin', en Brer Fox he lay low."

"'Tu'n me loose, of' I kick de natal stuffin' outen you,' sez Brer Rabbit, sezee; but de Tar-Baby she ain't sayin' nuthin'. She des hilt on, en den Brer Rabbit lose de use er his feet in de same way. Brer Fox he lay low. Den Brer Rabbit squall out dat ef de Tar-Baby don't tu'n 'im loose he butt 'er crank-sided. En den he butted, en his head got stuck. Den Brer Fox he santered fort', lookin' des ez innercent ez wunner yo' mammy's mockin'-birds."

"'Howdy, Brer Rabbit?' sez Brer Fox, sezee. 'You look sorter stuck up dis mawnin',' sezee; en den he rolled on de groun', en laft en laft twel he couldn't laff no mo'. 'I speck you'll take dinner wid me dis time, Brer Rabbit. I done laid in some calamus-root, en I ain't gwineter take no skuse,' sez Brer Fox, sezee."

Here Uncle Remus paused, and drew a two-pound yam out of the ashes.

"Did the fox eat the rabbit?" asked the little boy to whom the story had been told.

"Dat's all de fur de tale goes," replied the old man. "He mout, en den ag'in he moutent. Some say Jedge B'ar come 'long en loosed 'im; some say he didn't. I hear Miss Sally callin'. You better run 'long."…

"Uncle Remus," said the little boy one evening, when he had found the old man with little or nothing to do, "did the fox kill and eat the rabbit when he caught him with the Tar-Baby?"

"Law, honey, ain't I tell you 'bout dat?" replied the old darky, chuckling slyly. "I 'clar ter grashus I ought er tole you dat; but ole man Nod wuz ridin' on my eyelids twel a leetle mo'n I'd 'a' dis'member'd my own name, en den on to dat here come yo' mammy hollerin' atter you."

"W'at I tell you w'en I fus' begin? I tole you Brer Rabbit

Brer Rabbit and a night owl

wuz a monstus soon beas'; leas'ways dat's w'at I laid out fer ter tell you. Well, den, honey, don't you go en make no udder kalkalashuns, kaze in dem days Brer Rabbit en his family wuz at de head er de gang w'en enny racket wuz on han', en dar dey stayed. 'Fo' you begins fer ter wipe yo' eyes 'bout Brer Rabbit, you wait en see whar'bouts Brer Rabbit gwineter fetch up at. But dat's needer yer ner dar.

"W'en Brer Fox fine Brer Rabbit mixt up wid de Tar-Baby, he feel mighty good, en he roll on de groun' en laff. Bimeby he up 'n' say, sezee:"

"Well, I speck I got you dis time, Brer Rabbit,' sezee; 'maybe I ain't but I speck I is. You been runnin' roun' here sassin' atter me a mighty long time, but I speck you done come ter de een' er de row. You bin cuttin' up yo' capers en bouncin' roun' in dis naberhood ontwel you come ter b'leeve yo'se'f de boss er de whole gang. En den youer allers some'rs whar you got no bizness,' sez Brer Fox, sezee. 'Who ax you fer ter come en strike up a 'quaintence wid dish yer Tar-Baby? En who stuck you up dar whar you iz? Nobody in de roun' worril. You des tuck en jam yo'se'f on dat Tar-Baby widout waitin' fer enny invite,' sez Brer Fox, sezee – ' en dar you is, en dar you'll stay twel I fixes up a bresh-pile and fires her up, kaze I'm gwineter bobbycue you dis day, sho',' sez Brer Fox, sezee."

"Den Brer Rabbit talk mighty 'umble."

"'I don't keer w'at you do wid me, Brer Fox,' sezee, 'so you don't fling me in dat brier-patch. Roas' me, Brer Fox,' sezee, 'but don't fling me in dat brier-patch,' sezee."

"'Hit's so much trouble fer ter kindle a fier,' sez Brer Fox, sezee, 'dat I speck I'll hatter hang you,' sezee."

"'Hang me des ez high ez you please, Brer Fox,' sez Brer Rabbit, sezee, 'but do fer de Lord's sake don't fling me in dat brier-patch,' sezee."

"'I ain't got no string,' sez Brer Fox, sezee, 'en now I speck I'll hatter drown you,' sezee."

"'Drown me ez deep ez you please, Brer Fox,' sez Brer Rabbit, sezee, 'but don't fling me in dat brier-patch,' sezee.

"'Dey ain't no water nigh,' sez Brer Fox, sezee, 'en now I speck I'll hatter skin you,' sezee."

"'Skin me, Brer Fox,' sez Brer Rabbit, sezee, 'snatch out my eyeballs, t'ar out my years by de roots, en cut off my legs,' sezee, 'but do please, Brer Fox, don't fling me in dat brier-patch,' sezee."

"Co'se Brer Fox wanter hurt Brer Rabbit bad ez he kin,

The Brer Rabbit stories were written down by Robert Roosevelt (uncle of the US president Theodore Roosevelt who loved hearing the tales as a child.). 'Uncle Remus' was popularized by Joel Chandler Harris who made the stories immortal in the late 1800s when he wrote up and published many of the erstwhile oral versions that he had heard in Georgia. The stories were also retold for children by Enid Blyton, the English children's writer.

so he cotch him by de behime legs en slung 'im right in de middle er de brier-patch. Dar wuz a considerbul flutter whar Brer Rabbit struck de bushes, en Brer Fox sorter hung roun' fer ter see what wuz gwineter happen. Bimeby he hear somebody call 'im, en way up de hill he see Brer Rabbit settin' cross-legged on a chinkapin log koamin' de pitch outen his har wid a chip. Den Brer Fox know dat he bin swop off mighty bad. Brer Rabbit wuz bleedzed fer ter fling back some er his sass, en he holler out:"

"Bred en bawn in a briar-patch, Brer Fox; bred en bawn."

This statue honours the rabbit's wit, courage and cunning

BRER RABBIT
BORN AND BRED
IN THE BRIARPATCH
HE SURVIVES FOREVER BY HIS WIT
HIS COURAGE AND HIS CUNNING

The Adventures of Pinocchio

Written first as a serial (not necessarily for children) in 1881-1883, this magical adventure is set in Tuscany, Italy, with characters that include the long-nosed naughty puppet himself as well as a fairy with turquoise hair, a friendly talking cricket, a scheming fox and cat, and a giant dogfish-shark. 'The original story had an unhappy ending, with Pinocchio being hanged. However the final version, pleading the case for honesty and a good education, does allow for reform and rescue, as Pinocchio at last becomes a real boy.

CHAPTER 1

Centuries ago there lived –
"A king!" my little readers will say immediately.
No, children, you are mistaken. Once upon a time there was a piece of wood. It was not an expensive piece of wood. Far from it. Just a common block of firewood, one of those thick, solid logs that are put on the fire in winter to make cold rooms cozy and warm.

I do not know how this really happened, yet the fact remains that one fine day this piece of wood found itself in the shop of an old carpenter. His real name was Mastro Antonio, but everyone called him Mastro Cherry, for the tip of his nose was so round and red and shiny that it looked like a ripe cherry.

As soon as he saw that piece of wood, Mastro Cherry was filled with joy. Rubbing his hands together happily, he mumbled half to himself:

"This has come in the nick of time. I shall use it to make the leg of a table."

He grasped the hatchet quickly to peel off the bark and shape the wood. But as he was about to give it the first blow, he stood still with arm uplifted, for he had heard a wee, little voice say in a beseeching tone: "Please be careful! Do not hit me so hard!"

What a look of surprise shone on Mastro Cherry's face! His funny face became still funnier.

He turned frightened eyes about the room to find out where that wee, little voice had come from and he saw no one! He looked under the bench – no one! He peeped inside the closet – no one! He searched among the shavings – no one! He opened the door to look up and down the street – and still no one!

"Oh, I see!" he then said, laughing and scratching his

Geppetto cuts and shapes the wood into a marionette

Wig. "It can easily be seen that I only thought I heard the tiny voice say the words! Well, well – to work once more."

He struck a most solemn blow upon the piece of wood.

"Oh, oh! You hurt!" cried the same far-away little voice. Mastro Cherry grew dumb, his eyes popped out of his head, his mouth opened wide, and his tongue hung down on his chin.

As soon as he regained the use of his senses, he said, trembling and stuttering from fright:

"Where did that voice come from, when there is no one around? Might it be that this piece of wood has learned to weep and cry like a child? I can hardly believe it. Here it is – a piece of common firewood, good only to burn in the stove, the same as any other. Yet – might someone be hidden in it? If so, the worse for him. I'll fix him!"

With these words, he grabbed the log with both hands and started to knock it about unmercifully. He threw it to the floor, against the walls of the room, and even up to the ceiling.

He listened for the tiny voice to moan and cry. He waited two minutes – nothing; five minutes – nothing; ten minutes – nothing.

"Oh, I see," he said, trying bravely to laugh and ruffling up his wig with his hand. "It can easily be seen I only imagined I heard the tiny voice! Well, well – to work once more!"

The poor fellow was scared half to death, so he tried to sing a gay song in order to gain courage. He set aside the hatchet and picked up the plane to make the wood smooth and even, but as he drew it to and fro, he heard the same tiny voice. This time it giggled as it spoke:

"Stop it! Oh, stop it! Ha, ha, ha! You tickle my stomach."

This time poor Mastro Cherry fell as if shot. When he opened his eyes, he found himself sitting on the floor.

His face had changed; fright had turned even the tip of his nose from red to deepest purple.

In Chapter 2 Mastro Cherry gives the piece of wood to his friend Geppetto, who takes it to make himself a Marionette that will dance, fence, and turn somersaults.
…Geppetto took the fine piece of wood, thanked Mastro Antonio, and limped away toward home.

CHAPTER 3

Little as Geppetto's house was, it was neat and comfortable. It was a small room on the ground floor, with a tiny window under the stairway. The furniture could not have been much simpler: a very old chair, a rickety old bed, and a tumble-down table. A fireplace full of burning logs was painted on the wall opposite the door. Over the fire, there was painted a pot full of something which kept boiling happily away and sending up clouds of what looked like real steam.

As soon as he reached home, Geppetto took his tools and began to cut and shape the wood into a Marionette.

"What shall I call him?" he said to himself. "I think I'll call him PINOCCHIO. This name will make his fortune. I knew a whole family of Pinocchi once – Pinocchio the father, Pinocchia the mother, and Pinocchi the children – and they were all lucky. The richest of them begged for his living."

After choosing the name for his Marionette, Geppetto set seriously to work to make the hair, the forehead, the eyes. Fancy his surprise when he noticed that these eyes moved and then stared fixedly at him. Geppetto, seeing this, felt insulted and said in a grieved tone:

"Ugly wooden eyes, why do you stare so?"

There was no answer.

After the eyes, Geppetto made the nose, which began to stretch as soon as finished. It stretched and stretched and stretched till it became so long, it seemed endless.

Poor Geppetto kept cutting it and cutting it, but the more he cut, the longer grew that impertinent nose. In despair he let it alone.

Next he made the mouth.

No sooner was it finished than it began to laugh and poke fun at him.

"Stop laughing!" said Geppetto angrily; but he might as well have spoken to the wall.

"Stop laughing, I say!" he roared in a voice of thunder.

The mouth stopped laughing, but it stuck out a long tongue.

Not wishing to start an argument, Geppetto made believe he saw nothing and went on with his work. After the mouth, he made the chin, then the neck, the shoulders, the stomach, the arms, and the hands.

As he was about to put the last touches on the finger tips,

A stamp commemorates Pinocchio and his nose

Geppetto felt his wig being pulled off. He glanced up and what did he see? His yellow wig was in the Marionette's hand. "Pinocchio, give me my wig!"

But instead of giving it back, Pinocchio put it on his own head, which was half swallowed up in it.

At that unexpected trick, Geppetto became very sad and downcast, more so than he had ever been before.

"Pinocchio, you wicked boy!" he cried out. "You are not yet finished, and you start out by being impudent to your poor old father. Very bad, my son, very bad!"

And he wiped away a tear.

The legs and feet still had to be made. As soon as they were done, Geppetto felt a sharp kick on the tip of his nose.

"I deserve it!" he said to himself. "I should have thought of this before I made him. Now it's too late!"

Many adventures lie ahead of the little wooden puppet

The little old man wanted to pull Pinocchio's ears. Think how he felt when, upon searching for them, he discovered that he had forgotten to make them!

All he could do was to seize Pinocchio by the back of the neck and take him home. As he was doing so, he shook him two or three times and said to him angrily:

"We're going home now. When we get home, then we'll settle this matter!"

Pinocchio, on hearing this, threw himself on the ground and refused to take another step. One person after another gathered around the two.

Some said one thing, some another.

"Poor Marionette," called out a man. "I am not surprised he doesn't want to go home. Geppetto, no doubt, will beat him unmercifully, he is so mean and cruel!"

"Geppetto looks like a good man," added another, "but with boys he's a real tyrant. If we leave that poor Marionette in his hands he may tear him to pieces!"

They said so much that, finally, the Carabineer ended matters by setting Pinocchio at liberty and dragging Geppetto to prison. The poor old fellow did not know how to defend himself, but wept and wailed like a child and said between his sobs: "Ungrateful boy! To think I tried so hard to make you a well-behaved Marionette! I deserve it, however! I should have given the matter more thought."

*"Catch him!" Geppetto shouts as the people
in the street stared*

He took hold of the Marionette under the arms and put him on the floor to teach him to walk.

Pinocchio's legs were so stiff that he could not move them, and Geppetto held his hand and showed him how to put out one foot after the other.

When his legs were limbered up, Pinocchio started walking by himself and ran all around the room. He came to the open door, and with one leap he was out into the street. Away he flew!

Poor Geppetto ran after him but was unable to catch him, for Pinocchio ran in leaps and bounds, his two wooden feet, as they beat on the stones of the street, making as much noise as twenty peasants in wooden shoes.

"Catch him! Catch him!" Geppetto kept shouting. But the people in the street, seeing a wooden Marionette running like the wind, stood still to stare and to laugh until they cried.

At last, by sheer luck, a Carabineer [policeman] happened along, who, hearing all that noise, thought that it might be a runaway colt, and stood bravely in the middle of the street, with legs wide apart, firmly resolved to stop it and prevent any trouble.

Pinocchio saw the Carabineer from afar and tried his best to escape between the legs of the big fellow, but without success.

The Carabineer grabbed him by the nose (it was an extremely long one and seemed made on purpose for that very thing) and returned him to Mastro Geppetto.

Wizard of Oz
The Cowardly Lion

This is an extract from the book written by Frank Baum and published in 1900. It inspired a stage musical in 1902 and the famous film starring Judy Garland in 1939. In total, there are fourteen books about the Land of Oz. Sales of the original novel have now reached over 5 million copies. Today, even if in poor condition, first editions can realize almost $3,000 at auction.

In an inscription in a book that Baum presented to his sister he comments: "I have learned to regard fame as a will-o'-the-wisp, which when caught, is not worth the possession; but to please a child is a sweet and lovely thing that warms one's heart and brings its own reward."

"I know I'm a coward," said the Lion, wiping a tear away

All this time Dorothy and her companions had been walking through the thick woods. The road was still paved with yellow brick, but these were much covered by dried branches and dead leaves from the trees, and the walking was not at all good.

There were few birds in this part of the forest, for birds love the open country where there is plenty of sunshine. But now and then there came a deep growl from some wild animal hidden among the trees. These sounds made the little girl's heart beat fast, for she did not know what made them; but Toto knew, and he walked close to Dorothy's side, and did not even bark in return.

"How long will it be," the child asked of the Tin Woodman, "before we are out of the forest?"

"I cannot tell," was the answer, "for I have never been to the Emerald City. But my father went there once, when I was a boy, and he said it was a long journey through a dangerous country, although nearer to the city where Oz dwells the country is beautiful. But I am not afraid so long as I have my oil-can, and nothing can hurt the Scarecrow, while you bear upon your forehead the mark of the Good

Witch's kiss, and that will protect you from harm."

"But Toto!" said the girl anxiously. "What will protect him?"

"We must protect him ourselves if he is in danger," replied the Tin Woodman.

Just as he spoke there came from the forest a terrible roar, and the next moment a great Lion bounded into the road. With one blow of his paw he sent the Scarecrow spinning over and over to the edge of the road, and then he struck at the Tin Woodman with his sharp claws. But, to the Lion's surprise, he could make no impression on the tin, although the Woodman fell over in the road and lay still.

Little Toto, now that he had an enemy to face, ran barking toward the Lion, and the great beast had opened his mouth to bite the dog, when Dorothy, fearing Toto would be killed, and heedless of danger, rushed forward and slapped the Lion upon his nose as hard as she could, while she cried out:

"Don't you dare to bite Toto! You ought to be ashamed of yourself, a big beast like you, to bite a poor little dog!"

"I didn't bite him," said the Lion, as he rubbed his nose

The Lion, the Scarecrow and the Tin Woodman help Dorothy to defeat the Wicked Witch of the West

with his paw where Dorothy had hit it.

"No, but you tried to," she retorted. "You are nothing but a big coward."

"I know it," said the Lion, hanging his head in shame. "I've always known it. But how can I help it?"

"I don't know, I'm sure. To think of your striking a stuffed man, like the poor Scarecrow!"

"Is he stuffed?" asked the Lion in surprise, as he watched her pick up the Scarecrow and set him upon his feet, while she patted him into shape again.

"Of course he's stuffed," replied Dorothy, who was still angry.

"That's why he went over so easily," remarked the Lion. "It astonished me to see him whirl around so. Is the other one stuffed also?"

"No," said Dorothy, "he's made of tin." And she helped the Woodman up again.

"That's why he nearly blunted my claws," said the Lion. "When they scratched against the tin it made a cold shiver run down my back. What is that little animal you are so tender of?"

"He is my dog, Toto," answered Dorothy.

"Is he made of tin, or stuffed?" asked the Lion.

"Neither. He's a – a – a meat dog," said the girl.

"Oh! He's a curious animal and seems remarkably small, now that I look at him. No one would think of biting such a little thing, except a coward like me," continued the Lion sadly.

"What makes you a coward?" asked Dorothy, looking at the great beast in wonder, for he was as big as a small horse.

"It's a mystery," replied the Lion. "I suppose I was born that way. All the other animals in the forest naturally expect me to be brave, for the Lion is everywhere thought to be the King of Beasts. I learned that if I roared very loudly every living thing was frightened and got out of my way.

Whenever I've met a man I've been awfully scared; but I just roared at him, and he has always run away as fast as he could go. If the elephants and the tigers and the bears had ever tried to fight me, I should have run myself – I'm such a coward; but just as soon as they hear me roar they all try to get away from me, and of course I let them go."

"But that isn't right. The King of Beasts shouldn't be a coward," said the Scarecrow.

"I know it," returned the Lion, wiping a tear from his eye with the tip of his tail. "It is my great sorrow, and makes my life very unhappy. But whenever there is danger, my heart begins to beat fast."

"Perhaps you have heart disease," said the Tin Woodman.

"It may be," said the Lion.

"If you have," continued the Tin Woodman, "you ought to be glad, for it proves you have a heart. For my part, I have no heart; so I cannot have heart disease."

"Perhaps," said the Lion thoughtfully, "if I had no heart I should not be a coward."

"Have you brains?" asked the Scarecrow.

"I suppose so. I've never looked to see," replied the Lion.

"I am going to the Great Oz to ask him to give me some," remarked the Scarecrow, "for my head is stuffed with straw."

"And I am going to ask him to give me a heart," said the Woodman.

"And I am going to ask him to send Toto and me back to Kansas," added Dorothy.

"Do you think Oz could give me courage?" asked the Cowardly Lion.

"Just as easily as he could give me brains," said the Scarecrow.

"Or give me a heart," said the Tin Woodman.

"Or send me back to Kansas," said Dorothy.

"Then, if you don't mind, I'll go with you," said the Lion,

"for my life is simply unbearable without a bit of courage."

"You will be very welcome," answered Dorothy, "for you will help to keep away the other wild beasts. It seems to me they must be more cowardly than you are if they allow you to scare them so easily."

"They really are," said the Lion, "but that doesn't make me any braver, and as long as I know myself to be a coward I shall be unhappy."

So once more the little company set off upon the journey, the Lion walking with stately strides at Dorothy's side. Toto did not approve this new comrade at first, for he could not forget how nearly he had been crushed between the Lion's great jaws. But after a time he became more at ease, and presently Toto and the Cowardly Lion had grown to be good friends.

During the rest of that day there was no other adventure to mar the peace of their journey. Once, indeed, the Tin Woodman stepped upon a beetle that was crawling along the road, and killed the poor little thing. This made the Tin Woodman very unhappy, for he was always careful not to hurt any living creature; and as he walked along he wept several tears of sorrow and regret. These tears ran slowly down his face and over the hinges of his jaw, and there they rusted. When Dorothy presently asked him a question the Tin Woodman could not open his mouth, for his jaws were tightly rusted together. He became greatly frightened at this and made many motions to Dorothy to relieve him, but she could not understand. The Lion was also puzzled to know what was wrong. But the Scarecrow seized the oil-can from Dorothy's basket and oiled the Woodman's jaws, so that after a few moments he could talk as well as before.

"This will serve me a lesson," said he, "to look where I step. For if I should kill another bug or beetle I should surely cry again, and crying rusts my jaws so that I cannot speak."

Thereafter he walked very carefully, with his eyes on the road, and when he saw a tiny ant toiling by he would step over it, so as not to harm it. The Tin Woodman knew very well he had no heart, and therefore he took great care never to be cruel or unkind to anything.

"You people with hearts," he said, "have something to guide you, and need never do wrong; but I have no heart, and so I must be very careful. When Oz gives me a heart of course I needn't mind so much."

The Tsarevna Frog or The Frog Princess

This Russian fairy tale – with various forms and several different titles – has percolated into Italian, Greek and other European nations' folklore. Andrew Lang included an Italian variant titled The Frog in *The Violet Fairy Book*. Traditionally Russian folktales and fairy stories have inspired beautiful illustrations and other media interpretations such as ballet and orchestral pieces.

In an old, old Russian tsarstvo [the domain of a tsar], I do not know when, there lived a sovereign prince with the princess his wife. They had three sons, all of them young, and such brave fellows that no pen could describe them. The youngest had the name of Ivan Tsarevitch. One day their father said to his sons:

"My dear boys, take each of you an arrow, draw your strong bow and let your arrow fly; in whatever court it falls, in that court there will be a wife for you."

The arrow of the oldest Tsarevitch fell on a boyar-house [a lord's house]; just in front of the terem [the ladies' rooms] where women live; the arrow of the second Tsarevitch flew to the red porch of a rich merchant, and on the porch there stood a sweet girl, the merchant's daughter. The youngest, the brave Tsarevitch Ivan, had the ill luck to send his arrow into the midst of a swamp, where it was caught by a croaking frog.

Ivan Tsarevitch came to his father: "How can I marry the frog?" complained the son. "Is she my equal? Certainly she is not."

"Never mind," replied his father, "you have to marry the frog, for such is evidently your destiny."

Thus the brothers were married: the oldest to a young boyarishnia, a nobleman's child; the second to the merchant's beautiful daughter, and the youngest, Tsarevitch Ivan, to a croaking frog.

After a while the sovereign prince called his three sons and said to them:

"Have each of your wives bake a loaf of bread by tomorrow morning."

Ivan returned home. There was no smile on his face, and his brow was clouded.

"C-R-O-A-K! C-R-O-A-K! Dear husband of mine, Tsarevitch Ivan, why so sad?" gently asked the frog. "Was there anything disagreeable in the palace?"

"Disagreeable indeed," answered Ivan Tsarevitch; "the

Tsar, my father, wants you to bake a loaf of white bread by tomorrow."

"Do not worry, Tsarevitch. Go to bed; the morning hour is a better adviser than the dark evening."

The Tsarevitch, taking his wife's advice, went to sleep.

Young Ivan's arrow flew into a swamp and was caught by a croaking frog

Then the frog threw off her frogskin and turned into a beautiful, sweet girl, Vassilissa by name. She now stepped out on the porch and called aloud:

"Nurses and waitresses, come to me at once and prepare a loaf of white bread for tomorrow morning, a loaf exactly like those I used to eat in my royal father's palace."

In the morning Tsarevitch Ivan awoke with the crowing cocks, and you know the cocks and chickens are never late. Yet the loaf was already made, and so fine it was that nobody could even describe it, for only in fairyland one finds such marvelous loaves. It was adorned all about with pretty figures, with towns and fortresses on each side, and within it was white as snow and light as a feather.

The Tsar father was pleased and the Tsarevitch received his special thanks.

"Now there is another task," said the Tsar smilingly. "Have each of your wives weave a rug by tomorrow."

Tsarevitch Ivan came back to his home. There was no smile on his face and his brow was clouded.

"C-R-O-A-K! C-R-O-A-K! Dear Tsarevitch Ivan, my husband and master, why so troubled again? Was not father pleased?"

"How can I be otherwise? The Tsar, my father, has ordered a rug by tomorrow."

"Do not worry, Tsarevitch. Go to bed; go to sleep. The morning hour will bring help."

Again the frog turned into Vassilissa, the wise maiden, and again she called aloud:

"Dear nurses and faithful waitresses, come to me for new work. Weave a silk rug like the one I used to sit upon in the palace of the king, my father."

Once said, quickly done. When the cocks began their early "cock-a-doodle-doo," Tsarevitch Ivan awoke, and lo! there lay the most beautiful silk rug before him, a rug that no one could begin to describe. Threads of silver and gold were interwoven among bright-colored silken ones, and the rug was too beautiful for anything but to admire.

The Tsar father was pleased, thanked his son Ivan, and issued a new order. He now wished to see the three wives of his handsome sons, and they were to present their brides on the next day.

The Tsarevitch Ivan returned home. Cloudy was his brow, more cloudy than before.

"C-R-O-A-K! C-R-O-A-K! Tsarevitch, my dear husband and master, why so sad? Hast thou heard anything unpleasant at the palace?"

"Unpleasant enough, indeed! My father, the Tsar, ordered all of us to present our wives to him. Now tell me, how could I dare go with thee?"

"It is not so bad after all, and might be much worse," answered the frog, gently croaking. "Thou shalt go alone and I will follow thee. When thou hearest a noise, a great noise, do not be afraid; simply say: 'There is my miserable froggy coming in her miserable box.'"

The two elder brothers arrived first with their wives, beautiful, bright, and cheerful, and dressed in rich garments. Both the happy bridegrooms made fun of the Tsarevitch Ivan.

"Why alone, brother?" they laughingly said to him. "Why didst thou not bring thy wife along with thee? Was there no rag to cover her? Where couldst thou have gotten such a beauty? We are ready to wager that in all the swamps in the dominion of our father it would be hard to find another one like her." And they laughed and laughed.

Lo! what a noise! The palace trembled, the guests were all frightened. Tsarevitch Ivan alone remained quiet and said:

"No danger; it is my froggy coming in her box."

To the red porch came flying a golden carriage drawn by six splendid white horses, and Vassilissa, beautiful beyond all description, gently reached her hand to her husband. He led her with him to the heavy oak tables, which were covered with snow-white linen and loaded with many wonderful dishes such as are known and eaten only in the land of fairies and never anywhere else. The guests were eating and chatting gayly.

Vassilissa drank some wine, and what was left in the tumbler she poured into her left sleeve. She ate some of the fried swan, and the bones she threw into her right sleeve. The wives of the two elder brothers watched her and did exactly the same.

When the long, hearty dinner was over, the guests began dancing and singing. The beautiful Vassilissa came forward, as bright as a star, bowed to her sovereign, bowed to the honorable guests and danced with her husband, the happy Tsarevitch Ivan.

While dancing, Vassilissa waved her left sleeve and a pretty lake appeared in the midst of the hall and cooled the air. She waved her right sleeve and white swans swam on the water. The Tsar, the guests, the servants, even the gray cat sitting in the corner, all were amazed and wondered at the beautiful Vassilissa. Her two sisters-in-law alone envied her. When their turn came to dance, they also waved their left sleeves as Vassilissa had done, and, oh, wonder! they sprinkled wine all around. They waved their right sleeves,

As beautiful Vassilissa danced, she waved her sleeves to create a lake
that cooled the air and white swans that swam upon the water

and instead of swans the bones flew in the face of the Tsar father. The Tsar grew very angry and bade them leave the palace. In the meantime Ivan Tsarevitch watched a moment to slip away unseen. He ran home, found the frogskin, and burned it in the fire.

Vassilissa, when she came back, searched for the skin, and when she could not find it her beautiful face grew sad and her bright eyes filled with tears. She said to Tsarevitch Ivan, her husband:

"Oh, dear Tsarevitch, what hast thou done? There was but a short time left for me to wear the ugly frogskin. The moment was near when we could have been happy together forever. Now I must bid thee good-bye. Look for me in a far-away country to which no one knows the roads, at the palace of Kostshei the Deathless;" and Vassilissa turned into a white swan and flew away through the window.

Tsarevitch Ivan wept bitterly. Then he prayed to the almighty God, and making the sign of the cross northward, southward, eastward, and westward, he went on a mysterious journey.

No one knows how long his journey was, but one day he met an old, old man. He bowed to the old man, who said:

"Good-day, brave fellow. What art thou searching for, and whither art thou going?"

Tsarevitch Ivan answered sincerely, telling all about his misfortune without hiding anything.

"And why didst thou burn the frogskin? It was wrong to do so. Listen now to me. Vassilissa was born wiser than her own father, and as he envied his daughter's wisdom he condemned her to be a frog for three long years. But I pity thee and want to help thee. Here is a magic ball. In whatever direction this ball rolls, follow without fear."

Ivan Tsarevitch thanked the good old man, and followed his new guide, the ball. Long, very long, was his road. One day in a wide, flowery field he met a bear, a big Russian bear. Ivan Tsarevitch took his bow and was ready to shoot the bear.

"Do not kill me, kind Tsarevitch," said the bear. "Who knows but that I may be useful to thee?" And Ivan did not shoot the bear.

Above in the sunny air there flew a duck, a lovely white duck. Again the Tsarevitch drew his bow to shoot it. But the duck said to him:

"Do not kill me, good Tsarevitch. I certainly shall be useful to thee some day."

And this time he obeyed the command of the duck and passed by. Continuing his way he saw a blinking hare. The Tsarevitch prepared an arrow to shoot it, but the gray, blinking hare said:

"Do not kill me, brave Tsarevitch. I shall prove myself grateful to thee in a very short time."

The Tsarevitch did not shoot the hare, but passed by. He walked farther and farther after the rolling ball, and came to the deep blue sea. On the sand there lay a fish. I do not remember the name of the fish, but it was a big fish, almost dying on the dry sand.

"O Tsarevitch Ivan!" prayed the fish, "have mercy upon me and push me back into the cool sea."

The Tsarevitch did so, and walked along the shore. The ball, rolling all the time, brought Ivan to a hut, a queer, tiny hut standing on tiny hen's feet.

"Izboushka! Izboushka!" – for so in Russia do they name small huts – "Izboushka, I want thee to turn thy front to me," cried Ivan, and lo! the tiny hut turned its front at once. Ivan stepped in and saw a witch, one of the ugliest witches he could imagine.

"Ho! Ivan Tsarevitch! What brings thee here?" was his greeting from the witch.

"O, thou old mischief!" shouted Ivan with anger. "Is it the way in holy Russia to ask questions before the tired guest gets something to eat, something to drink, and some hot water to wash the dust off?"

Baba Yaga, the witch, gave the Tsarevitch plenty to eat and drink, besides hot water to wash the dust off. Tsarevitch Ivan felt refreshed. Soon he became talkative, and related the wonderful story of his marriage. He told how he had lost his dear wife, and that his only desire was to find her.

"I know all about it," answered the witch. "She is now at the palace of Kostshei the Deathless, and thou must understand that Kostshei is terrible. He watches her day and night and no one can ever conquer him. His death depends on a magic needle. That needle is within a hare; that hare is within a large trunk; that trunk is hidden in the branches of an old oak tree; and that oak tree is watched by Kostshei as closely as Vassilissa herself, which means closer than any treasure he has."

Then the witch told Ivan Tsarevitch how and where to find the oak tree. Ivan hastily went to the place. But when he perceived the oak tree he was much discouraged, not knowing what to do or how to begin the work. Lo and behold! that old acquaintance of his, the Russian bear, came running along, approached the tree, uprooted it, and the trunk fell and broke. A hare jumped out of the trunk and began to run fast; but another hare, Ivan's friend, came running after, caught it and tore it to pieces. Out of the hare there flew a duck, a gray one which flew very high and was almost invisible, but the beautiful white duck followed the bird and struck its gray enemy, which lost an egg. That egg fell into the deep sea. Ivan meanwhile was anxiously watching his faithful friends helping him. But when the egg disappeared in the blue waters he could not help weeping. All of a sudden a big fish came swimming up, the same fish he had saved, and brought the egg in his mouth. How happy Ivan was when he took it! He broke it and found the needle inside, the magic needle upon which everything depended.

At the same moment Kostshei lost his strength and power forever. Ivan Tsarevitch entered his vast dominions, killed him with the magic needle, and in one of the palaces found his own dear wife, his beautiful Vassilissa. He took her home and they were very happy ever after.

Princess Belle-Etoile

Written by Madame D'Aulnoy in 1892, this story that tells how a poverty-stricken queen and her three daughters help an old woman who turns out to be a fairy and promises to grant their wishes. In due course the sisters marry the king's admiral, the king's brother, and the king himself – much to the anger of the king's mother who wrecks the marriages and gets rid of her grandchildren. The story involves pirates, a singing apple, a dragon and the little Princess Belle-Etoile. The following section is from the middle of the story.

The jealous queen plots to have her grandchildren strangled and buried but the maid Feintise secretly goes against her orders . . .

She had a boat brought to the sea-shore, and put the four children in one cradle into it, and some jewelled necklaces, so that if fate led them to the hands of any one kind-hearted enough to bring them up, he might be rewarded.

Driven before a high wind, Feintise soon lost sight of the boat, and in the same instant the waves grew bigger, the sun was hidden, the clouds and water seemed to meet, and thunderclaps resounded on every side. She never doubted but the frail craft was upset, and felt glad that the poor innocents were no more, because she had dreaded something extraordinary happening in their favour.

The gods took pity on the princes and the princess in the boat. The fairy who protected them, instead of rain, caused milk to fall into their little mouths, and the terrible storm that had so suddenly arisen did not do them the least injury. After drifting along for seven days and seven nights in open sea as gently as if they had been on a lake, they fell in with a pirate ship. The captain, struck even at a distance by the brilliant light of the stars on their foreheads, felt sure the boat must be full of precious stones. He verily found some in it, but was even more delighted with the beauty of the four marvellous children. The desire of saving them made him return home in order to give them to his wife, who was childless, but ardently wished for sons and daughters.

She was troubled to see him return so soon, because he had intended making a long voyage; but she was overjoyed when he delivered to her keeping such an important treasure. Together they wondered at the marvel of the stars, the gold chains that could not be removed from their necks, and their long hair. Their astonishment increased when the woman combed their hair, and every second there fell from it pearls, rubies, diamonds, and emeralds, of various sizes and all perfect; she told her husband about it, and he was equally surprised.

"I am," he said, "very tired of being a pirate if these little children's locks continue to give us such treasures, I will no longer scour the ocean, and my property will be as great as that of our chief captain's." The pirate's wife, whose name was Corsine, was delighted at her husband's determination, and loved the children all the more in consequence. She named the princess, Belle-Etoile, her elder brother, Petit-Soleil; the younger, Heureux; and the princess's son, Chéri. So superior in beauty to the other two was Chéri that, although he had neither star nor necklace, Corsine loved him best.

As she could not rear them without the aid of a nurse, she asked her husband, who was fond of hunting, to catch her some very young fawns. He easily succeeded, because the forest in which they dwelt was very large. Corsine exposed them on the weather side, and the hinds scenting them, hastened up to suckle them. Corsine then hid them, and put the children in their stead, who eagerly drank the hind's milk. Twice every day four of them came to Corsine's house in search of the princes and the princess whom they took for fawns.

Thus passed the princes' early childhood; the pirate and his wife loved them so passionately that they gave them every care. The man had been well educated, and it was less from inclination than from the frowardness of fortune that he had become a pirate. He had met Corsine in the house of a princess, where her mind had been properly cultivated; she was well-bred, and, although she inhabited a kind of desert, where they subsisted on the booty he brought home from his voyages, she had not forgotten the usages of society. Thus their joy that they were no longer forced to expose themselves to all the dangers inseparable from a pirate's life, was very great, and they were getting rich all the same. About every three days, there fell, as I have already mentioned, a quantity of precious stones from the hair of the princess and her brothers; those Corsine sold at the nearest town, and brought back all manner of pretty things for her little ones.

When they had passed their earliest infancy, the pirate began seriously to cultivate the charming dispositions heaven had endowed them with. As he never doubted that a great mystery attached to their origin, and his finding them, he wished to show his gratitude to the gods by giving the children a good education, so that, after rendering his house more comfortable, he brought there clever men who taught them the various branches of knowledge with an ease that vastly surprised those learned persons.

The pirate and his wife had never told any one the story of the finding of the four children. They passed for theirs, although their actions proved they sprung from a more illustrious stock. They were extremely fond of one another, which was only natural and polite, but Prince Chéri's affection for Princess Belle-Etoile was more eager and ardent than that of the other two; no sooner did she express a wish for anything than he attempted even the impossible to procure her what she wanted. He scarcely ever left her; when she went hunting, he accompanied her; when she stayed at home, he always found an excuse for remaining with her. Petit-Soleil and Heureux treated her with less affection and respect. She noticed the difference, but Chéri quite made up for it, and she loved him more than the others.

As they grew older their mutual affection increased, and at first they derived only pleasure from the fact.

The captain of a pirate ship rescued the four hapless infants afloat on the ocean

"My dear brother," said Belle-Etoile, "if my wishes could make you happy, you should be one of the greatest kings on the earth."

"Alas my sister," he replied, "do not grudge me the happiness I find in being near you. I would rather spend an hour with you than possess the high honour you wish for me. When she made a like speech to her brothers, they

very naturally replied that they would like nothing better, and to prove them further she added: "I should like you to sit on the greatest throne in the world, even if I were never to see you". They immediately said "You are right, my sister; the one is worth much more than the other". "You would then be willing, she said, "never to see me again?" "Certainly," they replied, "we should be quite content to hear from you occasionally."

When she was alone she examined these different ways of loving, and felt her own heart was just like theirs, for although she was fond of Petit-Soleil and Heureux, she did not desire to remain with them all her life, but she burst into tears whenever she thought their father might possibly send Chéri to sea, or put him into the army. Thus love, under the guise of a beautiful disposition, grew up in these young hearts. But at the age of fourteen, Belle-Etoile began to reproach herself for the injustice she thought she was doing her brothers in not loving them equally. She imagined Chéri's attentions and caresses were the cause, and forbade him to seek further means of making himself beloved. "You have found only too many," she said, pleasantly, "and you have succeeded in causing me to make a great difference between you and them." When she spoke thus his joy was intense; far from lessening his love, she increased it, and every day he showed her some fresh gallantry.

They had no idea what their affection tended to, nor did they know its meaning, when one day Belle-Etoile received some new books. She took the first that came to her hand; it contained the story of two young lovers, whose passion began when they thought themselves brother and sister, but afterwards their relatives recognised them and discovered to them that such was not the case, and after many troubles they were married. As Chéri read extremely well, intelligently, and with expression, she asked him to read the tale to her while she finished a piece of needlework she was anxious to complete.

He read the story, and it was not without some emotion that he recognised in it a perfect description of his own feelings. Belle-Etoile was equally surprised; it seemed as if the author had divined all that was passing in her mind...

Later the story continues

One day the three princes had gone hunting. Belle-Etoile shut herself up in a little room that she liked because it was dark, and she could indulge her dreams there with less interruption than elsewhere; she made no noise at all. This room was only divided from that of Corsine by a partition wall. Corsine thought the girl was out walking, and Belle-Etoile heard her say to the pirate: "Belle-Etoile is now old enough to be married: if we knew who she was, we should try to find her a husband suited to her rank, or if we could think those who pass for her brothers, were not so, we could give her one of them, for where can she hope to find any one more perfect?"

"When I found them," said the pirate, "there was nothing

to give me any clue to their rank. The precious stones placed in their cradle pointed to the fact that they must belong to wealthy people, but the strange thing was that they all seemed to be of exactly the same age, and it is not usual to have four children at one birth."

"I doubt," said Corsine, "if Chéri is their brother; he has neither star nor necklace."

"That is true," replied her husband, "but the diamonds fall from his hair as from that of the others, and considering all the wealth we have amassed by means of these dear children, I have nothing further to wish for than to discover their origin."

"We must leave everything to the gods," said Corsine, "who gave them to us, and will, doubtless, at the right time reveal to us the secret."

Belle-Etoile listened attentively to this conversation. Her joy at the hope she might be of illustrious birth cannot be expressed for although she had never been wanting in respect to those she believed to be her parents, she had all the same been sorry to know herself the daughter of a pirate. But what delighted her even more was the hope that Chéri was not her brother. She burned with impatience to talk to him, and tell him so strange a circumstance.

She mounted a light bay horse, whose black mane was tied up with diamond buckles, for she had only to comb her hair once to provide the whole hunt with jewels. Her green velvet saddle-cloth was studded with diamonds and embroidered with rubies. She rode swiftly towards the forest in search of her brothers. The sound of horns and the baying of hounds signified to her where they were, and in a moment she had joined them. At sight of her, Chéri left the others and went to meet her. "What a delightful surprise,' he exclaimed. "Belle-Etoile! at length you come to the hunt, you who can never for a moment be persuaded to leave the joys of music and the sciences."

"I have so many things to say to you," she replied, "that wishing to be alone with you, I came in search of you."

"Alas! my sister, he said, sighing, what do you want of me? It seems to me that for some while past you have been avoiding me." She blushed, cast down her eyes, and remained on her horse, sad and pondering, without replying a word. When her brothers came up she started as from deep slumber, and jumped to the ground, walking on in front. They all followed her, and in the midst of a grass-plot, shaded by trees, she said "Let us stay here, and I will tell you what I have just heard."

She related to them the conversation between the pirate and his wife, and how they were not their children. The surprise of the three princes was enormous, and they discussed what they ought to do. One wished to depart without saying anything about it; another preferred remaining where he was, and the last wanted to go, but at the same time to tell the pirate of their intention. ...

... They joined the pirate and Corsine with a mingled expression of joy and anxiety on their countenances.

"We do not come," said Petit-Soleil, who was spokesman,

"to deny the affection, gratitude, and respect we owe you; although we have learnt that you are not our father and mother, the pity that induced you to rescue us, the noble education you have given us, all the care and kindness with which you have surrounded us, have formed such close ties that nothing in the world could free us from them. We come, therefore, to renew our sincerest thanks, to beg you to tell us the strange story, and give us your advice, so that guided by you we may have no cause to reproach ourselves."

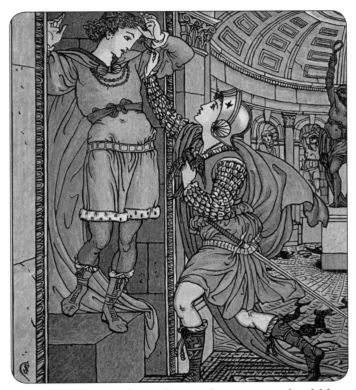

"If my wishes could make you happy, you should be one of the greatest kings on the earth"

The pirate and Corsine were much surprised that a thing they had so carefully concealed should have been discovered. "You have been only too well informed," they said, "and we cannot hide the fact that you are not our children, and came into our possession by the merest chance. We know nothing of your rank, but the precious stones that were in your cradle prove that your parents are either great nobles or very rich. Now how can we advise you? If you consult our affections for you, you would then remain with us and console our old age with your pleasant society. If you do not like the castle we have built here, or if living in this solitude wearies you, we would go wherever you pleased, provided it was not to the court. A long experience has made it hateful to us, and would make it equally hateful to you if you knew the continual agitation, hypocrisy, envy, the disparity of rank, the real evil and the pretended good to be found there. We would say more but you would think our advice interested; and so it is, my children, for we want to keep you in this peaceful retreat, although you are at liberty to quit it when you like. Do not, however, fail to remember that here you are in the harbour, and that you go to the stormy sea, and that there trouble is nearly always in excess of joy; that the period of our lives is but short, and we often have to leave the world in the midst of our career; that the great things of the earth are counterfeit stones by which through a strange fatality we allow ourselves to he dazzled, and that the most enduring of all goods is to be able to limit our desires, to enjoy tranquillity, and become wise."

The pirate would have spoken longer had not Prince Heureux interrupted him. "My dear father," he said, "we are too anxious to clear up the mystery of our birth to bury ourselves in a desert. Your teaching is excellent and I wish we were capable of following it, but some indescribable fatality calls us else where. Permit us to fulfil our destiny; we shall return and tell you our adventures." The pirate and his wife began to weep. The princes felt very sorry, especially Belle-Etoile, who had a charming disposition and would never have thought of leaving the desert if she had been sure that Chéri would always stay with her.

The decision made, they thought only of preparing for their embarkation, for as they had been found on the sea they hoped to receive there some revelation of what they desired to know. They took on board their ship a horse for each, and after combing their hair violently in order to leave Corsine as many precious stones as possible, they asked her to give them in exchange the diamond chains found in their cradle. She fetched them from her closet, where she had carefully put them, and fastened them to Belle-Etoile's gown. She could not leave off embracing her, moistening her face with her tears.

Never was there a sadder parting; the pirate and his wife thought they could not survive it. Their sorrow did not arise from interested motives, for they had amassed such a quantity of treasure that they did not want an more. Petit-Soleil, Heureux, Chéri, and Belle-Etoile got into the ship. The pirate had had built for them a very stout and magnificent vessel; the mast was of ebony and cedar, the rigging of green silk mixed with gold, the sails of green and gold cloth, and the decorations beautiful. When it began to move, Cleopatra with her Antony and even the whole of Venus's crew would have lowered their flag before it. The princess was seated under a rich canopy on the poop, her two brothers and her cousin near her, and brighter than the constellations of heaven their stars gave forth long dazzling rays of light. They determined to go to the place where the pirate had found them. They prepared for a great sacrifice to the gods and fairies to obtain their protection and their guidance to the place of their birth. They caught a dove to sacrifice, but the princess finding it beautiful, took pity on it and saved its life, and to protect it from such a fate let it fly away. "Go," she said, "bird of Venus, and if some day I have need of you, do not forget the benefit you owe me."

The dove flew away. When the sacrifice was ended, they began so charming a concert, that it seemed as if all nature kept silence to listen; the waves of the sea were at rest, not a wind blew, zephyr alone gently stirred the princess's hair and veil. Then there came forth from the water a mermaid, who sang so well that the princess and her brothers were enchanted. After singing a few songs, she turned towards them and exclaimed: "Cease to disturb yourselves; let your ship go as it listeth; disembark where it stops, and let all who love continue to love."

Belle-Etoile and Chéri were charmed with the mermaid's words. They had no doubt these were meant for them, and expressing this belief in their glances, their hearts conversed, and neither Petit-Soleil nor Heureux perceived any thing of it. The ship sailed on at the will of the winds and waves; the voyage was uneventful, the weather was always fine, and the sea always calm. They were three months at sea, and during the time Prince Chéri often talked with the princess. "What delightful hopes I have, charming star," he said to her one day. "I am not your brother; this heart that owns your power and will never recognise that of another is not born for crime, and it would be one to love you as I do, if you were my sister. But the kindly mermaid, who gave us counsel, confirmed what I already thought." "Ah! my brother," she replied, "do not put too much trust in a thing still so obscure that we cannot see it clearly. What would our fate be if we vexed the gods by feelings they disapproved? The mermaid's words were so vague, that if we apply them to ourselves, it only proves that we wish to give them that meaning." "Cruel girl," said the distressed prince; "you say that less out of fear of the gods than out of hatred for me." Belle-Etoile did not reply, but raising her eyes to the heavens, she heaved so deep a sigh that he could not help regarding it as a favourable sign.

It was the season of the year when the days are long and hot. Towards evening the princess and her brothers came on deck to watch the sun sink into the sea. She sat down, the princes placed themselves near her; they took their instruments, and began a delightful concert. But the ship, driven by a fresh breeze, seemed to sail more swiftly, and quickly doubled a small cape that hid a part of the most beautiful town imaginable; and when it stood fully revealed, the sight surprised our young people. All the palaces were of marble, with gilded roofs, and the rest of the houses were of very fine porcelain. Some evergreen trees mingled their enamelled leaves with the various colours of the marble, gold, and porcelain. They hoped their ship would enter the harbour, but feared it would scarcely find room there, for the number of masts made it look like a floating forest.

Their wish was granted; the ship ran into the harbour, and the quay was immediately crowded with people, who had noticed the magnificent ship. The vessel built by the Argonauts for the quest of the Golden Fleece was not so splendid. The stars, and the beauty of the wondrous children, enchanted all beholders, and the king was informed of the new arrivals.

Ricky of the Tuft

This story by Charles Perrault is a French fairy tale about an ugly but wise prince. The tale was adapted to make a film in 1908 and has also been performed as a puppet play.

Once upon a time there was a queen who bore a son so ugly and misshapen that for some time it was doubtful if he would have human form at all. But a fairy who was present at his birth promised that he should have plenty of brains, and added that by virtue of the gift which she had just bestowed upon him he would be able to impart to the person whom he should love best the same degree of intelligence which he possessed himself.

This somewhat consoled the poor queen, who was greatly disappointed at having brought into the world such a hideous brat. And indeed, no sooner did the child begin to speak than his sayings proved to be full of shrewdness, while all that he did was somehow so clever that he charmed everyone.

I forgot to mention that when he was born he had a little tuft of hair upon his head. For this reason he was called Ricky of the Tuft, Ricky being his family name.

Some seven or eight years later the queen of a neighboring kingdom gave birth to twin daughters. The first one to come into the world was more beautiful than the dawn, and the queen was so overjoyed that it was feared her great excitement might do her some harm. The same fairy who had assisted at the birth of Ricky of the Tuft was present, and in order to moderate the transports of the queen she declared that this little princess would have no sense at all, and would be as stupid as she was beautiful. The queen was deeply mortified, and a moment or two later her chagrin became greater still, for the second daughter proved to be extremely ugly.

"Do not be distressed, Madam," said the fairy. "Your daughter shall be recompensed in another way. She shall have so much good sense that her lack of beauty will scarcely be noticed."

"May Heaven grant it!" said the queen. "But is there no means by which the elder, who is so beautiful, can be endowed with some intelligence?"

"In the matter of brains I can do nothing for her, Madam," said the fairy, "but as regards beauty I can do a great deal. As there is nothing I would not do to please you, I will bestow upon her the power of making beautiful any person who shall greatly please her."

As the two princesses grew up their perfections increased, and everywhere the beauty of the elder and the wit of the younger were the subject of common talk.

It is equally true that their defects also increased as they became older. The younger grew uglier every minute, and the elder daily became more stupid. Either she answered nothing at all when spoken to, or replied with some idiotic remark. At the same time she was so awkward that she could not set four china vases on the mantelpiece without breaking one of them, nor drink a glass of water without spilling half of it over her clothes.

Now although the elder girl possessed the great advantage which beauty always confers upon youth, she was nevertheless outshone in almost all company by her younger sister. At first everyone gathered round the beauty to see and admire her, but very soon they were all attracted by the graceful and easy conversation of the clever one. In a very short time the elder girl would be left entirely alone, while everybody clustered round her sister.

The elder princess was not so stupid that she was not aware of this, and she would willingly have surrendered all her beauty for half her sister's cleverness. Sometimes she was ready to die of grief for the queen, though a sensible woman, could not refrain from occasionally reproaching her for her stupidity.

The princess had retired one day to a wood to bemoan her misfortune, when she saw approaching her an ugly little man, of very disagreeable appearance, but clad in magnificent attire.

This was the young prince Ricky of the Tuft. He had fallen in love with her portrait, which was everywhere to be seen, and had left his father's kingdom in order to have the pleasure of seeing and talking to her.

Delighted to meet her thus alone, he approached with every mark of respect and politeness. But while he paid her the usual compliments he noticed that she was plunged in melancholy.

"I cannot understand, madam," he said, "how anyone with your beauty can be so sad as you appear. I can boast of having seen many fair ladies, and I declare that none of them could compare in beauty with you."

"It is very kind of you to say so, sir," answered the princess; and stopped there, at a loss what to say further.

"Beauty," said Ricky, "is of such great advantage that everything else can be disregarded; and I do not see that the possessor of it can have anything much to grieve about."

To this the princess replied, "I would rather be as plain as you are and have some sense, than be as beautiful as I am and at the same time stupid."

"Nothing more clearly displays good sense, madam, than a belief that one is not possessed of it. It follows, therefore, that the more one has, the more one fears it to be wanting."

"I am not sure about that," said the princess; "but I know only too well that I am very stupid, and this is the reason of the misery which is nearly killing me."

"If that is all that troubles you, madam, I can easily put an end to your suffering."

"How will you manage that?" said the princess.

"I am able, madam," said Ricky of the Tuft, "to bestow as much good sense as it is possible to possess on the person whom I love the most. You are that person, and it therefore rests with you to decide whether you will acquire so much intelligence. The only condition is that you shall consent to marry me."

The princess was dumfounded, and remained silent.

"I can see," pursued Ricky, "that this suggestion perplexes you, and I am not surprised. But I will give you a whole year to make up your mind to it."

The princess had so little sense, and at the same time desired it so ardently, that she persuaded herself the end of this year would never come. So she accepted the offer which had been made to her. No sooner had she given her word to Ricky that she would marry him within one year from that very day, than she felt a complete change come over her. She found herself able to say all that she wished with the greatest ease, and to say it in an elegant, finished, and natural manner. She at once engaged Ricky in a brilliant and lengthy conversation, holding her own so well that Ricky feared he had given her a larger share of sense than he had retained for himself.

On her return to the palace amazement reigned throughout the court at such a sudden and extraordinary change. Whereas formerly they had been accustomed to hear her give vent to silly, pert remarks, they now heard her express herself sensibly and very wittily.

The entire court was overjoyed. The only person not too pleased was the younger sister, for now that she had no longer the advantage over the elder in wit, she seemed nothing but a little fright in comparison.

The king himself often took her advice, and several times held his councils in her apartment.

The news of this change spread abroad, and the princes of the neighboring kingdoms made many attempts to captivate her. Almost all asked her in marriage. But she found none with enough sense, and so she listened to all without promising herself to any.

At last came one who was so powerful, so rich, so witty, and so handsome, that she could not help being somewhat attracted by him. Her father noticed this, and told her she could make her own choice of a husband. She had only to declare herself. Now the more sense one has, the more difficult it is to make up one's mind in an affair of this kind. After thanking her father, therefore, she asked for a little time to think it over. In order to ponder quietly what she

had better do she went to walk in a wood – the very one, as it happened, where she had encountered Ricky of the Tuft.

While she walked, deep in thought, she heard beneath her feet a thudding sound, as though many people were running busily to and fro. Listening more attentively she heard voices. "Bring me that boiler," said one; then another, "Put some wood on that fire!"

At that moment the ground opened, and she saw

The court greatly admired the beauty of the first-born princess but she was very sad for she knew herself to be stupid

below what appeared to be a large kitchen full of cooks and scullions, and all the train of attendants which the preparation of a great banquet involves. A gang of some twenty or thirty spit-turners emerged and took up their positions round a very long table in a path in the wood. They all wore their cook's caps on one side, and with their basting implements in their hands they kept time together as they worked, to the lilt of a melodious song.

The princess was astonished by this spectacle, and asked for whom their work was being done.

"For Prince Ricky of the Tuft, madam," said the foreman of the gang. ''His wedding is tomorrow."

At this the princess was more surprised than ever. In a flash she remembered that it was a year to the very day since she had promised to marry Prince Ricky of the Tuft, and was taken aback by the recollection. The reason she had forgotten was that when she made the promise she was still without sense, and with the acquisition of that intelligence which the prince had bestowed upon her, all memory of her former stupidities had been blotted out.

She had not gone another thirty paces when Ricky of the Tuft appeared before her, gallant and resplendent, like a prince upon his wedding day.

"As you see, madam," he said, "I keep my word to the minute. I do not doubt that you have come to keep yours, and by giving me your hand to make me the happiest of men."

"I will be frank with you," replied the princess. "I have

Ricky of the Tuft, arriving with his train
of porters, met the pretty princess
when she was walking in the woods

not yet made up my mind on the point, and I am afraid I shall never be able to take the decision you desire."

"You astonish me, madam," said Ricky of the Tuft.

"I can well believe it," said the princess, "and undoubtedly, if I had to deal with a clown, or a man who lacked good sense, I should feel myself very awkwardly situated. 'A princess must keep her word,' he would say, 'and you must marry me because you promised to!' But I am speaking to a man of the world, of the greatest good sense, and I am sure that he will listen to reason. As you are aware, I could not make up my mind to marry you even when I was entirely without sense; how can you expect that today, possessing the intelligence you bestowed on me, which makes me still more difficult to please than formerly, I should take a decision which I could not take then? If you wished so much to marry me, you were very wrong to relieve me of my stupidity, and to let me see more clearly than I did."

"If a man who lacked good sense," replied Ricky of the Tuft, "would be justified, as you have just said, in

reproaching you for breaking your word, why do you expect, madam, that I should act differently where the happiness of my whole life is at stake? Is it reasonable that people who have sense should be treated worse than those who have none? Would you maintain that for a moment – you, who so markedly have sense, and desired so ardently to have it? But, pardon me, let us get to the facts. With the exception of my ugliness, is there anything about me which displeases you? Are you dissatisfied with my breeding, my brains, my disposition, or my manners?"

"In no way," replied the princess. "I like exceedingly all that you have displayed of the qualities you mention."

"In that case," said Ricky of the Tuft, "happiness will be mine, for it lies in your power to make me the most attractive of men."

"How can that be done?" asked the princess.

"It will happen of itself," replied Ricky of the Tuft, "if you love me well enough to wish that it be so. To remove your doubts, madam, let me tell you that the same fairy who on the day of my birth bestowed upon me the power of endowing with intelligence the woman of my choice, gave to you also the power of endowing with beauty the man whom you should love, and on whom you should wish to confer this favor."

"If that is so," said the princess, "I wish with all my heart that you may become the handsomest and most attractive prince in the world, and I give you without reserve the boon which it is mine to bestow."

No sooner had the princess uttered these words than Ricky of the Tuft appeared before her eyes as the handsomest, most graceful and attractive man that she had ever set eyes on.

Some people assert that this was not the work of fairy enchantment, but that love alone brought about the transformation. They say that the princess, as she mused upon her lover's constancy, upon his good sense, and his many admirable qualities of heart and head, grew blind to the deformity of his body and the ugliness of his face; that his humpback seemed no more than was natural in a man who could make the courtliest of bows, and that the dreadful limp which had formerly distressed her now betokened nothing more than a certain diffidence and charming deference of manner. They say further that she found his eyes shine all the brighter for their squint, and that this defect in them was to her but a sign of passionate love; while his great red nose she found naught but martial and heroic.

However that may be, the princess promised to marry him on the spot, provided only that he could obtain the consent of her royal father.

The king knew Ricky of the Tuft to be a prince both wise and witty, and on learning of his daughter's regard for him, he accepted him with pleasure as a son-in-law.

The wedding took place upon the morrow, just as Ricky of the Tuft had foreseen, and in accordance with the arrangements he had long ago put in train.

The Blue Bird

Here follows the beginning and the
end of one of the best-known works
by Madame D'Aulnoy who wrote an
impressive number of fairy tales. This
one from 1697 bears some similarities
to *Cinderella* with a jealous sister and
conniving stepmother and also, like
Sing a Song of Sixpence has birds
singing in a pie.

Once upon a time there lived a King who was immensely rich. He had broad lands, and sacks overflowing with gold and silver; but he did not care a bit for all his riches, because the Queen, his wife, was dead. He shut himself up in a little room and knocked his head against the walls for grief, until his courtiers were really afraid that he would hurt himself. So they hung feather-beds between the tapestry and the walls, and then he could go on knocking his head as long as it was any consolation to him without coming to much harm. All his subjects came to see him, and said whatever they thought would comfort him: some were grave, even gloomy with him; and some agreeable, even gay; but not one could make the least impression upon him. Indeed, he hardly seemed to hear what they said. At last came a lady who was wrapped in a black mantle, and seemed to be in the deepest grief. She wept and sobbed until even the King's attention was attracted; and when she said that, far from coming to try and diminish his grief, she, who had just lost a good husband, was come to add her tears to his, since she knew what he must be feeling; the King redoubled his lamentations. Then he told the sorrowful lady long stories about the good qualities of his departed Queen, and she in her turn recounted all the virtues of her departed husband; and this passed the time so agreeably that the King quite forgot to thump his head against the feather-beds, and the lady did not need to wipe the tears from her great blue eyes as often as before. By degrees they came to talking about other things in which the King took an interest, and in a wonderfully short time the whole kingdom was astonished by the news that the King was married again to the sorrowful lady.

Now the King had one daughter, who was just fifteen years old. Her name was Fiordelisa, and she was the prettiest and most charming Princess imaginable, always merry. Now the new Queen also had a daughter and very

soon sent for her to come to the palace. Turritella, for that was her name, had been brought up by her godmother, the Fairy Mazilla, but in spite of all the care bestowed upon her, she was neither beautiful nor gracious. Indeed, when the Queen saw how ill-tempered and ugly she appeared beside Fiordelisa she was in despair, and did everything in her power to turn the King against his own daughter.

One day the King said that it was time Fiordelisa and Turritella were married, so he would give one of them to the first suitable prince who visited his court. The Queen answered:

"My daughter certainly ought to be the first to be married; she is older than yours, and a thousand times more charming!"

The King, who hated disputes, said, "Very well, it's no affair of mine, settle it your own way."

Very soon after came the news that King Charming, who was the most handsome and magnificent King in all the country round, was on his way to visit them. As soon as the Queen heard this, she set all her jewellers, tailors, weavers, and embroiderers to work upon splendid dresses and ornaments for Turritella, but she told the King that Fiordelisa had no need of anything new, and the night before King Charming was to arrive, she bribed her waiting woman to steal away all the princess's own dresses and jewels, so that when the day came, and Fiordelisa wished to adorn herself as became her high rank, not even a ribbon could she find.

However, as she easily guessed who had played her such a trick, she made no complaint, but sent to the merchants for some rich stuffs. But they said that the Queen had expressly forbidden them to supply her with any, and they dared not disobey. So the Princess had nothing left to put on but the little white frock she had been wearing the day before; and dressed in that, she went down when the time of the King's arrival came, and sat in a corner hoping to escape notice. The Queen received her guest with great ceremony, and presented him to her daughter, who was gorgeously attired, but so much splendour only made her ugliness more noticeable, and the King, after one glance at her, looked the other way. The Queen, however, only thought that he was bashful, and took pains to keep Turritella in full view. King Charming then asked it there was not another Princess, called Fiordelisa.

"Yes," said Turritella, pointing with her finger, "there she is, trying to keep out of sight because she is not fit to be seen."

At this Fiordelisa blushed, and looked so shy and so lovely, that the King was fairly astonished. He rose, and bowing low before her, said –

"Madam, your incomparable beauty needs no adornment."

"Sire," answered the Princess, "I assure you that I am not in the habit of wearing dresses as crumpled and untidy as this one, so I should have been better pleased if you had not seen me at all."

"Impossible!" cried King Charming. "Wherever such a marvellously beautiful Princess appears I can look at nothing else."

Here the Queen broke in, saying sharply –

"I assure you, Sire, that Fiordelisa is vain enough already. Pray make her no more flattering speeches."

The King quite understood that she was not pleased, but that did not matter to him, so he admired Fiordelisa to his heart's content, and talked to her for three hours without stopping.

The Queen was in despair, and so was Turritella, when they saw how much King Charming preferred Fiordelisa. They complained bitterly to the King, and begged and teased him, until he at last consented to have the Princess shut up somewhere out of sight while King Charming's visit lasted. So that night, as she went to her room, she was seized by four masked figures, and carried up into the topmost room of a high tower, where they left her in the deepest dejection. She easily guessed that she was to be kept out of sight for fear the young King should fall in love with her; but then, how disappointing that was, for she already liked him very much, and would have been quite willing to be chosen for his bride!

After several attempts at trickery by the new stepmother queen and King Charming's rejection of her daughter, the wicked queen has the young king transformed into a blue bird for seven years – with a crown of white feathers adorning his head. In this guise is able to visit Fiordelisa in the tower and to help her but is wounded just as Fiordelisa inherits her throne and believes she has betrayed him. The young queen is set free from the tower and heads homeward. Meanwhile her beloved King Charming is granted one year's release from his blue bird enchantment.

. . . Fiordelisa, disguised as a poor peasant girl, wearing a great straw hat that concealed her face, and carrying an old sack over her shoulder, had set out upon her weary journey, and had travelled far, sometimes by sea and sometimes by land; sometimes on foot, and sometimes on horseback, but not knowing which way to go. She feared all the time that every step she took was leading her farther from her lover. One day as she sat, quite tired and sad, on the bank of a little brook, cooling her white feet in the clear running water, and combing her long hair that glittered like gold in the sunshine, a little bent old woman passed by, leaning on a stick. She stopped, and said to Fiordelisa:

"What, my pretty child, are you all alone?"

"Indeed, good mother, I am too sad to care for company," she answered; and the tears ran down her cheeks.

"Don't cry," said the old woman, "but tell me truly what is the matter. Perhaps I can help you."

Fiordelisa told her willingly all that had happened, and how she was seeking the Blue Bird. Thereupon the little old woman suddenly stood up straight, and grew tall, and young, and beautiful, and said with a smile to the astonished Fiordelisa:

"The King whom you seek is no longer a bird. My sister Mazilla has given his own form back to him, and he is in his own kingdom. Do not be afraid, you will reach him, and will prosper. Take these four eggs; if you break one when you are in any great difficulty, you will find aid."

So saying, she disappeared, and Fiordelisa, feeling much encouraged, put the eggs into her bag and turned her steps towards Charming's kingdom. After walking on and on for eight days and eight nights, she came at last to a tremendously high hill of polished ivory, so steep that it was impossible to get a foothold upon it. Fiordelisa tried a thousand times, and scrambled and slipped, but always in the end found herself exactly where she started from. At last she sat down at the foot of it in despair, and then suddenly bethought herself of the eggs. Breaking one quickly, she found in it some little gold hooks, and with these fastened to her feet and hands, she mounted the ivory hill without further trouble, for the little hooks saved her from slipping. As soon as she reached the top a new difficulty presented itself, for all the other side, and indeed the whole valley, was one polished mirror, in which thousands and thousands of people were admiring their reflections. For this was a magic mirror, in which people saw themselves just as they wished to appear, and pilgrims came to it from the four corners of the world. But nobody had ever been able to reach the top of the hill, and when they saw Fiordelisa standing there, they raised a terrible outcry, declaring that if she set foot upon their glass she would break it to pieces. Not knowing what to do, for Fiordelisa saw it would be dangerous to try to go down, broke the second egg, and out came a chariot, drawn by two white doves, and Fiordelisa got into it, and was floated softly away. After a night and a day the doves alighted outside the gate of King Charming's kingdom. Here Fiordelisa got out of the chariot, and kissed the doves and thanked them, and then with a beating heart she walked into the town, asking the people she met where she could see the King. But they only laughed at her, crying:

"See the King? And pray, why do you want to see him, my little kitchen-maid? You had better go and wash your face first, your eyes are not clear enough to see him!" For Fiordelisa had disguised herself, and pulled her hair down about her eyes, that no one might know her. As they would not tell her, she went on farther, and presently asked again, and this time the people answered that to-morrow she might see the King driving through the streets with the Princess Turritella, as it was said that at last he had consented to marry her. This was indeed terrible news to Fiordelisa. Had she come all this weary way only to find Turritella had succeeded in making King Charming forget her?

She was too tired and miserable to walk another step, so she sat down in a doorway and cried bitterly all night long. As soon as it was light she hastened to the palace, and after being sent away fifty times by the guards, she got in at last, and saw the thrones set in the great hall for the King and Turritella, who was already looked upon as Queen.

Fiordelisa hid herself behind a marble pillar, and very soon saw Turritella make her appearance, richly dressed, but as ugly as ever, and with her came the King, more handsome and splendid even than Fiordelisa had remembered him. When Turritella had seated herself upon

The young Prince was transformed into a blue bird with a white crown of feathers

the throne, Fiordelisa approached her.

"Who are you, and how dare you come near my high-mightiness, upon my golden throne?" said Turritella, frowning fiercely at her.

"They call me the little kitchen-maid," she replied, "and I come to offer some precious things for sale," and with that she searched in her old sack, and drew out the emerald bracelets Prrince Charming had given her.

"Ho, ho!" said Turritella, "those are pretty bits of glass. I suppose you would like five silver pieces for them."

"Show them to someone who understands such things, Madam," answered the Fiordelisa; "after that we can decide upon the price."

Turritella, who really loved King Charming as much as she could love anybody, and was always delighted to get a chance of talking to him, now showed him the bracelets, asking how much he considered them worth. As soon as he saw them he remembered those he had given to Fiordelisa, and turned very pale and sighed deeply, and fell into such sad thought that he quite forgot to answer her. Presently she asked him again, and then he said, with

a great effort:

"I believe these bracelets are worth as much as my kingdom. I thought there was only one such pair in the world; but here, it seems, is another."

Then Turritella went back to little kitchen-maid, and asked her what was the lowest price she would take for them.

"More than you would find it easy to pay, Madam," answered she; "but if you will manage for me to sleep one night in the Chamber of Echoes, I will give you the emeralds."

"By all means, my little kitchen-maid," said Turritella, highly delighted.

The King did not try to find out where the bracelets had come from, not because he did not want to know, but because the only way would have been to ask Turritella, and he disliked her so much that he never spoke to her if he could possibly avoid it. It was he who had told Fiordelisa about the Chamber of Echoes, when he was a Blue Bird. It was a little room below the his own bed-chamber, and was so ingeniously built that the softest whisper in it was plainly heard in his room. Fiordelisa wanted to reproach him for his faithlessness, and could not imagine a better way than this. So when, by Turritella's orders, she was left there she began to weep and lament, and never ceased until daybreak.

The pages told Turritella, when she asked them, what a sobbing and sighing they had heard, and so she asked Fiordelisa what it was all about. The unhappy girl answered that she often dreamed and talked aloud.

But the King heard nothing of all this, for he took a sleeping draught every night before he lay down, and did not wake up until the sun was high.

"If he did hear me," Fiordelisa wondered, "could he remain so cruelly indifferent? But if he did not hear me, what can I do to get another chance? I have plenty of jewels, it is true, but nothing remarkable enough to catch Turritella's fancy."

Just then she thought of the eggs, and broke one, out of which came a little carriage of polished steel ornamented with gold, drawn by six green mice. The coachman was a rose-coloured rat, the postilion a grey one, and the carriage was occupied by the tiniest and most charming figures, who could dance and do wonderful tricks. Fiordelisa clapped her hands and danced for joy when she saw this triumph of magic art, and as soon as it was evening, went to a shady garden-path down which she knew Turritella would pass, and then she made the mice gallop, and the tiny people show off their tricks, and sure enough Turritella came, and the moment she saw it all cried:

"Little kitchen-maid, little kitchen-maid, what will you take for your mouse-carriage?"

And Fiordelisa answered:

"Let me sleep once more in the Chamber of Echoes."

"I won't refuse your request, poor creature," said Turritella condescendingly.

And then she turned to her ladies and whispered "The silly creature does not know how to profit by her chances;

so much the better for me."

When night came Fiordelisa said all the loving words she could think of, but alas! with no better success than before, for the King slept heavily after his draught. One of the pages said:

"This peasant girl must be crazy;" but another answered, "Yet what she says sounds very sad and touching."

As for Fiordelisa, she thought the King must have a very hard heart if he could hear how she grieved and yet pay her no attention. She had but one more chance, and on breaking the last egg she found to her great delight that it contained a more marvellous thing than ever. It was a pie made of six birds, cooked to perfection, and yet they were all alive, and singing and talking, and they answered questions and told fortunes in the most amusing way. Taking this treasure Fiordelisa once more set herself to wait in the great hall through which Turritella was sure to pass, and as she sat there one of the pages came by, and said to her:

Fiordelisa made the Queen a pie filled with pretty little singing birds

"Well, little kitchen-maid, it is a good thing that the King always takes a sleeping draught, for if not he would be kept awake all night by your sighing and lamenting."

Then Fiordelisa knew why he had not heeded her, and taking a handful of pearls and diamonds out of her sack, she said, "If you can promise me that to-night the King shall not have his sleeping draught, I will give you all these jewels."

"Oh! I promise that willingly," said the page.

At this moment Turritella appeared, and at the first sight of the savoury pie, with the pretty little birds all singing and chattering, she cried: –

"That is an admirable pie, little kitchen-maid. Pray what will you take for it?"

"The usual price," she answered. "To sleep once more in the Chamber of Echoes."

"By all means, only give me the pie," said the greedy Turritella. And when night was come, Fiordelisa waited until she thought everybody in the palace would be asleep, and then began to lament as before.

"Ah, Charming!" she said, "what have I ever done that you should forsake me and marry Turritella? If you could only know all I have suffered, and what a weary way I have come to seek you."

Now the page had faithfully kept his word, and given King Charming a glass of water instead of his usual sleeping draught, so there he lay wide awake, and heard every word Fiordelisa said, and even recognised her voice, though he could not tell where it came from.

"Ah, Fiordelisa!" he said, "how could you betray me to our cruel enemies when I loved you so dearly?"

Fiordelisa heard him, and answered quickly:

"Find out the little kitchen-maid, and she will explain everything."

Then the King in a great hurry sent for his pages and said:

"If you can find the little kitchen-maid, bring her to me at once."

"Nothing could be easier, Sire," they answered, "for she is in the Chamber of Echoes."

The King was very much puzzled when he heard this. How could the lovely young Queen Fiordelisa be a little kitchen-maid? or how could a little kitchen-maid have Fiordelisa's own voice? So he dressed hastily, and ran down a little secret staircase which led to the Chamber of Echoes. There, upon a heap of soft cushions, sat his lovely young Queen. She had laid aside all her ugly disguises and wore a white silken robe, and her golden hair shone in the soft lamp-light. King Charming was overjoyed at the sight, and rushed to throw himself at her feet, and asked her a thousand questions without giving her time to answer one. Fiordelisa was equally happy to be with him once more. But at this moment in came the Enchanter, and with him the fairy who had given Fiordelisa the eggs. After greeting King Charming and Queen, they said that as they were united in wishing to help King, the Fairy Mazilla had no longer any power against him, and he might marry Fiordelisa as soon as he pleased. Their great joy may be imagined, and soon the news spread through the palace, and everybody who saw Fiordelisa loved her directly. When Turritella heard what had happened she was terribly angry but before she could say a word the Enchanter and the Fairy changed her into a big brown owl, and she floated away out of one of the palace windows, hooting dismally. Then the wedding was held with great splendour and King Charming and Queen Fiordelisa lived happily ever after.

The Phoenix and the Carpet

Edith Nesbit's tale of magic begins when a nursery carpet turns out to be the flying variety and a golden egg once rolled up inside falls into the fire and releases a phoenix – a symbol of rebirth that appears in European, Central American, Egyptian and Asian myths and was said to live for 500 years before burning itself and its nest. Hans Christian Anderson wrote a story about the phoenix and one appears in J.K. Rowling's 'Harry Potter' series.

They locked the front door and they locked the back door, and they fastened all the windows. They moved the table and chairs off the carpet, and Anthea swept it.

"We must show it a little attention," she said kindly. "We'll give it tea-leaves next time. Carpets like tea-leaves."

Then everyone put on their outdoor things, because as Cyril said, they didn't know where they might be going, and it makes people stare if you go out of doors in November in pinafores and without hats.

Then Robert gently awoke the Phoenix, who yawned and stretched itself, and allowed Robert to lift it on to the middle of the carpet, where it instantly went to sleep again with its crested head tucked under its golden wing as before. Then every one sat down on the carpet.

"Where shall we go?" was of course the question, and it was warmly discussed. Anthea wanted to go to Japan. Robert and Cyril voted for America, and Jane wished to go to the seaside.

"Because there are donkeys there," said she.

"Not in November, silly," said Cyril; and the discussion got warmer and warmer, and still nothing was settled.

"I vote we let the Phoenix decide," said Robert, at last. So they stroked it till it woke. "We want to go somewhere abroad," they said, "and we can't make up our minds where."

"Let the carpet make up its mind, if it has one," said the Phoenix. "Just say you wish to go abroad."

So they did; and the next moment the world seemed to spin upside down, and when it was right way up again and they were ungiddy enough to look about them, they were out of doors.

Out of doors – this is a feeble way to express where they were. They were out of – out of the earth, or off it. In fact, they were floating steadily, safely, splendidly, in the crisp clear air, with the pale bright blue of the sky above them, and far down below the pale bright sun-diamonded waves of the sea. The carpet had stiffened itself somehow, so that it was square and firm like a raft, and it steered itself so beautifully and kept on its way so flat and fearless that no one was at all afraid of tumbling off. In front of them lay land.

"The coast of France," said the Phoenix, waking up and pointing with its wing. "Where do you wish to go? I should always keep one wish, of course – for emergencies – otherwise you may get into an emergency from which you can't emerge at all."

But the children were far too deeply interested to listen.

"I tell you what," said Cyril: "let's let the thing go on and on, and when we see a place we really want to stop at – why, we'll just stop. Isn't this ripping?"

"It's like trains," said Anthea, as they swept over the low-lying coast-line and held a steady course above orderly fields and straight roads bordered with poplar trees – "like express trains, only in trains you never can see anything because of grown-ups wanting the windows shut; and then they breathe on them, and it's like ground glass, and nobody can see anything, and then they go to sleep."

"It's like tobogganing," said Robert, "so fast and smooth, only there's no door-mat to stop short on – it goes on and on."

"You darling Phoenix," said Jane, "it's all your doing. Oh, look at that ducky little church and the women with flappy cappy things on their heads."

"Don't mention it," said the Phoenix, with sleepy politeness.

"Oh!" said Cyril, summing up all the rapture that was in every heart. "Look at it all – look at it – and think of the Kentish Town Road!"

Every one looked and every one thought. And the glorious, gliding, smooth, steady rush went on, and they looked down on strange and beautiful things, and held their breath and let it go in deep sighs, and said "Oh!" and "Ah!" till it was long past dinner-time.

It was Jane who suddenly said, "I wish we'd brought that jam tart and cold mutton with us. It would have been jolly to have a picnic in the air."

The jam tart and cold mutton were, however, far away, sitting quietly in the larder of the house in Camden Town which the children were supposed to be keeping. A mouse was at that moment tasting the outside of the raspberry jam part of the tart (she had nibbled a sort of gulf, or bay, through the pastry edge) to see whether it was the sort of dinner she could ask her little mouse-husband to sit down to. She had had a very good dinner herself. It is an ill wind that blows nobody any good.

"We'll stop as soon as we see a nice place," said Anthea. "I've got threepence, and you boys have the fourpence each that your trams didn't cost the other day, so we can buy things to eat. I expect the Phoenix can speak French."

The carpet was sailing along over rocks and rivers and trees and towns and farms and fields. It reminded everybody of a certain time when all of them had had wings, and had flown up to the top of a church tower, and had had a feast there of chicken and tongue and new bread and soda-water. And this again reminded them how hungry they were. And just as they were all being reminded of this very strongly indeed, they saw ahead of them some ruined walls on a hill, and strong and upright, and really, to look at, as good as new – a great square tower.

"The top of that's just the exactly same size as the carpet," said Jane. "I think it would be good to go to the top of that, because then none of the Abby-what's-its-names – I mean natives – would be able to take the carpet away even if they wanted to. And some of us could go out and get things to eat – buy them honestly, I mean, not take them out of larder windows."

"I think it would be better if we went –" Anthea was beginning; but Jane suddenly clenched her hands.

"I don't see why I should never do anything I want, just because I'm the youngest. I wish the carpet would fit itself in at the top of that tower – so there!"

The carpet made a disconcerting bound, and next moment it was hovering above the square top of the tower. Then slowly and carefully it began to sink under them. It was like a lift going down with you at the Army and Navy Stores.

"I don't think we ought to wish things without all agreeing to them first," said Robert, huffishly. "Hullo! What on earth?"

For unexpectedly and greyly something was coming up all round the four sides of the carpet. It was as if a wall were being built by magic quickness. It was a foot high – it was two feet high – three, four, five. It was shutting out the light – more and more.

Anthea looked up at the sky and the walls that now rose six feet above them.

"We're dropping into the tower," she screamed. "There wasn't any top to it. So the carpet's going to fit itself in at the bottom."

Robert sprang to his feet.

"We ought to have – Hullo! an owl's nest." He put his knee on a jutting smooth piece of grey stone, and reached his hand into a deep window slit – broad to the inside of the tower, and narrowing like a funnel to the outside.

"Look sharp!" cried every one, but Robert did not look sharp enough. By the time he had drawn his hand out of the owl's nest – there were no eggs there – the carpet had sunk eight feet below him.

"Jump, you silly cuckoo!" cried Cyril, with brotherly anxiety.

But Robert couldn't turn round all in a minute into a jumping position. He wriggled and twisted and got on to the broad ledge, and by the time he was ready to jump

the walls of the tower had risen up thirty feet above the others, who were still sinking with the carpet, and Robert found himself in the embrasure of a window; alone, for even the owls were not at home that day. The wall was smoothish; there was no climbing up, and as for climbing down – Robert hid his face in his hands, and squirmed back and back from the giddy verge, until the back part of him was wedged quite tight in the narrowest part of the window slit.

He was safe now, of course, but the outside part of his window was like a frame to a picture of part of the other side of the tower. It was very pretty, with moss growing between the stones and little shiny gems; but between him and it there was the width of the tower, and nothing in it but empty air. The situation was terrible. Robert saw in a flash that the carpet was likely to bring them into just the same sort of tight places that they used to get into with the wishes the Psammead granted them.

And the others – imagine their feelings as the carpet sank slowly and steadily to the very bottom of the tower, leaving Robert clinging to the wall. Robert did not even try to imagine their feelings – he had quite enough to do with his own; but you can.

As soon as the carpet came to a stop on the ground at the bottom of the inside of the tower it suddenly lost that raft-like stiffness which had been such a comfort during the journey from Camden Town to the topless tower, and spread itself limply over the loose stones and little earthy mounds at the bottom of the tower, just exactly like any ordinary carpet. Also it shrank suddenly, so that it seemed to draw away from under their feet, and they stepped quickly off the edges and stood on the firm ground, while the carpet drew itself in till it was its proper size, and no longer fitted exactly into the inside of the tower, but left quite a big space all round it.

Then across the carpet they looked at each other, and then every chin was tilted up and every eye sought vainly to see where poor Robert had got to. Of course, they couldn't see him.

"I wish we hadn't come," said Jane.

"You always do," said Cyril, briefly. "Look here, we can't leave Robert up there. I wish the carpet would fetch him down."

The carpet seemed to awake from a dream and pull itself together. It stiffened itself briskly and floated up between the four walls of the tower. The children below craned their heads back, and nearly broke their necks in doing it. The carpet rose and rose. It hung poised darkly above them for an anxious moment or two; then it dropped down again, threw itself on the uneven floor of the tower, and as it did so it tumbled Robert out on the uneven floor of the tower.

"Oh, glory!" said Robert, "that was a squeak. You don't know how I felt. I say, I've had about enough for a bit. Let's wish ourselves at home again and have a go at that jam tart and mutton. We can go out again afterwards."

"Righto!" said every one, for the adventure had shaken

*The Phoenix told the children how the carpet had been given to him by a prince and princess
who had flown on it into the wilderness but now had no further use for it!*

The Phoenix is a mystical bird who rises from the ashes and flames to begin a new life

"It isn't necessary. Birds always take what they want. It is not regarded as stealing, except in the case of magpies."

The children were glad to find they had been right in supposing this to be the case, on the day when they had wings, and had enjoyed somebody else's ripe plums.

"Yes; let the Phoenix get us something to eat, anyway," Robert urged – ("If it will be so kind you mean," corrected Anthea, in a whisper); "if it will be so kind, and we can be thinking while it's gone."

So the Phoenix fluttered up through the grey space of the tower and vanished at the top, and it was not till it had quite gone that Jane said,

"Suppose it never comes back."

The carpet sinks inside a tall square tower, trapping the children inside

the nerves of all. So they all got on to the carpet again, and said –

"I wish we were at home."

And lo and behold, they were no more at home than before. The carpet never moved. The Phoenix had taken the opportunity to go to sleep. Anthea woke it up gently.

"Look here," she said.

"I'm looking," said the Phoenix.

"We wished to be at home, and we're still here," complained Jane.

"No," said the Phoenix, looking about it at the high dark walls of the tower. "No; I quite see that."

"But we wished to be at home," said Cyril.

"No doubt," said the bird, politely.

"And the carpet hasn't moved an inch," said Robert.

"No," said the Phoenix, "I see it hasn't."

"But I thought it was a wishing carpet?"

"So it is," said the Phoenix.

"Then why – ?" asked the children, altogether.

"I did tell you, you know," said the Phoenix, "only you are so fond of listening to the music of your own voices. It is, indeed, the most lovely music to each of us, and therefore –"

"You did tell us what?"

"Why, that the carpet only gives you three wishes a day and you've had them."

There was a heartfelt silence.

"Then how are we going to get home?" said Cyril, at last.

"I haven't any idea," replied the Phoenix, kindly. "Can I fly out and get you any little thing?"

"How could you carry the money to pay for it?"

131

Boots and the Troll

Boots and the Troll is a fairy tale from
Norwegian Folktales collected by Peter
Christen Asbjørnsen who walked on
foot the length and breadth of Norway,
adding to his pot of stories and by
Jørgen Moe who, quite independently,
had begun a search for national folklore.
The two friends compared their results
and then set out together to complete
their mission

Once on a time there was a poor man who had three sons. When he died, the two elder set off into the world to try their luck, but the youngest they wouldn't have with them at any price.

"As for you," they said, "you're fit for nothing but to sit and poke about in the ashes."

So the two went off and got places at a palace – the one under the coachman, and the other under the gardener. But Boots, he set off too, and took with him a great kneading-trough, which was the only thing his parents left behind them, but which the other two would not bother themselves with. It was heavy to carry, but he did not like to leave it behind, and so, after he had trudged a bit, he too came to the palace, and asked for a place. So they told him they did not want him, but he begged so prettily that at last he got leave to be in the kitchen, and carry in wood and water for the kitchen maid. He was quick and ready, and in a little while every one liked him; but the two others were dull, and so they got more kicks than half pence, and grew quite envious of Boots, when they saw how much better he got on.

Just opposite the palace, across a lake, lived a Troll, who had seven silver ducks which swam on the lake, so that they could be seen from the palace. These the king had often longed for; and so the two elder brothers told the coachman:

"If our brother only chose, he has said he could easily get the king those seven silver ducks."

You may fancy it wasn't long before the coachman told this to the king; and the king called Boots before him, and said, –

"Your brothers say you can get me the silver ducks; so now go and fetch them."

"I'm sure I never thought or said anything of the kind," said the lad.

"You did say so, and you shall fetch them," said the king, who would hold his own.

"Well, well," said the lad; "needs must, I suppose; but give me a bushel of rye and a bushel of wheat, and I'll try what I can do."

So he got the rye and the wheat, and put them into the kneading-trough he had brought with him from home, got in, and rowed across the lake. When he reached the other side he began to walk along the shore, and to sprinkle and strew the grain, and at last he coaxed the ducks into his kneading-trough, and rowed back as fast as ever he could.

When he got half over, the Troll came out of his house and set eyes on him.

"Halloa!" roared out the Troll; "is it you that has gone off with my seven silver ducks?"

"Ay! ay!" said the lad.

"Shall you be back soon?" asked the Troll.

"Very likely," said the lad.

So when he got back to the king, with the seven silver ducks, he was more liked than ever, and even the king was pleased to say, "Well done!" But at this his brothers grew more and more spiteful and envious; and so they went and told the coachman that their brother had said if he chose, he was man enough to get the king the Troll's bed-quilt, which had a gold patch and a silver patch, and a silver

The troll owned seven silver ducks that had flown down to swim upon the lake

patch and a gold patch; and this time, too, the coachman was not slow in telling all this to the king. So the king said to the lad, how his brothers had said he was good to steal the Troll's bed-quilt, with gold and silver patches; so now he must go and do it, or lose his life.

Boots answered, he had never thought or said any such thing; but when he found there was no help for it, he begged for three days to think over the matter.

So when the three days were gone, he rowed over in his kneading-trough, and went spying about. At last, he saw those in the Troll's cave come out and hang the quilt out to air, and as soon as ever they had gone back into the face of the rock, Boots pulled the quilt down, and rowed away with it as fast as he could.

And when he was half across, out came the Troll and set eyes on him, and roared out, –

"Halloa! It is you who took my seven silver ducks?"

"Ay! ay!" said the lad.

"And now, have you taken my bed-quilt, with silver patches and gold patches, and gold patches and silver patches?"

"Ay! ay!" said the lad.

"Shall you come back again?"

"Very likely," said the lad.

But when he got back with the gold and silver patchwork quilt every one was fonder of him than ever and he was made the king's body-servant.

At this the other two were still more vexed, and to be revenged, they went and told the coachman, –

"Now, our brother has said he is man enough to get the king the gold harp which the Troll has, and that harp is of such a kind that all who listen when it is played grow glad, however sad they may be."

Yes; the coachman went and told the king, and he said to the lad, –

"If you have said this you shall do it. If you do it you shall have the Princess and half the kingdom. If you don't, you shall lose your life."

"I'm sure I never thought or said anything of the kind," said the lad; "but if there's no help for it, I may as well try; but I must have six days to think about it."

Yes, he might have six days, but when they were over he must set out.

Then he took a tenpenny nail, a birch-pin, and a waxen taper-end in his pocket, and rowed across, and walked up and down before the Troll's cave, looking stealthily about him. So when the Troll came out he saw him at once.

"HO, HO!" roared the Troll; "is it you who took my seven silver ducks?"

"Ay! ay!" said the lad.

"And it is you who took my bed-quilt, with the gold and silver patches?" asked the Troll.

"Ay! ay!" said the lad.

So the Troll caught hold of him at once, and took him off into the cave in the face of the rock.

"Now, daughter dear," said the Troll, "I've caught the fellow who stole the silver ducks and my bed-quilt with gold and silver patches; put him into the fattening coop, and when he's fat we'll kill him, and make a feast for our friends."

She was willing enough, and put him at once into the fattening coop, and there he stayed eight days, fed on the best, both in meat and drink, and as much as he could cram. So, when the eight days were over, the Troll said to his daughter to go down and cut him in his little finger, that they might see if he were fat. Down she came to the coop.

"Out with your little finger!" she said.

But Boots stuck out his tenpenny nail, and she cut at it.

"Nay, nay! he's as hard as iron still," said the Troll's daughter, when she got back to her father; "we can't take, him yet."

After another eight days the same thing happened, and this time Boots stuck out his birchen pin.

"Well, he's a little better," she said, when she got back to the Troll; "but still he'll be as hard as wood to chew."

But when another eight days were gone, the Troll told his daughter to go down and see if he wasn't fat now.

"Out with your little finger," said the Troll's daughter, when she reached the coop, and this time Boots stuck out the taper end.

"Now he'll do nicely," she said.

"Will he?" said the Troll. "Well, then, I'll just set off and ask the guests; meantime you must kill him, and roast half

"HO, HO!" roared the ugly Troll, "Halloa!
Is it you who took my seven silver ducks?"

and boil half."

So when the Troll had been gone a little while, the daughter began to sharpen a great long knife.

"Is that what you're going to kill me with?" asked the lad.

"Yes, it is," said she.

"But it isn't sharp," said the lad. "Just let me sharpen it for you, and then you'll find it easier work to kill me."

So she let him have the knife, and he began to rub and sharpen it on the whetstone.

"Just let me try it on one of your hair plaits; I think it's about right now."

So he got leave to do that; but at the same time that he

grasped the plait of hair he pulled back her head, and at one gash cut off the Troll's daughter's head; and half of her he roasted and half of her he boiled, and served it all up.

After that he dressed himself in her clothes, and sat away in the corner.

So when the Troll came home with his guests, he called out to his daughter – for he thought all the time it was his daughter – to come and take a snack.

"No, thank, you," said the lad, "I don't care for food, I'm so sad and downcast."

"Oh!" said the Troll, "if that's all, you know the cure; take the harp, and play a tune on it."

"Yes!" said the lad; "but where has it got to; I can't find it."

"Why, you know well enough," said the Troll; "you used it last; where should it be but over the door yonder?"

The lad did not wait to be told twice; he took down the harp, and went in and out playing tunes; but, all at once he shoved off the kneading-trough, jumped into it, and rowed off, so that the foam flew around the trough.

After a while the Troll thought his daughter was a long while gone, and went out to see what ailed her; and then he saw the lad in the trough, far, far out on the lake.

"Halloa! Is it you," he roared, "that took my seven silver ducks?"

"Ay, ay!" said the lad.

"Is it you that took my bed-quilt, with the gold and silver patches?"

"Yes!" said the lad.

"And now you have taken off my gold harp?" screamed the Troll.

"Yes!" said the lad; "I've got it, sure enough."

"And haven't I eaten you up after all, then?"

"No, no! 'twas your own daughter you ate," answered the lad.

But when the Troll heard that, he was so sorry, he burst; and then Boots rowed back, and took a whole heap of gold and silver with him, as much as the trough could carry. And so, when he came to the palace with the gold harp he got the Princess and half the kingdom, as the king had promised him; and, as for his brothers, he treated them well, for he thought they had only wished his good when they said what they had said.

Hansel and Grethel

First published in 1812 by Brothers Grimm, this is a tale of how two forsaken children outwit a fearsome cannibalistic witch who has enticed them into her house made of sweetmeats, cake and confectionery. She enslaves the little girl and plans to fatten up the lad until he is fit to eat. In the late 1800s composer Engelbert Humperdinck wrote an opera based on the story – often performed at Christmas time.

Once upon a time there dwelt near a large wood a poor woodcutter, with his wife and two children by his former marriage, a little boy called Hansel, and a girl named Grethel. He had little enough to break or bite; and once, when there was a great famine in the land, he could not procure even his daily bread; and as he lay thinking in his bed one evening, rolling about for trouble, he sighed, and

The two children discover a house made of bread and cakes with sugar window panes

said to his wife, "What will become of us? How can we feed our children, when we have no more than we can eat ourselves?"

"Know, then, my husband," answered she, "we will lead them away, quite early in the morning, into the thickest part of the wood, and there make them a fire, and give them each a little piece of bread; then we will go to our work, and leave them alone, so they will not find the way home again, and we shall be freed from them." "No, wife," replied he, "that I can never do. How can you bring your heart to leave my children all alone in the wood, for the wild beasts will soon come and tear them to pieces?"

"Oh, you simpleton!" said she, "then we must all four die of hunger; you had better plane the coffins for us." But she left him no peace till he consented, saying, "Ah, but I shall regret the poor children."

The two children, however, had not gone to sleep for very hunger, and so they overheard what the stepmother said to their father. Grethel wept bitterly, and said to Hansel, "What will become of us?" "Be quiet, Grethel," said he; "do not cry – I will soon help you." And as soon as their parents had fallen asleep, he got up, put on his coat, and, unbarring the back door, slipped out. The moon shone brilliantly, and the white pebbles which lay before the door seemed like silver pieces, they glittered so brightly. Hansel stooped down, and put as many into his pocket as it would hold; and then going back, he said to Grethel, "Be comforted, dear sister, and sleep in peace; God will not forsake us." And so saying, he went to bed again.

The next morning, before the sun arose, the wife went and awoke the two children. "Get up, you lazy things; we are going into the forest to chop wood." Then she gave them each a piece of bread, saying, "There is something for your dinner; do not eat it before the time, for you will get nothing else." Grethel took the bread in her apron, for Hansel's pocket was full of pebbles; and so they all set out upon their way. When they had gone a little distance, Hansel stood still, and peeped back at the house; and this he repeated several times, till his father said, "Hansel, what are you peeping at, and why do you lag behind? Take care, and remember your legs."

"Ah, father," said Hansel, "I am looking at my white cat sitting upon the roof of the house, and trying to say good-bye." "You simpleton!" said the wife, "that is not a cat; it is only the sun shining on the white chimney." But in reality Hansel was not looking at a cat; but every time he stopped, he dropped a pebble out of his pocket upon the path.

When they came to the middle of the forest, the father

The door opened and a very old woman hobbled out

told the children to collect wood, and he would make them a fire, so that they should not be cold. So Hansel and Grethel gathered together quite a little mountain of twigs. Then they set fire to them; and as the flame burnt up high, the wife said, "Now, you children, lie down near the fire, and rest yourselves, while we go into the forest and chop wood; when we are ready, I will come and call you."

Hansel and Grethel sat down by the fire, and when it was noon, each ate the piece of bread; and because they could hear the blows of an axe, they thought their father was near: but it was not an axe, but a branch which he had bound to a withered tree, so as to be blown to and fro by the wind. They waited so long that at last their eyes closed from weariness, and they fell fast asleep. When they awoke, it was quite dark, and Grethel began to cry, "How shall we get out of the wood?" But Hansel tried to comfort her by saying, "Wait a little while till the moon rises, and then we will quickly find the way." The moon soon shone forth, and Hansel, taking his sister's hand, followed the pebbles, which glittered like new-coined silver pieces, and showed them the path. All night long they walked on, and as day broke they came to their father's house. They knocked at the door, and when the wife opened it, and saw Hansel and Grethel, she exclaimed, "You wicked children! why did you sleep so long in the wood? We thought you were never coming home again." But their father was very glad, for it had grieved his heart to leave them all alone.

Not long afterward there was again great scarcity in every corner of the land; and one night the children overheard their stepmother saying to their father, "Everything is again consumed; we have only half a loaf left, and then the food is ended: the children must be sent away. We will take them deeper into the wood, so that they may not find the way out again; it is the only means of escape for us."

But her husband felt heavy at heart, and thought, "It were better to share the last crust with the children." His wife, however, would listen to nothing that he said, and scolded and reproached him without end.

He who says A must say B too; and he who consents the first time must also the second.

The children, however, had heard the conversation as they lay awake, and as soon as the old people went to sleep Hansel got up, intending to pick up some pebbles as before; but the wife had locked the door, so that he could not get out. Nevertheless, he comforted Grethel, saying, "Do not cry; sleep in quiet; the good God will not forsake us."

Early in the morning the stepmother came and pulled them out of bed, and gave them each a slice of bread, which was still smaller than the former piece. On the way, Hansel broke his in his pocket, and, stooping every now and then, dropped a crumb upon the path. "Hansel, why do you stop and look about?" said the father; "keep in the path." "I am looking at my little dove," answered Hansel, "nodding a good-bye to me." "Simpleton!" said the wife, "that is no dove, but only the sun shining on the chimney." But Hansel still kept dropping crumbs as he went along.

The mother led the children deep into the wood, where they had never been before, and there making an immense fire, she said to them, "Sit down here and rest, and when you feel tired you can sleep for a little while. We are going into the forest to hew wood, and in the evening, when we are ready, we will come and fetch you."

When noon came Grethel shared her bread with Hansel, who had strewn his on the path. Then they went to sleep; but the evening arrived and no one came to visit the poor children, and in the dark night they awoke, and Hansel comforted his sister by saying, "Only wait, Grethel, till the moon comes out, then we shall see the crumbs of bread which I have dropped, and they will show us the way home." The moon shone and they got up, but they could not see any crumbs, for the thousands of birds which had been flying about in the woods and fields had picked them all up. Hansel kept saying to Grethel, "We will soon find the way"; but they did not, and they walked the whole night long and the next day, but still they did not come out of the wood; and they got so hungry, for they had nothing to eat but the berries which they found upon the bushes. Soon they got so tired that they could not drag themselves along, so they lay down under a tree and went to sleep.

It was now the third morning since they had left their father's house, and they still walked on; but they only got deeper and deeper into the wood, and Hansel saw that if help did not come very soon they would die of hunger. At about noonday they saw a beautiful snow-white bird sitting upon a bough, which sang so sweetly that they stood still and listened to it. It soon ceased, and spreading its wings flew off; and they followed it until it arrived at a cottage, upon the roof of which it perched; and when they went close up to it they saw that the cottage was made of bread and cakes, and the window-panes were of clear sugar.

"We will go in there," said Hansel, "and have a glorious feast. I will eat a piece of the roof, and you can eat the window. Will they not be sweet?" So Hansel reached up and broke a piece off the roof, in order to see how it tasted, while Grethel stepped up to the window and began to bite it. Then a sweet voice called out in the room, "Tip-tap, tip-tap, who raps at my door?" and the children answered, "the wind, the wind, the child of heaven"; and they went on eating without interruption. Hansel thought the roof tasted very nice, so he tore off a great piece; while Grethel broke a large round pane out of the window, and sat down quite contentedly. Just then the door opened, and a very old woman, walking upon crutches, came out. Hansel and Grethel were so frightened that they let fall what they had in their hands; but the old woman, nodding her head, said, "Ah, you dear children, what has brought you here? Come in and stop with me, and no harm shall befall you"; and so saying she took them both by the hand, and led them into her cottage. A good meal of milk and pancakes, with sugar, apples, and nuts, was spread on the table, and in the back room were two nice little beds, covered with white, where Hansel and Grethel laid themselves down, and thought themselves in heaven. The old woman behaved very kindly to them, but in reality she was a wicked witch who waylaid children, and built the bread-house in order to entice them in, but as soon as they were in her power she killed them, cooked and ate them, and made a great festival of the day. Witches have red eyes, and cannot see very far; but they have a fine sense of smelling, like wild beasts, so that they know when children approach them. When Hansel and Grethel came near the witch's house she laughed wickedly, saying, "Here come two who shall not escape me." And early in the morning, before they awoke, she went up to them, and saw how lovingly they lay sleeping, with their chubby red cheeks, and she mumbled to herself, "That will be a good bite." Then she took up Hansel with her rough hands, and shut him up in a little cage with a lattice-door; and although he screamed loudly

Grethel pushed the horrid witch into the oven and then released Hansel from his prison. At last the two children were free and could live happily ever after

it was of no use. Grethel came next, and, shaking her till she awoke, the witch said, "Get up, you lazy thing, and fetch some water to cook something good for your brother, who must remain in that stall and get fat; when he is fat enough I shall eat him." Grethel began to cry, but it was all useless, for the old witch made her do as she wished. So a nice meal was cooked for Hansel, but Grethel got nothing but a crab's claw.

Every morning the old witch came to the cage and said, "Hansel, stretch out your finger that I may feel whether you are getting fat." But Hansel used to stretch out a bone, and the old woman, having very bad sight, thought it was his finger, and wondered very much that he did not get fatter. When four weeks had passed, and Hansel still kept quite lean, she lost all her patience, and would not wait any longer. "Grethel," she called out in a passion, "get some water quickly; be Hansel fat or lean, this morning I will kill and cook him." Oh, how the poor little sister grieved, as she was forced to fetch the water, and fast the tears ran down her cheeks! "Dear good God, help us now!" she exclaimed. "Had we only been eaten by the wild beasts in the wood, then we should have died together." But the old witch called out, "Leave off that noise; it will not help you a bit."

So early in the morning Grethel was forced to go out

and fill the kettle, and make a fire. "First, we will bake, however," said the old woman; "I have already heated the oven and kneaded the dough"; and so saying, she pushed poor Grethel up to the oven, out of which the flames were burning fiercely. "Creep in," said the witch, "and see if it is hot enough, and then we will put in the bread"; but she intended when Grethel got in to shut up the oven and let her bake, so that she might eat her as well as Hansel. Grethel perceived what her thoughts were, and said, "I do not know how to do it; how shall I get in?" "You stupid goose," said she, "the opening is big enough. See, I could even get in myself!" and she got up, and put her head into the oven. Then Grethel gave her a push, so that she fell right in, and then shutting the iron door she bolted it! Oh! how horribly she howled; but Grethel ran away, and left the ungodly witch to burn to ashes.

Now she ran to Hansel, and, opening his door, called out, "Hansel, we are saved; the old witch is dead!" So he sprang out, like a bird out of his cage when the door is opened; and they were so glad that they fell upon each other's neck, and kissed each other over and over again. And now, as there was nothing to fear, they went into the witch's house, where in every corner were caskets full of pearls and precious stones. "These are better than pebbles," said Hansel, putting as many into his pocket as it would hold; while Grethel thought, "I will take some too," and filled her apron full. "We must be off now," said Hansel, "and get out of this enchanted forest." But when they had walked for two hours they came to a large piece of water. "We cannot get over," said Hansel; "I can see no bridge at all." "And there is no boat, either," said Grethel; "but there swims a white duck, and I will ask her to help us over." And she sang:

"Little Duck, good little Duck,
Grethel and Hansel, here we stand;
There is neither stile nor bridge,
Take us on your back to land."

So the duck came to them, and Hansel sat himself on, and bade his sister sit behind him. "No," answered Grethel, "that will be too much for the duck; she shall take us over one at a time." This the good little bird did, and when both were happily arrived on the other side, and had gone a little way, they came to a well-known wood, which they knew the better every step they went, and at last they perceived their father's house. Then they began to run, and, bursting into the house, they fell into their father's arms. He had not had one happy hour since he had left the children in the forest; and his wife was dead. Grethel shook her apron, and the pearls and precious stones rolled out upon the floor, and Hansel threw down one handful after the other out of his pocket. Then all their sorrows were ended, and they lived together in great happiness.

Little Ida's Flowers

This story by Hans Christian Andersen encompasses the enchanting notion that some of the most beautiful butterflies were once flowers but have flown off their stalks into the air. It was first published in 1835 in an unbound 61-page booklet – costing 24 shillings (some £3 or US$5) – to launch his first collection.

From *Fairy Tales Told for Children*:

"My poor flowers are quite dead," said little Ida, "they were so pretty yesterday evening, and now all the leaves are hanging down quite withered. What do they do that for," she asked, of the student who sat on the sofa; she liked him very much, he could tell the most amusing stories, and cut out the prettiest pictures; hearts, and ladies dancing, castles with doors that opened, as well as flowers; he was a delightful student. "Why do the flowers look so faded to-day?" she asked again, and pointed to her nosegay, which was quite withered.

"Don't you know what is the matter with them?" said the student. "The flowers were at a ball last night, and therefore, it is no wonder they hang their heads."

"But flowers cannot dance?" cried little Ida.

The student told Little Ida many amusing stories

"Yes indeed, they can," replied the student. "When it grows dark, and everybody is asleep, they jump about quite merrily. They have a ball almost every night."

"Can children go to these balls?"

"Yes," said the student, "little daisies and lilies of the valley."

"Where do the beautiful flowers dance?" asked little Ida.

"Have you not often seen the large castle outside the gates of the town, where the king lives in summer, and where the beautiful garden is full of flowers? And have you not fed the swans with bread when they swam towards you? Well, the flowers have capital balls there, believe me."

"I was in the garden out there yesterday with my mother," said Ida, "but all the leaves were off the trees, and there was not a single flower left. Where are they? I used to see so many in the summer."

"They are in the castle," replied the student. "You must know that as soon as the king and all the court are gone into the town, the flowers run out of the garden into the castle, and you should see how merry they are. The two most beautiful roses seat themselves on the throne, and are called the king and queen, then all the red cockscombs range themselves on each side, and bow, these are the lords-in-waiting. After that the pretty flowers come in, and there is a grand ball. The blue violets represent little naval cadets, and dance with hyacinths and crocuses which they call young ladies. The tulips and tiger-lilies are the old ladies who sit and watch the dancing, so that everything may be conducted with order and propriety."

"But," said little Ida, "is there no one there to hurt the flowers for dancing in the king's castle?"

"No one knows anything about it," said the student. "The old steward of the castle, who has to watch there at night, sometimes comes in; but he carries a great bunch of keys, and as soon as the flowers hear the keys rattle, they run and hide themselves behind the long curtains, and stand quite still, just peeping their heads out. Then the old steward says, 'I smell flowers here,' but he cannot see them."

"Oh how capital," said little Ida, clapping her hands. "Should I be able to see these flowers?"

"Yes," said the student, "mind you think of it the next time you go out, no doubt you will see them, if you peep through the window. I did so to-day, and I saw a long yellow lily lying stretched out on the sofa. She was a court lady."

"Can the flowers from the Botanical Gardens go to these balls?" asked Ida. "It is such a distance!"

"Oh yes," said the student "whenever they like, for they can fly. Have you not seen those beautiful red, white, and yellow butterflies, that look like flowers? They were flowers once. They have flown off their stalks into the air, and flap their leaves as if they were little wings to make

The flowers fly off to a grand ball at the castle. Some may turn into butterflies

them fly. Then, if they behave well, they obtain permission to fly about during the day, instead of being obliged to sit still on their stems at home, and so in time their leaves become real wings. It may be, however, that the flowers in the Botanical Gardens have never been to the king's palace, and, therefore, they know nothing of the merry doings at night, which take place there. I will tell you what to do, and the botanical professor, who lives close by here, will be so surprised. You know him very well, do you not? Well, next time you go into his garden, you must tell one of the flowers that there is going to be a grand ball at the castle, then that flower will tell all the others, and they will fly away to the castle as soon as possible. And when the professor walks into his garden, there will not be a single flower left. How he will wonder what has become of them!"

"But how can one flower tell another? Flowers cannot speak?"

"No, certainly not," replied the student; "but they can make signs. Have you not often seen that when the wind blows they nod at one another, and rustle all their green leaves?"

"Can the professor understand the signs?" asked Ida.

"Yes, to be sure he can. He went one morning into his garden, and saw a stinging nettle making signs with its leaves to a beautiful red carnation. It was saying, 'You are so pretty, I like you very much.' But the professor did not

"I wonder," thought Ida, "If my flowers have danced in the king's garden."

approve of such nonsense, so he clapped his hands on the nettle to stop it. Then the leaves, which are its fingers, stung him so sharply that he has never ventured to touch a nettle since."

"Oh how funny!" said Ida, and she laughed.

"How can anyone put such notions into a child's head?" said a tiresome lawyer, who had come to pay a visit, and sat on the sofa. He did not like the student, and would grumble when he saw him cutting out droll or amusing pictures. Sometimes it would be a man hanging on a gibbet and holding a heart in his hand as if he had been stealing hearts. Sometimes it was an old witch riding through the air on a broom and carrying her husband on her nose. But the lawyer did not like such jokes, and he would say as he had just said, "How can anyone put such nonsense into a child's head! what absurd fancies they are!"

But to little Ida, all these stories which the student told her about the flowers, seemed very droll, and she thought over them a great deal. The flowers did hang their heads, because they had been dancing all night, and were very tired, and most likely they were ill. Then she took them into the room where a number of toys lay on a pretty little table, and the whole of the table drawer besides was full of beautiful things. Her doll Sophy lay in the doll's bed asleep, and little Ida said to her, "You must really get up Sophy, and be content to lie in the drawer to-night; the poor flowers are ill, and they must lie in your bed, then perhaps they will get well again." So she took the doll out, who looked quite cross, and said not a single word, for she was angry at being turned out of her bed.

Ida placed the flowers in the doll's bed, and drew the quilt over them. Then she told them to lie quite still and be good, while she made some tea for them, so that they might be quite well and able to get up the next morning. And she drew the curtains close round the little bed, so that the sun might not shine in their eyes.

During the whole evening she could not help thinking of what the student had told her. And before she went to bed herself, she was obliged to peep behind the curtains into the garden where all her mother's beautiful flowers grew, hyacinths and tulips, and many others. Then she whispered to them quite softly, "I know you are going to a ball to-night." But the flowers appeared as if they did not understand, and not a leaf moved; still Ida felt quite sure she knew all about it.

She lay awake a long time after she was in bed, thinking how pretty it must be to see all the beautiful flowers dancing in the king's garden. "I wonder if my flowers have really been there," she said to herself, and then she fell asleep. In the night she awoke; she had been dreaming of the flowers and of the student, as well as of the tiresome lawyer who found fault with him. It was quite still in Ida's bedroom; the night-lamp burnt on the table, and her father and mother were asleep.

"I wonder if my flowers are still lying in Sophy's bed," she thought to herself; "how much I should like to know."

She raised herself a little, and glanced at the door of the room where all her flowers and playthings lay; it was partly open, and as she listened, it seemed as if some one in the room was playing the piano, but softly and more prettily than she had ever before heard it.

"Now all the flowers are certainly dancing in there," she thought, "oh how much I should like to see them," but she did not dare move for fear of disturbing her father and mother. "If they would only come in here," she thought; but they did not come, and the music continued to play so beautifully, and was so pretty, that she could resist no longer. She crept out of her little bed, went softly to the door and looked into the room. Oh what a splendid sight there was to be sure!

The student tells Little Ida that butterflies were once flowers but have flown away from their stalks

There was no night-lamp burning, but the room appeared quite light, for the moon shone through the window upon the floor, and made it almost like day. All the hyacinths and tulips stood in two long rows down the room, not a single flower remained in the window, and the flower-pots were all empty. The flowers were dancing gracefully on the floor, making turns and holding each other by their long green leaves as they swung round. At the piano sat a large yellow lily which little Ida was sure she had seen in the summer, for she remembered the student saying she was very much like Miss Lina, one of Ida's friends. They all laughed at him then, but now it seemed to little Ida as if the tall, yellow flower was really like the young lady. She had just the same manners while playing, bending her long yellow face from side to side, and nodding in time to the beautiful music. Then she saw a large purple crocus jump into the middle of the table where the playthings stood, go up to the doll's bedstead and draw back the curtains; there lay the sick flowers, but they got up directly, and nodded to the others as a sign that they wished to dance with them. The old rough doll, with the broken mouth, stood up and bowed to the pretty flowers. They did not look ill at all now, but jumped about and were very merry, yet none of them noticed little Ida.

Presently it seemed as if something fell from the table. Ida looked that way, and saw a slight carnival rod jumping down among the flowers as if it belonged to them; it was, however, very smooth and neat, and a little wax doll with a broad brimmed hat on her head, like the one worn by the lawyer, sat upon it. The carnival rod hopped about among the flowers on its three red stilted feet, and stamped quite loud when it danced the Mazurka; the flowers could not perform this dance, they were too light to stamp in that manner.

All at once the wax doll which rode on the carnival rod seemed to grow larger and taller, and it turned round and said to the paper flowers, "How can you put such things in a child's head? they are all foolish fancies;" and then the doll was exactly like the lawyer with the broad brimmed hat, and looked as yellow and as cross as he did; but the paper dolls struck him on his thin legs, and he shrunk up again and became quite a little wax doll. This was very amusing, and Ida could not help laughing. The carnival rod went on dancing, and the lawyer was obliged to dance also. It was no use, he might make himself great and tall, or remain a little wax doll with a large black hat; still he must dance. Then at last the other flowers interceded for him, especially those who had lain in the doll's bed, and the carnival rod gave up his dancing. At the same moment a loud knocking was heard in the drawer, where Ida's doll Sophy lay with many other toys. Then the rough doll ran to the end of the table, laid himself flat down upon it, and began to pull the drawer out a little way. Then Sophy raised herself, and looked round quite astonished, "There must be a ball here to-night," said Sophy. "Why did not somebody tell me?"

"Will you dance with me?" said the rough doll.

"You are the right sort to dance with, certainly," said she, turning her back upon him. Then she seated herself on the edge of the drawer, and thought that perhaps one of the flowers would ask her to dance; but none of them came. Then she coughed, "Hem, hem, a-hem;" but for all that not one came. The shabby doll now danced quite alone, and not very badly, after all.

As none of the flowers seemed to notice Sophy, she let herself down from the drawer to the floor, so as to make a very great noise. All the flowers came round her directly, and asked if she had hurt herself, especially those who had lain in her bed. But she was not hurt at all, and Ida's flowers thanked her for the use of the nice bed, and were very kind to her. They led her into the middle of the room, where the moon shone, and danced with her, while all the other flowers formed a circle round them. Then Sophy was very happy, and said they might keep her bed; she did not mind lying in the drawer at all.

But the flowers thanked her very much, and said, – "We cannot live long. To-morrow morning we shall be quite dead; and you must tell little Ida to bury us in the garden, near to the grave of the canary; then, in the summer we shall wake up and be more beautiful than ever."

"No, you must not die," said Sophy, as she kissed the flowers. Then the door of the room opened, and a number of beautiful flowers danced in. Ida could not imagine where they could come from, unless they were the flowers from the king's garden. First came two lovely roses, with little golden crowns on their heads; these were the king and queen. Beautiful stocks and carnations followed, bowing to every one present. They had also music with them. Large poppies and peonies had pea-shells for instruments, and blew into them till they were quite red in the face. The bunches of blue hyacinths and the little white snowdrops jingled their bell-like flowers, as if they were real bells. Then came many more flowers: blue violets, purple heart's-ease, daisies, and lilies of the valley, and they all danced together, and kissed each other. It was very beautiful to behold.

At last the flowers wished each other good-night. Then little Ida crept back into her bed again, and dreamt of all she had seen.

When she arose the next morning, she went quickly to the little table, to see if the flowers were still there. She drew aside the curtains of the little bed. There they all lay, but quite faded; much more so than the day before. Sophy was lying in the drawer where Ida had placed her; but she looked very sleepy.

"Do you remember what the flowers told you to say to me?" said little Ida. But Sophy looked quite stupid, and said not a single word. "You are not kind at all," said Ida; "and yet they all danced with you." Then she took a little paper box, on which were painted beautiful birds, and laid the dead flowers in it. "This shall be your pretty coffin," she said; "and by and by, when my cousins come to visit me, they shall help me to bury you out in the garden; so that next summer you may grow up again more beautiful than ever."

Her cousins were two good-tempered boys, whose names were James and Adolphus. Their father had given them each a bow and arrow, and they had brought them to show Ida. She told them about the poor flowers which were dead; and as soon as they obtained permission, they went with her to bury them. The two boys walked first, with their crossbows on their shoulders, and little Ida followed, carrying the pretty box containing the dead flowers. They dug a little grave in the garden. Ida kissed her flowers and then laid them, with the box, in the earth. James and Adolphus then fired their crossbows over the grave, as they had neither guns nor cannons.

Peer Gynt

Per Gynt was the original fairy tale from which Norwegian dramatist Henrik Ibsen based his five-act verse play, a production which was complemented by the striking incidental music by Edvard Grieg – that premiered along with the play in 1876

Once upon a time thre was a little boy named Peer Gynt. He was a bad boy. He stole things, played tricks, never helped his mother and was generally a wild and naughty lad. Nobody really liked Peer Gynt.

One day, Peer Gynt was invited to a wedding. There he met the most beautiful girl in the world. The very first moment he saw Soveig, he knew that that he was in love and that day he would marry this wonderful girl. However Soveig's parents had hear all about the antics of the rascally Peer Gynt and so they determined that on no account should he be allowed to marry their beloved daughter. They told Peer to leave Soveig alone because she would not marry him.

Poor Peer's heart was broken. He knew that he could not stay in the village because seeing Soveig would be always be too painful if he was not allowed to love her. So he ran away, up high and into the mountains where he could be alone forever. But little did Peer know that along his way he would have many adventures.

First he arrived at the Hall of the Mountain King where he was immediately then surrounded by many fierce-looking trolls, some of the most ugly creatures imaginable.

The king of the trolls decided that Peer Gynt was just the person to marry his daughter whom was beautiful but not as pretty as Soveig. The king described what Peer would have to do to marry his daughter. The things he would have to do were: grow a tail, not see the light of day for the rest of his life, and, last but not least, slit his eyes to see the world as a troll does. Peer was not about to become a troll.

After saying "NO" the trolls started to surround Peer. Peer started to step backwards and he heard church bells ringing. When the sounds hit the eardrums of the ugly, hairy trolls, they melted away to never be seen or heard from again.

Peer's next adventure was to Mongolia where he found a white stallion and a beautiful red robe. He put on the robe and rode the stallion into the nearest village. There, he was greeted by a couple of men.

He was invited to a village supper that was in his honor. There were many dances to be danced, there were also belly dancers. Peer had never been happier in his life.

There was one dancer that Peer watched very closely. She was the chief's daughter. Peer loved her so much, more than anyone ever.

Towards the end of the dance, Peer started to remember his home and his mother, Ace. Peer was homesick. After the dinner, Peer rode out of town on the stallion and rode for home.

When Peer returned home, he rode straight for his mother's house. But when he arrived at the house, his mother wasn't there. Peer later learned that after he left, his mother seached night and day for him for she missed him so much. After seaching for years, Ace finally died of a broken heart.

Peer was sad, his heart had ripped in two. Peer walked through the streets of the village, wondering what he should do next. He walked until he was in front of an old house. Peer knew whose house this was!

This was where his sweetheart, Soveig, used to live. Peer ran up to the door, his heart pounding. Who was to answer the door but none other than Soveig.

At first Soveig didn't belive that this was Peer, but when Peer told her his story, she knew that this was Peer and only Peer.

Peer and Soveig were married and lived together in Peer's house for many happy years to come.

The king of the trolls wants Peer Gynt to marry his daughter

The White Snake

This Illyrian-Slovenish story is among the sixty gathered in by Reverend A H Wratislaw in his in 1890 collection. His biography was penned by his nephew Theodore William Graf Wratislaw (1871-1933) – a Count of the Holy Roman Empire, educated at Rugby School – who was also a renowned poet. One of their ancestors, Baron Vratislav von Mitrovitz, had in the 1500s been a galley slave to the Turks when he was only about 15 years old.

A terrible snake wound its way up the burning pile

Once upon a time snakes multiplied so prodigiously in the district of Osojani (Ossiach), that every place swarmed with them. The peasants in that district were in evil case. The snakes crept into the parlours, the churches, the dairies, and the beds. People had not even quiet at table, for the hungry snakes made their way into the dish. But the greatest terror was caused by a frightfully large white snake, which was several times seen attacking the cattle at Ososcica (Görlitz Alpe). The peasants did not know how to help themselves; they instituted processions, and went on pilgrimages, that God might please to remove that terrible scourge from them. But neither did that help them.

When the poor people were in the greatest distress, and knew not how to act to rid themselves of this plague, one day an unknown man came into the district, who promised to put an end to every one of the snakes, provided they could assure him that they had seen no great white snake. "We have not seen one at all," was the reply of some of the number that had collected round the stranger.

Then he caused a great pile to be constructed round a tall fir, and when he had climbed to the top of the fir, he ordered them to set the whole pile on fire on all sides, and afterwards to run quickly aside.

When the flame had risen on all sides against the tall fir, the unknown man took a bone pipe out of his pocket, and began to blow it so powerfully that everybody's ears tingled. Quickly up rushed and crowded from all quarters a vast number of snakes, lizards, and salamanders to the pile, and, driven by some strange force, all sprang into the fire and perished there. But all at once a mightier and shriller hiss was heard from Ososcica, so that all present were seized with fear and dread. The man on the fir, at hearing it, trembled with terror: "Woe is me! there is no help for me!" so said he. "I have heard a white snake hiss; why did you thus mislead me? But be so compassionate as not to forget every year to give alms to the poor on my behalf."

Scarcely had the poor man uttered these words, when a terrible snake wound its way up with a great noise, like a furious torrent, over the sharp rocks, and plunged into the lake, so that the foam flew up. It soon swam to the other side of the lake, and, all exasperated, rushed to the burning pile, reared itself up against the fir, and pushed the poor man into the fire. The snake itself struggled and hissed terribly in the fire, but the strong fire soon overpowered it.

Thus perished, along with the whole lizard race, the monstrous snake which had done so much harm to the cattle. The peasants were again able without fear to carry on their occupations, and the shepherds at Ososcica to pasture their cattle without anxiety. The grateful people have not up to the present time forgotten the promise of their ancestors, and every year on that selfsame day distribute gifts of corn to the poor.

Just So Stories

First published in 1902, these stories written and illustrated by Rudyard Kipling are animal fantasies about how each animal came to have particular features – with some magic and a good deal of logic and morality involved. Kipling also wrote *The Jungle Book* and *Kim*. Kipling was born in Bombay but his parents had met and courted at Rudyard Lake in Staffordshire, England, and named their firstborn after this beautiful place.

How the Camel got his Hump

Now this is the next tale, and it tells how the Camel got his big hump.

In the beginning of years, when the world was so new and all, and the Animals were just beginning to work for Man, there was a Camel, and he lived in the middle of a Howling Desert because he did not want to work; and besides, he was a Howler himself. So he ate sticks and thorns and tamarisks and milkweed and prickles, most 'scruciating idle; and when anybody spoke to him he said "Humph!" Just "Humph!" and no more.

Presently the Horse came to him on Monday morning, with a saddle on his back and a bit in his mouth, and said, "Camel, O Camel, come out and trot like the rest of us."

"Humph!" said the Camel; and the Horse went away and told the Man.

Presently the Dog came to him, with a stick in his mouth, and said, "Camel, O Camel, come and fetch and carry like the rest of us."

"Humph!" said the Camel; and the Dog went away and told the Man.

Presently the Ox came to him, with the yoke on his neck and said, "Camel, O Camel, come and plough like the rest of us."

"Humph!" said the Camel; and the Ox went away and told the Man.

At the end of the day the Man called the Horse and the Dog and the Ox together, and said, "Three, O Three, I'm very sorry for you (with the world so new-and-all); but

that Humph-thing in the Desert can't work, or he would have been here by now, so I am going to leave him alone, and you must work double-time to make up for it."

That made the Three very angry (with the world so new-and-all), and they held a palaver, and an indaba, and a punchayet, and a pow-wow on the edge of the Desert; and the Camel came chewing on milkweed most 'scruciating idle, and laughed at them. Then he said "Humph!" and went away again.

Presently there came along the Djinn in charge of All Deserts, rolling in a cloud of dust (Djinns always travel that way because it is Magic), and he stopped to palaver

This is the picture of the Djinn making the beginnings of the Magic that brought the Humph to the Camel. First he drew a line in the air with his finger, and it became solid: and then he made a cloud, and then he made an egg and then there was a magic pumpkin that turned into a big white flame. Then the Djinn took his magic fan and fanned that flame till the flame turned into a magic by itself. It was a good Magic and a very kind Magic really, though it had to give the Camel a Humph because the Camel was lazy. The Djinn in charge of All Deserts was one of the nicest of the Djinns, so he would never do anything really unkind.

and pow-pow with the Three.

"Djinn of All Deserts," said the Horse, "is it right for any one to be idle, with the world so new-and-all?"

"Certainly not," said the Djinn.

"Well," said the Horse, "there's a thing in the middle of your Howling Desert (and he's a Howler himself) with a long neck and long legs, and he hasn't done a stroke of work since Monday morning. He won't trot."

"Whew!" said the Djinn, whistling, "that's my Camel, for all the gold in Arabia! What does he say about it?"

"He says 'Humph!' " said the Dog; "and he won't fetch and carry."

"Does he say anything else?"

"Only 'Humph!'; and he won't plough," said the Ox.

"Very good," said the Djinn. "I'll humph him if you will kindly wait a minute."

The Djinn rolled himself up in his dust-cloak, and took a bearing across the desert, and found the Camel most 'scruciatingly idle, looking at his own reflection in a pool of water.

"My long and bubbling friend," said the Djinn, "what's this I hear of your doing no work, with the world so new-and-all?"

"Humph!" said the Camel.

The Djinn sat down, with his chin in his hand, and began to think a Great Magic, while the Camel looked at his own reflection in the pool of water.

"You've given the Three extra work ever since Monday morning, all on account of your 'scruciating idleness," said the Djinn; and he went on thinking Magics, with his chin in his hand.

"Humph!" said the Camel.

"I shouldn't say that again if I were you," said the Djinn; "you might say it once too often. Bubbles, I want you to work."

And the Camel said "Humph!" again; but no sooner had he said it than he saw his back, that he was so proud of, puffing up and puffing up into a great big lolloping humph.

"Do you see that?" said the Djinn. "That's your very own humph that you've brought upon your very own self by not working. To-day is Thursday, and you've done no work since Monday, when the work began. Now you are going to work."

"How can I," said the Camel, "with this humph on my back?"

"That's made a-purpose," said the Djinn, "all because you missed those three days. You will be able to work now for three days without eating, because you can live on your humph; and don't you ever say I never did anything for you. Come out of the Desert and go to the Three, and behave. Humph yourself!"

And the Camel humphed himself, humph and all, and went away to join the Three. And from that day to this the Camel always wears a humph (we call it "hump" now, not to hurt his feelings); but he has never yet caught up with the three days that he missed at the beginning of the world, and he has never yet learned how to behave.

The Camel's hump is an ugly lump
  Which well you may see at the Zoo;
But uglier yet is the hump we get
  From having too little to do.

Kiddies and grown-ups too-oo-oo,
  If we haven't enough to do-oo-oo,
    We get the hump –
    Cameelious hump –
The hump that is black and blue!

We climb out of bed with a frouzly head
  And a snarly-yarly voice.
We shiver and scowl and we grunt and we growl
  At our bath and our boots and our toys;

And there ought to be a corner for me
  (And I know there is one for you)
    When we get the hump –
    Cameelious hump –
The hump that is black and blue!

The cure for this ill is not to sit still,
  Or frowst with a book by the fire;
But to take a large hoe and a shovel also,
  And dig till you gently perspire;

And then you will find that the sun and the wind,
  And the Djinn of the Garden too,
    Have lifted the hump –
    The horrible hump –
The hump that is black and blue!

I get it as well as you-oo-oo –
  If I haven't enough to do-oo-oo –
    We all get hump –
    Cameelious hump –
Kiddies and grown-ups too!

The Djinn fanned the flame with his magic fan

How the Rhinoceros got his Skin

Once upon a time, on an uninhabited island on the shores of the Red Sea, there lived a Parsee from whose hat the rays of the sun were reflected in more-than-oriental splendour. And the Parsee lived by the Red Sea with nothing but his hat and his knife and a cooking-stove of the kind that you must particularly never touch. And one day he took flour and water and currants and plums and sugar and things, and made himself one cake which was two feet across and three feet thick. It was indeed a Superior Comestible (that's magic), and he put it on the stove because he was allowed to cook on that stove, and he baked it and he baked it till it was all done brown and smelt most sentimental. But just as he was going to eat it there came down to the beach from the Altogether Uninhabited Interior one Rhinoceros with a horn on his nose, two piggy eyes, and few manners. In those days the Rhinoceros's skin fitted him quite tight. There were no wrinkles in it anywhere. He looked exactly like a Noah's Ark Rhinoceros, but of course much bigger. All the same, he had no manners then, and he has no manners now, and he never will have any manners. He said, 'How!' and the Parsee left that cake and climbed to the top of a palm tree with nothing on but his hat, from which the rays of the sun were always reflected in more-than-oriental splendour. And the Rhinoceros upset the oil-stove with his nose, and the cake rolled on the sand, and he spiked that cake on the horn of his nose, and he ate it, and he went away, waving his tail, to the desolate and Exclusively Uninhabited Interior which abuts on the islands of Mazanderan, Socotra, and the Promontories of the Larger Equinox. Then the Parsee came down from his palm-tree and put the stove on its legs and recited the following Sloka, which, as you have not heard, I will now proceed to relate:

> Them that takes cakes
> Which the Parsee-man bakes
> Makes dreadful mistakes.

And there was a great deal more in that than you would think.

Because, five weeks later, there was a heat wave in the Red Sea, and everybody took off all the clothes they had. The Parsee took off his hat; but the Rhinoceros took off his skin and carried it over his shoulder as he came down to the beach to bathe. In those days it buttoned underneath with three buttons and looked like a waterproof. He said nothing whatever about the Parsee's cake, because he had eaten it all; and he never had any manners, then, since, or henceforward. He waddled straight into the water and blew bubbles through his nose, leaving his skin on the beach.

Presently the Parsee came by and found the skin, and he smiled one smile that ran all round his face two times.

This is the picture of the Parsee beginning to eat his cake on the Uninhabited Island in the Red Sea on a very hot day; and of the Rhinoceros coming down from the Altogether Uninhabited Interior, which, as you can truthfully see, is all rocky. The Rhinoceros's skin is quite smooth, and the three buttons that button it up are underneath, so you can't see them. The squiggly things on the Parsee's hat are the rays of the sun reflected in more-than-oriental splendour; because if I had drawn real rays they would have filled up all the picture. The cake has currants in it; and the wheel-thing lying on the sand in front belonged to one of Pharaoh's chariots when he tried to cross the Red Sea. The Parsee found it, and kept it to play with. The Parsee's name was Pestonjee Bomonjee, and the Rhinoceros was called Strorks, because he breathed through his mouth instead of his nose. I wouldn't ask anything about the cooking-stove if I were you.

Then he danced three times round the skin and rubbed his hands. Then he went to his camp and filled his hat with cake-crumbs, for the Parsee never ate anything but cake, and never swept out his camp. He took that skin, and he shook that skin, and he scrubbed that skin, and he rubbed that skin just as full of old, dry, stale, tickly cake-crumbs and some burned currants as ever it could possibly hold. Then he climbed to the top of his palm-tree and waited for the Rhinoceros to come out of the water and put it on.

And the Rhinoceros did. He buttoned it up with the three buttons, and it tickled like cake crumbs in bed. Then he wanted to scratch, but that made it worse; and then he lay down on the sands and rolled and rolled and rolled, and every time he rolled the cake crumbs tickled him worse and worse and worse. Then he ran to the palm-tree and rubbed and rubbed and rubbed himself against it. He rubbed so much and so hard that he rubbed his skin into a great fold over his shoulders, and another fold underneath, where the buttons used to be (but he rubbed the buttons off), and he rubbed some more folds over his legs. And it spoiled his temper, but it didn't make the least difference to the cake-crumbs. They were inside his skin and they tickled. So he went home, very angry indeed and horribly scratchy; and from that day to this every rhinoceros has great folds in his skin and a very bad temper, all on account of the cake-crumbs inside.

But the Parsee came down from his palm-tree, wearing his hat, from which the rays of the sun were reflected in more-than-oriental splendour, packed up his cooking-stove, and went away in the direction of Orotavo, Amygdala, the Upland Meadows of Anantarivo, and the Marshes of Sonaput.

Poem by Rudyard Kipling

This Uninhabited Island
Is off Cape Gardafui,
By the Beaches of Socotra
And the Pink Arabian Sea:
But it's hot – too hot from Suez
For the likes of you and me
Ever to go
In a P. and O.
And call on the Cake-Parsee!

The Elephant's Child

In the High and Far-Off Times the Elephant, O Best Beloved, had no trunk. He had only a blackish, bulgy nose, as big as a boot, that he could wriggle about from side to side; but he couldn't pick up things with it. But there was one Elephant – a new Elephant – an Elephant's Child – who was full of 'satiable curtiosity, and that means he asked ever so many questions. And he lived in Africa, and he filled all Africa with his 'satiable curtiosities. He asked his tall aunt, the Ostrich, why her tail-feathers grew just so, and his tall aunt the Ostrich spanked him with her hard, hard claw. He asked his tall uncle, the Giraffe, what made his skin spotty, and his tall uncle, the Giraffe, spanked him with his hard, hard hoof. And still he was full of 'satiable curtiosity! He asked his broad aunt, the Hippopotamus, why her eyes were red, and his broad aunt, the Hippopotamus, spanked him with her broad, broad hoof; and he asked his hairy uncle, the Baboon, why melons tasted just so, and his hairy uncle, the Baboon, spanked him with his hairy, hairy paw. And still he was full of 'satiable curtiosity! He asked questions about everything that he saw, or heard, or felt, or smelt, or touched, and all his uncles and his aunts spanked him. And still he was full of 'satiable curtiosity!

One fine morning in the middle of the Precession of the Equinoxes this 'satiable Elephant's Child asked a new fine question that he had never asked before. He asked, "What does the Crocodile have for dinner?" Then everybody said, "Hush!" in a loud and dretful tone, and they spanked him immediately and directly, without stopping, for a long time.

By and by, when that was finished, he came upon Kolokolo Bird sitting in the middle of a wait-a-bit thorn-bush, and he said, "My father has spanked me, and my mother has spanked me; all my aunts and uncles have spanked me for my 'satiable curtiosity; and still I want to know what the Crocodile has for dinner!"

Then Kolokolo Bird said, with a mournful cry, "Go to the banks of the great grey-green, greasy Limpopo River, all set about with fever-trees, and find out."

That very next morning, when there was nothing left of the Equinoxes, because the Precession had preceded according to precedent, this 'satiable Elephant's Child took a hundred pounds of bananas (the little short red kind), and a hundred pounds of sugar-cane (the long purple kind), and seventeen melons (the greeny-crackly kind), and said to all his dear families, "Goodbye. I am going to the great grey-green, greasy Limpopo River, all

This is the Elephant's Child having his nose pulled by the Crocodile. He is much surprised and astonished and hurt, and he is talking through his nose and saying, "Led go! You are hurtig be!" He is pulling very hard, and so is the Crocodile: but the Bi-Coloured-Python-Rock-Snake is hurrying through the water to help the Elephant's Child. All that black stuff is the banks of the great grey-green greasy Limpopo River (but I am not allowed to paint these pictures), and the bottly-tree with the twisty roots and the eight leaves is one of the fever-trees that grow there.

set about with fever-trees, to find out what the Crocodile has for dinner." And they all spanked him once more for luck, though he asked them most politely to stop.

Then he went away, a little warm, but not at all astonished, eating melons, and throwing the rind about, because he could not pick it up.

He went from Graham's Town to Kimberley, and from Kimberley to Khama's Country, and from Khama's Country he went east by north, eating melons all the time, till at last he came to the banks of the great grey-green, greasy

Limpopo River, all set about with fever-trees, precisely as Kolokolo Bird had said.

Now you must know and understand, O Best Beloved, that till that very week, and day, and hour, and minute, this 'satiable Elephant's Child had never seen a Crocodile, and did not know what one was like. It was all his 'satiable curtiosity.

The first thing that he found was a Bi-Coloured-Python-Rock-Snake curled round a rock.

"'Scuse me," said the Elephant's Child most politely, "but have you seen such a thing as a Crocodile in these promiscuous parts?"

"Have I seen a Crocodile?" said the Bi-Coloured-Python-Rock-Snake, in a voice of dretful scorn. "What will you ask me next?"

"'Scuse me," said the Elephant's Child, "but could you kindly tell me what he has for dinner?"

Then the Bi-Coloured-Python-Rock-Snake uncoiled himself very quickly from the rock, and spanked the Elephant's Child with his scalesome, flailsome tail.

"That is odd," said the Elephant's Child, "because my father and my mother, and my uncle and my aunt, not to mention my other aunt, the Hippopotamus, and my other uncle, the Baboon, have all spanked me for my 'satiable curtiosity – and I suppose this is the same thing."

So he said good-bye very politely to the Bi-Coloured-Python-Rock-Snake, and helped to coil him up on the rock again, and went on, a little warm, but not at all astonished, eating melons, and throwing the rind about, because he could not pick it up, till he trod on what he thought was a log of wood at the very edge of the great grey-green, greasy Limpopo River, all set about with fever-trees.

But it was really the Crocodile, O Best Beloved, and the Crocodile winked one eye – like this!

"'Scuse me," said the Elephant's Child most politely, "but do you happen to have seen a Crocodile in these promiscuous parts?"

Then the Crocodile winked the other eye, and lifted half his tail out of the mud; and the Elephant's Child stepped back most politely, because he did not wish to be spanked again.

"Come hither, Little One," said the Crocodile. "Why do you ask such things?"

"'Scuse me," said the Elephant's Child most politely, "but my father has spanked me, my mother has spanked me, not to mention my tall aunt, the Ostrich, and my tall uncle, the Giraffe, who can kick ever so hard, as well as my broad aunt, the Hippopotamus, and my hairy uncle, the Baboon, and including the Bi-Coloured-Python-Rock-Snake, with the scalesome, flailsome tail, just up the bank, who spanks harder than any of them; and so, if it's quite all the same to you, I don't want to be spanked any more."

"Come hither, Little One," said the Crocodile, "for I am the Crocodile," and he wept crocodile-tears to show it was quite true.

Then the Elephant's Child grew all breathless, and panted, and kneeled down on the bank and said, "You are the very person I have been looking for all these long days.

Will you please tell me what you have for dinner?"

"Come hither, Little One," said the Crocodile, "and I'll whisper."

Then the Elephant's Child put his head down close to the Crocodile's musky, tusky mouth, and the Crocodile caught him by his little nose, which up to that very week, day, hour, and minute, had been no bigger than a boot, though much more useful.

"I think," said the Crocodile – and he said it between his teeth, like this – 'I think to-day I will begin with Elephant's Child!"

At this, O Best Beloved, the Elephant's Child was much annoyed, and he said, speaking through his nose, like this, "Led go! You are hurtig be!"

Then the Bi-Coloured-Python-Rock-Snake scuffled down from the bank and said, "My young friend, if you do not now, immediately and instantly, pull as hard as ever you can, it is my opinion that your acquaintance in the large-pattern leather ulster" (and by this he meant the Crocodile) "will jerk you into yonder limpid stream before you can say Jack Robinson."

This is the way Bi-Coloured-Python-Rock-Snakes always talk.

Then the Elephant's Child sat back on his little haunches, and pulled, and pulled, and pulled, and his nose began to stretch. And the Crocodile floundered into the water, making it all creamy with great sweeps of his tail, and he pulled, and pulled, and pulled.

And the Elephant's Child's nose kept on stretching; and the Elephant's Child spread all his little four legs and pulled, and pulled, and pulled, and his nose kept on stretching; and the Crocodile threshed his tail like an oar, and he pulled, and pulled, and pulled, and at each pull the Elephant's Child's nose grew longer and longer – and it hurt him hijjus!

Then the Elephant's Child felt his legs slipping, and he said through his nose, which was now nearly five feet long, "This is too butch for be!"

Then the Bi-Coloured-Python-Rock-Snake came down from the bank, and knotted himself in a double-clove-hitch round the Elephant's Child's hind legs, and said, "Rash and inexperienced traveller, we will now seriously devote ourselves to a little high tension, because if we do not, it is my impression that yonder self-propelling man-of-war with the armour-plated upper deck" (and by this, O Best Beloved, he meant the Crocodile), "will permanently vitiate your future career."

That is the way all Bi-Coloured-Python-Rock-Snakes always talk.

So he pulled, and the Elephant's Child pulled, and the Crocodile pulled; but the Elephant's Child and the Bi-Coloured-Python-Rock-Snake pulled hardest; and at last the Crocodile let go of the Elephant's Child's nose with a plop that you could hear all up and down the Limpopo.

Then the Elephant's Child sat down most hard and sudden; but first he was careful to say "Thank you" to the

Bi-Coloured-Python-Rock-Snake; and next he was kind to his poor pulled nose, and wrapped it all up in cool banana leaves, and hung it in the great grey-green, greasy Limpopo to cool.

"What are you doing that for?" said the Bi-Coloured-Python-Rock-Snake.

"'Scuse me," said the Elephant's Child, "but my nose is badly out of shape, and I am waiting for it to shrink."

"Then you will have to wait a long time," said the Bi-Coloured-Python-Rock-Snake. "Some people do not know what is good for them."

The Elephant's Child sat there for three days waiting for his nose to shrink. But it never grew any shorter, and, besides, it made him squint. For, O Best Beloved, you will see and understand that the Crocodile had pulled it out into a really truly trunk same as all Elephants have to-day.

At the end of the third day a fly came and stung him on the shoulder, and before he knew what he was doing he lifted up his trunk and hit that fly dead with the end of it.

"'Vantage number one!" said the Bi-Coloured-Python-Rock-Snake. "You couldn't have done that with a mere-smear nose. Try and eat a little now."

Before he thought what he was doing the Elephant's Child put out his trunk and plucked a large bundle of grass, dusted it clean against his fore-legs, and stuffed it into his own mouth.

"'Vantage number two!" said the Bi-Coloured-Python-Rock-Snake. "You couldn't have done that with a mere-smear nose. Don't you think the sun is very hot here?"

"It is," said the Elephant's Child, and before he thought what he was doing he schlooped up a schloop of mud from the banks of the great grey-green, greasy Limpopo, and slapped it on his head, where it made a cool schloopy-sloshy mud-cap all trickly behind his ears.

"'Vantage number three!" said the Bi-Coloured-Python-Rock-Snake. "You couldn't have done that with a mere-smear nose. Now how do you feel about being spanked again?"

"'Scuse me," said the Elephant's Child, "but I should not like it at all."

"How would you like to spank somebody?" said the Bi-Coloured-Python-Rock-Snake.

"I should like it very much indeed," said the Elephant's Child.

"Well," said the Bi-Coloured-Python-Rock-Snake, "you will find that new nose of yours very useful to spank people with."

"Thank you," said the Elephant's Child, "I'll remember that; and now I think I'll go home to all my dear families and try."

So the Elephant's Child went home across Africa frisking and whisking his trunk. When he wanted fruit to eat he pulled fruit down from a tree, instead of waiting for it to fall as he used to do. When he wanted grass he plucked grass up from the ground, instead of going on his knees as he used to do. When the flies bit him he broke off the branch of a tree and used it as fly-whisk; and he made himself a new, cool, slushy-squshy mud-cap whenever the sun was hot. When he felt lonely walking through Africa he sang to himself down his trunk, and the noise was louder than several brass bands.

He went especially out of his way to find a broad Hippo-potamus (she was no relation of his), and he spanked her very hard, to make sure that the Bi-Coloured-Python-Rock-Snake had spoken the truth about his new trunk. The rest of the time he picked up the melon rinds that he had dropped on his way to the Limpopo – for he was a Tidy Pachyderm.

One dark evening he came back to all his dear families, and he coiled up his trunk and said, "How do you do?" They were very glad to see him, and immediately said, "Come here and be spanked for your 'satiable curtiosity."

"Pooh," said the Elephant's Child. "I don't think you peoples know anything about spanking; but I do, and I'll show you." Then he uncurled his trunk and knocked two of his dear brothers head over heels.

"O Bananas!" said they, "where did you learn that trick, and what have you done to your nose?"

"I got a new one from the Crocodile on the banks of the great grey-green, greasy Limpopo River," said the Elephant's Child. "I asked him what he had for dinner, and he gave me this to keep."

"It looks very ugly," said his hairy uncle, the Baboon.

"It does," said the Elephant's Child. "But it's very useful," and he picked up his hairy uncle, the Baboon, by one hairy leg, and hove him into a hornet's nest.

Then that bad Elephant's Child spanked all his dear families for a long time, till they were very warm and greatly astonished. He pulled out his tall Ostrich aunt's tail-feathers; and he caught his tall uncle, the Giraffe, by the hind-leg, and dragged him through a thorn-bush; and he shouted at his broad aunt, the Hippopotamus, and blew bubbles into her ear when she was sleeping in the water after meals; but he never let any one touch Kolokolo Bird.

At last things grew so exciting that his dear families went off one by one in a hurry to the banks of the great grey-green, greasy Limpopo River, all set about with fever-trees, to borrow new noses from the Crocodile. When they came back nobody spanked anybody any more; and ever since that day, O Best Beloved, all the Elephants you will ever see, besides all those that you won't, have trunks precisely like the trunk of the 'satiable Elephant's Child.

Poem by Rudyard Kipling

I keep six honest serving-men:
(They taught me all I knew)
Their names are What and Where and When
And How and Why and Who.
I send them over land and sea,
I send them east and west;
But after they have worked for me,
I give them all a rest.

Poems by Robert Louis Stevenson

Robert Louis Stevenson who said :
"... every child can remember laying his
head in the grass, staring into the
infinitesimal forest and seeing it grow
populous with fairy armies ..."

Happy Thought

The world is so full of a number of things,
I'm sure we should all be as happy as kings.

Fairy Bread

Come up here, O dusty feet!
Here is fairy bread to eat.
Here in my retiring room,
Children, you may dine
On the golden smell of broom
And the shade of pine;
And when you have eaten well,
Fairy stories hear and tell.

There are fairies for every season

Young Night-Thought

All night long and every night,
When my mama puts out the light,
I see the people marching by,
As plain as day before my eye.

Armies and emperor and kings,
All carrying different kinds of things,
And marching in so grand a way,
You never saw the like by day.

So fine a show was never seen
At the great circus on the green;
For every kind of beast and man
Is marching in that caravan.

As first they move a little slow,
But still the faster on they go,
And still beside me close I keep
Until we reach the town of Sleep.

The Unseen Playmate

When children are playing alone on the green,
In comes the playmate that never was seen.
When children are happy and lonely and good,
The Friend of the Children comes out of the wood.

Nobody heard him, and nobody saw,
His is a picture you never could draw,
But he's sure to be present, abroad or at home,
When children are happy and playing alone.

He lies in the laurels, he runs on the grass,
He sings when you tinkle the musical glass;
Whene'er you are happy and cannot tell why,
The Friend of the Children is sure to be by!

He loves to be little, he hates to be big,
'Tis he that inhabits the caves that you dig;
'Tis he when you play with your soldiers of tin
That sides with the Frenchmen and never can win.

'Tis he, when at night you go off to your bed,
Bids you go to sleep and not trouble your head;
For wherever they're lying, in cupboard or shelf,
'Tis he will take care of your playthings himself!

The fairies dance at night while children sleep and dream

The Little Land

When at home alone I sit
And am very tired of it,
I have just to shut my eyes
To go sailing through the skies....
To go sailing far away
To the pleasant Land of Play;
To the fairy land afar
Where the Little People are;
Where the clover-tops are trees,
And the rain-pools are the seas,
And the leaves, like little ships,
Sail about on tiny trips;
And above the Daisy tree
Through the grasses,
High o'erhead the Bumble Bee
Hums and passes.

In that forest to and fro
I can wander, I can go;
See the spider and the fly,

*". . . To the fairy land afar
Where the Little People are"*

And the ants go marching by,
Carrying parcels with their feet
Down the green and grassy street.
I can in the sorrel sit
Where the ladybird alit.
I can climb the jointed grass
And on high
And my tiny self I see,
Painted very clear and neat
On the rain-pool at my feet.
Should a leaflet come to land
Drifting near to where I stand,
Straight I'll board that tiny boat
Round the rain-pool sea to float.

Little thoughtful creatures sit
On the grassy coasts of it;
Little things with lovely eyes
See me sailing with surprise.
Some are clad in armour green....
(These have sure to battle been!)....
Some are pied with ev'ry hue,
Black and crimson, gold and blue;
Some have wings and swift are gone....
But they all look kindly on.

When my eyes I once again
Open, and see all things plain:
High bare walls, great bare floor;
Great big knobs on drawer and door;
Great big people perched on chairs,
Stitching tucks and mending tears,
Each a hill that I could climb,
And talking nonsense all the time....
O dear me,
That I could be
A sailor on a the rain-pool sea,
A climber in the clover tree,
And just come back a sleepy-head,
Late at night to go to bed.

Why the Sea is Salt

A Norwegian tale, gathered by
Peter Christen Asbjørnsen and
Jørgen Moe in their *Popular
Tales from the Norse*. There are
various versions in other countries,
including Iceland, Denmark,
Germany and Greece and it was
included in Andrew Lang's *The
Blue Fairy Book*. The bribe may
be a ham or bacon or a lamb.

Once upon a time, long, long ago, there were two brothers, the one rich and the other poor. When Christmas Eve came, the poor one had not a bite in the house, either of meat or bread; so he went to his brother, and begged him, in God's name, to give him something for Christmas Day. It was by no means the first time that the brother had been forced to give something to him, and he was not better pleased at being asked now than he generally was.

"If you will do what I ask you, you shall have a whole ham," said he. The poor one immediately thanked him, and promised this.

"Well, here is the ham, and now you must go straight to Dead Man's Hall," said the rich brother, throwing the ham to him.

"Well, I will do what I have promised," said the other, and he took the ham and set off. He went on and on for the livelong day, and at nightfall he came to a place where there was a bright light.

"I have no doubt this is the place," thought the man with the ham.

An old man with a long white beard was standing in the outhouse, chopping Yule logs.

"Good-evening," said the man with the ham.

"Good-evening to you. Where are you going at this late hour?" said the man.

"I am going to Dead Man's Hall, if only I am on the right track," answered the poor man.

"Oh! yes, you are right enough, for it is here," said the old man. "When you get inside they will all want to buy your ham, for they don't get much meat to eat there; but you must not sell it unless you can get the hand-mill which stands behind the door for it. When you come out again I will teach you how to stop the hand-mill, which is useful for almost everything."

So the man with the ham thanked the other for his good advice, and rapped at the door.

When he got in, everything happened just as the old man had said it would: all the people, great and small, came round him like ants on an ant-hill, and each tried to outbid the other for the ham.

"By rights my old woman and I ought to have it for our Christmas dinner, but, since you have set your hearts upon it, I must just give it up to you," said the man. "But, if I sell it, I will have the hand-mill which is standing there behind the door."

At first they would not hear to this, and haggled and bargained with the man, but he stuck to what he had said, and the people were forced to give him the hand-mill. When the man came out again into the yard, he asked the old wood-cutter how he was to stop the hand-mill, and when he had learned that, he thanked him and set off home with all the speed he could, but did not get there until after the clock had struck twelve on Christmas Eve.

"Where in the world have you been?" said the old woman. "Here I have sat waiting hour after hour, and have not even two sticks to lay across each other under the Christmas porridge-pot."

"Oh! I could not come before; I had something of importance to see about, and a long way to go, too; but now you shall just see!" said the man, and then he set the hand-mill on the table, and bade it first grind light, then a table-cloth, and then meat, and beer, and everything else that was good for a Christmas Eve's supper; and the mill ground all that he ordered. "Bless me!" said the old woman

The magical hand-mill ground away to produce all the man ordered – meat, beer and all good things

as one thing after another appeared; and she wanted to know where her husband had got the mill from, but he would not tell her that.

"Never mind where I got it; you can see that it is a good one, and the water that turns it will never freeze," said the man. So he ground meat and drink, and all kinds of good things, to last all Christmas-tide, and on the third day he invited all his friends to come to a feast.

Now when the rich brother saw all that there was at the banquet and in the house, he was both vexed and angry, for he grudged everything his brother had. "On Christmas Eve he was so poor that he came to me and begged for a trifle, for God's sake, and now he gives a feast as if he were both a count and a king!" thought he. "But, for heaven's sake, tell me where you got your riches from," said he to his brother.

"From behind the door," said he who owned the mill, for he did not choose to satisfy his brother on that point; but later in the evening, when he had taken a drop too much, he could not refrain from telling how he had come by the hand-mill. "There you see what has brought me all my wealth!" said he, and brought out the mill, and made it grind first one thing and then another. When the brother saw that, he insisted on having the mill, and after a great deal of persuasion got it; but he had to give three hundred dollars for it, and the poor brother was to keep it till the haymaking was over, for he thought: "If I keep it as long as that, I can make it grind meat and drink that will last many a long year." During that time you may imagine that the mill did not grow rusty, and when hay-harvest came the rich brother got it, but the other had taken good care not to teach him how to stop it. It was evening when the rich man got the mill home, and in the morning he bade the old woman go out and spread the hay after the mowers, and he would attend to the house himself that day, he said.

So, when dinner-time drew near, he set the mill on the kitchen-table, and said: "Grind herrings and milk pottage, and do it both quickly and well."

So the mill began to grind herrings and milk pottage, and first all the dishes and tubs were filled, and then it came out all over the kitchen-floor. The man twisted and turned it, and did all he could to make the mill stop, but, howsoever he turned it and screwed it, the mill went on grinding, and in a short time the pottage rose so high that the man was like to be drowned. So he threw open the parlor door, but it was not long before the mill had ground the parlor full too, and it was with difficulty and danger that the man could go through the stream of pottage and get hold of the door-latch. When he got the door open, he did not stay long in the room, but ran out, and the herrings and pottage came after him, and it streamed out over both farm and field. Now the old woman, who was out spreading the hay, began to think dinner was long in coming, and said to the women and the mowers: "Though the master does not call us home, we may as well go. It may be that he finds he is not good at making pottage and I should do well to help him." So they began to straggle homeward, but when they had got a little

The old man had been chopping Yule logs

way up the hill they met the herrings and pottage and bread, all pouring forth and winding about one over the other, and the man himself in front of the flood. "Would to heaven that each of you had a hundred stomachs! Take care that you are not drowned in the pottage!" he cried as he went by them as if Mischief were at his heels, down to where his brother dwelt. Then he begged him, for God's sake, to take the mill back again, and that in an instant, for, said he: "If it grind one hour more the whole district will be destroyed by herrings and pottage." But the brother would not take it until the other paid him three hundred dollars, and that he was obliged to do. Now the poor brother had both the money and the mill again. So it was not long before he had a farmhouse much finer than that in which his brother lived, but the mill ground him so much money that he covered it with plates of gold; and the farmhouse lay close by the sea-shore, so it shone and glittered far out to sea. Everyone who sailed by there now had to be put in to visit the rich man in the gold farmhouse, and everyone wanted to see the wonderful mill, for the report of it spread far and wide, and there was no one who had not heard tell of it.

After a long, long time came also a skipper who wished to see the mill. He asked if it could make salt. "Yes, it could make salt," said he who owned it, and when the skipper heard that, he wished with all his might and main to have the mill, let it cost what it might, for, he thought, if he had it, he would get off having to sail far away over the perilous sea for freights of salt. At first the man would not hear of parting with it, but the skipper begged and prayed, and at last the man sold it to him, and got many, many thousand dollars for it. When the skipper had got the mill on his back he did not stay there long, for he was so afraid that the man would change his mind, and he had no time to ask how he was to stop it grinding, but got on board his ship as fast as he could.

When he had gone a little way out to sea he took the mill on deck. "Grind salt, and grind both quickly and well," said the skipper. So the mill began to grind salt, till it spouted out like water, and when the skipper had got the ship filled he wanted to stop the mill, but whichsoever way he turned it, and how much soever he tried, it went on grinding, and the heap of salt grew higher and higher, until at last the ship sank. There lies the mill at the bottom of the sea, and still, day by day, it grinds on; and that is why the sea is salt.

The Knights of the Fish

This Spanish fairy tale was collected
by Fernan Caballaro in *Cuentos:
Oraciones y Adivinas* and appears
in Andrew Lang's *Brown Fairy
Book*, *A Book of Enchantments*
by Ruth Manning-Sanders and *The
Goldenrod Fairy Book* by Esther
Singleton. It tells how a man catches
a magical fish and of his two sons
and their great adventures with a
dragon, a witch and a princess.

*A beautiful princess was to be offered
to the dreadful fiery dragon*

Once upon a time there lived an old cobbler who worked hard at his trade from morning till night, and scarcely gave himself a moment to eat. But, industrious as he was, he could hardly buy bread and cheese for himself and his wife, and they grew thinner and thinner daily.

For a long while whey pretended to each other that they had no appetite, and that a few blackberries from the hedges were a great deal nicer than a good strong bowl of soup. But at length there came a day when the cobbler could bear it no longer, and he threw away his last, and

borrowing a rod from a neighbour he went out to fish.

Now the cobbler was as patient about fishing as he had been about cobbling. From dawn to dark he stood on the banks of the little stream, without hooking anything better than an eel, or a few old shoes, that even he, clever though he was, felt were not worth mending. At length his patience began to give way, and as he undressed one night he said to himself: "Well, I will give it one more chance; and if I don't catch a fish to-morrow, I will go and hang myself."

He had not cast his line for ten minutes the next morning before he drew from the river the most beautiful fish he had ever seen in his life. But he nearly fell into the water from surprise, when the fish began to speak to him, in a small, squeaky voice:

"Take me back to your hut and cook me; then cut me up, and sprinkle me over with pepper and salt. Give two of the pieces to your wife, and bury two more in the garden."

The cobbler did not know what to make of these strange words; but he was wiser than many people, and when he did not understand, he thought it was well to obey. His children wanted to eat all the fish themselves, and begged their father to tell them what to do with the pieces he had put aside; but the cobbler only laughed, and told them it was no business of theirs. And when they were safe in bed he stole out and buried the two pieces in the garden.

By and by two babies, exactly alike, lay in a cradle, and in the garden were two tall plants, with two brilliant shields on the top.

Years passed away, and the babies were almost men. They were tired of living quietly at home, being mistaken for each other by everybody they saw, and determined to set off in different directions, to seek adventures.

So, one fine morning, the two brothers left the hut, and walked together to the place where the great road divided. There they embraced and parted, promising that if anything remarkable had happened to either, he would return to the cross roads and wait till his brother came.

The youth who took the path that ran eastwards arrived presently at a large city, where he found everybody standing at the doors, wringing their hands and weeping bitterly.

"What is the matter?" asked he, pausing and looking round. And a man replied, in a faltering voice, that each year a beautiful girl was chosen by lot to be offered up to a dreadful fiery dragon, who had a mother even worse than himself, and this year the lot had fallen on their peerless princess.

"But where IS the princess?" said the young man once more, and again the man answered him: "She is standing under a tree, a mile away, waiting for the dragon."

This time the Knight of the Fish did not stop to hear more, but ran off as fast as he could, and found the princess

The old cobbler worked so hard he scarcely had time to eat

bathed in tears, and trembling from head to foot.

She turned as she heard the sound of his sword, and removed her handkerchief from his eyes.

"Fly," she cried; "fly while you have yet time, before that monster sees you."

She said it, and she mean it; yet, when he had turned his back, she felt more forsaken than before. But in reality it was not more than a few minutes before he came back, galloping furiously on a horse he had borrowed, and carrying a huge mirror across its neck.

155

"I am in time, then," he cried, dismounting very carefully, and placing the mirror against the trunk of a tree.

"Give me your veil," he said hastily to the princess. And when she had unwound it from her head he covered the mirror with it.

"The moment the dragon comes near you, you must tear off the veil," cried he; "and be sure you hide behind the mirror. Have no fear; I shall be at hand."

He and his horse had scarcely found shelter amongst some rocks, when the flap of the dragon's wings could be plainly heard. He tossed his head with delight at the sight of her, and approached slowly to the place where she stood, a little in front of the mirror. Then, still looking the monster steadily in the face, she passed one hand behind her back and snatched off the veil, stepping swiftly behind the tree as she did so.

The princess had not known, when she obeyed the orders of the Knight of the Fish, what she expected to happen. Would the dragon with snaky locks be turned to stone, she wondered, like the dragon in an old story her nurse had told her; or would some fiery spark dart from the heart of the mirror, and strike him dead? Neither of these things occurred, but, instead, the dragon stopped short with surprise and rage when he saw a monster before him as big and strong as himself. He shook his mane with rage and fury; the enemy in front did exactly the same. He lashed his tail, and rolled his red eyes, and the dragon opposite was no whit behind him. Opening his mouth to its very widest, he gave an awful roar; but the other dragon only roared back. This was too much, and with another roar which made the princess shake in her shoes, he flung himself upon his foe. In an instant the mirror lay at his feet broken into a thousand pieces, but as every piece reflected part of himself, the dragon thought that he too had been smashed into atoms.

It was the moment for which the Knight of the Fish had watched and waited, and before the dragon could find out that he was not hurt at all, the young man"s lance was down his throat, and he was rolling, dead, on the grass.

Oh! what shouts of joy rang through the great city, when the youth came riding back with the princess sitting behind him, and dragging the horrible monster by a cord. Everybody cried out that the king must give the victor the hand of the princess; and so he did, and no one had ever seen such balls and feasts and sports before. And when they were all over the young couple went to the palace prepared for them, which was so large that it was three miles round.

The first wet day after their marriage the bridegroom begged the bride to show him all the rooms in the palace, and it was so big and took so long that the sun was shining brightly again before they stepped on to the roof to see the view.

"What castle is that out there," asked the knight; "it seems to be made of black marble?"

"It is called the castle of Albatroz," answered the princess.

"It is enchanted, and no one that has tried to enter it has ever come back."

Her husband said nothing, and began to talk of something else; but the next morning he ordered his horse, took his spear, called his bloodhound, and set off for the castle.

It needed a brave man to approach it, for it made your hair stand on end merely to look at it; it was as dark as the night of a storm, and as silent as the grave. But the Knight of the Fish knew no fear, and had never turned his back on an enemy; so he drew out his horn, and blew a blast.

The sound awoke all the sleeping echoes in the castle, and was repeated now loudly, now softly; now near, and now far. But nobody stirred for all that.

"Is there anyone inside?" cried the young man in his loudest voice; "anyone who will give a knight hospitality? Neither governor, nor squire, not even a page?"

"Not even a page!" answered the echoes. But the young man did not heed them, and only struck a furious blow at the gate.

Then a small grating opened, and there appeared the tip of a huge nose, which belonged to the ugliest old woman that ever was seen.

"What do you want?" said she.

"To enter," he answered shortly. "Can I rest here this night? Yes or No?"

"No, No, No!" repeated the echoes.

Between the fierce sun and his anger at being kept waiting, the Knight of the Fish had grown so hot that he lifted his visor, and when the old woman saw how handsome he was, she began fumbling with the lock of the gate.

"Come in, come in," said she, "so fine a gentleman will do us no harm."

"Harm!" repeated the echoes, but again the young man paid no heed.

"Let us go in, ancient dame," but she interrupted him.

"You must call me the Lady Berberisca," she answered, sharply; "and this is my castle, to which I bid you welcome. You shall live here with me and be my husband." But at these words the knight let his spear fall, so surprised was he.

"I marry YOU? why you must be a hundred at least!" cried he. "You are mad! All I desire is to inspect the castle and then go." As he spoke he heard the voices give a mocking laugh; but the old woman took no notice, and only bade the knight follow her.

Old though she was, it seemed impossible to tire her. There was no room, however small, she did not lead him into, and each room was full of curious things he had never seen before.

At length they came to a stone staircase, which was so dark that you could not see your hand if you held it up before your face.

"I have kept my most precious treasure till the last," said the old woman; "but let me go first, for the stairs are steep, and you might easily break your leg." So on she went, now and then calling back to the young man in the darkness. But he did not know that she had slipped aside into a recess, till suddenly he put his foot on a trap door which gave way under him, and he fell down, down, as many good knights had done before him, and his voice joined the echoes of theirs.

"So you would not marry me!" chuckled the old witch. "Ha! ha! Ha! ha!"

Meanwhile his brother had wandered far and wide, and at last he wandered back to the same great city where the other young knight had met with so many adventures. He noticed, with amazement, that as he walked through the streets the guards drew themselves up in line, and saluted him, and the drummers played the royal march; but he was still more bewildered when several servants in livery ran up to him and told him that the princess was sure something terrible had befallen him, and had made herself ill with weeping. At last it occurred to him that once more he had been taken for his brother. "I had better say nothing," thought he; "perhaps I shall be able to help him after all."

So he suffered himself to be borne in triumph to the palace, where the princess threw herself into his arms.

"And so you did go to the castle?" she asked.

"Yes, of course I did," answered he.

The long-nosed witch peered out at the Knight

"And what did you see there?"

"I am forbidden to tell you anything about it, until I have returned there once more," replied he.

"Must you really go back to that dreadful place?" she asked wistfully. "You are the only man who has ever come back from it."

"I must," was all he answered. And the princess, who was a wise woman, only said: "Well, go to bed now, for I am sure you must be very tired."

But the knight shook his head. "I have sworn never to lie in a bed as long as my work in the castle remains standing."

The Knight struck the dragon with his lance

And the princess again sighed, and was silent.

Early next day the young man started for the castle, feeling sure that some terrible thing must have happened to his brother.

At the blast of his horn the long nose of the old woman appeared at the grating, but the moment she caught sight of his face, she nearly fainted from fright, as she thought it was the ghost of the youth whose bones were lying in the dungeon of the castle.

"Lady of all the ages," cried the new comer, "did you not give hospitality to a young knight but a short time ago?"

"A short time ago!" wailed the voices.

"And how have you ill-treated him?" he went on.

"Ill-treated him!" answered the voices. The woman did not stop to hear more; she turned to fly; but the knight"s sword entered her body.

"Where is my brother, cruel hag?" asked he sternly.

"I will tell you," said she; "but as I feel that I am going to die I shall keep that piece of news to myself, till you have brought me to life again."

The young man laughed scornfully. "How do you propose that I should work that miracle?"

"Oh, it is quite easy. Go into the garden and gather the flowers of the everlasting plant and some of dragon"s blood. Crush them together and boil them in a large tub of water, and then put me into it."

The knight did as the old witch bade him, and, sure enough, she came out quite whole, but uglier than ever. She then told the young man what had become of his brother, and he went down into the dungeon, and brought up his body and the bodies of the other victims who lay there, and when they were all washed in the magic water their strength was restored to them.

And, besides these, he found in another cavern the bodies of the girls who had been sacrificed to the dragon, and brought them back to life also.

As to the old witch, in the end she died of rage at seeing her prey escape her; and at the moment she drew her last breath the castle of Albatroz fell into ruins with a great noise.

The Water of Life

The pool of the Water of Life lay in a hollow near the mountain peak

This Spanish Catalan fairy story was collected by D. Francisco de S. Maspous y Labros, in *Cuentos Populars Catalans*. It also appeared in Andrew Lang's *Pink Fairy Book*

Three brothers and one sister lived together in a small cottage, and they loved one another dearly. One day the eldest brother, who had never done anything but amuse himself from sunrise to sunset, said to the rest, "Let us all work hard, and perhaps we shall grow rich, and be able to build ourselves a palace."

And his brothers and sister answered joyfully, "Yes, we will all work!"

So they fell to working with all their might, till at last they became rich, and were able to build themselves a beautiful palace; and everyone came from miles round to see its wonders, and to say how splendid it was. No one thought of finding any faults, till at length an old woman, who had been walking through the rooms with a crowd of people, suddenly exclaimed, "Yes, it is a splendid palace, but there is still something it needs!"

"And what may that be?"

"A church."

When they heard this the brothers set to work again to earn some more money, and when they had got enough they set about building a church, which should be as large and beautiful as the palace itself.

And after the church was finished greater numbers of people than ever flocked to see the palace and the church and vast gardens and magnificent halls.

But one day, as the brothers were as usual doing the honours to their guests, an old man turned to them and said, "Yes, it is all most beautiful, but there is still something it needs!"

"And what may that be?"

"A pitcher of the water of life, a branch of the tree the smell of whose flowers gives eternal beauty, and the talking bird."

"And where am I to find all those?"

"Go to the mountain that is far off yonder, and you will find what you seek."

After the old man had bowed politely and taken farewell of them the eldest brother said to the rest, "I will go in search of the water of life, and the talking bird, and the tree of beauty."

"But suppose some evil thing befalls you?" asked his sister. "How shall we know?"

"You are right," he replied; "I had not thought of that!"

Then they followed the old man, and said to him, "My eldest brother wishes to seek for the water of life, and the tree of beauty, and the talking bird, that you tell him are needful to make our palace perfect. But how shall we know if any evil thing befall him?"

So the old man took them a knife, and gave it to them, saying, "Keep this carefully, and as long as the blade is bright all is well; but if the blade is bloody, then know that evil has befallen him."

The brothers thanked him, and departed, and went straight to the palace, where they found the young man making ready to set out for the mountain where the treasures he longed for lay hid.

And he walked, and he walked, and he walked, till he had gone a great way, and there he met a giant.

"Can you tell me how much further I have still to go before I reach that mountain yonder?"

"And why do you wish to go there?"

"I am seeking the water of life, the talking bird, and a branch of the tree of beauty."

"Many have passed by seeking those treasures, but none have ever come back; and you will never come back either, unless you mark my words. Follow this path, and when you reach the mountain you will find it covered with stones. Do not stop to look at them, but keep on your way. As you go you will hear scoffs and laughs behind you; it will be the stones that mock. Do not heed them; above all, do not turn round. If you do you will become as one of them. Walk straight on till you get to the top, and then take all you wish for."

The young man thanked him for his counsel, and walked, and walked, and walked, till he reached the mountain. And as he climbed he heard behind him scoffs and jeers, but he kept his ears steadily closed to them. At last the noise grew so loud that he lost patience, and he stooped to pick up a stone to hurl into the midst of the clamour, when suddenly his arm seemed to stiffen, and the next moment he was a stone himself!

The three brothers and
their sister built themselves a splendid palace

At last she reached the tree of beauty

*The giant had seen both the brothers
making their way to the mountain*

That day his sister, who thought her brother's steps were long in returning, took out the knife and found the blade was red as blood. Then she cried out to her brothers that something terrible had come to pass.

"I will go and find him," said the second. And he went. And he walked, and he walked, and he walked, till he met the giant, and asked him if he had seen a young man travelling towards the mountain.

And the giant answered, "Yes, I have seen him pass, but I have not seen him come back. The spell must have worked upon him."

"Then what can I do to disenchant him, and find the water of life, the talking bird, and a branch of the tree of beauty?"

"Follow this path, and when you reach the mountain you will find it covered with stones. Do not stop to look at them, but climb steadily on. Above all, heed not the laughs and scoffs that will arise on all sides, and never turn round. And when you reach the top you can then take all you desire."

The young man thanked him for his counsel, and set out for the mountain. But no sooner did he reach it than loud jests and gibes broke out on every side, and almost deafened him. For some time he let them rail, and pushed boldly on, till he had passed the place which his brother had gained; then suddenly he thought that among the scoffing sounds he heard his brother's voice. He stopped and looked back; and another stone was added to the number.

Meanwhile the sister left at home was counting the days when her two brothers should return to her. The time seemed long, and it would be hard to say how often she took out the knife and looked at its polished blade to make sure that this one at least was still safe. The blade was always bright and clear; each time she looked she had the happiness of knowing that all was well, till one evening, tired and anxious, as she frequently was at the end of the day, she took it from its drawer, and behold! the blade was red with blood. Her cry of horror brought her youngest brother to her, and, unable to speak, she held out the knife!

"I will go," he said.

So he walked, and he walked, and he walked, until he met the giant, and he asked, "Have two young men, making for yonder mountain, passed this way?"

And the giant answered, "Yes, they have passed by, but they never came back, and by this I know that the spell has fallen upon them."

"Then what must I do to free them, and to get the water of life, and the talking bird, and the branch of the tree of beauty?"

"Go to the mountain, which you will find so thickly covered with stones that you will hardly be able to place your feet, and walk straight forward, turning neither to the right hand nor to the left, and paying no heed to the laughs and scoffs which will follow you, till you reach the top, and then you may take all that you desire."

The young man thanked the giant for his counsel, and set forth to the mountain. And when he began to climb there burst forth all around him a storm of scoffs and jeers; but he thought of the giant's words, and looked neither to the right hand nor to the left, till the mountain top lay straight before him. A moment now and he would have gained it, when, through the groans and yells, he heard his brothers' voices. He turned, and there was one stone the more.

And all this while his sister was pacing up and down the palace, hardly letting the knife out of her hand, and dreading what she knew she would see, and what she did see. The blade grew red before her eyes, and she said, "Now it is my turn."

So she walked, and she walked, and she walked till she came to the giant, and prayed him to tell her if he had seen three young men pass that way seeking the distant mountain.

"I have seen them pass, but they have never returned, and by this I know that the spell has fallen upon them."

"And what must I do to set them free, and to find the water of life, and the talking bird, and a branch of the tree of beauty?"

"You must go to that mountain, which is so full of stones that your feet will hardly find a place to tread, and as you climb you will hear a noise as if all the stones in the world were mocking you; but pay no heed to anything you may hear, and, once you gain the top, you have gained everything."

The girl thanked him for his counsel, and set out for the mountain; and scarcely had she gone a few steps upwards when cries and screams broke forth around her, and she felt as if each stone she trod on was a living thing. But she remembered the words of the giant, and knew not what had befallen her brothers, and kept her face steadily towards the mountain top, which grew nearer and nearer every moment. But as she mounted the clamour increased sevenfold: high above them all rang the voices of her three brothers. But the girl took no heed, and at last her feet stood upon the top.

Then she looked round, and saw, lying in a hollow, the pool of the water of life. And she took the brazen pitcher that she had brought with her, and filled it to the brim. By the side of the pool stood the tree of beauty, with the talking bird on one of its boughs; and she caught the bird, and placed it in a cage, and broke off one of the branches.

After that she turned, and went joyfully down the hill again, carrying her treasures, but her long climb had tired her out, and the brazen pitcher was very heavy, and as she walked a few drops of the water spilt on the stones, and as it touched them they changed into young men and maidens, crowding about her to give thanks for their deliverance.

So she learnt by this how the evil spell might be broken, and she carefully sprinkled every stone till there was not one left – only a great company of youths and girls who followed her down the mountain.

When they arrived at the palace she did not lose a moment in planting the branch of the tree of beauty and watering it with the water of life. And the branch shot up into a tree, and was heavy with flowers, and the talking bird nestled in its branches.

Now the fame of these wonders was noised abroad, and the people flocked in great numbers to see the three marvels, and the maiden who had won them; and among the sightseers came the king's son, who would not go till everything was shown him, and till he had heard how it had all happened. And the prince admired the strangeness and beauty of the treasures in the palace, but more than all he admired the beauty and courage of the maiden who had brought them there. So he went home and told his parents, and gained their consent to wed her for his wife.

Then the marriage was celebrated in the church adjoining the palace. Then the bridegroom took her to his own home, where they lived happy for ever after.

The talking bird nestled in the branches of a tree as people came from miles around to see the three marvels – including a prince who married the maiden and took her back to his own fine palace

East of the Sun and West of the Moon

Once upon a time there was a poor peasant who had so many children that he did not have enough of either food or clothing to give them. Pretty children they all were, but the prettiest was the youngest daughter, who was so lovely there was no end to her loveliness.

One day – it was on a Thursday evening late in the fall – the weather was wild and rough outside, and it was cruelly dark. The rain was falling and the wind blowing, until the walls of the cottage shook. They were all sitting around the fire busy with this thing and that. Then all at once something gave three taps on the window. The father went out to see what was the matter. Outside, what should he see but a great big white bear.

"Good evening to you," said the white bear.

"The same to you," said the man.

"Will you give me your youngest daughter? If you will, I'll make you as rich as you are now poor," said the bear.

Well, the man would not be at all sorry to be so rich; but still he thought he must have a bit of a talk with his daughter first; so he went in and told them how there was a great white bear waiting outside, who had given his word to make them so rich if he could only have the youngest daughter.

The girl said "No!" outright. Nothing could get her to say anything else; so the man went out and settled it with the white bear, that he should come again the next Thursday evening and get an answer. Meantime he talked to his daughter, and kept on telling her of all the riches they would get, and how well off she herself would be. At last she agreed to it, so she washed and mended her rags, and made herself as smart as she could. Soon she was ready for the trip, for she didn't have much to take along.

The next Thursday evening came the white bear to fetch her. She got on his back with her bundle, and off they went. After they had gone a good way, the white bear said, "Are you afraid?"

No, she wasn't.

"Just hold tight to my shaggy coat, and there's nothing to be afraid of," said the bear.

She rode a long, long way, until they came to a large steep cliff. The white bear knocked on it. A door opened, and they came into a castle, where there were many rooms all lit up; rooms gleaming with silver and gold. Further, there was a table set there, and it was all as grand as grand could be. Then the white bear gave her a silver bell; and when she wanted anything, she only had to ring it, and she would get it at once.

Well, after she had eaten, and it became evening, she felt

The great white bear was lonely when the lovely girl left him to visit her family

sleepy from her journey, and thought she would like to go to bed, so she rang the bell. She had barely rung it before she found herself in a room, where there was a bed made as fair and white as anyone would wish to sleep in, with silken pillows and curtains, and gold fringe. All that was in the room was gold or silver. After she had gone to bed, and put out the light, a man came and laid himself alongside her. It was the white bear, who cast off his pelt at night; but she never saw him, for he always came after she had put out the light. Before the day dawned he was up and off again. Things went on happily for a while, but at last she became quiet and sad. She was alone all day long, and she became very homesick to see her father and mother and brothers and sisters. So one day, when the white bear asked what was wrong with her, she said it was so lonely there, and how she longed to go home to see her father and mother and brothers and sisters, and that was why she was so sad, because she couldn't get to them.

"Well," said the bear, "that can happen all right, but you must promise me, not to talk alone with your mother, but only when the others are around to hear. She will want to take you by the hand and lead you into a room to talk alone with her. But you must not do that, or else you'll bring bad luck on both of us."

So one Sunday the white bear came and said they could now set off to see her father and mother. Off they went, she sitting on his back; and they went far and long. At last they came to a grand house. Her bothers and sisters were outside running about and playing. Everything was so pretty, it was a joy to see.

"This is where your father and mother live now," said the white bear. "Now don't forget what I told you, else you'll make us both unhappy."

No, heaven forbid, she'd not forget. When they reached the house, the white bear turned around and left her.

She went in to see her father and mother, and there was

In the middle of the night she arose and lit the candle

such joy, that there was no end to it. None of them could thank her enough for all she had done for them. They now had everything they could wish for, as good as good could be. Then they wanted to know how she was.

Well, she said, it was very good to live where she did; she had all she wished. I don't know what else she said, but I don't think she told any of them the whole story. That afternoon, after they had eaten dinner, everything happened as the white bear had said it would. Her mother

wanted to talk with her alone in her bedroom; but she remembered what the white bear had said, and wouldn't go with her.

"What we have to talk about we can talk about any time," she said, and put her mother off. But somehow or other, her mother got to her at last, and she had to tell her the whole story. She told her, how every night, after she had gone to bed, a man came and lay down beside her as soon as she had put out the light, and how she never saw him, because he was always up and away before the morning dawned; and how she was terribly sad, for she wanted so much to see him, and how she was by herself all day long, and how dreary, and lonesome it was.

"Oh dear," said her mother; "it may well be a troll you are sleeping with! But now I'll give you some good advice how to see him. I'll give you a candle stub, which you can carry home in your bosom; just light it while he is asleep, but be careful not to drop any tallow on him."

Yes, she took the candle, and hid it in her bosom, and that evening the white bear came and took her away.

But when they had gone a piece, the white bear asked if all hadn't happened as he had said.

She couldn't deny that it had.

"Take care," said he, "if you have listened to your mother's advice, you will bring bad luck on us both, and it will be finished with the two of us."

No, by no means!

So when she reached home, and had gone to bed, it was the same as before. A man came and lay down beside her; but in the middle of the night, when she heard that he was fast asleep, she got up and lit the candle. She let the light shine on him, and saw that he was the most handsome prince one ever set eyes on. She fell so deeply in love with him, that she thought she couldn't live if she didn't give him a kiss at once. And so she did, but as she kissed him

*The long-nosed princess desperately
wanted the golden apple*

she let three drops of hot tallow drip onto his shirt, and he woke up.

"What have you done?" he cried; "now you have made us both unlucky, for had you held out only this one year, I would have been free! I have a stepmother who has bewitched me, so that I am a white bear by day, and a man by night. But now all ties are broken between us. Now I must leave you for her. She lives in a castle east of the sun and west of the moon, and there, too, is a princess, one with a nose three yards long, and now I will have to marry her."

She cried and grieved, but there was no help for it; he had to go.

Then she asked if she could go with him.

No, she could not.

"Tell me the way, then" she said, "so I can look for you; surely I may do that."

Yes, she could do that, but there was no way leading to the place. It lay east of the sun and west of the moon, and she'd never find her way there.

The next morning, when she woke up, both the prince and the castle were gone, and she was lying on a little green patch, in the midst of the thick, dark forest, and by her side lay the same bundle of rags she had brought with her from her old home.

When she had rubbed the sleep out of her eyes, and cried until she was tired, she set out on her way, and walked many, many days, until she came to a high cliff. An old woman sat under it, and played with a golden apple which she tossed about. The girl asked her if she knew the way to the prince, who lived with his stepmother in the castle east of the sun and west of the moon, and who was to marry the princess with a nose three yards long.

"How did you come to know about him?" asked the old woman. "Maybe you are the girl who should have had him?"

Yes, she was.

"So, so; it's you, is it?" said the old woman. "Well, all I know about him is, that he lives in the castle east of the sun and west of the moon, and that you'll get there too late or never; but still you may borrow my horse, and you can ride him to my next neighbor. Maybe she'll be able to tell you; and when you get there just give the horse a switch under the left ear, and beg him to be off home. And you can take this golden apple along with you."

So she got on the horse, and rode a long, long time, until she came to another cliff, under which sat another old woman, with a golden carding comb. The girl asked her if she knew the way to the castle that lay east of the sun and west of the moon, and she answered, like the first old woman, that she knew nothing about it, except that it was east of the sun and west of the moon.

"And you'll get there too late or never; but you can borrow my horse to my next neighbor; maybe she'll tell you all about it; and when you get there, just switch the horse under the left ear, and beg him to be off for home."

This old woman gave her the golden carding comb; she might find some use for it, she said. So the girl got up on

the horse, and again rode a long, long way. At last she came to another great cliff, under which sat another old woman, spinning with a golden spinning wheel. She asked her, as well, if she knew the way to the prince, and where the castle was that lay east of the sun and west of the moon. But it was the same thing over again.

"Perhaps you are the one who should have had the prince?" said the old woman.

Yes, that she was.

But she didn't know the way any better than the other two. She knew it was east of the sun and west of the moon, but that was all.

"And you'll get there too late or never; but I'll lend you my horse, and then I think you'd best ride to the east wind and ask him; maybe he knows his way around those parts,

She walked for many days until she came to a high cliff

and can blow you there. When you get to him, just give the horse a switch under the left ear, and he'll trot home by himself."

She too gave her her golden spinning wheel. "Maybe you'll find a use for it," said the old woman.

She rode many weary days, before she got to the east wind's house, but at last she did reach it, and she asked the east wind if he could tell her the way to the prince who lived east of the sun and west of the moon. Yes, the east wind had often heard tell of it, the prince and the castle, but he didn't know the way there, for he had never blown so far.

"But, if you want, I'll go with you to my brother the west wind. Maybe he knows, for he's much stronger. If you will just get on my back I'll carry you there."

Yes, she got on his back, and off they went in a rush.

When they arrived at the west wind's house, the east wind said the girl he had brought was the one who was supposed to have had the prince who lived in the castle east of the sun and west of the moon. She had set out to find him, and he had brought her here, and would be glad to know if the west wind knew how to get to the castle.

"No," said the west wind, "I've never blown so far; but if you want, I'll go with you to our brother the south wind, for he's much stronger than either of us, and he has flown far and wide. Maybe he'll tell you. Get on my back, and I'll carry you to him."

Yes, she got on his back, and so they traveled to the south wind, and I think it didn't take long at all.

When they got there, the west wind asked him if he could tell her the way to the castle that lay east of the sun and west of the moon, for she was the one who was supposed to have had the prince who lived there.

"Is that so?" said the south wind. "Is she the one? Well, I have visited a lot of places in my time, but I have not yet blown there. If you want, I'll take you to my brother the north wind; he is the oldest and strongest of us all, and if he doesn't know where it is, you'll never find anyone in the world to tell you. Get on my back, and I'll carry you there."

Yes, she got on his back, and away he left his house at a good clip. They were not long underway. When they reached the north wind's house he was so wild and cross, that he blew cold gusts at them from a long way off. "Blast you both, what do you want?" he roared at them from afar, so that it struck them with an icy shiver.

"Well," said the south wind, "you don't need to bluster so, for here I am, your brother, the south wind, and here is the girl who was supposed to have had the prince who lives in the castle that lies east of the sun and west of the moon, and now she wants to ask you if you ever were there, and can show her the way, for she wants so much to find him again."

"Yes, I know where it is," said the north wind; "a single time I blew an aspen leaf there, but afterward I was so tired that I couldn't blow a puff for many days. But if you really wish to go there, and aren't afraid to come along with me, I'll take you on my back and see if I can blow you there."

Yes, with all her heart; she wanted to and had to get there if it were at all possible; and she wouldn't be afraid, however madly he went.

"Very well, then," said the north wind, "but you must sleep here tonight, for we must have the whole day before us, if we're to get there at all."

Early next morning the north wind woke her, and puffed himself up, and blew himself out, and made himself so stout and big that he was gruesome to look at. Off they went high up through the air, as if they would not stop until they reached the end of the world.

Here on earth there was a terrible storm; acres of forest and many houses were blown down, and when it swept over the sea, ships wrecked by the hundred.

They tore on and on – no one can believe how far they went – and all the while they still went over the sea, and the north wind got more and more weary, and so out of breath he could barely bring out a puff, and his wings drooped and drooped, until at last he sunk so low that the tops of the waves splashed over his heels.

"Are you afraid?" said the north wind.

No, she wasn't.

They weren't very far from land by now, and the north wind had enough strength left that he managed to throw her up on the shore under the windows of the castle which lay east of the sun and west of the moon. But then he was so weak and worn out, that he had to stay there and rest many days before he could go home again.

The next morning the girl sat down under the castle window, and began to play with the golden apple. The first person she saw was the long-nosed princess who was to have the prince.

"What do you want for your golden apple, you girl?" said the long-nosed one, as she opened the window.

"It's not for sale, for gold or money," said the girl.

"If it's not for sale for gold or money, what is it that you will sell it for? You may name your own price," said the princess.

"Well, you can have it, if I may get to the prince, who lives here, and be with him tonight," said the girl whom the north wind had brought.

Yes, that could be done. So the princess took the golden apple; but when the girl came up to the prince's bedroom that night, he was fast asleep. She called him and shook him, and cried and grieved, but she could not wake him up. The next morning. as soon as day broke, the princess with the long nose came and drove her out.

That day she sat down under the castle windows and began to card with her golden carding comb, and the same thing happened. The princess asked what she wanted for it. She said it wasn't for sale for gold or money, but if she could have permission to go to the prince and be with him that night, the princess could have it. But when she went to his room she found him fast asleep again, and however much she called, and shook, and cried, and prayed, she couldn't get life into him. As soon as the first gray peep of day came, the princess with the long nose came, and chased her out again.

That day the girl sat down outside under the castle window and began to spin with her golden spinning wheel, and the princess with the long nose wanted to have it as well. She opened the window and asked what she wanted for it. The girl said, as she had said twice before, that it wasn't for sale for gold or money, but if she could go to the prince who was there, and be alone with him that night she could have it.

Yes, she would be welcome to do that. But now you must know that there were some Christians who had been taken there, and while they were sitting in their room, which was next to the prince's, they had heard how a woman had been in there, crying, praying, and calling to him for two nights in a row, and they told this to the prince.

That evening, when the princess came with a sleeping potion, the prince pretended to drink it, but threw it over his shoulder, for he could guess it was a sleeping potion. So, when the girl came in, she found the prince wide awake, and then she told him the whole story of how she had come there.

"Yes, you are the girl for me," said the prince. Now at last the prince and princess would be together and live happily ever after – despite the old troll woman's scheming

"Ah," said the prince, "you've come in the very nick of time, for tomorrow is to be our wedding day. But now I won't have the long-nose, and you are the only woman in the world who can set me free. I'll say that I want to see what my wife is fit for, and beg her to wash the shirt which has the three spots of tallow on it. She'll agree, for she doesn't know that you are the one who put them there. Only Christians, and not such a pack of trolls, can wash them out again. I'll say that I will marry only the woman who can wash them out, and ask you to try it."

So there was great joy and love between them all the night. But next day, when the wedding was planned, the prince said, "First of all, I'd like to see what my bride is fit for."

"Yes!" said the stepmother, with all her heart.

"Well," said the prince, "I've got a fine shirt which I'd like for my wedding shirt, but somehow or other it got three spots of tallow on it, which I must have washed out. I have sworn to marry only the woman who is able to do that. If she can't, then she's not worth having."

Well, that was no big thing they said, so they agreed, and the one with the long nose began to wash away as hard as she could, but the more she rubbed and scrubbed, the bigger the spots grew.

"Ah!" said the old troll woman, her mother, "you can't wash. Let me try."

But she had hardly touched the shirt, before it got far worse than before, and with all her rubbing, and wringing, and scrubbing, the spots grew bigger and blacker, and the shirt got ever darker and uglier.

Then all the other trolls began to wash, but the longer it lasted, the blacker and uglier the shirt grew, until at last it was as black all over as if it been up the chimney.

"Ah!" said the prince, "none of you is worth a straw; you can't wash. Why there, outside, sits a beggar girl, I'll bet she knows how to wash better than the whole lot of you. Come in, girl!" he shouted.

She came in.

"Can you wash this shirt clean, girl, you?" he said.

"I don't know," she said, "but I think I can."

And almost before she had taken it and dipped it into the water, it was as white as driven snow, and whiter still.

"Yes, you are the girl for me," said the prince.

At that the old troll woman flew into such a rage, she exploded on the spot, and the princess with the long nose after her, and the whole pack of trolls after her – at least I've never heard a word about them since.

As for the prince and princess, they set free all the poor Christians who had been captured and shut up there; and they took with them all the silver and gold, and flew away as far as they could from the castle that lay east of the sun and west of the moon.

The Vain Little Mouse

This popular Spanish tale has many variants. In most the mouse ends up being eaten by the cat on her wedding night but she sometimes escapes this fate. The vain 'heroine may be represented by an ant or a cockroach, rather than a mouse. From its oral origins, the tale was later included in *Lagrimas* (1839) and *La Gaviota* (1856), with the complete tale appearing later in *Cuentos, oraciones, adivinanzas y refranes populares* (1877). *The Little Roach* is also found in the folklore of Costa Rica, Cuba, Mexico and Panama.

"Oh no, I should be frightened by that noise," said the mouse.

The next to appear was a dog.

"My dear little mouse, you are so beautiful; will you marry me?" he said, to which the mouse replied, "I do not know. What will you do at night?"

"I will bark like this," said the dog "Wow, wow!"

"Oh no, I will not marry you," said the mouse, "That noise terrifies me."

The next to appear was a pig.

"My dear little mouse, you are so beautiful; will you marry me?" asked the pig.

And the mouse said, "I really do not know. What will you do at night?"

"I will grunt like this," said the pig, "Oink, oink!"

"Oh no, I will not marry you," said the vain little mouse, "That sound is so very common."

Once upon a time, there was a mouse who was very vain. One day when she was sweeping her neat little house she suddenly spotted something glittering on the floor. It was a gold coin.

The mouse picked it up and began to wonder what she might purchase with this money. "I know I'll buy some sugar candy ... but, no, no, that would be bad for my nice sharp teeth. Well, I'll buy a cake instead but, no, no, that might give me tummy ache. I know … I'll buy a lovely red bow for my tail."

The mouse popped the coin into her purse and then off she went to the market. There she asked the shopkeeper for a piece of his best red ribbon. She paid for it quickly and ran back to her house.

The next day the mouse tied the ribbon in a pretty bow around her tail and sat upon her balcony. Just then a rooster appeared and said, "My dear little mouse, you are so beautiful; will you marry me?"

The mouse said, "I do not know. Tell me first, what will you do at night?"

"I will go cock-a-doodle-doo," replied the rooster. "Just like this … Cock-a-doodle-doo!"

"Oh no, I will not marry you," said the mouse, "I do not like the loud noise you make."

The next to appear was a donkey.

"My dear little mouse, you do look so pretty," said the donkey. "Will you marry me?"

And the mouse asked, "What will you do at night?"

"I will bray like this," said the donkey. And he brayed, "Hee-haw!"

The vain little mouse scampered everywhere, cleaning her house

Then the pig trotted away and met a fine white cat that soon came to call upon the vain little mouse, saying, "You are so pretty, my dear little mouse; will you marry me?"

And the mouse said, "I cannot decide. What sound do you make at night?"

And the cat sang a beautiful song with a soft, sweet voice, "Meow, meow, meow!"

"Oh yes, I will marry you." cried the little mouse, "You sing the sweetest song I have ever heard."

And so they were married straight away – that vain little mouse and the soft-singing cat. And yes, the two did live together happily ever after but the little vain mouse had the worst of their shared life . . . for the cat had gobbled her up!

The Princess Nobody
A Tale of Fairyland

This charming tale by Andrew Lang dates from 1884. A timeless classic, it describes how Prince Comical seeks the beautiful nameless Princess after she has been banished to a distant place by the Water Fairy Queen – to protect her from an ugly dwarf. The cast of characters includes fairies, dwarfs, sprites and other tiny creatures set in the diminutive fairy world. The text is peppered with capital letters, as was the style at that time.

Once upon a time, when Fairies were much more common than they are now, there lived a King and a Queen. Their country was close to Fairy Land, and very often the little Elves would cross over the border, and come into the King's fields and gardens. The girl-fairies would swing out of the bells of the fuschias, and loll on the leaves, and drink the little drops of dew that fell down the stems. Here you may see some Fairies making themselves merry at a picnic on a fuschia, and an ugly little Dwarf is climbing up the stalk.

Now the King and Queen of the country next to Fairy Land were very rich, and very fond of each other; but one thing made them unhappy. They had no child, neither boy nor girl, to sit on the Throne when they were dead and gone. Often the Queen said she wished she had a child, even if it were no bigger than her thumb; and she hoped the Fairies might hear her and help her. But they never took any notice. One day, when the King had been counting out his money all day (the day when the tributes were paid in), he grew very tired. He took off his crown, and went into his garden. Then he looked all round his kingdom, and said, "Ah! I would give it all for a Baby!"

No sooner had the King said this, than he heard a little squeaking voice near his foot: "You shall have a lovely Baby, if you will give me what I ask."

The King looked down, and there was the funniest little Dwarf that ever was seen. He had a high red cap like a flower. He had a big moustache, and a short beard that curled outwards. His cloak was red, like his cap, and his coat was green, and he rode on a green Frog. Many people would have been frightened, but the King was used to Fairies.

"You shall have a beautiful Baby, if you will give me what I ask," said the Dwarf again.

"I'll give you anything you like," said the King.

"Then promise to give me Niente," said the Dwarf.

"Certainly," said the King (who had not an idea what Niente meant). "How will you take it?"

"I will take it," said the Dwarf, "in my own way, on my own day."

With that he set spurs to his Frog, which cleared the garden path at one bound, and he was soon lost among the flowers.

Well, next day, a dreadful war broke out between the Ghosts and the Giants, and the King had to set forth and fight on the side of his friends the Giants. A long, long time he was away; nearly a year. At last he came back to his own country, and he heard all the church bells ringing merrily. "What can be the matter?" said the King, and hurried to his Palace, where all the Courtiers rushed out and told him the Queen had got a Baby.

"Girl or a boy?" says the King.

"A Princess, your Majesty," says the Nurse, with a low curtsey, correcting him.

Well, you may fancy how glad the King was, though he would have preferred a boy.

"What have you called her?" he asked.

"Till your Majesty's return, we thought it better not to christen the Princess," said the Nurse, "so we have called her by the Italian name for Nothing: Niente; the Princess Niente, your Majesty."

When the King heard that, and remembered that he had promised to give Niente to the Dwarf, he hid his face in his hands and groaned. Nobody knew what he meant, or why he was sad, so he thought it best to keep it to himself. He went in and kissed the Queen, and comforted her, and looked at the Baby. Never was there a Baby so beautiful; she was like a Fairy's child, and so light, she could sit on a flower and not crush it. She had little wings on her back; and all the birds were fond of her. The peasants and common people (who said they "could not see why the first Royal baby should be called 'Ninety'") always spoke of her as the Princess Nobody. Only the Courtiers called her Niente. The Water Fairy was her Godmother, but (for a Fairy reason) they concealed her real name, and of course, she was not christened Niente. Next you may see her sitting teaching the little Birds to sing. They are all round her in a circle, each of them singing his very best. Great fun she and all her little companions had with the Birds; here they are, riding on them, and tumbling off when the Bird kicks.

The baby Princess is riding a Parrot, while one of her Maids of Honour teases an Owl. Never was there such a happy country; all Birds and Babies, playing together, singing, and as merry as the day was long.

Well, this joyful life went on till the Princess Niente was growing quite a big girl; she was nearly fourteen. Then, one day, came a tremendous knock at the Palace gates. Out rushed the Porter, and saw a little Dwarf, in a red cap, and a red cloak, riding a green Frog.

"Tell the King he is wanted," said the Dwarf.

The Porter carried this rude message, and the King went trembling to the door.

"I have come to claim your promise; you give me Niente," said the Dwarf, in his froggy voice.

Now the King had spoken long ago about his foolish promise, to the Queen of the Water Fairies, a very powerful person, and Godmother of his child.

"The Dwarf must be one of my people, if he rides a Frog," the Queen of the Water Fairies had said. "Just send him to me, if he is troublesome."

The King remembered this when he saw the Dwarf, so he put a bold face on it.

"That's you, is it?" said the King to the Dwarf. "Just you go to the Queen of the Water Fairies; she will have a word to say to you."

When the Dwarf heard that, it was his turn to tremble. He shook his little fist at the King; he half-drew his sword.

"I'll have Niente yet," he said, and he set spurs to his Frog, and bounded off to see the Queen of the Water Fairies.

It was night by the time the Dwarf reached the stream where the Queen lived, among the long flags and rushes and reeds of the river.

Here you see him by the river; how tired his Frog looks! He is talking to the Water Fairy. Well, he and the Water Fairy had a long talk, and the end of it was that the Fairy found only one way of saving the Princess. She flew to the King, and said, "I can only help you by making the Princess vanish clean away. I have a bird here on whose back she can fly away in safety. The Dwarf will not get her, but you will never see her again, unless a brave Prince can find her where she is hidden, and guarded by my Water Fairies."

Then the poor mother and father cried dreadfully, but they saw there was no hope. It was better that the Princess should vanish away, than that she should be married to a horrid rude Dwarf, who rode on a Frog. So they sent for the Princess, and kissed her, and embraced her, and wept over her, and (gradually she faded out of their very arms, and vanished clean away) then she flew away on the bird's back.

In Mushroom Land

Now all the Kingdom next Fairy Land was miserable, and all the people were murmuring, and the King and Queen were nearly melted in tears. They thought of all ways to recover their dear daughter, and at last the Queen hit on a plan.

"My dear," she said to the King, "let us offer to give our daughter for a wife, to any Prince who will only find her and bring her home."

"Who will want to marry a girl he can't see?" said the

The Elves dance at dusk in Mushroom Land

The Elves know that it is midnight when the mushrooms begin to grow

169

Girl-fairies swing from the bells of the fuschias

Land! They saw a great Snail race, the Snails running so fast, that some of the Fairy jockeys fell off on the grass. They saw a Fairy boy dancing with a Squirrel, and they found all the birds, and all the beasts, quite friendly and kind, and able to talk like other people. This was the way in old times, but now no beasts talk, and no birds, except Parrots only.

Now among all this gallant army of Princes, one was ugly, and he looked old, and odd, and the rest laughed at him, and called him the Prince Comical. But he had a kind heart. One day, when he was out walking alone, and thinking what he could do to find the Princess, he saw three bad little boys teasing a big Daddy Long Legs. They had got hold of one of his legs, and were pulling at it with all their might. When the Prince Comical saw this, he ran up and drove the bad boys away, and rubbed the limb of the Daddy Long Legs, till he gave up groaning and crying. Then the Daddy Long Legs sat up, and said in a weak voice, "You have been very kind to me; what can I do for you?"

"Oh, help me," said the Prince, "to find the Princess Niente! You fly everywhere; don't you know where she is?"

"I don't know," said the Daddy Long Legs, mournfully. "I have never flown so far. But I know that you are all in a very dangerous part of Fairy Land. And I will take you to an aged Black Beetle, who can give you the best advice."

So saying the Daddy Long Legs walked off with the Prince till they came to the Black Beetle.

"Can you tell this Prince," said the Daddy Long Legs, "where the Princess Niente is hidden?"

"I know it is in Mushroom Land," said the Beetle; "but he will want a guide."

"Will you be my guide?" asked the Prince.

"Yes," said the Beetle; "but what about your friends, the other Princes?" "Oh, they must come too; it would not be fair to leave them behind," said the Prince Comical.

He was the soul of honour; and though the others laughed at him, he would not take advantage of his luck, and run away from them.

"Well, you are a true Knight," said the Black Beetle; "but before we go into the depths of Mushroom Land, just you come here with me."

Then the Black Beetle pointed out to the Prince a great smooth round red thing, a long way off.

"That is the first Mushroom in Mushroom Land," said the Beetle. "Now come with me, and you shall see, what you shall see."

So the Prince followed the Beetle, till they came to the Mushroom.

"Climb up and look over," said the Beetle.

So the Prince climbed up, and looked over. There he saw a crowned King, sound asleep. Here is the Prince Comical (you see he is not very handsome!); and here is the King so sound asleep.

"Try to waken him," said the Beetle; "just try."

So the Prince tried to waken the King, but it was of no use.

King. "If they have not married pretty girls they can see, they won't care for poor Niente."

"Never mind; we can only try," said the Queen. So she sent out messengers into all the world, and sent the picture of the Princess everywhere, and proclaimed that the beautiful Princess Niente, and no less than three-quarters of the Kingdom would be given to the Prince that could find the Princess and bring her home. And there was to be a great tournament, or sham fight, at the Palace, to amuse all the Princes before they went on the search. So many Princes gathered together, all full of hope; and they rode against each other with spears and swords, and knocked each other about, and afterwards dined, and danced, and made merry. Some Fairy Knights, too, came over the border, and they fought with spears, riding Beetles and Grasshoppers, instead of horses. By all these warlike exercises, they increased their courage till they felt brave enough to fight all the Ghosts, and all the Giants, if only they could save the beautiful Princess.

Well, the tournaments were over, and off all the Princes went into Fairy Land. What funny sights they saw in Fairy

"Now, take warning by that," said the Black Beetle, "and never go to sleep under a Mushroom in Mushroom country. You will never wake, if you do, till the Princess Niente is found again."

Well, the Prince Comical said he would remember that, and he and the Beetle went off and found the other Princes. They were disposed to laugh at being led by a Black Beetle; but one of them, who was very learned, reminded them that armies had been led before by Woodpeckers, and Wolves, and Humming Birds.

So they all moved on, and at night they were very tired.

Now there were no houses, and not many trees, in Mushroom Land, and when night came all the Princes wanted to lie down under a very big Mushroom.

It was in vain that the Black Beetle and Prince Comical warned them to beware.

As they marched through Mushroom Land the twilight came upon them, and the Elves began to come out for

A green bower was full of fairy folk and butterflies

their dance, for Elves only dance at dusk, and they could not help joining them, which was very imprudent, as they had plenty to do the next day, and it would have been wiser if they had gone to sleep.

The Elves went on with their play till midnight, and exactly at midnight the Elves stopped their play, and undressed, and got up into the boughs of a big tree and went to sleep. You may wonder how the Elves know when it is midnight, as there are no clocks in Mushroom Land, of course. But they cannot really help knowing, as it is exactly at twelve that the Mushrooms begin to grow, and the little Mushrooms come up.

Now the Elves covered every branch of the tree, and the Princes did not know where to lie down. At last they decided to lie down under a very big Mushroom.

"Nonsense," they said. "You may sleep out in the open air, if you like; we mean to make ourselves comfortable here."

So they all lay down under the shelter of the Mushroom, and Prince Comical slept in the open air. In the morning he wakened, feeling very well and hungry and off he set

to call his friends. But he might as well have called the Mushroom itself. There they all lay under its shade; and though some of them had their eyes open, not one of them could move. The Prince shook them, dragged them, shouted at them, and pulled their hair. But the more he shouted and dragged, the louder they snored; and the worst of it was, that he could not pull them out of the shadow of the Magic Mushroom. So there he had to leave them, sound asleep.

The Prince thought the Elves could help him perhaps, so he went and asked them how to waken his friends. They were all awake, and their Fairies were dressing the Baby Elves. But they only said, "Oh! it's their fault for sleeping under a Mushroom. Anybody would know that is a stupid thing to do. Besides, we have no time to attend to them, as the sun will be up soon, and we must get these Babies dressed and be off before then."

"Why, where are you going to?" said the Prince.

"Ah! nobody knows where we go to in the day time," said the Elves.

And nobody does.

"Well, what am I to do now?" said the Prince to the Black Beetle.

"I don't know where the Princess is," said the Beetle; "but the Blue Bird is very wise, and he may know. Now your best plan will be to steal two of the Blue Bird's eggs, and not give them back till he tells you all he can."

Book cover from about 1884

So off they set for the Blue Bird's nest; and, to make a long story short, the Prince stole two of the eggs, and would not give them back, till the Bird promised to tell him all it knew. And the end of it was, that the Bird carried him to the Court of the Queen of Mushroom Land. She was sitting, in her Crown, on a Mushroom, and she looked very funny and mischievous.

The Prince took his hat off, kissed the Queen's hair and asked for the Princess.

"Oh, she's quite safe," said the Queen of Mushroom Land; "but what a funny boy you are. You are not half handsome enough for the Princess Niente."

The poor Prince blushed. "They call me Prince Comical," said he; "I know I'm not half good enough!"

"You are good enough for anything," said the Queen of Mushroom Land; "but you might be prettier."

Then she touched him with her wand, and he became as handsome a Prince as ever was seen, in a beautiful red silk doublet, slashed with white, and a long gold-coloured robe.

"Now you will do for my Princess Niente," said the Queen of Mushroom Land. "Blue Bird" (and she whispered in the Bird's ear), "take him away to the Princess Niente."

So they flew, and they flew, all day and all night, and next day they came to a green bower, all full of Fairies, and Butterflies, and funny little people. And there, with all her long yellow hair round her, there sat the Princess Niente. And the Prince Charming laid his Crown at her feet, and knelt on one knee, and asked the Princess to be his love and his lady. And she did not refuse him, so they were married in the Church of the Elves, and the Glowworm sent his torches, and all the bells of all the flowers made a message. And soon they were to travel home, to the King and the Queen.

Lost and Found

Now the Prince had found the Princess, and you might think that they had nothing to do but go home again. The father and mother of the Princess were wearying very much to hear about her. Every day they climbed to the bartizan of the Castle, and looked across the plain, hoping to see dust on the road, and some brave Prince riding back with their daughter. But she never came, and their hair grew grey with sorrow and time. The parents of the other Princes, too, who were all asleep under the Mushroom, were alarmed about their sons, and feared that they had all been taken prisoners, or perhaps eaten up by some Giant. But Princess Niente and Prince Charming were lingering in the enchanted land, too happy to leave the flowers, the brooks, and the Fairies.

The faithful Black Beetle often whispered to the Prince that it was time to turn homewards, but the Prince paid no more attention to his ally than if he had been an Ear-wig. So there, in the Valley Magical, the Prince and Princess might be wandering to this day but for a very sad accident. The night they were married, the Princess had said to the Prince, "Now you may call me Niente, or any pet name you

like; but never call me by my own name."

"But I don't know it," said the Prince. "Do tell me what it is?"

"Never," said the Princess; "you must never seek to know it."

"Why not?" said the Prince.

"Something dreadful will happen," said the Princess, "if ever you find out my name, and call me by it."

And she looked quite as if she could be very angry.

Now ever after this, the Prince kept wondering what his wife's real name could be, till he made himself quite unhappy.

"Is it Margaret?" he would say, when he thought the Princess was off her guard; or, "is it Joan?" "Is it Dorothy?" "It can't be Sybil, can it?"

But she would never tell him.

Now, one morning, the Princess awoke very early, but she felt so happy that she could not sleep. She lay awake and listened to the Birds singing and then she watched a

An evening ride

Fairy-boy teasing a Bird, which sang (so the boy said) out of tune, and another Fairy-baby riding on a Fly.

At last the Princess, who thought the Prince was sound asleep, began to croon softly a little song she had made about him and her. She had never told him about the song, partly because she was shy, and partly for another reason. So she crooned and hummed to herself,

Oh, hand in hand with Gwendoline,
While yet our locks are gold,
He'll fare among the forests green,
And through the gardens old;
And when, like leaves that lose their green,
Our gold has turned to grey,
Then, hand in hand with Gwendoline,
He'll fade and pass away!

"Oh, Gwendoline is your name, is it?" said the Prince, who had been wide awake, and listening to her song. And he began to laugh at having found out her secret, and tried to kiss her.

But the Princess turned very, very cold, and white like marble, so that the Prince began to shiver, and he sat down on a fallen Mushroom, and hid his face in his hands, and, in a moment, all his beautiful hair vanished, and his splendid clothes, and his gold train, and his Crown. He wore a red cap, and common clothes, and was Prince Comical once more. But the Princess arose, and she vanished swiftly away.

The poor Prince cried, and the Princess vanished away, and thus he was punished for being curious and prying. It is natural, you will say, that a man should like to call his wife by her name. But the Fairies would not allow it, and, what is more, there are still some nations who will not allow a woman to mention the name of her husband.

Well, here was a sad state of things! The Princess was lost as much as ever, and Prince Charming was changed back into Prince Comical.

Black Beetle sighed day and night, and mingled his tears with those of the Prince. But neither of them knew what to do. They wandered about the Valley Magical, and though it was just as pretty as ever, it seemed quite ugly and stupid to them. The worst of it was, that the Prince felt so foolish. After winning the greatest good fortune, and the dearest bride in the world, he had thrown everything away. He walked about crying, "Oh, Gwen – I mean oh, Niente! dear Niente! return to your own Prince Comical, and all will be forgiven!"

It is impossible to say what would have happened; and probably the Prince would have died of sorrow and hunger (for he ate nothing), if the Black Beetle had not one day met a Bat, which was the favourite charger of Puck. Now Puck, as all the world knows, is the Jester at the Court of Fairy Land. He can make Oberon and Titania – the King and Queen – laugh at the tricks he plays, and therefore they love him so much that there is nothing they would not do for him. So the Black Beetle began to talk about his master, the Prince, to the Bat Puck commonly rode; and the Bat, a good-natured creature, told the whole story to Puck. Now Puck was also in a good humour, so he jumped at once on his Bat's back, and rode off to consult the King and Queen of Fairy Land. Well, they were sorry for the Prince – he had only broken one little Fairy law after all – and they sent Puck back to tell him what he was to do. This was to find the Blue Bird again, and get the Blue Bird to guide him to the home of the Water Fairy, the Godmother of the Princess.

Long and far the Prince wandered, but at last he found the Blue Bird once more. And the Bird (very good-naturedly) promised to fly in front of him till he led him to the beautiful stream, where the Water Fairy held her court. So they reached it at last, and then the Blue Bird harnessed himself to the chariot of the Water Fairy, arid the chariot was the white cup of a Water Lily. Then he pulled, and pulled at the chariot, till he brought her where the Prince was waiting.

At first, when she saw him, she was rather angry. "Why did you find out my God-daughter's name?" she said; and the Prince had no excuse to make. He only turned red, and sighed. This rather pleased the Water Fairy.

"Do you love the Princess very much?" said she.

"Oh, more than all the world," said the Prince.

"Then back you go to Mushroom Land, and you will find her in the old place. But perhaps she will not be pleased to forgive you at first."

The Prince thought he would chance that, but he did not say so. He only bowed very low, and thanked the Water Fairy. Then off he set, with the Blue Bird to guide him, in search of Mushroom Land. At long and at last he reached it, and glad he was to see the little sentinel on the border of the country.

All up and down Mushroom Land the Prince searched, and at last he saw his own Princess, and he rushed up, and knelt at her feet, and held out his hands to ask pardon for having disobeyed the Fairy law.

But she was still rather cross, and down she jumped and ran round the Mushroom, and he ran after her.

So he chased her for a minute or two, and at last she laughed, and popped up her head over the Mushroom, and pursed up her lips into a cherry. And he kissed her across the Mushroom, and knew he had won back his own dear Princess, and they felt even happier than if they had never been parted.

"Journeys end in lovers meeting," and so do Stories. The Prince has his Princess once again, and I can tell you they did not wait long, this time, in the Valley Magical. Off they went, straight home, and the Black Beetle guided them, flying in a bee-line. Just on the further border of Mushroom Land, they came to all the Princes fast asleep. But when the Princess drew near, they all wakened, and jumped up, and they slapped the fortunate Prince on the back, and wished him luck, and cried, "Hullo, Comical, old chap; we hardly knew you! Why, you've grown quite handsome!" And so he had; he was changed into Prince Charming again, but he was so happy he never noticed it, for he was not conceited. But the Princess noticed it, and she loved him all the better. Then they all made a procession, with the Black Beetle marching at the head; indeed, they called him "Black Rod" now, and he was quite a Courtier.

So with flags flying, and music playing, they returned to the home of the Princess. And the King and Queen met them at the park gates, and fell on the neck of the Prince and Princess, and kissed them, and laughed, and cried for joy, and kissed them again. You may be sure the old Nurse was out among the foremost, her face quite shining with pleasure, and using longer words than the noblest there. And she admired the Prince very much, and was delighted that "her girl," as she called the Princess, had got such a good husband. So here we leave them, and that country remained always happy, and so it has neither history nor geography. Therefore you won't find it on any map, nor can you read about it in any book..

As to the Black Beetle, he was appointed to a place about the Court, but he never married, he had no children, and there are no other Black Beetles, consequently, in the country where the Prince and Princess became King and Queen.

Rapunzel

The Brothers Grimm first published
this story in 1812 as part of
Children's and Household Tales
but it was derived from the fairy
tale *Persinette* and originally
published in 1698 by Charlotte-
Rose de Caumont de La Force
(or Mademoiselle de La Force) – a
novelist and poet who was dauphine
to King Louis XIV of France.

A prince, riding through the wood,
heard Rapunzel singing in the tower

Once upon a time there lived a man and his wife who were very unhappy because they had no children. These good people had a little window at the back of their house, which looked into the most lovely garden, full of all manner of beautiful flowers and vegetables; but the garden was surrounded by a high wall, and no one dared to enter it, for it belonged to a witch of great power, who was feared by the whole world. One day the woman stood at the window overlooking the garden, and saw there a bed full of the finest rampion: the leaves looked so fresh and green that she longed to eat them. The desire grew day by day, and just because she knew she couldn't possibly get any, she pined away and became quite pale and wretched. Then her husband grew alarmed and said:

"What ails you, dear wife?"

"Oh," she answered, "if I don't get some rampion to eat out of the garden behind the house, I know I shall die."

The man, who loved her dearly, thought to himself, "Come! rather than let your wife die you shall fetch her some rampion, no matter the cost." So at dusk he climbed over the wall into the witch's garden, and, hastily gathering a handful of rampion leaves, he returned with them to his wife. She made them into a salad, which tasted so good that her longing for the forbidden food was greater than ever. If she were to know any peace of mind, there was nothing for it but that her husband should climb over the garden wall again, and fetch her some more. So at dusk over he got, but when he reached the other side he drew back in terror, for there, standing before him, was the old witch.

"How dare you," she said, with a wrathful glance, "climb into my garden and steal my rampion like a common thief? You shall suffer for your foolhardiness."

"Oh!" he implored, "pardon my presumption; necessity alone drove me to the deed. My wife saw your rampion from her window, and conceived such a desire for it that she would certainly have died if her wish had not been gratified." Then the Witch's anger was a little appeased, and she said:

"If it's as you say, you may take as much rampion away with you as you like, but on one condition only – that you give me the child your wife will shortly bring into the world. All shall go well with it, and I will look after it like a mother."

The man in his terror agreed to everything she asked, and as soon as the child was born the Witch appeared, and having given it the name of Rapunzel, which is the same as rampion, she carried it off with her.

Rapunzel was the most beautiful child under the sun. When she was twelve years old the Witch shut her up in a tower, in the middle of a great wood, and the tower had neither stairs nor doors, only high up at the very top a small window. When the old Witch wanted to get in she stood underneath and called out:

"Rapunzel, Rapunzel, Let down your golden hair," for Rapunzel had wonderful long hair, and it was as fine as spun gold. Whenever she heard the Witch's voice she unloosed her plaits, and let her hair fall down out of the window about twenty yards below, and the old Witch climbed up by it.

After they had lived like this for a few years, it happened one day that a Prince was riding through the wood and passed by the tower. As he drew near it he heard someone singing so sweetly that he stood still spell-bound, and listened. It was Rapunzel in her loneliness trying to while away the time by letting her sweet voice ring out into the wood. The Prince longed to see the owner of the voice, but he sought in vain for a door in the tower. He rode home, but he was so haunted by the song he had heard that he returned every day to the wood and listened. One day, when he was standing thus behind a tree, he saw the old Witch approach and heard her call out:

"Rapunzel, Rapunzel, Let down your golden hair."

Then Rapunzel let down her plaits, and the Witch climbed up by them.

"So that's the staircase, is it?" said the Prince. "Then I too will climb it and try my luck."

Rapunzel forgot her fear, and when he asked her to marry him she consented at once. "For," she thought, "he is young and handsome, and I'll certainly be happier with him than with the old Witch." So she put her hand in his and said:

"Yes, I will gladly go with you, only how am I to get down out of the tower? Every time you come to see me you must bring a skein of silk with you, and I will make a ladder of them, and when it is finished I will climb down by it, and you will take me away on your horse."

They arranged that till the ladder was ready, he was to come to her every evening, because the old woman was with her during the day. The old Witch, of course, knew nothing of what was going on, till one day Rapunzel, not thinking of what she was about, turned to the Witch and said:

"How is it, good mother, that you are so much harder to pull up than the young Prince? He is always with me in a moment."'

"Oh! you wicked child," cried the Witch. "What is this

German stamps show various scenes from the story of "Rapunzel"

So on the following day, at dusk, he went to the foot of the tower and cried:

"Rapunzel, Rapunzel, Let down your golden hair," and as soon as she had let it down the Prince climbed up.

At first Rapunzel was terribly frightened when a man came in, for she had never seen one before; but the Prince spoke to her so kindly, and told her at once that his heart had been so touched by her singing, that he felt he should know no peace of mind till he had seen her. Very soon

I hear? I thought I had hidden you safely from the whole world, and in spite of it you have managed to deceive me."

In her wrath she seized Rapunzel's beautiful hair, wound it round and round her left hand, and then grasping a pair of scissors in her right, snip snap, off it came, and the beautiful plaits lay on the ground. And, worse than this, she was so hard-hearted that she took Rapunzel to a lonely desert place, and there left her to live in loneliness and misery.

But on the evening of the day in which she had driven poor

Rapunzel away, the Witch fastened the plaits on to a hook in the window, and when the Prince came and called out:

"Rapunzel, Rapunzel, Let down your golden hair,"

she let them down, and the Prince climbed up as usual, but instead of his beloved Rapunzel he found the old Witch, who fixed her evil, glittering eyes on him, and cried mockingly:

"Ah, ah! you thought to find your lady love, but the pretty bird has flown and its song is dumb; the cat caught it, and will scratch out your eyes too. Rapunzel is lost to you for ever – you will never see her more."

The Prince was beside himself with grief, and in his despair he jumped right down from the tower, and, though he escaped with his life, the thorns among which he fell pierced his eyes out. Then he wandered, blind and miserable, through the wood, eating nothing but roots and berries, and weeping and lamenting the loss of his lovely bride. So he wandered about for some years, as wretched and unhappy as he could well be, and at last he came to the desert place where Rapunzel was living. Of a sudden he heard a voice which seemed strangely familiar to him. He walked eagerly in the direction of the sound, and when he was quite close, Rapunzel recognised him and fell on his neck and wept. But two of her tears touched his eyes, and in a moment they became quite clear again, and he saw as well as he had ever done. Then he led her to his kingdom, where they were received and welcomed with great joy, and they lived happily ever after.

As soon as Rapunzel had let down her amazingly long hair, the witch was able to climb up to her window

Fairy Things

Poem (written 1927) by Marion St John Webb (1888-1930)

There's fairy things,
An' things that isn't fairy;
An' if you look carefully to see
You sometimes think that something isn't fairy –
An' really it's as fairy as can be.

The fairy things
Have all belonged to fairies
Who've flowned away an' left the things behind.
Like Mother's little thimble in her workbox,
An' Daddy's watch – the one he lets me wind.

A fairy place
Is where there's been a fairy;
An' when you're there you always want to sing,
Like in the little tool-shed in the garden –
You feel as happy there as anything.

The other things,
The things that isn't fairy,
Are mizzerable, an' things that you can't bear,
Like when you go in Aunt Priscilla's parlour.
You know there isn't any fairies there!

The Elves and the Shoemaker

In this story the little elves are industrious, helpful fellows who come to the aid of a poor cobbler. Their tale was first included in a set of three elf stories in the Grimm Brothers' *Die Wichtelmänner*. There have been various cartoon versions including one with Elmer Fudd as the King of industrial Elves.

There was once a shoemaker, who worked very hard and was very honest: but still he could not earn enough to live upon; and at last all he had in the world was gone, save just leather enough to make one pair of shoes.

Then he cut his leather out, all ready to make up the next day, meaning to rise early in the morning to his work. His conscience was clear and his heart light amidst all his troubles; so he went peaceably to bed, left all his cares to Heaven, and soon fell asleep. In the morning after he had said his prayers, he sat himself down to his work; when, to his great wonder, there stood the shoes all ready made, upon the table. The good man knew not what to say or think at such an odd thing happening. He looked at the workmanship; there was not one false stitch in the whole job; all was so neat and true, that it was quite a masterpiece.

The same day a customer came in, and the shoes suited him so well that he willingly paid a price higher than usual for them; and the poor shoemaker, with the money, bought leather enough to make two pairs more. In the evening he cut out the work, and went to bed early, that he might get up and begin betimes next day; but he was saved all the trouble, for when he got up in the morning the work was done ready to his hand. Soon in came buyers, who paid him handsomely for his goods, so that he bought leather enough for four pair more. He cut out the work again overnight and found it done in the morning, as before; and so it went on for some time: what was got ready in the evening was always done by daybreak, and the good man soon became thriving and well off again.

One evening, about Christmas-time, as he and his wife were sitting over the fire chatting together, he said to her, "I should like to sit up and watch tonight, that we may see who it is that comes and does my work for me." The wife liked the thought; so they left a light burning, and hid themselves in a corner of the room, behind a curtain that was hung up there, and watched what would happen.

As soon as it was midnight, there came in two little naked dwarfs; and they sat themselves upon the shoemaker's bench, took up all the work that was cut out, and began to ply with their little fingers, stitching and rapping and tapping away at such a rate, that the shoemaker was all wonder, and could not take his eyes off them. And on they went, till the job was quite done, and the shoes stood ready for use upon the table. This was long before daybreak; and then they bustled away as quick as lightning.

The next day the wife said to the shoemaker. "These little wights have made us rich, and we ought to be thankful to them, and do them a good turn if we can. I am quite sorry to see them run about as they do; and indeed it is not very decent, for they have nothing upon their backs to keep off the cold. I'll tell you what, I will make each of them a shirt, and a coat and waistcoat, and a pair of pantaloons into the bargain; and do you make each of them a little pair of shoes."

The thought pleased the good cobbler very much; and one evening, when all the things were ready, they laid them on the table, instead of the work that they used to cut out, and then went and hid themselves, to watch what the little elves would do.

About midnight in they came, dancing and skipping, hopped round the room, and then went to sit down to their work as usual; but when they saw the clothes lying for them, they laughed and chuckled, and seemed mightily delighted.

Then they dressed themselves in the twinkling of an eye, and danced and capered and sprang about, as merry as could be; till at last they danced out at the door, and away over the green.

The good couple saw them no more; but everything went well with them from that time forward, as long as they lived.

The old shoemaker and his wife hid and watched the elves at work

The Red Shoes

This Hans Christian Andersen tale was first published in 1845 and republished in 1849. The story is about a girl forced to dance continually in her red shoes. It was adapted by Michael Powell and Emeric Pressburger into what would become one of the BFI's Top 10 British films (starring Moira Shearer). It has also been a Broadway musical and inspired the title song for a 1993 Kate Bush album.

There was once a little girl, very nice and very pretty, but so poor that she had to go barefooted all summer. And in winter she had to wear thick wooden shoes that chafed her ankles until they were red, oh, as red as could be.

In the middle of the village lived "Old Mother Shoemaker." She took some old scraps of red cloth and did her best to make them into a little pair of shoes. They were a bit clumsy, but well meant, for she intended to give them to the little girl. Karen was the little girl's name.

The first time Karen wore her new red shoes was on the very day when her mother was buried. Of course, they were not right for mourning, but they were all she had, so she put them on and walked barelegged after the plain wicker coffin.

The beautiful red leather shoes had been made for a count's daughter

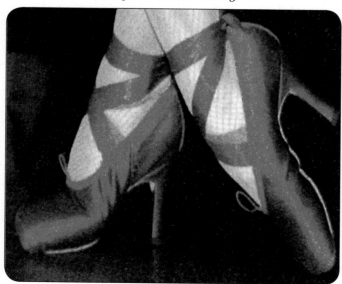

Just then a large old carriage came by, with a large old lady inside it. She looked at the little girl and took pity upon her. And she went to the parson and said: "Give the little girl to me, and I shall take good care of her."

Karen was sure that this happened because she wore red shoes, but the old lady said the shoes were hideous, and ordered them burned. Karen was given proper new clothes. She was taught to read, and she was taught to sew. People said she was pretty, but her mirror told her, "You are more than pretty. You are beautiful."

It happened that the Queen came travelling through the country with her little daughter, who was a Princess. Karen went with all the people who flocked to see them at the castle. The little Princess, all dressed in white, came to the window to let them admire her. She didn't wear a train, and she didn't wear a gold crown, but she did wear a pair of splendid red morocco shoes. Of course, they were much nicer than the ones "Old Mother Shoemaker" had put together for little Karen, but there's nothing in the world like a pair of red shoes!

When Karen was old enough to be confirmed, new clothes were made for her, and she was to have new shoes. They went to the house of a thriving shoemaker, to have him take the measure of her little feet. In his shop were big glass cases, filled with the prettiest shoes and the shiniest boots. They looked most attractive but, as the old lady did not see very well, they did not attract her. Among the shoes there was a pair of red leather ones which were just like those the Princess had worn. How perfect they were! The shoemaker said he had made them for the daughter of a count, but that they did not quite fit her.

"They must be patent leather to shine so," said the old lady.

"Yes, indeed they shine," said Karen. As the shoes fitted Karen, the old lady bought them, but she had no idea they were red. If she had known that, she would never have let Karen wear them to confirmation, which is just what Karen did.

Every eye was turned toward her feet. When she walked up the aisle to the chancel of the church, it seemed to her as if even those portraits of bygone ministers and their wives, in starched ruffs and long black gowns – even they fixed their eyes upon her red shoes. She could think of nothing else, even when the pastor laid his hands upon her head and spoke of her holy baptism, and her covenant with God, and her duty as a Christian. The solemn organ rolled, the children sang sweetly, and the old choir leader sang too, but Karen thought of nothing except her red shoes.

Once she began, her feet kept on dancing – over fields and valleys, in rain and sun, all day and all night

THE · RED SHOES

Before the afternoon was over, the old lady had heard from everyone in the parish that the shoes were red. She told Karen it was naughty to wear red shoes to church. Highly improper! In the future she was always to wear black shoes to church, even though they were her old ones.

Next Sunday there was holy communion. Karen looked at her black shoes. She looked at her red ones. She kept looking at her red ones until she put them on.

It was a fair, sunny day. Karen and the old lady took the path through the cornfield, where it was rather dusty. At

psalm. She forgot to say the Lord's Prayer.

Then church was over, and the old lady got into her carriage. Karen was lifting her foot to step in after her when the old soldier said, "Oh, what beautiful shoes for dancing!"

Karen couldn't resist taking a few dancing steps, and once she began her feet kept on dancing. It was as if the shoes controlled her. She danced round the corner of the church – she simply could not help it. The coachman had to run after her, catch her, and lift her into the carriage. But even there her feet went on dancing so that she gave

The angel had warned her that she would be forced to dance for ever

the church door they met an old soldier, who stood with a crutch and wore a long, curious beard. It was more reddish than white. In fact it was quite red. He bowed down to the ground, and asked the old lady if he might dust her shoes. Karen put out her little foot too.

"Oh, what beautiful shoes for dancing," the soldier said. "Never come off when you dance," he told the shoes, as he tapped the sole of each of them with his hand.

The old lady gave the soldier a penny, and went on into the church with Karen. All the people there stared at Karen's red shoes, and all the portraits stared too. When Karen knelt at the altar rail, and even when the chalice came to her lips, she could think only of her red shoes. It was as if they kept floating around in the chalice, and she forgot to sing the

the good old lady a terrible kicking. Only when she took her shoes off did her legs quiet down. When they got home the shoes were put away in a cupboard, but Karen would still go and look at them.

Shortly afterwards the old lady was taken ill, and it was said she could not recover. She required constant care and faithful nursing, and for this she depended on Karen. But a great ball was being given in the town, and Karen was invited. She looked at the old lady, who could not live in any case. She looked at the red shoes, for she thought there was no harm in looking. She put them on, for she thought there was no harm in that either. But then she went to the ball and began dancing. When she tried to turn to the right, the shoes turned to the left. When she wanted to dance up the ballroom, her shoes danced down. They danced down the stairs, into the street, and out through the gate of the town. Dance she did, and dance she must, straight into the dark woods.

Suddenly something shone through the trees, and she thought it was the moon, but it turned out to be the red-bearded soldier. He nodded and said, "Oh, what beautiful shoes for dancing."

She was terribly frightened, and tried to take off her shoes. She tore off her stockings, but the shoes had grown fast to her feet. And dance she did, for dance she must, over fields and valleys, in the rain and in the sun, by day and night. It was most dreadful by night. She danced over an unfenced graveyard, but the dead did not join her dance. They had better things to do. She tried to sit on a pauper's grave, where the bitter fennel grew, but there was no rest or peace for her there. And when she danced toward the open doors of the church, she saw it guarded by an angel with long white robes and wings that reached from his shoulders down to the ground. His face was grave and stern, and in his hand he held a broad, shining sword.

"Dance you shall!" he told her. "Dance in your red shoes until you are pale and cold, and your flesh shrivels down to the skeleton. Dance you shall from door to door, and wherever there are children proud and vain you must knock at the door till they hear you, and are afraid of you. Dance you shall. Dance always."

"Have mercy upon me!" screamed Karen. But she did not hear the angel answer. Her shoes swept her out through the gate, and across the fields, along highways and byways, forever and always dancing.

One morning she danced by a door she knew well. There was the sound of a hymn, and a coffin was carried out covered with flowers. Then she knew the old lady was dead. She was all alone in the world now, and cursed by the angel of God.

Dance she did and dance she must, through the dark night. Her shoes took her through thorn and briar that scratched her until she bled. She danced across the wastelands until she came to a lonely little house. She knew that this was where the executioner lived, and she tapped with her finger on his window pane.

"Come out!" she called. "Come out! I can't come in, for I am dancing."

The executioner said, "You don't seem to know who I am. I strike off the heads of bad people, and I feel my ax beginning to quiver."

"Don't strike off my head, for then I could not repent of my sins," said Karen. "But strike off my feet with the red shoes on them."

She confessed her sin, and the executioner struck off her feet with the red shoes on them. The shoes danced away with her little feet, over the fields into the deep forest. But he made wooden feet and a pair of crutches for her. He taught her a hymn that prisoners sing when they are sorry for what they have done. She kissed his hand that held the

ax, and went back across the wasteland.

"Now I have suffered enough for those red shoes," she said. "I shall go and be seen again in the church." She hobbled to church as fast as she could, but when she got there the red shoes danced in front of her, and she was frightened and turned back.

All week long she was sorry, and cried many bitter tears. But when Sunday came again she said, "Now I have suffered and cried enough. I think I must be as good as many who sit in church and hold their heads high." She started out unafraid, but the moment she came to the church gate she saw her red shoes dancing before her. More frightened than ever, she turned away, and with all her heart she really repented.

She went to the pastor's house, and begged him to give her work as a servant. She promised to work hard, and do all that she could. Wages did not matter, if only she could have a roof over her head and be with good people. The pastor's wife took pity on her, and gave her work at the parsonage. Karen was faithful and serious. She sat quietly in the evening, and listened to every word when the pastor read the Bible aloud. The children were devoted to her, but when they spoke of frills and furbelows, and of being as beautiful as a queen, she would shake her head.

When they went to church next Sunday they asked her to go too, but with tears in her eyes she looked at her crutches, and shook her head. The others went to hear the word of God, but she went to her lonely little room, which was just big enough to hold her bed and one chair. She sat with her hymnal in her hands, and as she read it with a contrite heart she heard the organ roll. The wind carried the sound from the church to her window. Her face was wet with tears as she lifted it up, and said, "Help me, O Lord!"

Then the sun shone bright, and the white-robed angel stood before her. He was the same angel she had seen that night, at the door of the church. But he no longer held a sharp sword. In his hand was a green branch, covered with roses. He touched the ceiling with it. There was a golden star where it touched, and the ceiling rose high. He touched the walls and they opened wide. She saw the deep-toned organ. She saw the portraits of ministers and their wives. She saw the congregation sit in flower-decked pews, and sing from their hymnals. Either the church had come to the poor girl in her narrow little room, or it was she who had been brought to the church. She sat in the pew with the pastor's family. When they had finished the hymn, they looked up and nodded to her.

"It was right for you to come, little Karen," they said.

"It was God's own mercy," she told them.

The organ sounded and the children in the choir sang, softly and beautifully. Clear sunlight streamed warm through the window, right down to the pew where Karen sat. She was so filled with the light of it, and with joy and with peace, that her heart broke. Her soul travelled along the shaft of sunlight to heaven, where no one questioned her about the red shoes.

The Bremen Town Musicians

This story is from *The Fairy Book* by Miss Mulock but it was also part of the Brothers Grimm collection. There have been many cartoons and animated versions of the story and even a *Muppets Musicians of Bremen.* Statues modeled after the Town Musicians of Bremen statue have been set up in front of each of the five German veterinary schools.

"You crow loud enough to deafen one,"
said the donkey

There was a man who owned a donkey, which had carried his sacks to the mill industriously for many years, but whose strength had come to an end, so that the poor beast grew more and more unfit for work. The master determined to stop his food, but the donkey, discovering that there was no good intended to him, ran away and took the road to Bremen: "There," thought he, "I can turn Town Musician."

When he had gone a little way, he found a hound lying on the road and panting, like one who was tired with running. "Hollo! what are you panting so for, worthy Seize 'em?" asked the donkey.

"Oh!" said the dog, "just because I am old, and get weaker every day, and cannot go out hunting, my master wanted to kill me, so I have taken leave of him; but how shall I gain my living now?"

"I'll tell you what," said the donkey, "I am going to Bremen to be Town Musician; come with me and take to music too. I will play the lute, and you shall beat the drum."

The dog liked the idea, and they traveled on. It was not long before they saw a cat sitting by the road, making a face like three rainy days.

"Now then, what has gone wrong with you old Whiskers?" said the donkey.

"Who can be merry when his neck is in danger?" answered the cat. "Because I am advanced in years, and my teeth are blunt, and I like sitting before the fire and purring better than chasing the mice about, my mistress wanted to drown me. I have managed to escape, but good advice is scarce; tell me where I shall go to?"

"Come with us two to Bremen; you understand serenading; you also can become a Town Musician."

The cat thought it a capital idea, and went with them. Soon after the three runaways came to a farmyard, and there sat a cock on the gate, crowing with might and main.

"You crow loud enough to deafen one," said the donkey; "what is the matter with you?"

"I prophesied fair weather," said the cock, "because it is our good mistress's washing-day, and she wants to dry the clothes; but because to-morrow is Sunday, and company is coming, the mistress has no pity on me, and has told the cook to put me into the soup to-morrow, and I must have my head cut off to-night: so now I am crowing with all my might as long as I can."

"O you old Redhead," said the donkey, "you had better come with us; we are going to Bremen, where you will certainly find something better than having your head cut off; you have a good voice, and if we all make music together, it will be something striking."

The cock liked the proposal, and they went on, all four together.

But they could not reach the city of Bremen in one day, and they came in the evening to a wood, where they agreed to spend the night. The donkey and the dog laid themselves down under a great tree, but the cat and the cock went higher – the cock flying up to the topmost branch, where he was safest. Before he went to sleep he looked round towards all the four points of the compass, and he thought he saw a spark shining in the distance. He called to his companions that there must be a house not far off; for he could see a light. The donkey said: "Then we must rise and go to it, for the lodgings here are very bad;" and the dog said, "Yes; a few bones with a little flesh on them would do me good." So they took the road in the direction where the light was, and soon saw it shine brighter; and it got larger and larger till they came to a brilliantly-illumined robber's house. The donkey, being the biggest, got up at the window and looked in.

What do you see, Greybeard?" said the cock.

"What do I see?" answered the donkey: "a table covered with beautiful food and drink, and robbers are sitting round it and enjoying themselves."

Stamps depict all the animal musicians

"That would do nicely for us," said the cock.

"Yes, indeed, if we were only there," replied the donkey.

The animals then consulted together how they should manage to drive out the robbers, till at last they settled on a plan. The donkey was to place himself with his forefeet on the window-sill, the dog to climb on the donkey's back, and the cat on the dog's, and, at last, the cock was to fly up and perch himself on the cat's head. When that was done, at a signal they began their music all together: the donkey brayed, the dog barked, the cat mewed, and the cock crowed; then, with one great smash, they dashed through the window into the room, so that the glass clattered down. The robbers jumped up at this dreadful

noise, thinking that nothing less than a ghost was coming in, and ran away into the wood in a great fright. The four companions then sat down at the table, quite content with what was left there, and ate as if they were expecting to fast for a month to come.

When the four musicians had finished, they put out the light, and each one looked out for a suitable and comfortable sleeping-place. The donkey lay down on the dunghill, the dog behind the door, the cat on the hearth near the warm ashes, and the cock set himself on the hen-roost; and, as they were all tired with their long journey, they soon went to sleep. Soon after midnight, as the robbers in the distance could see that no more lights were burning in the house, and as all seemed quiet, the captain said, "We ought not to have let ourselves be scared so easily," and sent one of them to examine the house. The messenger found everything quiet, went into the kitchen to light a candle, and, thinking the cat's shining fiery eyes were live coals, he held a match to them to light it. But the cat did not understand the joke, flew in his face, spat at him, and scratched. He was dreadfully frightened, ran away, and was going out of the back door; when the dog, who was lying there, jumped up and bit him in the leg. As he ran through the yard, past the dunghill, the donkey gave him a good kick with his hind-foot; and the cock being awakened, and made quite lively by the noise, called out from the hen-roost "Cock-a-doodle-doo!"

The robber ran as hard as he could, back to the captain, and said: "Oh, dear! in the house sits a horrid old witch, who blew at me, and scratched my face with her long fingers; and by the door stands a man with a knife, who stabbed me in the leg; and in the yard lies a black monster, who hit me with a club; and up on the roof there sits the judge, who called out, 'Bring the rascal up here' – so I made the best of my way off."

From that time the robbers never trusted themselves again in the house; but the four musicians liked it so well that they could not make up their minds to leave it, and spent there the remainder of their days, as the last person who told the story is ready to avouch for a fact.

A vet's sign shows the animals one atop another

The animals never actually reach Bremen despite the title of the tale!

Jack and the Beanstalk

First published in 1807, the
story has oral tradition dating
back centuries A similar tale
called *Jack Spriggins and the
Enchanted Bean* was published
in 1734, and another beanstalk
tale, *The History of Mother
Twaddle*, arrived in 1807. The
notion of a ladder reaching up
into the sky has Biblical origins,
of course – with Jacob's ladder
and the Tower of Babel – while the
theme of rags to riches permeated
many a fairy tale. This is the story
as told by Joseph Jacobs.

There was once upon a time a poor widow who had an only son named Jack, and a cow named Milky-White. And all they had to live on was the milk the cow gave every morning, which they carried to the market and sold. But one morning Milky-White gave no milk, and they didn't know what to do.

"What shall we do, what shall we do?" said the widow, wringing her hands.

"Cheer up, mother, I'll go and get work somewhere," said Jack.

"We've tried that before, and nobody would take you," said his mother. "We must sell Milky-White and with the money start a shop, or something."

"All right, mother," says Jack. "It's market day today, and I'll soon sell Milky-White, and then we'll see what we can do."

So he took the cow's halter in his hand, and off he started. He hadn't gone far when he met a funny-looking old man, who said to him, "Good morning, Jack."

"Good morning to you," said Jack, and wondered how he knew his name.

"Well, Jack, and where are you off to?" said the man.

"I'm going to market to sell our cow there."

"Oh, you look the proper sort of chap to sell cows," said the man. "I wonder if you know how many beans make five."

"Two in each hand and one in your mouth," says Jack, as sharp as a needle.

"Right you are," says the man, "and here they are, the very beans themselves," he went on, pulling out of his pocket a number of strange-looking beans. "As you are so sharp," says he, "I don't mind doing a swap with you – your cow for these beans."

"Go along," says Jack. "Wouldn't you like it?"

"Ah! You don't know what these beans are," said the man. "If you plant them overnight, by morning they grow right up to the sky."

"Really?" said Jack. "You don't say so."

"Yes, that is so. And if it doesn't turn out to be true you can have your cow back."

"Right," says Jack, and hands him over Milky-White's halter and pockets the beans.

Back goes Jack home, and as he hadn't gone very far it wasn't dusk by the time he got to his door.

"Back already, Jack?" said his mother. "I see you haven't got Milky-White, so you've sold her. How much did you get for her?"

"You'll never guess, mother," says Jack.

"No, you don't say so. Good boy! Five pounds? Ten? Fifteen? No, it can't be twenty."

"I told you you couldn't guess. What do you say to these beans? They're magical. Plant them overnight and – "

"What!" says Jack's mother. "Have you been such a fool, such a dolt, such an idiot, as to give away my Milky-White, the best milker in the parish, and prime beef to boot, for

Jack scrambled up the tall beanstalk

a set of paltry beans? Take that! Take that! Take that! And as for your precious beans here they go out of the window. And now off with you to bed. Not a sup shall you drink, and not a bit shall you swallow this very night."

So Jack went upstairs to his little room in the attic, and sad and sorry he was, to be sure, as much for his mother's sake as for the loss of his supper.

At last he dropped off to sleep.

When he woke up, the room looked so funny. The sun was shining into part of it, and yet all the rest was quite dark and shady. So Jack jumped up and dressed himself and went to the window. And what do you think he saw? Why, the beans his mother had thrown out of the window into the garden had sprung up into a big beanstalk which went up and up and up till it reached the sky. So the man spoke truth after all.

The beanstalk grew up quite close past Jack's window, so all he had to do was to open it and give a jump onto the beanstalk which ran up just like a big ladder. So Jack climbed, and he climbed, and he climbed, and he climbed, and he climbed, and he climbed, and he climbed till at last he reached the sky. And when he got there he found a long broad road going as straight as a dart. So he walked along, and he walked along, and he walked along till he came to a great big tall house, and on the doorstep there was a great big tall woman.

"Good morning, mum," says Jack, quite polite-like. "Could you be so kind as to give me some breakfast?" For he hadn't had anything to eat, you know, the night before, and was as hungry as a hunter.

"It's breakfast you want, is it?" says the great big tall woman. "It's breakfast you'll be if you don't move off from here. My man is an ogre and there's nothing he likes better than boys broiled on toast. You'd better be moving on or he'll be coming."

"Oh! please, mum, do give me something to eat, mum. I've had nothing to eat since yesterday morning, really and truly, mum," says Jack. "I may as well be broiled as die of hunger."

Well, the ogre's wife was not half so bad after all. So she took Jack into the kitchen, and gave him a hunk of bread and cheese and a jug of milk. But Jack hadn't half finished these when thump! thump! thump! the whole house began to tremble with the noise of someone coming.

"Goodness gracious me! It's my old man," said the ogre's wife. "What on earth shall I do? Come along quick and jump in here." And she bundled Jack into the oven just as the ogre came in.

He was a big one, to be sure. At his belt he had three calves strung up by the heels, and he unhooked them and threw them down on the table and said, "Here, wife, broil me a couple of these for breakfast. Ah! what's this I smell?

Fee-fi-fo-fum,

I smell the blood of an Englishman,

Be he alive, or be he dead,

I'll have his bones to grind my bread."

"Nonsense, dear," said his wife. "You're dreaming. Or perhaps you smell the scraps of that little boy you liked so much for yesterday's dinner. Here, you go and have a wash and tidy up, and by the time you come back your breakfast'll be ready for you."

So off the ogre went, and Jack was just going to jump out of the oven and run away when the woman told him not. "Wait till he's asleep," says she; "he always has a doze after breakfast."

Well, the ogre had his breakfast, and after that he goes to a big chest and takes out a couple of bags of gold, and down he sits and counts till at last his head began to nod and he began to snore till the whole house shook again.

Then Jack crept out on tiptoe from his oven, and as he was passing the ogre, he took one of the bags of gold under his arm, and off he pelters till he came to the beanstalk, and then he threw down the bag of gold, which, of course, fell into his mother's garden, and then he climbed down

The giant slept deeply while Jack stole his gold

and climbed down till at last he got home and told his mother and showed her the gold and said, "Well, mother, wasn't I right about the beans? They are really magical, you see."

So they lived on the bag of gold for some time, but at last they came to the end of it, and Jack made up his mind to try his luck once more at the top of the beanstalk. So one fine morning he rose up early, and got onto the beanstalk, and he climbed, and he climbed, and he climbed, and he climbed, and he climbed, and he climbed till at last he came out onto the road again and up to the great tall house he had been to before. There, sure enough, was the great tall woman a-standing on the doorstep.

"Good morning, mum," says Jack, as bold as brass, "could you be so good as to give me something to eat?"

"Go away, my boy," said the big tall woman, "or else my man will eat you up for breakfast. But aren't you the youngster who came here once before? Do you know, that very day my man missed one of his bags of gold."

"That's strange, mum," said Jack, "I dare say I could tell you something about that, but I'm so hungry I can't speak till I've had something to eat."

Well, the big tall woman was so curious that she took him in and gave him something to eat. But he had scarcely begun munching it as slowly as he could when thump! thump! they heard the giant's footstep, and his wife hid Jack away in the oven.

All happened as it did before. In came the ogre as he did before, said, "Fee-fi-fo-fum," and had his breakfast off three broiled oxen.

Then he said, "Wife, bring me the hen that lays the golden eggs." So she brought it, and the ogre said, "Lay," and it laid an egg all of gold. And then the ogre began to nod his head, and to snore till the house shook.

Then Jack crept out of the oven on tiptoe and caught hold of the golden hen, and was off before you could say "Jack Robinson." But this time the hen gave a cackle which woke the ogre, and just as Jack got out of the house he heard him calling, "Wife, wife, what have you done with my golden hen?"

And the wife said, "Why, my dear?"

But that was all Jack heard, for he rushed off to the beanstalk and climbed down like a house on fire. And when he got home he showed his mother the wonderful hen, and said "Lay" to it; and it laid a golden egg every time he said "Lay."

Well, Jack was not content, and it wasn't long before he determined to have another try at his luck up there at the top of the beanstalk. So one fine morning he rose up early and got to the beanstalk, and he climbed, and he climbed, and he climbed, and he climbed till he got to the top.

But this time he knew better than to go straight to the ogre's house. And when he got near it, he waited behind a bush till he saw the ogre's wife come out with a pail to get some water, and then he crept into the house and got into the copper. He hadn't been there long when he heard thump! thump! thump! as before, and in came the ogre and his wife.

"Fee-fi-fo-fum, I smell the blood of an Englishman," cried out the ogre. "I smell him, wife, I smell him."

"Do you, my dearie?" says the ogre's wife. "Then, if it's that little rogue that stole your gold and the hen that laid the golden eggs he's sure to have got into the oven." And they both rushed to the oven.

But Jack wasn't there, luckily, and the ogre' s wife said, "There you are again with your fee-fi-fo-fum. Why, of course, it's the boy you caught last night that I've just broiled for your breakfast. How forgetful I am, and how careless you are not to know the difference between live and dead after all these years."

So the ogre sat down to the breakfast and ate it, but every now and then he would mutter, "Well, I could have sworn –" and he'd get up and search the larder and the cupboards and everything, only, luckily, he didn't think of the copper.

After breakfast was over, the ogre called out, "Wife, wife, bring me my golden harp."

So she brought it and put it on the table before him. Then he said, "Sing!" and the golden harp sang most beautifully. And it went on singing till the ogre fell asleep,

and commenced to snore like thunder.

Then Jack lifted up the copper lid very quietly and got down like a mouse and crept on hands and knees till he came to the table, when up he crawled, caught hold of the golden harp and dashed with it towards the door.

But the harp called out quite loud, "Master! Master!" and the ogre woke up just in time to see Jack running off with his harp.

Jack ran as fast as he could, and the ogre came rushing after, and would soon have caught him, only Jack had a start and dodged him a bit and knew where he was going. When he got to the beanstalk the ogre was not more than twenty yards away when suddenly he saw Jack disappear like, and when he came to the end of the road he saw Jack underneath climbing down for dear life. Well, the ogre didn't like trusting himself to such a ladder, and he stood and waited, so Jack got another start.

But just then the harp cried out, "Master! Master!" and the ogre swung himself down onto the beanstalk, which shook with his weight. Down climbs Jack, and after him climbed the ogre.

By this time Jack had climbed down and climbed down and climbed down till he was very nearly home. So he called out, "Mother! Mother! bring me an ax, bring me an ax." And his mother came rushing out with the ax in her hand, but when she came to the beanstalk she stood stock still with fright, for there she saw the ogre with his legs just through the clouds.

But Jack jumped down and got hold of the ax and gave a chop at the beanstalk which cut it half in two. The ogre felt the beanstalk shake and quiver, so he stopped to see what was the matter. Then Jack gave another chop with the ax, and the beanstalk was cut in two and began to topple over. Then the ogre fell down and broke his crown, and the beanstalk came toppling after.

Then Jack showed his mother his golden harp, and what with showing that and selling the golden eggs, Jack and his mother became very rich, and he married a great princess, and they lived happy ever after.

Illustration of Jack with the singing harp by Walter Crane

The Field of Boliauns

In Ireland a leprechaun is traditionally a little old man, whose presence marks a spot where buried treasure or a crock of gold lie concealed, often at the end of a rainbow. Many an excited farmer has tried to mark the place where he saw the little fellow and presumed treasure to be hidden but the guile of the leprechaun generally wins through and the treasure proves elusive. Here the cunning creature is, in fact, a clurichaun, an Irish fairy often described as the night-time version of the leprechaun, who goes out to drink after finishing his daily chores.

Tom Fitzpatrick was the eldest son of a comfortable farmer who lived at Ballincollig. Tom was just turned of nine-and-twenty, when he met the following adventure, and was as clever, clean, tight, good-looking a boy as any in the whole county Cork. One fine day in harvest – it was indeed Lady-day in harvest, that every body knows to be one of the greatest holidays in the year – Tom was taking a ramble through the ground, and went sauntering along the sunny side of a hedge, thinking in himself, where would be the great harm if people, instead of idling and going about doing nothing at all, were to shake out the hay, and bind and stook the oats that was lying on the ledge, especially as the weather had been rather broken of late, he all of a sudden heard a clacking sort of noise a little before him, in the hedge.

"Dear me," said Tom, "but isn't it surprising to hear the stonechatters singing so late in the season?" So Tom stole on, going on the tops of his toes to try if he could get a sight of what was making the noise, to see if he was right in his guess. The noise stopped; but as Tom looked sharply through the bushes, what should he see in a nook of the hedge but a brown pitcher that might hold about a gallon and a half of liquor; and by and by a little wee diny dony bit of an old man, with a little motty of a cocked hat stuck upon the top of his head, and a deeshy daushy leather apron hanging

before him, pulled out a little wooden stool, and stood up upon it and dipped a little piggin into the pitcher, and took out the full of it, and put it beside the stool, and then sat down under the pitcher, and began to work at putting a heel-piece on a bit of a brogue just fitting for himself. " Well, by the powers!" said Tom to himself, "I often heard tell of the Cluricaune; and, to tell God's truth, I never rightly believed in them – but here's one of them in real earnest. If I go knowingly to work, I'm a made man. They say a body must never take their eyes off them, or they'll escape."

Tom now stole on a little farther, with his eye fixed on the little man just as a cat does with a mouse, or, as we read in hooks, the rattle-snake does with the birds he wants to enchant. So when he got up quite close to him, "God bless your work, neighbour," said Tom.

The little man raised up his head, and "Thank you kindly," said he.

"I wonder you'd be working on the holy-day?" said Tom.

"That's my own business, not yours," was the reply.

"Well, may be you 'd be civil enough to tell us what you've got in the pitcher there?" said Tom.

"That I will, with pleasure," said he: "It's good beer."

"Beer!" said Tom: "Thunder and fire! Where did you get it?"

A traditional Irish leprechaun

"Where did I get it, is it? Why, I made it. And what do you think I made it of?"

"Devil a one of me knows," said Tom, "but of malt, I suppose; what else?"

"There you're out. I made it of heath."

"Of heath!" said Tom, bursting out laughing: "Sure you don't think me to be such a fool as to believe that?"

"Do as you please," said he, "but what I tell you is the truth. Did you never hear tell of the Danes?"

"And that I did," said Tom: "weren't them the fellows we gave such a licking when they thought to take Limerick from us?"

"Hem!" said the little man drily "is that all you know about the matter?"

"Well, but about them Danes?" said Tom.

"Why, all the about them there is, is that when they were here they taught us to make beer out of the heath, and the secret's in my family ever since."

"Will you give a body a taste of your beer?" said Tom.

"I'll tell you what it is, young man – it would be fitter for you to be looking after your father's property than to be bothering decent, quiet people with your foolish questions. There now, while you're idling away your time here, there's the cows have broke into the oats, and are knocking the corn all about."

Tom was taken so by surprise with this, that he was just on the very point of turning round when he recollected himself; so, afraid that the like might happen again, he made a grab at the Cluricaune, and caught him up in his hand; but in his hurry he overset the pitcher, and spilt all the beer, so that he could not get a taste of it to tell what sort it was. He then swore what he would not do to him if he did not show him where his money was. Tom looked so wicked and so bloody-minded, that the little man was quite frightened; so, says he, "Come along with me a couple of fields off, and I'll show you a crock of gold." So they went, and Tom held the Cluricaune fast in his hand, and never took his eyes from off him, though they had to cross hedges, and ditches, and a crooked bit of bog (for the Cluricaune seemed, out of pure mischief, to pick out the hardest and most contrary way), till at last they came to a great field all full of boliaun buies [ragweed], and the Cluricaune pointed to a big boliaun, and, says he, "Dig under that boliaun, and you'll get the great crock all full of guineas."

Tom in his hurry had never minded the bringing a spade with him, so he thought to run home and fetch one; and that he might know the place again, he took off one of his red garters, and tied it round the boliaun.

"I suppose," said the Cluricaune, very civilly, "you've no farther occasion for me?"

"No," says Tom "You may go away now, if you please, and God speed you, and may good luck attend you wherever you go."

"Well, goodbye to you, Tom Fitzpatrick," said the Cluricaune, "and much good may do you, with what you'll get."

So Tom ran, for the dear life, till he came home, and got a spade, and then away with him, as hard as he could go, back to the field of boliauns; but when he got there, lo, and behold! not a boliaun in the field but had a red garter, the very identical model of his own, tied about it; and as to digging up the whole field, that was all nonsense, for there was more than forty good Irish acres in it. So Tom came home again with his spade on his shoulder, a little cooler than he went; and many's the hearty curse he gave the Cluricaune every time he thought of the neat turn he had served him.

The Cluricaune promised Tom he would show him a crock of gold

Tom cursed the Cluricaune every time he remembered the trick the little fellow had played

The Glass Mountain

This Polish fairy story was collected by Hermann Kletke and included in Andrew Lang's *Yellow Fairy Book*. It tells how a young but sharp-witted lad succeeds in surmounting obstacles to win the princess where many a brave knight has failed. The Brothers Grimm also had a Glassberg (glass mountain) story.

Once upon a time there was a Glass Mountain at the top of which stood a castle made of pure gold, and in front of the castle there grew an apple-tree on which there were golden apples.

Anyone who picked an apple gained admittance into the golden castle, and there in a silver room sat an enchanted Princess of surpassing fairness and beauty. She was as rich too as she was beautiful, for the cellars of the castle were full of precious stones, and great chests of the finest gold stood round the walls of all the rooms.

Many knights had come from afar to try their luck, but it was in vain they attempted to climb the mountain. In spite of having their horses shod with sharp nails, no one managed to get more than half-way up, and then they all fell back right down to the bottom of the steep slippery hill. Sometimes they broke an arm, sometimes a leg, and many a brave man had broken his neck even.

The beautiful Princess sat at her window and watched the bold knights trying to reach her on their splendid horses. The sight of her always gave men fresh courage, and they flocked from the four quarters of the globe to attempt the work of rescuing her. But all in vain, and for seven years the Princess had sat now and waited for some one to scale the Glass Mountain.

A heap of corpses both of riders and horses lay round the mountain, and many dying men lay groaning there unable to go any farther with their wounded limbs. The whole neighbourhood had the appearance of a vast churchyard. In three more days the seven years would be at an end, when a knight in golden armour and mounted on a spirited steed was seen making his way towards the fatal hill.

Sticking his spurs into his horse he made a rush at the mountain, and got up half-way, then he calmly turned his horse's head and came down again without a slip or stumble. The following day he started in the same way; the horse trod on the glass as if it had been level earth, and sparks of fire flew from its hoofs. All the other knights gazed in astonishment, for he had almost gained the summit, and in another moment he would have reached the apple-tree; but of a sudden a huge eagle rose up and spread its mighty wings, hitting as it did so the knight's horse in the eye.

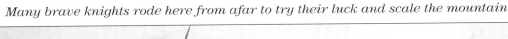

Many brave knights rode here from afar to try their luck and scale the mountain

189

The beast shied, opened its wide nostrils and tossed its mane, then rearing high up in the air, its hind feet slipped and it fell with its rider down the steep mountain side. Nothing was left of either of them except their bones, which rattled in the battered golden armour like dry peas in a pod.

And now there was only one more day before the close of the seven years. Then there arrived on the scene a mere schoolboy – a merry, happy-hearted youth, but at the same time strong and well-grown. He saw how many knights had broken their necks in vain, but undaunted he approached the steep mountain on foot and began the ascent.

For long he had heard his parents speak of the beautiful Princess who sat in the golden castle at the top of the Glass Mountain. He listened to all he heard, and determined that he too would try his luck. But first he went to the forest

he was so worn out, and his mouth was parched by thirst. A huge black cloud passed over his head, but in vain did he beg and beseech her to let a drop of water fall on him. He opened his mouth, but the black cloud sailed past and not as much as a drop of dew moistened his dry lips.

He caught a lynx and cut off its sharp claws

His feet were torn and bleeding, and he could only hold on now with his hands. Evening closed in, and he strained his eyes to see if he could behold the top of the mountain. Then he gazed beneath him, and what a sight met his eyes! A yawning abyss, with certain and terrible death at the bottom, reeking with half-decayed bodies of horses and riders! And this had been the end of all the other brave men who like himself had attempted the ascent.

It was almost pitch dark now, and only the stars lit up the Glass Mountain. The poor boy still clung on as if glued to

A merry schoolboy arrived on the very last day

The eagle kept a sharp look-out over the golden apple tree

and caught a lynx, and cutting off the creature's sharp claws, he fastened them on to his own hands and feet.

Armed with these weapons he boldly started up the Glass Mountain.

The sun was nearly going down, and the youth had not got more than half-way up. He could hardly draw breath

the glass by his blood-stained hands. He made no struggle to get higher, for all his strength had left him, and seeing no hope he calmly awaited death. Then all of a sudden he fell into a deep sleep, and forgetful of his dangerous position, he slumbered sweetly. But all the same, although he slept, he had stuck his sharp claws so firmly into the glass that he was quite safe not to fall.

The enchanted princess married the happy youth

remained in his flesh, and put the peel of one of the golden apples on the wound, and in one moment it was healed and well again. He pulled several of the beautiful apples and put them in his pocket; then he entered the castle. The door was guarded by a great dragon, but as soon as he threw an apple at it, the beast vanished.

At the same moment a gate opened, and the youth perceived a courtyard full of flowers and beautiful trees, and on a balcony sat the lovely enchanted Princess with her retinue.

As soon as she saw the youth, she ran towards him and greeted him as her husband and master. She gave him all her treasures, and the youth became a rich and mighty ruler. But he never returned to the earth, for only the mighty eagle, who had been the guardian of the Princess and of the castle, could have carried on his wings the enormous treasure down to the world. But as the eagle had lost its feet it died, and its body was found in a wood on the Glass Mountain.

One day when the youth was strolling about in the palace garden with the Princess, his wife, he looked down over the edge of the Glass Mountain and saw to his astonishment a great number of people gathered there. He blew his silver whistle, and the swallow who acted as messenger in the golden castle flew past.

'Fly down and ask what the matter is,' he said to the little bird, who sped off like lightning and soon returned saying:

'The blood of the eagle has restored all the people below to life. All those who have perished on this mountain are awakening up to-day, as it were from a sleep, and are mounting their horses, and the whole population are gazing on this unheard-of wonder with joy and amazement.'

Now the golden apple-tree was guarded by the eagle which had overthrown the golden knight and his horse. Every night it flew round the Glass Mountain keeping a careful look-out, and no sooner had the moon emerged from the clouds than the bird rose up from the apple-tree, and circling round in the air, caught sight of the sleeping youth.

Greedy for carrion, and sure that this must be a fresh corpse, the bird swooped down upon the boy. But he was awake now, and perceiving the eagle, he determined by its help to save himself.

The eagle dug its sharp claws into the tender flesh of the youth, but he bore the pain without a sound, and seized the bird's two feet with his hands. The creature in terror lifted him high up into the air and began to circle round the tower of the castle. The youth held on bravely. He saw the glittering palace, which by the pale rays of the moon looked like a dim lamp; and he saw the high windows, and round one of them a balcony in which the beautiful Princess sat lost in sad thoughts. Then the boy saw that he was close to the apple-tree, and drawing a small knife from his belt, he cut off both the eagle's feet. The bird rose up in the air in its agony and vanished into the clouds, and the youth fell on to the broad branches of the apple-tree.

Then he drew out the claws of the eagle's feet that had

They lived together in the palace on the mountain top

The Little Match Girl

First published in 1845, this rather sad story (as are quite a few Hans Christian Andersen tales) tells of a dying child's hopes and dreams. It was inspired by a woodcut of a poor little girl selling matches by Johan Thomas Lundbye that appeared in an 1843 calendar.

It was terribly cold and nearly dark on the last evening of the old year, and the snow was falling fast. In the cold and darkness, a poor little girl with bare head and naked feet, roamed thru the streets. It is true she had on a pair of slippers when she left home, but they were not of much use. They were very large, so large, indeed, for they had belonged to her Mother and the poor little girl had lost them in running across the street to avoid two carriages that were rolling at a terrible rate.

One of the slippers she could not find, and a boy seized the other and ran away with it saying he could use it as a cradle when he had children of his own. So the little girl went on with her little naked feet, which were quite red and blue with the cold. In an old apron she carried a number of matches, and had a bundle of them in her hands. No one had bought anything of her the whole day, nor had anyone given her even a penny. Shivering with cold and hunger, she crept along, looking like the picture of misery. The snowflakes fell on her fair hair, which hung

The little girl shivered with cold

in curls on her shoulders, but she regarded them not.

Lights were shining from every window, and there was a savory smell of roast goose, for it was New-year's eve, yes, she remembered that. In a corner, between two houses one of which projected beyond the other, she sank down and huddled herself together. She had drawn her little feet under her, but could not keep off the cold. And she dared not go home, for she had sold no matches.

Her father would certainly beat her; besides, it was almost as cold at home as here, for they had only the roof to cover them. Her little hands were almost frozen with the

Snowflakes fell as she huddled against the wall

cold. Ah! perhaps a burning match might be some good, if she could draw it from the bundle and strike it against the wall, just to warm her fingers. She drew one out – "scratch!" how it sputtered as it burnt. It gave a warm, bright light, like a little candle, as she held her hand over it. It was really a wonderful light. It seemed as though she was sitting by a large iron stove. How the fire burned! And seemed so beautifully warm that the child stretched out her feet as if to warm them, when, lo! the flame of the match went out!

The stove vanished, and she had only the remains of the half-burnt match in her hand.

She rubbed another match on the wall. It burst into a flame, and where its light fell upon the wall it became as transparent as a veil, and she could see into the room. The table was covered with a snowy white table cloth on which stood a splendid dinner service and a steaming roast goose stuffed with apples and dried plums. And what was still more wonderful, the goose jumped down from the dish and waddled across the floor, with a knife and fork in its beak, to the little girl. Then the match went out, and there remained nothing but the thick, damp, cold wall before her.

Her grandmother and she would be together at last

By the light of the match she saw a beautiful Christmas tree

She lighted another match, and then she found herself sitting under a beautiful Christmas tree. It was larger and more beautifully decorated than the one she had seen through the rich merchant's glass door. Thousands of tapers were burning upon the green branches, and colored pictures, like those she had seen in the shop-windows, looked down upon it all. The little one stretched out her hand towards them, and the match went out.

The Christmas lights rose higher and higher till they looked to her like the stars in the sky. Then she saw a star fall, leaving behind it it a bright streak of fire. "Someone is dying," thought the little girl, for her old grandmother, the only one who had ever loved her, and who was now in Heaven had told her that when a star falls, a soul was going up to God.

She again rubbed a match on the wall, and the light shone round her; in the brightness stood her old grandmother, clear and shining, yet mild and loving in her appearance.

"Grandmother," cried the little one, "O take me with you; I know you will go away when the match burns out; you will vanish like the warm stove, the roast goose, and the large glorious Christmas-tree." And she made haste to light the whole bundle of matches, for she wished to keep her grandmother there. And the matches glowed with a light that was brighter than the noon-day and her grandmother had never appeared so large or so beautiful. She took the little girl in her arms, and they both flew upwards in brightness and joy far above the earth, where there was neither cold nor hunger nor pain, for they were with God.

In the dawn of morning there lay the poor little one, with pale cheeks and smiling mouth, leaning against the wall. She had been frozen on the last evening of the year; and the New-year's sun rose and shone upon a little child. The child still sat, holding the matches in her hand, one bundle of which was burnt.

"She tried to warm herself," said some. No one imagined what beautiful things she had seen, nor into what glory she had entered with her grandmother, on New-year's day.

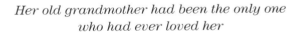

Her old grandmother had been the only one who had ever loved her

The Golden Goose

Part of the Brothers Grimm collection, this is a simple fun story about how the youngest of three sons, called *Dummerly* (little fool) inadvertently makes a princess laugh and thus wins her hand in marriage.

There was once a man who had three sons. The youngest was called Dummerly, and was on all occasions scorned and ill-treated by the whole family. It happened that the eldest took it into his head one day to go into the forest to cut wood; and his mother gave him a delicious meat pie and a bottle of wine to take with him, that he might sustain himself at his work. As he went into the forest, a little old man bid him good day, and said, "Give me a little bit of meat from your plate, and a little wine out of your flask; I am very hungry and thirsty." But this clever young man said, "Give you my meat and wine! No, I thank you; there would not be enough left for me;" and he went on his way. He soon began to chop down a tree; but he had not worked long before he missed his stroke, and cut himself, and was obliged to go home and have the wound bound up. Now, it was the little old man who caused him this mischief.

Next the second son went out to work; and his mother gave him, too, a meat pie and a bottle of wine. And the same little old man encountered him also, and begged him for something to eat and drink. But he, too, thought himself extremely clever, and said, "Whatever you get, I shall be without; so go your way!" The little man made sure that he should have his reward; and the second stroke that he struck at a tree, hit him on the leg, so that he too was compelled to go home.

Then Dummerly said, "Father, I should like to go and cut fuel too." But his father replied, "Your brothers have both maimed themselves; you had better stop at home, for you know nothing of the job." But Dummerly was very urgent; and at last his father said, "Go your way; you will be wiser when you have suffered for your foolishness." And his mother gave him only some dry bread, and a bottle of sour ale; but when he went into the forest, he met the little old man, who said, "Give me some meat and drink, for I am very hungry and thirsty."

Dummerly said, "I have nothing but dry bread and sour beer; if that will do for you, we will sit down and eat it together." So they sat down, and when the lad took out his bread, behold it was turned into a splendid meat pie, and his sour beer became delicious wine! They ate and drank

In the hollow under the roots sat a golden goose

heartily, and when they had finished, the little man said, "As you have a kind heart, and have been willing to share everything with me I will bring good to you. There stands an old tree; chop it down, and you will find something at the root." Then he took his leave and went his way.

Dummerly set to work, and cut down the tree; and when it fell, he discovered in a hollow under the roots a goose with plumage of pure gold. He took it up, and went on to an inn, where he proposed sleep for the night. The landlord had three daughters, and when they saw the goose, they were very curious to find out what this wonderful bird could be, and wished very much to pluck one of the feathers out of its tail.

At last the eldest said, "I must and will have a feather." So she waited till his back was turned, and then caught hold of the goose by the wing; but to her great surprise, there she stuck, for neither hand nor finger could she pull away again. Presently in came the second sister, and thought to have a feather too; but the instant she touched her sister, there she too hung fast. At last came the third, and desired a feather; but the other two cried out, "Keep away! for heaven's sake, keep away!" However, she did not understand what they meant. "If they are there," thought she, "I may as well be there too," so she went up to them. But the moment she touched her sisters she stuck fast, and hung to the goose as they did. And so they abode with the goose all night.

The next morning Dummerly carried off the goose under his arm, and took no heed of the three girls, but went out with them sticking fast behind; and wherever he journeyed, the three were obliged to follow, whether they wished or not, as fast as their legs could carry them.

In the middle of a field the parson met them; and when he saw the procession, he said, "Are you not ashamed of yourselves, you bold girls, to run after the young man like that over the fields? Is that proper behavior?"

Then he took the youngest by the hand to lead her away; but the moment he touched her he, too, hung fast, and followed in the procession.

Presently up came the clerk; and when he saw his master, the parson, running after the three girls, he was greatly surprised, and said, "Hollo! hollo! your reverence! whither so fast! There is a christening to-day."

Then he ran up, and caught him by the gown, and instantly he was fast too.

As the five were thus trudging along, one after another, they met two laborers with their mattocks coming from work; and the parson called out to them to set him free. But hardly had they touched him, when they, too, joined the ranks, and so made seven, all running after Dummerly and his goose.

At last they came to a city, where reigned a King who had an only daughter. The princess was of so thoughtful and serious a turn of mind that no one could make her laugh; and the King had announced to all the world that whoever could make her laugh should have her for his wife. When the young man heard this, he went to her with the goose and all

The sisters all stuck fast behind the golden goose

its followers; and as soon as she saw the seven all hanging together, and running about, treading on each other's heels, she could not help bursting into a long and loud laugh.

Then Dummerly claimed her for his bride; the wedding took place, and he was heir to the kingdom, and lived long and happily with his wife.

Fairy Thoughts

As Peter Pan said – according to James Matthew Barrie 1st Baronet, OM (1860 –1937):

When the first baby laughed for the first time, the laugh broke into a thousand pieces and they all went skipping about, and that was the beginning of fairies. And now when every new baby is born its first laugh becomes a fairy. So there ought to be one fairy for every boy or girl.

They [fairies] live in nests on the tops of trees; and the mauve ones are boys and the white ones are girls, and the blue ones are just little sillies who are not sure what they are.

And, from an unknown source:

And as the season come and go
Here's something you might like to know ...
There are fairies everywhere
Under bushes, in the air
Playing games just like you play,
Singing through their busy day.
So listen, touch, and look around –
In the air and on the ground.
And if you watch all nature's things,
You might just see a fairy's wing."

The Hare and the Hedgehog

The son of a schoolmaster, writer and newspaper editor Wilhelm Schröder first noted this tale in 1840 and three years later it was taken up by the Brothers Grimm (Jacob 1785–1863 and Wilhelm 1786–1859), too. It has similarities to the Aesop's fable of *The Hare and the Tortoise* and a good deal of humour in its telling.

This story, my dear young folks, seems to be false, but it really is true, for my grandfather, from whom I have it, used always, when relating it, to say, it must be true, my son, or else no one could tell it to you. The story is as follows.

One Sunday morning about harvest time, just as the buckwheat was in bloom, the sun was shining brightly in heaven, the east wind was blowing warmly over the stubble-fields, the larks were singing in the air, the bees buzzing among the buckwheat, the people in their Sunday clothes were all going to church, and all creatures were happy, and the hedgehog was happy too. The hedgehog, however, was standing by his door with his arms akimbo, enjoying the morning breezes, and slowly trilling a little song to himself, which was neither better nor worse than the songs which hedgehogs are in the habit of singing on a blessed sunday morning.

Whilst he was thus singing half aloud to himself, it suddenly occurred to him that, while his wife was washing and drying the children, he might very well take a walk into the field, and see how his turnips were getting on. The turnips, in fact, were close beside his house, and he and his family were accustomed to eat them, for which reason he looked upon them as his own.

No sooner said than done. The hedgehog shut the house-door behind him, and took the path to the field. He had not gone very far from home, and was just turning round the sloe-bush which stands there outside the field, to go up into the turnip-field, when he observed the hare who had gone out on business of the same kind, namely, to visit his cabbages. When the hedgehog caught sight of the hare, he bade him a friendly good morning. But the hare, who was in his own way a distinguished gentleman, and frightfully haughty, did not return the hedgehog's greeting, but said to him, assuming at the same time a very contemptuous manner, "How do you happen to be running about here in

The hedgehog's wife helped him to trick the hare

the field so early in the morning?"

"I am taking a walk," said the hedgehog.

"A walk," said the hare, with a smile. "It seems to me that you might use your legs for a better purpose."

This answer made the hedgehog furiously angry, for he can bear anything but a reference to his legs, just because they are crooked by nature. So now the hedgehog said to the hare, "You seem to imagine that you can do more with your legs than I with mine."

"That is just what I do think," said the hare.

"That can be put to the test," said the hedgehog. "I wager that if we run a race, I will outstrip you."

"That is ridiculous. You with your short legs, said the hare, but for my part I am willing, if you have such a monstrous fancy for it. What shall we wager?"

"A golden louis-d'or and a bottle of brandy," said the hedgehog.

"Done," said the hare. "Shake hands on it, and then we may as well begin at once."

"Nay," said the hedgehog, "There is no such great hurry. I am still fasting, I will go home first, and have a little breakfast. In half-an-hour I will be back again at this place." Hereupon the hedgehog departed, for the hare was quite satisfied with this.

On his way the hedgehog thought to himself, the hare relies on his long legs, but I will contrive to get the better of him. He may be a great man, but he is a very silly fellow, and he shall pay for what he has said. So when the hedgehog reached home, he said to his wife, wife, "Dress yourself quickly; you must go out to the field with me."

"What is going on, then?" asked his wife.

"I have made a wager with the hare, for a gold louis-d'or and a bottle of brandy. I am to run a race with him, and you must be present."

"Good heavens, husband," the wife now cried, "Are you not right in your mind, have you completely lost your wits. What can make you want to run a race with the hare."

"Hold your tongue, woman," said the hedgehog, "That is my affair. Don't begin to discuss things which are matters for men. Be off, dress yourself, and come with me."

What could the hedgehog's wife do. She was forced to obey him, whether she liked it or not. So when they had set out on their way together, the hedgehog said to his wife, "Now pay attention to what I am going to say. Look you, I will make the long field our race-course. The hare shall run in one furrow, and when the hare arrives at the end of the furrow on the other side of you, you must cry out to him, I am here already." Then they reached the field, and the hedgehog showed his wife her place, and then walked up the field. When he reached the top, the hare was already there.

"Shall we start?" asked the hare.

"Certainly," said the hedgehog.

Then each placed himself in his own furrow. The hare counted, once, twice, thrice, and away, and went off like a whirlwind down the field. The hedgehog, however, only ran

Both the hedgehogs went home, delighted to have scored against the exhausted hare

about three paces, and then he crouched down in the furrow, and stayed quietly where he was. When the hare therefore arrived at full speed at the lower end of the field, the hedgehog's wife met him with the cry, "I am here already."

The hare was shocked but thought no other than that it was the hedgehog himself who was calling to him, for the hedgehog's wife looked just like her husband. The hare, however, thought to himself, that has not been done fairly, and cried, "It must be run again, let us have it again!" And once more he went off like the wind in a storm, so that he seemed to fly. But the hedgehog's wife stayed quietly in her place. So when the hare reached the top of the field, the hedgehog himself cried out to him, "I am here already."

The hare, however, quite beside himself with anger, cried, "It must be run again, we must have it again!"

"All right," answered the hedgehog, "For my part I am happy to race just as often as you choose."

So the hare ran seventy-three times more, and the hedgehog always held out against him, and every time the hare reached either the top or the bottom, either the hedgehog or his wife said, "I am here already."

At the seventy-fourth time, however, the hare could no longer reach the end. In the middle of the field he fell to the ground, blood streamed out of his mouth, and he lay dead on the spot. But the hedgehog took the louis-d'or which he had won and the bottle of brandy, called his wife out of the furrow, and both went home together in great delight, and if they are not dead, they are living there still.

The moral of this story is, firstly, that no one, however great he may be, should permit himself to jest at any one beneath him, even if he be only a hedgehog. And, secondly, it teaches, that when a man marries, he should take a wife in his own position, who looks just as he himself looks. So whosoever is a hedgehog let him see to it that his wife is a hedgehog also, and so forth.

Struwwelpeter

Intending to buy a picture book as a Christmas present for his three-year-old son, Heinrich Hoffmann (1809–1894) was disappointed at the lack of inspiring stories so instead he wrote and illustrated his own. Thus were born the cautionary tales of *Struwwelpeter* – published first in 1845. The book became very popular throughout Europe and in many languages with Mark Twain responsible for its English translation as *"Slovenly Peter"*. It is listed among the 'top ten must-reads' for children so while there are no fairies involved, we have included it as representation of the Victorian-style morals that so strongly threaded their way into children's 1800s literature.

The Dreadful Story of Harriet and the Matches

It almost makes me cry to tell
What foolish Harriet befell.
Mamma and Nurse went out one day
And left her all alone at play.
Now, on the table close at hand,
A box of matches chanced to stand;
And kind Mamma and Nurse had told her,
That, if she touched them, they would scold her.
But Harriet said: "Oh, what a pity!
For, when they burn, it is so pretty;
They crackle so, and spit, and flame:
Mamma, too, often does the same."

Merry Stories And Funny Pictures

When the children have been good,
That is, be it understood,
Good at meal-times, good at play,
Good all night and good all day—
They shall have the pretty things
Merry Christmas always brings.

Naughty, romping girls and boys
Tear their clothes and make a noise,
Spoil their pinafores and frocks,
And deserve no Christmas-box.
Such as these shall never look
At this pretty Picture-book

Strewwelpeter (Shock-headed Peter)

Just look at him! there he stands,
With his nasty hair and hands.
See! his nails are never cut;
They are grimed as black as soot;
And the sloven, I declare,
Never once has combed his hair;
Anything to me is sweeter
Than to see Shock-headed Peter.

The pussy-cats heard this,
And they began to hiss,
And stretch their claws,
And raise their paws;
"Me-ow," they said, "me-ow, me-o,
You'll burn to death, if you do so."

But Harriet would not take advice:
She lit a match, it was so nice!

It crackled so, it burned so clear—
Exactly like the picture here.
She jumped for joy and ran about
And was too pleased to put it out.

The Pussy-cats saw this
And said: "Oh, naughty, naughty Miss!"
And stretched their claws,
And raised their paws:
"'Tis very, very wrong, you know,
Me-ow, me-o, me-ow, me-o,
You will be burnt, if you do so."

And see! oh, what dreadful thing!
The fire has caught her apron-string;
Her apron burns, her arms, her hair—
She burns all over everywhere.

Then how the pussy-cats did mew—
What else, poor pussies, could they do?
They screamed for help, 'twas all in vain!
So then they said: "We'll scream again;
Make haste, make haste, me-ow, me-o,
She'll burn to death; we told her so."

So she was burnt, with all her clothes,
And arms, and hands, and eyes, and nose;
Till she had nothing more to lose
Except her little scarlet shoes;
And nothing else but these was found
Among her ashes on the ground.

And when the good cats sat beside
The smoking ashes, how they cried!
"Me-ow, me-oo, me-ow, me-oo,
What will Mamma and Nursey do?"
Their tears ran down their cheeks so fast,
They made a little pond at last.

The Story of Augustus, who would not have any Soup

Augustus was a chubby lad;
Fat ruddy cheeks Augustus had:
And everybody saw with joy
The plump and hearty, healthy boy.
He ate and drank as he was told,
And never let his soup get cold.
But one day, one cold winter's day,
He screamed out "Take the soup away!
O take the nasty soup away!
I won't have any soup today."

Next day, now look, the picture shows
How lank and lean Augustus grows!
Yet, though he feels so weak and ill,

The naughty fellow cries out still
"Not any soup for me, I say:
O take the nasty soup away!
I won't have any soup today."

The third day comes: Oh what a sin!
To make himself so pale and thin.
Yet, when the soup is put on table,
He screams, as loud as he is able,
"Not any soup for me, I say:
O take the nasty soup away!
I WON'T have any soup today."

Look at him, now the fourth day's come!
He scarcely weighs a sugar-plum;
He's like a little bit of thread,
And, on the fifth day, he was—dead!

The Story of Fidgety Philip

"Let me see if Philip can
Be a little gentleman;
Let me see if he is able
To sit still for once at table":
Thus Papa bade Phil behave;
And Mamma looked very grave.
But fidgety Phil,
He won't sit still;
He wriggles,
And giggles,
And then, I declare,
Swings backwards and forwards,

And tilts up his chair,
Just like any rocking horse—
"Philip! I am getting cross!"

See the naughty, restless child
Growing still more rude and wild,
Till his chair falls over quite.
Philip screams with all his might,
Catches at the cloth, but then
That makes matters worse again.
Down upon the ground they fall,
Glasses, plates, knives, forks, and all.
How Mamma did fret and frown,
When she saw them tumbling down!
And Papa made such a face!
Philip is in sad disgrace.

Where is Philip, where is he?
Fairly covered up you see!
Cloth and all are lying on him;
He has pulled down all upon him.
What a terrible to-do!
Dishes, glasses, snapt in two!
Here a knife, and there a fork!
Philip, this is cruel work.
Table all so bare, and ah!
Poor Papa, and poor Mamma
Look quite cross, and wonder how
They shall have their dinner now.

The Story of Johnny Head-in-Air

As he trudged along to school,
It was always Johnny's rule
To be looking at the sky
And the clouds that floated by;
But what just before him lay,
In his way,
Johnny never thought about;
So that every one cried out
"Look at little Johnny there,
Little Johnny Head-In-Air!"

Running just in Johnny's way
Came a little dog one day;
Johnny's eyes were still astray
Up on high,
In the sky;
And he never heard them cry
"Johnny, mind, the dog is nigh!"
Bump!
Dump!
Down they fell, with such a thump,
Dog and Johnny in a lump!

Once, with head as high as ever,
Johnny walked beside the river.
Johnny watched the swallows trying
Which was cleverest at flying.
Oh! what fun!
Johnny watched the bright round sun
Going in and coming out;
This was all he thought about.
So he strode on, only think!
To the river's very brink,
Where the bank was high and steep,
And the water very deep;
And the fishes, in a row,
Stared to see him coming so.

One step more! oh! sad to tell!
Headlong in poor Johnny fell.
And the fishes, in dismay,
Wagged their tails and swam away.

There lay Johnny on his face,
With his nice red writing-case;
But, as they were passing by,
Two strong men had heard him cry;
And, with sticks, these two strong men
Hooked poor Johnny out again.

Oh! you should have seen him shiver
When they pulled him from the river.
He was in a sorry plight!
Dripping wet, and such a fright!
Wet all over, everywhere,
Clothes, and arms, and face, and hair:
Johnny never will forget
What it is to be so wet.

And the fishes, one, two, three,
Are come back again, you see;
Up they came the moment after,
To enjoy the fun and laughter.
Each popped out his little head,
And, to tease poor Johnny, said
"Silly little Johnny, look,
You have lost your writing-book!"

The Crow

This is a Polish fairy tale but can also
be found in *The Yellow Fairy Book*
by Andrew Lang.

Once upon a time there were three Princesses who were all three young and beautiful; but the youngest, although she was not fairer than the other two, was the most lovable of them all.

About half a mile from the palace in which they lived there stood a castle, which was uninhabited and almost a ruin, but the garden which surrounded it was a mass of blooming flowers, and in this garden the youngest Princess used often to walk.

One day when she was pacing to and fro under the lime trees, a black crow hopped out of a rose-bush in front of her. The poor beast was all torn and bleeding, and the kind little Princess was quite unhappy about it. When the crow saw this it turned to her and said:

'I am not really a black crow, but an enchanted Prince, who has been doomed to spend his youth in misery. If you only liked, Princess, you could save me. But you would have to say good-bye to all your own people and come and be my constant companion in this ruined castle. There is one habitable room in it, in which there is a golden bed; there you will have to live all by yourself, and don't forget that whatever you may see or hear in the night you must not scream out, for if you give as much as a single cry my sufferings will be doubled.'

The good-natured Princess at once left her home and her family and hurried to the ruined castle, and took possession of the room with the golden bed.

When night approached she lay down, but though she shut her eyes tight sleep would not come. At midnight she heard to her great horror some one coming along the passage, and in a minute her door was flung wide open and a troop of strange beings entered the room. They at once proceeded to light a fire in the huge fireplace; then they placed a great cauldron of boiling water on it. When they had done this, they approached the bed on which the trembling girl lay, and, screaming and yelling all the time, they dragged her towards the cauldron. She nearly died with fright, but she never uttered a sound. Then of a sudden the cock crew, and all the evil spirits vanished.

At the same moment the crow appeared and hopped all round the room with joy. It thanked the Princess most heartily for her goodness, and said that its sufferings had already been greatly lessened.

Now one of the Princess's elder sisters, who was very inquisitive, had found out about everything, and went to pay her youngest sister a visit in the ruined castle. She implored her so urgently to let her spend the night with her in the golden bed, that at last the good-natured little Princess consented. But at midnight, when the odd folk appeared, the elder sister screamed with terror, and from this time on the youngest Princess insisted always on keeping watch alone.

So she lived in solitude all the daytime, and at night she would have been frightened, had she not been so brave; but every day the crow came and thanked her for her endurance, and assured her that his sufferings were far less than they had been.

And so two years passed away, when one day the crow came to the Princess and said: "In another year I shall be freed from the spell I am under at present, because then the seven years will be over. But before I can resume my natural form, and take possession of the belongings of my forefathers, you must go out into the world and take service as a maidservant."

The young Princess consented at once, and for a whole year she served as a maid; but in spite of her youth and beauty she was very badly treated, and suffered many things. One evening, when she was spinning flax, and had worked her little white hands weary, she heard a rustling beside her and a cry of joy. Then she saw a handsome youth standing beside her; who knelt down at her feet and kissed the little weary white hands.

"I am the Prince," he said, "who you in your goodness, when I was wandering about in the shape of a black crow, freed from the most awful torments. Come now to my castle with me, and let us live there happily together."

So they went to the castle where they had both endured so much. But when they reached it, it was difficult to believe that it was the same, for it had all been rebuilt and done up again. And there they lived for a hundred years, a hundred years of joy and happiness.

The Three Brothers

This is a Polish fairy tale included in Andrew Lang's (1844–1912) *The Yellow Fairy Book* and tells how the youngest of three brothers kills an evil witch as well as a great serpent and rescues a fair maiden.

There was once upon a time a witch, who in the shape of a hawk used every night to break the windows of a certain village church. In the same village there lived three brothers, who were all determined to kill the mischievous hawk. But in vain did the two eldest mount guard in the church with their guns; as soon as the bird appeared high above their heads, sleep overpowered them, and they only awoke to hear the windows crashing in.

Then the youngest brother took his turn of guarding the windows, and to prevent his being overcome by sleep he placed a lot of thorns under his chin, so that if he felt drowsy and nodded his head, they would prick him and keep him awake.

The witch assumed the shape of a great hawk

The moon was already risen, and it was as light as day, when suddenly he heard a fearful noise, and at the same time a terrible desire to sleep overpowered him.

His eyelids closed, and his head sank on his shoulders, but the thorns ran into him and were so painful that he awoke at once. He saw the hawk swooping down upon the church, and in a moment he had seized his gun and shot at the bird. The hawk fell heavily under a big stone, severely wounded in its right wing. The youth ran to look at it, and saw that a huge abyss had opened below the stone. He went at once to fetch his brothers, and with their help dragged a lot of pine-wood and ropes to the spot. They fastened some of the burning pine-wood to the end of the rope, and let it slowly down to the bottom of the abyss. At first it was quite dark, and the flaming torch only lit up dirty gray stone walls. But the youngest brother determined to explore the abyss, and letting himself down by the rope he soon reached the bottom. Here he found a

A great abyss had opened below the stone

lovely meadow full of green trees and exquisite flowers.

In the middle of the meadow stood a huge stone castle, with an iron gate leading to it, which was wide open. Everything in the castle seemed to be made of copper, and the only inhabitant he could discover was a lovely girl, who was combing her golden hair; and he noticed that whenever one of her hairs fell on the ground it rang out like pure metal. The youth looked at her more closely, and saw that her skin was smooth and fair, her blue eyes bright and sparkling, and her hair as golden as the sun. He fell in love with her on the spot, and kneeling at her feet, he implored her to become his wife.

The lovely girl accepted his proposal gladly; but at the same time she warned him that she could never come up to the world above till her mother, the old witch, was dead. And she went on to tell him that the only way in which the old creature could be killed was with the sword that hung up in the castle; but the sword was so heavy that no one could lift it.

Then the youth went into a room in the castle where everything was made of silver, and here he found another beautiful girl, the sister of his bride. She was combing her silver hair, and every hair that fell on the ground rang out like pure metal. The second girl handed him the sword,

Inside the castle was a lovely girl with golden hair

but though he tried with all his strength he could not lift it. At last a third sister came to him and gave him a drop of something to drink, which she said would give him the needful strength. He drank one drop, but still he could not lift the sword; then he drank a second, and the sword began to move; but only after he had drunk a third drop was he able to swing the sword over his head.

Then he hid himself in the castle and awaited the old witch's arrival. At last as it was beginning to grow dark she

The hawk landed and changed into a woman

appeared. She swooped down upon a big apple tree, and after shaking some golden apples from it, she pounced down upon the earth. As soon as her feet touched the ground she became transformed from a hawk into a woman. This was the moment the youth was waiting for, and he swung his mighty sword in the air with all his strength and the witch's head fell off, and her blood spurted up on the walls.

Without fear of any further danger, he packed up all the treasures of the castle into great chests, and gave his brothers a signal to pull them up out of the abyss. First the treasures were attached to the rope and then the three lovely girls. And now everything was up above and only he himself remained below. But as he was a little suspicious of his brothers, he fastened a heavy stone on to the rope and let them pull it up. At first they heaved with a will, but when the stone was half way up they let it drop suddenly,

and it fell to the bottom broken into a hundred pieces.

"So that's what would have happened to my bones had I trusted myself to them," said the youth sadly; and he began to cry bitterly, not because of the treasures, but because of the lovely girl with her swanlike neck and golden hair.

For a long time he wandered sadly all through the beautiful underworld, and one day he met a magician who asked him the cause of his tears. The youth told him all that had befallen him, and the magician said:

"Do not grieve, young man! If you will guard the children who are hidden in the golden apple tree, I will bring you at once up to the earth. Another magician who lives in this land always eats my children up. It is in vain that I have hidden them under the earth and locked them into the castle. Now I have hidden them in the apple tree; hide yourself there too, and at midnight you will see my enemy."

The youth climbed up the tree, and picked some of the beautiful golden apples, which he ate for his supper.

At midnight the wind began to rise, and a rustling sound was heard at the foot of the tree. The youth looked down and beheld a long thick serpent beginning to crawl up the tree. It wound itself round the stem and gradually got higher and higher. It stretched its huge head, in which the eyes glittered fiercely, among the branches, searching for the nest in which the little children lay. They trembled with terror when they saw the hideous creature, and hid themselves beneath the leaves.

Then the youth swung his mighty sword in the air, and with one blow cut off the serpent's head. He cut up the rest of the body into little bits and strewed them to the four winds.

The father of the rescued children was so delighted over the death of his enemy that he told the youth to get on his back, and in this way he carried him up to the world above.

With what joy did he hurry now to his brothers' house! He burst into a room where they were all assembled, but no one knew who he was. Only his bride, who was serving as cook to her sisters, recognized her lover at once.

His brothers, who had quite believed he was dead, yielded him up his treasures at once, and flew into the woods in terror. But the good youth forgave them all they had done, and divided his treasures with them. Then he built himself a big castle with golden windows, and there he lived happily with his golden haired wife till the end of their lives.

The eyes of the serpent glittered fiercely

The Tiger,
the Brahman and the Jackal

There are more than a hundred versions of this very popular Indian tale that has spread right across the world and has an incredibly ancient history – some scholars believe it may have been composed as early as the 3rd century BCE. Its many variants include one that appeared in the Joseph Jacobs (1854–1916) *Indian Fairy Tales* collection. In some stories the released animal is a crocodile, in some it becomes a snake, a tiger, or a wolf.

Once upon a time, a tiger was caught in a trap. He tried in vain to get out through the bars, and rolled and bit with rage and grief when he failed.

By chance a poor Brahman came by.

"Let me out of this cage, oh pious one!" cried the tiger.

"Nay, my friend," replied the Brahman mildly, "you would probably eat me if I did."

"Not at all!" swore the tiger with many oaths; "on the contrary, I should be for ever grateful, and serve you as a slave!"

Now when the tiger sobbed and sighed and wept and swore, the pious Brahman's heart softened, and at last he consented to open the door of the cage. Out popped the tiger, and, seizing the poor man, cried, "What a fool you are! What is to prevent my eating you now, for after being cooped up so long I am just terribly hungry!"

In vain the Brahman pleaded for his life; the most he could gain was a promise to abide by the decision of the first three things he chose to question as to the justice of the tiger's action.

So the Brahman first asked a pipal tree what it thought of the matter, but the pipal tree replied coldly, "What have you to complain about? Don't I give shade and shelter to every one who passes by, and don't they in return tear down my branches to feed their cattle? Don't whimper – be a man!"

Then the Brahman, sad at heart, went further afield till he saw a buffalo turning a well-wheel; but he fared no better from it, for it answered, "You are a fool to expect gratitude! Look at me! Whilst I gave milk they fed me on cotton-seed and oil-cake, but now I am dry they yoke me here, and give me refuse as fodder!"

The Brahman, still more sad, asked the road to give him its opinion.

"My dear sir," said the road, "how foolish you are to expect anything else! Here am I, useful to everybody, yet all, rich and poor, great and small, trample on me as they

"Pooh!" interrupted the tiger, "what a fool you are! I was in the cage."

go past, giving me nothing but the ashes of their pipes and the husks of their grain!"

On this the Brahman turned back sorrowfully, and on the way he met a jackal, who called out, "Why, what's the matter, Mr. Brahman? You look as miserable as a fish out of water!"

The Brahman told him all that had occurred. "How very confusing!" said the jackal, when the recital was ended; "would you mind telling me over again, for everything has got so mixed up?"

The Brahman told it all over again, but the jackal shook his head in a distracted sort of way, and still could not understand.

"It's very odd," said he, sadly, "but it all seems to go in at one ear and out at the other! I will go to the place where it all happened, and then perhaps I shall be able to give a judgment."

So they returned to the cage, by which the tiger was waiting for the Brahman, and sharpening his teeth and claws.

The jackal asked to hear the story again

Brahman, and the cage came walking by – no, that's not it, either! Well, don't mind me, but begin your dinner, for I shall never understand!"

"Yes, you shall!" returned the tiger, in a rage at the jackal's stupidity; "I'll make you understand! Look here – I am the tiger –"

"Yes, my lord!"

"And that is the Brahman –"

"Yes, my lord!"

"And that is the cage –"

"Yes, my lord!"

"And I was in the cage – do you understand?"

"Yes – no – Please, my lord –"

"Well?" cried the tiger impatiently.

"Please, my lord! how did you get in?"

"How! Why in the usual way, of course!"

"Oh, dear me! – my head is beginning to whirl again! Please don't be angry, my lord, but what is the usual way?"

At this the tiger lost patience, and, jumping into the cage, cried, "This way! Now do you understand how it was?"

"Perfectly!" grinned the jackal, as he dexterously shut the door, "and if you will permit me to say so, I think matters will remain as they were!"

The Brahman let the tiger out of the trap

"You've been away a long time!" growled the savage beast, "but now let us begin our dinner."

"Our dinner!" thought the wretched Brahman, as his knees knocked together with fright; "what a remarkably delicate way of putting it!"

"Give me five minutes, my lord!" he pleaded, " in order that I may explain matters to the jackal here, who is somewhat slow in his wits."

The tiger consented, and the Brahman began the whole story over again, not missing a single detail, and spinning as long a yarn as possible.

"Oh, my poor brain! oh, my poor brain!" cried the jackal, wringing its paws. "Let me see! How did it all begin? You were in the cage, and the tiger came walking by –"

"Pooh!" interrupted the tiger, "what a fool you are! I was in the cage."

"Of course!" cried the jackal, pretending to tremble with fright; "yes! I was in the cage – no I wasn't – dear! dear! where are my wits? Let me see – the tiger was in the

The impatient tiger jumped back into the cage

The Velveteen Rabbit
or How toys become real

This tale, published first in 1922, tells how a toy rabbit became real through the love of his owner. English-American author Margery Williams Bianco (1881 to 1944) began writing professionally at the age of nineteen and regarded the poet Walter de la Mare as her spiritual mentor.

There was once a velveteen rabbit, and in the beginning he was really splendid. He was fat and bunchy, as a rabbit should be; his coat was spotted brown and white, he had real thread whiskers, and his ears were lined with pink sateen. On Christmas morning, when he sat wedged in the top of the Boy's stocking, with a sprig of holly between his paws, the effect was charming.

There were other things in the stocking, nuts and oranges and a toy engine, and chocolate almonds and a clockwork mouse, but the Rabbit was quite the best of all. For at least two hours the Boy loved him, and then Aunts and Uncles came to dinner, and there was a great rustling of tissue paper and unwrapping of parcels, and in the excitement of looking at all the new presents the Velveteen Rabbit was forgotten.

Christmas morning

For a long time he lived in the toy cupboard or on the nursery floor, and no one thought very much about him. He was naturally shy, and being only made of velveteen, some of the more expensive toys quite snubbed him. The mechanical toys were very superior, and looked down upon every one else; they were full of modern ideas, and pretended they were real. The model boat, who had lived through two seasons and lost most of his paint, caught the tone from them and never missed an opportunity of referring to his rigging in technical terms. The Rabbit could not claim to be a model of anything, for he didn't know that real rabbits existed; he thought they were all stuffed with sawdust like himself, and he understood that sawdust was quite out-of-date and should never be mentioned in modern circles. Even Timothy, the jointed wooden lion, who was made by the disabled soldiers, and should have had broader views, put on airs and pretended he was connected with Government. Between them all the poor little Rabbit was made to feel himself very insignificant and commonplace, and the only person who was kind to him at all was the Skin Horse.

The Skin Horse had lived longer in the nursery than any of the others. He was so old that his brown coat was bald in patches and showed the seams underneath, and most of the hairs in his tail had been pulled out to string bead necklaces. He was wise, for he had seen a long succession of mechanical toys arrive to boast and swagger, and by-and-by break their mainsprings and pass away, and he knew that they were only toys, and would never turn into anything else. For nursery magic is very strange and wonderful, and only those playthings that are old and wise and experienced like the Skin Horse understand all about it.

"What is REAL?" asked the Rabbit one day, when they were lying side by side near the nursery fender, before Nana came to tidy the room. "Does it mean having things that buzz inside you and a stick-out handle?"

"Real isn't how you are made," said the Skin Horse. "It's a thing that happens to you. When a child loves you for a long, long time, not just to play with, but REALLY loves you, then you become Real."

"Does it hurt?" asked the Rabbit.

"Sometimes," said the Skin Horse, for he was always truthful. "When you are Real you don't mind being hurt."

"Does it happen all at once, like being wound up," he asked, "or bit by bit?"

"It doesn't happen all at once," said the Skin Horse. "You become. It takes a long time. That's why it doesn't happen often to people who break easily, or have sharp edges, or who have to be carefully kept. Generally, by the time you are Real, most of your hair has been loved off, and your eyes drop out and you get loose in the joints and very shabby. But these things don't matter at all, because once you are Real you can't be ugly, except to people who don't understand."

"I suppose you are real?" said the Rabbit. And then he

The Skin Horse tells his story

wished he had not said it, for he thought the Skin Horse might be sensitive. But the Skin Horse only smiled.

"The Boy's Uncle made me Real," he said. "That was a great many years ago; but once you are Real you can't become unreal again. It lasts for always."

The Rabbit sighed. He thought it would be a long time before this magic called Real happened to him. He longed to become Real, to know what it felt like; and yet the idea of growing shabby and losing his eyes and whiskers was rather sad. He wished that he could become it without these uncomfortable things happening to him.

There was a person called Nana who ruled the nursery. Sometimes she took no notice of the playthings lying about, and sometimes, for no reason whatever, she went swooping about like a great wind and hustled them away in cupboards. She called this "tidying up," and the playthings all hated it, especially the tin ones. The Rabbit didn't mind it so much, for wherever he was thrown he came down soft.

One evening, when the Boy was going to bed, he couldn't find the china dog that always slept with him. Nana was in a hurry, and it was too much trouble to hunt for china dogs at bedtime, so she simply looked about her, and seeing that the toy cupboard door stood open, she made a swoop.

"Here," she said, "take your old Bunny! He'll do to sleep with you!" And she dragged the Rabbit out by one ear, and put him into the Boy's arms.

That night, and for many nights after, the Velveteen Rabbit slept in the Boy's bed. At first he found it rather uncomfortable, for the Boy hugged him very tight, and sometimes he rolled over on him, and sometimes he pushed him so far under the pillow that the Rabbit could scarcely breathe. And he missed, too, those long moonlight hours in the nursery, when all the house was silent, and his talks with the Skin Horse. But very soon he grew to like it, for the Boy used to talk to him, and made nice tunnels for him under the bedclothes that he said were like the burrows the real rabbits lived in. And they had splendid games together, in whispers, when Nana had gone away to her supper and left the night-light burning on the mantelpiece. And when the Boy dropped off to sleep, the Rabbit would snuggle down close under his little warm chin and dream, with the Boy's hands clasped close round him all night long.

And so time went on, and the little Rabbit was very happy – so happy that he never noticed how his beautiful velveteen fur was getting shabbier and shabbier, and his tail becoming unsewn, and all the pink rubbed off his nose where the Boy had kissed him.

Spring came, and they had long days in the garden, for wherever the Boy went the Rabbit went too. He had rides in the wheelbarrow, and picnics on the grass, and lovely fairy huts built for him under the raspberry canes behind the flower border. And once, when the Boy was called away suddenly to go out to tea, the Rabbit was left out on the lawn until long after dusk, and Nana had to come and look for him with the candle because the Boy couldn't go to sleep unless he was there. He was wet through with the dew and quite earthy from diving into the burrows the Boy had made for him in the flower bed, and Nana grumbled as she rubbed him off with a corner of her apron.

Spring Time

"You must have your old Bunny!" she said. "Fancy all that fuss for a toy!"

The Boy sat up in bed and stretched out his hands.

"Give me my Bunny!" he said. "You mustn't say that. He isn't a toy. He's REAL!"

When the little Rabbit heard that he was happy, for he knew that what the Skin Horse had said was true at last. The nursery magic had happened to him, and he was a toy no longer. He was Real. The Boy himself had said it.

That night he was almost too happy to sleep, and so much love stirred in his little sawdust heart that it almost burst. And into his boot-button eyes, that had long ago lost

That was a wonderful Summer!

their polish, there came a look of wisdom and beauty, so that even Nana noticed it next morning when she picked him up, and said, "I declare if that old Bunny hasn't got quite a knowing expression!"

Near the house where they lived there was a wood, and in the long June evenings the Boy liked to go there after tea to play. He took the Velveteen Rabbit with him, and before he wandered off to pick flowers, or play at brigands among the trees, he always made the Rabbit a little nest somewhere among the bracken, where he would be quite cosy, for he was a kind-hearted little boy and he liked Bunny to be comfortable. One evening, while the Rabbit was lying there alone, watching the ants that ran to and fro between his velvet paws in the grass, he saw two strange beings creep out of the tall bracken near him.

They were rabbits like himself, but quite furry and brand-new. They must have been very well made, for their seams didn't show at all, and they changed shape in a queer way when they moved; one minute they were long and thin and the next minute fat and bunchy, instead of always staying the same like he did. Their feet padded softly on the ground, and they crept quite close to him, twitching their noses, while the Rabbit stared hard to see which side the clockwork stuck out, for he knew that people who jump generally have something to wind them up. But he couldn't see it. They were evidently a new kind of rabbit altogether.

They stared at him, and the little Rabbit stared back. And all the time their noses twitched.

"Why don't you get up and play with us?" one of them asked.

"I don't feel like it," said the Rabbit, for he didn't want to explain that he had no clockwork.

"Ho!" said the furry rabbit. "It's as easy as anything," And he gave a big hop sideways and stood on his hind legs.

"I don't believe you can!" he said.

"I can!" said the little Rabbit. "I can jump higher than anything!" He meant when the Boy threw him, but of course he didn't want to say so.

"Can you hop on your hind legs?" asked the furry rabbit.

That was a dreadful question, for the Velveteen Rabbit had no hind legs at all! The back of him was made all in one piece, like a pincushion. He sat still in the bracken, and hoped that the other rabbits wouldn't notice.

"I don't want to!" he said again.

But the wild rabbits have very sharp eyes. And this one stretched out his neck and looked.

"He hasn't got any hind legs!" he called out. "Fancy a rabbit without any hind legs!" And he began to laugh.

"I have!" cried the little Rabbit. "I have got hind legs! I am sitting on them!"

"Then stretch them out and show me, like this!" said the wild rabbit. And he began to whirl round and dance, till the little Rabbit got quite dizzy.

"I don't like dancing," he said. "I'd rather sit still!"

But all the while he was longing to dance, for a funny new tickly feeling ran through him, and he felt he would give anything in the world to be able to jump about like these rabbits did.

The strange rabbit stopped dancing, and came quite close. He came so close this time that his long whiskers brushed the Velveteen Rabbit's ear, and then he wrinkled his nose suddenly and flattened his ears and jumped backwards.

"He doesn't smell right!" he exclaimed. "He isn't a rabbit at all! He isn't real!"

"I am Real!" said the little Rabbit. "I am Real! The Boy said so!" And he nearly began to cry.

Just then there was a sound of footsteps, and the Boy ran past near them, and with a stamp of feet and a flash of white tails the two strange rabbits disappeared.

"Come back and play with me!" called the little Rabbit. "Oh, do come back! I know I am Real!"

But there was no answer, only the little ants ran to and fro, and the bracken swayed gently where the two strangers had passed. The Velveteen Rabbit was all alone.

"Oh, dear!" he thought. "Why did they run away like that? Why couldn't they stop and talk to me?"

For a long time he lay very still, watching the bracken, and hoping that they would come back. But they never returned, and presently the sun sank lower and the little white moths fluttered out, and the Boy came and carried him home.

Weeks passed, and the little Rabbit grew very old and shabby, but the Boy loved him just as much. He loved him so hard that he loved all his whiskers off, and the pink lining to his ears turned grey, and his brown spots faded. He even began to lose his shape, and he scarcely looked like a rabbit any more, except to the Boy. To him he was always beautiful, and that was all that the little Rabbit cared about. He didn't mind how he looked to other people, because the nursery magic had made him Real, and when you are Real shabbiness doesn't matter.

And then, one day, the Boy was ill.

His face grew very flushed, and he talked in his sleep, and his little body was so hot that it burned the Rabbit when he held him close. Strange people came and went in the nursery, and a light burned all night and through it all the little Velveteen Rabbit lay there, hidden from sight under the bedclothes, and he never stirred, for he was afraid that if they found him some one might take him away, and he knew that the Boy needed him.

It was a long weary time, for the Boy was too ill to play, and the little Rabbit found it rather dull with nothing to do all day long. But he snuggled down patiently, and looked forward to the time when the Boy should be well again, and they would go out in the garden amongst the flowers and the butterflies and play splendid games in the raspberry thicket like they used to. All sorts of delightful things he planned, and while the Boy lay half asleep he crept up close to the pillow and whispered them in his ear. And presently the fever turned, and the Boy got better. He was able to sit up in bed and look at picture-books, while the little Rabbit cuddled close at his side. And one day, they let him get up and dress.

It was a bright, sunny morning, and the windows stood wide open. They had carried the Boy out on to the balcony, wrapped in a shawl, and the little Rabbit lay tangled up among the bedclothes, thinking.

The Boy was going to the seaside to-morrow. Everything was arranged, and now it only remained to carry out the doctor's orders. They talked about it all, while the little Rabbit lay under the bedclothes, with just his head peeping out, and listened. The room was to be disinfected, and all the books and toys that the Boy had played with in bed must be burnt.

"Hurrah!" thought the little Rabbit. "To-morrow we shall go to the seaside!" For the boy had often talked of the seaside, and he wanted very much to see the big waves coming in, and the tiny crabs, and the sand castles.

Just then Nana caught sight of him.

"How about his old Bunny?" she asked.

"That?" said the doctor. "Why, it's a mass of scarlet fever germs! – Burn it at once. What? Nonsense! Get him a new one. He mustn't have that any more!"

Anxious Times

And so the little Rabbit was put into a sack with the old picture-books and a lot of rubbish, and carried out to the end of the garden behind the fowl-house. That was a fine place to make a bonfire, only the gardener was too busy just then to attend to it. He had the potatoes to dig and the green peas to gather, but next morning he promised to come quite early and burn the whole lot.

That night the Boy slept in a different bedroom, and he had a new bunny to sleep with him. It was a splendid bunny, all white plush with real glass eyes, but the Boy was too excited to care very much about it. For to-morrow he was going to the seaside, and that in itself was such a wonderful thing that he could think of nothing else.

And while the Boy was asleep, dreaming of the seaside, the little Rabbit lay among the old picture-books in the corner behind the fowl-house, and he felt very lonely. The sack had been left untied, and so by wriggling a bit he was able to get his head through the opening and look out. He was shivering a little, for he had always been used to sleeping in a proper bed, and by this time his coat had worn so thin and threadbare from hugging that it was no longer any protection to him. Near by he could see the thicket of raspberry canes, growing tall and close like a tropical jungle, in whose shadow he had played with the Boy on bygone mornings. He thought of those long sunlit hours in the garden – how happy they were – and a great sadness came over him. He seemed to see them all pass before him, each more beautiful than the other, the fairy huts in the flower-bed, the quiet evenings in the wood when he lay in the bracken and the little ants ran over his paws; the wonderful day when he first knew that he was Real. He thought of the Skin Horse, so wise and gentle, and all that he had told him. Of what use was it to be loved and lose one's beauty and become Real if it all ended like this? And a tear, a real tear, trickled down his little shabby velvet nose and fell to the ground.

And then a strange thing happened. For where the tear had fallen a flower grew out of the ground, a mysterious flower, not at all like any that grew in the garden. It had slender green leaves the colour of emeralds, and in the centre of the leaves a blossom like a golden cup. It was so beautiful that the little Rabbit forgot to cry, and just lay there watching it. And presently the blossom opened, and out of it there stepped a fairy.

She was quite the loveliest fairy in the whole world. Her dress was of pearl and dew-drops, and there were flowers round her neck and in her hair, and her face was like the most perfect flower of all. And she came close to the little Rabbit and gathered him up in her arms and kissed him on his velveteen nose that was all damp from crying.

"Little Rabbit," she said, "don't you know who I am?"

The Rabbit looked up at her, and it seemed to him that he had seen her face before, but he couldn't think where.

"I am the nursery magic Fairy," she said. "I take care of all the playthings that the children have loved. When they are old and worn out and the children don't need them any more, then I come and take them away with me and turn them into Real."

"Wasn't I Real before?" asked the little Rabbit.

"You were Real to the Boy," the Fairy said, "because he loved you. Now you shall be Real to every one."

The Fairy Flower

And she held the little Rabbit close in her arms and flew with him into the wood.

It was light now, for the moon had risen. All the forest was beautiful, and the fronds of the bracken shone like frosted silver. In the open glade between the tree-trunks the wild rabbits danced with their shadows on the velvet grass, but when they saw the Fairy they all stopped dancing and stood round in a ring to stare at her.

"I've brought you a new playfellow," the Fairy said. "You must be very kind to him and teach him all he needs to know in Rabbit-land, for he is going to live with you for ever and ever!"

And she kissed the little Rabbit again and put him down on the grass.

"Run and play, little Rabbit!" she said.

But the little Rabbit sat quite still for a moment and never moved. For when he saw all the wild rabbits dancing around him he suddenly remembered about his hind legs, and he didn't want them to see that he was made all in one piece. He did not know that when the Fairy kissed him that last time she had changed him altogether. And he might have sat there a long time, too shy to move, if just then something hadn't tickled his nose, and before he thought what he was doing he lifted his hind toe to scratch it.

And he found that he actually had hind legs! Instead of dingy velveteen he had brown fur, soft and shiny, his ears twitched by themselves, and his whiskers were so long that they brushed the grass. He gave one leap and the joy of using those hind legs was so great that he went springing about the turf on them, jumping sideways and whirling round as the others did, and he grew so excited that when at last he did stop to look for the Fairy she had gone.

He was a Real Rabbit at last, at home with the other rabbits.

At Last! At Last!

Autumn passed and Winter, and in the Spring, when the days grew warm and sunny, the Boy went out to play in the wood behind the house. And while he was playing, two rabbits crept out from the bracken and peeped at him. One of them was brown all over, but the other had strange markings under his fur, as though long ago he had been spotted, and the spots still showed through. And about his little soft nose and his round black eyes there was something familiar, so that the Boy thought to himself:

"Why, he looks just like my old Bunny that was lost when I had scarlet fever!"

But he never knew that it really was his own Bunny, come back to look at the child who had first helped him to be Real.

Original book cover

Rabbits and hares

Rabbits and hares have always been seen as wily, clever survivors and the keeping of a rabbit's foot as a good luck charm goes back to the ancient Greeks. The clever hare is considered one of the most respected animals in the Zodiac while the rabbit represents speed, strength and a kind heart. People born in the year of the rabbit are said to be intelligent, love work, be romantic – and occasionally sly. They are modest, merciful, opportunistic and utterly charming. From *Alice in Wonderland's* white rabbit and Mad March Hare to many a Beatrix Potter tale, these animals are ever present in fairy stories!

Babes in the Wood

This is a traditional children's tale, which often serves as a Christmas pantomime theme, despite its original unhappy content, often combining with Robin Hood and Maid Marion who come to their rescue. Today the term may refer to inexperienced innocents entering potentially dangerous situations and some child murder cases have been referred to as *Babes in the Wood* crimes. Folklore relates the tale to Wayland Wood in Norfolk, England, where the 'wicked uncle' lived at nearby Griston Hall. Local village signs depict the story and the ghosts of the children are said to haunt the woodland.

The two babes are abandoned in the forest

Now ponder well, you parents deare,
These wordes which I shall write;
A doleful story you shall heare,
In time brought forth to light.
A gentleman of good account
In Norfolke dwelt of late.
Who did in honour far surmount
Most men of his estate.

Sore sicke he was, and like to dye,
No helpe his life could save;
His wife by him as sicke did lye,
And both possest one grave.
No love between these two was lost,
Each was to other kinde;
In love they liv'd, in love they dyed,
And left two babes behinde:

The one a fine and pretty boy,
Not passing three yeares olde;
The other a girl more young than he
And fram'd in beautye's molde.
The father left his little son,
As plainlye doth appeare,
When he to perfect age should come
Three hundred poundes a yeare.

And to his little daughter Jane
Five hundred poundes in gold,
To be paid downe on marriage-day,
Which might not be controll'd:
But if the children chanced to dye,
Ere they to age should come,
Their uncle should possesse their wealth;
For so the wille did run.

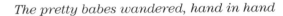

The pretty babes wandered, hand in hand

"Now, brother," said the dying man,
"Look to my children deare;
Be good unto my boy and girl,
No friendes else have they here:
 "To God and you I do commend
My children deare this daye;
But little while be sure we have
Within this world to staye.

"You must be father and mother both,
And uncle all in one;
God knowes what will become of them,
When I am dead and gone."
With that bespake their mother deare:
"O brother kinde," quoth shee,
You are the man must bring our babes
To wealth or miserie:

The children home he takes,
And bringes them straite unto his house,
Where much of them he makes.
He had not kept these pretty babes
A twelvemonth and a daye,
But, for their wealth, he did devise
To make them both awaye.

He bargain'd with two ruffians strong,
Which were of furious mood,
That they should take the children young,
And slaye them in a wood.
He told his wife an artful tale,
He would the children send
To be brought up in faire London,
With one that was his friend.

*The dying man asked his brother to care
for the children*

*Two ruffians took away the children,
who were happy to ride on a horse*

"And if you keep them carefully,
Then God will you reward;
But if you otherwise should deal,
God will your deedes regard."
With lippes as cold as any stone.
They kist the children small:
'God bless you both, my children deare;'
With that the teares did fall.

These speeches then their brother spake
To this sicke couple there:
"The keeping of your little ones,
Sweet sister, do not feare:
 "God never prosper me nor mine,
Nor aught else that I have,
If I do wrong your children deare,
When you are layd in grave."
The parents being dead and gone,

Away then went those pretty babes,
Rejoycing at that tide,
Rejoycing with a merry minde,
They should on cock-horse ride.
They prate and prattle pleasantly
As they rode on the waye,
To those that should their butchers be,
And work their lives' decaye:

So that the pretty speeche they had,
Made murderers' heart relent:
And they that undertooke the deed,
Full sore did now repent.
Yet one of them, more hard of heart,
Did vow to do his charge,
Because the wretch, that hired him,
Had paid him very large.
The other would not agree thereto,

So here they fell to strife;
With one another they did fight,
About the children's life:
And he that was of mildest mood,
Did slaye the other there,
Within an unfrequented wood,
Where babes did quake for feare!

He took the children by the hand,
While teares stood in their eye,
And bade them come and go with him,
And look they did not crye:
And two long miles he ledd them on,
While they for food complaine:
"Stay here," quoth he, "I'll bring ye bread,
When I come back againe."

These prettye babes, with hand in hand,
Went wandering up and downe;
But never more they sawe the man
Approaching from the town.
Their prettye lippes with blackberries
Were all besmear'd and dyed;
And when they sawe the darksome night,
They sat them downe and cryed.

Thus wandered these two prettye babes,
Till death did end their grief;
In one another's armes they dyed,
As babes wanting relief.
No burial these prettye babes
Of any man receives,
Till Robin-redbreast painfully
Did cover them with leaves

The ruffians fell into a fight

As dark night came the two babes died in the forest

Oh! Where Do Fairies Hide Their Heads?

Thomas Haynes Bayly (1797–1839)

OH! where do fairies hide their heads
  When snow lies on the hills,
When frost has spoil'd their mossy beds,
  And crystalliz'd their rills?
Beneath the moon they cannot trip
  In circles o'er the plain;
And draughts of dew they cannot sip
  Till green leaves come again.

Perhaps, in small, blue diving-bells,
  They plunge beneath the waves,
  Inhabiting the wreathed shells

That lie in coral caves;
  Perhaps, in red Vesuvius,
  Carousals they maintain;
And cheer their little spirits thus,
  Till green leaves come again.

When they return there will be mirth,
  And music in the air,
And fairy wings upon the earth,
  And mischief everywhere.
The maids, to keep the elves aloof,
  Will bar the doors in vain;
No key-hole will be fairy-proof,
  When green leaves come again.

The Enchanted Pig

This is the Andrew Lang (1844–1912) version (from *The Red Fairy Book*) of a Romanian story collected in *Rumanische Märchen*. Like many another fairy tale, it describes a princess's search for her lost prince who has been subject to enchantment and transformation.

Once upon a time there lived a King who had three daughters. Now it happened that he had to go out to battle, so he called his daughters and said to them:

"My dear children, I am obliged to go to the wars. The enemy is approaching us with a large army. It is a great grief to me to leave you all. During my absence take care of yourselves and be good girls; behave well and look after everything in the house. You may walk in the garden, and you may go into all the rooms in the palace, except the room at the back in the right-hand corner; into that you must not enter, for harm would befall you."

Once upon a time there lived a king who had three daughters . . .

"You may keep your mind easy, father," they replied. "We have never been disobedient to you. Go in peace, and may heaven give you a glorious victory!"

When everything was ready for his departure, the King gave them the keys of all the rooms and reminded them once more of what he had said. His daughters kissed his hands with tears in their eyes, and wished him prosperity, and he gave the eldest the keys.

Now when the girls found themselves alone they felt so sad and dull that they did not know what to do. So, to pass the time, they decided to work for part of the day, to read for part of the day, and to enjoy themselves in the garden for part of the day. As long as they did this all went well with them. But this happy state of things did not last long. Every day they grew more and more curious, and you will see what the end of that was.

"Sisters," said the eldest Princess, "all day long we sew, spin, and read. We have been several days quite alone, and there is no corner of the garden that we have not explored. We have been in all the rooms of our father's palace, and have admired the rich and beautiful furniture: why should not we go into the room that our father forbad us to enter?"

A big open book lay upon the table

"Sister," said the youngest, "I cannot think how you can tempt us to break our father's command. When he told us not to go into that room he must have known what he was saying, and have had a good reason for saying it."

"Surely the sky won't fall about our heads if we DO go in," said the second Princess. "Dragons and such like monsters that would devour us will not be hidden in the room. And how will our father ever find out that we have gone in?"

While they were speaking thus, encouraging each other, they had reached the room; the eldest fitted the key into the lock, and snap! the door stood open.

The three girls entered, and what do you think they saw?

The room was quite empty, and without any ornament, but in the middle stood a large table, with a gorgeous cloth, and on it lay a big open book.

Now the Princesses were curious to know what was written in the book, especially the eldest, and this is what she read:

The youngest princess was horrified to read that she would marry a pig

"The eldest daughter of this King will marry a prince from the East."

Then the second girl stepped forward, and turning over the page she read:

"The second daughter of this King will marry a prince from the West."

The girls were delighted, and laughed and teased each other.

But the youngest Princess did not want to go near the table or to open the book. Her elder sisters however left her no peace, and willy-nilly, they dragged her up to the table, and in fear and trembling she turned over the page and read:

"The youngest daughter of this King will be married to a pig from the North."

Now if a thunderbolt had fallen upon her from heaven it would not have frightened her more.

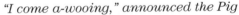

"I come a-wooing," announced the Pig

She almost died of misery, and if her sisters had not held her up, she would have sunk to the ground and cut her head open.

When she came out of the fainting fit into which she had fallen in her terror, her sisters tried to comfort her, saying:

"How can you believe such nonsense? When did it ever happen that a king's daughter married a pig?"

"What a baby you are!" said the other sister; "has not our father enough soldiers to protect you, even if the disgusting creature did come to woo you?"

The youngest Princess would fain have let herself be convinced by her sisters' words, and have believed what they said, but her heart was heavy. Her thoughts kept turning to the book, in which stood written that great happiness waited her sisters, but that a fate was in store for her such as had never before been known in the world.

Besides, the thought weighed on her heart that she had

The Pig's dwelling stood in a thick wood

been guilty of disobeying her father. She began to get quite ill, and in a few days she was so changed that it was difficult to recognise her; formerly she had been rosy and merry, now she was pale and nothing gave her any pleasure. She gave up playing with her sisters in the garden, ceased to gather flowers to put in her hair, and never sang when they sat together at their spinning and sewing.

In the meantime the King won a great victory, and having completely defeated and driven off the enemy, he hurried home to his daughters, to whom his thoughts had constantly turned. Everyone went out to meet him with cymbals and fifes and drums, and there was great rejoicing over his victorious return. The King's first act on reaching home was to thank Heaven for the victory he had gained over the enemies who had risen against him. He then entered his palace, and the three Princesses stepped forward to meet him. His joy was great when he saw that they were all well, for the youngest did her best not to appear sad.

In spite of this, however, it was not long before the King noticed that his third daughter was getting very thin and sad-looking. And all of a sudden he felt as if a hot iron were entering his soul, for it flashed through his mind that she had disobeyed his word. He felt sure he was right; but to be quite certain he called his daughters to him, questioned them, and ordered them to speak the truth. They confessed everything, but took good care not to say which had led the other two into temptation.

The King was so distressed when he heard it that he was almost overcome by grief. But he took heart and tried to comfort his daughters, who looked frightened to death. He saw that what had happened had happened, and that a thousand words would not alter matters by a hair's-breadth.

Well, these events had almost been forgotten when one fine day a prince from the East appeared at the Court and asked the King for the hand of his eldest daughter. The King gladly gave his consent. A great wedding banquet was prepared, and after three days of feasting the happy pair were accompanied to the frontier with much ceremony and rejoicing.

After some time the same thing befell the second daughter, who was wooed and won by a prince from the West.

Now when the young Princess saw that everything fell out exactly as had been written in the book, she grew very sad. She refused to eat, and would not put on her fine clothes nor go out walking, and declared that she would rather die than become a laughing-stock to the world. But the King would not allow her to do anything so wrong, and he comforted her in all possible ways.

So the time passed, till lo and behold! one fine day an enormous pig from the North walked into the palace, and going straight up to the King said, "Hail! oh King. May your life be as prosperous and bright as sunrise on a clear day!"

"I am glad to see you well, friend," answered the King, "but what wind has brought you hither?"

"I come a-wooing," replied the Pig.

Now the King was astonished to hear so fine a speech from a Pig, and at once it occurred to him that something strange was the matter. He would gladly have turned the Pig's thoughts in another direction, as he did not wish to give him the Princess for a wife; but when he heard that the Court and the whole street were full of all the pigs in the world he saw that there was no escape, and that he must give his consent. The Pig was not satisfied with mere promises, but insisted that the wedding should take place within a week, and would not go away till the King had sworn a royal oath upon it.

The King then sent for his daughter, and advised her to submit to fate, as there was nothing else to be done. And he added:

"My child, the words and whole behaviour of this Pig are quite unlike those of other pigs. I do not myself believe that he always was a pig. Depend upon it some magic or witchcraft has been at work. Obey him, and do everything that he wishes, and I feel sure that Heaven will shortly send you release."

"If you wish me to do this, dear father, I will do it," replied the girl.

In the meantime the wedding-day drew near. After the marriage, the Pig and his bride set out for his home in one of the royal carriages. On the way they passed a great bog, and the Pig ordered the carriage to stop, and got out and rolled about in the mire till he was covered with mud from head to foot; then he got back into the carriage and told his wife to kiss him. What was the poor girl to do? She bethought herself of her father's words, and, pulling out her pocket handkerchief, she gently wiped the Pig's snout and kissed it.

By the time they reached the Pig's dwelling, which stood in a thick wood, it was quite dark. They sat down quietly for a little, as they were tired after their drive; then they

The witch told the princess that she understood magic

had supper together, and lay down to rest. During the night the Princess noticed that the Pig had changed into a man. She was not a little surprised, but remembering her father's words, she took courage, determined to wait and see what would happen.

And now she noticed that every night the Pig became a man, and every morning he was changed into a Pig before she awoke. This happened several nights running, and the Princess could not understand it at all. Clearly her husband must be bewitched. In time she grew quite fond of him, he was so kind and gentle.

One fine day as she was sitting alone she saw an old witch go past. She felt quite excited, as it was so long since she had seen a human being, and she called out to the old woman to come and talk to her. Among other things the witch told her that she understood all magic arts, and that she could foretell the future, and knew the healing powers of herbs and plants.

"I shall be grateful to you all my life, old dame," said the Princess, "if you will tell me what is the matter with my husband. Why is he a Pig by day and a human being by night?"

"I was just going to tell you that one thing, my dear, to show you what a good fortune-teller I am. If you like, I will give you a herb to break the spell."

"If you will only give it to me," said the Princess, "I will give you anything you choose to ask for, for I cannot bear to see him in this state."

"Here, then, my dear child," said the witch, "take this thread, but do not let him know about it, for if he did it would lose its healing power. At night, when he is asleep, you must get up very quietly, and fasten the thread round his left foot as firmly as possible; and you will see in the morning he will not have changed back into a Pig, but will still be a man. I do not want any reward. I shall be sufficiently repaid by knowing that you are happy. It almost breaks my heart to think of all you have suffered, and I only wish I had known it sooner, as I should have come to your rescue at once."

When the old witch had gone away the Princess hid the thread very carefully, and at night she got up quietly, and with a beating heart she bound the thread round her husband's foot. Just as she was pulling the knot tight there was a crack, and the thread broke, for it was rotten.

Her husband awoke with a start, and said to her, "Unhappy woman, what have you done? Three days more and this unholy spell would have fallen from me, and now, who knows how long I may have to go about in this disgusting shape? I must leave you at once, and we shall not meet again until you have worn out three pairs of iron shoes and blunted a steel staff in your search for me." So saying he disappeared.

Now, when the Princess was left alone she began to weep and moan in a way that was pitiful to hear; but when she saw that her tears and groans did her no good, she got up, determined to go wherever fate should lead her.

On reaching a town, the first thing she did was to order three pairs of iron sandals and a steel staff, and having made these preparations for her journey, she set out in search of her husband. On and on she wandered over nine seas and across nine continents; through forests with trees whose stems were as thick as beer-barrels; stumbling and knocking herself against the fallen branches, then picking herself up and going on; the boughs of the trees hit her face, and the shrubs tore her hands, but on she went, and never looked back. At last, wearied with her long journey and worn out and overcome with sorrow, but still with hope at her heart, she reached a house.

Now who do you think lived there? The Moon.

The Princess knocked at the door, and begged to be let in that she might rest a little. The mother of the Moon, when she saw her sad plight, felt a great pity for her, and took her in and nursed and tended her. And while she was here the Princess had a little baby.

One day the mother of the Moon asked her:

"How was it possible for you, a mortal, to get hither to the house of the Moon?"

Then the poor Princess told her all that happened to her, and added "I shall always be thankful to Heaven for leading me hither, and grateful to you that you took pity on me and on my baby, and did not leave us to die. Now I beg one last favour of you; can your daughter, the Moon, tell me where my husband is?"

"She cannot tell you that, my child," replied the goddess, "but, if you will travel towards the East until you reach the dwelling of the Sun, he may be able to tell you something."

She wandered through forests of thick trees and slept, exhausted

Then she gave the Princess a roast chicken to eat, and warned her to be very careful not to lose any of the bones, because they might be of great use to her.

When the Princess had thanked her once more for her hospitality and for her good advice, and had thrown away one pair of shoes that were worn out, and had put on a second pair, she tied up the chicken bones in a bundle, and taking her baby in her arms and her staff in her hand, she set out once more on her wanderings.

On and on and on she went across bare sandy deserts, where the roads were so heavy that for every two steps that she took forwards she fell back one; but she struggled on till she had passed these dreary plains; next she crossed

Tongues of fire flared up from mountains of flint

high rocky mountains, jumping from crag to crag and from peak to peak. Sometimes she would rest for a little on a mountain, and then start afresh always farther and farther on. She had to cross swamps and to scale mountain peaks covered with flints, so that her feet and knees and elbows were all torn and bleeding, and sometimes she came to a precipice across which she could not jump, and she had to crawl round on hands and knees, helping herself along with her staff. At length, wearied to death, she reached the palace in which the Sun lived. She knocked and begged for admission. The mother of the Sun opened the door, and was astonished at beholding a mortal from the distant earthly shores, and wept with pity when she heard of all she had suffered. Then, having promised to ask her son about the Princess's husband, she hid her in the cellar, so that the Sun might notice nothing on his return home, for he was always in a bad temper when he came in at night. The next day the Princess feared that things would not go well with her, for the Sun had noticed that some one from the other world had been in the palace. But his mother had soothed him with soft words, assuring him that this was not so. So the Princess took heart when she saw how kindly she was treated, and asked:

"But how in the world is it possible for the Sun to be angry? He is so beautiful and so good to mortals."

"This is how it happens," replied the Sun's mother. "In the morning when he stands at the gates of paradise he is happy, and smiles on the whole world, but during the day he gets cross, because he sees all the evil deeds of men, and that is why his heat becomes so scorching; but in the evening he is both sad and angry, for he stands at the gates of death; that is his usual course. From there he comes back here."

She then told the Princess that she had asked about her husband, but that her son had replied that he knew nothing about him, and that her only hope was to go and inquire of the Wind.

Before the Princess left the mother of the Sun gave her a roast chicken to eat, and advised her to take great care of the bones, which she did, wrapping them up in a bundle.

She then threw away her second pair of shoes, which were quite worn out, and with her child on her arm and her staff in her hand, she set forth on her way to the Wind.

In these wanderings she met with even greater difficulties than before, for she came upon one mountain of flints after another, out of which tongues of fire would flame up; she passed through woods which had never been trodden by human foot, and had to cross fields of ice and avalanches of snow. The poor woman nearly died of these hardships, but she kept a brave heart, and at length she reached an enormous cave in the side of a mountain. This was where the Wind lived. There was a little door in the railing in front of the cave, and here the Princess knocked and begged for admission. The mother of the Wind had pity on her and took her in, that she might rest a little. Here too she was hidden away, so that the Wind might not notice her.

The next morning the mother of the Wind told her that her husband was living in a thick wood, so thick that no axe had been able to cut a way through it; here he had built himself a sort of house by placing trunks of trees together and fastening them with withes and here he lived alone, shunning human kind.

After the mother of the Wind had given the Princess a chicken to eat, and had warned her to take care of the bones, she advised her to go by the Milky Way, which at night lies across the sky, and to wander on till she reached her goal.

Having thanked the old woman with tears in her eyes for her hospitality, and for the good news she had given her, the Princess set out on her journey and rested neither night nor day, so great was her longing to see her husband again. On and on she walked until her last pair of shoes fell in pieces. So she threw them away and went on with bare feet, not heeding the bogs nor the thorns that wounded her, nor the stones that bruised her. At last she reached a beautiful green meadow on the edge of a wood. Her heart was cheered by the sight of the flowers and the soft cool grass, and she sat down and rested for a little. But hearing the birds chirping to their mates among the trees made her think with longing of her husband, and she wept bitterly, and taking her child in her arms, and her bundle of chicken bones on her shoulder, she entered the wood.

For three days and three nights she struggled through it, but could find nothing. She was quite worn out with weariness and hunger, and even her staff was no further help to her, for in her many wanderings it had become quite blunted. She almost gave up in despair, but made one last great effort, and suddenly in a thicket she came upon the sort of house that the mother of the Wind had described. It had no windows, and the door was up in the roof. Round the house she went, in search of steps, but could find none. What was she to do? How was she to get in? She thought and thought, and tried in vain to climb up to the door. Then suddenly she be-thought her of the chicken bones that she had dragged all that weary way, and she said to herself: "They would not all have told me to take such good care of these bones if they had not had some good reason for doing so. Perhaps now, in my hour of need, they may be of use to me."

So she took the bones out of her bundle, and having thought for a moment, she placed the two ends together. To her surprise they stuck tight; then she added the other bones, till she had two long poles the height of the house; these she placed against the wall, at a distance of a yard from one another. Across them she placed the other bones, piece by piece, like the steps of a ladder. As soon as one step was finished she stood upon it and made the next one, and then the next, till she was close to the door. But just as she got near the top she noticed that there were no

The prince told her, "I slew the youngest dragon."

bones left for the last rung of the ladder. What was she to do? Without that last step the whole ladder was useless. She must have lost one of the bones. Then suddenly an idea came to her. Taking a knife she chopped off her little finger, and placing it on the last step, it stuck as the bones had done. The ladder was complete, and with her child on her arm she entered the door of the house. Here she found everything in perfect order. Having taken some food, she laid the child down to sleep in a trough that was on the floor, and sat down herself to rest.

When her husband, the Pig, came back to his house, he was startled by what he saw. At first he could not believe his eyes, and stared at the ladder of bones, and at the little

finger on the top of it. He felt that some fresh magic must be at work, and in his terror he almost turned away from the house; but then a better idea came to him, and he changed himself into a dove, so that no witchcraft could have power over him, and flew into the room without touching the ladder. Here he found a woman rocking a child. At the sight of her, looking so changed by all that she had suffered for his sake, his heart was moved by such love and longing and by so great a pity that he suddenly became a man.

The Princess stood up when she saw him and her heart beat with fear, for she did not know him. But when he had told her who he was, in her great joy she forgot all her sufferings, and they seemed as nothing to her. He was a very handsome man, as straight as a fir tree. They sat down together and she told him all her adventures, and he wept with pity at the tale. And then he told her his own history.

"I am a King's son. Once when my father was fighting against some dragons, who were the scourge of our country, I slew the youngest dragon. His mother, who was a witch, cast a spell over me and changed me into a Pig. It was she who in the disguise of an old woman gave you the thread to bind round my foot. So that instead of the three days that had to run before the spell was broken, I was forced to remain a Pig for three more years. Now that we have suffered for each other, and have found each other again, let us forget the past."

And in their joy they kissed one another.

Next morning they set out early to return to his father's kingdom. Great was the rejoicing of all the people when they saw him and his wife; his father and his mother embraced them both, and there was feasting in the palace for three days and three nights.

Then they set out to see her father. The old King nearly went out of his mind with joy at beholding his daughter again. When she had told him all her adventures, he said to her:

"Did not I tell you that I was quite sure that that creature who wooed and won you as his wife had not been born a Pig? You see, my child, how wise you were in doing what I told you."

And as the King was old and had no heirs, he put them on the throne in his place. And they ruled as only kings rule who have suffered many things. And if they are not dead they are still living and ruling happily.

"The witch cast a spell and changed me into a pig"

The Snake Prince

This is a Punjabi Indian fairy tale collected by Major Campbell Feroshepore and included by Andrew Lang (1844–1912) in his *The Olive Fairy Book*. It tells of enchantment, the impact of insatiable curiosity and how, in the end, love, determination and bravery overcomes all.

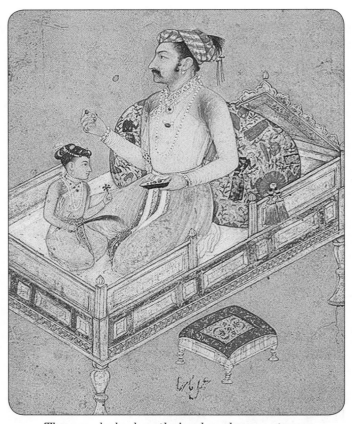

The new baby boy thrived and grew strong

Once upon a time there lived by herself, in a city, an old woman who was desperately poor. One day she found that she had only a handful of flour left in the house, and no money to buy more nor hope of earning it. Carrying her little brass pot, very sadly she made her way down to the river to bathe and to obtain some water, thinking afterwards to come home and make herself an unleavened cake of what flour she had left; and after that she did not know what was to become of her.

Whilst she was bathing she left her little brass pot on the river bank covered with a cloth, to keep the inside nice and clean; but when she came up out of the river and took the cloth off to fill the pot with water, she saw inside it the glittering folds of a deadly snake. At once she popped the cloth again into the mouth of the pot and held it there; and then she said to herself:

They locked the necklace in the queen's special chest

"Ah, kind death! I will take thee home to my house, and there I will shake thee out of my pot and thou shalt bite me and I will die, and then all my troubles will be ended."

With these sad thoughts in her mind the poor old woman hurried home, holding her cloth carefully in the mouth of the pot; and when she got home she shut all the doors and. windows, and took away the cloth, and turned the pot upside down upon her hearthstone. What was her surprise to find that, instead of the deadly snake which she expected to see fall out of it, there fell out with a rattle and a clang a most magnificent necklace of flashing jewels!

For a few minutes she could hardly think or speak, but stood staring; and then with trembling hands she picked the necklace up, and folding it in the corner of her veil, she hurried off to the king's hall of public audience.

"A petition, O king!" she said. "A petition for thy private ear alone!" And when her prayer had been granted, and she found herself alone with the king, she shook out her veil at his feet, and there fell from it in glittering coils the splendid necklace. As soon as the king saw it he was filled with amazement and delight; and the more he looked at it the more he felt that he must possess it at once. So he gave the old woman five hundred silver pieces for it, and put it straightway into his pocket. Away she went full of happiness; for the money that the king had given her would be enough to keep her for the rest of her life.

As soon as be could leave his business the king hurried off and showed his wife his prize, with which she was as pleased as he, if not more so; and, as soon as they had finished admiring the wonderful necklace, they locked it up in the great chest where the queen's jewellery was kept, the key of which hung always round the king's neck.

A short while afterwards, a neighbouring king sent a message to say that a most lovely girl baby had been born to him; and he invited his neighbours to come to a great feast in honour of the occasion. The queen told her husband that of course they must be present at the banquet, and she would wear the new necklace which he had given her. They had only a short time to prepare for the journey, and at the last moment the king went to the jewel chest to take out the necklace for his wife to wear, but he could see no necklace at all, only, in its place, a fat little boy baby crowing and shouting. The king was so astonished that he nearly fell backwards, but presently he found his voice, and called for his wife so loudly that she came running, thinking that the necklace must at least have been stolen.

"Look here! Look!" cried the king, "Haven't we always longed for a son? And now heaven has sent us one!"

"What do you mean?" cried the queen. "Are you mad?"

"Mad? No, I hope not," shouted the king, dancing in excitement round the open chest. "Come here, and look! Look what we've got instead of that necklace!"

Just then the baby let out a great crow of joy, as though he would like to jump up and dance with the king; and the

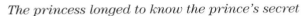

The princess longed to know the prince's secret

A long time passed and the lonely princess sorely missed her prince

queen gave a cry of surprise, and ran up and looked into the chest.

"Oh!" she gasped, as she looked at the baby, "What an adorable little child! Where could he have come from?"

"I'm sure I can't say," said the king; "All I know is that we locked up a necklace in the chest, and when I unlocked it just now there was no necklace, but a baby, and as fine a baby as ever was seen."

By this time the queen had the baby in her arms. "Oh, the blessed one!" she cried, "Fairer ornament for the bosom of a queen than any necklace that ever was wrought. Write," she continued, "write to our neighbour and say that we cannot come to his feast, for we have a feast of our own, and a baby of our own! Oh, happy day!"

So the visit was given up; and, in honour of the new baby, the bells of the city, and its guns, and its trumpets, and its people, small and great, had hardly any rest for a week; there was such a ringing, and banging, and blaring, and such fireworks, and feasting, and rejoicing, and merry-making, as had never been seen before.

A few years went by; and, as the king's boy baby and his neighbour's girl baby grew and throve, the two kings arranged that as soon as they were old enough they should marry; and so, with much signing of papers and agreements, and wagging of wise heads, and stroking of grey beards, the compact was made, and signed, and sealed, and lay waiting for its fulfilment. And this too came to pass; for, as soon as the prince and princess were eighteen years of age, the kings agreed that it was time for the wedding; and the young prince journeyed away to the neighbouring kingdom for his bride, and was there married to her with great and renewed rejoicings.

Now, I must tell you that the old woman who had sold the king the necklace had been called in by him to be the nurse of the young prince; and although she loved her charge dearly, and. was a most faithful servant, she could not help talking just a little, and so, by-and-by, it began to be rumoured that there was some magic about the young prince's birth; and the rumour of course had come in due time to the ears of the parents of the princess. So now that she was going to be the wife of the prince, her mother (who was curious, as many other people are) said to her daughter on the eve of the ceremony:

"Remember that the first thing you must do is to find out what this story is about the prince. And, in order to do it, you must not speak a word to him whatever he says until he asks you why you are silent; then you must ask him what the truth is about his magic birth; and until he tells you, you must not speak to him again."

And the princess promised that she would follow her mother's advice.

Therefore when they were married, and the prince spoke to his bride, she did not answer him. He could not think what was the matter, but even about her old home she would not utter a word. At last he asked why she would not speak; and then she said:

"Tell me the secret of your birth."

Then the prince was very sad and displeased, and although she pressed him sorely he would not tell her, but always reply:

"If I tell you, you will repent that ever you asked me."

For several months they lived together; and it was not such a happy time for either as it ought to have been, for the secret was still a secret, and lay between them like a cloud between the sun and the earth, making what should be fair, dull and sad.

At length the prince could bear it no longer; so he said to his wife one day: "At midnight I will tell you my secret if you still wish it; but you will repent it all your life." However, the princess was overjoyed that she had succeeded, and paid no attention to his warnings.

That night the prince ordered horses to be ready for the princess and himself a little before midnight. He placed her on one, and mounted the other himself, and they rode together down to the river to the place where the old woman had first found the snake in her brass pot. There the prince drew rein and said sadly: "Do you still insist that I should tell you my secret?" And the princess answered "Yes."

"If I do," answered the prince, "remember that you will regret it all your life." But the princess only replied, "Tell

me!" "Then," said the prince, "know that I am the son of the king of a far country, but by enchantment I was turned into a snake."

The word "snake" was hardly out of his lips when he disappeared, and the princess heard a rustle and saw a ripple on the water; and in the faint moonlight she beheld a snake swimming into the river. Soon it disappeared and she was left alone. In vain she waited with beating heart for something to happen, and for the prince to come back to her. Nothing happened and no one came; only the wind mourned through the trees on the riverbank, and the night birds cried, and a jackal howled in the distance, and the river flowed black and silent beneath her.

In the morning they found her, weeping and dishevelled, on the riverbank; but no word could they learn from her or from anyone as to the fate of her husband. At her wish they built on the riverbank a little house of black stone; and there she lived in mourning, with a few servants and guards to watch over her.

The huge scaly Queen Snake swayed before her

A long, long time passed by, and still the princess lived in mourning for her prince, and saw no one, and went nowhere away from her house on the river bank and the garden that surrounded it. One morning, when she woke up, she found a stain of fresh mud upon the carpet. She sent for the guards, who watched outside the house day and night, and asked them who had entered her room while she was asleep. They declared that no one could have entered, for they kept such careful watch that not even a bird could fly in without their knowledge; but none of them could explain the stain of mud. The next morning, again, the princess found another stain of wet mud, and she questioned everyone most carefully; but none could say how the mud came there. The third night the princess determined to lie awake herself and watch; and, for fear that she might fall asleep, she cut her finger with a penknife and rubbed salt into the cut, that the pain of it might keep her from sleeping. So she lay awake, and at midnight she saw a snake come wriggling along the ground with some mud from the river in its mouth; and when it came near the bed, it reared up its head and dropped its muddy head on the bedclothes. She was very frightened, but tried to control her fear, and called out:

"Who are you, and what do you here?"

And the snake answered:

"I am the prince, your husband, and I am come to visit you."

Then the princess began to weep; and the snake continued:

"Alas! Did I not say that if I told you my secret you would repent it? And have you not repented?"

"Oh, indeed!" cried the poor princess, "I have repented it, and shall repent it all my life! Is there nothing I can do?"

And the snake answered:

"Yes, there is one thing, if you dared to do it."

"Only tell me," said the princess, "and I will do anything!"

"Then," replied the snake, "on a certain night you must put a large bowl of milk and sugar in each of the four corners of this room. All the snakes in the river will come out to drink the milk, and the one that leads the way will be the queen of the snakes. You must stand in her way at the door, and say: 'Oh, Queen of Snakes, Queen of Snakes, give me back my husband!' and perhaps she will do it. But if you are frightened, and do not stop her, you will never see me again." And he glided away.

On the night of which the snake had told her, the princess got four large bowls of milk and sugar, and put one in each corner of the room, and stood in the doorway waiting. At midnight there was a great hissing and rustling from the direction of the river, and presently the ground appeared to be alive with horrible writhing forms of snakes, whose eyes glittered and forked tongues quivered as they moved on in the direction of the princess's house. Foremost among them was a huge, repulsive scaly creature that led the dreadful procession. The guards were so terrified that they all ran away; but the princess stood in the doorway, as white as death, and with her hands clasped tight together for fear she should scream or faint, and fail to do her part. As they came closer and saw her in the way, all the snakes raised their horrid heads and swayed them to and fro, and looked at her with wicked beady eyes, while their breath seemed to poison the very air. Still the princess stood firm, and, when the leading snake was within a few feet of her, she cried: "Oh, Queen of Snakes, Queen of Snakes, give me back my husband!" Then all the rustling, writhing crowd of snakes seemed to whisper to one another "Her husband? Her husband?" But the queen of snakes moved on until her head was almost in the princess's face, and her little eyes seemed to flash fire. And still the princess stood in the doorway and never moved, but cried again: "Oh, Queen of Snakes, Queen of Snakes, give me back my husband!"

Then the queen of snakes replied: "To-morrow you shall have him – to-morrow!

When she heard these words and knew that she had conquered, the princess staggered from the door, and sank upon her bed and fainted. As in a dream, she saw that her room was full of snakes, all jostling and squabbling over the bowls of milk until it was finished. And then they went away. In the morning the princess was up early, and took off the mourning dress which she had worn for five whole years, and put on gay and beautiful clothes. And she swept the house and cleaned it, and adorned it with garlands and nosegays of sweet flowers and ferns, and prepared it as though she were making ready for her wedding. And when night fell she lit up the woods and gardens with lanterns, and spread a table as for a feast, and lit in the house a thousand wax candles. Then she waited for her husband, not knowing in what shape he would appear. And at midnight there came striding from the river the prince, laughing but with tears in his eyes; and she ran to meet him and threw herself into his arms, crying and laughing too.

So the prince came home; and the next day they two went back to the palace, and the old king wept with joy to see them. And the bells, so long silent, were set a-ringing again, and the guns firing, and the trumpets blaring, and there was fresh feasting and rejoicing.

And the old woman who had been the prince's nurse became nurse to the prince's children – at least she was called so; though she was far too old to do anything for them but love them. Yet she still thought that she was useful, and knew that she was happy. And happy, indeed, were the prince and princess, who in due time became king and queen, and lived and ruled long and prosperously.

The old king wept with joy when the happy pair returned to the palace

Snow White

There are countless versions of this much-loved fairy tale but the best known is the German one collected by the Brothers Grimm (Jacob 1785–1863 and Wilhelm 1786–1859) which includes the magic mirror and the seven dwarfs – first given individual names in the 1912 Broadway play and then given yet another set of names in Disney's 1937 film *Snow White and the Seven Dwarfs*. In the first Grimm edition, the jealous villain was Snow White's own mother, rather than her stepmother but in some versions, it is two jealous sisters who try to kill her. Sometimes the dwarfs are robbers, and in one story the princess lives with forty dragons. In two Albanian versions a ring causes her death-like sleep.

It was in the middle of winter, when the broad flakes of snow were falling around, that a certain queen sat working at her window, the frame of which was made of fine black ebony; and, as she was looking out upon the snow, she pricked her finger, and three drops of blood fell upon it. Then she gazed thoughtfully down on the red drops which sprinkled the white snow and said, "Would that my little daughter may be as white as that snow, as red as the blood, and as black as the ebony window-frame!" And so the little girl grew up; her skin was a white as snow, her cheeks as rosy as blood, and her hair as black as ebony; and she was called Snow-White.

But this queen died; and the king soon married another wife, who was very beautiful, but so proud that she could not bear to think that any one could surpass her. She had a magical looking-glass, to which she used to go and gaze upon herself in it, and say –

"Tell me, glass, tell me true!
Of all the ladies in the land,
Who is fairest? tell me who?"

And the glass answered, "Thou, Queen, art fairest in the land"

But Snow-White grew more and more beautiful; and when she was seven years old, she was as bright as the day, and fairer than the queen herself. Then the glass one day answered queen, when she went to consult it as usual –

"Thou, Queen, may'st fair and beauteous be,
But Snow-White is lovelier far than thee?"

When the queen heard this she turned pale with rage and envy; and calling to one of her servants said, "Take Snow-White away into the wide wood, that I may never see her more." Then the servant led the little girl away; but his heart melted when she begged him to spare her life, and he said, "I will not hurt thee, thou pretty child." So he left her there alone; and though he thought it most likely that the wild beasts would tear her to pieces, he felt as if a great weight were taken off his heart when he had made up his mind not to kill her, but leave her to her fate.

Then poor Snow-White wandered along through the wood in great fear; and the wild beasts roared around, but none did her any harm. In the evening she came to a little cottage, and went in there to rest, for her weary feet would carry her no further. Everything was spruce and neat in the cottage: on the table was spread a white cloth, and there

Snow-White took good care of the dwarfs and their little house

were seven little plates with seven little loaves and seven little glasses with wine in them; and knives and forks laid in order, and by the wall stood seven little beds. Then, as she was exceedingly hungry, she picked a little piece off each loaf, and drank a very little wine out of each glass; and after that she thought she would lie down and rest. So she tried all the little beds; and one was too long, and another was too short, till, at last, the seventh suited her; and there she laid herself down and went to sleep. Presently in came the masters of the cottage, who were seven little dwarfs that lived among the mountains, and dug and searched about for gold. They lighted up their seven lamps, and saw directly that all was not right. The first said, "Who has been sitting on my stool?" The second, "Who has been eating off my plate?" The third, "Who has been picking at my bread?" The fourth, "Who has been meddling with my spoon?" The fifth, "Who has been handling my fork?" The sixth, "Who has been cutting with my knife?" The seventh, "Who has been drinking my wine?" Then the first looked around and said, "Who has been lying on my bed?" And the rest came running to him, and every one cried out that somebody had been upon his bed. But the seventh saw Snow-White, and called upon his brethren to come and look at her; and they cried out with wonder and astonishment, and brought their lamps and gazing upon her, they said, "Good heavens! What a lovely child she is!" And they were delighted to see her, and took care not to waken her; and the seventh dwarf

The pedlar woman showed Snow-White the fine wares she had to sell

slept an hour with each of the other dwarfs in turn, till the night was gone.

In the morning Snow-White told them all her story, and they pitied her, and said if she would keep all things in order, and cook and wash, and knit and spin for them, she might stay where she was, and they would take good care of her. Then they went out all day long to their work, seeking for gold and silver in the mountains; and Snow-White remained at home; and they warned her, saying, "The queen will soon find out where you are, so take care and let no one in." But the queen, now that she thought Snow-White was dead, believed that she was certainly the handsomest lady in the land; so she went to her glass and said –

"Tell me, glass, tell me true!
Of all the ladies in the land,
Who is fairest? Tell me who?"
And the glass answered –
"Thou, Queen, thou are fairest in all this land;
But over the Hills, in the greenwood shade,
Where the seven dwarfs their dwelling have made,
There Snow-White is hiding; and she
Is lovelier far, O Queen, than thee."

Then the queen was very much alarmed; for she knew that the glass always spoke the truth, and she was sure that the servant had betrayed her. And as she could not bear to think that any one lived who was more beautiful than she was, she disguised herself as an old pedlar woman and went her way over the hills to the place where the dwarfs dwelt. Then she knocked at the door and cried, "Fine wares to sell!" Snow-White looked out of the window, and said, "Good day, good woman; what have you to sell?" "Good wares, fine wares," replied she; "'laces and bobbins of all colors." "I will let the old lady in; she seems to be a very good sort of a body," thought Snow-White; so she ran down, and unbolted the door. "Bless me!" said the woman, "how badly your stays are laced. Let me lace them up with one of my nice new laces." Snow-White did not dream of any mischief; so she stood up before the old woman who set to work so nimbly, and pulled the lace so tightly that Snow-White lost her breath, and fell down as if she were dead. "There's an end of all thy beauty," said the spiteful queen, and went away home.

In the evening the seven dwarfs returned; and I need not say how grieved they were to see their faithful Snow-White stretched upon the ground motionless, as if she were quite dead. However, they lifted her up, and when they found what was the matter, they cut the lace; and in a little time she began to breathe, and soon came to herself again. Then they said, "The old woman was the queen; take care another time, and let no one in when we are away."

When the queen got home, she went to her glass, and spoke to it, but to her surprise it replied in the same words as before.

Then the blood ran cold in her heart with spite and malice to hear that Snow-White still lived; and she dressed herself up again in a disguise, but very different from the one she wore before, and took with her a poisoned comb. When she reached the dwarfs' cottage, she knocked at the door, and cried, "Fine wares to sell!" but Snow-White said, "I dare not let any one in." Then the queen said, "Only look at my beautiful combs;" and gave her the poisoned one. And it looked so pretty that the little girl took it up and put it into her hair to try it; but the moment it touched her head the poison was so powerful that she fell down senseless. "There you may lie," said the queen, and went her way. But

Some scholars think that the
legendary Snow-White was
inspired by the beautiful Margarete
von Waldeck (1533–1554) wooed
by Philip II of Spain but poisoned
so that she died when only twenty-
one. She had grown up in the
mining town of Waldeck where
small children known as "dwarfs"
worked in the mines. The Bavarian
city of Lohr also claims to be the
birthplace of another potential
Snow-White figure, Maria Sophia
Margaretha Catharina von Erthal.

All the dwarfs and the woodland animals loved her

by good luck the dwarfs returned very early that evening;
and when they saw Snow-White lying on the ground, they
thought what had happened, and soon found the poisoned
comb. And when they took it away, she recovered, and told
them all that had passed; and they warned her once more
not to open the door to any one.

The surprised dwarfs found Snow-White upstairs

Meantime the queen went home to her glass, and
trembled with rage when she received exactly the same
answer as before; and she said, "Snow-White shall die, if
it costs me my life." So she went secretly into a chamber,
and prepared a poisoned apple: the outside looked very
rosy and tempting, but whosoever tasted it was sure to

die. Then she dressed herself up as a peasant's wife,
and travelled over the hills to the dwarfs' cottage, and
knocked at the door; but Snow-White put her head out of
the window, and said, "I dare not let any one in, for the
dwarfs have told me not to." "Do as you please," said the
old woman, "but at any rate take this pretty apple; I will
make you a present of it." "No," said Snow-White, "I dare
not take it." "You silly girl!" answered the other, "What are
you afraid of? Do you think it is poisoned? Come! Do you
eat one part, and I will eat the other." Now the apple was
so prepared that one side was good, though the other side
was poisoned. Then Snow-White was very much tempted
to taste, for the apple looked exceedingly nice; and when
she saw the old woman eat, she could refrain no longer.
But she had scarcely put the piece into her mouth when
she fell down dead upon the ground. "This time nothing
will save thee," said the queen; and she went home to her
glass, and at last it said – "Thou, Queen, art the fairest of
all the fair." And then her envious heart was glad, and as
happy as such a heart could be.

When evening came, and the dwarfs returned home, they
found Snow-White lying on the ground; no breath passed
her lips, and they were afraid that she was quite dead.
They lifted her up, and combed her hair, and washed her
face with wine and water; but all was in vain. So they laid
her down upon a bier, and all seven watched and bewailed
her three whole days; and then they proposed to bury her;
but her cheeks were still rosy, and her face looked just as
it did while she was alive; so they said, "We will never bury

her in the cold ground." And they made a coffin of glass so that they might still look at her, and wrote her name upon it in golden letters, and that she was a king's daughter. Then the coffin was placed upon the hill, and one of the dwarfs always sat by it and watched. And the birds of the air came, too, and bemoaned Snow-White. First of all came an owl, and then a raven, but at last came a dove.

And thus Snow-White lay for a long, long time, and still only looked as though she were asleep; for she was even now as white as snow, and as red as blood, and as black as ebony. At last a prince came and called at the dwarfs' house; and he saw Snow-White and read what was written in golden letters. Then he offered the dwarfs money, and earnestly prayed them to let him take her away; but they said, "We will not part with her for all the gold in the world." At last, however, they had pity on him, and gave him the coffin; but the moment he lifted it up to carry it home with him, the piece of apple fell from between her lips, and Snow-White awoke, and exclaimed, "Where am I!" And the prince answered, "Thou art safe with me." Then he told her all that had happened, and said, "I love you better than all the world; come with me to my father's palace, and you shall be my wife." Snow-White consented, and went home with the prince; and everything was prepared with great pomp and splendor for their wedding.

It seemed so long ago that she had been
lost in the woods

To the feast was invited, among the rest, Snow-White's old enemy, the queen; and as she was dressing herself in fine, rich clothes, she looked in the glass and said, "Tell me, glass, tell me true! Of all the ladies in the land, Who is fairest? Tell me who?" And the glass answered, "Thou, lady, art the loveliest here, I ween; But lovelier far is the new-made queen."

When she heard this, the queen started with rage; but her envy and curiosity were so great, that she could not help setting out to see the bride. And when she arrived, and saw that it was no other than Snow-White, whom she thought had been dead a long while, she choked with passion, and

fell ill and died; but Snow-White and the prince lived and reigned happily over that land, many, many years.

"Snow-White" remains one of the most
popular bedtime stories

The Snow White story has been enjoyed in many languages:

Albanian – Borebardha
Arabic – Bayad-Althalj
Bengali –Tusar Konna
Bosnian – Snježana
Bulgarian – Снежанка – Snezhanka
Catalan – Blanca Neus
Chinese – Báixuě Gōngzhǔ
Croatian –Snjeguljica
Czech – Sněhurka
Danish – Snehvide
Dutch – Sneeuwwitje
English – Snow-White
Estonian – Lumivalgeke
Finnish – Lumikki
French – Blanche-Neige
German – Schneewittchen
Greek – Χιονάτη – Chionáti
Hebrew – Shilgia
Hindi – Himgauri
Hungarian – Hófehérke
Icelandic – Mjallhvít
Indonesian – Putih Salju or Putri Salju (Snow Princess)
Irish – Sneachta Bán
Italian – Biancaneve
Japanese – Shirayuki-hime
Korean – Baegseol Gongju
Latvian – Sniegbaltīte
Marathi – Himgauri
Montenegrin – Snježana
Norwegian – Snehvit
Oriya – Dhola gori
Persian – Sefid Barfi
Polish – Królewna Śnieżka
Portuguese – Branca de Neve
Romanian – Albă ca Zăpada
Russian – Белоснежка – Belosnezhka
Scottish/Gaelic – Sneachd Bàn

The Swineherd

In this Hans Christian Andersen (1805–1875) story a prince disguises himself as a swineherd in order to woo a vain princess. The tale was first published in 1841 and seems to be all Andersen's own although some similar stories do exist. A ballet called *The Hundred Kisses* has been based on the tale and in the 1950s, Soviet-Russian composer Boris Tchaikovsky (no relation to his more famous predecessor) wrote a suite of music to accompany a radio presentation of the tale.

"Tell him he can have my ten kisses but must collect the rest from my maids-in-waiting"

Once there was a poor Prince. He had a kingdom; it was very tiny. Still it was large enough to marry upon, and on marriage his heart was set.

Now it was certainly rather bold of him to say, "Will you have me?" to the Emperor's own daughter. But he did, for his name was famous, and far and near there were hundreds of Princesses who would have said, "Yes!" and "Thank you!" too. But what did the Emperor's daughter say? Well, we'll soon find out.

A rose tree grew over the grave of the Prince's father. It was such a beautiful tree. It bloomed only once in five long years, and then it bore but a single flower. Oh, that was a rose indeed! The fragrance of it would make a man forget all of his sorrows and his cares. The Prince had a nightingale too. It sang as if all the sweet songs of the world were in its little throat. The nightingale and the rose were to be gifts to the Princess. So they were sent to her in two large silver cases.

The Emperor ordered the cases carried before him, to the great hall where the Princess was playing at "visitors," with her maids-in waiting. They seldom did anything else. As soon as the Princess saw that the large cases contained presents, she clapped her hands in glee. "Oh," she said, "I do hope I get a little pussy-cat." She opened a casket and there was the splendid rose.

"Oh, how pretty it is," said all the maids-in-waiting.

"It's more than pretty," said the Emperor. "It's superb."

But the Princess poked it with her finger, and she almost started to cry. "Oh fie! Papa," she said, "it isn't artificial. It is natural."

"Oh, fie," said all her maids-in-waiting, "it's only natural."

"Well," said the Emperor, "before we fret and pout, let's see what's in the other case." He opened it, and out came the nightingale, which sang so sweetly that for a little while no one could think of a single thing to say against it.

"Superbe!" "Charmant!" said the maids-in-waiting with their smattering of French, each one speaking it worse than the next.

"How the bird does remind me of our lamented Empress's music box," said one old courtier. "It has just the same tone, and the very same way of trilling."

The Emperor wept like a child. "Ah me," he said.

"Bird?" said the Princess. "You mean to say it's real?"

"A real live bird," the men who had brought it assured her.

"Then let it fly and begone," said the Princess, who refused to hear a word about the Prince, much less to see him.

But it was not so easy to discourage him. He darkened his face both brown and black, pulled his hat down over his eyes, and knocked at the door.

228

"Hello, Emperor," he said. "How do you do? Can you give me some work about the palace?"

"Well," said the Emperor, "people are always looking for jobs, but let me see. I do need somebody to tend the pigs, because we've got so many of them."

So the Prince was appointed "Imperial Pig Tender." He was given a wretched little room down by the pigsties, and there he had to live. All day long he sat and worked, as busy as could be, and by evening he had made a neat little kettle with bells all around the brim of it. When the kettle boiled, the bells would tinkle and play the old tune:

"Oh, dear Augustin,

All is lost, lost, lost."

But that was the least of it. If anyone put his finger in the steam from this kettle he could immediately smell whatever there was for dinner in any cooking-pot in town. No rose was ever like this!

Now the Princess happened to be passing by with all of her maids-in-waiting. When she heard the tune she stopped and looked pleased, for she too knew how to play "Oh, dear Augustin." It was the only tune she did know, and she played it with one finger.

The prince was appointed "Imperial Pig Tender"

"Why, that's the very same tune I play. Isn't the swineherd highly accomplished? I say," she ordered, "go and ask him the price of the instrument."

So one of the maids had to go, in among the pigsties, but she put on her overshoes first.

"What will you take for the kettle?" she asked.

"I'll take ten kisses from the Princess," said the swineherd.

"Oo, for goodness' sakes!" said the maid.

"And I won't take less," said the swineherd.

"Well, what does he say?" the Princess wanted to know.

"I can't tell you," said the maid. "He's too horrible."

"Then whisper it close to my ear." She listened to what the maid had to whisper. "Oo, isn't he naughty!" said the Princess and walked right away from there. But she had not gone very far when she heard the pretty bells play again:

"Oh, dear Augustin,

All is lost, lost, lost."

"I say," the Princess ordered, "ask him if he will take his ten kisses from my maids-in-waiting."

"No, I thank you," said the swineherd. "Ten kisses from the Princess, or I keep my kettle."

"Now isn't that disgusting!" said the Princess. "At least stand around me so that no one can see."

So her maids stood around her, and spread their skirts wide, while the swineherd took his ten kisses. Then the kettle was hers.

And then the fun started. Never was a kettle kept so busy. They boiled it from morning till night. From the chamberlain's banquet to the cobbler's breakfast, they knew all that was cooked in town. The maids-in-waiting danced about and clapped their hands.

"We know who's having sweet soup and pancakes. We know who's having porridge and cutlets. Isn't it interesting?"

"Most interesting," said the head lady of the bedchamber.

"Now, after all, I'm the Emperor's daughter," the Princess reminded them. "Don't you tell how I got it."

"Goodness gracious, no!" said they all.

But the swineherd – that's the Prince, for nobody knew he wasn't a real swineherd – was busy as he could be. This time he made a rattle. Swing it around, and it would play all the waltzes, jigs, and dance tunes that have been heard since the beginning of time.

"Why it's superb!" said the Princess as she came by. "I never did hear better music. I say, go and ask him the price of that instrument. But mind you – no more kissing!"

"He wants a hundred kisses from the Princess," said the maid-in-waiting who had been in to ask him.

"I believe he's out of his mind," said the Princess, and she walked right away from there. But she had not gone very far when she said, "After all, I'm the Emperor's daughter, and it's my duty to encourage the arts. Tell him he can have ten kisses, as he did yesterday, but he must collect the rest from my maids-in-waiting."

"Oh, but we wouldn't like that," said the maids.

"Fiddlesticks," said the Princess, "If he can kiss me he certainly can kiss you. Remember, I'm the one who gives you board and wages." So the maid had to go back to the swineherd.

"A hundred kisses from the Princess," the swineherd told her, "or let each keep his own."

"Stand around me," said the Princess, and all her maids-in-waiting stood in a circle to hide her while the swineherd began to collect.

"What can have drawn such a crowd near the pigsties?" the Emperor wondered, as he looked down from his balcony. He rubbed his eyes, and he put on his spectacles. "Bless my soul if those maids-in-waiting aren't up to mischief again. I'd better go see what they are up to now."

He pulled his easy slippers up over his heels, though ordinarily he just shoved his feet in them and let them flap.

Nobody knew that the swinherd was really a prince with a kingdom of his own

Then, my! How much faster he went. As soon as he came near the pens he took very soft steps. The maids-in-waiting were so busy counting kisses, to see that everything went fair and that he didn't get too many or too few, that they didn't notice the Emperor behind them. He stood on his tiptoes.

"Such naughtiness!" he said when he saw them kissing, and he boxed their ears with his slipper just as the swineherd was taking his eighty-sixth kiss.

"Be off with you!" the Emperor said in a rage. And both the Princess and the swineherd were turned out of his empire. And there she stood crying. The swineherd scolded, and the rain came down in torrents.

"Poor little me," said the Princess. "If only I had married the famous Prince! Oh, how unlucky I am!"

The swineherd slipped behind a tree, wiped the brown and black off his face, threw off his ragged clothes, and showed himself in such princely garments that the Princess could not keep from curtsying.

"I have only contempt for you," he told her. "You turned down a Prince's honest offer, and you didn't appreciate the rose or the nightingale, but you were all too ready to kiss a swineherd for a tinkling toy to amuse you. You are properly punished."

Then the Prince went home to his kingdom, and shut and barred the door. The Princess could stay outside and sing to her heart's content:

"Oh, dear Augustin,

All is lost, lost, lost."

The vain princess would regret her unkind treatment of the prince – now disguised as a swineherd

The Bended Rocks

This Native American tale relates
how Niagara Falls began and was
taken from *American Indian
Fairy Tales* by Margaret Compton
(1852–1903), published in 1907
but with an oral tradition dating
back into the mists of time.

*The spirit of
Cloud and Rain
took Bending
Willow into his
lodge*

Bending willow was the most beautiful girl in a tribe noted for its handsome women. She had many suitors, but she refused them all; for her love was given to a young warrior of a distant nation, who, she felt sure, would some day return to throw a red deer at her feet in token that he wished to marry her.

Among her suitors was a hideous old Indian, a chief who was very rich. He was scarred and wrinkled and his hair was as gray as the badger that burrows in the forest. He was cruel also, for when the young men were put to the torture to prove themselves worthy to be warriors, he devised tests more dreadful than any that the tribe had ever known. But the chief, who was rightly named No Heart, declared that he would marry Bending Willow, and, as he was powerful, her parents did not dare to refuse him. Bending Willow begged and pleaded in vain.

On the night before the day set for the marriage, she went into the woods, and throwing herself on the ground, sobbed as if her heart would break. All night she lay there, listening to the thunder of the great cataract of Niagara, which was but a woman's journey from the village. At last it suggested to her a sure means of escape.

Early in the morning before any one was stirring, she went back to her father's wigwam, took his canoe and dragged it to the edge of the river. Then stepping into it she set it adrift and it headed quickly towards the Falls. It soon reached the rapids and was tossed like a withered branch on the white-crested billows, but went on, on, swiftly and surely to the edge of the great fall.

For a moment only, she saw the bright, green water, and then she felt herself lifted and was borne on great, white wings which held her above the rocks. The water divided and she passed into a dark cave behind the rainbow.

The spirit of Cloud and Rain had gone to her rescue and had taken her into his lodge. He was a little, old man, with a white face and hair and beard of soft, white mist, like that which rises day and night from the base of the Falls. The

Bending Willow sobbed as if her heart would break

Night and day a fine mist rose from the great falls

231

door of his lodge was the green wave of Niagara, and the walls were of gray rock studded with white stone flowers.

Cloud and Rain gave her a warm wrapper and seated her on a heap of ermine skins in a far corner of the lodge where the dampness was shut out by a magic fire. This is the fire that runs beneath the Falls, and throws its yellow-and-green flames across the water, forming the rainbow.

He brought her dainty fish to eat and delicate jelly made from mosses which only the water spirits can find or prepare.

When she was rested he told her that he knew her story, and if she would stay with him he would keep her until her ugly old suitor was dead. "A great serpent," added he, "lies beneath the village, and is even now poisoning the spring from which No Heart draws all the water that he uses, and he will soon die."

Bending Willow was grateful, and said that she would gladly remain all her life in such a beautiful home and with such a kind spirit.

Cloud and Rain smiled; but he knew the heart of a young girl would turn towards her own home when it was safe for her to return. He needed no better proof of this than the questions she asked about the serpent which caused so much sickness among her people.

He told her that this serpent had lain there many years. When he once tasted human blood he could never be satisfied. He crept beneath a village and cast a black poison into the springs from which people drew water. When any one died the serpent stole out at night and drank his blood. That made him ravenous for more. So when one death occurred more followed until the serpent was gorged and went to sleep for a time.

"When you return," said Cloud and Rain, "persuade your people to move their camp. Let them come near me, and should the serpent dare to follow I will defend them."

Bending Willow stayed four months with Cloud and Rain, and he taught her much magic, and showed her the herbs which would cure sickness.

One day when he came in from fishing he said to her: "No Heart is dead. This night I will throw a bridge from the foot of the waters across the Falls to the high hills. You must climb it without fear, for I will hold it firmly until you are on the land."

When the moon rose and lighted all the river, Cloud and Rain caused a gentle wind to raise the spray until it formed a great, white arch reaching from his cave to the distant hills. He led Bending Willow to the foot of this bridge of mist and helped her to climb until she was assured of her safety and could step steadily.

All the tribe welcomed her, and none were sorry that she had not married No Heart. She told them of the good spirit, Cloud and Rain, of his wonderful lodge, of his kindness, and of the many things he had taught her.

At first they would not entertain the idea of moving their village, for there were pleasant fishing-grounds where they lived, and by the Falls none but spirits could catch the fish.

But when strong men sickened and some of the children of the Chief died, they took down their lodge poles and sought the protection of the good spirit.

For a long time they lived in peace and health; but after many moons the serpent discovered their new camp and made his way thither.

Cloud and Rain was soon aware of his arrival, and was very angry because the serpent dared to come so near his lodge.

He took a handful of the magic fire and molded it into thunderbolts which he hurled at the monster. The first stunned him, the second wounded him severely, and the third killed him.

Cloud and Rain told them to drag the body to the rapids and hurl it into the water. It took all the women of the tribe to move it, for it was longer than the flight of twenty arrows. As it tossed upon the water, it looked as though a mountain had fallen upon the waves, and it drifted but slowly to the edge of the Great Fall. There it was drawn between the rocks and became wedged so firmly that it could not be dislodged, but coiled itself as if it had lain down to sleep. Its weight was so great that it bent the rocks, and they remain curved like a drawn bow to this day. The serpent itself was gradually washed to pieces and disappeared.

In the Moon of Flowers the young warrior whom Bending Willow loved came and cast a red deer at her feet, and they were happy ever after.

Cloud and Rain attacked the monster with thunderbolts

The young warrior gave Bending Willow a red deer

The Boy and the Wolves

This Native American story is drawn from the rich source of their ancient culture and was included in the Andrew Lang (1844–1912) fairy tale collections in his 1894 *The Yellow Fairy Book*. It is sometimes called *The Broken Promise*.

Once upon a time an Indian hunter built himself a house in the middle of a great forest, far away from all his tribe; for his heart was gentle and kind, and he was weary of the treachery and cruel deeds of those who had been his friends. So he left them, and took his wife and three children, and they journeyed on until they found a spot near to a clear stream, where they began to cut down trees, and to make ready their wigwam. For many years they lived peacefully and happily in this

The young boy crept out to eat what the wolves had left behind

sheltered place, never leaving it except to hunt the wild animals, which served them both for food and clothes. At last, however, the strong man felt sick, and before long he knew he must die.

So he gathered his family round him, and said his last words to them. "You, my wife, the companion of my days, will follow me ere many moons have waned to the island of the blest. But for you, O my children, whose lives are but newly begun, the wickedness, unkindness, and ingratitude from which I fled are before you. Yet I shall go hence in peace, my children, if you will promise always to love each

other, and never to forsake your youngest brother."

"Never!" they replied, holding out their hands. And the hunter died content.

Scarcely eight moons had passed when, just as he had said, the wife went forth, and followed her husband; but before leaving her children she bade the two elder ones think of their promise never to forsake the younger, for he was a child, and weak. And while the snow lay thick upon the ground, they tended him and cherished him; but when the earth showed green again, the heart of the young man stirred within him, and he longed to see the wigwams of the village where his father's youth was spent.

Having no friends, he sought the company of animals and soon the wolves knew him and gave him food

Therefore he opened all his heart to his sister, who answered: "My brother, I understand your longing for our fellow-men, whom here we cannot see. But remember our father's words. Shall we seek not our own pleasures; should we forget the little one?"

But he would not listen, and, making no reply, he took his bow and arrows and left the hut. The snows fell and melted, yet he never returned; and at last the heart of the

When the snows melted the boy went down to the shore near where his family were living

girl grew cold and hard, and her little boy became a burden in her eyes, till one day she spoke thus to him: "See, there is food for many days to come. Stay here within the shelter of the hut. I go to seek our brother, and when I have found him I shall return hither."

But when, after hard journeying, she reached the village where her brother dwelt, and saw that he had a wife and was happy, and when she, too, was sought by a young brave, then she also forgot the boy alone in the forest, and thought only of her husband.

Now as soon as the little boy had eaten all the food which his sister had left him, he went out into the woods, and gathered berries and dug up roots, and while the sun shone he was contented and had his fill. But when the snows began and the wind howled, then his stomach felt empty and his limbs cold, and he hid in trees all the night, and only crept out to eat what the wolves had left behind. And by-and-by, having no other friends, he sought their company, and sat by while they devoured their prey, and they grew to know him, and gave him food. And without them he would have died in the snow.

But at last the snows melted, and the ice upon the great lake, and as the wolves went down to the shore, the boy went after them. And it happened one day that his big brother was fishing in his canoe near the shore, and he heard the voice of a child singing in the Indian way:

"My brother, my brother! I am becoming a wolf, I am becoming a wolf!"

And when he had so sung he howled as wolves howl.

Then the heart of the elder sunk, and he hastened towards him, crying, "Brother, little brother, come to me!" but he, being half a wolf, only continued his song. And the louder the elder called him, "Brother, little brother, come to me," the swifter he fled after his brothers the wolves, and the heavier grew his skin, till, with a long howl, he vanished into the depths of the forest.

So, with shame and anguish in his soul, the elder brother went back to his village, and, with his sister, mourned the little boy and the broken promise till the end of his life.

Even his sister had deserted him

The Nightingale

This 1843 story about an emperor and his preference for a toy bird's tinkling to the song of a real nightingale is said to have been inspired by the unrequited love of Hans Christian Andersen (1805–1875) for singer, Jenny Lind, known as the 'Swedish Nightingale'. He wrote it in two days. Over the years, the tale has inspired many adaptations including a Stravinsky opera, a Russian ballet with sets by Matisse, puppet presentations, an animated film, a musical play starring Sarah Brightman and a television drama with Mick Jagger as the Emperor.

In China, as you know, the Emperor is a Chinaman, and all those about him him are Chinamen too. It is many years since the story I am going to tell you happened, but that is all the more reason for telling it, lest it should be forgotten. The emperor's palace was the most beautiful thing in the world; it was made entirely of the finest porcelain, very costly, but at the same time so fragile that it could only be touched with the very greatest care. There were the most extraordinary flowers to be seen in the garden; the most beautiful ones had little silver bells tied to them, which tinkled perpetually, so that one should not pass the flowers without looking at them. Every little detail in the garden had been most carefully thought out, and it was so big, that even the gardener himself did not know where it ended. If one went on walking, one came to beautiful woods with lofty trees and deep lakes. The wood extended to the sea, which was deep and blue, deep enough for large ships to sail right under the branches of the trees. Among these trees lived a nightingale, which sang so deliciously, that even the poor fisherman, who had plenty of other things to do, lay still to listen to it, when he was out at night drawing his nets. "Heavens, how beautiful it is!" he said, but then he had to attend to his business and forgot it. The next night when he heard it again exclaim, "Heavens, how beautiful it is!"

Travellers came to the emperor's capital, from every country in the world. They admired everything very much, especially the palace and the gardens, but when they heard the nightingale they all said, "This is better than anything!"

When they got home they described it, and the learned ones wrote many books about the town, the palace and the garden, but nobody forgot the nightingale, it was always put above everything else. Those among them who were poets wrote the most beautiful poems, all about the nightingale in the woods by the deep blue sea. These books went all over the world, and in course of time some of them reached the emperor. He sat in his golden chair reading and reading, and nodding his head, well pleased to hear such beautiful descriptions of the town, the palace and the garden. "But the nightingale is the best of all," he read.

"What is this?" said the emperor. "The nightingale? Why, I know nothing about it. Is there such a bird in my kingdom, and in my own garden into the bargain, and I have never heard of it? Imagine my having to discover this from a book?"

Then he called his gentleman-in-waiting, who was so grand that when any one of a lower rank dared to speak to him, or to ask him a question, he would only answer, 'P,' which means nothing at all.

"There is said to be a very wonderful bird called a nightingale here," said the emperor. "They say that it is better than anything else in all my kingdom! Why have I never been told anything about it?"

"I have never heard it mentioned,' said the gentleman-in-waiting. "It has never been presented at court."

"I wish it to appear here this evening to sing to me," said

The Emperor had a vast and beautiful garden

The Emperor lay near to death, pale and cold

the emperor. "The whole world knows what I am possessed of, and I know nothing about it!"

"I have never heard it mentioned before," said the gentleman-in-waiting. "I will seek it, and I will find it!" But where was it to be found? The gentleman-in-waiting ran upstairs and downstairs and in and out of all the rooms and corridors. No one of all those men had ever heard anything about the nightingale, so the gentleman-in-waiting ran back to the emperor, and said that it must be a myth, invented by the writers of the books. "Your imperial majesty must not believe everything that is written. Books are often mere inventions, even if they do not belong to what we call the black art!"

"But the book in which I read it is sent to me by the powerful Emperor of Japan, so it can't be untrue. I will hear this nightingale. I insist upon its being here tonight. I extend my most gracious protection to it, and if it is not forthcoming, I will have the whole court trampled upon after supper!"

"Tsing-pe!" said the gentleman-in-waiting, and away he ran again, up and down all the stairs, in and out of all the rooms and corridors. Half the court ran with him, for none of them wished to be trampled on. There was much questioning about the nightingale, which was known to all the outside world, but to no one at court. At last they found a poor little maid in the kitchen. She said, "Oh heavens,

the nightingale? I know it very well. Yes, indeed it can sing. Every evening I am allowed to take broken meat to my poor sick mother: she lives down by the shore. On my way back, when I am tired, I can rest awhile in the wood, and then I hear the nightingale. Its song brings the tears into my eyes. I feel as if my mother were kissing me!"

"Little kitchen-maid," said the gentleman-in-waiting, "I will procure you a permanent position in the kitchen, and permission to see the emperor dining, if you will take us to the nightingale. It is commanded to appear at court tonight."

Then they all went out into the wood where the nightingale usually sang. Half the court was there. As they were going along at their best pace a cow began to bellow.

"Oh!' said the young courtier, "there we have it. What wonderful power for such a little creature; I have certainly heard it before."

"No, those are cows bellowing; we are a long way yet from the place." Then the frogs began to croak in the marsh.

"Beautiful!' said the Chinese chaplain. "It is just like the tinkling of church bells."

"No, those are the frogs!" said the little kitchen-maid. But I think we shall soon hear it now!"

Then the nightingale began to sing.

"There it is!" said the little girl. "Listen, listen, there it sits!" and she pointed to a little grey bird up among the branches.

"Is it possible?" said the gentleman-in-waiting. "I should never have thought it was like that. How common it looks! Seeing so many grand people must have frightened all its colours away."

"Little nightingale!" called the kitchen-maid quite loud, "our gracious emperor wishes you to sing to him!"

"With the greatest of pleasure!" said the nightingale, warbling away in the most delightful fashion.

"It is just like crystal bells," said the gentleman-in-waiting. "Look at its little throat, how active it is. It is extraordinary that we have never heard it before! I am sure it will be a great success at court!"

"Shall I sing again to the emperor?" said the nightingale, who thought he was present.

"My precious little nightingale," said the gentleman-in-waiting, "I have the honour to command your attendance at the court festival tonight, where you will charm his gracious majesty the emperor with your fascinating singing."

"It sounds best among the trees," said the nightingale, but it went with them willingly when it heard that the emperor wished it.

The palace had been brightened up for the occasion. The walls and the floors, which were all of china, shone by the light of many thousand golden lamps. The most beautiful flowers, all of the tinkling kind, were arranged in the corridors; there was hurrying to and fro, and a great draught, but this was just what made the bells ring; one's ears were full of tinkling. In the middle of the large reception-room where the emperor sat a golden rod had been fixed, on which the nightingale was to perch. The whole court assembled, and the little kitchen-maid had been permitted to stand behind the door, as she now had the actual title of cook. They were all dressed in their best; everbody's eyes were turned towards the little grey bird at which the emperor was nodding. The nightingale sang delightfully, and the tears came into the emperor's eyes, nay, they rolled down his cheeks; and then the nightingale sang more beautifully than ever, its notes touched all hearts. The emperor was charmed, and said the nightingale should have his gold slipper to wear round its neck. But the nightingale declined with thanks; it had already been sufficiently rewarded.

The real nightingale sang in the woods by the shore

"I have seen tears in the eyes of the emperor; that is my richest reward. The tears of an emperor have a wonderful power! God knows I am sufficiently recompensed!" and then it again burst into its sweet heavenly song.

"That is the most delightful coquetting I have ever seen!" said the ladies, and they took some water into their mouths to try and make the same gurgling when any one spoke to them, thinking so to equal the nightingale. Even the lackeys and the chamber-maids announced that they were satisfied, and that is saying a great deal; they are always the most difficult people to please. Yes, indeed, the nightingale had made a sensation. It was to stay at court now, and to have its own cage, as well as liberty to walk out twice a day, and once at night. It always had twelve footmen, with each one holding a ribbon which was tied round its leg. There was not much pleasure in an outing of that sort.

The whole town talked about the marvellous bird, and if two people met, one said to the other, "Night," and the other answered, "Gale," and they sighed, perfectly understanding each other. Eleven cheesemongers' children were called after it, but they had not got a voice among them.

One day a large parcel came for the emperor; outside was written the word "Nightingale."

"Here we have another new book about this celebrated bird," said the emperor. But it was no book; it was a little work of art in a box, an artificial nightingale, exactly like the living one, but it was studded all over with diamonds, rubies and sapphires.

When the bird was wound up it could sing one of the songs the real one sang, and it wagged its tail, which glittered with silver and gold. A ribbon was tied round its neck on which was written, "The Emperor of Japan's nightingale is very poor compared to the Emperor of China's."

Everybody said, "Oh, how beautiful!" And the person who brought the artificial bird immediately received the title of Imperial Nightingale-Carrier in Chief.

"Now, they must sing together; what a duet that will be."

Then they had to sing together, but they did not get on very well, for the real nightingale sang in its own way, and the artificial one could only sing waltzes.

"There is no fault in that," said the music-master; "it is perfectly in time and correct in every way!"

Then the artificial bird had to sing alone. It was just as great a success as the real one, and then it was so much prettier to look at; it glittered like bracelets and breast-pins.

It sang the same tune three and thirty times over, and yet it was not tired; people would willingly have heard it from the beginning again, but the emperor said that the real one must have a turn now – but where was it? No one had noticed that it had flown out of the open window, back to

The music master had insisted that the song of the artificial bird was better than the real nightingale's

its own green woods.

"But what is the meaning of this?" said the emperor.

All the courtiers railed at it, and said it was a most ungrateful bird.

"We have got the best bird though," said they, and then the artificial bird had to sing again, and this was the thirty-fourth time that they heard the same tune, but they did not know it thoroughly even yet, because it was so difficult.

The music-master praised the bird tremendously, and insisted that it was much better than the real nightingale, not only as regarded the outside with diamonds, but the inside too.

"Because you see, my ladies and gentlemen, and the emperor before all, in the real nightingale you never know what you will hear, but in the artificial one everything is decided beforehand! So it is, and so it must remain, it can't be otherwise. You can account for things, you can open it and show the human ingenuity in arranging the waltzes, how they go, and how one note follows upon another!"

"Those are exactly my opinions," they all said, and the music-master got leave to show the bird to the public next Sunday. They were also to hear it sing, said the emperor. So they heard it, and all became as enthusiastic over it as if they had drunk themselves merry on tea.

Then they all said, "Oh," and stuck their forefingers in the air and nodded their heads; but the poor fisherman who had heard the real nightingale said, "It sounds very nice, and it is very like the real one, but there is something wanting, we don't know what." The real nightingale was banished from the kingdom.

The artificial bird had its place on silken cushion, close to the emperor's bed: all the presents it had received of gold and precious jewels were scattered round it. Its title had risen to be Chief Imperial Singer of the Bed-Chamber, in rank number one, on the left side; for the emperor reckoned that side the important one, where the heart was seated. And even an emperor's heart is on the left side. The music-master wrote five-and-twenty volumes about the artificial bird; the treatise was very long and written in all the most difficult Chinese characters. Everybody said they had read and understood it, for otherwise they would have been reckoned stupid, and then their bodies would have been trampled upon.

Things went on in this way for a whole year. The emperor, the court, and all the other Chinamen knew every little gurgle in the song of the artificial bird by heard; but they liked it all the better for this, and they could all join in the song themselves. Even the street boys sang, "zizizi," and "cluck, cluck, cluck," and the emperor sang it too.

But one evening when the bird was singing its best, and the emperor was lying in bed listening to it, something gave way inside the bird with a, "whizz." Then a spring burst, "whirr," went all the wheels, and the music stopped. The emperor jumped out of bed and sent for his private physicians, but what good could they do? Then they sent for the watchmaker, and after a good deal of talk and

The gentleman-in-waiting commanded the nightingale to attend the court

examination he got the works so as to be sure of the tune. This was a great blow! They only dared to let the artificial bird sing once a year, and hardly that; but then the music-master made a little speech, using all the most difficult words. He said it was just as good as ever, and his saying it made it so.

Five years now passed, and then a great grief came upon the nation, for they were all very fond of their emperor, and he was ill and could not live, it was said. A new emperor was already chosen, and people stood about in the street, and asked the gentleman-in-waiting how their emperor was going on.

"Pooh," answered he, shaking his head.

The emperor lay pale and cold in his gorgeous bed, the courtiers thought he was dead, and they all went off to pay their respects to their new emperor. The lackeys ran off to talk matters over, and the chambermaids gave a great coffee-party. Cloth had been laid down in all the rooms and corridors so as to deaden the sound of footsteps, so it was very, very quiet. But the emperor was not dead yet. He lay stiff and pale in the gorgeous bed with its velvet hangings and heavy golden tassel. There was an open window high above him, and the moon streamed in upon the emperor, and the artificial bird beside him.

The poor emperor could hardly breathe. He seemed to have a weight on his chest. He opened is eyes, and then he saw that it was Death sitting upon his chest, wearing his golden crown. In one hand he held the emperor's golden sword, and in the other his imperial banner. Round about, from among the folds of the velvet hangings peered many curious faces: some were hideous, others gentle and pleasant. They were all the emperor's good and bad deeds, which now looked him in the face when Death was weighing him down.

"Do you remember that?" whispered one after the other; "Do you remember this?" and they told him so many things that the perspiration poured down his face.

"I never knew that," said the emperor. "Music, music! Sound the great Chinese drums!" he cried, "that I may not hear what they are saying." But they went on and on, and Death sat nodding his head, just like a Chinaman, at everything that was said.

"Music, music!" shrieked the emperor. "You precious little golden bird, sing, sing! I have loaded you with precious stones, and even hung my own golden slipper round your neck; sing, I tell you, sing!"

Death knelt upon his chest, wearing his golden crown

But the bird stood silent; there was nobody to wind it up, so of course it could not go. Death continued to fix the great empty socket of his eyes upon the emperor, and all was silent, so terribly silent.

Suddenly, close to the window, there was a burst of lovely song; it was the living nightingale, perched on a branch outside. It had heard of the emperor's need, and had come to bring comfort and hope to him. As it sang the faces round became fainter and fainter, and the blood coursed with feeble limbs. Even Death himself listened to the song and said, "Go on, little nightingale, go on!"

"Yes, if you give me the gorgeous golden sword; yes, if you give me the imperial banner; yes, if you give me the emperor's crown," said the bird.

And Death gave back each of these treasures for a song, and the nightingale went on singing. It sang about the quiet churchyard, when the roses bloom, where the elderflower scents the air, and where the fresh grass is ever moistened anew by the tears of the mourners. This song brought to Death a longing for his own garden, and, like a cold grey mist, he passed out of the window.

"Thanks, thanks!" said the emperor; "you heavenly little bird, I know you! I banished you from my kingdom, and yet you have charmed the evil visions away from my bed by your song, and even Death away from my heart! How can I ever repay you?"

"You have rewarded me," said the nightingale. "I brought tears to your eyes, the very first time I ever sang to you, and I shall never forget it! Those are the jewels which gladden the heart of a singer; but sleep now, and wake up fresh and strong and well again! I will sing to you!"

Then it sang again, and the emperor fell into a sweet refreshing sleep. The sun shone in at his window, when he awoke refreshed and well; none of his attendants had yet come back to him, for they thought he was dead, but the nightingale still sat there singing.

"You must always stay with me!" said the emperor. "You shall sing only when you like, and I will break the artificial bird into a thousand pieces!"

"Don't do that!" said the nightingale, "it did all the good it could! Keep it as you have always done! I can't build my nest and live in this palace, but let me come whenever I like, then I will sit on the branch in the evening and sing to you. I will sing to cheer you and to make you thoughtful too; I will sing to you of the happy ones, and of those that suffer too. I will sing about the good and the evil, which are kept hidden from you. The little singing bird flies far and wide, to the poor fisherman, and the peasant's home, to numbers who are far from you and your court. I love your heart better than your crown, and yet something holy lingers round that also. I will come, and I will sing to you! But you must promise me one thing!"

"Everything!" said the emperor, who stood there in his imperial robes which he had just put on and held the sword heavy with gold pressed upon his heart.

"One thing only I ask you!" replied the nightingale, "Tell no one that you have a little bird who tells you everything; it will be better so!"

Then the nightingale flew away. The attendants came in to look after their dead emperor and, to their astonishment, lo! there he stood, bidding them, "Good morning!"

The Storks

This tale by Hans Christian Andersen (1805–1875) describes how the young storks learn about their world and how to tolerate teasing from the children below (and take their revenge) before their flight to Egypt. The notion that storks deliver new-born babies to parents may derive from Greek mythology as the goddess Hera changed her enemy Gerana into a stork, who then tried to abduct Hera's child. Moreover, storks like to live on rooftops, a convenient place from which to deliver a baby. In many regions they are fertility symbols associated with springtime and birth and in some areas, it is thought a woman may become pregnant simply because a stork has looked at her.

O N the last house in a little village stood a stork's nest. The Mother Stork sat in it with her four young ones, who stretched out their heads with the pointed black beaks, for their beaks had not yet turned red. A little way off stood the Father Stork, all alone on the ridge of the roof, quite upright and stiff; he had drawn up one of his legs, so as not to be quite idle while he stood sentry. One would have thought he had been carved out of wood, so still did he stand. He thought, "It must look very grand, that my wife has a sentry standing by her nest. They can't tell that it is her husband. They certainly think I have been commanded to stand here. That looks so aristocratic!" And he went on standing on one leg.

Below in the street a whole crowd of children were playing; and when they caught sight of the storks, one of the boldest of the boys, and afterwards all of them, sang the old verse about the Storks. But they only sang it just as he could remember it:

"Stork, stork, fly away,
Stand not on one leg, I pray,
See your wife is in her nest,
With her little ones at rest.
They will hang one,
And fry another;
They will shoot a third,
And roast his brother."

"Just hear what those boys are saying!" said the little stork children. "They say we're to be hanged and killed."

"You're not to care for that!" said the Mother Stork. "Don't listen to it, and then it won't matter."

But the boys went on singing, and pointed at the storks mockingly with their fingers; only one boy, whose name was Peter, declared that it was a sin to make a jest of animals, and he would not join in it at all.

The Mother Stork comforted her children. "Don't you mind it at all," she said; "see how quiet your father stands, though it's only on one leg."

"We are very much afraid," said the young storks; and they drew their heads far back into the nest.

Now to-day, when the children came out again to play, and saw the storks, they sang their song:

"The first he will be hanged,
The second will be hit."

"Shall we be hanged and beaten?" asked the young storks.

"No, certainly not," replied the mother. "You shall learn to fly; I'll exercise you; then we shall fly into the meadows and pay a visit to the frogs; they will bow before us in the water, and sing 'Co-ax! co-ax!' and then we shall eat them up. That will be a real pleasure."

"And what then?" asked the young storks.

*Mother and Father Stork were very proud
of their new young ones*

"Then all the storks will assemble, all that are here in the whole country, and the autumn exercises begin: then one must fly well, for that is highly important, for whoever cannot fly properly will be thrust dead by the general's beak; so take care and learn well when the exercising begins."

"But then we shall be killed, as the boys say – and only listen, now they're singing again."

"Listen to me, and not to them," said the Mother Stork. "After the great review we shall fly away to the warm countries, far away from here, over mountains and forests. We shall fly to Egypt, where there are three covered houses of stone, which curl in a point and tower above the clouds; they are called pyramids, and are older than a stork can imagine. There is a river in that country which runs out of its bed, and then all the land is turned to mud. One walks about in the mud, and eats frogs."

"Oh!" cried all the young ones.

"Yes! It is glorious there! One does nothing all day long but eat; and while we are so comfortable over there, here there is not a green leaf on the trees; here it is so cold that the clouds freeze to pieces, and fall down in little white rags!"

It was the snow that she meant, but she could not explain it in any other way.

"And do the naughty boys freeze to pieces?" asked the young storks.

"No, they don't freeze to pieces; but they are not far from it, and must sit in the dark room and cower. You, on the other hand, can fly about in foreign lands, where there are flowers, and the sun shines warm."

Now some time had elapsed, and the nestlings had grown so large that they could stand upright in the nest and

Father Stork perched on the rooftop like a sentry standing guard

look far around; and the Father Stork came every day with delicious frogs, little snakes, and all kinds of stork-dainties as he found them. Oh! it looked funny when he performed feats before them. He laid his head quite back upon his tail, and clapped with his beak as if he had been a little clapper; and then he told them stories, all about the marshes.

"Listen! Now you must learn to fly," said the Mother Stork one day; and all the four young ones had to go out on the ridge of the roof. O, how they tottered! How they balanced themselves with their wings, and yet they were nearly falling down.

"Only look at me," said the mother. "Thus you must hold your heads! Thus you must pitch your feet! One, two! one, two! That's what will help you on in the world."

Then she flew a little way, and the young ones made a little clumsy leap. Bump! – There they lay, for their bodies were too heavy.

"I will not fly!" said one of the young Storks, and crept back into the nest. "I don't care about getting to the warm countries."

"Do you want to freeze to death here, when the winter comes? Are the boys to come and hang you, and singe you, and roast you? Now I'll call them."

"Oh no!" cried the young Stork, and hopped out on to the roof again like the rest.

On the third day they could actually fly a little, and then they thought they could also soar and hover in the air. They tried it, but – bump! – Down they tumbled, and they had to shoot their wings again quickly enough. Now the boys came into the street again and sang their chant:

"Stork, stork, long-legged stork!
Stork, stork, long-legged stork!

"Shall we fly down and pick their eyes out?" asked the young Storks.

"No," replied the mother, "Let them alone. Only listen to me; that's far more important. One, two, three! – now we fly round to the right. One, two, three! – Now to the left round the chimney! See, that was very good! The last kick with the feet was so neat and correct that you shall have permission to-morrow to fly with me to the marsh! Several nice stork families go there with their young: show them that mine are the nicest, and that you can start proudly; that looks well, and will get you consideration."

"But are we not to take revenge on the rude boys?" asked the young Storks.

"Let them scream as much as they like. You will fly up to the clouds, and get to the land of the pyramids, when they will have to shiver, and not have a green leaf or a sweet apple."

"Yes, we will revenge ourselves!" they whispered to one another; and then the practice went on.

Among all the boys down in the street, the one most bent upon singing the teasing song was he who had begun it, and he was quite a little boy. He could hardly be more than six years old. The young storks certainly thought he was a hundred, for he was much bigger than their mother and father; and how should they know how old children

Mother Stork told her babies that they would soon all fly away to Egypt and see the pyramids

and grown-up people can be! Their revenge was to come upon this boy, for it was he who had begun, and he always kept on. The young storks were very angry; and as they grew bigger they were less inclined to bear it: at last their mother had to promise them that they should be revenged, but not till the last day of their stay.

"We must first see how you behave at the grand review. If you get through badly, so that the general stabs you through the chest with his beak, the boys will be right, at least in one way. Let us see."

"Yes, you shall see!" cried the young storks; and then they took all imaginable pains. They practiced every day, and flew so neatly and so lightly that it was a pleasure to see them.

Now the autumn came on; all the storks began to assemble, to fly away to the warm countries while it is winter here. That was a review. They had to fly over forests and villages, to show how well they could soar, for it was a long journey they had before them. The young storks did their parts so well that they got as a mark, "Remarkably well, with frogs and snakes." That was the highest mark; and they might eat the frogs and snakes; and that is what they did.

"Now we will be revenged!" they said.

"Yes, certainly!" said the Mother Stork. "What I have thought of will be the best. I know the pond in which all the little mortals lie till the stork comes and brings them to their parents. The pretty little babies lie there and dream so sweetly as they never dream afterwards. All parents are glad to have such a child, and all children want to have a sister or a brother. Now we will fly to the pond, and bring one for each of the children who have not sung the naughty song and laughed at the storks."

"But he who began to sing, that naughty, ugly boy!" screamed the young Storks; "What shall we do with him?"

"There is a little dead child in the pond, one that has dreamed itself to death; we will bring that for him. Then he will cry because we have brought him a little dead brother. But that good boy – you have not forgotten him, the one who said, 'It is wrong to laugh at animals!' – for him we will bring a brother and a sister too. And as his name is Peter, all of you shall be called Peter too."

And it was done as she said; all the storks were named Peter, and so they are all called even now.

The Well of the World's End

This story in the collection made by
Joseph Jacobs (1854–1916) is a similar
story to the Brothers Grimm's first tale
The Frog Prince but here the young maid
is far less haughty – perhaps because she
is not a royal princess in the first place
but of humble birth. A well of this name
occurs also in the Scottish version, *Three
Heads of the Well* while the sieve-bucket
task is widespread – from the Danaids of
the Greeks to the little rabbits of Uncle
Remus, who, "… fill it wid moss en
dob it wid clay."

Once upon a time, and a very good time it was, though it wasn't in my time, nor in your time, nor anyone else's time, there was a girl whose mother had died, and her father married again. And her stepmother hated her because she was more beautiful than herself, and she was very cruel to her. She used to make her do all the servant's work, and never let her have any peace. At last, one day, the stepmother thought to get rid of her altogether; so she handed her a sieve and said to her: "Go, fill it at the Well of the World's End and bring it home to me full, or woe betide you." For she thought she would never be able to find the Well of the World's End, and, if she did, how could she bring home a sieve full of water?

Well, the girl started off, and asked everyone she met to tell her where was the Well of the World's End. But nobody knew, and she didn't know what to do, when a queer little old woman, all bent double, told her where it was, and how she could get to it. So she did what the old woman told her, and at last arrived at the Well of the World's End. But when she dipped the sieve in the cold, cold water, it all ran out again. She tried and tried again, but every time it was the same; and at last she sate down and cried as if her heart would break.

Suddenly she heard a croaking voice, and she looked up and saw a great frog with goggle eyes looking at her and speaking to her.

"What's the matter, dearie?" it said.

"Oh, dear, oh dear," she said, "my stepmother has sent me all this long way to fill this sieve with water from the Well of the World's End, and I can't fill it no how at all."

"Well," said the frog, "if you promise me to do whatever I bid you for a whole night long, I'll tell you how to fill it."

So the girl agreed, and the frog said:

"Stop it with moss and daub it with clay
And then it will carry the water away"

. . . and then it gave a hop, skip, and jump, and went flop into the Well of the World's End.

So the girl looked about for some moss, and lined the bottom of the sieve with it, and over that she put some clay, and then she dipped it once again into the Well of the World's End; and this time, the water didn't run out, and she turned to go away.

Just then the frog popped up its head out of the Well of the World's End, and said: "Remember your promise."

"All right," said the girl; for thought she, "What harm can a frog do me?"

So she went back to her stepmother, and brought the sieve full of water from the Well of the World's End. The stepmother was angry as angry, but she said nothing at all.

That very evening they heard something tap-tapping at

The frog told the girl that he could help her fill the sieve with water

the door low down, and a voice cried out:

"Open the door, my hinny, my heart
Open the door, my own darling;
Mind you the words that you and I spoke,
Down in the meadow, at the World's End Well."

"Stop it with moss, and daub it with clay"

Well, she didn't mind doing that, so she got it a bowl of milk and bread, and fed it well. And when the frog had finished, it said:

"Go with me to bed, my hinny, my heart,
Go with me to bed, my own darling;
Mind you the words you spake to me,
Down by the cold well, so weary."

But that the girl wouldn't do, till her stepmother said: "Do what you promised, girl; girls must keep their promises. Do what you're bid, or out you go, you and your froggie."

So the girl took the frog with her to bed, and kept it as far away from her as she could. Well, just as the day was beginning to break what should the frog say but:

"Chop off my head, my hinny, my heart
Chop off my head, my own darling;
Remember the promise you made to me,
Down by the cold well, so weary."

At first the girl wouldn't, for she thought of what the frog had done for her at the Well of the World's End. But when the frog said the words over again she went and took an axe and chopped off its head, and lo! and behold, there stood before her a handsome young prince, who told her that he had been enchanted by a wicked magician, and he could never be 'unspelled' till some girl would do his bidding for a whole night, and chop off his head at the end of it.

The stepmother was surprised indeed when she found

"Whatever can that be?" cried out the stepmother, and the girl had to tell her about it, and what she had promised the frog.

"Girls must keep their promises," said the stepmother. "Go and open the door this instant." For she was glad the girl would have to obey a nasty frog.

So the girl went and opened the door, and there was the frog from the Well of the World's End. And it hopped, and it hopped, and it jumped, till it reached the girl, and then it said:

"Lift me to your knee, my hinny, my heart;
Lift me to your knee, my own darling;
Remember the words you and I spake,
Down in the meadow, by the World's End Well."

But the girl didn't like to, till her stepmother said: "Lift it up this instant, you hussy! Girls must keep their promises!"

So at last she lifted the frog up on to her lap, and it lay there for a time, till at last it said:

"Give me some supper, my hinny, my heart,
Give me some supper, my darling;
Remember the words you and I spake,
In the meadow, by the Well of the World's End."

The prince married the stepdaughter, delighted that she had 'unspelled' him

the young prince instead of the nasty frog, and she wasn't best pleased, you may be sure, when the prince told her that he was going to marry her stepdaughter because she had 'unspelled' him. But married they were, and went away to live in the castle of the king, his father, and all the stepmother had to console her was that it was all through her that her stepdaughter was married to a prince.

The Cat's Elopement

The Cat's Elopement is a Japanese fairy tale collected by David Brauns in *Japanische Marchen und Sagen* and by Andrew Lang (1844–1912) for his *The Pink Fairy Book*. It tells how two cats fall in love but since neither owner will part with their own pet, the animals decide to elope. As the story proceeds, a prince, princess and snake are also involved.

Once upon a time there lived a cat of marvellous beauty, with a skin as soft and shining as silk, and wise green eyes, that could see even in the dark. His name was Gon, and he belonged to a music teacher, who was so fond and proud of him that he would not have parted with him for anything in the world.

Now not far from the music master's house there dwelt a lady who possessed a most lovely little pussy cat called Koma. She was such a little dear altogether, and blinked her eyes so daintily, and ate her supper so tidily, and when she had finished she licked her pink nose so delicately with her little tongue, that her mistress was never tired of saying, "Koma, Koma, what should I do without you?"

Well, it happened one day that these two, when out for an evening stroll, met under a cherry tree, and in one moment fell madly in love with each other. Gon had long felt that it was time for him to find a wife, for all the ladies in the neighbourhood paid him so much attention that it made him quite shy; but he was not easy to please, and did not care about any of them. Now, before he had time to think, Cupid had entangled him in his net, and he was filled with love towards Koma. She fully returned his passion, but, like any woman, she saw the difficulties in the way, and consulted sadly with Gon as to the means of overcoming them. Gon entreated his master to set matters right by buying Koma, but her mistress would not part from her. Then the music master was asked to sell Gon to the lady, but he declined to listen to any such suggestion, so everything remained as before.

At length the love of the couple grew to such a pitch that they determined to please themselves, and to seek their fortunes together. So one moonlight night they stole away, and ventured out into an unknown world. All day long they marched bravely on through the sunshine, till they had left their homes far behind them, and towards evening they found themselves in a large park. The wanderers by this time were very hot and tired, and the grass looked very soft and inviting, and the trees cast cool deep shadows, when suddenly an ogre appeared in this Paradise, in the shape of a big, big dog! He came springing towards them showing all his teeth, and Koma shrieked, and rushed up a cherry tree. Gon, however, stood his ground boldly, and prepared to give battle, for he felt that Koma's eyes were upon him, and that he must not run away. But, alas! His courage would have availed him nothing had his enemy once touched him, for he was large and powerful, and very fierce. From her perch in the tree Koma saw it all, and screamed with all her might, hoping that someone would hear, and come to help. Luckily a servant of the princess to whom the park belonged was walking by, and he drove

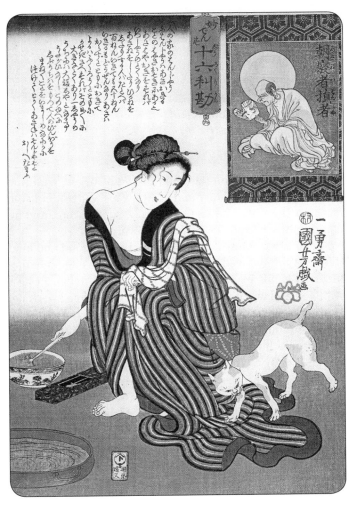

The princess adored her new pet

off the dog, and picking up the trembling Gon in his arms, carried him to his mistress.

So poor little Koma was left alone, while Gon was borne away – very troubled, not in the least knowing what to

245

*Poor little Koma was left all alone while
Gon lived in the palace*

world stretched out before him, and saw in the distance a big ruffian of a cat teasing and ill-treating quite a little one. He jumped up, full of rage, and chased away the big cat, and then he turned to comfort the little one, when his heart nearly burst with joy to find that it was Koma. At first Koma did not know him again, he had grown so large and stately; but when it dawned upon her who it was, her happiness knew no bounds. And they rubbed their heads and their noses again and again, while their purring might have been heard a mile off.

Paw in paw they appeared before the princess, and told her the story of their life and its sorrows. The princess wept for sympathy, and promised that they should never more be parted, but should live with her to the end of their days. By-and-bye the princess herself got married, and brought a prince to dwell in the palace in the park. And she told him all about her two cats, and how brave Gon had been, and how he had delivered her from her enemy the serpent.

And when the prince heard, he swore they should never leave them, but should go with the princess wherever she went. So it all fell out as the princess wished; and Gon and Koma had many children, and so had the princess, and they all played together, and were friends to the end of their lives.

do. Even the attention paid him by the princess, who was delighted with his beauty and pretty ways, did not console him, but there was no use in fighting against fate, and he could only wait and see what would turn up.

The princess, Gon's new mistress, was so good and kind that everybody loved her, and she would have led a happy life, had it not been for a serpent who had fallen in love with her, and was constantly annoying her by his presence. Her servants had orders to drive him away as often as he appeared; but as they were careless, and the serpent very sly, it sometimes happened that he was able to slip past them, and to frighten the princess by appearing before her. One day she was seated in her room, playing on her favourite musical instrument, when she felt something gliding up her sash, and saw her enemy making his way to kiss her cheek. She shrieked and threw herself backwards, and Gon, who had been curled up on a stool at her feet, understood her terror, and with one bound seized the snake by his neck. He gave him one bite and one shake, and flung him on the ground, where he lay, never to worry the princess any more. Then she took Gon in her arms, and praised and caressed him, and saw that he had the nicest bits to eat, and the softest mats to lie on; and he would have had nothing in the world to wish for if only he could have seen Koma again.

Time passed on, and one morning Gon lay before the house door, basking in the sun. He looked lazily at the

*The prince and princess were happily married and
had many children – as did Gon and Koma*

246

The Star Maiden

Here are two Native American tales with the same title. The first one tells how the Star Maiden chooses to live among the water lilies on the lake where young braves paddle their canoes. It was collected by Margaret Compton (1852–1903) and included in her *American Indian Fairy Tales*, published in 1907. Its roots, however, go back considerably further into ancient storytelling.

The Ojibways were a great nation whom the fairies loved. Their land was the home of many spirits, and as long as they lived on the shores of the great lakes the woods in that country were full of fairies. Some of them dwelt in the moss at the roots or on the trunks of trees. Others hid beneath the mushrooms and toadstools. Some changed themselves into bright-winged butterflies or tinier insects with shining wings. This they did that they might be near the children they loved and play with them where they could see and be seen.

But there were also evil spirits in the land. These burrowed in the ground, gnawed at the roots of the loveliest flowers and destroyed them. They breathed upon the corn and blighted it. They listened whenever they heard men talking, and carried the news to those with whom it would make most mischief.

It is because of these wicked fairies that the Indian must be silent in the woods and must not whisper confidences in the camp unless he is sure the spirits are fast asleep under the white blanket of the snow.

The Ojibways looked well after the interests of the good spirits. They shielded the flowers and stepped carefully aside when moss or flower was in their path. They brushed no moss from the trees, and they never snared the sunbeams, for on them thousands of fairies came down from the sky. When the chase was over they sat in the doorways of their wigwams smoking, and as they watched the blue circles drift and fade into the darkness of the evening, they listened to the voices of the fairies and the insects' hum and the thousand tiny noises that night always brings.

One night as they were listening they saw a bright light shining in the top of the tallest trees. It was a star brighter than all the others, and it seemed very near the earth. When they went close to the tree they found that it was really caught in the topmost branches.

The wise men of the tribe were summoned and for three nights they sat about the council fire, but they came to no conclusion about the beautiful star. At last one of the young warriors went to them and told them that the truth had come to him in a dream.

While asleep the west wind had lifted the curtains of his wigwam and the light of the star fell full upon him. Suddenly a beautiful maiden stood at his side. She smiled upon him, and as he gazed speechless she told him that her home was in the star and that in wandering over all the earth she had seen no land so fair as the land of the Ojibways. Its flowers, its sweet-voiced birds, its rivers, its beautiful lakes, the mountains clothed in green, these had charmed her, and she wished to be no more a wanderer. If they would welcome her she would make her home among them, and she asked them to choose a place in which she might dwell.

The council were greatly pleased; but they could not agree upon what was best to offer the Star Maiden, so they decided to ask her to choose for herself.

She searched first among the flowers of the prairie. There she found the fairies' ring, where the little spirits

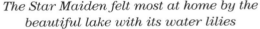

The Star Maiden felt most at home by the beautiful lake with its water lilies

danced on moonlight nights. "Here," thought she, "I will rest." But as she swung herself backwards and forwards on the stem of a lovely blossom, she heard a terrible noise and fled in great fear. A vast herd of buffaloes came and took possession of the fairies' ring, where they rolled over one another, and bellowed so they could be heard far on the trail. No gentle star maiden could choose such a resting-place.

She next sought the mountain rose. It was cool and pleasant, the moss was soft to her dainty feet, and she could talk to the spirits she loved, whose homes were in the stars. But the mountain was steep, and huge rocks hid from her view the nation that she loved.

She was almost in despair, when one day as she looked down from the edge of the wild rose leaf she saw a white flower with a heart of gold shining on the waters of the lake below her. As she looked a canoe steered by the young warrior who had told her wishes to his people, shot past, and his strong, brown hand brushed the edge of the flower.

"That is the home for me," she cried, and half-skipping, half-flying down the side of the mountain, she quickly made her way to the flower and hid herself in its bosom. There she could watch the stars as well as when she looked upward from the cup of the mountain rose; there she could talk to the star spirits, for they bathed in the clear lake; and best of all, there she could watch the people whom she loved, for their canoes were always upon the water.

> This second Star Maiden tale comes from *The Red Indian Fairy Book* by Frances Jenkins Olcott, published in 1917. Here the Star Maiden takes her young Indian brave up to visit her home in the Sky Land before returning to live with him on Earth.

LISTEN to the Wyandot Grandmother, as she tells of the lovely Star Maiden:

In the olden days when the Earth was young, an Indian brave sat at the door of his lodge, not far from a lake. Soon faint and distant sounds of music came to his ears. He looked on all sides, but could not tell from whence the sounds came. Then they grew clearer and louder, and seemed to fall from the sky to the lake.

The young man listened closely, and thought he heard voices by the water. So he crept through the grasses and reeds that grew along the shore. And when he parted the reeds, he saw seven lovely maidens singing and dancing, hand in hand, upon the beach.

They were as beautiful as Starlight, and one was more lovely than the rest. And as the young man crept nearer,

a pebble slipped beneath his hand, and at the sound the maidens sprang into a large osier basket, that rose with them to the sky. And so they disappeared from his sight.

The young man returned in sorrow to his lodge. All that night he did not sleep, but thought of the maiden who was lovelier than the rest. And all the next day he wandered about lonely and sad. But when evening came, he went down again to the water, and hid among the reeds.

Soon he heard the music falling sweetly from the sky, and the osier basket came floating downward. The Seven Maidens stepped out on the beach, and began to dance and sing as before. And as the young man watched them, his delight was so great that he exclaimed with joy. The maidens heard the sound, and sprang into the basket, that rose with them to the sky.

Again on the third night, the young man watched, and the maidens came. And as they danced to and fro, he rushed in among them. Filled with terror, they ran to their basket, and six of them sprang in, and the basket began to rise. But the young man caught the loveliest maiden by her girdle, as she clung to the side of the basket; and they were both lifted into the air. Soon she lost her hold, and they fell gently to the ground.

Then the young man led her to his lodge and begged her to become his bride. Very grieved she was, but not angry. "We are the Seven Star Sisters," she said, "the Singing Maidens. We have always lived together in the Sky Land where you have seen us dancing above you. If you will go with me to the lodge of the Sun, I will become your bride."

So the next night, when the basket descended again, the Star Maiden took the young man with her into the Sky Land, and there he saw many wonderful things. After which they returned once more to the Earth, and the Star Maiden became his bride.

That is why today the Indian children see only six Singing Maidens among the Pleiades; and why sometimes the shadow of the seventh is faintly seen.

The Star Maidens danced upon the beach

The Goblin Spider

In Japanese folklore, a goblin-spider is supposed to have the magical ability to take human shape when it suits it in order to trick people – and may even become a beautiful seductive woman. This famous Japanese story about such a creature also involves samurai and goblins.

The samisen changed into a monstrous spider web

In very ancient books it is said that there used to be many goblin-spiders in Japan.

Some folks declare there are still some goblin-spiders. During the daytime they look just like common spiders; but very late at night, when everybody is asleep, and there is no sound, they become very, very big, and do awful things. Goblin-spiders are supposed also to have the magical power of taking human shape – so as to deceive people. And there is a famous Japanese story about such a spider.

There was once, in some lonely part of the country, a haunted temple. No one could live in the building because of the goblins that had taken possession of it. Many brave samurai went to that place at various times for the purpose of killing the goblins. But they were never heard of again after they had entered the temple.

At last one who was famous for his courage and his prudence, went to the temple to watch during the night. And he said to those who accompanied him there: "If in the morning I am still alive, I shall drum upon the drum of the temple." Then he was left alone, to watch by the light of a lamp.

As the night advanced he crouched down under the altar, which supported a dusty image of Buddha. He saw nothing strange and heard no sound till after mid night. Then there came a goblin, having but half a body and one eye, and said: "Hitokusai!" [There is the smell of a man.] But the samurai did not move. The goblin went away.

Then there came a priest and played upon a samisen so wonderfully that the samurai felt sure it was not the playing of a man. So he leaped up with his sword drawn. The priest, seeing him, burst out laughing, and said: "So you thought I was a goblin? Oh no! I am only the priest of this temple; but I have to play to keep off the goblins. Does not this samisen sound well? Please play a little."

And he offered the instrument to the samurai who grasped it very cautiously with his left hand. But instantly the samisen changed into a monstrous spider web, and the priest into a goblin and the warrior found himself caught fast in the web by the left hand. He struggled bravely, and struck at the spider with his sword, and wounded it; but he soon became entangled still more in the net, and could not move.

However, the wounded spider crawled away, and the sun rose, in a little while the people came and found the samurai in the horrible web, and freed him. They saw tracks of blood upon the floor, and followed the tracks out of the temple to a hole in the deserted garden. Out of the hole issued a frightful sound of groaning. They found the wounded goblin in the hole, and killed it.

The samurai fought the great spider bravely

The One Tree

This is an excerpt from a fairy tale by Pierz Hugo (born 1947). It tells of the One Tree and how it shares its wisdom and love for the natural world and changing seasons with a sad little boy, comforting him and easing his loneliness. The story reflects both on the importance of friendship and the cycle of life since time immemorial.

Not far from anywhere . . .
and quite near somewhere,
by a rock near the top of a small hill, stood a tall, lone tree.

This tree, the One Tree, could see for miles, across the hills, over the river, down to the sea.

Looking from its highest branch, the One Tree could not see any other trees.

When the wind blew, the One Tree sighed and bent, but always stood bravely, by the rock on the hill . . .

Not far from anywhere
and quite near somewhere.

One day a boy struggled up the hill and sat down on the rock under the One Tree.

The boy sat down on a rock under the One Tree

The boy was crying, so the One Tree lowered a long branch and patted him on the shoulder to comfort him.

"Why are you crying?" asked the One Tree.

"Because I feel all alone," said the boy. "Are you lonely, too?" asked the boy, for he had noticed the One Tree was all alone.

"No, I am never lonely," said the One Tree. "The birds come and nest in my branches.

The foxes come wandering around my trunk at night, when the moon is out.

The winds blow and the rain comes and quenches my thirst.

The worms wriggle into their holes between my roots. Sometimes that tickles. But I am never alone or sad," said the One Tree.

They talked together for a long time. The sun set. The sky was turning dark.

"It's getting late," said the boy. "Will you be here if I come back tomorrow?"

"Of course," said the One Tree . . . "I will always be here."

Each day after school, the boy would climb up the hill to sit on the rock under the One Tree, and they would talk.

As they talked, the boy began to realise a little more each day that the One Tree always saw the good side of everything.

The One Tree explained:

"I like the wind because it helps seeds to spread to other places and take root, and because it helps the birds to fly long distances to other lands.

I like the rain, because water helps me to grow taller by feeding my roots.

And I even like the snow in winter, because it keeps me warm like a blanket when the wind blows cold."

The One Tree explained to the boy that trees breathe out oxygen, which is in the air that people need to survive on Earth.

And that trees breathe in carbon dioxide, a gas that people breathe out.

The One Tree said: "I help to keep the air clean on our planet Earth.

And if we look after Earth, then it will look after us."

The One Tree told the boy that it loved:

The change of the seasons.

The rhythm of the rain.

The music of the stream.

The soft touch of the snow.

The music in the wind.

The singing of the birds.

The movement of the clouds.

After several weeks of his talks each day with the One Tree, the boy no longer felt lonely.

Every day after school, the boy looked forward to

climbing up the hill and sitting on the rock, near the top of the small hill, under the spreading branches of his friend, the One Tree . . .

Not far from anywhere

and quite near somewhere.

Eventually the boy discovers that his family are to move away, to a new town in another land but when the boy goes to see his friend for the last time, to say goodbye, he discovers that the One Tree has been cut down. It is no longer there.

Then the boy sat on the rock and wept.

Although the man sailed away across the widest oceans he always remembered the One Tree

His tears ran down the rock between his feet and into the hole where the roots of the One Tree had been. The boy sat on the rock for hours. He kept closing his eyes. He hoped that when he opened them he would find that his friend, the One Tree, was still standing there, brave and tall.

He hoped that the One Tree would pat him gently on the shoulder with a branch and comfort him, as he had on that first day when they became friends.

But there was no touch on his shoulder.

All the boy could hear was the sound of the wind.

At last, the boy went slowly down the hill to his home.

Many years passed. The boy became a man; the man grew older and older. Then at last one day he came back . . .

The old man sat on the rock, looking at the ground. He began to cry.

His tears ran down the rock, just as had all those years before. The old man cried and cried.

His tears flowed down the rock and into the hole where the One Tree had stood.

Suddenly, a small green leaf pushed its way out of the ground, right before his eyes.

"Thank you," said a voice from the earth between the old man's feet:

"I have been waiting so long for you to come and give

me your tears of friendship to feed the roots that were left when my trunk was torn away. I knew you would not let me down. I knew that one day you would come and help me to grow back into a tall strong tree."

While he listened to the words from the earth, the old man had stopped crying. Now he wept again. This time with tears of joy as he recognised the voice of his old friend, the One Tree.

As he wept, his tears of friendship provided more strength to feed the green shoot that had sprung from the Earth at that special place . . .

Not far from anywhere

and quite near somewhere.

If you could go there now, if you could find that special place, near the top of a small hill, you would have to search hard to find the rock where the boy first talked to his friend, the One Tree.

For now, all around, a forest has grown, with plants and animals and birds and insects living among many, many trees, near where the boy and the One Tree first met and talked.

And if you could be in the trees where this forest has grown, you might catch a glimpse of the shape of the shadow of an old man moving in and out of the trees.

And if you could look into the old man's eyes, you would see an image of the boy who never stopped believing in his friend, the One Tree, and the time they shared together –

The timeless time that all the Earth's people share . . .

Not far from anyone

and quite near everyone.

Not far from anywhere

and quite near somewhere.

If you could look into the old man's eyes you would see an image of the boy who trusted his friend

The Crab and the Monkey

This tale (sometimes called *The Quarrel of the Monkey and the Crab*) is a Japanese fairy tale, as related by Andrew Lang (1844–1912) and published 1902. Its themes are revenge and justice. There are some quite violent elements here that may be 'toned down' in some modern versions.

exchange. So the monkey went off with his rice, and the crab returned to her hole with the kernel.

For some time the crab saw no more of the monkey, who had gone to pay a visit on the sunny side of the mountain; but one morning he happened to pass by her hole, and found her sitting under the shadow of a beautiful kaki tree.

"Good day," he said politely, "you have some very fine fruit there! I am very hungry, could you spare me one or two?"

"Oh, certainly," replied the crab, "but you must forgive me if I cannot get them for you myself. I am no tree-climber."

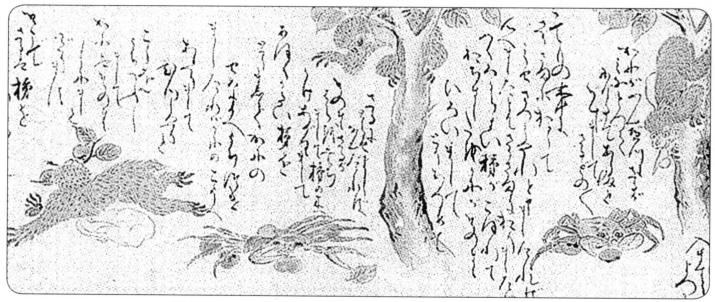

The monkey seized the ripest kakis and ran away with them

There was once a crab who lived in a hole on the shady side of a mountain. She was a very good housewife, and so careful and industrious that there was no creature in the whole country whose hole was so neat and clean as hers, and she took great pride in it.

One day she saw lying near the mouth of her hole a handful of cooked rice which some pilgrim must have let fall when he was stopping to eat his dinner. Delighted at this discovery, she hastened to the spot, and was carrying the rice back to her hole when a monkey, who lived in some trees near by, came down to see what the crab was doing. His eyes shone at the sight of the rice, for it was his favourite food, and like the sly fellow he was, he proposed a bargain to the crab. She was to give him half the rice in exchange for the kernel of a sweet red kaki fruit which he had just eaten. He half expected that the crab would laugh in his face at this impudent proposal, but instead of doing so she only looked at him for a moment with her head on one side and then said that she would agree to the

"Pray do not apologise," answered the monkey. "Now that I have your permission I can get them myself quite easily." And the crab consented to let him go up, merely saying that he must throw her down half the fruit.

In another moment he was swinging himself from branch to branch, eating all the ripest kakis and filling his pockets with the rest, and the poor crab saw to her disgust that the few he threw down to her were either not ripe at all or else quite rotten.

"You are a shocking rogue," she called in a rage; but the monkey took no notice, and went on eating as fast as he could. The crab understood that it was no use her scolding, so she resolved to try what cunning would do.

"Sir Monkey," she said, "you are certainly a very good climber, but now that you have eaten so much, I am quite sure you would never be able to turn one of your somersaults." The monkey prided himself on turning better somersaults than any of his family, so he instantly went head over heels three times on the bough on which

The monkey was a rogue but luckily the crab had friends who helped her

he was sitting, and all the beautiful kakis that he had in his pockets rolled to the ground. Quick as lightning the crab picked them up and carried a quantity of them into her house, but when she came up for another the monkey sprang on her, and treated her so badly that he left her for dead. When he had beaten her till his arm ached he went his way.

It was a lucky thing for the poor crab that she had some friends to come to her help or she certainly would have died then and there. The wasp flew to her, and took her back to bed and looked after her, and then he consulted with a rice-mortar and an egg which had fallen out of a nest near by, and they agreed that when the monkey returned, as he was sure to do, to steal the rest of the fruit, that they would punish him severely for the manner in which he had behaved to the crab. So the mortar climbed up to the beam over the front door, and the egg lay quite still on the ground, while the wasp set down the water-bucket in a corner. Then the crab dug itself a deep hole in the ground, so that not even the tip of her claws might be seen.

Soon after everything was ready the monkey jumped down from his tree, and creeping to the door began a long hypocritical speech, asking pardon for all he had done. He waited for an answer of some sort, but none came. He listened, but all was still; then he peeped, and saw no one; then he went in. He peered about for the crab, but in vain; however, his eyes fell on the egg, which he snatched up and set on the fire. But in a moment the egg had burst into a thousand pieces, and its sharp shell struck him in the face and scratched him horribly. Smarting with pain he ran to the bucket and stooped down to throw some water over his head. As he stretched out his hand up started the wasp and stung him on the nose. The monkey shrieked and ran to the door, but as he passed through down fell the mortar and struck him dead. After that the crab lived happily for many years, and at length died in peace under her own kaki tree.

When the monkey grabbed the bucket of water the wasp stung him

The Story of the Three Little Pigs

There are several stories about the pig and a Big Bad Wolf in a much-loved English fairy tale. Here follows the version by Joseph Jacobs (1854–1916). There are printed versions from the 1840s, but the story itself is thought to be much older with its phrases and morals enshrined in western culture. Andrew Lang also included it in his *The Green Fairy Book* and Joel Chandler Harris (Uncle Remus) also used the storyline but replaced the pigs with Brer Rabbit. There has been a Walt Disney cartoon version – and a stage musical.

O nce upon a time when pigs spoke rhyme
    And monkeys chewed tobacco,
      And hens took snuff to make them tough,
And ducks went quack, quack, quack, O!

There was an old sow with three little pigs, and as she had not enough to keep them, she sent them out to seek their fortune.

The first that went off met a man with a bundle of straw, and said to him:

"Please, man, give me that straw to build me a house."

Which the man did, and the little pig built a house with it. Presently came along a wolf, and knocked at the door, and said:

"Little pig, little pig, let me come in."

To which the pig answered:

"No, no, by the hair of my chinny chin chin."

The wolf then answered to that:

"Then I'll huff, and I'll puff, and I'll blow your house in."

So he huffed, and he puffed, and he blew his house in, and ate up the little pig.

The second little pig met a man with a bundle of furze, and said:

"Please, man, give me that furze to build a house."

Which the man did, and the pig built his house. Then along came the wolf, and said:

"Little pig, little pig, let me come in."

"No, no, by the hair of my chiny chin chin."

"Then I'll puff, and I'll huff, and I'll blow your house in."

So he huffed, and he puffed, and he puffed, and he huffed, and at last he blew the house down, and he ate up the little pig.

The third little pig met a man with a load of bricks, and said:

"Please, man, give me those bricks to build a house with."

So the man gave him the bricks, and he built his house with them. So the wolf came, as he did to the other little pigs, and said:

The old sow sent the young pigs off into the world

The straw house quickly collapsed

"Little pig, little pig, let me come in."

"No, no, by the hair of my chiny chin chin."

"Then I'll huff, and I'll puff, and I'll blow your house in."

Well, he huffed, and he puffed, and he huffed and he puffed, and he puffed and huffed; but he could NOT get the house down. When he found that he could not, with all his huffing and puffing, blow the house down, he said:

"Little pig, I know where there is a nice field of turnips."

"Where?" said the little pig.

"Oh, in Mr. Smith's Home-field, and if you will be ready tomorrow morning I will call for you, and we will go together, and get some for dinner."

"Very well," said the little pig, "I will be ready. What time do you mean to go?"

"Oh, at six o'clock."

Well, the little pig got up at five, and got the turnips before the wolf came (which he did about six) and who said:

"Little Pig, are you ready?"

The little pig said: "Ready! I have been and come back again, and got a nice potful for dinner."

The wolf felt very angry at this, but thought that he would be up to the little pig somehow or other, so he said:

"Little pig, I know where there is a nice apple-tree."

"Where?" said the pig.

"Down at Merry-garden," replied the wolf, "and if you will not deceive me I will come for you, at five o'clock tomorrow and get some apples."

Well, the little pig bustled up the next morning at four o'clock, and went off for the apples, hoping to get back before the wolf came; but he had further to go, and had to climb the tree, so that just as he was coming down from it, he saw the wolf coming, which, as you may suppose, frightened him very much. When the wolf came up he said:

"Little pig, what! are you here before me? Are they nice apples?"

"Yes, very," said the little pig. "I will throw you down one."

And he threw it so far, that, while the wolf was gone to pick it up, the little pig jumped down and ran home. The next day the wolf came again, and said to the little pig:

"Little pig, there is a fair at Shanklin this afternoon, will you go?"

"Oh yes," said the pig, "I will go; what time shall you be ready?"

"At three," said the wolf. So the little pig went off before the time as usual, and got to the fair, and bought a butter-churn, which he was going home with, when he saw the wolf coming. Then he could not tell what to do. So he got into the churn to hide, and by so doing turned it round, and it rolled down the hill with the pig in it, which frightened the wolf so much, that he ran home without going to the fair. He went to the little pig's house, and told him how frightened he had been by a great round thing which came down the hill past him. Then the little pig said:

"Hah, I frightened you, then. I had been to the fair and bought a butter-churn, and when I saw you, I got into it, and rolled down the hill."

Then the wolf was very angry indeed, and declared he WOULD eat up the little pig, and that he would get down the chimney after him. When the little pig saw what he was about, he hung on the pot full of water, and made up a blazing fire, and, just as the wolf was coming down, took off the cover, and in fell the wolf; so the little pig put on the cover again in an instant, boiled him up, and ate him for supper, and lived happy ever afterwards.

The brick house was strong and sturdy

Down tumbled the fox into the pot

The Owl and the Pussycat

This nonsense poem by Edward Lear (1812–1888) was first published in 1871, having been initially penned for Janet Symonds, the three-year-old daughter of fellow poet John Addington Symonds. Lear invented the term *'runcible spoon'* for this poem and then went on to use it in several other works. The animals featured are an owl, cat, a pig and a turkey.

Edward Lear had begun to pen the sequel, The Children of The Owl and the Pussycat, but sections of the poem still remained incomplete at the time of his death in 1888. The portion that was complete, was published posthumously in 1938.

A pea-green boat

The marriage

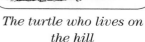
The turtle who lives on the hill

The old man with a beard

The Owl and the Pussy-Cat went to sea
In a beautiful pea-green boat:
They took some honey,
and plenty of money
Wrapped up in a five-pound note.

The Owl looked up to the stars above,
And sang to a small guitar,
"O lovely Pussy, O Pussy, my love,
What a beautiful Pussy you are,
You are,
You are!
What a beautiful Pussy you are!"

Pussy said to the Owl, "You elegant fowl,
How charmingly sweet you sing!
Oh! let us be married;
too long we have tarried:
But what shall we do for a ring?"
They sailed away, for a year and a day,
To the land where the bong-tree grows;
And there in a wood a Piggy-wig stood,
With a ring at the end of his nose,
His nose,
His nose,
With a ring at the end of his nose.

"Dear Pig, are you willing to sell for one shilling
Your ring?" Said the Piggy, "I will."
So they took it away, and were married next day
By the Turkey who lives on the hill.
They dined on mince and slices of quince,
Which they ate with a runcible spoon;
And hand in hand on the edge of the sand
They danced by the light of the moon,
The moon,
The moon,
They danced by the light of the moon.

The Children of the Owl and the Pussycat

Our mother was the Pussy-cat,
our father was the Owl,
And so we're partly little beasts
and partly little fowl,

The brothers of our family
have feathers and they hoot,
While all the sisters dress in fur
and have long tails to boot.

He wrote many limericks too such as

There was an Old Man with a beard,
Who said, "It is just as I feared!
Two Owls and a Hen,
Four Larks and a Wren,
Have all built their nests in my beard!"

The twentieth child of Jeremiah Lear, a London stockbroker, and his wife Ann, Lear was also a talented painter – of both landscapes and birds – and gave England's Queen Victoria drawing lessons.

The Fountain of Youth

Lafcadio Hearn (1850-1904) translated five volumes of *Japanese Fairy Tales*, including this one about an old couple living in the mountains whose lives are changed irrecoverably when they find a magic spring that restores their long-lost youth.

Long, long ago there lived somewhere among the mountains of Japan a poor woodcutter and his wife. They were very old, and had no children. Every day the husband went, alone to the forest to cut wood, while the wife sat weaving at home.

One day the old man went further into the forest than was his custom, to seek a certain kind of wood; and he suddenly found himself at the edge of a little spring he had never seen before. The water was strangely clear and cold, and he was thirsty; for the day was hot, and he had been working hard. So he doffed his huge straw-hat, knelt down, and took a long drink.

That water seemed to refresh him in a most extraordinary way. Then he caught sight of his own face in the spring, and started back. It was certainly his own face, but not at all as he was accustomed to see it in the bronze mirror at home. It was the face of a very young man! He could not believe his eyes. He put up both hands to his head which had been quite bald only a moment before, when he had wiped it with the little blue towel he always carried with him. But now it was covered with thick black hair. And his face had become smooth as a boy's: every wrinkle was gone. At the same moment he discovered himself full of new strength. He stared in astonishment at the limbs that had been so long withered by age: they were now

The old man's wife did not recognise him at all and was frightened

shapely and hard with dense young muscle. Unknowingly he had drunk of the Fountain of Youth; and that draught had transformed him.

First he leaped high and shouted for joy; then he ran home faster than he had ever run before in his life. When he entered his house his wife was frightened – because she took him for a stranger – and when he told her the wonder, she could not at once believe him. But after a long time he

The old woman became younger and younger but she had drunk too deeply and there was no way of stopping the magic

was able to convince her that the young man she now saw before her was really her husband; and he told her where the spring was, and asked her to go there with him.

Then she said, "You have become so handsome and so young that you cannot continue to love an old woman – so I must drink some of that water immediately. But it will never do for both of us to be away from the house at the same time. Do you wait here, while I go." And she ran to the woods all by herself.

She found the spring and knelt down, and began to drink. Oh! how cool and sweet that water was! She drank and drank and drank, and stopped for breath only to begin again.

Her husband waited for her impatiently; he expected to see her come back changed into a pretty slender girl. But she did not come back at all. He got anxious, shut up the house, and went to look for her.

When he reached the spring, he could not see her. He was just on the point of returning when he heard a little wail in the high grass near the spring. He searched there and discovered his wife's clothes and a baby – a very small baby, perhaps six months old.

For the old woman had drunk too deeply of the magical water; she had drunk herself far back beyond the time of youth into the period of speechless infancy.

He took up the child in his arms. It looked at him in a sad wondering way. He carried it home – murmuring to it – thinking strange melancholy thoughts.

Little Red Hen

This is a very old folk tale, probably of Russian origin, and it became highly popular in the USA during the 1880s as a primer for teaching children to read and then again through its mass-market publication during the 1940s. It tells of laziness, greediness and how the other animals get their 'come-uppance' when the hard-working little hen finally eats her well-deserved, delicious, freshly-baked bread.

an idea. She would plant the grains – but it would be good to have some help.

The little red hen asked her friends, "Who will help me plant the corn?"

"Not I," grunted the pig from his muddy patch in the garden.

"Not I," barked the dog on the doorstep.

"Not I," purred the sleepy cat.

"Not I," quacked the noisy yellow duck.

"Then I will do it myself," said the little red hen. So the little red hen planted the corn all by herself.

During the summer the grains of corn grew. First they sprouted into tall green stalks, then they ripened in the

While the cat and the other animals rested, the little red hen worked very hard all day

Once upon a time, there was a little red hen who lived on a farm with a pig, a rather lazy dog, a sleepy cat, and a very noisy quacking yellow duck. The little red hen liked to keep everything clean and tidy and worked hard at her jobs all day. The others never helped. They meant to, of course, but somehow never got around to it. Instead, the pig would grunt in the mud outside, the dog would sleep on the doorstep, the duck swam in the pond all day, and the cat enjoyed lying in the sun, purring.

One day the little red hen was working in the garden when she found some grains of corn. The little red hen had

summer warmth until they had turned as gold as the sun itself. The little red hen saw that the corn was ready for cutting.

"Who will help me cut the corn?" asked the little red hen.

"Not I," grunted the pig from his muddy patch in the garden.

"Not I," barked the dog on the doorstep.

"Not I," quacked the duck from her pond.

"Not I," purred the cat from his place in the sun.

"Very well then, I will cut it myself," said the little red hen. Carefully she cut the stalks and took out all the grains of corn from the husks.

When all the wheat was cut, the little red hen asked her friends, "Who will help me to take the wheat to the mill to be ground into flour?"

"Not I," grunted the pig from his muddy patch in the garden.

"Not I," barked the dog on the doorstep.

"Not I," quacked the duck from her pond.

"Not I," purred the cat from his place in the sun.

"Very well then, I will take it myself," said the little red hen. So the little red hen carried the wheat to the mill all by herself and then watched as the miller ground it into flour. Then she carried the heavy sack of flour back to the farm.

The tired little red hen asked her friends, "Who will help me bake the bread?"

"Not I," grunted the pig from his muddy patch in the garden.

"Not I," barked the dog on the doorstep.

the corners of the house and drifted out into the garden.

The pig ambled into the kitchen from his muddy patch in the garden. The dog had a scratch and then left the warm doorstep to follow his nose into the kitchen. The duck waddled in from the pond. The cat yawned and stretched and then pattered inside. When the little red hen opened the oven door the dough had risen up and had turned into the most wonderful crusty loaf of bread any of them had ever seen.

"Who is going to eat this bread?" asked the little red hen.

"I will," grunted the pig.

"I will," barked the dog.

"I will," quacked the duck.

"I will," purred the cat.

"Oh no, you won't," said the little red hen. "I planted the seed, I cut the corn. I took it to the mill to be ground into flour into flour. I carried back the heavy sack. I kneaded

At last she took the wheat to the mill to be ground into flour to make bread

All the other animals came running to share the loaf that they could smell baking in the oven

"Not I," quacked the duck from her pond.

"Not I," purred the cat from his place in the sun.

"Very well then, I will bake it myself," said the little red hen.

So the little red hen baked the bread all by herself. She went into her neat little kitchen. She mixed the flour into dough. She kneaded the dough and put it into the oven to bake. Soon the delicious smell of hot fresh bread filled all

the dough and I made the bread and cooked it in the oven – all by myself. So now I shall eat the loaf, too – all by myself, all on my owny-own."

The pig, the dog, the duck and the cat all stood and watched with their mouths watering as the little red hen ate the loaf of bread all by herself. It was delicious and she enjoyed it, right to the very last crumb.

The Fish and the Ring

This story is one from Joseph Jacobs (1854–1916) *English Fairy Tales* which was published in 1890. There are many parallel tales about rings in the literature and folklore of various cultures including stories about Polycrates, Solomon, and the Sanskrit drama of *Sakuntala* while the notion of "Letters to kill bearer" can be traced from Homer and the Greek *Iliad* onwards and have also been found in India. This particular romance has a Byzantine source, having travelled from Ethiopia and Constantinople. It seems probable that the tale was brought from Byzantium to France and thence to England from whence an Irish version also emerged.

Once upon a time, there was a mighty baron in the North Country who was a great magician and knew everything that would come to pass. So one day, when his little boy was four years old, he looked into the Book of Fate to see what would happen to him. And to his dismay, he found that his son would wed a lowly maid that had just been born in a house under the shadow of York Minster. Now

The baron put the baby in the river but she was washed ashore

the Baron knew the father of the little girl was very, very poor, and he had five children already. So he called for his horse, and rode into York, and passed by the father's house, and saw him sitting by the door, sad and doleful. So he dismounted and went up to him and said: "What is the matter, my good man?" And the man said: "Well, your

honour, the fact is, I've five children already, and now a sixth's come, a little lass, and where to get the bread from to fill their mouths, that's more than I can say."

"Don't be downhearted, my man," said the Baron. "If that's your trouble, I can help you. I'll take away the last little one, and you won't have to bother about her."

"Thank you kindly, sir," said the man; and he went in

The baron wrote a letter ordering the girl's death

and brought out the lass and gave her to the Baron, who mounted his horse and rode away with her. And when he got by the bank of the River Ouse, he threw the little thing into the river, and rode off to his castle.

But the little lass didn't sink; her clothes kept her up for a time, and she floated, and she floated, till she was cast ashore just in front of a fisherman's hut. There the fisherman found her, and took pity on the poor little thing and took her into his house, and she lived there till she was fifteen years old, and a fine handsome girl.

One day it happened that the Baron went out hunting with some companions along the banks of the River Ouse, and stopped at the fisherman's hut to get a drink, and the girl came out to give it to them. They all noticed her beauty, and one of them said to the Baron: "You can read fates, Baron, whom will she marry, d'ye think?"

"Oh! that's easy to guess," said the Baron; "some yokel

A band of robbers read the letter

or other. But I'll cast her horoscope. Come here, girl, and tell me on what day you were born."

"I don't know, sir," said the girl, "I was picked up just here after having been brought down by the river about fifteen years ago."

Then the Baron knew who she was, and when they went away, he rode back and said to the girl: "Hark ye, girl, I will make your fortune. Take this letter to my brother in Scarborough, and you will be settled for life." And the girl took the letter and said she would go. Now this is what he had written in the letter:

"DEAR BROTHER,

Take the bearer and put her to death immediately.

Yours affectionately,

HUMPHREY."

Soon after the girl set out for Scarborough, and slept for the night at a little inn. Now that very night a band

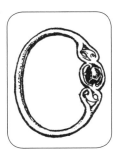

The gold ring
was
swallowed by
a fish

of robbers broke into the inn, and searched the girl, who had no money, and only the letter. So they opened this and read it, and thought it a shame. The captain of the robbers took a pen and paper and wrote this letter:

"DEAR BROTHER,

Take the bearer and marry her to my son immediately.

Yours affectionately,

HUMPHREY."

And then he gave it to the girl, bidding her begone. So she went on to the Baron's brother at Scarborough, a noble knight, with whom the Baron's son was staying. When she gave the letter to his brother, he gave orders for the wedding to be prepared at once, and they were married that very day.

Soon after, the Baron himself came to his brother's castle, and what was his surprise to find the very thing he had plotted against had come to pass. But he was not to be put off that way; and he took the girl out for a walk, as he said, along the cliffs. And when he got her all alone, he took her by the arms, and was going to throw her over. But she begged hard for her life.

"I have not done anything," she said: "if you will only spare me, I will do whatever you wish. I will never see you or your son again till you desire it."

Then the Baron took off his gold ring and threw it into the sea, saying: "Never let me see your face till you can show me that ring!" – and he let her go.

The poor girl wandered on and on, till at last she came

to a great noble's castle, and she asked to have some work given to her; and they made her the scullion girl of the castle, for she had been used to such work in the fisherman's hut.

Now one day, who should she see coming up to the noble's house but the Baron and his brother and his son, her husband. She didn't know what to do; but thought they would not see her in the castle kitchen. So she went back to her work with a sigh, and set to cleaning a huge big fish that was to be boiled for their dinner. And, as she was cleaning it, she saw something shine inside it, and. what do you think she found? Why, there was the Baron's ring, the very one he had thrown over the cliff at Scarborough. She was glad indeed to see it, you may be sure. Then she cooked the fish as nicely as she could, and served it up.

Well, when the fish came on the table, the guests liked it so well that they asked the noble who cooked it. He said he didn't know, but called to his servants:

"Ho, there, send the cook who cooked that fine fish."

So they went down to the kitchen and told the girl she was wanted in the hall.

When the banqueters saw such a young and beautiful cook they were surprised. But the Baron was in a tower of temper, and started up as if he would do her some violence. So the girl went up to him with her hand before her with the ring on it; and she put it down before him on the table. Then at last the Baron saw that no one could fight against Fate, and he handed her to a seat and announced to all the company that this was his son's true wife; and he took her and his son home to his castle; and they all lived happy as could be ever afterwards.

The girl showed the baron the ring

The Flying Trunk

First published in 1839, *The Flying Trunk* is a fairy tale by Hans Christian Andersen (1786–1859) that tells of a young man whose magical trunk carries him to Turkey where he visits the Sultan's daughter. The tale is reminiscent of the flying carpets in *The Arabian Nights*, a collection Andersen read and loved as a child and from which he drew great inspiration.

There once was a merchant so wealthy that he could have paved a whole street with silver, and still have had enough left over to pave a little alley. But he did nothing of the sort. He knew better ways of using his money than that. If he parted with pennies they came back to him as crowns. That's the sort of merchant he was – and then he died.

Now his son got all the money, and he led a merry life, went to masquerades every night, made paper dolls out of banknotes, and played ducks and drakes at the lake with gold pieces instead of pebbles. This makes the money go, and his inheritance was soon gone. At last he had only four pennies, and only a pair of slippers and a dressing gown to wear.

Now his former friends didn't care for him any more, as he could no longer appear in public with them, but one of them was so good as to send him an old trunk, with the hint that he pack and be off. This was all very well, but he had nothing to pack, so he sat himself in it.

It was no ordinary trunk. Press on the lock and it would fly. And that's just what it did. Whisk! It flew up the chimney, and over the clouds, and away through the skies. The bottom of it was so creaky that he feared he would fall through it, and what a fine somersault he would have made then! Good gracious! But at long last he came down safely, in the land of the Turks. He hid his trunk under some dry leaves in the woods, and set off toward the nearest town. He could do so very well, for the Turks all wear dressing gowns and slippers, just as he did.

When he passed a nurse with a child, he said, "Hello, Turkish nurse. Tell me, what's that great big palace at the edge of town? The one that has its windows up so high."

"That's where the Sultan's daughter lives," said the nurse. "It has been foretold that she will be unhappy

He told the princess amazing fairy tales

262

when she falls in love, so no one is ever permitted to visit her except in the presence of her mother and father."

"Thank you," said the merchant's son. Back he went to the woods, sat in his trunk, and whisked off to the roof of the palace. From there, he climbed in at the Princess's window.

She lay fast asleep on a sofa, and she looked so lovely that the merchant's son couldn't help kissing her. She woke up and was terribly frightened, but he told her he was a Turkish prophet, who had sailed through the air just to see her. This pleased her very much.

As they sat there, side by side, he told her stories about her eyes. He said they were beautifully dark, deep lakes in which her thoughts went swimming by like mermaids. He told her about her forehead, which he compared to

The lovely princess lay sleeping on a sofa

a snow-covered mountainside with its many wonderful halls and pictures. Then he told her about the stork, which brings lovely little children from over the sea. Oh, they were such pretty stories! Then he asked her to marry him, and the Princess said yes, right away.

"But you must come on Saturday," she told him, "when my mother and father will be here to have tea with me. They will be so proud when I tell them I am going to marry a prophet. But be sure you have a really pretty tale to tell them, for both my parents love stories. My mother likes them to be elevating and moral, but my father likes them merry, to make him laugh."

"I shall bring no other wedding present than a fairy tale," he told her, and so they parted. But first the Princess made him a present of a gold sabre all covered with gold pieces, and this came in very handy.

He flew away, bought himself a new dressing gown, and went to the woods to invent a fairy tale. That wasn't so easy. However, he had it ready promptly on Saturday. The Sultan, his wife and the whole court awaited him at the Princess's tea party. They gave him a splendid reception.

"Won't you tell us a story?" said the Sultan's wife. "One that is instructive and thoughtful."

*The flying trunk soared over the clouds and
the world far below*

"One that will make us laugh, too," said the Sultan.

"To be sure," he said, and started his story. Now listen closely:

"There once was a bundle of matches, and they were particularly proud of their lofty ancestry. Their family tree – that is to say, the great pine tree of which they were little splinters – had been a great old tree in the forest. As the matches lay on the kitchen shelf, they talked of their younger days to the tinder box and an old iron pot beside them.

'When we were a part of the green branches,' they said, 'then we really were on a green branch! Every morning and evening we were served the diamond tea that is called dew drops. We had sunshine all day long, and the little birds had to tell us stories. It was plain to see that we were wealthy, for while the other trees' garments lasted only the summer, our family could afford to wear green clothes all the year round. But then the woodcutters came, there was a big revolution, and our family was broken up. The chief support of our family got a place as the mainmast of a fine ship, that could sail around the world if need be. The other branches were scattered in different directions, and now our task is to bring light to the lower classes. That's the reason we distinguished people came to this kitchen.'

'My lot has been quite different,' said the iron pot, who stood next to the matches. 'From the moment I came into this world, I've known little but cooking and scouring, day in, day out. I look after the solid and substantial part, and am in fact the most important thing in the house. My only amusement comes when dinner is over. Then, clean and tidy, I take my place here to have a sound conversation with my associates. But except for the watering pot, who now and then makes excursions into the yard, we always live indoors. Our only source of news is the market basket, and he speaks most alarmingly about the government and the people. Why, just the other day an old conservative pot was so upset that he fell down and burst. That basket is a liberal, I tell you!'

'You talk too much,' the tinder box flashed sparks from his flint. 'Let's have a pleasant evening.'

'Yes, let's talk about who among us is most aristocratic,' said the matches.

'No. I don't like to talk about myself,' said the earthenware crock. 'Let's have some entertainment this evening. I'll begin. I'll tell you the sort of things we already know. That won't tax our imaginations, and it is so amusing. By the Baltic sea, by the beech trees of Denmark –'

'That's a very pretty beginning,' the plates chattered. 'That's just the kind of story we like.'

'There I passed my youth in a quiet home, where they polished the furniture, and swept the floor, and hung up fresh curtains every fourteenth day!'

'How well you tell a story!' said the broom. 'You can hear right away that it's a woman who tells it. There's not a speck of dirt in it.'

'Yes, one feels that,' said the water pail, and made a happy little jump so the water splashed on the floor.

The crock went on with her story, and the end was as good as the beginning.

All the plates clattered for joy. The broom made a wreath of parsley to crown the crock, because she knew how that would annoy the others. And the broom thought, 'If I crown her tonight, she will crown me tomorrow.'

'Now I'll do a dance,' said the fire tongs, and dance she did. Yes, good heavens, how she could kick one of her legs up in the air! The old chair cover in the corner split to see it. 'Will you crown me too?' said the tongs, so they gave her a wreath.

'What a common mob,' said the matches.

The tea pot was asked to sing, but she had a cold in her throat. She said nothing short of boiling water could make her sing, but that was sheer affectation. She wished to sing only for the ladies and gentlemen in the drawing room.

On the window sill was an old quill pen that the servant used. There was nothing remarkable about him except that he had been dipped too deep in the ink, but in that difference he took pride.

'The tea pot can sing or not, as she pleases,' he declared. 'In a cage, outside my window, there's a nightingale who will sing for us. He hasn't practiced for the occasion, but tonight we won't be too critical.'

'I find it highly improper,' said the tea kettle, who was the official kitchen singer, and a half-sister of the tea pot. 'Why should we listen to a foreign bird? Is that patriotic? Let the market basket make the decision.'

'I am most annoyed,' said the market basket. 'I am more annoyed than anyone can imagine. Is this any way to spend an evening? Wouldn't it be better to call the house to order? Everyone take his appointed place, and I shall run the whole game. That will be something quite different.'

'Yes. Let us all make a noise,' they clamored.

Just then the servant opened the door, and they stood stock-still. Not one had a word to say. But there was not a pot among them who did not know what he could do, and how well qualified he was. 'If I had wanted to,' each one thought, 'we could have a gay evening. No question about it!'

The servant girl took the matches and struck a light with them. My stars, how they sputtered and flared!

'Now,' they thought, 'everyone can see we are the first. How brilliant we are! What a light we spread.' Then they burned out."

"That was a delightful story," said the Sultan's wife. "I felt myself right in the kitchen with the matches. My dear prophet, thou shalt certainly marry our daughter."

"Yes indeed," said the Sultan. "Thou shalt marry her on Monday." They said "Thou" to him now, for he was soon to be one of the family.

So the wedding day was set, and on the evening that preceded it the whole city was gay with lights. Cookies and cakes were thrown among the people. The boys in the street stood on tiptoe. They shouted, "Hurrah!" and whistled through their fingers. It was all so grand.

"I suppose I really ought to do something too," said the merchant's son. So he bought firecrackers, and rockets, and fireworks of every sort, loaded his trunk with them, and flew over the town.

Pop! went the crackers, and swoosh! went the rockets. The Turks jumped so high that their slippers flopped over their ears. Such shooting stars they never had seen. Now they could understand that it was the prophet of the Turks himself who was to marry their Princess.

As soon as the merchant's son came down in the woods, he thought, "I'll go straight to the town to hear what sort of impression I made." It was the natural thing to do.

Oh, what stories they told! Every last man he asked had his own version, but all agreed it had been fine. Very fine!

"I saw the prophet himself," said one. "His eyes shone like stars, and his beard foamed like water."

"He was wrapped in a fiery cloak," said another. "The heads of beautiful angels peeped out of the folds of it."

Yes, he heard wonderful things, and his wedding was to be on the following day. He went back to the woods to rest in his trunk-but what had become of it? The trunk was burned! A spark from the fireworks had set it on fire, and now the trunk was burned to ashes. He couldn't fly any more. He had no way to reach his bride. She waited for him on the roof, all day long. Most likely she is waiting there still. But he wanders through the world, telling tales which are not half so merry as that one he told about the matches.

The Valiant Little Tailor

This is a Brothers Grimm (Jacob 1785–1863 and Wilhelm 1786–1859) tale that tells how a brave little fellow uses guile instead of brute strength to achieve his aims, with his technique of tricking the giants into fighting each other – not dissimilar to the technique used in Greek mythology by Cadmus to deal with the warriors who sprang up when he sowed dragon's teeth.

One fine day a tailor was sitting on his bench by the window in very high spirits, sewing away most diligently, and presently up the street came a country woman, crying, "Good jams for sale! Good jams for sale!" This call attracted the tailor's attention and, poking his diminutive head out of the window, he called, "Here, my good woman, just bring your jams in here!"

The woman mounted the three steps up to the tailor's

The little tailor set out on his travels and soon met a giant

house with her large basket, and began to open all the pots together before him. He looked at them all, held them up to the light, smelt them, and at last said, "These jams seem to me to be very nice, so you may weigh me out two ounces, my good woman; I don't object even if you make it a quarter of a pound." The woman, who hoped to have met with a good customer, gave him all he wished, and went off grumbling, and in a very bad temper.

"Now!" exclaimed the tailor, "Heaven will send me a

blessing on this jam, and give me fresh strength and vigor;" and, taking the bread from the cupboard, he cut himself a slice the size of the whole loaf, and spread the jam upon it. "I am sure that will taste very good," said he; "but, before I take a bite, I will just finish this waistcoat." So he put the bread on the table and stitched away, making larger and larger stitches every time for joy. Meanwhile the smell of the jam rose to the ceiling, where many flies were sitting, and enticed them down, so that soon a great swarm of them had pitched on the bread. "Holloa! Who asked you?" exclaimed the tailor, driving away the uninvited visitors; but the flies, not understanding his words, would not be

The courtiers were jealous of the tailor and all the attention he was attracting

driven off, and came back in greater numbers than before. This put the little man in a great passion, and, snatching up in his anger a bag of cloth, he brought it down with a merciless swoop upon them. When he raised it again he counted as many as seven lying dead before him with outstretched legs.

"What a fellow you are!" said he to himself, astonished at his own bravery. "The whole town must hear of this." In great haste he cut himself out a band, hemmed it, and then put on it in large letters, "SEVEN AT ONE BLOW!"

"Ah," said he, "not one city alone, the whole world shall hear it!" and his heart danced with joy, like a puppy-dog's tail.

The little tailor bound the belt around his body, and made ready to travel forth into the wide world, feeling the workshop too small for his great deeds. Before he set out, however, he looked about his house to see if there were anything he could carry with him, but he found only an old cheese, which he pocketed, and observing a bird which was caught in the bushes before the door, he captured it, and put that in his pocket also. Soon after he set out boldly on his travels; and, as he was light and active, he felt no fatigue. His road led him up a hill, and when he arrived at the highest point of it he found a great giant sitting there, who was gazing about him very composedly.

But the little tailor went boldly up, and said, "Good day, friend; truly you sit there and see the whole world stretched below you. I also am on my way thither to seek my fortune. Are you willing to go with me?"

The giant looked with scorn at the little tailor, and said, "You rascal! You wretched creature!"

The clever tailor tricked one giant after another

"Perhaps so," replied the tailor; "but here may be seen what sort of a man I am;" and, unbuttoning his coat, he showed the giant his belt. The giant read, "SEVEN AT ONE BLOW"; and supposing they were men whom the tailor had killed, he felt some respect for him. Still he meant to try him first; so taking up a pebble, he squeezed it so hard that water dropped out of it.

"Do as well as that," said he to the other, "if you have the strength."

"If it be nothing harder than that," said the Tailor, "that's child's play." And, diving into his pocket, he pulled out the cheese and squeezed it till the whey ran out of it, and said, "Now, I fancy that I have done better than you."

The giant wondered what to say, and could not believe it of the little man; so, catching up another pebble, he flung it so high that it almost went out of sight, saying, "There, you pigmy, do that if you can."

"Well done," said the tailor; "but your pebble will fall down again to the ground. I will throw one up which will not come down;" and, dipping into his pocket, he took out the bird and threw it into the air. The bird, glad to be free, flew straight up, and then far away, and did not come back. "How does that little performance please you, friend?" asked the tailor.

"You can throw well," replied the giant; "Now truly we will see if you are able to carry something uncommon." So saying, he took him to a large oak tree, which lay upon the ground, and said, "If you are strong enough, now help me to carry this tree out of the forest."

"With pleasure," replied the Tailor; "You may hold the trunk upon your shoulder, and I will lift the boughs and branches, they are the heaviest, and carry them."

The giant took the trunk upon his shoulder, but the tailor sat down on one of the branches, and the giant, who could not look round, was compelled to carry the whole tree and the tailor also. He being behind, was very cheerful, and laughed at the trick, and presently began to sing the song, "There rode three tailors out at the gate," as if the carrying of trees were a trifle. The giant, after he had staggered a very short distance with his heavy load, could go no further, and called out, "Do you hear? I must drop the tree."

The tailor, jumping down, quickly embraced the tree with both arms, as if he had been carrying it, and said to the giant, "Are you such a big fellow, and yet cannot you carry a tree by yourself?"

Then they travelled on further, and as they came to a cherry-tree, the giant seized the top of the tree where the ripest cherries hung, and, bending it down, gave it to the tailor to hold, telling him to eat. But the tailor was far too weak to hold the tree down, and when the giant let go, the tree flew up in the air, and the tailor was taken with it. He came down on the other side, however, unhurt, and the giant said, "What does that mean? Are you not strong enough to hold that twig?"

"My strength did not fail me," said the Tailor; "Do you imagine that that was a hard task for one who has slain seven at one blow? I sprang over the tree simply because the hunters were shooting down here in the thicket. Jump after me if you can." The giant made the attempt, but could not clear the tree, and stuck fast in the branches; so that in this affair, too, the tailor had the advantage.

Then the giant said, "Since you are such a brave fellow, come with me to my house, and stop a night with me." The tailor agreed, and followed him; and when they came to

The tailor dropped one stone after another onto the sleeping giants

the cave, there sat by the fire two other giants, each with a roast sheep in his hand, of which he was eating. The tailor sat down thinking. "Ah, this is very much more like the world than is my workshop." And soon the Giant pointed out a bed where he could lie down and go to sleep. The bed, however, was too large for him, so he crept out of it, and lay down in a corner. When midnight came, and the giant fancied the tailor would be in a sound sleep, he got up, and taking a heavy iron bar, beat the bed right through at one stroke, and believed he had thereby given the tailor his death-blow. At the dawn of day the giants went out into the forest, quite forgetting the tailor, when presently up he came, quite cheerful, and showed himself before them. The giants were frightened, and, dreading he might kill them all, they ran away in a great hurry.

The tailor travelled on, always following his nose, and after he had journeyed some long distance, he came into the courtyard of a royal palace; and feeling very tired he laid himself down on the ground and went to sleep. Whilst he lay there the people came and viewed him on all sides, and read upon his belt, "Seven at one blow." "Ah," they said, "what does this great warrior here in time of peace? This must be some valiant hero." So they went and told the King, knowing that, should war break out, here was a valuable and useful man, whom one ought not to part with at any price. The King took advice, and sent one of his courtiers to the tailor to beg for his fighting services, if he should be awake. The messenger stopped at the sleeper's side, and waited till he stretched out his limbs and unclosed his eyes, and then he mentioned to him his message. "Solely for that reason did I come here," was his answer; "I am quite willing to enter into the King's service." Then he was taken away with great honor, and a fine house was appointed him to dwell in.

The courtiers, however, became jealous of the tailor, and wished him at the other end of the world. "What will happen?" said they to one another. "If we go to war with him, when he strikes out seven will fall at one stroke, and nothing will be left for us to do." In their anger they came to the determination to resign, and they went all together to the King, and asked his permission, saying, "We are not prepared to keep company with a man who kills seven at one blow." The King was sorry to lose all his devoted servants for the sake of one, and wished that he had never seen the tailor, and would gladly have now been rid of him. He dared not, however dismiss him, because he feared the tailor might kill him and all his subjects, and seat himself upon the throne. For a long time he deliberated, till finally he came to a decision; and, sending for the tailor, he told him that, seeing he was so great a hero, he wished to beg a favor of him. "In a certain forest in my kingdom," said the King, "there are two giants, who, by murder, rapine, fire, and robbery, have committed great damage, and no one approaches them without endangering his own life. If you overcome and slay both these giants, I will give you my only daughter in marriage, and half of my kingdom for

a dowry: a hundred knights shall accompany you, too, in order to render you assistance."

"Ah, that is something for a man like me," thought the tailor to himself: "a lovely Princess and half a kingdom are not offered to one every day." "Oh, yes," he replied, "I will soon settle these two giants, and a hundred horsemen are not needed for that purpose; he who kills seven at one blow has no fear of two."

The unicorn rushed against the tree but its horn became stuck in the trunk

Speaking thus, the little tailor set out, followed by the hundred knights, to whom he said, immediately they came to the edge of the forest, "You must stay here; I prefer to meet these giants alone."

Then he ran off into the forest, peering about him on all sides; and after a while he saw the two giants sound asleep under a tree, snoring so loudly that the branches above them shook violently. The tailor, bold as a lion, filled both his pockets with stones and climbed up the tree. When he got to the middle of it he crawled along a bough, so that he sat just above the sleepers, and then he let fall one stone after another upon the body of one of them. For some time the giant did not move, until, at last awaking, he pushed his companion, and said, "Why are you hitting me?"

"You have been dreaming," he answered; "I did not touch you."

So they laid themselves down again to sleep, and presently the tailor threw a stone down upon the other. "What is that?" he cried. "Why are you knocking me about?"

"I did not touch you; you are dreaming," said the first. So they argued for a few minutes; but, both being very weary with the day's work, they soon went to sleep again. Then the tailor began his fun again, and, picking out the largest stone, threw it with all his strength upon the chest of the first giant. "This is too bad!" he exclaimed; and, jumping up like a madman, he fell upon his companion, who considered himself equally injured, and they set to in such good earnest, that they rooted up trees and beat one another about until they both fell dead upon the ground. Then the tailor jumped down, saying, "What a piece of luck they did not pull up the tree on which I sat, or else I must have jumped on another like a squirrel, for I am not used to flying." Then he drew his sword, and, cutting a deep wound in the breast of both, he went to the horsemen and said, "The deed is done; I have given each his death-stroke; but it was a tough job, for in their defence they uprooted trees to protect themselves with; still, all that is of no use when such an one as I come, who slew seven at one stroke."

"And are you not wounded?" they asked.

"How can you ask me that? They have not injured a hair of my head," replied the little man. The knights could hardly believe him, till, riding into the forest, they found the giants lying dead, and the uprooted trees around them.

Then the tailor demanded the promised reward of the King; but he repented of his promise, and began to think of some new plan to shake off the hero. "Before you receive my daughter and the half of my kingdom," said he to him, "you must execute another brave deed. In the forest there lives a unicorn that commits great damage, you must first catch him."

"I fear a unicorn less than I did two giants! Seven at one blow is my motto," said the tailor. So he carried with him a rope and an axe and went off to the forest, ordering those, who were told to accompany him, to wait on the outskirts. He had not to hunt long, for soon the unicorn approached, and prepared to rush at him as if it would pierce him on the spot. "Steady! steady!" he exclaimed, "that is not done so easily"; and, waiting till the animal was close upon him, he sprang nimbly behind a tree. The unicorn, rushing with all its force against the tree, stuck its horn so fast in the trunk that it could not pull it out again, and so it remained prisoner.

"Now I have got him," said the tailor; and coming from behind the tree, he first bound the rope around its neck, and then cutting the horn out of the tree with his axe, he arranged everything, and, leading the unicorn, brought it before the King.

The King, however, would not yet deliver over the promised reward, and made a third demand, that, before the marriage, the tailor should capture a wild boar which did much damage, and he should have the huntsmen to help him. "With pleasure," was the reply; "it is a mere nothing." The huntsmen, however, he left behind, to their great joy, for this wild boar had already so often hunted them, that they saw no fun in now hunting it. As soon as the boar perceived the tailor, it ran at him with gaping mouth and glistening teeth, and tried to throw him down on the ground; but our flying hero sprang into a little chapel which stood near, and out again at a window, on the other side, in a moment. The boar ran after him, but he, skipping around, closed the door behind it, and there the furious beast was caught, for it was much too unwieldy and heavy to jump out of the window.

The tailor now ordered the huntsmen up, that they might see his prisoner with their own eyes; then our hero presented himself before the King, who was obliged at last, whether he would or no, to keep his word, and surrender his daughter and the half of his kingdom.

If he had known that it was no warrior, but only a tailor, who stood before him, it would have grieved him still more.

So the wedding was celebrated with great magnificence, though with little rejoicing, and out of a tailor there was made a King.

A short time afterwards the young Queen heard her husband talking in his sleep, saying, "Boy, make me a coat, and then stitch up these trousers, or I will lay the yard-measure over your shoulders!" Then she understood of what condition her husband was, and complained in the morning to her father, and begged he would free her from her husband, who was nothing more than a tailor. The King comforted her by saying, "This night leave your chamber-door open: my servants shall stand outside, and when he is asleep they shall come in, bind him, and carry him away to a ship, which shall take him out into the wide world." The wife was pleased with the proposal; but the King's armor-bearer, who had overheard all, went to the young King and revealed the whole plot.

"I will soon put an end to this affair," said the valiant little tailor. In the evening at their usual time they went to bed, and when his wife thought he slept she got up, opened the door, and laid herself down again.

The tailor, however, only pretended to be asleep, and began to call out in a loud voice, "Boy, make me a coat, and then stitch up these trousers, or I will lay the yard-measure about your shoulders. Seven have I slain with one blow, two giants have I killed, a unicorn have I led captive, and a wild boar have I caught, and shall I be afraid of those who stand outside my room?"

When the men heard these words spoken by the tailor, a great fear came over them, and they ran away as if wild huntsmen were following them; neither afterwards dared any man venture to oppose him. Thus the tailor became a king, and so he lived for the rest of his life.

Henny-penny

Sometimes this story is called *Chicken Licken* or *Chicken Little* (especially in the USA) while an Irish version had the title *The End of the World*. The story tells of a hen that believes the end of the world is imminent when an acorn falls onto her head. The term 'The sky is falling!' is now often used to refer to any mistaken belief that disaster is imminent. This version was apparently told to Joseph Jacobs (1854–1916) in Australia in 1860 and published in his *English Fairy Tales* some thirty years later.

One day Henny-penny was picking up corn in the courtyard when – whack! – something hit her upon the head. "Goodness gracious me!" said Henny-penny; "The sky's a-going to fall; I must go and tell the king."

So she went along and she went along and she went along till she met Cocky-locky. "Where are you going, Henny-penny?" says Cocky-locky. "Oh! I'm going to tell the king the sky's a-falling," says Henny-penny. "May I come with you?" says Cocky-locky. "Certainly," says Henny-penny. So Henny-penny and Cocky-locky went to tell-the king the sky was falling.

They went along, and they went along, and they went along, till they met Ducky-daddles. "Where are you going to, Henny-penny and Cocky-locky?" says Ducky-daddles. "Oh! we're going to tell the king the sky's a-falling," said Henny-penny and Cocky-locky. "May I come with you?" says Ducky-daddles. "Certainly," said Henny-penny and Cocky-locky. So Henny-penny, Cocky-locky and Ducky-daddles went to tell the king the sky was a-falling.

So they went along, and they went along, and they went along, till they met Goosey-poosey, "Where are you going to, Henny-penny, Cocky-locky and Ducky-daddles?" said Goosey-poosey. "Oh! we're going to tell the king the sky's a-falling," said Henny-penny and Cocky-locky and Ducky-daddles. "May I come with you," said Goosey-poosey. "Certainly," said Henny-penny, Cocky-locky and Ducky-daddles. So Henny-penny, Cocky-locky, Ducky-daddles and Goosey-poosey went to tell the king the sky was a-falling.

So they went along, and they went along, and they went along, till they met Turkey-lurkey. "Where are you going, Henny-penny, Cocky-locky, Ducky-daddles, and Goosey-poosey?" says Turkey-lurkey. "Oh! we're going to tell the king the sky's a-falling," said Henny-penny, Cocky-locky, Ducky-daddles and Goosey-poosey. "May I come with you? Henny-penny, Cocky-locky, Ducky-daddles and Goosey-poosey?" said Turkey-lurkey. "Why, certainly, Turkey-lurkey," said Henny-penny, Cocky-locky, Ducky-daddles, and Goosey-poosey. So Henny-penny, Cocky- locky, Ducky-daddles, Goosey-poosey and Turkey-lurkey all went to tell the king the sky was a-falling.

So they went along, and they went along, and they went along, till they met Foxy-woxy, and Foxy-woxy said to Henny-penny, Cocky-locky, Ducky-daddles, Goosey-poosey and Turkey-lurkey: "Where are you going, Henny-penny, Cocky-locky, Ducky-daddles, Goosey-poosey, and Turkey-lurkey?" And Henny-penny, Cocky-locky, Ducky-daddles, Goosey-poosey, and Turkey-lurkey said to Foxy-woxy: "We're going to tell the king the sky's a-falling."

"Oh! but this is not the way to the king, Henny-penny, Cocky-locky, Ducky-daddles, Goosey-poosey and Turkey-lurkey," says Foxy-woxy; "I know the proper way; shall I show it you?" "Why certainly, Foxy-woxy," said Henny-penny, Cocky-locky, Ducky-daddles, Goosey-poosey, and Turkey-lurkey. So Henny-penny, Cocky-locky, Ducky-daddles, Goosey-poosey, Turkey-lurkey, and Foxy-woxy all went to tell the king the sky was a-falling.

So they went along, and they went along, and they went along, till they came to a narrow and dark hole. Now this was the door of Foxy-woxy's cave. But Foxy-woxy said to Henny-penny, Cocky-locky, Ducky-daddles, Goosey-poosey, and Turkey-lurkey: "This is the short way to the king's palace you'll soon get there if you follow me. I will go first and you come after, Henny-penny, Cocky-locky, Ducky daddles, Goosey-poosey, and Turkey-lurkey."

"Why of course, certainly, without doubt, why not?" said Henny-Penny, Cocky-locky, Ducky-daddles, Goosey-poosey, and Turkey-lurkey.

So Foxy-woxy went into his cave, and he didn't go very far but turned round to wait for Henny-Penny, Cocky-locky, Ducky-daddles, Goosey-poosey and Turkey-lurkey. So first Turkey-lurkey went through the dark hole into the cave. He hadn't got far when "Hrumph," Foxy-woxy snapped off Turkey-lurkey's head and threw his body over his left shoulder. Then Goosey-poosey went in, and "Hrumph," off went her head and Goosey-poosey was thrown beside Turkey-lurkey. Then Ducky-daddles waddled down, and "Hrumph," snapped Foxy-woxy, and Ducky-daddles' head was off and Ducky-daddles was thrown alongside Turkey-lurkey and Goosey-poosey. Then Cocky-locky strutted down into the cave and he hadn't gone far when "Snap, Hrumph!" went Foxy-woxy and Cocky-locky was thrown alongside of Turkey-lurkey, Goosey-poosey and Ducky-daddles.

But Foxy-woxy had made two bites at Cocky-locky, and when the first snap only hurt Cocky-locky, but didn't kill him, he called out to Henny-penny. So she turned tail and ran back home, so she never told the king the sky was a-falling.

Henny-penny was picking up corn in the farm courtyard

The Steadfast Tin Soldier

This literary fairy tale was written by Hans Christian Andersen (1805–1875) and published in 1838. It describes how a tin soldier falls in love with a paper ballerina but ultimately both perish in a fire. The was the first of Andersen's stories not to be based upon a folk tale or a literary model and marks a new independence in his writing.

There were once five-and-twenty tin soldiers, who were all brothers, for they had been made out of the same old tin spoon. They shouldered arms and looked straight before them, and wore a splendid uniform, red and blue. The first thing in the world they ever heard were the words, "Tin soldiers!" uttered by a little boy, who clapped his hands with delight when the lid of the box, in which they lay, was taken off. They were given him for a birthday present, and he stood at the table to set them up. The soldiers were all exactly alike, excepting one, who had only one leg; he had been left to the last, and then there was not enough of the melted tin to finish him, so they made him to stand firmly on one leg, and this caused him to be very remarkable.

The table on which the tin soldiers stood, was covered with other playthings, but the most attractive to the eye was a pretty little paper castle. Through the small windows the rooms could be seen. In front of the castle a number of little trees surrounded a piece of looking-glass, which was intended to represent a transparent lake. Swans, made of wax, swam on the lake, and were reflected in it. All this was very pretty, but the prettiest of all was a tiny little lady, who stood at the open door of the castle; she, also, was made of paper, and she wore a dress of clear muslin, with a narrow blue ribbon over her shoulders just like a scarf. In front of these was fixed a glittering tinsel rose, as large as her whole face. The little lady was a dancer, and she stretched out both her arms, and raised one of her legs so high, that the tin soldier could not see it at all, and he thought that she, like himself, had only one leg. "That is the wife for me," he thought; "but she is too grand, and lives in a castle, while I have only a box to live in, five-and-twenty of us altogether, that is no place for her. Still I must try and make her acquaintance." Then he laid himself at full length on the table behind a snuff-box that stood upon it, so that he could peep at the little delicate lady, who continued to stand on one leg without losing her balance. When evening came, the other tin soldiers were all placed in the box, and the people of the house went to bed. Then the playthings began to have their own games together, to pay visits, to have sham fights, and to give balls. The tin soldiers rattled in their box; they wanted to get out and join the amusements, but they could not open the lid. The nut-crackers played at leap-frog, and the pencil jumped about the table. There was such a noise that the canary woke up and began to talk, and in poetry too. Only the tin soldier and the dancer remained in their places. She stood on tiptoe, with her legs stretched out, as firmly as he did on his one leg. He never took his eyes from her for even a moment. The clock struck twelve, and, with a bounce, up sprang the lid of the snuff-box; but, instead of snuff, there jumped up a little black goblin; for the snuff-box was a toy puzzle.

"Tin soldier," said the goblin, "don't wish for what does not belong to you."

The tin soldier thought that the ballerina, like him, had only one leg

But the tin soldier pretended not to hear.

"Very well; wait till to-morrow, then," said the goblin.

When the children came in the next morning, they placed the tin soldier in the window. Now, whether it was the goblin who did it, or the draught, is not known, but the window flew open, and out fell the tin soldier, heels over head, from the third story, into the street beneath. It was a terrible fall; for he came head downwards, his helmet and his bayonet stuck in between the flagstones, and his one leg up in the air. The servant maid and the little boy went down stairs directly to look for him; but he was nowhere to be seen, although once they nearly trod upon him. If he had called out, "Here I am," it would have been all right, but he was too proud to cry out for help while he wore a uniform.

Presently it began to rain, and the drops fell faster and faster, till there was a heavy shower. When it was over, two boys happened to pass by, and one of them said, "Look, there is a tin soldier. He ought to have a boat to sail in."

So they made a boat out of a newspaper, and placed the tin soldier in it, and sent him sailing down the gutter, while the two boys ran by the side of it, and clapped their hands. Good gracious, what large waves arose in that gutter! and how fast the stream rolled on! for the rain had been very heavy. The paper boat rocked up and down, and turned itself round sometimes so quickly that the tin soldier trembled; yet he remained firm; his countenance did not change; he looked straight before him, and shouldered his musket. Suddenly the boat shot under a bridge which formed a part of a drain, and then it was as dark as the tin soldier's box.

"Where am I going now?" thought he. "This is the black goblin's fault, I am sure. Ah, well, if the little lady were only here with me in the boat, I should not care for any darkness."

Suddenly there appeared a great water-rat, who lived in the drain.

"Have you a passport?" asked the rat, "Give it to me at once." But the tin soldier remained silent and held his musket tighter than ever. The boat sailed on and the rat followed it. How he did gnash his teeth and cry out to the bits of wood and straw, "Stop him, stop him; he has not paid toll, and has not shown his pass." But the stream rushed on stronger and stronger. The tin soldier could already see daylight shining where the arch ended. Then he heard a roaring sound quite terrible enough to frighten the bravest man. At the end of the tunnel the drain fell into a large canal over a steep place, which made it as dangerous for him as a waterfall would be to us. He was too close to it to stop, so the boat rushed on, and the poor tin soldier could only hold himself as stiffly as possible, without moving an eyelid, to show that he was not afraid. The boat whirled round three or four times, and then filled with water to the very edge; nothing could save it from sinking. He now stood up to his neck in water, while deeper and deeper sank the boat, and the paper became soft and loose with the wet, till at last the water closed over the soldier's head. He thought of the elegant little dancer whom he should never see again, and the words of the song sounded in his ears –

"Farewell, warrior! ever brave,
Drifting onward to thy grave."

Then the paper boat fell to pieces, and the soldier sank into the water and immediately afterwards was swallowed up by a great fish. Oh how dark it was inside the fish! A great deal darker than in the tunnel, and narrower too, but the tin soldier continued firm, and lay at full length shouldering his musket. The fish swam to and fro, making

When evening came the toys played their own games

the most wonderful movements, but at last he became quite still. After a while, a flash of lightning seemed to pass through him, and then the daylight approached, and a voice cried out, "I declare here is the tin soldier." The fish had been caught, taken to the market and sold to the cook, who took him into the kitchen and cut him open with a large knife. She picked up the soldier and held him by the waist between her finger and thumb, and carried him into the room. They were all anxious to see this wonderful soldier who had travelled about inside a fish; but he was not at all proud. They placed him on the table, and – how many curious things do happen in the world! – there he was in the very same room from the window of which he had fallen, there were the same children, the same playthings, standing on the table, and the pretty castle with the elegant little dancer at the door; she still balanced herself on one leg, and held up the other, so she was as firm as himself. It touched the tin soldier so much to see her that he almost wept tin tears, but he kept them back. He only looked at her and they both remained silent. Presently one of the little boys took up the tin soldier, and threw him into the stove. He had no reason for doing so, therefore it must have been the fault of the black goblin who lived in the snuff-box. The flames lighted up the tin soldier, as he stood, the heat was very terrible, but whether it proceeded from the real fire or from the fire of love he could not tell. Then he could see that the bright colors were faded from his uniform, but whether they had been washed off during his journey or from the effects of his sorrow, no one could say. He looked at the little lady, and she looked at him. He felt himself melting away, but he still remained firm with his gun on his shoulder. Suddenly the door of the room flew open and the draught of air caught up the little dancer, she fluttered like a sylph right into the stove by the side of the tin soldier, and was instantly in flames and was gone. The tin soldier melted down into a lump, and the next morning, when the maid servant took the ashes out of the stove, she found him in the shape of a little tin heart. But of the little dancer nothing remained but the tinsel rose, which was burnt black as a cinder.

The Goose-Girl

This Brothers Grimm (Jacob 1785–1863 and Wilhelm 1786–1859) tale was published in 1819 in *Children's and Household Tales* and translated into English in 1884. Andrew Lang (1844–1912) included it in *The Blue Fairy Book*. It tells how a sweet-hearted princess is betrayed by her greedy maid and has to work as a common goose girl. There have been many film adaptations of the story in Germany.

Tricked by her cheating maid, the princess has to work as a goose girl

An old queen, whose husband had been dead some years, had a beautiful daughter. When she grew up, she was betrothed to a prince who lived a great way off; and as the time drew near for her to be married, she got ready to set off on her journey to his country. Then the queen, her mother, packed up a great many costly things – jewels, and gold, and silver, trinkets, fine dresses, and in short, everything that became a royal bride; for she loved her child very dearly; and she gave her a waiting-maid to ride with her, and give her into the bridegroom's hands; and each had a horse for the journey. Now the princess' horse was called Falada, and could speak.

When the time came for them to set out, the old queen went into her bed-chamber, and took a little knife, and cut off a lock of her hair, and gave it to her daughter, saying, "Take care of it, dear child; for it is a charm that may be of use to you on the road." Then they took a sorrowful leave of each other, and the princess put the lock of her mother's hair into her bosom, got upon her horse, and set off on her journey to her bridegroom's kingdom.

One day, as they were riding along by the side of a brook, the princess began to feel very thirsty, and said to her maid, "Pray get down and fetch me some water in my golden cup out of yonder brook, for I want to drink."

"Nay," said the maid, "if you are thirsty, get down yourself, and lie down by the water and drink; I shall not be your waiting-maid any longer."

The princess was so thirsty that she got down, and knelt over the little brook and drank, for she was frightened, and dared not bring out her golden cup; and then she wept, and said, "Alas! What will become of me?" And the lock of hair answered her, and said:

"Alas! Alas! If thy mother knew it,
Sadly, sadly her heart would rue it."

But the princess was very humble and meek, so she said nothing about her maid's ill behavior, but got upon her horse again.

Then all rode further on their journey, till the day grew so warm, and the sun so scorching, that the bride began to feel very thirsty again; and at last, when they came to a river, she forgot her maid's rude speech, and said, "Pray get down and fetch me some water to drink in my golden cup."

But the maid answered her, and even spoke more haughtily than before, "Drink if you will, but I shall not be your waiting-maid."

Then the princess was so thirsty that she got off her horse and lay down, and held her head over the running stream, and cried, and said, "What will become of me?" And the lock of hair answered her again:

"Alas! Alas! If thy mother knew it,
Sadly, sadly her heart would rue it."

And as she leaned down to drink, the lock of hair fell from her bosom and floated away with the water, without her seeing it, she was so much frightened. But her maid saw it, and was very glad, for she knew the charm, and saw that the poor bride would be in her power now that she had lost the hair. So when the bride had finished drinking, and would have got upon Falada again, the maid said, "I shall ride upon Falada, and you may have my horse instead," so she was forced to give up her horse, and soon afterwards to take off her royal clothes, and put on her maid's shabby ones.

At last, as they drew near the end of the journey, this treacherous servant threatened to kill her mistress if she ever told anyone what had happened. But Falada saw it all, and marked it well. Then the waiting-maid got upon Falada, and the real bride was set upon the other horse, and they went on in this way till at last they came to the royal court. There was great joy at their coming, and the prince hurried to meet them, and lifted the maid from her horse, thinking she was the one who was to be his wife; and she was led upstairs to the royal chamber, but the true princess was told to stay in the court below.

However, the old king happened to be looking out of the window, and saw her in the yard below; and as she looked very pretty, and too delicate for a waiting-maid, he went into the royal chamber to ask the bride whom it was she had brought with her, that was thus left standing in the court below.

"I brought her with me for the sake of her company on the road," said she. "Pray give the girl some work to do, that she may not be idle."

The old king could not for some time think of any work for her, but at last he said, "I have a lad who takes care of my geese; she may go and help him." Now the name of this lad, that the real bride was to help in watching the king's geese, was Curdken.

Soon after, the false bride said to the prince, "Dear husband, pray do me one piece of kindness."

"That I will," said the prince.

"Then tell one of your slaughterers to cut off the head of the horse I rode upon, for it was very unruly, and plagued me sadly on the road." But the truth was, she was very much afraid lest Falada should speak, and tell all she had done to the princess. She carried her point, and the faithful Falada was killed; but when the true princess heard of it she wept, and begged the man to nail up Falada's head against a large dark gate in the city through which she had to pass every morning and evening, that there she might still see him sometimes. Then the slaughterer said

he would do as she wished, so he cut off the head and nailed it fast under the dark gate.

Early the next morning, as the princess and Curdken went out through the gate, she said sorrowfully:

"Falada, Falada, there thou art hanging!"

and the head answered:

"Bride, bride, there thou are ganging!
Alas! Alas! If thy mother knew it,

Each day the princess took the geese into the meadow

Sadly, sadly her heart would rue it."

Then they went out of the city, driving the geese. And when they came to the meadow, the princess sat down upon a bank there and let down her waving locks of hair, which were all of pure gold; and when Curdken saw it glitter in the sun, he ran up, and would have pulled some of the locks out; but she cried:

"Blow, breezes, blow!
Let Curdken's hat go!
Blow breezes, blow!
Let him after it go!
O'er hills, dales, and rocks,
Away be it whirl'd,
Till the golden locks
Are all comb'd and curl'd!"

Then there came a wind, so strong that it blew off Curdken's hat, and away it flew over the hills, and he after it; till, by the time he came back, she had done combing and curling her hair, and put it up again safely. Then he was very angry and sulky, and would not speak to her at all; but they watched the geese until it grew dark in the evening, and then drove them homewards.

The next morning, as they were going through the dark gate, the poor girl looked up at Falada's head, and cried –

"Falada, Falada, there thou art hanging!"

and it answered:

The wind whirled away Curdken's hat

"Bride, bride, there thou are ganging!
Alas! Alas! If thy mother knew it,
Sadly, sadly her heart would rue it."

Then she drove on the geese and sat down again in the meadow, and began to comb out her hair as before, and Curdken ran up to her, and wanted to take of it; but she cried out quickly –

"Blow, breezes, blow!
Let Curdken's hat go!
Blow breezes, blow!
Let him after it go!
O'er hills, dales, and rocks,
Away be it whirl'd,
Till the golden locks
Are all comb'd and curl'd!"

Then the wind came and blew off his hat, and off it flew a great distance over the hills and far away, so that he had to run after it: and when he came back, she had done up her hair again, and all was safe. So they watched the geese till it grew dark.

In the evening, after they came home, Curdken went to the old king, and said, "I cannot have that strange girl to help me to keep the geese any longer."

"Why?" inquired the king.

"Because she does nothing but tease me all day long."

Then the king made him tell him all that had passed.

And Curdken said, "When we go in the morning through the dark gate with our flock of geese, she weeps, and talks with the head of a horse that hangs upon the wall, and says –

"Falada, Falada, there thou art hanging!"

and the head answers –

"Bride, bride, there thou are ganging!
Alas! alas! if thy mother knew it,
Sadly, sadly her heart would rue it."

And Curdken went on telling the king what had happened upon the meadow where the geese fed; and how his hat was blown away, and he was forced to run after it, and leave his flock. But the old king told him to go out again as usual the next day: and when morning came, he placed himself behind the dark gate, and heard how the princess spoke, and how Falada answered; and then he went into the field and hid himself in a bush by the meadow's side, and soon saw with his own eyes how they drove the flock of geese, and how, after a little time, she let down her hair that glittered in the sun; and then he heard her say:

"Blow, breezes, blow!
Let Curdken's hat go!
Blow breezes, blow!
Let him after it go!
O'er hills, dales, and rocks,
Away be it whirl'd,
Till the golden locks
Are all comb'd and curl'd!"

And soon came a gale of wind, and carried away Curdken's hat, while the girl went on combing and curling her hair.

All this the old king saw; so he went home without being seen; and when the goose-girl came back in the evening, he called her aside, and asked her why she did so; but she burst into tears, and said, "That I must not tell you or any man, or I shall lose my life."

But the old king begged so hard that she had no peace till she had told him all, word for word: and it was very lucky for her that she did so, for the king ordered royal clothes to be put upon her, and he gazed with wonder, she was so beautiful.

Then he called his son, and told him that he had only the false bride, for that she was merely a waiting-maid, while the true one stood by.

And the young king rejoiced when he saw her beauty, and heard how meek and patient she had been; and without saying anything, he ordered a great feast to be prepared for all his court.

The bridegroom sat at the top, with the false princess on one side, and the true one on the other; but nobody knew her, for she was quite dazzling to their eyes, and was not at all like the little goose-girl, now that she had on her brilliant dress.

When they had eaten and drunk, and were very merry, the old king told all the story, as one that he had once heard of, and asked the true waiting-maid what she thought ought to be done to anyone who would behave thus.

"Nothing better," said this false bride, "than that she should be thrown into a cask stuck around with sharp nails, and that two white horses should be put to it, and should drag it from street to street till she is dead."

"Thou art she!" said the old king; "and since thou hast judged thyself, it shall be so done to thee."

Then the young king was married to his true wife, and they reigned over the kingdom in peace and happiness all their lives.

Mother Holle

This tale, first published in 1812, was originally known as *Frau Holle* and is sometimes called *Mother Hulda*. The story involves a rich widow, her favoured daughter and misused stepdaughter who leaps into a well to retrieve a spindle and finds herself in another world. Its origins may lie in Norse mythology; in Germany, the name Holle may be a reference to Hell (Hölle) and also Hel, the queen of the Norse underworld as well as goddess of peace, marriage and fertility. She was one of the wives of the chief god Odin and mother to Thor. Over time, Scandinavian paganism was absorbed into rural folklore, in which the character of Mother Hulda survived – often said to dwell at the bottom of a well, ride a wagon, and to be responsible for teaching mortals how to make linen from flax. Hulda is the goddess to whom dead infants go and she may be called the Dark Grandmother. The legend survived in Hesse, in Central Germany, and was told to the Brothers Grimm (Jacob 1785–1863 and Wilhelm 1786–1859) by Henriette Dorothea Wild (whom Wilhelm Grimm married in 1825). People in Hesse still say that "Hulda is making her bed" when it is snowing!

Every time she made the bed she shook it well so that the feathers flew like snowflakes

Once upon a time there was a widow who had two daughters; one of them was beautiful and industrious, the other ugly and lazy. The mother, however, loved the ugly and lazy one best, because she was her own daughter, and so the other, who was only her stepdaughter, was made to do all the work of the house, and was quite the Cinderella of the family. Her stepmother sent her out every day to sit by the well in the high road, there to spin until she made her fingers bleed. Now it chanced one day that some blood fell on to the spindle, and as the girl stopped over the well to wash it off, the spindle suddenly sprang out of her hand and fell into the well. She ran home crying to tell of her misfortune, but her stepmother spoke harshly to her, and after giving her a violent scolding, said unkindly, "As you have let the spindle fall into the well you may go yourself and fetch it out."

The girl went back to the well not knowing what to do, and at last in her distress she jumped into the water after the spindle.

She remembered nothing more until she awoke and found herself in a beautiful meadow, full of sunshine, and with countless flowers blooming in every direction.

She walked over the meadow, and presently she came upon a baker's oven full of bread, and the loaves cried out to her, "Take us out, take us out, or alas! we shall be burnt to a cinder; we were baked through long ago." So she took the bread-shovel and drew them all out.

She went on a little farther, till she came to a tree full of apples. "Shake me, shake me, I pray," cried the tree; "My apples, one and all, are ripe." So she shook the tree, and the apples came falling down upon her like rain; but she continued shaking until there was not a single apple left upon it. Then she carefully gathered the apples together in a heap and walked on again.

The next thing she came to was a little house, and there she saw an old woman looking out, with such large teeth, that she was terrified, and turned to run away. But the old woman called after her, "What are you afraid of, dear

277

child? Stay with me; if you will do the work of my house properly for me, I will make you very happy. You must be very careful, however, to make my bed in the right way, for I wish you always to shake it thoroughly, so that the feathers fly about; then they say, down there in the world, that it is snowing; for I am Mother Holle." The old woman spoke so kindly, that the girl summoned up courage and agreed to enter into her service.

She took care to do everything according to the old woman's bidding and every time she made the bed she shook it with all her might, so that the feathers flew about like so many snowflakes. The old woman was as good as her word: she never spoke angrily to her, and gave her roast and boiled meats every day.

So she stayed on with Mother Holle for some time, and then she began to grow unhappy. She could not at first tell why she felt sad, but she became conscious at last of great longing to go home; then she knew she was homesick, although she was a thousand times better off with Mother Holle than with her stepmother and sister. After waiting awhile, she went to Mother Holle and said, "I am so homesick, that I cannot stay with you any longer, for although I am so happy here, I must return to my own people."

Then Mother Holle said, "I am pleased that you should want to go back to your own people, and as you have served me so well and faithfully, I will take you home myself."

Thereupon she led the girl by the hand up to a broad gateway. The gate was opened, and as the girl passed through, a shower of gold fell upon her, and the gold clung to her, so that she was covered with it from head to foot.

"That is a reward for your industry," said Mother Holle, and as she spoke she handed her the spindle which she had dropped into the well.

The gate was then closed, and the girl found herself back in the old world close to her mother's house. As she entered the courtyard, the cock who was perched on the well, called out:

"Cock-a-doodle-doo!
Your golden daughter's come back to you."

Then she went in to her stepmother and sister, and as she was so richly covered with gold, they gave her a warm welcome. She related to them all that had happened, and when the mother heard how she had come by her great riches, she thought she should like her ugly, lazy daughter to go and try her fortune. So she made the sister go and sit by the well and spin, and the girl pricked her finger and thrust her hand into a thorn-bush, so that she might drop some blood on to the spindle; then she threw it into the well, and jumped in herself.

Like her sister she awoke in the beautiful meadow, and walked over it till she came to the oven. "Take us out, take us out, or alas! we shall be burnt to a cinder; we were baked through long ago," cried the loaves as before. But the lazy girl answered, "Do you think I am going to dirty my hands for you?" and walked on.

Presently she came to the apple-tree. "Shake me, shake

The girl worked hard and did everything according to the old woman's wishes

me, I pray; my apples, one and all, are ripe," it cried. But she only answered, "A nice thing to ask me to do, one of the apples might fall on my head," and passed on.

At last she came to Mother Holle's house, and as she had heard all about the large teeth from her sister, she was not afraid of them, and engaged herself without delay to the old woman.

The first day she was very obedient and industrious, and exerted herself to please Mother Holle, for she thought of the gold she should get in return. The next day, however, she began to dawdle over her work, and the third day she was more idle still; then she began to lie in bed in the mornings and refused to get up. Worse still, she neglected to make the old woman's bed properly, and forgot to shake it so that the feathers might fly about. So Mother Holle very soon got tired of her, and told her she might go. The lazy girl was delighted at this, and thought to herself, "The gold will soon be mine." Mother Holle led her, as she had led her sister, to the broad gateway; but as she was passing through, instead of the shower of gold, a great bucketful of pitch came pouring over her.

"That is in return for your services," said the old woman, and she shut the gate.

So the lazy girl had to go home covered with pitch, and the cock on the well called out as she saw her:

"Cock-a-doodle-doo!
Your dirty daughter's come back to you."

But, try what she would, she could not get the pitch off and it stuck to her as long as she lived.

The Six Swans

The Six Swans is a Brothers Grimm (Jacob 1785–1863 and Wilhelm 1786–1859) tale with a wicked-stepmother theme. Six brothers from a king's first marriage have been turned into swans by their hateful stepmother (the young and beautiful but evil daughter of a witch). Ultimately the evil stepmother is burned at the stake and the King, Queen, and her six erstwhile-swan brothers live happily ever after.

"My good woman," said he to her, "Can you not show me the way out of the forest?"

"Oh, yes, my lord King," she replied; "I can do that very well, but upon one condition, which if you do not fulfil, you will never again get out of the wood, but will die of hunger."

"What, then, is this condition?" asked the King.

"I have a daughter," said the old woman, "who is as beautiful as any one you can find in the whole world, and well deserves to be your bride. Now, if you will make her your Queen, I will show you your way out of the wood."

In the anxiety of his heart, the King consented, and the old woman led him to her cottage, where the daughter

A King was once hunting in a large wood, and pursued his game so hotly that none of his courtiers could follow him. But when evening approached he stopped, and looking around him perceived that he had lost himself. He sought a path out of the forest but could not find one, and presently he saw an old woman, with a nodding head, who came up to him.

The king saw that the old woman's daughter was beautiful but not to be trusted

The brothers had been changed into swans

was sitting by the fire. She received the King as if she had expected him, and he saw at once that she was very beautiful, but yet she did not quite please him, for he could not look at her without a secret shuddering. However, he took the maiden upon his horse, and the old woman showed him the way, and the King arrived safely at his palace, where the wedding was to be celebrated.

The King had been married once before, and had seven children by his first wife, six boys and a girl, whom he loved above everything else in the world. He became afraid, soon, that the step-mother might not treat his children very well, and might even do them some great injury, so he took them away to a lonely castle which stood in the midst of a forest. The castle was so entirely hidden, and the way to it was so difficult to discover, that he himself could not have found it if a wise woman had not given him a ball of cotton which had the wonderful property, when he threw it before him, of unrolling itself and showing him the right path. The King went, however, so often to see his dear children, that the Queen, noticing his absence, became inquisitive, and wished to know what he went to fetch out of the forest. So she gave his servants a great quantity of money, and they disclosed to her the secret, and also told her of the ball of cotton which alone could show her the way. She had now no peace until she discovered where this ball was concealed, and then she made some fine silken shirts, and, as she had learnt of her mother, she sewed within each a charm.

One day soon after, when the King was gone out hunting, she took the little shirts and went into the forest, and the cotton showed her the path. The children, seeing someone coming in the distance, thought it was their dear father, and ran out full of joy. Then she threw over each of them a shirt, that, as it touched their bodies, changed them into Swans, which flew away over the forest. The Queen then went home quite contented, and thought she was free of her step-children; but the little girl had not met her with the brothers, and the Queen did not know of her.

The following day the King went to visit his children, but he found only the maiden. "Where are your brothers?" asked he.

"Ah, dear father," she replied, "they are gone away and have left me alone"; and she told him how she had looked out of the window and seen them changed into swans, which had flown over the forest; and then she showed him the feathers which they had dropped in the courtyard, and which she had collected together. The King was much grieved, but he did not think that his wife could have done this wicked deed, and, as he feared the girl might also be stolen away, he took her with him. She was, however, so much afraid of the step-mother, that she begged him not to stop more than one night in the castle.

The poor maiden thought to herself, "This is no longer my place; I will go and seek my brothers"; and when night came she escaped and went quite deep into the wood. She walked all night long, and a great part of the next day, until she could go no further from weariness. Just then she saw a rough-looking hut, and going in, she found a room with six little beds, but she dared not get into one, so crept under, and laying herself upon the hard earth, prepared to pass the night there. Just as the sun was setting, she heard a rustling, and saw six white swans come flying in at the window. They settled on the ground and began blowing one another until they had blown all their feathers off, and their swan's down slipped from them like a shirt. Then the maiden knew them at once for her brothers, and gladly crept out from under the bed, and the brothers were not less glad to see their sister, but their joy was of short duration.

"Here you must not stay," said they to her; "This is a

The maiden crept out from under the bed, delighted to see her brothers again

robbers' hiding-place; if they should return and find you here, they would murder you."

"Can you not protect me, then?" inquired the sister.

"No," they replied; "for we can only lay aside our swan's feathers for a quarter of an hour each evening, and for that time we regain our human form, but afterwards we resume our changed appearance."

Their sister then asked them, with tears, "Can you not be restored again?"

"Oh, no," replied they; "the conditions are too difficult. For six long years you must neither speak nor laugh, and during that time you must sew together for us six little shirts of star-flowers, and should there fall a single word from your lips, then all your labor will be in vain." Just as the brothers finished speaking, the quarter of an hour elapsed, and they all flew out of the window again like swans.

The little sister, however, made a solemn resolution to rescue her brothers, or die in the attempt; and she left the cottage, and, penetrating deep into the forest, passed the night amid the branches of a tree. The next morning she went out and collected the star-flowers to sew together. She had no one to converse with and no reason to laugh, so there up in the tree she sat, intent upon her work.

After she had passed some time there, it happened that the King of that country was hunting in the forest, and

The king and his huntsmen saw the girl in the tree

his huntsmen came beneath the tree on which the maiden sat. They called to her and asked, "Who art thou?" But she gave no answer. "Come down to us," continued they; "we will do thee no harm." She simply shook her head, and when they pressed her further with questions, she threw down to them her gold necklace, hoping therewith to satisfy them. They did not, however, leave her, and she threw down her girdle, but in vain! and even her rich dress did not make them desist. At last the huntsman himself climbed the tree and brought down the maiden, and took her before the King.

The King asked her, "Who art thou? What dost thou upon that tree?" But she did not answer; and then he questioned her in all the languages that he knew, but she remained dumb to all, as a fish. Since, however, she was so beautiful, the King's heart was touched, and he conceived for her a strong affection. Then he put around her his cloak, and, placing her before him on his horse, took her to his castle. There he ordered rich clothing to be made for her, and, although her beauty shone as the sunbeams, not a word escaped her. The King placed her by his side at table, and there her dignified mien and manners so won upon him, that he said, "This maiden will I marry, and no other in the world," and after some days he wedded her.

Now, the King had a wicked step-mother, who was discontented with his marriage, and spoke evil of the young Queen. "Who knows whence the wench comes?" said she. "She who cannot speak is not worthy of a king." A year after, when the Queen brought her first-born into the world, the old woman took him away. Then she went to the King and complained that the Queen was a murderess. The King, however, would not believe it, and suffered no one to do any injury to his wife, who sat composedly sewing at her shirts and paying attention to nothing else. When a second child was born, the false stepmother used the same deceit, but the King again would not listen to her words, saying, "She is too pious and good to act so; could she but speak and defend herself, her innocence would come to light." But when again, the old woman stole away the third child, and then accused the Queen, who answered not a word to the accusation, the King was obliged to give her up to be tried, and she was condemned to suffer death by fire.

When the time had elapsed, and the sentence was to be carried out, it happened that the very day had come round when her dear brothers should be set free; the six shirts were also ready, all but the last, which yet wanted the left sleeve. As she was led to the scaffold, she placed the shirts upon her arm, and just as she had mounted it, and the fire was about to be kindled, she looked around, and saw six swans come flying through the air. Her heart leapt for joy as she perceived her deliverers approaching, and soon the swans, flying towards her, alighted so near that she was enabled to throw over them the shirts, and as soon as she had done so, their feathers fell off and the brothers stood up alive and well; but the youngest was without his left arm, instead of which he had a swan's wing. They embraced and kissed each other, and the Queen, going to the King, who was thunderstruck, began to say, "Now may I speak, my dear husband, and prove to you that I am innocent and falsely accused," and then she told him how the wicked woman had stolen away and hidden her three children. When she had concluded, the King was overcome with joy, and the wicked stepmother was led to the scaffold and bound to the stake and burnt to ashes. The King and Queen for ever after lived in peace and prosperity with their six brothers.

Mr. Vinegar

Mr. and Mrs. Vinegar lived in a vinegar bottle. Now, one day, when Mr. Vinegar was from home, Mrs. Vinegar, who was a very good housewife, was busily sweeping her house, when an unlucky thump of the broom brought the whole house cutter-clatter, cutter-clatter, about her ears. In an agony of grief she rushed forth to meet her husband. On seeing him she exclaimed, "O Mr. Vinegar, Mr. Vinegar, we are ruined, we are ruined: I have knocked the house down, and it is all to pieces!"

Mr. Vinegar then said: "My dear, let us see what can be done. Here is the door; I will take it on my back, and we will go forth to seek our fortune."

They walked all that day, and at nightfall entered a thick forest. They were both very, very tired, and Mr. Vinegar said: "My love, I will climb up into a tree, drag up the door, and you shall follow."

He accordingly did so, and they both stretched their weary limbs on the door, and fell asleep. In the middle of the night, Mr. Vinegar was disturbed by the sound of voices underneath and to his horror and dismay found that it was a band of thieves met to divide their booty. "Here, Jack," said one, "there's five pounds for you; here, Bill, here's ten pounds for you; here, Bob, there's three pounds for you."

Mr. Vinegar could listen no longer; his terror was so great that he trembled and trembled, and shook down the door on their heads. Away scampered the thieves, but Mr. Vinegar dared not quit his retreat till broad daylight. He then scrambled out of the tree, and went to lift up the door. What did he see but a number of golden guineas.

"Come down, Mrs. Vinegar," he cried; "come down, I say; our fortune's made, our fortune's made! Come down, I say."

Mrs. Vinegar got down as fast as she could, and when she saw the money, she jumped for joy. "Now, my dear," said she, "I'll tell you what you shall do. There is a fair at the neighbouring town; you shall take these forty guineas and buy a cow. I can make butter and cheese, which you shall sell at market, and we shall then be able to live very comfortably."

Mr. Vinegar joyfully agrees, takes the money, and off he goes to the fair. When he arrived, he walked up and down, and at length saw a beautiful red cow. It was an excellent milker, and perfect in every way. "Oh!" thought Mr. Vinegar, "if I had but that cow, I should be the happiest man alive."

So he offered the forty guineas for the cow, and the owner said that, as he was a friend, he'd oblige him. So the bargain was made, and he got the cow and he drove it backwards and forwards to show it. By and by he saw a man playing the bagpipes – Tweedle-dum, tweedle-dee. The children followed him about, and he appeared to be pocketing money on all sides.

"Well," thought Mr. Vinegar, "if I had but that beautiful instrument I should be the happiest man alive my fortune would be made." So he went up to the man. "Friend," says he, "what a beautiful instrument that is, and what a deal of money you must make."

"Why, yes," said the man, "I make a great deal of money, to be sure, and it is a wonderful instrument."

"Oh!" cried Mr. Vinegar, "how I should like to possess it!"

"Well," said the man, "as you are a friend, I don't much mind parting with it: you shall have it for that red cow."

"Done!" said the delighted Mr. Vinegar. So the beautiful red cow was given for the bagpipes. He walked up and down with his purchase; but it was in vain he tried to play a tune, and instead of pocketing pence, the boys followed him hooting, laughing, and pelting.

Poor Mr. Vinegar, his fingers grew very cold, and, just as he was leaving the town, he met a man with a fine thick pair of gloves. "Oh, my fingers are so very cold," said Mr. Vinegar to himself. "Now if I had but those beautiful gloves I should be the happiest man alive."

He went up to the man, and said to him: "Friend, you seem to have a capital pair of gloves there."

"Yes, truly," cried the man; "and my hands are as warm as possible this cold November day."

"Well," said Mr. Vinegar, "I should like to have them."

"What will you give?" said the man; "as you are a friend, I don't much mind letting you have them for those bagpipes."

"Done!" cried Mr. Vinegar. He put on the gloves, and felt perfectly happy as he trudged homewards.

At last he grew very tired, when he saw a man coming towards him with a good stout stick in his hand.

"Oh," said Mr. Vinegar, "that I had but that stick! I should then be the happiest man alive." He said to the man: "Friend, what a rare good stick you have got!"

"Yes," said the man; "I have used it for many a long mile, and a good friend it has been; but if you have a fancy for it, as you are a friend, I don't mind giving it to you for that

Mr. Vinegar would, in due course, squander the riches he had found when the thieves ran away

pair of gloves."

Mr. Vinegar's hands were so warm, and his legs so tired, that he gladly made the exchange. As he drew near to the wood where he had left his wife, he heard a parrot on a tree calling out his name: "Mr. Vinegar, you foolish man, you blockhead, you simpleton; you went to the fair, and laid out all your money in buying a cow. Not content with that, you changed it for bagpipes, on which you could not play, and which were not worth one-tenth of the money. You fool, you had no sooner got the bagpipes than you changed them for the gloves, which were not worth one-

quarter of the money; and when you had got the gloves, you changed them for a poor miserable stick; and now for your forty guineas, cow, bagpipes, and gloves, you have nothing to show but that poor miserable stick, which you might have cut in any hedge."

On this the bird laughed and laughed, and Mr. Vinegar, falling into a violent rage, threw the stick at its head. The stick lodged in the tree, and he returned to his wife without money, cow, bagpipes, gloves, or stick, and she instantly gave him such a sound cudgelling that she almost broke every bone in his skin.

The Little Brother and Sister

The Brothers Grimm (Jacob 1785–1863 and Wilhelm 1786–1859) wrote this story about of the cruel mistreatment of a brother and sister who run away from their wicked witch stepmother and have to spend spent the night in the woods. The brother drinks enchanted water and turns into a deer but ultimately their faith in each other and the true uncompromising love of the king for the sister overcomes the evil magic, and family fidelity triumphs over adversity and separation!

There was once a little brother who took his sister by the hand, and said, "Since our own dear mother's death we have not had one happy hour; our stepmother beats us every day, and, when we come near her, kicks us away with her foot. Come, let us wander forth into the wide world." So all day long they travelled over meadows, fields, and stony roads. By the evening they came into a large forest, and laid themselves down in a hollow tree, and went to sleep. When they awoke the next morning, the sun had already risen high in the heavens, and its beams made the tree so hot that the little boy said to his sister, "I am so very thirsty, that if I knew where there was a brook, I would go and drink. Ah! I think I hear one running;" and so saying, he got up, and taking his sister's hand they went to look for the brook.

The wicked stepmother, however, was a witch, and had witnessed the departure of the two children: so, sneaking after them secretly, as is the habit of witches, she had enchanted all the springs in the forest.

Presently they found a brook, which ran trippingly over the pebbles, and the brother would have drunk out of it, but the sister heard how it said as it ran along, "Who drinks of me will become a tiger!"

So the sister exclaimed, "I pray you, Brother, drink not, or you will become a tiger, and tear me to pieces!" So the brother did not drink, although his thirst was very great, and he said, "I will wait till the next brook." As they came to the second, the sister heard it say, "Who drinks of me becomes a wolf!" The sister ran up crying, "Brother, do not, pray do not drink, or you will become a wolf and eat me up!" Then the brother did not drink, saying, "I will wait until we come to the next spring, but then I must drink, you may say what you will; my thirst is much too great." Just as they reached the third brook, the sister heard the voice saying, "Who drinks of me will become a fawn – who drinks of me will become a fawn!" So the sister said, "Oh,

The brother drank the enchanted water and turned into a fawn

my Brother do not drink, or you will be changed into a fawn, and run away from me!" But he had already kneeled down, and he drank of the water, and, as the first drops passed his lips, his shape took that of a fawn.

At first the sister wept over her little, changed brother, and he wept too, and knelt by her, very sorrowful; but at last the maiden said, "Be still, dear little fawn, and I will never forsake you!" and, taking off her golden garter, she placed it around his neck, and, weaving rushes, made a girdle to lead him with. This she tied to him, and taking the other end in her hand, she led him away, and they travelled deeper and deeper into the forest. After they had gone a long distance they came to a little hut, and the maiden, peeping in, found it empty, and thought, "Here we can stay and dwell." Then she looked for leaves and moss to make a soft couch for the fawn, and every morning she went out and collected roots and berries and nuts for herself, and tender grass for the fawn. In the evening when the sister was tired, and had said her prayers, she laid her head upon the back of the fawn, which served for a pillow, on which she slept soundly. Had but the brother regained his own proper form, their lives would have been happy indeed.

Thus they dwelt in this wilderness, and some time had elapsed when it happened that the King of the country had a great hunt in the forest; and now sounded through the trees the blowing of horns, the barking of dogs, and the lusty cry of the hunters, so that the little fawn heard them, and wanted very much to join in. "Ah!" said he to his sister, "let me go to the hunt, I cannot restrain myself any longer;" and he begged so hard that at last she consented. "But," she told him," "return again in the evening, for I shall shut my door against the wild huntsmen, and, that I may know you, do you knock, and say, 'sister, dear, let me in,' and if you do not speak I shall not open the door."

As soon as she had said this, the little fawn sprang off quite glad and merry in the fresh breeze. The King and his huntsmen perceived the beautiful animal, and pursued him; but they could not catch him, and when they thought they certainly had him, he sprang away over the bushes, and got out of sight. Just as it was getting dark, he ran up to the hut, and, knocking, said, "Sister mine, let me in."

Then she unfastened the little door, and he went in, and rested all night long upon his soft couch. The next morning the hunt was commenced again, and as soon as the little fawn heard the horns and the tally-ho of the sportsmen he could not rest, and said, "Sister, dear, open the door; I must be off."

The sister opened it, saying, "Return at evening, mind, and say the words as before." When the King and his huntsmen saw him again, the fawn with the golden necklace, they followed him, close, but he was too nimble and quick for them. The whole day long they kept up with him, but towards evening the huntsmen made a circle around him, and one wounded him slightly in the hinder foot, so that he could run but slowly. Then one of them slipped after him to the little hut, and heard him say, "Sister, dear, open the door," and saw that the door was opened and immediately shut behind him. The huntsman, having observed all this, went and told the King what he had seen and heard, and he said, "On the morrow I will pursue him once again."

The sister, however, was terribly afraid when she saw that her fawn was wounded, and, washing off the blood, she put herbs upon the foot, and said, "Go and rest upon your bed, dear fawn, that your wound may heal." It was so slight, that the next morning he felt nothing of it, and

when he heard the hunting cries outside, he exclaimed, "I cannot stop away – I must be there, and none shall catch me so easily again!" The sister wept very much and told him, "Soon will they kill you, and I shall be here alone in this forest, forsaken by all the world: I cannot let you go."

"I shall die here in vexation," answered the fawn, "if you do not, for when I hear the horn, I think I shall jump out of my skin." The sister, finding she could not prevent him, opened the door, with a heavy heart, and the fawn jumped out, quite delighted, into the forest. As soon as the King perceived him, he said to his huntsmen, "Follow him all day long till the evening, but let no one do him any harm." Then when the sun had set, the King asked his huntsman to show him the hut; and as they came to it he knocked at the door and said, "Let me in, dear Sister." Upon this the door opened, and, stepping in, the King saw a maiden more beautiful than he had ever beheld before. She was frightened when she saw not her fawn, but a man enter, who had a golden crown upon his head. But the King, looking at her with a kindly glance, held out to her his hand, saying, "Will you go with me to my castle, and be my dear wife?"

"Oh, yes," replied the maiden; "but the fawn must go too:

The sister married the king but the fawn remained with her

him I will never forsake." The King replied, "He shall remain with you as long as you live, and shall never want."

The King took the beautiful maiden upon his horse, and rode to his castle, where the wedding was celebrated with great splendor and she became Queen, and they lived together a long time; while the fawn was taken care of and played about the castle garden.

The wicked stepmother, however, on whose account the children had wandered forth into the world, had supposed that long ago the sister had been torn into pieces by the wild beasts, and the little brother in his fawn's shape hunted to death by the hunters. As soon, therefore, as she heard how happy they had become, and how everything

How sad the sister was that her brother was still a fawn and that they had stolen her baby away

prospered with them, envy and jealousy were aroused in her wicked heart, and left her no peace; and she was always thinking in what way she could bring misfortune upon them.

Her own daughter, who was as ugly as night, and had but one eye, for which she was continually reproached, said, "The luck of being a Queen has never happened to me."

"Be quiet, now," replied the old woman, "and make yourself contented: when the time comes I will help and assist you."

As soon, then, as the time came when the Queen gave birth to a beautiful little boy, which happened when the King was out hunting, the old witch took the form of a chambermaid, and got into the room where the Queen was lying, and said to her, "The bath is ready, which will restore you and give you fresh strength; be quick before it gets cold." Her daughter being at hand, they carried the weak Queen between them into the room, and laid her in the bath, and then, shutting the door, they ran off; but first they made up an immense fire in the stove, which must soon suffocate the poor young Queen.

When this was done, the old woman took her daughter, and, putting a cap upon her head, laid her in the bed in the Queen's place. She gave her, too, the form and appearance of the real Queen, as far as she was able; but she could not restore the lost eye, and, so that the King might not notice it, she turned her upon that side where there was no eye.

When midnight came, and every one was asleep, the nurse, who sat by herself, wide awake, near the cradle, in the nursery, saw the door open and the true Queen come in. She took the child in her arms, and rocked it a while, and then, shaking up its pillow, laid it down in its cradle, and covered it over again. She did not forget the fawn, either, but going to the corner where he was, stroked his head, and then went silently out of the door. The nurse asked in the morning of the guards if any one had passed into the castle during the night; but they answered, "No, we have not seen anybody." For many nights afterwards she came constantly, but never spoke a word; and the nurse saw her always, but she would not trust herself to speak about it to any one.

When some time had passed away, the Queen one night began to speak, and said:

"How fares my child! how fares my fawn?
Twice more will I come, but never again."

The nurse made no reply; but, when she had disappeared, went to the King, and told him. The King exclaimed, "Oh, mercy! what does this mean? The next night I will watch myself by the child."

So in the evening he went into the nursery, and about midnight the Queen appeared, and said:

"How fares my child! how fares my fawn?
Once more will I come, but never again."

And she nursed the child, as she usually did, and then disappeared. The King dared not speak; but he watched the following night, and this time she said:

"How fares my child! how fares my fawn?
This time have I come, but never again."

At these words the King could hold back no longer, but, springing up, cried, "You can be no other than my dear wife!"

Then she answered, "Yes, I am your dear wife;" and at that moment her life was restored by God's mercy, and she was again as beautiful and charming as ever. She told the King the fraud which the witch and her daughter had practised upon him, and he had them both tried, and sentence was pronounced against them. The little fawn was disenchanted, and received once more his human form; and the brother and sister lived happily together to the end of their days.

Diamonds and Toads

The young daughter told the royal hunting party all that had happened to her

Sometimes called *The Fairies (Les Fées)*, this is a French fairy tale by Charles Perrault (1628–1703) and one which Andrew Lang (1844–1912) included in *The Blue Fairy Book* (published 1889.) Here the archetypal kind girl is the stepdaughter, not the initial daughter – perhaps to make it different to *Cinderella*. That jewels may fall from a good person is a theme in several other tales.

There was once upon a time a widow who had two daughters. The eldest was so much like her in the face and humor that whoever looked upon the daughter saw the mother. They were both so disagreeable and so proud that there was no living with them.

The youngest, who was the very picture of her father for courtesy and sweetness of temper, was withal one of the most beautiful girls ever seen. As people naturally love their own likeness, this mother even doted on her eldest daughter and at the same time had a horrible aversion for the youngest – she made her eat in the kitchen and work continually.

Among other things, this poor child was forced twice a

Her mother was amazed to see so many diamonds

day to draw water above a mile and a-half off the house, and bring home a pitcher full of it. One day, as she was at this fountain, there came to her a poor woman, who begged of her to let her drink.

"Oh! ay, with all my heart, Goody," said this pretty little girl; and rinsing immediately the pitcher, she took up some water from the clearest place of the fountain, and gave it to her, holding up the pitcher all the while, that she might drink the easier.

The good woman, having drunk, said to her:

"You are so very pretty, my dear, so good and so mannerly, that I cannot help giving you a gift." For this was a fairy, who had taken the form of a poor country woman, to see

how far the civility and good manners of this pretty girl would go. "I will give you for a gift," continued the Fairy, "that, at every word you speak, there shall come out of your mouth either a flower or a jewel."

When this pretty girl came home her mother scolded her for staying so long at the fountain.

"I beg your pardon, mamma," said the poor girl, "for not making more haste."

And in speaking these words there came out of her mouth two roses, two pearls, and two diamonds

"What is it I see there?" said the mother, quite astonished. "I think I see pearls and diamonds come out of the girl's mouth! How happens this, child?"

This was the first time she had ever called her child.

The poor creature told her frankly all the matter, not without dropping out infinite numbers of diamonds.

"In good faith," cried the mother, "I must send my child thither. Come hither, Fanny; look what comes out of thy sister's mouth when she speaks. Wouldst not thou be glad, my dear, to have the same gift given thee? Thou hast nothing else to do but go and draw water out of the fountain, and when a certain poor woman asks you to let her drink, to give it to her very civilly."

"It would be a very fine sight indeed," said this ill-bred minx, "to see me go draw water."

"You shall go, hussy!" said the mother; "and this minute."

So away she went, but grumbling all the way, taking with her the best silver tankard in the house.

She was no sooner at the fountain than she saw coming out of the wood a lady most gloriously dressed, who came up to her, and asked to drink. This was, you must know, the very fairy who appeared to her sister, but now had taken the air and dress of a princess, to see how far this girl's rudeness would go.

"Am I come hither," said the proud, saucy one, "to serve you with water, pray? I suppose the silver tankard was brought purely for your ladyship, was it? However, you may drink out of it, if you have a fancy."

"You are not over and above mannerly," answered the

When the saucy daughter opened her mouth, vipers and toads popped out

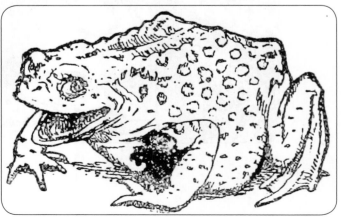

A poor old woman came up to the fountain and begged for a drink

Fairy, without putting herself in a passion. "Well, then, since you have so little breeding, and are so disobliging, I give you for a gift that at every word you speak there shall come out of your mouth a snake or a toad."

So soon as her mother saw her coming she cried out: "Well, daughter?"

"Well, mother?" answered the pert hussy, throwing out of her mouth two vipers and two toads.

"Oh! mercy," cried the mother; "What is it I see? Oh! It is that wretch her sister who has occasioned all this; but she shall pay for it"; and immediately she ran to beat her. The poor child fled away from her, and went to hide herself in the forest, not far from thence.

The King's son, then on his return from hunting, met her, and seeing her so very pretty, asked her what she did there alone and why she cried.

"Alas! sir, my mamma has turned me out of doors."

The King's son, who saw five or six pearls and as many diamonds come out of her mouth, desired her to tell him how that happened. She thereupon told him the whole story; and so the King's son fell in love with her, and, considering himself that such a gift was worth more than any marriage portion, conducted her to the palace of the King his father, and there married her.

As for the sister, she made herself so much hated that her own mother turned her off; and the miserable wretch, having wandered about a good while without finding anybody to take her in, went to a corner of the wood, and there died.

Speak roughly to your little boy

Lewis Carroll (1832–1898)

As sung by the Duchess (as well as the the cook and the baby) in *Alice's Adventures in Wonderland*, Chapter VI

'Speak roughly to your little boy,
And beat him when he sneezes:
He only does it to annoy,
Because he knows it teases.'

CHORUS.
'Wow! wow! wow!'

'I speak severely to my boy,
I beat him when he sneezes;
For he can thoroughly enjoy
The pepper when he pleases!'

CHORUS.
'Wow! wow! wow!'

The Fir Tree
A Christmas story

The Fir Tree by Hans Christian Andersen (1805–1875) was first published in 1844 and underlines the problems that arise when someone (or something) is over-anxious for greater things to the degree that the value of the present moment fails to be appreciated. This was the first of Andersen's fairy tales to express his deep pessimism – and is a very sad story.

Out in the woods stood such a pretty little fir tree. It grew in a good place, where it had plenty of sun and plenty of fresh air. Around it stood many tall comrades, both fir trees and pines.

The little fir tree was in a headlong hurry to grow up. It didn't care a thing for the warm sunshine, or the fresh air, and it took no interest in the peasant children who ran about chattering when they came to pick strawberries or raspberries. Often when the children had picked their pails full, or had gathered long strings of berries threaded on straws, they would sit down to rest near the little fir. "Oh, isn't it a nice little tree?" they would say. "It's the baby of the

The hare could hop right over the tiny fir tree

woods." The little tree didn't like their remarks at all.

Next year it shot up a long joint of new growth, and the following year another joint, still longer. You can always tell how old a fir tree is by counting the number of joints it has.

"I wish I were a grown-up tree, like my comrades," the little tree sighed. "Then I could stretch out my branches and see from my top what the world is like. The birds would make me their nesting place, and when the wind

blew I could bow back and forth with all the great trees."

It took no pleasure in the sunshine, nor in the birds. The glowing clouds, that sailed overhead at sunrise and sunset, meant nothing to it.

In winter, when the snow lay sparkling on the ground, a hare would often come hopping along and jump right over the little tree. Oh, how irritating that was! That happened for two winters, but when the third winter came the tree was so tall that the hare had to turn aside and hop around it.

"Oh, to grow, grow! To get older and taller," the little tree thought. "That is the most wonderful thing in this world."

In the autumn, woodcutters came and cut down a few of the largest trees. This happened every year. The young fir was no longer a baby tree, and it trembled to see how those stately great trees crashed to the ground, how their limbs were lopped off, and how lean they looked as the naked trunks were loaded into carts. It could hardly recognize the trees it had known, when the horses pulled them out of the woods.

Where were they going? What would become of them?

In the springtime, when swallows and storks came back, the tree asked them, "Do you know where the other trees

It was nearly Christmas time and snow fell

went? Have you met them?"

The swallows knew nothing about it, but the stork looked thoughtful and nodded his head. "Yes, I think I met them," he said. "On my way from Egypt I met many new ships, and some had tall, stately masts. They may well have been the trees you mean, for I remember the smell of fir. They wanted to be remembered to you."

"Oh, I wish I were old enough to travel on the sea. Please

People came to choose the most beautiful trees

tell me what it really is, and how it looks."

"That would take too long to tell," said the stork, and off he strode.

"Rejoice in your youth," said the sunbeams. "Take pride in your growing strength and in the stir of life within you."

And the wind kissed the tree, and the dew wept over it, for the tree was young and without understanding.

When Christmas came near, many young trees were cut down. Some were not even as old or as tall as this fir tree of ours, who was in such a hurry and fret to go traveling. These young trees, which were always the handsomest ones, had their branches left on them when they were loaded on carts and the horses drew them out of the woods.

"Where can they be going?" the fir tree wondered. "They are no taller than I am. One was really much smaller than I am. And why are they allowed to keep all their branches? "Where can they be going?"

"We know! We know!" the sparrows chirped. "We have been to town and peeped in the windows. We know where

The children wanted to hear the
story of Humpty-Dumpty

they are going. The greatest splendor and glory you can imagine awaits them. We've peeped through windows. We've seen them planted right in the middle of a warm room, and decked out with the most splendid things – gold apples, good gingerbread, gay toys, and many hundreds of candles."

"And then?" asked the fir tree, trembling in every twig. "And then? What happens then?"

"We saw nothing more. And never have we seen anything that could match it."

"I wonder if I was created for such a glorious future?" The fir tree rejoiced. "Why, that is better than to cross the sea. I'm tormented with longing. Oh, if Christmas would only come! I'm just as tall and grown-up as the trees they chose last year. How I wish I were already in the cart, on

my way to the warm room where there's so much splendor and glory. Then – then something even better, something still more important is bound to happen, or why should they deck me so fine? Yes, there must be something still grander! But what? Oh, how I long: I don't know what's the matter with me."

"Enjoy us while you may," the air and sunlight told him. "Rejoice in the days of your youth, out here in the open."

But the tree did not rejoice at all. It just grew. It grew and was green both winter and summer – dark evergreen. People who passed it said, "There's a beautiful tree!" And when Christmas time came again they cut it down first. The axe struck deep into its marrow. The tree sighed as it fell to the ground. It felt faint with pain. Instead of the happiness it had expected, the tree was sorry to leave the home where it had grown up. It knew that never again would it see its dear old comrades, the little bushes and the flowers about it – and perhaps not even the birds. The departure was anything but pleasant.

The tree did not get over it until all the trees were unloaded in the yard, and it heard a man say, "That's a splendid one. That's the tree for us." Then two servants came in fine livery, and carried the fir tree into a big splendid drawing-room. Portraits were hung all around the walls. On either side of the white porcelain stove stood great Chinese vases, with lions on the lids of them. There were easy chairs, silk-covered sofas and long tables strewn with picture books, and with toys that were worth a mint of money, or so the children said.

The fir tree was planted in a large tub filled with sand, but no one could see that it was a tub, because it was wrapped in a gay green cloth and set on a many-colored carpet. How the tree quivered! What would come next? The servants and even the young ladies helped it on with its fine decorations. From its branches they hung little nets cut out of colored paper, and each net was filled with candies. Gilded apples and walnuts hung in clusters as if they grew there, and a hundred little white, blue, and even red, candles were fastened to its twigs. Among its green branches swayed dolls that it took to be real living people, for the tree had never seen their like before. And up at its very top was set a large gold tinsel star. It was splendid, I tell you, splendid beyond all words!

"Oh," thought the tree, "if tonight would only come! If only the candles were lit! And after that, what happens then? Will the trees come trooping out of the woods to see me? Will the sparrows flock to the windows? Shall I take root here, and stand in fine ornaments all winter and summer long?"

That was how much it knew about it. All its longing had gone to its bark and set it to arching, which is as bad for a tree as a headache is for us.

Now the candles were lighted. What dazzling splendor! What a blaze of light! The tree quivered so in every bough that a candle set one of its twigs ablaze. It hurt terribly.

"Mercy me!" cried every young lady, and the fire was

quickly put out. The tree no longer dared rustle a twig – it was awful! Wouldn't it be terrible if it were to drop one of its ornaments? Its own brilliance dazzled it.

Suddenly the folding doors were thrown back, and a whole flock of children burst in as if they would overturn the tree completely. Their elders marched in after them, more sedately. For a moment, but only for a moment, the young ones were stricken speechless. Then they shouted till the rafters rang. They danced about the tree and plucked off one present after another.

"What are they up to?" the tree wondered. "What will happen next?"

This story, although sad, has been very popular for over one hundred and fifty years

As the candles burned down to the bark they were snuffed out, one by one, and then the children had permission to plunder the tree. They went about it in such earnest that the branches crackled and, if the tree had not been tied to the ceiling by the gold star at top, it would have tumbled headlong.

The children danced about with their splendid playthings. No one looked at the tree now, except an old nurse who peered in among the branches, but this was only to make sure that not an apple or fig had been overlooked.

"Tell us a story! Tell us a story!" the children clamored, as they towed a fat little man to the tree. He sat down beneath it and said, "Here we are in the woods, and it will do the tree a lot of good to listen to our story. Mind you, I'll tell only one. Which will you have, the story of Ivedy-Avedy, or the one about Humpty-Dumpty who tumbled downstairs, yet ascended the throne and married the Princess?"

"Ivedy-Avedy," cried some. "Humpty-Dumpty," cried the others. And there was a great hullabaloo. Only the fir tree held its peace, though it thought to itself, "Am I to be left out of this? Isn't there anything I can do?" For all the fun of the evening had centered upon it, and it had played its part well.

The fat little man told them all about Humpty-Dumpty, who tumbled downstairs, yet ascended the throne and married the Princess. And the children clapped and shouted, "Tell us another one! Tell us another one!" For they wanted to hear about Ivedy-Avedy too, but after Humpty-Dumpty the story telling stopped. The fir tree stood very still as it pondered how the birds in the woods had never told it a story to equal this.

"Humpty-Dumpty tumbled downstairs, yet he married the Princess. Imagine! That must be how things happen in the world. You never can tell. Maybe I'll tumble downstairs and marry a princess too," thought the fir tree, who believed every word of the story because such a nice man had told it.

The tree looked forward to the following day, when they would deck it again with fruit and toys, candles and gold. "Tomorrow I shall not quiver," it decided. "I'll enjoy my splendor to the full. Tomorrow I shall hear about Humpty-Dumpty again, and perhaps about Ivedy-Avedy too." All night long the tree stood silent as it dreamed its dreams, and next morning the butler and the maid came in with their dusters.

"Now my splendor will be renewed," the fir tree thought. But they dragged it upstairs to the garret, and there they left it in a dark corner where no daylight ever came. "What's the meaning of this?" the tree wondered. "What am I going to do here? What stories shall I hear?" It leaned against the wall, lost in dreams. It had plenty of time for dreaming, as the days and the nights went by. Nobody came to the garret. And when at last someone did come, it was only to put many big boxes away in the corner. The tree was quite hidden. One might think it had been entirely forgotten.

"It's still winter outside," the tree thought. "The earth is too hard and covered with snow for them to plant me now. I must have been put here for shelter until springtime comes. How thoughtful of them! How good people are! Only, I wish it weren't so dark here, and so very, very lonely. There's not even a little hare. It was so friendly out in the woods when the snow was on the ground and the hare came hopping along. Yes, he was friendly even when he jumped right over me, though I did not think so then. Here it's all so terribly lonely."

"Squeak, squeak!" said a little mouse just then. He crept

across the floor, and another one followed him. They sniffed the fir tree, and rustled in and out among its branches.

"It is fearfully cold," one of them said. "Except for that, it would be very nice here, wouldn't it, you old fir tree?"

"I'm not at all old," said the fir tree. "Many trees are much older than I am."

"Where did you come from?" the mice asked him. "And what do you know?" They were most inquisitive creatures.

"Tell us about the most beautiful place in the world. Have you been there? Were you ever in the larder, where there are cheeses on shelves and hams that hang from the rafters? It's the place where you can dance upon tallow candles – where you can dart in thin and squeeze out fat."

"I know nothing of that place," said the tree. "But I know the woods where the sun shines and the little birds sing."

just this winter, and I'm really in the prime of life, though at the moment my growth is suspended."

"How nicely you tell things," said the mice. The next night they came with four other mice to hear what the tree had to say. The more it talked, the more clearly it recalled things, and it thought, "Those were happy times. But they may still come back-they may come back again. Humpty-Dumpty fell downstairs, and yet he married the Princess. Maybe the same thing will happen to me." It thought about a charming little birch tree that grew out in the woods. To the fir tree she was a real and lovely Princess.

"Who is Humpty-Dumpty?" the mice asked it. So the fir tree told them the whole story, for it could remember it word by word. The little mice were ready to jump to the top of the tree for joy. The next night many more mice

The tree had felt faint with pain when the axe felled it to the ground

Now the tree gloried in its dazzling spendour as its candles glowed and ornaments shone

Then it told them about its youth. The little mice had never heard the like of it. They listened very intently, and said, "My! How much you have seen! And how happy it must have made you."

"I?" the fir tree thought about it. "Yes, those days were rather amusing." And he went on to tell them about Christmas Eve, when it was decked out with candies and candles.

"Oh," said the little mice, "how lucky you have been, you old fir tree!"

"I am not at all old," it insisted. "I came out of the woods

came to see the fir tree, and on Sunday two rats paid it a call, but they said that the story was not very amusing. This made the little mice so sad that they began to find it not so very interesting either.

"Is that the only story you know?" the rats asked.

"Only that one," the tree answered. "I heard it on the happiest evening of my life, but I did not know then how happy I was."

"It's a very silly story. Don't you know one that tells about bacon and candles? Can't you tell us a good larder story?"

"No," said the tree.

"Then good-bye, and we won't be back," the rats said, and went away.

At last the little mice took to staying away too. The tree sighed, "Oh, wasn't it pleasant when those gay little mice sat around and listened to all that I had to say. Now that, too, is past and gone. But I will take good care to enjoy myself, once they let me out of here."

When would that be? Well, it came to pass on a morning when people came up to clean out the garret. The boxes were moved, the tree was pulled out and thrown – thrown hard – on the floor. But a servant dragged it at once to the stairway, where there was daylight again.

"Now my life will start all over," the tree thought. It felt the fresh air and the first sunbeam strike it as if it came out into the courtyard. This all happened so quickly and there was so much going around it, that the tree forgot to give even a glance at itself. The courtyard adjoined a garden, where flowers were blooming. Great masses of fragrant roses hung over the picket fence. The linden trees were in blossom, and between them the swallows skimmed past, calling, "Tilira-lira-lee, my love's come back to me." But it was not the fir tree of whom they spoke.

"Now I shall live again," it rejoiced, and tried to stretch out its branches. Alas, they were withered, and brown, and brittle. It was tossed into a corner, among weeds and nettles. But the gold star that was still tied to its top sparkled bravely in the sunlight.

Several of the merry children, who had danced around the tree and taken such pleasure in it at Christmas, were playing in the courtyard. One of the youngest seized upon it and tore off the tinsel star.

"Look what is still hanging on that ugly old Christmas tree," the child said, and stamped upon the branches until they cracked beneath his shoes.

The tree saw the beautiful flowers blooming freshly in the garden. It saw itself, and wished that they had left it in the darkest corner of the garret. It thought of its own young days in the deep woods, and of the merry Christmas Eve, and of the little mice who had been so pleased when it told them the story of Humpty-Dumpty.

"My days are over and past," said the poor tree. "Why didn't I enjoy them while I could? Now they are gone – all gone."

A servant came and chopped the tree into little pieces. These heaped together quite high. The wood blazed beautifully under the big copper kettle, and the fir tree moaned so deeply that each groan sounded like a muffled shot. That's why the children who were playing near-by ran to make a circle around the flames, staring into the fire and crying, "Pif! Paf!" But as each groan burst from it, the tree thought of a bright summer day in the woods, or a starlit winter night. It thought of Christmas Eve and thought of Humpty-Dumpty, which was the only story it ever heard and knew how to tell. And so the tree was burned completely away.

The children played on in the courtyard. The youngest child wore on his breast the gold star that had topped the tree on its happiest night of all. But that was no more, and the tree was no more, and there's no more to my story. No more, nothing more. All stories come to an end.

Fairies in the woods

American Transcendentalist poet, philosopher, lecturer and essayist Ralph Waldo Emerson (1803-1882) wrote:

"A lady, with whom I was riding in the forest, said to me, that the woods always seemed to her to wait, as if the genii who inhabit them suspended their deeds until the wayfarer has passed onward: a thought which poetry has celebrated in the dance of the fairies, which breaks off on the approach of human feet."

Fairy funerals

Poet, painter, and printmaker William Blake (1757–1827) claimed to have seen a fairy funeral:

"Did you ever see a fairy's funeral, madam?" he asked of a lady who happened to sit next to him. "Never, Sir!" said the lady. "I have," said Blake, "but not before last night." And he went on to tell how, in his garden, he had seen "a procession of creatures of the size and colour of green and grey grasshoppers, bearing a body laid out on a rose-leaf, which they buried with songs, and then disappeared". They are believed to be an omen of death.

Jack the Giant Killer

First printed in 1711, this tale is set during the reign of King Arthur and tells how brave young Jack, a clever farmer's son, outwits various giants. Its sources are unknown but the tale possibly sprang from Norse mythology and also has parallels with French fairy tales and Grimm's *The Valiant Little Tailor*. Child psychologists will claim that such stories are ever popular because children can identify with the tricking of giants as being equivalent to outsmarting grown-ups!

When good King Arthur reigned, there lived near the Land's End of England, in the county of Cornwall, a farmer who had one only son called Jack. He was brisk and of a ready lively wit, so that nobody or nothing could worst him.

In those days the Mount of Cornwall was kept by a huge giant named Cormoran. He was eighteen feet in height, and about three yards round the waist, of a fierce and grim countenance, the terror of all the neighbouring towns and villages. He lived in a cave in the midst of the Mount, and whenever he wanted food he would wade over to the mainland, where he would furnish himself with whatever came in his way. Everybody at his approach ran out of their houses, while he seized on their cattle, making nothing of carrying half-a-dozen oxen on his back at a time; and as for their sheep and hogs, he would tie them round his waist like a bunch of tallow-dips. He had done this for many years, so that all Cornwall was in despair.

One day Jack happened to be at the town hall when the magistrates were sitting in council about the Giant. He asked: "What reward will be given to the man who kills Cormoran?"

"The giant's treasure," they said, "will be the reward."

Quoth Jack: "Then let me undertake it."

So he got a horn, shovel, and pickaxe, and went over to the Mount in the beginning of a dark winter's evening, when he fell to work, and before morning had dug a pit twenty-two feet deep, and nearly as broad, covering it over with long sticks and straw. Then he strewed a little mould over it, so that it appeared like plain ground. Jack then placed himself on the opposite side of the pit, farthest

from the giant's lodging, and, just at the break of day, he put the horn to his mouth, and blew, Tantivy, Tantivy. This noise roused the giant, who rushed from his cave, crying: "You incorrigible villain, are you come here to disturb my rest? You shall pay dearly for this. Satisfaction I will have, and this it shall be, I will take you whole and broil you for breakfast."

He had no sooner uttered this, than he tumbled into the pit, and made the very foundations of the Mount to shake.

"Oh, Giant," quoth Jack, "where are you now? Oh, faith, you are gotten now into Lob's Pound, where I will surely plague you for your threatening words: what do you think now of broiling me for your breakfast? Will no other diet serve you but poor Jack?" Then having tantalised the giant for a while, he gave him a most weighty knock with his pickaxe on the very crown of his head, and killed him on the spot.

Jack then filled up the pit with earth, and went to search the cave, which he found contained much treasure. When

Jack met many giants, including one with two heads

the magistrates heard of this they made a declaration he should henceforth be presented him with a sword and a belt, on which were written these words embroidered in letters of gold:

> "Here's the right valiant Cornish man,
> Who slew the giant Cormoran."

The news of Jack's victory soon spread over all the West of England, so that another giant, named Blunderbore, hearing of it, vowed to be revenged on Jack, if ever he should light on him. This giant was the lord of an enchanted castle situated in the midst of a lonesome wood. Now Jack, about four months afterwards, walking near this wood in his journey to Wales, being weary, seated himself near a pleasant fountain and fell fast asleep. While he was sleeping, the giant, coming there for water, discovered him, and knew him to be the far-famed Jack the Giant-killer by the lines written on the belt. Without ado, he took Jack on his shoulders and carried him towards his castle. Now, as they passed through a thicket, the rustling of the boughs awakened Jack, who was strangely surprised to find himself in the clutches of the giant. His terror was

HISTORY OF
JACK
THE
GIANT KILLER.

CONTAINING

His Birth and Parentage—His meeting with the King's Son—His noble Conquests over many monstrous Giants —and, his relieving a beautiful Lady, whom he afterwards married; &c.

GLASGOW:
PRINTED FOR THE BOOKSELLERS.
62.

This story was first printed in 1711

only begun, for, on entering the castle, he saw the ground strewed with human bones, and the giant told him his own would ere long be among them. After this the giant locked poor Jack in an immense chamber, leaving him there while he went to fetch another giant, his brother, living in the same wood, who might share in the meal on Jack.

After waiting some time Jack, on going to the window beheld afar off the two giants coming towards the castle.

"Now," quoth Jack to himself, "my death or my deliverance is at hand."

Now, there were strong cords in a corner of the room in which Jack was, and two of these he took, and made a strong noose at the end; and while the giants were unlocking the iron gate of the castle he threw the ropes over each of their heads. Then he drew the other ends across a beam, and pulled with all his might, so that he throttled them. Then, when he saw they were black in the face, he slid down the rope, and drawing his sword, slew them both. Then, taking the giant's keys, and unlocking the rooms, he found three fair ladies tied by the hair of their heads, almost starved to death.

"Sweet ladies," quoth Jack, "I have destroyed this monster and his brutish brother, and obtained your liberties." This said he presented them with the keys, and so proceeded on his journey to Wales.

Jack made the best of his way by travelling as fast as he could, but lost his road, and was benighted, and could not find any habitation until, coming into a narrow valley, he found a large house, and in order to get shelter took courage to knock at the gate. But what was his surprise when there came forth a monstrous giant with two heads; yet he did not appear so fiery as the others were, for he was a Welsh giant, and what he did was by private and secret malice under the false show of friendship. Jack, having told his condition to the giant, was shown into a bedroom, where, in the dead of night, he heard his host in another apartment muttering these words:

"Though here you lodge with me this night,
You shall not see the morning light
My club shall dash your brains outright!"

"Say'st thou so," quoth Jack; "that is like one of your Welsh tricks, yet I hope to be cunning enough for you." Then, getting out of bed, he laid a billet in the bed in his stead, and hid himself in a corner of the room. At the dead time of the night in came the Welsh giant, who struck several heavy blows on the bed with his club, thinking he had broken every bone in Jack's skin. The next morning Jack, laughing in his sleeve, gave him hearty thanks for his night's lodging.

"How have you rested?" quoth the giant; "did you not feel anything in the night?" "No," quoth Jack, "nothing but a rat, which gave me two or three slaps with her tail." With that, greatly wondering, the giant led Jack to breakfast, bringing him a bowl containing four gallons of hasty pudding. Being loth to let the giant think it too much for him, Jack put a large leather bag under his loose coat, in such a way that he could convey the pudding into it without its being perceived. Then, telling the giant he would show him a trick, taking a knife, Jack ripped open the bag, and out came all the hasty pudding. Whereupon, saying, "Odds splutters hur nails, hur can do that trick hurself," the monster took the knife, and ripping open his belly, fell down dead.

Now, it happened in these days that King Arthur's only son asked his father to give him a large sum of money, in order that he might go and seek his fortune in the principality of

Jack relied upon his wit and guile to trick many of the giants around at the time of King Arthur

Wales, where lived a beautiful lady possessed with seven evil spirits. The king did his best to persuade his son from it, but in vain; so at last gave way and the prince set out with two horses, one loaded with money, the other for himself to ride upon. Now, after several days' travel, he came to

Two fierce griffins guarded the castle gate

a market-town in Wales, where he beheld a vast crowd of people gathered together. The prince asked the reason of it, and was told that they had arrested a corpse for several large sums of money which the deceased owed when he died. The prince replied that it was a pity creditors should be so cruel, and said: "Go bury the dead, and let his creditors come to my lodging, and there their debts shall be paid."

They came, in such great numbers that before night he had only twopence left for himself.

Now Jack the Giant-Killer, coming that way, was so taken with the generosity of the prince, that he desired to be his servant. This being agreed upon, the next morning they set forward on their journey together, when, as they were riding out of the town, an old woman called after the prince, saying, "He has owed me twopence these seven years; pray pay me as well as the rest."

Putting his hand to his pocket, the prince gave the woman all he had left, so that after their day's food, which cost what small spell Jack had by him, they were without a penny between them.

When the sun got low, the king's son said: "Jack, since we have no money, where can we lodge this night?"

But Jack replied: "Master, we'll do well enough, for I have an uncle lives within two miles of this place; he is a huge and monstrous giant with three heads; he'll fight five hundred men in armour, and make them to fly before him."

"Alas!" quoth the prince, "what shall we do there? He'll certainly chop us up at a mouthful. Nay, we are scarce enough to fill one of his hollow teeth!"

"It is no matter for that," quoth Jack; "I myself will go before and prepare the way for you; therefore stop here and wait till I return."

Jack then rode away at full speed, and coming to the gate of the castle, he knocked so loud that he made the neighbouring hills resound. The giant roared out at this like thunder: "Who's there?"

Jack answered: "None but your poor cousin Jack."

Quoth he: "What news with my poor cousin Jack?"

He replied: "Dear uncle, heavy news, God wot!"

"Prithee," quoth the giant, "what heavy news can come to me? I am a giant with three heads, and besides thou knowest I can fight five hundred men in armour, and make them fly like chaff before the wind."

"Oh, but," quoth Jack, "here's the king's son a-coming with a thousand men in armour to kill you and destroy all that you have!"

"Oh, cousin Jack," said the giant, "this is heavy news indeed! I will immediately run and hide myself, and thou shalt lock, bolt, and bar me in, and keep the keys until the prince is gone." Having secured the giant, Jack fetched his master, when they made themselves heartily merry whilst the poor giant lay trembling in a vault under the ground.

The giant, Galligantua (sometimes called Galligantus) was beheaded and blew away in a whirlwind

Early in the morning Jack furnished his master with a fresh supply of gold and silver, and then sent him three miles forward on his journey, at which time the prince was pretty well out of the smell of the giant. Jack then returned, and let the giant out of the vault, who asked what he should give him for keeping the castle from destruction.

"Why," quoth Jack, "I want nothing but the old coat and cap, together with the old rusty sword and slippers which are at your bed's head."

Quoth the giant: "You know not what you ask; they are the most precious things I have. The coat will keep you invisible, the cap will tell you all you want to know, the sword cuts asunder whatever you strike, and the shoes are of extraordinary swiftness. But you have been very serviceable to me, therefore take them with all my heart."

Jack thanked his uncle, and then went off with them. He soon overtook his master and they quickly arrived at the house of the lady the prince sought, who, finding the prince to be a suitor, prepared a splendid banquet for him. After the repast was concluded, she told him she had a task for him. She wiped his mouth with a handkerchief, saying: "You must show me that handkerchief to-morrow morning, or else you will lose your head."

With that she put it in her bosom. The prince went to bed

A fierce giant brandishes a knobbly club

in great sorrow, but Jack's cap of knowledge informed him how it was to be obtained. In the middle of the night she called upon her familiar spirit to carry her to Lucifer. But Jack put on his coat of darkness and his shoes of swiftness, and was there as soon as she was. When she entered the place of the Old One, she gave the handkerchief to old Lucifer, who laid it upon a shelf, whence Jack took it and brought it to his master, who showed it to the lady next day, and so saved his life. On that day, she gave the prince a kiss and told him he must show her the lips to-morrow morning that she kissed last night, or lose his head.

"Ah!" he replied, "if you kiss none but mine, I will."

"That is neither here nor there," said she; "if you do not, death's your portion!"

At midnight she went as before, and was angry with old Lucifer for letting the handkerchief go. "But now," quoth she, "I will be too hard for the king's son, for I will kiss thee, and he is to show me thy lips."

Which she did, and Jack, when she was not standing by, cut off Lucifer's head and brought it under his invisible coat to his master, who the next morning pulled it out by

the horns before the lady. This broke the enchantment and the evil spirit left her, and she appeared in all her beauty. They were married the next morning, and soon after went to the court of King Arthur, where Jack for his many great exploits, was made one of the Knights of the Round Table.

Jack soon went searching for giants again, but he had not ridden far, when he saw a cave, near the entrance of which he beheld a giant sitting upon a block of timber, with a knotted iron club by his side. His goggle eyes were like flames of fire, his countenance grim and ugly, and his cheeks like a couple of large flitches of bacon, while the bristles of his beard resembled rods of iron wire, and the locks that hung down upon his brawny shoulders were like curled snakes or hissing adders. Jack alighted from his horse, and, putting on the coat of darkness, went up close to the giant, and said softly: "Oh! are you there? It will not be long before I take you fast by the beard."

The giant all this while could not see him, on account of his invisible coat, so that Jack, coming up close to the monster, struck a blow with his sword at his head, but, missing his aim, he cut off the nose instead. At this, the giant roared like claps of thunder, and began to lay about him with his iron club like one stark mad. But Jack, running behind, drove his sword up to the hilt in the giant's back, so that he fell down dead. This done, Jack cut off the

Some of the giants Jack met were living in Cornwall

Jack remained undaunted by the giant's size

coffers, he shared the gold and silver equally amongst them and took them to a neighbouring castle, where they all feasted and made merry over their deliverance.

But in the midst of all this mirth a messenger brought news that one Thunderdell, a giant with two heads, having heard of the death of his kinsmen, had come from the northern dales to be revenged on Jack, and was within a mile of the castle, the country people flying before him like chaff. But Jack was not a bit daunted, and said: "Let him come! I have a tool to pick his teeth; and you, ladies and gentlemen, walk out into the garden, and you shall witness this giant Thunderdell's death and destruction."

The castle was situated in the midst of a small island surrounded by a moat thirty feet deep and twenty feet wide, over which lay a drawbridge. So Jack employed men to cut through this bridge on both sides, nearly to the middle; and then, dressing himself in his invisible coat, he marched against the giant with his sword of sharpness. Although the giant could not see Jack, he smelt his approach, and cried out in these words:

"Fee, fi, fo, fum!
I smell the blood of an Englishman!
Be he alive or be he dead,
I'll grind his bones to make me bread!"

"Say'st thou so," said Jack; "then thou art a monstrous miller indeed."

The giant cried out again: "Art thou that villain who killed my kinsmen? Then I will tear thee with my teeth, suck thy blood, and grind thy bones to powder."

giant's head, and sent it, with his brother's also, to King Arthur, by a Wagoner he hired for that purpose.

Jack now resolved to enter the giant's cave in search of his treasure, and, passing along through a great many windings and turnings, he came at length to a large room paved with freestone, at the upper end of which was a boiling caldron, and on the right hand a large table, at which the giant used to dine. Then he came to a window, barred with iron, through which he looked and beheld a vast number of miserable captives, who, seeing him, cried out: "Alas! young man, art thou come to be one amongst us in this miserable den?"

"Ay," quoth Jack, "but pray tell me what is the meaning of your captivity?"

"We are kept here," said one, "till such time as the giants have a wish to feast, and then the fattest among us is slaughtered! And many are the times they have dined upon murdered men!"

"Say you so," quoth Jack, and straightway unlocked the gate and let them free, who all rejoiced like condemned men at sight of a pardon. Then searching the giant's

Cormoran lived in a cave by the Mount of Cornwall

The giant Cormoran and his wife, giantess Cormelian, are especially associated with St Michael's Mount in Cornwall, England, while Blunderbore (or Blunderboar, Thunderbore, Blunderbus, or Blunderbuss) is also associated with Cornwall and was said to terrorize travellers heading towards St Ives.

301

"You'll have to catch me first," quoth Jack, and throwing off his invisible coat, so that the giant might see him, and putting on his shoes of swiftness, he ran from the giant, who followed like a walking castle, so that the very foundations of the earth seemed to shake at every step. Jack led him a long dance, in order that the gentlemen and ladies might see; and at last to end the matter, ran lightly over the drawbridge, the giant, in full speed, pursuing him with his club. Then, coming to the middle of the bridge, the giant's great weight broke it down, and he tumbled headlong into the water, where he rolled and wallowed like a whale. Jack, standing by the moat, laughed at him all the while; but though the giant foamed to hear him scoff, and plunged from place to place in the moat, yet he could not get out to be revenged. Jack at length got a cart-rope and cast it over the two heads of the giant, and drew him ashore by a team of horses, and then cut off both his heads with his sword of sharpness, and sent them to King Arthur.

After some time spent in mirth and pastime, Jack, taking leave of the knights and ladies, set out for new adventures. Through many woods he passed, and came at length to the foot of a high mountain. Here, late at night, he found a lonesome house, and knocked at the door, which was opened by an aged man with a head as white as snow.

"Father," said Jack, "can you lodge a benighted traveller that has lost his way?"

"Yes," said the old man; "you are right welcome to my poor cottage."

Whereupon Jack entered, and down they sat together, and the old man began to speak as follows: "Son, I see by your belt you are the great conqueror of giants, and behold, my son, on the top of this mountain is an enchanted castle, this is kept by a giant named Galligantua, and he by the help of an old conjurer, betrays many knights and ladies into his castle, where by magic art they are transformed into sundry shapes and forms. But above all, I grieve for a duke's daughter, whom they fetched from her father's garden, carrying her through the air in a burning chariot drawn by fiery dragons, when they secured her within the castle, and transformed her into a white hind. And though many knights have tried to break the enchantment, and work her deliverance, yet no one could accomplish it, on

Jack and those he had rescued were taken
to King Arthur's court

account of two dreadful griffins which are placed at the castle gate and which destroy every one who comes near. But you, my son, may pass by them undiscovered, where on the gates of the castle you will find engraven in large letters how the spell may be broken." Jack gave the old man his hand, and promised that in the morning he would venture his life to free the lady.

In the morning Jack arose and put on his invisible coat and magic cap and shoes, and prepared himself for the fray. Now, when he had reached the top of the mountain he soon discovered the two fiery griffins, but passed them without fear, because of his invisible coat. When he had got beyond them, he found upon the gates of the castle a golden trumpet hung by a silver chain, under which these lines were engraved:

"Whoever shall this trumpet blow,
Shall soon the giant overthrow,
And break the black enchantment straight;
So all shall be in happy state."

Jack had no sooner read this but he blew the trumpet, at which the castle trembled to its vast foundations, and the giant and conjurer were in horrid confusion, biting their thumbs and tearing their hair, knowing their wicked reign was at an end. Then the giant stooping to take up his club, Jack at one blow cut off his head; whereupon the conjurer, mounting up into the air, was carried away in a whirlwind. Then the enchantment was broken, and all the lords and ladies who had so long been transformed into birds and beasts returned to their proper shapes, and the castle vanished away in a cloud of smoke. This being done, the head of Galligantua was likewise, in the usual manner, conveyed to the Court of King Arthur, where, the very next day, Jack followed, with the knights and ladies who had been delivered. Whereupon, as a reward for his good services, the king prevailed upon the duke to bestow his daughter in marriage on honest Jack. So married they were, and the whole kingdom was filled with joy at the wedding.

Furthermore, the king bestowed on Jack a noble castle, with a very beautiful estate thereto belonging, where he and his lady lived in great joy and happiness all the rest of their days.

The Snow Queen

What follows here is how it all began, with an excerpt that includes the first two stories and some of the third:

FIRST STORY

Which Treats of a Mirror and of the Splinters

Now then, let us begin. When we are at the end of the story, we shall know more than we know now: but to begin.

Once upon a time there was a wicked sprite, indeed he was the most mischievous of all sprites. One day he was in a very good humor, for he had made a mirror with the power of causing all that was good and beautiful when it was reflected therein, to look poor and mean; but that which was good-for-nothing and looked ugly was shown magnified and increased in ugliness. In this mirror the most beautiful landscapes looked like boiled spinach, and the best persons were turned into frights, or appeared to stand on their heads; their faces were so distorted that they were not to be recognised; and if anyone had a mole, you might be sure that it would be magnified and spread over both nose and mouth.

"That's glorious fun!" said the sprite. If a good thought passed through a man's mind, then a grin was seen in the mirror, and the sprite laughed heartily at his clever discovery. All the little sprites who went to his school – for he kept a sprite school – told each other that a miracle had happened; and that now only, as they thought, it would be possible to see how the world really looked. They ran about with the mirror; and at last there was not a land or a person who was not represented distorted in the mirror. So then they thought they would fly up to the sky, and have a joke there. The higher they flew with the mirror, the more terribly it grinned: they could hardly hold it fast. Higher and higher still they flew, nearer and nearer to the stars, when suddenly the mirror shook so terribly with grinning, that it flew out of their hands and fell to the earth, where it was dashed in a hundred million and more pieces. And now it worked much more evil than before; for some of these pieces were hardly so large as a grain of sand, and they flew about in the wide world, and when they got into people's eyes, there they stayed; and then people saw everything perverted, or only had an eye for that which was evil. This happened because the very smallest bit had the same power which the whole mirror had possessed.

The Snow Queen casts her spell upon the child

Some persons even got a splinter in their heart, and then it made one shudder, for their heart became like a lump of ice. Some of the broken pieces were so large that they were used for windowpanes, through which one could not see one's friends. Other pieces were put in spectacles; and that was a sad affair when people put on their glasses to see well and rightly. Then the wicked sprite laughed till he almost choked, for all this tickled his fancy. The fine splinters still flew about in the air: and now we shall hear what happened next.

Silver coinage depicts the characters from this story

SECOND STORY
A Little Boy and a Little Girl

In a large town, where there are so many houses, and so many people, that there is no roof left for everybody to have a little garden; and where, on this account, most persons are obliged to content themselves with flowers in pots; there lived two little children, who had a garden somewhat larger than a flower-pot. They were not brother

they grew splendidly. They now thought of placing the boxes across the gutter, so that they nearly reached from one window to the other, and looked just like two walls of flowers. The tendrils of the peas hung down over the boxes; and the rose-trees shot up long branches, twined round the windows, and then bent towards each other: it was almost like a triumphant arch of foliage and flowers. The boxes were very high, and the children knew that they must not creep over them; so they often obtained permission to get out of the windows to each other, and to sit on their little stools among the roses, where they could play delightfully. In winter there was an end of this pleasure. The windows were often frozen over; but then

The Snow Queen was a beautiful enchantress

The child rode upon a reindeer

and sister; but they cared for each other as much as if they were. Their parents lived exactly opposite. They inhabited two garrets; and where the roof of the one house joined that of the other, and the gutter ran along the extreme end of it, there was to each house a small window: one needed only to step over the gutter to get from one window to the other.

The children's parents had large wooden boxes there, in which vegetables for the kitchen were planted, and little rosetrees besides: there was a rose in each box, and

they heated copper farthings on the stove, and laid the hot farthing on the windowpane, and then they had a capital peep-hole, quite nicely rounded; and out of each peeped a gentle friendly eye – it was the little boy and the little girl who were looking out. His name was Kay, hers was Gerda. In summer, with one jump, they could get to each other; but in winter they were obliged first to go down the long stairs, and then up the long stairs again: and out-of-doors there was quite a snow-storm.

"It is the white bees that are swarming," said Kay's old grandmother.

"Do the white bees choose a queen?" asked the little boy; for he knew that the honey-bees always have one.

"Yes," said the grandmother, "she flies where the swarm hangs in the thickest clusters. She is the largest of all; and she can never remain quietly on the earth, but goes up again into the black clouds. Many a winter's night she flies through the streets of the town, and peeps in at the windows; and they then freeze in so wondrous a manner that they look like flowers."

"Yes, I have seen it," said both the children; and so they knew that it was true.

"Can the Snow Queen come in?" said the little girl.

"Only let her come in!" said the little boy. "Then I'd put her on the stove, and she'd melt."

And then his grandmother patted his head and told him other stories.

In the evening, when little Kay was at home, and half undressed, he climbed up on the chair by the window, and peeped out of the little hole. A few snow-flakes were falling, and one, the largest of all, remained lying on the edge of a flower-pot.

The flake of snow grew larger and larger; and at last it was like a young lady, dressed in the finest white gauze, made of a million little flakes like stars. She was so beautiful

"The rose in the valley is blooming so sweet,
And angels descend there the children to greet."

And the children held each other by the hand, kissed the roses, looked up at the clear sunshine, and spoke as though they really saw angels there. What lovely summer-days those were! How delightful to be out in the air, near the fresh rose-bushes, that seem as if they would never finish blossoming!

Kay and Gerda looked at the picture-book full of beasts and of birds; and it was then – bthe clock in the church-tower was just striking five – that Kay said, "Oh! I feel such a sharp pain in my heart; and now something has got into my eye!"

The little girl put her arms around his neck. He winked his eyes; now there was nothing to be seen.

"I think it is out now," said he; but it was not. It was just one of those pieces of glass from the magic mirror that had got into his eye; and poor Kay had got another piece right in his heart. It will soon become like ice. It did not hurt any longer, but there it was.

"What are you crying for?" asked he. "You look so ugly! There's nothing the matter with me. Ah," said he at once, "that rose is cankered! And look, this one is quite crooked! After all, these roses are very ugly! They are just like the box they are planted in!" And then he gave the box a good kick with his foot, and pulled both the roses up.

Wicked sprites cavort and make mischief

*Kay's old grandmother explained
all about bees and snowflakes*

and delicate, but she was of ice, of dazzling, sparkling ice; yet she lived; her eyes gazed fixedly, like two stars; but there was neither quiet nor repose in them. She nodded towards the window, and beckoned with her hand. The little boy was frightened, and jumped down from the chair; it seemed to him as if, at the same moment, a large bird flew past the window.

The next day it was a sharp frost – and then the spring came; the sun shone, the green leaves appeared, the swallows built their nests, the windows were opened, and the little children again sat in their pretty garden, high up on the leads at the top of the house.

"What are you doing?" cried the little girl; and as he perceived her fright, he pulled up another rose, got in at the window, and hastened off from dear little Gerda.

Afterwards, when she brought her picture-book, he asked, "What horrid beasts have you there?" And if his grandmother told them stories, he always interrupted her; besides, if he could manage it, he would get behind her, put on her spectacles, and imitate her way of speaking; he copied all her ways, and then everybody laughed at

The magical world of "The Snow Queen" has inspired wonderful illustrations and been the subject of some lively stamps, as well as opera and ballet

The story explores the battle between good and evil

him. He was soon able to imitate the gait and manner of everyone in the street. Everything that was peculiar and displeasing in them – that Kay knew how to imitate: and at such times all the people said, "The boy is certainly very clever!" But it was the glass he had got in his eye; the glass that was sticking in his heart, which made him tease even little Gerda, whose whole soul was devoted to him.

His games now were quite different to what they had formerly been, they were so very knowing. One winter's day, when the flakes of snow were flying about, he spread the skirts of his blue coat, and caught the snow as it fell.

"Look through this glass, Gerda," said he. And every flake seemed larger, and appeared like a magnificent flower, or beautiful star; it was splendid to look at!

"Look, how clever!" said Kay. "That's much more interesting than real flowers! They are as exact as possible; there is not a fault in them, if they did not melt!"

It was not long after this, that Kay came one day with large gloves on, and his little sledge at his back, and bawled right into Gerda's ears, "I have permission to go

out into the square where the others are playing"; and off he was in a moment.

There, in the market-place, some of the boldest of the boys used to tie their sledges to the carts as they passed by, and so they were pulled along, and got a good ride. It was so capital! Just as they were in the very height of their amusement, a large sledge passed by: it was painted quite white, and there was someone in it wrapped up in a rough white mantle of fur, with a rough white fur cap on his head. The sledge drove round the square twice, and Kay tied on his sledge as quickly as he could, and off he drove with it. On they went quicker and quicker into the next street; and the person who drove turned round to Kay, and nodded to him in a friendly manner, just as if they knew each other. Every time he was going to untie his sledge, the person nodded to him, and then Kay sat quiet; and so on they went till they came outside the gates of the town. Then the snow began to fall so thickly that the little boy could not see an arm's length before him, but still on he went: when suddenly he let go the string he held in his hand in order to get loose from the sledge, but it was of no use; still the little vehicle rushed on with the quickness of the wind. He then cried as loud as he could, but no one beard him; the snow drifted and the sledge flew on, and sometimes it gave a jerk as though they were driving over hedges and ditches. He was quite frightened, and he tried to repeat the Lord's Prayer; but all he could do, he was only able to remember the multiplication table.

The snow-flakes grew larger and larger, till at last they looked just like great white fowls. Suddenly they flew on one side; the large sledge stopped, and the person who drove rose up. It was a lady; her cloak and cap were of snow. She was tall and of slender figure, and of a dazzling whiteness. It was the Snow Queen.

"We have travelled fast," said she; "but it is freezingly cold. Come under my bearskin." And she put him in the sledge beside her, wrapped the fur round him, and he felt as though he were sinking in a snow-wreath.

"Are you still cold?" asked she; and then she kissed his forehead. Ah! it was colder than ice; it penetrated to his very heart, which was already almost a frozen lump; it seemed to him as if he were about to die – but a moment more and it was quite congenial to him, and he did not remark the cold that was around him.

"My sledge! Do not forget my sledge!" It was the first thing he thought of. It was there tied to one of the white chickens, who flew along with it on his back behind the large sledge. The Snow Queen kissed Kay once more, and then he forgot little Gerda, grandmother, and all whom he had left at his home.

"Now you will have no more kisses," said she, "or else I should kiss you to death!"

Kay looked at her. She was very beautiful; a more clever, or a more lovely countenance he could not fancy to himself; and she no longer appeared of ice as before, when she sat outside the window, and beckoned to him; in his eyes she was perfect, he did not fear her at all, and told her that he could calculate in his head and with fractions, even; that he knew the number of square miles there were in the different countries, and how many inhabitants they contained; and she smiled while he spoke. It then seemed to him as if what he knew was not enough, and he looked upwards in the large huge empty space above him, and on she flew with him; flew high over,the black clouds, while the storm moaned and whistled as though it were singing some old tune. On they flew over woods and lakes, over seas, and many lands; and beneath them the chilling storm rushed fast, the wolves howled, the snow crackled; above them flew large screaming crows, but higher up appeared the moon, quite large and bright; and it was on it that Kay gazed during the long long winter's night; while by day he slept at the feet of the Snow Queen.

THE FIRST PART OF THE THIRD STORY
Of the Flower-Garden At the Old Woman's Who Understood Witchcraft

But what became of little Gerda when Kay did not return? Where could he be? Nobody knew; nobody could give any intelligence. All the boys knew was, that they had seen him tie his sledge to another large and splendid one, which drove down the street and out of the town. Nobody knew where he was; many sad tears were shed, and little Gerda wept long and bitterly; at last she said he must be dead; that he had been drowned in the river which flowed close to the town. Oh! those were very long and dismal winter evenings!

At last spring came, with its warm sunshine.

"Kay is dead and gone!" said little Gerda.

"That I don't believe," said the Sunshine.

"Kay is dead and gone!" said she to the Swallows.

"That I don't believe," said they: and at last little Gerda did not think so any longer either.

"I'll put on my red shoes," said she, one morning; "Kay has never seen them, and then I'll go down to the river and ask there."

It was quite early; she kissed her old grandmother, who was still asleep, put on her red shoes, and went alone to the river.

"Is it true that you have taken my little playfellow? I will make you a present of my red shoes, if you will give him back to me."

And, as it seemed to her, the blue waves nodded in a

strange manner; then she took off her red shoes, the most precious things she possessed, and threw them both into the river. But they fell close to the bank, and the little waves bore them immediately to land; it was as if the stream would not take what was dearest to her; for in reality it had not got little Kay; but Gerda thought that she had not thrown the shoes out far enough, so she clambered into a boat which lay among the rushes, went to the farthest end, and threw out the shoes. But the boat was not fastened, and the motion which she occasioned, made it drift from the shore. She observed this, and hastened to get back; but before she could do so, the boat was more than a yard from the land, and was gliding quickly onward.

Little Gerda was very frightened, and began to cry; but no one heard her except the sparrows, and they could not carry her to land; but they flew along the bank, and sang as if to comfort her, "Here we are! Here we are!" The boat drifted with the stream, little Gerda sat quite still without shoes, for they were swimming behind the boat, but she could not reach them, because the boat went much faster than they did.

The banks on both sides were beautiful; lovely flowers, venerable trees, and slopes with sheep and cows, but not a human being was to be seen.

"Perhaps the river will carry me to little Kay," said she; and then she grew less sad. She rose, and looked for many hours at the beautiful green banks. Presently she sailed by a large cherry-orchard, where was a little cottage with curious red and blue windows; it was thatched, and before it two wooden soldiers stood sentry, and presented arms when anyone went past.

Gerda called to them, for she thought they were alive; but they, of course, did not answer. She came close to them, for the stream drifted the boat quite near the land.

Gerda called still louder, and an old woman then came out of the cottage, leaning upon a crooked stick. She had a large broad-brimmed hat on, painted with the most splendid flowers.

"Poor little child!" said the old woman. "How did you get upon the large rapid river, to be driven about so in the wide world!" And then the old woman went into the water, caught hold of the boat with her crooked stick, drew it to the bank, and lifted little Gerda out.

And Gerda was so glad to be on dry land again; but she was rather afraid of the strange old woman.

"But come and tell me who you are, and how you came here," said she.

And Gerda told her all; and the old woman shook her head and said, "A-hem! a-hem!" and when Gerda had told her everything, and asked her if she had not seen little Kay, the woman answered that he had not passed there, but he no doubt would come; and she told her not to be cast down, but taste her cherries, and look at her flowers, which were finer than any in a picture-book, each of which could tell a whole story. She then took Gerda by the hand, led her into the little cottage, and locked the door.

The queen in "The Lion, the Witch and the Wardrobe" may have been inspired by the Snow Queen

The windows were very high up; the glass was red, blue, and green, and the sunlight shone through quite wondrously in all sorts of colors. On the table stood the most exquisite cherries, and Gerda ate as many as she chose, for she had permission to do so. While she was eating, the old woman combed her hair with a golden comb, and her hair curled and shone with a lovely golden color around that sweet little face, which was so round and so like a rose.

"I have often longed for such a dear little girl," said the old woman. "Now you shall see how well we agree together"; and while she combed little Gerda's hair, the child forgot her foster-brother Kay more and more, for the old woman understood magic; but she was no evil being, she only practised witchcraft a little for her own private amusement, and now she wanted very much to keep little Gerda. She therefore went out in the garden, stretched out her crooked stick towards the rose-bushes, which, beautifully as they were blowing, all sank into the earth and no one could tell where they had stood. The old woman feared that if Gerda should see the roses, she would then think of her own, would remember little Kay, and run away from her.

There are seven 'stories':
About the Mirror and its Pieces
A Little Boy and a Little Girl
The Flower Garden of the Woman Who
Knew Magic
The Prince and Princess
The Little Robber Girl
The Lapp Woman and the Finn Woman
What Happened at the Snow Queen's Palace
and What happened Afterwards

The Three Golden Hairs

A charcoal burner had a cottage deep in the forest

There was once a king who took great delight in hunting. One day he followed a stag a great distance into the forest. He went on and on until he lost his way. Night fell and the king by happy chance came upon a clearing where a charcoal-burner had a cottage. The king asked the charcoal-burner to lead him out of the forest and offered to pay him handsomely.

"I'd be glad to go with you," the charcoal-burner said, "but my wife is expecting the birth of a child and I cannot leave her. It is too late for you to start out alone. Won't you spend the night here? Lie down on some hay in the garret and tomorrow I'll be your guide."

The king had to accept this arrangement. He climbed into the garret and lay down on the floor. Soon afterwards a son was born to the charcoal-burner.

At midnight the king noticed a strange light in the room below him. He peeped through a chink in the boards and saw the charcoal-burner asleep, his wife lying in a dead faint, and three old women, all in white, standing over the baby, each holding a lighted taper in her hand.

The first old woman said: "My gift to this boy is that he shall encounter great dangers."

The second said: "My gift to him is that he shall go safely through them all, and live long."

The third one said: "And I give him for wife the baby daughter born this night to the king who lies upstairs on the straw."

The three old women blew out their tapers and all was quiet. They were the Fates.

The king felt as though a sword had been thrust into his heart. He lay awake till morning trying to think out some plan by which he could thwart the will of the three old Fates.

When day broke the child began to cry and the charcoal-burner woke up. Then he saw that his wife had died during the night.

"Ah, my poor motherless child," he cried, "what shall I do with you now?"

"Give me the baby," the king said. "I'll see that he's looked after properly and I'll give you enough money to keep you the rest of your life."

The charcoal-burner was delighted with this offer and the king went away promising to send at once for the baby.

A few days later when he reached his palace he was met with the joyful news that a beautiful little baby daughter had been born to him. He asked the time of her birth, and of course it was on the very night when he saw the Fates.

The king's servant put the baby into the river

Instead of being pleased at the safe arrival of the baby princess, the king frowned.

Then he called one of his stewards and said to him: "Go into the forest in a direction that I shall tell you. You will find there a cottage where a charcoal-burner lives. Give him this money and get from him a little child. Take the child and on your way back drown it. Do as I say or I shall have you drowned."

The steward went, found the charcoal-burner, and took the child. He put it into a basket and carried it away. As he was crossing a broad river he dropped the basket into the water.

"Goodnight to you, little son-in-law that nobody wanted!" the king said when he heard what the steward had done.

He supposed of course that the baby was drowned. But it wasn't. Its little basket floated in the water like a cradle, and the baby slept as if the river were singing it a lullaby. It floated down with the current past a fisherman's cottage. The fisherman saw it, got into his boat, and went after it. When he found what the basket contained he was overjoyed. At once he carried the baby to his wife and said:

"You have always wanted a little son and here you have one. The river has given him to us."

The fisherman's wife was delighted and brought up the child as her own. They named him Plavachek, which means a little boy who has come floating on the water.

The river flowed on and the days went by and Plavachek grew from a baby to a boy and then into a handsome youth, the handsomest by far in the whole countryside.

One day the king happened to ride that way unattended. It was hot and he was thirsty. He beckoned to the fisherman to get him a drink of fresh water. Plavachek brought it to him. The king looked at the handsome youth in astonishment.

"You have a fine lad," he said to the fisherman. "Is he your own son?"

"He is, yet he isn't," the fisherman answered. "Just twenty years ago a little baby in a basket floated down the river. We took him in and he has been ours ever since."

A mist rose before the king's eyes and he went deathly pale, for he knew at once that Plavachek was the child that he had ordered drowned.

Soon he recovered himself and jumping from his horse he said: "I need a messenger to send to my palace and I have no one with me. Could this youth go for me?"

"Your majesty has but to command," the fisherman said,

The king loved to go hunting. One day he left the others to follow a stag and was soon lost in the deep woods

311

"and Plavachek will go."

The king sat down and wrote a letter to the queen. This is what he said:

"Have the young man who delivers this letter run through with a sword at once. He is a dangerous enemy. Let him be dispatched before I return. Such is my will."

He folded the letter, made it secure, and sealed it with his own signet.

Plavachek took the letter and started out with it at once. He had to go through a deep forest where he missed the path and lost his way. He struggled on through underbrush and thicket until it began to grow dark. Then he met an old woman who said to him:

"Where are you going, Plavachek?"

"I'm carrying this letter to the king's palace and I've lost my way. Can you put me on the right road, mother?"

"You can't get there today," the old woman said. "It's dark now. Spend the night with me. You won't be with a stranger, for I'm your old godmother."

Plavachek allowed himself to be persuaded and presently he saw before him a pretty little house that seemed at that moment to have sprung out of the ground.

During the night while Plavachek was asleep, the old woman took the letter out of his pocket and put in another that read as follows:

"Have the young man who delivers this letter married to our daughter at once. He is my destined son-in-law. Let the wedding take place before I return. Such is my will."

The next day Plavachek delivered the letter and as soon as the queen read it, she gave orders at once for the wedding. Both she and her daughter were much taken with the handsome youth and gazed at him with tender eyes. As for Plavachek he fell instantly in love with the princess and was delighted to marry her.

Some days after the wedding the king returned and when he heard what had happened he flew into a violent rage at the queen.

"But," protested the queen, "you yourself ordered me to have him married to our daughter before you came back. Here is your letter."

The king took the letter and examined it carefully. The handwriting, the seal, the paper – all were his own.

He called his son-in-law and questioned him.

Plavachek related how he had lost his way in the forest and spent the night with his godmother.

"What does your godmother look like?" the king asked.

The city – that had once been great – was now in a state of decay

Plavachek described her.

From the description the king recognized her as the same old woman who had promised the princess to the charcoal-burner's son twenty years before.

He looked at Plavachek thoughtfully and at last he said:

"What's done can't be undone. However, young man, you can't expect to be my son-in-law for nothing. If you want my daughter you must bring me for dowry three of the golden hairs of old Grandfather Knowitall."

He thought to himself that this would be an impossible task and so would be a good way to get rid of an undesirable son-in-law.

Plavachek took leave of his bride and started off. He didn't know which way to go. Who would know? Everybody talked about old Grandfather Knowitall, but nobody seemed to know where to find him. Yet Plavachek had a Fate for a godmother, so it wasn't likely that he would miss the right road.

He traveled long and far, going over wooded hills and desert plains and crossing deep rivers. He came at last to a black sea.

There he saw a boat and an old ferryman.

"God bless you, old ferryman!" he said.

"May God grant that prayer, young traveler! Where are you going?"

"I'm going to old Grandfather Knowitall to get three of his golden hairs."

"Oho! I have long been hunting for just such a messenger as you! For twenty years I have been ferrying people across this black sea and nobody has come to relieve me. If you promise to ask Grandfather Knowitall when my work will end, I'll ferry you over."

Plavachek promised and the boatman took him across.

Plavachek traveled on until he came to a great city that was in a state of decay. Before the city he met an old man who had a staff in his hand, but even with the staff he could scarcely crawl along.

"God bless you, old grandfather!" Plavachek said.

"May God grant that prayer, handsome youth! Where are you going?"

"I am going to old Grandfather Knowitall to get three of his golden hairs."

"Indeed! We have been waiting a long time for just such a messenger as you! I must lead you at once to the king."

So he took him to the king and the king said: "Ah, so you are going on an errand to Grandfather Knowitall! We have an apple-tree here that used to bear apples of youth. If any one ate one of those apples, no matter how aged he was, he'd become young again. But, alas, for twenty years now our tree has borne no fruit. If you promise to ask Grandfather Knowitall if there is any help for us, I will reward you handsomely."

Plavachek gave the king his promise and the king bid him godspeed.

Plavachek traveled on until he reached another great city that was half in ruins. Not far from the city a man was

"If I ate one of those apples I should be young again" said the king

burying his father, and tears as big as peas were rolling down his cheek.

"God bless you, mournful grave-digger!" Plavachek said.

"May God grant that prayer, kind traveler! Where are you going?"

"I'm going to old Grandfather Knowitall to get three of his golden hairs."

"To Grandfather Knowitall! What a pity you didn't come sooner! Our king has long been waiting for just such a messenger as you! I must lead you to him."

So he took Plavachek to the king and the king said to him: "So you're going on an errand to Grandfather Knowitall. We have a well here that used to flow with the water of life. If any one drank of it, no matter how sick he was, he would get well. Nay, if he were already dead, this water, sprinkled upon him, would bring him back to life. But, alas, for twenty years now the well has gone dry. If you promise to ask Grandfather Knowitall if there is help for us, I will reward you handsomely."

Plavachek gave the king his promise and the king bid him godspeed.

After that Plavachek traveled long and far into a black forest. Deep in the forest he came upon a broad green meadow full of beautiful flowers and in its midst a golden palace glittering as though it were on fire. This was the palace of Grandfather Knowitall.

Plavachek entered and found nobody there but an old woman who sat spinning in a corner.

"Welcome, Plavachek," she said. "I am delighted to see you again."

He looked at the old woman and saw that she was his godmother with whom he had spent the night when he was carrying the letter to the palace.

"What has brought you here, Plavachek?" she asked.

"The king, godmother. He says I can't be his son-in-law for nothing. I have to give a dowry. So he has sent me to old

The Sun rode out in glorious light

Grandfather Knowitall to get three of his golden hairs."

The old woman smiled and said: "Do you know who Grandfather Knowitall is? Why, he's the bright Sun who goes everywhere and sees everything. I am his mother. In the morning he's a little lad, at noon he's a grown man, and in the evening an old grandfather. I will get you three of the golden hairs from his golden head, for I must not be a godmother for nothing! But, my lad, you mustn't remain where you are. My son is kind, but if he comes home hungry he might want to roast you and eat you for his supper. There's an empty tub over there and I'll just cover you with it."

Plavachek begged his godmother to get from Grandfather Knowitall the answers for the three questions he had promised to ask.

"I will," said the old woman, "and do you listen carefully to what he says."

Suddenly there was the rushing sound of a mighty wind outside and the Sun, an old grandfather with a golden head, flew in by the western window. He sniffed the air suspiciously.

"Phew! Phew!" he cried. "I smell human flesh! Have you any one here, mother?"

"Star of the day, whom could I have here without your seeing him? The truth is you've been flying all day long over God's world and your nose is filled with the smell of human flesh. That's why you still smell it when you come home in the evening."

The old man said nothing more and sat down to his supper.

After supper he laid his head on the old woman's lap and fell sound asleep. The old woman pulled out a golden hair and threw it on the floor. It twanged like the string of a violin.

"What is it, mother?" the old man said. "What is it?"

"Nothing, my boy, nothing. I was asleep and had a wonderful dream."

"What did you dream about, mother?"

"I dreamt about a city where they had a well of living water. If any one drank of it, no matter how sick he was, he would get well. Nay, if he were already dead, this water, sprinkled on him, would bring him back to life. For the last twenty years the well has gone dry. Is there anything to be done to make it flow again?"

"Yes. There's a frog sitting on the spring that feeds the well. Let them kill the frog and clean out the well and the water will flow as before."

When he fell asleep again the old woman pulled out another golden hair and threw it on the floor.

"What is it, mother?"

"Nothing, my boy, nothing. I was asleep again and I had a wonderful dream. I dreamt of a city where they had an apple-tree that bore apples of youth. If any one ate one of those apples, no matter how aged he was, he'd become young again. But for twenty years the tree has borne no fruit. Can anything be done about it?"

"Yes. In the roots of the tree there is a snake that takes its strength. Let them kill the snake and transplant the tree. Then it will bear fruit as before."

He fell asleep again and the old woman pulled out a third golden hair.

"Why won't you let me sleep, mother?" he complained, and started to sit up.

"Lie still, my boy, lie still. I didn't intend to wake you, but a heavy sleep fell upon me and I had another wonderful dream. I dreamt of a boatman on the black sea. For twenty years he has been ferrying that boat and no one has offered to relieve him. When will he be relieved?"

The horses were as white as swans and laden with gold and silver

"Ah, but that boatman is the son of a stupid mother! Why doesn't he thrust the oar into the hand of some one else and jump ashore himself? Then the other man would have to be ferryman in his place. But now let me be quiet. I must get up early tomorrow morning and go and dry the tears which the king's daughter sheds every night for her husband, the charcoal-burner's son, whom the king has

Back at the palace, the king was amazed to see the three golden hairs

sent to get three of my golden hairs."

In the morning there was again the rushing sound of a mighty wind outside and a beautiful golden child – no longer an old man – awoke on his mother's lap. It was the glorious Sun. He bade his mother farewell and flew out by an eastern window.

The old woman turned over the tub and said to Plavachek: "Here are the three golden hairs for you. You also have Grandfather Knowitall's answers to your three questions.

Now good-by. As you will need me no more, you will never see me again."

Plavachek thanked his godmother most gratefully and departed.

When he reached the first city the king asked him what news he brought.

"Good news!" Plavachek said. "Have the well cleaned out and kill the frog that sits on its spring. If you do this the water will flow again as it used to."

The king ordered this to be done at once and when he saw the water beginning to bubble up and flow again, he made Plavachek a present of twelve horses, white as swans, laden with as much gold and silver as they could carry.

When Plavachek came to the second city and the king of that city asked him what news he brought, he said:

"Good news! Have the apple tree dug up. At its roots you will find a snake. Kill the snake and replant the tree. Then it will bear fruit as it used to."

The king had this done at once and during the night the tree burst into bloom and bore great quantities of fruit. The king was delighted and made Plavachek a present of twelve horses, black as ravens, laden with as much riches as they could carry.

Plavachek traveled on and when he came to the black sea, the boatman asked him had he the answer to his question.

"Yes, I have," said Plavachek, "but you must ferry me over before I tell you."

The boatman wanted to hear the answer at once, but Plavachek was firm. So the old man ferried him across with his twelve white horses and his twelve black horses.

When Plavachek was safely landed, he said: "The next person who comes to be ferried over, thrust the oar into his hand and do you jump ashore. Then the other man will have to be boatman in your place."

Plavachek traveled home to the palace. The king could scarcely believe his eyes when he saw the three golden hairs of Grandfather Knowitall. The princess wept again, not for sorrow this time but for joy at her bridegroom's return.

"But, Plavachek," the king gasped, "where did you get these beautiful horses and all these riches?"

"I earned them," said Plavachek proudly. Then he related how he helped one king who had a tree of the apples of youth and another king who had a well of the water of life.

"Apples of youth! Water of life!" the king kept repeating softly to himself. "If I ate one of those apples I should become young again! If I were dead the water of life would restore me!"

He lost no time in starting out in quest of the apples of youth and the water of life. And do you know, he hasn't come back yet!

So Plavachek, the charcoal-burner's son, became the king's son-in-law as the old Fate foretold.

As for the king, well, I fear he's still ferrying that boat across the black sea!

Twelve Dancing Princesses

This story has various names including *The Worn-Out Dancing Shoes* or *The Shoes that were Danced to Pieces* and is a German tale by the Brothers Grimm (Jacob 1785–1863 and Wilhelm 1786–1859) originally published in 1812. The Grimms heard their version from the Haxthausens, a family of friends, who themselves had heard the tale in Munster. The version of the tale from Hesse has only one princess who wears out twelve pairs of shoes every night. Twelve apprentices are required to replace the pairs each day. In another version, three princesses wear out their shoes.

was travelling through a wood, he met an old woman, who asked him where he was going.

"I hardly know where I am going, or what I had better do," said the soldier; "but I think I would like to find out where it is that the princesses dance, and then in time I might be a king."

"Well," said the old woman, "that is not a very hard task: only take care not to drink any of the wine which one of the princesses will bring to you in the evening; and as soon as she leaves you pretend to be fast asleep."

Then she gave him a cloak, and said, "As soon as you put that on you will become invisible, and you will then be able to follow the princesses wherever they go." When the soldier heard all this good advice, he was determined to try his luck, so he went to the king, and said he was willing to undertake the task.

He was as well received as the others had been, and the

Every evening the princesses slipped down into a secret world – to dance all night

There was once a king who had twelve beautiful daughters. They slept in twelve beds all in one room and when they went to bed, the doors were shut and locked up. However, every morning their shoes were found to be quite worn through as if they had been danced in all night. Nobody could find out how it happened, or where the princesses had been.

So the king made it known to all the land that if any person could discover the secret and find out where it was that the princesses danced in the night, he would have the one he liked best to take as his wife, and would be king after his death. But whoever tried and did not succeed, after three days and nights, they would be put to death.

A king's son soon came. He was well entertained, and in the evening was taken to the chamber next to the one where the princesses lay in their twelve beds. There he was to sit and watch where they went to dance; and, in order that nothing could happen without him hearing it, the door of his chamber was left open. But the king's son soon fell asleep; and when he awoke in the morning he found that the princesses had all been dancing, for the soles of their shoes were full of holes.

The same thing happened the second and third night and so the king ordered his head to be cut off.

After him came several others; but they all had the same luck, and all lost their lives in the same way.

Now it happened that an old soldier, who had been wounded in battle and could fight no longer, passed through the country where this king reigned, and as he

king ordered fine royal robes to be given him; and when the evening came he was led to the outer chamber.

Just as he was going to lie down, the eldest of the princesses brought him a cup of wine; but the soldier threw it all away secretly, taking care not to drink a drop. Then he laid himself down on his bed, and in a little while began to snore very loudly as if he was fast asleep.

When the twelve princesses heard this they laughed heartily; and the eldest said, "This fellow too might have done a wiser thing than lose his life in this way!" Then they rose and opened their drawers and boxes, and took out all their fine clothes, and dressed themselves at the mirror, and skipped about as if they were eager to begin dancing.

But the youngest said, "I don't know why it is, but while you are so happy I feel very uneasy; I am sure some mischance will befall us."

"You simpleton," said the eldest, "you are always afraid; have you forgotten how many kings sons have already watched in vain? And as for this soldier, even if I had not given him his sleeping draught, he would have slept soundly enough."

When they were all ready, they went and looked at the soldier; but he snored on, and did not stir hand or foot: so they thought they were quite safe.

Then the eldest went up to her own bed and clapped her hands, and the bed sank into the floor and a trap-door flew open. The soldier saw them going down through the trap-door one after another, the eldest leading the way; and thinking he had no time to lose, he jumped up, put on the cloak which the old woman had given him, and followed them.

However, in the middle of the stairs he trod on the gown of the youngest princess, and she cried out to her sisters, "All is not right; someone took hold of my gown."

"You silly creature!" said the eldest, "it is nothing but a nail in the wall."

Down they all went, and at the bottom they found themselves in a most delightful grove of trees; and the leaves were all of silver, and glittered and sparkled beautifully. The soldier wished to take away some token of the place; so he broke off a little branch, and there came a loud noise from the tree. Then the youngest daughter said again, "I am sure all is not right – did not you hear that noise? That never happened before."

But the eldest said, "It is only our princes, who are shouting for joy at our approach."

They came to another grove of trees, where all the leaves were of gold; and afterwards to a third, where the leaves were all glittering diamonds. And the soldier broke a branch from each; and every time there was a loud noise, which made the youngest sister tremble with fear. But the eldest still said it was only the princes, who were crying for joy.

They went on till they came to a great lake; and at the side of the lake there lay twelve little boats with twelve handsome princes in them, who seemed to be waiting there for the princesses.

One of the princesses went into each boat, and the soldier stepped into the same boat as the youngest. As they were rowing over the lake, the prince who was in the boat with the youngest princess and the soldier said, "I do not know why it is, but though I am rowing with all my might we do not get on so fast as usual, and I am quite tired: the boat seems very heavy today."

"It is only the heat of the weather," said the princess, "I am very warm, too."

On the other side of the lake stood a fine, illuminated castle from which came the merry music of horns and trumpets. There they all landed, and went into the castle, and each prince danced with his princess; and the soldier, who was still invisible, danced with them too. When any of the princesses had a cup of wine set by her, he drank it all up, so that when she put the cup to her mouth it was empty. At this, too, the youngest sister was terribly frightened, but the eldest always silenced her.

They danced on till three o'clock in the morning, and then all their shoes were worn out, so that they were obliged to leave. The princes rowed them back again over the lake (but this time the soldier placed himself in the boat with the eldest princess); and on the opposite shore they took leave of each other, the princesses promising to come again the next night.

When they came to the stairs, the soldier ran on before the princesses, and laid himself down. And as the twelve, tired sisters slowly came up, they heard him snoring in his bed and they said, "Now all is quite safe". Then they undressed themselves, put away their fine clothes, pulled off their shoes, and went to bed.

In the morning the soldier said nothing about what had happened, but determined to see more of this strange adventure, and went again on the second and third nights. Everything happened just as before: the princesses danced till their shoes were worn to pieces, and then returned home. On the third night the soldier carried away one of the golden cups as a token of where he had been.

As soon as the time came when he was to declare the secret, he was taken before the king with the three branches and the golden cup; and the twelve princesses stood listening behind the door to hear what he would say.

The king asked him. "Where do my twelve daughters dance at night?"

The soldier answered, "With twelve princes in a castle underground." And then he told the king all that had happened, and showed him the three branches and the golden cup which he had brought with him.

The king called for the princesses, and asked them whether what the soldier said was true and when they saw that they were discovered, and that it was of no use to deny what had happened, they confessed it all.

So the king asked the soldier which of the princesses he would choose for his wife; and he answered, "I am not very young, so I will have the eldest." – and they were married that very day, and the soldier was chosen to be the king's heir.

The Water Babies

The Water-Babies, A Fairy Tale for a Land Baby is a children's novel by the Reverend Charles Kingsley, published first as a serial and then in its entirety in 1863. It tells how a young chimney sweep, Tom, falls into a river and is transformed into a "water baby". He has many adventures and learns important lessons in this new world – both from the water creatures there and the fairies – before he earns the right to return to human form. The following excerpt is from Chapter III.

Tom was very happy in the water. He had been sadly overworked in the land-world; and so now, to make up for that, he had nothing but holidays in the water-world for a long, long time to come. He had nothing to do now but enjoy himself, and look at all the pretty things which are to be seen in the cool clear water-world, where the sun is never too hot, and the frost is never too cold.

And what did he live on? Water-cresses, perhaps; or

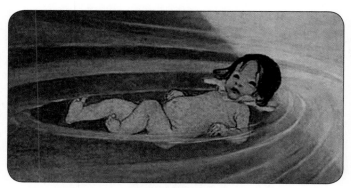

He felt how comfortable it was to have nothing on him but himself.

perhaps water-gruel, and water-milk; too many land-babies do so likewise. But we do not know what one-tenth of the water-things eat; so we are not answerable for the water-babies.

Sometimes he went along the smooth gravel water-ways, looking at the crickets which ran in and out among the stones, as rabbits do on land; or he climbed over the ledges of rock, and saw the sand-pipes hanging in thousands, with every one of them a pretty little head and legs peeping out; or he went into a still corner, and

watched the caddises eating dead sticks as greedily as you would eat plum-pudding, and building their houses with silk and glue. Very fanciful ladies they were; none of them would keep to the same materials for a day. One would begin with some pebbles; then she would stick on a piece of green wood; then she found a shell, and stuck it on too; and the poor shell was alive, and did not like at all being taken to build houses with: but the caddis did not let him have any voice in the matter, being rude and selfish, as vain people are apt to be; then she stuck on a piece of rotten wood, then a very smart pink stone, and so on, till she was patched all over like an Irishman's coat. Then she found a long straw, five times as long as herself, and said, "Hurrah! My sister has a tail, and I'll have one too;" and she stuck it on her back, and marched about with it quite proud, though it was very inconvenient indeed. And, at that, tails became all the fashion among the caddis-baits in that pool, as they were at the end of the Long Pond last May, and they all toddled about with long straws sticking out behind, getting between each other's legs, and tumbling over each other, and looking so ridiculous, that Tom laughed at them till he cried, as we did. But they were quite right, you know; for people must always follow the fashion, even if it be spoon-bonnets.

Then sometimes he came to a deep still reach; and there he saw the water-forests. They would have looked to you only little weeds: but Tom, you must remember, was so little that everything looked a hundred times as big to him as it does to you, just as things do to a minnow, who sees and catches the little water-creatures which you can only see in a microscope.

And in the water-forest he saw the water-monkeys and water-squirrels (they had all six legs, though; everything almost has six legs in the water, except efts and water-babies); and nimbly enough they ran among the branches. There were water-flowers there too, in thousands; and Tom tried to pick them: but as soon as he touched them, they drew themselves in and turned into knots of jelly; and then Tom saw that they were all alive — bells, and stars, and wheels, and flowers, of all beautiful shapes and colours; and all alive and busy, just as Tom was. So now he found that there was a great deal more in the world than he had fancied at first sight.

There was one wonderful little fellow, too, who peeped out of the top of a house built of round bricks. He had two big wheels, and one little one, all over teeth, spinning round and round like the wheels in a thrashing-machine;

*Tom meets the fairies, Mrs. Bedonebyasyoudid and
Mrs. Doasyouwouldbedoneby*

and Tom stood and stared at him, to see what he was going to make with his machinery. And what do you think he was doing? Brick-making. With his two big wheels he swept together all the mud which floated in the water: all that was nice in it he put into his stomach and ate; and all the mud he put into the little wheel on his breast, which really was a round hole set with teeth; and there he spun it into a neat hard round brick; and then he took it and stuck it on the top of his house-wall, and set to work to make another. Now was not he a clever little fellow?

Tom thought so: but when he wanted to talk to him the brick-maker was much too busy and proud of his work to take notice of him.

Now you must know that all the things under the water talk; only not such a language as ours; but such as horses, and dogs, and cows, and birds talk to each other; and Tom soon learned to understand them and talk to them; so that he might have had very pleasant company if he had only been a good boy. But I am sorry to say, he was too like some other little boys, very fond of hunting and tormenting creatures for mere sport. Some people say that boys cannot help it; that it is nature, and only a proof that we are all originally descended from beasts of prey. But whether it is nature or not, little boys can help it, and must help it. For if they have naughty, low, mischievous tricks in their nature, as monkeys have, that is no reason why they should give way to those tricks like monkeys, who know no better. And therefore they must not torment dumb creatures; for if they do, a certain old lady who is coming will surely give them exactly what they deserve.

But Tom did not know that; and he pecked and hounded the poor water-things about sadly, till they were all afraid of him, and got out of his way, or crept into their shells; so he had no one to speak to or play with.

The water-fairies, of course, were very sorry to see him so unhappy, and longed to take him, and tell him how naughty he was, and teach him to be good, and to play and romp with him too: but they had been forbidden to do that. Tom had to learn his lesson for himself by sound and sharp experience, as many another foolish person has to do, though there may be many a kind heart yearning over them all the while, and longing to teach them what they can only teach themselves.

At last one day he found a caddis, and wanted it to peep out of its house: but its house-door was shut. He had never seen a caddis with a house-door before: so what must he do, the meddlesome little fellow, but pull it open, to see what the poor lady was doing inside. What a shame! How should you like to have any one breaking your bedroom-door in, to see how you looked when you where in bed? So Tom broke to pieces the door, which was the prettiest little grating of silk, stuck all over with shining bits of crystal; and when he looked in, the caddis poked out her head, and it had turned into just the shape of a bird's. But when Tom spoke to her she could not answer; for her mouth and face were tight tied up in a new night-cap of neat pink skin.

However, if she didn't answer, all the other caddises did; for they held up their hands and shrieked like the cats in Struwelpeter: "Oh, you nasty horrid boy; there you are at it again! And she had just laid herself up for a fortnight's sleep, and then she would have come out with such beautiful wings, and flown about, and laid such lots of eggs: and now you have broken her door, and she can't mend it because her mouth is tied up for a fortnight, and she will die. Who sent you here to worry us out of our lives?"

So Tom swam away. He was very much ashamed of himself, and felt all the naughtier; as little boys do when they have done wrong and won't say so.

Then he came to a pool full of little trout, and began tormenting them, and trying to catch them: but they slipped through his fingers, and jumped clean out of water in their fright. But as Tom chased them, he came close to a great dark hover under an alder root, and out floushed a huge old brown trout ten times as big as he was, and ran right against him, and knocked all the breath out of his body; and I don't know which was the more frightened of the two.

Then he went on sulky and lonely, as he deserved to be; and under a bank he saw a very ugly dirty creature sitting, about half as big as himself; which had six legs, and a big stomach, and a most ridiculous head with two great eyes and a face just like a donkey's.

"Oh," said Tom, "you are an ugly fellow to be sure!" and he began making faces at him; and put his nose close to him, and halloed at him, like a very rude boy.

When, hey presto; all the thing's donkey-face came off in a moment, and out popped a long arm with a pair of pincers at the end of it, and caught Tom by the nose. It did not hurt him much; but it held him quite tight.

"Yah, ah! Oh, let me go!" cried Tom.

"Then let me go," said the creature. "I want to be quiet. I want to split."

Tom promised to let him alone, and he let go.

"Why do you want to split?" said Tom.

"Because my brothers and sisters have all split, and turned into beautiful creatures with wings; and I want to split too. Don't speak to me. I am sure I shall split. I will split!"

Tom stood still, and watched him. And he swelled himself, and puffed, and stretched himself out stiff, and at last – crack, puff, bang – he opened all down his back, and then up to the top of his head.

And out of his inside came the most slender, elegant, soft creature, as soft and smooth as Tom: but very pale and weak, like a little child who has been ill a long time in a dark room. It moved its legs very feebly; and looked about it half ashamed, like a girl when she goes for the first time into a ballroom; and then it began walking slowly up a grass stem to the top of the water.

Tom was so astonished that he never said a word but he stared with all his eyes. And he went up to the top of the water too, and peeped out to see what would happen.

And as the creature sat in the warm bright sun, a

wonderful change came over it. It grew strong and firm; the most lovely colours began to show on its body, blue and yellow and black, spots and bars and rings; out of its back rose four great wings of bright brown gauze; and its eyes grew so large that they filled all its head, and shone like ten thousand diamonds.

"Oh, you beautiful creature!" said Tom; and he put out his hand to catch it.

But the thing whirred up into the air, and hung poised on its wings a moment, and then settled down again by Tom quite fearless.

"No!" it said, "you cannot catch me. I am a dragon-fly now, the king of all the flies; and I shall dance in the sunshine, and hawk over the river, and catch gnats, and have a beautiful

There were great fish and many tiny creatures, too

wife like myself. I know what I shall do. Hurrah!" And he flew away into the air, and began catching gnats.

"Oh! come back, come back," cried Tom, "you beautiful creature. I have no one to play with, and I am so lonely here. If you will but come back I will never try to catch you."

"I don't care whether you do or not," said the dragon-fly; "for you can't. But when I have had my dinner, and looked a little about this pretty place, I will come back, and have a little chat about all I have seen in my travels. Why, what a huge tree this is! and what huge leaves on it!"

It was only a big dock: but you know the dragon-fly had never seen any but little water-trees; starwort, and milfoil, and water-crowfoot, and such like; so it did look very big

to him. Besides, he was very short-sighted, as all dragon-flies are; and never could see a yard before his nose; any more than a great many other folks, who are not half as handsome as he.

The dragon-fly did come back, and chatted away with Tom. He was a little conceited about his fine colours and his large wings; but you know, he had been a poor dirty ugly creature all his life before; so there were great excuses for him. He was very fond of talking about all the wonderful things he saw in the trees and the meadows; and Tom liked to listen to him, for he had forgotten all about them. So in a little while they became great friends.

And I am very glad to say, that Tom learned such a lesson that day, that he did not torment creatures for a long time after. And then the caddises grew quite tame, and used to tell him strange stories about the way they built their houses, and changed their skins, and turned at last into winged flies; till Tom began to long to change his skin, and have wings like them some day.

And the trout and he made it up (for trout very soon forget if they have been frightened and hurt). So Tom used to play with them at hare and hounds, and great fun they had; and he used to try to leap out of the water, head over heels, as they did before a shower came on; but somehow he never could manage it. He liked most, though, to see them rising at the flies, as they sailed round and round under the shadow of the great oak, where the beetles fell flop into the water, and the green caterpillars let themselves down from the boughs by silk ropes for no reason at all; and then changed their foolish minds for no reason at all either; and hauled themselves up again into the tree, rolling up the rope in a ball between their paws; which is a very clever rope-dancer's trick, and neither Blondin nor Leotard could do it: but why they should take so much trouble about it no one can tell; for they cannot get their living, as Blondin and Leotard do, by trying to break their necks on a string.

And very often Tom caught them just as they touched the water; and caught the alder-flies, and the caperers, and the cock-tailed duns and spinners, yellow, and brown, and claret, and gray, and gave them to his friends the trout. Perhaps he was not quite kind to the flies; but one must do a good turn to one's friends when one can.

And at last he gave up catching even the flies; for he made acquaintance with one by accident and found him a very merry little fellow. And this was the way it happened; and it is all quite true.

He was basking at the top of the water one hot day in July, catching duns and feeding the trout, when he saw a new sort, a dark gray little fellow with a brown head. He was a very little fellow indeed: but he made the most of himself, as people ought to do. He cocked up his head, and he cocked up his wings, and he cocked up his tail, and he cocked up the two whisks at his tail-end, and, in short, he looked the cockiest little man of all little men. And so he proved to be; for instead of getting away, he hopped upon

"Oh, you beautiful creature!" said Tom to the dragon-fly

Tom's finger, and sat there as bold as nine tailors; and he cried out in the tiniest, shrillest, squeakiest little voice you ever heard,

"Much obliged to you, indeed; but I don't want it yet."

"Want what?" said Tom, quite taken aback by his impudence.

"Your leg, which you are kind enough to hold out for me to sit on. I must just go and see after my wife for a few minutes. Dear me! what a troublesome business a family is!" (though the idle little rogue did nothing at all, but left his poor wife to lay all the eggs by herself). "When I come back, I shall be glad of it, if you'll be so good as to keep it sticking out just so;" and off he flew.

Tom thought him a very cool sort of personage; and still more so, when, in five minutes he came back, and said – "Ah, you were tired waiting? Well, your other leg will do as well."

And he popped himself down on Tom's knee, and began chatting away in his squeaking voice.

"So you live under the water? It's a low place. I lived there for some time; and was very shabby and dirty. But I didn't choose that that should last. So I turned respectable, and came up to the top, and put on this gray suit. It's a very business-like suit, you think, don't you?"

"Very neat and quiet indeed," said Tom.

"Yes, one must be quiet and neat and respectable, and all that sort of thing for a little, when one becomes a family man. But I'm tired of it, that's the truth. I've done quite enough business, I consider, in the last week, to last me my life. So I shall put on a ball dress, and go out and be a smart man, and see the gay world, and have a dance or two. Why shouldn't one be jolly if one can?"

"And what will become of your wife?"

"Oh! she is a very plain stupid creature, and that's the truth; and thinks about nothing but eggs. If she chooses to come, why she may; and if not, why I go without her; – and here I go."

And, as he spoke, he turned quite pale, and then quite white.

"Why, you're ill!" said Tom. But he did not answer.

"You're dead," said Tom, looking at him as he stood on his knee as white as a ghost.

"No, I ain't!" answered a little squeaking voice over his head. "This is me up here, in my ball-dress; and that's my skin. Ha, ha! you could not do such a trick as that!"

And no more Tom could, nor Houdin, nor Robin, nor Frikell, nor all the conjurors in the world. For the little rogue had jumped clean out of his own skin, and left it standing on Tom's knee, eyes, wings, legs, tail, exactly as if it had been alive.

"Ha, ha!" he said, and he jerked and skipped up and down, never stopping an instant, just as if he had St. Vitus's dance. "Ain't I a pretty fellow now?"

And so he was; for his body was white, and his tail orange, and his eyes all the colours of a peacock's tail. And what was the oddest of all, the whisks at the end of his tail had grown five times as long as they were before.

"Ah!" said he, "now I will see the gay world. My living, won't cost me much, for I have no mouth, you see, and no inside; so I can never be hungry nor have the stomach-ache neither."

No more he had. He had grown as dry and hard and empty as a quill, as such silly shallow-hearted fellows deserve to grow.

But, instead of being ashamed of his emptiness, he was quite proud of it, as a good many fine gentlemen are, and began flirting and flipping up and down, and singing –

"My wife shall dance, and I shall sing,
So merrily pass the day;
For I hold it for quite the wisest thing,
To drive dull care away."

And he danced up and down for three days and three nights, till he grew so tired, that he tumbled into the water, and floated down. But what became of him Tom never knew, and he himself never minded; for Tom heard him singing to the last, as he floated down –

"To drive dull care away-ay-ay!"

And if he did not care, why nobody else cared either.

The Battle of the Birds

This story was first collected 'officially' by John Francis Campbell (1821–1885) who had recorded it from a fisherman near Inverary. Joseph Jacobs (1854–1916) then published this version in his *Celtic Fairy Tales* in 1892, adding some of the humorous Gaelic end pieces. It was also included in *The Lilac Fairy Book* by Andrew Lang and Alan Garner's *A Book of British Fairy Tales*. The plot is remarkably similar to the classical myth of Jason and Medea, with its forest, mountain, and river obstacles reflecting the boundaries of Hades. This may be one of the oldest folk-tales in existence and was part of ancient Aryan lore. It developed in its modern form in Scandinavia (as in *The Master Maid* by Asbjörnsen), having probably reached this part of the world via the Celts and early Irish monks. The tale also spread into India and the Buddhistic world, and thence to the South Seas and Madagascar. Here the giants, who may be supposed to be somewhat old-fashioned in their language and attitudes still say 'thou' rather than 'you'!

She put out the hand without a little finger

Will I tell you a story about the wren? There was once a farmer who was seeking a servant, and the wren met him and said: "What are you seeking?"

"I am seeking a servant," said the farmer to the wren.

"Will you take me?" said the wren.

"You, you poor creature, what good would you do?"

"Try me," said the wren.

So he engaged him, and the first work he set him to do was threshing in the barn. The wren threshed (what did he thresh with? Why a flail to be sure), and he knocked off one grain. A mouse came out and she eats that.

"I'll trouble you not to do that again," said the wren.

He struck again, and he struck off two grains. Out came the mouse and she eats them. So they arranged a contest to see who was strongest, and the wren brings his twelve birds, and the mouse her tribe.

"You have your tribe with you," said the wren.

"As well as yourself," said the mouse, and she struck out her leg proudly. But the wren broke it with his flail, and there was a pitched battle on a set day.

When every creature and bird was gathering to battle, the son of the king of Tethertown said that he would go to see the battle, and that he would bring sure word home to his father the king, who would be king of the creatures this year. The battle was over before he arrived all but one fight, between a great black raven and a snake. The snake was twined about the raven's neck, and the raven held the snake's throat in his beak, and it seemed as if the snake would get the victory over the raven. When the king's son saw this he helped the raven, and with one blow takes the head off the snake. When the raven had taken breath, and saw that the snake was dead, he said, "For thy kindness to me this day, I will give thee a sight. Come up now on the root of my two wings." The king's son put his hands about the raven before his wings, and, before he stopped, he took him over nine Bens, and nine Glens, and nine Mountain Moors.

"Now," said the raven, "see you that house yonder? Go now to it. It is a sister of mine that makes her dwelling in it; and I will go bail that you are welcome. And if she asks you, 'Were you at the battle of the birds?' say you were. And if she asks, 'Did you see any one like me?' say you did, but be sure that you meet me tomorrow morning here, in this place." The king's son got good and right good treatment that night. Meat of each meat, drink of each drink, warm water to his feet, and a soft bed for his limbs.

On the next day the raven gave him the same sight over six Bens, and six Glens, and six Mountain Moors. They saw a bothy far off, but, though far off, they were soon there. He got good treatment this night, as before – plenty of meat and drink, and warm water to his feet, and a soft bed to his limbs – and on the next day it was the same thing, over three Bens and three Glens, and three Mountain Moors.

On the third morning, instead of seeing the raven as at the other times, who should meet him but the handsomest lad he ever saw, with gold rings in his hair, with a bundle in his hand. The king's son asked this lad if he had seen a big black raven.

Said the lad to him, "You will never see the raven again, for I am that raven. I was put under spells by a bad druid; it was meeting you that loosed me, and for that you shall get this bundle. Now," said the lad, "you must turn back on the self-same steps, and lie a night in each house as before; but you must not loose the bundle which I gave ye, till in the place where you would most wish to dwell."

The king's son turned his back to the lad, and his face to his father's house; and he got lodging from the raven's sisters, just as he got it when going forward. When he was nearing his father's house he was going through a close wood. It seemed to him that the bundle was growing heavy, and he thought he would look what was in it.

When he loosed the bundle he was astonished. In a twinkling he sees the very grandest place he ever saw. A great castle, and an orchard about the castle, in which was every kind of fruit and herb. He stood full of wonder and regret for having loosed the bundle – for it was not in his power to put it back again – and he would have wished this pretty place to be in the pretty little green hollow that was opposite his father's house; but he looked up and saw a great giant coming towards him.

"Bad's the place where you have built the house, king's son," says the giant.

"Yes, but it is not here I would wish it to be, though it happens to be here by mishap," says the king's son.

"What's the reward for putting it back in the bundle as it was before?"

"What's the reward you would ask?" says the king's son.

"That you will give me the first son you have when he is seven years of age," says the giant.

"If I have a son you shall have him," said the king's son.

In a twinkling the giant put each garden, and orchard, and castle in the bundle as they were before.

"Now," says the giant, "take your own road, and I will take mine; but mind your promise, and if you forget I will remember."

The king's son took to the road, and at the end of a few days he reached the place he was fondest of. He loosed the bundle, and the castle was just as it was before. And when he opened the castle door he sees the handsomest maiden he ever cast eye upon.

"Advance, king's son," said the pretty maid; "everything is in order for you, if you will marry me this very day."

"It's I that am willing," said the king's son. And on the same day they married.

But at the end of a day and seven years, who should be seen coming to the castle but the giant. The king's son was reminded of his promise to the giant, and till now he had not told his promise to the queen.

"Leave the matter between me and the giant," says the queen.

"Turn out your son," says the giant; "mind your promise."

The giant's daughter was called Auburn Mary

"You shall have him," says the king, "when his mother puts him in order for his journey."

The queen dressed up the cook's son, and she gave him to the giant by the hand. The giant went away with him but he had not gone far when he put a rod in the hand of the little laddie. The giant asked him – "If thy father had that rod what would he do with it?"

"If my father had that rod he would beat the dogs and the cats, so that they shouldn't be going near the king's meat," said the little laddie.

"Thou'rt the cook's son," said the giant. He catches him by the two small ankles and knocks him against the stone that was beside him. The giant turned back to the castle in rage and madness, and he said that if they did not send out the king's son to him, the highest stone of the castle would be the lowest.

Said the queen to the king, "We'll try it yet; the butler's son is of the same age as our son."

She dressed up the butler's son, and she gives him to the giant by the hand. The giant had not gone far when he put the rod in his hand.

"If thy father had that rod," says the giant, "what would he do with it?"

He would beat the dogs and the cats when they would be coming near the king's bottles and glasses."

"Thou art the son of the butler," says the giant and dashed his brains out too. The giant returned in a very great rage and anger. The earth shook under the sole of his feet, and the castle shook and all that was in it.

"OUT HERE WITH THY SON," says the giant, "or in a twinkling the stone that is highest in the dwelling will be the lowest." So they had to give the king's son to the giant.

When they were gone a little bit from the earth, the giant showed him the rod that was in his hand and said: "What would thy father do with this rod if he had it?"

The king's son said: "My father has a braver rod than that."

And the giant asked him, "Where is thy father when he has that brave rod?"

And the king's son said: "He will be sitting in his kingly chair."

The magpie's nest

Then the giant understood that he had the right one.

The giant took him to his own house, and he reared him as his own son. On a day of days when the giant was from home, the lad heard the sweetest music he ever heard in a room at the top of the giant's house. At a glance he saw the finest face he had ever seen. She beckoned to him to come a bit nearer to her, and she said her name was Auburn Mary but she told him to go this time, but to be sure to be at the same place about that dead midnight.

And as he promised he did. The giant's daughter was at his side in a twinkling, and she said, "Tomorrow you will get the choice of my two sisters to marry; but say that you will not take either, but me. My father wants me to marry the son of the king of the Green City, but I don't like him." On the morrow the giant took out his three daughters, and he said:

"Now, son of the king of Tethertown, thou hast not lost by living with me so long. Thou wilt get to wife one of the two eldest of my daughters, and with her leave to go home with her the day after the wedding."

"If you will give me this pretty little one," says the king's son, "I will take you at your word."

The giant's wrath kindled, and he said: "Before thou gett'st her thou must do the three things that I ask thee to do."

"Say on," says the king's son.

The giant took him to the byre.

"Now," says the giant, "a hundred cattle are stabled here, and it has not been cleansed for seven years. I am going from home to-day, and if this byre is not cleaned before night comes, so clean that a golden apple will run from end to end of it, not only thou shalt not get my daughter, but 'tis only a drink of thy fresh, goodly, beautiful blood that will quench my thirst this night."

He begins cleaning the byre, but he might just as well to keep baling the great ocean. After midday when sweat was blinding him, the giant's youngest daughter came where he was, and she said to him:

"You are being punished, king's son."

"I am that," says the king's son.

"Come over," says Auburn Mary, "and lay down your weariness."

"I will do that," says he, "there is but death awaiting me, at any rate." He sat down near her. He was so tired that he fell asleep beside her. When he awoke, the giant's daughter was not to be seen, but the byre was so well cleaned that a golden apple would run from end to end of it and raise no stain. In comes the giant, and he said:

"Mast thou cleaned the byre, king's son?"

"I have cleaned it," says he.

"Somebody cleaned it," says the giant.

"You did not clean it, at all events," said the king's son.

"Well, well!" says the giant, "since thou wert so active today, thou wilt get to this time tomorrow to thatch this byre with birds' down, from birds with no two feathers of one colour."

There was a wonderful wedding when everyone danced and made merry

The king's son was on foot before the sun; he caught up his bow and his quiver of arrows to kill the birds. He took to the moors, but if he did, the birds were not so easy to take. He was running after them till the sweat was blinding him. About mid-day who should come but Auburn Mary.

"You are exhausting yourself, king's son," says she.

"I am," said he.

"There fell but these two blackbirds, and both of one colour."

"Come over and lay down your weariness on this pretty hillock," says the giant's daughter.

"It's I am willing," said he.

He thought she would aid him this time, too, and he sat down near her, and he was not long there till he fell asleep.

When he awoke, Auburn Mary was gone. He thought he would go back to the house, and he sees the byre thatched with feathers. When the giant came home, he said:

"Hast thou thatched the byre, king's son?"

"I thatched it," says he.

"Somebody thatched it," says the giant.

"You did not thatch it," says the king's son.

"Yes, yes!" says the giant. "Now," says the giant, "there is a fir tree beside that loch down there, and there is a magpie's nest in its top. The eggs thou wilt find in the nest.

I must have them for my first meal. Not one must be burst or broken, and there are five in the nest."

Early in the morning the king's son went where the tree was, and that tree was not hard to hit upon. Its match was not in the whole wood. From the foot to the first branch was five hundred feet. The king's son was going all round the tree. She came who was always bringing help to him.

"You are losing the skin of your hands and feet."

"Ach! I am," says he. "I am no sooner up than down."

"This is no time for stopping," says the giant's daughter. "Now you must kill me, strip the flesh from my bones, take all those bones apart, and use them as steps for climbing the tree. When you are climbing the tree, they will stick to the bark as if they had grown out of it; but when you are coming down, and have put your foot on each one, they will drop into your hand when you touch them. Be sure and stand on each bone, leave none untouched; if you do, it will stay behind. Put all my flesh into this clean cloth by the side of the spring at the roots of the tree. When you come to the earth, arrange my bones together, put the flesh over them, sprinkle it with water from the spring, and I shall be alive before you. But don't forget a bone of me on the tree."

"How could I kill you," asked the king's son, "after what you have done for me?"

"If you won't obey, you and I are done for," said Auburn Mary. "You must climb the tree, or we are lost; and to climb the tree you must do as I say."

The king's son obeyed. He killed Auburn Mary, cut the flesh from her body, and unjointed the bones, as she had told him.

As he went up, the king's son put the bones of Auburn Mary's body against the side of the tree, using them as steps, till he came under the nest and stood on the last bone.

Then he took the eggs, and coming down, put his foot on every bone, then took it with him, till he came to the last bone, which was so near the ground that he failed to touch it with his foot.

He now placed all the bones of Auburn Mary in order again at the side of the spring, put the flesh on them, sprinkled it with water from the spring. She rose up before him, and said: " Didn't I tell you not to leave a bone of my body without stepping on it? Now I am lame for life! You left my little finger on the tree without touching it, and I have but nine fingers."

"Now," says she, "go home with the eggs quickly, and you will get me to marry tonight if you can know me. I and my two sisters will be arrayed in the same garments, and made like each other, but look at me when my father says, 'Go to thy wife, king's son;' and you will see a hand without a little finger."

He gave the eggs to the giant.

"Yes, yes!" says the giant, "be making ready for your marriage."

Then, indeed, there was a wedding, and it was a wedding! Giants and gentlemen, and the son of the king of the Green

City was in the midst of them. They were married, and the dancing began, that was a dance! The giant's house was shaking from top to bottom.

But bed time came, and the giant said, "It is time for thee to go to rest, son of the king of Tethertown; choose thy bride to take with thee from amidst those."

She put out the hand off which the little finger was, and he caught her by the hand.

"Thou hast aimed well this time too; but there is no knowing but we may meet thee another way," said the giant.

But to rest they went. "Now," says she, "sleep not, or else you are a dead man. We must fly quick, quick, or for certain my father will kill you."

Out they went, and on the blue grey filly in the stable they mounted. "Stop a while," says she, "and I will play a trick to the old hero." She jumped in, and cut an apple into nine shares, and she put two shares at the head of the bed, and two shares at the foot of the bed, and two shares at the door of the kitchen, and two shares at the big door, and one outside the house.

The giant awoke and called, "Are you asleep?"

"Not yet," said the apple that was at the head of the bed.

At the end of a while he called again.

"Not yet," said the apple that was at the foot of the bed.

A while after this he called again: "Are you asleep?

"Not yet," said the apple at the kitchen door. The giant called again.

The apple that was at the big door answered.

"You are now going far from me," says the giant.

"Not yet," says the apple that was outside the house.

"You are flying," says the giant. The giant jumped on his feet, and to the bed he went, but it was cold-empty.

"My own daughter's tricks are trying me," said the giant. "Here's after them," says he.

At the mouth of day, the giant's daughter said that her father's breath was burning her back.

"Put your hand, quick," said she, "in the ear of the grey filly, and whatever you find in it, throw it behind us."

"There is a twig of sloe tree," said he.

"Throw it behind us," said she.

No sooner did he that, than there were twenty miles of blackthorn wood, so thick that scarce a weasel could go through it.

The giant came headlong, and there he is fleecing his head and neck in the thorns.

"My own daughter's tricks are here as before," said the giant; "but if I had my own big axe and wood knife here, I would not be long making a way through this."

He went home for the big axe and the wood knife, and sure he was not long on his journey, behind the big axe. He was not long making a way through the blackthorn.

"I will leave the axe and the wood knife here till I return," says he.

"If you leave 'em, leave 'em," said a hoodie that was in a tree, "we'll steal 'em, steal 'em."

"If you will do that," says the giant, "I must take them

The shoemaker was preparing fine shoes, ready for the prince's wedding

home." He returned home and left them at the house.

At the heat of day the giant's daughter felt her father's breath burning her back.

"Put your finger in the filly's ear, and throw behind whatever you find in it."

He got a splinter of grey stone, and in a twinkling there were twenty miles, by breadth and height, of great grey rock behind them.

The giant came full pelt, but past the rock he could not go.

"The tricks of my own daughter are the hardest things that ever met me," says the giant; "but if I had my lever and my mighty mattock, I would not be long in making my way through this rock also."

There was no help for it, but to turn the chase for them; and be the boy to split the stones. He was not long in making a road through the rock.

"I will leave the tools here, and I will return no more."

"If you leave 'em, leave 'em," says the hoodie, "we will steal 'em, steal 'em."

"Do that if you will; there is no time to go back."

At the time of breaking the watch, the giant's daughter said that she felt her father's breath burning her back.

"Look in the filly's ear, king's son, or else we are lost."

He did so, and it was a bladder of water that was in her ear this time. He threw it behind him and there was a fresh-water loch, twenty miles in length and breadth, behind them.

The giant came on, but with the speed he had on him, he was in the middle of the loch, and he went under, and he rose no more.

On the next day the young companions were come in sight of his father's house. "Now," says she, "my father is drowned, and he won't trouble us any more; but before we go further," says she, "go you to your father's house, and tell that you have the likes of me; but let neither man nor creature kiss you, for if you do, you will not remember that you have ever seen me."

Every one he met gave him welcome and luck, and he charged his father and mother not to kiss him; but as mishap was to be, an old greyhound was indoors, and she knew him, and jumped up to his mouth, and after that he did not remember the giant's daughter.

She was sitting at the well's side as he left her, but the king's son was not coming. In the mouth of night she climbed up into a tree of oak that was beside the well, and she lay in the fork of that tree all night. A shoemaker had a house near the well, and about mid-day on the morrow, the shoemaker asked his wife to go for a drink for him out of the well. When the shoemaker's wife reached the well, and when she saw the shadow of her that was in the tree, thinking it was her own shadow, and she never thought till now that she was so handsome – she gave a cast to the dish that was in her hand, and it was broken on the ground, and she took herself to the house without vessel or water.

"Where is the water, wife?" said the shoemaker.

"You shambling, contemptible old carle, without grace, I have stayed too long your water and wood thrall."

"I think, wife, that you have turned crazy. Go you, daughter, quickly, and fetch a drink for your father."

His daughter went, and in the same way so it happened to her. She never thought till now that she was so lovable, and she took herself home.

"Up with the drink," said her father.

"You home-spun shoe carle, do you think I am fit to be your thrall?"

The poor shoemaker thought that they had taken a turn in their understandings, and he went himself to the well. He saw the shadow of the maiden in the well, and he looked up to the tree, and he sees the finest woman he ever saw.

"Your seat is wavering, but your face is fair," said the shoemaker. "Come down, for there is need of you for a short while at my house."

The shoemaker understood that this was the shadow that had driven his people mad. The shoemaker took her to his house, and he said that he had but a poor bothy, but that she should get a share of all that was in it.

One day, the shoemaker had shoes ready, for on that very day the king's son was to be married. The shoemaker was going to the castle with the shoes of the young people, and the girl said to the shoemaker, "I would like to get a sight of the king's son before he marries."

"Come with me," says the shoemaker, "I am well acquainted with the servants at the castle, and you shall get a sight of the king's son and all the company."

And when the gentles saw the pretty woman that was here they took her to the wedding-room, and they filled for her a glass of wine. When she was going to drink what is in it, a flame went up out of the glass, and a golden pigeon and a silver pigeon sprang out of it. They were flying about when three grains of barley fell on the floor. The silver pigeon sprung, and ate that up.

Said the golden pigeon to him, "If you remembered when I cleared the byre, you would not eat that without giving me a share."

Again there fell three other grains of barley, and the silver pigeon sprung, and ate that up as before.

If you remembered when I thatched the byre, you would not eat that without giving me my share," says the golden pigeon.

Three other grains fall, and the silver pigeon sprung, and ate that up.

"If you remembered when I harried the magpie's nest, you would not eat that without giving me my share," says the golden pigeon; "I lost my little finger bringing it down, and I want it still."

The king's son minded, and he knew who it was that was before him.

"Well," said the king's son to the guests at the feast, "when I was a little younger than I am now, I lost the key of a casket that I had. I had a new key made, but after it was brought to me I found the old one. Now, I'll leave it to any one here to tell me what I am to do. Which of the keys should I keep?"

My advice to you," said one of the guests, "is to keep the old key, for it fits the lock better and you're more used to it."

Then the king's son stood up and said "I thank you for a wise advice and an honest word. This is my bride the daughter of the giant who saved my life at the risk of her own. I'll have her and no other woman."

So the king's son married Auburn Mary and the wedding lasted long and all were happy. But all I got was butter on a live coal, porridge in a basket, and they sent me for water to the stream, and the paper shoes came to an end.

The giant asked the lad "What is the reward for putting it all back into the bundle?"

The Black Bull of Norroway

The Black Bull of Norroway was collected by Joseph Jacobs (1854–1916) and formed part of his *More English Fairy Tales* although it is clearly a Scottish tale rather than an English one. It was also included in *The Blue Fairy Book* by Andrew Lang (1844 –1912) and mentioned by J. R. R. Tolkein (1892 – 1973) in his essay "On Fairy Stories" as a good example of a 'eucatastrophe' – a term he coined to describe a sudden turn of events at the end of a tale that helps the hero or heroine. He formed the word by affixing the Greek prefix eu, meaning good, to catastrophe, Here the story tells how the three daughters set out to seek their fortunes, meeting a washerwoman witch along the way. It is the third daughter that finds a black bull.

The term langsyne in the first line is reminiscent of the Hogmanay (Scottish New Year) song Auld Lang Syne

In Norroway, langsyne, there lived a certain lady, and she had three dochters. The auldest o' them said to her mither: "Mither, bake me a bannock, and roast me a collop, for I'm gaun awa' to seek my fortune." Her mither did sae; and the dochter gaed awa' to an auld witch washerwife and told her purpose. The auld wife bade her stay that day, and gang and look out o' her back door, and see what she could see. She saw nocht the first day. The second day she did the same, and saw nocht. On the third day she looked again, and saw a coach-and-six coming along the road. She ran in and telled the auld wife what she saw.

A coach-and-four was coming along the road

"Aweel," quo' the auld wife, "yon's for you."

Sae they took her into the coach, and galloped aff.

The second dochter next says to her mither: "Mither, bake me a bannock, and roast me a collop, fur I'm gaun awa' to seek my fortune."

Her mither did sae; and awa' she gaed to the auld wife, as her sister had dune. On the third day she looked out o' the back door, and saw a coach-and-four coming along the road.

"Aweel," quo' the auld wife, "yon's for you."

Sae they took her in, and aff they set.

The third dochter says to her mither: "Mither, bake me a bannock, and roast me a collop, for I'm gaun awa' to seek my fortune."

Her mither did sae; and awa' she gaed to the auld witch-wife. She bade her look out o' her back door, and see what she could see. She did sae; and when she came back said she saw nocht. The second day she did the same, and saw nocht. The third day she looked again, and on coming back said to the auld wife she saw nocht but a muckle Black Bull coming roaring alang the road.

"Aweel," quo' the auld wife, "yon's for you."

On hearing this she was next to distracted wi' grief and terror; but she was lifted up and set on his back, and awa' they went.

Aye they traveled, and on they traveled, till the lady grew faint wi' hunger.

"Eat out o' my right lug," says the Black Bull, "and drink out o' my left lug, and set by your leavings."

Sae she did as he said, and was wonderfully refreshed. And lang they gaed, and sair they rade, till they came in sight o' a very big and bonny castle. "Yonder we maun be this night," quo' the bull; "for my auld brither lives yonder"; and presently they were at the place. They lifted her aff his back, and took her in, and sent him away to a park for the night. In the morning, when they brought the bull hame, they took the lady into a fine shining parlor, and gave her a beautiful apple, telling her no to break it till she was in the greatest strait ever mortal was in in the world, and that wad bring her o't. Again she was lifted on the bull's back, and after she had ridden far, and farer than I can tell, they came in sight o' a far bonnier castle, and far farther awa' than the last.

Says the bull till her: "Yonder we maun be the night, for my second brither lives yonder"; and they were at the place directly. They lifted her down and took her in, and sent the bull to the field for the night. In the morning they took the lady into a fine and rich room, and gave her the finest pear she had ever seen, bidding her no to break it till she was in the greatest strait ever mortal could be in, and that wad get her out o't. Again she was lifted and set on his back, and awa' they went. And lang they gaed, and sair they rade, till they came in sight o' the far biggest castle, and far farthest aff, they had yet seen. "We maun be yonder the night," says the bull, "for my young brither lives yonder"; and they were there directly. They lifted her down, took her in, and sent the bull to the field for the night. In the morning they took her into a room, the finest of a', and gied her a plum, telling her no to break it till she was in the greatest strait mortal could be in, and that wad get her out o't. Presently they brought hame the bull, set the lady on his back, and awa' they went.

that had given in some bluidy sarks to wash, and whaever washed thae sarks was to be his wife. The auld wife had washed till she was tired, and then she set to her dochter, and baith washed, and they washed, and they better washed, in hopes of getting the young knight; but a' they could do they couldna bring out a stain. At length they set the stranger damosel to wark; and whenever she began the stains came out pure and clean, but the auld wife made the knight believe it was her dochter had washed the sarks. So the knight and the eldest dochter were to be married, and the stranger damosel was distracted at the thought of it,

The third daughter was set upon the Black Bull's back

A beautiful apple and fine pear would serve her well

And aye they gaed, and on they rade, till they came to a dark and ugsome glen, where they stopped, and the lady lighted down. Says the bull to her: "Here ye maun stay till I gang and fight the deil. Ye maun seat yoursel' on that stane, and move neither hand nor fit till I come back, else I'll never find ye again. And if everything round about ye turns blue I hae beated the deil; but should a' things turn red he'll hae conquered me."

She set hersel' down on the stane, and by-and-by a' round her turned blue. O'ercome wi' joy, she lifted the ae fit and crossed it owre the ither, sae glad was she that her companion was victorious. The bull returned and sought for but never could find her.

Lang she sat, and aye she grat, till she wearied. At last she rase and gaed awa', she kedna whaur till. On she wandered till she came to a great hill o' glass, that she tried a' she could to climb, bat wasna able. Round the bottom o' the hill she gaed, sabbing and seeking a passage owre, till at last she came to a smith's house; and the smith promised, if she wad serve him seven years, he wad make her iron shoon, wherewi' she could climb owre the glassy hill. At seven years' end she got her iron shoon, clamb the glassy hill, and chanced to come to the auld washerwife's habitation. There she was telled of a gallant young knight

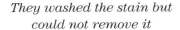

They washed the stain but could not remove it

331

for she was deeply in love wi' him. So she bethought her of her apple, and breaking it, found it filled with gold and precious jewelry, the richest she had ever seen.

"All these," she said to the eldest dochter, "I will give you, on condition that you put off your marriage for ae day, and allow me to go into his room alone at night." So the lady consented; but meanwhile the auld wife had prepared a sleeping-drink, and given it to the knight, wha drank it, and never wakened till next morning. The lee-lang night ther damosel sabbed and sang:

"Seven lang years I served for thee.
The glassy hill I clamb for thee,

She set herself down upon the stone and waited

The bluidy shirt I wrang for thee;
And wilt thou no wauken and turn to me?"

Next day she kentna what to do for grief. She then brak the pear, and found it filled wi' jewelry far richer than the contents o' the apple. Wi' thae jewels she bargained for permission to be a second night in the young knight's chamber; but the auld wife gied him anither sleeping-drink, and he again sleepit till morning. A' night she kept sighing and singing as before:

"Seven lang years I served for thee.
The glassy hill I clamb for thee,

The bluidy shirt I wrang for thee;
And wilt thou no wauken and turn to me?"

Still he sleepit, and she nearly lost hope a'thegither. But that day when he was out at the hunting, somebody asked him what noise and moaning was yon they heard all last night in his bedchamber. He said he heardna ony noise. But they assured him there was sae; and he resolved to keep waking that night to try what he could hear. That being the third night, and the damosel being between hope and despair, she brak her plum, and it held far the richest jewelry of the three. She bargained as before; and the auld wife, as before, took in the sleeping-drink to the young knight's chamber; but he told her he couldna drink it that night without sweetening. And when she gaed awa' for some honey to sweeten it wi', he poured out the drink, and sae made the auld wife think he had drunk it. They a' went to bed again, and the damosel began, as before, singing:

"Seven lang years I served for thee.
The glassy hill I clamb for thee,
The bluidy shirt I wrang for thee;
And wilt thou no wauken and turn to me?"

He heard, and turned to her. And she told him a' that had befa'en her, and he told her a' that had happened to him. And he caused the auld washerwife and her dochter to be burned. And they were married, and he and she are living happy till this day, for aught I ken.

*After seven years the damsel would at last
be reunited with her knight*

Eva's Visit to Fairyland

This is an extract from a book by the American author, Louisa May Alcott (1832–1888) who is most widely known for *Little Women* published in 1868. She could afford no other than to work at an early age and found employment as a teacher, seamstress, governess, domestic helper and ultimately as a writer. Her first book was *Flower Fables* (1849), a selection of tales originally written for Ellen Emerson, daughter of Ralph Waldo Emerson.

between the Elves. "Now I can go with you," said she, "but see, I can no longer step from the bank to yonder stone, for the brook seems now like a great river, and you have not given me wings like yours."

But the Fairies took each a hand, and flew lightly over the stream. The Queen and her subjects came to meet her, and all seemed glad to say some kindly word of welcome to the little stranger. They placed a flower-crown upon her head, laid their soft faces against her own, and soon it seemed as if the gentle Elves had always been her friends.

"Now must we go home," said the Queen, "and you shall go with us, little one."

Then there was a great bustle, as they flew about on shining wings, some laying cushions of violet leaves in

Down among the grass and fragrant clover lay little Eva by the brook-side, watching the bright waves, as they went singing by under the drooping flowers that grew on its banks. As she was wondering where the waters went, she heard a faint, low sound, as of far-off music. She thought it was the wind, but not a leaf was stirring, and soon through the rippling water came a strange little boat.

It was a lily of the valley, whose tall stem formed the mast, while the broad leaves that rose from the roots, and drooped again till they reached the water, were filled with gay little Elves, who danced to the music of the silver lily-bells above, that rang a merry peal, and filled the air with their fragrant breath.

On came the fairy boat, till it reached a moss-grown rock; and here it stopped, while the Fairies rested beneath the violet-leaves, and sang with the dancing waves.

Eva looked with wonder on their gay faces and bright garments, and in the joy of her heart sang too, and threw crimson fruit for the little folks to feast upon.

They looked kindly on the child, and, after whispering long among themselves, two little bright-eyed Elves flew over the shining water, and, lighting on the clover-blossoms, said gently, "Little maiden, many thanks for your kindness; and our Queen bids us ask if you will go with us to Fairy-Land, and learn what we can teach you."

"Gladly would I go with you, dear Fairies," said Eva, "but I cannot sail in your little boat. See! I can hold you in my hand, and could not live among you without harming your tiny kingdom, I am so large."

Then the Elves laughed gayly, as they folded their arms about her, saying, "You are a good child, dear Eva, to fear doing harm to those weaker than yourself. You cannot hurt us now. Look in the water and see what we have done."

Eva looked into the brook, and saw a tiny child standing

Fairies are not idle, wilful spirits but busy as can be

the boat, others folding the Queen's veil and mantle more closely round her, lest the falling dews should chill her.

The cool waves' gentle plashing against the boat, and the sweet chime of the lily-bells, lulled little Eva to sleep, and when she woke it was in Fairy-Land. A faint, rosy light, as of the setting sun, shone on the white pillars of the Queen's palace as they passed in, and the sleeping flowers leaned gracefully on their stems, dreaming beneath their soft green curtains. All was cool and still, and the Elves glided silently about, lest they should break their slumbers. They led Eva to a bed of pure white leaves, above which

*Fairies soothed the insects with gentle hands
and loving words*

drooped the fragrant petals of a crimson rose.

"You can look at the bright colors till the light fades, and then the rose will sing you to sleep," said the Elves, as they folded the soft leaves about her, gently kissed her, and stole away.

Long she lay watching the bright shadows, and listening to the song of the rose, while through the long night dreams of lovely things floated like bright clouds through her mind; while the rose bent lovingly above her, and sang in the clear moonlight.

With the sun rose the Fairies, and, with Eva, hastened away to the fountain, whose cool waters were soon filled with little forms, and the air ringing with happy voices, as the Elves floated in the blue waves among the fair white lilies, or sat on the green moss, smoothing their bright

locks, and wearing fresh garlands of dewy flowers. At length the Queen came forth, and her subjects gathered round her, and while the flowers bowed their heads, and the trees hushed their rustling, the Fairies sang their morning hymn to the Father of birds and blossoms, who had made the earth so fair a home for them.

Then they flew away to the gardens, and soon, high up among the tree-tops, or under the broad leaves, sat the Elves in little groups, taking their breakfast of fruit and pure fresh dew; while the bright-winged birds came fearlessly among them, pecking the same ripe berries, and dipping their little beaks in the same flower-cups, and the Fairies folded their arms lovingly about them, smoothed their soft bosoms, and gayly sang to them.

"Now, little Eva," said they, "you will see that Fairies are not idle, wilful Spirits, as mortals believe. Come, we will show you what we do."

They led her to a lovely room, through whose walls of deep green leaves the light stole softly in. Here lay many wounded insects, and harmless little creatures, whom cruel hands had hurt; and pale, drooping flowers grew beside urns of healing herbs, from whose fresh leaves came a faint, sweet perfume.

Eva wondered, but silently followed her guide, little Rose-Leaf, who with tender words passed among the delicate blossoms, pouring dew on their feeble roots, cheering them with her loving words and happy smile.

Then she went to the insects; first to a little fly who lay in a flower-leaf cradle.

"Do you suffer much, dear Gauzy-Wing?" asked the Fairy. "I will bind up your poor little leg, and Zephyr shall rock you to sleep." So she folded the cool leaves tenderly about the poor fly, bathed his wings, and brought him refreshing drink, while he hummed his thanks, and forgot his pain, as Zephyr softly sung and fanned him with her waving wings.

They passed on, and Eva saw beside each bed a Fairy, who with gentle hands and loving words soothed the suffering insects. At length they stopped beside a bee, who lay among sweet honeysuckle flowers, in a cool, still place, where the summer wind blew in, and the green leaves rustled pleasantly. Yet he seemed to find no rest, and murmured of the pain he was doomed to bear. " Why must I lie here, while my kindred are out in the pleasant fields, enjoying the sunlight and the fresh air, and cruel hands have doomed me to this dark place and bitter pain when I have done no wrong? Uncared for and forgotten, I must stay here among these poor things who think only of themselves. Come here, Rose-Leaf, and bind up my wounds, for I am far more useful than idle bird or fly."

Then said the Fairy, while she bathed the broken wing, –

"Love-Blossom, you should not murmur. We may find happiness in seeking to be patient even while we suffer. You are not forgotten or uncared for, but others need our care more than you, and to those who take cheerfully the pain and sorrow sent, do we most gladly give our help. You need not be idle, even though lying here in darkness and sorrow; you can be taking from your heart all sad and discontented feelings, and if love and patience blossom there, you will be better for the lonely hours spent here. Look on the bed beside you; this little dove has suffered far greater pain than you, and all our care can never ease it; yet through the long days he hath lain here, not an unkind word or a repining sigh hath he uttered. Ah, Love-Blossom, the gentle bird can teach a lesson you will be wiser and better for."

Then a faint voice whispered, "Little Rose-Leaf, come quickly, or I cannot thank you as I ought for all your loving care of me."

So they passed to the bed beside the discontented bee, and here upon the softest down lay the dove, whose gentle eyes looked gratefully upon the Fairy, as she knelt beside the little couch, smoothed the soft white bosom, folded her arms about it and wept sorrowing tears, while the bird still whispered its gratitude and love.

"Dear Fairy, the fairest flowers have cheered me with their sweet breath, fresh dew and fragrant leaves have been ever ready for me, gentle hands to tend, kindly hearts to love; and for this I can only thank you and say farewell."

They took Eva to the Flower Palace and Fairy Court

Then the quivering wings were still, and the patient little dove was dead; but the bee murmured no longer, and the dew from the flowers fell like tears around the quiet bed.

Sadly Rose-Leaf led Eva away, saying, "Lily-Bosom shall have a grave tonight beneath our fairest blossoms, and you shall see that gentleness and love are prized far above gold or beauty, here in Fairy-Land. Come now to the Flower Palace, and see the Fairy Court."

Beneath green arches, bright with birds and flowers, beside singing waves, went Eva into a lofty hall. The roof of pure white lilies rested on pillars of green clustering vines, while many-colored blossoms threw their bright shadows on the walls, as they danced below in the deep green moss, and their low, sweet voices sounded softly through the sunlit palace, while the rustling leaves kept time.

Beside the throne stood Eva, and watched the lovely forms around her, as they stood, each little band in its own color, with glistening wings, and flower wands.

Suddenly the music grew louder and sweeter, and the Fairies knelt, and bowed their heads, as on through the crowd of loving subjects came the Queen, while the air was filled with gay voices singing to welcome her.

She placed the child beside her, saying, "Little Eva, you shall see now how the flowers on your great earth bloom so brightly. A band of loving little gardeners go daily forth from Fairy-Land, to tend and watch them, that no harm may befall the gentle spirits that dwell beneath their leaves. This is never known, for like all good it is unseen by mortal eyes, and unto only pure hearts like yours do we make known our secret. The humblest flower that grows is visited by our messengers, and often blooms in fragrant beauty unknown, unloved by all save Fairy friends, who seek to fill the spirits with all sweet and gentle virtues, that they may not be useless on the earth; for the noblest mortals stoop to learn of flowers. Now, Eglantine, what have you to tell us of your rosy namesakes on the earth?"

From a group of Elves, whose rose-wreathed wands showed the flower they loved, came one bearing a tiny urn, and, answering the Queen, she said –

"Over hill and valley they are blooming fresh and fair as summer sun and dew can make them. No drooping stem or withered leaf tells of any evil thought within their fragrant bosoms, and thus from the fairest of their race have they gathered this sweet dew, as a token of their gratitude to one whose tenderness and care have kept them pure and happy; and this, the loveliest of their sisters, have I brought to place among the Fairy flowers that never pass away."

Eglantine laid the urn before the Queen, and placed the fragrant rose on the dewy moss beside the throne, while a murmur of approval went through the hall, as each elfin wand waved to the little Fairy who had toiled so well and faithfully, and could bring so fair a gift to their good Queen.

Then came forth an Elf bearing a withered leaf, while her many-colored robe and the purple tulips in her hair told her name and charge.

"Dear Queen," she sadly said, "I would gladly bring as pleasant tidings as my sister, but, alas! my flowers are proud and wilful, and when I went to gather my little gift of colored leaves for royal garments, they bade me bring this withered blossom, and tell you they would serve no longer one who will not make them Queen over all the other flowers. They would yield neither dew nor honey, but proudly closed their leaves and bid me go."

"Your task has been too hard for you," said the Queen kindly, as she placed the drooping flower in the urn Eglantine had given, "you will see how this dew from a sweet, pure heart will give new life and loveliness even to this poor faded one. So can you, dear Rainbow, by loving words and gentle teachings, bring back lost purity and peace to those whom pride and selfishness have blighted. Go once again to the proud flowers, and tell them when

Child elves studied the tender buds

they are queen of their own hearts they will ask no fairer kingdom. Watch more tenderly than ever over them, see that they lack neither dew nor air, speak lovingly to them, and let no unkind word or deed of theirs anger you. Let them see by your patient love and care how much fairer they might be, and when next you come, you will be laden with gifts from humble, loving flowers."

Thus they told what they had done, and received from their Queen some gentle chiding or loving word of praise.

"You will be weary of this," said little Rose-Leaf to Eva; "come now and see where we are taught to read the tales written on flower-leaves, and the sweet language of the birds, and all that can make a Fairy heart wiser and better."

Then into a cheerful place they went, where were many groups of flowers, among whose leaves sat the child Elves, and learned from their flower-books all that Fairy hands had written there. Some studied how to watch the tender buds, when to spread them to the sunlight, and when to shelter them from rain; how to guard the ripening seeds, and when to lay them in the warm earth or send them on the summer wind to far off hills and valleys, where other Fairy hands would tend and cherish them, till a sisterhood of happy flowers sprang up to beautify and gladden the lonely spot where they had fallen. Others learned to heal the wounded insects, whose frail limbs a breeze could shatter, and who, were it not for Fairy hands, would die ere half their happy summer life had gone. Some learned how by pleasant dreams to cheer and comfort mortal hearts, by whispered words bf love to save from evil deeds those who had gone astray, to fill young hearts with gentle thoughts and pure affections, that no sin might mar the beauty

of the human flower; while others, like mortal children, learned the Fairy alphabet. Thus the Elves made loving friends by care and love, and no evil thing could harm them, for those they helped to cherish and protect ever watched to shield and save them.

Eva nodded to the gay little ones, as they peeped from among the leaves at the stranger, and then she listened to the Fairy lessons. Several tiny Elves stood on a broad leaf while the teacher sat among the petals of a flower that bent beside them, and asked questions that none but Fairies would care to know.

"Twinkle, if there lay nine seeds within a flower-cup and the wind bore five away, how many would the blossom have?" "Four," replied the little one.

"Rosebud, if a Cowslip opens three leaves in one day and four the next, how many rosy leaves will there be when the whole flower has bloomed?"

"Seven," sang the gay little Elf.

"Harebell, if a silkworm spin one yard of Fairy cloth in an hour, how many will it spin in a day?"

"Twelve," said the Fairy child.

"Primrose, where lies Violet Island?"

"In the Lake of Ripples."

"Lilla, you may bound Rose Land."

"On the north by Ferndale, south by Sunny Wave River, east by the hill of Morning Clouds, and west by the Evening Star."

"Now, little ones," said the teacher, "you may go to your painting, that our visitor may see how we repair the flowers that earthly hands have injured."

Then Eva saw how, on large, white leaves, the Fairies learned to imitate the lovely colors, and with tiny brushes to brighten the blush on the anemone's cheek, to deepen the blue of the violet's eye, and add new light to the golden cowslip.

"You have stayed long enough," said the Elves at length, "we have many things to show you. Come now and see what is our dearest work."

So Eva said farewell to the child Elves, and hastened with little Rose-Leaf to the gates. Here she saw many bands of Fairies, folded in dark mantles that mortals might not know them, who, with the child among them, flew away over hill and valley. Some went to the cottages amid the hills, some to the sea-side to watch above the humble fisher folks; but little Rose-Leaf and many others went into the noisy city.

Eva wondered within herself what good the tiny Elves could do in this great place; but she soon learned, for the Fairy band went among the poor and friendless, bringing pleasant dreams to the sick and old, sweet, tender thoughts of love and gentleness to the young, strength to the weak, and patient cheerfulness to the poor and lonely.

Then the child wondered no longer, but deeper grew her love for the tender-hearted Elves, who left their own happy home to cheer and comfort those who never knew what hands had clothed and fed them, what hearts had given of their own joy, and brought such happiness to theirs.

The Wolf and the Seven Little Kids

This German fairy tale was collected by the Brothers Grimm (Jacob 1785–1863 and Wilhelm 1786–1859). A mother goat warns her children to be wary of the wolf while she is out shopping. As predicted, the wily wolf appears and claims to be their mother but with somewhat non-maternal motives! Maine and Alsace both have their own versions of this wolf story as do Transylvania and Greece.

There was once an old goat who had seven little ones, and was as fond of them as ever a mother was of her children. One day she had to go into the wood to fetch food for them, so she called them all round her.

"Dear children," said she, "I am going out into the wood; and while I am gone, be on your guard against the wolf, for if he were once to get inside he would eat you up, skin, bones, and all. The wretch often disguises himself, but he may always be known by his hoarse voice and black paws."

"Dear mother," answered the kids, "you need not be afraid, we will take good care of ourselves." And the mother bleated good-bye, and went on her way with an easy mind.

It was not long before some one came knocking at the house-door, and crying out: "Open the door, my dear children, your mother is come back, and has brought each of you something."

But the little kids knew it was the wolf by the hoarse voice. "We will not open the door," cried they; "you are not our mother, she has a delicate and sweet voice, and your voice is hoarse; you must be the wolf."

Then off went the wolf to a shop and bought a big lump of chalk, and ate it up to make his voice soft. And then he came back, knocked at the house-door, and cried: "Open the door, my dear children, your mother is here, and has brought each of you something."

But the wolf had put up his black paws against the window, and the kids seeing this, cried out, "We will not open the door; our mother has no black paws like you; you must be the wolf."

The wolf then ran to a baker. "Baker," said he, "I am hurt in the foot; pray spread some dough over the place." And when the baker had plastered his feet, he ran to the miller.

"Miller," said he, "strew me some white meal over my paws." But the miller refused, thinking the wolf must be meaning harm to some one. "If you don't do it," cried the wolf, "I'll eat you up!" And the miller was afraid and did as he was told. And that just shows what men are like!.

And now came the rogue the third time to the door and knocked.

"Open, children!" cried he. "Your dear mother has come home, and brought you each something from the wood."

"First show us your paws," said the kids, "so that we may know if you are really our mother or not." And he put up his paws against the window, and when they saw that they were white, all seemed right, and they opened the door. And when he was inside they saw it was the wolf, and they were terrified and tried to hide themselves. One ran under the table, the second got into the bed, the third into the oven, the fourth in the kitchen, the fifth in the cupboard,

They filled the wolf's tummy with heavy stones

the sixth under the sink, the seventh in the clock-case. But the wolf found them all, and gave them short shrift; one after the other he swallowed down, all but the youngest, who was hid in the clock-case. And so the wolf, having got what he wanted, strolled forth into the green meadows, and laying himself down under a tree, he fell asleep.

Not long after, the mother goat came back from the wood; and, oh! what a sight met her eyes! the door was standing wide open, table, chairs, and stools, all thrown about, dishes broken, quilt and pillows torn off the bed. She sought her children; they were nowhere to be found. She called to each of them by name, but nobody answered, until she came to the name of the youngest. "Here I am, mother," a little voice cried, "here, in the clock case." And so she helped him out, and heard how the wolf had come, and eaten all the rest. And you may think how she cried for the loss of her dear children.

The wolf bought a big lump of chalk

The kids opened the door and in ran the wolf

At last in her grief she wandered out of doors, and the youngest kid with her; and when they came into the meadow, there they saw the wolf lying under a tree, and snoring so that the branches shook. The mother goat looked at him carefully on all sides and she noticed how something inside his body was moving and struggling. Dear me! thought she, can it be that my poor children that he devoured for his evening meal are still alive? And she sent the little kid back to the house for a pair of shears, and needle, and thread. Then she cut the wolf's body open, and no sooner had she made one snip than out came the head of one of the kids, and then another snip, and then one after the other the six little kids all jumped out alive and well, for in his greediness the rogue had swallowed them down whole. How delightful this was! so they comforted their dear mother and hopped about like tailors at a wedding.

"Now fetch some good hard stones," said the mother, "and we will fill his body with them, as he lies asleep." And so they fetched some in all haste, and put them inside him, and the mother sewed him up so quickly again that he was none the wiser.

When the wolf at last awoke, and got up, the stones inside him made him feel very thirsty, and as he was going to the brook to drink, they struck and rattled one against another. And so he cried out:

"What is this I feel inside me?
Knocking hard against my bones?
How should such a thing betide me!
They were kids, and now they're stones."

So he came to the brook, and stooped to drink, but the heavy stones weighed him down, so he fell over into the water and was drowned. And when the seven little kids saw it they came up running.

"The wolf is dead, the wolf is dead!" they cried, and taking hands, they danced with their mother all about the place.

*A German stamp
depicts the story*

338

A Frog he would a Wooing go

The first known appearance of this folk song is in *Wedderburn's Complaynt of Scotland* (1548/9) as "The frog came to the myl dur" – in Scots in rather than English. There is a reference in the London Company of Stationer's Register of 1580 to "A Moste Strange Weddinge of the Frogge and the Mouse." but the oldest known musical version is in *Melismata* by Thomas Ravenscroft (1582 or 1592–1635) in 1611. It may, indeed, have been a satire about how Queen Elizabeth I of England called her ministers animal nicknames with Sir Walter Raleigh dubbed her 'fish', the French Ambassador her 'ape' and the Duc d'Alencon her 'frog'. The 1580 version recorded with the London Company of Stationers may have been revised from the older song, at the time of the proposed marriage of Queen Elizabeth I to the Duc d'Alencon. Tom and Jerry and Bob Dylan and Kermit the (Muppet) Frog have all been responsible for more recent versions. Whatever the origins of this ancient tale, the wedding certainly turned into a riotous party!

Melismata - Musicall Phansies Fitting the Court, Citie, and Countrey Humours, To 3, 4, and 5 Voyces. (London, 1611)

Twas the Frogge in the well, humble dum, humble, dum.
And the merrie Mouse in the Mill, tweedle, tweedle, twino.
The Frogge he would a woing ride, humble dum, humble, dum.
Sword and a buckler by his side, tweedle, tweedle, twino.
When he was upon his high horse set, humble dum, humble, dum,
His boots they shone as blacke as jet, tweedle, tweedle, twino.
When he came to a merry mill pin, humble dum, humble dum,
"Lady Mouse beene you within?" Tweedle, tweedle, twino.
Then came out the dusty Mouse, humble dum, humble dum.
"I am Lady of this house," tweedle, tweedle, twino.
"Hast thou any minde of me?" humble dum, humble dum.
"I have e'ne greate minde of thee," tweedle, tweedle, twino.
"Who shall this marriage make?" humble dum, humble dum.
"Our Lord which is the rat," tweedle, tweedle, twino.
"What shall we have to our supper?" humble dum, humble dum.
"Three beanes in a pound of butter," tweedle, tweedle, twino.
When supper they were at, humble dum, humble dum.
The Frog, the Mouse, and even the Rat, tweedle, tweedle, twino.
Then came in gib our cat, humble dum, humble dum,
And catcht the mouse even by the backe, tweedle, tweedle, twino.
Then did they separate, humble dum, humble dum,
And the frog leapt on the floore so flat, tweedle, tweedle, twino.
Then came in Dicke our Drake, humble dum, humble dum,
And drew the frogge even to the lake, tweedle, tweedle, twino.
The Rat run up the wall, humble dum, humble dum.
A goodly company, the divell goe with all, tweedle, tweedle, twino.

Mrs. Mouse gave them beer so Froggy and Rowley had good cheer

Original drawings by Randolph Caldecott

A frog he would a wooing go
Illustrations by Randolph Caldecott (1846-1886).

A Frog he would a wooing go,
Heigh-ho, says Rowley,
A Frog he would a-wooing go,
Whether this mother would let him or no,
With a Roley, Poley, Gammon and Spinach,
Heigh-ho says Anthony Rowley.

He saddled and bridled a great black snail,
Heigh-ho, says Rowley,
He saddled and bridled a great black snail,
And rode between the horns and the tail,
With a Roley, Poley, Gammon and Spinach,
Heigh-ho says Anthony Rowley.

So off he set with his opera hat,
Heigh-ho, says Rowley,
So off he set with his opera hat,
And on the way he met with a rat,
With a Roley, Poley, Gammon and Spinach,
Heigh-ho says Anthony Rowley.

They rode till they came to Mousey Hall,
Heigh-ho, says Rowley,
They rode till they came to Mousey Hall,
And there they both did knock and call,
With a Roley, Poley, Gammon and Spinach,
Heigh-ho says Anthony Rowley.

"Pray, Mrs. Mouse, are you within?"
Heigh-ho, says Rowley,
"Pray, Mrs. Mouse, are you within?"
"Oh yes, sir, here I sit and spin."
With a Roley, Poley, Gammon and Spinach,
Heigh-ho says Anthony Rowley.

Then Mrs. Mouse she did come down,
Heigh-ho, says Rowley,
Then Mrs. Mouse she did come down,
All smartly dressed in a russet gown,
With a Roley, Poley, Gammon and Spinach,
Heigh-ho says Anthony Rowley.

"Pray, Mrs. Mouse, can you give us some beer,"
Heigh-ho, says Rowley,
"Pray, Mrs. Mouse, can you give us some beer,
That froggy and I may have good cheer?"
With a Roley, Poley, Gammon and Spinach,
Heigh-ho says Anthony Rowley.

She had not been sitting long to spin,
Heigh-ho, says Rowley,
She had not been sitting long to spin,
When the cat and the kittens came tumbling in,
With a Roley, Poley, Gammon and Spinach,
Heigh-ho says Anthony Rowley.

The cat she seized Master Rat by the crown,
Heigh-ho, says Rowley,
The cat she seized Master Rat by the crown,
The kitten she pulled Miss Mousey down,
With a Roley, Poley, Gammon and Spinach,
Heigh-ho says Anthony Rowley.

This put Mr. Frog in a terrible fright,
Heigh-ho, says Rowley,
This put Mr. Frog in a terrible fright,
He took up his hat and he wished them "Good night!"
With a Roley, Poley, Gammon and Spinach,
Heigh-ho says Anthony Rowley.

And as he was passing over the brook,
Heigh-ho, says Rowley,
And as he was passing over the brook,
A lily white duck came and gobbled him up,
With a Roley, Poley, Gammon and Spinach,
Heigh-ho says Anthony Rowley.

So there's an end of one, two, and three,
Heigh-ho, says Rowley,
So there's an end of one, two, and three,
The Rat, the Mouse, and little Froggy,
With a Roley, Poley, Gammon and Spinach,
Heigh-ho says Anthony Rowley.

The Wind in the Willows

The Wind in the Willows was published in 1908 when its author Kenneth Grahame retired from his position as secretary of the Bank of England and moved to the country, where he spent his time by the River Thames and often, as the book says, "simply messing about in boats". This has become is a classic of children's literature, encompassing all the enchantment of talking animals and the English countryside – with large servings of humour to add to the magic in a wonderful blend of mysticism, adventure, morality, and camaraderie. A. A. Milne used the characters in his stage version, *Toad of Toad Hall* in 1929. Here follows an extract from Chapter 6.

Then Toad burst out laughing. "All right, Ratty," he said. "It's only my way, you know. And it's not such a very bad house, is it? You know you rather like it yourself. Now, look here. Let's be sensible. You are the very animals I wanted. You've got to help me. It's most important!"

"It's about your rowing, I suppose," said the Rat, with an innocent air. "You're getting on fairly well, though you splash a good bit still. With a great deal of patience, and any quantity of coaching, you may –"

"O, pooh! boating!" interrupted the Toad, in great disgust. "Silly boyish amusement. I've given that up *long* ago. Sheer waste of time, that's what it is. It makes me downright sorry to see you fellows, who ought to know better, spending all your energies in that aimless manner. No, I've discovered the real thing, the only genuine occupation for a life time. I propose to devote the remainder of mine to it, and can only regret the wasted years that lie behind me, squandered in trivialities. Come with me, dear Ratty, and your amiable friend also, if he will be so very good, just as far as the stable-yard, and you shall see what you shall see!"

He led the way to the stable-yard accordingly, the Rat following with a most mistrustful expression; and there, drawn out of the coach house into the open, they saw a gipsy caravan, shining with newness, painted a canary-yellow picked out with green, and red wheels.

"There you are!" cried the Toad, straddling and expanding himself. "There's real life for you, embodied in that little cart. The open road, the dusty highway, the heath, the common, the hedgerows, the rolling downs! Camps, villages, towns, cities! Here to-day, up and off to somewhere else to-morrow! Travel, change, interest, excitement! The whole world before you, and a horizon that's always changing! And mind! this is the very finest cart of its sort that was ever built, without any exception. Come inside and look at the arrangements. Planned 'em all myself, I did!"

The Mole was tremendously interested and excited, and followed him eagerly up the steps and into the interior of the caravan. The Rat only snorted and thrust his hands deep into his pockets, remaining where he was.

It was indeed very compact and comfortable. Little sleeping bunks – a little table that folded up against the wall – a cooking-stove, lockers, bookshelves, a bird-cage with a bird in it; and pots, pans, jugs and kettles of every size and variety.

"All complete!" said the Toad triumphantly, pulling open a locker. "You see – biscuits, potted lobster, sardines – everything you can possibly want. Soda-water here – baccy there – letter-paper, bacon, jam, cards and dominoes – you'll find," he continued, as they descended the steps again, "you'll find that nothing whatever has been forgotten, when

A gaunt tree and clouds set the scene on the title piece

we make our start this afternoon."

"I beg your pardon," said the Rat slowly, as he chewed a straw, "but did I overhear you say something about "*we*," and "*start*," and "*this afternoon?*""

"Now, you dear good old Ratty," said Toad, imploringly, "don't begin talking in that stiff and sniffy sort of way, because you know you've got to come. I can't possibly manage without you, so please consider it settled, and don't argue – it's the one thing I can't stand. You surely don't mean to stick to your dull fusty old river all your life, and just live in a hole in a bank, and boat? I want to show you the world! I'm going to make an animal of you, my boy!"

"I don't care," said the Rat, doggedly. "I'm not coming, and that's flat. And I am going to stick to my old river, and live in a hole, and boat, as I've always done. And what's more, Mole's going to stick to me and do as I do, aren't you, Mole?"

"Of course I am," said the Mole, loyally. "I'll always stick to you, Rat, and what you say is to be – has got to be. All

"Come along in, and have some lunch," he said, diplomatically, "and we'll talk it over. We needn't decide anything in a hurry. Of course, I don't really care. I only want to give pleasure to you fellows. 'Live for others!' That's my motto in life."

During luncheon – which was excellent, of course, as everything at Toad Hall always was – the Toad simply let himself go. Disregarding the Rat, he proceeded to play upon the inexperienced Mole as on a harp. Naturally a voluble animal, and always mastered by his imagination, he painted the prospects of the trip and the joys of the open life and the roadside in such glowing colours that

The open road and dusty highway lay before them

The Piper at the Gates of Dawn

the same, it sounds as it might have been – well, rather fun, you know!" he added, wistfully. Poor Mole! The Life Adventurous was so new a thing to him, and so thrilling; and this fresh aspect of it was so tempting; and he had fallen in love at first sight with the canary-coloured cart and all its little fitments.

The Rat saw what was passing in his mind, and wavered. He hated disappointing people, and he was fond of the Mole, and would do almost anything to oblige him. Toad was watching both of them closely.

the Mole could hardly sit in his chair for excitement. Somehow, it soon seemed taken for granted by all three of them that the trip was a settled thing; and the Rat, though still unconvinced in his mind, allowed his good-nature to over-ride his personal objections. He could not bear to disappoint his two friends, who were already deep in schemes and anticipations, planning out each day's separate occupation for several weeks ahead.

When they were quite ready, the now triumphant Toad led his companions to the paddock and set them to capture the old grey horse, who, without having been consulted, and to his own extreme annoyance, had been told off by Toad for the dustiest job in this dusty expedition. He frankly preferred the paddock, and took a deal of catching. Meantime Toad packed the lockers still tighter with necessaries, and hung nosebags, nets of onions, bundles of hay, and baskets from the bottom of the cart. At last the horse was caught and harnessed, and they set off, all talking at once, each animal either trudging by the side of the cart or sitting on the shaft, as the humour took him. It was a golden afternoon. The smell of the dust they kicked up was rich and satisfying; out of thick orchards

Toad talked big about all he was going to do in the days to come, while stars grew fuller and larger all around them, and a yellow moon, appearing suddenly and silently from nowhere in particular, came to keep them company and listen to their talk. At last they turned in to their little bunks in the cart; and Toad, kicking out his legs, sleepily said, "Well, good night, you fellows! This is the real life for a gentleman! Talk about your old river!"

"I *don't* talk about my river," replied the patient Rat. "You *know* I don't, Toad. But I *think* about it," he added pathetically, in a lower tone: "I think about it – all the time!"

Rat peeped out at the world

Rat said that he was going to stick to his old river

on either side the road, birds called and whistled to them cheerily; good-natured wayfarers, passing them, gave them "Good-day," or stopped to say nice things about their beautiful cart; and rabbits, sitting at their front doors in the hedgerows, held up their fore-paws, and said, "O my! O my! O my!"

Late in the evening, tired and happy and miles from home, they drew up on a remote common far from habitations, turned the horse loose to graze, and ate their simple supper sitting on the grass by the side of the cart.

The Mole reached out from under his blanket, felt for the Rat's paw in the darkness, and gave it a squeeze. "I'll do whatever you like, Ratty," he whispered. "Shall we run away tomorrow morning, quite early – very early – and go back to our dear old hole on the river?"

"No, no, we'll see it out," whispered back the Rat. "Thanks awfully, but I ought to stick by Toad till this trip is ended. It wouldn't be safe for him to be left to himself. It won't take very long. His fads never do. Good night!"

The end was indeed nearer than even the Rat suspected.

After so much open air and excitement the Toad slept very soundly, and no amount of shaking could rouse him out of bed next morning. So the Mole and Rat turned to, quietly and manfully, and while the Rat saw to the horse, and lit a fire, and cleaned last night's cups and platters, and got things ready for breakfast, the Mole trudged off to the nearest village, a long way off, for milk and eggs and various necessaries the Toad had, of course, forgotten to provide. The hard work had all been done, and the two animals were resting, thoroughly exhausted, by the time Toad appeared on the scene, fresh and gay, remarking what a pleasant easy life it was they were all leading now, after the cares and worries and fatigues of housekeeping at home.

They had a pleasant ramble that day over grassy downs and along narrow by-lanes, and camped as before, on a common, only this time the two guests took care that Toad should do his fair share of work. In consequence, when the time came for starting next morning, Toad was by no means so rapturous about the simplicity of the primitive life, and indeed attempted to resume his place in his bunk, whence he was hauled by force. Their way lay, as before, across country by narrow lanes, and it was not till the afternoon that they came out on the high-road, their first high-road; and there disaster, fleet and unforeseen, sprang out on them – disaster momentous indeed to their expedition, but simply overwhelming in its effect on the after-career of Toad.

They were strolling along the high-road easily, the Mole by the horse's head, talking to him, since the horse had complained that he was being frightfully left out of it, and nobody considered him in the least; the Toad and the Water Rat walking behind the cart talking together – at least Toad was talking, and Rat was saying at intervals, "Yes, precisely; and what did you say to him?" – and thinking all the time of something very different, when far behind them they heard a faint warning hum; like the drone of a distant bee. Glancing back, they saw a small cloud of dust, with a dark centre of energy, advancing on them at incredible speed, while from out the dust a faint "Poop-poop!" wailed like an uneasy animal in pain. Hardly regarding it, they turned to resume their conversation, when in an instant (as it seemed) the peaceful scene was changed, and with a blast of wind and a whirl of sound that made them jump for the nearest ditch, It was on them! The "Poop-poop" rang with a brazen shout in their ears, they had a moment's glimpse of an interior of glittering plate-glass and rich morocco, and the magnificent motor-car, immense, breath-snatching, passionate, with its pilot tense and hugging his wheel, possessed all earth and air for the fraction of a second, flung an enveloping cloud of dust that blinded and enwrapped them utterly, and then dwindled to a speck in the far distance, changed back into a droning bee once more.

The old grey horse, dreaming, as he plodded along, of his quiet paddock, in a new raw situation such as this simply abandoned himself to his natural emotions. Rearing,

plunging, backing steadily, in spite of all the Mole's efforts at his head, and all the Mole's lively language directed at his better feelings, he drove the cart backwards towards the deep ditch at the side of the road. It wavered an instant – then there was a heartrending crash – and the canary-coloured cart, their pride and their joy, lay on its side in the ditch, an irredeemable wreck.

The Rat danced up and down in the road, simply transported with passion. "You villains!" he shouted, shaking both fists, "You scoundrels, you highwaymen, you – you – roadhogs! – I'll have the law on you! I'll report you! I'll take you through all the Courts!" His home-sickness had quite slipped away from him, and for the moment he was the skipper of the canary-coloured vessel driven on a shoal by the reckless jockeying of rival mariners, and he was trying to recollect all the fine and biting things he used to say to masters of steam-launches when their wash, as they drove too near the bank, used to flood his parlour-carpet at home.

Toad sat straight down in the middle of the dusty road, his legs stretched out before him, and stared fixedly in the direction of the disappearing motor-car. He breathed short, his face wore a placid satisfied expression, and at intervals he faintly murmured "Poop-poop!"

The Mole was busy trying to quiet the horse, which he succeeded in doing after a time. Then he went to look at the cart, on its side in the ditch. It was indeed a sorry sight. Panels and windows smashed, axles hopelessly bent, one wheel off, sardine-tins scattered over the wide world, and the bird in the bird-cage sobbing pitifully and calling to be let out.

The Rat came to help him, but their united efforts were not sufficient to right the cart. "Hi! Toad!" they cried. "Come and bear a hand, can't you!"

The Toad never answered a word, or budged from his seat in the road; so they went to see what was the matter with him. They found him in a sort of a trance, a happy smile on his face, his eyes still fixed on the dusty wake of their destroyer. At intervals he was still heard to murmur "Poop-poop!"

The Rat shook him by the shoulder. "Are you coming to help us, Toad?" he demanded sternly.

"Glorious, stirring sight!" murmured Toad, never offering to move. "The poetry of motion! The *real* way to travel! The *only* way to travel! Here today – in next week tomorrow! Villages skipped, towns and cities jumped – always somebody else's horizon! O bliss! O poop-poop! O my! O my!"

"O *stop* being an ass, Toad!" cried the Mole despairingly.

"And to think I never *knew*!" went on the Toad in a dreamy monotone. "All those wasted years that lie behind me, I never knew, never even *dreamt*! But *now* – but now that I know, now that I fully realise! O what a flowery track lies spread before me, henceforth! What dust-clouds shall spring up behind me as I speed on my reckless way! What carts I shall fling carelessly into the ditch in the wake of my magnificent onset! Horrid little carts – common carts – canary-coloured carts!"

"What are we to do with him?" asked the Mole of the Water Rat.

"Nothing at all," replied the Rat firmly. "Because there is really nothing to be done. You see, I know him from of old. He is now possessed. He has got a new craze, and it always takes him that way, in its first stage. He'll continue like that for days now, like an animal walking in a happy dream, quite useless for all practical purposes. Never mind him. Let's go and see what there is to be done about the cart."

A careful inspection showed them that, even if they succeeded in righting it by themselves, the cart would travel no longer. The axles were in a hopeless state, and the missing wheel was shattered into pieces.

The Rat knotted the horse's reins over his back and took him by the head, carrying the bird cage and its hysterical occupant in the other hand. "Come on!" he said grimly to the Mole. "It's five or six miles to the nearest town, and we shall just have to walk it. The sooner we make a start the better."

"But what about Toad?" asked the Mole anxiously, as they set off together. "We can't leave him here, sitting in the middle of the road by himself, in the distracted state he's in! It's not safe. Supposing another Thing were to come along?"

"O, *bother* Toad," said the Rat savagely; "I've done with him!"

They had not proceeded very far on their way, however, when there was a pattering of feet behind them, and Toad caught them up and thrust a paw inside the elbow of each of them; still breathing short and staring into vacancy.

"Now, look here, Toad!" said the Rat sharply: "as soon as we get to the town, you'll have to go straight to the police-station, and see if they know anything about that motor-car and who it belongs to, and lodge a complaint against it. And then you'll have to go to a blacksmith's or a wheelwright's and arrange for the cart to be fetched and mended and put to rights. It'll take time, but it's not quite a hopeless smash. Meanwhile, the Mole and I will go to an inn and find comfortable rooms where we can stay till the cart's ready, and till your nerves have recovered their shock."

"Police-station! Complaint!" murmured Toad dreamily. "Me *complain* of that beautiful, that heavenly vision that has been vouchsafed me! *Mend the cart*! I've done with carts for ever. I never want to see the cart, or to hear of it, again. O, Ratty! You can't think how obliged I am to you for consenting to come on this trip! I wouldn't have gone without you, and then I might never have seen that – that swan, that sunbeam, that thunderbolt! I might never have heard that entrancing sound, or smelt that bewitching smell! I owe it all to you, my best of friends!"

The Rat turned from him in despair. "You see what it is?" he said to the Mole, addressing him across Toad's head: "He's quite hopeless. I give it up – when we get to the

Toad said, "I've done with carts for ever."

town we'll go to the railway station, and with luck we may pick up a train there that'll get us back to riverbank to-night. And if ever you catch me going a-pleasuring with this provoking animal again!"

He snorted, and during the rest of that weary trudge addressed his remarks exclusively to Mole.

On reaching the town they went straight to the station and deposited Toad in the second-class waiting-room, giving a porter twopence to keep a strict eye on him. They then left the horse at an inn stable, and gave what directions they could about the cart and its contents. Eventually, a slow train having landed them at a station not very far from Toad Hall, they escorted the spell-bound, sleep-walking Toad to his door, put him inside it, and instructed his housekeeper to feed him, undress him, and put him to bed. Then they got out their boat from the boat-house, sculled down the river home, and at a very late hour sat down to supper in their own cosy riverside parlour, to the Rat's great joy and contentment.

The following evening the Mole, who had risen late and taken things very easy all day, was sitting on the bank fishing, when the Rat, who had been looking up his friends and gossiping, came strolling along to find him. "Heard the news?" he said. "There's nothing else being talked about, all along the river bank. Toad went up to Town by an early train this morning. And he has ordered a large and very expensive motor-car."

The Magic Fishbone

This 1867 story by Charles Dickens 1812–1870 tells how Alicia, age seven, is the oldest of nineteen children and lives with her mother and father, King Watkins I. Alicia takes care of all the princes and princesses, and they all take care of the baby. Dickens attributed the story to a seven-year-old, Miss Alice Rainbird, but she was most likely a literary device, not a real girl.

A Holiday Romance from the Pen of Miss Alice Rainbird Aged 7

There was once a King, and he had a Queen; and he was the manliest of his sex, and she was the loveliest of hers. The King was, in his private profession, Under Government. The Queen's father had been a medical man out of town.

The Princess Alicia looked after all the other children including the baby

They had nineteen children, and were always having more. Seventeen of these children took care of the baby; and Alicia, the eldest, took care of them all. Their ages varied from seven years to seven months.

Let us now resume our story.

One day the King was going to the office, when he stopped at the fishmonger's to buy a pound and a half of salmon not too near the tail, which the Queen (who was a careful housekeeper) had requested him to send home. Mr. Pickles, the fishmonger, said, "Certainly, sir, is there any other article, Good-morning."

The King went on towards the office in a melancholy mood, for quarter day was such a long way off, and several of the dear children were growing out of their clothes. He had not proceeded far, when Mr. Pickles's errand-boy came running after him, and said, "Sir, you didn't notice the old lady in our shop."

"What old lady?" enquired the King. "I saw none."

Now, the King had not seen any old lady, because this old lady had been invisible to him, though visible to Mr. Pickles's boy. Probably because he messed and splashed the water about to that degree, and flopped the pairs of soles down in that violent manner, that, if she had not been visible to him, he would have spoilt her clothes.

Just then the old lady came trotting up. She was dressed in shot-silk of the richest quality, smelling of dried lavender.

"King Watkins the First, I believe?" said the old lady.

"Watkins," replied the King, "is my name."

"Papa, if I am not mistaken, of the beautiful Princess Alicia?" said the old lady.

"And of eighteen other darlings," replied the King.

"Listen. You are going to the office," said the old lady.

It instantly flashed upon the King that she must be a Fairy, or how could she know that?

"You are right," said the old lady, answering his thoughts, "I am the Good Fairy Grandmarina. Attend. When you return home to dinner, politely invite the Princess Alicia to have some of the salmon you bought just now."

"It may disagree with her," said the King.

The old lady became so very angry at this absurd idea, that the King was quite alarmed, and humbly begged her pardon.

"We hear a great deal too much about this thing disagreeing, and that thing disagreeing," said the old lady, with the greatest contempt it was possible to express. "Don't be greedy. I think you want it all yourself."

The King hung his head under this reproof, and said he wouldn't talk about things disagreeing, any more.

"Be good, then," said the Fairy Grandmarina, "and don't! When the beautiful Princess Alicia consents to partake of the salmon – as I think she will – you will find she will leave a fish-bone on her plate. Tell her to dry it, and to rub it, and to polish it till it shines like mother-of-pearl, and to take care of it as a present from me."

"Is that all?" asked the King.

"Don't be impatient, sir," returned the Fairy Grandmarina, scolding him severely. "Don't catch people

Princess Alicia entertained the children, hoping their mother would soon be well again

short, before they have done speaking. Just the way with you grown-up persons. You are always doing it."

The King again hung his head, and said he wouldn't do so any more.

"Be good then," said the Fairy Grandmarina, "and don't! Tell the Princess Alicia, with my love, that the fish-bone is a magic present which can only be used once; but that it will bring her, that once, whatever she wishes for, provided she wishes for it at the right time. That is the message. Take care of it."

The King was beginning, "Might I ask the reason?" when the Fairy became absolutely furious.

"Will you be good, sir?" she exclaimed, stamping her foot on the ground. "The reason for this, and the reason for that, indeed! You are always wanting the reason. No reason. There! Hoity-toity me! I am sick of your grown-up reasons."

The King was extremely frightened by the old lady's flying into such a passion, and said he was very sorry to have offended her, and he wouldn't ask for reasons any more.

"Be good then," said the old lady, "and don't!"

With those words, Grandmarina vanished, and the King went on and on and on, till he came to the office. There he wrote and wrote and wrote, till it was time to go home again. Then he politely invited the Princess Alicia, as the

Fairy had directed him, to partake of the salmon. And when she had enjoyed it very much, he saw the fish-bone on her plate, as the Fairy had told him he would, and he delivered the Fairy's message, and the Princess Alicia took care to dry the bone, and to rub it, and to polish it till it shone like mother-of-pearl.

And so when the Queen was going to get up in the morning, she said, "O, dear me, dear me; my head, my head!" and then she fainted away.

The Princess Alicia, who happened to be looking in at the chamber-door, asking about breakfast, was very much alarmed when she saw her Royal Mamma in this state, and she rang the bell for Peggy, which was the name of the Lord Chamberlain. But remembering where the smelling-bottle was, she climbed on a chair and got it, and after that she climbed on another chair by the bedside and held the smelling-bottle to the Queen's nose, and after that she jumped down and got some water, and after that she

"Be good then", said Fairy Grandmarina

jumped up again and wetted the Queen's forehead, and, in short, when the Lord Chamberlain came in, that dear old woman said to the little Princess, "What a Trot you are! I couldn't have done it better myself!"

But that was not the worst of the good Queen's illness. O, no! She was very ill indeed, for a long time. The Princess Alicia kept the seventeen young Princes and Princesses quiet, and dressed and undressed and danced the baby, and made the kettle boil, and heated the soup, and swept the hearth, and poured out the medicine, and nursed the Queen, and did all that ever she could, and was as busy busy busy, as busy could be. For there were not many servants at that Palace, for three reasons; because the King was short of money, because a rise in his office never seemed to come, and because quarter day was so far off that it looked almost as far off and as little as one of the stars.

But on the morning when the Queen fainted away, where was the magic fish-bone? Why, there it was in the Princess

Alicia's pocket. She had almost taken it out to bring the Queen to life again, when she put it back, and looked for the smelling-bottle.

After the Queen had come out of her swoon that morning, and was dozing, the Princess Alicia hurried up-stairs to tell a most particular secret to a most particularly confidential friend of hers, who was a Duchess. People did suppose her to be a Doll; but she was really a Duchess, though nobody knew it except the Princess.

This most particular secret was a secret about the magic fish-bone, the history of which was well known to the Duchess, because the Princess told her everything. The Princess kneeled down by the bed on which the Duchess was lying, full-dressed and wide awake, and whispered the secret to her. The Duchess smiled and nodded. People might have supposed that she never smiled and nodded, but she often did, though nobody knew it except the Princess.

Then the Princess Alicia hurried downstairs again, to keep watch in the Queen's room. She often kept watch by herself in the Queen's room; but every evening, while the illness lasted, she sat there watching with the King. And every evening the King sat looking at her with a cross look, wondering why she never brought out the magic fish-bone. As often as she noticed this, she ran up-stairs, whispered the secret to the Duchess over again, and said to the Duchess besides, "They think we children never have a reason or a meaning!" And the Duchess, though the most fashionable Duchess that ever was heard of, winked her eye.

"Alicia," said the King, one evening when she wished him Good Night.

"Yes, Papa."

"What is become of the magic fish-bone?"

"In my pocket, Papa."

"I thought you had lost it?"

"O, no, Papa."

"Or forgotten it?"

"No, indeed, Papa."

And so another time the dreadful little snapping pug-dog next door made a rush at one of the young Princes as he stood on the steps coming home from school, and terrified him out of his wits and he put his hand through a pane of glass, and bled bled bled. When the seventeen other young Princes and Princesses saw him bleed bleed bleed, they were terrified out of their wits too, and screamed themselves black in their seventeen faces all at once. But the Princess Alicia put her hands over all their seventeen mouths, one after another, and persuaded them to be quiet because of the sick Queen. And then she put the wounded Prince's hand in a basin of fresh cold water, while they stared with their twice seventeen are thirty-four put down four and carry three eyes, and then she looked in the hand for bits of glass, and there were fortunately no bits of glass there. And then she said to two chubby-legged Princes who were sturdy though small, "Bring me in the Royal rag-bag; I must snip and stitch and cut and contrive." So those two young Princes tugged at the Royal rag-bag and lugged it in, and the Princess Alicia sat down on the floor with a large pair of scissors and a needle and thread, and snipped and stitched and cut and contrived, and made a bandage and put it on, and it fitted beautifully, and so when it was all done she saw the King her Papa looking on by the door.

"Alicia."

"Yes, Papa."

"What have you been doing?"

"Snipping stitching cutting and contriving, Papa."

"Where is the magic fish-bone?"

"In my pocket, Papa."

"I thought you had lost it?"

"O, no, Papa."

"Or forgotten it?"

"No, indeed, Papa."

After that, she ran up-stairs to the Duchess and told her what had passed, and told her the secret over again, and the Duchess shook her flaxen curls and laughed with her rosy lips.

Well! and so another time the baby fell under the grate. The seventeen young Princes and Princesses were used to it, for they were almost always falling under the grate or down the stairs, but the baby was not used to it yet, and it gave him a swelled face and a black eye. The way the poor little darling came to tumble was, that he slid out of the Princess Alicia's lap just as she was sitting in a great coarse apron that quite smothered her, in front of the kitchen-fire, beginning to peel the turnips for the broth for dinner; and the way she came to be doing that was, that the King's cook had run away that morning with her own true love who was a very tall but very tipsy soldier. Then, the seventeen young Princes and Princesses, who cried at everything that happened, cried and roared. But the Princess Alicia (who couldn't help crying a little herself) quietly called to them to be still, on account of not throwing back the Queen up-stairs, who was fast getting well, and said, "Hold your tongues, you wicked little monkeys, every one of you, while I examine baby!" Then she examined baby, and found that he hadn't broken anything, and she held cold iron to his poor dear eye, and smoothed his poor dear face, and he presently fell asleep in her arms. Then, she said to the seventeen Princes and Princesses, "I am afraid to lay him down yet, lest he should wake and feel pain, be good, and you shall all be cooks."

They jumped for joy when they heard that, and began making themselves cooks' caps out of old newspapers. So to one she gave the salt-box, and to one she gave the barley, and to one she gave the herbs, and to one she gave the turnips, and to one she gave the carrots, and to one she gave the onions, and to one she gave the spice-box, till they were all cooks, and all running about at work, she sitting in the middle smothered in the great coarse apron, nursing baby. By and by the broth was done, and the baby woke up smiling like an angel, and was trusted to the sedatest Princess to hold, while the other Princes and Princesses were squeezed into a far-off corner to look at the Princess

Alicia turning out the saucepan-full of broth, for fear (as they were always getting into trouble) they should get splashed and scalded. When the broth came tumbling out, steaming beautifully, and smelling like a nosegay good to eat, they clapped their hands. That made the baby clap his hands; and that, and his looking as if he had a comic toothache, made all the Princes and Princesses laugh. So the Princess Alicia said, "Laugh and be good, and after dinner we will make him a nest on the floor in a corner, and he shall sit in his nest and see a dance of eighteen cooks." That delighted the young Princes and Princesses, and they ate up all the broth, and washed up all the plates and dishes, and cleared away, and pushed the table into a corner, and then they in their cooks' caps, and the Princess Alicia in the smothering coarse apron that belonged to the cook that had run away with her own true love that was the very tall but very tipsy soldier, danced a dance of eighteen cooks before the angelic baby, who forgot his swelled face

With seventeen young Princes and Princesses there were always plenty of games to play

and his black eye, and crowed with joy.

And so then, once more the Princess Alicia saw King Watkins the First, her father, standing in the doorway looking on, and he said: "What have you been doing, Alicia?"

"Cooking and contriving, Papa."

"What else have you been doing, Alicia?"

"Keeping the children light-hearted, Papa."

"Where is the magic fish-bone, Alicia?"

"In my pocket, Papa."

"I thought you had lost it?"

"O, no, Papa."

"Or forgotten it?"

"No, indeed, Papa."

The King then sighed so heavily, and seemed so low-spirited, and sat down so miserably, leaning his head upon his hand, and his elbow upon the kitchen table pushed away in the corner, that the seventeen Princes and Princesses crept softly out of the kitchen, and left him alone with the Princess Alicia and the angelic baby.

"What is the matter, Papa?"

"I am dreadfully poor, my child."

"Have you no money at all, Papa?"

"None my child."

"Is there no way left of getting any, Papa?"

"No way," said the King. "I have tried very hard, and I have tried all ways."

When she heard those last words, the Princess Alicia began to put her hand into the pocket where she kept the magic fish-bone.

Papa always asked if the magic fish-bone was safe

"Papa," said she, "when we have tried very hard, and tried all ways, we must have done our very very best?"

"No doubt, Alicia."

"When we have done our very very best, Papa, and that is not enough, then I think the right time must have come for asking help of others." This was the very secret connected with the magic fish-bone, which she had found out for herself from the good fairy Grandmarina's words, and which she had so often whispered to her beautiful and fashionable friend the Duchess.

So she took out of her pocket the magic fish-bone that had been dried and rubbed and polished till it shone like mother-of-pearl; and she gave it one little kiss and wished it was quarter day. And immediately it was quarter day; and the King's quarter's salary came rattling down the chimney, and bounced into the middle of the floor.

But this was not half of what happened, no not a quarter, for immediately afterwards the good fairy Grandmarina came riding in, in a carriage and four (Peacocks), with Mr. Pickles's boy up behind, dressed in silver and gold, with a cocked hat, powdered hair, pink silk stockings, a jewelled cane, and a nosegay. Down jumped Mr. Pickles's boy with his cocked hat in his hand and wonderfully polite (being entirely changed by enchantment), and handed Grandmarina out, and there she stood in her rich shot silk smelling of dried lavender, fanning herself with a sparkling fan.

"Alicia, my dear," said this charming old Fairy, "how do you do, I hope I see you pretty well, give me a kiss."

The Princess Alicia embraced her, and then Grandmarina turned to the King, and said rather sharply: "Are you good?"

The King said he hoped so.

"I suppose you know the reason, now, why my god-Daughter here," kissing the Princess again, "did not apply to the fish-bone sooner?" said the Fairy.

The King made her a shy bow.

"Ah! but you didn't then!" said the Fairy.

The King made her a shyer bow.

"Any more reasons to ask for?" said the Fairy.

The King said no, and he was very sorry.

"Be good then," said the Fairy, "and live happy ever afterwards."

Then, Grandmarina waved her fan, and the Queen came in most splendidly dressed, and the seventeen young Princes and Princesses, no longer grown out of their clothes, came in newly fitted out from top to toe, with tucks in everything to admit of its being let out. After that, the Fairy tapped the Princess Alicia with her fan, and the smothering coarse apron flew away, and she appeared exquisitely dressed, like a little Bride, with a wreath of orange-flowers and a silver veil. After that, the kitchen dresser changed of itself into a wardrobe, made of beautiful woods and gold and looking glass, which was full of dresses of all sorts, all for her and all exactly fitting her. After that, the angelic baby came in, running alone, with his face and eye not a bit the worse but much the better. Then, Grandmarina begged to be introduced to the Duchess, and, when the Duchess was brought down many compliments passed between them.

A little whispering took place between the Fairy and the Duchess, and then the Fairy said out loud, "Yes. I thought she would have told you." Grandmarina then turned to the King and Queen, and said, "We are going in search of Prince Certainpersonio. The pleasure of your company is requested at church in half an hour precisely." So she and the Princess Alicia got into the carriage, and Mr. Pickles's boy handed in the Duchess who sat by herself on the opposite seat, and then Mr. Pickles's boy put up the steps and got up behind, and the Peacocks flew away with their tails spread.

Grandmarina told Alicia that she would have thirty-five good and beautiful children

Prince Certainpersonio was sitting by himself, eating barley-sugar and waiting to be ninety. When he saw the Peacocks followed by the carriage, coming in at the window, it immediately occurred to him that something uncommon was going to happen.

"Prince," said Grandmarina, "I bring you your Bride."

The moment the Fairy said those words, Prince Certainpersonio's face left off being sticky, and his jacket and corduroys changed to peach-bloom velvet, and his hair curled, and a cap and feather flew in like a bird and settled on his head. He got into the carriage by the Fairy's invitation, and there he renewed his acquaintance with the Duchess, whom he had seen before.

In the church were the Prince's relations and friends, and the Princess Alicia's relations and friends, and the seventeen Princes and Princesses, and the baby, and a crowd of the neighbours. The marriage was beautiful beyond expression. The Duchess was bridesmaid, and beheld the ceremony from the pulpit where she was supported by the cushion of the desk.

Grandmarina gave a magnificent wedding feast afterwards, in which there was everything and more to eat, and everything and more to drink. The wedding cake was delicately ornamented with white satin ribbons, frosted silver and white lilies, and was forty-two yards round.

When Grandmarina had drunk her love to the young couple, and Prince Certainpersonio had made a speech, and everybody had cried Hip hip hip hurrah! Grandmarina announced to the King and Queen that in future there would be eight quarter days in every year, except in leap year, when there would be ten. She then turned to Certainpersonio and Alicia, and said, "My dears, you will have thirty-five children, and they will all be good and beautiful. Seventeen of your children will be boys, and eighteen will be girls. The hair of the whole of your children will curl naturally. They will never have the measles, and will have recovered from the whooping-cough before being born."

On hearing such good news, everybody cried out "Hip hip hip hurrah!" again.

"It only remains," said Grandmarina in conclusion, "to make an end of the fish-bone."

So she took it from the hand of the Princess Alicia, and it instantly flew down the throat of the dreadful little snapping pug-dog next door and choked him, and he expired in convulsions.

The Two Children and the Witch

This Portuguese tale is very reminiscent of *Hansel and Gretel* and was collected by Consiglieri Pedroso (1851–1910) and translated in 1882 for a USA publication. Pedroso was a man of many talents – a politician, ethnographer, essayist, writer, professor and company director. He wrote *Portuguese Folk Traditions, Contributions to a Portuguese Popular Mythology* and *Portuguese Folk Tales.*

There was once a woman who had a son and a daughter. The mother one day sent her son to buy five reis' worth of beans, and then said to both: "My children, go as far out on the road as you shall find shells of beans strewed on the path, and when you reach the wood you will find me there collecting fire-wood."

The children did as they were bid; and after the mother had gone out they went following the track of the beans which she went strewing along the road, but they did not find her in the wood or anywhere else. As night had come on they perceived in the darkness a light shining at a distance, easy of access. They walked on towards it, and they soon came up to an old woman who was frying cakes. The old woman was blind of one eye, and the boy went on the blind side and stole a cake, because he felt so hungry. Believing that it was her cat that had stolen the cake, she said, "You thief of a cat! Leave my cakes alone; they are not meant for you!"

The little boy now said to his sister, "You go now and take a cake."

But the little girl replied, "I cannot do so, as I am sure to laugh."

Still, as the boy persisted upon it and urged her to try, she had no other alternative but to do so. She went on the side of the old woman's blind eye and stole another of her cakes. The old woman, again thinking that it was her cat, said, "Be off! shoo, you old pussy cat; these cakes are not meant for you!"

The little girl now burst out into a fit of laughter, and the old hag turning round then, noticed the two children, and addressed them thus: "Ah! is it you, my dear grandchildren? Eat, eat away, and get fat!"

She then took hold of them and thrust them into a large box full of chestnuts, and shut them up. Next day she came close to the box and spoke to them thus: "Show me your little fingers, my pets, that I may be able to judge whether you have grown fat and sleek."

The children put out their little fingers as desired. But next day the old hag again asked them: "Show your little fingers, my little dears, that I may see if you have grown fat and plump!"

The children, instead of their little fingers, showed her the tail of a cat they had found inside the box. The old hag then said: "My pets, you can come out now, for you have grown nice and plump."

She took them out of the box, and told them they must go with her and gather sticks. The children went into the wood searching one way while the old hag took another direction. When they had arrived at a certain spot they met a fay. This fay said to them: "You are gathering sticks, my children, to heat the oven, but you do not know that the old hag wants to bake you in it."

She further told them that the old witch meant to order them to stand on the baker's peel, saying: "Stand on this peel, my little pets, that I may see you dance in the oven" but that they were to ask her to sit upon it herself first, that so they might learn the way to do it. The fay then went away. Shortly after they had met this good lady they found the old witch in the wood. They gathered together in bundles all the fire-sticks they had collected, and carried them home to heat the oven. When they had finished heating the oven, the old hag swept it carefully out, and then said to the little ones, "Sit here, my little darlings, on this peel, that I may see how prettily you dance in the oven!"

The children replied to the witch as the good fay had instructed them: "Sit you here, little granny, that we may first see you dance in the oven."

As the hag's intention was to bake the children, she sat on the peel first, so as to coax them to do the same after her; but the very moment the children saw her on the peel they thrust the peel into the oven with the witch upon it. The old hag gave a great start, and was burnt to a cinder immediately after. The children took possession of the shed and all it contained.

Two little children were lost in the forest where they met an old witch

The Buried Moon

Sometimes called *The Dead Moon* this unusual tale by Joseph Jacobs (1854–1916) has a mythological bent and was collected by Mrs. Balfour from the Lincolnshire Fens, England – where the marshes are a source of many strange legends. Indeed, the story may be evidence of moon worship and other such pagan goings-on!

Once upon a time the Carland was all bogs and water

Long ago, in my grandmother's time, the Carland was all in bogs, great pools of black water, and creeping trickles of green water, and squishy pools which squirted when you stepped on them.

Well, granny used to say how long before her time the Moon herself was once dead and buried in the marshes, and as she used to tell me, I'll tell you all about it.

The Moon up yonder shone and shone, just as she does now, and when she shone she lighted up the bog-pools, so that one could walk about almost as safe as in the day. But when she didn't shine, out came the Things that dwelt in the darkness and went about seeking to do evil and harm; Bogles and Crawling Horrors, all came out when the Moon didn't shine.

Well, the Moon heard of this, and being kind and good – as she surely is, shining for us in the night instead of taking her natural rest – she was main troubled. "I'll see for myself, I will," said she, "maybe it's not so bad as folks make out."

Sure enough, at the month's end down she stept, wrapped up in a black cloak, and a black hood over her yellow shining hair. Straight she went to the bog edge and looked about her. Water here and water there; waving tussocks and trembling pools, and great black snags all twisted and bent. Before her all was dark – dark but for the glimmer of the stars in the pools, and the light that came from her own white feet, stealing out of her black cloak.

The Moon drew her cloak faster about and trembled, but she wouldn't go back without seeing all there was to be seen; so on she went, stepping as light as the wind in summer from tuft to tuft between the greedy gurgling water holes. Just as she came near a big black pool her foot slipped and she was nigh tumbling in. She grabbed with both hands at a snag near by to steady herself with, but as she touched it, it twined itself round her wrists, like a pair of handcuffs, and gript her so that she couldn't move. She pulled and twisted and fought, but it was no good. She was fast, and must stay fast.

Presently as she stood trembling in the dark, wondering if help would come, she heard something calling in the distance, calling, calling, and then dying away with a sob, till the marshes were full of this pitiful crying sound; then she heard steps floundering along, squishing in the mud and slipping on the tufts, and through the darkness she saw a white face with great feared eyes.

'Twas a man strayed in the bogs. Mazed with fear he struggled on toward the flickering light that looked like help and safety. And when the poor Moon saw that he was coming nigher and nigher to the deep hole, further and further from the path, she was so mad and so sorry that she struggled and fought and pulled harder than ever. And though she couldn't get loose, she twisted and turned, till her black hood fell back off her shining yellow hair, and the beautiful light that came from it drove away the darkness.

Oh, but the man cried with joy to see the light again. And at once all evil things fled back into the dark corners, for they cannot abide the light. So he could see where he was, and where the path was, and how he could get out of the marsh. And he was in such haste to get away from the Quicks, and Bogles, and Things that dwelt there, that he scarce looked at the brave light that came from the beautiful shining yellow hair, streaming out over the black cloak and falling to the water at his feet. And the Moon herself was so taken up with saving him, and with rejoicing that he was back on the right path, that she clean forgot that she needed help herself, and that she was held fast by the Black Snag.

So off he went; spent and gasping, and stumbling and sobbing with joy, flying for his life out of the terrible bogs. Then it came over the Moon, she would most like to go with him. So she pulled and fought as if she were mad, till she fell on her knees, spent with tugging, at the foot of the

The moon shone and shone, just as she does now and lit up the bog-pools so people could walk safely

snag. And as she lay there, gasping for breath, the black hood fell forward over her head. So out went the blessed light and back came the darkness, with all its Evil Things, with a screech and a howl. They came crowding round her, mocking and snatching and beating; shrieking with rage and spite, and swearing and snarling, for they knew her for their old enemy, that drove them back into the corners, and kept them from working their wicked wills.

"Drat thee!" yelled the witch-bodies, "thou'st spoiled our spells this year agone!"

"And us thou sent'st to brood in the corners!" howled the Bogles.

And all the Things joined in with a great "Ho, ho!" till the very tussocks shook and the water gurgled. And they began again.

"We'll poison her – poison her!" shrieked the witches.

And "Ho, ho!" howled the Things again.

"We'll smother her – smother her!" whispered the Crawling Horrors, and twined themselves round her knees.

And "Ho, ho!" mocked the rest of them.

And again they all shouted with spite and ill-will. And the poor Moon crouched down, and wished she was dead and done with.

And they fought and squabbled what they should do with her, till a pale grey light began to come in the sky; and it drew nigh the dawning. And when they saw that, they were feared lest they shouldn't have time to work their

will; and they caught hold of her, with horrid bony fingers, and laid her deep in the water at the foot of the snag. And the Bogles fetched a strange big stone and rolled it on top of her, to keep her from rising. And they told two of the Will-o-the-wykes to take turns in watching on the black snag, to see that she lay safe and still, and couldn't get out to spoil their sport.

And there lay the poor Moon, dead and buried in the bog, till some one would set her loose; and who'd know where to look for her.

Well, the days passed, and 'twas the time for the new moon's coming, and the folk put pennies in their pockets and straws in their caps so as to be ready for her, and looked about, for the Moon was a good friend to the marsh folk, and they were main glad when the dark time was gone, and the paths were safe again, and the Evil Things were driven back by the blessed Light into the darkness and the waterholes.

But days and days passed, and the new Moon never came, and the nights were aye dark, and the Evil Things were worse than ever. And still the days went on, and the new Moon never came. Naturally the poor folk were strangely feared and mazed, and a lot of them went to the Wise Woman who dwelt in the old mill, and asked if so be she could find out where the Moon was gone.

"Well," said she, after looking in the brewpot, and in the mirror, and in the Book, "it be main queer, but I can't

The moon was caught by brambles that twined around her wrists

rightly tell ye what's happened to her. If ye hear of aught, come and tell me."

So they went their ways; and as days went by, and never a Moon came, naturally they talked – my word! I reckon they did talk! Their tongues wagged at home, and at the inn, and in the garth. But so came one day, as they sat on the great settle in the inn, a man from the far end of the bog lands was smoking and listening, when all at once he sat up and slapped his knee. "My faicks!" says he, "I'd clean forgot, but I reckon I kens where the Moon be!" and he told them of how he was lost in the bogs, and how, when he was nigh dead with fright, the light shone out, and he found the path and got home safe.

So off they all went to the Wise Woman, and told her about it, and she looked long in the pot and the Book again, and then she nodded her head.

"It's dark still, childer, dark!" says she, "and I can't rightly see, but do as I tell ye, and ye'll find out for yourselves. Go all of ye, just afore the night gathers, put a stone in your mouth, and take a hazel-twig in your hands, and say never a word till you're safe home again. Then walk on and fear not, far into the midst of the marsh, till ye find a coffin, a candle, and a cross. Then ye'll not be far from your Moon; look, and m'appen ye'll find her."

So came the next night in the darklings, out they went all together, every man with a stone in his mouth, and a hazel-twig in his hand, and feeling, thou may'st reckon, main feared and creepy. And they stumbled and stottered along the paths into the midst of the bogs; they saw nought, though they heard sighings and flutterings in their ears, and felt cold wet fingers touching them; but all at once, looking around for the coffin, the candle, and the cross, while they came nigh to the pool beside the great snag, where the Moon lay buried. And all at once they stopped, quaking and mazed and skeery, for there was the great stone, half in, half out of the water, for all the world like a strange big coffin; and at the head was the black snag, stretching out its two arms in a dark gruesome cross, and on it a tiddy light flickered, like a dying candle. And they all knelt down in the mud, and said, "Our Lord, first forward, because of the cross, and then backward, to keep off the Bogles; but without speaking out, for they knew that the Evil Things would catch them, if they didn't do as the Wise Woman told them."

Then they went nigher, and took hold of the big stone, and shoved it up, and afterwards they said that for one tiddy minute they saw a strange and beautiful face looking up at them glad-like out of the black water; but the Light came so quick and so white and shining, that they stept back mazed with it, and the very next minute, when they could see again, there was the full Moon in the sky, bright and beautiful and kind as ever, shining and smiling down at them, and making the bogs and the paths as clear as day, and stealing into the very corners, as though she'd have driven the darkness and the Bogles clean away if she could.

The Lion and the Crane

This is an Indian Hindu tale collected by Joseph Jacobs (1854–1916). This story describes a meeting between a Siberian crane and a lion in India. The crane frees a bone that has become stuck in the lion's mouth but is wise enough to be wary of the hungry lion, despite having helped him. It is similar in many ways to the Aesop fable of the wolf and the crane and in some versions the bird may be a heron, partridge or woodpecker.

The Bodhisatta was at one time born in the region of Himavanta as a white crane; now Brahmadatta was at that time reigning in Benares. Now it chanced that as a lion was eating meat a bone stuck in his throat. The throat became swollen, he could not take food, his suffering was terrible. The crane seeing him, as he was perched on a tree looking for food, asked, "What ails thee, friend?" He told him why. "I could free thee from that bone, friend, but dare not enter thy mouth for fear thou mightest eat me." "Don't be afraid, friend, I'll not eat thee; only save my life." "Very well," says he, and caused him to lie down on his left side. But thinking to himself, "Who knows what this fellow will do?" he placed a small stick upright between his two jaws that he could not close his mouth, and inserting his head inside his mouth struck one end of the bone with his beak. Whereupon the bone dropped and fell out. As soon as he had caused the bone to fall, he got out of the lion's mouth, striking the stick with his beak so that it fell out, and then settled on a branch. The lion gets well, and one day was eating a buffalo he had killed. The crane, thinking "I will sound him," settled on a branch just over him, and in conversation spoke this first verse:

"A service have we done thee
To the best of our ability,
King of the Beasts! Your Majesty!
What return shall we get from thee?"
In reply the Lion spoke the second verse:
"As I feed on blood,
And always hunt for prey,
'Tis much that thou art still alive
Having once been between my teeth."
Then in reply the crane said the two other verses:
"Ungrateful, doing no good,
Not doing as he would be done by,
In him there is no gratitude,
To serve him is useless.
His friendship is not won
By the clearest good deed.
Better softly withdraw from him,
Neither envying nor abusing."
And having thus spoken the crane flew away.

And when the great Teacher, Gautama the Buddha, told this tale, he used to add: "Now at that time the lion was Devadatta the Traitor, but the white crane was I myself."

The moral of this tale is that fierce beasts are not to be trusted and that life is not always fair!

Mermaids

Upon the shore a mermaid fair, with shimmering
seashells in her hair, whispers a secret from
the deep, and gently lulls me off to sleep.
Anon

Who would be
A mermaid fair,
Singing alone,
Combing her hair
Under the sea,
In a golden curl
With a comb of pearl,
On a throne?

I would be a mermaid fair;
I would sing to myself the whole of the day;
With a comb of pearl I would comb my hair;
"Who is it loves me? who loves not me?"

*From 'The Mermaid' by
Lord Alfred Tennyson (1809-1892)*

Thou rememb'rest
Since once I sat upon a promontory
And heard a mermaid, on a dolphin's back,
Uttering such dulcet and harmonious breath
That the rude sea grew civil at her song,
And certain stars shot madly from their spheres
To hear the sea-maid's music.

*From 'A Midsummer Night's Dream' by William
Shakespeare (1564–1616)*

Moonlight magic

In the fairy woods when the moonlight glows
The animals twirl, each up on their toes;
Fox fiddles a merry and magical tune
As the animals dance in the light of the moon.
All around they skip, like the pixies do,
Dreaming of wishes bound to come true
Bear bounces and laughs, the hares leap high,
Till stars grow dim and the dawn is nigh . . .
Then home they go, paws dimpling grass
Where dewdrops gleam like bubbles of glass.

Anon

Fontaine Fables
The Frog that Wished to be as Big as the Ox

The tenant of a bog,
An envious little frog,
Not bigger than an egg,
A stately bullock spies,
And, smitten with his size,
Attempts to be as big.
With earnestness and pains,
She stretches, swells, and strains,
And says, "Sister Frog, look here! see me!
Is this enough?" "No, no."

"Well, then, is this?" "Poh! poh!
Enough! you don't begin to be."
And thus the reptile sits,
Enlarging till she splits.
The world is full of folks
Of just such wisdom;—
The lordly dome provokes
The cit to build his dome;
And, really, there is no telling
How much great men set little ones a-swelling.

Fontaine Fables
The Fox and the Stork

Old Mister Fox was at expense, one day,
To dine old Mistress Stork.
The fare was light, was nothing, sooth to say,
Requiring knife and fork.
That sly old gentleman, the dinner-giver,
Was, you must understand, a frugal liver.
This once, at least, the total matter
Was thinnish soup served on a platter,
For madam's slender beak a fruitless puzzle,
Till all had passed the fox's lapping muzzle.
But, little relishing his laughter,
Old gossip Stork, some few days after,
Returned his Foxship's invitation.
Without a moment's hesitation,
He said he'd go, for he must own he
Never stood with friends for ceremony.
And so, precisely at the hour,

He hied him to the lady's bower;
Where, praising her politeness,
He finds her dinner right nice.
Its punctuality and plenty,
Its viands, cut in mouthfuls dainty,
Its fragrant smell, were powerful to excite,
Had there been need, his foxish appetite.
But now the dame, to torture him,
Such wit was in her,
Served up her dinner
In vases made so tall and slim,
They let their owner's beak pass in and out,
But not, by any means, the fox's snout!
All arts without avail,
With drooping head and tail,
As ought a fox a fowl had cheated,
The hungry guest at last retreated.

Fontaine Fables
The Wolf and the Fox in the Well

Jean de La Fontaine (1621–1695) was the most famous French writer of fables and one of the most widely read French poets from the 1600s. Possibly he meant his tales as an exploitation of ethics for an adult audience but his fables were soon regarded as providing an excellent education in morals for children and the first edition was dedicated to the six-year old Dauphin of France.

Why does Aesop give to the fox the reputation of excelling in all tricks of cunning? I have sought for a reason, but cannot find one. Does not the wolf, when he has need to defend his life or take that of another, display as much knowingness as the fox? I believe he knows more, and I dare, perhaps with some reason, to contradict my master in this particular.

Nevertheless, here is a case where undoubtedly all the honour fell to the dweller in burrows.

One evening a fox, who was as hungry as a dog, happened to see the round reflection of the moon in a well, and he believed it to be a fine cheese. There were two pails which alternately drew up the water. Into the uppermost of these the fox leapt, and his weight caused him to descend the well, where he at once discovered his mistake about the cheese. He became extremely worried and fancied his end approaching, for he could see no way to get up again but by some other hungry one, enticed by the same reflection, coming down in the same way that he had.

Two days passed without any one coming to the well. Time, which is always marching onward, had, during two nights, hollowed the outline of the silvery planet, and Reynard was in despair.

At last a wolf, parched with thirst, drew near, to whom the fox called from below, "Comrade, here is a treat for you! Do you see this? It is an exquisite cheese, made by Faunus from milk of the heifer Io. If Jupiter were ill and lost his appetite he would find it again by one taste of this. I have only eaten this piece out of it; the rest will be plenty for you. Come down in the pail up there. I put it there on purpose for you."

A rigmarole so cleverly told was easily believed by the fool of a wolf, who descended by his greater weight, which not only took him down, but brought the fox up.

We ought not to laugh at the wolf, for we often enough let ourselves be deluded with just as little cause. Everybody is ready to believe the thing he fears and the thing he desires.

The weight of the wolf took him down into the well

il faut considérer la

362

Fontaine Fables
The Grasshopper and the Ant

The fables of Jean de La Fontaine are both in straight text and in verse. This one tells the tale of an industrious ant and a happy-go-lucky grasshopper

The Grasshopper, singing

All summer long,
Now found winter stinging,
And ceased in his song.
Not a morsel or crumb in his cupboard–
So he shivered, and ceased in his song.

Miss Ant was his neighbor;
To her he went:
"O, you're rich from labor,
And I've not a cent.

Lend me some food, and I vow I'll return it,
Though at present I have not a cent."

The Ant's not a lender,
I must confess.
Her heart's far from tender
To one in distress.
So she said:
"Pray, how passed you the summer,
That in winter you come to distress?"

"I sang through the summer,"
Grasshopper said.
"But now I am glummer
Because I've no bread."
"So you sang!" sneered the Ant.
"That relieves me.
Now it's winter – go dance for your bread

The Lambikin

This traditional Indian tale involves a little lamb, a jackal, a vulture, a tiger, a wolf, an eagle and a Granny whose good intentions come to no avail.

Once upon a time there was a wee wee Lambikin, who frolicked about on his little tottery legs, and enjoyed himself amazingly.

Now one day he set off to visit his Granny, and was jumping with joy to think of all the good things he should get from her, when who should he meet but a Jackal, who looked at the tender young morsel and said: "Lambikin! Lambikin! I'll EAT YOU!"

But Lambikin only gave a little frisk, and said:

"To Granny's house I go,
Where I shall fatter grow,
Then you can eat me so."

The Jackal thought this reasonable, and let Lambikin pass.

By-and-by he met a Vulture, and the Vulture, looking hungrily at the tender morsel before him, said: "Lambikin! Lambikin! I'll EAT YOU!"

But Lambikin only gave a little frisk, and said:

"To Granny's house I go,
Where I shall fatter grow
Then you can eat me so."

The Vulture thought this reasonable, and let Lambikin pass.

And by-and-by he met a Tiger, and then a Wolf, and a Dog, and an Eagle; and all these, when they saw the tender little morsel, said: "Lambikin! Lambikin! I'll EAT YOU!"

But to all of them Lambikin replied, with a little frisk:

"To Granny's house I go,
Where I shall fatter grow,
Then you can eat me so."

At last he reached his Granny's house, and said, all in a great hurry, "Granny dear, I've promised to get very fat; so, as people ought to keep their promises, please put me into the corn-bin at once."

So his Granny said he was a good boy, and put him into the corn-bin, and there the greedy little Lambikin stayed for seven days, and ate, and ate, and ate, until he could scarcely waddle, and his Granny said he was fat enough for anything, and must go home. But cunning little Lambikin said that would never do, for some animal would be sure to eat him on the way back, he was so plump and tender.

"I'll tell you what you must do," said Master Lambikin; "you must make a little drumikin out of the skin of my little brother who died, and then I can sit inside and trundle along nicely, for I'm as tight as a drum myself.'

So his Granny made a nice little drumikin out of his brother's skin, with the wool inside, and Lambikin curled himself up snug and warm in the middle, and trundled away gaily. Soon he met with the Eagle, who called out:

"Drumikin! Drumikin!

Have you seen Lambikin?"

And Mr. Lambikin, curled up in his soft warm nest, replied:

"Fallen into the fire, and so will you

On little Drumikin. Tum-pa, tum-too!"

"How very annoying!" sighed the Eagle, thinking regretfully of the tender morsel he had let slip.

Meanwhile Lambikin trundled along, laughing to himself, and singing:

"Tum-pa, tum-too;
Tum-pa, tum-too!"

Every animal and bird he met asked him the same question:

"Drumikin! Drumikin!

Have you seen Lambikin?"

And to each of them the little slyboots replied:

"Fallen into the fire, and so will you

On little Drumikin. Tum-pa, tum-too;

Tum-pa, tum-too; Tum-pa, tum-too!"

Then they all sighed to think of the tender little morsel they had let slip.

At last the Jackal came limping along, for all his sorry looks as sharp as a needle, and he too called out:

"Drumikin! Drumikin!

Have you seen Lambikin?"

And Lambikin, curled up in his snug little nest, replied gaily:

"Fallen into the fire, and so will you

On little Drumikin! Tum-pa--"

But he never got any further, for the Jackal recognised his voice at once, and cried: "Hullo! you've turned yourself inside out, have you? Just you come out of that!"

Whereupon he tore open Drumikin and gobbled up Lambikin.

Snow-White and Rose-Red

The Brothers Grimm, Jacob (1785-1863) and Wilhelm (1786-1859) were born in Hanau, near Frankfurt, in the German state of Hesse. Their collection of over two hundred folk tales included this one. A shorter version called *The Ungrateful Dwarf* is probably the oldest variant of the tale, but the Grimm version remains the most popular.

There was once a poor widow who lived in a lonely cottage. In front of the cottage was a garden wherein stood two rose-trees, one of which bore white and the other red roses. She had two children who were like the two rose-trees, and one was called Snow-white, and the other Rose-red. They were as good and happy, as busy and cheerful as ever two children in the world were, only Snow-white was more quiet and gentle than Rose-red. Rose-red liked better to run about in the meadows and fields seeking flowers and catching butterflies; but Snow-white sat at home with her mother, and helped her with her housework, or read to her when there was nothing to do.

The two children were so fond of one another that they always held each other by the hand when they went out together, and when Snow-white said: "We will not leave each other," Rose-red answered: "Never so long as we live," and their mother would add: "What one has she must share with the other."

They often ran about the forest alone and gathered red berries, and no beasts did them any harm, but came close to them trustfully. The little hare would eat a cabbage-leaf out of their hands, the roe grazed by their side, the stag leapt merrily by them, and the birds sat still upon the boughs, and sang whatever they knew.

No mishap overtook them; if they had stayed too late in the forest, and night came on, they laid themselves down near one another upon the moss, and slept until morning came, and their mother knew this and did not worry on their account.

Once when they had spent the night in the wood and the dawn had roused them, they saw a beautiful child in a shining white dress sitting near their bed. He got up and looked quite kindly at them, but said nothing and went into the forest. And when they looked round they found that they had been sleeping quite close to a precipice, and would certainly have fallen into it in the darkness if they had gone only a few paces further. And their mother told them that it must have been the angel who watches over good children.

Snow-white and Rose-red kept their mother's little cottage so neat that it was a pleasure to look inside it. In the summer Rose-red took care of the house, and every morning laid a wreath of flowers by her mother's bed before she awoke, in which was a rose from each tree. In the winter Snow-white lit the fire and hung the kettle on the hob. The kettle was of brass and shone like gold, so brightly was it polished. In the evening, when the snowflakes fell, the mother said: "Go, Snow-white, and bolt the door," and then they sat round the hearth, and the mother took her spectacles and read aloud out of a large book, and the two girls listened as they sat and spun. And close by them lay a lamb upon the floor, and behind them upon a perch sat a white dove with its head hidden beneath its wings.

One evening, as they were thus sitting comfortably together, someone knocked at the door as if he wished to be let in. The mother said: "Quick, Rose-red, open the door, it must be a traveller who is seeking shelter." Rose-red went and pushed back the bolt, thinking that it was a poor man, but it was not; it was a bear that stretched his broad, black head within the door.

Rose-red screamed and sprang back, the lamb bleated, the dove fluttered, and Snow-white hid herself behind her mother's bed. But the bear began to speak and said: "Do not be afraid, I will do you no harm! I am half-frozen, and only want to warm myself a little beside you."

"Poor bear," said the mother, "lie down by the fire, only take care that you do not burn your coat." Then she cried: "Snow-white, Rose-red, come out, the bear will do you no harm, he means well." So they both came out, and by-and-by the lamb and dove came nearer, and were not afraid of him. The bear said: "Here, children, knock the snow out of my coat a little"; so they brought the broom and swept the bear's hide clean; and he stretched himself by the fire and growled contentedly and comfortably. It was not long before they grew quite at home, and played tricks with their clumsy guest. They tugged his hair with their hands, put their feet upon his back and rolled him about, or they took a hazel-switch and beat him, and when he growled they laughed. But the bear took it all in good part, only when they were too rough he called out:

"Leave me alive, children,
Snow-white, Rose-red,
 Will you beat your wooer dead?"

When it was bed-time, and the others went to bed, the mother said to the bear: "You can lie there by the hearth, and then you will be safe from the cold and the bad weather." As soon as day dawned the two children let him out, and he trotted across the snow into the forest.

Henceforth the bear came every evening at the same time, laid himself down by the hearth, and let the children amuse themselves with him as much as they liked; and

through; but now, when the sun has thawed and warmed the earth, they break through it, and come out to pry and steal; and what once gets into their hands, and in their caves, does not easily see daylight again."

Snow-white was quite sorry at his departure, and as she unbolted the door for him, and the bear was hurrying out, he caught against the bolt and a piece of his hairy coat was torn off, and it seemed to Snow-white as if she had seen

The dwarf was jumping up and down in the grass

they got so used to him that the doors were never fastened until their black friend had arrived.

When spring had come and all outside was green, the bear said one morning to Snow-white: "Now I must go away, and cannot come back for the whole summer." "Where are you going, then, dear bear?" asked Snow-white. "I must go into the forest and guard my treasures from the wicked dwarfs. In the winter, when the earth is frozen hard, they are obliged to stay below and cannot work their way

gold shining through it, but she was not sure about it. The bear ran away quickly, and was soon out of sight behind the trees.

A short time afterwards the mother sent her children into the forest to get firewood. There they found a big tree which lay felled on the ground, and close by the trunk something was jumping backwards and forwards in the grass, but they could not make out what it was. When they came nearer they saw a dwarf with an old withered face and a snow-white beard a yard long. The end of the beard was caught in a crevice of the tree, and the little fellow was jumping about like a dog tied to a rope, and did not know what to do.

The fierce-looking bear roared loudly

He glared at the girls with his fiery red eyes and cried: "Why do you stand there? Can you not come here and help me?" "What are you up to, little man?" asked Rose-red. "You stupid, prying goose!" answered the dwarf: "I was going to split the tree to get a little wood for cooking. The little bit of food that we people get is immediately burnt up with heavy logs; we do not swallow so much as you coarse, greedy folk. I had just driven the wedge safely in, and everything was going as I wished; but the cursed wedge was too smooth and suddenly sprang out, and the tree closed so quickly that I could not pull out my beautiful white beard; so now it is tight and I cannot get away, and the silly, sleek, milk-faced things laugh! Ugh! how odious you are!"

The children tried very hard, but they could not pull the beard out, it was caught too fast. "I will run and fetch someone," said Rose-red. "You senseless goose!" snarled the dwarf; "why should you fetch someone? You are already two too many for me; can you not think of something better?" "Don't be impatient," said Snow-white, "I will help you," and she pulled her scissors out of her pocket, and cut off the end of the beard.

As soon as the dwarf felt himself free he laid hold of a bag which lay amongst the roots of the tree, and which was full of gold, and lifted it up, grumbling to himself: "Uncouth people, to cut off a piece of my fine beard. Bad luck to you!" and then he swung the bag upon his back, and went off without even once looking at the children.

Some time afterwards Snow-white and Rose-red went to catch a dish of fish. As they came near the brook they saw something like a large grasshopper jumping towards the water, as if it were going to leap in. They ran to it and found it was the dwarf. "Where are you going?" said Rose-red; "you surely don't want to go into the water?" "I am not such a fool!" cried the dwarf; "don't you see that the accursed fish wants to pull me in?" The little man had been sitting there fishing, and unluckily the wind had tangled up his beard with the fishing-line; a moment later a big fish made a bite and the feeble creature had not strength to pull it out; the fish kept the upper hand and pulled the dwarf towards him. He held on to all the reeds and rushes, but it was of little good, for he was forced to follow the movements of the fish, and was in urgent danger of being dragged into the water.

The girls came just in time; they held him fast and tried to free his beard from the line, but all in vain, beard and line were entangled fast together. There was nothing to do but to bring out the scissors and cut the beard, whereby a small part of it was lost. When the dwarf saw that he screamed out: "Is that civil, you toadstool, to disfigure a man's face? Was it not enough to clip off the end of my

The children brushed the snow off the bear's back

beard? Now you have cut off the best part of it. I cannot let myself be seen by my people. I wish you had been made to run the soles off your shoes!" Then he took out a sack of pearls which lay in the rushes, and without another word he dragged it away and disappeared behind a stone.

It happened that soon afterwards the mother sent the two children to the town to buy needles and thread, and laces and ribbons. The road led them across a heath upon which huge pieces of rock lay strewn about. There they noticed a large bird hovering in the air, flying slowly round and round above them; it sank lower and lower, and at last settled near a rock not far away. Immediately they heard a loud, piteous cry. They ran up and saw with horror that the eagle had seized their old acquaintance the dwarf, and was going to carry him off.

The children, full of pity, at once took tight hold of the little man, and pulled against the eagle so long that at last he let his booty go. As soon as the dwarf had recovered from his first fright he cried with his shrill voice: "Could you not have done it more carefully! You dragged at my brown coat so that it is all torn and full of holes, you clumsy creatures!" Then he took up a sack full of precious stones, and slipped away again under the rock into his hole. The girls, who by this time were used to his ingratitude, went on their way and did their business in town.

As they crossed the heath again on their way home they surprised the dwarf, who had emptied out his bag of precious stones in a clean spot, and had not thought that anyone would come there so late. The evening sun shone upon the brilliant stones; they glittered and sparkled with all colours so beautifully that the children stood still and stared at them. "Why do you stand gaping there?" cried the dwarf, and his ashen-grey face became copper-red with rage. He was still cursing when a loud growling was heard, and a black bear came trotting towards them out of the forest. The dwarf sprang up in a fright, but he could not reach his cave, for the bear was already close. Then in the dread of his heart he cried: "Dear Mr. Bear, spare me, I will give you all my treasures; look, the beautiful jewels lying there! Grant me my life; what do you want with such a slender little fellow as I? you would not feel me between your teeth. Come, take these two wicked girls, they are tender morsels for you, fat as young quails; for mercy's sake eat them!" The bear took no heed of his words, but gave the wicked creature a single blow with his paw, and he did not move again.

The girls had run away, but the bear called to them: "Snow-white and Rose-red, do not be afraid; wait, I will come with you." Then they recognized his voice and waited, and when he came up to them suddenly his bearskin fell off, and he stood there a handsome man, clothed all in gold. "I am a king's son," he said, "and I was bewitched by that wicked dwarf, who had stolen my treasures; I have had to run about the forest as a savage bear until I was freed by his death. Now he has got his well-deserved punishment.

Snow-white was married to him, and Rose-red to his

brother, and they divided between them the great treasure which the dwarf had gathered together in his cave. The old mother lived peacefully and happily with her children for many years. She took the two rose-trees with her, and they stood before her window, and every year bore the most beautiful roses, white and red.

If they had stayed too late in the forest, and night came on, they laid themselves down near one another upon the moss, and slept safely until morning came

From a Railway Carriage

Published 1885 this poem is by Robert Louis Stevenson (1850–1894), the Scottish novelist, poet, essayist and travel writer. It begins with: "faster than fairies, faster than witches' and captures the joy of seeing glimpses of a world just out of reach, "Each a glimpse and gone forever" – just like magic!

Faster than fairies, faster than witches,
Bridges and houses, hedges and ditches;
And charging along like troops in a battle
All through the meadows the horses and cattle:
All of the sights of the hill and the plain
Fly as thick as driving rain;
And ever again, in the wink of an eye,
Painted stations whistle by.
Here is a child who clambers and scrambles,
All by himself and gathering brambles;
Here is a tramp who stands and gazes;
And here is the green for stringing the daisies!
Here is a cart runaway in the road
Lumping along with man and load;
And here is a mill, and there is a river:
Each a glimpse and gone forever!

Jack and his golden snuff-box

This gypsy fairy tale was collected by Joseph Jacobs (1854–1916). Parts of the tale might remind readers of Aladdin: there are little men who help as the genie did and a magically created castle plus a wish-giving snuffbox (equivalent to the lamp) that is stolen but regained. The tale is told with wry humour, adding to the fun.

Once upon a time, and a very good time it was, though it was neither in my time nor in your time nor in anyone else's time, there was an old man and an old woman, and they had one son, and they lived in a great forest. And their son never saw any other people in his life, but he knew that there were some more in the world besides his own father and mother, because he had lots of books, and he used to read every day about them. And when he read about charming princesses, he would go wild to see some of them; till one day, when his father was out cutting wood, he told his mother that he wished to go away to look for his living in some other country, and to see some other people beside them two. And he said: "I see nothing at all here but great trees around me; and if I stay here, maybe I shall go mad before I see anything." The young man's father was out all the time when this talk was going on between him and his poor old mother.

The old woman began by saying to her son before leaving: "Well, well, my poor boy, if you want to go, it's better for you to go, and God be with you." – (The old woman thought for the best when she said that.) – "But stop for a bit before you go. Which would you like best for me to make you, a little cake and bless you, or a big cake and curse you?"

"Dear, dear!" said he, "make me a big cake. Maybe I shall be hungry on the road." The old woman made the big cake, and she went to the top of the house, and she cursed him as far as she could see him.

He presently met with his father, and the old man said to him: "Where are you going, my poor boy?" when the son told the father the same tale as he told his mother. "Well," said his father, "I'm sorry to see you going away, but if you've made up your mind to go, it's better for you to go."

The poor lad had not gone far, when his father called him back; then the old man drew out of his pocket a golden snuff-box, and said to him: "Here, take this little box, and put it in your pocket, and be sure not to open it till you are near your death." And away went poor Jack upon his road, and walked till he was tired and hungry, for he had eaten all his cake upon the road; and by this time night was upon him, so he could hardly see his way before him. He could see some light a long way before him, and he made up to it, and found the back door and knocked at it, till one of the maid-servants came and asked him what he wanted. He said that night was on him, and he wanted to get some place to sleep. The maid-servant called him in to the fire, and gave him plenty to eat, good meat and bread and beer; and as he was eating his food by the fire, there came the young lady to look at him, and she loved him well and he loved her. And the young lady ran to tell her father, and said there was

The magical golden snuff box

a pretty young man in the back kitchen; and immediately the gentleman came to him, and questioned him, and asked what work he could do. Jack said, the silly fellow, that he could do anything. (He meant that he could do any foolish bit of work, that would be wanted about the house.)

"Well," says the gentleman to him, "if you can do anything, at eight o'clock in the morning I must have a great lake and some of the largest man-of-war vessels sailing before my mansion, and one of the largest vessels must fire a royal salute, and the last round must break the leg of the bed where my young daughter is sleeping. And if you don't do that, you will have to forfeit your life."

"All right," said Jack; and away he went to his bed, and said his prayers quietly, and slept till it was near eight o'clock, and he had hardly any time to think what he was to do, till all of a sudden he remembered about the little golden box that his father gave him. And he said to himself:

"Well, well, I never was so near my death as I am now"; and then he felt in his pocket, and drew the little box out. And when he opened it, out there hopped three little red men, and asked Jack: "What is your will with us?"

"Well," said Jack, "I want a great lake and some of the largest man-of-war vessels in the world before this mansion, and one of the largest vessels to fire a royal salute, and the last round to break one of the legs of the bed where this young lady is sleeping."

"All right," said the little men; "Go to sleep."

Jack had hardly time to bring the words out of his mouth, to tell the little men what to do, but what it struck eight o'clock, when Bang, Bang! went one of the largest man-of-war vessels; and it made Jack jump out of bed to look through the window; and I can assure you it was a wonderful sight for him to see, after being so long with his father and mother living in a wood.

By this time Jack dressed himself, and said his prayers, and came down laughing; for he was proud, he was, because the thing was done so well. The gentleman comes

Three little men popped out of the snuff box

to him, and says to him: "Well, my young man, I must say that you are very clever indeed. Come and have some breakfast." And the gentleman tells him, "Now there are two more things you have to do, and then you shall have my daughter in marriage." Jack took his breakfast, and had a good look at the young lady, and also she at him.

The other thing that the gentleman told him to do was to fell all the great trees for miles around by eight o'clock in the morning; and, to make my long story short, it was done, and it pleased the gentleman well. The gentleman said to him: "The other thing you have to do" – (and it was the last thing) – "you must get me a great castle standing on twelve golden pillars; and there must come regiments of soldiers and go through their drill. At eight o'clock the

commanding officer must say, "Shoulder up."

"All right," said Jack; when the third and last morning came the third great feat was finished, and he had the young daughter in marriage. But, oh dear! there was worse to come yet.

The gentleman now made a large hunting party, and invited all the gentlemen around the country to it, and to see the castle as well. And by this time Jack had a beautiful horse and a scarlet dress to go with them. On that morning his valet, when putting; clothes by, after changing them to go a-hunting, put his hand in one of Jack's waistcoat pockets, and pulled out the little golden snuff-box poor Jack had left behind by mistake. And that man opened the little box, and there hopped out the three little red men, and asked him what he wanted with them. "Well," said the valet to them, "I want this castle to be moved from this place far and far across the sea."

"All right," said the little red men to him: "do you wish to go with it?"

"Yes," said he.

"Well, get up," said they to him; and away they went far and far over the great sea.

Now the grand hunting party came back, and the castle upon the twelve golden pillars had disappeared, to the great disappointment of those gentlemen who did not see it before. Poor silly Jack was threatened to have his beautiful young wife taken from him, for deceiving them as he did. But the gentleman at last made an agreement with him, and he was to have a twelvemonths and a day to look for it; and off he went with a good horse and money in his pocket.

So off poor Jack starts in search of his missing castle, over hills, dales, valleys, and mountains, through woolly woods and sheepwalks, further than I can tell you or ever intend to tell you. Until at last he comes up to the place where lives the king of all the little mice in the world. There was one of the little mice on sentry at the front gate going up to the palace, and he did try to stop Jack from going in. Jack asked the little mouse: "Where does the king live? I should like to see him." This one sent another with him to show him the place; and when the king saw him, he called him in. And the king questioned him, and asked him where he was going that way. Well, Jack told him all the truth, that he had lost the great castle, and was going to look for it, and he had a whole twelvemonths and a day to find it out. And Jack asked him whether he knew anything about it, and the king said: "No, but I am the king of all the little mice in the world, and I will call them all up in the morning, and maybe they have seen something of it."

Then Jack got a good meal and bed, and in the morning he and the king went on to the fields: and the king called

Jack flew along and reached a beautiful castle

all the mice together, and asked them whether they had seen the great beautiful castle standing on golden pillars. And all the little mice said, No, there was none of them had seen it. The old king said to him that he had two other brothers: "One is the king of all the frogs; and my other brother, who is the oldest, he is the king of all the birds in the world. And if you go there, maybe they know something about the missing castle." The king said to him: "Leave your horse here with me till you come back, and take one of my best horses under you, and give this cake to

my brother; he will know then who you got it from. Mind and tell him I am well, and should like dearly to see him." And then the king and Jack shook hands together.

And when Jack was going through the gates, the little mouse asked him, should he go with him; and Jack said to him: "No, I shall get myself into trouble with the king." And the little thing told him: "It will be better for you to let me go with you; maybe I shall do some good to you sometime without you knowing it."

"Jump up, then." And the little mouse ran up the horse's leg,

The king of the mice promised to help Jack

Jack's adventures took him to many exciting places: he flew through the air and sailed across many a sea

and made it dance; and Jack put the mouse in his pocket.

Now Jack, after wishing good morning to the king and pocketing the little mouse which was on sentry, trudged on his way; and such a long way he had to go and this was his first day. At last he found the place; and there was one of the frogs on sentry, and gun upon his shoulder, and he did try to hinder Jack from going in; but when Jack said to him that he wanted to see the king, he allowed him to pass; and Jack made up to the door. The king came out, and asked him his business; and Jack told him all from beginning to end. "Well, well, come in." He got good entertainment that night; and in the morning the king made such a funny sound, and collected all the frogs in the world. And he asked them, did they know or see anything of a castle that stood upon twelve golden pillars; and they all made a curious sound, Kro-kro, kro-kro, and said, No.

Jack had to take another horse, and a cake to this king's brother, who is the king of all the fowls of the air; and as Jack was going through the gates, the little frog that was on sentry asked him should he go with him. Jack refused him for a bit; but at last he told him to jump up, and Jack put him in his other waistcoat pocket. And away he went again on his great long journey; it was three times as long this time as it was the first day; however, he found the place, and there was a fine bird on sentry. And Jack passed him, and he never said a word to him: and he talked with the king, and told him everything, all about the castle. "Well," said the king to him, "you shall know in the morning from my birds whether they know anything or not."

Jack put up his horse in the stable, and then went to bed, after having something to eat. And when he got up in the morning the king and he went on to the fields, and there

the king made some funny noises, and there came all the fowls that there were in the world. And the king asked them: "Did they see a fine castle?" and all the birds answered,

Out came Jack's young wife to meet him with a fine, jolly, bonny, young son

No. "Well," said the king, "where is the great bird?" They had to wait then for a long time for the eagle to make his appearance, when at last he came all in a perspiration, after two little birds had been sent high up in the sky to whistle on him to make all the haste he possibly could. The king asked the great bird, Did he see the great castle? and the bird said: "Yes, I came from there where it now is."

"Well," said the king to him, "this gentleman has lost it, and you must go with him back to it; but stop till you get a bit of something to eat first."

They killed a calf, and sent the best part of it to feed the eagle on his journey over the seas, and he had to carry Jack on his back. Now when they came in sight of the castle, they did not know what to do to get the little golden box. Well, the little mouse said to them: "Leave me down, and I will get the little box for you." So the mouse stole into the castle, and got hold of the box; and when he was coming down the stairs, it fell down, and he was very near being caught. He came running out with it, laughing his best. "Have you got it?" Jack said to him. He said: "Yes"; and off they went back again, and left the castle behind.

As they were all of them (Jack, mouse, frog and eagle) passing over the great sea, they fell to quarrelling about which it was that got the little box, till down it slipped into the water. (It was by their looking at it and handing it from one hand to the other that they dropped the little box to the bottom of the sea.) "Well, well," said the frog, "I knew that I would have to do something, so you had better let me go down in the water." And they let him go, and he was down for three days and three nights; and up he comes, and shows his nose and little mouth out of the water; and all of them asked him, Did he get it? and he told them, No. "Well, what are you doing there, then?" "Nothing at all," he said, "only I want my full breath"; and the poor little frog went down the second time, and he was down for a day and a night, and up he brings it.

And away they did go, after being there four days and nights; and after a long tug over seas and mountains, arrived at the palace of the old king, who is the master of all the birds in the world. And the king was very proud to see them, and had a hearty welcome and a long conversation. Jack opened the little box, and "told the men to go back and to bring the castle here to them, "and all of you make as much haste back again as you possibly can".

The three little men went off; and when they came near the castle they were afraid to go to it till the gentleman and lady and all the servants were gone out to some dance. And there was no one left behind there, only the cook and another maid with her; and the little red men asked them which would they rather – go, or stop behind? and they both said: "I will go with you"; and the little men told them to run upstairs quick. They were no sooner up and in one of the drawing-rooms than there came just in sight the gentleman and lady and all the servants; but it was too late. Off the castle went at full speed, with the women laughing at them through the window, while they made motions for them to stop, but all to no purpose.

They were nine days on their journey, in which they did try to keep the Sunday holy, when one of the little men turned to be the priest, the other the clerk, and third preside at the organ, and the women were the singers, for they had a grand chapel in the castle already. Strange to say, there was a discord made in the music, and one of the little men ran up one of the organ-pipes to see where the bad sound came from, when he found out it only happened to be that the two women were laughing at the little red man stretching his little legs full length on the bass pipes, also his two arms the same time, with his little red nightcap, which he never forgot to wear, a sight they never witnessed before, and which could not help making them laugh long and loud and heartily. And poor things! through their not going on with what they begun, they very near came to danger, as the castle was once all but sinking in the middle of the sea.

At length, after a merry journey, they came again to Jack and the king. The king was quite struck with the sight of the castle; and going up the golden stairs, went to see the inside.

The king was very much pleased with the castle, but poor Jack's time of twelvemonths and a day was drawing to a close; and he, wishing to go home to his young wife, gave orders to the three little men to get ready by the next morning at eight o'clock to be off to the next brother, and to stop there for one night; also to proceed from there to the last or the youngest brother, the master of all the mice in the world, in such place where the castle should be left under his care until it's sent for. Jack took a farewell of the king, thanking him very much for his hospitality.

Away went Jack and his castle again, and stopped one night in that place; and away they went again to the third king, and there they left the castle under his care. As Jack had to leave the castle behind, he had to take his own horse, which he left there when he first started.

So our poor Jack leaves his castle behind and faces towards home; and after having so much merriment with the three brothers every night Jack became sleepy on horseback, and would have lost the road if it was not for the little men a-guiding him. At last he arrived weary and tired, and they did not seem to receive him with any kindness whatever, because he had not found the stolen castle; and to make it worse, he was disappointed in not seeing his young and beautiful wife come out to meet him, hindered as she was by her parents. But that did not stop long. Jack put full power on and set off with the three little men to bring on the castle, and they soon got there.

Jack shook hands with the king, and returned many thanks for his kingly kindness in minding the castle for him; and then Jack instructed the little men to spur up and put speed on. And off they went, and were not long before they reached their journey's end, when out comes the young wife to meet him with a fine jolly, bonny young son, and they all lived happy ever afterwards

Good Little Henry

day the poor mother fell sick. They knew no doctor and besides they had no money to pay for one. Poor Henry did not know how to cure her. He brought her fresh cool water for he had nothing else to give her, he stayed by her night and day and ate his little morsel of dry bread at the foot of her bed. When she slept he looked at her sadly and wept. The sickness increased from day to day and at last the poor woman was almost in a dying condition. She could neither speak nor swallow and she no longer knew her little Henry, who was sobbing on his knees near her bed. In his despair, he cried out: "Fairy Bienfaisante, come to my help! Save my mother!"

Henry had scarcely pronounced these words, when a window opened and a lady richly dressed entered and in a

Henry resolved to ascend a mountain so dangerous that none who attempted it ever reached the summit

The Poor Sick Mother

There was a poor woman, a widow, who lived alone with her little son Henry. She loved him tenderly and she had good reason to do so, for no one had ever seen a more charming child. Although he was but seven years old, he kept the house while his good mother labored diligently and then left home to sell her work and buy food for herself and her little Henry. He swept, he washed the floor, he cooked, he dug and cultivated the garden and when all this was done he seated himself to mend his clothes or his mother's shoes and to make stools and tables – in short, to do everything his strength would enable him to do.

The house in which they lived belonged to them, but it was very lonesome. In front of their dwelling there was a lofty mountain so high that no one had ever ascended to its summit, and besides it was surrounded by a rushing torrent, by high walls and insurmountable precipices.

The mother and her little boy were happy but alas! one

soft voice, said to him: "What do you wish of me, my little friend? You called me – here I am!"

"Madam," cried Henry, throwing himself on his knees and clasping his hands, "if you are the fairy Bienfaisante, save my poor mother who is about to die and leave me alone in the world."

The good fairy looked at Henry most compassionately and then, without saying a word, she approached the poor woman, bent over her, examined her attentively, breathed upon her and said: "It is not in my power, my poor child, to cure your mother; her life depends upon you alone, if you have the courage to undertake the journey I will point out to you."

"Speak, madam! I entreat you to speak! there is nothing I will not undertake to save the life of my dear mother."

The fairy replied, "You must go and seek the plant of life, which grows on top of the mountain that you see from this window. When you have obtained this plant, press its juice into the mouth of your mother and she will be immediately restored to health."

"I will start out immediately, madam. But who will take care of my poor mother during my absence? And, moreover," said he, sobbing bitterly, "she will be dead before my return."

"Do not worry, my dear child. If you go to seek the plant of life, your mother will need nothing before your return; she will remain precisely in the condition in which you leave her. But you must dare many dangers and endure many things before you pluck the plant of life. Great courage and great perseverance are necessary on your part."

"I fear nothing, madam, my courage and perseverance shall not fail. Tell me only how I shall know this plant amongst all the others which cover the top of the mountain."

"When you reach the summit, call the doctor who has charge of this plant, inform him that I have sent you and he will give you a branch of the plant of life."

Henry kissed the good fairy's hands and thanked her heartily, took a sorrowful leave of his mother, covering her with kisses, put some bread in his pocket and set out, after saluting the fairy respectfully.

The fairy smiled encouragingly at this poor child who so bravely resolved to ascend a mountain so dangerous that none of those who had attempted it had ever reached the summit.

Little Henry marched resolutely onwards and has many adventures along the way.

The Vintage

Henry began to walk rapidly and perceived with great delight that every step brought him nearer to the summit of the mountain. In three hours he had walked two-thirds of the way. But suddenly he found himself arrested by a very high wall which he had not perceived before. He walked around it, and found, after three days' diligent advance, that this wall surrounded the entire mountain and that there was no door, not the smallest opening by which he could enter.

Henry seated himself on the ground, to reflect upon his situation. He resolved to wait patiently—he sat there forty-five days. At the end of this time he said:

"I will not go back if I have to wait here a hundred years."

He had scarcely uttered these words when a part of the wall crumbled away with a terrible noise and he saw in the opening a giant, brandishing an enormous cudgel.

"You have then a great desire to pass here, my boy? What are you seeking beyond my wall?"

"I am seeking the plant of life, Master Giant, to cure my poor mother who is dying. If it is in your power and you will allow me to pass this wall, I will do anything for you that you may command."

"Is it so? Well, listen! Your countenance pleases me. I am one of the genii of this mountain. I will allow you to pass this wall if you will fill my wine-cellar. Here are all my

vines. Gather the grapes, crush them, put the juice in the casks and arrange them well in my wine-cellar. You will find all the implements necessary at the foot of this wall. When it is done, call me."

The Giant disappeared, closing the wall behind him. Henry looked around him and as far as he could see, the vines of the Giant were growing luxuriously.

A part of the wall crumbled away with a terrible noise and he saw in the opening a giant

"Well, well," said Henry to himself, "I cut all the wheat of the little old man—I can surely also gather the grapes of the big Giant. It will not take me so long and it will not be as difficult to make wine of these grapes as to make bread of the wheat."

Henry took off his coat, picked up a pruning-knife which he saw at his feet and began to cut the grapes and throw them into the vats. It took him thirty days to gather this crop. When all was finished, he crushed the grapes, poured the juice into the casks and ranged them in the cellar, which they completely filled. He was ninety days making the wine.

When the wine was ready and everything in the cellar in complete order, Henry called the Giant who immediately appeared, examined the casks, tasted the wine, then turned towards Henry and said:

"You are a brave little man and I wish to pay you for your trouble. It shall not be said that you worked gratis for the Giant of the mountain."

He drew a thistle from his pocket, gave it to Henry and said: "After your return home, whenever you desire anything, smell this thistle."

Henry did not think the Giant very generous but he received the thistle with an amiable smile.

Then the Giant whistled so loudly that the mountain trembled and the wall and Giant disappeared entirely and Henry was enabled to continue his journey.

The Chase

Henry was within a half-hour's walk of the summit of the mountain when he reached a pit so wide that he could not possibly jump to the other side and so deep that it seemed bottomless. Henry did not lose courage, however. He followed the borders of the pit till he found himself where he started from and knew that this yawning pit surrounded the mountain.

"Alas! What shall I do?" said poor Henry; "I scarcely overcome one obstacle when another more difficult seems to rise up before me. How shall I ever pass this pit?"

The poor child felt for the first time that his eyes were

Henry sprang upon the Wolf's back

filled with tears. He looked around for some means of passing over but saw no possible chance and seated himself sadly on the brink of the precipice. Suddenly he heard a terrible growl. He turned and saw within ten steps of him an enormous Wolf gazing at him with flaming eyes.

"What are you seeking in my kingdom?" said the Wolf, in a threatening voice.

"Master Wolf, I am seeking the plant of life which alone can save my dear mother who is about to die. If you will assist me to cross this pit, I will be your devoted servant and will obey any command you may give me."

"Well, my boy, if you will catch all the game which is in my forests, birds and beasts, and make them up into pies

and nice roasts, by the faith of the genius of the mountain, I will pass you over to the other side. You will find near this tree all the instruments necessary to catch the game and to cook it. When your work is done, call me."

Saying these words, he disappeared.

Henry took courage. He lifted a bow and arrow which he saw on the ground, and began to shoot at the partridges, woodcocks, pheasants and game of all kinds which abounded there. But, alas! He did not understand it and killed nothing.

During eight days he was shooting right and left in vain and was at last wearied and despairing, when he saw near him the Crow whose life he had saved in the commencement of his journey.

"You rescued me from mortal danger," said the Crow, "and I told you I should see you again. I have come to redeem my promise. If you do not fulfil your promise to the Wolf, he will change you into some terrible wild beast. Follow me. I am going a-hunting and you have only to gather the game and cook it."

Saying these words, the Crow flew above the trees of the forest and with his beak and his claws killed all the game to be found. In fact, during one hundred and fifty days he caught one million eight hundred and sixty thousand seven hundred and twenty-six animals and birds, squirrels, moor-cocks, pheasants, and quails. As the Crow killed them, Henry plucked the feathers, skinned them, cut them up and cooked them in roasts or pies. When all was cooked he arranged them neatly and then the Crow said to him:

"Adieu, Henry. There remains one obstacle yet to overcome but in that difficulty I cannot aid you. But do not be discouraged. The good fairies protect filial love."

Before Henry had time to thank the Crow, he had disappeared. He then called the Wolf and said to him: "Master Wolf, here is all the game of your forest. I have prepared it as you ordered and now will you assist me to pass this precipice?"

The Wolf examined a pheasant, crunched a roast squirrel and a pie, licked his lips and said to Henry: "You are a brave and good boy. I will pay you for your trouble. It shall not be said that you have worked for the Wolf of the mountain without receiving your reward."

Saying these words, he gave Henry a staff which he cut in the forest and said to him: "When you have gathered the plant of life and wish yourself transported to any part of the world, mount the stick and it will be your horse."

Henry was on the point of throwing this useless stick into the woods but he wished to be polite, and receiving it smilingly, he thanked the Wolf cordially.

"Get on my back, Henry," said the Wolf.

Henry sprang upon the Wolf's back and he made a bound so prodigious that they landed immediately on the other side of the precipice.

Henry dismounted, thanked the Wolf and walked on vigorously.

The Fishing

At last, after so many labors and perils, Henry saw the lattice of the garden in which the plant of life was growing and his heart bounded for joy. He looked always upward as he walked, and went on as rapidly as his strength would permit, when suddenly he fell into a hole. He sprang backwards, looked anxiously around him and saw a ditch full of water, large and long, so long indeed that he could not see either end.

"Without doubt this is that last obstacle of which the Crow spoke to me," said Henry to himself. "Since I have overcome all my other difficulties with the help of the good fairy Bienfaisante, she will assist me to surmount this also. It was surely she who sent me the Cock, the Crow and the Old Man, the Giant and the Wolf. I will wait patiently till it shall please her to assist me this time."

On saying these words, Henry began to walk along the ditch, hoping to find the end. He walked on steadily two days and found himself at the end of that time just where he had started. Henry would not give way to distress, he would not be discouraged; he seated himself on the borders of the ditch and said: "I will not move from this spot till the genius of the mountain allows me to pass this ditch."

Henry had just uttered these words when an enormous Cat appeared before him and began to mew so horribly that he was almost deafened by the sound. The Cat said to him: "What are you doing here? Do you not know that I could tear you to pieces with one stroke of my claws?"

"I do not doubt your power, Mr. Cat, but you will not do so when you know that I am seeking the plant of life to save my poor mother who is dying. If you will permit me to pass your ditch, I will do anything in my power to please you."

"Will you?" said the Cat. "Well, then, listen; your countenance pleases me. If, therefore, you will catch all the fish in this ditch and salt and cook them, I will pass you over to the other side, on the faith of a Cat!"

Henry advanced some steps and saw lines, fish-hooks, bait, and nets on the ground. He took a net, and hoped that by one vigorous haul he would take many fish and that he would succeed much better than with a line and hook. He threw the net and drew it in with great caution. But alas! he had caught nothing!

Disappointed, Henry thought he had not been adroit. He threw the net again and drew it very softly: still nothing!

Henry was patient. For ten days he tried faithfully without having caught a single fish. Then he gave up the net and tried the hook and line. He waited an hour, two hours;– not a single fish bit at the bait! He moved from place to place, till he had gone entirely around the ditch. He tried diligently fifteen days and caught not a single fish. He knew not now what to do. He thought of the good fairy Bienfaisante, who had abandoned him at the end of his undertaking. He seated himself sadly and gazed intently

at the ditch when suddenly the water began to boil and he saw the head of a Frog appear.

"Henry," said the Frog, "you saved my life – I wish now to save yours in return. If you do not execute the orders of the Cat of the mountain he will eat you for his breakfast. You cannot catch the fish because the water is so deep and they take refuge at the bottom. But allow me to act for you. Light your fire for cooking and prepare your vessels

*Henry saw that the waves were
agitated and boiling up*

for salting. I will bring you the fish."

Saying these words, the Frog plunged back into the water. Henry saw that the waves were agitated and boiling up, as if a grand contest was going on at the bottom of the ditch. In a moment, however, the Frog reappeared, sprang ashore and deposited a superb salmon which he had caught. Henry had scarcely time to seize the salmon when the Frog leaped ashore with a carp. During sixty days the Frog continued his labors. Henry cooked the large fish and threw the little ones into the casks to be salted. Finally, at the end of two months, the Frog leaped towards Henry and said:

"There is not now a single fish in the ditch. You can call the Cat of the mountain."

Henry thanked the Frog heartily, who extended his wet foot towards him, in sign of friendship. Henry pressed it affectionately and gratefully and the Frog disappeared.

It took Henry fifteen days to arrange properly all the large fish he had cooked and all the casks of small fish he had salted. He then called the Cat, who appeared immediately.

"Mr. Cat," said Henry, "Here are all your fish cooked and salted. Will you now keep your promise and pass me over to the other side?"

The Cat examined the fish and the casks; tasted a salted

and a cooked fish, licked his lips, smiled and said to Henry: "You are a brave boy! I will recompense your fortitude and patience. It shall never be said that the Cat of the mountain does not pay his servants."

Saying these words, the Cat tore off one of his own claws and said, handing it to Henry: "When you are sick or feel yourself growing old, touch your forehead with this claw. Sickness, suffering and old age will disappear. This miraculous claw will have the same virtue for all that you love and all who love you."

Henry thanked the Cat most warmly, took the precious claw and wished to try its powers immediately, as he felt painfully weary. The claw had scarcely touched his brow when he felt as fresh and vigorous as if he had just left his bed.

The Cat looked on smiling, and said: "Now get on my tail."

Henry obeyed. He was no sooner seated on the Cat's tail than he saw the tail lengthen itself till it reached across the ditch.

The plant of life

When he had saluted the Cat respectfully, Henry ran towards the garden of the plant of life, which was only a hundred steps from him. He trembled lest some new obstacle should retard him but he reached the garden lattice without any difficulty. He sought the gate and found it readily, as the garden was not large. But, alas! the garden was filled with innumerable plants utterly unknown to him and it was impossible to know how to distinguish the plant of life. Happily he remembered that the good fairy Bienfaisante had told him that when he reached the summit of the mountain he must call the Doctor who cultivated the garden of the fairies. He called him then with a loud voice. In a moment he heard a noise among the plants near him and saw issue from them a little man, no taller than a hearth brush. He had a book under his arm, spectacles on his crooked little nose and wore the great black cloak of a doctor.

What are you seeking, little one?" said the Doctor; "and how is it possible that you have gained this summit?"

"Doctor, I come from the fairy Bienfaisante, to ask the plant of life to cure my poor sick mother, who is about to die."

"All those who come from the fairy Bienfaisante," said the little Doctor, raising his hat respectfully, "are most welcome. Come, my boy, I will give you the plant you seek."

The Doctor then buried himself in the botanical garden where Henry had some trouble in following him, as he was so small as to disappear entirely among the plants. At last they arrived near a bush growing by itself. The Doctor drew a little pruning-knife from his pocket, cut a bunch and gave it to Henry, saying: "Take this and use it as the good fairy Bienfaisante directed but do not allow it to leave your hands. If you lay it down under any circumstances it will escape from you and you will never recover it."

Henry was about to thank him but the little man had disappeared in the midst of his medicinal herbs, and he found himself alone.

"What shall I do now in order to arrive quickly at home? If I encounter on my return the same obstacles which met me as I came up the mountain, I shall perhaps lose my plant, my dear plant, which should restore my dear mother to life."

Happily Henry now remembered the stick which the Wolf had given him.

"Well, let us see," said he, "if this stick has really the power to carry me home."

Saying this, he mounted the stick and wished himself at home. In the same moment he felt himself raised in the air, through which he passed with the rapidity of lightning and found himself almost instantly by his mother's bed.

Henry sprang to his mother and embraced her tenderly. But she neither saw nor heard him. He lost no time, but pressed the plant of life upon her lips. At the same moment she opened her eyes, threw her arms around Henry's neck and exclaimed: "My child! My dear Henry! I have been very sick but now I feel almost well. I am hungry."

Then, looking at him in amazement, she said: "How you have grown, my darling! How is this? How can you have changed so in a few days?"

Henry had indeed grown a head taller. Two years, seven months and six days had passed away since he left his home. He was now nearly ten years old. Before he had time to answer, the window opened and the good fairy Bienfaisante appeared. She embraced Henry and, approaching the couch of his mother, related to her all that little Henry had done and suffered, the dangers he had dared, the fatigues he endured; the courage, the patience, the goodness he had manifested. Henry blushed on hearing himself thus praised by the fairy. His mother pressed him to her heart, and covered him with kisses. After the first moments of happiness and emotion had passed away, the fairy said: "Now, Henry, you can make use of the present of the little Old Man and the Giant of the mountain."

Henry drew out his little box and opened it. Immediately there issued from it a crowd of little workmen, not larger than bees, who filled the room. They began to work with such promptitude that in a quarter of an hour they had built and furnished a beautiful house in the midst of a lovely garden with a thick wood on one side and a beautiful meadow on the other.

"All this is yours, my brave Henry," said the fairy. "The Giant's thistle will obtain for you all that is necessary. The Wolf's staff will transport you where you wish. The Cat's claw will preserve your health and your youth and also that of your dear mother. Adieu, Henry! Be happy and never forget that virtue and filial love are always recompensed."

Henry threw himself on his knees before the fairy who gave him her hand to kiss, smiled upon him and disappeared.

Henry's mother had a great desire to arise from her

bed and admire her new house, her garden, her woods and her meadow. But, alas! She had no dress. During her first illness she had made Henry sell all that she possessed, as they were suffering for lack of bread.

"Alas! alas! My child, I cannot leave my bed. I have neither dresses nor shoes."

"You shall have all those things, dear mother," exclaimed Henry.

Drawing his thistle from his pocket, he smelled it while he wished for dresses, linen, shoes for his mother and himself and also for linen for the house. At the same moment the presses were filled with linen, his mother was dressed in a good and beautiful robe of merino and Henry completely clothed in blue cloth, with good, substantial shoes. They both uttered a cry of joy. His mother sprang from her bed to run through the house with Henry. Nothing was wanting. Everywhere the furniture was good and comfortable. The kitchen was filled with pots and kettles; but there was nothing in them.

Henry again put his thistle to his nose and desired to have a good dinner served up.

A table soon appeared, with good smoking soup, a splendid leg of lamb, a roasted pullet and good salad. They took seats at the table with the appetite of those who had not eaten for three years. The soup was soon swallowed, the leg of lamb entirely eaten, then the pullet, then the salad.

When their hunger was thus appeased, the mother, aided by Henry, took off the cloth, washed and arranged all the dishes and then put the kitchen in perfect order. They then made up their beds with the sheets they found in the presses and went happily to bed, thanking God and the good fairy Bienfaisante. The mother also gave grateful thanks for her dear son Henry.

They lived thus most happily, they wanted nothing – the thistle provided everything. They did not grow old or sick – the claw cured every ill. They never used the staff, as they were too happy at home ever to desire to leave it.

Henry asked of his thistle only two cows, two good horses and the necessaries of life for every day. He wished for nothing superfluous, either in clothing or food and thus he preserved his thistle as long as he lived. It is not known when they died. It is supposed that the Queen of the Fairies made them immortal and transported them to her palace, where they still are.

"What are you seeking, little one?"
said the Doctor; "and how is it possible
that you have gained this summit?"

Butterfairies

Some people say that butterflies
Are really fairies in disguise
And sometimes to your
great surprise
They dance before your very eyes.
Oh, do not catch them in a net
Oh, do not ever, ever let
Collecting be your only aim
As little fairies you might maim.

Intent to catch a butterfly
You might not hear the fairy cry,
"My gentle wings bruise easily
Please allow me to go free.
Oh, do not pin me to a board
For then three wishes you're assured."
She waves her wand to make a spell
And whispers softly, "Fare thee well!"
Then Butterfairy flutters high
And disappears into the sky.

Donkey Skin

This is one of the fairy
tales recorded by Charles
Perrault (1628–1703) and
then retold by Andrew Lang,
(1844–1912) in his *The
Grey Fairy Book*. A king had
a beautiful wife , a fine castle,
and a wonderful donkey –
whose droppings were gold!

*She requested the skin of the king's
donkey*

There was once upon a time a king who was so much beloved by his subjects that he thought himself the happiest monarch in the whole world, and he had everything his heart could desire. His palace was filled with the rarest of curiosities, and his gardens with the sweetest flowers, while in the marble stalls of his stables stood a row of milk-white Arabs, with big brown eyes.

Strangers who had heard of the marvels which the king had collected, and made long journeys to see them, were, however, surprised to find the most splendid stall of all occupied by a donkey, with particularly large and drooping ears. It was a very fine donkey; but still, as far as they could tell, nothing so very remarkable as to account for the care with which it was lodged; and they went away wondering, for they could not know that every night, when it was asleep, bushels of gold pieces tumbled out of its ears, which were picked up each morning by the attendants.

After many years of prosperity a sudden blow fell upon the king in the death of his wife, whom he loved dearly. But before she died, the queen, who had always thought first of his happiness, gathered all her strength, and said to him:

"Promise me one thing: you must marry again, I know, for the good of your people, as well as of yourself. But do not set about it in a hurry. Wait until you have found a woman more beautiful and better formed than myself."

"Oh, do not speak to me of marrying," sobbed the king; "rather let me die with you!" But the queen only smiled faintly, and turned over on her pillow and died.

For some months the king's grief was great; then gradually he began to forget a little, and, besides, his counsellors were always urging him to seek another wife. At first he refused to listen to them, but by-and-by he allowed himself to be persuaded to think of it, only stipulating that the bride should be more beautiful and attractive than the late queen, according to the promise he had made her.

Overjoyed at having obtained what they wanted, the counsellors sent envoys far and wide to get portraits of all the most famous beauties of every country. The artists were very busy and did their best, but, alas! nobody could even pretend that any of the ladies could compare for a moment with the late queen.

At length, one day, when he had turned away discouraged from a fresh collection of pictures, the king's eyes fell on his adopted daughter, who had lived in the palace since she was a baby, and he saw that, if a woman existed on the whole earth more lovely than the queen, this was she! He at once made known what his wishes were, but the young girl, who was not at all ambitious, and had not the faintest desire to marry him, was filled with dismay, and begged for time to think about it. That night, when everyone was asleep, she started in a little cart drawn by a big sheep, and went to consult her fairy godmother.

"I know what you have come to tell me," said the fairy, when the maiden stepped out of the cart; "and if you don't wish to marry him, I will show you how to avoid it. Ask him to give you a dress that exactly matches the sky. It will be impossible for him to get one, so you will be quite safe." The girl thanked the fairy and returned home again.

The next morning, when her father (as she had always called him) came to see her, she told him that she could give him no answer until he had presented her with a dress the colour of the sky. The king, overjoyed at this answer, sent for all the choicest weavers and dressmakers

presence, the girl told him what she wanted.

"Madam, I can refuse you nothing," said he; and he ordered the dress to be ready in twenty-four hours, or every man should be hanged.

They set to work with all their might, and by dawn next day, the dress of moonbeams was laid across her bed. The girl, though she could not help admiring its beauty, began to cry, till the fairy, who heard her, came to her help.

"Well, I could not have believed it of him!" said she; "but ask for a dress of sunshine, and I shall be surprised indeed if he manages that!"

The goddaughter did not feel much faith in the fairy after her two previous failures; but not knowing what else

*That night she slipped out of the palace and
went to consult her godmother*

*When she saw her reflection she was ashamed
and plunged into the pool*

in the kingdom, and commanded them to make a robe the colour of the sky without an instant's delay, or he would cut off their heads at once. Dreadfully frightened at this threat, they all began to dye and cut and sew, and in two days they brought back the dress, which looked as if it had been cut straight out of the heavens! The poor girl was thunderstruck, and did not know what to do; so in the night she harnessed her sheep again, and went in search of her godmother.

"The king is cleverer than I thought," said the fairy; "but tell him you must have a dress of moonbeams."

And the next day, when the king summoned her into his

to do, she told her father what she was bid.

The king made no difficulties about it, and even gave his finest rubies and diamonds to ornament the dress, which was so dazzling, when finished, that it could not be looked at save through smoked glasses!

When the princess saw it, she pretended that the sight hurt her eyes, and retired to her room, where she found the fairy awaiting her, very much ashamed of herself.

"There is only one thing to be done now," cried she; "you must demand the skin of the ass he sets such store by. It is from that donkey he obtains all his vast riches, and I am sure he will never give it to you."

Kings arrived for the wedding in rich carriages and litters. Some rode on elephants, tigers, or eagles

The princess was not so certain; however, she went to the king, and told him she could never marry him till he had given her the ass's skin.

The king was both astonished and grieved at this new request, but did not hesitate an instant. The ass was sacrificed, and the skin laid at the feet of the princess.

The poor girl, seeing no escape from the fate she dreaded, wept afresh, and tore her hair; when, suddenly, the fairy stood before her.

"Take heart," she said, "all will now go well! Wrap yourself in this skin, and leave the palace and go as far as you can. I will look after you. Your dresses and your jewels shall follow you underground, and if you strike the earth whenever you need anything, you will have it at once. But go quickly: you have no time to lose."

Messengers went everywhere, asking if anyone has seen the missing princess

The busy tailors made a yellow-gold dress of glittering sunshine

So the princess clothed herself in the ass's skin, and slipped from the palace without being seen by anyone.

Directly she was missed there was a great hue and cry, and every corner, possible and impossible, was searched. Then the king sent out parties along all the roads, but the fairy threw her invisible mantle over the girl when they approached, and none of them could see her.

The princess walked on a long, long way, trying to find someone who would take her in, and let her work for them; but though the cottagers, whose houses she passed, gave her food from charity, the ass's skin was so dirty they would not allow her to enter their houses. For her flight had been so hurried she had had no time to clean it.

Tired and disheartened at her ill-fortune, she was wandering, one day, past the gate of a farmyard, situated just outside the walls of a large town, when she heard a voice calling to her. She turned and saw the farmer's wife standing among her turkeys, and making signs to her to come in.

"I want a girl to wash the dishes and feed the turkeys, and

386

clean out the pig-sty," said the women, "and, to judge by your dirty clothes, you would not be too fine for the work."

The girl accepted her offer with joy, and she was at once set to work in a corner of the kitchen, where all the farm servants came and made fun of her, and the ass's skin in which she was wrapped. But by-and-by they got so used to the sight of it that it ceased to amuse them, and she worked so hard and so well, that her mistress grew quite fond of her. And she was so clever at keeping sheep and herding turkeys that you would have thought she had done nothing else during her whole life!

One day she was sitting on the banks of a stream bewailing her wretched lot, when she suddenly caught sight of herself in the water. Her hair and part of her face was quite concealed by the sass's head, which was drawn right over like a hood, and the filthy matted skin covered her whole body. It was the first time she had seen herself as other people saw her, and she was filled with shame at the spectacle. Then she threw off her disguise and jumped into the water, plunging in again and again, till she shone like ivory. When it was time to go back to the farm, she was forced to put on the skin which disguised her, and now seemed more dirty than ever; but, as she did so, she comforted herself with the thought that to-morrow was a holiday, and that she would be able for a few hours to forget that she was a farm girl, and be a princess once more.

So, at break of day, she stamped on the ground, as the fairy had told her, and instantly the dress like the sky lay across her tiny bed. Her room was so small that there was no place for the train of her dress to spread itself out, but she pinned it up carefully when she combed her beautiful hair and piled it up on the top of her head, as she had always worn it. When she had done, she was so pleased with herself that she determined never to let a chance pass of putting on her splendid clothes, even if she had to wear them in the fields, with no one to admire her but the sheep and turkeys.

Now the farm was a royal farm, and, one holiday, when "Donkey Skin" (as they had nicknamed the princess) had locked the door of her room and clothed herself in her dress of sunshine, the king's son rode through the gate, and asked if he might come and rest himself a little after hunting. Some food and milk were set before him in the garden, and when he felt rested he got up, and began to explore the house, which was famous throughout the whole kingdom for its age and beauty. He opened one door after the other, admiring the old rooms, when he came to a handle that would not turn. He stooped and peeped through the keyhole to see what was inside, and was greatly astonished at beholding a beautiful girl, clad in a dress so dazzling that he could hardly look at it.

The dark gallery seemed darker than ever as he turned away, but he went back to the kitchen and inquired who slept in the room at the end of the passage. The scullery maid, they told him, whom everybody laughed at, and called Donkey Skin; and though he perceived there was some strange mystery about this, he saw quite clearly there was nothing to be gained by asking any more questions. So he rode back to the palace, his head filled with the vision he had seen through the keyhole.

All night long he tossed about, and awoke the next morning in a high fever. The queen, who had no other child, and lived in a state of perpetual anxiety about this one, at once gave him up for lost, and indeed his sudden illness puzzled the greatest doctors, who tried the usual remedies in vain. At last they told the queen that some secret sorrow must be at the bottom of all this, and she threw herself on her knees beside her son's bed, and implored him to confide his trouble to her. If it was ambition to be king, his father would gladly resign the cares of the crown, and suffer him to reign in his stead; or, if it was love, everything should be sacrificed to get for him the wife he desired, even if she were daughter of a king with whom the country was at war at present!

"Madam," replied the prince, whose weakness would hardly allow him to speak, "do not think me so unnatural as to wish to deprive my father of his crown. As long as he lives I shall remain the most faithful of his subjects! And as to the princesses you speak of, I have seen none that I should care for as a wife, though I would always obey your wishes, whatever it might cost me."

"Ah! my son," cried she, "we will do anything in the world to save your life – and ours too, for if you die, we shall die also."

"Well, then," replied the prince, "I will tell you the only thing that will cure me – a cake made by the hand of Donkey Skin."

"Donkey Skin?" exclaimed the queen, who thought her son had gone mad; "and who or what is that?"

"Madam," answered one of the attendants present, who had been with the prince at the farm, "Donkey Skin is, next to the wolf, the most disgusting creature on the face of the earth. She is a girl who wears a black, greasy skin, and lives at your farmer's as hen-wife."

"Never mind," said the queen; "my son seems to have eaten some of her pastry. It is the whim of a sick man, no doubt; but send at once and let her bake a cake."

The attendant bowed and ordered a page to ride with the message.

Now it is by no means certain that Donkey Skin had not caught a glimpse of the prince, either when his eyes looked through the keyhole, or else from her little window, which was over the road. But whether she had actually seen him or only heard him spoken of, directly she received the queen's command, she flung off the dirty skin, washed herself from head to foot, and put on a skirt and bodice of shining silver. Then, locking herself into her room, she took the richest cream, the finest flour, and the freshest eggs on the farm, and set about making her cake.

As she was stirring the mixture in the saucepan a ring that she sometimes wore in secret slipped from her finger and fell into the dough. Perhaps Donkey Skin saw it, or perhaps she did not; but, any way, she went on stirring, and soon the cake was ready to be put in the oven. When it was nice and brown she took off her dress and put on her dirty skin, and gave the cake to the page, asking at the same time for news of the prince. But the page turned his head aside, and would not even condescend to answer.

The page rode like the wind, and as soon as he arrived at the palace he snatched up a silver tray and hastened to present the cake to the prince. The sick man began to eat it so fast that the doctors thought he would choke; and, indeed, he very nearly did, for the ring was in one of the bits which he broke off, though he managed to extract it from his mouth without anyone seeing him.

The moment the prince was left alone he drew the ring from under his pillow and kissed it a thousand times. Then he set his mind to find how he was to see the owner---for even he did not dare to confess that he had only beheld Donkey Skin through a keyhole, lest they should laugh at this sudden passion. All this worry brought back the fever, which the arrival of the cake had diminished for the time; and the doctors, not knowing what else to say, informed the queen that her son was simply dying of love. The queen, stricken with horror, rushed into the king's presence with the news, and together they hastened to their son's bedside.

"My boy, my dear boy!" cried the king, "who is it you want to marry? We will give her to you for a bride; even if she is the humblest of our slaves. What is there in the whole world that we would not do for you?"

The prince, moved to tears at these words, drew the ring, which was an emerald of the purest water, from under his pillow.

"Ah, dear father and mother, let this be a proof that she whom I love is no peasant girl. The finger which that ring fits has never been thickened by hard work. But be her condition what it may, I will marry no other."

The king and queen examined the tiny ring very closely, and agreed, with their son, that the wearer could be no mere farm girl. Then the king went out and ordered heralds and trumpeters to go through the town, summoning every maiden to the palace. And she whom the ring fitted would some day be queen.

First came all the princesses, then all the duchesses" daughters, and so on, in proper order. But not one of them could slip the ring over the tip of her finger, to the great joy of the prince, whom excitement was fast curing. At last, when the high-born damsels had failed, the shopgirls and chambermaids took their turn; but with no better fortune.

"Call in the scullions and shepherdesses," commanded the prince; but the sight of their fat, red fingers satisfied everybody.

"There is not a woman left, your Highness," said the chamberlain; but the prince waved him aside.

"Have you sent for Donkey Skin, who made me the cake?" asked he, and the courtiers began to laugh, and replied that they would not have dared to introduce so dirty a creature into the palace.

"Let some one go for her at once," ordered the king. " I commanded the presence of every maiden, high or low, and I meant it."

The princess had heard the trumpets and the proclamations, and knew quite well that her ring was at the bottom of it all. She, too, had fallen in love with the prince in the brief glimpse she had had of him, and trembled with fear lest someone else's finger might be as small as her own. When, therefore, the messenger from the palace rode up to the gate, she was nearly beside herself with delight. Hoping all the time for such a summons, she had dressed herself with great care, putting on the garment of moonlight, whose skirt was scattered over with emeralds. But when they began calling to her to come down, she hastily covered herself with her donkey-skin and announced she was ready to present herself before his Highness. She was taken straight into the hall, where the prince was awaiting her, but at the sight of the donkey-skin his heart sank. Had he been mistaken after all?

"Are you the girl," he said, turning his eyes away as he spoke, "are you the girl who has a room in the furthest corner of the inner court of the farmhouse?"

"Yes, my lord, I am," answered she.

"Hold out your hand then," continued the prince, feeling that he must keep his word, whatever the cost, and, to the astonishment of every one present, a little hand, white and delicate, came from beneath the black and dirty skin. The ring slipped on with the utmost ease, and, as it did so, the skin fell to the ground, disclosing a figure of such beauty that the prince, weak as he was, fell on his knees before her, while the king and queen joined their prayers to his. Indeed, their welcome was so warm, and their caresses so bewildering, that the princess hardly knew how to find words to reply, when the ceiling of the hall opened, and the fairy godmother appeared, seated in a cart made entirely of white lilac. In a few words she explained the history of the princess, and how she came to be there, and, without losing a moment, preparations of the most magnificent kind were made for the wedding.

The kings of every country in the earth were invited, including, of course, the princess's adopted father (who by this time had married a widow), and not one refused.

But what a strange assembly it was! Each monarch travelled in the way he thought most impressive; and some came borne in litters, others had carriages of every shape and kind, while the rest were mounted on elephants, tigers, and even upon eagles. So splendid a wedding had never been seen before; and when it was over the king announced that it was to be followed by a coronation, for he and the queen were tired of reigning, and the young couple must take their place. The rejoicings lasted for three whole months, then the new sovereigns settled down to govern their kingdom, and made themselves so much beloved by their subjects, that when they died, a hundred years later, each man mourned them as his own father and mother.

The Sprig of Rosemary

This is a Spanish tale from Cuentos Populars Catalans collected by Dr. D. Francisco de S. Maspons y Labros. It was published in 1885 and then, in 1897, appeared in *The Pink Fairy Book* by Andrew Lang (1844–1912). Here it is a prince who changes back into an animal rather than a frog becoming a prince. Once again elemental forces (here the Sun, Moon and Wind) help her along the way but the first two magical treasures have to be sold to her rival in order to help the heroine win back her prince – just in time.

Once upon a time there lived a man with one daughter and he made her work hard all the day. One morning, when she had finished everything he had set her to do, he told her to go out into the woods and get some dry leaves and sticks to kindle a fire.

The girl went out, and soon collected a large bundle, and then she plucked at a sprig of sweet-smelling rosemary for herself. But the harder she pulled the firmer seemed the plant, and at last, determined not to be beaten, she gave one great tug, and the rosemary remained in her hands.

Then she heard a voice close to her saying, "Well?" and turning she saw before her a handsome young man, who asked why she had come to steal his firewood.

The girl, who felt much confused, only managed to stammer out as an excuse that her father had sent her.

"Very well," replied the young man; "then come with me."

So he took her through the opening made by the torn-up root, and they travelled till they reached a beautiful palace, splendidly furnished, but only lighted from the top. And when they had entered he told her that he was a great lord, and that never had he seen a maiden so beautiful as she, and that if she would give him her heart they would be married and live happy for ever after.

And the maiden said "yes, she would," and so they were married.

The next day the old dame who looked after the house handed her all the keys, but pointed her out one that she would do well never to use, for if she did the whole palace would fall to the ground, and the grass would grow over it, and the damsel herself would be remembered no more.

The bride promised to be careful, but in a little while, when there was nothing left for her to do, she began to wonder what could be in the chest, which was opened by the key. As everybody knows, if we once begin to think we soon begin to do, and it was not very long before the key was no longer in the maiden's hand but in the lock of the chest.

But the lock was stiff and resisted all her efforts, and in the end she had to break it. And what was inside after all? Why, nothing but a serpent's skin, which her husband, who was, unknown to her, a magician, put on when he was at work; and at the sight of it the girl was turning away in disgust, when the earth shook violently under her feet, the palace vanished as if it had never been, and the bride found herself in the middle of a field, not knowing where she was or whither to go.

She burst into a flood of bitter tears, partly at her own folly, but more for the loss of her husband, whom she dearly loved. Then, breaking a sprig of rosemary off a bush hard by, she resolved, cost what it might, to seek him through the world till she found him.

So she walked and she walked and she walked, till she arrived at a house built of straw. And she knocked at the door, and asked if they wanted a servant. The mistress said she did, and if the girl was willing she might stay. But day by day the poor maiden grew more and more sad, till at last her mistress begged her to say what the matter. Then she told her story-how she was going through the world seeking after her husband.

And her mistress answered her, "Where he is, none can tell better than the Sun, the Moon, Sand the Wind, for they go everywhere!"

On hearing these words the damsel set forth once more, and walked till she reached the Golden Castle, where lived the Sun. And she knocked boldly at the door, saying, "All hail, O Sun! I have come to ask it, of your charity, you will help me in my need. By my own fault have I fallen into these straits, and I am weary, for I seek my husband through the wide world."

"Indeed!" spoke the Sun. "Do you, rich as you are, need help? But though you live in a palace without windows, the Sun enters everywhere, and he knows you."

Then the bride told him the whole story, and did not hide her own ill-doing. And the Sun listened, and was sorry for her; and though he could not tell her where to go, he gave her a nut, and bid her open it in a time of great distress. The damsel thanked him with all her heart, and departed, and walked and walked and walked, till she came to another castle, and knocked at the door, which was opened by an old woman.

"All hail!" said the girl. "I have come, of your charity, to ask your help!"

"It is my mistress, the Moon, you seek. I will tell her of your prayer."

So the Moon came out, and when she saw the maid she knew her again, for she had watched her sleeping both in the cottage and in the palace. And she spake to her and said:

"Do you, rich as you are, need help?"

Then the girl told her the whole story, and the Moon listened, and was sorry for her; and though she could not tell her where to find her husband, she gave her an almond, and told her to crack it when she was in great need. So the damsel thanked her, and departed, and walked and walked and walked till she came to another castle. And she knocked at the door, and said:

"All hail! I have come to ask if, of your charity, you will help me in my need."

Inside the mysterious chest lay a serpent's skin

"It is my lord, the Wind, that you want," answered the old woman who opened it. "I will tell him of your prayer."

And the Wind looked on her and knew her again, for he had seen her in the cottage and in the palace, and he spake to her and said:

"Do you, rich as you are, want help?"

And she told him the whole story. And the Wind listened, and was sorry for her, and he gave her a walnut that she was to eat in time of need. But the girl did not go as the Wind expected. She was tired and sad and knew not where to turn, so she began to weep bitterly. The Wind wept too for company, and said:

"Don't be frightened; I will go and see if I can find out something."

And the Wind departed with a great noise and fuss, and in the twinkling of an eye he was back again, beaming with delight.

"From what one person and another have let fall," he exclaimed, "I have contrived to learn that he is in the palace of the king, who keeps him hidden lest anyone should see him; and that to-morrow he is to marry the princess, who, ugly creature that she is, has not been able to find any man to wed her."

Who can tell the despair which seized the poor maiden when she heard this news! As soon as she could speak she implored the Wind to do all he could to get the wedding

The young girl had collected a bundle of sticks

put off for two or three days, for it would take all that time to reach the palace of the king.

The Wind gladly promised to do what he could, and as he travelled much faster than the maiden he soon arrived at the palace, where he found five tailors working night and day at the wedding clothes of the princess.

Down came the Wind right in the middle of their lace and satin and trimmings of pearl! Away they all went whiz! through the open windows, right up into the tops of the trees, across the river, among the dancing ears of corn! After them ran the tailors, catching, jumping, climbing, but all to no purpose! The lace was torn, the satin stained, the pearls knocked off! There was nothing for it but to go to the shops to buy fresh, and to begin all over again! It was plainly quite impossible that the wedding clothes could be ready next day.

However, the king was much too anxious to see his daughter married to listen to any excuses, and he declared that a dress must be put together somehow for the bride to wear. But when he went to look at the princess, she was such a figure that he agreed that it would be unfitting for someone in her position to be seen in such a gown, and he ordered the ceremony and the banquet to be postponed for a few hours, so that the tailors might take the dress to pieces and make it fit.

But by this time the maiden had arrived footsore and weary at the castle, and as soon as she reached the door she cracked her nut and drew out of it the most beautiful

The wedding dress was made of satin, lace and pearl trimmings

mantle in the world. Then she rang the bell, and asked:

"Is not the princess to be married today?"

"Yes, she is."

"Ask her if she would like to buy this mantle."

And when the princess saw the mantle she was delighted, for her wedding mantle had been spoilt with all the other things, and it was too late to make another. So she told the maiden to ask what price she would, and it should be given her.

The maiden fixed a large sum, many pieces of gold, but the princess had set her heart on the mantle, and gave it readily.

Now the maiden hid her gold in the pocket of her dress, and turned away from the castle. The moment she was out of sight she broke her almond, and drew from it the most magnificent petticoats that ever were seen. Then she went back to the castle, and asked if the princess wished to buy any petticoats. No sooner did the princess cast her eyes on the petticoats than she declared they were even more beautiful than the mantle, and that she would give the maiden whatever price she wanted for them. And the maiden named many pieces of gold, which the princess paid her gladly, so pleased was she with her new possessions.

Then the girl went down the steps where none could watch her and cracked her walnut, and out came the most splendid court dress that any dressmaker had ever invented; and, carrying it carefully in her arms, she knocked at the door, and asked if the princess wished to buy a court dress.

When the message was delivered the princess sprang to her feet with delight, for she had been thinking that after all it was not much use to have a lovely mantle and elegant petticoats if she had no dress, and she knew the tailors would never be ready in time. So she sent at once to say she would buy the dress, and what sum did the maiden want for it.

This time the maiden answered that the price of the dress was the permission to see the bridegroom.

The princess was not at all pleased when she heard the maiden's reply, but, as she could not do without the dress, she was forced to give in, and contented herself with thinking that after all it did not matter much.

So the maiden was led to the rooms which had been given to her husband. And when she came near she touched him with the sprig of rosemary that she carried; and his memory came back, and he knew her, and kissed her, and declared that she was his true wife, and that he loved her and no other.

Then they went back to the maiden's home, and grew to be very old, and lived happy all the days of their life.

The Princess and the Goblin

This fantasy published in 1872 (and its sequel, *The Princess and Curdie*) were written by George MacDonald. Not unlike some of Lewis Carroll's tales with their symbolism and wry humour, these are fairytales that become stranger by the minute as the Princess discovers her great, great, great grandmother, whom only she can see, a miner boy who can navigate through the dark, and warring goblins in an imaginative world where understanding and trust are vital for survival.

Why the Princess has a Story about Her

There was once a little princess whose father was king over a great country full of mountains and valleys. His palace was built upon one of the mountains, and was very grand and beautiful. The princess, whose name was Irene, was born there, but she was sent soon after her birth, because her mother was not very strong, to be brought up by country people in a large house, half castle, half farmhouse, on the side of another mountain, about halfway between its base and its peak.

The princess was a sweet little creature, and at the time my story begins, was about eight years old, I think, but she got older very fast. Her face was fair and pretty, with eyes like two bits of night-sky, each with a star dissolved in the blue. Those eyes you would have thought must have known they came from there, so often were they turned up in that direction. The ceiling of her nursery was blue, with stars in it, as like the sky as they could make it. But I doubt if ever she saw the real sky with the stars in it, for a reason which I had better mention at once. These mountains were full of hollow places underneath; huge caverns, and winding ways, some with water running through them, and some shining with all colours of the rainbow when a light was taken in. There would not have been much known about them, had there not been mines there, great deep pits, with long galleries and passages running off from them, which had been dug to get at the ore of which the mountains were full. In the course of digging, the miners came upon many of these natural caverns. A few of them had far-off openings out on the side of a mountain, or into a ravine.

Now in these subterranean caverns lived a strange race of beings, called by some gnomes, by some kobolds, by some goblins. There was a legend current in the country, that at one time they lived above ground, and were very like other people. But for some reason or other, concerning which there were different legendary theories, the king had laid what they thought too severe taxes upon them, or had required observances of them they did not like, or had begun to treat them with more severity, in some way or other, and impose stricter laws; and the consequence was that they had all disappeared from the face of the country. According to the legend, however, instead of going to some other country, they had all taken refuge in the subterranean caverns, whence they never came out but at night, and then seldom showed themselves in any numbers, and never to many people at once.

It was only in the least frequented and most difficult parts of the mountains that they were said to gather even at night in the open air. Those who had caught sight of any of them said that they had greatly altered in the course of generations; and no wonder, seeing they lived away from the sun, in cold and wet and dark places. They were now, not ordinarily ugly, but either absolutely hideous, or ludicrously grotesque both in face and form. There was no invention, they said, of the most lawless imagination expressed by pen or pencil, that could surpass the extravagance of their appearance. But I suspect those who said so, had mistaken some of their animal companions for the goblins themselves – of which more by and by. The goblins themselves were not so far removed from the human as such a description would imply. And as they grew misshapen in body, they had grown in knowledge and cleverness, and now were able to do things no mortal could see the possibility of. But as they grew in cunning, they grew in mischief, and their great delight was in every way they could think of to annoy the people who lived in the open-air-storey above them. They had enough of affection left for each other, to preserve them from being absolutely cruel for cruelty's sake to those that came in their way; but still they so heartily cherished the ancestral grudge against those who occupied their former possessions, and especially against the descendants of the king who had caused their expulsion, that they sought every opportunity of tormenting them in ways that were as odd as their inventors; and although dwarfed and misshapen, they had strength equal to their cunning. In the process of time they had got a king and a government of their own, whose chief business, beyond their own simple affairs, was to devise trouble for their neighbours. It will now be pretty evident why the little princess had never seen the sky at night. They were much too afraid of the goblins to let her out of the house then, even in company with ever so many attendants; and they had good reason, as we shall see by and by.

Princess Irene was feeling thoroughly miserable

The Princess loses Herself

I have said the Princess Irene was about eight years old when my story begins. And this is how it begins. One very wet day, when the mountain was covered with mist which was constantly gathering itself together into raindrops, and pouring down on the roofs of the great old

house, whence it fell in a fringe of water from the eaves all round about it, the princess could not of course go out. She got very tired, so tired that even her toys could no longer amuse her. You would wonder at that if I had time to describe to you one half of the toys she had. But then you wouldn't have the toys themselves, and that makes all the difference: you can't get tired of a thing before you have it. It was a picture, though, worth seeing – the princess sitting in the nursery with the sky ceiling over her head, at a great table covered with her toys. If the artist would like to draw this, I should advise him not to meddle with the toys. I am afraid of attempting to describe them, and I think he had better not try to draw them. He had better not. He can do a thousand things I can't, but I don't think he could draw those toys. No man could better make the princess herself than he could, though – leaning with her back bowed into the back of the chair, her head hanging down, and her hands in her lap, very miserable as she would say herself, not even knowing what she would like, except it were to go out and get thoroughly wet, and catch a particularly nice cold, and have to go to bed and take gruel. The next moment after you see her sitting there, her nurse goes out of the room.

Even that is a change, and the princess wakes up a little, and looks about her. Then she tumbles off her chair, and runs out of the door, not the same door the nurse went out of, but one which opened at the foot of a curious old stair of worm-eaten oak, which looked as if never anyone had set foot upon it. She had once before been up six steps, and that was sufficient reason, in such a day, for trying to find out what was at the top of it.

Up and up she ran – such a long way it seemed to her! until she came to the top of the third flight. There she found the landing was the end of a long passage. Into this she ran. It was full of doors on each side. There were so many that she did not care to open any, but ran on to the end, where she turned into another passage, also full of doors. When she had turned twice more, and still saw doors and only doors about her, she began to get frightened. It was so silent! And all those doors must hide rooms with nobody in them! That was dreadful. Also the rain made a great trampling noise on the roof. She turned and started at full speed, her little footsteps echoing through the sounds of the rain – back for the stairs and her safe nursery. So she thought, but she had lost herself long ago. It doesn't follow that she was lost, because she had lost herself, though. . . .

The Twelve-headed Griffin

This traditional Romanian story tells of a magnificent prince, an only son who rescues a princess from a monster, and a magical bull who can restore life to his owner.

Once upon a time there lived a king and queen whose greatest blessing from God was an only child of fifteen, named Theodor.

This boy from his childhood had learnt to ride, and to shoot with the bow, and had become a great proficient in both arts.

He had learned to use a bow and arrow when very young

One day while practising archery, one of his arrows shot out of sight. The boy having marked the direction which it took, went to his father to request his swiftest horse, and money to go in search of his arrow.

His father gave him money, and permission to take the best horse in his stables.

With joy the boy mounted swiftly, and set off at a gallop.

After riding long and far, so far that the sun was disappearing from the horizon, he found himself in a vast prairie full of flowers. Stopping his horse, standing up in his stirrups, and shading his eyes with his hand, he perceived his arrow sticking in the ground. Dismounting he went quickly to the spot, seized the arrow with both hands, and with difficulty drew it out, leaving a great hole in the earth where it had penetrated. On looking down this hole, he saw at the bottom of it, a fine bull, and on the bull's back, a sword and a letter.

In great surprise at all these strange surroundings, he opened the letter and read, "Whomsoever will take this bull and will give it three pecks of wheat and a gallon of wine, and continue to do so daily, the bull will have power to bring back to life the man who does this, no matter how many times he may die. This sword will turn into stone any living or inanimate object."

Leading the bull, and strapping on the sword, the boy went on his way.

Towards night he reached a city and asked food and shelter of an old woman whom he met with. For himself a draught of water, for the bull a gallon of wine. The old woman fed him and his animals, and gave the requisite wine to the bull. Water she said she had none, for in the whole city there was but one fountain, and that at the outskirts of the town; and that this fountain was guarded by a twelve-headed monster. Whomsoever needed water must sacrifice a young maiden to his appetite.

She told him that the next day it was the king's turn to give his daughter, and that this said King had made a proclamation to the effect, that whosoever would kill this monster and save his daughter, immense riches, and the hand of his daughter in marriage would be the reward.

The youth hearing all this, requested the old woman to awake him very early next morning, and to give him her water-jars, saying he would fill them without giving anything to the monster. She promised this, and he soon fell into a sound sleep.

According to her promise, the next morning she aroused him, and taking his sword, his bow and arrows, and the water-jars, set off for the well. Arriving there, he found the King's daughter weeping, and waiting to be eaten by the monster. Said the youth to her, "I have come to deliver you from the fangs of the monster, on one condition, that is,

Bulls have been revered as sacred or magical beasts since ancient times

that you let me sit down by your side, lay my head on your lap, and if I should fall asleep, not to awake me until the monster shows himself."

The young girl acquiesced with joy, and sitting down beside her, the youth laid his head on her lap, and soon fell asleep. When the monster made his appearance, the girl was so overwhelmed with terror that she could not awake the youth, but cried so plentifully that the scalding tears fell on his face. Jumping up, he saw the monster before him. Charging his bow, he placed himself in front of the maiden; the monster seeing this, exclaimed, "Stand aside, and let me take my right," but the youth refused; at the same time he drew the string of his bow and sent an arrow into the head which was stretched forth for his destruction.

The monster writhed with pain, and projected a second head, and then began a terrible strife. The youth's only defence was his courage and his bow, but the monster had his twelve heads, and his poisoned breath.

All that long summer's day they fought until evening; as night fell the boy could hardly stand from fatigue, had broken his bow, and had but one arrow in his quiver. But,

on the other hand, the monster remained with only one head left out of the twelve.

The bull had miraculous powers and could bring the dead back to life

At length, the youth took from the maiden's head, a long mesh of her rich hair – she, more dead than alive from terror, and with it bound his broken bow together, and the fight recommenced. Eventually the youth was victorious, but fell down faint from loss of blood. While both these young creatures lay fainting by the well side, there came up a Tzigan, in the service of the king, to fetch water. Seeing the monster annihilated, he sought the young princess, and finding that she was not dead, but only in a swoon, he threw water over her, and she quickly returned to her senses. The Tzigan enquired of her who had killed the monster, and the maiden pointed to the apparently dead Theodor. Quick as thought the Tzigan seized the youth's sword, and cut his body into hundreds of pieces.

Then, collecting the twelve heads and tongues of the

"It is true," said his daughter, tremulously.

Though the king was sorely grieved that the deliverer of his child was a gypsy, and a slave, yet he felt bound to fulfill the promise that she should be given him to wife.

While Theodor was lying hewed in morsels, by the side of the well, the old woman, his hostess, went to her stable to feed and give drink to the bull. On seeing her, he refused all nourishment, telling her that "he was thirsting after water, and not after wine, and that she must lead him to the public well; as now that the monster existed no longer, all the world could drink water in peace."

He bade her take with them a lump of salt, and soon they arrived at the well.

When the woman saw the morsels of what had once been the brave youth, she began to cry aloud; but the bull

The king asked his daughter if Tzigan was telling the truth

The king was sad but knew he must keep his word

monster, and charging the maiden not to tell to the king who had performed this mighty deed, he accompanied her to her father's palace.

Without the knowledge of the Tzigan, the maid let fall a ring, and a handkerchief, beside the remains of the slaughtered youth.

When the king saw his daughter approach, he was overwhelmed with joy, and demanded the name of her deliverer. "I, mighty King," replied the Tzigan, with pride.

"Can this be true?" enquired the King.

said to her, "Don't distress yourself in that way, but do as I tell you: take up piece by piece, limb by limb, and place them together, as they were in life."

Obeying him, she put the different members once more together again. The bull licked well the lump of salt, then breathed over, and licked the youth. Wherever his tongue passed over, the marks of the sword disappeared, and when he once more breathed into his face, Theodor opened his eyes and exclaimed: "Have I slept long?"

"You would have slept longer," said the woman, "if your

bull had not brought you to life."

All was as a dream to him, and it was only after the bull had explained all that had occurred, that he understood why the maiden was no longer by his side.

On looking around him he saw the ring and the handkerchief which she had dropped; he took possession of them, and they returned to the old woman's dwelling.

The following day the king caused a proclamation to be issued to the effect that the nuptials of his beloved daughter, with Burcea, the Tzigan, would take place in eight days. Burcea her deliverer, inviting the neighbouring kings and nobles to come and do honour to the ceremony.

He sent for the court tailor, and commanded for his future son-in-law, clothing befitting his new rank. He ordered his treasurer to pay to Burcea any sum of money which he might demand.

On the appointed day, the guests were assembled in the Imperial Palace; but all were melancholy, and angry that an ugly, uneducated gypsy should have gained such a high-born, lovely bride.

Amongst them all, the king was the most grieved, with the exception, perhaps, of his daughter, who reproached herself for not having told the truth to the king, her father. Burcea, the Tzigan, alone, was joyful.

In those days, it was the custom at the marriage of a king's daughter, for each subject to offer a present, according to his means; so Theodor begged the old woman to make him a cake, which she should take to the palace as his offering. She willingly agreed, and began to make the cake. When it was ready for the oven, the youth slipped the ring into the middle of the cake, and covered the paste over it.

The cake was baked, and wrapped in a clean napkin, and taken by the old woman to the gate of the palace. Her dress was so old and so patched that the servants forbade her to enter; but the princess looking from the window, gave orders that she should be admitted and brought into her presence.

This was quickly done, and the cake was offered with humble wishes for her future happiness. The Princess took the cake and broke it; imagine her surprise when she found her ring in the middle of it!

"Where is the person who put this ring here?" asked she of the old woman. "It must be the handsome boy that is at my cottage," said she, "he who was hewn to pieces by your slave, and was restored to life and health by his friendly bull."

"Take this purse of money for yourself," said the princess," and return quickly to your home; tell my deliverer to come here, for I am awaiting him."

The woman sped swiftly on her errand. Full of joy, the youth seized his sword and, taking the handkerchief, set off for the Imperial palace.

On reaching the reception ball, he saw a crowd of nobles, and in their centre, Burcea the Tzigan, swelling with pride, and thinking himself as powerful as a Grand Vizier.

The youth passed speedily on, until he reached an apartment where the princess was resting. Seeing him, she sprang up, and flung herself into his arms, crying out, "This is my deliverer, this is my deliverer."

A crowd quickly surrounded them, and Theodor, in a clear voice, said: "It is true that I am the deliverer of this maiden, who would have been eaten by the monster of the well. I killed him, and she was free; but when I was faint from fatigue and loss of blood, a slave of the king's come to the well, and, seeing me in this state, hewed me to pieces with my own sword and threatened the maiden with death, if she avowed the truth. At the same time he possessed himself with the proofs of the monster's destruction. Had it not been for a bull, endowed with a miraculous power of bringing the dead to life, I should now be ready for my grave. Seeing that many wise men are here, and knowing that there is wisdom in numbers, I entreat all present to judge and condemn the one who is guilty."

"To death! to death!" cried the crowd.

The king, calling his servants, ordered them to bring two horses from his stables, one bred in the mountains, the other bred in the plains, and to tie the limbs of Burcea, the Tzigan, to these two animals; his order was obeyed, the horses were let loose, and setting off in a gallop in different directions, the body of the slave was torn limb from limb.

And now, indeed, there was a real rejoicing; but the marriage, and the court festivities were all postponed, until the arrival of the parents of Theodor, who embraced him, and wept for joy and pride, that he had so nobly distinguished himself.

They built for him, and his young bride, a magnificent palace; at the entrance to the court-yard, there was also a well of purest water, apparently guarded and watched over by a gigantic bull in marble.

A magnificent well was built in the palace courtyard

The Flower Queen's Daughter

This Romanian story is from a traditional Bukovinan fairy tale collected by Dr Heinrich von Wlislocki (1856–1907) and told by Andrew Lang (1844–1912) in his *The Yellow Fairy Book*. The most beautiful daughter of the Flower Queen has been kidnapped by dragons and a prince comes to her rescue helped by a bell: one ring will bring the King of the Eagles; two rings – the King of the Foxes; and three, the King of the Fishes.

A young prince was riding one day through a meadow that stretched for miles in front of him, when he came to a deep open ditch. He was turning aside to avoid it, when he heard the sound of someone crying in the ditch. He dismounted from his horse, and stepped along in the direction the sound came from. To his astonishment he found an old woman, who begged him to help her out of the ditch. The prince bent down and lifted her out of her living grave, asking her at the same time how she had managed to get there.

"My son," answered the old woman, "I am a very poor woman, and soon after midnight I set out for the neighbouring town in order to sell my eggs in the market on the following morning; but I lost my way in the dark, and fell into this deep ditch, where I might have remained for ever but for your kindness."

Then the prince said to her, "You can hardly walk; I will put you on my horse and lead you home. Where do you live?"

"Over there, at the edge of the forest in the little hut you see in the distance," replied the old woman.

The prince lifted her on to his horse, and soon they reached the hut, where the old woman got down, and turning to the prince said, "Just wait a moment, and I will give you something." And she disappeared into her hut, but returned very soon and said, "You are a mighty prince, but at the same time you have a kind heart, which deserves to be rewarded. Would you like to have the most beautiful woman in the world for your wife?"

"Most certainly I would," replied the prince.

So the old woman continued, "The most beautiful woman in the whole world is the daughter of the Queen of the Flowers, who has been captured by a dragon. If you wish to marry her, you must first set her free, and this I will help you to do. I will give you this little bell: if you ring it once, the King of the Eagles will appear; if you ring it twice, the King of the Foxes will come to you; and if you ring it three times, you will see the King of the Fishes by your side. These will help you if you are in any difficulty. Now farewell, and heaven prosper your undertaking." She handed him the little bell, and there disappeared hut and all, as though the earth had swallowed her up.

Then it dawned on the prince that he had been speaking to a good fairy, and putting the little bell carefully in his pocket, he rode home and told his father that he meant to set the daughter of the Flower Queen free, and intended setting out on the following day into the wide world in search of the maid.

Flower Queen's daughter was most beautiful

So the next morning the Prince mounted his fine horse and left his home. He had roamed round the world for a whole year, and his horse had died of exhaustion, while he himself had suffered much from want and misery, but still he had come on no trace of her he was in search of. At last one day he came to a hut, in front of which sat a very old man. The prince asked him, "Do you not know where the Dragon lives who keeps the daughter of the Flower Queen prisoner?"

"No, I do not," answered the old man. "But if you go straight along this road for a year, you will reach a hut where my father lives, and possibly he may be able to tell you."

The Prince thanked him for his information, and continued his journey for a whole year along the same road, and at the end of it came to the little hut, where he found a very old man. He asked him the same question, and the old man answered, "No, I do not know where the Dragon lives. But go straight along this road for another year, and you will come to a hut in which my father lives. I know he can tell you."

And so the prince wandered on for another year, always on the same road, and at last reached the hut where he found the third old man. He put the same question to him as he had put to his son and grandson; but this time

*The prince led the Mother Dragon's mare
out into the meadows*

the old man answered, "The Dragon lives up there on the mountain, and he has just begun his year of sleep. For one whole year he is always awake, and the next he sleeps. But if you wish to see the Flower Queen's daughter go

up the second mountain: the Dragon's old mother lives there, and she has a ball every night, to which the Flower Queen's daughter goes regularly."

So the prince went up the second mountain, where he found a castle all made of gold with diamond windows. He opened the big gate leading into the courtyard, and was just going to walk in, when seven dragons rushed on him and asked him what he wanted?

The prince replied, "I have heard so much of the beauty and kindness of the Dragon's Mother, and would like to enter her service."

This flattering speech pleased the dragons, and the eldest of them said, "Well, you may come with me, and I will take you to the Mother Dragon."

They entered the castle and walked through twelve splendid halls, all made of gold and diamonds. In the twelfth room they found the Mother Dragon seated on a diamond throne. She was the ugliest woman under the sun, and, added to it all, she had three heads. Her appearance was a great shock to the prince, and so was her voice, which was like the croaking of many ravens. She asked him, "Why have you come here?"

The prince answered at once, "I have heard so much of your beauty and kindness, that I would very much like to enter your service."

"Very well," said the Mother Dragon; "but if you wish to enter my service, you must first lead my mare out to the meadow and look after her for three days; but if you don't bring her home safely every evening, we will eat you up."

The Prince undertook the task and led the mare out to the meadow.

But no sooner had they reached the grass than she vanished. The prince sought for her in vain, and at last in despair sat down on a big stone and contemplated his sad fate. As he sat thus lost in thought, he noticed an eagle flying over his head. Then he suddenly bethought him of his little bell, and taking it out of his pocket he rang it once. In a moment he heard a rustling sound in the air beside him, and the King of the Eagles sank at his feet.

"I know what you want of me," the bird said. "You are looking for the Mother Dragon's mare who is galloping about among the clouds. I will summon all the eagles of the air together, and order them to catch the mare and bring her to you." And with these words the King of the Eagles flew away. Towards evening the prince heard a mighty rushing sound in the air, and when he looked up he saw thousands of eagles driving the mare before them. They sank at his feet on to the ground and gave the mare over to him. Then the prince rode home to the old Mother Dragon, who was full of wonder when she saw him, and said, "You have succeeded today in looking after my mare, and as a reward you shall come to my ball tonight." She gave him at the same time a cloak made of copper, and led him to a big room where several young he-dragons and she-dragons were dancing together. Here, too, was the Flower Queen's beautiful daughter. Her dress was woven out of the most lovely flowers in the world, and her complexion was like lilies and roses. As the prince was dancing with her he managed to whisper in her ear, "I have come to set you free!"

Then the beautiful girl said to him, "If you succeed in bringing the mare back safely the third day, ask the Mother

The brave prince rescued the princess from her dragon captor

Dragon to give you a foal of the mare as a reward."

The ball came to an end at midnight, and early next morning the prince again led the Mother Dragon's mare out into the meadow. But again she vanished before his eyes. Then he took out his little bell and rang it twice.

In a moment the King of the Foxes stood before him and said: "I know already what you want, and will summon all the foxes of the world together to find the mare who has hidden herself in a hill."

With these words the King of the Foxes disappeared, and

in the evening many thousand foxes brought the mare to the prince.

Then he rode home to the Mother-Dragon, from whom he received this time a cloak made of silver, and again she led him to the ball-room.

The Flower Queen's daughter was delighted to see him safe and sound, and when they were dancing together she whispered in his ear: "If you succeed again to-morrow, wait for me with the foal in the meadow. After the ball we will fly away together."

On the third day the prince led the mare to the meadow again; but once more she vanished before his eyes. Then the prince took out his little bell and rang it three times.

In a moment the King of the Fishes appeared, and said to him: "I know quite well what you want me to do, and I will summon all the fishes of the sea together, and tell them to bring you back the mare, who is hiding herself in a river."

Towards evening the mare was returned to him, and when he led her home to the Mother Dragon she said to him:

"You are a brave youth, and I will make you my body-servant. But what shall I give you as a reward to begin with?"

The prince begged for a foal of the mare, which the Mother Dragon at once gave him, and over and above, a cloak made of gold, for she had fallen in love with him because he had praised her beauty.

So in the evening he appeared at the ball in his golden cloak; but before the entertainment was over he slipped away, and went straight to the stables, where he mounted his foal and rode out into the meadow to wait for the Flower Queen's daughter. Towards midnight the beautiful girl appeared, and placing her in front of him on his horse, the Prince and she flew like the wind till they reached the Flower Queen's dwelling. But the dragons had noticed their flight, and woke their brother out of his year's sleep. He flew into a terrible rage when he heard what had happened, and determined to lay siege to the Flower Queen's palace; but the Queen caused a forest of flowers as high as the sky to grow up round her dwelling, through which no one could force a way.

When the Flower Queen heard that her daughter wanted to marry the prince, she said to him: "I will give my consent to your marriage gladly, but my daughter can only stay with you in summer. In winter, when everything is dead and the ground covered with snow, she must come and live with me in my palace underground." The prince consented to this, and led his beautiful bride home, where the wedding was held with great pomp and magnificence. The young couple lived happily together till winter came, when the Flower Queen's daughter departed and went home to her mother. In summer she returned to her husband, and their life of joy and happiness began again, and lasted till the approach of winter, when the Flower Queen's daughter went back again to her mother. This coming and going continued all her life long, and in spite of it they always lived happily together.

The Transformed Children

This is a Polish folk tale that tells of an evil stepmother, many enchantments and a very brave heroine who rescues her brothers, despite many trials. It is similar to *The Six Swans* by the Brothers Grimm.

There was once a king, who had lost his wife. They had a family of thirteen twelve gallant sons, and one daughter, who was exquisitely beautiful. For twelve years after his wife's death the king grieved very much; he used to go daily to her tomb, and there weep, and pray, and give away alms to the poor. He thought never to marry again; for he had promised his dying wife never to give her children a stepmother.

One day, when visiting his dead wife's grave as usual, he saw beside him a maiden so entrancingly fair, that he fell in love with her, and soon made her his second queen. But before long he found out that he had made a great mistake. Though she was so beautiful she turned out to be

The queen was transformed into a basilisk

401

a wicked sorceress, and not only made the king himself unhappy, but proved most unkind to his children, whom she wished out of the way, so that her own little son might inherit the kingdom.

One day, when the king was far away, at war against his enemies, the queen went into her stepchildren's apartments, and pronounced some magical words on which every one of the twelve princes flew away in the shape of eagles, and the princess was changed into a dove. The queen looked out of the window, to see in what direction they would fly, when she saw right under the window an old man, with a beard as white as snow. "What

The princes were changed into eagles

are you here for, old man?" she asked.

"To be witness of your deed," he answered.

"Then you saw it?"

"I saw it."

"Then be what I command!" She whispered some magical words. The old man disappeared in a blaze of sunshine; and the queen, as she stood there, dumb with terror, was changed into a basilisk. The basilisk ran off in fright; trying to hide herself underground. But her glance was so deadly, that it killed every one she looked at; so that all the people in the palace were soon dead, including her own son, whom she slew by merely looking at him. And this once populous and happy royal residence quickly became

an uninhabited ruin, which no one dared approach, for fear of the basilisk lurking in its underground vaults.

Meanwhile the princess, who had been changed into a dove, flew after her brothers the eagles, but not being able to overtake them, she rested under a wayside cross, and began cooing mournfully.

"What are you grieving for, pretty dove?" asked an old man, with a snow-white beard, who just then came by.

"I am grieving for my poor dear father, who is fighting in the wars far away; for my loved brothers, who have flown away from me into the clouds. I am grieving also for myself. Not long ago I was a happy princess; and now I must wander over the world as a dove, to hide from the birds of prey and be parted for ever from my dear father and brothers!"

"You may grieve and weep, little dove; but do not lose hope," said the old man. "Sorrow is only for a time, and all will come right in the end." So saying he stroked the little dove, and she at once regained her natural shape. She kissed the old man's hand in her gratitude, saying: "How can I ever thank you enough! But since you are so kind, will you not tell me how to rescue my brothers?"

The old man gave her an everlasting loaf, and said: "This loaf is enough to sustain, not only you, but a thousand people for a thousand years, without ever diminishing. Go towards the sunset, and weep your tears into this little bottle. And when it is full . . ."

And then the old man told her what else to do, blessed her, and disappeared. The princess travelled on towards the sunset; and in about a year she reached the boundary of the next world, and stood before an iron door, where Death was keeping guard with his scythe. "Stop, princess!" he said; "You can proceed no further, for you are not yet parted by death from your own world."

"But what am I to do?" she asked. "Must I go back without my poor brothers?"

"Your brothers," said Death, "fly here every day in the guise of eagles. They want to reach the other side of this door, which leads into the other world; for they hate the one they live in; nevertheless they, and you also, must remain there, until your time be come. Therefore every day I must compel them to go back, which they can do, because they are eagles. But how are you going to get back yourself? Look about you!"

The princess looked around her, and wept bitterly. For though she had not perceived this before, nor seen how she got there, she saw now that she was in a deep abyss, shut in on all sides by such high precipices, that she wondered how her brothers, even with eagle wings, could fly to the top. But remembering what the mysterious old man had said she took courage, and began to pray and weep, till she had filled the little bottle with her tears.

Soon she heard the sound of wings over her head, and saw twelve eagles flying. The eagles dashed themselves against the iron portal, beating their wings upon it, and imploring Death to open it to them. But Death only threatened them with his scythe, saying: "Hence! ye enchanted princes! You must fulfil your penance on earth, till I come for you myself."

The eagles were about to turn and fly, when all at once they perceived their sister. They came round her, and caressed her hands lovingly with their beaks. She at once began to sprinkle them with her tears from the bottle; and in one moment the twelve eagles were changed back into the twelve princes, and joyfully embraced their sister. The princess then fed them well from her everlasting loaf; but once their hunger was appeased they began to be troubled as to how they were to ascend from the abyss, since they had no longer eagle wings to fly.

And all at once there shot down from heaven to the depth of the abyss a ray of sunshine, on which descended a gigantic bird, with rainbow wings, a bright sparkling crest, and peacock's eyes all over his body, a golden tail, and silvery breast.

"What are your commands, princess?" asked the bird.

"Carry us from this threshold of eternity to our own world."

"I will, but you must know, princess, that before I can reach the top of this precipice with you on my back, three days and nights must pass; and I must have food on the way, or my strength will fail me, and I shall fall down with you to the bottom, and we shall all perish."

The basilisk had a deadly glance that killed everyone in the palace

But the princess knelt down and prayed:
"Bird of heavenly pity here
By each labour, prayer and tear
Come in thine unvanquished power,
Come and aid us in this hour!"

"I have an everlasting loaf, which will suffice both for you and ourselves," replied the princess.

"Then climb upon my back, and whenever I look round, give me some bread to eat."

The bird was so large that all the princes, and the

The gigantic bird was strong enough to carry the princess and all the princes

princess in the midst of them, could easily find place on his back, and he began to fly upwards. He flew higher and higher, and whenever he looked round at her, she gave him bits of the loaf, and he flew on, and upwards.

So they went on steadily for two nights and days; but upon the third day, when they were hoping in a short time to view the summit of the precipice, and to land upon the borders of this world, the bird looked round as usual for a piece of the loaf. The princess was just going to break off some to give him, when a sudden violent gust of wind from the bottom of the abyss snatched the loaf from her hand, and sent it whistling downwards. Not having received his usual meal the bird became sensibly weaker, and looked round once more. The princess trembled with fear; she had nothing more to give him, and she felt that he was becoming exhausted.

In utter desperation she cut off a piece of her flesh, and gave it to him. Having eaten this the bird recovered strength, and flew upwards faster than before; but after an hour or two he looked round once more. So she cut off another piece of her flesh; the bird seized it greedily, and flew on so fast that in a few minutes he reached the ground at the top of the precipice.

When they alighted, and he asked her: "Princess, what were those two delicious morsels you gave me last? I never ate anything so good before."

"They were part of my flesh, I had nothing else for you," replied the princess in a faint voice, for she was swooning away with pain and loss of blood. But then the bird breathed upon her wounds; and the flesh at once healed over, and grew again as before. Then he flew up again to heaven, and was lost in the clouds.

The princess and her brothers resumed their journey, this time towards the sunrise, and at last arrived in their own country, where they met their father, returning from the wars. The king had proved victorious over his enemies, and was on his way home had first heard of the sudden disappearance of his children and of the queen, and how his palace was tenanted only by a basilisk with a death-dealing glance. He was therefore most surprised and overjoyed to meet his dear children once more, and on the way his daughter told him all that had come to pass.

When they got back to the palace the king sent one of his nobles with a looking-glass down into the underground vaults. The basilisk saw herself reflected in this mirror, and her own glance slew her immediately. They gathered up the remains of the basilisk, and burnt them in a great fire in the courtyard, afterwards scattering the ashes to the four winds.

When this was done the king, his sons, and his daughter, returned to live in their former home and were all as happy as could be ever after.

Through the Telescope

This is a fairy tale from Poland.
When enchantment sends all
to sleep, the princess (unlike
Sleeping Beauty) remains
awake, ready to fight the evil king
of the Underworld Realm, helped
by the prince of her dreams.

The dragon raged and writhed about

Far away, in the wide ocean there was once a green island where lived the most beautiful princess in the world, named Miranda. She had lived there ever since her birth, and was queen of the island. Nobody knew who were her parents, or how she had come there. But she was not alone; for there were twelve beautiful maidens, who had grown up with her on the island, and were her ladies-in-waiting. A few strangers had visited the island, and spoken of the princess's great beauty; and many more came over the years Some stayed to become her subjects and built a magnificent city, in the middle of which the princess had a splendid palace of white marble.

In the course of time a great many young princes came to woo her. But she did not care to marry any of them; and if anyone persisted, and tried to compel her by force to be his wife, she could turn him and all his soldiers into ice, by merely fixing her eyes upon them.

One day the wicked Kosciey, the king of the Underworld Realm, came out into the upper world, and began to gaze all around it with his telescope. Various empires and kingdoms passed in review before him; and at last he saw the green island, and the rich city upon it; and the marble palace in this city, and in this palace the twelve beautiful young ladies- of-honour, and among them he beheld, lying on a rich couch of swansdown, the Princess Miranda asleep.

She slept like an innocent child, but she was dreaming of a young knight, wearing a golden helmet, on a gallant steed, and carrying an invisible mace, that could fight all by itself – and she loved him better than life.

Kosciey stared at her, delighted by her beauty; he struck the earth three times, and stood upon the green island.

Princess Miranda immediately called together her brave army, and led them into the field, to fight the wicked Kosciey. But he, blowing on them with his poisonous breath, sent them all fast asleep and was just about to lay hands upon the princess, when she, throwing a glance of scorn at him, changed him into a lump of ice, and fled to her capital.

Kosciey did not long remain ice. As soon as the princess was on her way, he freed himself from the power of her glance, and regaining his usual form, followed her to her city. Then he sent all the inhabitants of the island to sleep – including amongst them the princess's twelve faithful damsels. She was the only one whom he could not injure; but being afraid of her glances, he surrounded the castle which stood upon a high hill with an iron rampart, and placed a dragon with twelve heads on guard before the gate. Then he waited for the princess to give herself up of her own accord. The days passed by, then weeks, then months, while her kingdom became a desert. All her people were asleep, and her faithful soldiers also lay snoring on the open fields, their steel armour all rusted, and wild plants growing over them undisturbed.

Her twelve maidens were all asleep in different rooms of the palace, just where they happened to be at the time; and she herself, all alone, kept walking sadly to and fro in a little room up in a tower, where she had taken refuge, wringing her white hands, weeping, heaving heavy sighs.

Around her all were silent, as though dead; only every now and then, Kosciey, not daring to encounter her angry glance, knocked at the door asking her to surrender,

The island was very green and beautiful

promising to make her queen of his Underworld Realm. But it was all of no use; the princess was silent, and only threatened him with her looks. But, grieving in her lonely prison, Princess Miranda could not forget the lover of whom she had been dreaming; she saw him just as he had appeared to her in her dream. She looked up with her blue eyes to heaven and, seeing a cloud floating by, she said:

"O cloud! through the bright sky flying!
Stay, and hearken my piteous sighing!
In my sorrow I call upon thee;
Oh! where is my loved one? say!
Oh! where do his footsteps stray?

And does he now think of me?"

"I know not?" the cloud replied. "Ask the wind."

"And she looked out into the wide plain, and seeing how the wind was blowing freely, she said:

"O wind! o'er the wide world flying!

Do thou pity my grief and crying!

Have pity on me!

Oh! where is my loved one? say!

Oh! where do his footsteps stray?

And does he now think of me?"

"Ask the stars," the wind replied; "they know more than I do."

So she cried to the stars:

"O stars! with your bright beams glowing!

Look down on my tears fast flowing!

Have pity, have pity on me!

Oh! where is my loved one? say!

Oh! where do his footsteps stray?

And does he now think of me? "

"Ask the moon," said the stars; "who being nearer to the earth, knows more of what happens there than we do."

So she said to the moon:

"Bright moon, as your watch you keep,

From the starry skies, o'er this land of sleep,

Look down now, and pity me!

Oh! where is my loved one? say!

Where? where do his footsteps stray?

And does he now think of me?"

"I know nothing about your loved one, princess," replied the moon; "but here comes the sun, who will surely be able to tell you." And the sun rose up in the dawn, and at noontide stood just over the princess's tower, and she said:

"Thou soul of the world! bright sun!

Look on me, in this prison undone!

Have pity on me!

Oh! where is my loved one? say!

Through what lands do his footsteps stray?

And does he now think of me?"

"Princess Miranda," said the sun; "dry your tears, comfort your heart; your lover is hastening to you, from the bottom of the deep sea, from under the coral reefs; he has won the enchanted ring; when he puts it on his finger, his army will increase by thousands, regiment after regiment, with horse and foot; the drums are beating, the sabres gleaming, the colours flying, the cannon roaring, they are bearing down on the empire of Kosciey. But he cannot conquer him by force of mortal weapons. I will teach him a surer way; and there is good hope that he will be able to deliver you from Kosciey, and save your country. I will hasten to your prince. Farewell."

The sun stood over a wide country, beyond the deep seas, beyond high mountains, where Prince Hero in a golden helmet, on a gallant horse, was drawing up his army, and preparing to march against Kosciey, the besieger of the fair princess. He had seen her three times in a dream, and had heard much about her, for her beauty was famous

This horse was the wonder of the world

throughout the world.

"Dismiss your army," said the sun. "No army can conquer Kosciey, no bullet can reach him; you can only free Princess Miranda by killing him, and how you are to do it, you must learn from the old woman Jandza; I can only tell you where you will find the horse, that must carry you to her. Go hence towards the East; you will come to a green meadow, in which there are three oak trees; and among them you will find hidden in the ground an iron door, with a brazen padlock; behind this door you will find a battle charger, and a mace; the rest you will learn afterwards; . . . farewell!"

Prince Hero was most surprised; but he took off his enchanted ring and threw it into the sea; with it all his great army vanished directly into mist, leaving no trace behind. He turned to the East and travelled onwards. After three days he came to the green meadow, where he found the three oak trees, and the iron door, as he had been told. It opened upon a narrow, crooked stairway, going downwards, leading into a deep dungeon, where he found another iron door, closed by a heavy iron padlock. Behind this he heard a horse neighing, so loudly that it made the door fall to the ground, and at the same moment eleven other doors flew open and there came out a war-horse, which had been shut up there for ages by a wizard.

The prince whistled to the horse; the horse tugged at his fastenings, and broke twelve chains by which he had been fettered. He had eyes like stars, flaming nostrils, and a mane like a thunder-cloud; . . . he was a horse of horses, the wonder of the world.

"Prince Hero! "said the horse, "I have long waited for such a rider as you, and I am ready to serve you for ever. Mount on my back, take that mace in your hand, which you see hanging to the saddle; you need not fight with it yourself, for it will strike wherever you command it, and beat a whole army. I know the way everywhere; tell me where you want to go, and you will presently be there."

The prince told him everything; took the self-fighting mace in his hand, and sprang on his back. The horse reared, snorted, spurned the ground, and they flew over mountains and forests, higher than the flying clouds, over rapid rivers, and deep seas; but when they flew along the ground the charger's light feet never trampled down a blade of grass, nor raised an atom of dust on the sandy soil.

Before sunset Prince Hero had reached the primeval forest in which the old woman Jandza lived. He was amazed at the size and age of the mighty oaks, pine trees and firs, where there reigned a perpetual twilight. And there was absolute silence not a leaf or a blade of grass stirring; and no living thing, not so much as a bird, or the hum of an insect; only amidst this grave-like stillness the sound of his horse's hoofs. The prince stopped before a little house, supported on crooked legs, and said:

"Little house, move

On your crooked legs free:

Turn your back to the wood,

And your front to me."

Princess Miranda lived in a splendid palace

The house turned round, with the door towards him; the prince went in, and the old woman Jandza asked him: "How did you get here, Prince Hero, where no living soul has penetrated till now?"

"Don't ask me; but welcome your guest politely."

So the old woman gave the prince food and drink, made up a soft bed for him, to rest on after his journey, and left him for the night. Next morning he told her all, and what he had come for.

"You have undertaken a great and splendid task, prince; so I will tell you how to kill Kosciey. In the Ocean-Sea, on the island of Everlasting Life, there is an old oak tree; under this tree is buried a coffer bound with iron; in this coffer is a hare; under the hare sits a grey duck; this duck carries within her an egg; and in this egg is enclosed the life of Kosciey. When you break the egg he will die at once. Now good-bye, prince; and good luck go with you; your horse will show you the way."

The prince leaped back upon the horse and they soon left the forest behind them, and came to the shore of the ocean. On the beach was a fisherman's net, and in the net was a great fish, who when he saw the prince, cried out piteously: "Prince Hero! take me out of the net, and throw me back into the sea; I will repay you!"

The prince took the fish out of the net, and threw it into the sea; it splashed in the water, and vanished. The prince looked over the sea, and saw the island in the grey distance, far, far away; but how was he to get there? He leaned upon his mace, deep in thought.

"What are you thinking of, prince?" asked the horse.

"I am thinking how I am to get to the island, when I cannot swim over that breadth of sea."

"Sit on my back, prince, and hold fast."

So the prince sat firm on the horse's back, and held fast by the thick mane; a wind arose, and the sea was somewhat rough; but rider and horse pushed on, through the billows, and at last came to shore on the island of Everlasting Life.

The prince took off his horse's bridle, and let him loose to feed in a meadow of luxuriant grass, and walked on quickly to a high hill, where grew the old oak tree. Taking it in both hands he tugged at it; the oak resisted all his efforts; he tugged again, the oak began to creak, and moved a little; he mustered all his strength, and tugged again. The oak fell with a crash to the ground, with its roots uppermost, and there, where they had stood firmly fixed so many hundred years, was a deep hole. Looking down he saw the iron-bound coffer; he fetched it up, broke open the lock with a stone, raised the lid, picked up the hare lying in it by its ears; but at that moment the duck, which had been sitting under the hare, took the alarm, and flew off straight to sea.

The prince fired a shot after her; the bullet hit the duck; she gave one loud quack, and fell; but in that same instant the egg fell from her down to the bottom of the sea. The prince gave a cry of despair; but just then a great fish came swimming, dived down to the depths of the sea, and coming to the shore, with the egg in its jaws, left it on the sand. The fish swam away; but the prince, taking up the egg, mounted his horse once more; and they swam till they reached Princess Miranda's island, where they saw a great iron wall stretching all round her white marble palace.

There was only one entrance through this iron wall to the palace, and before this lay the monstrous dragon with the twelve heads, six of which kept guard alternately; when the one half slept the other six remained awake. If anyone were to approach the gate he could not escape the horrid jaws. Nobody could hurt the dragon; his death could be wrought only by his own actions. The prince stood on the hill before that gate, and commanded his self-fighting mace, which could become invisible, to go and clear an entrance to the palace.

The invisible, self-fighting mace fell upon the dragon and began to thunder on all his horrid heads with such force, that the beast's eyes became bloodshot, and he began to hiss fiercely; he shook his twelve heads, and stretched wide his twelve horrid jaws; he spread out his forest of claws; but this helped him not at all, the mace kept on smiting him, moving about so fast, that not a single head escaped, as he hissed, groaned, and shrieked wildly!

Now it had given a thousand blows, the blood gushed from a thousand wounds, and there was no help for the dragon; he raged, writhed about, and squealed in despair; finally, as blow followed blow, and he could not see who gave them, he gnashed his teeth, belched forth flame, and at length turned his claws upon himself, plunging them deep into his own flesh, struggled, writhed, twisted himself round, and in and out; his blood flowed freely from his wounds.

Now, at last, it was all over for the dragon. The prince, seeing this, went into the courtyard of the palace, put his horse into the stable, and went up by a winding stair, towards the tower, whence the Princess Miranda, having seen him, addressed him: "Welcome, Prince Hero! I saw how you disposed of the dragon; but do be careful, for my enemy, Kosciey, is in this palace; he is most powerful, both through his own strength, and through his sorceries; and if he kill you I can live no longer."

"Princess Miranda, do not trouble about me." the prince assured her. "I have the life of Kosciey in this egg." Then he called out: "Invisible self-fighting mace, go into the palace and beat Kosciey. The mace bestirred itself quickly, battered in the iron doors, and set upon Kosciey; it smote him on the neck, till he crouched and cowered as sparks flew from his eyes, and there was a noise like a thousand mills in his ears.

If he had been an ordinary mortal it would have been all over with him at once; as it was, he was horribly tormented, and puzzled, feeling all these blows and never seeing whence they came. He sprang about, raving and raging, till the whole island resounded with his roaring. At last he looked through the window, and behold there he

All the while Princess Miranda dreamed of how her prince would rescue her

saw Prince Hero.

"Ah! that is all your doing!" he exclaimed; and sprang out into the courtyard, to rush straight at him, and beat him to a jelly! But the prince held the egg in one hand ready; and he squeezed it so hard, that the shell cracked and the yolk and the white were all spilled together . . . and Kosciey fell lifeless!

And so, with the death of the enchanter all his evil charms were dissolved at once; all the people in the island who were asleep began to stir. The soldiers woke from sleep, and as the drums began to beat; they formed their ranks, massed themselves in order, and began to march towards the palace.

Meanwhile in the palace there was great joy; for Princess Miranda came towards the prince, gave him her white hand, and thanked him warmly. Then they went to the throne-room. There, following the princess's example, her twelve waiting-maids linked hands with twelve young officers of the army, and the couples grouped themselves around the throne, on which the prince and princess were sitting.

A priest, arrayed in all his finest vestments, came in at the open door, and the prince and princess exchanged rings, and were married. And all the other couples were married at the same time! After the wedding there was a feast, dancing, and music, which it is a pleasure to think of. Everywhere there was great rejoicing.

Handsome is as Handsome Does

This story from Romania begins in a similar way to Hansel and Gretel with two children being sent out into the forest – but marking their way as they go in order to be able to return home safely. However, their adventures then take a rather different turn with adventures in a giant's castle . . .

Once on a time, there lived an old man and an old woman; each had two children by previous marriages. The wife took good care of her own children, feeding them well, and giving them good clothes; while the children, of the husband were neglected, and left almost without food. Not content with thus ill-treating them, and seeing that they were better looking, and better behaved, than her own, she made up her mind to get rid of them.

So one day she said to her husband, "Your boy and girl are too lazy and good-for-nothing, you must send them from here, or I will not eat bread and salt out of the same platter with you again.

"Where can I take them to?" asked he.

"Where you please, so long as I am no longer troubled with them."

Finding no other way of pacifying his wife, he determined to take them next day to a wood and leave them there. The boy overheard the conversation, and repeated it to his sister; so they took their precautions, and next morning they each filled a canvas bag, one with ashes, the other with corn flour, before their father called them to accompany him, and on the way, the boy scattered the ashes. On arriving at the four cross roads, the father bade them wait there for him, as he was going further into the forest to cut down some branches.

Giving them some food, he disappeared amongst the thickets, and tying a hollow gourd to a tree, he returned by another way to his cottage.

When the wind blew, it struck the gourd against the tree, and produced a sound like wood-chopping, so when the children heard this they said, "Hark, to father, cutting wood!"

The fox begged the boy not to shoot him

410

Bears lived deep in the forest

*The last band snapped and
the giant was free*

Waiting half the day, and seeing that their father did not come, they set off to search him from whence the sound came. On reaching the tree from whence the noise proceeded they found only the gourd; so they began to cry, but by the aid of the traces of the ashes, found their home again.

The parents, with the wife's children were sitting round the fire eating long white loaves, the outside of which being burnt, the wife said to her husband, "Where are your children that they may eat these spoiled pieces?"

"Here we are!" cried they, entering the cottage, and beginning to eat the burnt bread.

A few days passed, and again the wife told her husband to take away his children; the second journey had the same result as the first, for the girl scattered some, and so found their way home again.

Seeing that he could not live in peace with his wife, he determined to take them to a greater distance, and on a road quite unknown to them. The girl had still some malain left, which she scattered as before, but this time rain fell, and made it into a paste, which was greedily eaten up by the little birds. So they walked all day until evening, and seeing no signs of their home they climbed into a tree, and made themselves a bed amongst the branches, and slept until daybreak. When morning came, they again

411

The boy confronted his sister angrily but she seemed oblivious to her treachery

began their wanderings through the forest. After a time hunger seized them, and they had nothing to eat; but at last the boy cut himself a pliant stick, and taking a mesh of his sister's hair, with it and the stick made himself a bow. Soon he shot some birds, while his sister procured a fire by rubbing two pieces of wood together and setting alight some dry branches. Thus they lived for some days, until in their wanderings they met with a fox; the boy was on the point of adjusting his bow, when the fox cried "Do not shoot me, and then I will give you one of my cubs, who will be useful to you," so, taking the cub, the boy continued his way.

Further on he encountered a she-wolf; he was again about to draw his bow when the wolf begged him to spare her life, and she would give him one of her young ones, who would be useful to him. Taking with him the young wolf, as well as the cub-fox, he went along.

Soon on his path he encountered a bear, and the same form of words and acts was gone through as with the fox and the wolf. When evening approached, the children, followed by the young animals, came suddenly on a fine palace. Entering fearlessly, the boy found in the lodge a bundle of keys; thinking that they were the keys of the palace, he took them and began to open the various doors. At length he reached a very fine carved steel door, and opening it he found there, a huge giant, bound to the wall by three iron bands. When the giant saw him he called, "Youngster, bring me a jug of water, for I am dying of thirst." Instead of doing this he went in search of his sister. Giving her all the keys, he told her she might enter every room excepting the one with the steel door, but if she went into that one a misfortune would befall her.

Thus saying, he set out for the chase, followed by his three young animals.

After his departure the girl began exploring the palace, and arriving at the steel door, she said to herself, "I wonder why my brother has forbidden me this chamber! perhaps there are treasures in it which he wants for himself alone-- why should he do this, seeing that I am his sister?"

So trying the lock, she turned the key and entered. At sight of her, the giant cried, "Maiden, bring me a jug of water, and I will be of great service to you." She went quickly, and returned with the water. After the giant had drunk it, one of his irons snapped and fell asunder.

Again the giant cried, "Maiden bring me another jug of water, and you shall not have cause to repent it." Quickly she came with the water, the giant drank it eagerly, and the second band fell away.

A third time he cried, "Maiden bring me but one more jug, then I shall be free, I am weary of being bound for so many years, and I will do whatsoever thou desirest."

She brought him water for the third time, and after he had drunk that also, the last band snapped and fell away. The giant finding himself free, said to the maiden, "Where is your brother?"

"Nenna is gone shooting," said she.

Childhood love forgotten, she betrayed her brother

"I should like to kill your brother," said he, "and to keep you to live with me here in this splendid palace, will you consent to this? Tell me so, for you have grown so dear to me, that I cannot live without you."

"How can you kill him?" said she, "He has always his fox and his wolf and his bear with him."

Said the giant, "The next time he goes out, you must manœuvre to keep his beasts at home, and then I can go and swallow him up." The maiden consented, and the giant returned to his chamber.

When Nenna arrived from the forest, his sister was very loving and caressing to him; and after eating their supper they retired to rest. Next morning by daybreak, the boy was again ready to set out for the chase, but his sister fondling him, and showing signs of great affection said, "Brother, you amuse yourself in the forest, while I am alone all day! Leave me your beasts to play with." With reluctance he consented and set off alone.

Shortly after his departure, the giant came out and bade the maiden shut up the animals securely in the room with the steel door, and to roll a heavy stone against it. Then the giant set off in pursuit of the boy, who, when he saw the giant, like a moving cloud in the distance, knew that his sister had disobeyed him, and set the giant free.

Climbing a lofty tree, he waited the approach of the giant, who was soon at the foot of the tree, calling him to come down so that he might eat him up. The boy flung him his sheep-skin cap, and called to him to gnaw at that until he had time to sing a song.

This was what he sang.

"Il! N'ande! N'a vede!

N'a grenlu pamentului,

Ilsurelulu campului,
Ca ve pere stapanalu."

The fox heard this song, and said, "Hark! our master is in danger."

"Shut your woollen ears," said the other two.

The giant had got to the last morsel of the sheepskin cap, so the boy flung one of his sandals and told him to eat that also, as he had not yet finished his song.

Beginning again his song, this time the wolf heard him, but the bear said, "Be quiet, sharp ears."

By this time the sandal was devoured, and the giant in a loud voice called him to descend, but the boy flung the other sandal, and entreated time to sing one more song.

This time the bear also heard him, and said, "In truth, our master is in great peril, but how can we get to him? For we are locked in here."

Said the fox, "I will make an opening," and forced himself with all his strength against the door, without success. Tthe wolf had no greater success – but when the bear put his broad back there, the door flow open, and the stone rolled twenty paces away.

Finding themselves at liberty, the wolf said, "Shall we go like wind, or as quick as thought?"

"Like the wind!" said the bear, "For if we travel as quick as thought, we shall be breathless, and incapable of fighting when we arrive."

So, like the wind they went and soon arrived to help their master. The giant, seeing their approach, transformed himself into a log of wood.

The boy cried to his beasts, "You must eat up all this wood for me, and leave for my share, only its heart and its liver."

They made no difficulty about it, so the boy, seizing the heart and the liver, returned home, to the great astonishment and vexation of his sister.

The boy made a wooden spit, and thrusting the liver and the heart on it, bade his sister prepare this food. When it was cooked he seized the spit, and striking his sister with it said, "This is because you set the giant free, and consented to my death – do you see?"

"I see as if I were looking through a sieve!"

Striking her again, he said, "Can you see now?"

"I see as through a mist," she replied.

Placing over her head nine casks, one above the other, and covering her completely with them, he said, "You will see clear when you have filled these nine casks with your tears;" and so he went on his way and left his cheating sister to die.

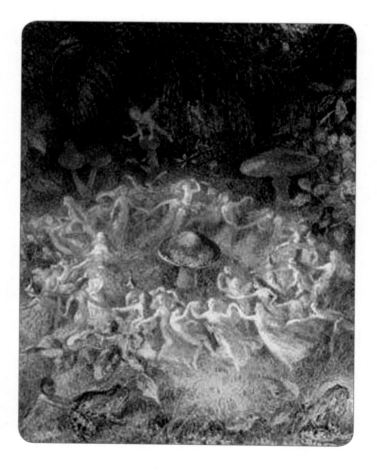

Fairy dance

They hold their great balls in the open air, in what is called a fairy-ring. For weeks afterward you can see the ring on the grass. It is not there when they begin, but they make it by waltzing round and round. Sometimes you will find mushrooms inside the ring, and these are fairy chairs that the servants have forgotten to clear away. The chairs and the rings are the only tell-tale marks these little people leave behind them, and they would remove even these were they not so fond of dancing that they toe it till the very moment of the opening of the gates."

Sir James M Barrie (Author of Peter Pan)

Of all the minor creatures of mythology, fairies are the most beautiful, the most numerous, the most memorable.

Andrew Lang (1844–1912)

Every time a new story is told, a faery is born.

Anon

How the Raja's son won the Princess

An Indian prince sets out on an adventure, hoping to find a beautiful princess. This tale was retold by Joseph Jacobs who was Australian born (1854–1916). Jacobs studied in Sydney, then at Cambridge in England and finally at the University of Berlin but settled permanently in the United States.

Just one parrot, called Hiraman, remained

In a country there was a Raja who had an only son who every day went out to hunt. One day the Rani, his mother, said to him, "You can hunt wherever you like on these three sides; but you must never go to the fourth side." This she said because she knew if he went on the fourth side he would hear of the beautiful Princess Labam, and that then he would leave his father and mother and seek for the princess.

The young prince listened to his mother, and obeyed her for some time; but one day, when he was hunting on the three sides where he was allowed to go, he remembered what she had said to him about the fourth side, and he determined to go and see why she had forbidden him to hunt on that side. When be got there, he found himself in a jungle, and nothing in the jungle but a quantity of parrots, who lived in it. The young Raja shot at some of them, and at once they all flew away up to the sky. All, that is, but one, and this was their Raja, who was called Hiraman parrot.

When Hiraman parrot found himself left alone, he called out to the other parrots, "Don't fly away and leave me alone when the Raja's son shoots. If you desert me like this, I will tell the Princess Labam."

Then the parrots all flew back to their Raja, chattering. The prince was greatly surprised, and said, "Why, these birds can talk!" Then he said to the parrots, "Who is the Princess Labam? Where does she live?" But the parrots would not tell him where she lived. "You can never get to the Princess Labam's country." That is all they would say.

The prince grew very sad when they would not tell him anything more; and he threw his gun away and went home. When he got home, he would not speak or eat, but lay on his bed for four or five days, and seemed very ill.

At last he told his father and mother that he wanted to go and see the Princess Labam. "I must go," be said; "I must see what she is like. Tell me where her country is."

"We do not know where it is," answered his father and mother.

"Then I must go and look for it," said the prince.

"No, no," they said, "you must not leave us. You are our only son. Stay with us. You will never find the Princess Labam."

His mother loved him dearly and wanted him to be safe

" I must try and find her," said the prince. "Perhaps God will show me the way. If I live and I find her, I will come back to you; but perhaps I shall die, and then I shall never see you again. Still I must go."

So they had to let him go, though they cried very much at parting with him. His father gave him fine clothes to wear, and a fine horse. And he took his gun, and his bow and arrows, and a great many other weapons; "for," he said, "I may want them." His father too, gave him plenty of rupees.

Then he himself got his horse all ready for the journey, and

he said goodbye to his father and mother; and his mother took her handkerchief and wrapped some sweetmeats in it, and gave it to her son. "My child," she said to him, "when you are hungry eat some of these sweetmeats."

He then set out on his journey, and rode on and on till he came to a jungle in which were a pool and shady trees. He bathed himself and his horse in the pool, and then sat down under a tree. "Now," he said to himself, "I will eat some of the sweetmeats my mother gave me, and I will drink some water, and then I will continue my journey." He opened his handkerchief and took out a sweetmeat. He found an ant in it. He took out another. There was an ant in that one too. So he laid the two sweetmeats on the ground, and he took out another, and another, and another, until he had taken them all out; but in, each he found an ant. "Never mind," he said, "I won't eat the sweetmeats; the ants shall eat them." Then the Ant-Raja came and stood before him and said, "You have been good to us. If ever you are in trouble, think of me and we will come to you."

The Raja's son thanked him, mounted his horse and continued his journey. He rode on and on until he came to another jungle, and there he saw a tiger who had a thorn in his foot, and was roaring loudly from the pain.

"Why do you roar like that?' said the young Raja. "What is the matter with you?"

"I have had a thorn in my foot for twelve years," answered the tiger, "and it hurts me so; that is why I roar."

"Well," said the Raja's son, "I will take it out for you. But perhaps, as you are a tiger, when I have made you well, you will eat me?"

"Oh no," said the tiger, "I won't eat you. Do make me well."

Then the prince took a little knife from his pocket and cut the thorn out of the tiger's foot; but when he cut, the tiger roared louder than ever – so loud that his wife heard him in the next jungle, and came bounding along to see what was the matter. The tiger saw her coming, and hid the prince in the jungle, so that she should not see him.

"What man hurt you that you roared so loud?" said the wife.

"No one hurt me," answered the husband; "but a Raja's son came and took the thorn out of my foot."

"Where is he? Show him to me," said his wife.

"If you promise not to kill him, I will call him," said the tiger.

"I won't kill him; only let me see him," answered his wife.

Then the tiger called the Raja's son, and when he came the tiger and his wife made him a great many salaams. Then they gave him a good dinner, and he stayed with them for three days. Every day he looked at the tiger's foot, and the third day it was quite healed. Then he said good-bye to the tigers, and the tiger said to him, "If ever you are in trouble, think of me, and we will come to you."

The Raja's son rode on and on till he came to a third jungle. Here he found four fakirs whose teacher and master had died, and had left four things,--a bed, which carried whoever sat on it whithersoever he wished to go; a bag, that gave its owner whatever he wanted, jewels, food or clothes; a stone bowl that gave its owner as much water as he wanted, no matter how far he might be from a tank; and a stick and rope, to which its owner had only to say, if any one came to make war on him, "Stick, beat as many men and soldiers as are here," and the stick would beat them and the rope would tie them up.

The four fakirs were quarrelling over these four things. One said, "I want this;" another said,." You cannot have it, for I want it;" and so on.

The Raja's son said to them, "Do not quarrel for these things. I will shoot four arrows in four different directions. Whichever of you gets to my first arrow, shall have the first thing – the bed. Whosoever gets to the second arrow, shall have the second thing – the bag. He who gets to the third arrow, shall have the third thing – the bowl. And he who gets to the fourth arrow, shall have the last things – the stick and rope." To this they agreed. And the prince shot off his first arrow. Away raced the fakirs to get it. When they brought it back to him he shot off the second, and when they had found and brought it to him he shot off his third, and when they had brought him the third he shot off the fourth.

While they were away looking for the fourth arrow the Raja's son let his horse loose in the jungle and sat on the bed, taking the bowl, the stick and rope, and the bag with him. Then he said, "Bed, I wish to go to the Princess Labam's country." The little bed instantly rose up into the air and began to fly, and it flew and flew till it came to the Princess Labam's country, where it settled on the ground. The Raja's son asked some men he saw, "Whose country is this?"

"The Princess Labam's country," they answered. Then the prince went on till he came to a house where he saw an old woman.

"Who are you? "she said. "Where do you come from?"

"I come from a far country," he said; "do let me stay with you to-night."

"No," she answered, "I cannot let you stay with me; for our king has ordered that men from other countries may not stay in his country. You cannot stay in my house."

"You are my aunty," said the prince; "Let me remain with you for this one night. You see it is evening, and if I go into the jungle, then the wild beasts will eat me."

"Well," said the old woman, "you may stay here tonight; but to-morrow morning you must go away, for if the king hears you have passed the night in my house, he will have me seized and put into prison."

Then she took him into her house, and the Raja's son was very glad. The old woman began preparing dinner, but he stopped her. "Aunty," he said, " I will give you food." He put his hand into his bag, saying, "Bag, I want some dinner," and the. bag gave him instantly a delicious dinner, served up on two gold plates. The old woman and the Raja's son then dined together.

When they had finished eating, 'the old woman said, "Now I will fetch some water."

"Don't go," said the prince. "You shall have plenty of water directly." So he took his bowl and said to it, "Bowl, I want some water," and then it filled with water. When it was full, the prince cried out, "Stop, bowl!" and the bowl stopped filling. "See, aunty," he said, "with this bowl I can always get as much water as I want."

By this time night had come. "Aunty," said the Raja's son, "why don't you light a lamp?"

"There is no need," she said. "Our king has forbidden

The tiger promised not to eat the Raja's son

Nobody knew the prince had come in the night and put it all there.

In the morning the old woman came to the Raja's son. "Now it is morning," she said, "and you must go; for if the king finds out all I have done for you, he will seize me."

"I am ill to-day, dear aunty," said the prince; "do let me stay till to-morrow morning."

"Good," said the old woman. So he stayed, and they took their dinner out of the bag, and the bowl gave them water.

When night came the princess got up and sat on her roof, and at twelve o'clock, when every one was in bed, she went to her bed-room, and was soon fast asleep. Then the Raja's son sat on his bed, and it carried him to the princess. He took his bag and said, "Bag, I want a most lovely shawl;" It gave him a splendid shawl, and he spread it over the princess as she lay asleep. Then he went back to the old woman's house and slept till morning.

In the morning, when the princess saw the shawl she was delighted. "See, mother," she said; "Khuda must have given me this shawl, it is so beautiful." Her mother was very glad too. "Yes, my child," she said; "Khuda must have given you this splendid shawl."

When it was morning the old woman said to the Raja's son, "Now you must really go."

the people in his country to light any lamps; for, as soon as it is dark, his daughter, the Princess Labam, comes and sits on her roof, and she shines so that she lights up all the country and our houses, and we can see to do our work as if it were day."

When it was quite black night the princess got up. She dressed herself in her rich clothes and jewels, and rolled up her hair, and across her head she put a band of diamonds and pearls. Then she shone like the moon and her beauty made night day. She came out of her room and sat on the roof of her palace. In the daytime she never came out of her house; she only came out at night. All the people in her father's country then went about their work and finished it.

The Raja's son watched the princess quietly, and was very happy. He said to himself, "How lovely she is!"

At midnight, when everybody had gone to bed, the princess came down from her roof and went to her room; and when she was in bed and asleep, the Raja's son got up softly and sat on his bed. "Bed," he said to it, "I want to go to the Princess Labam's bed-room." So the little bed carried him to the room where she lay fast asleep.

The young Raja took his bag and said, "I want a great deal of betel-leaf," and it at once gave him quantities of betel-leaf. This he laid near the princess's bed, and then his little bed carried him back to the old woman's house.

Next morning all the princess's servants found the betel-leaf, and began to eat it.

"Where did you get all that betel-leaf?" asked the princess.

"We found it near your bed," answered the servants.

Many brave rajas and sons of rajas had been killed in their pursuit of the lovely princess

The princess rode on an elephant to their magnificent wedding

"Aunty," he answered, "I am not well enough yet. Let me stay a few days longer. I will remain hidden in your house, so that no one may see me." So the old woman let him stay.

When it was black night, the princess put on her lovely. clothes and jewels and sat on her roof. At midnight she went to her room and went to sleep. Then the Raja's son sat on his bed and flew to her bed-room. There he said to his bag, "Bag, I want a very, very beautiful ring." The bag gave him a glorious ring. Then he took the Princess Labam's hand gently to put on the ring, and she started up very much frightened.

"Who are you?" she said to the prince. "Where do you come from? Why do you come to my room?"

"Do not be afraid, princess," he said; "I am no thief. I am a great Raja's son. Hiraman parrot, who lives in the jungle where I went to hunt, told me your name, and then I left my father and mother and came to see you."

"Well," said the princess, "as you are the son of such a great kaja, I will not have you killed, and I will tell my father and mother that I wish to marry you."

The prince then returned to the old woman's house; and when morning came the princess said to her mother, "The son of a great Raja has come to this country, and I wish to marry him." Her mother told this to the king.

"Good," said the king; "but if this Raja's son wishes to marry my daughter, he must first do whatever I bid him. If he fails I will kill him. I will give him eighty pounds weight of mustard seed, and out of this he must crush the oil in one day. If he cannot do this he shall die."

In the morning the Raja's son told the old woman that he intended to marry the princess. "Oh," said the old woman, "go away from this country, and do not think of marrying her. A great many Rajas and Rajas' sons have come here to marry her, and her father has had them all killed. He says whoever wishes to marry his daughter must first do whatever he bids him. If he can, then he shall marry the princess; if he cannot, the king will have him killed. But no one can do the things the king tells him to do; so all the Rajas and Rajas' sons who have tried have been put to death. You will be killed too, if you try. Do go away." But

419

the prince would not listen to anything she said.

The king sent for the prince to the old woman's. house, and his servants brought the Raja's son to the king's courthouse to the king. There the king gave him eighty pounds of mustard seed, and told him to crush all the oil out of it that day, and bring it next morning to him to the courthouse. "Whoever wishes to marry my daughter." he said to the prince, "must first do all I tell him. If he cannot, then I have him killed. So if you cannot crush all the oil out of this mustard seed you will die."

The prince was very sorry when he heard this. "How can I crush the oil out of all this mustard seed in one thy?" he said to himself; "and if I do not, the king will kill me." He took the mustard seed to the old woman's house, and did not know what to do. At last he remembered the Ant-Raja, and the moment he did so, the Ant-Raja and his ants came to him. "Why do you look so sad?" said the Ant-Raja.

The prince showed him the mustard seed, and said to him, "How can I crush the oil out of all this mustard seed in one day? And if I do not take the oil to the king to-morrow morning, he will kill me."

"Be happy," said the Ant-Raja; "lie down and sleep; we will crush all the oil out for you during the day, and to-morrow morning you shall take it to the king." The Raja's son lay down and slept, and the ants crushed out the oil for him. The prince was very glad when he saw the oil.

The next morning he took it to the court-house to the king. But the king said," You cannot yet marry my daughter. If you wish to do so, you must first fight with my two demons, and kill them." The king a long time ago had caught two demons, and then, as he did not know what to do with them, he had shut them up in a cage. He was afraid to let them loose for fear they would eat up all the people in his country; and he did not know how to kill them. So all the kings and kings' sons who wanted to marry the Princess Labam had to fight with these demons; "for," said the king to himself, "perhaps the demons may be killed, and then I shall be rid of them."

When he heard of the demons the Raja's son was very sad. "What can I do?" he said to himself. "How can I fight with these two demons?" Then he thought of his tiger: and the tiger and his wife came to him and said, "Why are you so sad?" The Raja's son answered, "The king has ordered me to fight with his two demons and kill them. How can I do this? " "Do not be frightened," said the tiger. "Be happy. I and my wife will fight with them for you."

Then the Raja's son took out of his bag two splendid coats. They were all gold and silver, and covered with pearls and diamonds. These he put on the tigers to make them beautiful, and he took them to the king, and said to him,. "May these tigers fight your demons for me?"

"Yes," said' the king, who did not care in the least who

Princess Labam remembered how
she would sit on the rooftop and dream
of a prince who would win her hand

killed his demons, provided they were killed. "Then call your demons," said the Raja's son, "and these tigers will fight them." The king did so, and the tigers and the demons fought and fought until the tigers had killed the demons.

"That is good," said the king. "But you must do something else before I give you my daughter. Up in the sky I have a kettle-drum. You must go and beat it. If you cannot do this, I will kill you."

The Raja's son thought of his little bed; so he went to the old woman's house and sat on his bed. "Little bed!' he said, "up in the sky is the king's kettle-drum. I want to go to it." The bed flew up with him, and the Raja's son beat the drum, and the king heard him. Still, when he came down, the king would not give him his daughter. "You have," he said to the prince, "done the three things I told you to do; but you must do one thing more."

"If I can, I will," said the Raja's son.

Then the king showed him the trunk of a tree that was lying near his court-house. It was a very, very, thick trunk. He gave the prince a wax hatchet, and said, "Tomorrow morning you must cut this trunk in two with this wax hatchet."

The Raja's son went back to the old woman's house. He was very sad, and thought that now the Raja would certainly kill him. "I had his oil crushed out by the ants," he said to himself. "I had his demons killed by the tigers. My bed helped me to beat his kettle-drum. But now what can I do? How can I cut that thick tree-trunk in two with a wax hatchet?"

At night he went on his bed to see the princess. "To morrow," he said to her, "your father will kill me." "Why?" asked the princess.

"He has told me to cut a thick tree-trunk in two with a wax hatchet. How can I ever do that?" said the Raja's son. "Do not be afraid," said the princess; "do as I bid you, and you will cut it in two quite easily."

Then she pulled out a hair from her head and gave it to the prince. "To-morrow," she said, "when no one is near you, you must say to the tree-trunk, 'The Princess Labam commands you to let yourself be cut in two by this hair. Then stretch the hair down the edge of the wax hatchet's blade."

The prince next day did exactly as the princess had told him; and the minute the hair that was stretched down the edge of the hatchet-blade touched the tree-trunk it split into two pieces.

The king said, "Now you can marry my daughter." Then the wedding took place. All the Rajas and kings of the countries round were asked to come to it, and there were great rejoicings. After a few days the prince's son said to his wife, "Let us go to my father's country." The Princess Labam's father gave them a quantity of camels and horses and rupees and servants; and they travelled in great state to the prince's country, where they lived happily.

The prince always kept his bag, bowl, bed, and stick; only, as no one ever came to make war on him, he never needed to use the stick.

The Daughter of the Rose

True love wins through in this Romanian tale that hints at a beautiful sweet maiden's seduction and tells of a prince who sees sense and makes her his own.

IN days gone by, there dwelt a King and a Queen in Jassy, who, to keep their only son at home with them, were always making him fine promises, which they never fulfilled.

One day this young prince, Marin by name, went to his mother's apartments, and announced to her, that if she did not speedily bring to him the beautiful princess from foreign parts which she had promised him to wife, he should set off in search of her himself. After waiting some weeks, finding that this promise was not likely to be fulfilled, he called for his horse and his retainers, and set off on his travels. He rode along until he came to a vast prairie, studded with the most beautiful flowers, through which meandered a silvery rivulet of pure water.

By the side of this rivulet grew a large rose tree with spreading branches, under which Marin stretched himself, and was trying to seek repose when he heard issuing from the tree these words:

"I pray thee sweet and loved rose tree
Open thy bark and let me free,
To seek the brook's refreshing wave,
To cool my face, my limbs to bathe,
To cull sweet flowers to deck my brow,
Then know'st my soul is pure as snow."

The rose tree unfolded, and from its centre came a fair golden-haired maiden, so dazzling, that to see her was brighter than sunlight. When Prince Marin cast his eyes upon her, he was stunned by the sight of her beauty; but recovering his confidence he approached her and said, "Lovely maiden, if you will give me a flower from your girdle, I will give you a nest in my palace; if you will give me a flower from your lips to kiss, I will dig up your rose tree and transplant it in the garden of my palace; if you will give me your love, I will make you Princess." The maiden, like most other young maidens, believed this flattery, and gave to Marin all that he asked and desired.

After sitting hand in hand, talking of love, they drifted off to sleep. Marin awoke before the maiden, mounted his horse, and went on his way with his followers, leaving only a bunch of flowers in the lap of the sleeping girl. Journeying on, the young prince arrived at length at a golden palace studded with jewels. He enquired of the first man whom he met, whether in that palace there dwelt a young princess? It so happened that it was the owner of the palace to whom he had addressed himself, and who immediately boasted of possessing a most charming daughter. He had heard of the good looks – and of the riches – of this Prince of Jassy, and readily came to the conclusion that this could be no other but the young Marin, so he replied willingly, "Yes, here dwells the Princess Lexandra, and I am her father." Marin heard this with joy, and requested to be admitted into the palace, with the view of seeking the hand of the young Lexandra.

The invitation was given, and after some days' sojourn, and finding that the princess was as lovely as she was good, and that he had found favour in her eyes, he set off with his future father-in-law and intended bride, in a chariot to present her to his parents at Jassy.

Meanwhile, the rose maiden on awaking, finding herself alone, and with but a bunch of flowers for her only companions, sighed and said, "Dear little flowers, why have you made me sleep so long, and why have you separated me from my beloved?" Rising from the ground, she went up to the rose tree, and striking it, said:

"I pray thee, sweet and loved rose tree,
Open thy bark, make place for me."

But the rose tree would not unfold itself, and only answered, "Go away, my pretty maiden, for you have sinned and can no more enter here."

Weeping, she turned aside, and seeing that she could no more be received in the bosom of the rose tree, seizing a staff she set off on the same road as that which the young Marin had taken. After going some distance she met with a monk, and entreated him to exchange with her his rough frock and cowl, in return for her rich dress. He accepted willingly; the maiden wrapped herself in his garment and went on her way. In the confines of a wood, being very weary, she seated herself under the shade of a large elm, in order to take a little rest; shortly after, she saw in the distance a chariot drawn by eight horses approaching, and as it drew near, she recognised her faithless lover.

"Good day, young monk," said Marin. "I thank thee, Highness," said the monk, approaching the carriage. "From whence come you?" said Marin.

"From the valley," said the Monk. "What did you see there?" asked the Prince.

"Nothing, very extraordinary," said the monk, "only near to a large rose tree, there was a beautiful girl weeping, and on my enquiring the cause of her grief, she told me her history."

The lovely maiden awoke to find that the handsome
young prince had vanished, leaving only the
flowers to keep her company

"Repeat it to us," said Marin, visibly moved.

"This was what she told me," said the Monk, "that her home had been in a rose tree, where she was loved and nurtured; that coming out one day in search of flowers, she met with a young prince, who begged a flower from her waist, which she gave him."

Now the monk looked fixedly at the prince, but the latter bade him go on with the story. "Then he asked a flower from her mouth to kiss, and then for her love, and she gave even that also."

"Go on," said the Prince.

"Sitting hand in hand amongst the flowers, sleep overtook them; but when the maiden awoke she found herself deserted, and only a bunch of flowers on her lap. Going to the rose tree, she repeated the rhyme which would open its bark to admit her into its body; but the rose tree remained solid and firm, because she was no longer worthy to enter within, and for this the young girl was weeping alone, and in misery."

"Is that all?" said the Prince.

"So far as I know, for I left her crying in the field."

"To what town are you going, my good monk?" asked the Prince.

"To the same as your Highness, to Jassy," said he.

"Jump into our carriage, then," said the prince, opening the door and making place for him. The monk accepted readily, and during the whole of their journey, the Prince questioned him for further news of the young maiden.

Arrived in the capital, and at the home of Marin, he invited the Monk to be his guest, and gave him a room next to his own in the palace. Yet in three days his marriage with the Princess Lexandra was to take place, and still Marin could not forget the rose maiden, and each evening on passing the door of the monk, he would stay to talk about her.

At length, as the wedding day approached, the monk disappeared.

The prince sought him out and stopped as usual at the monk's door, hoping to hear more of the deserted maiden; but for answer he only heard a muffled sigh! Breaking open the door, he saw the poor monk suspended by a cord to a large book on the wall. Swiftly the prince cut him down, and, underneath the monk's frock, saw the golden hair and the pale face of the rose maiden. Then he called the King and Queen-his parents, and exclaimed, "Look! this is my Princess! Do what you will with the other."

So the Princess Lexandra was sent back home with her father – with great riches, enough for her dower, and the rose maiden was married to Prince Marin, and they had many children and lived very happily ever after.

She disguised herself as a monk and set out to find Prince Marin again

The Old Man and his Grandson

This is a very short moralistic tale by the Brothers Grimm (Jacob 1785–1863 and Wilhelm 1786–1859) serving to remind all of us that age is inevitable and that we should do unto others as we should wish to be done by! Back in the 1700s and 1800s, long before the invention of the "happy ending," folk tales for children often doubled as lessons in morality – with quite dark themes and undercurrents.

There was once a very old man, whose eyes had become dim, his ears dull of hearing, his knees trembled, and when he sat at table he could hardly hold the spoon, and spilt the broth upon the table-cloth or let it run out of his mouth. His son and his son's wife were disgusted at this, so the old grandfather at last had to sit in the corner behind the stove, and they gave him his food in an earthenware bowl, and not even enough of it. And he used to look towards the table with his eyes full of tears. Once, too, his trembling hands could not hold the bowl, and it fell to the ground and broke. The young wife scolded him, but he said nothing and only sighed. Then they brought him a wooden bowl for a few half-pence, out of which he had to eat.

They were once sitting thus when the little grandson of four years old began to gather together some bits of wood upon the ground. "What are you doing there?" asked the father. "I am making a little trough," answered the child, "for father and mother to eat out of when I am big."

The man and his wife looked at each other for a while, and presently began to cry. Then they took the old grandfather to the table, and henceforth always let him eat with them, and likewise said nothing if he did spill a little of anything.

The wise four-year-old boy understood far better than his parents that his grandfather could not help the effects of growing old and frail and that in due course his mother and father, too, would suffer the impact of the passing years

The Black Horse

Fairy cups often appear in Scandinavian
tales while a garron means an undersized
or clumsy (and generally much-despised)
horse or pony. Here a youngest prince
exchanges his garron for an amazing
magical black horse and had many
adventures thereafter. This tale is by
Joseph Jacobs (1854–1916) and appeared
in *More Celtic Fairy Tales* published
in 1894. The original J. F. Campbell's
manuscript was collected in Gaelic in
1862 by Hector MacLean, from Roderick
MacNeill, in the island of Menglay who in
turn had heard the story in about 1840
from a Barra man.

ONCE there was a king and he had three sons, and when the king died, they did not give a shade of anything to the youngest son, but an old white limping garron.

"If I get but this," quoth he, "it seems that I had best go with this same."

He was going with it right before him, sometimes walking, sometimes riding. When he had been riding a good while he thought that the garron would need a while of eating, so he came down to earth, and what should he see coming out of the heart of the western airt towards him but a rider riding high, well, and right well.

"All hail, my lad," said he.

"Hail, king's son," said the other.

"What's your news?" said the king's son.

"I have got that," said the lad who came. "I am after breaking my heart riding this ass of a horse; but will you give me the limping white garron for him?"

"No," said the prince; "it would be a bad business for me."

"You need not fear," said the man that came, "there is no saying but that you might make better use of him than I. He has one value, there is no single place that you can think of in the four parts of the wheel of the world that the black horse will not take you there."

So the king's son got the black horse, and he gave the limping white garron.

Where should he think of being when he mounted but in the Realm Underwaves. He went, and before sunrise on the morrow he was there. What should he find when he got there but the son of the King Underwaves holding a Court, and the people of the realm gathered to see if there was any one who would undertake to go to seek the daughter of the King of the Greeks to be the prince's wife. No one came forward, when who should come up but the rider of the black horse.

"You, rider of the black horse," said the prince, "I lay you under crosses and under spells to have the daughter of the King of the Greeks here before the sun rises to-morrow."

He went out and he reached the black horse and leaned his elbow on his mane, and he heaved a sigh.

"Sigh of a king's son under spells!". said the horse; "but have no care; we shall do the thing that was set before you." And so off they went.

"Now," said the horse, "when we get near the great town of the Greeks, you will notice that the four feet of a horse never went to the town before. The king's daughter will see me from the top of the castle looking out of a window, and she will not be content without a turn of a ride upon me. Say that she may have that, but the horse will suffer no man but you to ride before a woman on him."

They came near the big town, and he fell to horsemanship; and the princess was looking out of the windows, and noticed the horse. The horsemanship pleased her, and she came out just as the horse had come.

"Give me a ride on the horse," said she.

"You shall have that," said he, "but the horse will let no man ride him before a woman but me."

"I have a horseman of my own," said she.

"If so, set him in front," said he.

Before the horseman mounted at all, when he tried to get up, the horse lifted his legs and kicked him off.

"Come then yourself and mount before me," said she; "I won't leave the matter so."

He mounted the horse and she behind him, and before she glanced from her she was nearer sky than earth. He was in Realm Underwaves with her before sunrise.

"You are come," said Prince Underwaves.

"I am come," said he.

"There you are, my hero," said the prince. "You are the son of a king, but I am a son of success. Anyhow, we shall have no delay or neglect now, but a wedding."

"Just gently," said the princess; "your wedding is not so short a way off as you suppose. Till I get the silver cup that my grandmother had at her wedding, and that my mother had as well, I will not marry, for I need to have it at my own wedding."

"You, rider of the black horse," said the Prince Underwaves, "I set you under spells and under crosses unless the silver cup is here before dawn to-morrow."

Out he went and reached the horse and leaned his elbow on his mane, and he heaved a sigh.

"Sigh of a king's son under spells!" said the horse; "mount and you shall get the silver cup. The people of the realm are gathered about the king tonight, for he has missed his daughter, and when you get to the palace go in and leave me without; they will have the cup there going round the

The prince sighed but the horse said, "Have no care;
we shall do the task set before you."
And off they rode together

427

The prince hid the beautiful silver cup under his oxter (armpit)

company. Go in and sit in their midst. Say nothing, and seem to be as one of the people of the place. But when the cup comes round to you, take it under your oxter, and come out to me with it, and we'll go."

Away they went and they got to Greece, and he went in to the palace and did as the black horse bade. He took the cup and came out and mounted, and before sunrise he was in the Realm Underwaves.

"You are come," said Prince Underwaves.

"I am come," said he.

"We had better get married now," said the prince to the Greek princess.

"Slowly and softly," said she. "I will not marry till I get the silver ring that my grandmother and my mother wore when they were wedded."

"You, rider of the black horse," said the Prince Underwaves, "do that. Let's have that ring here to-morrow at sunrise."

The lad went to the black horse and put his elbow on his crest and told him how it was.

"There never was a matter set before me harder than this matter which has now been set in front of me," said the horse, " but there is no help for it at any rate. Mount me. There is a snow mountain and an ice mountain and a mountain of fire between us and the winning of that ring. It is right hard for us to pass them."

Thus they went as they were, and about a mile from the snow mountain they were in a bad case with cold. As they came near it he struck the horse, and with the bound he gave the black horse was on the top of the snow mountain; at the next bound he was on the top of the ice mountain; at the third bound he went through the mountain of fire. When he had passed the mountains he was dragging at the horse's neck, as though he were about to lose himself. He went on before him down to a town below.

"Go down," said the black horse, "to a smithy; make an iron spike for every bone end in me."

Down he went as the horse desired, and he got the spikes made, and back he came with them.

"Stick them into me," said the horse, "every spike of them in every bone end that I have."

That he did; he stuck the spikes into the horse.

"There is a loch here," said the horse, "four miles long and four miles wide, and when I go out into it the loch will take fire and blaze. If you see the Loch of Fire going out before the sun rises, expect me, and if not, go your way."

Out went the black horse into the lake, and the lake became flame. Long was he stretched about the lake, beating his palms and roaring. Day came, and the loch did not go out.

But at the hour when the sun was rising out of the water the lake went out.

And the black horse rose in the middle of the water with one single spike in him, and the ring upon its end.

He came on shore, and down he fell beside the loch.

Then down went the rider. He got the ring, and he dragged the horse down to the side of a hill. He fell to sheltering him with his arms about him, and as the sun was rising he got better and better, till about. midday, when he rose on his feet.

"Mount," said the horse, "and let us begone."

He mounted on the black horse, and away they went. He reached the mountains, and he leaped the horse at the fire mountain and was on the top. From the mountain of fire he leaped to the mountain of ice, and from the mountain of ice to the mountain of snow. He put the mountains past him, and by morning he was in realm under the waves.

"You are come," said the prince.

"I am," said he.

*The black horse and his fine young brother-in-law
were but one and the same, cast under a spell*

"That's true," said Prince Underwaves. "A king's son are you, but a son of success am I. We shall have no more mistakes and delays, but a wedding this time."

"Go easy," said the Princess of the Greeks. "Your wedding is not so near as you think yet. Till you make a castle, I won't marry you. Not to your father's castle nor to your mother's will I go to dwell; but make me a castle for which your father's castle will not make washing water."

"You, rider of the black horse, make that," said Prince Underwaves, "before the morrow's sun rises."

The lad went out to the horse and leaned his elbow on his neck and sighed, thinking that this castle never could be made for ever.

"There never came a turn in my road yet that is easier for me to pass than this," said the black horse.

Glance that the lad gave from him he saw all that there were, and ever so many wrights and stone masons at work, and the castle was ready before the sun rose.

He shouted at the Prince Underwaves, and he saw the castle. He tried to pluck out his eye, thinking that it was a false sight.

"Son of King Underwaves," said the rider of the black horse, "don't think that you have a false sight; this is a true sight."

"That's true," said the prince. "You are a son of success, but I am a son of success too. There will be no more mistakes and delays, but a wedding now."

"No," said she. "The time is come. Should we not go to look at the castle? There's time enough to get married before the night comes."

They went to the castle and it seemed that the castle was without a fault.

"I see one," said the prince. "One want at least to be made good. A well to be made inside, so that water may not be far to fetch when there is a feast or a wedding in the castle."

"That won't be long undone," said the rider of the black horse.

The well was made, and it was seven fathoms deep and two or three fathoms wide, and they looked at the well on the way to the wedding.

"It is very well made," said she, "but for one little fault yonder."

"Where is it?" said Prince Underwaves.

"There," said she.

He bent him down to look. She came out, and she put her two hands at his back, and cast him in.

"Be thou there," said she. "If I go to be married, thou art not the man; but the man who did each exploit that has been done, and, if he chooses, him will I have."

Away she went with the rider of the little black horse to the wedding.

And at the end of three years after that so it was that he first remembered the black horse or where he left him.

He got up and went out, and he was very sorry for his neglect of the black horse. He found him just where he left him.

"Good luck to you, gentleman," said the horse. "You seem as if you had got something that you like better than me."

"I have not got that, and I won't; but it came over me to forget you," said he.

"I don't mind," said the horse, "it will make no difference. Raise your sword and smite off my head."

"Fortune will not allow that I should do that," said he.

"Do it instantly, or I will do it to you," said the horse.

So the lad drew his sword and smote off the horse's head; then he lifted his two palms and uttered a doleful cry.

What should he hear behind him but "All hail, my brother-in-law."

He looked behind him, and there was the finest man he ever set eyes upon.

"What set you weeping for the black horse?" said he.

"This," said the lad, "that there never was born of man or beast a creature in this world that I was fonder of."

"Would you take me for him?" said the stranger.

"If I could think you the horse, I would; but if not, I would rather the horse," said the rider.

"I am the black horse," said the lad, "and if I were not, how should you have all these things that you went to seek in my father's house. Since I went under spells, many a man have I ran at before you met me. They had but one word amongst them: they could not keep me, nor manage me, and they never kept me a couple of days. But when I fell in with you, you kept me till the time ran out that was to come from the spells. And now you shall go home with me, and we will make a wedding in my father's house."

The Little Peasant

This tale is by the Brothers Grimm (Jacob 1785–1863 and Wilhelm 1786–1859) Other stories with this 'trading places' theme include the Norwegian *Big Peter and Little Peter* collected by Peter Christen Asbjørnsen and Jørgen Engebretsen Moe and Hans Christian Andersen's *Little Claus and Big Claus*.

Now the peasant and his wife owned, at last, the cow for which they had longed

There was a certain village wherein no one lived but really rich peasants, and just one poor one, whom they called the little peasant. He had not even so much as a cow, and still less money to buy one, and yet he and his wife did so wish to have one. One day he said to her: "Listen, I have a good idea, there is our kinsman the carpenter, he shall make us a wooden calf, and paint it brown, so that it looks like any other, and in time it will certainly get big and be a cow." The woman also liked the idea, and their kinsman the carpenter cut and planed the calf, and painted it as it ought to be, and made it with its head hanging down as if it were eating.

Next morning when the cows were being driven out, the little peasant called the cow-herd in and said: "Look, I have a little calf there, but it is still small and has to be carried." The cow-herd said: "All right," and took it in his arms and carried it to the pasture, and set it among the grass. The little calf always remained standing like one which was eating, and the cow-herd said: "It will soon run by itself, just look how it eats already!"

At night when he was going to drive the herd home again, he said to the calf: "If you can stand there and eat your fill, you can also go on your four legs; I don't care to drag you home again in my arms." But the little peasant stood at his door, and waited for his little calf, and when the cow-herd drove the cows through the village, and the calf was missing, he inquired where it was.

The cow-herd answered: "It is still standing out there eating. It would not stop and come with us." But the little peasant said: "Oh, but I must have my beast back again." Then they went back to the meadow together, but someone had stolen the calf, and it was gone. The cow-herd said: "It must have run away." The peasant, however, said: "Don't tell me that," and led the cow-herd before the mayor, who for his carelessness condemned him to give the peasant a cow for the calf which had run away.

And now the little peasant and his wife had the cow for which they had so long wished, and they were heartily glad, but they had no food for it, and could give it nothing to eat, so it soon had to be killed. They salted the flesh, and the peasant went into the town and wanted to sell the skin there, so that he might buy a new calf with the proceeds.

On the way he passed by a mill, and there sat a raven with broken wings, and out of pity he took him and wrapped him in the skin. But as the weather grew so bad and there was a storm of rain and wind, he could go no farther, and turned back to the mill and begged for shelter. The miller's wife was alone in the house, and said to the peasant: "Lay yourself on the straw there," and gave him a slice of bread and cheese. The peasant ate it, and lay down with his skin beside him, and the woman thought: "He is tired and has gone to sleep." In the meantime came the parson; the miller's wife received him well, and said: "My husband is out, so we will have a feast." The peasant listened, and when he heard them talk about feasting he was vexed that he had been forced to make shift with a slice of bread and cheese. Then the woman served up four different things, roast meat, salad, cakes, and wine.

Just as they were about to sit down and eat, there was a knocking outside. The woman said: "Oh, heavens! It is my husband!" she quickly hid the roast meat inside the tiled stove, the wine under the pillow, the salad on the bed, the cakes under it, and the parson in the closet on the porch. Then she opened the door for her husband, and said: "Thank heaven, you are back again! There is such a storm, it looks as if the world were coming to an end." The miller saw the peasant lying on the straw, and asked,

peasant pinched the raven's head, so that he croaked and made a noise like krr, krr. The miller said: "What did he say?" The peasant answered: "In the first place, he says that there is some wine hidden under the pillow." "Bless

This was a prosperous village: almost everyone had good food to eat and friends, but not all were generous

"What is that fellow doing there?"

"Ah," said the wife, "the poor knave came in the storm and rain, and begged for shelter, so I gave him a bit of bread and cheese, and showed him where the straw was." The man said: "I have no objection, but be quick and get me something to eat." The woman said: "But I have nothing but bread and cheese."

"I am contented with anything," replied the husband, "so far as I am concerned, bread and cheese will do," and looked at the peasant and said: "Come and eat some more with me." The peasant did not require to be invited twice, but got up and ate. After this the miller saw the skin in which the raven was, lying on the ground, and asked: "What have you there?" The peasant answered: "I have a soothsayer inside it."

"Can he foretell anything to me?" said the miller. "Why not?" answered the peasant: "but he only says four things, and the fifth he keeps to himself." The miller was curious, and said: "Let him foretell something for once." Then the

me!" cried the miller, and went there and found the wine. "Now go on," said he. The peasant made the raven croak again, and said: "In the second place, he says that there is some roast meat in the tiled stove."

"Upon my word!" cried the miller, and went thither, and found the roast meat. The peasant made the raven prophesy still more, and said: "Thirdly, he says that there is some salad on the bed." "That would be a fine thing!" cried the miller, and went there and found the salad. At last the peasant pinched the raven once more till he croaked, and said: "Fourthly, he says that there are some cakes under the bed."

"That would be a fine thing!" cried the miller, and looked there, and found the cakes.

And now the two sat down to the table together, but the miller's wife was frightened to death, and went to bed and took all the keys with her. The miller would have liked much to know the fifth, but the little peasant said: "First, we will quickly eat the four things, for the fifth is something

The peasant passed a mill where he would later seek shelter in a storm

bad." So they ate, and after that they bargained how much the miller was to give for the fifth prophecy, until they agreed on three hundred talers. Then the peasant once more pinched the raven's head till he croaked loudly. The miller asked: "What did he say?" The peasant replied: "He says that the Devil is hiding outside there in the closet on the porch." The miller said: "The Devil must go out," and opened the house-door; then the woman was forced to give up the keys, and the peasant unlocked the closet. The parson ran out as fast as he could, and the miller said: "It was true; I saw the black rascal with my own eyes." The peasant, however, made off next morning by daybreak with the three hundred talers.

At home the small peasant gradually launched out; he built a beautiful house, and the peasants said: "The small peasant has certainly been to the place where golden snow falls, and people carry the gold home in shovels." Then the small peasant was brought before the mayor, and bidden to say from whence his wealth came. He answered: "I sold my cow's skin in the town, for three hundred talers." When the peasants heard that, they too wished to enjoy this great profit, and ran home, killed all their cows, and stripped off their skins in order to sell them in the town to the greatest advantage. The mayor, however, said: "But my servant must go first." When she came to the merchant in the town, he did not give her more than two talers for a skin, and when the others came, he did not give them so much, and said: "What can I do with all these skins?"

Then the peasants, vexed that the small peasant should have thus outwitted them, wanted to take vengeance on him, and accused him of this treachery before the major. The innocent little peasant was unanimously sentenced

The village folk were amazed to see the fine flock of sheep that the poor peasant said he had found in sweet meadows at the bottom of the barrel

to death, and was to be rolled into the water, in a barrel pierced full of holes. He was led forth, and a priest was brought who was to say a mass for his soul. The others were all obliged to retire to a distance, and when the peasant looked at the priest, he recognized the man who had been with the miller's wife. He said to him: "I set you free from the closet, set me free from the barrel." At this same moment up came, with a flock of sheep, the very shepherd whom the peasant knew had long been wishing to be mayor, so he cried with all his might: "No, I will not do it; if the whole world insists on it, I will not do it!" The shepherd hearing that, came up to him, and asked: "What are you about? What is it that you will not do?" The peasant said: "They want to make me mayor, if I will but put myself in the barrel, but I will not do it." The shepherd said: "If nothing more than that is needful in order to be mayor, I would get into the barrel at once." The peasant said: "If you will get in, you will be mayor." The shepherd was willing, and got in, and the peasant shut the top down on him; then he took the shepherd's flock for himself, and drove it away.

The parson went to the crowd, and declared that the mass had been said. Then they came and rolled the barrel towards the water. When the barrel began to roll, the shepherd cried: "I am quite willing to be mayor." They believed no otherwise than that it was the peasant who was saying this, and answered: "That is what we intend,

but first you shall look about you a little down below there," and they rolled the barrel down into the water.

After that the peasants went home, and as they were entering the village, the small peasant also came quietly in, driving a flock of sheep and looking quite contented. Then the peasants were astonished, and said: "Peasant, from whence do you come? Have you come out of the water?"

"Yes, truly," replied the peasant, "I sank deep, deep down, until at last I got to the bottom; I pushed the bottom out of the barrel, and crept out, and there were pretty meadows on which a number of lambs were feeding, and from thence I brought this flock away with me." Said the peasants: "Are there any more there?"

"Oh, yes," said he, "more than I could want." Then the peasants made up their minds that they too would fetch some sheep for themselves, a flock apiece, but the mayor said: "I come first." So they went to the water together, and just then there were some of the small fleecy clouds in the blue sky, which are called little lambs, and they were reflected in the water, whereupon the peasants cried: "We already see the sheep down below!" The mayor pressed forward and said: "I will go down first, and look about me, and if things promise well I'll call you." So he jumped in; splash! went the water; it sounded as if he were calling them, and the whole crowd plunged in after him as one man. Then the entire village was dead, and the small peasant, as sole heir, became a rich man.

Sweetheart Roland

This is German tale number 56 of those collected by the Grimm brothers (Jacob 1785–1863 and Wilhelm 1786–1859). As with many other stories it describes how an abandoned first love reclaims her suitor just as he is about to marry someone else. And, as ever, scant attention is given here to the feelings of the other bride-to-be who is deserted at the final moment!

There was once upon a time a woman who was a real witch and had two daughters, one ugly and wicked, and this one she loved because she was her own daughter, and one beautiful and good, and this one she hated, because she was her stepdaughter. The stepdaughter once had a pretty apron, which the other fancied so much that she became envious, and told her mother that she must and would have that apron. "Be quiet, my child," said the old woman, "and you shall have

When Roland played his magical music on the fiddle the witch was forced to dance

434

it. Your stepsister has long deserved death; tonight when she is asleep I will come and cut her head off. Only be careful that you are at the far side of the bed, and push her well to the front." It would have been all over with the poor girl if she had not just then been standing in a corner, and heard everything. All day long she dared not go out of doors, and when bedtime had come, the witch's daughter got into bed first, so as to lie at the far side, but when she was asleep, the other pushed her gently to the front, and took for herself the place at the back, close by the wall. In the night, the old woman came creeping in, she held an axe in her right hand, and felt with her left to see if anyone were lying at the outside, and then she grasped the axe with both hands, and cut her own child's head off.

When she had gone away, the girl got up and went to her sweetheart, who was called Roland, and knocked at his door. When he came out, she said to him: "Listen, dearest Roland, we must fly in all haste; my stepmother wanted to kill me, but has struck her own child. When daylight comes, and she sees what she has done, we shall be lost."

"But," said Roland, "I counsel you first to take away her magic wand, or we cannot escape if she pursues us." The maiden fetched the magic wand, and she took the dead girl's head and dropped three drops of blood on the ground, one in front of the bed, one in the kitchen, and one on the stairs. Then she hurried away with her lover.

When the old witch got up next morning, she called her daughter, and wanted to give her the apron, but she did not come. Then the witch cried: "Where are you?"

"Here, on the stairs, I am sweeping," answered the first drop of blood. The old woman went out, but saw no one on the stairs, and cried again: "Where are you?"

"Here in the kitchen, I am warming myself," cried the second drop of blood. She went into the kitchen, but found no one. Then she cried again: "Where are you?"

"Ah, here in the bed, I am sleeping," cried the third drop of blood. She went into the room to the bed. What did she see there? Her own child, whose head she had cut off, bathed in her blood. The witch fell into a passion, sprang to the window, and as she could look forth quite far into the world, she perceived her stepdaughter hurrying away with her sweetheart Roland. "That shall not help you," cried she, "even if you have got a long way off, you shall still not escape me." She put on her many-league boots, in which she covered an hour's walk at every step, and it was not long before she overtook them. The girl, however, when she saw the old woman striding towards her, changed, with her magic wand, her sweetheart Roland into a lake, and herself into a duck swimming in the middle of it. The witch placed herself on the shore, threw breadcrumbs in, and went to endless trouble to entice the duck; but the duck did not let herself be enticed, and the old woman had to go home at night as she had come. At this the girl and her sweetheart Roland resumed their natural shapes again, and they walked on the whole night until daybreak. Then the maiden changed herself into a beautiful flower which

stood in the midst of a briar hedge, and her sweetheart Roland into a fiddler. It was not long before the witch came striding up towards them, and said to the musician: "Dear musician, may I pluck that beautiful flower for myself?" "Oh, yes," he replied, "I will play to you while you do it." As she was hastily creeping into the hedge and was just going to pluck the flower, knowing perfectly well who the flower was, he began to play, and whether she would or not, she was forced to dance, for it was a magical dance. The faster he played, the more violent springs was she forced to make, and the thorns tore her clothes from her body, and pricked her and wounded her till she bled, and as he did not stop, she had to dance till she lay dead on the ground.

As they were now set free, Roland said: "Now I will go to my father and arrange for the wedding." "Then in the

When Roland forsook his sweetheart she changed her-self into a flower, expecting to be trampled upon

meantime I will stay here and wait for you," said the girl, "and that no one may recognize me, I will change myself into a red stone landmark." Then Roland went away, and the girl stood like a red landmark in the field and waited for her beloved. But when Roland got home, he fell into the snares of another, who so fascinated him that he forgot the maiden. The poor girl remained there a long time, but at length, as he did not return at all, she was sad, and changed herself into a flower, and thought: "Someone will surely come this way, and trample me down."

It befell, however, that a shepherd kept his sheep in the field and saw the flower, and as it was so pretty, plucked it, took it with him, and laid it away in his chest. From that time forth, strange things happened in the shepherd's house. When he arose in the morning, all the work was already done, the room was swept, the table and benches cleaned, the fire in the hearth was lighted, and the water was fetched, and at noon, when he came home, the table was laid, and a good dinner served. He could not conceive how this came to pass, for he never saw a human being in

Fiddle music has long been associated with magic – and the Devil is said to be an excellent player

his house, and no one could have concealed himself in it. He was certainly pleased with this good attendance, but still at last he was so afraid that he went to a wise woman and asked for her advice. The wise woman said: "There is some enchantment behind it, listen very early some morning if anything is moving in the room, and if you see anything, no matter what it is, throw a white cloth over it, and then the magic will be stopped."

The shepherd did as she bade him, and next morning just as day dawned, he saw the chest open, and the flower come out. Swiftly he sprang towards it, and threw a white cloth over it. Instantly the transformation came to an end, and a beautiful girl stood before him, who admitted to him that she had been the flower, and that up to this time

she had attended to his house-keeping. She told him her story, and as she pleased him he asked her if she would marry him, but she answered: "No," for she wanted to remain faithful to her sweetheart Roland, although he had deserted her. Nevertheless, she promised not to go away, but to continue keeping house for the shepherd.

And now the time drew near when Roland's wedding was to be celebrated, and then, according to an old custom in the country, it was announced that all the girls were to be present at it, and sing in honour of the bridal pair. When the faithful maiden heard of this, she grew so sad that she thought her heart would break, and she would not go thither, but the other girls came and took her. When it came to her turn to sing, she stepped back, until at last she was the only one left, and then she could not refuse. But when she began her song, and it reached Roland's ears, he sprang up and cried: "I know the voice, that is the true bride, I will have no other!" Everything he had forgotten, and which had vanished from his mind, had suddenly come home again to his heart. Then the faithful maiden held her wedding with her sweetheart Roland, and grief came to an end and joy began.

At last Roland recognized the sweet maiden as his own true love and their joyful wedding was held

Reynard and Bruin

The Reynard cycle includes French, Dutch, English and German allegorical fables that feature the trickster red fox, Reynard. In this story from *European Folk and Fairy Tales* collected by Joseph Jacobs 1854–1916 Reynard knows that Bruin has a closely guarded beehive full of honeycomb so some ingenuity and cunning will be needed if he is to help himself to any.

You must know that once upon a time Reynard the Fox and Bruin the Bear went into partnership and kept house together. Would you like to know the reason? Well, Reynard knew that Bruin had a beehive full of honeycomb, and that was what he wanted. But Bruin kept so close a guard upon his honey that Master Reynard didn't know how to get away from him and get hold of the honey.

So one day he said to Bruin, "Pardner, I have to go and be gossip – that means godfather, you know – to one of my old friends."

"Why, certainly," said Bruin. So off Reynard goes into the woods, and after a time he crept back and uncovered the beehive and had such a feast of honey.

Then he went back to Bruin, who asked him what name had been given to the child. Reynard had forgotten all about the christening and could only say, "Just-Begun."

"What a funny name," said Master Bruin.

A little while after, Reynard thought he would like another feast of honey. So he told Bruin that he had to go to another christening. And off he went. And when he came back and Bruin asked him what was the name given to the child, Reynard said, "Half-Eaten."

The third time the same thing occurred, and this time the name given by Reynard to the child that didn't exist was "All-Gone." You can guess why.

A short time afterwards, Master Bruin thought he would like to eat up some of his honey and asked Reynard to come and join him in the feast. When they got to the beehive, Bruin was so surprised to find that there was no honey left, and he turned round to Reynard and said, "Just-Begun, Half-Eaten, All-Gone. So that is what you meant. You have eaten my honey."

"Why no," said Reynard. "How could that be?" I have never stirred from your side except when I went a-gossiping [serving as godfather], and then I was far away from here. You must have eaten the honey yourself, perhaps when you were asleep. At any rate we can easily tell. Let us lie down here in the sunshine, and if either of us has eaten the honey, the sun will soon sweat it out of us."

No sooner said than done, and the two lay side by side in the sunshine. Soon Master Bruin commenced to doze, and Mr. Reynard took some honey from the hive and smeared it round Bruin's snout. Then he woke him up and said, "See, the honey is oozing out of your snout. You must have eaten it when you were asleep."

Reynard the Fox and Bruin the Bear joined together in their hunt for honey

Three Czech Tales

Many of the Czech fairy tales are different from the ones we know, and the legends are not often found in conventional story books or are variations on ones we may have read. For example, the Czech version of Goldilocks (seen below) is much different from ours – no bears!! These two tales were collected by Karel Jaromír Erben in the mid-1800s.

Princess Goldie

Once upon a time in the ancient land of Bohemia, there lived an old woman. One day, she went to the palace gates and requested an audience with the king. She appeared so aged and so frail, and yet so wise, that the guards allowed her inside. Once alone with the king, the woman uncovered the basket she was carrying and uncovered the snake it held. "Have your cook prepare the snake for your dinner," she said. "Once you have eaten it, you will be able to understand all that is said by the birds, the beasts, and the fish."

The king was delighted to have such a gift, and excited to know he could have knowledge no one else could have. He quickly ordered his cook and servant Georgie to prepare the 'fish' for his table. "Don't you dare taste any of the 'fish' yourself, Boy," warned the king, "or you shall pay for it with your life!"

Georgie found this all very strange. "I've never seen such a fish in all my life," he muttered to himself on the way to the kitchen. "It looks more like a snake! And, what kind of cook would I be if I did not taste the dish I was preparing?" When the fish was finished, Georgie put the tiniest little bit in his mouth just to taste it. At that very moment, he heard a buzzing noise close to his ear. The voice said, "Give us some, too. We would like to have some."

Georgie looked all around the room to see who was talking, but all he saw were a couple of flies buzzing around the kitchen. Then, he heard a wheezing voice shouting in the street, "Where shall we go? Where shall we go?" A shriller voice answered, "To the miller's barley field, we can eat there." Georgie stuck his head out the window and saw a gander with a flock of geese making their way

to the field. "So!" he thought, "it's a magic fish!"

He had figured out what was going on and he popped another little piece into his mouth before carrying the snake to the king. After dinner, the king asked Georgie to accompany him on a horse ride. Georgie went to saddle the two horses. The king rode in front with Georgie following behind. As they were crossing the meadow, Georgie's horse reared slightly and neighed, "Oh, I am so happy! I could jump over the mountains!"

"Well, that's fine for you," neighed the king's horse, "I have an old man on my back. If I were to jump, he would fall off and break his neck."

"So what? Let him fall!" Georgie's horse replied. "Then, you can carry a young man rather than an old boy!" Georgie thought this conversation was quite funny and laughed quietly to himself. He didn't want the king to know he had understood what the horses were saying. Of course, the king also understood what had been said. He turned around and noticed a grin on Georgie's face. "What are you grinning about?" he demanded. "Oh, nothing of importance," Georgie lied. "It was just a passing thought."

Nonetheless, the king was suspicious, and he didn't trust the horses either. He decided to go back to the palace. When they reached the palace, the king was thirsty and asked Georgie to pour him a glass of wine. "I want the wine right up to the brim," he ordered. "If you pour a drop too little or a drop too much, you'll pay for it with your head." Georgie lifted the bottle of wine and started to pour. Just then, two little birds flew in through the window. The first had three golden hairs in its beak and was being chased by the other bird. "Hand them over!" the second bird chirped. "They're mine!" "No, they're not," chirped the lead bird. "I found them, and I picked them up off the ground. They're mine." "But, I saw them fall when Goldie was combing her hair. Couldn't you give me a couple at least?" "No, not a single one!" insisted the first bird. "They're mine, and that's that."

The bird in pursuit then seized the free end of the golden hairs in its beak, and they both tugged and pulled and fluttered about until each was left with one, while the third hair dropped to the floor with a tinkling sound. All this caught Georgie's attention and he spilled a drop of wine.

"You've forfeited you life to me!" the king cried, "But, I shall be merciful if you find the golden-haired maiden and bring her to me to be my bride."

What could Georgie do? To save his life, he had to find Goldie, but he had no idea where to look for her. With a

Every morning at sunrise
Princess Goldie combed her golden hair

438

Georgie rode on through the dark forest

sigh, he saddled his horse and set off. As he approached a dark forest, he noticed a small bush burning at the side of the path. There were sparks falling on an anthill and ants were rushing about, trying to escape, carrying little white eggs on their backs. "Oh, help us, help us!" they pleaded. "We are being burnt alive, and our young ones are still in the egg!" Georgie leapt from his horse, cut down the bush and stamped out the fire.

"Oh, thank you, thank you!" cried the ants. "If you ever need us, think of us and we shall be there to help you." Georgie rode on through the forest until he came to a tall fir tree with a raven's nest in its crown. On the ground below sat two baby ravens, squealing pitifully. "Our mother and father have flown away and we are all alone! How can we find food for ourselves, poor fledglings that we are, when we can't even fly yet! Oh, help us, please, help us! Find us something to eat, or we shall die of hunger!"

Georgie only hesitated a moment. He jumped off his horse and killed it with his sword, so the young ravens would have ample food. "Thank you, Georgie," they cawed happily, "if you ever need us, think of us and we'll be there to help you!" Now, Georgie had to continue on foot. He walked for a long time, when, at last, he left the forest behind, and he came to a great wide sea. Two fishermen were quarrelling on the shore. They had caught a huge golden fish in their net, and each wanted it for himself. "The net is mine, so the fish is mine, too," one said. "What good is your net without my boat and my help?" asked the other. "The next time we catch such a fish, it can be yours!" "Certainly not! I'll have this one and you can wait for the next!"

"I'll settle your quarrel," Georgie said. "Sell the fish to me, I'll pay you handsomely and you can split the money between you." He pulled out his purse with the money the king had given him for the journey, and handed it over. He did not keep a single coin for himself. The fishermen were delighted to get such a high price for their catch, and Georgie let the fish go back into the sea. It splashed merrily and dived down, but its head reappeared once more before it swam away. "Thank you, Georgie, thank you!" the fish cried. "If you ever need me, think of me and I'll be there."

"Where are you going?" the fishermen asked. "I am searching for Goldie, the golden-haired maiden, but I have no idea where to find her. My master, the old king, wants her for his bride."

"We can help you," the fishermen said. "Goldie is a princess, and she is the daughter of the king who lives in the crystal palace on the island over there. Every morning, as the sun rises, she combs her golden hair, and its glow

440

The princess had a necklace of precious pearls

spreads across the sky and the sea. As you have settled our quarrel, we'll row you across the island. Be sure you choose the right princess. The king has twelve daughters, but only one with the golden hair."

When Georgie reached the island, he went straight to the king in the crystal palace and asked for his golden-haired daughter as a bride for his own king and master.

"I'll give her to you," the king agreed, "but first you must earn the princess. I shall give you three tasks, and you must accomplish one each day. Now rest until tomorrow." The next morning, the king assigned his first task. "My daughter had a necklace of precious pearls. The string broke and the pearls have scattered in the long grass in our meadow. Now, go and find them, every single one." Georgie walked to the meadow, which was very big. He knelt down in the long grass and began to look for the pearls. Though he searched all morning, he could not find one pearl. "Oh, if only my ant friends were here. Perhaps they would help me," he sighed.

"We're here and ready to help," cried a chorus of tiny voices. And, there they were, crawling all around him. "What would you like us to do?"

"I have to collect the pearls spilled in this meadow, and I can't seem to see a single one."

"Wait a minute, Georgie, and we'll find them all!" said

the ants. True to their word, in a few minutes there was a whole piles of pearls at Georgie's feet. All he had to do was string them onto the golden thread. He was just about to fasten the thread when a tiny ant came limping towards him. It was lame, for it had lost its leg in the anthill fire. "Wait, oh please, wait!" the little ant cried. "Here is another one!"

Georgie took the pearls to the king, and when the king had counted them, not a single one was missing. "You have done well," he said. "Tomorrow, I shall set you to another task."

The following morning, the king turned to Georgie and said, "When my daughter, Goldie, bathed in the sea, she lost a gold ring. Go find it."

Georgie went to the sea and walked sadly along the shoreline. Though the water was clear, it was so deep, he could not see the sea bed. What chance had he of ever finding the ring? "Oh, if only the golden fish were here," he sighed. Suddenly, there was a flash of light in the sea and the golden fish shot from the depths to the surface. "I'm right here to help you!" it said. "What do you want of me?"

"I'm suppose to find a gold ring lost in the sea, and I can't even see the bottom."

"Why, I swam past a pike wearing a gold ring on its fin only a moment ago! I'll be back in a minute."

In no time at all, the fish was back with the pike in her mouth. The gold ring was indeed on the pike's fin.

Again, the king praised Georgie for completing the task. On the third morning, he said, "If you want me to give you my daughter, Goldie, as a bride for your king, you must bring her the water of life and the water of death. She will need them both." Georgie had no idea where to look and he wandered about at random until he came to a deep, dark forest. "Oh, if only my young raven friends were here," he sighed. "Perhaps they could help me." Suddenly, something flew through the air, and there sat the two ravens on a branch above his head. "We are right here," they said. "How can we help you?"

"I've been ordered to fetch the water of death and the water of life, and I don't know where to find them."

"We know where they are. Be patient, we will be back in a little while with the waters." In no time at all, the little birds returned, each carrying a gourd. One contained the water of life, the other the water of death. Georgie was thrilled with his good fortune, and hastened back to the palace.

As he was coming out of the forest, he noticed a spider's web stretched from tree to tree, with a big, fat spider sitting in the middle, about to munch on a fly. Georgie took the gourd filled with the water of death and sprinkled a few drops over the spider. It fell dead to the ground like an over-ripe cherry. Then, he sprinkled the dead fly with the water of life, and soon the fly was wriggling about until it scrambled out of the spider's web and buzzed around Georgie's head joyfully. "Lucky for you, Georgie, that you revived me," it buzzed. "Without me, you would never

Each princess was beautiful but only one had truly golden hair – soon to be hidden behind a veil

be able to guess which of the twelve princesses is the one you want."

When the king saw that Georgie had accomplished the third task, he agreed to give him princess Goldie. "But," he warned, "you must pick her out yourself." Then, he led them into a big hall with a big round table in the center. The twelve lovely maidens were seated, all exactly alike. Each had her head covered with a long white veil which fell to the ground, so that it was impossible to see whether her hair was dark or fair. "Here are my daughters," said the king. "Guess which one is Goldie and she shall be yours and you will be able to depart with her at once. If your guess is wrong, you must leave without her."

Georgie was so afraid, he did not know what to do. Just then, someone whispered in his ear, "Walk around the table, and I'll tell you which one to choose." It was the fly he had revived! "Not this one, nor this one, nor this, but . . . this is the one! She is Goldie!"

"Give me this daughter!" Georgie stated. "She is the one I have earned for my master."

"You have guessed rightly," said the king. The princess rose from the table, took off her veil, and her golden locks fell in thick waves from her head to the floor, shining like the morning sun, until they dazzled Georgie's eyes and warmed his heart. The king gave his daughter a fitting dowry, and Georgie returned with her to his master. The old king's eyes nearly popped out of his head and he jumped for joy upon seeing the lovely princess. Straightaway, he gave orders for their wedding preparations to be made. "I was going to have you hanged for your disobedience," the king said to Georgie, "and leave your carcass for the

crows. But, as you have served me well, I shall only have you beheaded and I shall give you an honorable funeral."

After Georgie's execution, Goldie begged the old king to give her the head and body of the dead servant. The king could not deny his golden-haired daughter anything, and he consented. Goldie placed Georgie's severed head close to his body and sprinkled him with the water of death, and the two grew together at once without leaving a scar. Then, she sprinkled the corpse with the water of life, and Georgie sprang to his feet. It was if he had been reborn, with youth and health shining in his face. "Oh, how soundly I have slept," he said, rubbing his eyes.

"How true," Goldie replied, "you slept soundly indeed, and had it not been for me, you would have stayed asleep for all time."

When the old king saw that Georgie had not only been brought back to life, but that he was younger and more handsome than before, the king decided that he, too, would like to grow young and handsome again. At once he gave the order for his head to be cut off and then for his body and head to be sprinkled with the water. So, the servants cut off his head and sprinkled him with the water of life; they kept on sprinkling him until they used up all the water, but the head just would not knit with the body. Only then did they try the water of death, and the two grew together at once. But, the king was still dead, and he remained dead, for there was no more water of life left to revive him. As the kingdom could not be without a king, and there was no one as wise as Georgie, who understood the language of all animals, he was crowned king, with Goldie as his queen.

Three Roses

ONCE upon a time there was a mother who had three daughters. There was to be a market in the next town, and she said she would go to it. She asked the daughters what she should bring them back. Two of them named a great number of things; she must buy all of them, they said. You know the sort of women, and the sort of things they would want. Well, when they had asked for more than enough, the mother asked the third daughter:

"And you, don't you want anything?"

"No, I don't want anything; but, if you like, you can bring me three roses, please."

The fine palace had a large garden full of the most beautiful roses

The basilisk demanded that she cut off his head and then from his body a long serpent emerged, hissing horribly

If she wanted no more than that, her mother was ready to bring them.

When the mother knew all she wanted, she went off to market. She bought all she could, piled it all on her back, and started for home. But she was overtaken by nightfall, and the poor mother completely lost her way and could go no farther. She wandered through the forest till she was quite worn out, and at last she came to a palace, though she had never before heard of any palace there. There was a large garden full of roses, so beautiful that no painter alive could paint them, and all the roses were smiling at her. So she remembered her youngest daughter, who had wished for just such roses. She had forgotten it entirely till then. Surely that was because she was so old! Now she thought: "There are plenty of roses here, so I will take these three."

So she went into the garden and took the roses. At once a basilisk came and demanded her daughter in exchange for the roses. The mother was terrified and wanted to throw the flowers away. But the basilisk said that wouldn't be any use, and he threatened to tear her to pieces. So she had to promise him her daughter. There was no help for it, and so she went home.

She took the three roses to her daughter and said: "Here are the roses, but I had to pay dearly for them. You must go to yonder castle in payment for them, and I don't even know whether you will ever come back."

But Mary seemed as though she didn't mind at all, and she said she would go. So the mother took her to the castle. There was everything she wanted there. Soon the basilisk appeared and told Mary that she must nurse him in her lap for three hours every day. There was no way out, do it she must, and so the basilisk came and she nursed him for three hours. Then he went out, but he came next day and the day after that. On the third day he brought a sword and told poor Mary to cut his head off.

She protested that she wasn't used to doing things like that, and do it she could not. But the basilisk said in a rage that, if that was so, he would tear her to pieces. As there was no choice, she went up to him and cut his head off. And as the basilisk's head rolled on the ground, there came forth from his body a long serpent, hissing horribly. He asked her to cut his head off again. Mary did not hesitate this time, but cut his head off at once.

The serpent (by the way, he held the golden keys of that palace in his mouth) was immediately changed into a beautiful youth, and he said in a pleasant voice: "This castle belongs to me, and, as you have delivered me, there is no help for it: I must marry you."

So there was a great wedding, the castle was full of their attendants, and they all had to play and dance. But the floor was of paper, so I fell through it, and here I am now.

So there was a great wedding, with the castle full of guests and attendants, who played and danced

A Clever Lass

ONCE upon a time there was a shepherd. He used to pasture his sheep upon a hill, and one day he saw something glittering on the opposite hill. So he went there to see what it was. It was a golden mortar. He took it up and said to his daughter: "I will give this mortar to our king."

But she said: "Don't do that. If you give him the mortar, you won't have the pestle, and he is sure to ask for it, and then you will get into trouble."

The shepherd presented the king with a golden mortar he had discovered in the hills

But the shepherd thought that she was only a silly girl. He took the mortar, and, when he came before the king, he said: "Begging your pardon, Mr. King, I want to give you this mortar."

The king answered him roughly: "If you give me the mortar, I must have the pestle as well. Unless the pestle is here within three days, your life will be forfeit."

The shepherd began to lament: "My daughter was right when she said that when you had got the mortar you would want the pestle too. I wouldn't listen to her, so it

serves me right."

"Have you such a clever daughter as that?" asked the king.

"Indeed I have," said the shepherd.

"Then tell your daughter that I will marry her, if she comes neither walking nor riding, clothed nor unclothed, neither by day nor by night, neither at noon nor in the morning. And I won't ask for the pestle either."

The shepherd went home and said: "You can get me out of this, if you go to Mr. King neither clothed nor unclothed," and the rest of it.

But the daughter wasn't a bit frightened. She came with the fall of dusk (and that was neither at noon nor in the morning); she dressed herself in fishing-nets; she took a goat, and she partly rode on the goat and partly she walked.

And when the king saw that she had only a fishing-net on, that she came with the approach of dusk, and that she was partly walking, partly riding on the goat, he was bound to marry her. But he said to her: "You will be my wife so long as you don't give advice to anybody; but if you do, you must part with me."

Well, she didn't give advice to anybody until one day there was a market in the town, and a farmer's mare had a foal at the market. The foal ran away to another farmer, who was there with a gelding, and the farmer said: "This foal belongs to me."

They went to law about it, and at last the matter came before the king. And the king, considering that every

*The clever lass
could not help herself but to give advice
when there was a dispute over a runaway foal*

animal ought to run to its mother, decided that a gelding had had a foal.

The farmer who owned the mare went down the stairs, saying over and over again: "The gelding has foaled! the gelding has foaled!"

The queen heard him, and she said: "Man, you are talking nonsense."

So he told her that he had been at the market, that his mare had foaled, but the foal ran to another farmer who was there with a gelding. "And now," he said, "it has been decided that the gelding has foaled." So he thought there could be no mistake; at any rate, he couldn't help it.

When the queen heard this story she said: "To-morrow, my lord the king will go out for a stroll. Take a fishing-net, and begin fishing on the road in front of him. The king will ask you: 'Why are you fishing on a dry road?' And you must answer: 'Why not? it's as hopeful as expecting a gelding to foal.' But you must not say who gave you this advice."

So it was. As the king was walking along he saw the farmer fishing on the dry road. He asked him why he was fishing there.

"Why not?" said he, "It's as hopeful as expecting a gelding to foal."

The king at once began to berate the farmer. "That's not out of your own head," he said, and he kept at the farmer until he let the secret out.

So the king came home, summoned the queen, and said to her: "You have been with me for a long time, and you have given advice in spite of all, so you must go to-morrow. But I will allow you to take with you the thing you like best."

It was no good arguing. So the king invited all his courtiers and prepared a splendid banquet. When the banquet was finished, the queen said to the king: "Before we part, you must drink this glass of wine to my health," and she had put some opium into the wine on the sly.

The king drank it at a draught and fell asleep at once. A carriage was got ready, and the queen put the king in it and drove to her father's old hut. There she laid the king on the straw, and, when he woke up, he asked where he was.

"You are with me. Didn't you tell me that I could take the thing I liked best with me?"

The king saw how clever she was, and he said: "Now you can give advice to anybody you like."

And so they drove home again, and he was king and she queen again.

The king invited all his courtiers to a magnificent banquet

The Littlest One: His Book

Verses by Marion St John Webb
1888–1930.

Telling Fairy Tales

When Mother tells me fairy tales
(She tells me one each night)
She puts in all the little bits
And always tells them right.
The tales I like the best of all
She tells me lots of times
Like how Jack's beanstalk grows and grows
An' up the stalk he climbs!

She makes the proper voices for
The story of Three Bears
And taps her foot for Cinderella
Runnin' down the stairs.
An' when about the story of
Dick Whittington she tells,
We always push the window up
An' listen for Bow Bells!

When Daddy tells a fairy tale
He doesn't make it long.
He leaves out all the little bits
An' always tells it wrong.
An' so I have to 'member him
To say it right, you see,
An' tell him how it really goes,
So's he can tell it me.

Andy

Andy says there isn't any fairies!
I never knowed before
Andy knows most ev'rything – he's thirteen
Andy is the boy who lives next door.

Andy says of course there isn't fairies!
An' when I ask him why,
Andy laughs and says, "Because there isn't!
Never has been! There now – go on – cry!"

'Course I wouldn't cry about the fairies!
I tole him, "I don't care!"
But when Mother tucked me up at bedtime
Ev'rything seemed dreffuly unfair. . . .

Mother said, "Who says there isn't any fairies?
Why Andy should be shook!"
Don't I 'member when we felt a fairy
Round the corner but we didn't look?

Mother says of course there is the fairies,
An Mother says she knows
If you think there's none you never find them
Silly Andy must be one of those!

Buttercup

I've got a fairy in a box;
I made her all myself.
I always keep her safe away
On Mother's shelf.

I thought of her an' cut her out
But Mother sewed her up.
An' then I picked a name for her –
It's Buttercup.

I musn't tell you what she's like,
She asked me not to say
In case you tried to make her, if
You knew the way.

And then she'd not know which to be
If there were two of her, you see.

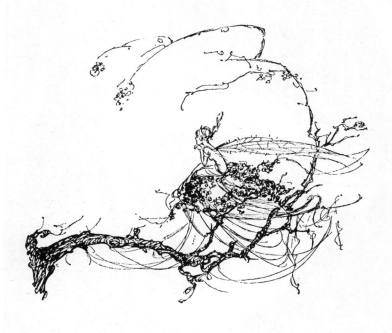

The Snow Man

This literary fairy tale by Hans Christian Andersen (1805–1875) tells how a snowman falls in love with a stove. First published in Copenhagen in 1861, its poignancy is similar to his Christmas tale of *The Fir Tree* and would, much later, be echoed in Raymond Briggs' snowman story of 1978.

"It is so delightfully cold," said the Snow Man, "that it makes my whole body crackle. This is just the kind of wind to blow life into one. How that great red thing up there is staring at me!" He meant the sun, who was just setting. "It shall not make me wink. I shall manage to keep the pieces."

He had two triangular pieces of tile in his head, instead of eyes; his mouth was made of an old broken rake, and was, of course, furnished with teeth. He had been brought into existence amidst the joyous shouts of boys, the jingling of sleigh-bells, and the slashing of whips. The sun went down, and the full moon rose, large, round, and clear, shining in the deep blue.

"There it comes again, from the other side," said the Snow Man, who supposed the sun was showing himself once more. "Ah, I have cured him of staring, though; now he may hang up there, and shine, that I may see myself. If I only knew how to manage to move away from this place,- I should so like to move. If I could, I would slide along yonder on the ice, as I have seen the boys do; but I don't understand how; I don't even know how to run."

"Away, away," barked the old yard-dog. He was quite hoarse, and could not pronounce "Bow wow" properly. He had once been an indoor dog, and lay by the fire, and he had been hoarse ever since. "The sun will make you run some day. I saw him, last winter, make your predecessor

The happy boys loved playing in the winter snow and had built a fine tall Snow Man

A bright fire gleamed merrily in the housekeeper's stove

run, and his predecessor before him. Away, away, they all have to go."

"I don't understand you, comrade," said the Snow Man. "Is that thing up yonder to teach me to run? I saw it running itself a little while ago, and now it has come creeping up from the other side.

"You know nothing at all," replied the yard-dog; "but then, you've only lately been patched up. What you see yonder is the moon, and the one before it was the sun. It will come again to-morrow, and most likely teach you to run down into the ditch by the well; for I think the weather is going to change. I can feel such pricks and stabs in my left leg; I am sure there is going to be a change."

"I don't understand him," said the Snow Man to himself; "but I have a feeling that he is talking of something very disagreeable. The one who stared so just now, and whom he calls the sun, is not my friend; I can feel that too."

"Away, away," barked the yard-dog, and then he turned

round three times, and crept into his kennel to sleep.

There was really a change in the weather. Towards morning, a thick fog covered the whole country round, and a keen wind arose, so that the cold seemed to freeze one's bones; but when the sun rose, the sight was splendid. Trees and bushes were covered with hoar frost, and looked like a forest of white coral; while on every twig glittered frozen dew-drops. The many delicate forms concealed in summer by luxuriant foliage, were now clearly defined, and looked like glittering lace-work. From every twig glistened a white radiance. The birch, waving in the wind, looked full of life, like trees in summer; and its appearance was wondrously beautiful. And where the sun shone, how everything glittered and sparkled, as if diamond dust had been strewn about; while the snowy carpet of the earth appeared as if covered with diamonds, from which countless lights gleamed, whiter than even the snow itself.

"This is really beautiful," said a young girl, who had come

into the garden with a young man; and they both stood still near the Snow Man, and contemplated the glittering scene. "Summer cannot show a more beautiful sight," she exclaimed, while her eyes sparkled.

"And we can't have such a fellow as this in the summer time," replied the young man, pointing to the Snow Man; "he is capital."

The girl laughed, and nodded at the Snow Man, and then tripped away over the snow with her friend. The snow creaked and crackled beneath her feet, as if she had been treading on starch.

"Who are these two?" asked the Snow Man of the yard-dog. "You have been here longer than I have; do you know them?"

"Of course I know them," replied the yard-dog; "she has stroked my back many times, and he has given me a bone of meat. I never bite those two."

"But what are they?" asked the Snow Man.

"They are lovers," he replied; "they will go and live in the same kennel by-and-by, and gnaw at the same bone. Away, away!"

"Are they the same kind of beings as you and I?" asked the Snow Man.

"Well, they belong to the same master," retorted the yard-dog. "Certainly people who were only born yesterday know very little. I can see that in you. I have age and experience. I know every one here in the house, and I know there was once a time when I did not lie out here in the cold, fastened to a chain. Away, away!"

"The cold is delightful," said the Snow Man; "but do tell me tell me; only you must not clank your chain so; for it jars all through me when you do that."

"Away, away!" barked the yard-dog; "I'll tell you; they said I was a pretty little fellow once; then I used to lie in a velvet-covered chair, up at the master's house, and sit in the mistress's lap. They used to kiss my nose, and wipe my paws with an embroidered handkerchief, and I was called 'Ami, dear Ami, sweet Ami.' But after a while I grew too big for them, and they sent me away to the housekeeper's room; so I came to live on the lower storey. You can look into the room from where you stand, and see where I was master once; for I was indeed master to the housekeeper. It was certainly a smaller room than those up stairs; but I was more comfortable; for I was not being continually taken hold of and pulled about by the children as I had been. I received quite as good food, or even better. I had my own cushion, and there was a stove – it is the finest thing in the world at this season of the year. I used to go under the stove, and lie down quite beneath it. Ah, I still dream of that stove. Away, away!"

"Does a stove look beautiful?" asked the Snow Man, "is it at all like me?"

"It is just the reverse of you,' said the dog; "it's as black as a crow, and has a long neck and a brass knob; it eats firewood, so that fire spurts out of its mouth. We should keep on one side, or under it, to be comfortable. You can see it through the window, from where you stand."

Then the Snow Man looked, and saw a bright polished thing with a brazen knob, and fire gleaming from the lower part of it. The Snow Man felt quite a strange sensation come over him; it was very odd, he knew not what it meant, and he could not account for it. But there are people who are not men of snow, who understand what it is. "And why did you leave her?" asked the Snow Man, for it seemed to him that the stove must be of the female sex. "How could you give up such a comfortable place?"

"I was obliged," replied the yard-dog. "They turned me out of doors, and chained me up here. I had bitten the youngest of my master's sons in the leg, because he kicked away the bone I was gnawing. 'Bone for bone,' I thought; but they were so angry, and from that time I have been fastened with a chain, and lost my bone. Don't you hear how hoarse I am. Away, away! I can't talk any more like other dogs. Away, away, that is the end of it all."

But the Snow Man was no longer listening. He was looking into the housekeeper's room on the lower storey; where the stove stood on its four iron legs, looking about the same size as the Snow Man himself. "What a strange crackling I feel within me," he said. "Shall I ever get in there? It is an innocent wish, and innocent wishes are sure to be fulfilled. I must go in there and lean against her, even if I have to break the window."

"You must never go in there," said the yard-dog, "for if you approach the stove, you'll melt away, away."

"I might as well go," said the Snow Man, "for I think I am breaking up as it is."

During the whole day the Snow Man stood looking in through the window, and in the twilight hour the room became still more inviting, for from the stove came a gentle glow, not like the sun or the moon; no, only the bright light which gleams from a stove when it has been well fed. When the door of the stove was opened, the flames darted out of its mouth; this is customary with all stoves. The light of the flames fell directly on the face and breast of the Snow Man with a ruddy gleam. "I can endure it no longer," said he; "how beautiful it looks when it stretches out its tongue?" The night was long, but did not appear so to the Snow Man, who stood there enjoying his own reflections, and crackling with the cold. In the morning, the window-panes of the housekeeper's room were covered with ice. They were the most beautiful ice-flowers any Snow Man could desire, but they concealed the stove. These window-panes would not thaw, and he could see nothing of the stove, which he pictured to himself, as if it had been a lovely human being. The snow crackled and the wind whistled around him; it was just the kind of frosty weather a Snow Man might thoroughly enjoy. But he did not enjoy it; how, indeed, could he enjoy anything when he was "stove sick?" "That is terrible disease for a Snow Man," said the yard-dog; "I have suffered from it myself, but I got over it. Away, away," he barked and then he added, "the weather is going to change." And the weather did change; it began to thaw.

As the warmth increased, the Snow Man decreased. He said nothing and made no complaint, which is a sure sign. One morning he broke, and sunk down altogether; and, behold, where he had stood, something like a broomstick remained sticking up in the ground. It was the pole round which the boys had built him up. "Ah, now I understand why he had such a great longing for the stove," said the yard-dog. "Why, there's the shovel that is used for cleaning out the stove, fastened to the pole." The Snow Man had a stove scraper in his body; that was what moved him so.

"But it's all over now. Away, away." And soon the winter passed. "Away, away," barked the hoarse yard-dog. But the girls in the house sang,

"Come from your fragrant home, green thyme;
Stretch your soft branches, willow-tree;
The months are bringing the sweet spring-time,
When the lark in the sky sings joyfully.
Come gentle sun, while the cuckoo sings,
And I'll mock his note in my wanderings."
And nobody thought any more of the Snow Man.

When the thaw came the Snow Man melted away, leaving behind the pole around which he had been built

Maud Keary Verse

These poems are by Maud Keary, a Victorian poet born in the 1820s. Her great aunts Annie and Eliza Keary also wrote verse which Maud added to the publication of her own material. Her inspiration was the countryside and its myriad flowers that so often are associated with fairy folk.

Do harebells ring an hourly chime?

Wild Flowers

Yellow Kingcup, is it true
That Fairie Kings drink out of you,
Golden Kingcup full of dew?
"My cup is filled," the flower replies,
"For Kings and Queens and butterflies."

Creeping scarlet Pimpernel,
With your closed or opened bell,
Do you shower and shine foretell?
"Low lying on the dusty grass,
I am the poor man's weather glass."

Fiery Golans, you who glow
Like suns upon the marshes low,
From earth or heaven do you grow?
"A giant dropped us from his car,
Flakes of the sun's own fire we are."

Daisy, with a yellow breast,
More beautiful than all the rest,
'Tis you can say who loves us best.
"I rise and spread beneath your feet,
In silver leaves, my portents sweet."

The Rainbow

Can that fairy place be found
Where the rainbow touches ground?
Will you tell me, driver, pray,
Is it many miles away?

Somewhere there must be a spot
Shining like a coloured blot,
Pink and purple, blue and green,
Like a transformation scene.

What must all the cattle think
When the grass and flowers turn pink?
Woolly sheep, what do you do
When the daisied field shines blue?

Happy must those children be,
Who the rainbow's end can see,
Who can play and dance and sing
In the rainbow's shining ring!

She kisses every folded flower and every silent bird

The Moon

There is a lovely lady,
Whom I have often seen,
She's fair and bright and beautiful,
And she was born a queen.

She looks both mild and gentle,
Though she lives in regal state,
And her attendant nobles
In countless myriads wait.

Her mien is humble, and with them
Her dignity she shares,
She would not that her lustrous eye
Should dim the light of theirs.

Upon the ground her beaming smiles
And blessings fall unheard,
She kisses every folded flower
And every silent bird.

If, when we draw our curtains,
We draw them not too tight,
She steals a glance into our room
And wishes us good-night!

Fairyland is an enchanted place where grasses whisper and daisies sing

The Snow Queen's throne is built of green ice where glittering icebergs shine

Fairyland

A Fairy's house stands in a wood,
Midst fairy trees and flowers,
Where daisies sing like little birds
Between the sun and showers,
And grasses whisper tiny things
About this world of ours.

Such flowers are there beside the way,
Lilies and hollyhocks:
Blow off their stalks to tell the time
Tall dandelion clocks;
While harebells ring an hourly chime
Like a wound music box.

Some day shall we two try to find
This strange enchanted place?
Go hand in hand through flower lit woods
Where living trees embrace—
And suddenly, as in a dream,
Behold a fairy's face!

The Snow Queen

Where the wild bear clasps the ice
Over the hanging precipice,
Where the glittering icebergs shine
Within the sunset, red as wine,
Where the reindeer lick the snow,
To see what there may be below,
Where the shades are blue and green,
There lives, they say, the great Snow Queen.
Wild her eyes are as the sea
When northern winds blow lustily.
Her queenly robes are white as snow,
But flaming diamonds on them glow,
And many a precious stone.
Of green ice builded is her throne:
Polar bears her watch dogs are—
Her only lamp, an evening star.

Enchanted Tulips

Tulips white and tulips red,
Sweeter than a violet bed!
Say, old Mother Bailey, say
Why your tulips look so gay,
Why they smell so sweet, and why
They bloom on when others die?

"By the pixies' magic power
Do my tulips always flower,
By the pixies' magic spell
Do they give so sweet a smell!
Tulips, tulips, red and white,
Fill the pixies with delight!

"Pixy women, pixy men,
Seek my tulips from the glen;
Midnight come, they may be heard
Singing sweet as any bird,
Singing their wee babes to rest
In the tulips they love best!"

Rhys at the Fairy Dance

Rhys and David hastened home,
For the night was well-nigh come,
And their tired and heavy tread
Woke the birds who'd gone to bed.

The tired moon leaned on the hill,
Tired, the soft wind had grown still,
Bats and beetles were about,
And the stars peeped shyly out …

When Rhys stopped and said, "Why, hark!
Who is singing like a lark?
Listen! for more joyful things
Never woke from fiddle-strings!

"It were madness to pass by
Such a sweet festivity.
Dance I must, and dance I will –
Go you, David, up the hill!"

*Pixies sing their wee babes to rest in the tulips
they love best*

*Crowds of little folk were singing and
dancing, hand in hand*

With wild hair and strange faces, the elfin folk danced in a fairy ring

"Stay!" cried David, struck with fear,
"There's no music in my ear –
I hear nothing but the call
Of yon valley's waterfall!"

Ah! too late, poor Rhys was gone;
David shouted, but went on.
When in bed, uneasy dreams
Crossed his sleep with evil gleams.

David saw Rhys all that night
Dancing by a shady light,
Dancing while he seemed to sing,
Dancing in a fairy ring!

Crowds of little folk were there –
(Strange their faces, wild their hair) –
Singing, dancing hand-in-hand,
As they do in fairyland!

David woke from sleep at last,
But his wild dreams held him fast;
So he dressed and hastened out,
Hoping to see Rhys about.

Carefully he searched the hill,
Thinking Rhys might lie there still,
Sleeping under hedge or wall.
There was no sign of him at all!

But they found a ring of grass,
Green as mountain-ash it was,
And the mark of tiny heels
Showed where elves had trod their reels!

Though many a year has passed away,
None have seen Rhys since that day!
Does he dance and does he sing
For ever in a Fairy Ring?

When foolish Jack Frost reached the North Pole the three great icebergs turned into three tall men

Jack Frost

Now listen: Once upon a time,
There lived a foolish boy,
Who would not be contented
With any pretty toy.

But one thing he did wish for,
You'll think it very droll –
For sure enough he wanted
To see the great North Pole.

He rode upon a donkey,
Once in the summer weather,
These two fit companions
Went on their way together.

They travelled through great deserts,
And forests that were greater;
They waded through the seas, and then
Jumped over the Equator.

And so they journeyed Northward,
A long, long, weary way;
It was a toilsome journey
For the longest summer day.

At last they reached the great North Pole,
And it, with age, was white;
To see it there so stiff and still
It was a wondrous sight.

Then, foolish boy, he touched it
With one finger – only one –
But quickly he repented
What he had rashly done!

For three tall icebergs round him,
Each shook its great white head,
And then there were no icebergs there,
But three tall men instead.

"Foolish little boy," said one,
"You shall be always cold."
The second said, "And you shall live
Till you are very old."

The third said, "You may tremble,
For all we say is true,
And everything you breathe upon
Shall be as cold as you."

It seemed as if the picture came alive – the sea took breath, the clouds awoke,
the fisherman bent to his oar and the small boat neared the shore

And so it is – we always know
When that little boy is near,
And when our lips are pinched and blue,
We say, "Jack Frost is here."

He walks about at nightfall,
And kills the poor field-mice;
He breathes upon the rivers,
And they are turned to ice.

He passes through our gardens, –
We see where he has been,
For every little blade of grass
Is white instead of green;

And if a foolish snowdrop
Lifts up too soon its head,
He holds it in his prickly hand
Till the little thing is dead.

He stays here all the winter,
Sometimes till almost May,
Then come the gentle summer winds
And blow him quite away.

Ole Luk-Oie

A picture hung beside my bed,
Wherein the boat was painted red,
And in the blue sea and rusty frame
From day to day were just the same,
Till one night Ole Luk-Oie spread
His big umbrella o'er my head.
And then like magic swift and strange
Within the picture came a change –
It seemed as if the sea took breath,
The clouds awoke, as though from death,
The fisherman bent to his oar,
And the small boat drew near the shore.
The waves foamed white upon the sands,
Some children ran and clapped their hands,
And little ships from far away
Came sailing towards the painted bay;
All this and such-like wondrous things
Ole Luk-Oie's umbrella brings!

A House Of Sweets

Build me a house of fairy ginger-bread,
Covered with candied fruits and sugarplums –
Fruits that decay not when November comes –
Sparkling and juicy, purple and gold and red.
Thatch me the roof with chips of cocoa-nut,
Sugared and white, as are December snows:
Around the eaves hang toffee-drops in rows.
With golden-syrup fill the water-butt.
Then in the flower garden dig deep wells
Of cowslip wine and bubbling lemonade;
Let the house walls with chocolate be laid,
And pave the floors with coloured caramels.

So, I contented there would often spend
My happy days, and give to every child
Bits of my house, for this, whene'er they smiled,
Should of its own self grow again and mend!

Build me a house of fairy ginger-bread
with chocolate walls and
caramel floors

Fashion

There was a King of England once,
I shall not tell his name,
But what this King of England thought,
The people thought the same.
All that he said they listened to,
And called it wondrous wise;
On everything in earth or heaven
They looked with courtiers' eyes.
To every one of his commands
They said, "So let it be."
There never yet a monarch was
More absolute than he.
One day within his presence-hall
Two men stood forth together –
One dressed in velvet and in gold,
The other clad in leather.

The King said to his people,
"Remember what you're told,
You may kick the man in leather,
You must kiss the man in gold."
Whilst on a country walk one day,
The King espied a frog.
"Why, here," said he, "I've found a most
Peculiar kind of dog!
He shall have meat for breakfast,
Of milk three saucers full,
A golden collar for his neck,
And a bed of cotton-wool."
Then every courtier kept a frog
And called it a peculiar dog!

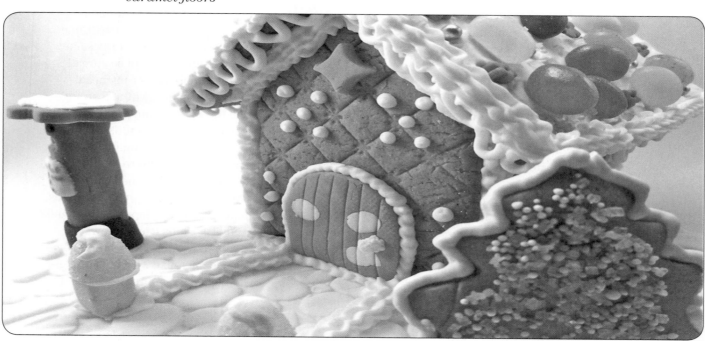

The Snowdrop

In this story by Hans Christian Andersen, (1805–1875) a young flower develops from a bulb, bursts into bloom early, while winter winds still blow harshly, and finally, having been plucked by a young woman, ends her days as a pressed bookmark in a poetry book, relatively contented with her ultimate fate. The message seems to be not to seek glory prematurely, before you are ready for this but that if your heart is pure and good, faith and perseverance will ultimately be rewarded.

The young flower shot forth from under the snow and lifted itself into the bright world

It was winter-time; the air was cold, the wind was sharp, but within the closed doors it was warm and comfortable, and within the closed door lay the Flower; it lay in the bulb under the snow-covered earth.

One day rain fell. The drops penetrated through the snowy covering down into the earth, and touched the flower-bulb, and talked of the bright world above. Soon the Sunbeam pierced its way through the snow to the root, and within the root there was a stirring.

"Come in," said the Flower.

"I cannot," said the Sunbeam. "I am not strong enough to unlock the door! When the summer comes I shall be strong!"

"When will it be summer?" asked the Flower, and she repeated this question each time a new sunbeam made its way down to her. But the summer was yet far distant. The snow still lay upon the ground, and there was a coat of ice on the water every night.

"What a long time it takes! what a long time it takes!" said the Flower. "I feel a stirring and striving within me; I must stretch myself, I must unlock the door, I must get out, and must nod a good morning to the summer, and what a happy time that will be!"

And the Flower stirred and stretched itself within the thin rind which the water had softened from without, and the snow and the earth had warmed, and the Sunbeam had knocked at; and it shot forth under the snow with a greenish-white blossom on a green stalk, with narrow thick leaves, which seemed to want to protect it. The snow was cold, but was pierced by the Sunbeam, therefore it was easy to get through it, and now the Sunbeam came with greater strength than before.

"Welcome, welcome!" sang and sounded every ray, and the Flower lifted itself up over the snow into the brighter world. The Sunbeams caressed and kissed it, so that it opened altogether, white as snow, and ornamented with green stripes. It bent its head in joy and humility.

"Beautiful Flower!" said the Sunbeams, "how graceful and delicate you are! You are the first, you are the only one! You are our love! You are the bell that rings out for summer, beautiful summer, over country and town. All the snow will melt; the cold winds will be driven away; we shall rule; all will become green, and then you will have companions, syringas, laburnums, and roses; but you are the first, so graceful, so delicate!"

That was a great pleasure. It seemed as if the air were singing and sounding, as if rays of light were piercing through the leaves and the stalks of the Flower. There it stood, so delicate and so easily broken, and yet so strong in its young beauty; it stood there in its white dress with the green stripes, and made a summer. But there was a

long time yet to the summer-time. Clouds hid the sun, and bleak winds were blowing.

"You have come too early," said Wind and Weather. "We have still the power, and you shall feel it, and give it up to us. You should have stayed quietly at home and not have run out to make a display of yourself. Your time is not come yet!"

It was a cutting cold! The days which now came brought not a single sunbeam. It was weather that might break such a little Flower in two with cold. But the Flower had more strength than she herself knew of. She was strong in joy and in faith in the summer, which would be sure to come, which had been announced by her deep longing and confirmed by the warm sunlight; and so she remained standing in confidence in the snow in her white garment, bending her head even while the snow-flakes fell thick and heavy, and the icy winds swept over her.

"You'll break!" they said, "and fade, and fade! What did you want out here? Why did you let yourself be tempted? The Sunbeam only made game of you. Now you have what you deserve, you summer gauk."

"Summer gauk!" she repeated in the cold morning hour.

"O summer gauk!" cried some children rejoicingly; "yonder stands one – how beautiful, how beautiful! The first one, the only one!"

These words did the Flower so much good, they seemed to her like warm sunbeams. In her joy the Flower did not even feel when it was broken off. It lay in a child's hand, and was kissed by a child's mouth, and carried into a warm room, and looked on by gentle eyes, and put into water. How strengthening, how invigorating! The Flower thought she had suddenly come upon the summer.

The daughter of the house, a beautiful little girl, was confirmed, and she had a friend who was confirmed, too. He was studying for an examination for an appointment. "He shall be my summer gauk," she said; and she took the delicate Flower and laid it in a piece of scented paper, on which verses were written, beginning with summer gauk and ending with summer gauk. "My friend, be a winter gauk." She had twitted him with the summer. Yes, all this was in the verses, and the paper was folded up like a letter, and the Flower was folded in the letter, too. It was dark around her, dark as in those days when she lay hidden in the bulb. The Flower went forth on her journey, and lay in the post-bag, and was pressed and crushed, which was

As summer came and went and then another summer came again, the Snowdrop thought of how the bright shining Sunbeams had called her the first, the only one

not at all pleasant; but that soon came to an end.

The journey was over; the letter was opened, and read by the dear friend. How pleased he was! He kissed the letter, and it was laid, with its enclosure of verses, in a box, in which there were many beautiful verses, but all of them without flowers; she was the first, the only one, as the Sunbeams had called her; and it was a pleasant thing to think of that.

She had time enough, moreover, to think about it; she thought of it while the summer passed away, and the long winter went by, and the summer came again, before she appeared once more. But now the young man was not pleased at all. He took hold of the letter very roughly, and threw the verses away, so that the Flower fell on the ground. Flat and faded she certainly was, but why should she be thrown on the ground? Still, it was better to be here than in the fire, where the verses and the paper were being burnt to ashes. What had happened? What happens so often – the Flower had made a gauk of him, that was a jest; the girl had made a fool of him, that was no jest, she had, during the summer, chosen another friend.

Next morning the sun shone in upon the little flattened Snowdrop, that looked as if it had been painted upon the floor. The servant girl, who was sweeping out the room, picked it up, and laid it in one of the books which were upon the table, in the belief that it must have fallen out while the room was being arranged. Again the Flower lay among verses – printed verses – and they are better than written ones – at least, more money has been spent upon them.

And after this years went by. The book stood upon the book-shelf, and then it was taken up and somebody read out of it. It was a good book; verses and songs by the old Danish poet, Ambrosius Stub, which are well worth reading. The man who was now reading the book turned over a page.

"Why, there's a Flower!" he said; "a snowdrop, a summer gauk, a poet gauk! That Flower must have been put in there with a meaning! Poor Ambrosius Stub! He was a summer fool too, a poet fool; he came too early, before his time, and therefore he had to taste the sharp winds, and wander about as a guest from one noble landed proprietor to another, like a Flower in a glass of water, a Flower in rhymed verses! Summer fool, winter fool, fun and folly – but the first, the only, the fresh young Danish poet of those days. Yes, thou shalt remain as a token in the book, thou little Snowdrop: thou hast been put there with a meaning."

And so the Snowdrop was put back into the book, and felt equally honored and pleased to know that it was a token in the glorious book of songs, and that he who was the first to sing and to write had been also a snowdrop, had been a summer gauk, and had been looked upon in the winter-time as a fool. The Flower understood this, in her way, as we interpret everything in our way.

That is the story of the Snowdrop.

The Windmill

Hans Christian Andersen (1805–1875) was brought up as an only child but had a half-sister, Karen Marie whom he scarcely knew. He had already published his first story, *The Ghost at Palnatoke's Grave*, in 1822 but attended school at Elsinore until 1827. He wrote *The Windmill* in 1865.

A windmill stood upon the hill, proud to look at, and it was proud too.

"I am not proud at all," it said, "but I am very much enlightened without and within. I have sun and moon for my outward use, and for inward use too; and into the bargain I have stearin candles, train oil and lamps, and tallow candles. I may well say that I'm enlightened. I'm a thinking being, and so well constructed that it's quite delightful. I have a good windpipe in my chest, and I have four wings that are placed outside my head, just beneath my hat. The birds have only two wings, and are obliged to carry them on their backs. I am a Dutchman by birth, that may be seen by my figure – a flying Dutchman. They are considered supernatural beings, I know, and yet I am quite natural. I have a gallery round my chest, and house-room beneath it; that's where my thoughts dwell. My strongest thought, who rules and reigns, is called by others 'The Man in the Mill.' He knows what he wants, and is lord over the meal and the bran; but he has his companion, too, and she calls herself 'Mother.' She is the very heart of me. She does not run about stupidly and awkwardly, for she knows what she wants, she knows what she can do, she's as soft as a zephyr and as strong as a storm; she knows how to begin a thing carefully, and to have her own way. She is my soft temper, and the father is my hard one. They are two, and yet one; they each call the other 'My half.' These two have some little boys, young thoughts, that can grow. The little ones keep everything in order. When, lately, in my wisdom, I let the father and the boys examine my throat and the hole in my chest, to see what was going on there, – for something in me was out of order, and it's well to examine one's self, – the little ones made a tremendous noise. The youngest jumped up into my hat, and shouted so there that it tickled me. The little thoughts may grow – I know that very well; and out in the world thoughts come too, and not only of my kind, for as far as I can see, I cannot discern anything like myself; but the wingless houses, whose throats make no noise, have thoughts too, and these come to my thoughts, and make love to them, as it is called. It's wonderful enough – yes, there are many wonderful things. Something has come over me, or into me, – something has changed in the mill-work. It seems as if the one half, the father, had altered, and had received a better temper and a more affectionate helpmate – so young and good, and yet the same, only more gentle and good through the course of time. What was bitter has passed away, and the whole is much more comfortable.

"The days go on, and the days come nearer and nearer to clearness and to joy; and then a day will come when it will be over with me; but not over altogether. I must be pulled down that I may be built up again; I shall cease, but yet shall live on. To become quite a different being, and yet remain the same! That's difficult for me to understand, however enlightened I may be with sun, moon, stearin, train oil, and tallow. My old wood-work and my old brick-work will rise again from the dust!

"I will hope that I may keep my old thoughts, the father in the mill, and the mother, great ones and little ones – the family; for I call them all, great and little, the company of thoughts, because I must, and cannot refrain from it.

"And I must also remain 'myself,' with my throat in my chest, my wings on my head, the gallery round my body; else I should not know myself, nor could the others know me, and say, 'There's the mill on the hill, proud to look at, and yet not proud at all.' "

That is what the mill said. Indeed, it said much more, but that is the most important part.

And the days came, and the days went, and yesterday was the last day.

Then the mill caught fire. The flames rose up high, and beat out and in, and bit at the beams and planks, and ate them up. The mill fell, and nothing remained of it but a heap of ashes. The smoke drove across the scene of the conflagration, and the wind carried it away.

Whatever had been alive in the mill remained, and what had been gained by it has nothing to do with this story.

The miller's family – one soul, many thoughts, and yet only one – built a new, a splendid mill, which answered its purpose. It was quite like the old one, and people said, "Why, yonder is the mill on the hill, proud to look at!" But this mill was better arranged, more according to the time than the last, so that progress might be made. The old beams had become worm-eaten and spongy – they lay in dust and ashes. The body of the mill did not rise out of the dust as they had believed it would do. They had taken it literally, and all things are not to be taken literally.

*Little knowing that his end was nigh, the fine old windmill boasted of his excellent sails
(which he called his 'wings') as well as his glowing candles and his gallery*

The Pink

Sometimes called *The Carnation*, this story was tale number 76 found by the Brothers Grimm (Jacob 1785–1863 and Wilhelm 1786–1859) and tells how a childless queen prays for a baby. Her wish is granted but later she is falsely accused of killing her son and her troubles are only just beginning!

and told him the joyful tidings, and when the time was come she gave birth to a son, and the king was filled with gladness.

Every morning she went with the child to the garden where the wild beasts were kept, and washed herself there in a clear stream. It happened once when the child was a little older, that it was lying in her arms and she fell asleep. Then came the old cook, who knew that the child had the power of wishing, and stole it away, and he took a hen,

Carnations are such intricate beautiful flowers. In this story a pink transforms into a lovely maiden as the king stares, amazed

Heavenly angels attended the queen

The two white doves were angels

There was once upon a time a queen to whom God had given no children. Every morning she went into the garden and prayed to God in heaven to bestow on her a son or a daughter. Then an angel from heaven came to her and said: "Be at rest, you shall have a son with the power of wishing, so that whatsoever in the world he wishes for, that shall he have." Then she went to the king,

and cut it in pieces, and dropped some of its blood on the queen's apron and on her dress. Then he carried the child away to a secret place, where a nurse was obliged to suckle it, and he ran to the king and accused the queen of having allowed her child to be taken from her by the wild beasts. When the king saw the blood on her apron, he believed this, fell into such a passion that he ordered a high tower to be built, in which neither sun nor moon could be seen and had his wife put into it, and walled up. Here she was to stay for seven years without meat or drink, and die of hunger. But God sent two angels from heaven in the shape of white doves, which flew to her twice a day, and carried her food until the seven years were over.

The cook, however, thought to himself: "If the child has the power of wishing, and I am here, he might very easily get me into trouble." So he left the palace and went to the boy, who was already big enough to speak, and said to him: "Wish for a beautiful palace for yourself with a garden, and all else that pertains to it." Scarcely were the words out of the boy's mouth, when everything was there that he had wished for. After a while the cook said to him: "It is not well for you to be so alone, wish for a pretty girl as a companion." Then the king's son wished for one, and

said: "Tonight when the boy is asleep, go to his bed and plunge this knife into his heart, and bring me his heart and tongue, and if you do not do it, you shall lose your life." Thereupon he went away, and when he returned next day she had not done it, and said: "Why should I shed the blood of an innocent boy who has never harmed anyone?" The cook once more said: "If you do not do it, it shall cost you your own life." When he had gone away, she had a little hind brought to her, and ordered her to be killed, and took her heart and tongue, and laid them on a plate, and when she saw the old man coming, she said to the boy: "Lie down in your bed, and draw the clothes over you." Then the wicked wretch came in and said: "Where are the boy's heart and tongue?" The girl reached the plate to him, but the king's son threw off the quilt, and said: "You old sinner, why did you want to kill me? Now will I pronounce

she immediately stood before him, and was more beautiful than any painter could have painted her. The two played together, and loved each other with all their hearts, and the old cook went out hunting like a nobleman. The thought occurred to him, however, that the king's son might some day wish to be with his father, and thus bring him into great peril. So he went out and took the maiden aside, and

thy sentence. You shall become a black poodle and have a gold collar round your neck, and shall eat burning coals, till the flames burst forth from your throat." And when he had spoken these words, the old man was changed into a poodle dog, and had a gold collar round his neck, and the cooks were ordered to bring up some live coals, and these he ate, until the flames broke forth from his throat.

The wicked old cook was changed into a black poodle with a gold collar and was made to eat live coals

The king's son remained there a short while longer, and he thought of his mother, and wondered if she were still alive. At length he said to the maiden: "I will go home to my own country; if you will go with me, I will provide for you." "Ah," she replied, "the way is so long, and what shall I do in a strange land where I am unknown?" As she did not seem quite willing, and as they could not be parted from each other, he wished that she might be changed into a beautiful pink, and took her with him. Then he went away to his own country, and the poodle had to run after him. He went to the tower in which his mother was confined, and as it was so high, he wished for a ladder which would reach up to the very top. Then he mounted up and looked inside, and cried: "Beloved mother, Lady Queen, are you still alive, or are you dead?" She answered: "I have just eaten, and am still satisfied," for she thought the angels were there. Said he: "I am your dear son, whom the wild beasts were said to have torn from your arms; but I am alive still, and will soon set you free." Then he descended again, and went to his father, and caused himself to be announced as a strange huntsman, and asked if he could offer him service. The king said yes, if he was skilful and could get game for him, he should come to him, but

that deer had never taken up their quarters in any part of the district or country. Then the huntsman promised to procure as much game for him as he could possibly use at the royal table. So he summoned all the huntsmen together, and bade them go out into the forest with him. And he went with them and made them form a great circle, open at one end where he stationed himself, and began to wish. Two hundred deer and more came running inside the circle at once, and the huntsmen shot them. Then they were all placed on sixty country carts, and driven home to the king, and for once he was able to deck his table with game, after having had none at all for years.

Now the king felt great joy at this, and commanded that his entire household should eat with him next day, and made a great feast. When they were all assembled together, he said to the huntsman: "As you are so clever, you shall sit by me." He replied: "Lord King, your majesty must excuse me, I am a poor huntsman." But the king insisted on it, and said: "You shall sit by me," until he did it. Whilst he was sitting there, he thought of his dearest mother, and wished that one of the king's principal servants would begin to speak of her, and would ask how it was faring with the queen in the tower, and if she were alive still, or had perished.

The king ordered a great feast to be held that all might dine on the fine venison and game

Hardly had he formed the wish than the marshal began, and said: "Your majesty, we live joyously here, but how is the queen living in the tower? Is she still alive, or has she died?" But the king replied: "She let my dear son be torn to pieces by wild beasts; I will not have her named." Then the huntsman arose and said: "Gracious lord father she is alive still, and I am her son, and I was not carried away by wild beasts, but by that wretch the old cook, who tore me from her arms when she was asleep, and sprinkled her apron with the blood of a chicken." Thereupon he took the dog with the golden collar, and said: "That is the wretch!" and caused live coals to be brought, and these the dog was compelled to devour before the sight of all, until flames burst forth from its throat. On this the huntsman asked the king if he would like to see the dog in his true shape, and wished him back into the form of the cook, in the which he stood immediately, with his white apron, and his knife by his side. When the king saw him he fell into a passion, and ordered him to be cast into the deepest dungeon. Then the huntsman spoke further and said: "Father, will you see the maiden who brought me up so tenderly and who was afterwards to murder me, but did not do it, though her own life depended on it?" The king replied: "Yes, I would

like to see her." The son said: "Most gracious father, I will show her to you in the form of a beautiful flower," and he thrust his hand into his pocket and brought forth the pink, and placed it on the royal table, and it was so beautiful that the king had never seen one to equal it. Then the son said: "Now will I show her to you in her own form," and wished that she might become a maiden, and she stood there looking so beautiful that no painter could have made her look more so.

And the king sent two waiting-maids and two attendants into the tower, to fetch the queen and bring her to the royal table. But when she was led in she ate nothing, and said: "The gracious and merciful God who has supported me in the tower, will soon set me free." She lived three days more, and then died happily, and when she was buried, the two white doves which had brought her food to the tower, and were angels of heaven, followed her body and seated themselves on her grave. The aged king ordered the cook to be torn in four pieces, but grief consumed the king's own heart, and he soon died. His son married the beautiful maiden whom he had brought with him as a flower in his pocket, and whether they are still alive or not, is known to God.

The Races

This 1858 tale by Hans Christian Andersen (1805–1875) explores the issues of fairness, motive and the rationale of judgment over who wins a race and why. Here are the hare and the snail, a fence-rail and a swallow, a mule, a fly and an earthworm – while a wild rose and a boundary post also give their opinions.

A prize, or rather two prizes, a great one and a small one, had been awarded for the greatest swiftness in running, – not in a single race, but for the whole year.

"I obtained the first prize," said the hare. "Justice must still be carried out, even when one has relations and good friends among the prize committee; but that the snail should have received the second prize, I consider almost an insult to myself"

"No," said the fence-rail, who had been a witness at the distribution of prizes; "there should be some consideration for industry and perseverance. I have heard many respectable people say so, and I can quite understand it. The snail certainly took half a year to get over the threshold of the door; but he injured himself, and broke his collar-bone by the haste he made. He gave himself up entirely to the race, and ran with his house on his back, which was all, of course, very praiseworthy; and therefore he obtained the second prize."

"I think I ought to have had some consideration too," said the swallow. "I should imagine no one can be swifter in soaring and flight than I am; and how far I have been! far, far away."

"Yes, that is your misfortune," said the fence-rail; "you are so fickle, so unsettled; you must always be travelling about into foreign lands when the cold commences here. You have no love of fatherland in you. There can be no consideration for you."

"But now, if I have been lying the whole winter in the moor," said the swallow, "and suppose I slept the whole time, would that be taken into account?" "Bring a certificate from the old moor-hen," said he, "that you have slept away half your time in fatherland; then you will be treated with some consideration."

"I deserved the first prize, and not the second," said the snail. "I know so much, at least, that the hare only ran from cowardice, and because he thought there was danger in delay. I, on the other hand, made running the business of my life, and have become a cripple in the service. If any one had a first prize, it ought to have been myself. But I do not understand chattering and boasting; on the contrary, I despise it." And the snail spat at them with contempt.

"I am able to affirm with word of oath, that each prize – at least, those for which I voted – was given with just and proper consideration," said the old boundary post in the wood, who was a member of the committee of judges. "I always act with due order, consideration, and calculation. Seven times have I already had the honor to be present at the distribution of the prizes, and to vote; but to-day is the first time I have been able to carry out my will. I always reckon the first prize by going through the alphabet from the beginning, and the second by going through from the end. Be so kind as to give me your attention, and I will explain to you how I reckon from the beginning. The eighth letter from A is H, and there we have H for hare; therefore I awarded to the hare the first prize. The eighth letter from the end of the alphabet is S, and therefore the snail received the second prize. Next year, the letter I will have its turn for the first prize, and the letter R for the second."

"I should really have voted for myself," said the mule, "if I had not been one of the judges on the committee. Not only the rapidity with which advance is made, but every other quality should have due consideration; as, for instance, how much weight a candidate is able to draw; but I have not brought this quality forward now, nor the sagacity of the hare in his flight, nor the cunning with which he suddenly springs aside and doubles, to lead people on a false track, thinking he has concealed himself. No; there is something else on which more stress should be laid, and which ought not be left unnoticed. I mean that which mankind call the beautiful. It is on the beautiful that I particularly fix my eyes. I observed the well-grown ears of the hare; it is a pleasure to me to observe how long they are. It seemed as if I saw myself again in the days of my childhood; and so I voted for the hare."

"Buzz," said the fly; "there, I'm not going to make a long speech; but I wish to say something about hares. I have really overtaken more than one hare, when I have been seated on the engine in front of a railway train. I often do so. One can then so easily judge of one's own swiftness. Not long ago, I crushed the hind legs of a young hare. He had been running a long time before the engine; he had no idea that I was travelling there. At last he had to stop in his career, and the engine ran over his hind legs, and crushed them; for I set upon it. I left him lying there, and rode on farther. I call that conquering him; but I do not want the prize."

"It really seems to me," thought the wild rose, though she did not express her opinion aloud – it is not in her nature to do so, – though it would have been quite as well if she had; "it certainly seems to me that the sunbeam ought to have had the honor of receiving the first prize. The sunbeam flies in a few minutes along the immeasurable path from the sun to us. It arrives in such strength, that all nature awakes to loveliness and beauty; we roses blush and exhale fragrance in its presence. Our worshipful judges don't appear to have noticed this at all. Were I the sunbeam, I would give each one of them a sun stroke; but that would only make them mad, and they are mad enough already. I only hope," continued the rose, "that peace may reign in the wood. It is glorious to bloom, to be fragrant, and to live; to live in story and in song. The sunbeam will outlive us all."

"What is the first prize?" asked the earthworm, who had overslept the time, and only now came up.

"It contains a free admission to a cabbage-garden," replied the mule. "I proposed that as one of the prizes. The hare most decidedly must have it; and I, as an active and thoughtful member of the committee, took especial care that the prize should be one of advantage to him; so now he is provided for. The snail can now sit on the fence, and lick up moss and sunshine. He has also been appointed one of the first judges of swiftness in racing. It is worth much to know that one of the numbers is a man of talent in the thing men call a 'committee.' I must say I expect much in the future; we have already made such a good beginning."

The hare was certain he had won the first prize (free admission to the cabbage garden) and also that the second prize should on no account be given to – in his opinion – the undeserving snail

Bruno Liljefors.

Tooth Fairies

In many societies a child's loss of baby teeth was said to be graced by the attendance of fairies – and long before that stage in their lives, a tooth-gift was often given to a baby on the cutting of his or her first tooth.

The legendary tooth fairy gives a child money or a gift in exchange for a baby tooth (or milk tooth) that has fallen out – making room for the adult teeth to grow. Children place the tooth under their pillow at night and the fairy is said to take the tooth from under the pillow and replace it with money once the youngster has fallen asleep.

It was traditional in early times in Europe to bury baby teeth that fell out and it is still common here for young children to believe in the Tooth Fairy. When a child's sixth tooth falls out, it is customary for the tooth fairy to pop a gift (or money) under the child's pillow but to leave the tooth as a reward for the child growing strong. Some parents will add to the illusion by leaving trails of so-called "fairy dust" on the floor of the child's room.

In northern Europe payment was paid when a child cut their first tooth and this is mentioned in writings in early Nordic and Northern European mythologies. Many centuries later different tooth fairies were described in the United States in about 1900. The value of the monetary gifts for lost teeth varies according to the family's fortune but the largest gift reported was in Manhattan where US$1.2 million was offered for one child's first tooth, with a sliding scale for each subsequent tooth lost.

Hammaspeikko, (the Finnish word for the tooth troll) is a metaphorical device for explaining tooth decay to children. It suggests that eating candy lures tooth trolls, who drill holes into teeth. Evidently, brushing the teeth scares them away.

In Norway Hammaspeikko is a fictional character – an adaptation from a book published in 1949, which introduces two characters Karius (meaning caries or tooth decay) and Bactus (standing for bacteria). The book was translated into Finnish as *Satu hammaspeikoista* (*A Tale about Tooth Trolls*) and published in 1961. Similar spirits were believed to cause toothache in the old Finnish religion.

Tooth fairies fly like gossamer
As they make their nightly rounds
They tiptoe in your bedroom
And never make a single sound.

They build their marble palaces
And pave many a glistening street
With all the teeth they've gathered
When their searches are complete.

Some leave a present on the pillow
Some slip coins there as you sleep
But you never see them come and go
Even if you try to peep.

New teeth will follow shortly
But it is very good to understand
That your old teeth will be useful
And have a place in Fairyland.

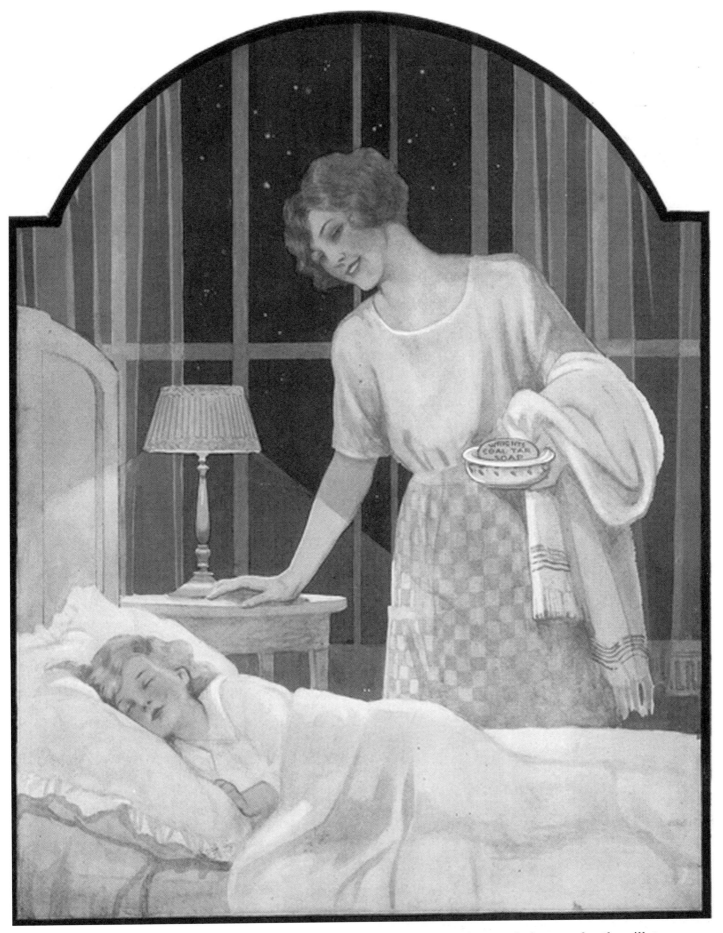

Tradition has it in many countries that fairies collect children's first teeth from under the pillow

The Old Street Lamp

This is another story from the prolific pen of Hans Christian Andersen (1805–1875). It tells of an old street lamp facing retirement and a new way of life

Did you ever hear the story of the old street lamp? It is not remarkably interesting, but for once in a way you may as well listen to it. It was a most respectable old lamp, which had seen many, many years of service, and now was to retire with a pension. It was this evening at its post for the last time, giving light to the street. His feelings were something like those of an old dancer at the theatre, who is dancing for the last time, and knows that on the morrow she will be in her garret, alone

For many a long year the old street lamp had shone brightly

and forgotten. The lamp had very great anxiety about the next day, for he knew that he had to appear for the first time at the town hall, to be inspected by the mayor and the council, who were to decide if he were fit for further service or not; – whether the lamp was good enough to be used to light the inhabitants of one of the suburbs, or in the country, at some factory; and if not, it would be sent at once to an iron foundry, to be melted down. In this latter case it might be turned into anything, and he wondered very much whether he would then be able to remember that he had once been a street lamp, and it troubled him exceedingly. Whatever might happen, one thing seemed certain, that he would be separated from the watchman and his wife, whose family he looked upon as his own. The lamp had first been hung up on that very evening that the watchman, then a robust young man, had entered upon the duties of his office. Ah, well, it was a very long time since one became a lamp and the other a watchman. His wife had a little pride in those days; she seldom condescended to glance at the lamp, excepting when she passed by in the evening, never in the daytime. But in later years, when all these – the watchman, the wife, and the lamp – had grown old, she had attended to it, cleaned it, and supplied it with oil. The old people were thoroughly honest, they had never cheated the lamp of a single drop of the oil provided for it.

This was the lamp's last night in the street, and to-morrow he must go to the town-hall – two very dark things to think of. No wonder he did not burn brightly. Many other thoughts also passed through his mind. How many persons he had lighted on their way, and how much he had seen; as much, very likely, as the mayor and corporation themselves! None of these thoughts were uttered aloud, however; for he was a good, honorable old lamp, who would not willingly do harm to any one, especially to those in authority. As many things were recalled to his mind, the light would flash up with sudden brightness; he had, at such moments, a conviction that he would be remembered. "There was a handsome young man once," thought he; "it is certainly a long while ago, but I remember he had a little note, written on pink paper with a gold edge; the writing was elegant, evidently a lady's hand: twice he read it through, and kissed it, and then looked up at me, with eyes that said quite plainly, 'I am the happiest of men!' Only he and I know what was written on this his first letter from his lady-love. Ah, yes, and there was another pair of eyes that I remember – it is really wonderful how the thoughts jump from one thing to another! A funeral passed through the street; a young and beautiful woman lay on a bier, decked with garlands of flowers, and attended by torches, which quite overpowered my light. All along the street stood the people from the houses, in crowds, ready to join the procession. But when the torches had passed from before me, and I could look round, I saw one person alone, standing, leaning against my post, and weeping. Never shall I forget the sorrowful eyes that looked up at me." These and similar reflections occupied the old street lamp, on this the last time that his light would shine. The sentry, when he is relieved from his post, knows at least who will succeed him, and may whisper a few words to him, but the lamp did not know his successor, or he could have given him a few hints respecting rain, or mist, and could have informed him how far the moon's rays would rest on the pavement, and from which side the wind generally blew, and so on.

On the bridge over the canal stood three persons, who wished to recommend themselves to the lamp, for they thought he could give the office to whomsoever he chose. The first was a herring's head, which could emit light in the darkness. He remarked that it would be a great saving of oil if they placed him on the lamp-post. Number two was a piece of rotten wood, which also shines in the dark. He considered himself descended from an old stem, once the pride of the forest. The third was a glow-worm, and how he found his way there the lamp could not imagine, yet there he was, and could really give light as well as the others. But the rotten wood and the herring's head declared most solemnly, by all they held sacred, that the glow-worm only gave light at certain times, and must not be allowed to compete with themselves. The old lamp assured them that not one of them could give sufficient light to fill the position of a street lamp; but they would believe nothing he said. And when they discovered that he had not the power of naming his successor, they said they were very glad to hear it, for the lamp was too old and worn-out to make a proper choice.

At this moment the wind came rushing round the corner of the street, and through the air-holes of the old lamp. "What is this I hear?" said he; "that you are going away to-morrow? Is this evening the last time we shall meet? Then I must present you with a farewell gift. I will blow into your brain, so that in future you shall not only be able to remember all that you have seen or heard in the past, but your light within shall be so bright, that you shall be able to understand all that is said or done in your presence."

"Oh, that is really a very, very great gift," said the old lamp; "I thank you most heartily. I only hope I shall not be melted down."

"That is not likely to happen yet," said the wind; "and I will also blow a memory into you, so that should you receive other similar presents your old age will pass very pleasantly."

"That is if I am not melted down," said the lamp. "But should I in that case still retain my memory?"

"Do be reasonable, old lamp," said the wind, puffing away.

At this moment the moon burst forth from the clouds. "What will you give the old lamp?" asked the wind.

At that moment the moon burst forth from the clouds

"I can give nothing," she replied; "I am on the wane, and no lamps have ever given me light while I have frequently shone upon them." And with these words the moon hid herself again behind the clouds, that she might be saved from further importunities. Just then a drop fell upon the lamp, from the roof of the house, but the drop explained that he was a gift from those gray clouds, and perhaps the best of all gifts. "I shall penetrate you so thoroughly," he said, "that you will have the power of becoming rusty, and, if you wish it, to crumble into dust in one night."

But this seemed to the lamp a very shabby present, and the wind thought so too. "Does no one give any more? Will no one give any more?" shouted the breath of the wind, as loud as it could. Then a bright falling star came down, leaving a broad, luminous streak behind it.

"What was that?" cried the herring's head. "Did not a star fall? I really believe it went into the lamp. Certainly, when such high-born personages try for the office, we may as well say 'Good-night,' and go home."

And so they did, all three, while the old lamp threw a wonderfully strong light all around him.

"This is a glorious gift," said he; "the bright stars have

A bright star came falling down from the sky above the city

always been a joy to me, and have always shone more brilliantly than I ever could shine, though I have tried with my whole might; and now they have noticed me, a poor old lamp, and have sent me a gift that will enable me to see clearly everything that I remember, as if it still stood before me, and to be seen by all those who love me. And herein lies the truest pleasure, for joy which we cannot share with others is only half enjoyed."

"That sentiment does you honor," said the wind; "but for this purpose wax lights will be necessary. If these are not lighted in you, your particular faculties will not benefit others in the least. The stars have not thought of this; they suppose that you and every other light must be a wax taper: but I must go down now." So he laid himself to rest.

"Wax tapers, indeed!" said the lamp, "I have never yet had these, nor is it likely I ever shall. If I could only be sure of not being melted down!"

The next day. Well, perhaps we had better pass over the next day. The evening had come, and the lamp was resting in a grandfather's chair, and guess where! Why, at the old watchman's house. He had begged, as a favor, that the mayor and corporation would allow him to keep the street lamp, in consideration of his long and faithful service, as he had himself hung it up and lit it on the day he first commenced his duties, four-and-twenty years

ago. He looked upon it almost as his own child; he had no children, so the lamp was given to him. There it lay in the great arm-chair near to the warm stove. It seemed almost as if it had grown larger, for it appeared quite to fill the chair. The old people sat at their supper, casting friendly glances at the old lamp, whom they would willingly have admitted to a place at the table. It is quite true that they dwelt in a cellar, two yards deep in the earth, and they had to cross a stone passage to get to their room, but within it was warm and comfortable and strips of list had been nailed round the door. The bed and the little window had curtains, and everything looked clean and neat. On the window seat stood two curious flower-pots which a sailor, named Christian, had brought over from the East or West Indies. They were of clay, and in the form of two elephants, with open backs; they were hollow and filled with earth, and through the open space flowers bloomed. In one grew some very fine chives or leeks; this was the kitchen garden. The other elephant, which contained a beautiful geranium, they called their flower garden. On the wall hung a large colored print, representing the congress of Vienna, and all the kings and emperors at once. A clock, with heavy weights, hung on the wall and went "tick, tick," steadily enough; yet it was always rather too fast, which, however, the old people said was better than being too slow. They were now eating their supper, while the old street lamp, as we have heard, lay in the grandfather's arm-chair near the stove. It seemed to the lamp as if the whole world had turned round; but after a while the old watchman looked at the lamp, and spoke of what they had both gone through together, – in rain and in fog; during the short bright nights of summer, or in the long winter nights, through the drifting snow-storms, when he longed to be at home in the cellar. Then the lamp felt it was all right again. He saw everything that had happened quite clearly, as if it were passing before him. Surely the wind had given him an excellent gift. The old people were very active and industrious, they were never idle for even a single hour. On Sunday afternoons they would bring out some books, generally a book of travels which they were very fond of. The old man would read aloud about Africa, with its great forests and the wild elephants, while his wife would listen attentively, stealing a glance now and then at the clay elephants, which served as flower-pots.

"I can almost imagine I am seeing it all," she said; and then how the lamp wished for a wax taper to be lighted in him, for then the old woman would have seen the smallest detail as clearly as he did himself. The lofty trees, with their thickly entwined branches, the naked negroes on horseback, and whole herds of elephants treading down bamboo thickets with their broad, heavy feet.

"What is the use of all my capabilities," sighed the old lamp, "when I cannot obtain any wax lights; they have only oil and tallow here, and these will not do." One day a great heap of wax-candle ends found their way into the cellar. The larger pieces were burnt, and the smaller ones the old woman kept for waxing her thread. So there were now candles enough, but it never occurred to any one to put a little piece in the lamp.

"Here I am now with my rare powers," thought the lamp, "I have faculties within me, but I cannot share them; they do not know that I could cover these white walls with beautiful tapestry, or change them into noble forests, or, indeed, to anything else they might wish for." The lamp, however, was always kept clean and shining in a corner where it attracted all eyes. Strangers looked upon it as lumber, but the old people did not care for that; they loved the lamp. One day – it was the watchman's birthday – the old woman approached the lamp, smiling to herself, and said, "I will have an illumination to-day in honor of my old man." And the lamp rattled in his metal frame, for he thought, "Now at last I shall have a light within me," but after all no wax light was placed in the lamp, but oil as usual. The lamp burned through the whole evening, and began to perceive too clearly that the gift of the stars would remain a hidden treasure all his life. Then he had a dream; for, to one with his faculties, dreaming was no difficulty. It appeared to him that the old people were dead, and that he had been taken to the iron foundry to be melted down. It caused him quite as much anxiety as on the day when he had been called upon to appear before the mayor and the council at the town-hall. But though he

had been endowed with the power of falling into decay from rust when he pleased, he did not make use of it. He was therefore put into the melting-furnace and changed into as elegant an iron candlestick as you could wish to see, one intended to hold a wax taper. The candlestick was in the form of an angel holding a nosegay, in the centre of which the wax taper was to be placed. It was to stand on a green writing table, in a very pleasant room; many books were scattered about, and splendid paintings hung on the walls. The owner of the room was a poet, and a man of intellect; everything he thought or wrote was pictured around him. Nature showed herself to him sometimes in the dark forests, at others in cheerful meadows where the storks were strutting about, or on the deck of a ship sailing across the foaming sea with the clear, blue sky above, or at night the glittering stars. "What powers I possess!" said the lamp, awaking from his dream; "I could almost wish to be melted down; but no, that must not be while the old people live. They love me for myself alone, they keep me bright, and supply me with oil. I am as well off as the picture of the congress, in which they take so much pleasure." And from that time he felt at rest in himself, and not more so than such an honorable old lamp really deserved to be.

Soon the poet would replace his old lamp with the new elegant iron candlestick

Lily and the Lion

This Grimm Brothers (Jacob 1785–1863 and Wilhelm 1786–1859) story bears some similarities to *Beauty and the Beast* but involves a lion, a dragon and a griffin, too!

A merchant, who had three daughters, was once setting out upon a journey; but before he went he asked each daughter what gift he should bring back for her. The eldest wished for pearls; the second for jewels; but the third, who was called Lily, said, "Dear father, bring me a rose." Now it was no easy task to find a rose, for it was the middle of winter; yet as she was his prettiest daughter, and was very fond of flowers, her father said he would try what he could do. So he kissed all three, and bid them goodbye.

And when the time came for him to go home, he had bought pearls and jewels for the two eldest, but he had sought everywhere in vain for the rose; and when he went into any garden and asked for such a thing, the people laughed at him, and asked him whether he thought roses grew in snow. This grieved him very much, for Lily was his dearest child; and as he was journeying home, thinking what he should bring her, he came to a fine castle; and around the castle was a garden, in one half of which it seemed to be summer-time and in the other half winter. On one side the finest flowers were in full bloom, and on the other everything looked dreary and buried in the snow. "A lucky hit!" said he, as he called to his servant, and told him to go to a beautiful bed of roses that was there, and bring him away one of the finest flowers.

This done, they were riding away well pleased, when up sprang a fierce lion, and roared out, "Whoever has stolen my roses shall be eaten up alive!" Then the man said, "I knew not that the garden belonged to you; can nothing save my life?" "No!" said the lion, "nothing, unless you undertake to give me whatever meets you on your return home; if you agree to this, I will give you your life, and the rose too for your daughter." But the man was unwilling to do so and said, "It may be my youngest daughter, who loves me most, and always runs to meet me when I go home." Then the servant was greatly frightened, and said, "It may perhaps be only a cat or a dog." And at last the man yielded with a heavy heart, and took the rose; and said he would give the lion whatever should meet him first on his return.

And as he came near home, it was Lily, his youngest and dearest daughter, that met him; she came running, and kissed him, and welcomed him home; and when she saw that he had brought her the rose, she was still more glad. But her father began to be very sorrowful, and to weep, saying, "Alas, my dearest child! I have bought this flower at a high price, for I have said I would give you to a wild lion; and when he has you, he will tear you in pieces, and eat you." Then he told her all that had happened, and said she should not go, let what would happen.

But she comforted him, and said, "Dear father, the word you have given must be kept; I will go to the lion, and soothe him: perhaps he will let me come safe home again."

The next morning she asked the way she was to go, and took leave of her father, and went forth with a bold heart into the wood. But the lion was an enchanted prince. By day he and all his court were lions, but in the evening they took their right forms again. And when Lily came to the castle, he welcomed her so courteously that she agreed

The servant fetched some beautiful roses for the merchant to give his youngest daughter, as promised.

The roaring beast was actually an enchanted prince; by day he and all his court became lions.

When the light shone upon the prince he turned into a dove and flew away from his bride

him no rest, and said she would take care no light should fall upon him. So at last they set out together, and took with them their little child; and she chose a large hall with thick walls for him to sit in while the wedding-torches were lighted; but, unluckily, no one saw that there was a crack in the door. Then the wedding was held with great pomp, but as the train came from the church, and passed with the torches before the hall, a very small ray of light fell upon the prince. In a moment he disappeared, and when his wife came in and looked for him, she found only a white dove; and it said to her, "Seven years must I fly up and down over the face of the earth, but every now and then I will let fall a white feather, that will show you the way I am going; follow it, and at last you may overtake and set me free."

This said, he flew out at the door, and poor Lily followed; and every now and then a white feather fell, and showed her the way she was to journey. Thus she went roving on through the wide world, and looked neither to the right hand nor to the left, nor took any rest, for seven years. Then she began to be glad, and thought to herself that the time was fast coming when all her troubles should end; yet repose was still far off, for one day as she was travelling on she missed the white feather, and when she lifted up her eyes she could nowhere see the dove. "Now," thought she to herself, "no aid of man can be of use to me." So she went to the sun and said, "Thou shinest everywhere, on the hill's top and the valley's depth – hast thou anywhere seen my white dove?" "No," said the sun, "I have not seen it; but I will give thee a casket – open it when thy hour of need comes."

So she thanked the sun, and went on her way till eventide; and when the moon arose, she cried unto it, and said, "Thou shinest through the night, over field and grove – hast thou nowhere seen my white dove?" "No," said the moon, "I cannot help thee but I will give thee an egg – break it when need comes."

Then she thanked the moon, and went on till the night-wind blew; and she raised up her voice to it, and said, "Thou blowest through every tree and under every leaf – hast thou not seen my white dove?" "No," said the night-wind, "but I will ask three other winds; perhaps they have seen it." Then the east wind and the west wind came, and said they too had not seen it, but the south wind said, "I have seen the white dove – he has fled to the Red Sea, and is changed once more into a lion, for the seven years are passed away, and there he is fighting with a dragon; and the dragon is an enchanted princess, who seeks to separate him from you." Then the night-wind said, "I will give thee counsel. Go to the Red Sea; on the right shore stand many rods – count them, and when thou comest to the eleventh, break it off, and smite the dragon with it; and so the lion will have the victory, and both of them will appear to you in their own forms. Then look round and thou wilt see a griffin, winged like bird, sitting by the Red Sea; jump on to his back with thy beloved one as quickly

to marry him. The wedding-feast was held, and they lived happily together a long time. The prince was only to be seen as soon as evening came, and then he held his court; but every morning he left his bride, and went away by himself, she knew not whither, till the night came again.

After some time he said to her, "Tomorrow there will be a great feast in your father's house, for your eldest sister is to be married; and if you wish to go and visit her my lions shall lead you thither." Then she rejoiced much at the thoughts of seeing her father once more, and set out with the lions; and everyone was overjoyed to see her, for they had thought her dead long since. But she told them how happy she was, and stayed till the feast was over, and then went back to the wood.

Her second sister was soon after married, and when Lily was asked to go to the wedding, she said to the prince, "I will not go alone this time—you must go with me." But he would not, and said that it would be a very hazardous thing; for if the least ray of the torch-light should fall upon him his enchantment would become still worse, for he should be changed into a dove, and be forced to wander about the world for seven long years. However, she gave

The dragon was an enchanted princess who aimed to steal away the prince.

as possible, and he will carry you over the waters to your home. I will also give thee this nut," continued the night-wind. "When you are half-way over, throw it down, and out of the waters will immediately spring up a high nut-tree on which the griffin will be able to rest, otherwise he would not have the strength to bear you the whole way; if, therefore, thou dost forget to throw down the nut, he will let you both fall into the sea."

So our poor wanderer went forth, and found all as the night-wind had said; and she plucked the eleventh rod, and smote the dragon, and the lion forthwith became a prince, and the dragon a princess again. But no sooner was the princess released from the spell, than she seized the prince by the arm and sprang on to the griffin's back, and went off carrying the prince away with her.

Thus the unhappy traveller was again forsaken and forlorn; but she took heart and said, "As far as the wind blows, and so long as the cock crows, I will journey on, till I find him once again." She went on for a long, long way, till at length she came to the castle whither the princess had carried the prince; and there was a feast got ready, and she heard that the wedding was about to be held. "Heaven

aid me now!" said she; and she took the casket that the sun had given her, and found that within it lay a dress as dazzling as the sun itself. So she put it on, and went into the palace, and all the people gazed upon her; and the dress pleased the bride so much that she asked whether it was to be sold. "Not for gold and silver." said she, "but for flesh and blood." The princess asked what she meant, and she said, "Let me speak with the bridegroom this night in his chamber, and I will give thee the dress." At last the princess agreed, but she told her chamberlain to give the prince a sleeping draught, that he might not hear or see her. When evening came, and the prince had fallen asleep, she was led into his chamber, and she sat herself down at his feet, and said: "I have followed thee seven years. I have been to the sun, the moon, and the night-wind, to seek thee, and at last I have helped thee to overcome the dragon. Wilt thou then forget me quite?" But the prince all the time slept so soundly, that her voice only passed over him, and seemed like the whistling of the wind among the fir-trees.

Then poor Lily was led away, and forced to give up the golden dress; and when she saw that there was no help for

The griffin helped the pair to escape across the waters of the Red Sea

her, she went out into a meadow, and sat herself down and wept. But as she sat she bethought herself of the egg that the moon had given her; and when she broke it, there ran out a hen and twelve chickens of pure gold, that played about, and then nestled under the old one's wings, so as to form the most beautiful sight in the world. And she rose up and drove them before her, till the bride saw them from her window, and was so pleased that she came forth and asked her if she would sell the brood. "Not for gold or silver, but for flesh and blood: let me again this evening speak with the bridegroom in his chamber, and I will give thee the whole brood."

Then the princess thought to betray her as before, and agreed to what she asked: but when the prince went to his chamber he asked the chamberlain why the wind had whistled so in the night. And the chamberlain told him all – how he had given him a sleeping draught, and how a poor maiden had come and spoken to him in his chamber, and

was to come again that night. Then the prince took care to throw away the sleeping draught; and when Lily came and began again to tell him what woes had befallen her, and how faithful and true to him she had been, he knew his beloved wife's voice, and sprang up, and said, "You have awakened me as from a dream, for the strange princess had thrown a spell around me, so that I had altogether forgotten you; but Heaven hath sent you to me in a lucky hour."

And they stole away out of the palace by night unawares, and seated themselves on the griffin, who flew back with them over the Red Sea. When they were half-way across Lily let the nut fall into the water, and immediately a large nut-tree arose from the sea, whereon the griffin rested for a while, and then carried them safely home. There they found their child, now grown up to be comely and fair; and after all their troubles they lived happily together to the end of their days.

The Last Pearl

The Last Pearl by Hans Christian Andersen (1805–1875) was published in 1854 and reminds us that childbirth was once a really risky procedure and used so often to leave sorrowing families bereft of their mothers

We are in a rich, happy house, where the master, the servants, the friends of the family are full of joy and felicity. For on this day a son and heir has been born, and mother and child are doing well. The lamp in the bed-chamber had been partly shaded, and the windows were covered with heavy curtains of some costly silken material. The carpet was thick and soft, like a covering of moss. Everything invited to slumber, everything had a charming look of repose; and so the nurse had discovered, for she slept; and well she might sleep, while everything around her told of happiness and blessing. The guardian angel of the house leaned against the head of the bed; while over the child was spread, as it were, a net of shining stars, and each star was a pearl of happiness. All the good stars of life had brought their gifts to the newly born; here sparkled health, wealth, fortune, and love; in short, there seemed to be everything for which man could wish on earth.

"Everything has been bestowed here," said the guardian angel.

"No, not everything," said a voice near him – the voice of the good angel of the child; "one fairy has not yet brought her gift, but she will, even if years should elapse, she will bring her gift; it is the last pearl that is wanting."

"Wanting!" cried the guardian angel; "nothing must be wanting here; and if it is so, let us fetch it; let us seek the powerful fairy; let us go to her."

"She will come, she will come some day unsought!"

"Her pearl must not be missing; it must be there, that the crown, when worn, may be complete. Where is she to be found? Where does she dwell?" said the guardian angel. "Tell me, and I will procure the pearl."

"Will you do that?" replied the good angel of the child. "Then I will lead you to her directly, wherever she may be. She has no abiding place; she rules in the palace of the emperor, sometimes she enters the peasant's humble cot; she passes no one without leaving a trace of her presence. She brings her gift with her, whether it is a world or a bauble. To this child she must come. You think that to wait for this time would be long and useless. Well, then, let us go for this pearl – the only one lacking amidst all this wealth."

Then hand-in-hand they floated away to the spot where the fairy was now lingering. It was in a large house with dark windows and empty rooms, in which a peculiar stillness reigned. A whole row of windows stood open, so that the rude wind could enter at its pleasure, and the long white curtains waved to and fro in the current of air. In the centre of one of the rooms stood an open coffin, in which lay the body of a woman, still in the bloom of youth and

It is every guardian angel's duty – and wish – to protect the little children in their care

very beautiful. Fresh roses were scattered over her. The delicate folded hands and the noble face glorified in death by the solemn, earnest look, which spoke of an entrance into a better world, were alone visible. Around the coffin stood the husband and children, a whole troop, the youngest in the father's arms. They were come to take a last farewell look of their mother. The husband kissed her hand, which now lay like a withered leaf, but which a short time before had been diligently employed in deeds of love for them all. Tears of sorrow rolled down their cheeks, and fell in heavy drops on the floor, but not a word was spoken. The silence which reigned here expressed a world of grief. With silent steps, still sobbing, they left the room. A burning light remained in the room, and a long, red wick rose far above the flame, which fluttered in the draught of air. Strange men came in and placed the lid of the coffin over the dead, and drove the nails firmly in; while the blows of the hammer resounded through the house, and echoed in the hearts that were bleeding.

"Whither art thou leading me?" asked the guardian angel. "Here dwells no fairy whose pearl could be counted amongst the best gifts of life."

"Yes, she is here; here in this sacred hour," replied the angel, pointing to a corner of the room; and there,

– where in her life-time, the mother had taken her seat amidst flowers and pictures: in that spot, where she, like the blessed fairy of the house, had welcomed husband, children, and friends, and, like a sunbeam, had spread joy and cheerfulness around her, the centre and heart of them all, – there, in that very spot, sat a strange woman, clothed in long, flowing garments, and occupying the place of the dead wife and mother. It was the fairy, and her name was "Sorrow." A hot tear rolled into her lap, and formed itself into a pearl, glowing with all the colors of the rainbow. The angel seized it: the, pearl glittered like a star with seven-fold radiance. The pearl of Sorrow, the last, which must not be wanting, increases the lustre, and explains the meaning of all the other pearls.

"Do you see the shimmer of the rainbow, which unites earth to heaven?" So has there been a bridge built between this world and the next. Through the night of the grave we gaze upwards beyond the stars to the end of all things. Then we glance at the pearl of Sorrow, in which are concealed the wings which shall carry us away to eternal happiness.

The Pearl of Sorrow is the most beautiful and shimmers like a rainbow

The Fox and the Horse

This tale by The Brothers Grimm (Jacob 1785–1863 and Wilhelm 1786–1859) shows how a cunning fox outwits both a lion and the farmer in order to help an old horse who has been treated most unfairly.

Then up he sprang, and moved off, dragging the lion behind him. The beast began to roar and bellow, till all the birds of the wood flew away for fright; but the horse let him sing on, and made his way quietly over the fields to his master's house.

"Here he is, master," said he, "I have got the better of him": and when the farmer saw his old servant, his heart relented, and he said. "Thou shalt stay in thy stable and be well taken care of." And so the poor old horse had plenty to eat, and lived – till he died.

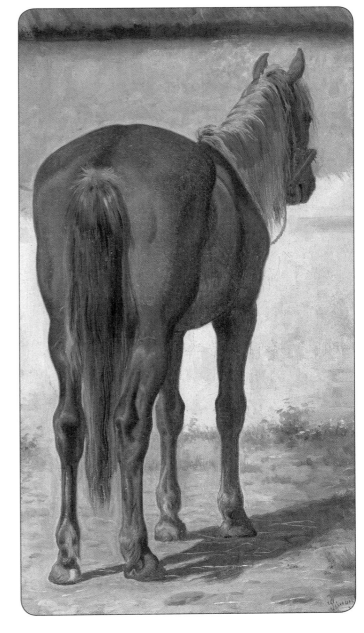

The poor old horse was turned out of his stable into the chill wind and rain

A farmer had a horse that had been an excellent faithful servant to him: but he was now grown too old to work; so the farmer would give him nothing more to eat, and said, "I want you no longer, so take yourself off out of my stable; I shall not take you back again until you are stronger than a lion." Then he opened the door and turned him adrift.

The poor horse was very melancholy, and wandered up and down in the wood, seeking some little shelter from the cold wind and rain. Presently a fox met him: "What's the matter, my friend?" said he, "why do you hang down your head and look so lonely and woe-begone?" "Ah!" replied the horse, "justice and avarice never dwell in one house; my master has forgotten all that I have done for him so many years, and because I can no longer work he has turned me adrift, and says unless I become stronger than a lion he will not take me back again; what chance can I have of that? he knows I have none, or he would not talk so."

However, the fox bid him be of good cheer, and said, "I will help you; lie down there, stretch yourself out quite stiff, and pretend to be dead." The horse did as he was told, and the fox went straight to the lion who lived in a cave close by, and said to him, "A little way off lies a dead horse; come with me and you may make an excellent meal of his carcase." The lion was greatly pleased, and set off immediately; and when they came to the horse, the fox said, "You will not be able to eat him comfortably here; I'll tell you what – I will tie you fast to his tail, and then you can draw him to your den, and eat him at your leisure."

This advice pleased the lion, so he laid himself down quietly for the fox to make him fast to the horse. But the fox managed to tie his legs together and bound all so hard and fast that with all his strength he could not set himself free. When the work was done, the fox clapped the horse on the shoulder, and said, "Up! Dobbin! Up!"

The Blue Light

The Brothers Grimm (Jacob 1785–1863 and Wilhelm 1786–1859) wrote this tale which is similar in some ways to Andersen's *The Tinder Box* – and to *Aladdin*, too, with the blue light serving as a magic lamp but summoning a dwarf rather than a genie!

The soldier made the beautiful princess work harder than any servant.

There was once upon a time a soldier who for many years had served the king faithfully, but when the war came to an end could serve no longer because of the many wounds which he had received. The king said to him: "You may return to your home, I need you no longer, and you will not receive any more money, for he only receives wages who renders me service for them." Then the soldier did not know how to earn a living, went away greatly troubled, and walked the whole day, until in the evening he entered a forest. When darkness came on, he saw a light, which he went up to, and came to a house wherein lived a witch. "Do give me one night's lodging, and a little to eat and drink," said he to her, "or I shall starve." "Oho!" she answered, "who gives anything to a run-away soldier? Yet will I be compassionate, and take you in, if you will do what I wish." "What do you wish?" said the soldier. "That you should dig all round my garden for me, tomorrow." The soldier consented, and next day laboured with all his strength, but could not finish it by the evening. "I see well enough," said the witch, "that you can do no more today, but I will keep you yet another night, in payment for which you must tomorrow chop me a load of wood, and chop it small." The soldier spent the whole day in doing it, and in the evening the witch proposed that he should stay one night more. "Tomorrow, you shall only do me a very trifling piece of work. Behind my house, there is an old dry well, into which my light has fallen, it burns blue, and never goes out, and you shall bring it up again." Next day the old woman took him to the well, and let him down in a basket. He found the blue light, and made her a signal to draw him up again. She did draw him up, but when he came near the edge, she stretched down her hand and wanted to take the blue light away from him. "No," said he, perceiving her evil intention, "I will not give you the light until I am standing with both feet upon the ground." The witch fell into a passion, let him fall again into the well, and went away.

The poor soldier fell without injury on the moist ground, and the blue light went on burning, but of what use was that to him? He saw very well that he could not escape death. He sat for a while very sorrowfully, then suddenly he felt in his pocket and found his tobacco pipe, which was still half full. "This shall be my last pleasure," thought he, pulled it out, lit it at the blue light and began to smoke. When the smoke had circled about the cavern, suddenly a little black dwarf stood before him, and said: "Lord, what are your commands?" "What my commands are?" replied the soldier, quite astonished. "I must do everything you bid me," said the little man. "Good," said the soldier; "then in the first place help me out of this well." The little man took him by the hand, and led him through an underground passage, but he did not forget to take the blue light with him. On the way the dwarf showed him the treasures which the witch had collected and hidden there, and the soldier took as much gold as he could carry. When he was above, he said to the little man: "Now go and bind the old witch, and carry her before the judge." In a short time she came by like the wind, riding on a wild tom-cat and screaming frightfully. Nor was it long before the little man reappeared. "It is all done," said he, "and the witch is

*The landlord of the best inn in town offered
the soldier a handsome room*

already hanging on the gallows. What further commands has my lord?" inquired the dwarf. "At this moment, none," answered the soldier; "you can return home, only be at hand immediately, if I summon you." "Nothing more is needed than that you should light your pipe at the blue light, and I will appear before you at once." Thereupon he vanished from his sight.

The soldier returned to the town from which he came. He went to the best inn, ordered himself handsome clothes, and then bade the landlord furnish him a room as handsome as possible. When it was ready and the soldier had taken possession of it, he summoned the little black manikin and said: "I have served the king faithfully, but

he has dismissed me, and left me to hunger, and now I want to take my revenge." "What am I to do?" asked the little man. "Late at night, when the king's daughter is in bed, bring her here in her sleep, she shall do servant's work for me." The manikin said: "That is an easy thing for me to do, but a very dangerous thing for you, for if it is discovered, you will fare ill." When twelve o'clock had struck, the door sprang open, and the manikin carried in the princess. "Aha! are you there?" cried the soldier, "get to your work at once! Fetch the broom and sweep the chamber." When she had done this, he ordered her to come to his chair, and then he stretched out his feet and said: "Pull off my boots," and then he threw them in her face, and made her pick them up again, and clean and brighten them. She, however, did everything he bade her, without opposition, silently and with half-shut eyes. When the first cock crowed, the manikin carried her back to the royal palace, and laid her in her bed.

Next morning when the princess arose she went to her father, and told him that she had had a very strange dream. "I was carried through the streets with the rapidity of lightning," said she, "and taken into a soldier's room,

The soldier was thrown into a dungeon

and I had to wait upon him like a servant, sweep his room, clean his boots, and do all kinds of menial work. It was only a dream, and yet I am just as tired as if I really had done everything." "The dream may have been true," said the king. "I will give you a piece of advice. Fill your pocket full of peas, and make a small hole in the pocket, and then if you are carried away again, they will fall out and leave a track in the streets." But unseen by the king, the manikin was standing beside him when he said that, and heard all. At night when the sleeping princess was again carried through the streets, some peas certainly did fall out of her pocket, but they made no track, for the crafty manikin had just before scattered peas in every street there was. And again the princess was compelled to do servant's work until cock-crow.

Next morning the king sent his people out to seek the track, but it was all in vain, for in every street poor children were sitting, picking up peas, and saying: "It must have rained peas, last night." "We must think of something else," said the king; "keep your shoes on when you go to bed, and before you come back from the place where you are taken, hide one of them there, I will soon contrive to find it." The black manikin heard this plot, and at night when the soldier again ordered him to bring the

The fierce wee dwarf had served his master well and had helped him to win a princess and a kingdom

princess, revealed it to him, and told him that he knew of no expedient to counteract this stratagem, and that if the shoe were found in the soldier's house it would go badly with him. "Do what I bid you," replied the soldier, and again this third night the princess was obliged to work like a servant, but before she went away, she hid her shoe under the bed.

Next morning the king had the entire town searched for his daughter's shoe. It was found at the soldier's, and the soldier himself, who at the entreaty of the dwarf had gone outside the gate, was soon brought back, and thrown into prison. In his flight he had forgotten the most valuable things he had, the blue light and the gold, and had only one ducat in his pocket. And now loaded with chains, he was standing at the window of his dungeon, when he chanced to see one of his comrades passing by. The soldier tapped at the pane of glass, and when this man came up, said to him: "Be so kind as to fetch me the small bundle I have left lying in the inn, and I will give you a ducat for doing it." His comrade ran thither and brought him what he wanted. As soon as the soldier was alone again, he lighted his pipe and summoned the black manikin. "Have no fear," said the latter to his master. "Go wheresoever they take you, and let them do what they will, only take the blue light with you." Next day the soldier was tried, and though he had done nothing wicked, the judge condemned him to death. When he was led forth to die, he begged a last favour of the king. "What is it?" asked the king. "That I may smoke one more pipe on my way." "You may smoke three," answered the king, "but do not imagine that I will spare your life." Then the soldier pulled out his pipe and lighted it at the blue light, and as soon as a few wreaths of smoke had ascended, the manikin was there with a small cudgel in his hand, and said: "What does my lord command?" "Strike down to earth that false judge there, and his constable, and spare not the king who has treated me so ill." Then the manikin fell on them like lightning, darting this way and that way, and whosoever was so much as touched by his cudgel fell to earth, and did not venture to stir again. The king was terrified; he threw himself on the soldier's mercy, and merely to be allowed to live at all, gave him his kingdom for his own, and his daughter to wife.

The Conceited Apple-Branch

The Conceited Apple-Branch, penned by Hans Christian Andersen (1805–1875) and published in 1852, is another of the ones in which Andersen explores vanity and humility.

It was the month of May. The wind still blew cold; but from bush and tree, field and flower, came the welcome sound, "Spring is come." Wild-flowers in profusion covered the hedges. Under the little apple-tree, Spring seemed busy, and told his tale from one of the branches which hung fresh and blooming, and covered with delicate pink blossoms that were just ready to open. The branch well knew how beautiful it was; this knowledge exists as much in the leaf as in the blood; I was therefore not surprised when a nobleman's carriage, in which sat the young countess, stopped in the road just by. She said that an apple-branch was a most lovely object, and an emblem of spring in its most charming aspect. Then the branch was broken off for her, and she held it in her delicate hand, and sheltered it with her silk parasol. Then they drove to the castle, in which were lofty halls and splendid drawing-rooms. Pure white curtains fluttered before the open windows, and beautiful flowers stood in shining, transparent vases; and in one of them, which looked as if it had been cut out of newly fallen snow, the apple-branch was placed, among some fresh, light twigs of beech. It was a charming sight. Then the branch became proud, which was very much like human nature.

People of every description entered the room, and, according to their position in society, so dared they to express their admiration. Some few said nothing, others expressed too much, and the apple-branch very soon got to understand that there was as much difference in the characters of human beings as in those of plants and

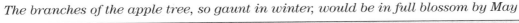

The branches of the apple tree, so gaunt in winter, would be in full blossom by May

The sunbeam kissed the humble dandelions as well as the rich garden flowers

flowers. Some are all for pomp and parade, others have a great deal to do to maintain their own importance, while the rest might be spared without much loss to society. So thought the apple-branch, as he stood before the open window, from which he could see out over gardens and fields, where there were flowers and plants enough for him to think and reflect upon; some rich and beautiful, some poor and humble indeed.

"Poor, despised herbs," said the apple-branch; "there is really a difference between them and such as I am. How unhappy they must be, if they can feel as those in my position do! There is a difference indeed, and so there ought to be, or we should all be equals."

And the apple-branch looked with a sort of pity upon them, especially on a certain little flower that is found in fields and in ditches. No one bound these flowers together in a nosegay; they were too common; they were even known to grow between the paving-stones, shooting up everywhere, like bad weeds; and they bore the very ugly name of "dog-flowers" or "dandelions."

"Poor, despised plants," said the apple-bough, "it is not your fault that you are so ugly, and that you have such an ugly name; but it is with plants as with men, – there must be a difference."

"A difference!" cried the sunbeam, as he kissed the blooming apple-branch, and then kissed the yellow dandelion out in the fields. All were brothers, and the sunbeam kissed them – the poor flowers as well as the rich.

The apple-bough had never thought of the boundless love of God, which extends over all the works of creation, over everything which lives, and moves, and has its being in Him; he had never thought of the good and beautiful which are so often hidden, but can never remain forgotten by Him, – not only among the lower creation, but also among men. The sunbeam, the ray of light, knew better.

"You do not see very far, nor very clearly," he said to the apple-branch. "Which is the despised plant you so specially pity?"

"The dandelion," he replied. "No one ever places it in a nosegay; it is often trodden under foot, there are so many of them; and when they run to seed, they have flowers like wool, which fly away in little pieces over the roads, and cling to the dresses of the people. They are only weeds; but of course there must be weeds. O, I am really very thankful that I was not made like one of these flowers."

There came presently across the fields a whole group of children, the youngest of whom was so small that it had to be carried by the others; and when he was seated on the grass, among the yellow flowers, he laughed aloud with joy, kicked out his little legs, rolled about, plucked the yellow flowers, and kissed them in childlike innocence. The elder children broke off the flowers with long stems, bent the stalks one round the other, to form links, and made first a chain for the neck, then one to go across the shoulders, and hang down to the waist, and at last a wreath to wear round the head, so that they looked quite splendid in their garlands of green stems and golden flowers. But the eldest among them gathered carefully the faded flowers, on the stem of which was grouped together the seed, in the form of a white feathery coronal. These loose, airy wool-flowers are very beautiful, and look like fine snowy feathers or down. The children held them to their mouths, and tried to blow away the whole coronal with one puff of the breath. They had been told by their grandmothers that who ever did so would be sure to have new clothes before the end of the year. The despised flower was by this raised to the position of a prophet or foreteller of events.

"Do you see," said the sunbeam, "do you see the beauty of these flowers? do you see their powers of giving pleasure?"

"Yes, to children," said the apple-bough.

By-and-by an old woman came into the field, and, with a blunt knife without a handle, began to dig round the roots of some of the dandelion-plants, and pull them up. With some of these she intended to make tea for herself; but the rest she was going to sell to the chemist, and obtain some money.

"But beauty is of higher value than all this," said the apple-tree branch; "only the chosen ones can be admitted into the realms of the beautiful. There is a difference between plants, just as there is a difference between men."

Then the sunbeam spoke of the boundless love of God, as seen in creation, and over all that lives, and of the equal distribution of His gifts, both in time and in eternity.

"That is your opinion," said the apple-bough.

Then some people came into the room, and, among them, the young countess, – the lady who had placed the apple-bough in the transparent vase, so pleasantly beneath the rays of the sunlight. She carried in her hand something that seemed like a flower. The object was hidden by two or three great leaves, which covered it like a shield, so that no draught or gust of wind could injure it, and it was carried more carefully than the apple-branch had ever been. Very cautiously the large leaves were removed, and there appeared the feathery seed-crown of the despised dandelion. This was what the lady had so carefully plucked, and carried home so safely covered, so that not one of the delicate feathery arrows of which its mist-like shape was so lightly formed, should flutter away. She now drew it forth quite uninjured, and wondered at its beautiful form, and airy lightness, and singular construction, so soon to be blown away by the wind.

"See," she exclaimed, "how wonderfully God has made this little flower. I will paint it with the apple-branch together. Every one admires the beauty of the apple-bough; but this humble flower has been endowed by Heaven with another kind of loveliness; and although they differ in appearance, both are the children of the realms of beauty."

Then the sunbeam kissed the lowly flower, and he kissed the blooming apple-branch, upon whose leaves appeared a rosy blush.

The Raven

This tale was number 93
collected by The Brothers
Grimm (Jacob 1785–1863
and Wilhelm 1786–1859)
and involves an enchanted
princess, robbers, a giant
and a cloak of invisibility

There was once a queen who had a little daughter, still too young to run alone. One day the child was very troublesome, and the mother could not quiet it, do what she would. She grew impatient, and seeing the ravens flying round the castle, she opened the window,

*The man did intend to help the raven but each
time succumbed to hunger or thirst*

and said: "I wish you were a raven and would fly away, then I should have a little peace." Scarcely were the words out of her mouth, when the child in her arms was turned into a raven, and flew away from her through the open window. The bird took its flight to a dark wood and remained there for a long time, and meanwhile the parents could hear nothing of their child.

Long after this, a man was making his way through the wood when he heard a raven calling, and he followed the sound of the voice. As he drew near, the raven said, "I am by birth a king's daughter, but am now under the spell of some enchantment; you can, however, set me free." "What am I to do?" he asked. She replied, "Go farther into the wood until you come to a house, wherein lives an old woman; she will offer you food and drink, but you must not take of either; if you do, you will fall into a deep sleep, and will not be able to help me. In the garden behind the house is a large tan-heap, and on that you must stand and watch for me. I shall drive there in my carriage at two o'clock in the afternoon for three successive days; the first day it will be drawn by four white, the second by four chestnut, and the last by four black horses; but if you fail to keep awake and I find you sleeping, I shall not be set free."

The man promised to do all that she wished, but the raven said, "Alas! I know even now that you will take something from the woman and be unable to save me." The man assured her again that he would on no account touch a thing to eat or drink.

When he came to the house and went inside, the old woman met him, and said, "Poor man! how tired you are! Come in and rest and let me give you something to eat and drink."

"No," answered the man, "I will neither eat not drink."

But she would not leave him alone, and urged him saying, "If you will not eat anything, at least you might take a draught of wine; one drink counts for nothing," and at last he allowed himself to be persuaded, and drank.

As it drew towards the appointed hour, he went outside into the garden and mounted the tan-heap to await the raven. Suddenly a feeling of fatigue came over him, and unable to resist it, he lay down for a little while, fully determined, however, to keep awake; but in another minute his eyes closed of their own accord, and he fell into such a deep sleep, that all the noises in the world would not have awakened him. At two o'clock the raven came driving along, drawn by her four white horses; but even before she reached the spot, she said to herself, sighing, "I know he has fallen asleep." When she entered the garden, there she found him as she had feared, lying on the tan-heap, fast asleep. She got out of her carriage and went to him; she called him and shook him, but it was all in vain,

The raven arrived in a black coach drawn by black horses

he still continued sleeping.

The next day at noon, the old woman came to him again with food and drink which he at first refused. At last, overcome by her persistent entreaties that he would take something, he lifted the glass and drank again.

Towards two o'clock he went into the garden and on to the tan-heap to watch for the raven. He had not been there long before he began to feel so tired that his limbs seemed hardly able to support him, and he could not stand upright any longer; so again he lay down and fell fast asleep. As the raven drove along her four chestnut horses, she said sorrowfully to herself, "I know he has fallen asleep." She went as before to look for him, but he slept, and it was impossible to awaken him.

The following day the old woman said to him, "What is this? You are not eating or drinking anything, do you want to kill yourself?"

He answered, "I may not and will not either eat or drink."

But she put down the dish of food and the glass of wine in front of him, and when he smelt the wine, he was unable to resist the temptation, and took a deep draught.

When the hour came round again he went as usual on to the tan-heap in the garden to await the king's daughter, but he felt even more overcome with weariness than on the two previous days, and throwing himself down, he slept like a log. At two o'clock the raven could be seen approaching, and this time her coachman and everything about her, as well as her horses, were black.

She was sadder than ever as she drove along, and said mournfully, "I know he has fallen asleep, and will not be able to set me free." She found him sleeping heavily, and all her efforts to awaken him were of no avail. Then she placed beside him a loaf, and some meat, and a flask of wine, of such a kind, that however much he took of them, they would never grow less. After that she drew a gold ring, on which her name was engraved, off her finger, and put it upon one of his. Finally, she laid a letter near him, in which, after giving him particulars of the food and drink she had left for him, she finished with the following words: "I see that as long as you remain here you will never be able to set me free; if, however, you still wish to do so, come to the golden castle of Stromberg; this is well within your power to accomplish." She then returned to her carriage and drove to the golden castle of Stromberg.

When the man awoke and found that he had been sleeping, he was grieved at heart, and said, "She has no doubt been here and driven away again, and it is now too late for me to save her." Then his eyes fell on the things

*The princess left her beautiful ring
upon the young man's finger*

which were lying beside him; he read the letter, and knew from it all that had happened. He rose up without delay, eager to start on his way and to reach the castle of Stromberg, but he had no idea in which direction he ought to go. He travelled about a long time in search of it and came at last to a dark forest, through which he went on walking for fourteen days and still could not find a way out. Once more the night came on, and worn out he lay down under a bush and fell asleep. Again the next day he pursued his way through the forest, and that evening, thinking to rest again, he lay down as before, but he heard such a howling and wailing that he found it impossible to sleep. He waited till it was darker and people had begun to light up their houses, and then seeing a little glimmer ahead of him, he went towards it.

He found that the light came from a house which looked smaller than it really was, from the contrast of its height with that of an immense giant who stood in front of it. He thought to himself, "If the giant sees me going in, my life will not be worth much." However, after a while he summoned up courage and went forward. When the giant saw him, he called out, "It is lucky for me that you have come, for I have not had anything to eat for a long time. I can have you now for my supper." "I would rather you let that alone," said the man, "for I do not willingly give myself up to be eaten; if you are wanting food I have enough to satisfy your hunger." "If that is so," replied the giant, "I will leave you in peace; I only thought of eating you because I had nothing else."

So they went indoors together and sat down, and the man brought out the bread, meat, and wine, which although he had eaten and drunk of them, were still unconsumed. The giant was pleased with the good cheer, and ate and drank to his heart's content. When he had finished his supper the man asked him if he could direct him to the castle of Stromberg. The giant said, "I will look on my map; on it are marked all the towns, villages, and houses." So he fetched his map, and looked for the castle, but could not find it. "Never mind," he said, "I have larger maps upstairs in the cupboard, we will look on those," but they searched in vain, for the castle was not marked even on these. The man now thought he should like to continue his journey, but the giant begged him to remain for a day or two longer until the return of his brother, who was away in search of provisions. When the brother came home, they asked him about the castle of Stromberg, and he told them he would look on his own maps as soon as he had eaten and appeased his hunger. Accordingly, when he had finished his supper, they all went up together to his room and looked through his maps, but the castle was not to be found. Then he fetched other older maps, and they went on looking for the castle until at last they found it, but it was many thousand miles away. "How shall I be able to get there?" asked the man. "I have two hours to spare," said the giant, "and I will carry you into the neighbourhood of the castle; I must then return to look after the child who is in our care."

The giant, thereupon, carried the man to within about a hundred leagues of the castle, where he left him, saying, "You will be able to walk the remainder of the way yourself." The man journeyed on day and night till he reached the golden castle of Stromberg. He found it situated, however, on a glass mountain, and looking up from the foot he saw the enchanted maiden drive round her castle and then go inside. He was overjoyed to see her, and longed to get to the top of the mountain, but the sides were so slippery that every time he attempted to climb he fell back again. When he saw that it was impossible to reach her, he was greatly grieved, and said to himself, "I will remain here and wait for her," so he built himself a little hut, and there he sat and watched for a whole year, and every day he saw the king's daughter driving round her castle, but still was unable to get nearer to her.

Looking out from his hut one day he saw three robbers fighting and he called out to them, "God be with you." They stopped when they heard the call, but looking round and seeing nobody, they went on again with their fighting, which now became more furious. "God be with you," he cried again, and again they paused and looked about, but seeing no one went back to their fighting. A third time he called out, "God be with you," and then thinking he should like to know the cause of dispute between the three men, he went out and asked them why they were fighting so angrily with one another. One of them said that he had found a stick, and that he had but to strike it against any door through which he wished to pass, and it immediately flew open. Another told him that he had found a cloak which rendered its wearer invisible; and the third had caught a horse which would carry its rider over any obstacle, and even up the glass mountain. They had been unable to decide whether they would keep together

The giant could stride across thousands of miles in just a few hours

and have the things in common, or whether they would separate. On hearing this, the man said, "I will give you something in exchange for those three things; not money, for that I have not got, but something that is of far more value. I must first, however, prove whether all you have told me about your three things is true." The robbers, therefore, made him get on the horse, and handed him the stick and the cloak, and when he had put this round him he was no longer visible. Then he fell upon them with the stick and beat them one after another, crying, "There, you idle vagabonds, you have got what you deserve; are you satisfied now!"

After this he rode up the glass mountain. When he reached the gate of the castle, he found it closed, but he gave it a blow with his stick, and it flew wide open at once

and he passed through. He mounted the steps and entered the room where the maiden was sitting, with a golden goblet full of wine in front of her. She could not see him for he still wore his cloak. He took the ring which she had given him off his finger, and threw it into the goblet, so that it rang as it touched the bottom. "That is my own ring," she exclaimed, "and if that is so the man must also be here who is coming to set me free."

She sought for him about the castle, but could find him nowhere. Meanwhile he had gone outside again and mounted his horse and thrown off the cloak. When therefore she came to the castle gate she saw him, and cried aloud for joy. Then he dismounted and took her in his arms; and she kissed him, and said, "Now you have indeed set me free, and tomorrow we will celebrate our marriage."

The Bell

Published in 1845, *The Bell* is by Hans
Christian Andersen (1805–1875) who
broke new ground for Danish literature
with his most memorable characters and
many of his tales inspired by the folk tales
he had learned as a child. They do not all
end happily but are always sincere and
poignant as the world is seen through
his characters' eyes – whether a tree, a
matchstick girl or an ugly duckling.

In the narrow streets of a large town people often heard
in the evening, when the sun was setting, and his last
rays gave a golden tint to the chimney-pots, a strange
noise which resembled the sound of a church bell; it only
lasted an instant, for it was lost in the continual roar of
traffic and hum of voices which rose from the town. "The
evening bell is ringing," people used to say; "the sun is
setting!" Those who walked outside the town, where the
houses were less crowded and interspersed by gardens and

*Ordinary church bells are all too easy to locate in their belfries, of course,
but the source of this sweet ringing proved elusive*

little fields, saw the evening sky much better, and heard the sound of the bell much more clearly. It seemed as though the sound came from a church, deep in the calm, fragrant wood, and thither people looked with devout feelings.

A considerable time elapsed: one said to the other, "I really wonder if there is a church out in the wood. The bell has indeed a strange sweet sound! Shall we go there and see what the cause of it is?" The rich drove, the poor walked, but the way seemed to them extraordinarily long, and when they arrived at a number of willow trees on the border of the wood they sat down, looked up into the great branches and thought they were now really in the wood. A confectioner from the town also came out and put up a stall there; then came another confectioner who hung a bell over his stall, which was covered with pitch to protect it from the rain, but the clapper was wanting.

When people came home they used to say that it had been very romantic, and that really means something else than merely taking tea. Three persons declared that they had gone as far as the end of the wood; they had always heard the strange sound, but there it seemed to them as if it came from the town. One of them wrote verses about the bell, and said that it was like the voice of a mother speaking to an intelligent and beloved child; no tune, he said, was sweeter than the sound of the bell.

The emperor of the country heard of it, and declared that he who would really find out where the sound came from should receive the title of 'Bellringer to the World,' even if there was no bell at all.

Now many went out into the wood for the sake of this splendid berth; but only one of them came back with some sort of explanation. None of them had gone far enough, nor had he, and yet he said that the sound of the bell came from a large owl in a hollow tree. It was a wisdom owl, which continually knocked its head against the tree, but he was unable to say with certainty whether its head or the hollow trunk of the tree was the cause of the noise.

He was appointed 'Bellringer to the World,' and wrote every year a short dissertation on the owl, but by this means people did not become any wiser than they had been before.

It was just confirmation-day. The clergyman had delivered a beautiful and touching sermon, the candidates were deeply moved by it; it was indeed a very important day for them; they were all at once transformed from mere children to grown-up people; the childish soul was to fly over, as it were, into a more reasonable being.

The sun shone most brightly; and the sound of the great unknown bell was heard more distinctly than ever. They had a mind to go thither, all except three. One of them wished to go home and try on her ball dress, for this very dress and the ball were the cause of her being confirmed this time, otherwise she would not have been allowed to go. The second, a poor boy, had borrowed a coat and a pair of boots from the son of his landlord to be confirmed in, and he had to return them at a certain time. The third

said that he never went into strange places if his parents were not with him; he had always been a good child, and wished to remain so, even after being confirmed, and they ought not to tease him for this; they, however, did it all the same. These three, therefore did not go; the others went on. The sun was shining, the birds were singing, and the confirmed children sang too, holding each other by the hand, for they had no position yet, and they were all equal in the eyes of God. Two of the smallest soon became tired and returned to the town; two little girls sat down and made garlands of flowers, they, therefore, did not go on. When the others arrived at the willow trees, where the confectioner had put up his stall, they said: "Now we

It was suggested that the sound of the bell might come from a wise owl in a hollow tree

are out here; the bell does not in reality exist – it is only something that people imagine!"

Then suddenly the sound of the bell was heard so beautifully and solemnly from the wood that four or five made up their minds to go still further on. The wood was very thickly grown. It was difficult to advance: wood lilies and anemones grew almost too high; flowering convolvuli and brambles were hanging like garlands from tree to tree; while the nightingales were singing and the sunbeams played. That was very beautiful! But the way was unfit for the girls; they would have torn their dresses. Large rocks, covered with moss of various hues, were lying about; the fresh spring water rippled forth with a peculiar sound. "I don't think that can be the bell," said one of the confirmed children, and then he lay down and listened. "We must

*Many people, rich and poor alike, made excursions into the
countryside and woodlands, hoping to find the mysterious bell*

try to find out if it is!" And there he remained, and let the others walk on.

They came to a hut built of the bark of trees and branches; a large crab-apple tree spread its branches over it, as if it intended to pour all its fruit on the roof, upon which roses were blooming; the long boughs covered the gable, where a little bell was hanging. Was this the one they had heard? All agreed that it must be so, except one who said that the bell was too small and too thin to be heard at such a distance, and that it had quite a different sound to that which had so touched men's hearts.

He who spoke was a king's son, and therefore the others said that such a one always wishes to be cleverer than other people.

Therefore they let him go alone; and as he walked on, the solitude of the wood produced a feeling of reverence in his breast; but still he heard the little bell about which the others rejoiced, and sometimes, when the wind blew in that direction, he could hear the sounds from the confectioner's stall, where the others were singing at tea. But the deep sounds of the bell were much stronger; soon it seemed to him as if an organ played an accompaniment – the sound came from the left, from the side where the heart is. Now something rustled among the bushes, and a little boy stood before the king's son, in wooden shoes and such a short jacket that the sleeves did not reach to his wrists. They knew each other: the boy was the one

who had not been able to go with them because he had to take the coat and boots back to his landlord's son. That he had done, and had started again in his wooden shoes and old clothes, for the sound of the bell was too enticing – he felt he must go on.

"We might go together," said the king's son. But the poor boy with the wooden shoes was quite ashamed; he pulled at the short sleeves of his jacket, and said that he was afraid he could not walk so fast; besides, he was of opinion that the bell ought to be sought at the right, for there was all that was grand and magnificent.

"Then we shall not meet," said the king's son, nodding to the poor boy, who went into the deepest part of the wood, where the thorns tore his shabby clothes and scratched his hands, face, and feet until they bled. The king's son also received several good scratches, but the sun was shining on his way, and it is he whom we will now follow, for he was a quick fellow. "I will and must find the bell," he said, "if I have to go to the end of the world."

Ugly monkeys sat high in the branches and clenched their teeth. "Shall we beat him?" they said. "Shall we thrash him? He is a king's son!"

But he walked on undaunted, deeper and deeper into the wood, where the most wonderful flowers were growing; there were standing white star lilies with blood-red stamens, sky-blue tulips shining when the wind moved them; apple-trees covered with apples like large glittering

The great majestic sea rolled its long waves against the shore, all golden as the sun glowed like a bright altar

soap bubbles: only think how resplendent these trees were in the sunshine! All around were beautiful green meadows, where hart and hind played in the grass. There grew magnificent oaks and beech-trees; and if the bark was split of any of them, long blades of grass grew out of the clefts; there were also large smooth lakes in the wood, on which the swans were swimming about and flapping their wings. The king's son often stood still and listened; sometimes he thought that the sound of the bell rose up to him out of one of these deep lakes, but soon he found that this was a mistake, and that the bell was ringing still farther in the wood. Then the sun set, the clouds were as red as fire; it became quiet in the wood; he sank down on his knees, sang an evening hymn and said: "I shall never find what I am looking for! Now the sun is setting, and the night, the dark night, is approaching. Yet I may perhaps see the round sun once more before he disappears beneath the horizon. I will climb up these rocks, they are as high as the highest trees!" And then, taking hold of the creepers and roots, he climbed up on the wet stones, where water-snakes were wriggling and the toads, as it were, barked at

him: he reached the top before the sun, seen from such a height, had quite set. "Oh, what a splendour!" The sea, the great majestic sea, which was rolling its long waves against the shore, stretched out before him, and the sun was standing like a large bright altar and there where sea and heaven met – all melted together in the most glowing colours; the wood was singing, and his heart too. The whole of nature was one large holy church, in which the trees and hovering clouds formed the pillars, the flowers and grass the woven velvet carpet, and heaven itself was the great cupola; up there the flame colour vanished as soon as the sun disappeared, but millions of stars were lighted; diamond lamps were shining, and the king's son stretched his arms out towards heaven, towards the sea, and towards the wood. Then suddenly the poor boy with the short-sleeved jacket and the wooden shoes appeared; he had arrived just as quickly on the road he had chosen. And they ran towards each other and took one another's hand, in the great cathedral of nature and poesy, and above them sounded the invisible holy bell; happy spirits surrounded them, singing hallelujahs and rejoicing.

Doctor Knowall

This is a German fairy tale collected by the Brothers Grimm (Jacob 1785–1863 and Wilhelm 1786–1859) and was tale number 98 in their collection. It is all about being in the right place at the right time and maximizing opportunity. A peasant named Crabb saw how well a doctor ate and asked how to become one; he then set about the deception and ultimately is rewarded through a chance misinterpretation of his words and intentions.

There was once upon a time a poor peasant called Crabb, who drove with two oxen a load of wood to the town, and sold it to a doctor for two talers. When the money was being counted out to him, it so happened that the doctor was sitting at table, and when the peasant saw how well he ate and drank, his heart desired what he saw, and would willingly have been a doctor too. So he remained standing a while, and at length inquired if he too could not be a doctor. "Oh, yes," said the doctor, "that is soon managed." "What must I do?" asked the peasant. "In the first place buy yourself an A B C book of the kind which has a cock on the frontispiece; in the second, turn your cart and your two oxen into money, and get yourself some clothes, and whatsoever else pertains to medicine; thirdly, have a sign painted for yourself with the words: "I am Doctor Knowall," and have that nailed up above your house-door." The peasant did everything that he had been told to do. When he had doctored people awhile, but not long, a rich and great lord had some money stolen. Then he was told about Doctor Knowall who lived in such and such a village, and must know what had become of the money. So the lord had the horses harnessed to his carriage, drove out to the village, and asked Crabb if he were Doctor Knowall. Yes, he was, he said. Then he was to go with him and bring

The doctor explained to the peasant what a simple matter it was to persuade people that you were a knowledgeable man whose opinions mattered

Crabb and his wife Grete sat down at the nobleman's table, ready to eat fine fare

back the stolen money. "Oh, yes, but Grete, my wife, must go too." The lord was willing, and let both of them have a seat in the carriage, and they all drove away together. When they came to the nobleman's castle, the table was spread, and Crabb was told to sit down and eat. "Yes, but my wife, Grete, too," said he, and he seated himself with her at the table. And when the first servant came with a dish of delicate fare, the peasant nudged his wife, and said: "Grete, that was the first," meaning that was the servant who brought the first dish. The servant, however, thought he intended by that to say: "That is the first thief," and as he actually was so, he was terrified, and said to his comrade outside: "The doctor knows all: we shall fare ill, he said I was the first." The second did not want to go in at all, but was forced. So when he went in with his dish, the peasant nudged his wife, and said: "Grete, that is the second." This servant was equally alarmed, and he got out as fast as he could. The third fared no better, for the peasant again said: "Grete, that is the third." The fourth had to carry in a dish that was covered, and the lord told the doctor that he was to show his skill, and guess what was beneath the cover. Actually, there were crabs. The doctor looked at the dish, had no idea what to say, and cried: "Ah, poor Crabb." When the lord heard that, he cried: "There! he

knows it; he must also know who has the money!"

On this the servants looked terribly uneasy, and made a sign to the doctor that they wished him to step outside for a moment. When therefore he went out, all four of them confessed to him that they had stolen the money, and said that they would willingly restore it and give him a heavy sum into the bargain, if he would not denounce them, for if he did they would be hanged. They led him to the spot where the money was concealed. With this the doctor was satisfied, and returned to the hall, sat down to the table, and said: "My lord, now will I search in my book where the gold is hidden." The fifth servant, however, crept into the stove to hear if the doctor knew still more. But the doctor sat still and opened his A B C book, turned the pages backwards and forwards, and looked for the cock. As he could not find it immediately he said: "I know you are there, so you had better come out!" Then the fellow in the stove thought that the doctor meant him, and full of terror, sprang out, crying: "That man knows everything!" Then Doctor Knowall showed the lord where the money was, but did not say who had stolen it, and received from both sides much money in reward, and became a renowned man.

The Butterfly

Published in 1861, this story by Hans Christian Andersen (1805–1875) tells how being too particular over finding a partner can ultimately mean ending up with no-one at all. His final comment reveals a somewhat cynical view of humanity, "One can't very well trust these plants in pots; they have too much to do with mankind."

There was once a butterfly who wished for a bride, and, as may be supposed, he wanted to choose a very pretty one from among the flowers. He glanced, with a very critical eye, at all the flower-beds, and found that the flowers were seated quietly and demurely on their stalks, just as maidens should sit before they are engaged; but there was a great number of them, and it appeared as if his search would become very wearisome. The butterfly did not like to take too much trouble, so he flew off on a visit to the daisies. The French call this flower "Marguerite," and they say that the little daisy can prophesy. Lovers pluck off the leaves, and as they pluck each leaf, they ask a question about their lovers; thus: "Does he or she love me?- Ardently? Distractedly? Very much? A little? Not at all?" and so on. Every one speaks these words in his own language. The butterfly came also to Marguerite to inquire, but he did not pluck off her leaves; he pressed a kiss on each of them, for he thought there was always more to be done by kindness.

"Darling Marguerite daisy," he said to her, "you are the wisest woman of all the flowers. Pray tell me which of the flowers I shall choose for my wife. Which will be my bride? When I know, I will fly directly to her, and propose."

But Marguerite did not answer him; she was offended that he should call her a woman when she was only a girl; and there is a great difference. He asked her a second time, and then a third; but she remained dumb, and answered

When a butterfly is caught by a collector and stuck upon a pin, it is unable to move and must remain perched upon its stalk like a flower.

not a word. Then he would wait no longer, but flew away, to commence his wooing at once. It was in the early spring, when the crocus and the snowdrop were in full bloom.

"They are very pretty," thought the butterfly; "charming little lasses; but they are rather formal."

Then, as the young lads often do, he looked out for the elder girls. He next flew to the anemones; these were rather sour to his taste. The violet, a little too sentimental. The lime-blossoms, too small, and besides, there was such a large family of them. The apple-blossoms, though they looked like roses, bloomed to-day, but might fall off to-morrow, with the first wind that blew; and he thought that a marriage with one of them might last too short a time. The pea-blossom pleased him most of all; she was white and red, graceful and slender, and belonged to those domestic maidens who have a pretty appearance, and can yet be useful in the kitchen. He was just about to make her an offer, when, close by the maiden, he saw a pod, with a withered flower hanging at the end.

"Who is that?" he asked.

"That is my sister," replied the pea-blossom.

"Oh, indeed; and you will be like her some day," said he; and he flew away directly, for he felt quite shocked.

A honeysuckle hung forth from the hedge, in full bloom; but there were so many girls like her, with long faces and sallow complexions. No; he did not like her. But which one did he like?

Spring went by, and summer drew towards its close; autumn came; but he had not decided. The flowers now appeared in their most gorgeous robes, but all in vain; they had not the fresh, fragrant air of youth. For the heart asks for fragrance, even when it is no longer young; and there is very little of that to be found in the dahlias or the dry chrysanthemums; therefore the butterfly turned to the mint on the ground. You know, this plant has no blossom; but it is sweetness all over,- full of fragrance from head to foot, with the scent of a flower in every leaf.

"I will take her," said the butterfly; and he made her an offer. But the mint stood silent and stiff, as she listened to him. At last she said,-

"Friendship, if you please; nothing more. I am old, and you are old, but we may live for each other just the same; as to marrying- no; don't let us appear ridiculous at our age."

And so it happened that the butterfly got no wife at all. He had been too long choosing, which is always a bad plan. And the butterfly became what is called an old bachelor.

It was late in the autumn, with rainy and cloudy weather. The cold wind blew over the bowed backs of the willows, so that they creaked again. It was not the weather for flying about in summer clothes; but fortunately the butterfly was not out in it. He had got a shelter by chance. It was in a room heated by a stove, and as warm as summer. He could exist here, he said, well enough.

"But it is not enough merely to exist," said he, "I need freedom, sunshine, and a little flower for a companion."

Then he flew against the window-pane, and was seen and admired by those in the room, who caught him, and stuck him on a pin, in a box of curiosities. They could not do more for him.

"Now I am perched on a stalk, like the flowers," said the butterfly. "It is not very pleasant, certainly; I should imagine it is something like being married; for here I am stuck fast." And with this thought he consoled himself a little.

"That seems very poor consolation," said one of the plants in the room, that grew in a pot.

"Ah," thought the butterfly, "one can't very well trust these plants in pots; they have too much to do with mankind."

The butterfly thought that the Marguerite daisy was the wisest of flowers

The Salad

As a merry young huntsman was once going briskly along through a wood, there came up a little old woman, who said to him, "Good day, good day; you seem merry enough, but I am hungry and thirsty; do pray give me something to eat." The huntsman took pity on her, and put his hand in his pocket and gave her what he had. Then he wanted to go his way; but she took hold of him, and said, "Listen, my friend, to what I am going to tell you; I will reward you for your kindness; go your way, and after a little time you will come to a tree where you will see nine birds sitting on a cloak. Shoot into the midst of them, and one will fall down dead: the cloak will fall too; take it, it is a wishing-cloak, and when you wear it you will find yourself at any place where you may wish to be. Cut open the dead bird, take out its heart and keep it, and you will find a piece of gold under your pillow every morning when you rise. It is the bird's heart that will bring you this good luck."

The huntsman thanked her, and thought to himself, "If all this does happen, it will be a fine thing for me." When he had gone a hundred steps or so, he heard a screaming and chirping in the branches over him, and looked up and saw a flock of birds pulling a cloak with their bills and feet; screaming, fighting, and tugging at each other as if each wished to have it himself. "Well," said the huntsman, "this is wonderful; this happens just as the old woman said"; then he shot into the midst of them so that their feathers flew all about. Off went the flock chattering away; but one fell down dead, and the cloak with it. Then the huntsman did as the old woman told him, cut open the bird, took out the heart, and carried the cloak home with him.

The next morning when he awoke he lifted up his pillow, and there lay the piece of gold glittering underneath; the same happened next day, and indeed every day when he arose. He heaped up a great deal of gold, and at last thought to himself, "Of what use is this gold to me whilst I am at home? I will go out into the world and look about me."

Then he took leave of his friends, and hung his bag and bow about his neck, and went his way. It so happened that his road one day led through a thick wood, at the end of which was a large castle in a green meadow, and at one of the windows stood an old woman with a very beautiful young lady by her side looking about them. Now the old woman was a witch, and said to the young lady, "There is a young man coming out of the wood who carries a wonderful prize; we must get it away from him, my dear child, for it is more fit for us than for him. He has a bird's heart that brings a piece of gold under his pillow every morning." Meantime the huntsman came nearer and looked at the lady, and said to himself, "I have been travelling so long that I should like to go into this castle and rest myself, for I have money enough to pay for anything I want"; but the real reason was, that he wanted to see more

When a young huntsmen gave food to a hungry old woman, he was rewarded with a magical cloak and gold

There were greens and cabbages growing everywhere – but no fruit

of the beautiful lady. Then he went into the house, and was welcomed kindly; and it was not long before he was so much in love that he thought of nothing else but looking at the lady's eyes, and doing everything that she wished. Then the old woman said, "Now is the time for getting the bird's heart." So the lady stole it away, and he never found any more gold under his pillow, for it lay now under the young lady's, and the old woman took it away every morning; but he was so much in love that he never missed his prize.

"Well," said the old witch, "we have got the bird's heart, but not the wishing-cloak yet, and that we must also get." "Let us leave him that," said the young lady; "he has already lost his wealth." Then the witch was very angry, and said, "Such a cloak is a very rare and wonderful thing, and I must and will have it." So she did as the old woman told her, and set herself at the window, and looked about the country and seemed very sorrowful; then the huntsman said, "What makes you so sad?" "Alas! dear sir," said she, "yonder lies the granite rock where all the costly diamonds grow, and I want so much to go there, that whenever I think of it I cannot help being sorrowful, for who can reach it? only the birds and the flies – man cannot." "If that's all your grief," said the huntsman, "I'll take you there with all my heart"; so he drew her under his cloak, and the moment he wished to be on the granite mountain they were both there. The diamonds glittered so on all sides that they were delighted with the sight and picked up the finest. But the old witch made a deep sleep come upon him, and he said to the young lady, "Let us sit down and rest ourselves a little, I am so tired that I cannot stand any longer." So they sat down, and he laid his head in her lap and fell asleep; and whilst he was sleeping on she took the cloak from his shoulders, hung it on her own, picked up the diamonds, and wished herself home again.

When he awoke and found that his lady had tricked him, and left him alone on the wild rock, he said, "Alas! what roguery there is in the world!" and there he sat in great grief and fear, not knowing what to do. Now this rock belonged to fierce giants who lived upon it; and as he saw three of them striding about, he thought to himself, "I can only save myself by feigning to be asleep"; so he laid himself down as if he were in a sound sleep. When the giants came up to him, the first pushed him with his foot, and said, "What worm is this that lies here curled up?" "Tread upon him and kill him," said the second. "It's not worth the trouble," said the third; "let him live, he'll go climbing higher up the mountain, and some cloud will come rolling and carry him away." And they passed on. But the huntsman had heard all they said; and as soon as they were gone, he climbed to the top of the mountain, and when he had sat there a short time a cloud came rolling around him, and caught him in a whirlwind and bore him along for some time, till it settled in a garden, and he fell quite gently to the ground amongst the greens and cabbages.

Then he looked around him, and said, "I wish I had something to eat, if not I shall be worse off than before; for here I see neither apples nor pears, nor any kind of fruits, nothing but vegetables." At last he thought to himself, "I can eat salad, it will refresh and strengthen me." So he picked out a fine head and ate of it; but scarcely had he swallowed two bites when he felt himself quite changed, and saw with horror that he was turned into an ass. However, he still felt very hungry, and the salad tasted very nice; so he ate on till he came to another kind of salad, and scarcely had he tasted it when he felt another change come over him, and soon saw

Before the huntsman set off again he broke off some of the good – and the bad – salad heads

that he was lucky enough to have found his old shape again.

Then he laid himself down and slept off a little of his weariness; and when he awoke the next morning he broke off a head both of the good and the bad salad, and thought to himself, "This will help me to my fortune again, and enable me to pay off some folks for their treachery." So he went away to try and find the castle of his friends; and after wandering about a few days he luckily found it. Then he stained his face all over brown, so that even his mother would not have known him, and went into the castle and asked for a lodging; "I am so tired," said he, "that I can go no farther." "Countryman," said the witch, "who are you? and what is your business?" "I am," said he, "a messenger sent by the king to find the finest salad that grows under the sun. I have been lucky enough to find it, and have brought it with me; but the heat of the sun scorches so that it begins to wither, and I don't know that I can carry it farther."

When the witch and the young lady heard of his beautiful salad, they longed to taste it, and said, "Dear countryman, let us just taste it." "To be sure," answered he; "I have two heads of it with me, and will give you one"; so he opened his bag and gave them the bad. Then the witch herself took it into the kitchen to be dressed; and when it was ready she could not wait till it was carried up, but took a few leaves immediately and put them in her mouth, and scarcely were they swallowed when she lost her own form and ran braying down into the court in the form of an ass. Now the servant-maid came into the kitchen, and seeing the salad ready, was going to carry it up; but on the way she too felt a wish to taste it as the old woman had done, and ate some leaves; so she also was turned into an ass and ran after the other, letting the dish with the salad fall on the ground. The messenger sat all this time with the beautiful young lady, and as nobody came with the salad and she longed to taste it, she said, "I don't know where the salad can be." Then he thought something must have happened, and said, "I will go into the kitchen and see." And as he went he saw two asses in the court running about, and the salad lying on the ground. "All right!" said

The old woman, the servant and the young lady were now turned into donkeys

he; "those two have had their share." Then he took up the rest of the leaves, laid them on the dish and brought them to the young lady, saying, "I bring you the dish myself that you may not wait any longer." So she ate of it, and like the others ran off into the court braying away.

Then the huntsman washed his face and went into the court that they might know him. "Now you shall be paid for your roguery," said he; and tied them all three to a rope and took them along with him till he came to a mill and knocked at the window. "What's the matter?" said the miller. "I have three tiresome beasts here," said the other; "if you will take them, give them food and room, and treat them as I tell you, I will pay you whatever you ask." "With all my heart," said the miller; "but how shall I treat them?" Then the huntsman said, "Give the old one stripes three times a day and hay once; give the next (who was the servant-maid) stripes once a day and hay three times; and give the youngest (who was the

beautiful lady) hay three times a day and no stripes": for he could not find it in his heart to have her beaten. After this he went back to the castle, where he found everything he wanted.

Some days after, the miller came to him and told him that the old ass was dead; "The other two," said he, "are alive and eat, but are so sorrowful that they cannot last long." Then the huntsman pitied them, and told the miller to drive them back to him, and when they came, he gave them some of the good salad to eat. And the beautiful young lady fell upon her knees before him, and said, "O dearest huntsman! forgive me all the ill I have done you; my mother forced me to it, it was against my will, for I always loved you very much. Your wishing-cloak hangs up in the closet, and as for the bird's heart, I will give it you too." But he said, "Keep it, it will be just the same thing, for I mean to make you my wife." So they were married, and lived together very happily till they died.

The Daisy

Hans Christian Andersen (1805–1875) published this story in 1838. It follows the pattern of so many of his tales that feature a simple kind-hearted creature as hero or heroine, surrounded by the pride and derision of others.

Now listen! In the country, close by the high road, stood a farmhouse; perhaps you have passed by and seen it yourself. There was a little flower garden with painted wooden palings in front of it; close by was a ditch, on its fresh green bank grew a little daisy; the sun shone as warmly and brightly upon it as on the magnificent garden flowers, and therefore it thrived well. One morning it had quite opened, and its little snow-white petals stood round the yellow centre, like the rays of the sun. It did not mind that nobody saw it in the grass, and that it was a poor despised flower; on the contrary, it was quite happy, and turned towards the sun, looking upward and listening to the song of the lark high up in the air.

The little daisy was as happy as if the day had been a great holiday, but it was only Monday. All the children were at school, and while they were sitting on the forms and learning their lessons, it sat on its thin green stalk and learnt from the sun and from its surroundings how kind God is, and it rejoiced that the song of the little lark expressed so sweetly and distinctly its own feelings. With a sort of reverence the daisy looked up to the bird that could fly and sing, but it did not feel envious. "I can see and hear," it thought; "the sun shines upon me, and the forest kisses me. How rich I am!"

In the garden close by grew many large and magnificent flowers, and, strange to say, the less fragrance they had the haughtier and prouder they were. The peonies puffed themselves up in order to be larger than the roses, but size is not everything! The tulips had the finest colours, and they knew it well, too, for they were standing bolt upright like candles, that one might see them the better. In their pride they did not see the little daisy, which looked over to them and thought, "How rich and beautiful they are! I am sure the pretty bird will fly down and call upon them. Thank God, that I stand so near and can at least see all the splendour." And while the daisy was still thinking, the lark came flying down, crying "Tweet," but not to the peonies and tulips – no, into the grass to the poor daisy. Its joy was

so great that it did not know what to think. The little bird hopped round it and sang, "How beautifully soft the grass is, and what a lovely little flower with its golden heart and silver dress is growing here." The yellow centre in the daisy did indeed look like gold, while the little petals shone as brightly as silver.

How happy the daisy was! No one has the least idea. The bird kissed it with its beak, sang to it, and then rose

Snow-white petals stood around the happy daisy's yellow centre like the rays of the sun

The daisy was delighted to be friends with the lark and so pleased that, as a common plant,
she was unlikely to be cut and put into a vase

again up to the blue sky. It was certainly more than a quarter of an hour before the daisy recovered its senses. Half ashamed, yet glad at heart, it looked over to the other flowers in the garden; surely they had witnessed its pleasure and the honour that had been done to it; they understood its joy. But the tulips stood more stiffly than ever, their faces were pointed and red, because they were vexed. The peonies were sulky; it was well that they could

not speak, otherwise they would have given the daisy a good lecture. The little flower could very well see that they were ill at ease, and pitied them sincerely.

Shortly after this a girl came into the garden, with a large sharp knife. She went to the tulips and began cutting them off, one after another. "Ugh!" sighed the daisy, "that is terrible; now they are done for."

The girl carried the tulips away. The daisy was glad that it was outside, and only a small flower – it felt very grateful. At sunset it folded its petals, and fell asleep, and dreamt all night of the sun and the little bird.

On the following morning, when the flower once more stretched forth its tender petals, like little arms, towards

Sadly, the lark had been caught and was now in a cage where it sang of happier days

the air and light, the daisy recognised the bird's voice, but what it sang sounded so sad. Indeed the poor bird had good reason to be sad, for it had been caught and put into a cage close by the open window. It sang of the happy days when it could merrily fly about, of fresh green corn in the fields, and of the time when it could soar almost up to the clouds. The poor lark was most unhappy as a prisoner in a cage. The little daisy would have liked so much to help it, but what could be done? Indeed, that was very difficult for such a small flower to find out. It entirely forgot how beautiful everything around it was, how warmly the sun was shining, and how splendidly white its own petals were.

It could only think of the poor captive bird, for which it could do nothing. Then two little boys came out of the garden; one of them had a large sharp knife, like that with which the girl had cut the tulips. They came straight towards the little daisy, which could not understand what they wanted.

"Here is a fine piece of turf for the lark," said one of the boys, and began to cut out a square round the daisy, so that it remained in the centre of the grass.

"Pluck the flower off" said the other boy, and the daisy trembled for fear, for to be pulled off meant death to it; and it wished so much to live, as it was to go with the square of turf into the poor captive lark's cage.

"No let it stay," said the other boy, "it looks so pretty".

And so it stayed, and was brought into the lark's cage. The poor bird was lamenting its lost liberty, and beating its wings against the wires; and the little daisy could not speak or utter a consoling word, much as it would have liked to do so. So the forenoon passed.

"I have no water," said the captive lark, "they have all gone out, and forgotten to give me anything to drink. My throat is dry and burning. I feel as if I had fire and ice within me, and the air is so oppressive. Alas! I must die, and part with the warm sunshine, the fresh green meadows, and all the beauty that God has created." And it thrust its beak into the piece of grass, to refresh itself a little. Then it noticed the little daisy, and nodded to it, and kissed it with its beak and said: "You must also fade in here, poor little flower. You and the piece of grass are all they have given me in exchange for the whole world, which I enjoyed outside. Each little blade of grass shall be a green tree for me, each of your white petals a fragrant flower. Alas! you only remind me of what I have lost."

"I wish I could console the poor lark," thought the daisy. It could not move one of its leaves, but the fragrance of its delicate petals streamed forth, and was much stronger than such flowers usually have: the bird noticed it, although it was dying with thirst, and in its pain tore up the green blades of grass, but did not touch the flower.

The evening came, and nobody appeared to bring the poor bird a drop of water; it opened its beautiful wings, and fluttered about in its anguish; a faint and mournful "Tweet, tweet," was all it could utter, then it bent its little head towards the flower, and its heart broke for want and longing. The flower could not, as on the previous evening, fold up its petals and sleep; it dropped sorrowfully. The boys only came the next morning; when they saw the dead bird, they began to cry bitterly, dug a nice grave for it, and adorned it with flowers. The bird's body was placed in a pretty red box; they wished to bury it with royal honours. While it was alive and sang they forgot it, and let it suffer want in the cage; now, they cried over it and covered it with flowers. The piece of turf, with the little daisy in it, was thrown out on the dusty highway. Nobody thought of the flower which had felt so much for the bird and had so greatly desired to comfort it.

King Grisly-Beard

The Brothers Grimm (Jacob 1785–1863 and Wilhelm 1786–1859) penned this tale about a haughty princess who called one of her suitors Grisly-beard, and said his whiskers were like an old mop.

A great king of a land far away in the East had a daughter who was very beautiful, but so proud, and haughty, and conceited, that none of the princes who came to ask her in marriage was good enough for her, and she only made sport of them.

Once upon a time the king held a great feast, and asked thither all her suitors; and they all sat in a row, ranged according to their rank—kings, and princes, and dukes, and earls, and counts, and barons, and knights. Then the princess came in, and as she passed by them she had something spiteful to say to every one. The first was too fat: "He"s as round as a tub," said she. The next was too tall: "What a maypole!" said she. The next was too short: "What a dumpling!" said she. The fourth was too pale, and she called him "Wallface." The fifth was too red, so she called him "Coxcomb." The sixth was not straight enough; so she said he was like a green stick, that had been laid to dry over a baker's oven. And thus she had some joke to crack upon every one: but she laughed more than all at a good king who was there. "Look at him," said she; "his beard is like an old mop; he shall be called Grisly-beard." So the king got the nickname of Grisly-beard.

But the old king was very angry when he saw how his daughter behaved, and how she ill-treated all his guests; and he vowed that, willing or unwilling, she should marry the first man, be he prince or beggar, that came to the door.

Two days after there came by a travelling fiddler, who began to play under the window and beg alms; and when the king heard him, he said, "Let him come in." So they brought in a dirty-looking fellow; and when he had sung before the king and the princess, he begged a boon. Then the king said, "You have sung so well, that I will give you my daughter for your wife." The princess begged and prayed; but the king said, "I have sworn to give you to the first comer, and I will keep my word." So words and tears were of no avail; the parson was sent for, and she was married to the fiddler. When this was over the king said, "Now get

ready to go – you must not stay here – you must travel on with your husband."

Then the fiddler went his way, and took her with him, and they soon came to a great wood. "Pray," said she, "whose is this wood?" "It belongs to King Grisly-beard," answered he; "hadst thou taken him, all had been thine." "Ah! unlucky wretch that I am!" sighed she; "would that I had married King Grisly-beard!" Next they came to some fine meadows. "Whose are these beautiful green meadows?" said she. "They belong to King Grisly-beard, hadst thou taken him, they had all been thine." "Ah! unlucky wretch that I am!" said she; "would that I had married King Grisly-beard!"

The king was very angry with his daughter and vowed to punish her rude behaviour to her suitors, especially Grisly-beard

Then they came to a great city. "Whose is this noble city?" said she. "It belongs to King Grisly-beard; hadst thou taken him, it had all been thine." "Ah! wretch that I am!" sighed she; "why did I not marry King Grisly-beard?" "That is no business of mine," said the fiddler: "why should you wish for another husband? Am not I good enough for you?"

The king was very angry with his daughter and vowed to punish her rude behaviour to her suitors, especially Grisly-beard

At last they came to a small cottage. "What a paltry place!" said she; "to whom does that little dirty hole belong?" Then the fiddler said, "That is your and my house, where we are to live." "Where are your servants?" cried she. "What do we want with servants?" said he; "you must do for yourself whatever is to be done. Now make the fire, and put on water and cook my supper, for I am very tired." But the princess knew nothing of making fires and cooking, and the fiddler was forced to help her. When they had eaten a very scanty meal they went to bed; but the fiddler called her up very early in the morning to clean the house. Thus they lived for two days: and when they had eaten up all there was in the cottage, the man said, "Wife, we can't go on thus, spending money and earning nothing. You must learn to weave baskets." Then he went out and cut willows, and brought them home, and she began to weave; but it made her fingers very sore. "I see this work won't do," said he: "try and spin; perhaps you will do that better." So she sat down and tried to spin; but the threads cut her tender fingers till the blood ran. "See now," said the fiddler, "you are good for nothing; you can do no work: what a bargain I have got! However, I'll try and set up a trade in pots and pans, and you shall stand in the market and sell them." "Alas!" sighed she, "if any of my father's court should pass by and see me standing in the market, how they will laugh at me!"

But her husband did not care for that, and said she must work, if she did not wish to die of hunger. At first the

The princess was forced to marry the fiddler

trade went well; for many people, seeing such a beautiful woman, went to buy her wares, and paid their money without thinking of taking away the goods. They lived on this as long as it lasted; and then her husband bought a fresh lot of ware, and she sat herself down with it in the corner of the market; but a drunken soldier soon came by, and rode his horse against her stall, and broke all her goods into a thousand pieces. Then she began to cry, and knew not what to do. "Ah! what will become of me?" said she; "what will my husband say?" So she ran home and told him all. "Who would have thought you would have been so silly," said he, "as to put an earthenware stall in the corner of the market, where everybody passes? But let us have no more crying; I see you are not fit for this sort of work, so I have been to the king's palace, and asked if they did not want a kitchen-maid; and they say they will take you, and there you will have plenty to eat."

Thus the princess became a kitchen-maid, and helped the cook to do all the dirtiest work; but she was allowed to carry home some of the meat that was left, and on this they lived.

She had not been there long before she heard that the king's eldest son was passing by, going to be married; and she went to one of the windows and looked out. Everything was ready, and all the pomp and brightness of the court was there. Then she bitterly grieved for the pride and folly which had brought her so low. And the servants gave her some of the rich meats, which she put into her basket to take home.

All on a sudden, as she was going out, in came the king's son in golden clothes; and when he saw a beautiful woman at the door, he took her by the hand, and said she should be his partner in the dance; but she trembled for fear, for she saw that it was King Grisly-beard, who was making sport of her. However, he kept fast hold, and led her in; and the cover of the basket came off, so that the meats in it fell about. Then everybody laughed and jeered at her; and she

The princess became a kitchen maid in the palace where she had to do all the hardest, dirtiest work

was so abashed, that she wished herself a thousand feet deep in the earth. She sprang to the door to run away; but on the steps King Grisly-beard overtook her, and brought her back and said, "Fear me not! I am the fiddler who has lived with you in the hut. I brought you there because I really loved you. I am also the soldier that overset your stall. I have done all this only to cure you of your silly pride, and to show you the folly of your ill-treatment of me. Now all is over: you have learnt wisdom, and it is time to hold our marriage feast."

Then the chamberlains came and brought her the most beautiful robes; and her father and his whole court were there already, and welcomed her home on her marriage. Joy was in every face and every heart. The feast was grand; they danced and sang; all were merry; and I only wish that you and I had been of the party.

514

The Golden Treasure

Hans Christian Andersen (1805–1875) wrote this tale about a child born with extraordinary qualities: Peter has a great ability for music, especially for playing the drum. When he grows older he plays the drum as the army matches to war, and his music is with him in his heart when he falls in love – and when he later achieves fame and wealth.

The drummer's wife went into the church. She saw the new altar with the painted pictures and the carved angels. Those upon the canvas and in the glory over the altar were just as beautiful as the carved ones; and they were painted and gilt into the bargain. Their hair gleamed golden in the sunshine, lovely to behold; but the real sunshine was more beautiful still. It shone redder, clearer through the dark trees, when the sun went down. It was lovely thus to look at the sunshine of heaven. And she looked at the red sun, and she thought about it so deeply, and thought of the little one whom the stork was to bring, and the wife of the drummer was very cheerful, and looked and looked, and wished that the child might have a gleam of sunshine given to it, so that it might at least become like one of the shining angels over the altar.

And when she really had the little child in her arms, and held it up to its father, then it was like one of the angels in the church to behold, with hair like gold – the gleam of the setting sun was upon it.

"My golden treasure, my riches, my sunshine!" said the mother; and she kissed the shining locks, and it sounded like music and song in the room of the drummer; and there was joy, and life, and movement. The drummer beat a roll – a roll of joy. And the Drum said, the Fire-drum, that was beaten when there was a fire in the town:

"Red hair! the little fellow has red hair! Believe the drum, and not what your mother says! Rub-a dub, rub-a dub!"

And the town repeated what the Fire-drum had said.

The boy was taken to church, the boy was christened. There was nothing much to be said about his name; he was called Peter. The whole town, and the Drum too, called him Peter the drummer's boy with the red hair; but his mother kissed his red hair, and called him her golden treasure.

In the hollow way in the clayey bank, many had scratched their names as a remembrance.

"Celebrity is always something!" said the drummer; and so he scratched his own name there, and his little son's name likewise.

Peter, the drummer's son, could sing like a bird

And the swallows came. They had, on their long journey, seen more durable characters engraven on rocks, and on the walls of the temples in Hindostan, mighty deeds of great kings, immortal names, so old that no one now could read or speak them. Remarkable celebrity!

In the clayey bank the martens built their nest. They bored holes in the deep declivity, and the splashing rain and the thin mist came and crumbled and washed the names away, and the drummer's name also, and that of his little son.

"Peter's name will last a full year and a half longer!" said the father.

"Fool!" thought the Fire-drum; but it only said, "Dub, dub, dub, rub-a-dub!"

He was a boy full of life and gladness, this drummer's son with the red hair. He had a lovely voice. He could sing, and he sang like a bird in the woodland. There was melody, and yet no melody.

"He must become a chorister boy," said his mother. "He

515

shall sing in the church, and stand among the beautiful gilded angels who are like him!"

"Fiery cat!" said some of the witty ones of the town.

The Drum heard that from the neighbours' wives.

"Don't go home, Peter," cried the street boys. "If you sleep in the garret, there'll be a fire in the house, and the fire-drum will have to be beaten."

"Look out for the drumsticks," replied Peter; and, small as he was, he ran up boldly, and gave the foremost such a punch in the body with his fist, that the fellow lost his legs and tumbled over, and the others took their legs off with themselves very rapidly.

The town musician was very genteel and fine. He was the son of the royal plate-washer. He was very fond of Peter, and would sometimes take him to his home; and he gave him a violin, and taught him to play it. It seemed as if the whole art lay in the boy's fingers; and he wanted to be more than a drummer – he wanted to become musician to the town.

"I'll be a soldier," said Peter; for he was still quite a little lad, and it seemed to him the finest thing in the world to carry a gun, and to be able to march one, two- one, two, and to wear a uniform and a sword.

"Ah, you learn to long for the drum-skin, drum, dum, dum!" said the Drum.

"Yes, if he could only march his way up to be a general!" observed his father; "but before he can do that, there must be war."

"Heaven forbid!" said his mother.

"We have nothing to lose," remarked the father.

"Yes, we have my boy," she retorted.

"But suppose he came back a general!" said the father.

"Without arms and legs!" cried the mother. "No, I would rather keep my golden treasure with me."

"Drum, dum, dum!" The Fire-drum and all the other drums were beating, for war had come. The soldiers all set out, and the son of the drummer followed them. "Red-head. Golden treasure!"

The mother wept; the father in fancy saw him "famous;" the town musician was of opinion that he ought not to go to war, but should stay at home and learn music.

"Red-head," said the soldiers, and little Peter laughed; but when one of them sometimes said to another, "Foxey," he would bite his teeth together and look another way-into the wide world. He did not care for the nickname.

The boy was active, pleasant of speech, and good-humored; that is the best canteen, said his old comrades.

And many a night he had to sleep under the open sky, wet through with the driving rain or the falling mist; but his good humor never forsook him. The drum-sticks sounded, "Rub-a-dub, all up, all up!" Yes, he was certainly born to be a drummer.

The drummer's son went into battle, as bullets and shells flew overhead

The day of battle dawned. The sun had not yet risen, but the morning was come. The air was cold, the battle was hot; there was mist in the air, but still more gunpowder-smoke. The bullets and shells flew over the soldiers' heads, and into their heads- into their bodies and limbs; but still they pressed forward. Here or there one or other of them would sink on his knees, with bleeding temples and a face as white as chalk. The little drummer still kept his healthy color; he had suffered no damage; he looked cheerfully at the dog of the regiment, which was jumping along as merrily as if the whole thing had been got up for his amusement, and as if the bullets were only flying about that he might have a game of play with them.

"March! Forward! March!" This, was the word of command for the drum. The word had not yet been given to fall back, though they might have done so, and perhaps there would have been much sense in it; and now at last the word "Retire" was given; but our little drummer beat "Forward! march!" for he had understood the command thus, and the soldiers obeyed the sound of the drum. That was a good roll, and proved the summons to victory for the men, who had already begun to give way.

Life and limb were lost in the battle. Bombshells tore away the flesh in red strips; bombshells lit up into a terrible glow the strawheaps to which the wounded had dragged themselves, to lie untended for many hours, perhaps for all the hours they had to live.

It's no use thinking of it; and yet one cannot help thinking of it, even far away in the peaceful town. The drummer and his wife also thought of it, for Peter was at the war.

"Now, I'm tired of these complaints," said the Fire-drum.

Again the day of battle dawned; the sun had not yet risen, but it was morning. The drummer and his wife were asleep. They had been talking about their son, as, indeed, they did almost every night, for he was out yonder in God's hand. And the father dreamt that the war was over, that the soldiers had returned home, and that Peter wore a silver cross on his breast. But the mother dreamt that she had gone into the church, and had seen the painted pictures and the carved angels with the gilded hair, and her own dear boy, the golden treasure of her heart, who was standing among the angels in white robes, singing so sweetly, as surely only the angels can sing; and that he had soared up with them into the sunshine, and nodded so kindly at his mother.

"My golden treasure!" she cried out; and she awoke. "Now the good God has taken him to Himself!" She folded her hands, and hid her face in the cotton curtains of the bed, and wept. "Where does he rest now? among the many in the big grave that they have dug for the dead? Perhaps he's in the water in the marsh! Nobody knows his grave; no holy words have been read over it!" And the Lord's Prayer went inaudibly over her lips; she bowed her head, and was so weary that she went to sleep.

And the days went by, in life as in dreams!

It was evening. Over the battle-field a rainbow spread, which touched the forest and the deep marsh.

It has been said, and is preserved in popular belief, that where the rainbow touches the earth a treasure lies buried, a golden treasure; and here there was one. No one but his mother thought of the little drummer, and therefore she dreamt of him.

And the days went by, in life as in dreams!

Not a hair of his head had been hurt, not a golden hair.

"Drum-ma-rum! drum-ma-rum! there he is!" the Drum might have said, and his mother might have sung, if she had seen or dreamt it.

By the evening it was known that a great victory had been won

With hurrah and song, adorned with green wreaths of victory, they came home, as the war was at an end, and peace had been signed. The dog of the regiment sprang on in front with large bounds, and made the way three times as long for himself as it really was.

And days and weeks went by, and Peter came into his parents' room. He was as brown as a wild man, and his eyes were bright, and his face beamed like sunshine. And his mother held him in her arms; she kissed his lips, his forehead, and his red hair. She had her boy back again; he had not a silver cross on his breast, as his father had dreamt, but he had sound limbs, a thing the mother had not dreamt. And what a rejoicing was there! They laughed and they wept; and Peter embraced the old Fire-drum.

"There stands the old skeleton still!" he said.

And the father beat a roll upon it.

"One would think that a great fire had broken out here," said the Fire-drum. "Bright day! fire in the heart! golden treasure! skrat! skr-r-at! skr-r-r-at!"

And what then? What then! – Ask the town musician.

"Peter's far outgrowing the drum," he said. "Peter will be greater than I."

And yet he was the son of a royal plate-washer; but all that he had learned in half a lifetime, Peter learned in half a year.

There was something so merry about him, something so truly kind-hearted. His eyes gleamed, and his hair gleamed too- there was no denying that!

"He ought to have his hair dyed," said the neighbour's wife. "That answered capitally with the policeman's daughter, and she got a husband."

"But her hair turned as green as duckweed, and was always having to be colored up."

"She knows how to manage for herself," said the neighbours, "and so can Peter. He comes to the most genteel houses, even to the burgomaster's where he gives Miss Charlotte piano-forte lessons."

He could play! He could play, fresh out of his heart, the most charming pieces, that had never been put upon music-paper. He played in the bright nights, and in the dark nights, too. The neighbors declared it was unbearable, and the Fire-drum was of the same opinion.

He played until his thoughts soared up, and burst forth in great plans for the future:

"To be famous!"

And burgomaster's Charlotte sat at the piano. Her delicate fingers danced over the keys, and made them ring into Peter's heart. It seemed too much for him to bear; and this happened not once, but many times; and at last one day he seized the delicate fingers and the white hand, and kissed it, and looked into her great brown eyes. Heaven knows what he said; but we may be allowed to guess at it. Charlotte blushed to guess at it. She reddened from brow to neck, and answered not a single word; and then strangers came into the room, and one of them was the state councillor's son. He had a lofty white forehead, and

*When Charlotte sat at the piano
her fingers danced over the keys*

carried it so high that it seemed to go back into his neck. And Peter sat by her a long time, and she looked at him with gentle eyes.

At home that evening he spoke of travel in the wide world, and of the golden treasure that lay hidden for him in his violin.

"To be famous!"

"Tum-me-lum, tum-me-lum, tum-me-lum!" said the Fire-drum. "Peter has gone clear out of his wits. I think there must be a fire in the house."

Next day the mother went to market.

"Shall I tell you news, Peter?" she asked when she came home. "A capital piece of news. Burgomaster's Charlotte has engaged herself to the state councillor's son; the betrothal took place yesterday evening."

"No!" cried Peter, and he sprang up from his chair. But his mother persisted in saying "Yes." She had heard it from the baker's wife, whose husband had it from the burgomaster's own mouth

And Peter became as pale as death, and sat down again.

"Good Heaven! what's the matter with you?" asked his mother.

"Nothing, nothing; only leave me to myself," he answered but the tears were running down his cheeks.

"My sweet child, my golden treasure!" cried the mother, and she wept; but the Fire-drum sang, not out loud, but inwardly.

"Charlotte's gone! Charlotte's gone! and now the song is done."

But the song was not done; there were many more verses in it, long verses, the most beautiful verses, the golden treasures of a life.

Peter lost his sweetheart but won great fame and always remained secure, supported by the great love of his parents

"She behaves like a mad woman," said the neighbor's wife. "All the world is to see the letters she gets from her golden treasure, and to read the words that are written in the papers about his violin playing. And he sends her money too, and that's very useful to her since she has been a widow."

"He plays before emperors and kings," said the town musician. "I never had that fortune, but he's my pupil, and he does not forget his old master."

And his mother said,

"His father dreamt that Peter came home from the war with a silver cross. He did not gain one in the war, but it is still more difficult to gain one in this way. Now he has the cross of honor. If his father had only lived to see it!"

"He's grown famous!" said the Fire-drum, and all his native town said the same thing, for the drummer's son, Peter with the red hair – Peter whom they had known as a little boy, running about in wooden shoes, and then as a drummer, playing for the dancers – was become famous!

"He played at our house before he played in the presence of kings," said the burgomaster's wife. "At that time he was quite smitten with Charlotte. He was always of an aspiring turn. At that time he was saucy and an enthusiast. My husband laughed when he heard of the foolish affair, and now our Charlotte is a state councillor's wife."

A golden treasure had been hidden in the heart and soul of the poor child, who had beaten the roll as a drummer- a roll of victory for those who had been ready to retreat. There was a golden treasure in his bosom, the power of sound; it burst forth on his violin as if the instrument had been a complete organ, and as if all the elves of a midsummer night were dancing across the strings. In its sounds were heard the piping of the thrush and the full clear note of the human voice; therefore the sound brought rapture to every heart, and carried his name triumphant through the land. That was a great firebrand- the firebrand of inspiration.

"And then he looks so splendid!" said the young ladies and the old ladies too; and the oldest of all procured an album for famous locks of hair, wholly and solely that she might beg a lock of his rich splendid hair, that treasure, that golden treasure.

And the son came into the poor room of the drummer, elegant as a prince, happier than a king. His eyes were as clear and his face was as radiant as sunshine; and he held his mother in his arms, and she kissed his mouth, and wept as blissfully as any one can weep for joy; and he nodded at every old piece of furniture in the room, at the cupboard with the tea-cups, and at the flower-vase. He nodded at the sleeping-bench, where he had slept as a little boy; but the old Fire-drum he brought out, and dragged it into the middle of the room, and said to it and to his mother:

"My father would have beaten a famous roll this evening. Now I must do it!"

And he beat a thundering roll-call on the instrument, and the Drum felt so highly honored that the parchment burst with exultation.

"He has a splendid touch!" said the Drum. "I've a remembrance of him now that will last. I expect that the same thing will happen to his mother, from pure joy over her golden treasure."

And this is the story of the Golden Treasure.

Iron Hans

The Brothers Grimm (Jacob 1785–1863 and Wilhelm 1786–1859) first incorporated this story into their *Children's and Household Tales* in 1850. It is also known as *The Wild Man*, *Goldener*, or *The Golden Boy* and versions can be found in many European countries. It tells how a king's forest is inhabited by a mysterious creature that kills all who enter.

hawk flying over it. This lasted for many years, when an unknown huntsman announced himself to the king as seeking a situation, and offered to go into the dangerous forest. The king, however, would not give his consent, and said: "It is not safe in there; I fear it would fare with you no better than with the others, and you would never come out again." The huntsman replied: "Lord, I will venture it at my own risk, of fear I know nothing."

The huntsman therefore betook himself with his dog to

The great forest became known as a dangerous place for many people had vanished there

There was once upon a time a king who had a great forest near his palace, full of all kinds of wild animals. One day he sent out a huntsman to shoot him a roe, but he did not come back. "Perhaps some accident has befallen him," said the king, and the next day he sent out two more huntsmen who were to search for him, but they too stayed away. Then on the third day, he sent for all his huntsmen, and said: "Scour the whole forest through, and do not give up until you have found all three." But of these also, none came home again, none were seen again. From that time forth, no one would any longer venture into the forest, and it lay there in deep stillness and solitude, and nothing was seen of it, but sometimes an eagle or a

the forest. It was not long before the dog fell in with some game on the way, and wanted to pursue it; but hardly had the dog run two steps when it stood before a deep pool, could go no farther, and a naked arm stretched itself out of the water, seized it, and drew it under. When the huntsman saw that, he went back and fetched three men to come with buckets and bale out the water. When they could see to the bottom there lay a wild man whose body was brown like rusty iron, and whose hair hung over his face down to his knees. They bound him with cords, and led him away to the castle. There was great astonishment over the wild man; the king, however, had him put in an iron cage in his courtyard, and forbade the door to be opened on pain of death, and the queen herself was to take the key into her keeping. And from this time forth everyone could again go into the forest with safety.

The king had a son of eight years, who was once playing in the courtyard, and while he was playing, his golden ball fell into the cage. The boy ran thither and said: "Give me my ball out." "Not till you have opened the door for me," answered the man. "No," said the boy, "I will not do that; the king has forbidden it," and ran away. The next day he again went and asked for his ball; the wild man said: "Open my door," but the boy would not. On the third day the king had ridden out hunting, and the boy went once more and said: "I cannot open the door even if I wished, for I have not the key." Then the wild man said: "It

The wild man took the prince deep into the forest where he slept on a bed of moss

lies under your mother's pillow, you can get it there." The boy, who wanted to have his ball back, cast all thought to the winds, and brought the key. The door opened with difficulty, and the boy pinched his fingers. When it was open the wild man stepped out, gave him the golden ball, and hurried away. The boy had become afraid; he called and cried after him: "Oh, wild man, do not go away, or I shall be beaten!" The wild man turned back, took him up, set him on his shoulder, and went with hasty steps into the forest. When the king came home, he observed the empty cage, and asked the queen how that had happened. She knew nothing about it, and sought the key, but it was gone. She called the boy, but no one answered. The king sent out people to seek for him in the fields, but they did not find him. Then he could easily guess what had happened, and much grief reigned in the royal court.

When the wild man had once more reached the dark forest, he took the boy down from his shoulder, and said to him: "You will never see your father and mother again, but I will keep you with me, for you have set me free, and I have compassion on you. If you do all I bid you, you shall fare well. Of treasure and gold have I enough, and more than anyone in the world." He made a bed of moss for the

boy on which he slept, and the next morning the man took him to a well, and said: "Behold, the gold well is as bright and clear as crystal, you shall sit beside it, and take care that nothing falls into it, or it will be polluted. I will come every evening to see if you have obeyed my order." The boy placed himself by the brink of the well, and often saw a golden fish or a golden snake show itself therein, and took care that nothing fell in. As he was thus sitting, his finger hurt him so violently that he involuntarily put it in the water. He drew it quickly out again, but saw that it was quite gilded, and whatsoever pains he took to wash the gold off again, all was to no purpose. In the evening Iron Hans came back, looked at the boy, and said: "What has happened to the well?" "Nothing nothing," he answered, and held his finger behind his back, that the man might not see it. But he said: "You have dipped your finger into the water, this time it may pass, but take care you do not again let anything go in." By daybreak the boy was already sitting by the well and watching it. His finger hurt him again and he passed it over his head, and then unhappily a hair fell down into the well. He took it quickly out, but it was already quite gilded. Iron Hans came, and already knew what had happened. "You have let a hair fall into the well," said he. "I will allow you to watch by it once more, but if this happens for the third time then the well is polluted and you can no longer remain with me."

On the third day, the boy sat by the well, and did not stir his finger, however much it hurt him. But the time was long to him, and he looked at the reflection of his face on the surface of the water. And as he still bent down more and more while he was doing so, and trying to look straight into the eyes, his long hair fell down from his shoulders into the water. He raised himself up quickly, but the whole of the hair of his head was already golden and shone like the sun. You can imagine how terrified the poor boy was! He took his pocket-handkerchief and tied it round his head, in order that the man might not see it. When he came he already knew everything, and said: "Take the handkerchief off." Then the golden hair streamed forth, and let the boy excuse himself as he might, it was of no use. "You have not stood the trial and can stay here no longer. Go forth into the world, there you will learn what poverty is. But as you have not a bad heart, and as I mean well by you, there is one thing I will grant you; if you fall into any difficulty, come to the forest and cry: "Iron Hans," and then I will come and help you. My power is great, greater than you think, and I have gold and silver in abundance."

Then the king's son left the forest, and walked by beaten and unbeaten paths ever onwards until at length he reached a great city. There he looked for work, but could find none, and he learnt nothing by which he could help himself. At length he went to the palace, and asked if they would take him in. The people about court did not at all know what use they could make of him, but they liked him, and told him to stay. At length the cook took him into his service, and said he might carry wood and water, and rake the cinders together. Once when it so happened that no one else was at hand, the cook ordered him to carry the food to the royal table, but as he did not like to let his golden hair be seen, he kept his little cap on. Such a thing as that had never yet come under the king's notice, and he said: "When you come to the royal table you must take your hat off." He answered: "Ah, Lord, I cannot; I have a bad sore place on my head." Then the king had the cook called before him and scolded him, and asked how he could take such a boy as that into his service; and that he was to send him away at once. The cook, however, had pity on him, and exchanged him for the gardener"s boy.

And now the boy had to plant and water the garden,

The boy had to work in the palace gardens –
digging and hoeing in all weathers

hoe and dig, and bear the wind and bad weather. Once in summer when he was working alone in the garden, the day was so warm he took his little cap off that the air might cool him. As the sun shone on his hair it glittered and flashed so that the rays fell into the bedroom of the king's daughter, and up she sprang to see what that could be. Then she saw the boy, and cried to him: "Boy, bring me a wreath of flowers." He put his cap on with all haste, and gathered wild field-flowers and bound them together.

When he was ascending the stairs with them, the gardener met him, and said: "How can you take the king's daughter a garland of such common flowers? Go quickly, and get another, and seek out the prettiest and rarest." "Oh, no," replied the boy, "the wild ones have more scent, and will please her better." When he got into the room, the king's daughter said: "Take your cap off, it is not seemly to keep it on in my presence." He again said: "I may not, I have a sore head." She, however, caught at his cap and pulled it off, and then his golden hair rolled down on his shoulders, and it was splendid to behold. He wanted to run out, but she held him by the arm, and gave him a handful of ducats. With these he departed, but he cared nothing for the gold pieces. He took them to the gardener, and said: "I present them to your children, they can play with them." The following day the king's daughter again called to him that he was to bring her a wreath of field-flowers, and then he went in with it, she instantly snatched at his cap, and wanted to take it away from him, but he held it fast with both hands. She again gave him a handful of ducats, but he would not keep them, and gave them to the gardener for playthings for his children. On the third day things went just the same; she could not get his cap away from him, and he would not have her money.

Not long afterwards, the country was overrun by war. The king gathered together his people, and did not know whether or not he could offer any opposition to the enemy, who was superior in strength and had a mighty army. Then said the gardener's boy: "I am grown up, and will go to the wars also, only give me a horse." The others laughed, and said: "Seek one for yourself when we are gone, we will leave one behind us in the stable for you." When they had gone forth, he went into the stable, and led the horse out; it was lame of one foot, and limped hobblety jib, hobblety jib; nevertheless he mounted it, and rode away to the dark forest. When he came to the outskirts, he called "Iron Hans" three times so loudly that it echoed through the trees. Thereupon the wild man appeared immediately, and said: "What do you desire?" "I want a strong steed, for I am going to the wars." "That you shall have, and still more than you ask for." Then the wild man went back into the forest, and it was not long before a stable-boy came out of it, who led a horse that snorted with its nostrils, and could hardly be restrained, and behind them followed a great troop of warriors entirely equipped in iron, and their swords flashed in the sun. The youth made over his three-legged horse to the stable-boy, mounted the other, and rode at the head of the soldiers. When he got near the battlefield a great part of the king's men had already fallen, and little was wanting to make the rest give way. Then the youth galloped thither with his iron soldiers, broke like a hurricane over the enemy, and beat down all who opposed him. They began to flee, but the youth pursued, and never stopped, until there was not a single man left. Instead of returning to the king, however, he conducted his troop by byways back to the forest, and called forth Iron Hans.

"What do you desire?" asked the wild man. "Take back your horse and your troops, and give me my three-legged horse again." All that he asked was done, and soon he was riding on his three-legged horse. When the king returned to his palace, his daughter went to meet him, and wished him joy of his victory. "I am not the one who carried away the victory," said he, "but a strange knight who came to my assistance with his soldiers." The daughter wanted to hear who the strange knight was, but the king did not know, and said: "He followed the enemy, and I did not see him again." She inquired of the gardener where his boy was, but he smiled, and said: "He has just come home on his three-legged horse, and the others have been mocking him, and crying: "Here comes our hobblety jib back again!" They asked, too: "Under what hedge have you been lying sleeping all the time?" So he said: "I did the best of all, and it would have gone badly without me." And then he was still more ridiculed."

The king said to his daughter: "I will proclaim a great feast that shall last for three days, and you shall throw a golden apple. Perhaps the unknown man will show himself." When the feast was announced, the youth went out to the forest, and called Iron Hans. "What do you desire?" asked he. "That I may catch the king's daughter's golden apple." "It is as safe as if you had it already," said Iron Hans. "You shall likewise have a suit of red armour for the occasion, and ride on a spirited chestnut-horse." When the day came, the youth galloped to the spot, took his place amongst the knights, and was recognized by no one. The king's daughter came forward, and threw a golden apple to the knights, but none of them caught it but he, only as soon as he had it he galloped away.

On the second day Iron Hans equipped him as a white knight, and gave him a white horse. Again he was the only one who caught the apple, and he did not linger an instant, but galloped off with it. The king grew angry, and said: "That is not allowed; he must appear before me and tell his name." He gave the order that if the knight who caught the apple, should go away again they should pursue him, and if he would not come back willingly, they were to cut him down and stab him.

On the third day, he received from Iron Hans a suit of black armour and a black horse, and again he caught the apple. But when he was riding off with it, the king's attendants pursued him, and one of them got so near him that he wounded the youth's leg with the point of his sword. The youth nevertheless escaped from them, but his horse leapt so violently that the helmet fell from the youth's head, and they could see that he had golden hair. They rode back and announced this to the king.

The following day the king's daughter asked the gardener about his boy. "He is at work in the garden; the queer creature has been at the festival too, and only came home yesterday evening; he has likewise shown my children three golden apples which he has won."

The king had him summoned into his presence, and he came and again had his little cap on his head. But the king's daughter went up to him and took it off, and then his golden hair fell down over his shoulders, and he was so handsome that all were amazed. "Are you the knight who came every day to the festival, always in different colours, and who caught the three golden apples?" asked the king. "Yes," answered he, "and here the apples are," and he took them out of his pocket, and returned them to the king. "If you desire further proof, you may see the wound which your people gave me when they followed me. But I am likewise the knight who helped you to your victory over

Iron Hans gave him a suit of black armour and a fine black horse

your enemies." "If you can perform such deeds as that, you are no gardener's boy; tell me, who is your father?" "My father is a mighty king, and gold have I in plenty as great as I require." "I well see," said the king, "that I owe my thanks to you; can I do anything to please you?" "Yes," answered he, "that indeed you can. Give me your daughter to wife." The maiden laughed, and said: "He does not stand much on ceremony, but I have already seen by his golden hair that he was no gardener's boy," and then she went and kissed him. His father and mother came to the wedding, and were in great delight, for they had given up all hope of ever seeing their dear son again. And as they were sitting at the marriage-feast, the music suddenly stopped, the doors opened, and a stately king came in with a great retinue. He went up to the youth, embraced him and said: "I am Iron Hans, and was by enchantment a wild man, but you have set me free; all the treasures which I possess, shall be your property."

Changelings

There are many folk stories and legends about changelings – fairy children that are left in the place of stolen human babies. The changeling theme is common among medieval literature – perhaps because in those days small children were so vulnerable to illness and affliction.

Sometimes older people might also be abducted by the little people, especially if they had succumbed to the temptation to eat fairy food which made them captive forever: some went on to live a merry life among the fairy folk while others pined for their lost families and human friends. Occasionally, very elderly fairy folk people would be exchanged for human babies so that the old fairy could live in comfort, made much of by its adopted human parents.

Sometimes the name refers to a human child who has been snatched away but generally a changeling is the offspring of a fairy, troll, elf or other such magical creature that has been secretly left in the place of a human child. Changelings might also describe an enchanted piece of wood that would soon appear to grow sick and die.

The motive for taking a human child might be to use the infant as a servant, or because the child was beautiful and beloved, or it might be merely mischief or an act of malice.

Some Norwegian tales suggest that the change was made to prevent inbreeding: both trolls and the human communities were strengthened by an injection of new blood and humans might be given children with enormous strength as a reward. There were ways to ward off the risk of such an exchange: an inverted coat or open iron scissors left where the child slept were thought to act as safety charms but a constant watch over the child was considered the wisest precaution.

Changelings were not always fit and healthy despite their voracious appetites; often they were ill-tempered, awkward, cried piteously and were slightly green or very pale . Their vast vocabularies betrayed a superhuman intelligence and in Scotland they were said to love playing the pipes and to be very musical.

Aesop's fables

A Town Mouse and a Country mouse

A Town Mouse and a Country Mouse were acquaintances, and the Country Mouse one day invited his friend to come and see him at his home in the fields. The Town Mouse came, and they sat down to a dinner of barleycorns and roots, the latter of which had a distinctly earthy flavour. The fare was not much to the taste of the guest, and presently he broke out with "My poor dear friend, you live here no better than the ants. Now, you should just see how I fare! My larder is a regular horn of plenty. You must come and stay with me, and I promise you you shall live on the fat of the land." So when he returned to town he took the Country Mouse with him, and showed him into a larder containing flour and oatmeal and figs and honey and dates. The Country Mouse had never seen anything like it, and sat down to enjoy the luxuries his friend provided: but before they had well begun, the door of the larder opened and some one came in. The two Mice scampered off and hid themselves in a narrow and exceedingly uncomfortable hole. Presently, when all was quiet, they ventured out again; but some one else came in, and off they scuttled again. This was too much for the visitor. "Good-bye," said he, "I'm off. You live in the lap of luxury, I can see, but you are surrounded by dangers; whereas at home I can enjoy my simple dinner of roots and corn in peace."

Clearly these are not fairy tales but have been included because they were the earliest of writings for children and marked the launch of the moral themes which have inspired many a fairy tale since. Aesop may not have written the fables for which he is so famous. This tongue-tied slave from Ancient Greece is traditionally given the credit as their author but no actual works by him survive. Numerous stories under his name were gathered across the centuries and translated into many languages in true storytelling tradition. Many of his animal characters speak and have human traits and failings. They were published in English by Caxton in 1484 and have become one of the most enduring elements of European culture.

The Hare and the Tortoise

A Hare was one day making fun of a Tortoise for being so slow upon his feet. "Wait a bit," said the Tortoise; "I'll run a race with you, and I'll wager that I win." "Oh, well," replied the Hare, who was much amused at the idea, "let's try and see"; and it was soon agreed that the Fox should set a course for them, and be the judge. When the time came both started off together, but the Hare was soon so far ahead that he thought he might as well have a rest: so down he lay and fell fast asleep. Meanwhile the Tortoise kept plodding on, and in time reached the goal. At last the Hare woke up with a start, and dashed on at his fastest, but only to find that the Tortoise had already won the race.

Slow and steady wins.

The Fox and the Crow

A Crow was sitting on a branch of a tree with a piece of cheese in her beak when a Fox observed her and set his wits to work to discover some way of getting the cheese. Coming and standing under the tree he looked up and said, "What a noble bird I see above me! Her beauty is without equal, the hue of her plumage exquisite. If only her voice is as sweet as her looks are fair, she ought without doubt to be Queen of the Birds." The Crow was hugely flattered by this, and just to show the Fox that she could sing she gave a loud caw. Down came the cheese, of course, and the Fox, snatching it up, said, "You have a voice, madam, I see: what you want is wits."

The Lion and the Mouse

A Lion asleep in his lair was waked up by a Mouse running over his face. Losing his temper he seized it with his paw and was about to kill it. The Mouse, terrified, piteously entreated him to spare its life. "Please let me go," it cried, "and one day I will repay you for your kindness." The idea of so insignificant a creature ever being able to do anything for him amused the Lion so much that he laughed aloud, and good-humouredly let it go. But the Mouse's chance came, after all. One day the Lion got entangled in a net which had been spread for game by some hunters, and the Mouse heard and recognised his roars of anger and ran to the spot. Without more ado it set to work to gnaw the ropes with its teeth, and succeeded before long in setting the Lion free. "There!" said the Mouse, "you laughed at me when I promised I would repay you: but now you see, even a Mouse can help a Lion."

The Goose that laid the Golden Eggs

A Man and his Wife had the good fortune to possess a Goose which laid a Golden Egg every day. Lucky though they were, they soon began to think they were not getting rich fast enough, and, imagining the bird must be made of gold inside, they decided to kill it in order to secure the whole store of precious metal at once. But when they cut it open they found it was just like any other goose. Thus, they neither got rich all at once, as they had hoped, nor enjoyed any longer the daily addition to their wealth. Much wants more and loses all.

Cinderella or The Little Glass Slipper

One of the oldest versions of the Cinderella story was actually ninth-century Chinese and then the slipper was gold! Some historians believe that Cinderella's glass slipper was originally fur (*vair*) in France and mistranslated as glass (*verre*).

Once there was a gentleman who married, for his second wife, the proudest and most haughty woman that was ever seen. She had, by a former husband, two daughters of her own, who were, indeed, exactly like her in all things. He had likewise, by another wife, a young daughter, but of unparalleled goodness and sweetness of temper, which she took from her mother, who was the best creature in the world.

No sooner were the ceremonies of the wedding over but the stepmother began to show herself in her true colors. She could not bear the good qualities of this pretty girl, and the less because they made her own daughters appear the more odious. She employed her in the meanest work of the house. She scoured the dishes, scrubbed tables and cleaned madam's chamber, and those of misses, her daughters. She slept in a sorry garret, on a wretched straw bed, while her sisters slept in fine rooms, with floors all inlaid, on beds of the very newest fashion, and where they had looking glasses so large that they could see themselves at their full length from head to foot.

The poor girl bore it all patiently, and dared not tell her father, who would have scolded her; for his wife governed him entirely. When she had done her work, she used to go to the chimney corner, and sit down there in the cinders and ashes, which caused her to be called Cinderwench. Only the younger sister, who was not so rude and uncivil as the older one, called her Cinderella. However, Cinderella, notwithstanding her coarse apparel, was a hundred times more beautiful than her sisters, although they were always dressed very richly.

It happened that the king's son gave a ball, and invited all persons of fashion to it. Our young misses were also invited, for they cut a very grand figure among those of quality. They were mightily delighted at this invitation, and wonderfully busy in selecting the gowns, petticoats, and hair dressing that would best become them. This was a new difficulty for Cinderella; for it was she who ironed her sister's linen and pleated their ruffles. They talked all day long of nothing but how they should be dressed.

"For my part," said the eldest, "I will wear my red velvet suit with French trimming."

"And I," said the youngest, "shall have my usual petticoat; but then, to make amends for that, I will put on my gold-flowered cloak, and my diamond stomacher, which is far from being the most ordinary one in the world."

They sent for the best hairdresser they could get to make up their headpieces and adjust their hairdos, and they had their red brushes and patches from Mademoiselle de la Poche.

They also consulted Cinderella in all these matters, for she had excellent ideas, and her advice was always good.

As Cinderella sobs, her fairy godmother appears

Indeed, she even offered her services to fix their hair, which they very willingly accepted. As she was doing this, they said to her, "Cinderella, would you not like to go to the ball?"

"Alas!" said she, "you only jeer me; it is not for such as I am to go to such a place."

"You are quite right," they replied. "It would make the people laugh to see a Cinderwench at a ball."

Anyone but Cinderella would have fixed their hair awry, but she was very good, and dressed them perfectly well. They were so excited that they hadn't eaten a thing for almost two days. Then they broke more than a dozen laces trying to have themselves laced up tightly enough to give them a fine slender shape. They were continually in front of their looking glass. At last the happy day came. They went to court, and Cinderella followed them with her eyes as long as she could. When she lost sight of them, she started to cry.

Her godmother, who saw her all in tears, asked her what was the matter.

"I wish I could. I wish I could." She was not able to speak the rest, being interrupted by her tears and sobbing.

This godmother of hers, who was a fairy, said to her, "You wish that you could go to the ball; is it not so?"

"Yes," cried Cinderella, with a great sigh.

"Well," said her godmother, "be but a good girl, and I will contrive that you shall go." Then she took her into her chamber, and said to her, "Run into the garden, and bring me a pumpkin."

Cinderella went immediately to gather the finest she could get, and brought it to her godmother, not being able to imagine how this pumpkin could help her go to the ball. Her godmother scooped out all the inside of it, leaving nothing but the rind. Having done this, she struck the pumpkin with her wand, and it was instantly turned into a fine coach, gilded all over with gold.

She then went to look into her mousetrap, where she found six mice, all alive, and ordered Cinderella to lift up a little the trapdoor. She gave each mouse, as it went out, a little tap with her wand, and the mouse was that moment turned into a fine horse, which altogether made a very fine set of six horses of a beautiful mouse colored dapple gray.

Being at a loss for a coachman, Cinderella said, "I will go and see if there is not a rat in the rat trap that we can turn into a coachman."

"You are right," replied her godmother, "Go and look."

Cinderella brought the trap to her, and in it there were three huge rats. The fairy chose the one which had the largest beard, touched him with her wand, and turned him into a fat, jolly coachman, who had the smartest whiskers that eyes ever beheld.

After that, she said to her, "Go again into the garden, and you will find six lizards behind the watering pot. Bring them to me."

She had no sooner done so but her godmother turned them into six footmen, who skipped up immediately behind

the coach, with their liveries all bedaubed with gold and silver, and clung as close behind each other as if they had done nothing else their whole lives. The fairy then said to Cinderella, "Well, you see here an equipage fit to go to the ball with; are you not pleased with it?"

"Oh, yes," she cried; "But must I go in these nasty rags?"

Her godmother then touched her with her wand, and, at the same instant, her clothes turned into cloth of gold and silver, all beset with jewels. This done, she gave her a pair of glass slippers, the prettiest in the whole world. Being thus decked out, she got up into her coach; but her godmother, above all things, commanded her not to stay past midnight, telling her, at the same time, that if she stayed one moment longer, the coach would be a pumpkin again, her horses mice, her coachman a rat, her footmen lizards, and that her clothes would become just as they were before.

She promised her godmother to leave the ball before midnight; and then drove away, scarcely able to contain herself for joy. The king's son, who was told that a great princess, whom nobody knew, had arrived, ran out to receive her. He gave her his hand as she alighted from the coach, and led her into the hall, among all the company. There was immediately a profound silence. Everyone stopped dancing, and the violins ceased to play, so entranced was everyone with the singular beauties of the unknown newcomer.

Nothing was then heard but a confused noise of, "How beautiful she is! How beautiful she is!"

The king himself, old as he was, could not help watching her, and telling the queen softly that it was a long time since he had seen so beautiful and lovely a creature.

All the ladies were busied in considering her clothes and headdress, hoping to have some made the next day after the same pattern, provided they could find such fine materials and as able hands to make them.

The king's son led her to the most honorable seat, and afterwards took her out to dance with him. She danced so very gracefully that they all more and more admired her. A fine meal was served up, but the young prince ate not a morsel, so intently was he busied in gazing on her.

She went and sat down by her sisters, showing them a thousand civilities, giving them part of the oranges and citrons which the prince had presented her with, which very much surprised them, for they did not know her. While Cinderella was thus amusing her sisters, she heard the clock strike eleven and three-quarters, whereupon she immediately made a courtesy to the company and hurried away as fast as she could.

Arriving home, she ran to seek out her godmother, and, after having thanked her, she said she could not but heartily wish she might go to the ball the next day as well, because the king's son had invited her.

As she was eagerly telling her godmother everything that had happened at the ball, her two sisters knocked at the door, which Cinderella ran and opened.

"You stayed such a long time!" she cried, gaping, rubbing her eyes and stretching herself as if she had been sleeping; she had not, however, had any manner of inclination to sleep while they were away from home.

"If you had been at the ball," said one of her sisters, "you would not have been tired with it. The finest princess was there, the most beautiful that mortal eyes have ever seen. She showed us a thousand civilities, and gave us oranges and citrons."

Cinderella seemed very indifferent in the matter. Indeed, she asked them the name of that princess; but they told

As the clock strikes midnight Cinderella flees

her they did not know it, and that the king's son was very uneasy on her account and would give all the world to know who she was. At this Cinderella, smiling, replied, "She must, then, be very beautiful indeed; how happy you have been! Could not I see her? Ah, dear Charlotte, do lend me your yellow dress which you wear every day."

"Yes, to be sure!" cried Charlotte; "lend my clothes to such a dirty Cinderwench as you are! I should be such a fool."

Cinderella, indeed, well expected such an answer, and was very glad of the refusal; for she would have been sadly put to it, if her sister had lent her what she asked for jestingly.

The next day the two sisters were at the ball, and so was Cinderella, but dressed even more magnificently than before. The king's son was always by her, and never ceased

his compliments and kind speeches to her. All this was so far from being tiresome to her, and, indeed, she quite forgot what her godmother had told her. She thought that it was no later than eleven when she counted the clock striking twelve. She jumped up and fled, as nimble as a deer. The prince followed, but could not overtake her. She left behind one of her glass slippers, which the prince picked up most carefully. She reached home, but quite out of breath, and in her nasty old clothes, having nothing left of all her finery but one of the little slippers, the mate to the one that she had dropped.

The guards at the palace gate were asked if they had not seen a princess go out. They replied that they had seen nobody leave but a young girl, very shabbily dressed, and who had more the air of a poor country wench than a gentlewoman.

When the two sisters returned from the ball Cinderella asked them if they had been well entertained, and if the fine lady had been there.

They told her, yes, but that she hurried away immediately when it struck twelve, and with so much haste that she dropped one of her little glass slippers, the prettiest in the world, which the king's son had picked up; that he had done nothing but look at her all the time at the ball, and that most certainly he was very much in love with the beautiful person who owned the glass slipper.

What they said was very true; for a few days later, the king's son had it proclaimed, by sound of trumpet, that he would marry her whose foot this slipper would just fit. They began to try it on the princesses, then the duchesses and all the court, but in vain; it was brought to the two sisters, who did all they possibly could to force their foot into the slipper, but they did not succeed.

Cinderella, who saw all this, and knew that it was her slipper, said to them, laughing, "Let me see if it will not fit me."

Her sisters burst out laughing, and began to banter with her. The gentleman who was sent to try the slipper looked earnestly at Cinderella, and, finding her very handsome, said that it was only just that she should try as well, and that he had orders to let everyone try.

He had Cinderella sit down, and, putting the slipper to her foot, he found that it went on very easily, fitting her as if it had been made of wax. Her two sisters were greatly astonished, but then even more so, when Cinderella pulled out of her pocket the other slipper, and put it on her other foot. Then in came her godmother and touched her wand to Cinderella's clothes, making them richer and more magnificent than any of those she had worn before.

And now her two sisters found her to be that fine, beautiful lady whom they had seen at the ball. They threw themselves at her feet to beg pardon for all the ill treatment they had made her undergo. Cinderella took them up, and, as she embraced them, said that she forgave them with all her heart, and wanted them always to love her.

She was taken to the young prince, dressed as she was.

The slipper fits!

He thought she was more charming than before, and, a few days after, married her. Cinderella, who was no less good than beautiful, gave her two sisters lodgings in the palace, and that very same day matched them with two great lords of the court.

Moral: Beauty in a woman is a rare treasure that will always be admired. Graciousness, however, is priceless and of even greater value. This is what Cinderella's godmother gave to her when she taught her to behave like a queen. Young women, in the winning of a heart, graciousness is more important than a beautiful hairdo. It is a true gift of the fairies. Without it nothing is possible; with it, one can do anything.

Another moral: Without doubt it is a great advantage to have intelligence, courage, good breeding, and common sense. These, and similar talents come only from heaven, and it is good to have them. However, even these may fail to bring you success, without the blessing of a godfather or a godmother.

This internationally popular story translates as follows

Cinderella (United Kingdom)
Cendrillon (France)
Cenicienta (Spain and Latin America)
Cenerentola (Italy)
Cenușăreasa (Romania)
Aschenputtel (Germany)
Assepoester (Nethrlands)
Askungen (Sweden)
Askepot (Denmark)
Askepott (Norway)
Золушка Zolushka (Russia)
Пепеляшка Pepelyashka (Bulgaria)
Pepeljuga   (Serbia and Croatia)
Σταχτοπούτα (Greece and Cyprus)
Popelka (Czech Republic)
Pelenė (Lithuania)

The Emperor's New Clothes

Penned by Hans Christian Andersen in 1837, this tale exhibits children in a rather better light than the adults surrounding them – as having a straightforward honest attitude and unlike the gullible crowd who follow what the others do and say or the fawning flatterers who dupe the Emperor or the Emperor himself, puffed up by pride but then humiliated.

Many years ago there was an Emperor so exceedingly fond of new clothes that he spent all his money on being well dressed. He cared nothing about reviewing his soldiers, going to the theatre, or taking a ride in his carriage, except to show off his new clothes. He had a coat for every hour of the day, and instead of saying, as one might, about any other ruler, "The King's in council," here they always said, "The Emperor's in his dressing room."

In the great city where he lived, life was always gay. Every day many strangers came to town, and among them one day came two swindlers. They let it be known they were weavers, and they said they could weave the most magnificent fabrics imaginable. Not only were their colors and patterns uncommonly fine, but clothes made of this cloth had a wonderful way of becoming invisible to anyone who was unfit for his office, or who was unusually stupid.

"Those would be just the clothes for me," thought the Emperor. "If I wore them I would be able to discover which men in my empire are unfit for their posts. And I could tell the wise men from the fools. Yes, I certainly must get some of the stuff woven for me right away." He paid the two swindlers a large sum of money to start work at once.

They set up two looms and pretended to weave, though there was nothing on the looms. All the finest silk and the purest gold thread which they demanded went into their travelling bags, while they worked the empty looms far into the night.

"I'd like to know how those weavers are getting on with the cloth," the Emperor thought, but he felt slightly uncomfortable when he remembered that those who were unfit for their position would not be able to see the fabric. It couldn't have been that he doubted himself, yet he thought he'd rather send someone else to see how things were going. The whole town knew about the cloth's peculiar power, and all were impatient to find out how stupid their neighbours were.

"I'll send my honest old minister to the weavers," the Emperor decided. "He'll be the best one to tell me how the material looks, for he's a sensible man and no one does his duty better."

So the honest old minister went to the room where the two swindlers sat working away at their empty looms.

"Heaven help me," he thought as his eyes flew wide open, "I can't see anything at all." But he did not say so.

Both the swindlers begged him to be so kind as to come near to approve the excellent pattern, the beautiful colours. They pointed to the empty looms, and the poor old minister stared as hard as he dared. He couldn't see anything, because there was nothing to see. "Heaven have mercy," he thought. "Can it be that I'm a fool? I'd have never guessed it, and not a soul must know. Am I unfit to be the minister? It would never do to let on that I can't see the cloth."

"Don't hesitate to tell us what you think of it," said one of the weavers.

"Oh, it's beautiful – it's enchanting." The old minister peered through his spectacles. "Such a pattern, what colours!" I'll be sure to tell the Emperor how delighted I am with it."

"We're pleased to hear that," the swindlers said. They proceeded to name all the colours and to explain the intricate pattern. The old minister paid the closest attention, so that he could tell it all to the Emperor. And so he did.

The weavers flatter the Emperor

The swindlers are paid

The swindlers at once asked for more money, more silk and more gold thread – to get on with the weaving. But it all went into their pockets. Not a thread went into the looms, though they worked at their weaving as hard as ever.

The Emperor presently sent another trustworthy official to see how the work progressed and how soon it would be ready. The same thing happened to him that had happened to the minister. He looked and he looked, but as there was nothing to see in the looms he couldn't see anything.

"Isn't it a beautiful piece of goods?" the swindlers asked him, as they displayed and described their imaginary pattern.

"I know I'm not stupid," the man thought, "so it must be that I'm unworthy of my good office. That's strange. I mustn't let anyone find it out, though." So he praised the material he did not see. He declared he was delighted with the beautiful colours and the exquisite pattern. To the Emperor he said, "It held me spellbound."

All the town was talking of this splendid cloth, and the Emperor wanted to see it for himself while it was still in the looms. Attended by a band of chosen men, among whom were his two old trusted officials – the ones who had been to the weavers – he set out to see the two swindlers. He found them weaving with might and main, but without a thread in their looms.

"Magnificent," said the two officials already duped. "Just look, Your Majesty, what colours! What a design!" They pointed to the empty looms, each supposing that the others could see the stuff.

"What's this?" thought the Emperor. "I can't see anything. This is terrible! Am I a fool? Am I unfit to be the Emperor? What a thing to happen to me of all people! – Oh! It's very pretty," he said. "It has my highest approval." And he nodded approbation at the empty loom. Nothing could make him say that he couldn't see anything.

His whole retinue stared and stared. One saw no more than another, but they all joined the Emperor in exclaiming, "Oh! It's very pretty," and they advised him to wear clothes made of this wonderful cloth especially for the great procession he was soon to lead. "Magnificent! Excellent! Unsurpassed!" were bandied from mouth to mouth, and everyone did his best to seem well pleased. The Emperor gave each of the swindlers a cross to wear in his buttonhole, and the title of "Sir Weaver."

Before the procession the swindlers sat up all night and burned more than six candles, to show how busy they were finishing the Emperor's new clothes. They pretended to take the cloth off the loom. They made cuts in the air with huge scissors. And at last they said, "Now the Emperor's new clothes are ready for him."

Then the Emperor himself came with his noblest noblemen, and the swindlers each raised an arm as if they were holding something. They said, "These are the trousers, here's the coat, and this is the mantle," naming each garment. "All of them are as light as a spider web. One would almost think he had nothing on, but that's what makes them so fine."

"Exactly," all the noblemen agreed, though they could see nothing, for there was nothing to see.

"If Your Imperial Majesty will condescend to take your clothes off," said the swindlers, "we will help you on with your new ones here in front of the long mirror."

The Emperor undressed, and the swindlers pretended to put his new clothes on him, one garment after another. They took him around the waist and seemed to be fastening something – that was his train – as the Emperor turned round and round before the looking glass.

"How well Your Majesty's new clothes look. Aren't they becoming!" He heard on all sides, "That pattern, so perfect! Those colours, so suitable! It is a magnificent outfit."

Then the minister of public processions announced: "Your Majesty's canopy is waiting outside."

"Well, I'm supposed to be ready," the Emperor said, and turned again for one last look in the mirror. "It is a remarkable fit, isn't it?" He seemed to regard his costume with the greatest interest.

The noblemen who were to carry his train stooped low and reached for the floor as if they were picking up his mantle. Then they pretended to lift and hold it high. They didn't dare admit they had nothing to hold.

So off went the Emperor in procession under his splendid canopy. Everyone in the streets and the windows said, "Oh, how fine are the Emperor's new clothes! Don't they fit him to perfection? And see his long train!" No one would confess that he couldn't see anything, for that would prove him either unfit for his position, or a fool. No costume the Emperor had worn before was ever such a complete success.

"But he hasn't got anything on," a little child said.

"Did you ever hear such innocent prattle?" said its father. And one person whispered to another what the child had said, "He hasn't anything on. A child says he hasn't anything on."

"But he hasn't got anything on!" the whole town cried out at last.

The Emperor shivered, for he suspected they were right. But he thought, "This procession has got to go on." So he walked more proudly than ever, as his noblemen held high the train that wasn't there at all.

The little boy shouts that the Emperor is naked!

Millers and fairies

Millers were thought by many local people (especially in Scotland) to be rather clever folk able to use and control the forces of nature, such as fire in the kiln and water in the millstream. Meanwhile, their whirring machinery and the mutation of plant material into flour suggested mysterious changes – an almost magical transition.

As a result the more superstitious folk in the community sometimes believed that the miller must be in league with the fairies. In Scotland, because fairies were often mischievous and to be feared, no one dared to set foot in the mill or kiln at night, as it was known that the fairies brought their corn to be milled after dark. Millers made no attempt to deny this, secure in the knowledge that so long as the locals believed this then they could sleep soundly, confident that their stores were not being robbed.

John Fraser, the miller of Whitehill, claimed to have hidden and watched the fairies trying unsuccessfully to work the mill. He said he decided to come out of hiding and help them, upon which one of the fairy women gave him a double handful of meal and told him to put it in his empty store, saying that the store would remain full for a long time, no matter how much he took out from it.

It is also said in some circles that to know the name of a particular fairy could summon it to you and force it to do your bidding. Depending on the circumstances, using the fairy's name might serve as an insult towards the fairy or to persuade it to grant powers and gifts to the user.

Fairies were said to bring their corn to the miller to be dealt with after dark so superstitious folk kept well clear at night

The Miser in the Bush

In this story by the Brothers Grimm (Jacob 1785–1863 and Wilhelm 1786–1859), a magic fiddle makes people dance interminably – not unlike the red shoes. This is a tale that sees a poor man's wishes spent wisely and justice meted out to those who cheat and steal.

A farmer had a faithful and diligent servant, who had worked hard for him three years, without having been paid any wages. At last it came into the man"s head that he would not go on thus without pay any longer; so he went to his master, and said, "I have worked hard for you a long time, I will trust to you to give me what I deserve to have for my trouble." The farmer was a sad miser, and knew that his man was very simple-hearted; so he took out threepence, and gave him for every year"s service a penny. The poor fellow thought it was a great deal of money to have, and said to himself, "Why should I work hard, and live here on bad fare any longer? I can now travel into the wide world, and make myself merry." With that he put his money into his purse, and set out, roaming over hill and valley.

As he jogged along over the fields, singing and dancing, a little dwarf met him, and asked him what made him so merry. "Why, what should make me down-hearted?" said he; "I am sound in health and rich in purse, what should I care for? I have saved up my three years" earnings and have it all safe in my pocket." "How much may it come to?" said the little man. "Full threepence," replied the countryman. "I wish you would give them to me," said the other; "I am very poor." Then the man pitied him, and gave him all he had; and the little dwarf said in return, "As you have such a kind honest heart, I will grant you three wishes – one for every penny; so choose whatever you like." Then the countryman rejoiced at his good luck, and said, "I like many things better than money: first, I will have a bow that will bring down everything I shoot at; secondly, a fiddle that will set everyone dancing that hears me play upon it; and thirdly, I should like that everyone should grant what I ask." The dwarf said he should have his three wishes; so he gave him the bow and fiddle, and went his way.

Our honest friend journeyed on his way too; and if he was merry before, he was now ten times more so. He had not gone far before he met an old miser: close by them stood a tree, and on the topmost twig sat a thrush

The servant asked for a bow that would always hit its target

singing away most joyfully. "Oh, what a pretty bird!" said the miser; "I would give a great deal of money to have such a one." "If that's all," said the countryman, "I will soon bring it down." Then he took up his bow, and down fell the thrush into the bushes at the foot of the tree. The miser crept into the bush to find it; but directly he had got into the middle, his companion took up his fiddle and played away, and the miser began to dance and spring about, capering higher and higher in the air. The thorns soon began to tear his clothes till they all hung in rags about him, and he himself was all scratched and wounded, so that the blood ran down. "Oh, for heaven's sake!" cried the miser, "Master! master! pray let the fiddle alone. What have I done to deserve this?" "Thou hast shaved many a poor soul close enough," said the other; "thou art only meeting thy reward": so he played up another tune. Then the miser began to beg and promise, and offered money for his liberty; but he did not come up to the musician's price for some time, and he danced him along brisker and brisker, and the miser bid higher and higher, till at last he

The fiddle was magic and wherever it was played, no-one could stop dancing

offered a round hundred of florins that he had in his purse, and had just gained by cheating some poor fellow. When the countryman saw so much money, he said, "I will agree to your proposal." So he took the purse, put up his fiddle, and travelled on very pleased with his bargain.

Meanwhile the miser crept out of the bush half-naked and in a piteous plight, and began to ponder how he should take his revenge, and serve his late companion some trick. At last he went to the judge, and complained that a rascal had robbed him of his money, and beaten him into the bargain; and that the fellow who did it carried a bow at his back and a fiddle hung round his neck. Then the judge sent out his officers to bring up the accused wherever they should find him; and he was soon caught and brought up to be tried.

The miser began to tell his tale, and said he had been robbed of his money. "No, you gave it me for playing a tune to you." said the countryman; but the judge told him that was not likely, and cut the matter short by ordering him off to the gallows.

So away he was taken; but as he stood on the steps he said, "My Lord Judge, grant me one last request." "Anything but thy life," replied the other. "No," said he, "I do not ask my life; only to let me play upon my fiddle for the last time." The miser cried out, "Oh, no! no! for heaven's sake

don"t listen to him! don't listen to him!" But the judge said, "It is only this once, he will soon have done." The fact was, he could not refuse the request, on account of the dwarf's third gift.

Then the miser said, "Bind me fast, bind me fast, for pity's sake." But the countryman seized his fiddle, and struck up a tune, and at the first note judge, clerks, and jailer were in motion; all began capering, and no one could hold the miser. At the second note the hangman let his prisoner go, and danced also, and by the time he had played the first bar of the tune, all were dancing together—judge, court, and miser, and all the people who had followed to look on. At first the thing was merry and pleasant enough; but when it had gone on a while, and there seemed to be no end of playing or dancing, they began to cry out, and beg him to leave off; but he stopped not a whit the more for their entreaties, till the judge not only gave him his life, but promised to return him the hundred florins.

Then he called to the miser, and said, "Tell us now, you vagabond, where you got that gold, or I shall play on for your amusement only," "I stole it," said the miser in the presence of all the people; "I acknowledge that I stole it, and that you earned it fairly." Then the countryman stopped his fiddle, and left the miser to take his place at the gallows.

The Changeling

by Charlotte Mew (1869 –1928)

Toll no bell for me, dear Father, dear Mother,
Waste no sighs;
There are my sisters, there is my little brother
Who plays in the place called Paradise,
Your children all, your children for ever;
But I, so wild,
Your disgrace, with the queer brown face, was never,
Never, I know, but half your child!

In the garden at play, all day, last summer,
Far and away I heard
The sweet "tweet-tweet" of a strange new-comer,
The dearest, clearest call of a bird.
It lived down there in the deep green hollow,
My own old home, and the fairies say
The word of a bird is a thing to follow,
So I was away a night and a day.

One evening, too, by the nursery fire,
We snuggled close and sat round so still,
When suddenly as the wind blew higher,
Something scratched on the window-sill.
A pinched brown face peered in – I shivered;
No one listened or seemed to see;
The arms of it waved and the wings of it quivered
Whoo – I knew it had come for me!
Some are as bad as bad can be!
All night long they danced in the rain,
Round and round in a dripping chain,
Threw their caps at the window-pane,
Tried to make me scream and shout
And fling the bedclothes all about:
I meant to stay in bed that night,
And if only you had left a light
They would never have got me out!

Sometimes I would speak, you see,
Or answer when you spoke to me,
Because in the long, still dusks of Spring
You can hear the whole world whispering;
The shy green grasses making love,
The feathers grow on the dear grey dove,
The tiny heart of the redstart beat,
The patter of the squirrel's feet,
The pebbles pushing in the silver streams,
The rushes talking in their dreams,
The swish-swish of the bat's black wings,
The wild-wood bluebell's sweet ting-tings,

Humming and hammering at your ear,
Everything there is to hear
In the heart of hidden things.
But not in the midst of the nursery riot,
That's why I wanted to be quiet,
Couldn't do my sums, or sing,
Or settle down to anything.
And when, for that, I was sent upstairs
I did kneel down to say my prayers;
But the King who sits on your high Church steeple
Has nothing to do with us fairy people!

'Times I pleased you, dear Father, dear Mother,
Learned all my lessons and liked to play,
And dearly I loved the little pale brother
Whom some other bird must have called away.
Why did they bring me here to make me
Not quite bad and not quite good,
Why, unless They're wicked, do They want,
in spite, to take me
Back to Their wet, wild wood?
Now, every night I shall see the windows shining,
The gold lamp's glow, and the fire's red gleam,
While the best of us are twining twigs and the rest of us
are whining
In the hollow by the stream.
Black and chill are Their nights on the wold
And They live so long and They feel no pain:
I shall grow up, but never grow old,
I shall always, always be very cold,I shall never come
back again!

This is an Arthur Rackham painting of fairies with a changeling

Little Red Riding Hood

The earliest form of this story was told by French peasants in the 1300s when wolves were a real threat in European forests. Several versions appeared in Italy, with one called *The False Grandmother*. Perrault and the Brothers Grimm related this popular tale, which may have sprung from an Oriental one called *Grandaunt Tiger*. In one version the child is saved not by the huntsman but because when the wolf tried to eat her, his jaws were burned by the enchanted golden hood she wore.

Once upon a time there lived in a certain village a little country girl, the prettiest creature was ever seen. Her mother was excessively fond of her; and her grandmother doted on her still more. This good woman had made for her a little red riding hood; which became the girl so extremely well that everybody called her Little Red Riding Hood.

One day her mother, having made some custards, said to her:

"Go, my dear, and see how thy grandmamma does, for I hear she has been very ill; carry her a custard, and this little pot of butter."

Little Red Riding Hood set out immediately to go to her grandmother, who lived in another village.

As she was going through the wood, she met with Gaffer Wolf, who had a very great mind to eat her up, but he dared not, because of some faggot-makers hard by in the forest. He asked her whither she was going. The poor child, who did not know that it was dangerous to stay and hear a wolf talk, said to him:

"I am going to see my grandmamma and carry her a custard and a little pot of butter from my mamma."

"Does she live far off?" said the Wolf.

"Oh! ay," answered Little Red Riding Hood; "it is beyond that mill you see there, at the first house in the village."

"Well," said the Wolf, "and I'll go and see her too. I'll go this way and you go that, and we shall see who will be there soonest."

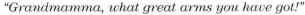

"Grandmamma, what great arms you have got!"

The Wolf began to run as fast as he could, taking the nearest way, and the little girl went by that farthest about, diverting herself in gathering nuts, running after butterflies, and making nosegays of such little flowers as she met with. The Wolf was not long before he got to the old woman's house. He knocked at the door – tap, tap.

"Who's there?"

"Your grandchild, Little Red Riding Hood," replied the Wolf, counterfeiting her voice; "who has brought you a custard and a little pot of butter sent you by mamma."

The good grandmother, who was in bed, because she was somewhat ill, cried out

"Pull the bobbin, and the latch will go up."

The Wolf pulled the bobbin, and the door opened, and then presently he fell upon the good woman and ate her up in a moment, for it was above three days that he had not touched a bit. He then shut the door and went into the grandmother's bed, expecting Little Red Riding Hood, who came some time afterward and knocked at the door – tap, tap.

"Who's there?"

Little Red Riding Hood, hearing the big voice of the Wolf, was at first afraid; but believing her grandmother had got a cold and was hoarse, answered:

"'Tis your grandchild, Little Red Riding-Hood, who has brought you a custard and a little pot of butter mamma

sends you."

The Wolf cried out to her, softening his voice as much as he could:

"Pull the bobbin, and the latch will go up."

Little Red Riding Hood pulled the bobbin, and the door opened.

The Wolf, seeing her come in, said to her, hiding himself under the bed-clothes:

"Put the custard and the little pot of butter upon the stool, and come and lie down with me."

Little Red Riding Hood undressed herself and went into bed, where, being greatly amazed to see how her grandmother looked in her night-clothes, she said to her:

"Grandmamma, what great arms you have got!"

"That is the better to hug thee, my dear."

"Grandmamma, what great legs you have got!"

"That is to run the better, my child."

"Grandmamma, what great ears you have got!"

"That is to hear the better, my child."

"Grandmamma, what great eyes you have got!"

"It is to see the better, my child."

"Grandmamma, what great teeth you have got!"

"That is to eat thee up."

And, saying these words, this wicked wolf fell upon Little Red Riding-Hood, and ate her all up.

"Tis your grandchild, Little Red Riding Hood, who has brought you a present," said the child

Perrault's 1697 story ends here but in the Grimm Brothers 1812
***Little Red Cap* version, the ending is a happier one, as follows:**

As soon as the wolf had finished this tasty bite, he climbed back into bed, fell asleep, and began to snore very loudly.

A huntsman was just passing by. He thought it strange that the old woman was snoring so loudly, so he decided to take a look. He stepped inside, and in the bed there lay the Wolf that he had been hunting for such a long time. "He has eaten the grandmother, but perhaps she still can be saved. I won't shoot him," thought the huntsman. So he took a pair of scissors and cut open his belly.

He had cut only a few strokes when he saw the red cap shining through. He cut a little more, and the girl jumped out and cried, "Oh, I was so frightened! It was so dark inside the Wolf's body!"

And then the grandmother came out alive as well. Then Little Red Cap fetched some large heavy stones. They filled the Wolf's body with them, and when he woke up and tried to run away, the stones were so heavy that he fell down dead.

The three of them were happy. The huntsman took the wolf's pelt. The grandmother ate the cake and drank the wine that Little Red Cap had brought. And Little Red Cap thought to herself, "As long as I live, I will never leave the path and run off into the woods by myself if mother tells me not to."

Puss in Boots or The Master Cat

This story first arrived in 1697 in *Tales of Mother Goose* by Perrault (1628–1703). The cat also appears in the ballet of *The Sleeping Beauty* by Tchaikovsky but stories of the trickster cat had been around for centuries and found their way into all parts of Europe and into Siberia, India, Indonesia and the Philippines. It also travelled with colonists from Europe to Africa and into American Indian culture.

There was a miller who left no more estate to the three sons he had than his mill, his ass, and his cat. The partition was soon made. Neither scrivener nor attorney was sent for. They would soon have eaten up all the poor patrimony. The eldest had the mill, the second the ass, and the youngest nothing but the cat. The poor young fellow was quite comfortless at having so poor a lot.

Puss in Boots pretended to be dead

"My brothers," said he, "may get their living handsomely enough by joining their stocks together; but for my part, when I have eaten up my cat, and made me a muff of his skin, I must die of hunger."

The Cat, who heard all this, but made as if he did not, said to him with a grave and serious air:

"Do not thus afflict yourself, my good master. You have nothing else to do but to give me a bag and get a pair of boots made for me that I may scamper through the dirt and the brambles, and you shall see that you have not so bad a portion in me as you imagine."

The Cat's master did not build very much upon what he said. He had often seen him play a great many cunning tricks to catch rats and mice, as when he used to hang by the heels, or hide himself in the meal, and make as if he were dead; so that he did not altogether despair of his affording him some help in his miserable condition. When the Cat had what he asked for he booted himself very gallantly, and putting his bag about his neck, he held the strings of it in his two forepaws and went into a warren where was great abundance of rabbits. He put bran and sow-thistle into his bag, and stretching out at length, as if he had been dead, he waited for some young rabbits, not yet acquainted with the deceits of the world, to come and rummage his bag for what he had put into it.

Scarce was he lain down but he had what he wanted. A rash and foolish young rabbit jumped into his bag, and Monsieur Puss, immediately drawing close the strings, took and killed him without pity. Proud of his prey, he went with it to the palace and asked to speak with his majesty. He was shown upstairs into the King's apartment, and, making a low reverence, said to him:

"I have brought you, sir, a rabbit of the warren, which my noble lord the Marquis of Carabas" (for that was the title which puss was pleased to give his master) "has commanded me to present to your majesty from him."

"Tell thy master," said the King, "that I thank him and that he does me a great deal of pleasure."

Another time he went and hid himself among some standing corn, holding still his bag open, and when a brace of partridges ran into it he drew the strings and so caught them both. He went and made a present of these to the King, as he had done before of the rabbit which he took in the warren. The King, in like manner, received the partridges with great pleasure, and ordered him some money for drink.

The Cat continued for two or three months thus to carry his Majesty, from time to time, game of his master's

Puss in Boots helps his young master attain riches

taking. One day in particular, when he knew for certain that he was to take the air along the river-side, with his daughter, the most beautiful princess in the world, he said to his master:

"If you will follow my advice your fortune is made. You have nothing else to do but go and wash yourself in the river, in that part I shall show you, and leave the rest to me."

The Marquis of Carabas did what the Cat advised him to, without knowing why or wherefore. While he was washing the King passed by, and the Cat began to cry out:

"Help! help! My Lord Marquis of Carabas is going to be drowned."

Puss in Boots uses guile and subterfuge to help his new friend

At this noise the King put his head out of the coach-window, and, finding it was the Cat who had so often brought him such good game, he commanded his guards to run immediately to the assistance of his Lordship the Marquis of Carabas. While they were drawing the poor Marquis out of the river, the Cat came up to the coach and told the King that, while his master was washing, there came by some rogues, who went off with his clothes, though he had cried out: "Thieves! thieves!" several times, as loud as he could.

This cunning Cat had hidden them under a great stone. The King immediately commanded the officers of his

wardrobe to run and fetch one of his best suits for the Lord Marquis of Carabas.

The King caressed him after a very extraordinary manner, and as the fine clothes he had given him extremely set off his good mien (for he was well made and very handsome in his person), the King's daughter took a secret inclination to him, and the Marquis of Carabas had no sooner cast two or three respectful and somewhat tender glances but she fell in love with him to distraction. The King would needs have him come into the coach and take part of the airing. The Cat, quite overjoyed to see his project begin to succeed, marched on before, and, meeting with some countrymen, who were mowing a meadow, he said to them:

"Good people, you who are mowing, if you do not tell the King that the meadow you mow belongs to my Lord Marquis of Carabas, you shall be chopped as small as herbs for the pot."

The King did not fail asking of the mowers to whom the meadow they were mowing belonged.

"To my Lord Marquis of Carabas," answered they altogether, for the Cat's threats had made them terribly afraid.

"You see, sir," said the Marquis, "this is a meadow which never fails to yield a plentiful harvest every year."

The Master Cat, who went still on before, met with some reapers, and said to them:

"Good people, you who are reaping, if you do not tell the King that all this corn belongs to the Marquis of Carabas, you shall be chopped as small as herbs for the pot."

The King, who passed by a moment after, would needs know to whom all that corn, which he then saw, did belong.

"To my Lord Marquis of Carabas," replied the reapers, and the King was very well pleased with it, as well as the Marquis, whom he congratulated thereupon. The Master Cat, who went always before, said the same words to all he met, and the King was astonished at the vast estates of my Lord Marquis of Carabas.

Monsieur Puss came at last to a stately castle, the master of which was an ogre, the richest had ever been known; for all the lands which the King had then gone over belonged to this castle. The Cat, who had taken care to inform himself who this ogre was and what he could do, asked to speak with him, saying he could not pass so near his castle without having the honor of paying his respects to him.

The ogre received him as civilly as an ogre could do, and made him sit down.

"I have been assured," said the Cat, "that you have the gift of being able to change yourself into all sorts of creatures you have a mind to; you can, for example, transform yourself into a lion, or elephant, and the like."

"That is true," answered the ogre very briskly; "and to convince you, you shall see me now become a lion."

Puss was so sadly terrified at the sight of a lion so near him that he immediately got into the gutter, not without abundance of trouble and danger, because of his boots,

The ogre – somewhat foolishly – turned himself into a mouse

which were of no use at all to him in walking upon the tiles. A little while after, when Puss saw that the ogre had resumed his natural form, he came down, and owned he had been very much frightened.

"I have been, moreover, informed," said the Cat, "but I know not how to believe it, that you have also the power to take on you the shape of the smallest animals; for example, to change yourself into a rat or a mouse; but I must own to you I take this to be impossible."

"Impossible!" cried the ogre; "you shall see that presently." And at the same time he changed himself into a mouse, and began to run about the floor. Puss no sooner perceived this but he fell upon him and ate him up.

Meanwhile the King, who saw, as he passed, this fine castle of the ogre's, had a mind to go into it. Puss, who heard the noise of his Majesty's coach running over the draw-bridge, ran out, and said to the King:

"Your Majesty is welcome to this castle of my Lord Marquis of Carabas."

"What! my Lord Marquis," cried the King, "and does this castle also belong to you? There can be nothing finer than this court and all the stately buildings which surround it; let us go into it, if you please."

The Marquis gave his hand to the Princess, and followed the King, who went first. They passed into a spacious hall, where they found a magnificent collation, which the ogre had prepared for his friends, who were that very day to visit him, but dared not to enter, knowing the King was there. His Majesty was perfectly charmed with the good qualities of my Lord Marquis of Carabas, as was his daughter, who had fallen violently in love with him, and, seeing the vast estate he possessed, said to him, after having drunk five or six glasses:

"It will be owing to yourself only, my Lord Marquis, if you are not my son-in-law."

The Marquis, making several low bows, accepted the honour which his Majesty conferred upon him, and forthwith, that very same day, married the Princess.

Puss became a great lord, and never ran after mice any more but only for his diversion.

The Boy who could Keep a Secret

This traditional Hungarian story appeared in Andrew Lang's (1844–1912) *The Crimson Fairy Book* and is a folk tale of the Magyars.

The boy found a sword sticking out of the garden soil

Once upon a time there lived a poor widow who had one little boy. At first sight you would not have thought that he was different from a thousand other little boys; but then you noticed that by his side hung the scabbard of a sword, and as the boy grew bigger the scabbard grew bigger too. The sword which belonged to the scabbard was found by the little boy sticking out of the ground in the garden, and every day he pulled it up to see if it would go into the scabbard. But though it was plainly becoming longer and longer, it was some time before the two would fit.

However, there came a day at last when it slipped in quite easily. The child was so delighted that he could hardly believe his eyes, so he tried it seven times, and each time it slipped in more easily than before. But pleased though the boy was, he determined not to tell anyone about it, particularly not his mother, who never could keep anything from her neighbours.

Still, in spite of his resolutions, he could not hide altogether that something had happened, and when he went in to breakfast his mother asked him what was the matter.

'Oh, mother, I had such a nice dream last night,' said he; 'but I can't tell it to anybody.'

'You can tell it to me,' she answered. 'It must have been a nice dream, or you wouldn't look so happy.'

'No, mother; I can't tell it to anybody,' returned the boy, 'till it comes true.'

'I want to know what it was, and know it I will,' cried she, 'and I will beat you till you tell me.'

But it was no use, neither words nor blows would get the secret out of the boy; and when her arm was quite tired and she had to leave off, the child, sore and aching, ran into the garden and knelt weeping beside his little sword. It was working round and round in its hole all by itself, and if anyone except the boy had tried to catch hold of it, he would have been badly cut. But the moment he stretched out his hand it stopped and slid quietly into the scabbard.

For a long time the child sat sobbing, and the noise was heard by the king as he was driving by. 'Go and see who it is that is crying so,' said he to one of his servants, and the man went. In a few minutes he returned saying: 'Your Majesty, it is a little boy who is kneeling there sobbing because his mother has beaten him.'

'Bring him to me at once,' commanded the monarch, 'and tell him that it is the king who sends for him, and that he has never cried in all his life and cannot bear anyone else to do so.' On receiving this message the boy dried his tears and went with the servant to the royal carriage. 'Will you be my son?' asked the king.

'Yes, if my mother will let me,' answered the boy. And the king bade the servant go back to the mother and say that if she would give her boy to him, he should live in the palace and marry his prettiest daughter as soon as he was a man.

The widow's anger now turned into joy, and she came running to the splendid coach and kissed the king's hand. 'I hope you will be more obedient to his Majesty than you were to me,' she said; and the boy shrank away half-frightened. But when she had gone back to her cottage, he asked the king if he might fetch something that he had left

The youngest princess was the prettiest of all

546

in the garden, and when he was given permission, he pulled up his little sword, which he slid into the scabbard.

Then he climbed into the coach and was driven away.

After they had gone some distance the king said: 'Why were you crying so bitterly in the garden just now?'

'Because my mother had been beating me,' replied the boy.

'And what did she do that for?' asked the king again.

'Because I would not tell her my dream.'

'And why wouldn't you tell it to her?'

'Because I will never tell it to anyone till it comes true,' answered the boy.

'And won't you tell it to me either?' asked the king in surprise.

'No, not even to you, your Majesty,' replied he.

'Oh, I am sure you will when we get home,' said the king smiling, and he talked to him about other things till they came to the palace.

'I have brought you such a nice present,' he said to his daughters, and as the boy was very pretty they were delighted to have him and gave him all their best toys.

'You must not spoil him,' observed the king one day, when he had been watching them playing together. He has a secret which he won't tell to anyone.'

'He will tell me,' answered the eldest princess; but the boy only shook his head.

'He will tell me,' said the second girl.

'Not I,' replied the boy.

'He will tell me,' cried the youngest, who was the prettiest too.

'I will tell nobody till it comes true,' said the boy, as he had said before; 'and I will beat anybody who asks me.'

The king was very sorry when he heard this, for he loved the boy dearly; but he thought it would never do to keep anyone near him who would not do as he was bid. So he commanded his servants to take him away and not to let him enter the palace again until he had come to his right senses.

The sword clanked loudly as the boy was led away, but the child said nothing, though he was very unhappy at being treated so badly when he had done nothing. However, the servants were very kind to him, and their children brought him fruit and all sorts of nice things, and he soon grew merry again, and lived amongst them for many years till his seventeenth birthday.

Meanwhile the two eldest princesses had become women, and had married two powerful kings who ruled over great countries across the sea. The youngest one was old enough to be married too, but she was very particular, and turned up her nose at all the young princes who had sought her hand.

One day she was sitting in the palace feeling rather dull and lonely, and suddenly she began to wonder what the servants were doing, and whether it was not more amusing down in their quarters. The king was at his council and the queen was ill in bed, so there was no one to stop the princess, and she hastily ran across the gardens to the houses where the servants lived. Outside she noticed a youth who was handsomer than any prince she had ever seen, and in a moment she knew him to be the little boy she had once played with.

'Tell me your secret and I will marry you,' she said to him; but the boy only gave her the beating he had promised her long ago, when she asked him the same question. The girl was very angry, besides being hurt, and ran home to complain to her father.

'If he had a thousand souls, I would kill them all,' swore the king.

That very day a gallows was built outside the town, and all the people crowded round to see the execution of the young man who had dared to beat the king's daughter. The prisoner, with his hands tied behind his back, was brought out by the hangman, and amidst dead silence his sentence was being read by the judge when suddenly the sword clanked against his side. Instantly a great noise was heard and a golden coach rumbled over the stones, with a white flag waving out of the window. It stopped underneath the gallows, and from it stepped the king of the Magyars, who begged that the life of the boy might be spared.

'Sir, he has beaten my daughter, who only asked him to tell her his secret. I cannot pardon that,' answered the princess's father.

'Give him to me, I'm sure he will tell me the secret; or, if not, I have a daughter who is like the Morning Star, and he is sure to tell it to her.'

The sword clanked for the third time, and the king said angrily: 'Well, if you want him so much you can have him; only never let me see his face again.' And he made a sign to the hangman. The bandage was removed from the young man's eyes, and the cords from his wrists, and he took his seat in the golden coach beside the king of the Magyars. Then the coachman whipped up his horses, and they set out for Buda.

The king talked very pleasantly for a few miles, and when he thought that his new companion was quite at ease with him, he asked him what was the secret which had brought him into such trouble. ' That I cannot tell you,' answered the youth, 'until it comes true.'

'You will tell my daughter,' said the king, smiling.

'I will tell nobody,' replied the youth, and as he spoke the sword clanked loudly. The king said no more, but trusted to his daughter's beauty to get the secret from him.

The journey to Buda was long, and it was several days before they arrived there. The beautiful princess happened to be picking roses in the garden, when her father's coach drove up.

'Oh, what a handsome youth! Have you brought him from fairyland?' cried she, when they all stood upon the marble steps in front of the castle.

'I have brought him from the gallows,' answered the king; rather vexed at his daughter's words, as never before had she consented to speak to any man.

'I don't care where you brought him from,' said the spoilt girl. 'I will marry him and nobody else, and we will live together till we die.'

'You will tell another tale,' replied the king, 'when you ask him his secret. After all he is no better than a servant.'

'That is nothing to me,' said the princess, 'for I love him. He will tell his secret to me, and will find a place in the middle of my heart.'

But the king shook his head, and gave orders that the lad was to be lodged in the summer-house.

One day, about a week later, the princess put on her finest dress, and went to pay him a visit. She looked so beautiful that, at the sight of her, the book dropped from his hand, and he stood up speechless. 'Tell me,' she said, coaxingly, 'what is this wonderful secret? Just whisper it in my ear, and I will give you a kiss.'

'My angel,' he answered, 'be wise, and ask no questions, if you wish to get safely back to your father's palace; I have kept my secret all these years, and do not mean to tell it now.'

However, the girl would not listen, and went on pressing him, till at last he slapped her face so hard that her nose bled. She shrieked with pain and rage, and ran screaming back to the palace, where her father was waiting to hear if she had succeeded. 'I will starve you to death, you son of a dragon,' cried he, when he saw her dress streaming with blood; and he ordered all the masons and bricklayers in the town to come before him.

'Build me a tower as fast as you can,' he said, 'and see that there is room for a stool and a small table, and for nothing else. The men set to work, and in two hours the tower was built, and they proceeded to the palace to inform the king that his commands were fulfilled. On the way they met the princess, who began to talk to one of the masons, and when the rest were out of hearing she asked if he could manage to make a hole in the tower, which nobody could see, large enough for a bottle of wine and some food to pass through.

'To be sure I can,' said the mason, turning back, and in a few minutes the hole was bored.

At sunset a large crowd assembled to watch the youth being led to the tower, and after his misdeeds had been proclaimed he was solemnly walled up. But every morning the princess passed him in food through the hole, and every third day the king sent his secretary to climb up a ladder and look down through a little window to see if he was dead. But the secretary always brought back the report that he was fat and rosy.

'There is some magic about this,' said the king.

This state of affairs lasted some time, till one day a messenger arrived from the Sultan bearing a letter for the king, and also three canes. 'My master bids me say,' said the messenger, bowing low, 'that if you cannot tell him which of these three canes grows nearest the root, which in the middle, and which at the top, he will declare war against you.

The king was very much frightened when he heard this, and though he took the canes and examined them closely, he could see no difference between them. He looked so sad that his daughter noticed it, and inquired the reason.

'Alas! my daughter,' he answered, 'how can I help being sad? The Sultan has sent me three canes, and says that if I cannot tell him which of them grows near the root, which in the middle, and which at the top, he will make war upon me. And you know that his army is far greater than mine.'

'Oh, do not despair, my father,' said she. 'We shall be sure to find out the answer'; and she ran away to the tower, and told the young man what had occurred.

'Go to bed as usual,' replied he, 'and when you wake, tell your father that you have dreamed that the canes must be placed in warm water. After a little while one will sink to the bottom; that is the one that grows nearest the root. The one which neither sinks nor comes to the surface is the cane that is cut from the middle; and the one that floats is from the top.'

So, the next morning, the princess told her father of her dream, and by her advice he cut notches in each of the canes when he took them out of the water, so that he might make no mistake when he handed them back to the messenger. The Sultan could not imagine how he had found out, but he did not declare war.

The following year the Sultan again wanted to pick a quarrel with the king of the Magyars, so he sent another messenger to him with three foals, begging him to say which of the animals was born in the morning, which at noon, and which in the evening. If an answer was not ready in three days, war would be declared at once. The king's heart sank when he read the letter. He could not expect his daughter to be lucky enough to dream rightly a second time, and as a plague had been raging through the country, and had carried off many of his soldiers, his army was even weaker than before. At this thought his face became so gloomy that his daughter noticed it, and inquired what was the matter.

'I have had another letter from the Sultan,' replied the king, 'and he says that if I cannot tell him which of three foals was born in the morning, which at noon, and which in the evening, he will declare war at once.'

'Oh, don't be cast down,' said she, 'something is sure to happen'; and she ran down to the tower to consult the youth.

'Go home, idol of my heart, and when night comes, pretend to scream out in your sleep, so that your father hears you. Then tell him that you have dreamt that he was just being carried off by the Turks because he could not answer the question about the foals, when the lad whom he had shut up in the tower ran up and told them which was foaled in the morning, which at noon, and which in the evening.'

So the princess did exactly as the youth had bidden her; and no sooner had she spoken than the king

The little princesses grew up into fine royal ladies; soon the two eldest were married to rich kings across the sea

ordered the tower to be pulled down, and the prisoner brought before him.

'I did not think that you could have lived so long without food,' said he, 'and as you have had plenty of time to repent your wicked conduct, I will grant you pardon, on condition that you help me in a sore strait. Read this letter from the Sultan; you will see that if I fail to answer his question about the foals, a dreadful war will be the result.'

The youth took the letter and read it through. 'Yes, I can help you,' replied he; 'but first you must bring me three troughs, all exactly alike. Into one you must put oats, into another wheat, and into the third barley. The foal which eats the oats is that which was foaled in the morning; the foal which eats the wheat is that which was foaled at noon; and the foal which eats the barley is that which was foaled at night.' The king followed the youth's directions, and, marking the foals, sent them back to Turkey, and there was no war that year.

Now the Sultan was very angry that both his plots to get possession of Hungary had been such total failures, and he sent for his aunt, who was a witch, to consult her as to what he should do next.

'It is not the king who has answered your questions,' observed the aunt, when he had told his story. 'He is far too stupid ever to have done that! The person who has found out the puzzle is the son of a poor woman, who, if he lives, will become King of Hungary. Therefore, if you want the crown yourself, you must get him here and kill him.'

After this conversation another letter was written to the Court of Hungary, saying that if the youth, now in the palace, was not sent to Turkey within three days, a large army would cross the border. The king's heart was sorrowful as he read, for he was grateful to the lad for what he had done to help him; but the boy only laughed, and bade the king fear nothing, but to search the town instantly for two youths just like each other, and he would paint himself a mask that was just like them. And the sword at his side clanked loudly.

After a long search twin brothers were found, so exactly resembling each other that even their own mother could not tell the difference. The youth painted a mask that was the precise copy of them, and when he had put it on, no one would have known one boy from the other. They set out at once for the Sultan's palace, and when they reached it, they were taken straight into his presence. He made a sign for them to come near; they all bowed low in greeting. He asked them about their journey; they answered his questions all together, and in the same words. If one sat down to supper, the others sat down at the same instant. When one got up, the others got up too, as if there had been only one body between them. The Sultan could not detect any difference between them, and he told his aunt that he would not be so cruel as to kill all three.

'Well, you will see a difference to-morrow,' replied the witch, 'for one will have a cut on his sleeve. That is the youth you must kill.' And one hour before midnight, when witches are invisible, she glided into the room where all three lads were sleeping in the same bed. She took out a pair of scissors and cut a small piece out of the boy's coat-sleeve which was hanging on the wall, and then crept silently from the room. But in the morning the youth saw the slit, and he marked the sleeves of his two companions in the same way, and all three went down to breakfast with the Sultan. The old witch was standing in the window and pretended not to see them; but all witches have eyes in the backs of their heads, and she knew at once that not one sleeve but three were cut, and they were all as alike as before. After breakfast, the Sultan, who was getting tired of the whole affair and wanted to be alone to invent some other plan, told them they might return home. So, bowing low with one accord, they went.

The princess welcomed the boy back joyfully, but the

Gallows were raised outside the town ready for the young man's execution

The king needed to know which foal was born at which time of day

poor youth was not allowed to rest long in peace, for one day a fresh letter arrived from the Sultan, saying that he had discovered that the young man was a very dangerous person, and that he must be sent to Turkey at once, and alone. The girl burst into tears when the boy told her what was in the letter which her father had bade her to carry to him. 'Do not weep, love of my heart,' said the boy, 'all will be well. I will start at sunrise to-morrow.'

So next morning at sunrise the youth set forth, and in a few days he reached the Sultan's palace. The old witch was waiting for him at the gate, and whispered as he passed: 'This is the last time you will ever enter it.' But the sword clanked, and the lad did not even look at her. As he crossed the threshold fifteen armed Turks barred his way, with the Sultan at their head. Instantly the sword darted forth and cut off the heads of everyone but the Sultan, and then went quietly back to its scabbard. The witch, who was looking on, saw that as long as the youth had possession of the sword, all her schemes would be in vain, and tried to steal the sword in the night, but it only jumped out of its scabbard and sliced off her nose, which was of iron. And in the morning, when the Sultan brought a great army to capture the lad and deprive him of his sword, they were all cut to pieces, while he remained without a scratch.

Meanwhile the princess was in despair because the days slipped by, and the young man did not return, and she never rested until her father let her lead some troops against the Sultan. She rode proudly before them, dressed in uniform; but they had not left the town more than a mile behind them, when they met the lad and his little sword. When he told them what he had done they shouted for joy, and carried him back in triumph to the palace; and the king declared that as the youth had shown himself worthy to become his son-in-law, he should marry the princess and succeed to the throne at once, as he himself was getting old, and the cares of government were too much for him. But the young man said he must first go and see his mother, and the king sent him in state, with a troop of soldiers as his bodyguard.

The old woman was quite frightened at seeing such an array draw up before her little house, and still more surprised when a handsome young man, whom she did not know, dismounted and kissed her hand, saying: 'Now, dear mother, you shall hear my secret at last! I dreamed that I should become King of Hungary, and my dream has come true. When I was a child, and you begged me to tell you, I had to keep silence, or the Magyar king would have killed me. And if you had not beaten me nothing would have happened that has happened, and I should not now be King of Hungary.

Shortshanks

This is a Norwegian
tale by Peter Christen
Asbjørnsen (1812-
1885) and Jørgen Moe (1813-
1882) and which was also
included in Andrew Lang's
fairy tale collections in the *Red
Fairy Book* where it was called
Mannikins.

Once on a time there was a poor couple who lived in a tumble-down hut, in which there was nothing but black want, so that they hadn't a morsel to eat, nor a stick to burn. But though they had next to nothing of other things, they had God's blessing in the way of children, and every year they had another babe. Now, when this story begins, they were just looking out for a new child; and, to tell the truth, the husband was rather cross, and he was always going about grumbling and growling, and saying, "For his part, he thought one might have too many of these God's gifts." So when the time came that the babe was to be born, he went off into the wood to fetch fuel, saying, "He didn't care to stop and see the young squaller; he'd be sure to hear him soon enough, screaming for food."

Now, when her husband was well out of the house, his wife gave birth to a beautiful boy, who began to look about the room as soon as ever he came into the world.

"Oh, dear mother!" he said, "Give me some of my brother's cast-off clothes, and a few days' food, and I'll go out into the world and try my luck; you have children enough as it is, that I can see."

"God help you, my son!" answered his mother; "That can never be, you are far too young yet."

But the tiny one stuck to what he said, and begged and prayed till his mother was forced to let him have a few old rags, and a little food tied up in a bundle, and off he went right merrily and manfully into the wide world. But he was scarce out of the house before his mother had another boy, and he too looked about him and said, "Oh, dear mother! Give me some of my brother's old clothes, and a few days' food, and I'll go out into the world to find my twin-brother; you have children enough already on your hands, that I can see."

"God help you, my poor little fellow!" said his mother;

"You are far too little, this will never do."

But it was no good; the tiny one begged and prayed so hard, till he got some old tattered rags and a bundle of food; and so he wandered out into the world like a man, to find his twin-brother. Now, when the younger had walked a while, he saw his brother a good bit on before him, so he called out to him to stop.

"Halloa! Can't you stop? Why, you lay legs to the ground

He was a very beautiful bright child

as if you were running a race. But you might just as well have stayed to see your youngest brother before set you off into the world in such a hurry."

So the elder stopped and looked round; and when the younger had come up to him and told him the whole story, and how he was his brother, he went on to say:

"But let's sit down here and see what our mother has given us for food." So they sat down together, and were soon great friends.

Now when they had gone a bit farther on their way they

came to a brook which ran through a green meadow, and the youngest said now the time was come to give one another names; "Since we set off in such a hurry that we hadn't time to do it at home, we may as well do it here."

"Well," said the elder, "and what shall your name be?"

"Oh!" said the younger, "my name shall be Shortshanks; and yours, what shall it be?"

"I will be called King Sturdy," answered the eldest.

So they christened each other in the brook, and went on; but when they had walked a while they came to a cross road, and agreed they should part there, and each take his own road. So they parted, but they hadn't gone half a mile before their roads met again. So they parted the second time, and took each a road; but in a little while the same thing happened, and they met again, they scarce knew how; and the same thing happened a third time also. Then they agreed that they should each choose a quarter of the heavens, and one was to go east and the other west; but before they parted, the elder said:

"If you ever fall into misfortune or need, call three times on me, and I will come and help you; but mind you don't call on me till you are at the last pinch."

"Well!" said Shortshanks, "if that's to be the rule, I don't think we shall meet again very soon."

After that they bade each other good-bye, and Shortshanks went east and King Sturdy west.

Now, you must know when Shortshanks had gone a good bit alone, he met an old, old, crook-backed hag who had only one eye, and Shortshanks snapped it up.

"Oh! Oh!" screamed the hag, "what has become of my eye?"

"What will you give me," asked Shortshanks, "if you get

The brothers reached a brook running through a green meadow

The old hag gave him a tiny ship which grew bigger and bigger until it was the size of a real sailing ship

your eye back?"

"I'll give you a sword, and such a sword! It will put a whole army to flight, be it ever so great," answered the old woman.

"Out with it, then!" said Shortshanks.

So the old hag gave him the sword, and got her eye back again. After that Shortshanks wandered on a while, and another old, old, crook-backed hag met him who had only one eye, which Shortshanks stole before she was aware of him.

"Oh! Oh! Whatever has become of my eye?" screamed the hag.

"What will you give me to get your eye back?" asked Shortshanks.

"I'll give you a ship," said the woman, "which can sail over fresh water and salt water, and over high hills and deep dales."

"Well, out with it!" said Shortshanks.

So the old woman gave him a little tiny ship, no bigger than he could put in his pocket, and she got her eye back again, and they each went their way. But when he had wandered on a long, long way, he met a third time an old, old, crook-backed hag, with only one eye. This eye too, Shortshanks stole; and when the hag screamed and made a great to-do,

bawling out what had become of her eye, Shortshanks said, "What will you give me to get back your eye?"

Then she answered, "I'll give you the art how to brew a hundred lasts of malt at one strike."

Well, for teaching that art the old hag got back her eye, and they each went their way.

But when Shortshanks had walked a little way, he thought it might be worth while to try his ship; so he took it out of his pocket, and put first one foot into it, and then the other; and as soon as ever he set one foot into it began to grow bigger and bigger, and by the time he set the other foot into it, it was as big as other ships that sail on the sea. Then Shortshanks said, "Off and away, over fresh water and salt water, over high hills and deep dales, and don't stop till you come to the king's palace."

And lo! away went the ship as swiftly as a bird through the air, till it came down a little below the king's palace, and there it stopped. From the palace windows people had stood and seen Shortshanks come sailing along, and they were all so amazed that they ran down to see who it could be that came sailing in a ship through the air. But while they were running down, Shortshanks had stepped out of his ship and put it into his pocket again; for as soon as he stepped out of it, it became as small as it was when he got

The ship landed beside a rich palace

it from the old woman. So those who had run down from the palace saw no one but a ragged little boy standing down there by the strand. Then the king asked whence he came, but the boy said he didn't know, nor could he tell them how he had got there. There he was, and that was all they could get out of him; but he begged and prayed so prettily to get a place in the king's palace, saying, if there was nothing else for him to do he could carry in wood and water for the kitchen-maid, that their hearts were touched, and he got leave to stay there.

Now when Shortshanks came up to the palace he saw how it was all hung with black, both outside and in, wall and roof; so he asked the kitchen-maid what all that mourning meant.

"Don't you know?" said the kitchen-maid; "I'll soon tell

There was a mound of gold and silver rings on the ship

you: the king's daughter was promised away a long time ago to three Ogres, and next Thursday evening one of them is coming to fetch her. Ritter Red, it is true, has given out that he is man enough to set her free, but God knows if he can do it; and now you know why we are all in grief and sorrow."

So when Thursday evening came, Ritter Red led the Princess down to the strand, for there it was she was to meet the Ogre, and he was to stay by her there and watch; but he wasn't likely to do the Ogre much harm, I reckon, for as soon as ever the Princess had sat down on the strand Ritter Red climbed up into a great tree that stood there, and hid himself as well as he could among the boughs. The Princess begged and prayed him not to leave her, but Ritter Red turned a deaf ear to her, and all he said was, "'Tis better for one to lose life than for two."

That was what Ritter Red said.

Meantime Shortshanks went to the kitchen-maid, and asked her so prettily if he mightn't go down to the strand for a bit.

"And what should take you down to the strand?" asked the kitchen-maid. "You know you've no business there."

"Oh, dear friend," said Shortshanks, "do let me go! I should so like to run down there and play a while with the other children; that I should."

"Well, well!" said the kitchen-maid, "off with you; but don't let me catch you staying there a bit over the time when the brose for supper must be set on the fire, and the roast put on the spit; and let me see, when you come back mind you bring a good armful of wood with you."

Yes, Shortshanks would mind all that; so off he ran down to the strand.

But just as he reached the spot where the Princess sat, what should come but the Ogre tearing along in his ship, so that the wind roared and howled after him. He was so tall and stout it was awful to look on him, and he had five heads of his own.

"Fire and flame!" screamed the Ogre.

"Fire and flame yourself!" said Shortshanks.

"Can you fight?" roared the Ogre.

"If I can't, I can learn," said Shortshanks.

So the Ogre struck at him with a great thick iron club which he had in his fist, and the earth and stones flew up five yards into the air after the stroke.

"My!" said Shortshanks, "that was something like a blow, but now you shall see a stroke of mine."

Then he grasped the sword he had got from the old crook-backed hag, and cut at the Ogre; and away went all his five heads flying over the sand. So when the Princess saw she was saved, she was so glad that she scarce knew what to do, and she jumped and danced for joy. "Come, lie down, and sleep a little in my lap," she said to Shortshanks, and as he slept she threw over him a tinsel robe.

Now you must know it wasn't long before Ritter Red crept down from the tree, as soon as he saw there was nothing to fear in the way, and he went up to the Princess and threatened her, until she promised to say it was he who had saved her life; for if she wouldn't say so, he said he would kill her on the spot. After that he cut out the Ogre's lungs and tongue, and wrapped them up in his handkerchief, and so led the Princess back to the palace, and whatever honours he had not before he got then, for the king did not know how to find honour enough for him, and made him sit every day on his right hand at dinner.

As for Shortshanks, he went first of all on board the Ogre's ship, and took a whole heap of gold and silver rings, as large as hoops, and trotted off with them as hard as he could to the palace. When the kitchen-maid set her eyes on all that gold and silver, she was quite scared, and asked him, "But dear, good Shortshanks, wherever did you get all this from?" for she was rather afraid he hadn't come rightly by it.

The kitchen-maid was always very busy but was still willing to let
Shortshanks escape down to the harbour

The princess and Shortshanks were married and what a grand wedding it was!

"Oh!" answered Shortshanks, "I went home for a bit, and there I found these hoops, which had fallen off some old pails of ours, so I laid hands on them for you if you must know."

Well, when the kitchen-maid heard they were for her, she said nothing more about the matter, but thanked

Shortshanks and they were good friends again.

The next Thursday evening it was the same story over again; all were in grief and trouble, but Ritter Red said, as he had saved the Princess from one Ogre it was hard if he couldn't save her from another; and down he led her to the strand as brave as a lion. But he didn't do this Ogre much harm either, for when the time came that they looked for the Ogre he said, as he had said before, " 'Tis better one should lose life than two," and crept up into his tree again. But Shortshanks begged the kitchen-maid to let him go down to the strand for a little.

"Oh!" asked the kitchen-maid, "and what business have you down there?"

"Dear friend," said Shortshanks, "do pray let me go! I long so to run down and play a while with the other children."

Well, the kitchen-maid gave him leave to go, but he must promise to be back by the time the roast was turned, and he was to mind and bring a big bundle of wood with him. So Shortshanks had scarce got down to the strand when the Ogre came tearing along in his ship, so that the wind howled and roared around him; he was twice as big as the other Ogre, and he had ten heads on his shoulders.

"Fire and flame!" screamed the Ogre.

"Fire and flame yourself!" answered Shortshanks.

"Can you fight?" roared the Ogre.

"If I can't, I can learn," said Shortshanks.

Then the Ogre struck at him with his iron club; it was even bigger than that which the first Ogre had, and the earth and stones flew up ten yards into the air.

"My!" said Shortshanks, "that was something like a blow; now you shall see a stroke of mine." Then he grasped his sword, and cut off all the Ogre's ten heads at one blow, and sent them dancing away over the sand.

Then the Princess said again to him, "Lie down and sleep a little while on my lap;" and while Shortshanks lay there, she threw over him a silver robe. But as soon as Ritter Red marked that there was no more danger in the way he crept down from the tree, and threatened the Princess, till she was forced to give her word to say it was he who had set her free; after that he cut the lungs and tongue out of the Ogre, and wrapped them in his handkerchief, and led the Princess back to the palace. Then you may fancy what mirth and joy there was, and the king was at his wits' end to know how to show Ritter Red honour and favour enough.

This time, too, Shortshanks took a whole armful of gold and silver rings from the Ogre's ship, and when he came back to the palace the kitchen-maid clapped her hands in wonder, asking wherever he got all that gold and silver from. But Shortshanks answered that he had been home a while,

Everyone in the locality celebrated the fact that Shortshanks and his beautiful princess were to be married

and that the hoops had fallen off some old pails, so he had laid his hands on them for his friend the kitchen-maid.

So when the third Thursday evening came, everything happened as it had happened twice before; the whole palace was hung with black, and all went about mourning and weeping. But Ritter Red said he couldn't see what need they had to be so afraid; he had freed the Princess from two Ogres, and he could very well free her from a third; so he led her down to the strand, but when the time drew near for the Ogre to come up, he crept into his tree again and hid himself. The Princess begged and prayed, but it was no good, for Ritter Red said again,—

" 'Tis better that one should lose life than two."

That evening, too, Shortshanks begged for leave to go down to the strand.

"Oh!" said the kitchen-maid, "what should take you down there?"

But he begged and prayed so, that at last he got leave to go, only he had to promise to be back in the kitchen again when the roast was to be turned. So off he went, but he had scarce reached the strand when the Ogre came with the wind howling and roaring after him. He was much, much bigger than either of the other two, and he had fifteen heads on his shoulders.

"Fire and flame!" roared out the Ogre.

"Fire and flame yourself!" said Shortshanks.

"Can you fight?" screamed the Ogre.

"If I can't, I can learn," said Shortshanks.

"I'll soon teach you," screamed the Ogre, and struck at him with his iron club, so that the earth and stones flew up fifteen yards into the air.

"My!" said Shortshanks, "that was something like a blow; but now you shall see a stroke of mine."

As he said that, he grasped his sword, and cut off all the Ogre's fifteen heads at one blow, and sent them all dancing over the sand.

So the Princess was freed from all the Ogres, and she both blessed and thanked Shortshanks for saving her life.

"Sleep now a while on my lap," she said; and he laid his head on her lap, and while he slept she threw over him a golden robe.

"But how shall we let it be known that it is you that have saved me?" she asked, when he awoke.

"Oh, I'll soon tell you," answered Shortshanks. "When Ritter Red has led you home again, and given himself out as the man who has saved you, you know he is to have you to wife, and half the kingdom. Now, when they ask you, on your wedding-day, whom you will have to be your cup-bearer, you must say, 'I will have the ragged boy who does odd jobs in the kitchen, and carries in wood and water for the kitchen-maid.' So, when I am filling your cups, I will spill a drop on his plate, but none on yours; then he will be wroth and give me a blow; and the same thing will happen three times. But the third time you must mind and say, 'Shame on you! to strike my heart's darling; he it is who set me free, and him will I have.' "

After that Shortshanks ran back to the palace, as he had done before; but he went first on board the Ogre's ship, and took a whole heap of gold, silver, and precious stones, and out of them he gave the kitchen-maid another great armful of gold and silver rings.

Well, as for Ritter Red, as soon as ever he saw that all risk was over he crept down from his tree, and threatened the Princess till she was forced to promise she would say it was he who had saved her. After that he led her back to the palace, and all the honour shown him before was nothing to what he got now, for the king thought of nothing else than how he might best honour the man who had saved his daughter from the three Ogres. As for his marrying her, and having half the kingdom, that was a settled thing, the king said. But when the wedding-day came, the Princess begged she might have the ragged boy, who carried in wood and water for the cook, to be her cup-bearer at the bridal-feast.

"I can't think why you should want to bring that filthy beggar boy in here," said Ritter Red; but the Princess had a will of her own, and said she would have him, and no one else, to pour out her wine; so she had her way at last. Now everything went as it had been agreed between Shortshanks and the Princess; he spilled a drop on Ritter Red's plate, but none on hers, and each time Ritter Red got wroth and struck him. At the first blow Shortshanks' rags fell off which he had worn in the kitchen; at the second the tinsel robe fell off; and at the third the silver robe; and then he stood in his golden robe, all gleaming and glittering in the light. Then the Princess said, "Shame on you! to strike my heart's darling; he has saved me, and him will I have."

Ritter Red cursed and swore it was he who had set her free; but the king put in his word, and said, "The man who saved my daughter must have some token to show for it."

Yes! Ritter Red had something to show, and he ran off at once after his handkerchief with the lungs and tongues in it; and Shortshanks fetched all the gold and silver and precious things he had taken out of the Ogres' ships. So each laid his tokens before the king, and the king said, "The man who has such precious stores of gold, and silver, and diamonds, must have slain the Ogre, and spoiled his goods, for such things are not to be had elsewhere."

So Ritter Red was thrown into a pit full of snakes, and Shortshanks was to have the Princess and half the kingdom.

One day Shortshanks and the king were out walking, and Shortshanks asked the king if he hadn't any more children.

"Yes," said the king, "I had another daughter; but the Ogre has taken her away, because there was no one who could save her. Now you are going to have one daughter, but if you can set the other free, whom the Ogre has carried off, you shall have her too, with all my heart, and the other half of my kingdom."

"Well," said Shortshanks, "I may as well try; but I must have an iron cable, five hundred fathoms long, and five hundred men, and food for them to last fifteen weeks, for

I have a long voyage before me."

Yes, the king said he should have them, but he was afraid there wasn't a ship in his kingdom big enough to carry such a freight.

"Oh! if that's all," said Shortshanks, "I have a ship of my own."

With that he whipped out of his pocket the ship he had got from the old hag.

The king laughed, and thought it was all a joke; but Shortshanks begged him only to give him what he asked, and he should soon see if it was a joke. So they got together what he wanted, and Shortshanks bade him put the cable on board the ship first of all; but there was no one man who could lift it, and there wasn't room for more than one at a time round the tiny ship. Then Shortshanks took hold of the cable by one end, and laid a link or two into the ship; and as he threw in the links, the ship grew bigger and bigger, till at last it got so big that there was room enough and to spare in it for the cable, and the five hundred men, and their food, and Shortshanks, and all. Then he said to the ship, "Off and away, over fresh water and salt water, over high hill and deep dale, and don't stop till you come to where the king's daughter is." And away went the ship over land and sea, till the wind whistled after it.

So when they had sailed far, far away, the ship stood stock still in the middle of the sea.

"Ah!" said Shortshanks, "now we have got so far; but how we are to get back is another story."

Then he took the cable and tied one end of it round his waist, and said, "Now, I must go to the bottom, but when I give the cable a good tug, and want to come up again, mind you all hoist away with a will, or your lives will be lost as well as mine;" and with these words overboard he leapt, and dived down, so that the yellow waves rose round him in an eddy.

Well, he sank and sank, and at last he came to the bottom, and there he saw a great rock rising up with a door in it, so he opened the door and went in. When he got inside, he saw another Princess, who sat and sewed, but when she saw Shortshanks, she clasped her hands together and cried out, "Now, God be thanked! You are the first Christian man I've set eyes on since I came here."

"Very good," said Shortshanks; "but do you know I've come to fetch you?"

"Oh!" she cried, "you'll never fetch me; you'll never have that luck, for if the Ogre sees you, he'll kill you on the spot."

"I'm glad you spoke of the Ogre," said Shortshanks; " 'twould be fine fun to see him; whereabouts is he?"

Then the Princess told him the Ogre was out looking for some one who could brew a hundred lasts of malt at one strike, for he was going to give a great feast, and less drink wouldn't do.

"Well! I can do that," said Shortshanks.

"Ah!" said the Princess, "if only the Ogre wasn't so hasty, I might tell him about you; but he's so cross; I'm afraid

he'll tear you to pieces as soon as he comes in, without waiting to hear my story. Let me see what is to be done. Oh! I have it; just hide yourself in the side-room yonder, and let us take our chance."

Well, Shortshanks did as she told him, and he had scarce crept into the side-room before the Ogre came in.

"HUF!" said the Ogre; "what a horrid smell of Christian man's blood!"

"Yes!" said the Princess, "I know there is, for a bird flew over the house with a Christian man's bone in his bill, and let it fall down the chimney. I made all the haste I could to get it out again, but I daresay it's that you smell."

"Ah!" said the Ogre, "like enough."

Then the Princess asked the Ogre if he had laid hold of any one who could brew a hundred lasts of malt at one strike?

"No," said the Ogre, "I can't hear of any one who can do it."

"Well," she said, "a while ago, there was a chap in here who said he could do it."

"Just like you, with your wisdom!" said the Ogre; "why did you let him go away then, when you knew he was the very man I wanted?"

"Well, then, I didn't let him go," said the Princess; "but father's temper is a little hot, so I hid him away in the side-room yonder; but if father hasn't hit upon any one, here he is."

"Well," said the Ogre, "let him come in then."

So Shortshanks came in, and the Ogre asked him if it were true that he could brew a hundred lasts of malt at a strike.

"Yes, it is," said Shortshanks.

" 'Twas good luck then to lay hands on you," said the Ogre, "and now fall to work this minute; but heaven help you if you don't brew the ale strong enough."

"Oh," said Shortshanks, "never fear, it shall be stinging stuff;" and with that he began to brew without more fuss, but all at once he cried out, "I must have more of you Ogres to help in the brewing for these I have got ain't half strong enough."

Well, he got more – so many, that there was a whole swarm of them, and then the brewing went on bravely. Now when the sweet-wort was ready, they were all eager to taste it, you may guess; first of all the Ogre, and then all his kith and kin. But Shortshanks had brewed the wort so strong that they all fell down dead, one after another, like so many flies, as soon as they had tasted it. At last there wasn't one of them left alive but one vile old hag, who lay bed-ridden in the chimney corner.

"Oh, you poor old wretch!" said Shortshanks, "you may just as well taste the wort along with the rest."

So he went and scooped up a little from the bottom of the copper in a scoop, and gave her a drink, and so he was rid of the whole pack of them.

As he stood there and looked about him, he cast his eye on a great chest, so he took it and filled it with gold and silver; then he tied the cable round himself and the Princess and the chest, and gave it a good tug, and his men pulled them all up, safe and sound. As soon as ever Shortshanks was well up, he said to the ship, "Off and away, over fresh water and salt water, high hill and deep dale, and don't stop till you come to the king's palace;" and straightway the ship held on her course, so that the yellow billows foamed round her. When the people in the palace saw the ship sailing up, they were not slow in meeting them with songs and music, welcoming Shortshanks with great joy; but the gladdest of all was the king, who had now got his other daughter back again.

But now Shortshanks was rather down-hearted, for you must know that both the Princesses wanted to have him, and he would have no other than the one he had first saved, and she was the youngest. So he walked up and down, and thought and thought what he should do to get her, and yet do something to please her sister. Well, one day as he was turning the thing over in his mind, it struck him if he only had his brother King Sturdy, who was so like him that no one could tell the one from the other, he would give up to him the other princess and half the kingdom, for he thought one-half was quite enough.

Well, as soon as ever this came into his mind, he went outside the palace and called on King Sturdy, but no one came. So he called a second time a little louder, but still no one came. Then he called out the third time "King Sturdy!" with all his might, and there stood his brother before him.

"Didn't I say!" he said to Shortshanks, "didn't I say you were not to call me except in your utmost need! and here there is not so much as a gnat to do you any harm," and with that he gave him such a box on the ear that Shortshanks tumbled head over heels on the grass.

"Now shame on you to hit so hard!" said Shortshanks. "First of all I won a princess and half the kingdom, and then I won another princess and the other half of the kingdom; and now I'm thinking to give you one of the princesses and half the kingdom. Is there any rhyme or reason in giving me such a box on the ear?"

When King Sturdy heard that, he begged his brother to forgive him, and they were soon as good friends as ever again.

"Now," said Shortshanks, "you know, we are so much alike that no one can tell the one from the other; so just change clothes with me and go into the palace; then the princesses will think it is I that am coming in, and the one that kisses you first you shall have for your wife, and I will have the other for mine."

And he said this because he knew well enough that the elder king's daughter was the stronger, and so he could very well guess how things would go. As for King Sturdy, he was willing enough, so he changed clothes with his brother and went into the palace. But when he came into the Princesses' bower they thought it was Shortshanks, and both ran up to him to kiss him; but the elder, who was stronger and bigger, pushed her sister on one side, and threw her arms round King Sturdy's neck, and gave him a kiss; and so he got her for his wife, and Shortshanks got the younger Princess. Then they made ready for the wedding, and you may fancy what a grand one it was, when I tell you that the fame of it was noised abroad over seven kingdoms.

The wedding was celebrated right across the country

The Three Lemons

This story retold by Parker Fillmore (1878-1944) is a Czechoslovak fairy tale, first published in 1919. It describes the adventures of young prince in his search for a magic lemon tree and a bride.

what to do, an old woman suddenly appeared before him.

"Go," she said, "to the top of the Glass Hill, pluck the three lemons, and you will get a wife in whom your heart will delight." With that she disappeared as mysteriously as she had come.

Her words went through the prince's soul like a bright dart. Instantly he determined, come what might, to find the Glass Hill and to pluck the three lemons. He told his father his intention and the old king fitted him out for the journey and gave him his blessing.

Once upon a time there was an aged king who had an only son. One day he called the prince to him and said: "My son, you see that my head is white. Soon I shall be closing my eyes and you are not yet settled in life. Marry, my son, marry at once so that I can bless you before I die."

The prince made no answer but he took the king's words to heart and pondered them. He would gladly have done as his father wished but there was no young girl upon whom his affections were set.

One day when he was sitting in the garden, wondering

For a long time the prince wandered over wooded mountains and desert plains without seeing or even hearing anything of the Glass Hill and the three lemons. One day, worn out with his long journey, he threw himself down in the shade of a wide-spreading linden tree. As his father's sword, which he wore at his side, clanked on the ground, twelve ravens began cawing from the top of the tree. Frightened by the clanking of the sword, they raised their wings and flew off.

The prince jumped to his feet. "Those are the first living creatures I have seen for many a day. I'll go in the direction

Twelve ravens were cawing

they have taken," he said to himself, "and perhaps I'll have better luck."

So he traveled on and after three days and three nights a high castle came in view.

"Thank God!" he exclaimed, pushing joyfully ahead. "I shall soon have human companionship once more."

The castle was built entirely of lead. The twelve ravens circled above it and in front of it stood an old woman leaning on a long leaden staff. She was a Yezibaba. Now you must know that a Yezibaba is an ugly old witch with a hooked nose, a bristly face, and long scrawny hands. She's a bad old thing usually, but sometimes, if you take her fancy, she's kind.

This time when she looked the prince over she shook her head at him in a friendly way.

"Yi, yi, my boy, how did you get here? Why, not even a little bird or a tiny butterfly comes here, much less a human being! You'd better escape if life is dear to you, or my son, when he comes home, will eat you!"

"No, no, old mother, don't make me go," begged the prince.

"I have come to you for advice to know whether you can tell me anything about the glass hill and the three lemons."

"No, I have never heard a word about the Glass Hill," Yezibaba said. "But wait until my son comes. He may be able to tell you something. Yes, yes, I'll manage to save you somehow. Go hide under the besom and stay there until I call you."

The mountains rumbled and the castle trembled and Yezibaba whispered to the prince that her son was coming.

"Phew! Phew! I smell human meat! I'll eat it!" shouted Yezibaba's son while he was still in the doorway. He struck the ground with his leaden club and the whole castle shook.

"No, no, my son, don't talk that way. It's true there is a pretty youth here, but he's come to ask you about something."

"Well, if he wants to ask me something, let him come out and ask."

"Yes, my son, he will, but only when you promise me that

564

you will do nothing to him."

"Well, I won't do anything to him. Now let him come out."

The prince hidden under the besom was shaking like an aspen leaf, for when he peeped through the twigs he saw an ogre so huge that he himself would reach up only to his knees. Happily the ogre had guaranteed his life before Yezibaba ordered him out.

"Well, well, well, you little June bug!" shouted the ogre. "What are you afraid of? Where have you been? What do you want?"

"What do I want?" repeated the prince. "I have been wandering in these mountains a long time and I can't find what I'm seeking. So I've come to you to ask whether you can tell me something about the Glass Hill and the three lemons."

Yezibaba's son wrinkled his forehead. He thought for a moment and then, lowering his voice a little, he said: "I've never heard of any Glass Hill around here. But I can tell you what to do: go on to my brother in arms who lives in the Silver Castle and ask him. Maybe he'll be to tell you. But I can't let you go away hungry. That would never do! Hi, mother, bring out the dumplings!"

Old Yezibaba placed a large dish on the table and her giant son sat down.

"Well, come on! Eat!" he shouted to the prince.

When the prince took the first dumpling and bit into it, he almost broke two of his teeth, for the dumplings were made of lead.

"Well," shouted Yezibaba's son, "why don't you eat? Doesn't the dumpling taste good?"

"Oh, yes, very good," said the prince, politely, "but just now I'm not hungry."

"Well, if you're not hungry now you will be later. Put a few in your pocket and eat them on your journey."

So, whether he wanted them or not, the prince had to put some leaden dumplings into his pocket. Then he took his leave of Yezibaba and her son and traveled on.

He went on and on for three days and three nights. The farther he went, the more inhospitable became the country. Before him stretched a waste of mountains behind him a waste of mountains with no living creatures in sight.

Wearied with his long journey, he threw himself on the ground. His silver sword clanked sharply and at its sound twenty-four ravens circled above him, cawed in fright, and flew away.

"A good sign!" cried the prince. "I'll follow the ravens again!"

So on he went as fast as his legs could carry him until he came in sight of a tall castle. It was still far away, but even at that distance it shone and flashed for it was built of pure silver.

In front of the castle stood an old woman, bent with age, and leaning on a silver staff. This was the second Yezibaba.

"Yi, yi, my boy!" she cried. "How did you get here? Why, not even a little bird or a tiny butterfly comes here, much less a human being. You'd better escape if life is dear to you, or my son, when he comes home, will eat you!"

"No, no, old mother, he won't eat me. I bring greetings from his brother of the Leaden Castle."

"Well, if you bring greetings from the Leaden Castle you are safe enough. Come in, my boy, and tell me your business."

"My business? For a long time, old mother, I've been looking for the Glass Hill and the three lemons, but I can't find them. So I've some to ask you whether you could tell me something about them."

"No, my boy, I don't know anything about the Glass Hill. But wait until my son comes. Perhaps he can help you. In the meantime hide yourself under the bed and don't come out until I call you."

The mountains rumbled and the castle trembled and the prince knew that Yezibaba's son was coming home.

"Phew! Phew! I smell human meat! I'll eat it!" bellowed the mighty fellow. He stood in the doorway and banged the ground with his silver club until the whole castle shook.

"No, no, my son," said Yezibaba, "don't talk that way! A pretty little chap has come bringing you greetings from your brother of the Leaden Castle."

"Well, if he's been at the Leaden Castle and came to no harm, he'll have nothing to fear from me either. Where is he?"

The bent old woman warned the boy to escape

The prince slipped out from under the bed and stood before the ogre. Looking up at him was like looking at the top of the tallest pine tree.

"Well, little June bug, so you've been at my brother's eh?"

"Yes," said the prince. "See, I still have the dumplings he gave me for the journey."

"I believe you. Well, what do you want?"

"What do I want? I came to ask you whether you could tell me something about the Glass Hill and the three lemons."

"H'm, it seems to me I used to hear something about them, but I forget. I tell you what you do: go to my brother of the Golden Castle and ask him. But wait! I can't let you go away hungry. Hi, mother, bring out the dumplings!"

Yezibaba brought the dumplings on a large silver dish and put them on the table.

"Eat!" shouted her son.

The prince saw they were silver dumplings, so he said he wasn't hungry just then, but he'd like to take some with him for the journey.

"Take as many as you want," shouted the ogre. "And give my greetings to my brother and my aunt."

So the prince took some silver dumplings, made suitable thanks, and departed.

He journeyed on from the Silver Castle three days and three nights, through dense forests and over rough mountains, not knowing where he was nor which way to turn. At last all worn out he threw himself down in the shade of a beech tree to rest. As the sword clanked on the ground, its silver voice rang out and a flock of thirty-six ravens circled over his head.

"Caw! Caw!" they croaked. Then, frightened by the sound of the sword, they flew away.

"Praise God!" cried the prince. "The Golden Castle can't be far!"

He jumped up and started eagerly off in the direction the ravens had taken. As he left a valley and climbed a little hill he saw before him a beautiful wide meadow in the midst of which stood the Golden Castle shining like the sun. Before the gate of the castle stood a bent old Yezibaba leaning on a golden staff.

"Yi, yi, my boy," she cried to the prince, "how did you get here? Why, not even a little bird or a tiny butterfly comes here, much less a human being! You'd better escape if life is dear to you, or my son, when he comes, will eat you!"

"No, no, old mother, he won't eat me, for I bring him greetings from his brother of the Silver Castle!"

"Well, if you bring greetings from the Silver Castle you are safe enough. Come in, my boy, and tell me your business."

"My business, old mother? For a long time I've been wandering over these wild mountains in search of the Glass Hill and the three lemons. At the Silver Castle they

Yezibaba explained how the boy had come from the Leaden Castle

sent me to you because they thought you might know something about them."

"The Glass Hill? No, I don't know where it is. But wait until my son comes. He will advise you where to go and what to do. Hide under the table and stay there until I call you."

The mountains rumbled and the castle trembled and Yezibaba's son came home.

"Phew! Phew! I smell human meat! I'll eat it!" he roared. He stood in the doorway and pounded the ground with his golden club until the whole castle shook.

"No, no, my son," said Yezibaba, "don't talk that way! A pretty little fellow has come bringing you greetings from

"Take the dumplings!" shouted the ogre

your brother of the Silver Castle. If you won't harm him, I'll call him out."

"Well, if my brother didn't do anything to him, I won't either."

So the prince crawled out from under the table and stood before the giant. It was like standing beneath a high tower. He showed the ogre the silver dumplings as proof that he had been at the Silver Castle.

"Well, well, well, my little June bug," shouted the monstrous fellow, "tell me what it is you want! I'll advise you if I can! Don't be afraid!"

So the prince told him the purpose of his journey and asked him how to get to the Glass Hill and pluck the three lemons.

"Do you see that blackish lump over yonder?" the ogre said, pointing with his golden club. "That is the Glass Hill. On that hill stands a tree. From that tree hang three lemons which send out fragrance for seven miles around. You will climb the Glass Hill, kneel beneath the tree, and reach up your hands. If the lemons are destined for you they will fall into your hands of their own accord. If they are not destined for you, you will not be able to pluck them no matter what you do. As you return, if you are hungry or thirsty, cut open one of the lemons and you will have food and drink in plenty. Go now with God's blessing. But wait! I can't let you go away hungry! Hi, mother, bring out the dumplings!"

Yezibaba set a large golden dish on the table.

"Eat!" her son shouted. "Or, if you are not hungry just now, put some in your pocket and eat them on the way."

The prince said that he was not hungry but that he would be glad to take some of the golden dumplings with him and eat them later. Then he thanked the ogre most courteously for his hospitality and advice and took his leave.

He trudged quickly on the hill to dale, from dale to hill again, and never stopped until he reached the Glass Hill itself. Then he stood still as if turned into stone. The hill was high and steep and smooth with not so much as a scratch on its surface. Over its top spread out the branches of the magic tree upon which hung the three lemons. Their fragrance was so powerful that the prince almost fainted.

"Let it be as God wills!" he thought to himself. "But however the adventure is to come out, now that I'm here I must at least make the attempt."

So he began to claw his way up the smooth glass, but he hadn't gone many yards before his foot slipped and down he went so hard that he didn't know where he was or what had happened to him until he found himself sitting on the ground.

In his vexation he began to throw away the dumplings thinking that perhaps their weight had dragged him down. He took one and threw it straight at the hill. Imagine his surprise to see it fix itself firmly in the glass. He threw a second and third and there he had three steps on which he was able to stand with safety!

The prince was overjoyed. He threw dumpling after dumpling and each one became a step. First he threw the leaden ones, then the silver ones, and last of all the golden ones. On the steps made in this way he climbed higher and higher until he reached the very summit of the hill. Then he knelt under the magic tree, lifted up his hands, and into them the three lemons dropped of their own accord!

Instantly the tree disappeared, the Glass Hill sank until it was lost, and when the prince came to himself there was neither tree nor hill to be seen, but only a wide plain.

Delighted with the outcome of his adventure, the prince turned homewards. At first he was too happy even to eat or drink. By the third day his stomach began to protest and he discovered that he was so hungry that he would have fallen ravenously upon a leaden dumpling if he had one in his pocket. But his pocket, alas, was empty, and the country all about was as bare as the palm of his hand.

Then he remembered what the ogre of the Golden Castle had told him and he took out one of the three lemons. He cut it open, and what do you suppose happened? Out jumped a beautiful maiden fresh from the hand of God, who bowed low before him and exclaimed:

"Have you food ready for me? Have you drink ready for me? Have you pretty clothes ready for me?"

"Alas, beautiful creature," the prince sighed, "I have not. I have nothing for you to eat or to drink or to put on."

The lovely maiden clapped her hands three times, bowed before him and disappeared.

"Ah," said the prince, "now I know what kind of lemons you are! I'll think twice before opening one of you again!"

Of the one he had opened he ate and drank his fill, and so refreshed, went on. He traveled three days and three nights and by that time he began to feel three times hungrier than before.

"God help me!" thought he. "I must eat something! There are still two lemons and if I cut open one there would still be one left."

So he took out the second lemon, cut it in two, and lo, a maiden twice as beautiful as the first stood before him. She bowed low and said:

"Have you food ready for me? Have you drink ready for me? Have you pretty clothes ready for me?"

"No, lovely creature, I haven't! I haven't!"

The maiden clapped her hands thrice, bowed before him, and disappeared.

Now there was only one lemon left. The prince took it in his hand, looked at it, and said: "I won't cut you open until I'm safe at home in my father's house."

The sweet young maiden had been trapped inside a lemon in the enchanted tree

He took up his journey again and on the third day he came to his native town and his father's castle. He had been gone a long time and how he ever got back he didn't know himself.

Tears of joy rained down the old king's cheeks.

"Welcome home, my son, welcome a hundred times!" he cried, falling on the prince's neck.

The prince related the adventures of his journey and they at home told him how anxiously they had awaited his return.

On the next day a great feast was prepared. All the

nobles in the land were invited. The tables were spread with food and drink the most expensive in the world and many rich dresses embroidered in gold and studded with pearls were laid out.

The guests assembled, seated themselves at the tables, and waited. Music played and when all was ready, the prince took the last lemon and cut it in two. Out jumped a beautiful creature, three times lovelier than the others.

"Have you food ready for me?" she cried. "Have you drink ready for me? Have you pretty clothes ready for me?"

"I have indeed, dear heart!" the prince answered. "I have everything ready for you!"

He led her to the gorgeous clothes and she dressed herself in them and every one present marveled at her great beauty.

Soon the betrothal took place and after the betrothal a magnificent wedding.

So now the old king's wish was fulfilled. He blessed his son, gave the kingdom to him, and not long afterwards he died.

The first thing that faced the young king after his father's death was a war which a neighboring king stirred up against him. So the young king stirred up against him. So the young king had to bid farewell to the bride whom he had won so dearly and lead his men to battle. In order that nothing happen to his queen in his absence, he built a golden throne for her in the garden beside the lake. This throne was as high as a tower and no one could ascend it except those to whom the queen let down a silken cord.

Not far from the king's castle lived an old woman who, in the first place, had told him about the three lemons. She knew well enough how the young king had won his bride and she was deeply incensed that he had not invited her to the wedding and in fact and in fact had not even thanked her for her good advice.

Now this old woman had a gipsy for a servant whom she used to send to the lake for water. One day when this gipsy was filling her pitcher, she saw in the lake a beautiful reflection. She supposed it was a reflection of herself.

"Is it right," she cried out, "that so lovely a creature as I should carry water for that old witch?"

In a fury she threw the pitcher on the ground and broke it into a hundred pieces. Then she looked up and discovered that it wasn't her own reflection she had seen in the water but that of the beautiful queen.

Ashamed of herself, she picked up the broken pitcher and went home. The old woman, who knew beforehand what had happened, went out to meet her with a new pitcher.

"It's no matter about the pitcher," the old woman said. "Go back to the lake and beg the lovely lady to let down the silken cord and pull you up. Tell her you will comb her hair. When she pulls you up, comb her hair until she falls asleep. Then stick this pin into her head. After that you can dress yourself up in her clothes and sit there like a queen."

It was easy enough to persuade the gipsy. She took the pitcher and the pin and returned to the lake.

As she drew water she gazed at the lovely queen.

"Oh, how beautiful you are!" she whined, leering up at the queen with an evil eye. "How beautiful you are! Aye, but you'd be a hundred times more beautiful if you but let me comb out your lovely hair! Indeed, I would so twine those golden tresses that your lord would be delighted!"

With words like these she beguiled and coaxed the queen until she let down the silken cord and drew the gipsy up. Once on the throne, the wicked gipsy combed out the golden tresses and plaited them and arranged them until the queen fell sound asleep. Then the gipsy took the pin and stuck it into the queen's head. Instantly a beautiful white dove flew off the golden throne and not a trace was left of the lovely queen except her rich clothing. The gipsy dressed herself in this, sat in the queen's place, and gazed down into the lake. But in the lake no lovely reflection showed itself, for even in the queen's clothes the gipsy remained a gipsy.

The young king waged a successful war against his enemies and made peace. Scarcely had he got home when he hurried to the garden to see whether anything had happened to his heart's delight. Who can express in words his astonishment and horror when instead of his beautiful wife he saw the evil gipsy!

"Ah, my dearest one, how you have changed!" he murmured and tears flowed down his cheeks.

"Yes, my dear, I have changed, I know I have," the gipsy answered. "It was grief for you that has broken me."

She tried to fall on his neck but the king turned quickly away and left her.

From that time forth he had no peace but day and night he mourned the lost beauty of his wife and nothing consoled him.

Grieving in this way and thinking always the same sad thoughts, he was walking one day in the garden when suddenly a beautiful white dove flew down from a high tree and alighted on his hand. She looked up at him with eyes as mournful as his own.

"Ah, my poor dove," the king said, "why are you so sad? Has your mate also changed?"

As he spoke he stroked the dove gently on the back and on the head. On the head he felt a little lump. He blew aside the feathers and discovered the head of a pin. He pulled out the pin and instantly the sad dove changed into his own beautiful wife.

She told him what had happened to her, how the gipsy had deceived her and stuck the pin into her head. The king had the gipsy and old witch caught at once and burnt at the stake.

From that time on nothing happened to mar the king's happiness, neither the plots of his enemies nor the spite of evil people. He lived in love and peace with his beautiful wife and he ruled his kingdom wisely. In fact he's ruling it still if he hasn't died.

Vasilissa the Beautiful

This Russian fairy tale is one of the most well known that features the character of Baba Yaga (a hag who flies through the air in a mortar, using the pestle as a rudder and sweeping away the tracks behind her with a silver-birch broom). Aleksandr Rou made a movie of the story in 1939 – the first large-budget feature in the Soviet Union to employ elements of fantasy.

Beyond the highest mountains and deepest forests lay a Tsardom that encompassed three times nine kingdoms

In a certain Tsardom across three times nine kingdoms, beyond high mountain chains, there once lived a merchant. He had been married for twelve years, but in that time there had been born to him only one child, a daughter, who from her cradle was called Vasilissa the Beautiful. When the little girl was eight years old the mother fell ill, and before many days it was plain to be seen that she must die. So she called her little daughter to her, and taking a tiny wooden doll from under the blanket of the bed, put it into her hands and said:

"My little Vasilissa, my dear daughter, listen to what I say, remember well my last words and fail not to carry out my wishes. I am dying, and with my blessing, I leave to thee this little doll. It is very precious for there is no other like it in the whole world. Carry it always about with thee in thy pocket and never show it to anyone. When evil threatens thee or sorrow befalls thee, go into a corner, take it from thy pocket and give it something to eat and drink. It will eat and drink a little, and then thou mayest tell it thy trouble and ask its advice, and it will tell thee

*Vasilissa was sent into the deep forest on
many errands*

*The second rider was dressed in red and
rode a scarlet horse*

how to act in thy time of need." So saying, she kissed her little daughter on the forehead, blessed her, and shortly after died.

Little Vasilissa grieved greatly for her mother, and her sorrow was so deep that when the dark night came, she lay in her bed and wept and did not sleep. At length she bethought herself of the tiny doll, so she rose and took it from the pocket of her gown and finding a piece of wheat bread and a cup of kvass, she set them before it, and said: "There, my little doll, take it. Eat a little, and drink a little, and listen to my grief. My dear mother is dead and I am lonely for her."

Then the doll's eyes began to shine like fireflies, and suddenly it became alive. It ate a morsel of the bread and took a sip of the kvass, and when it had eaten and drunk, it said:

"Don't weep, little Vasilissa. Grief is worst at night. Lie down, shut thine eyes, comfort thyself and go to sleep. The morning is wiser than the evening." So Vasilissa the Beautiful lay down, comforted herself and went to sleep, and the next day her grieving was not so deep and her tears were less bitter.

Now after the death of his wife, the merchant sorrowed for many days as was right, but at the end of that time he began to desire to marry again and to look about him for a suitable wife. This was not difficult to find, for he had a fine house, with a stable of swift horses, besides being a good man who gave much to the poor. Of all the women he saw, however, the one who, to his mind, suited him best of all, was a widow of about his own age with two daughters of her own, and she, he thought, besides being a good housekeeper, would be a kind foster mother to his little Vasilissa.

So the merchant married the widow and brought her home as his wife, but the little girl soon found that her foster mother was very far from being what her father had thought. She was a cold, cruel woman, who had desired the merchant for the sake of his wealth, and had no love for his daughter. Vasilissa was the greatest beauty in the whole village, while her own daughters were as spare and homely as two crows, and because of this all three envied and hated her. They gave her all sorts of errands to run and difficult tasks to perform, in order that the toil might make her thin and worn and that her face might grow brown from sun and wind, and they treated her so cruelly as to leave few joys in life for her. But all this the little Vasilissa endured without complaint, and while the stepmother's two daughters grew always thinner and uglier, in spite of the fact that they had no hard tasks to do, never went out in cold or rain, and sat always with their arms folded like ladies of a Court, she herself had cheeks like blood and milk and grew every day more and more beautiful.

Now the reason for this was the tiny doll, without whose help little Vasilissa could never have managed to do all the work that was laid upon her. Each night, when everyone else was sound asleep, she would get up from her bed, take the doll into a closet, and locking the door, give it something to eat and drink, and say: "There, my little doll, take it. Eat a little, drink a little, and listen to my grief. I live in my father's house, but my spiteful stepmother wishes to drive me out of the white world. Tell me! How shall I act, and what shall I do?"

Then the little doll's eyes would begin to shine like glow-worms, and it would become alive. It would eat a little food, and sip a little drink, and then it would comfort her and tell her how to act. While Vasilissa slept, it would get ready all her work for the next day, so that she had only to rest in the shade and gather flowers, for the doll would have the kitchen garden weeded, and the beds of cabbage watered, and plenty of fresh water brought from the well, and the stoves heated exactly right. And, besides this, the little doll told her how to make, from a certain herb, an ointment which prevented her from ever being sunburnt. So all the joy in life that came to Vasilissa came to her through the tiny doll that she always carried in her pocket.

Years passed, till Vasilissa grew up and became of an age when it is good to marry. All the young men in the village, high and low, rich and poor, asked for her hand, while not one of them stopped even to look at the stepmother's two daughters, so ill-favored were they. This angered their mother still more against Vasilissa; she answered every gallant who came with the same words: "Never shall the younger be wed before the older ones!" and each time, when she had let a suitor out of the door, she would soothe her anger and hatred by beating her stepdaughter. So while Vasilissa grew each day more lovely and graceful, she was often miserable, and but for the little doll in her pocket, would have longed to leave the white world.

Now there came a time when it became necessary for the merchant to leave his home and to travel to a distant Tsardom. He bade farewell to his wife and her two daughters, kissed Vasilissa and gave her his blessing and departed, bidding them say a prayer each day for his safe return. Scarce was he out of sight of the village, however, when his wife sold his house, packed all his goods and moved with them to another dwelling far from the town, in a gloomy neighborhood on the edge of a wild forest. Here every day, while her two daughters were working indoors, the merchant's wife would send Vasilissa on one errand or other into the forest, either to find a branch of a certain rare bush or to bring her flowers or berries.

Now deep in this forest, as the stepmother well knew, there was a green lawn and on the lawn stood a miserable little hut on hens' legs, where lived a certain Baba Yaga, an old witch grandmother. She lived alone and none dared go near the hut, for she ate people as one eats chickens. The merchant's wife sent Vasilissa into the forest each day,

The third rider was dressed in black and rode a coal-black horse

hoping she might meet the old witch and be devoured; but always the girl came home safe and sound, because the little doll showed her where the bush, the flowers and the berries grew, and did not let her go near the hut that stood on hens' legs. And each time the stepmother hated her more and more because she came to no harm.

One autumn evening the merchant's wife called the three girls to her and gave them each a task. One of her daughters she bade make a piece of lace, the other to knit a pair of hose, and to Vasilissa she gave a basket of flax to be spun. She bade each finish a certain amount. Then she put out all the fires in the house, leaving only a single candle lighted in the room where the three girls worked, and she herself went to sleep.

They worked an hour, they worked two hours, they worked three hours, when one of the elder daughters took up the tongs to straighten the wick of the candle. She pretended to do this awkwardly (as her mother had bidden her) and put the candle out, as if by accident.

"What are we to do now?" asked her sister. "The fires are all out, there is no other light in all the house, and our tasks are not done."

"We must go and fetch fire," said the first. "The only house near is a hut in the forest, where a Baba Yaga lives. One of us must go and borrow fire from her."

"I have enough light from my steel pins," said the one who was making the lace, "and I will not go."

*The bony old witch swept her trail behind her
with a spindly broom*

"And I have plenty of light from my silver needles," said the other, who was knitting the hose, "and I will not go.

"Thou, Vasilissa," they both said, "shalt go and fetch the fire, for thou hast neither steel pins nor silver needles and cannot see to spin thy flax!" They both rose up, pushed Vasilissa out of the house and locked the door, crying:

"Thou shalt not come in till thou hast fetched the fire."

Vasilissa sat down on the doorstep, took the tiny doll from one pocket and from another the supper she had ready for it, put the food before it and said: "There, my little doll, take it. Eat a little and listen to my sorrow. I must go to the hut of the old Baba Yaga in the dark forest to borrow some fire and I fear she will eat me. Tell me! What shall I do?"

Then the doll's eyes began to shine like two stars and it became alive. It ate a little and said: "Do not fear, little Vasilissa. Go where thou hast been sent. While I am with thee no harm shall come to thee from the old witch." So Vasilissa put the doll back into her pocket, crossed herself and started out into the dark, wild forest.

Whether she walked a short way or a long way the telling is easy, but the journey was hard. The wood was very dark, and she could not help trembling from fear. Suddenly she heard the sound of a horse's hoofs and a man on horseback galloped past her. He was dressed all in white, the horse under him was milk-white and the harness was white, and just as he passed her it became twilight.

She went a little further and again she heard the sound of a horse's hoofs and there came another man on horseback galloping past her. He was dressed all in red, and the horse under him was blood-red and its harness was red, and just as he passed her the sun rose.

That whole day Vasilissa walked, for she had lost her way. She could find no path at all in the dark wood and she had no food to set before the little doll to make it alive.

But at evening she came all at once to the green lawn where the wretched little hut stood on its hens' legs. The wall around the hut was made of human bones and on its top were skulls. There was a gate in the wall, whose hinges were the bones of human feet and whose locks were jaw-bones set with sharp teeth. The sight filled Vasilissa with horror and she stopped as still as a post buried in the ground.

As she stood there a third man on horseback came galloping up. His face was black, he was dressed all in black, and the horse he rode was coal-black. He galloped up to the gate of the hut and disappeared there as if he had sunk through the ground and at that moment the night came and the forest grew dark.

But it was not dark on the green lawn, for instantly the eyes of all the skulls on the wall were lighted up and shone till the place was as bright as day. When she saw this Vasilissa trembled so with fear that she could not run away.

Then suddenly the wood became full of a terrible noise; the trees began to groan, the branches to creak and the dry leaves to rustle, and the Baba Yaga came flying from the forest. She was riding in a great iron mortar and driving it with the pestle, and as she came she swept away her trail behind her with a kitchen broom.

She rode up to the gate and stopping, said, "Little House, little House, Stand the way thy mother placed thee, Turn thy back to the forest and thy face to me!"

And the little hut turned facing her and stood still. Then smelling all around her, she cried: "Foo! Foo! I smell a smell that is Russian. Who is here?"

Vasilissa, in great fright, came nearer to the old woman and bowing very low, said: "It is only Vasilissa, grandmother. My stepmother's daughters sent me to thee to borrow some fire."

"Well," said the old witch, "I know them. But if I give thee the fire thou shalt stay with me some time and do some work to pay for it. If not, thou shalt be eaten for my supper." Then she turned to the gate and shouted: "Ho! Ye, my solid locks, unlock! Thou, my stout gate, open!" Instantly the locks unlocked, the gate opened of itself, and the Baba Yaga rode in whistling. Vasilissa entered behind her and immediately the gate shut again and the locks snapped tight.

When they had entered the hut the old witch threw herself down on the stove, stretched out her bony legs and said:

"Come, fetch and put on the table at once everything that is in the oven. I am hungry." So Vasilissa ran and lighted a splinter of wood from one of the skulls on the wall and took the food from the oven and set it before

The old woman bowed before the Tsar and then presented him with the fine soft linen

The skulls began to glitter and shine in the dark

her. There was enough cooked meat for three strong men. She brought also from the cellar kvass, honey, and red wine, and the Baba Yaga ate and drank the whole, leaving the girl only a little cabbage soup, a crust of bread and a morsel of suckling pig.

When her hunger was satisfied, the old witch, growing drowsy, lay down on the stove and said: "Listen to me well, and do what I bid thee. Tomorrow when I drive away, do thou clean the yard, sweep the floors and cook my supper. Then take a quarter of a measure of wheat from my store house and pick out of it all the black grains and the wild peas. Mind thou dost all that I have bade; if not, thou shalt be eaten for my supper."

Presently the Baba Yaga turned toward the wall and began to snore and Vasilissa knew that she was fast asleep. Then she went into the corner, took the tiny doll from her pocket, put before it a bit of bread and a little cabbage soup that she had saved, burst into tears and said: "There, my little doll, take it. Eat a little, drink a little, and listen to my grief. Here I am in the house of the old witch and the gate in the wall is locked and I am afraid. She has given me a difficult task and if I do not do all she has bade, she will eat me tomorrow. Tell me: What shall I do?"

Then the eyes of the little doll began to shine like two candles. It ate a little of the bread and drank a little of the soup and said: "Do not be afraid, Vasilissa the Beautiful. Be comforted. Say thy prayers, and go to sleep. The morning is wiser than the evening." So Vasilissa trusted the little doll and was comforted. She said her prayers, lay down on the floor and went fast asleep.

When she woke next morning, very early, it was still dark. She rose and looked out of the window, and she saw that the eyes of the skulls on the wall were growing dim. As she looked, the man dressed all in white, riding the milk-white horse, galloped swiftly around the corner of the hut, leaped the wall and disappeared, and as he went, it became quite light and the eyes of the skulls flickered and went out. The old witch was in the yard; now she began to whistle and the great iron mortar and pestle and the kitchen broom flew out of the hut to her. As she got into the mortar the man dressed all in red, mounted on the blood-red horse, galloped like the wind around the corner of the hut, leaped the wall and was gone, and at that moment the sun rose. Then the Baba Yaga shouted: "Ho! Ye, my solid locks, unlock! Thou, my stout gate, open!" And the locks unlocked and the gate opened and she rode away in the mortar, driving with the pestle and sweeping away her path behind her with the broom.

When Vasilissa found herself left alone, she examined the hut, wondering to find it filled with such an abundance of everything. Then she stood still, remembering all the work that she had been bidden to do and wondering what to begin first. But as she looked she rubbed her eyes, for the yard was already neatly cleaned and the floors were nicely swept, and the little doll was sitting in the storehouse picking the last black grains and wild peas out of the quarter-measure of wheat.

Vasilissa ran and took the little doll in her arms. "My dearest little doll!" she cried. "Thou hast saved me from my trouble! Now I have only to cook the Baba Yaga's supper, since all the rest of the tasks are done!"

"Cook it, with God's help," said the doll, "and then rest, and may the cooking of it make thee healthy!" And so saying it crept into her pocket and became again only a little wooden doll.

So Vasilissa rested all day and was refreshed; and when it

When Baba Yaga shouted her command, the locks unlocked and the stout gates swung open before her

grew toward evening she laid the table for the old witch's supper, and sat looking out of the window, waiting for her coming. After a while she heard the sound of a horse's hoofs and the man in black, on the coal-black horse, galloped up to the wall gate and disappeared like a great dark shadow, and instantly it became quite dark and the eyes of all the skulls began to glitter and shine. Then all at once the trees of the forest began to creak and groan and the leaves and the bushes to moan and sigh, and the Baba Yaga came riding out of the dark wood in the huge iron mortar, driving with the pestle and sweeping out the trail behind her with the kitchen broom. Vasilissa let her in; and the witch, smelling all around her, asked:

"Well, hast thou done perfectly all the tasks I gave thee to do, or am I to eat thee for my supper?"

"Be so good as to look for thyself, grandmother," answered Vasilissa.

The Baba Yaga went all about the place, tapping with her iron pestle, and carefully examining everything. But so well had the little doll done its work that, try as hard as she might, she could not find anything to complain of. There was not a weed left in the yard, nor a speck of dust on the floors, nor a single black grain or wild pea in the wheat.

The old witch was greatly angered, but was obliged to pretend to be pleased. "Well," she said, "thou hast done all well." Then, clapping her hands, she shouted: "Ho! my faithful servants! Friends of my heart! Haste and grind my wheat!" Immediately three pairs of hands appeared, seized the measure of wheat and carried it away.

The Baba Yaga sat down to supper, and Vasilissa put before her all the food from the oven, with kvass, honey, and red wine. The old witch ate it, bones and all, almost to the last morsel, enough for four strong men, and then, growing drowsy, stretched her bony legs on the stove and said: "Tomorrow do as thou hast done today, and besides these tasks take from my storehouse a half-measure of poppy seeds and clean them one by one. Someone has mixed earth with them to do me a mischief and to anger me, and I will have them made perfectly clean." So saying she turned to the wall and soon began to snore.

When she was fast asleep Vasilissa went into the corner, took the little doll from her pocket, set before it a part of the food that was left and asked its advice. And the doll, when it had become alive, and eaten a little food and sipped a little drink, said: "Don't worry, beautiful Vasilissa! Be comforted. Do as thou didst last night: say thy prayers and go to sleep." So Vasilissa was comforted. She said her prayers and went to sleep and did not wake till next morning when she heard the old witch in the yard whistling. She ran to the window just in time to see her take her place in the big iron mortar, and as she did so the man dressed all in red, riding on the blood red horse, leaped over the wall and was gone, just as the sun rose over the wild forest.

As it had happened on the first morning, so it happened

now. When Vasilissa looked she found that the little doll had finished all the tasks excepting the cooking of the supper. The yard was swept and in order, the floors were as clean as new wood, and there was not a grain of earth left in the half-measure of poppy seeds. She rested and refreshed herself till the afternoon, when she cooked the supper, and when evening came she laid the table and sat down to wait for the old witch's coming.

Soon the man in black, on the coal-black horse, galloped up to the gate, and the dark fell and the eyes of the skulls began to shine like day; then the ground began to quake, and the trees of the forest began to creak and the dry leaves to rustle, and the Baba Yaga came riding in her iron mortar, driving with her pestle and sweeping away her path with her broom.

When she came in she smelled around her and went all about the hut, tapping with the pestle; but pry and examine as she might, again she could see no reason to find fault and was angrier than ever. She clapped her hands and shouted:

"Ho! My trusty servants! Friends of my soul! Haste and press the oil out of my poppy seeds!" And instantly the three pairs of hands appeared, seized the measure of poppy seeds and carried it away.

Presently the old witch sat down to supper and Vasilissa brought all she had cooked, enough for five grown men, and set it before her, and brought beer and honey, and then she herself stood silently waiting. The Baba Yaga ate and drank it all, every morsel, leaving not so much as a crumb of bread; then she said snappishly: "Well, why dost thou say nothing, but stand there as if thou wast dumb?"

"I spoke not," Vasilissa answered, "because I dared not. But if thou wilt allow me, grandmother, I wish to ask thee some questions."

"Well," said the old witch, "only remember that every question does not lead to good. If thou knowest overmuch, thou wilt grow old too soon. What wilt thou ask?"

"I would ask thee," said Vasilissa, "of the men on horseback. When I came to thy hut, a rider passed me. He was dressed all in white and he rode a milk-white horse. Who was he?"

"That was my white, bright day," answered the Baba Yaga angrily. "He is a servant of mine, but he cannot hurt thee. Ask me more."

"Afterwards," said Vasilissa, "a second rider overtook me. He was dressed in red and the horse he rode was blood-red. Who was he?"

"That was my servant, the round, red sun," answered the Baba Yaga, "and he, too, cannot injure thee," and she ground her teeth. "Ask me more."

"A third rider," said Vasilissa, "came galloping up to the gate. He was black, his clothes were black and the horse was coal-black. Who was he?"

"That was my servant, the black, dark night," answered the old witch furiously; "but he also cannot harm thee. Ask me more."

But Vasilissa, remembering what the Baba Yaga had said, that not every question led to good, was silent.

"Ask me more!" cried the old witch. "Why dost thou not ask me more? Ask me of the three pairs of hands that serve me!"

But Vasilissa saw how she snarled at her and she answered: "The three questions are enough for me. As thou hast said, grandmother, I would not, through knowing over much, become too soon old."

"It is well for thee," said the Baba Yaga, "that thou didst not ask of them, but only of what thou didst see outside of this hut. Hadst thou asked of them, my servants, the three pairs of hands would have seized thee also, as they did the wheat and poppy seeds, to be my food. Now I would ask a question in my turn: How is it that thou hast been able, in a little time, to do perfectly all the tasks I gave thee? Tell me!"

Vasilissa was so frightened to see how the old witch ground her teeth that she almost told her of the little doll; but she bethought herself just in time, and answered: "The blessing of my dead mother helps me."

Then the Baba Yaga sprang up in a fury. "Get thee out of my house this moment!" she shrieked. "I want no one who bears a blessing to cross my threshold! Get thee gone!"

Vasilissa ran to the yard, and behind her she heard the old witch shouting to the locks and the gate. The locks opened, the gate swung wide, and she ran out on to the lawn. The Baba Yaga seized from the wall one of the skulls with burning eyes and flung it after her. "There," she howled, "is the fire for thy stepmother's daughters. Take it. That is what they sent thee here for, and may they have joy of it!"

Vasilissa put the skull on the end of a stick and darted away through the forest, running as fast as she could, finding her path by the skull's glowing eyes which went out only when morning came.

Whether she ran a long way or a short way, and whether the road was smooth or rough, towards evening of the next day, when the eyes in the skull were beginning to glimmer, she came out of the dark, wild forest to her stepmother's house.

When she came near to the gate, she thought, "Surely, by this time they will have found some fire," and threw the skull into the hedge; but it spoke to her, and said: "Do not throw me away, beautiful Vasilissa; bring me to thy stepmother." So, looking at the house and seeing no spark of light in any of the windows, she took up the skull again and carried it with her.

Now since Vasilissa had gone, the stepmother and her two daughters had had neither fire nor light in all the house. When they struck flint and steel the tinder would not catch and the fire they brought from the neighbors would go out immediately as soon as they carried it over the threshold, so that they had been unable to light or warm themselves or to cook food to eat. Therefore now, for the first time in her life, Vasilissa found herself welcomed. They opened the

door to her and the merchant's wife was greatly rejoiced to find that the light in the skull did not go out as soon as it was brought in. "Maybe the witch's fire will stay," she said, and took the skull into the best room, set it on a candlestick and called her two daughters to admire it.

But the eyes of the skull suddenly began to glimmer and to glow like red coals, and wherever the three turned or ran the eyes followed them, growing larger and brighter till they flamed like two furnaces, and hotter and hotter till the merchant's wife and her two wicked daughters took fire and were burned to ashes. Only Vasilissa the Beautiful was not touched.

In the morning Vasilissa dug a deep hole in the ground and buried the skull. Then she locked the house and set out to the village, where she went to live with an old woman who was poor and childless, and so she remained for many days, waiting for her father's return from the far-distant Tsardom.

But, sitting lonely, time soon began to hang heavy on her hands. One day she said to the old woman: "It is dull for me, grandmother, to sit idly hour by hour. My hands want work to do. Go, therefore, and buy me some flax, the best and finest to be found anywhere, and at least I can spin."

The old woman hastened and bought some flax of the best sort and Vasilissa sat down to work. So well did she spin that the thread came out as even and fine as a hair, and presently there was enough to begin to weave. But so fine was the thread that no frame could be found to weave it upon, nor would any weaver undertake to make one.

Then Vasilissa went into her closet, took the little doll from her pocket, set food and drink before it and asked its help. And after it had eaten a little and drunk a little, the doll became alive and said: "Bring me an old frame and an old basket and some hairs from a horse's mane, and I will arrange everything for thee." Vasilissa hastened to fetch all the doll had asked for and when evening came, said her prayers, went to sleep, and in the morning she found ready a frame, perfectly made, to weave her fine thread upon.

She wove one month, she wove two months – all the winter Vasilissa sat weaving, weaving her fine thread, till the whole piece of linen was done, of a texture so fine that it could be passed, like thread, through the eye of a needle. When the spring came she bleached it, so white that no snow could be compared with it. Then she said to the old woman: "Take thou the linen to the market, Grandmother, and sell it, and the money shall suffice to pay for my food and lodging." When the old woman examined the linen, however, she said:

"Never will I sell such cloth in the market place; no one should wear it except it be the Tsar himself, and tomorrow I shall carry it to the Palace."

Next day, accordingly, the old woman went to the Tsar's splendid Palace and fell to walking up and down before the windows. The servants came to ask her her errand but she answered them nothing, and kept walking up and down. At length the Tsar opened his window, and asked: "What dost thou want, old woman, that thou walkest here?"

"O Tsar's Majesty," the old woman answered, "I have with me a marvelous piece of linen stuff, so wondrously woven that I will show it to none but thee."

The Tsar bade them bring her before him and when he saw the linen he was struck with astonishment at its fineness and beauty. "What wilt thou take for it, old woman?" he asked.

"There is no price that can buy it, Little Father Tsar," she answered; "but I have brought it to thee as a gift." The Tsar could not thank the old woman enough. He took the linen and sent her to her house with many rich presents.

Seamstresses were called to make shirts for him out of the cloth; but when it had been cut up, so fine was it that no one of them was deft and skillful enough to sew it. The best seamstresses in all the Tsardom were summoned but none dared undertake it. So at last the Tsar sent for the old woman and said: "If thou didst know how to spin such thread and weave such linen, thou must also know how to sew me shirts from it."

And the old woman answered: "O Tsar's Majesty, it was not I who wove the linen; it is the work of my adopted daughter."

"Take it, then," the Tsar said, "and bid her do it for me." The old woman brought the linen home and told Vasilissa the Tsar's command: "Well I knew that the work would needs be done by my own hands," said Vasilissa, and, locking herself in her own room, began to make the shirts. So fast and well did she work that soon a dozen were ready. Then the old woman carried them to the Tsar, while Vasilissa washed her face, dressed her hair, put on her best gown and sat down at the window to see what would happen. And presently a servant in the livery of the Palace came to the house and entering, said: "The Tsar, our lord, desires himself to see the clever needlewoman who has made his shirts and to reward her with his own hands."

Vasilissa rose and went at once to the Palace, and as soon as the Tsar saw her, he fell in love with her with all his soul. He took her by her white hand and made her sit beside him. "Beautiful maiden," he said, "never will I part from thee and thou shalt be my wife."

So the Tsar and Vasilissa the Beautiful were married, and her father returned from the far-distant Tsardom, and he and the old woman lived always with her in the splendid Palace, in all joy and contentment. And as for the little wooden doll, she carried it about with her in her pocket all her life long.

The Enchanted Castle

An extract from the story by E. Nesbit (1858–1924)

Then came a glimmer of daylight that grew and grew, and presently ended in another arch that looked out over a scene so like a picture out of a book about Italy that everyone's breath was taken away, and they simply walked forward silent and staring. A short avenue of cypresses led, widening as it went, to a marble terrace that lay broad and white in the sunlight. The children, blinking, leaned their arms on the broad, flat balustrade and gazed. Immediately below them was a lake just like a lake in "The Beauties of Italy" a lake with swans and an island and weeping willows; beyond it were green slopes dotted with groves of trees, and amid the trees gleamed the white limbs of statues. Against a little hill to the left was a round white building with pillars, and to the right a waterfall came tumbling down among mossy stones to splash into the lake. Steps fed from the terrace to the water, and other steps to the green lawns beside it. Away across the grassy slopes deer were feeding, and in the distance where the groves of trees thickened into what looked almost a forest were enormous shapes of grey stone, like nothing that the children had ever seen before.

"It is an enchanted castle," said Kathleen.

"I don't see any castle," said Jimmy.

"What do you call that, then?" Gerald pointed to where, beyond a belt of lime-trees, white towers and turrets broke the blue of the sky.

"There doesn't seem to be anyone about," said Kathleen, "and yet it's all so tidy. I believe it is magic"

"Magic mowing machines," Jimmy suggested. "If we were in a book it would be an enchanted castle, certain to be," said Kathleen.

"It is an enchanted castle," said Gerald in hollow tones.

"But there aren't any" Jimmy was quite positive.

"How do you know? Do you think there's nothing in the world but what you've seen?" His scorn was crushing.

"I think magic went out when people began to have steam-engines," Jimmy insisted, "and newspapers, and telephones and wireless telegraphing."

"Wireless is rather like magic when you come to think of it," said Gerald.

"Oh, that sort!" Jimmy's contempt was deep.

"Perhaps there's given up being magic because people didn't believe in it any more," said Kathleen.

"Well, don't let's spoil the show with any silly old not believing," said Gerald with decision. "I'm going to believe in magic as hardest I can. This is an enchanted garden, and that's an enchanted castle, and I'm jolly well going to explore."

Why the Fish Laughed

This is part of the collection made by Joseph Jacobs (1854–1916) and was included in his *Indian Fairy Tales*, published in 1912. A clever girl can guess the answers to riddles. This kind of theme is spread widely in early Indian literature as well as in more recent European folk literature.

As a certain fisherwoman passed by a palace selling her fish, the Queen appeared at one of the windows and beckoned her to come near and show what she had. At that moment a very big fish jumped about in the bottom of the basket.

"Is it a he or a she?" inquired the Queen. "I wish to purchase a she-fish."

On hearing this the fish laughed aloud.

"It's a he," replied the fisherwoman, and proceeded on her rounds.

The Queen returned to her room in a great rage; and on coming to see her in the evening, the King noticed that something had disturbed her.

"Are you indisposed?" he said.

"No; but I am very much annoyed at the strange behaviour of a fish. A woman brought me one today, and on my inquiring whether it was a male or female, the fish laughed most rudely."

"A fish laugh! Impossible! You must be dreaming."

"I am not a fool. I speak of what I have seen with my own eyes and have heard with my own ears."

"Passing strange! Be it so. I will inquire, concerning it."

On the morrow the King repeated to his vizier what his wife had told him, and bade him investigate the matter, and be ready with a satisfactory answer within six months, on pain of death. The vizier promised to do his best, though he felt almost certain of failure. For five months he laboured indefatigably to find a reason for the laughter of the fish. He sought everywhere and from every one. The wise and learned, and they who were skilled in magic and in all manner of trickery, were consulted. Nobody, however, could explain the matter; and so he returned broken-

People called out to them and put some chapatis into their hands

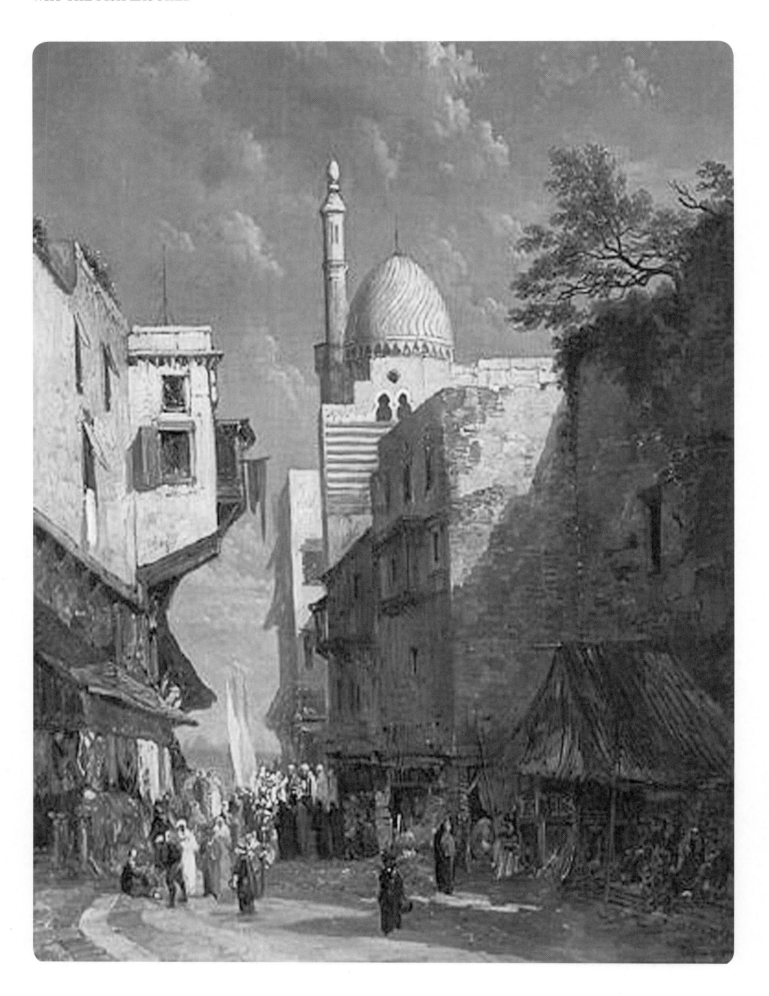

hearted to his house, and began to arrange his affairs in prospect of certain death, for he had had sufficient experience of the King to know that his Majesty would not go back from his threat. Amongst other things, he advised his son to travel for a time, until the King's anger should have somewhat cooled.

The young fellow, who was both clever and handsome, started off whithersoever Kismet might lead him. He had been gone some days, when he fell in with an old farmer, who also was on a journey to a certain village. Finding the old man very pleasant, he asked him if he might accompany him, professing to be on a visit to the same place. The old farmer agreed, and they walked along together. The day was hot, and the way was long and weary.

"Don't you think it would be pleasanter if you and I sometimes gave one another a lift?" said the youth.

"What a fool the man is!" thought the old farmer.

Presently they passed through a field of corn ready for the sickle, and looking like a sea of gold as it waved to and fro in the breeze.

"Is this eaten or not?" said the young man.

Not understanding his meaning, the old man replied, "I don't know."

After a little while the two travellers arrived at a big village, where the young man gave his companion a clasp-knife, and said, "Take this, friend, and get two horses with it; "but, mind and bring it back, for it is very precious."

The old man, looking half amused and half angry, pushed back the knife, muttering something to the effect that his friend was either a fool himself or else trying to play the fool with him. The young man pretended not to notice his reply, and remained almost silent till they reached the city, a short distance outside which was the old farmer's house. They walked about the bazaar and went to the mosque, but nobody saluted them or invited them to come in and rest.

"What a large cemetery!" exclaimed the young man.

"What does the man mean," thought the old farmer, "calling this largely populated city a cemetery?"

On leaving the city their way led through a cemetery. where a few people were praying beside a grave and distributing chapatis and kulchas to passers-by, in the name of their beloved dead. They beckoned to the two travellers and gave them as much as they would.

"What a splendid city this is!" said the young man.

"Now, the man must surely be demented!" thought the old farmer. "I wonder what he will do, next? He will be calling the land water, and the water land; and be speaking of light where there is darkness, and of darkness when it is light." However, he kept his thoughts to himself.

Presently, they had to wade through a stream that ran along the edge of the cemetery. The water was rather deep, so the old farmer took off his shoes and pajamas and crossed over; but the young man waded through it

They walked about the busy bazaar and
then went to the mosque

with his shoes and pajamas on.

"Well! I never did see such a perfect fool, both in word and in deed," said the old man to, himself.

However, he liked the fellow; and thinking that he would amuse his wife and daughter, he invited him to come and stay at his house as long as he had occasion to remain in the village.

"Thank you very much," the young man replied; "but let me first inquire, if you please, whether the beam of your house is strong."

The old farmer left him in despair, and entered his house laughing.

"There is a man in yonder field," he said, after returning their greetings. "He has come the greater part of the way with me, and I wanted him to put up here as long as he had to stay in this village. But the fellow is such a fool that I cannot make anything out of him. He wants to know if the beam of this house is all right. The man must be mad!" and saying this, he burst into a fit of laughter.

"Father," said the farmer's daughter, who was a very sharp and wise girl, "this man, whosoever he is, is no fool, as you deem him. He only wishes to know if you can afford to entertain him."

"Oh! Of course," replied, the farmer. "I see. Well, perhaps you can help me to solve some of his other mysteries. While we were walking together he asked whether he should carry me or I should carry him, as he thought that would be a pleasanter mode of proceeding."

"Most assuredly," said the girl. "He meant that one of you should tell a story to beguile the time."

"Oh yes. Well, we were passing through a corn-field, when he asked me whether it was eaten or not."

"And didn't you know the meaning of this, father? He simply wished to know if the man was in debt or not; because, if the owner of the field was in debt, then the produce of the field was as good as eaten to him; that is, it would have to go to his creditors."

"Yes, yes, yes, of course! Then, on entering a certain village, he bade me take his clasp-knife and get two horses with it, and bring back the knife again to him."

"Are not two stout sticks as good as two horses for helping one along on the road? He only asked you to cut a couple of sticks and be careful not to lose his knife."

"I see," said the farmer. "While we were walking over the city we did not see anybody that we knew, and not a soul gave us a scrap of anything to eat, till we were passing the cemetery; but there some people called to us and put into our hands some chapatis and kulchas; so my companion called the city a cemetery, and the cemetery a city."

"This also is to be understood, father, if one thinks of the city as the place where everything is to be obtained, and of inhospitable people as worse than the dead. The city, though crowded with people, was as if dead, as far as you were concerned; while, in the cemetery, which is crowded with the dead, you were saluted by kind friends and provided with bread."

While passing through a corn-field, he asked whether the crop was eaten or not, wishing to know if the man was in debt

The huge fish had jumped about in the bottom of the basket

The king repeated to the vizier what his wife had told him

She sent a servant to the young man with a basin of ghee, twelve chapatis, and a jar of milk

Happy crowds gathered to attend the wedding of the vizier's son

"True, true!" said' the astonished farmer. "Then, just now, when we were crossing the stream, he waded through it without taking off his shoes and pajamas."

"I admire his wisdom," replied the girl. "I have often thought how stupid people were to venture into that swiftly flowing stream and over those sharp stones with bare feet. The slightest stumble and they would fall, and be wetted from head to foot. This friend of yours is a most wise man. I should like to see him and speak to him."

"Very well," said the farmer; "I will go and find him, and bring him in."

"Tell him, father, that our beams are strong enough, and then he will come in. I'll send on, ahead a present to the man, to show him that we can afford to have him for our guest."

Accordingly she called a servant and sent him to the young man with a present of a basin of ghee, twelve chapatis, and a jar of milk, and the following message –" O friend, the moon is full; twelve months make a year, and

was shown to him, and he was treated in every way as if he were the son of a great man, although his humble host knew nothing of his origin. At length be told them everything – about the laughing of the fish, his father's threatened execution, and his own banishment – and asked their advice as to what he should do.

"The laughing of the fish," said the girl, "which seems to have been the cause of all this trouble, indicates that there is a man in the palace who is plotting against the King's life."

"Joy, joy!" exclaimed the vizier's son. "There is yet time for me to return and save my father from an ignominious and unjust death, and the King from danger."

The following day he hastened back to his own country, taking with him the farmer's daughter. Immediately on arrival he ran to the palace and informed his father of what he had heard. The poor vizier, now almost dead from the expectation of death, was at once carried to the King, to whom be repeated the news that his son had just brought.

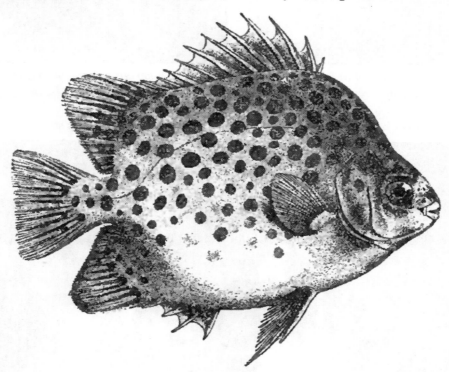

the sea is overflowing with water."

Halfway the bearer of this present and message met his little son, who, seeing what was in the basket, begged his father to give him some of the food. His father foolishly complied. Presently he saw the young man, and gave him the rest of the present and the message.

"Give your mistress my salaam," he replied, "and tell her that the moon is new, and that I can only find eleven months in the year, and the sea is by no means full."

Not understanding the meaning of these words, the servant repeated them word for word, as he had heard them, to his mistress; and thus his theft was discovered, and he was severely punished. After a little while the young man appeared with the old farmer. Great attention

"Never!" said the King.

"But it must be, so, your Majesty," replied the vizier; "and in order to prove the truth of what I have heard, I pray you to call together all the maids in your palace, and order them to jump over a pit, which must be dug. We'll soon find out whether there is any man there."

The King had the pit dug, and commanded all the maids belonging to the palace to try to jump it. All of them tried, but only one succeeded. That one was found to be a man!

Thus was the Queen satisfied, and the faithful old vizier saved.

Afterwards, as soon as could be, the vizier's son married the old farmer's daughter and a most happy marriage it was.

Thumbelina

This is a much-love tale by Hans Christian Andersen 1805–1875 which was published first in 1835 and tells of a tiny girl's adventures with toads, moles, and other small creatures before she falls in love with a flower-fairy prince who is just her size. The earliest English translation was in 1846 and since then this popular story has been adapted to various media, including song and animated film.

There was once a woman who wished very much to have a little child, but she could not obtain her wish. At last she went to a fairy, and said, "I should so very much like to have a little child; can you tell me where I can find one?"

"Oh, that can be easily managed," said the fairy. "Here is a barleycorn of a different kind to those which grow in the farmer's fields, and which the chickens eat; put it into a flower-pot, and see what will happen."

"Thank you," said the woman, and she gave the fairy twelve shillings, which was the price of the barleycorn. Then she went home and planted it, and immediately there grew up a large handsome flower, something like a tulip in appearance, but with its leaves tightly closed as if it were still a bud.

"It is a beautiful flower," said the woman, and she kissed the red and golden-colored leaves, and while she did so the flower opened, and she could see that it was a real tulip. Within the flower, upon the green velvet stamens, sat a very delicate and graceful little maiden. She was scarcely half as long as a thumb, and they gave her the name of Thumbelina, or Tiny, because she was so small. A walnut-shell, elegantly polished, served her for a cradle; her bed was formed of blue violet-leaves, with a rose-leaf for a counterpane. Here she slept at night, but during the day she amused herself on a table, where the woman had placed a plateful of water. Round this plate were wreaths of flowers with their stems in the water, and upon it floated a large tulip-leaf, which served Tiny for a boat. Here the little maiden sat and rowed herself from side to side, with two oars made of white horse-hair. It really was a very pretty sight. Tiny could; also, sing so softly and sweetly that nothing like her singing had ever before been heard.

One night, while she lay in her pretty bed, a large, ugly, wet toad crept through a broken pane of glass in the window, and leaped right upon the table where Tiny lay sleeping under her rose-leaf quilt. "What a pretty little wife this would make for my son," said the toad, and she took up the walnut-shell in which little Tiny lay asleep, and jumped through the window with it into the garden.

In the swampy margin of a broad stream in the garden lived the toad, with her son. He was uglier even than his mother, and when he saw the pretty little maiden in her elegant bed, he could only cry, "Croak, croak, croak."

"Don't speak so loud, or she will wake," said the toad, "and then she might run away, for she is as light as swan's down. We will place her on one of the water-lily

Tiny sat on the green leaf and wept, unable to bear the thought of an ugly toad as her husband

leaves out in the stream; it will be like an island to her, she is so light and small, and then she cannot escape; and, while she is away, we will make haste and prepare the state-room under the marsh, in which you are to live when you are married."

Far out in the stream grew a number of water-lilies, with broad green leaves, which seemed to float on the top of the water. The largest of these leaves appeared farther off than the rest, and the old toad swam out to it with the walnut-shell, in which little Tiny lay still asleep.

The tiny little creature woke very early in the morning, and began to cry bitterly when she found where she was, for she could see nothing but water on every side of the large green leaf, and no way of reaching the land.

Meanwhile the old toad was very busy under the marsh, decking her room with rushes and wild yellow flowers, to make it look pretty for her new daughter-in-law. Then she swam out with her ugly son to the leaf on which she had placed poor little Tiny. She wanted to fetch the pretty bed, that she might put it in the bridal chamber to be ready for her. The old toad bowed low to her in the water, and said, "Here is my son, he will be your husband, and you will live happily in the marsh by the stream."

"Croak, croak, croak," was all her son could say for

pretty, and it made them very sorry to think that she must go and live with the ugly toads. "No, it must never be!" So they assembled together in the water, round the green stalk which held the leaf on which the little maiden stood, and gnawed it away at the root with their teeth. Then the leaf floated down the stream, carrying Tiny far away out of reach of land.

Tiny sailed past many towns, and the little birds in the bushes saw her, and sang, "What a lovely little creature;" so the leaf swam away with her farther and farther, till it brought her to other lands.

A graceful little white butterfly constantly fluttered round her, and at last alighted on the leaf. Tiny pleased him, and she was glad of it, for now the toad could not possibly reach her, and the country through which she sailed was

"Croak, croak!" went the toad when he saw pretty Thumbelina

himself; so the toad took up the elegant little bed, and swam away with it, leaving Tiny all alone on the green leaf, where she sat and wept. She could not bear to think of living with the old toad, and having her ugly son for a husband.

The little fishes, who swam about in the water beneath, had seen the toad, and heard what she said, so they lifted their heads above the water to look at the little maiden. As soon as they caught sight of her, they saw she was very

beautiful, and the sun shone upon the water, till it glittered like liquid gold. She took off her girdle and tied one end of it round the butterfly, and the other end of the ribbon she fastened to the leaf, which now glided on much faster than ever, taking little Tiny with it as she stood.

Presently a large cockchafer flew by; the moment he caught sight of her, he seized her round her delicate waist with his claws, and flew with her into a tree. The green leaf floated away on the brook, and the butterfly flew with it,

The little fishes in the water beneath heard all about the little maiden and gathered to take a peep at her

for he was fastened to it, and could not get away.

Oh, how frightened little Tiny felt when the cockchafer flew with her to the tree! But especially was she sorry for the beautiful white butterfly which she had fastened to the leaf, for if he could not free himself he would die of hunger. But the cockchafer did not trouble himself at all about the matter. He seated himself by her side on a large green leaf, gave her some honey from the flowers to eat, and told her she was very pretty, though not in the least like a cockchafer.

After a time, all the cockchafers turned up their feelers, and said, "She has only two legs! how ugly that looks."

"She has no feelers," said another. "Her waist is quite slim. Pooh! she is like a human being."

"Oh! she is ugly," said all the lady cockchafers, although Tiny was very pretty. Then the cockchafer who had run away with her, believed all the others when they said she was ugly, and would have nothing more to say to her, and told her she might go where she liked. Then he flew down with her from the tree, and placed her on a daisy, and she wept at the thought that she was so ugly that even the cockchafers would have nothing to say to her. And all the while she was really the loveliest creature that one could imagine, and as tender and delicate as a beautiful rose-leaf.

During the whole summer poor little Tiny lived quite alone in the wide forest. She wove herself a bed with blades of grass, and hung it up under a broad leaf, to protect herself from the rain. She sucked the honey from the flowers for food, and drank the dew from their leaves every morning. So passed away the summer and the autumn, and then came the winter – the long, cold winter. All the birds who had sung to her so sweetly were flown away, and the trees and the flowers had withered. The large clover leaf under the shelter of which she had lived, was now rolled together and shrivelled up, nothing remained but a yellow withered stalk. She felt dreadfully cold, for her clothes were torn, and she was herself so frail and delicate, that poor little Tiny was nearly frozen to death.

It began to snow too; and the snow-flakes, as they fell upon her, were like a whole shovelful falling upon one of us, for we are tall, but she was only an inch high. Then she wrapped herself up in a dry leaf, but it cracked in the middle and could not keep her warm, and she shivered with cold.

Near the wood in which she had been living lay a corn-field, but the corn had been cut a long time; nothing remained but the bare dry stubble standing up out of the frozen ground. It was to her like struggling through a large wood. Oh! how she shivered with the cold.

She came at last to the door of a field-mouse, who had a little den under the corn-stubble. There dwelt the field-mouse in warmth and comfort, with a whole roomful of corn, a kitchen, and a beautiful dining room. Poor little Tiny stood before the door just like a little beggar-girl, and begged for a small piece of barley-corn, for she had been without a morsel to eat for two days.

"You poor little creature," said the field-mouse, who was really a good old field-mouse, "come into my warm room and dine with me." She was very pleased with Tiny, so she said, "You are quite welcome to stay with me all the winter, if you like; but you must keep my rooms clean and neat, and tell me stories, for I shall like to hear them very much."

And Tiny did all the field-mouse asked her, and found herself very comfortable.

"We shall have a visitor soon," said the field-mouse one day; "my neighbor pays me a visit once a week. He is better off than I am; he has large rooms, and wears a beautiful black velvet coat. If you could only have him for a husband, you would be well provided for indeed. But he is blind, so you must tell him some of your prettiest stories."

But Tiny did not feel at all interested about this neighbour, for he was a mole. However, he came and paid his visit dressed in his black velvet coat.

"He is very rich and learned, and his house is twenty times larger than mine," said the field-mouse.

He was rich and learned, no doubt, but he always spoke slightingly of the sun and the pretty flowers, because he had never seen them. Tiny was obliged to sing to him, "Lady-bird, lady-bird, fly away home," and many other pretty songs. And the mole fell in love with her because

The field mice had a cosy den below the corn stubble

*The cockchafers pronounced that, to their minds,
Thumbelina was very ugly*

*Thumbelina adored the pretty little birds who had
sung to her so merrily all summer*

she had such a sweet voice; but he said nothing yet, for he was very cautious.

A short time before, the mole had dug a long passage under the earth, which led from the dwelling of the field-mouse to his own, and here she had permission to walk with Tiny whenever she liked. But he warned them not to be alarmed at the sight of a dead bird which lay in the passage. It was a perfect bird, with a beak and feathers, and could not have been dead long, and was lying just where the mole had made his passage. The mole took a piece of phosphorescent wood in his mouth, and it glittered like fire in the dark; then he went before them to light them through the long, dark passage. When they came to the spot where lay the dead bird, the mole pushed his broad nose through the ceiling, the earth gave way, so that there was a large hole, and the daylight shone into the passage. In the middle of the floor lay a dead swallow, his beautiful wings pulled close to his sides, his feet and his head drawn up under his feathers; the poor bird had evidently died of the cold. It made little Tiny very sad to see it, she did so love the little birds; all the summer they had sung and twittered for her so beautifully. But the mole pushed it aside with his crooked legs, and said, "He will sing no more now. How miserable it must be to be born a little bird! I am thankful that none of my children will ever be birds, for they can do nothing but cry, 'Tweet, tweet,' and always die of hunger in the winter."

"Yes, you may well say that, as a clever man!" exclaimed

A little graceful white butterfly floated and flittered around her

The fish gnawed away at the leaf stem until the lily pad broke free and floated away

the field-mouse, "What is the use of his twittering, for when winter comes he must either starve or be frozen to death. Still birds are very high bred."

Tiny said nothing; but when the two others had turned their backs on the bird, she stooped down and stroked aside the soft feathers which covered the head, and kissed the closed eyelids. "Perhaps this was the one who sang to me so sweetly in the summer," she said; "and how much pleasure it gave me, you dear, pretty bird."

The mole now stopped up the hole through which the daylight shone, and then accompanied the lady home. But during the night Tiny could not sleep; so she got out of bed and wove a large, beautiful carpet of hay; then she carried it to the dead bird, and spread it over him; with some down from the flowers which she had found in the field-mouse's room. It was as soft as wool, and she spread some of it on each side of the bird, so that he might lie warmly in the cold earth.

"Farewell, you pretty little bird," said she, "farewell; thank you for your delightful singing during the summer, when all the trees were green, and the warm sun shone upon us." Then she laid her head on the bird's breast, but she was alarmed immediately, for it seemed as if something inside the bird went "thump, thump." It was the bird's heart; he was not really dead, only benumbed with the cold, and the warmth had restored him to life. In autumn, all the swallows fly away into warm countries, but if one

happens to linger, the cold seizes it, it becomes frozen, and falls down as if dead; it remains where it fell, and the cold snow covers it. Tiny trembled very much; she was quite frightened, for the bird was large, a great deal larger than herself – she was only an inch high. But she took courage, laid the wool more thickly over the poor swallow, and then took a leaf which she had used for her own counterpane, and laid it over the head of the poor bird.

The next morning she again stole out to see him. He was alive but very weak; he could only open his eyes for a moment to look at Tiny, who stood by holding a piece of decayed wood in her hand, for she had no other lantern.

"Thank you, pretty little maiden," said the sick swallow; "I have been so nicely warmed, that I shall soon regain my strength, and be able to fly about again in the warm sunshine."

"Oh," said she, "it is cold out of doors now; it snows and freezes. Stay in your warm bed; I will take care of you."

Then she brought the swallow some water in a flower-leaf, and after he had drank, he told her that he had

The little prince took off his gold crown and placed it on Thumbelina's head

wounded one of his wings in a thorn-bush, and could not fly as fast as the others, who were soon far away on their journey to warm countries. Then at last he had fallen to the earth, and could remember no more, nor how he came to be where she had found him.

The whole winter the swallow remained underground, and Tiny nursed him with care and love. Neither the mole nor the field-mouse knew anything about it, for they did not like swallows. Very soon the spring time came, and the sun warmed the earth. Then the swallow bade farewell to Tiny, and she opened the hole in the ceiling which the mole had made. The sun shone in upon them so beautifully, that the swallow asked her if she would go with him; she could sit on his back, he said, and he would fly away with her into the green woods. But Tiny knew it would make the field-mouse very grieved if she left her in that manner, so she said, "No, I cannot."

"Farewell, then, farewell, you good, pretty little maiden," said the swallow; and he flew out into the sunshine.

Tiny looked after him, and the tears rose in her eyes. She was very fond of the poor swallow.

"Tweet, tweet," sang the bird, as he flew out into the green woods, and Tiny felt very sad. She was not allowed to go out into the warm sunshine. The corn which had been sown in the field over the house of the field-mouse had grown up high into the air, and formed a thick wood to Tiny, who was only an inch in height.

"You are going to be married, Tiny," said the field-mouse. "My neighbour has asked for you. What good fortune for a poor child like you. Now we will prepare your wedding clothes. They must be both woollen and linen. Nothing must be wanting when you are the mole's wife."

Tiny had to turn the spindle, and the field-mouse hired four spiders, who were to weave day and night. Every evening the mole visited her, and was continually speaking of the time when the summer would be over. Then he would keep his wedding-day with Tiny; but now the heat of the sun was so great that it burned the earth, and made it quite hard, like a stone. As soon as the summer was over, the wedding should take place. But Tiny was not at all pleased; for she did not like the tiresome mole. Every morning when the sun rose, and every evening when it went down, she would creep out at the door, and as the wind blew aside the ears of corn, so that she could see the blue sky, she thought how beautiful and bright it seemed out there, and wished so much to see her dear swallow again. But he never returned; for by this time he had flown far away into the lovely green forest.

As everyone rejoiced, the little swallow sang at Thumbelina's wedding

When autumn arrived, Tiny had her outfit quite ready; and the field-mouse said to her, "In four weeks the wedding must take place."

Then Tiny wept, and said she would not marry the disagreeable mole.

"Nonsense," replied the field-mouse. "Now don't be obstinate, or I shall bite you with my white teeth. He is a very handsome mole; the queen herself does not wear more beautiful velvets and furs. His kitchen and cellars are quite full. You ought to be very thankful for such good fortune."

So the wedding-day was fixed, on which the mole was to fetch Tiny away to live with him, deep under the earth, and never again to see the warm sun, because he did not like it. The poor child was very unhappy at the thought of saying farewell to the beautiful sun, and as the field-mouse had given her permission to stand at the door, she went to look at it once more.

"Farewell bright sun," she cried, stretching out her arm towards it; and then she walked a short distance from the house; for the corn had been cut, and only the dry stubble remained in the fields. "Farewell, farewell," she repeated, twining her arm round a little red flower that grew just by her side. "Greet the little swallow from me, if you should see him again."

"Tweet, tweet," sounded over her head suddenly. She looked up, and there was the swallow himself flying close by. As soon as he spied Tiny, he was delighted; and then she told him how unwilling she felt to marry the ugly mole, and to live always beneath the earth, and never to see the bright sun any more. And as she told him she wept.

"Cold winter is coming," said the swallow, "and I am going to fly away into warmer countries. Will you go with me? You can sit on my back, and fasten yourself on with your sash. Then we can fly away from the ugly mole and his gloomy rooms – far away, over the mountains, into warmer countries, where the sun shines more brightly than here; where it is always summer, and the flowers bloom in greater beauty. Fly now with me, dear little Tiny; you saved my life when I lay frozen in that dark passage."

"Yes, I will go with you," said Tiny; and she seated herself on the bird's back, with her feet on his outstretched wings, and tied her girdle to one of his strongest feathers.

Then the swallow rose in the air, and flew over forest and over sea, high above the highest mountains, covered with eternal snow. Tiny would have been frozen in the cold air, but she crept under the bird's warm feathers, keeping her little head uncovered, so that she might admire the beautiful lands over which they passed.

At length they reached the warm countries, where the sun shines brightly, and the sky seems so much higher above the earth. Here, on the hedges, and by the wayside, grew purple, green, and white grapes; lemons and oranges hung from trees in the woods; and the air was fragrant with myrtles and orange blossoms. Beautiful children ran along the country lanes, playing with large gay butterflies;

and as the swallow flew farther and farther, every place appeared still more lovely.

At last they came to a blue lake, and by the side of it, shaded by trees of the deepest green, stood a palace of dazzling white marble, built in the olden times. Vines clustered round its lofty pillars, and at the top were many swallows' nests, and one of these was the home of the swallow who carried Tiny.

This is my house," said the swallow; "but it would not do for you to live there – you would not be comfortable. You must choose for yourself one of those lovely flowers, and I will put you down upon it, and then you shall have everything that you can wish to make you happy."

"That will be delightful," she said, and clapped her little hands for joy.

A large marble pillar lay on the ground, which, in falling, had been broken into three pieces. Between these pieces grew the most beautiful large white flowers; so the swallow flew down with Tiny, and placed her on one of the broad leaves. But how surprised she was to see in the middle of the flower, a tiny little man, as white and transparent as if he had been made of crystal! He had a gold crown on his head, and delicate wings at his shoulders, and was not much larger than Tiny herself. He was the angel of the flower; for a tiny man and a tiny woman dwell in every flower; and this was the king of them all.

"Oh, how beautiful he is!" whispered Tiny to the swallow.

The little prince was at first quite frightened at the bird, who was like a giant, compared to such a delicate little creature as himself; but when he saw Tiny, he was delighted, and thought her the prettiest little maiden he had ever seen. He took the gold crown from his head, and placed it on hers, and asked her name, and if she would be his wife, and queen over all the flowers.

This certainly was a very different sort of husband to the son of a toad, or the mole, with my black velvet and fur; so she said, "Yes," to the handsome prince. Then all the flowers opened, and out of each came a little lady or a tiny lord, all so pretty it was quite a pleasure to look at them. Each of them brought Tiny a present; but the best gift was a pair of beautiful wings, which had belonged to a large white fly and they fastened them to Tiny's shoulders, so that she might fly from flower to flower. Then there was much rejoicing, and the little swallow who sat above them, in his nest, was asked to sing a wedding song, which he did as well as he could; but in his heart he felt sad for he was very fond of Tiny, and would have liked never to part from her again. "You must not be called Tiny any more," said the spirit of the flowers to her. "It is an ugly name, and you are so very pretty. We will call you Maia."

"Farewell, farewell," said the swallow, with a heavy heart as he left the warm countries to fly back into Denmark. There he had a nest over the window of a house in which dwelt the writer of fairy tales. The swallow sang, "Tweet, tweet," and from his song came the whole story.

The Master Thief

Readers enjoy hearing about the adventures of clever, loveable rogues, here explored in this tale by Joseph Jacobs (1854–1916). The purse incident occurs in Brittany, Piedmont, Tuscany, the Tyrol and Iceland while the man twice hanged element is found in the folk tales of Norway, Ireland, Saxony, Tuscany and Germany. Other parts of the story are found in tales from Bengal, Brittany, Norway, Tuscany, Scotland, Flanders, the Basque and Catalan, Russia, Ireland, Lithuania and Serbia. In Iceland the persons carried away are a king and a queen. The three tests of the Master Thief are the stealing of a bed, a horse, and a priest. In some variants the Master Thief executes his tricks in order to gain the King's daughter but in most cases he does them to escape the impending punishment for his crimes.

Will set about learning to be a robber, crying, "Your purse or your life!"

There was once a farmer who had a son named Will, and he sent him out in the world to learn a trade and seek his fortune. Now he hadn't gone far when he was stopped by a band of robbers who called out to him, "Your purse or your life!"

So he gave them his purse and said: "That is an easy way of getting money, I'd like to be a robber myself."

So they agreed to take him into their band if he could show he was able to do a robber's work. They sent Will to see if he could rob the first person who went through the wood. So he went up to the man and said to him:

"Your purse or your life!"

The man gave him his purse, whereupon Will took all the money out of it and gave it back to the man and took the purse back to the robbers, who said, "Well, what luck?"

"Oh, I got his purse from him quite easily; here it is."

"Well, what about the money?" said they.

"Well, that I gave back to him. You only asked me to say, 'Your purse or your life."

At that the robbers roared with laughter and said: "You'll never be a thief."

Will was quite ashamed of making such a fool of himself and determined he would do better next time.

A herd of cattle were being driven to market

So one day he saw two farmers driving a herd of cattle to market, and told the robbers that he knew a way to take the cattle from them without fighting for them.

"If you do that," said they, "you will be a Master Thief."

Then Will went a little way ahead of the robbers with a stout cord, which he tied under his armpits and then fixed himself upon a branch of a tree over the road so that it looked as if he had been hanged.

When the farmers came with their cattle they said: "There's one of the robbers hung up for an example," and drove their cattle on farther.

Then Will got down and, running across a by-path made sure that he was once again in front of the farmers and hung himself up as before on a tree by the side of the road.

When the farmers came up to him one of them said: "Goodness gracious me, why there's the same robber hanged up here again."

"Oh, that's not the same robber," said the other.

"Yes, it is," said the first, "for I noticed he had a white horn button on his coat, and see, there it is. It must be the same man."

"How could that be?" said the other. "We left that one hanging up dead half a mile back."

"I am sure it is."

"I am certain it isn't."

"Well, give a good look at him, and we'll go back and see if it isn't the same."

So the farmers went back to look. Meanwhile Will took their cattle and drove them back to the robbers, who agreed that he was a Master Thief.

He stopped with them for several years and made much money, and then drove back in a carriage and pair to his father's farm.

When he came there his father came to the carriage and bowed to him and asked him, "What's your pleasure, sir?"

"Oh I want to make some inquiries about a young fellow named William who used to be on this farm. What has become of him?"

"Oh, I don't know; he was my son and I have not heard from him for many years; I am afraid he has come to no good."

"Look at me closely and see if you see any resemblance to him."

Then the farmer recognized Will and took him into the farmhouse and called Will's mother to come and welcome him back.

"So, Will, you've come back in a carriage and pair," said she. "How have you earned so much money?"

So Will told his mother that he had become a Master Thief but begged her not to mention it to anyone, but to tell them that he had been an explorer and had found gold.

Well, the very next day a neighbouring gossip called in upon Will's mother and asked her to tell her the news

Will returned home in a carriage and pair

about Will and what he had been doing.

So she said: "Oh, Will has been an exploiter, I mean explorer, but he really was a Master Thief. But you mustn't tell anybody; you'll promise, won't you?"

So the gossip promised, but of course the moment she got home she told all about Will, the Master Thief.

Now the lord of the village soon heard of this, and he called Will up to him and said: "I hear you are a Master Thief. You know that you deserve death for that. But if you can prove that you are really a master in your thievery I will let you go free. First let us see whether you can steal my horse out of my stable tonight."

To prevent his horse being stolen, the lord ordered it to be saddled and put a stable boy on it, telling him to stop there all night.

Will took two flasks of brandy into one of which he had poured a drug, and dressing himself as an old woman he went to the lord's stable late at night and asked to rest there as it was so cold and she was so tired.

The stable boy pointed to some straw in the corner and told the woman she might rest there for a time.

When she sat down she took one of the brandy flasks out of her pocket and drank it off, saying, "Ah, that warms one! Would you like to have a drink?"

And when the stable boy said "Yes," Will gave him the

other flask, and as soon as he had drunk it he fell dead asleep.

So Will lifted him off of the horse and put him on the crossbar of the stable as if he were riding, and then he got on the horse and rode away.

In the morning the lord went down to the stable and there he saw the stable boy riding the cross bar and his horse gone.

Then Will rode up to the stable on the lord's horse and said: "Am I not a Master Thief?"

"Oh, stealing my horse was not so hard. Let us see if you can steal the sheet from off my bed tonight. But, look out, if you come near my bedroom I shall shoot you."

That night Will took a dummy man and propped it up on a ladder, which he put up to the lord's bedroom.

And when the lord saw the dummy coming in at the window he shot his pistol at it and it fell down. He rushed downstairs and out into the open air, looking to see if he had shot Will.

Meanwhile Will went up to the lord's bedroom and, speaking in the lord's voice, said to his wife: "Give me the sheet, my dear, to wrap the body of that poor Master Thief in."

So she gave him the sheet and he went away.

Next morning Will brought up the sheet to the lord, who said: "That was a good trick, I must confess. But if you want really to prove that you are a Master Thief bring to me the priest in a bag, and then I will own your mastery."

So that night Will took a number of crabs and tied candle ends upon them and, taking them to the cemetery, lit the candle ends and let them loose.

When the priest of the village saw these lights moving over the cemetery he came to the door and watched them and called out, "What is that?"

Now Will had dressed himself up like an angel.

"It is the last day of judgment, and I have come for thee, Father Lawrence, to carry thee to heaven. Come within this bag, and in a short time thou wilt be in thine appointed place."

So Father Lawrence crept within the bag, and Will dragged him along, and when he bumped against the ground Father Lawrence said, "Oh, we must be going through purgatory."

And then Will took him to the hen-coops and threw him in among the chickens and ducks and geese, and Father Lawrence said, "We must be getting near the angels for I

The lord challenged Will to steal the horse from his stable

The young stable boy, set to watch at night, succumbed to the offer of a drink of brandy

Will propped a dummy man up on a ladder, set against the lord's bedroom

hear the rustling of their wings."

So Will went up to the lord's house and made him come down to the hen-coops and there showed him the priest in the bag, and the lord said, "I do not know how you do these things. I cannot tell if you are really a Master Thief unless you take my horse from under me. If you can do that I will call you the Master of all Master Thieves."

Well, next day, Will dressed himself up as an old woman and, taking a cart with an old horse, put in it a cask of beer – and then went driving along with his thumb in the bunghole.

Soon after he met the lord on horseback who asked him if he had seen a man like Will lurking about there in the forest.

"I think I have," said Will, "and could bring him to you if you wanted. But I can't leave this cask before the taps come out; I have to keep my thumb in the bunghole."

"Oh, I will do that," said the lord, "if you will only go and get that man. Take my horse and run him down."

So Will got on the lord's horse and rode off, leaving the nobleman with his thumb in the bunghole. He waited and he waited and he waited till at last he drove in the cart back to his house, and there he saw no less a person than Will himself riding his horse.

Then the noble said unto Will, "You are indeed a Master Thief. Go your way in peace."

The Language of Animals

Jack could understand all that the birds meant with their twitters and chirps

There was once a man who had a son named Jack, who was very simple in mind and backward in thought. So his father sent him away to school so that he might learn something; and after a year he came back from school.

"Well, Jack," asked his father, "what have you learnt at school?"

And Jack said, "I know what dogs mean when they bark."

"That's not much," said his father. "You must go to school again."

So he sent him to school for another year, and when he came back he asked him what he had learnt.

"Well, father," said the boy, "when frogs croak I know what they mean."

"You must learn more than that," said the father, and sent him once more to school.

And when he returned, after another year, he asked him once more what he had learnt.

"I know all that the birds say when they twitter and chirp, caw and coo, gobble and cluck."

"Well I must say," said the father, "that does not seem much for three years' schooling. But let us see if you have learnt your lessons properly. What does that bird say just above our heads in the tree there?"

Jack listened for some time but did not say anything.

"Well, Jack, what is it?" asked his father.

"I don't like to say, father."

"I don't believe you know or else you would say. Whatever it is I shall not mind."

Then the boy said, "The bird kept on saying as clear as could be, 'the time is not so far away when Jack's father will offer him water on bended knees for him to wash his hands; and his mother shall offer him a towel to wipe them with.' "

Thereupon the father grew very angry with Jack and his love for him changed to hatred, and one day he

When Jack stopped overnight at a castle he was able to warn the owner of an impending attack

spoke to a robber and promised him much money if he would take Jack away into the forest and kill him there and bring back his heart to show that he had done what he had promised. But instead of doing this the robber told Jack all about it and advised him to flee away, while the robber took back to Jack's father the heart of a deer saying that it was Jack's. Then Jack travelled on and on till one night he stopped at a castle on the way; and while they were all supping together in the castle hall the dogs in the courtyard began barking and baying. And Jack went up to the lord of the castle and said, "There will be an attack upon the castle tonight."

"How do you know that?" asked the lord.

"The dogs say so," said Jack.

At that the lord and his men laughed, but nevertheless put an extra guard around the castle that night, and, sure enough, the attack was made, which was easily beaten off because the men were prepared. So the lord gave Jack a great reward for warning him, and he went on his way with a fellow traveller who had heard him warn the lord.

Soon afterwards they arrived at another castle in which the lord's daughter was lying sick unto death; and a great reward had been offered to him that should cure her. Now Jack had been listening to the frogs as they were croaking in the moat which surrounded the castle. So Jack went to the lord of the castle and said, "I know what ails your daughter."

"What is it," asked the lord.

"She has dropped the holy wafer from her mouth and it has been swallowed by one of the frogs in the moat."

Jack travelled on to Rome where the Pope dwelt

"How do you know that?" said the lord.

"I heard the frogs say so."

At first the lord would not believe it; but in order to save his daughter's life he got Jack to point out the frog who was boasting of what he had swallowed, and, catching it, found what Jack had said was true. The frog was caught and killed, the wafer got back, and the girl recovered – so the lord gave Jack the reward which was promised, and he went on further with his companion and with another guest of the castle who had heard what Jack had said and done.

So Jack, with his two companions travelled on towards Rome, the city of cities, where dwelt the pope, in those days the head of all Christendom. And as they were resting by the road Jack said to his companions, "Who would have thought it? One of us is going to be the Pope of Rome."

And his comrades asked him how he knew.

And he said, "The birds above in the tree have said so."

And his comrades at first laughed at him but then remembered that what he had said before of the barking of dogs and of the croaking of frogs had turned out to be true.

Now when they arrived at Rome they found that the pope had just died and that they were about to select his successor. And it was decided that all the people should pass under an arch whereon was a bell and two doves, and

he upon whose shoulders the doves should alight, and for whom the bell should ring as he passed under the arch was to be the next pope. And when Jack and his companions came near the arch they all remembered his prophecy and wondered which of the three should receive the signs. And his first comrade passed under the arch and nothing happened, and then the second and nothing happened – but when Jack went through the doves descended and alighted upon his shoulder and the bell began to toll, so Jack was made Pope of all Christendom, and he took the name of Pope Sylvester.

After a while the new pope went upon his travels and came to the town where his father dwelt. And there was a great banquet held, to which Jack's father and mother were invited at his request. And when they came he ordered his servants to give to his father the basin of water, and to his mother the towel, wherewith the pope would wash his hands after dinner. Now this was, in those days, a great honour, and people wondered why Jack's father and mother should be so honoured. But after Jack's father had offered him the basin of water, and his mother the towel, Jack said to them, "Do you not know me, mother? Do you not know me, father?" and made himself known to them and reminded his father of what the bird had said. So he forgave his father and took him and his mother to live with him ever afterwards.

Inside Again

This is an Indian tale found by Joseph Jacobs (1854–1916) and is similar to *The Tiger, the Brahman, and the Jackal*. It occurs in both early and recent times in India, in classical and modern Greece, in the earliest mediaeval collection of popular tales by Petrus Alfonsi and also in the Reynard cycle – thus ranging over more than 2000 years, with countless versions that include one of America's *Uncle Remus* tales. The common thread is the ingratitude of a rescued animal (crocodile, snake, tiger and so on) which is thwarted by its being placed back in the situation from which it was initially rescued.

A man was walking through the forest one day when he saw a funny black thing like a whip wriggling about under a big stone. He was curious to know what it all meant. So he lifted up the stone and found there a huge black snake.

"That's well," said the snake. "I have been trying to get out for two days, and, oh, how hungry I am. I must have something to eat, and there is nobody around, so I must eat you."

"But that wouldn't be fair," said the man with a trembling voice. "But for me you would never have come out from under the stone."

"I do not care for that," said the snake. "Self preservation is the first law of life; you ask anybody if that isn't so."

"Anyone will tell you," said the man, "that gratitude is

A huge black snake had been trapped under the stone

The poor old limping hound was nearly blind

a person's first duty, and surely you owe me thanks for saving your life."

"But you haven't saved my life, if I am to die of hunger," said the snake.

"Oh yes, I have," said the man; "All you have to do is to wait till you find something to eat."

"Meanwhile I shall die, and what's the use of being saved!"

So they disputed and they disputed whether the case was to be decided by the claims of gratitude or the rights of self-preservation, till they did not know what to do.

"I tell you what I'll do," said the snake, "I'll let the first passer-by decide which is right."

"But I can't let my life depend upon the word of the first comer."

"Well, we'll ask the first two that pass by."

"Perhaps they won't agree," said the man; "What are we to do then? We shall be as badly off as we are now."

"Ah, well," said the snake, "let it be the first three. In all law courts it takes three judges to make a session. We'll follow the majority of votes."

So they waited till at last there came along an old, old horse. And they put the case to him, whether gratitude should ward off death.

"I don't see why it should," said the horse. "Here have I been slaving for my master for the last fifteen years, till I am thoroughly worn out, and only this morning I heard him say, 'Roger' – that's my name – 'is no use to me any longer; I shall have to send him to the knacker's and get a few pence for his hide and his hoofs.' There's gratitude for you."

So the horse's vote was in favor of the snake. And they waited till at last an old hound passed by limping on three legs, half blind with scarcely any teeth. So they put the case to him.

"Look at me," said he; "I have slaved for my master for ten years, and this very day he has kicked me out of his house because I am no use to him any longer, and he grudged me a few bones to eat. So far as I can see, nobody acts from gratitude."

"Well," said the snake, "there's two votes for me. What's the use of waiting for the third? he's sure to decide in my favor, and if he doesn't it's two to one. Come here and I'll eat you!"

"No, no," said the man, "a bargain's a bargain; perhaps the third judge will be able to convince the other two and my life will be saved."

So they waited and they waited, till at last a fox came

601

The man promised the fox a pair of fat chickens

trotting along; and they stopped him and explained to him both sides of the case. He sat up and scratched his left ear with his hind paw, and after a while he beckoned the man to come near him. And when he did so the fox whispered, "What will you give me if I get you out of this?"

The man whispered back, "A pair of fat chickens."

"Well," said the fox, "if I am to decide this case I must clearly understand the situation. Let me see! If I comprehend aright, the man was lying under the stone and the snake –"

"No, no," cried out the horse and the hound and the snake. "It was the other way."

"Ah, ha, I see! The stone was rolling down and the man sat on it, and then –"

"Oh, how stupid you are," they all cried; "It wasn't that way at all."

"Dear me, you are quite right. I am very stupid, but, really, you haven't explained the case quite clearly to me."

"I'll show you," said the snake, impatient from his long hunger; and he twisted himself again under the stone and wriggled his tail till at last the stone settled down upon him and he couldn't move out. "That's the way it was."

"And that's the way it will be," said the fox, and, taking the man's arm, he walked off, followed by the horse and the hound. "And now for my chickens."

"I'll go and get them for you," said the man, and went up to his house, which was near, and told his wife all about it.

"But," she said, "why waste a pair of chickens on a foxy old fox! I know what I'll do."

So she went into the back yard and unloosed the dog and put it into a meal-bag and gave it to the man, who took it down and gave it to the fox, who trotted off with it to his den.

But when he opened the bag out sprung the dog and gobbled him all up.

There's gratitude for you.

Day Dreaming

Now there was once a man at Baghdad who had seven sons, and when he died he left to each of them one hundred dirhems. His fifth son, called Alnaschar the Babbler, invested all this money in some glassware, and, putting it in a big tray, from which to show and sell it, he sat down on a raised bench, at the foot of a wall, against which he leant back, placing the tray on the ground in front of him.

As he sat he began day-dreaming and said to himself: "I have laid out a hundred dirhems on this glass. Now I will surely sell it for two hundred, and with it I will buy more glass and sell that for four hundred; nor will I cease to buy and sell till I become master of much wealth. With this I will buy all kinds of merchandise and jewels and perfumes and gain great profit on them till, God willing, I will make my capital a hundred thousand dinars or two million dirhems. Then I will buy a handsome house, together with slaves and horses and trappings of gold, and fine food to eat and drink; nor will there be a singing girl in the city but I will have her to sing to me."

This he said looking at the tray before him with glassware worth a hundred dirhems. Then he continued: "When I have amassed a hundred thousand dinars I will send out marriage-brokers to demand for me in marriage the hand of the Vizier's daughter, for I hear that she is perfect in

The day dreamer imagined how every singing girl in the city would serenade him

He imagined the palatial home in which he would live and command all his servants

beauty and of surpassing grace. I will give her a dowry of a thousand dinars, and if her father consent, 'tis well; if not, I will take her by force, in spite of him. When I return home, I will buy ten little slaves and clothes for myself such as are worn by kings and sultans and get a saddle of gold, set thick with precious jewels. Then I will mount and parade the city, with slaves before and behind me, while the people will salute me and call down blessings upon me: after which I will go to the Vizier, the girl's father, with slaves behind and before me, as well as on either hand. When the Vizier sees me, he will rise and seating me in his own place, sit down below me, because I am his son-in-law."

"Now I will have with me two slaves with purses, in each a thousand dinars, and I will give him the thousand dinars of the dowry and make him a present of another thousand dinars so that he may recognize my nobility and generosity and greatness of mind and the littleness of the world in my eyes; and for every ten words he will say to me, I will answer him only two. Then I will return to my house, and if anyone come to me on the bride's part, I will make him a present of money and clothe him in a robe of honour; but if he bring me a present I will return it to him and will not accept it so that they may know how great of soul I am."

After a while Alnaschar continued: "Then I will command them to bring the Vizier's daughter to me in state and will get ready my house in fine condition to receive her. When the time of the unveiling of the bride is come, I will put on my richest clothes and sit down on a couch of brocaded silk, leaning on a cushion and turning my eyes neither to the right nor to the left, to show the haughtiness of my mind and the seriousness of my character. My bride shall stand before me like the full moon, in her robes and ornaments, and I, out of my pride and my disdain, will not look at her, till all who are present shall say to me: 'O my lord, thy wife and thy handmaid stands before thee; deign to look upon her, for standing is irksome to her.' And they will kiss the earth before me many times, whereupon I will lift my eyes and give one glance at her, then bend down my head again. Then they will carry her to the bride-chamber, and meanwhile I will rise and change my clothes for a richer suit."

"When they bring in the bride for the second time, I will not look at her till they have implored me several times, when I will glance at her and bow down my head; nor will I cease doing thus, till they have made an end of parading and displaying her. Then I will order one of my slaves to fetch a purse, and, giving it to the tire-women, command them to lead her to the bride-chamber When they leave me alone with the bride, I will not look at her or speak to her, but will sit by her with averted face, that she may say I am high of soul."

"Presently her mother will come to me and kiss my head and hands and say to me: 'O my lord, look on thy handmaid, for she longs for thy favour, and heal her spirit.' But I will give her no answer; and when she sees this, she will come and kiss my feet and say, 'O my lord, verily my daughter is a beautiful girl, who has never seen man; and if thou show her this aversion, her heart will break; so do thou be gracious to her and speak to her.'"

"Then she will rise and fetch a cup of wine, and her daughter will take it and come to me; but I will leave her standing before me, while I recline upon a cushion of cloth of gold, and will not look at her to show the haughtiness of my heart, so that she will think me to be a sultan of exceeding dignity and will say to me: 'O my lord, for God's sake, do not refuse to take the cup from thy servant's hand, for indeed I am thy handmaid.' But I will not speak to her, and she will press me, saying: 'Needs must thou drink it,' and put it to my lips. Then I will shake my fist in her face and spurn her with my foot thus." So saying, he gave a kick with his foot and knocked over the tray of glass, which fell over to the ground, and all that was in it was broken.

In his mind's eye, he could see just how it would be when the Vizier invited him into the palace

The Fisherman and the Boyard's Daughter

This is a traditional Romanian folk tale about Mariola, a Boyard's daughter who falls in love with a handsome young fisherman but hurts his pride at their wedding banquet – an act that she soon greatly regrets. A Boyard was a member of a Russian aristocratic order eventually abolished by Peter the Great.

Once on a time there was a good-looking fisherman, young and intelligent. Every time that he went through the court of a certain Boyard, Mariola, the daughter of this Boyard, would call him to her, purchase his fish, and give him money to ten times its value. So much money did he gain in this way, that he began to be indifferent to its possession and yet each day Mariola would still be a customer.

On one of these occasions, while she was handing him the money, she touched his hand and gave it a squeeze; the fisherman grew as red as a beetroot, and looked down, but regaining confidence, began to give himself airs, and twirl his moustache.

Gradually they entered into conversation, and she learned that he was unmarried, and became altogether charmed with the replies she drew from him. Although he was but a fisherman, she fell desperately in love with him, and giving him a purse of gold, she bade him go and buy clothing suitable for a gentleman, and then to come back to her to show her if they were becoming to him.

After having bought a caftan, and other things fit for a real Boyard, he dressed himself in them, and came to exhibit himself to Mariola.

She almost failed to recognise him, for both his carriage and dress were far above one of his station, and she could no

The very handsome young fisherman attracted the attention of the Boyard's daughter

A grand wedding took place despite the Boyard's doubts about the match

longer restrain the love which she had for him in her heart, and gave him to understand that he might be her husband if he wished. The fisherman hesitated, knowing that he was no match for a Boyard's daughter; but finding that she still insisted, with much bashfulness, and twirling his caciula (cap) from hand to hand, he eventually consented.

On hearing this astounding intelligence, the Boyard was very angry, saying that a fisherman was no match for his child; but as he loved Mariola so tenderly, and seeing that her heart was set upon the marriage, eventually he consented to her prayer.

Mariola again gave a purse of gold to her intended, bidding him buy wedding garments and all that was necessary. Shortly he presented himself, clad in a rich suit embroidered thickly with gold; Mariola conducted him to her father's presence, and they were at once affianced.

Not many days after this, the wedding took place, and they took their seats at the banquet given in honour of the occasion.

There was a rule in those days, that the newly-married pair should each eat from one lightly boiled egg; the fisherman cut a thin slice of bread, and was going to dip it into the egg, when Mariola caught his arm, saying, "No! I must eat of it first; I am a Boyard's daughter, and you are only a fisherman."

No reply did he make, but rising quietly from the table, quitted the banqueting hall, to the astonishment of many of the guests, who did not know that he had been a fisherman.

The bride was very troubled at the mistake she had made, and sat biting her lips with dismay and chagrin. Being unable to support her position, she withdrew to her bedroom, and locked herself in.

All night long sleep would not come to her, and she could think only of her absent bridegroom.

At early morning she went to her father to demand permission to go in search of her husband. Her father tried to dissuade her from taking such a step, but in vain, and she set off on her errand.

She traversed the town, the country, villages, country again – again villages; until at length, in one of these small villages, she saw him meanly dressed, and acting as servant at a wayside inn. Approaching him quickly, she began to address him, but he would not appear to know her, and continued his occupation. She entreated him only to speak one word to her, but he only shrugged his shoulders, and turned away his head.

The master of the inn seeing this interruption, called, "How is it that you interfere with my servant, and prevent his working? Don't you see that he is dumb? If you are as respectable as your appearance would show, I advise you to go away and leave him alone."

"He is not dumb," cried she, "He is my husband, and left me for a simple misunderstanding."

The villagers, who had collected around, were astonished at what she said, for she did not look like one who would be poking fun at them.

The innkeeper was also incredulous, saying, that a man who was able to speak, would not remain a whole week without uttering a word. In truth, all around took him to be a mute, and used to converse with him by signs. He had already gained their goodwill by his usefulness and good temper.

Mariola seeing that no one would believe her story, offered to make a bet, that in three days she would make her husband speak, if she were allowed always to be at his side; that if she did not succeed she would consent to be hung. This bet was accepted and legalised by the Prefect of the village.

The following day was to be the first of the trial. The fisherman, at the beginning of this, knew nothing of the bet, though later on, he heard a whisper of it.

Mariola was constantly entreating for one little word. "My darling," she said, "I have been very wrong; I married you because I loved you. I bind myself never again, in all our life-time, to commit such a fault; soften your heart and speak one word to me." Yet no answer came – only a shrug of the shoulders, as if he did not understand what she was saying.

The first day passed – came the second day; that passed too, and yet not a sound.

On the third day, Mariola began to tremble with fear, and followed the fisherman wherever he went, still begging him to speak only one word to her. He, on the other hand, fearing to be overcome by her tears, fled from her presence.

Son the three days had passed; all the villagers were taken up with the affair of the dumb servant at the inn, and

Mariola finally found her husband working as a servant at a merry wayside inn

the pretty looking girl who had mistaken him for someone else and brought this misfortune on herself.

The scaffold was erected, the people had congregated together to see the end of this tragedy; the officials were there, who, against their will, were bound to carry out the punishment.

The executioner approached Mariola and led her to the scaffold, saying that as she had failed to make the dumb man speak, she must accept the forfeit of her life.

Sighing, she turned her head once more towards her impassive husband, but seeing no yielding from him, she prepared herself to die. Loosening her hair, making the sign of the cross, she commended herself in prayer to God. All the spectators were moved at the sight. On the steps of the scaffold, with the Priest at her side, once more she turned towards the fisherman, crying, "My dear husband, pray come to my rescue, one word from you will suffice." Shaking his head, he looked in another direction.

With the noose in his hand, the executioner waited; soon he adjusted it around Mariola's pretty neck. One more minute and all would have been over but suddenly the fisherman, stretching forth his hand, called – "Stop!"

All the people were struck with astonishment, and tears of joy rolled down their cheeks. The executioner withdrew the noose, and the fisherman, looking severely at Mariola, asked, "Will you again taunt me with being a fisherman?"

With great emotion she cried, "Forgive me, my dear husband, I own my fault, and will never wound your feelings again."

"Let her come down," said he, "for she is indeed my wife;" and taking her by the hand, he led her back to their home, where their life was one banquet of happiness and prosperity in future.

At last the couple were reunited and lived many happy years together

Pandora's Box

Pandora was the first woman on earth, according to classic Greek mythology and the gods gave her the gift of curiosity. Pandora was given a jar (or a box in many versions) which she was told not to open under any circumstance. However, impelled by the curiosity given to her by the gods, Pandora was unable to resist the desire to discover what lay inside.

The god Zeus created a beautiful woman from clay

A swarm of beastly things flew out, humming and buzzing and stinging Pandora

Long, long in ancient Greece there were two brothers called Epimetheus and Prometheus. They had upset the gods and annoyed the most powerful of all, Zeus, so he took away from them the power to make fire.

Now Prometheus was clever and he knew that the blacksmith Hephaestos kept a fire burning to keep his forge hot so Prometheus made his way over to Lemnos and stole the blacksmith's fire. Zeus was furious and decided that the human race should be had to be punished.

He set about creating a woman from clay. The goddess Athene helped him by breathing life into her while Aphrodite made her very beautiful and Hermes taught her how to be beguiling. Mightily pleased with their creation, Zeus called her Pandora and sent her as a gift to Epimetheus.

His brother Prometheus had warned him not to accept any presents from the gods but Epimetheus was truly delighted with his gift and thought Pandora was so beautiful that he wanted to marry her.

Meanwhile cunning Zeus presented Pandora with a fine wedding gift – a beautiful box – but then told her that she must never ever open it, not on any account. Pandora was very curious about the contents of the box; she longed to see what was inside but for a good while she kept her promise although she could think of nothing else. She ached to see what lay inside. Her fingers itched to open the lid.

At last, Pandora could stand it no longer. When she knew Epimetheus was away, she took the great key off the high shelf, fitted it into the box's lock and turned it. Then, at the last moment, suddenly afraid, she quickly locked it up again. Three more times she did this until, at last, she knew she just had to take one peep!

She took the key, slid it into the lock and turned it again. She took a deep breath, closed her eyes and slowly lifted up the heavy lid.

But there was no gold or treasure inside, no silks or velvets or fine crowns. Instead Zeus had filled the box with all the terrible things – the most evil, horrid, nasty things imaginable. Out of the box they poured – disease and poverty, misery, death, sorrow – a swarm of beastly things shaped like tiny insects came whirring and buzzing out.

The creatures stung Pandora again and again as she cried and tried to slam down the lid again. Epimetheus ran into the room to see what all the noise was about. Just one thing still remained trapped inside Pandora's box, begging to be released so, as they did not feel matters could be made much worse than they already were, at last Epimetheus and Pandora decided to open the lid just once more.

The only creature that had been left inside was Hope. It fluttered from the box like a beautiful dragonfly, touching and healing Pandora's wounds as it escaped.

Even though Pandora was so sad to have introduced pain and suffering to the world, she knew that at least she had also allowed Hope to follow them and the gods, meanwhile, knew that Pandora could not really help herself. She was who she was and her curiosity was of their own making.

The Gingerbread Man

This is a classic folk tale, with no known author but instead a strong oral tradition and repetition to add to the fun as the story progresses.

Once upon a time, there was an old woman and her husband who lived in a little old house at the edge of the forest. They were very happy together – except for one thing; the couple had no children.

So, feeling lonely, the woman decided to make a child of her own – from gingerbread. She carefully mixed the batter, rolled out the dough, and cut out a very fine-looking gingerbread man. She used sugar icing to make his hair, to paint a smiling mouth, and to suggest his clothes and then she gave him for candy eyes and buttons.

What a fine gingerbread man he was now so the old woman popped him into the oven to bake. Before very long the room smelled of gingerbread baking and so she opened the oven door to see if he was ready.

Up jumped the gingerbread man, and he ran out the door saying:

"Run, run, as fast as you can!

You can't catch me!

 I'm the Gingerbread Man!"

The old woman and the old man ran after him, but they could not catch the little rascal.

And so the Gingerbread Man ran and ran. Soon he passed the threshers in the barn and called out to them as he passed by:

"I have run away from a little old woman.

I have run away from a little old man.

Run, run, as fast as you can!

You can't catch me!

I'm the Gingerbread Man!"

The barn full of threshers set out to run after him. But, though they ran as quickly as they could, they were unable to catch him.

Soon he met some mowers, mowing the long green grass and called out to them as he passed by:

"I have run away from a little old woman.

I have run away from a little old man.

I have run away from the threshers threshing.

Run, run, as fast as you can!

You can't catch me!

I'm the Gingerbread Man!"

The mowers set off at once to run after him. But, though they ran as quickly as they could, they were unable to catch him.

Next he met a cow.

"Moo," said the cow. "You look very fresh! Fresh enough to eat!" And the cow started to chase after the little man.

But the Gingerbread Man ran faster, saying:

"I ran away from an old woman.

I ran away from an old man.

I ran away from the threshers and mowers too.

And I can run away from you, Cow, too!"

And he laughed, calling out:

"Run, run, as fast as you can!

You can't catch me!

I'm the Gingerbread Man!"

So now the cow too ran after the Gingerbread Man, but she could not catch him.

The Gingerbread Man kept running, faster than ever, and soon he met a horse.

"Neigh," said the horse, "You look incredibly tasty. I think that I would like to eat you."

"But you can't!" said the Gingerbread Man.

"I ran away from an old woman

I ran away from an old man.

I ran away from the threshers too.

And the mowers and a cow who goes Moo! Moo.

And I can run away from you, too!"

And so he ran singing,

"Run, run, as fast as you can!

You can't catch me!

I'm the Gingerbread Man!"

The horse ran after the Gingerbread Man but he could not catch him.

The Gingerbread Man ran and ran, laughing and singing.

While he was running, he met a chicken.

"Cluck, cluck," said the chicken, "You look good enough to peck at for my dinner. I'm going to eat you, Mr. Gingerbread Man."

But the Gingerbread Man just laughed and said.

"I ran away from an old woman

I ran away from an old man.

I ran away from the threshers too.

I ran away from the mowers mowing the field.

I ran away from a cow.

I ran away from a horse.

And I can run away from you, too!"

And so he ran off, singing,

"Run, run, as fast as you can!

You can't catch me!

I'm the Gingerbread Man!"

The chicken ran after the Gingerbread Man, but she could not catch him.

While he was running, he met a pig.

"Oink, Oink," said the pig "You look good enough for my trough. I'm going to eat you, Mr. Gingerbread Man."

But the Gingerbread Man just laughed and said.

"I ran away from an old woman

I ran away from an old man.

I ran away from the threshers too.

I ran away from the mowers mowing the field.

I ran away from a cow.

I ran away from a horse.

I ran away from a hen

And now I can run away from you, too!"

And so he ran off, singing,

"Run, run, as fast as you can!

You can't catch me!

I'm the Gingerbread Man!"

The pig ran after the Gingerbread Man, but he could not catch the little fellow.

How proud the Gingerbread Man was that he could run so fast.

"Nobody can catch me," he thought.

So he kept on running until he met a fox.

He just had to tell the fox how he had run faster than all the others.

"Mr. Fox," he said . . .

"As tasty as I appear to be,

No-one has caught and nibbled at me.

I ran away from an old woman.

I ran away from an old man.

I ran away from the threshers too.

I ran away from the mowers mowing the field.

I ran away from a cow.

I ran away from a horse.

I ran away from a chicken.

I ran away from the pig

And I can run away from you!

Just you watch me go!"

But Mr. Fox did not seem to care.

"Why ever should I want to bother about you?" asked Mr. Fox. "You don't even look that tasty to me. No, young man, however much the others might want to swallow you up, I don't want to eat you at all, not one scrap."

The Gingerbread Man was so relieved.

"Well, indeed, Mr. Fox," said the Gingerbread Man. "If you don't mind, I think I'll take a little rest here."

And the Gingerbread Man stopped running and stood still.

And as soon as he did so . . . Snap! went Mr. Fox's jaws right into the Gingerbread Man and he gobbled him right up, until every delicious crumb was gone.

Cap o' Rushes

This Joseph Jacobs tale is a Cinderella format story and is also similar to Perrault's *Peau d'Ane* (Donkey skin). There are said to be twenty-six variants of *Cap o' Rushes* scattered through Italy, Sweden, France, Spain, Portugal, Germany, Corsica and Belgium. Almost all of these contain the 'loving-like-salt' episode and the heroine disguise. The essence of the tale is similar to themes in Shakespeare's *King Lear*, with its king and three daughters.

Well, there was once a very rich gentleman, and he had three daughters, and he thought he'd see how fond they were of him. So he says to the first, "How much do you love me, my dear?"

"Why," says she, "as I love my life."

"That's good," says he.

So he says to the second, "How much do you love me, my dear?"

"Why," says she, "better nor all the world."

"That's good," says he.

So he says to the third, "How much do you love me, my dear?"

"Why, I love you as fresh meat loves salt," says she.

Well, but he was angry. "You don't love me at all," says he, "and in my house you stay no more." So he drove her out there and then, and shut the door in her face.

Well, she went away on and on till she came to a fen,

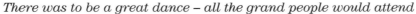

There was to be a great dance – all the grand people would attend

and there she gathered a lot of rushes and made them into a kind of a sort of a cloak with a hood, to cover her from head to foot, and to hide her fine clothes. And then she went on and on till she came to a great house.

"Do you want a maid?" says she.

"No, we don't," said they.

"I haven't anywhere to go," says she; "and I ask no wages, and do any sort of work," says she.

"Well," said they, "if you like to wash the pots and scrape the saucepans you may stay," said they.

So she stayed there and washed the pots and scraped the saucepans and did all the dirty work. And because she gave no name they called her "Cap o' Rushes".

Well, one day there was to be a great dance a little way off, and the servants were allowed to go and look on at the grand people. Cap o' Rushes said she was too tired to go, so she stayed at home.

But when they were gone, she offed with her cap o' rushes and cleaned herself, and went to the dance. And no one there was so finely dressed as she.

Well, who should be there but her master's son, and what should he do but fall in love with her the minute he set eyes on her. He wouldn't dance with anyone else.

But before the dance was done, Cap o' Rushes slipt off, and away she went home. And when the other maids came back, she was pretending to be asleep with her cap o' rushes on.

Well, next morning they said to her, "You did miss a sight, Cap o' Rushes!"

"What was that?" says she.

"Why, the beautifullest lady you ever see, dressed right gay and all. The young master, he never took his eyes off her."

"Well, I should have liked to have seen her," says Cap o' Rushes.

"Well, there's to be another dance this evening, and perhaps she'll be there."

But, come the evening, Cap o' Rushes said she was too tired to go with them. Howsoever, when they were gone, she offed with her Cap o' Rushes and cleaned herself, and away she went to the dance.

The master's son had been reckoning on seeing her, and he danced with no one else, and never took his eyes off her. But, before the dance was over, she slipt off, and home she went, and when the maids came back she pretended to be asleep with her Cap o' Rushes on.

Next day they said to her again, "Well, Cap o' Rushes, you should ha' been there to see the lady. There she was again, gay and all, and the young master he never took his eyes off her."

"Well, there," says she, "I should ha' liked to ha' seen her."

"Well," says they, "there's a dance again this evening, and you must go with us, for she's sure to be there."

Well, come this evening, Cap o' Rushes said she was too tired to go, and do what they would she stayed at home.

But when they were gone, she offed her cap o' rushes and cleaned herself, and away she went to the dance.

The master's son was rarely glad when he saw her. He danced with none but her and never took his eyes off her. When she wouldn't tell him her name, nor where she came from, he gave her a ring and told her if he didn't see her

She felt like Cinderella – the master's son would dance with no other lady

again he should die.

Well, before the dance was over, off she slipped, and home she went, and when the maids came home she was pretending to be asleep with her cap o' rushes on.

Well, next day they says to her, "There, Cap o' Rushes, you didn't come last night, and now you won't see the lady, for there's no more dances."

"Well, I should have rarely liked to have seen her," says she.

The master's son tried every way to find out where the lady was gone, but go where he might, and ask whom he

Eventually, her rich gentleman father would appreciate the importance of salt and his daughter

might he never heard anything about her. And he got worse and worse for the love of her till he had to keep his bed.

"Make some gruel for the young master," they said to the cook. "He's dying for the love of the lady." The cook set about making it when Cap o' Rushes came in.

"What are you a-doing of?" says she.

"I'm going to make some gruel for the young master," says the cook, "for he's dying for love of the lady."

"Let me make it," says Cap o' Rushes.

Well, the cook wouldn't at first, but at last she said yes, and Cap o' Rushes made the gruel. And when she had made it, she slipped the ring into it on the sly before the cook took it upstairs.

The young man he drank it and then he saw the ring at the bottom.

"Send for the cook," says he. So up she comes.

"Who made this gruel here?" says he.

"I did," says the cook, for she was frightened.

And he looked at her.

"No, you didn't," says he. "Say who did it, and you shanty be harmed."

"Well, then, twas Cap o' Rushes," says she.

"Send Cap o' Rushes here," says he.

So Cap o' Rushes came.

"Did you make my gruel?" says he.

"Yes, I did," says she.

"Where did you get this ring?" says he.

"From him that gave it me," says she.

"Who are you, then?" says the young man.

"I'll show you," says she. And she offed with her cap o' rushes, and there she was in her beautiful clothes.

Well, the master's son he got well very soon, and they were to be married in a little time. It was to be a very grand wedding, and everyone was asked far and near. And Cap o' Rushes father was asked. But she never told anybody who she was.

But before the wedding, she went to the cook, and says she:

Cap o' Rushes danced at the ball by night and cleaned the pots and pans by day

"I want you to dress every dish without a mite o' salt."

"That'll be rare nasty," says the cook.

"That doesn't signify," says she.

"Very well," says the cook.

Well, the wedding day came, and they were married. And after they were married, all the company sat down to the dinner. When they began to eat the meat, it was so tasteless they couldn't eat it. But Cap o' Rushes father tried first one dish and then another, and then he burst into tears.

"What is the matter?" said the master's son to him.

"Oh!" says he, "I had a daughter. And I asked her how much she loved me. And she said. "As much as fresh meat loves salt." And I turned her from my door, for I thought she didn't love me. And now I see she loved me best of all. And she may be dead for aught I know."

"No, father, here she is!" said Cap o' Rushes. And she goes up to him and puts her arms round him.

And so they were all happy ever after.

Androcles and the Lion

This is the Joseph Jacobs (1854–1916) version of a tale set in Ancient Rome that also inspired a witty play by George Bernard Shaw. Its beginning is similar to the Aesop fable (and appeared first in the fables of Phasdrus) but it ends very differently. There is a claim that the story is of Oriental origin, showing Buddhistic traits in the kindly relations between the slave and the lion but whatever its beginnings, the story has been with us for many centuries.

The Roman arena was a place for spectacle and blood sports

Poor Androcles was in despair; he had not strength to rise and run away, and there was the lion coming upon him. But when the great beast came up to him instead of attacking him it kept on moaning and groaning and looking at Androcles, who saw that the lion was holding out his right paw, which was covered with blood and much swollen. Looking more closely at it Androcles saw a great big thorn pressed into the paw, which was the cause of all the lion's trouble. Plucking up courage he seized hold of the thorn and drew it out of the lion's paw, who roared with pain when the thorn came out, but soon after found such relief from it that he fawned upon Androcles and showed, in every way that he knew, to whom he owed the relief. Instead of eating him up he brought him a young deer that he had slain, and Androcles managed to make a meal from it. For some time the lion continued to bring the game he had killed to Androcles, who became quite fond of the huge beast.

But one day a number of soldiers came marching through the forest and found Androcles, and as he could not explain what he was doing they took him prisoner and brought him back to the town from which he had fled. Here his master soon found him and brought him before the authorities, and he was condemned to death because he had fled from his master. Now it used to be the custom to throw murderers and other criminals to the lions in a huge circus, so that while the criminals were punished the public could enjoy the spectacle of a combat between them and the wild beasts.

So Androcles was condemned to be thrown to the lions, and on the appointed day he was led forth into the Arena and left there alone with only a spear to protect him from the lion. The Emperor was in the royal box that day and gave the signal for the lion to come out and attack Androcles. But when it came out of its cage and got near Androcles, what do you think it did? Instead of jumping upon him it fawned upon him and stroked him with its paw and made no attempt to do him any harm.

It was of course the lion which Androcles had met in the forest. The Emperor, surprised at seeing such a strange behavior in so cruel a beast, summoned Androcles to him

and asked him how it happened that this particular lion had lost all its cruelty of disposition. So Androcles told the Emperor all that had happened to him and how the lion was showing its gratitude for his having relieved it of the thorn. Thereupon the Emperor pardoned Androcles and ordered his master to set him free, while the lion was taken back into the forest and let loose to enjoy liberty once more.

The lion recognised the man who had helped him and, instead of attacking Androcles, stroked him

Will you show me the way to Fairyland?

There are many doors that lead to Fairyland or into other secret magical worlds – from wells and hollow trees to the wardrobe that leads to C.S Lewis's Narnia in *The Lion, the Witch and the Wardrobe*. Meanwhile dwarfs and trolls were often said to dwell in an Underworld, beneath us and many a cavern conceals a dragon.

The home of the elves in Norse mythology was Álfheim – a name which also appears in Scottish ballads as Elfhame (sometimes modernized as Elfland, Elfinland or Elvenland.

Author of *The Hobbit* and *Lord of the Rings*, J. R. Tolkein, anglicized Álfheim as Elvenhome, or Eldamar, set in a coastal region in the Uttermost West. The High King of the Elves in the West was Ingwë, not unlike Yngvi which was often used as a name for Frey, whose abode was in Álfheim.

However it may have been reached in fairy tales, whatever the secret portal, once over the threshold, many adventures await. Here is a world that fills children's dreams and stirs their imagination. Probably most of us in our infancy at some time hoped we might find a way into this wonderful place!

Will you show me the way to Fairyland?
There are secret doors they say
And if can you can find and open them
You'll discover the elfin ways.
Oh I do want to visit Fairyland
Will you take me there?
Will you help me to meet Aladdin
And fly on a carpet through the air?

Will you show me the way to Fairyland, Horse
If I ride upon your gleaming back?
Will you gallop away to where elves play
Along a secret forest track
Can you rise in the air like Pegasus
And gallop where rainbows shimmer?
Please will you take me to Fairyland
Where goblin lanterns glimmer.

Perhaps I should ride high on a unicorn
And stroke his gentle mane;
His horn is wonderfully magic
And spirals like sugarcane.
A unicorn grants wishes
And, although it is wild and free,
Will sleep in a maiden's lap –
How I wish one would visit me.

Oh who will show me the path to follow
Where fairies skip and dance,
Making rings in a mossy hollow
As little elves spring and prance?
How I wish I could find a snow-white bear
For I know that he would carry me there
And then if the journey he needs to share
I should soar on a goose up high in the air.

Will you help me to meet Aladdin and fly on a carpet through the air?

I should soar on a goose

If I could find a magic lamp
And a friendly genie too,
I should ride to an Eastern palace
Where every dream comes true;
With Turkish delight for supper
And a nightingale singing sweet,
I'd rest on billowing cloud-spun cushions
And turbaned princes meet.

How sweet it would be to see the stars
As a tortoise plods along,
And listen as high, up above in the sky,
Stars twinkle and sing sweet songs.

How exciting it is to ride like the wind
On a wolf that bounds without making a sound
With a prince close by as the trees fly by
And danger is all around.

Will you show me the way to Fairyland?
Can I meet the Fairy Queen?
Will she make me her special friend
Where blossom and bluebells gleam?
I must make a wish when the moon is new
Please make my Fairyland dreams come true.
Will you show me the way? Can we go today?
Do find me that door that will let me through.

Who killed Cock Robin?

The underlying theme of this English folksong may refer to the death of the legendary figure of Robin Hood or of William Rufus in the New Forest in 1100. Whatever its ancient origins, it seems that Robin was held in great esteem by the common folk. Although the song is not recorded until the 1700s there is some evidence that it might be much older and the rhyme is similar to John Skelton's *Phyllyp Sparowe* written by in about 1508. Meanwhile the use of the rhyme 'owl' with 'shovel', could suggest original older Middle English pronunciation. Versions appear in various other countries, including Germany.

"Who killed Cock Robin?"
"I," said the Sparrow,
"With my bow and arrow,
I killed Cock Robin."

"Who saw him die?"
"I," said the Fly,
"With my little eye,
I saw him die."

"Who caught his blood?"
"I," said the Fish,
"With my little dish,
I caught his blood."

"Who'll make the shroud?"
"I," said the Beetle,
"With my thread and needle,
I'll make the shroud."

"Who'll dig his grave?"
"I," said the Owl,
"With my pick and shovel,
I'll dig his grave."

"Who'll be the parson?"
"I," said the Rook,
"With my little book,
I'll be the parson."

"Who'll be the clerk?"
"I," said the Lark,
"If it's not in the dark,
I'll be the clerk."

"Who'll carry the link?"
"I," said the Linnet,
"I'll fetch it in a minute,
I'll carry the link."

"Who'll be chief mourner?"
"I," said the Dove,
"I mourn for my love,
I'll be chief mourner."

"Who'll carry the coffin?"
"I," said the Kite,
"If it's not through the night,
I'll carry the coffin."

"Who'll bear the pall?"
"We," said the Wren,
"Both the cock and the hen,
We'll bear the pall."

"Who'll sing a psalm?"
"I," said the Thrush,
As she sat on a bush,
"I'll sing a psalm."

"Who'll toll the bell?"
"I," said the bull,
"Because I can pull,
I'll toll the bell."

All the birds of the air
Fell a-sighing and a-sobbing,
When they heard the bell toll
For poor Cock Robin.

The Remarkable Rocket

This is a delightful fairy tale by Oscar Wilde (1854–1900) describing the celebrations at a royal wedding – including a grand display of fireworks at midnight.

The King's son was going to be married, so there were general rejoicings. He had waited a whole year for his bride, and at last she had arrived. She was a Russian Princess, and had driven all the way from Finland in a sledge drawn by six reindeer. The sledge was shaped like a great golden swan, and between the swan's wings lay the little Princess herself. Her long ermine-cloak reached right down to her feet, on her head was a tiny cap of silver tissue, and she was as pale as the Snow Palace in which she had always lived. So pale was she that as she drove through the streets all the people wondered. "She is like a white rose!" they cried, and they threw down flowers on her from the balconies.

At the gate of the Castle the Prince was waiting to receive her. He had dreamy violet eyes, and his hair was like fine gold. When he saw her he sank upon one knee, and kissed her hand.

"Your picture was beautiful," he murmured, "but you are more beautiful than your picture"; and the little Princess blushed.

"She was like a white rose before," said a young Page to his neighbour, "but she is like a red rose now"; and the whole Court was delighted.

For the next three days everybody went about saying, "White rose, Red rose, Red rose, White rose"; and the King gave orders that the Page's salary was to be doubled. As he received no salary at all this was not of much use to him, but it was considered a great honour, and was duly published in the Court Gazette.

When the three days were over the marriage was celebrated. It was a magnificent ceremony, and the bride and bridegroom walked hand in hand under a canopy of purple velvet embroidered with little pearls. Then there was a State Banquet, which lasted for five hours. The Prince and Princess sat at the top of the Great Hall and drank out of a cup of clear crystal. Only true lovers could drink out of this cup, for if false lips touched it, it grew grey and dull and cloudy.

"It's quite clear that they love each other," said the little Page, "as clear as crystal!" and the King doubled his salary a second time. "What an honour!" cried all the courtiers.

After the banquet there was to be a Ball. The bride and bridegroom were to dance the Rose-dance together, and the King had promised to play the flute. He played very badly, but no one had ever dared to tell him so, because he was the King. Indeed, he knew only two airs, and was never quite certain which one he was playing; but it made no matter, for, whatever he did, everybody cried out, "Charming! Charming!"

The last item on the programme was a grand display of fireworks, to be let off exactly at midnight. The little Princess had never seen a firework in her life, so the King had given orders that the Royal Pyrotechnist should be in attendance on the day of her marriage.

"What are fireworks like?" she had asked the Prince, one morning, as she was walking on the terrace.

"They are like the Aurora Borealis," said the King, who always answered questions that were addressed to other people, "only much more natural. I prefer them to stars myself, as you always know when they are going to appear, and they are as delightful as my own flute-playing. You must certainly see them."

So at the end of the King's garden a great stand had been set up, and as soon as the Royal Pyrotechnist had put everything in its proper place, the fireworks began to talk to each other.

"The world is certainly very beautiful," cried a little Squib. "Just look at those yellow tulips. Why! if they were real crackers they could not be lovelier. I am very glad I have travelled. Travel improves the mind wonderfully, and does away with all one's prejudices."

"The King's garden is not the world, you foolish squib," said a big Roman Candle; "the world is an enormous place, and it would take you three days to see it thoroughly."

"Any place you love is the world to you," exclaimed a pensive Catherine Wheel, who had been attached to an old deal box in early life, and prided herself on her broken heart; "but love is not fashionable any more, the poets

The princess arrived in a magnificent sledge, shaped like a swan

CHARLES ROBINSON

have killed it. They wrote so much about it that nobody believed them, and I am not surprised. True love suffers, and is silent. I remember myself once--But it is no matter now. Romance is a thing of the past."

"Nonsense!" said the Roman Candle, "Romance never dies. It is like the moon, and lives for ever. The bride and bridegroom, for instance, love each other very dearly. I heard all about them this morning from a brown-paper cartridge, who happened to be staying in the same drawer

the poor Catherine Wheel, who was still shaking her head, and murmuring, "Romance is dead."

"Order! order!" cried out a Cracker. He was something of a politician, and had always taken a prominent part in the local elections, so he knew the proper Parliamentary expressions to use.

"Quite dead," whispered the Catherine Wheel, and she went off to sleep.

As soon as there was perfect silence, the Rocket coughed

The royal wedding was celebrated with a magnificent firework display

as myself, and knew the latest Court news."

But the Catherine Wheel shook her head. "Romance is dead, Romance is dead, Romance is dead," she murmured. She was one of those people who think that, if you say the same thing over and over a great many times, it becomes true in the end.

Suddenly, a sharp, dry cough was heard, and they all looked round.

It came from a tall, supercilious-looking Rocket, who was tied to the end of a long stick. He always coughed before he made any observation, so as to attract attention.

"Ahem! ahem!" he said, and everybody listened except

a third time and began. He spoke with a very slow, distinct voice, as if he was dictating his memoirs, and always looked over the shoulder of the person to whom he was talking. In fact, he had a most distinguished manner.

"How fortunate it is for the King's son," he remarked, "that he is to be married on the very day on which I am to be let off. Really, if it had been arranged beforehand, it could not have turned out better for him; but, Princes are always lucky."

"Dear me!" said the little Squib, "I thought it was quite the other way, and that we were to be let off in the Prince's honour."

"It may be so with you," he answered; "indeed, I have no doubt that it is, but with me it is different. I am a very remarkable Rocket, and come of remarkable parents. My mother was the most celebrated Catherine Wheel of her day, and was renowned for her graceful dancing. When she made her great public appearance she spun round nineteen times before she went out, and each time that she did so she threw into the air seven pink stars. She was three feet and a half in diameter, and made of the

very best gunpowder. My father was a Rocket like myself, and of French extraction. He flew so high that the people were afraid that he would never come down again. He did, though, for he was of a kindly disposition, and he made a most brilliant descent in a shower of golden rain. The newspapers wrote about his performance in very flattering terms. Indeed, the Court Gazette called him a triumph of Pylotechnic art."

"Pyrotechnic, Pyrotechnic, you mean," said a Bengal Light; "I know it is Pyrotechnic, for I saw it written on my own canister."

Well, I said Pylotechnic," answered the Rocket, in a severe tone of voice, and the Bengal Light felt so crushed that he began at once to bully the little squibs, in order to show that he was still a person of some importance.

"I was saying," continued the Rocket, "I was saying – What was I saying?"

"You were talking about yourself," replied the Roman Candle.

"Of course; I knew I was discussing some interesting subject when I was so rudely interrupted. I hate rudeness and bad manners of every kind, for I am extremely sensitive. No one in the whole world is so sensitive as I am, I am quite sure of that."

"What is a sensitive person?" said the Cracker to the Roman Candle.

"A person who, because he has corns himself, always treads on other people's toes," answered the Roman Candle in a low whisper; and the Cracker nearly exploded with laughter.

"Pray, what are you laughing at?" inquired the Rocket; "I am not laughing."

"I am laughing because I am happy," replied the Cracker.

"That is a very selfish reason," said the Rocket angrily. "What right have you to be happy? You should be thinking about others. In fact, you should be thinking about me. I am always thinking about myself, and I expect everybody else to do the same. That is what is called sympathy. It is a beautiful virtue, and I possess it in a high degree. Suppose, for instance, anything happened to me to-night, what a misfortune that would be for every one! The Prince and Princess would never be happy again, their whole married life would be spoiled; and as for the King, I know he would not get over it. Really, when I begin to reflect on the importance of my position, I am almost moved to tears."

"If you want to give pleasure to others," cried the Roman Candle, "you had better keep yourself dry."

"Certainly," exclaimed the Bengal Light, who was now in better spirits; "that is only common sense."

"Common sense, indeed!" said the Rocket indignantly; "you forget that I am very uncommon, and very remarkable. Why, anybody can have common sense, provided that they have no imagination. But I have imagination, for I never think of things as they really are; I always think of them as being quite different. As for keeping myself dry, there is evidently no one here who can at all appreciate an emotional

nature. Fortunately for myself, I don't care. The only thing that sustains one through life is the consciousness of the immense inferiority of everybody else, and this is a feeling that I have always cultivated. But none of you have any hearts. Here you are laughing and making merry just as if the Prince and Princess had not just been married."

"Well, really," exclaimed a small Fire-balloon, "why not? It is a most joyful occasion, and when I soar up into the air I intend to tell the stars all about it. You will see them twinkle when I talk to them about the pretty bride."

"Ah! what a trivial view of life!" said the Rocket; "but it is only what I expected. There is nothing in you; you are hollow and empty. Why, perhaps the Prince and Princess may go to live in a country where there is a deep river, and perhaps they may have one only son, a little fair-haired boy with violet eyes like the Prince himself; and perhaps some day he may go out to walk with his nurse; and perhaps the nurse may go to sleep under a great elder-tree; and perhaps the little boy may fall into the deep river and be drowned. What a terrible misfortune! Poor people, to lose their only son! It is really too dreadful! I shall never get over it."

"But they have not lost their only son," said the Roman Candle; "no misfortune has happened to them at all."

"I never said that they had," replied the Rocket; "I said that they might. If they had lost their only son there would be no use in saying anything more about the matter. I hate people who cry over spilt milk. But when I think that they might lose their only son, I certainly am very much affected."

"You certainly are!" cried the Bengal Light. "In fact, you are the most affected person I ever met."

"You are the rudest person I ever met," said the Rocket, "and you cannot understand my friendship for the Prince."

"Why, you don't even know him," growled the Roman Candle.

"I never said I knew him," answered the Rocket. "I dare say that if I knew him I should not be his friend at all. It is a very dangerous thing to know one's friends."

"You had really better keep yourself dry," said the Fire-balloon. "That is the important thing."

"Very important for you, I have no doubt," answered the Rocket, "but I shall weep if I choose"; and he actually burst into real tears, which flowed down his stick like rain-drops, and nearly drowned two little beetles, who were just thinking of setting up house together, and were looking for a nice dry spot to live in.

"He must have a truly romantic nature," said the Catherine Wheel, "for he weeps when there is nothing at all to weep about"; and she heaved a deep sigh, and thought about the deal box.

But the Roman Candle and the Bengal Light were quite indignant, and kept saying, "Humbug! humbug!" at the top

The King had ordered that the firework expert, the Royal Pyrotechnist, should be in attendance on the day of the marriage

of their voices. They were extremely practical, and whenever they objected to anything they called it humbug.

Then the moon rose like a wonderful silver shield; and the stars began to shine, and a sound of music came from the palace.

The Prince and Princess were leading the dance. They danced so beautifully that the tall white lilies peeped in at the window and watched them, and the great red poppies nodded their heads and beat time.

Then ten o'clock struck, and then eleven, and then twelve, and at the last stroke of midnight every one came out on the terrace, and the King sent for the Royal Pyrotechnist.

"Let the fireworks begin," said the King; and the Royal Pyrotechnist made a low bow, and marched down to the end of the garden. He had six attendants with him, each of whom carried a lighted torch at the end of a long pole.

It was certainly a magnificent display.

Whizz! Whizz! went the Catherine Wheel, as she spun round and round. Boom! Boom! went the Roman Candle. Then the Squibs danced all over the place, and the Bengal Lights made everything look scarlet. "Good-bye," cried the Fire-balloon, as he soared away, dropping tiny blue sparks. Bang! Bang! answered the Crackers, who were enjoying themselves immensely. Every one was a great success except the Remarkable Rocket. He was so damp with crying that he could not go off at all. The best thing in him was the gunpowder, and that was so wet with tears that it was of no use. All his poor relations, to whom he would never speak, except with a sneer, shot up into the sky like wonderful golden flowers with blossoms of fire. Huzza! Huzza! cried the Court; and the little Princess laughed with pleasure.

"I suppose they are reserving me for some grand occasion," said the Rocket; "no doubt that is what it means," and he looked more supercilious than ever.

The next day the workmen came to put everything tidy. "This is evidently a deputation," said the Rocket; "I will receive them with becoming dignity" so he put his nose in the air, and began to frown severely as if he were thinking about some very important subject. But they took no notice of him at all till they were just going away. Then one of them caught sight of him. "Hallo!" he cried, "what a bad rocket!" and he threw him over the wall into the ditch.

"BAD Rocket? BAD Rocket?" he said, as he whirled through the air; "impossible! GRAND Rocket, that is what the man said. BAD and GRAND sound very much the same, indeed they often are the same"; and he fell into the mud.

"It is not comfortable here," he remarked, "but no doubt it is some fashionable watering-place, and they have sent me away to recruit my health. My nerves are certainly very much shattered, and I require rest."

Then a little Frog, with bright jewelled eyes, and a green mottled coat, swam up to him.

"A new arrival, I see!" said the Frog. "Well, after all there is nothing like mud. Give me rainy weather and a ditch, and I am quite happy. Do you think it will be a wet afternoon? I am sure I hope so, but the sky is quite blue and cloudless. What a pity!"

"Ahem! ahem!" said the Rocket, and he began to cough.

"What a delightful voice you have!" cried the Frog. "Really it is quite like a croak, and croaking is of course the most musical sound in the world. You will hear our glee-club this evening. We sit in the old duck pond close by the farmer's house, and as soon as the moon rises we begin. It is so entrancing that everybody lies awake to listen to us. In fact, it was only yesterday that I heard the farmer's wife say to her mother that she could not get a wink of sleep at night on account of us. It is most gratifying to find oneself so popular."

"Ahem! ahem!" said the Rocket angrily. He was very much annoyed that he could not get a word in.

"A delightful voice, certainly," continued the Frog; "I hope you will come over to the duck-pond. I am off to look for my daughters. I have six beautiful daughters, and I am so afraid the Pike may meet them. He is a perfect monster, and would have no hesitation in breakfasting off them. Well, good-bye: I have enjoyed our conversation very much, I assure you."

"Conversation, indeed!" said the Rocket. "You have talked the whole time yourself. That is not conversation."

"Somebody must listen," answered the Frog, "and I like to do all the talking myself. It saves time, and prevents arguments."

"But I like arguments," said the Rocket.

"I hope not," said the Frog complacently. "Arguments are extremely vulgar, for everybody in good society holds exactly the same opinions. Good-bye a second time; I see my daughters in the distance and the little Frog swam away.

"You are a very irritating person," said the Rocket, "and very ill-bred. I hate people who talk about themselves, as you do, when one wants to talk about oneself, as I do. It is what I call selfishness, and selfishness is a most detestable thing, especially to any one of my temperament, for I am well known for my sympathetic nature. In fact, you should take example by me; you could not possibly have a better model. Now that you have the chance you had better avail yourself of it, for I am going back to Court almost immediately. I am a great favourite at Court; in fact, the Prince and Princess were married yesterday in my honour. Of course you know nothing of these matters, for you are a provincial."

"There is no good talking to him," said a Dragon-fly, who was sitting on the top of a large brown bulrush; "no good at all, for he has gone away."

"Well, that is his loss, not mine," answered the Rocket. "I am not going to stop talking to him merely because he pays no attention. I like hearing myself talk. It is one of my greatest pleasures. I often have long conversations

Swimming up to him was a large white duck who was considered a great beauty on account of her fine waddle

all by myself, and I am so clever that sometimes I don't understand a single word of what I am saying."

"Then you should certainly lecture on Philosophy," said the Dragon- fly; and he spread a pair of lovely gauze wings and soared away into the sky.

"How very silly of him not to stay here!" said the Rocket. "I am sure that he has not often got such a chance of improving his mind. However, I don't care a bit. Genius like mine is sure to be appreciated some day"; and he sank down a little deeper into the mud.

After some time a large White Duck swam up to him. She had yellow legs, and webbed feet, and was considered a great beauty on account of her waddle.

"Quack, quack, quack," she said. "What a curious shape you are! May I ask were you born like that, or is it the result of an accident?"

"It is quite evident that you have always lived in the country," answered the Rocket, "otherwise you would know who I am. However, I excuse your ignorance. It would be unfair to expect other people to be as remarkable as oneself. You will no doubt be surprised to hear that I can fly up into the sky, and come down in a shower of golden rain."

"I don't think much of that," said the Duck, "as I cannot see what use it is to any one. Now, if you could plough the fields like the ox, or draw a cart like the horse, or look after the sheep like the collie-dog, that would be something."

"My good creature," cried the Rocket in a very haughty tone of voice, "I see that you belong to the lower orders. A person of my position is never useful. We have certain accomplishments, and that is more than sufficient. I have no sympathy myself with industry of any kind, least of all with such industries as you seem to recommend. Indeed, I have always been of opinion that hard work is simply the refuge of people who have nothing whatever to do."

"Well, well," said the Duck, who was of a very peaceable disposition, and never quarrelled with any one, "everybody has different tastes. I hope, at any rate, that you are going to take up your residence here."

"Oh! dear no," cried the Rocket. "I am merely a visitor, a distinguished visitor. The fact is that I find this place rather tedious. There is neither society here, nor solitude. In fact, it is essentially suburban. I shall probably go back to Court, for I know that I am destined to make a sensation in the world."

"I had thoughts of entering public life once myself," remarked the Duck; "there are so many things that need reforming. Indeed, I took the chair at a meeting some time ago, and we passed resolutions condemning everything that we did not like. However, they did not seem to have much effect. Now I go in for domesticity, and look after my family."

"I am made for public life," said the Rocket, "and so are all my relations, even the humblest of them. Whenever we appear we excite great attention. I have not actually appeared myself, but when I do so it will be a magnificent sight. As for domesticity, it ages one rapidly, and distracts one's mind from higher things."

"Ah! the higher things of life, how fine they are!" said the Duck; "and that reminds me how hungry I feel": and she swam away down the stream, saying, "Quack, quack, quack."

"Come back! come back!" screamed the Rocket, "I have a great deal to say to you"; but the Duck paid no attention to him. "I am glad that she has gone," he said to himself, "she has a decidedly middle-class mind"; and he sank a little deeper still into the mud, and began to think about the loneliness of genius, when suddenly two little boys in white smocks came running down the bank, with a kettle and some faggots.

"This must be the deputation," said the Rocket, and he tried to look very dignified.

"Hallo!" cried one of the boys, "look at this old stick! I wonder how it came here"; and he picked the rocket out of the ditch.

"OLD Stick!" said the Rocket, "impossible! GOLD Stick, that is what he said. Gold Stick is very complimentary. In fact, he mistakes me for one of the Court dignitaries!"

"Let us put it into the fire!" said the other boy, "it will help to boil the kettle."

So they piled the faggots together, and put the Rocket on top, and lit the fire.

"This is magnificent," cried the Rocket, "they are going to let me off in broad day-light, so that every one can see me."

"We will go to sleep now," they said, "and when we wake up the kettle will be boiled"; and they lay down on the grass, and shut their eyes.

The Rocket was very damp, so he took a long time to burn. At last, however, the fire caught him.

"Now I am going off!" he cried, and he made himself very stiff and straight. "I know I shall go much higher than the stars, much higher than the moon, much higher than the sun. In fact, I shall go so high that--"

Fizz! Fizz! Fizz! and he went straight up into the air.

"Delightful!" he cried, "I shall go on like this for ever. What a success I am!"

But nobody saw him.

Then he began to feel a curious tingling sensation all over him.

"Now I am going to explode," he cried. "I shall set the whole world on fire, and make such a noise that nobody will talk about anything else for a whole year." And he certainly did explode. Bang! Bang! Bang! went the gunpowder. There was no doubt about it.

But nobody heard him, not even the two little boys, for they were sound asleep.

Then all that was left of him was the stick, and this fell down on the back of a Goose who was taking a walk by the side of the ditch.

"Good heavens!" cried the Goose. "It is going to rain sticks"; and she rushed into the water.

"I knew I should create a great sensation," gasped the Rocket, and he went out.

Nursery Rhymes

Most nursery rhymes were not written down until the 1700s, when the publishing of children's books became more fully established.

The origins of many nursery rhymes reflect events in history and these oh-so-familiar songs from our infancy often conceal a comment on current affairs or topical issues. It is interesting to discover the underlying meanings behind the words we have so often taken for granted. Many of the lyrics parodied the famous figures of the day and royalty or political events at a time when direct dissent might have been construed as an act of treachery – with the gallows, guillotine or executioner's axe an all too realistic threat for acts against king, queen, lord or government.

Most of us are probably unaware of the historical events that relate to the songs sung in the nursery or learned in early schooldays; we take them at face value so it is interesting to give these rhymes a fresh look!

Ring-a-Ring-a-Roses

Ring-a-ring-a-roses,

A pocket full of posies;

A-tishoo! A-tishoo!

We all fall down.

This song refers to the bubonic plague and there are many versions – with some in Germany, Holland, and the USA.

A rosy rash was a symptom of the plague while posies of herbs were carried as protection and to ward off the smell of the disease. Coughing and sneezing were early symptoms and 'falling down' obviously refers to the victim's ultimate demise. Some versions include the line 'Ashes! Ashes!' and this may refer to the blackening of the skin or the burning of victims' houses and corpses.

The 'falling down' may refer to plague victims' ultimate demise

Humpty Dumpty

Humpty Dumpty sat on a wall.

Humpty Dumpty had a great fall.

All the king's horses and all the king's men

Couldn't put Humpty together again!

Humpty Dumpty was a term used in the 1400s to describe someone who was obese. Rather later, the image of Humpty Dumpty was made famous by the illustrations included in Alice through the Looking Glass by Lewis Carroll.

However, the Humpty Dumpty in the rhyme actually refers to a large cannon used during the 1600s English Civil War. During the Parliamentarian siege of the walled town of Colchester in 1648 a huge cannon called Humpty Dumpty was strategically placed on fortified St Mary's Church. When the Royalist fort and church tower was hit by the enemy, the top of the tower was blown off, sending the cannon tumbling to the ground. Naturally the infantry (the King's men) and the cavalry troops (the horses) tried to mend the vital cannon but their efforts were in vain.

Old Mother Goose

> Old Mother Goose
>
> When she wanted to wander
>
> Would fly through the air
>
> On a very fine gander.
>
> Mother Goose had a house;
>
> It stood in the wood
>
> Where an owl at the door
>
> As sentinel stood.

The familiar Mother Goose figure is the imaginary author of a collection fairy tales and rhymes and a Christmas pantomime character. She is generally depicted as an elderly country woman in a tall hat and shawl, a costume identical to the peasant costume worn in Wales in the 1900s, but is sometimes shown as a goose wearing a bonnet

Was Mother Goose meant to be a witch? The rhyme probably originates from the 1600s when there were many cruel witch hunts. As someone who was able to fly (albeit on a goose rather than a broomstick) her role as a witch is clear. Living alone in the woods with an owl as her 'familiar', Mother Goose may well have been the kind of old crone readily suspected of sorcery at that time.

Whatever, Mother Goose is the name given to an archetypal country woman like Mother Hubbard, already a stock figure in the 1500s.

Some say that that the original Mother Goose was Elizabeth Foster Goose (1665–1758) or Mary Goose (d. 1690) and her Boston grave is shown to tourists. The second wife of Isaac it is said that she used to sing songs and ditties to her grandchildren all day, and eventually, her son-in-law gathered her jingles together and printed them.

In *The Real Personages of Mother Goose* (1930), Katherine Elwes Thomas describes ancient legends of the wife of French king Robert II who is often referred to in French legends as spinning incredible tales that enraptured children.

In 1695, the initiator of the literary fairy tale genre, Charles Perrault, published a collection of fairy tales *Histoires ou contes du temps passés, avec des moralités*, which grew better known under its subtitle, *Contes de ma mère l'Oye* or *Tales of my Mother Goose*. Perrault's publication marks the first authenticated starting-point for Mother Goose stories that would not arrive in the New World until printer Isaiah Thomas reprinted Robert Samber's 1729 English volume in 1786.

The original Mother Goose may have been Elizabeth Foster Goose whose Boston grave is shown to tourists

Adam and Eve

> When Adam delved and Eve span
>
> Who was then a gentleman?

The Black Death had swept across Europe from Asia in the wake of the Crusades and killed a massive one third of the population and in its aftermath peasants suddenly realized their vital role and just how important their remaining core of workers was to the economy. Now they sought equality and this little jingle spread like wild fire, helping to fuel the resistance to their masters which culminated in the Peasants Revolt of 1381.

Adam and Eve and Pinch Me

This is a fun rhyme which children enjoy sharing – in order to have the invitation to pinch their friends! Writer Ruth Rendell used the name as the title for one of her mystery novels.

> Adam and Eve and Pinch Me
>
> Went down to the river to bathe
>
> Adam and Eve were drowned.
>
> Who do you think was saved?

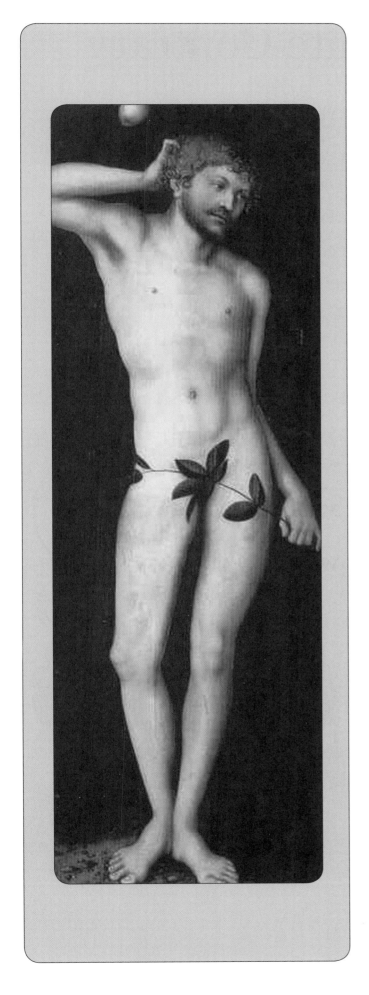

Mary, Mary, Quite Contrary

Mary, Mary, quite contrary,

How does your garden grow?

With silver bells and cockleshells,

And pretty maids all in a row.

This rhyme may refer to Mary Queen of Scots with "how does your garden grow" a comment on her reign, "silver bells" meaning Catholic cathedral bells and "cockle shells" a comment on her husband's infidelity. "Pretty maids all in a row" are probably her ladies-in-waiting.

It might also refer to Mary I of England with "How does your garden grow?" a mocking reference to her lack of heirs, or to her chief minister, Stephen Gardiner. "Quite contrary" could be a reference to her unsuccessful attempt to reverse the ecclesiastical changes implemented by her father Henry VIII while "pretty maids all in a row" may be a reference to her miscarriages – or her execution of Lady Jane Grey. "Rows and rows" may refer to her infamous burnings and executions of Protestants with the "silver bells and cockle shells" the callous instruments of torture that preceded their deaths.

Little Jack Horner

Little Jack Horner

Sat in the corner,

Eating a Christmas pie;

He put in his thumb,

And pulled out a plum,

And said "What a good boy am I!"

Ever associated with acts of opportunism, the poem has been said to refer to Prime Minister Robert Walpole. Alternatively it may mean the abbot of Glastonbury, Richard Whiting who, prior to the abbey's destruction under Henry VIII's Dissolution of the monasteries, sent Horner to London with a huge Christmas pie which had secreted inside the deeds to a dozen manors. During the journey Horner opened the pie and extracted the deeds of one manor. Records do indicate that Thomas Horner became the owner of the manor, paying for the title, but his descendants assert that the legend is untrue.

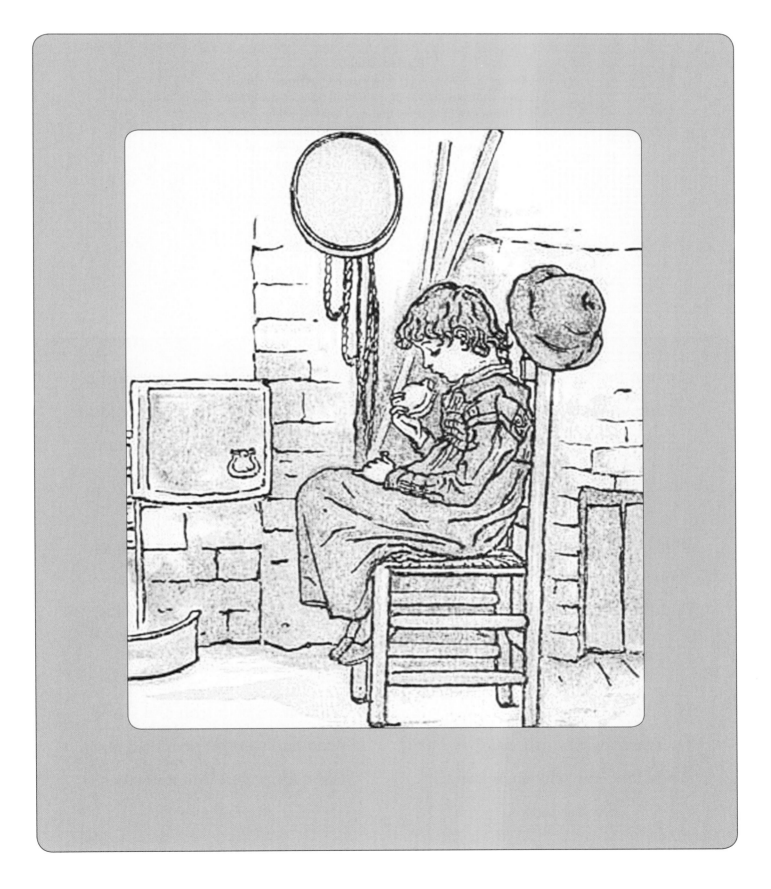

London Bridge is falling down

Buried alive!

One theory is that the song refers to the burying of children (perhaps while still alive) in the foundations of the bridge. Some 'primitive' cultures believed that a bridge would collapse unless the body of a human sacrifice were buried below. However, there is no archaeological evidence of human remains in London Bridge's foundations.

London Bridge is falling down,
Falling down, falling down.
London Bridge is falling down
My fair lady.

Build it up with wood and clay,
Wood and clay, wood and clay,
Build it up with wood and clay,
My fair lady.

Wood and clay will wash away,
Wash away, wash away,
Wood and clay will wash away,
My fair lady.

Build it up with bricks and mortar,
Bricks and mortar, bricks and mortar,
Build it up with bricks and mortar,
My fair lady.

Bricks and mortar will not stay,
Will not stay, will not stay,
Bricks and mortar will not stay,
My fair lady.

Build it up with iron and steel,
Iron and steel, iron and steel,
Build it up with iron and steel,
My fair lady.

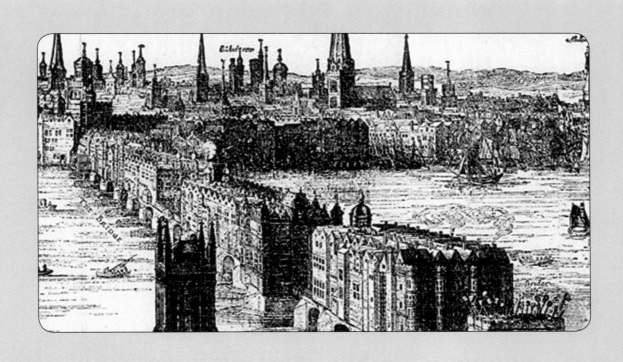

Iron and steel will bend and bow,

Bend and bow, bend and bow,

Iron and steel will bend and bow,

My fair lady.

Build it up with silver and gold,

Silver and gold, silver and gold,

Build it up with silver and gold,

My fair lady.

Silver and gold will be stolen away,

Stolen away, stolen away,

Silver and gold will be stolen away,

My fair lady.

Set a man to watch all night,

Watch all night, watch all night,

Set a man to watch all night,

My fair lady.

Suppose the man should fall asleep,

Fall asleep, fall asleep,

Suppose the man should fall asleep?

My fair lady.

Give him a pipe to smoke all night,

Smoke all night, smoke all night,

Give him a pipe to smoke all night,

My fair lady

Vikings attack the Bridge

One theory proposes that the rhyme relates to the destruction of London Bridge by Olaf II of Norway in the early 1000s; the nineteenth-century translation of the Norse saga the *Heimskringla* included a verse by Óttarr svarti that looks very similar to the nursery rhyme:

London Bridge is broken down. –

Gold is won, and bright renown.

Shields resounding,

War-horns sounding,

Hild is shouting in the din!

Arrows singing,

Mail-coats ringing –

Odin makes our Olaf win!

However, now it is believed that this was a very free translation and some historians doubt that the attack ever took place! In *The Truth About Mother Goose* (1957) by Walt Disney the rhyme refers to the deterioration of the original London Bridge which (built in 1176) had been considered a wonder of the world due to its great age and or impact of the 1666 Great Fire of London. This original bridge was finally ordered to be demolished in 1823.

Who was My Fair Lady?

Several attempts have been made to identify the 'fair lady', 'lady gay', or lady 'lee/lea' of the rhyme. She may have been Matilda of Scotland (*c*.1080–1118) consort to Henry I, who between 1110 and 1118 was responsible for the building of the series of bridges that carried the London-Colchester road across the River Lea and its side streams between Bow and Stratford. Or she was Eleanor of Provence (*c*.1223–91), Henry III's consort who had custody of the bridge revenues from 1269 to about 1281? Meanwhile a member of the Leigh family of Warwickshire had a family tradition that a human sacrifice lies under the building.

Other versions

Similar rhymes can be found across Europe, pre-dating English records. These include 'Knippelsbro Går Op og Ned' (Denmark), 'Die Magdeburger Brück' (Germany), 'pont chus' (1500s France); and 'Le porte', (1300s Italy) and the 'Podul de piatra' song and game from Romania. It is possible that the rhyme was acquired from one of these sources and then adapted to fit the most famous bridge in England.

The lion and the unicorn

The lion and the unicorn

Were fighting for the crown

The lion beat the unicorn

All around the town.

Some gave them white bread,

And some gave them brown;

Some gave them plum cake

and drummed them out of town

The legend of the two animals may have been intensified by the Acts of Union in 1707 and it was one year later that William King (1663–1712) recorded a verse very similar to the first stanza of the modern rhyme. This seems to have grown to include several other verses. Apart from those above only one survives:

And when he had beat him out,

He beat him in again;

He beat him three times over,

His power to maintain.

This rhyme was used by Lewis Carroll in *Through the Looking Glass* where they fought for the White King's crown. Here the traditional alert lion is replaced by a rather slow stupid one. Meanwhile, the Unicorn views Alice as a "monster", but promises to start believing in her if she will believe in him. Sir John Tenniel's illustrations caricature Benjamin Disraeli as the Unicorn and William Ewart Gladstone as the Lion, reflecting their parliamentary battles.

Sing a Song of Sixpence

Sing a song of sixpence

A pocket full of rye,

Four and twenty blackbirds

Baked in a pie.

When the pie was opened

The birds began to sing,

Oh wasn't that a dainty dish

To set before the king?

The king was in his counting house

Counting out his money,

The queen was in the parlour

Eating bread and honey

The maid was in the garden

Hanging out the clothes,

When down came a blackbird

And pecked off her nose!

Song birds (including blackbirds) were once eaten as a delicacy! It is known that a 16th century amusement was to place the live birds in a pie and an Italian cookbook from 1549 contained such a recipe: "to make pies so that birds may be alive in them and flie out when it is cut up". At the 1600 wedding of Henry IV of France shortly before the starter – when the guests sat down, and unfolded their napkins, songbirds flew out. The rhyme's ultimate origins are uncertain. Sir Toby Belch in Shakespeare's *Twelfth Night* tells a clown: "Come on; there is sixpence for you: let's have a song".

Some suggest that the queen symbolizes the moon, the king the sun, and the blackbirds the number of hours in a day; or the blackbirds may represent monks facing the Dissolution of the monasteries under King Henry VIII with Catherine of Aragon as the Queen and Anne Boleyn as the maid. The rye and the birds may have been seen to represent a tribute sent to Henry VII or the "pocketful of rye" may in fact refer to an older term of measurement.

Agatha Christie used the song's events as both plot theme and title in her 1929 murder mystery, *Sing a Song of Sixpence*.

The maid was in the garden, hanging out the clothes;

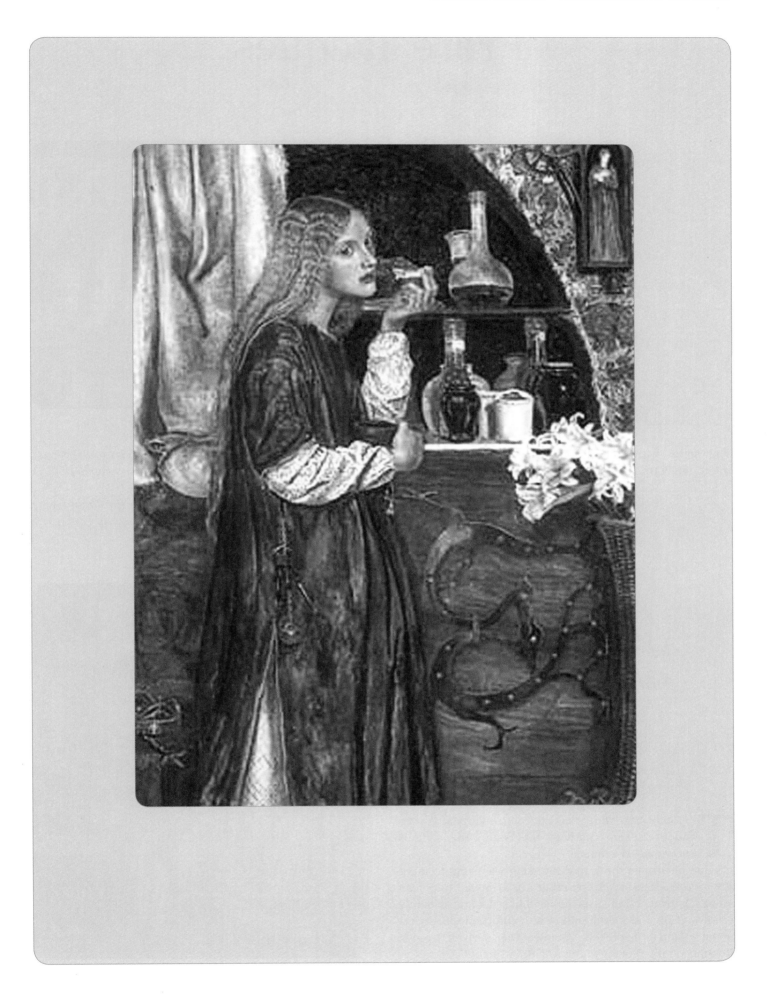

Frère Jacques

Frère Jacques,

Frère Jacques,

Dormez-vous?

Dormez-vous?

Sonnez les matines!

Sonnez les matines!

Din, dan, don.

Din, dan, don.

The song, with its tune first published in 1811, is traditionally translated into English as:

Are you sleeping?

Are you sleeping?

Brother John,

Brother John,

Morning bells are ringing!

Morning bells are ringing!

Ding, dang, dong.

Ding, dang, dong.

Bell-ringing remains a traditional part of worship and a skill that requires some diligent practice

The reputation of Dominican monks (or Jacobins) may have given rise to the song

The song has been translated into many languages and in Mexico (perhaps via Spain) the song is known as "Martinillo".

Some historians think that the song was sung to taunt Jews, Protestants or Martin Luther – or to mock Dominican monks, known in France as the Jacobin order and evidently renowned for their sloth and over-comfortable lifestyles. Some claimed that Frère Jacques was derived from a Russian seminary song about a "Father Theofil".

Ride a cock-horse to Banbury Cross

Ride a cock-horse to Banbury Cross

To see a fine lady upon a white horse;

Rings on her fingers and bells on her toes,

And she shall have music wherever she goes.

One version was printed in *Tommy Thumb's Pretty Song Book* (*c.*1744) while a 1784 version replaces the "fine lady" with "an old woman".

There is considerable speculation about the meaning of the rhyme. A medieval date had been argued for the rhyme on the grounds that the bells worn on the lady's toes refer to the fashion of wearing bells on the end of shoes in the fifteenth century. A "Cock Horse" can mean a high-spirited horse or the additional horse to assist pulling a cart or carriage up a hill. From the mid-sixteenth century it also meant a toy hobby horse.

Despite being absent or significantly different in many early versions, the "fine lady" has been associated with Queen Elizabeth. Banbury was set at the top of a steep hill and in order to help carriages up the steep incline during a royal visit a white cock horse (a large stallion) was made available to help with this task. When the Queen's carriage attempted to go up the hill a wheel broke and the Queen chose to mount the cock horse to reach Banbury cross.

Her visit was so important that the people of the town had decorated the cock horse with ribbons and bells

There is also one Celia Fiennes of Broughton Castle (with 'fine' perhaps being derived from her surname) who apparently rode side-saddle through every county in England and later published a journal about her travels.

Perhaps most famously the rhyme is thought to refer to Lady Godiva and, in some versions of the rhyme, Coventry rather than Banbury is mentioned. The wife of Earl Leofric of Mercia, she was said to have ridden naked, albeit cloaked with her long hair, through the Coventry streets – in order to gain a remission of the oppressive tax imposed by her husband on his tenants. The term 'peeping Tom' originates from later versions of this legend in which a man named Tom watched her ride and was struck blind or dead.

The nursery rhyme has been very popular for many years and was sung every day by British prime minister Gladstone to his children as they had "rides on his foot, slung over his knee".

The Queen of Hearts

The Queen of Hearts

She made some tarts,

All on a summer's day;

The Knave of Hearts

He stole those tarts,

And took them clean away.

The King of Hearts

Called for the tarts,

And beat the knave full sore;

The Knave of Hearts

Brought back the tarts,

And vowed he'd steal no more.

The queen on the playing card may represent the consort of England's Henry VII, Elizabeth of York (1466–1503). She is certainly wearing an early Tudor headdress under her crown.

The Queen may be a playing card, a character in *Alice in Wonderland* or possibly Elizabeth of Scotland, Queen of Bohemia (1596–1662) who was the eldest daughter of James VI and I, King of Scotland, England and Ireland.

Far right
The Queen of Bohemia may have inspired the nursery rhyme – her beauty attracted most of the royal suitors of Europe, giving rise to her nickname as the "Queen of Hearts"

Mr. Rabbit Nibbles up the Butter

This African-American
tale is from the pen of
Joel Chandler Harris
(1845–1908) and appears
in *The Complete Tales of
Uncle Remus.*

Uncle Remus tells the story of how the animals and the creatures just kept on getting more and more familiar with one another . . .

Now it happened like this: By and by Brer Rabbit and Brer Fox and Brer Possum got to sort of bunching their provisions together in the same shanty. And after a while the roof sort of began to leak, and one day Brer Rabbit and Brer Fox and Brer Possum gathered to see if they couldn't kind of patch it up. They had a big day's work in front

Uncle Remus tells how Brer Rabbit was unable to stop himself stealing butter

of them, and they fetched their dinner with them. They lumped the vittles up in one pile, and the butter that Brer Fox brought, they went and put it in the spring-house to keep it cool, and then they went to work, and it wasn't long before Brer Rabbit's stomach began to sort of growl and pester him. Brer Fox's butter sat heavy on his mind, and his mouth watered every time he remembered it.

Presently he said to himself that he would like to have a nip at the butter, and then he laid out his plans, he did. First thing you know, while they were working along, Brer Rabbit raised his head quickly and flung his ears forward, and hollered out, "Here I am. What do you want with me?" and off he went, like something was after him.

He sallied around, old Brer Rabbit did, and after he made sure that nobody was following, he bounced into the spring-house, and there he stayed until he got a helping of butter. Then he sauntered on back and went to work.

"Where have you been?" said Brer Fox.

"I heard my children calling me," said Brer Rabbit, "and I had to go see what they wanted. My old woman has gone and taken sick," he said.

They worked on until by and by the butter tasted so good that old Brer Rabbit wanted some more. Then he raised up his head, he did, and hollered out, "He-yo! Hold on! I'm a-coming!" And off he went.

This time he stayed a good while, and when he got back, Brer Fox asked him where he'd been.

"I've been to see my old woman, and she's sinking," he said.

Directly Brer Rabbit heard them calling him again, and off he went, and this time, bless your soul, he got the butter out so clean that he could see himself in the bottom of the bucket. He scraped it clean and licked it dry, and then he went back to work looking like a black man that had been picked up by the plantation patrol.

"How's your old woman this time?" said Brer Rabbit.

"I'm obliged to you, Brer Fox," said Brer Rabbit, "but I'm afraid that she's gone by now," and that sort of made Brer Fox and Brer Possum feel in mourning with Brer Rabbit.

By and by, when dinnertime came, they all got out their vittles, but Brer Rabbit kept on looking lonesome, and Brer Fox and Brer Possum, they sort of rustled around to see if they couldn't make Brer Rabbit feel sort of splimmy.

"What is that, Uncle Remus?" asked the little boy.

"Sort of splimmy-splammy [feeling fine], honey. Sort of like he was among friends, sort of like his old woman wasn't dead after all. You know what folks do when they are around people who are mourning?

The butter barrel proved an irresistible lure

Mr Rabbit as depicted in 1881

Brer Rabbit, Brer Fox and Brer Bear had many adventures together

Cartoon of the author Mr Joel Chandler Harris with Brer Rabbit watching him

The Brer Rabbit family

The little boy didn't know, fortunately for him, and Uncle Remus went on:

Brer Fox and Brer Possum rustled around, they did, getting out the vittles, and by and by Brer Fox, he said, "Brer Possum, you run down to the spring and fetch the butter, and I'll sail around you and set the table," he said.

Brer Possum, he loped off after the butter, and directly he came loping back with his ears a-trembling and his tongue a-hanging out.

"Brer Fox!" he hollered out.

"What's the matter now, Brer Possum?" he said.

"You all had better run, folks" said Brer Possum. "The last drop of that butter is gone."

"Where did it go?" said Brer Fox.

"It looks like it dried up," said Brer Possum.

Then Brer Rabbit, he looked sort of solemn, he did, and he up and said, "I suspect that the butter melted in somebody's mouth," he said.

Then they went down to the spring with Brer Possum, and sure enough, the butter was gone. While they were talking about the mystery, Brer Rabbit said that he could see tracks all around there, and he pointed out that if they would all go to sleep, he could catch the chap that stole the butter.

They all lay down, and Brer Fox and Brer Possum, they soon dropped off to sleep, but Brer Rabbit, he stayed awake, and when the time came, he got up easy, and smeared Brer Possum's mouth with the butter on his paws, and then he ran off and nibbled up the best of the dinner that they had left lying out, and then he came back and woke up Brer Fox and showed him the butter on Brer Possum's mouth. Then they woke up Brer Possum and told him about it, but of course Brer Possum denied it to the last.

Now Brer Fox, he's kind of a lawyer, and he argued this way: that Brer Possum was the first one at the butter, and the first one to miss it, and more than that, there were the signs on his mouth.

Brer Possum could see that they had him jammed up in a corner, and then he up and said that the way to catch the man that stole the butter was to build a big brush heap and set it on fire, and everyone would try to jump over it, and the one that fell in, that would be the chap that stole the butter.

Brer Rabbit and Brer Fox, they both agreed, they did, and they whirled in and built the brush heap, and they built it high, and they built it wide, and then they touched it off. When it got to blazing up good, Brer Rabbit he took the first turn. He sort of stepped back, and looked around and giggled, and over he went, just like a bird flying.

Then came Brer Fox. He got back a little further, and spit on his hands, and lit out and made the jump, and he came so close to falling in that his tail caught fire.

"Haven't you ever seen a fox, honey?" inquired Uncle Remus, in a tone that implied both conciliation and information.

The little boy thought probably he had, but he wouldn't commit himself.

"Well then, continued the old man, "next time you see one of them, you look right close and see if the end of his tail isn't white. It's just like I tell you. They bear the scar of that brush right down to this day. They are marked, that's what they are. They are marked."

"And what about Brother Possum?" asked the little boy.

"Old Brer Possum, he took a running start, he did, and he came lumbering along, and he lit – kerblam! –- right in the middle of the fire, and that was the last of old Brer Possum."

"But, Uncle Remus, Brother Possum didn't steal the butter after all," said the little boy, who was not at all satisfied with such summary injustice.

"That's what makes me say what I say, honey. In this world, lots of folks have to suffer for other folks' sins. It looks like it's mighty wrong, but it's just that way. Tribulation seems like it's a-waiting just around the corner to catch one and all of us, honey."

Brer Rabbit tells the youngsters just how tempting butter can be

The Star-Child

This fairy tale by Oscar Wilde is set in a winter forest and focusses on the difficulties faced by the hungry animals and birds in the coldest months as well as the hardship of poor woodcutters whose lives are changed by the arrival of a child that seems to have fallen from the stars.

They went down five brass steps into a garden filled with black poppies

O nce upon a time two poor Woodcutters were making their way home through a great pine-forest. It was winter, and a night of bitter cold. The snow lay thick upon the ground, and upon the branches of the trees: the frost kept snapping the little twigs on either side of them, as they passed: and when they came to the Mountain-Torrent she was hanging motionless in air, for the Ice-King had kissed her.

So cold was it that even the animals and the birds did not know what to make of it.

'Ugh!' snarled the Wolf, as he limped through the brushwood with his tail between his legs, 'this is perfectly monstrous weather. Why doesn't the Government look to it?'

'The Earth is going to be married, and this is her bridal dress,' whispered the Turtle-doves to each other. Their little pink feet were quite frost-bitten, but they felt that it was their duty to take a romantic view of the situation.

'Nonsense!' growled the Wolf. 'I tell you that it is all the fault of the Government, and if you don't believe me I shall eat you.' The Wolf had a thoroughly practical mind, and was never at a loss for a good argument.

'Well, for my own part,' said the Woodpecker, who was a born philosopher, 'I don't care an atomic theory for explanations. If a thing is so, it is so, and at present it is terribly cold.'

Terribly cold it certainly was. The little Squirrels, who lived inside the tall fir-tree, kept rubbing each other's noses to keep themselves warm, and the Rabbits curled themselves up in their holes, and did not venture even to look out of doors. The only people who seemed to enjoy it were the great horned Owls. Their feathers were quite stiff with rime, but they did not mind, and they rolled their large yellow eyes, and called out to each other across the forest, 'Tu-whit! Tu-whoo! Tu-whit! Tu-whoo! what delightful weather we are having!'

On and on went the two Woodcutters, blowing lustily upon their fingers, and stamping with their huge iron-shod boots upon the caked snow. Once they sank into a deep drift, and came out as white as millers are, when the stones are grinding; and once they slipped on the hard smooth ice where the marsh-water was frozen, and their faggots fell out of their bundles, and they had to pick them up and

Being weary she sat down under a chestnut tree to rest

bind them together again; and once they thought that they had lost their way, and a great terror seized on them, for they knew that the Snow is cruel to those who sleep in her arms. But they put their trust in the good Saint Martin, who watches over all travellers, and retraced their steps, and went warily, and at last they reached the outskirts of the forest, and saw, far down in the valley beneath them, the lights of the village in which they dwelt.

So overjoyed were they at their deliverance that they laughed aloud, and the Earth seemed to them like a flower of silver, and the Moon like a flower of gold.

Yet, after that they had laughed they became sad, for they remembered their poverty, and one of them said to the other, 'Why did we make merry, seeing that life is for the rich, and not for such as we are? Better that we had died of cold in the forest, or that some wild beast had fallen upon us and slain us.'

'Truly,' answered his companion, 'much is given to some, and little is given to others. Injustice has parcelled out the world, nor is there equal division of aught save of sorrow.'

But as they were bewailing their misery to each other this strange thing happened. There fell from heaven a very bright and beautiful star. It slipped down the side of the sky, passing by the other stars in its course, and, as they watched it wondering, it seemed to them to sink behind a clump of willow-trees that stood hard by a little sheepfold no more than a stone's-throw away.

'Why! there is a crook of gold for whoever finds it,' they cried, and they set to and ran, so eager were they for the gold.

And one of them ran faster than his mate, and outstripped him, and forced his way through the willows, and came out on the other side, and lo! there was indeed a thing of gold lying on the white snow. So he hastened towards it, and stooping down placed his hands upon it, and it was a cloak of golden tissue, curiously wrought with stars, and wrapped in many folds. And he cried out to his comrade that he had found the treasure that had fallen from the sky, and when his comrade had come up, they sat them down in the snow, and loosened the folds of the cloak that they might divide the pieces of gold. But, alas! no gold was in it, nor silver, nor, indeed, treasure of any kind, but only a little child who was asleep.

And one of them said to the other: 'This is a bitter ending to our hope, nor have we any good fortune, for what doth a child profit to a man? Let us leave it here, and go our way, seeing that we are poor men, and have children of our own whose bread we may not give to another.'

But his companion answered him: 'Nay, but it were an evil thing to leave the child to perish here in the snow, and though I am as poor as thou art, and have many mouths to

feed, and but little in the pot, yet will I bring it home with me, and my wife shall have care of it.'

So very tenderly he took up the child, and wrapped the cloak around it to shield it from the harsh cold, and made his way down the hill to the village, his comrade marvelling much at his foolishness and softness of heart.

And when they came to the village, his comrade said to him, 'Thou hast the child, therefore give me the cloak, for it is meet that we should share.'

But he answered him: 'Nay, for the cloak is neither mine nor thine, but the child's only,' and he bade him Godspeed, and went to his own house and knocked.

And when his wife opened the door and saw that her husband had returned safe to her, she put her arms round his neck and kissed him, and took from his back the bundle of faggots, and brushed the snow off his boots, and bade him come in.

But he said to her, 'I have found something in the forest, and I have brought it to thee to have care of it,' and he stirred not from the threshold.

'What is it?' she cried. 'Show it to me, for the house is bare, and we have need of many things.' And he drew the cloak back, and showed her the sleeping child.

'Alack, goodman!' she murmured, 'Have we not children of our own, that thou must needs bring a changeling to sit by the hearth? And who knows if it will not bring us bad fortune? And how shall we tend it?' And she was wroth against him.

'Nay, but it is a Star-Child,' he answered; and he told her the strange manner of the finding of it.

But she would not be appeased, but mocked at him, and spoke angrily, and cried: 'Our children lack bread, and shall we feed the child of another? Who is there who careth for us? And who giveth us food?'

'Nay, but God careth for the sparrows even, and feedeth them,' he answered.

'Do not the sparrows die of hunger in the winter?' she asked. 'And is it not winter now?'

And the man answered nothing, but stirred not from the threshold.

And a bitter wind from the forest came in through the open door, and made her tremble, and she shivered, and said to him: 'Wilt thou not close the door? There cometh a bitter wind into the house, and I am cold.'

'Into a house where a heart is hard cometh there not always a bitter wind?' he asked. And the woman answered him nothing, but crept closer to the fire.

And after a time she turned round and looked at him, and her eyes were full of tears. And he came in swiftly, and placed the child in her arms, and she kissed it, and laid it in a little bed where the youngest of their own children was lying. And on the morrow the Woodcutter took the curious cloak of gold and placed it in a great chest, and a chain of amber that was round the child's neck his wife took and set it in the chest also.

A bright and beautiful star fell from heaven

So the Star-Child was brought up with the children of the

Woodcutter, and sat at the same board with them, and was their playmate. And every year he became more beautiful to look at, so that all those who dwelt in the village were filled with wonder, for, while they were swarthy and black-haired, he was white and delicate as sawn ivory, and his curls were like the rings of the daffodil. His lips, also, were like the petals of a red flower, and his eyes were like violets by a river of pure water, and his body like the narcissus of a field where the mower comes not.

Yet did his beauty work him evil. For he grew proud, and cruel, and selfish. The children of the Woodcutter, and the other children of the village, he despised, saying that they were of mean parentage, while he was noble, being sprang from a Star, and he made himself master over them, and called them his servants. No pity had he for the poor, or for those who were blind or maimed or in any way afflicted, but would cast stones at them and drive them forth on to the highway, and bid them beg their bread elsewhere, so that none save the outlaws came twice to that village to ask for alms. Indeed, he was as one enamoured of beauty, and would mock at the weakly and ill-favoured, and make jest of them; and himself he loved, and in summer, when the winds were still, he would lie by the well in the priest's orchard and look down at the marvel of his own face, and laugh for the pleasure he had in his fairness.

Often did the Woodcutter and his wife chide him, and say: 'We did not deal with thee as thou dealest with those who are left desolate, and have none to succour them. Wherefore art thou so cruel to all who need pity?'

Often did the old priest send for him, and seek to teach him the love of living things, saying to him: 'The fly is thy brother. Do it no harm. The wild birds that roam through the forest have their freedom. Snare them not for thy pleasure. God made the blind-worm and the mole, and each has its place. Who art thou to bring pain into God's world? Even the cattle of the field praise Him.'

But the Star-Child heeded not their words, but would frown and flout, and go back to his companions, and lead them. And his companions followed him, for he was fair, and fleet of foot, and could dance, and pipe, and make music. And wherever the Star-Child led them they followed, and whatever the Star-Child bade them do, that did they. And when he pierced with a sharp reed the dim eyes of the mole, they laughed, and when he cast stones at the leper they laughed also. And in all things he ruled them, and they became hard of heart even as he was.

Now there passed one day through the village a poor beggar-woman. Her garments were torn and ragged, and her feet were bleeding from the rough road on which she had travelled, and she was in very evil plight. And being weary she sat her down under a chestnut-tree to rest.

But when the Star-Child saw her, he said to his companions, 'See! There sitteth a foul beggar-woman under that fair and green-leaved tree. Come, let us drive her hence, for she is ugly and ill-favoured.'

So he came near and threw stones at her, and mocked

her, and she looked at him with terror in her eyes, nor did she move her gaze from him. And when the Woodcutter, who was cleaving logs in a haggard hard by, saw what the Star-Child was doing, he ran up and rebuked him, and said to him: 'Surely thou art hard of heart and knowest not mercy, for what evil has this poor woman done to thee that thou shouldst treat her in this wise?'

And the Star-Child grew red with anger, and stamped his foot upon the ground, and said, 'Who art thou to question me what I do? I am no son of thine to do thy bidding.'

'Thou speakest truly,' answered the Woodcutter, 'yet did I show thee pity when I found thee in the forest.'

And when the woman heard these words she gave a loud cry, and fell into a swoon. And the Woodcutter carried her to his own house, and his wife had care of her, and when she rose up from the swoon into which she had fallen, they set meat and drink before her, and bade her have comfort.

But she would neither eat nor drink, but said to the Woodcutter, 'Didst thou not say that the child was found in the forest? And was it not ten years from this day?'

And the Woodcutter answered, 'Yea, it was in the forest that I found him, and it is ten years from this day.'

'And what signs didst thou find with him?' she cried. 'Bare he not upon his neck a chain of amber? Was not round him a cloak of gold tissue broidered with stars?'

'Truly,' answered the Woodcutter, 'it was even as thou sayest.' And he took the cloak and the amber chain from the chest where they lay, and showed them to her.

And when she saw them she wept for joy, and said, 'He is my little son whom I lost in the forest. I pray thee send for him quickly, for in search of him have I wandered over the whole world.'

So the Woodcutter and his wife went out and called to the Star-Child, and said to him, 'Go into the house, and there shalt thou find thy mother, who is waiting for thee.'

So he ran in, filled with wonder and great gladness. But when he saw her who was waiting there, he laughed scornfully and said, 'Why, where is my mother? For I see none here but this vile beggar-woman.'

And the woman answered him, 'I am thy mother.'

'Thou art mad to say so,' cried the Star-Child angrily. 'I am no son of thine, for thou art a beggar, and ugly, and in rags. Therefore get thee hence, and let me see thy foul face no more.'

'Nay, but thou art indeed my little son, whom I bare in the forest,' she cried, and she fell on her knees, and held out her arms to him. 'The robbers stole thee from me, and left thee to die,' she murmured, 'but I recognised thee when I saw thee, and the signs also have I recognised, the cloak of golden tissue and the amber chain. Therefore I pray thee come with me, for over the whole world have I

Only a little child who was asleep

Two poor woodcutters were making their way home through a great pine-forest

wandered in search of thee. Come with me, my son, for I have need of thy love.'

But the Star-Child stirred not from his place, but shut the doors of his heart against her, nor was there any sound heard save the sound of the woman weeping for pain.

And at last he spoke to her, and his voice was hard and bitter. 'If in very truth thou art my mother,' he said, 'it had been better hadst thou stayed away, and not come here to bring me to shame, seeing that I thought I was the child of some Star, and not a beggar's child, as thou tellest me that I am. Therefore get thee hence, and let me see thee no more.'

'Alas! my son,' she cried, 'wilt thou not kiss me before I go? For I have suffered much to find thee.'

'Nay,' said the Star-Child, 'but thou art too foul to look at, and rather would I kiss the adder or the toad than thee.'

So the woman rose up, and went away into the forest weeping bitterly, and when the Star-Child saw that she had gone, he was glad, and ran back to his playmates that he might play with them.

But when they beheld him coming, they mocked him and said, 'Why, thou art as foul as the toad, and as loathsome as the adder. Get thee hence, for we will not suffer thee to play with us,' and they drave him out of the garden.

And the Star-Child frowned and said to himself, 'What is this that they say to me? I will go to the well of water and look into it, and it shall tell me of my beauty.'

So he went to the well of water and looked into it, and lo! his face was as the face of a toad, and his body was sealed like an adder. And he flung himself down on the grass and wept, and said to himself, 'Surely this has come upon me by reason of my sin. For I have denied my mother, and driven her away, and been proud, and cruel to her. Wherefore I will go and seek her through the whole world, nor will I rest till I have found her.'

And there came to him the little daughter of the Woodcutter, and she put her hand upon his shoulder and said, 'What doth it matter if thou hast lost thy comeliness? Stay with us, and I will not mock at thee.'

And he said to her, 'Nay, but I have been cruel to my mother, and as a punishment has this evil been sent to me. Wherefore I must go hence, and wander through the world till I find her, and she give me her forgiveness.'

So he ran away into the forest and called out to his mother to come to him, but there was no answer. All day long he called to her, and, when the sun set he lay down to sleep on a bed of leaves, and the birds and the animals fled from him, for they remembered his cruelty, and he was alone save for the toad that watched him, and the slow adder that crawled past.

And in the morning he rose up, and plucked some bitter berries from the trees and ate them, and took his way through the great wood, weeping sorely. And of everything that he met he made inquiry if perchance they had seen his mother.

He said to the Mole, 'Thou canst go beneath the earth. Tell me, is my mother there?'

And the Mole answered, 'Thou hast blinded mine eyes. How should I know?'

He said to the Linnet, 'Thou canst fly over the tops of the tall trees, and canst see the whole world. Tell me, canst thou see my mother?'

And the Linnet answered, 'Thou hast clipt my wings for thy pleasure. How should I fly?'

And to the little Squirrel who lived in the fir-tree, and was lonely, he said, 'Where is my mother?'

And the Squirrel answered, 'Thou hast slain mine. Dost thou seek to slay thine also?'

And the Star-Child wept and bowed his head, and prayed forgiveness of God's things, and went on through the forest, seeking for the beggar-woman. And on the third day he came to the other side of the forest and went down into the plain.

And when he passed through the villages the children mocked him, and threw stones at him, and the carlots would not suffer him even to sleep in the byres lest he might bring mildew on the stored corn, so foul was he to look at, and their hired men drave him away, and there was none who had pity on him. Nor could he hear anywhere of the beggar-woman who was his mother, though for the space of three years he wandered over the world, and often seemed to see her on the road in front of him, and would call to her, and run after her till the sharp flints made his feet to bleed. But overtake her he could not, and those who dwelt by the way did ever deny that they had seen her, or any like to her, and they made sport of his sorrow.

For the space of three years he wandered over the world, and in theworld there was neither love nor loving-kindness nor charity for him, but it was even such a world as he had made for himself in the days of his great pride.

And one evening he came to the gate of a strong-walled city that stood by a river, and, weary and footsore though he was, he made to enter in. But the soldiers who stood on guard dropped their halberts across the entrance, and said roughly to him, 'What is thy business in the city?'

'I am seeking for my mother,' he answered, 'and I pray ye to suffer me to pass, for it may be that she is in this city.'

But they mocked at him, and one of them wagged a black beard, and set down his shield and cried, 'Of a truth, thy mother will not be merry when she sees thee, for thou art more ill-favoured than the toad of the marsh, or the adder that crawls in the fen. Get thee gone. Get thee gone. Thy mother dwells not in this city.'

And another, who held a yellow banner in his hand, said to him, 'Who is thy mother, and wherefore art thou seeking for her?'

And he answered, 'My mother is a beggar even as I am, and I have treated her evilly, and I pray ye to suffer me to pass that she may give me her forgiveness, if it be that she tarrieth in this city.' But they would not, and pricked him with their spears.

And, as he turned away weeping, one whose armour was inlaid with gilt flowers, and on whose helmet couched a lion that had wings, came up and made inquiry of the soldiers who it was who had sought entrance. And they said to him, 'It is a beggar and the child of a beggar, and we have driven him away.'

'Nay,' he cried, laughing, 'but we will sell the foul thing for a slave, and his price shall be the price of a bowl of sweet wine.'

And an old and evil-visaged man who was passing by called out, and said, 'I will buy him for that price,' and, when he had paid the price, he took the Star-Child by the hand and led him into the city.

And after that they had gone through many streets they came to a little door that was set in a wall that was covered with a pomegranate tree. And the old man touched the door with a ring of graved jasper and it opened, and they went down five steps of brass into a garden filled with black poppies and green jars of burnt clay. And the old man took then from his turban a scarf of figured silk, and bound with it the eyes of the Star-Child, and drove him in front of him. And when the scarf was taken off his eyes, the Star-Child found himself in a dungeon, that was lit by a lantern of horn.

And the old man set before him some mouldy bread on a trencher and said, 'Eat,' and some brackish water in a cup and said, 'Drink,' and when he had eaten and drunk, the old man went out, locking the door behind him and fastening it with an iron chain.

And on the morrow the old man, who was indeed the subtlest of the magicians of Libya and had learned his art from one who dwelt in the tombs of the Nile, came in to him and frowned at him, and said, 'In a wood that is nigh to the gate of this city of Giaours there are three pieces

The forest was a wonderful place for the woodcutters and their families in summer time but was bitter cold once winter arrived

of gold. One is of white gold, and another is of yellow gold, and the gold of the third one is red. To-day thou shalt bring me the piece of white gold, and if thou bringest it not back, I will beat thee with a hundred stripes. Get thee away quickly, and at sunset I will be waiting for thee at the door of the garden. See that thou bringest the white gold, or it shall go ill with thee, for thou art my slave, and I have bought thee for the price of a bowl of sweet wine.'

And he bound the eyes of the Star-Child with the scarf of figured silk, and led him through the house, and through the garden of poppies, and up the five steps of brass. And having opened the little door with his ring he set him in the street.

And the Star-Child went out of the gate of the city, and came to the wood of which the Magician had spoken to him.

Now this wood was very fair to look at from without, and seemed full of singing birds and of sweet-scented flowers, and the Star-Child entered it gladly. Yet did its beauty profit him little, for wherever he went harsh briars and thorns shot up from the ground and encompassed him, and evil nettles stung him, and the thistle pierced him with her daggers, so that he was in sore distress. Nor could he anywhere find the piece of white gold of which the Magician had spoken, though he sought for it from morn to noon, and from noon to sunset. And at sunset he set his face towards home, weeping bitterly, for he knew what fate was in store for him.

But when he had reached the outskirts of the wood, he heard from a thicket a cry as of some one in pain. And forgetting his own sorrow he ran back to the place, and saw there a little Hare caught in a trap that some hunter had set for it.

And the Star-Child had pity on it, and released it, and said to it, 'I am myself but a slave, yet may I give thee thy freedom.'

And the Hare answered him, and said: 'Surely thou hast given me freedom, and what shall I give thee in return?'

And the Star-Child said to it, 'I am seeking for a piece of white gold, nor can I anywhere find it, and if I bring it not to my master he will beat me.'

'Come thou with me,' said the Hare, 'and I will lead thee to it, for I know where it is hidden, and for what purpose.'

So the Star-Child went with the Hare, and lo! in the cleft of a great oak-tree he saw the piece of white gold that he was seeking. And he was filled with joy, and seized it, and said to the Hare, 'The service that I did to thee thou hast rendered back again many times over, and the kindness that I showed thee thou hast repaid a hundred-fold.'

'Nay,' answered the Hare, 'but as thou dealt with me, so I did deal with thee,' and it ran away swiftly, and the Star-Child went towards the city.

Now at the gate of the city there was seated one who was a leper. Over his face hung a cowl of grey linen, and through the eyelets his eyes gleamed like red coals. And when he saw the Star-Child coming, he struck upon a wooden bowl, and clattered his bell, and called out to him, and said, 'Give me a piece of money, or I must die of hunger. For they have thrust me out of the city, and there is no one who has pity on me.'

'Alas!' cried the Star-Child, 'I have but one piece of money in my wallet, and if I bring it not to my master he will beat me, for I am his slave.'

But the leper entreated him, and prayed of him, till the Star-Child had pity, and gave him the piece of white gold.

And when he came to the Magician's house, the Magician opened to him, and brought him in, and said to him, 'Hast thou the piece of white gold?' And the Star-Child answered, 'I have it not.' So the Magician fell upon him, and beat him, and set before him an empty trencher, and said, 'Eat,' and an empty cup, and said, 'Drink,' and flung him again into the dungeon.

And on the morrow the Magician came to him, and said, 'If to-day thou bringest me not the piece of yellow gold, I will surely keep thee as my slave, and give thee three hundred stripes.'

So the Star-Child went to the wood, and all day long he searched for the piece of yellow gold, but nowhere could he find it. And at sunset he sat him down and began to weep, and as he was weeping there came to him the little Hare that he had rescued from the trap,

And the Hare said to him, 'Why art thou weeping? And what dost thou seek in the wood?'

And the Star-Child answered, 'I am seeking for a piece of yellow gold that is hidden here, and if I find it not my master will beat me, and keep me as a slave.'

'Follow me,' cried the Hare, and it ran through the wood till it came to a pool of water. And at the bottom of the pool the piece of yellow gold was lying.

'How shall I thank thee?' said the Star-Child, 'for lo! this is the second time that you have succoured me.'

'Nay, but thou hadst pity on me first,' said the Hare, and it ran away swiftly.

And the Star-Child took the piece of yellow gold, and put it in his wallet, and hurried to the city. But the leper saw him coming, and ran to meet him, and knelt down and cried, 'Give me a piece of money or I shall die of hunger.'

And the Star-Child said to him, 'I have in my wallet but one piece of yellow gold, and if I bring it not to my master he will beat me and keep me as his slave.'

A woodcutter at work

But the leper entreated him sore, so that the Star-Child had pity on him, and gave him the piece of yellow gold.

And when he came to the Magician's house, the Magician opened to him, and brought him in, and said to him, 'Hast thou the piece of yellow gold?' And the Star-Child said to him, 'I have it not.' So the Magician fell upon him, and beat him, and loaded him with chains, and cast him again into the dungeon.

And on the morrow the Magician came to him, and said, 'If to-day thou bringest me the piece of red gold I will set thee free, but if thou bringest it not I will surely slay thee.'

So the Star-Child went to the wood, and all day long he searched for the piece of red gold, but nowhere could he find it. And at evening he sat him down and wept, and as he was weeping there came to him the little Hare.

And the Hare said to him, 'The piece of red gold that thou seekest is in the cavern that is behind thee. Therefore weep no more but be glad.'

'How shall I reward thee?' cried the Star-Child, 'for lo! this is the third time thou hast succoured me.'

'Nay, but thou hadst pity on me first,' said the Hare, and it ran away swiftly.

And the Star-Child entered the cavern, and in its farthest corner he found the piece of red gold. So he put it in his wallet, and hurried to the city. And the leper seeing him coming, stood in the centre of the road, and cried out, and said to him, 'Give me the piece of red money, or I must die,' and the Star-Child had pity on him again, and gave him the piece of red gold, saying, 'Thy need is greater than mine.' Yet was his heart heavy, for he knew what evil fate awaited him.

But lo! as he passed through the gate of the city, the guards bowed down and made obeisance to him, saying, 'How beautiful is our lord!' and a crowd of citizens followed him, and cried out, 'Surely there is none so beautiful in the whole world!' so that the Star- Child wept, and said to himself, 'They are mocking me, and making light of my misery.' And so large was the concourse of the people, that he lost the threads of his way, and found himself at last in a great square, in which there was a palace of a King.

And the gate of the palace opened, and the priests and the high officers of the city ran forth to meet him, and they abased themselves before him, and said, 'Thou art our lord for whom we have been waiting, and the son of our King.'

And the Star-Child answered them and said, 'I am no king's son, but the child of a poor beggar-woman. And how say ye that I am beautiful, for I know that I am evil to look at?'

Then he, whose armour was inlaid with gilt flowers, and on whose helmet crouched a lion that had wings, held up a shield, and cried, 'How saith my lord that he is not beautiful?'

And the Star-Child looked, and lo! his face was even as it had been, and his comeliness had come back to

him, and he saw that in his eyes which he had not seen there before.

And the priests and the high officers knelt down and said to him, 'It was prophesied of old that on this day should come he who was to rule over us. Therefore, let our lord take this crown and this sceptre, and be in his justice and mercy our King over us.'

But he said to them, 'I am not worthy, for I have denied the mother who bare me, nor may I rest till I have found her, and known her forgiveness. Therefore, let me go, for I must wander again over the world, and may not tarry here, though ye bring me the crown and the sceptre.' And as he spake he turned his face from them towards the street that led to the gate of the city, and lo! amongst the crowd that pressed round the soldiers, he saw the beggar-woman who was his mother, and at her side stood the leper, who had sat by the road.

And a cry of joy broke from his lips, and he ran over, and kneeling down he kissed the wounds on his mother's feet, and wet them with his tears. He bowed his head in the dust, and sobbing, as one whose heart might break, he said to her: 'Mother, I denied thee in the hour of my pride. Accept me in the hour of my humility. Mother, I gave thee hatred. Do thou give me love. Mother, I rejected thee. Receive thy child now.' But the beggar-woman answered him not a word.

And he reached out his hands, and clasped the white feet of the leper, and said to him: 'Thrice did I give thee of my mercy. Bid my mother speak to me once.' But the leper answered him not a word.

And he sobbed again and said: 'Mother, my suffering is greater than I can bear. Give me thy forgiveness, and let me go back to the forest.' And the beggar-woman put her hand on his head, and said to him, 'Rise,' and the leper put his hand on his head, and said to him, 'Rise,' also.

And he rose up from his feet, and looked at them, and lo! they were a King and a Queen.

And the Queen said to him, 'This is thy father whom thou hast succoured.'

And the King said, 'This is thy mother whose feet thou hast washed with thy tears.' And they fell on his neck and kissed him, and brought him into the palace and clothed him in fair raiment, and set the crown upon his head, and the sceptre in his hand, and over the city that stood by the river he ruled, and was its lord. Much justice and mercy did he show to all, and the evil Magician he banished, and to the Woodcutter and his wife he sent many rich gifts, and to their children he gave high honour. Nor would he suffer any to be cruel to bird or beast, but taught love and loving-kindness and charity, and to the poor he gave bread, and to the naked he gave raiment, and there was peace and plenty in the land.

Yet ruled he not long, so great had been his suffering, and so bitter the fire of his testing, for after the space of three years he died. And he who came after him ruled evilly.

The Old Woman and her Pig

This Joseph Jacobs (1894-1916) tale is another one that uses repetition and adds one more character to the list as the story goes along – a common theme in fairy and folk tales all around the world.

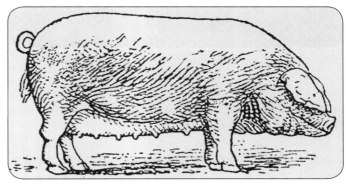

The pig refused to go over the stile

An old woman was sweeping her house, and she found a little crooked sixpence. "What," said she, "shall I do with this little sixpence? I will go to market, and buy a little pig."

As she was coming home, she came to a stile: but the piggy wouldn't go over the stile.

She went a little further, and she met a dog. So she said to the dog: "Dog! bite pig; piggy won't go over the stile; and I shan't get home to-night." But the dog wouldn't.

She went a little further, and she met a stick. So she said: "Stick! stick! beat dog! dog won't bite pig; piggy won't get over the stile; and I shan't get home to-night." But the stick wouldn't.

The old woman found a crooked sixpence and set off to buy a pig

She went a little further, and she met a fire. So she said: "Fire! fire! burn stick; stick won't beat dog; dog won't bite pig; piggy won't get over the stile; and I shan't get home to-night." But the fire wouldn't.

She went a little further, and she met some water. So she said: "Water, water! quench fire; fire won't burn stick; stick won't beat dog; dog won't bite pig; piggy won't get over the stile; and I shan't get home to-night." But the water wouldn't.

She went a little further, and she met an ox. So she said: "Ox! ox! drink water; water won't quench fire; fire won't burn stick; stick won't beat dog; dog won't bite pig; piggy won't get over the stile; and I shan't get home to-night." But the ox wouldn't.

She went a little further, and she met a butcher. So she said: "Butcher! butcher! kill ox; ox won't drink water; water won't quench fire; fire won't burn stick; stick won't beat dog; dog won't bite pig; piggy won't get over the stile; and I shan't get home to-night." But the butcher wouldn't.

She went a little further, and she met a rope. So she said: "Rope! rope! hang butcher; butcher won't kill ox; ox won't drink water; water won't quench fire; fire won't burn stick; stick won't beat dog; dog won't bite pig; piggy won't get over the stile; and I shan't get home to-night." But the rope wouldn't.

She went a little further, and she met a rat. So she said: "Rat! rat! gnaw rope; rope won't hang butcher; butcher won't kill ox; ox won't drink water; water won't quench fire; fire won't burn stick; stick won't beat dog; dog won't bite pig; piggy won't get over the stile; and I shan't get home to-night." But the rat wouldn't.

She went a little further, and she met a cat. So she said: "Cat! cat! kill rat; rat won't gnaw rope; rope won't hang butcher; butcher won't kill ox; ox won't drink water; water won't quench fire; fire won't burn stick; stick won't beat dog; dog won't bite pig; piggy won't get over the stile; and I shan't get home to-night." But the cat said to her, "If you will go to yonder cow, and fetch me a saucer of milk, I will kill the rat." So away went the old woman to the cow.

But the cow said to her: "If you will go to yonder hay-stack, and fetch me a handful of hay, I'll give you the

The old bent woman finally arrived home that night

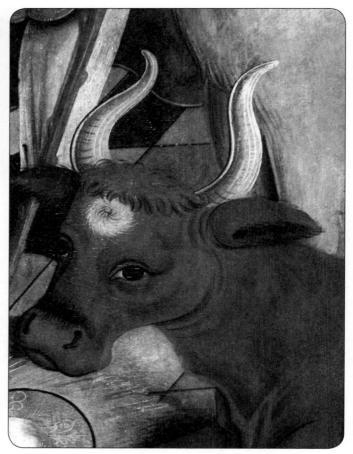

milk." So away went the old woman to the haystack and she brought the hay to the cow.

As soon as the cow had eaten the hay, she gave the old woman the milk; and away she went with it in a saucer to the cat.

As soon as the cat had lapped up the milk, the cat began to kill the rat; the rat began to gnaw the rope; the rope began to hang the butcher; the butcher began to kill the ox; the ox began to drink the water; the water began to quench the fire; the fire began to burn the stick; the stick began to beat the dog; the dog began to bite the pig; the little pig in a fright jumped over the stile, and so the old woman got home that night.

The ox would not drink the water

At long last the pig jumped over the stile

The Cat and the Mouse

In many respects this tale is similar to *The Old Woman and her Pig* with the same kind of repetition and run of names ending the story – in a way similar to how Bengali women end their folk-tales. This the Joseph Jacobs (1854–1916) version.

The cat and the mouse played in the malt-house:

 The cat bit the mouse's tail off.

 "Pray, Puss, give me my tail."

"No," says the cat, "I'll not give you your tail, till you go to the cow, and fetch me some milk."

First she leapt, and then she ran, till she came to the cow, and thus began:

"Pray, Cow, give me milk, that I may give cat milk, that cat may give me my own tail again."

"No," said the cow, "I will give you no milk, mouse, till you go to the farmer, and get me some hay."

First she leapt, and then she ran, till she came to the farmer, and thus began:

"Pray, Farmer, give me hay, that I may give cow hay, that cow may give me milk, that I may give cat milk, that cat may give me my own tail again."

"No," says the farmer, "I'll give you no hay, till you go to the butcher and fetch me some meat."

The mouse asked the farmer for hay

The mouse asked the baker for bread

At last the cat gave mouse her own tail back again

First the mouse leapt and then she ran

The farmer gave the hay

First she leapt, and then she ran, till she came to the butcher, and thus began:

"Pray, Butcher, give me meat, that I may give farmer meat, that farmer may give me hay, that I may give cow hay, that cow may give me milk, that I may give cat milk, that cat may give me my own tail again."

"No," says the butcher, "I'll give you no meat, till you go to the baker and fetch me some bread."

First she leapt, and then she ran, till she came to the baker, and thus began:

"Pray, Baker, give me bread, that I may give butcher bread, that butcher may give me meat, that I may give farmer meat, that farmer may give me hay, that I may give cow hay, that cow may give me milk, that I may give cat milk, that cat may give me my own tail again."

"Yes," says the baker, "I'll give you some bread but if you eat my meal, I'll cut off your head."

Then the baker gave mouse bread, and mouse gave butcher bread, and butcher gave mouse meat, and mouse gave farmer meat, and farmer gave mouse hay, and mouse gave cow hay, and cow gave mouse milk, and mouse gave cat milk, and cat gave mouse her own tail again.

The butcher gave mouse meat

The Old Woman who Lost her Dumpling

> Lafcadio Hearn (1850-1904)
> translated five volumes of
> *Japanese Fairy Tales* including
> this one about an old woman who
> drops her dumpling down a hole.
> While trying to recover it, she
> falls through the earth and finds
> herself in a strange country.

Long, long ago there was a funny old woman, who liked to laugh and to make dumplings of rice-flour.

One day, while she was preparing some dumplings for dinner, she let one fall; and it rolled into a hole in the earthen floor of her little kitchen and disappeared. The old woman tried to reach it by putting her hand down the hole, and all at once the earth gave way, and the old woman fell in.

She fell quite a distance, but was not a bit hurt; and when she got up on her feet again, she saw that she was standing on a road, just like the road before her house. It was quite light down there; and she could see plenty of rice-fields, but no one in them. How all this happened, I cannot tell you. But it seems that the old woman had fallen into another country. The road she had fallen upon sloped very much: so, after having looked for her dumpling in vain, she thought that it must have rolled farther away down the slope. She ran down the road to look, crying:

"My dumpling, my dumpling! Where is that dumpling of mine?"

After a little while she saw a stone Jizo standing by the roadside, and she said:

"O Lord Jizo, did you see my dumpling?" Jizo answered:

"Yes, I saw your dumpling rolling by me down the road. But you had better not go any farther, because there is a wicked Oni living down there, who eats people."

But the old woman only laughed, and ran on further down the road, crying: "My dumpling, my dumpling! Where is that dumpling of mine?" And she came to another statue of Jizo, and asked it:

"O kind Lord Jizo, did you see my dumpling?"

And Jizo said:

"Yes, I saw your dumpling go by a little while ago. But you must not run any further, because there is a wicked Oni down there, who eats people."

But she only laughed, and ran on, still crying out: "My dumpling, my dumpling! Where is that dumpling of mine?" And she came to a third Jizo, and asked it:

"O dear Lord Jizo, did you see my dumpling?"

But Jizo said:

"Don't talk about your dumpling now. Here is the Oni coming. Squat down here behind my sleeve, and don't make any noise."

Presently the Oni came very close, and stopped and bowed to Jizo, and said:

"Good-day, Jizo San!"

Jizo said good-day, too, very politely.

Then the Oni suddenly snuffed the air two or three times in a suspicious way, and cried out: "Jizo San, Jizo San! I smell a smell of mankind somewhere – don't you?"

"Oh!" said Jizo, "perhaps you are mistaken."

"No, no!" said the Oni after snuffing the air again, "I smell a smell of mankind."

Then the old woman could not help laughing, "Te he-he!" and the Oni immediately reached down his big hairy hand behind Jiao's sleeve, and pulled her out, still laughing, "Te-he-he!"

"Ah! ha!" cried the Oni.

Then Jizo said:

"What are you going to do with that good old woman? You must not hurt her."

"I won't," said the Oni. "But I will take her home with me to cook for us."

"Te-he-he!" laughed the old woman.

"Very well," said Jizo; "but you must really be kind to her. If you are not, I shall be very angry."

"I won't hurt her at all," promised the Oni; "and she will only have to do a little work for us every day. Good bye, Jizo San."

Then the Oni took the old woman far down the road, till they came to a wide deep river, where there was a boat. He put her into the boat, and took her across the river to his house. It was a very large house. He led her at once into

The funny old woman liked to laugh and to make rice-flour dumplings

the kitchen, and told her to cook some dinner for himself and the other Oni who lived with him. And he gave her a small wooden rice-paddle, and said:

"You must always put only one grain of rice into the pot, and when you stir that one grain of rice in the water with this paddle, the grain will multiply until the pot is full."

So the old woman put just one rice-grain into the pot, as the Oni told her, and began to stir it with the paddle; and, as she stirred, the one grain became two ... then four ... then eight ... then sixteen, thirty-two, sixty-four, and so on. Every time she moved the paddle the rice increased in quantity; and in a few minutes the great pot was full.

After that, the funny old woman stayed a long time in the house of the Oni, and every day cooked food for him and for all his friends. The Oni never hurt or frightened her, and her work was made quite easy by the magic paddle-although she had to cook a very, very great quantity of rice, because an Oni eats much more than any human being eats.

But she felt lonely, and always wished very much to go back to her own little house, and make her dumplings. And one day, when the Oni were all out somewhere, she thought she would try to run away.

She first took the magic paddle, and slipped it under her girdle; and then she went down to the river. No one saw her; and the boat was there. She got into it, and pushed off; and as she could row very well, she was soon far away from the shore.

But the river was very wide; and she had not rowed more than one-fourth of the way across, when the Oni, all of them, came back to the house.

They found that their cook was gone, and the magic paddle, too. They ran down to the river at once, and saw the old woman rowing away very fast.

Perhaps they could not swim: at all events they had no boat; and they thought the only way they could catch the funny old woman would be to drink up all the water of the river before she got to the other bank. So they knelt down, and began to drink so fast that before the old woman had got half way over, the water had become quite low.

But the old woman kept on rowing until the water had got so shallow that the Oni stopped drinking, and began to wade across. Then she dropped her oar, took the magic paddle from her girdle, and shook it at the Oni, and made such funny faces that the Oni all burst out laughing.

But the moment they laughed, they could not help throwing up all the water they had drunk, and so the river became full again. The Oni could not cross; and the funny old woman got safely over to the other side, and ran away up the road as fast as she could. She never stopped running until she found herself at home again.

After that she was very happy; for she could make dumplings whenever she pleased. Besides, she had the magic paddle to make rice for her. She sold her dumplings to her neighbors and passengers, and in quite a short time she became rich.

But the river was very wide; and she had not rowed more than one-fourth of the way across, when the *Oni*, all of them, came back to the house.

She fell into a strange land and asked everyone she met if they had seen her dumpling

This is the house that Jack built

This is the rat that ate the malt

A cumulative tale, this fun narrative describes all the various characters involved with Jack's house. Some believe that the rhyme is derived from an Aramaic hymn *Chad Gadya* (One Young Goat) first printed in 1590; but although this is an early cumulative tale that may have inspired the form, the lyrics are very different. Others think that the "priest all shaven and shorn" indicates that the English version may indeed be mid-1500s. The story was printed in numerous collections in the late 1700s and early 1800s, with Randolph Caldecott's illustrated version appearing in 1878.
A lovely old timber-framed house called Cherrington Manor in Shropshire, England, is reputed to be the actual house that Jack built and there is a former malt house in the grounds.

This is the house that Jack built.

This is the malt that lay in the house that Jack built.

This is the rat that ate the malt

That lay in the house that Jack built.

This is the cat that killed the rat

That ate the malt

That lay in the house that Jack built.

This is the dog that worried the cat

That killed the rat that ate the malt

That lay in the house that Jack built.

This is the cow with the crumpled horn

That tossed the dog that worried the cat

That killed the rat that ate the malt

That lay in the house that Jack built.

This is the maiden all forlorn

That milked the cow with the crumpled horn

That tossed the dog that worried the cat

That killed the rat that ate the malt

That lay in the house that Jack built.

This is the man all tattered and torn

That kissed the maiden all forlorn

That milked the cow with the crumpled horn

That tossed the dog that worried the cat

That killed the rat that ate the malt

That lay in the house that Jack built.

This is the priest all shaven and shorn

That married the man all tattered and torn

That kissed the maiden all forlorn

That milked the cow with the crumpled horn

That tossed the dog that worried the cat

That killed the rat that ate the malt

That lay in the house that Jack built.

This is the cock that crowed in the morn

That waked the priest all shaven and shorn

That married the man all tattered and torn

That kissed the maiden all forlorn

That milked the cow with the crumpled horn

That tossed the dog that worried the cat

That killed the rat that ate the malt

That lay in the house that Jack built.

This is the man all tattered and torn

This is the farmer sowing his corn

That kept the cock that crowed in the morn

That waked the priest all shaven and shorn

That married the man all tattered and torn

That kissed the maiden all forlorn

That milked the cow with the crumpled horn

That tossed the dog that worried the cat

That killed the rat that ate the malt

That lay in the house that Jack built.

This is the horse and the hound and the horn

That belonged to the farmer sowing his corn

That kept the cock that crowed in the morn

That waked the priest all shaven and shorn

That married the man all tattered and torn

That kissed the maiden all forlorn

That milked the cow with the crumpled horn

That tossed the dog that worried the cat

That killed the rat that ate the malt

That lay in the house that Jack built.

This is the house that Jack built!

This is the cock that crowed in the morn

The Red Swan

This is a traditional Native American tale and a wonderful combination of magic and heroism as a young brave accomplishes many tasks and finds wives for himself and his brothers. He meets several magicians, and a red swan who is actually a beautiful woman who becomes his wife. The story was discovered by Margaret Bemister (1877-) and there are several versions (one by Cornelius Mathews) with some different endings. This is the one by Margaret Compton (1852 – 1903), published in 1907. Such tales were often recited during the winter solstice to mark the return of the sun.

Great chief, Red Thunder, was travelling with his wife and three children to a council of the nations. When they were near the place appointed for the meeting, one of the children saw a beautiful white bird winging its way high in the air. He pointed upwards, clapping his hands with delight, for it was flying swiftly towards the earth and the sun was shining on its broad back and wings.

While the smile was on their faces the bird suddenly appeared above them, and in a moment struck their mother to the earth, driving her into the ground so that no portion of her body remained. The force of the blow was so great that the bird itself was broken in pieces and its plumes were scattered far and wide. The Indians assembled at the council, rushed forth eagerly to secure them; for a white feather is not easily procured and is highly prized in time of war.

Red Thunder stood speechless in his great agony. Then taking his little ones with him he hied into the forest, and no man ever saw him again. He built himself a lodge and never passed far from its doorway. When Winter shook his white locks and covered the land with snow, Red Thunder fell, shot by an unseen arrow.

Thus the three boys were left alone. Even the eldest was not large enough or strong enough to bring home much food, and all that they could do was to set snares for rabbits. The animals were sorry for them and took them in charge. The squirrels dropped nuts at their doorway, and a great brown bear kept guard over them at night. They were too young to remember much of their parents, and they were brave boys, who tried their best to learn how to hunt and fish. The eldest soon became skillful and he taught his brothers.

When they were all able to take care of themselves, the eldest wanted to leave them and go to see the world, to find other lodges and bring home wives for each of them. The younger ones would not hear of this, and said that they had gone along so far well without strangers, and they could still do without them. So they continued to live together and no more was said about any of them leaving.

One day they wanted new quivers for their arrows. One made his of otter, another chose sheep, and a third took wolf skin. Then they thought it well to make new arrows. They made many, some being of oak and a few, very precious, of the thigh-bone of the buck. It took them much longer to fashion the heads of flint and sandstone; but at last all were finished, and they were ready for a grand hunt. They laid wagers with one another as to who should come in first with game, each one agreeing to kill only the animal he was in the habit of taking, and not to meddle with what he knew belonged to his brother.

The youngest, named Deep Voice, had not gone far when he met a black bear, which according to the agreement he was not to kill. But the animal was so close to him that he could not refrain from taking aim. The bear fell dead at his feet. His scruples were gone then, so he began skinning it.

Soon his eyes troubled him and he rubbed them with his bloody hands, when, on looking up, everything appeared red. He went to the brook and washed his hands and face, but the same red hue was still on the trees, the ground, and even on the skin of the black bear. He heard a strange noise, and leaving the animal partly skinned, went to see whence it came.

By following the sound he came to the shore of a great lake, where he saw a beautiful swan swimming. Its feathers were not like those of any other swan he had ever seen, for they were a brilliant scarlet and glistened in the sun.

He drew one of his arrows and fired at it, but the arrow fell short of its mark. He shot again and again

The beautiful swan had brilliant scarlet feathers

until his quiver was empty. Still the swan remained dipping its long neck into the water, seemingly ignorant of the hunter's presence.

Then he remembered that three magic arrows which had belonged to his father were in the wigwam. At any other time he would not have thought of meddling with them; but he was determined to secure this beautiful bird. He ran quickly to the lodge, brought the arrows and fired them. The first went very near the bird, but did not strike it. The second also fell harmless in the water. The third struck the swan in the neck; but she rose immediately and flew towards the setting sun.

Deep Voice was disappointed, and knowing that his brothers would be angry about the loss of the arrows, he rushed into the water and secured the first two, but found that the third had been carried off by the red swan.

He thought that as the bird was wounded it could not fly far, so, placing the magic arrows in his quiver, he ran on to overtake it. Over hills and prairies, through the forests and out on the plain he went, till at last it grew dark and he lost sight of the swan.

On coming out of the forest he heard voices in the distance, and knew that people could not be far off. He looked about and saw a large town on a distant hill and heard the watchman, an old owl, call out, "We are visited," to which the people answered with a loud "Hallo!"

Deep Voice approached the watchman and told him that he came for no evil purpose, but merely to ask for shelter. The owl said nothing, but led him to the lodge of the Chief, and told him to enter.

"Come in, come in," said the Chief; "Sit there," he added, as the young man appeared. He was given food to eat and but few questions were asked him.

By and by the Chief, who had been watching him closely, said, "Daughter, take our son-in-law's moccasins, and if they need mending, do it for him."

Deep Voice was much astonished to find himself married at such short notice, but made up his mind to let one of his brothers have her for his wife. She was not good-looking and she proved herself bad-tempered by snatching the moccasins in such a surly manner that Deep Voice ran after her, took them from her and hung them up himself.

Being very tired he soon fell asleep. Early next morning he said to the girl: "Which way did the red swan go?"

"Do you think you can catch it?" she said, and turned angrily away.

Yes," he answered.

"Foolishness!" said the girl; but as he persisted, she went to the door and showed him the direction in which the bird had flown. It was still dark, and as the road was strange to him he travelled slowly. When daylight came he started to run and ran all day as fast as lie could. Towards night he was almost exhausted and was glad to find himself near another village, where he might be able to rest.

This village also had an owl for a watchman, a large, gray bird, who saw him at a distance and called to those in

afternoon, showed him the exact course it took and pointed out the shortest road to the prairie.

He went slowly until sunrise and then ran as before. He was a swift runner, for he could shoot an arrow and then pass it in its flight so that it would fall behind him. He did this many times on the second day, for it helped him to travel faster. Towards evening, not seeing any town, he went more leisurely, thinking that he would have to travel all night.

Soon after dark he saw a glow of light in the woods, and found when he went nearer that it came from a small, low lodge. He went cautiously on and looked in at the doorway.

The three magic arrows were still in the wigwam

The watchman was a wise old owl who called out, "We are visited!"

the camp, "Tu-who! We are visited."

Deep Voice was shown to the lodge of the Chief and treated exactly as on the first night. This time the Chief's daughter was beautiful and gentle in her ways. "She shall be for my elder brother," thought the boy, "for he has always been kind to me."

He slept soundly all night and it was nearly dawn when he awoke; but he lost no time, for the Chief's daughter was ready to answer his questions at once. She told him the red swan had passed about the middle of the previous

An old man was sitting by the fire, his head bent forward on his breast.

Although Deep Voice had not made the slightest noise the old man called out, "Come in, my grandson."

The boy entered.

"Take a seat there," said the old man, pointing to a corner opposite him by the fire. "Now dry your things, for you must be tired, and I will cook supper for you. My kettle of water stands near the fire."

Deep Voice had been looking about the fireplace, but

694

A great brown bear had kept guard over the three boys at night

had seen no kettle. Now there appeared a small earthen pot filled with water. The old man took one grain of corn and one whortleberry, dropped them into the pot and set it where it would boil. Deep Voice was hungry and thought to himself that there was small chance of a good supper.

When the water boiled the old man took the kettle off, handed him a dish and spoon made of the same material as the pot and told him to help himself. Deep Voice found the soup so good that he helped himself again and again until he had taken all there was. He felt ashamed, but he was still hungry.

Before he could speak, the old man said, "Eat, eat, my grandchild, help yourself," and motioned to the pot, which was immediately refilled.

Deep Voice again helped himself to all the soup and again the kettle was filled, and his hunger was satisfied. Then the pot vanished.

"My grandchild," said the old man, when Deep Voice had finished, "you have set out on a difficult journey, but you will succeed. Only be determined, and be prepared for whatever may happen. Tomorrow you will go on your way until the sun sets, when you will find one of my fellow-magicians. He will give you food and shelter and will tell you more than I am permitted to do. Only

be firm. On the day beyond to-morrow you will meet still another who will tell you all you wish to know and how you are to gain your wish."

Deep Voice lay down on the buffalo skins, which were white and soft, and slept soundly; for the old man's words made him very happy. The magician prepared his breakfast as he had done the supper, after which the boy went on his way. He found the second magician as he had been told, and was given a supper from a magic kettle, and a couch upon white buffalo robes.

The second magician did not seem so sure of the young man's success. "Many have gone this way before you," said he, "and none have ever come back. We shall see, we shall see."

This was said to try the courage of Deep Voice; but he remembered what the first magician had told him and was firm in his resolution.

After breakfast next day he ran forward quickly, for he was anxious to meet the third magician who should tell him all about the red swan. But though he ran all day he did not get to the third lodge any earlier than he had reached the others.

After a supper prepared as on the previous nights, the magician said to him: "My grandchild, to-morrow night you will come to the lodge of the Red Swan. She is not a bird, but a beautiful girl, the most beautiful that ever lived. Her father is a magician and rich in wampum. This wampum is of much value, for many of the shells were brought from the Great Salt Lake; but he prizes his daughter far more than all. The Red Swan loves her father, and all her life is spent in making him comfortable. The old man has met with a misfortune, having lost his cap of wampum which used to be fastened to his scalp and was never removed, night or day. A tribe of Indians, who had heard of it, one day sent to him, saying that their Chief's daughter was very ill and that but one thing could cure her – a sight of

groans, which he believed came from the lodge of the Red Swan.

It was not long before he reached a fine wigwam, and on entering saw the magician seated in the center, holding his head with both hands and moaning with pain.

The old man prepared supper, for no one was allowed to see the Red Swan, or even to know that she was in the wigwam. But Deep Voice saw a curtain dividing the lodge, and thought that he heard a rustle of wings.

His heart did not fail him, and he answered the old man's questions patiently and truthfully. When he told his dreams, the magician shook his head, saying, "No,

As he travelled on the tribes all made him welcome

this magic cap of wampum. The magician did not suspect the messengers, though he tried to persuade them to bring the maiden to him. They declared that she could not be moved; whereupon the old man tore off his cap, though it gave him much pain to do so, and sent it to the Chief. The story was all a pretence; and when they got the cap they made fun of it and placed it on a pole for the birds to peck at, and the stranger to ridicule. The old man is not strong enough to get the cap back; but he has been told that a young warrior shall some day procure it for him. The Red Swan goes forth in the Moon of Falling Leaves to seek for this Brave, and she has promised to be the wife of him who is successful. My grandchild, many have followed her and have failed, but I think you will be more favored. When you are seated in the lodge of the Red Swan, the magician will ask you many things. Tell him your dreams and what your guardian spirits have done for you. Then he will ask you to recover his cap of wampum and will show you what you are to do to find and punish the wicked possessors of it."

Deep Voice was greatly pleased to hear that he might win such a beautiful wife. He leaped and ran gaily through the forest the next day, and the idea that he might fail never entered his mind. Towards evening he heard deep

that is not the one, that is not it," to each, until Deep Voice thought he would not tell him any more. He was not willing, however, to give up the Red Swan, so at last he remembered a dream wholly different from the others, which he straightway told.

The magician became quite excited before he had finished his story, and exclaimed: "That's it, that's it! You will cause me to live! That is what I have been waiting for a young man to say. Will you go and get my cap for me?"

"Yes," said Deep Voice, "and on the day beyond to-morrow when you hear the voice of the night-hawk, you must put your head out of the door of the lodge. You will see me coming with the cap, which I will fasten on your head before I enter. The magic food that I have eaten has given me the power to change my form, so I shall come as a night-hawk, and will give the cry to let you know that I am successful. Have ready your war-club that I may seize it to strike with when I come."

Deep Voice had not known when he began speaking what he would say, but as the magician looked at him the words came. In spite of all the tales that he had heard about the young men who had gone before him, and the magician told him many that night, Deep Voice was anxious to begin his task. He rose early and went in the direction pointed out to him.

When he saw the cap at a distance he thought that no one was near it; but as he went nearer he found that those about it were as the hanging leaves for number. Knowing that he could not pass unharmed through so great a crowd, he changed himself into a humming-bird and flew close enough to the cap to examine it, but did not touch it, for fear an arrow might be aimed at him.

The cap was tied securely to a tall pole and no bird could unfasten it without his actions being noticed. Deep Voice, therefore, changed himself into the down of a dandelion and lighted on the cap itself. He thrust his silver fingers under and between the cords, untied them, and lifted the cap slowly, for it was a great weight for so small a thing to carry.

When the crowd below saw the cap moving, and that it was being carried away, they raised a great shout and ran after it, shooting clouds of arrows as they went. The wind which blew the arrows blew the down out of their reach; so it was soon far enough from them to be safe for Deep Voice to take the form of a bird. As a night-hawk he flew swiftly towards the magician's lodge, giving the call he had named as a signal.

The old man heard him and looked out. Deep Voice flew close to him and dropped the cap upon his head; then changing himself into a man, he seized the war-club which the magician had placed just outside the lodge, and with one powerful blow fastened the cap securely, but knocked the old man senseless. When he recovered, what was the surprise of Deep Voice to see, not the old magician who had entertained him, but a handsome young warrior who said to him, "Thank you, my friend, for the bravery and kindness by which you have restored my youth and strength."

He urged Deep Voice to remain in his lodge as his guest. They hunted together many days and became fast friends. At last Deep Voice wished to return to his brothers. The young magician then brought out gifts – buffalo robes and deer skin white as snow, strings and belts of wampum, as much as he could carry, enough to make him a great man in any country.

During all his stay nothing had been said about the Red Swan. This day, as they were smoking their farewell pipe, the young magician said to Deep Voice: "My brother, you know the reward that was to be for him who restored my cap of wampum. I have given you riches that will be all that you will want as long as you live. I now give you the best gift of all."

At this the Red Swan appeared.

"Take her," said the magician; "She is my sister, let her be your wife."

So Deep Voice and the Red Swan went home by the way he came, stopping at the lodges of the old magicians to take with them the wives for his brothers. The Red Swan far surpassed them in beauty and loveliness, and her daughters and their daughters have ever been known as the handsomest women of the tribe.

Deep Voice and the Red Swan went home but stopped at the lodges of the old magicians as they went

The Cottingley Fairies

In 1917 a series of photographs of fairies were said to have been taken by Elsie Wright and Frances Griffiths, two young cousins (Elsie was 16 years old and Frances was 10) who lived in Cottingley, England. The two girls often played together beside the stream at the bottom of the garden, many times returning home with wet feet and clothes. Frances and Elsie said they only went to the beck to see the fairies and, to prove it, Elsie borrowed her father's camera to record what they saw.

Their father was a keen amateur photographer with his own darkroom. The picture he developed showed Frances behind a bush in the foreground, on which four fairies appeared to be dancing. Knowing his daughter's artistic ability, and that she had spent some time working in a photographer's studio, he dismissed the figures as cardboard cutouts.

Two months later the girls borrowed his camera again, and this time returned with a photograph of Elsie sitting on the lawn holding out her hand to a gnome. Exasperated by what he believed to be "nothing but a prank", Arthur Wright refused to lend his camera to them again. His wife Polly, however, believed the photographs to be authentic. The fact that two young girls had not only been able to see fairies but had actually for the first time ever been able to record the images on a photographic plate caused great excitement as the news spread.

Photography expert Harold Snelling stated that "the two negatives are entirely genuine, unfaked photographs . . . [with] no trace whatsoever of studio work involving card or paper models . . . these are straight forward photographs of whatever was in front of the camera at the time".

In due course the photographs attracted the attention of Scottish physician and author of the "Sherlock Holmes" books, Sir Arthur Ignatius Conan Doyle (1859–1930), who used them to illustrate an article on fairies that he wrote for the Christmas 1920 edition of *The Strand Magazine*. Conan Doyle hoped the photographs might convince the public of the existence of fairies and that they might then more readily accept the other psychic phenomena in which he was deeply interested. He ended his article with the words:

"The recognition of their existence will jolt the material twentieth century mind out of its heavy ruts in the mud, and will make it admit that there is a glamour and mystery to life. Having discovered this, the world will not find it so difficult to accept that spiritual message supported by physical facts which has already been put before it.

Public reaction was mixed; some accepted the images as genuine, but others were convinced they had been faked. Despite the initial excitement and fuss, over the succeeding years interest in the Cottingley Fairies gradually declined – although there was a sudden flurry of interest again in the late 1960s and early 1970s. It was not until in the early 1980s that Elsie and Frances finally admitted that the photographs were faked – using cardboard cutouts of fairies copied from a popular children's book of the time.

"Two village kids and a brilliant man like Conan Doyle – well, we could only keep quiet." Frances said: "I never even thought of it as being a fraud – it was just Elsie and I having a bit of fun and I can't understand to this day why they were taken in – they wanted to be taken in."

However, Frances continued to claim that the fifth and final photograph was indeed genuine.

Prints of their photographs of the fairies, along with a few other items (including a first edition of Conan Doyle's book *The Coming of the Fairies*) were sold at auction in London for £21,620 in 1998.

The girls often played beside the stream at the bottom of the garden

The fairy photographs aroused enormous interest; what had begun as fun took on its own momentum

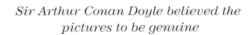

*Sir Arthur Conan Doyle believed the
pictures to be genuine*

Authors

Aesop

(African-Greek, 620 to 560 BC)

Hans Christian Andersen

(Danish, 1805–1875)

Aesop was, by tradition, a slave and story teller of African descent who lived in Ancient Greece. Little is known about him from credible records and some scholars deny his existence altogether. He is famous for *Aesop's Fables* – a collection of fables credited to him – which remain popular today as moral lessons and as the basis for children's plays and cartoons. *Aesop's Fables* has also become a blanket term for collections of brief fables that usually involve personified animals.

The Fox and the Grapes and *The Boy Who Cried Wolf* are examples of the fables which have become popular all over the world. Perhaps the most famous fable credited to him is the parable of *The Tortoise and the Hare*. In this story, a rabbit challenges a tortoise to a race. The rabbit is confident of its victory and as a result takes a nap or takes too many breaks. The slower tortoise wins because it persevered.

www.mythfolklore.net/aesopica/index.htm

Hans Christian Andersen was a author and poet from a humble background who became famous for his children's fairy tale stories. In contrast to the Brothers Grimm, who collected fairy tales and wrote them down, Andersen invented new ones such as *The Snow Queen*, *The Little Mermaid*, and *The Ugly Duckling*. During his lifetime he was was feted by royalty and acclaimed for delighting children worldwide. His poetry and stories have been translated into more than 150 languages and have inspired many movies, plays, ballets, and animated films.

Andersen's tales of fantasy with moral lessons are popular with children, but his best are written for adults as well – they take on different meanings to different readers, a feat only a great poet can accomplish.

The Brothers Grimm

(German, Jacob 1785–1863,

Wilhelm 1786–1859)

Lewis Carroll

(British, 1832–1898)

The Brothers Grimm were German academics, linguists and cultural researchers who became most famous for their collections of old folk tales and fairy tales. Their work popularized stories such as *Cinderella, Hansel and Gretel, Sleeping Beauty* and *Snow White*.

In later years their interest in old literature led them to study older languages and their relationship to modern German. The brothers also worked to document the relationship between similar words of related languages, such as the English *apple* and the German *Apfel*. Their creation of the rules for these relationships became known as *Grimm's Law*. The Grimm brothers' last years were spent in preparing a complete dictionary of the German language, tracing the origin of every word.

www.grimmstories.com

Lewis Carroll was the pseudonym of Charles Lutwidge Dodgson – a British writer, mathematician, Anglican clergyman, and photographer. He is most famous for his story *Alice's Adventures in Wonderland*. He outlined this story to a young friend, Alice Liddel, when he took the girl and her two sisters, Lorina and Edith, on a boat trip. Alice enjoyed the story and asked Dodgson to write it down, which he did much later. Carroll then wrote a second story about Alice called *Through the Looking Glass*. Both are still popular with people all over the world. Carroll also wrote the poems *The Hunting of the Snark* and *Jabberwocky*, and was well-known for his talent at word play, logic, and fantasy.

Charles Dickens

(British, 1812–1870)

Jean de La Fontaine

(French, 1621–1695)

Dickens was one of the most popular and influential writers of the Victorian era.

His life, like many of his characters, was one of rags to riches. At the age of nine he was fortunate to be sent to school. However, when his father was imprisoned for debt, his family was sent away and the young Charles was sent to work in a blacking factory. Here he endured loneliness and terrible working conditions. After three years he returned to school, but he never forgot his experiences and they served as the basis of ideas for many of his novels.

Dickens started his writing career as a journalist. From 1837 till 1860, he wrote popular novels with a concern for social reform: *Oliver Twist, Nicholas Nickelby, David Copperfield, Bleak House, A Tale of Two Cities and Great Expectations*. These were often first serialised in magazines and, unlike other authors, Dickens often wrote his episodes as they were being serialised. This meant his stories are punctuated by cliffhangers to keep the public looking forward to the next installment.

Dickens also campaigned against social injustice and hypocrisy in society. He travelled extensively, lecturing against slavery in the United States and touring Italy with companions.

The continuing popularity of his novels and short stories has meant that none of them have ever gone out of print.

Jean de La Fontaine was one of the most widely read poets of the 17th century. He is perhaps most famous for his fables of animals and everyday life which have become masterpieces of French literature.

These took their inspiration from Aesop, Horace and ancient Indian literature such as the Panchatantra. While he borrowed freely from ancient and modern writers, La Fontaine created a style and a poetic world which was personal, inimitable and accessible to all.

The first collection of 124 fables, *Choisies*, were published in 1668 and dedicated to Dauphin, the six-year-old grandson of Louis XIV. They were an immediate and enormous success. In style they are natural, easy, witty and knowing and cover a huge range of human experience. On the surface the fables seem to be children's literature but careful examination shows they are a sophisticated satire of conventional wisdom and morality.

New editions with more fables appeared at intervals throughout the rest of his life, the last edition in 1693. In 1683 he became a member of the Académie Française. He died in Paris, and is interred at Père Lachaise Cemetery. A set of postage stamps celebrating La Fontaine and the fables was issued by France in 1995.

James Halliwell-Phillipps

(British, 1820–1889)

James Orchard Halliwell-Phillipps was a collector of English nursery rhymes and fairy tales and a scholar of Shakespeare. He was born in London and educated at Jesus College, Cambridge where he studied early English literature.

In 1842 he published the first edition of *Nursery Rhymes of England* which were collected mainly from oral tradition. It became immediately popular and went through several editions in a very short time. It marks the start of the serious study of children's folklore and nursery rhymes. A second book of this type, *Nursery Rhymes and Nursery Tales*, appeared in 1849 and contained the first printed version of the *Three Little Pigs*.

Between them, these volumes contained tales such as *Jack and the Giants*, *The Story of Mr. Fox*, and *Chicken-Licken*, as well as nursery rhymes, proverbs, riddles, counting-out rhymes, games, tongue-twisters and songs.

From 1870 onwards he concentrated on the study and documentation of William Shakespeare and he was instrumental in the formation of the Shakespeare Museum in Stratford-upon-Avon.

Joel Chandler Harris

(American, 1845–1908)

Joel Chandler Harris was a journalist, fiction writer and folklorist best known for his collection of Uncle Remus stories.

Harris was born in Eatonton, Georgia to Mary Ann Harris. His father abandoned his family shortly after he was born and Harris was later schooled thanks to the help of neighbours. At the age of 13 he became an apprentice on a newspaper where he learned about writing, going on to work on newspapers in several Southern cities.

It was his work as a columnist that led to his creation of Uncle Remus, a venerable family servant who tells stories to a young boy on a Georgia plantation. The tales, collected in *Uncle Remus: His Songs and Sayings* (1880) are based on the Br'er Rabbit stories Harris heard told by the African-Americans on the plantations. Br'er Rabbit (a contraction of 'Brother Rabbit') is a trickster character who succeeds in the tales by his wits rather than his brawn, tweaking authority figures and bending social virtues as he sees fit.

Large sales and positive reviews led Harris to publish many other Uncle Remus tales and his stories had an important influence on children's writers such as Rudyard Kipling, A.A. Milne, Beatrix Potter and Enid Blyton.

705

Joseph Jacobs

(Australian, 1854–1816)

A folklorist, literary critic and important Jewish historian, Joseph Jacobs wrote extensively on the subject of folklore for journals and books and produced a popular series of fairy tales.

Jacobs was educated at Sydney Grammar School and at the University of Sydney, where he won a scholarship for classics, mathematics and chemistry. He completed his studies at St John's College, Cambridge and later studied at the University of Berlin.

In 1890 he edited *English Fairy Tales*, the first of his series of books of fairy tales published during the next 10 years. From 1899–1900 he edited the journal *Folklore*, and from 1890 to 1912 edited five collections of fairy tales: *English Fairy Tales*, *More English Fairy Tales*, *Celtic Fairy Tales*, *More Celtic Fairy Tales*, and *European Folk and Fairy Tales* which were accompanied by the fine illustrations of John Dickson Batten.

Jacobs was inspired by the Brothers Grimm and the romantic nationalism common in folklorists of his age. Until then, British children had read mainly French and German fairy tales. Joseph Jacobs ensured they had access to the tales of English and Celtic origin.

Charles Kingsley

(British, 1819–1875)

Charles Kingsley was a priest of the Church of England, university professor, historian and novelist. The son of a vicar in Holne, Devon, Kingsley was educated at King's College, London and Magdalene College, Cambridge, after which he pursued a ministry in the church. From 1844, he was rector of Eversley in Hampshire and from 1860 was Regius Professor of Modern History at the University of Cambridge.

He had a great concern for social reform. He was also sympathetic to the idea of evolution and was instantly supportive of Darwin's *On the Origin of Species*.

In 1850 Kingsley published his first novel, *Alton Locke*, in which he tried to expose the social injustice suffered by farm labourers and workers in the clothing trade. This was followed by the historical novel *Hypatia* in 1853 and *Two Years Ago* in 1857 – a novel about poor sanitary conditions and public apathy causing an outbreak of cholera.

His most famous novel, *The Water Babies* (1863), was written for his youngest son. It tells the story of a young chimney-sweep who, in running away from his cruel employer, falls into a river and is transformed into a water baby. He meets all sorts of creatures in the river and in the seas and learns a series of moral lessons.

Kingsley also wrote *Westward Ho!* (1855), *The Heroes* (1856), *Hereward the Wake* (1866) and *At Last* (1871).

Rudyard Kipling

(British, 1865–1936)

Andrew Lang

(British, 1844–1912)

Rudyard Kipling was a poet, short-story writer and novelist who celebrated the British Empire. He was born in Bombay but educated in England at the United Services College, at Westward Ho!, Devon. He returned to India in 1882 where he worked for Anglo-Indian newspapers. Kipling became a prolific writer and he quickly achieved fame as a writer of short stories and as poet of the British Empire.

In 1894 he published *The Jungle Book*, followed by *The Second Jungle Book* in 1895. These were collections of stories first published in magazines. The best-known of them are about the adventures of an abandoned 'man-cub' called Mowgli who is raised by wolves in the Indian jungle. The stories, which are fables that use animals in an anthropomorphic manner to give moral lessons, became a children's classics all over the world. Because of its moral tone, *The Jungle Book* was later used as a motivational book by the Cub Scouts. The 1967 Walt Disney animated film *The Jungle Book* was also incredibly popular, though it took many liberties with the characters and plot.

Kipling recieved many awards including the Nobel Prize for Literature in 1907 and the Gold Medal of the Royal Society of Literature in 1926.

A Scots poet, novelist, and literary critic and contributor to the field of anthropology, Andrew Lang is best known as a collector of folk and fairy tales. He was born in Selkirk in the Scottish Borders and educated in the Edinburgh Academy, St. Andrews University, Glasgow University and Balliol College Oxford. He later became a fellow at Merton College where he studied Anthropology until 1874.

From 1889–1907, Lang collected and adapted dozens of fairy tales in a lavishly colourful, twelve-book series of books now known collectively as *Andrew Lang's Fairy Books*. Though not collected directly from the oral tradition, they were an extremely influential collection with many of the tales translated for the first time into English. Lang made most of the selections but his wife, Leonora Blanche, and others did a large part of the work.

Ironically, for a man who wrote for a profession – literary criticism, fiction, poems, books and articles on anthropology, mythology, history, and travel – he is best known for the works he did not write.

Edward Lear

(British, 1812–1888)

Miss Mulock

(British, 1826–1887)

Edward Lear was an English artist, illustrator, author, and poet, famous today for his literary nonsense and his limericks. Born in Holloway, London, his father was a stockbroker and he was raised mainly by his sister Ann. He first became a draughtsman for the Zoological Society and then an artist for the British Museum.

From 1832 he worked for the Earl of Derby, making coloured drawings of the rare birds and animals in the menagerie at Knowsley Hall. The position also enabled Lear to travel to Italy, Albania and Illyria, Calabria, Corsica the Holy Land and Greece.

In 1846, Lear produced his first volume of nonsense poetry, *A Book of Nonsense*, which was written for the Earl of Derby's grandchildren. It was beautifully illustrated throughout and contained Lear's favourite poetic format, the limerick. *Nonsense Songs and Stories* was published in 1871 and his fame was secured by poems such as *The Owl and the Pussycat*.

His poetry is unique, inventive, ludicrous and fantastical. There is also an air of deep sadness in his nonsense verse – Lear suffered from depression and loneliness, despite the support of friends such as Alfred Tennyson's wife, Emily.

Dinah Maria Craik (born Dinah Maria Mulock and often credited as Miss Mulock) was an English novelist and poet born in Stoke-on-Trent and brought up in Newcastle-under-Lyme, Staffordshire.

When her mother died in 1845, she moved to London where she was determined to earn her living by writing. She began with children's fiction and slowly rose to become one of the foremost female novelists of the era.

She is perhaps best-known for her 1856 novel *John Halifax, Gentleman*. In 1858 she wrote *Woman's Thoughts about Women*, an advice book providing emotional support for middle class women who wished to become more self-sufficient, followed in 1859 by *A Life for a Life* which she considered to be the best of her novels.

In 1863 she compiled *The Fairy Book* which included versions of French, English and Grimms' tales. *The Adventures of a Brownie*, published in 1872, was a light-hearted story about the capers of a mischievous household elf. In 1875 she published *The Little Lame Prince and his Travelling Cloak* – one of the most original allegorical fantasies of the era. The young prince, whose legs are paralysed, is given a magical cloak by his fairy godmother which enables him to go on various adventures where he gains much wisdom and empathy.

Charles Perrault

(French, 1628–1703)

Sergei Prokoviev

(Russian, 1891–1953)

Charles Perrault was a French poet, prose writer and storyteller who laid foundations for what was a new literary genre at the time – the fairy tale. His best known tales, derived from pre-existing folk tales, include *Little Red Riding Hood, Sleeping Beauty, Puss in Boots, Cinderella* and *Bluebeard*.

From 1660 onwards, Perrault had a literary reputation for his light verse and love poetry. In 1695, when he was 67, he decided to dedicate himself to his children and published *Tales of Mother Goose* which included many of the most well-known tales. It suddenly made him well-known beyond his own circles. In the tales, he used imagery which surrounded him, such as the Chateau Ussé for *Sleeping Beauty* and in *Puss in Boots*, the Marquis of the Château d'Oiron, and contrasted his folktale subject matter with details and asides drawn from the world of fashion.

He spent the rest of his life promoting the study of literature and the arts and was a leading member of the Académie Française. Perrault's stories continue to be printed and have been adapted to opera, theatre, film and ballet (Tchaikovsky's Sleeping Beauty).

Prokofiev was born in Sontsovka in the Ukraine. He was a talented pianist and conductor, and one of the greatest composers of the twentieth century.

At the age of five he composed for piano and wrote an opera when he was nine. From 1904–1914 he attended the St. Petersburg Conservatory where he developed a reputation as a musical rebel, though when he graduated he won the Anton Rubinstein prize for best student pianist.

He mastered a wide range of genres – symphonies, ballets, concerti, operas and film music. He travelled widely, spending many years in London, Paris and the United States. He gained wide notoriety and his works were considered innovative and modern.

He returned permanently to the Soviet Union in 1936. He was soon commissioned by Moscow's Central Children's Theatre to write a symphony for children. Drawing on memories of his own childhood, Prokofiev wrote *Peter and the Wolf* in just 4 days, inventing the story and writing the narration himself. He wrote the music as a child's introduction to the orchestra, with each character represented by a different instrument.

The moral of the story – you can't be a hero if you don't take risks – delighted children and it was an instant success. It has been loved ever since by children all over the world.

William Shakespeare

(British, 1564–1616)

Jonathan Swift

(British, 1667–1745)

William Shakespeare was an English poet and playwright, widely considered the greatest writer and dramatist in the English language.

He was born in Stratford-upon-Avon, the son of a tanner, glove maker and high bailiff. He attended grammar school in Stratford-upon-Avon where he mainly studied Latin. At the age of 18, he married Anne Hathaway, with whom he had three children.

Between 1585 and 1592, he had a successful career in London as an actor, writer, and co-owner of a playing company. Shakespeare wrote most of his known works between 1589 and 1613 – about 38 plays, 154 sonnets and several poems. His early plays were mainly comedies and histories. He then wrote mainly tragedies until about 1608, including Hamlet, King Lear, Othello, and Macbeth. In his last phase, he wrote tragicomedies (or romances).

A Midsummer Night's Dream was one of Shakespeare's comedy plays, written between 1590 to 1596. Most of the play is set in a forest and depicts events surrounding the marriage of Theseus the Duke of Athens, and Hippolyta the Queen of the Amazons. These include the adventures of four young Athenian lovers and a group of amateur actors, who are manipulated by fairies in the forest. The play is one of Shakespeare's most popular and is widely performed across the world.

Jonathan Swift was an Anglo-Irish satirist, essayist, political pamphleteer and cleric who became Dean of St. Patrick's Cathedral. He is best known for writing *Gulliver's Travels*. Born in Dublin, his father died when he was very young, so he spent his first five years with a nanny in England.

In 1682 he attended university in Dublin. On graduating, Swift worked in the service of Sir William Temple before returning to university at Oxford. In 1694 he was ordained as an Anglican minister and returned to work for Sir William the following year. During this time, Swift completed *A Tale of a Tub*, a religious allegory, and *The Battle of the Books*, a short satire depicting a literal battle between books in the King's Library. From 1710, Swift became politically active and wrote sharp-tongued political satire. He was also editor of the Tory weekly *Examiner*.

In 1726, Swift published *Gulliver's Travels*, a satire on human nature and a parody of 'travellers' tales'. It follows Lemuel Gulliver and his journey to four countries: Lilliput, a land of little people; Brobdingnag, a land of big people; Laputa, a land of intelligent but useless people; and Houyhnhnm, a land of horses. The story was originally written for adults to show that some people and governments were wrong and to attempt to make them change. It has become a classic of English literature.

Oscar Wilde

(Irish, 1854–1900)

Albert Henry Wratislaw

(British, 1822–1892)

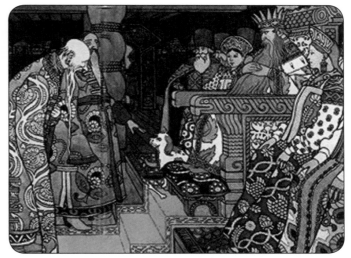

Oscar Wilde was an Irish novelist, playwright, poet and critic. Born in Dublin, his father was a surgeon and his mother a writer and literary hostess. He was educated at Trinity College, Dublin and Magdalen College, Oxford. While at Oxford, Wilde became involved in the aesthetic movement.

After graduating, he moved to London to pursue a literary career. A first volume of his poetry was published in 1881 and he contributed to publications such as the *Pall Mall Gazette*.

In 1888 Wilde published *The Happy Prince and Other Tales*, a collection of fairy tales for children which convey an appreciation for compassion, love and beauty. *The Happy Prince* is about a metal statue who befriends a migratory bird. Other stories included *The Nightingale and the Rose* and *The Selfish Giant*.

In 1891 he published his only novel, *The Picture of Dorian Gray*, a classic piece of gothic fiction. From 1892–1895 he produced a series of extremely popular comedy plays including *Lady Windermere's Fan*, *An Ideal Husband* and *The Importance of Being Earnest*. *Salomé*, a biblical tragedy, was performed in Paris in 1896.

Albert Henry Wratislaw was an English Slavonic scholar of Czech descent. He is best known for his collection of *Sixty Folk-Tales from Exclusively Slavonic Sources*.

He was born in Rugby, England, the son of William Ferdinand 'Count' Wratislaw von Mitro-vitz, a solicitor, and Charlotte Anne. He was educated at Rugby School, Trinity College, Cambridge and Christ's College, Cambridge.

In 1849 he visited Bohemia and studied the Czech language in Prague, later that year publishing *Bohemian Poems, Ancient and Modern, translated from the original Slavonic*.

In 1850, Wratislaw was appointed headmaster of Felsted School, and in 1855 he became headmaster of King Edward VI's Grammar School at Bury St. Edmund's.

In 1852, he published *The Queen's Court Manuscript with other Ancient Bohemian Poems* which he translated from Slavonic poems discovered in a church tower in 1817. In 1879 he resigned as headmaster and moved to Manorbier in Pembrokeshire where he wrote the notable *John Huss, the Commencement of Resistance to Papal Authority on the part of the Inferior Clergy*.

His last and best-known work was the charming collection of *Sixty Folk-Tales from exclusively Slavonic sources*. It displayed Wratislaw's impressive knowledge of the Slavonic languages and it has become the definitive translated anthology of eastern European folklore.

Alexander Afanasyev

(Russian, 1826–1871)

Asbjørnsen and Moe

Peter Christen Asbjørnsen (1812–1885)

Jørgen Moe (1813–1882) both Norwegian

Alexander Afanasyev was a folklorist who collected and published more than 600 Russian folktales and fairytales. He first became interested in the folktales that many of the women knew and remembered in his home town of Bobrov. He hoped that a reawakening of indigenous fairy tales would promote the Russian language over the French language, which had been adopted by the Russian aristocracy.

Afanasyev's first collection of eight volumes, modelled on the famous collection by the Brothers Grimm, was published from 1855–1863 and earned him the reputation of the Russian equivalent to the Brothers.

Afanasyev edited many other compilations which included *Russian Fairy Tales for Children*, a collection of animal, magic and amusing tales for children, and *Russian Folk Legends* which was ultimately banned in Russia because the church thought it was blasphemous.

Afanasyev's collections made an important contribution to the promotion and of Russian culture and their influence can be seen in the works of many writers and composers including Stravinsky and Rimsky-Korsakov.

Peter Christen Asbjørnsen, a teacher and scholar, and Jørgen Moe, a bishop, were collectors of Norwegian folklore. They met at school at the age of 14 and were to be closely united throughout their lives' work.

Asbjørnsen begun to collect and write down fairy tales and legends when he was 20. He later walked the length and breadth of Norway, adding to his stories.

From 1841, Moe spent his summer holidays travelling through the remote, mountainous parts of Norway, collecting stories and traditions. In 1842-1843 they published their first collection, *Norwegian Folk Tales*, which was very well received all over Europe. A second volume was published in 1844 and a new collection in 1871. Many of these tales were translated into English by Sir George Dasent in 1859.

Asbjørnsen and Moe's impact on Norwegian culture was enormous. In collecting and securing Norwegian fairy tales for common readers, they also contributed to the development of the Norwegian language.

L. Frank Baum

(American, 1856–1919)

Carlo Collodi

(Italian, 1826–1890)

Lyman Frank Baum was an American author of children's books, best known for writing *The Wonderful Wizard of Oz*.

The son of an affluent oil baron, Baum made his debut as a novelist in 1897 with *Mother Goose in Prose*, based on stories told to his own children. Its last chapter introduced the farm-girl Dorothy.

In 1900, *The Wonderful Wizard of Oz* was published, lavishly and colourfully illustrated by W. W. Denslow. The story followed the adventures of a girl called Dorothy in the Land of Oz. Thanks to a popular 1902 Broadway musical and the 1939 MGM film of the same name, it has become one of the best-known stories in American popular culture and has been widely translated theoughout the world.

Baum also wrote 13 Oz novel sequels, 9 other fantasy novels, 55 novels in total, 82 short stories and over 200 poems. In his fairy tales, Baum's intention was to write stories similar to those of Hans Christian Andersen the Brothers Grimm, but to introduce modern characters and to omit both the violence and the moral to which the violence was to point.

Carlo Collodi, who's real name was Carlo Lorenzini, was an Italian children's writer best known for the famous fairy tale *The Adventures of Pinocchio*. Born in Florence, Collodi served as a volunteer with the Tuscan army during the Wars of Independence in 1848 and 1860. He founded the satirical newspaper *Il Lampione* and wrote many satirical sketches and stories for various publications.

Collodi became fascinated by the idea of using a rascally but amiable character as a means of expressing his own convictions through allegory. In 1880, he began writing *The Adventures of Pinocchio* which was first serialised in the Italian newspaper for children, *Il Giornale dei Bambini*. The story is about the adventures of a mischievous animated puppet and his 'father,' a poor woodcarver called Geppetto. It has become a classic of children's literature, spawning many adaptations including Walt Disney's famous animation and establishing commonplace ideas such as a liar's long nose.

Collodi died in Florence in 1890 unaware of the fame and popularity that awaited Pinocchio. Just as in the allegory of the story, Pinocchio went on to lead its own independent life, distinct from that of the author.

Artists

William Wallace Denslow

1856 – 1915

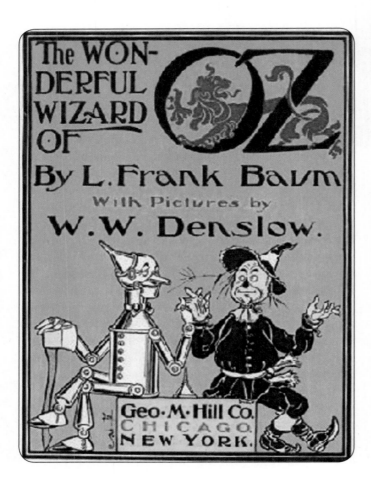

Philapdelphia-born W. W. Denslow is renowned mainly for his illustrations for *The Wonderful Wizard of Oz*. A caricaturist and cartoonist with an ardent interest in politics, Denslow quarrelled with the author Baum over royalty shares from the 1902 stage adaptation of *The Wizard of Oz*, for which Denslow had designed the sets and costumes, and they parted company. The American artist went on to illustrate an edition of traditional nursery rhymes Denslow's *Mother Goose* (1901), along with Denslow's *Night Before Christmas* (1902) and the 18-volume *Denslow's Picture Books* series (1903–04). Royalties from the print and stage versions of *The Wizard of Oz* gave him the wherewithal to purchase an island off Bermuda and there crown himself King Denslow I. Denslow had three wives and three divorces, drank his money away, and died in obscurity at the Knickerbocker Hospital in New York City.

Kate Greenaway

1846–1901

Anne Anderson

1874–1930

This prolific Scottish illustrator spent her childhood in Argentina. Anne brought her talents to bear upon many a children's book, often collaborating with her fellow-artist husband Alan Wright whom she married in June 1912. Her art nouveau style was featured on many fairy tale books but she also designed greeting cards, and was an accomplished painter and etcher.

John Bauer

1882–1918

John Bauer was born in Sweden, the third of four children, although his sister Anna died when John was only 11. At 16, John went to Stockholm to study art and was later accepted at The Royal Academy of Art, where he met his wife, Esther, whom he married in 1906. Esther was the model for The Fairy Princess and many of his later illustrations. John was also inspired by two years spent in Italy. His most famous work was for the eight volumes of *Bland tomtar och Troll (Among Gnomes and Trolls)*, a collection of tales written by Swedish authors and published in 1907. Sadly John, his wife Esther and their two-year-old son all drowned when a ferry they were travelling on to Stockholm capsized in stormy weather.

717

Ivan Yakovlevich Bilibin

1876–1942

Russian illustrator Ivan Bilibin was inspired by Slavic folk and fairy tales and the remoteness of the wildernesses that had given rise to these legends. Bilibin was born in St Petersburg, studied art in Munich and then explored northern Russia, becoming fascinated by its timber buildings, scenery and folklore. He was also influenced by traditional Japanese prints and during the Russian Revolution he drew revolutionary cartoons. An 1899 exhibition by Victor Vasnetsov was a turning point in Bilibin's life. His books include *The Tale of Ivan the Tsar's Son, The Firebird and the Grey Wolf, The Frog Princess, Maria Morevna, The Little White Duck* and *Vassilisa the Beautiful*. He was also a renowned stage and costume designer; he contributed to the Ballet Russes and collaborated with Rimsky-Korsakov. Bilibin had lived in Egypt and spent much time in Paris but in 1936 he returned to Soviet Russia where he died during the Siege of Leningrad six years later. His ability to bring a sense of reality to a world of ghosts and dreams brought reality and historical and geographical authenticity to a world of fantasy and folklore.

Walter Crane

1845–1915

This prolific and influential artist and book illustrator added greatly to nursery and children's illustrated literature in the latter 1800s with his colourful and beautifully detailed work. Participating in the Arts and Crafts movement, he produced an array of paintings, illustrations, children's books, ceramic tiles and other decorative arts. As a wood-engraver he studied the output of this contemporaries, including Pre-Raphaelites Rossetti and Millais, as well as John Tenniel's work for *Alice in Wonderland*. In the mid-1860s he began to collaborate with Edmund Evans on a nursery rhyme and fairy tale series and they were soon producing two or three sixpenny nursery rhyme titles a year as well as, in 1874, launching a fairy tale series beginning with *The Frog Prince* which showed the influence of Japanese art – and Crane's honeymoon visit to Italy in 1871. More stunningly illustrated children's books followed through the years with the lovely Goose Girl illustration taken from his beautiful *Household Stories from Grimm* (1882) being reproduced by William Morris in a tapestry. Crane also illustrated an elegant edition of Edmund Spenser's *Faerie Queene*.

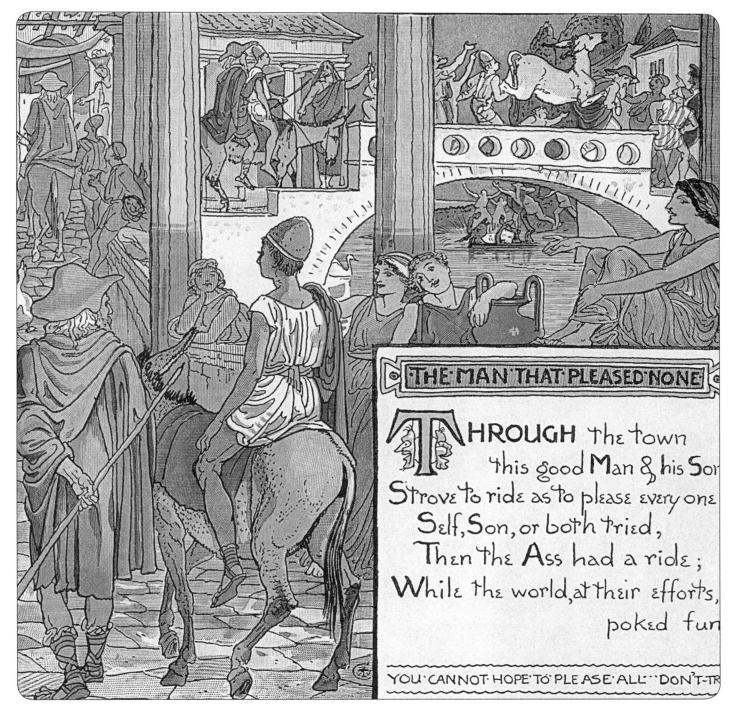

Arthur Rackham

1867–1939

Born September 19, 1867, in London, England, Arthur Rackham was brought up as one of twelve children. He studied at the Lambeth School of Art and was elected to membership in The Royal Watercolour Society and the Society Nationale des Beaux Arts. Eventually he became Master of the Art Workers' Guild. Rackham began his career as a journalist and illustrator but in due course concentrated on his artistic skills and developed into one of the most famous artists to illustrate books during the seven decades of the 'Golden Age' of illustration from 1870–1930. The many works he illustrated included Shakespeare's *A Midsummer Night's Dream* (1908) and *The Tempest* (1926), *Rip van Winkle* (1905), *Alice in Wonderland* (1907), *Fairy Tales of the Brothers Grimm* (1900 and 1909), *Aesop's Fables* (1912), *Fairy Tales by Hans Andersen* (1932) and countless other myths and fairy tales.

Randolph Caldecott

1846–1886

This artist worked on many children's books in the 1800s including nursery rhymes and *Babes in the Wood*. He counted Gaugin and Van Gogh among the admirers of his work. Randolph was born in Chester and grew up among 12 brothers and sisters from his father's two marriages. As a boy, Randolph loved drawing animals but on leaving school (aged 15) he initially worked in a bank. That year, however, he had a drawing published in the *Illustrated London News* and soon took the opportunity to study at the Manchester School of Art before moving to London in 1872, aged 26. Within two years he had become a successful magazine illustrator. He remained in London for seven years, mostly in lodgings just opposite the British Museum in Bloomsbury where he made friends with many artistic and literary people such as Rosetti, George du Maurier, Millais and Lord Leighton. He was elected to the Royal Institute of Watercolour Painting in 1872. In 1877 Randolph illustrated *The House that Jack Built* and from then on until he died eight years later, he produced two more titles each year, priced at one shilling each, for Christmas publication – with stories and rhymes of his own choosing.

Carl Offterdinger

1829–1889

German illustrator Carl Offterdinger, born 8 January 1829 in Stuttgart, was a pupil of Heinrich von Rustige who specialized in landscape, portraits and historic scenes. Offterdinger illustrated numerous children's books – adventures like *Robinson Crusoe* and *Gulliver's Travels* as well as some wonderful fairy tales, including *Cinderella*, *The Sleeping Beauty*, *Little Red Riding Hood*, *Snow White*, *Hansel and Gretel*, *Puss in Boots*, *The Valiant Little Tailor* and *The Wolf and the Seven Little Kids*.

Gustave Doré

1832–1883

This French illustrator and etcher was born in Strasbourg. His wonderful illustrations for over 100 books included works for the Bible, Perrault fairy tales, Don Quixote, and scenes from books by Rabelais, Balzac, Milton, Dante and Lord Byron. His work was perhaps valued more in England than in France and he worked there a good deal. His book, *London: A Pilgrimage*, included some darker elements – with scenes of the docklands and poverty. Doré's fairytale illustrations included *Puss in Boots*, *Little Red Riding Hood*, *La Fontaine fables*, *Tom Thumb* and *Cinderella*. At one time Doré had a forty-strong staff working with him to help reproduce his engravings. He died after a short illness in Paris when still in his early fifties.

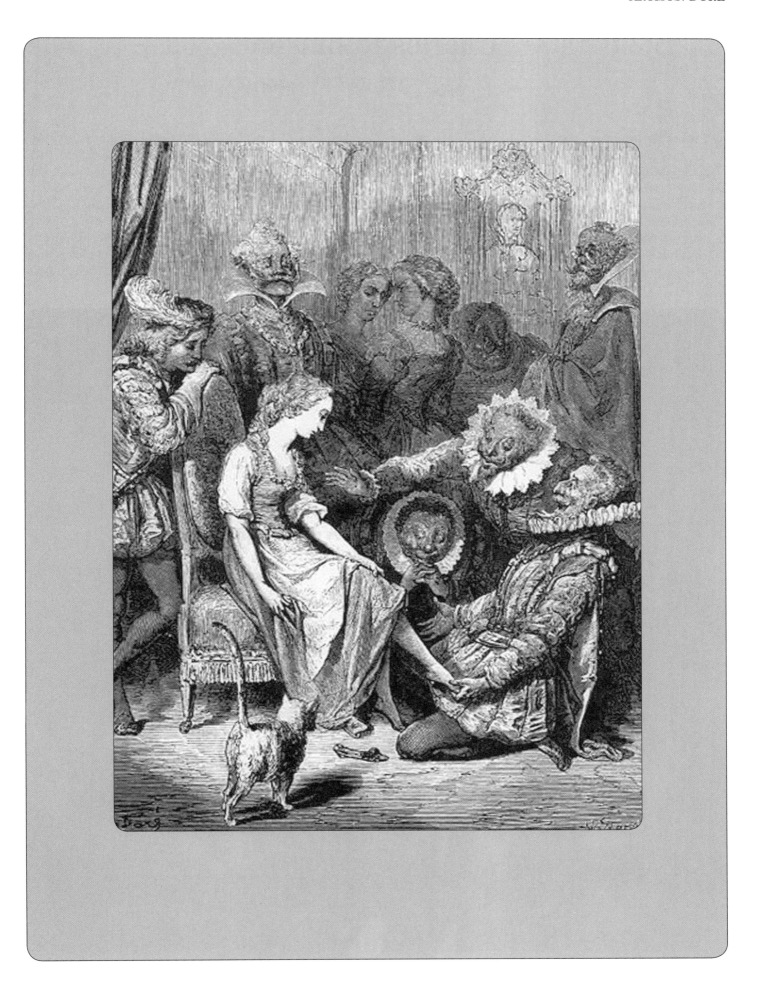

Charles Robinson

1870 –1937

Charles Robinson was born in 1870. His father was an illustrator and his grandfather engraved the work of magazine and newspaper illustrators. His older brother, Thomas Heath Robinson, was also a very talented illustrator, as was his younger brother, Thomas Heath Robinson. Charles was apprenticed to a printer where he worked the lithographic stones. During his seven years' indenture, he took art lessons in the evenings but finances kept him from taking advantage of entrance to the Royal Academy in 1892. As photographic reproduction progressed, stylistic variations took a huge step forward and suddenly images by Abbey, Beardsley, and Crane were able to be reproduced faithfully – just as drawn. Charles's first full book was Robert Louis Stevenson's *A Child's Garden of Verses* (1895) – filled with over a hundred pen-and-ink drawings. Meanwhile, children's magazines were proliferating with an ever-growing demand for

illustration. *Golden Sunbeams*, started in 1896, is a rich source of his work for the first dozen issues. Charles, Tom and William Robinson combined their efforts and styles on a version of Andersen's Fairy Tales. Robinson illustrated very many fairy tales and children's books throughout his career, often producing six or seven books a year to include: *Lullaby Land* (1897), *Alice's Adventures in Wonderland* (1907), *Grimm's Fairy Tales* (1910) and *The Secret Garden* (1911).

Jesse Wilcox Smith

1863–1935

Born in Philadelphia in 1863, Jesse originally trained as a kindergarten teacher before discovering a propensity for drawing when aged about 20. She studied at the Pennsylvania Academy of the Fine Arts where she was taught by Thomas Eakins. She found work in the production department of *The Ladies' Home Journal* and then in 1901, her illustration for *The Last of the Fairy Wands* appeared in the December issue of *Scribners Magazine*. She produced calendars while book and magazine commissions continued to flow in her direction, including the Scribners Classic edition of *A Child's Garden of Verses*. Perhaps her best-loved books are *A Child's Book of Stories* (1911), *The Water-Babies* (1916), *At the Back of the North Wind* (1919), *Boys and Girls of Bookland* (1923), *Dickens' Children* (1912) and *The Everyday Fairy Book* (1915). Her covers for *Good Housekeeping* created over 15 years made her, literally, a household name and she was probably America's premier female illustrator for most of her life.

Virginia Frances Sterrett

1900-1931

Virginia Frances Sterrett was born in Chicago, Illinois. She was an introverted child who preferred the world of imagination and drawing to playing with her friends. When her family moved to Missouri, she won several awards at the Kansas State Fair (*c.*1913), an event that encouraged her to concentrate on her artistic skills. Her first commission came in 1919 when, aged only nineteen, she was asked to illustrate the Comptesse de Ségur's *Old French Fairy Tales*. This was quickly followed by another commission for *Tanglewood Tales* from the same publisher, the Penn Publishing Company. In 1923, the family moved to the warmer climate of southern California. Here, despite suffering tuberculosis, she began the illustrations for *Arabian Nights* but this commission took three years to complete because of her state of health. This artwork was to comprise her last published works and the collection is considered her masterpiece. In 1930, Virginia began work on her final commission, a series of illustration for *Myths and Legends* but this undertaking was never completed; her health took a turn for the worse and she died in the June of 1931 – aged only 30 years' old.

John Tenniel

1820–1914

Born in London, Sir John Tenniel was the son of a dancing-master. He studied at The Royal Academy there but was disappointed in the standards of the teaching and so left in disgust. When he was aged only 16, his paintings were exhibited at the Suffolk Street Galleries and he soon received several commissions, including a fresco for the House of Lords. Soon he had cartoons in *Punch Magazine* and then began to work there. Despite being blind in one eye (after an accident when fencing with his father) he had amazing photographic memory. On one occasion he was invited to 10 Downing Street to study and depict William Gladstone's face. Tenniel's work as a book illustrator most famously included Lewis Carroll's two Alice stories – *Alice's Adventures in Wonderland* which soon became an instant best-seller – and *Through the Looking Glass*. Tenniel secured lasting fame as both books took their place among the most famous literary illustrations ever made. In 1893 an elderly Tenniel was honored as a living national treasure and knighted by Queen Victoria – the first such honour ever bequeathed on an illustrator or cartoonist. Tenniel had truly raised the status of his erstwhile lowly profession.

Victor Vasnetsov

1848–1926

An outstanding Russian painter, Viktor Mikhaylovich Vasnetsov was born in a remote village in Vyatka. His grandfather painted icons while his father, a village priest, was interested in astronomy, the natural sciences and painting. Viktor studied at the local seminary and at the Academy of Fine Arts. Soon his rich creativity embraced many a genre – book illustration, folk epics, history and religious subjects (his paintings graced Vladimir Cathedral in Kiev and the temple of the Resurrection in St. Petersburg). He became a key figure in the Russian Revivalist movement. While in Paris he studied classical and contemporary paintings, painted *Acrobats* (1877), and became fascinated with fairy-tale subjects, starting to work on *Riding a Grey Wolf* and *The Firebird*. In 1877 he returned to Moscow and illustrating Russian fairy tales including *Knight at the Crossroads* (1878), *Prince Igor's Battlefield* (1878) and *The Magic Carpet* (1880). He also worked on stage designs and costumes for Rimsky-Korsakov and was probably the first painter (as opposed to an artisan) to create theatre backdrops. In 1912, Vasnetsov was given a noble title by Czar Nicholas II but after the October Revolution, participated in the designing of a military uniform for the newly founded Red Army and is said to have designed the military hat that echoed the nation's ancient cone-shaped helmets!

A Worldwide Sweep – a timeline

600 BCE to AD

Aesop's fables

602-564 BCE Ancient Greece
Aesop's fables include *Androcles and the Lion*
Greek legends include *Pandora's Box*

100s BCE Greco-Egypt
Earliest version of *Cinderella*
recorded by Strabo

AD 100 to 1399

The Pied Piper

AD 100s Africa and Greece
Cupid and Psyche myth written by Lucius Apuleius
(born *c*.124 in northern Africa, educated Carthage and
Athens). Story is similar to *Beauty and the Beast*. Some
scholars consider this to be the first literary fairy tale

1200s-1300s
England or Germany or France
Gesta Romanorum – a Latin collection of tales
and anecdotes about the deeds of the Romans

1284 Germany
Hamelin suffers rat infestation giving
rise to *The Pied Piper* story

Late 1300s
The Canterbury Tales by Chaucer

There are many common elements in the countless fairy tales that have spread across the continents over the centuries; all the tales stem from shared human experience and revel in the magic they unfold. Similar plots, characters and motifs have flowed across many different cultures – often initially transmitted orally. In most cases it is hard to pin down their origins – the influences of the major collectors like Perrault, the Brothers Grimm, Hans Christian Andersen, and Joseph Jacobs is a good deal clearer. Different versions have mutated over the years, some having different endings and all reflecting the times, attitudes and fashions of both their historic setting and the nationality or location of the storyteller. This timeline of fairy tales attempts to take a worldwide view of the genre but there are strong European influences because this is the source of the most well-loved fairy stories in Western literature.

Asia and Australia

Africa and the Americas

c.2000 BCE Mesopotamia (Iraq)
Biblical tale of *Noah and the Ark* may derive from the ancient Sumerian epic tale of *Gilgamesh*

300s-200s BCE China
Zhuangzi and other Taoist philosophers recount fairy tales

1300 BCE Ancient Egypt
The oldest known written fairy tales stem from Ancient Egypt including the *Tale of Two Brothers*

6th century BCE onwards India
Many tales derive from ancient times and are an important part of Indian lore connected to Lord Gautama Buddha.
These include *Lambikin, The Lion and the Crane, How the Raja's son won Princess Labam, The Tiger, the Braham and the Jackal* and *Why the Fish Laughed*

200-300 Ancient India
The *Panchatantra*, a Hindu collection of tales from Ancient India – forerunners to some European fairy tales with animal fables in verse and prose

850-860 China
First-known literary version of *Cinderella*

Cinderella, one of the earliest tales

Europe including Scandinavia and Russia

1400 to 1499

1450 Germany
Johannes Gutenberg invents the printing press

1500 to 1699

1500s England
William Shakespeare *A Midsummer Night's Dream*

1590s England
Edmund Spenser
The Faerie Queen published 1590; 2nd section 1596

800s-1600s Middle East – and into Europe
A Thousand and One Nights/The Arabian Nights
Includes *Ali Baba and the Forty Thieves* and *Aladdin*

1548 Scotland
Frog Went A-Courtin'

1550 and 1553 Italy
The Pleasant Nights by Gianfrancesco Straparola.
The 1st volume is in France in 1560; the 2nd in 1573

1595 England
Babes in the Wood

1605 England
Dick Whittington and His Cat

1621 England and France
The History of Tom Thumb/Hop o' My Thumb
by Charles Perrault

1632-36 Italy
Giambattista Basile writes *The Tale of Tales*
1632 in dialect: translated into Italian 1747,
German in 1846, and English in 1848

1667 Ireland
Gulliver's Travels by Jonathan Swift

1690-1710 France
Fairy tales enjoyed in the French salons,
especially works by Marie-Catherine D'Aulnoy
that are translated into English in 1699

Babes in the Wood

Asia and Australia

The Americas

Tom Thumb

1500s Japan
The Samurai's Tale series

1600s to 1700s Asia
Asian fairy tales include inspiring tales from
China, Japan, the Ottoman Empire (Turkey)
and kingdoms in Korea and Indonesia

1500s and 1600s North and South America
In the wake of Columbus arriving in the West Indies
(1492) many Europeans land in the Americas,
bringing with them stories from Spain, Portugal,
England, the Netherlands and other such cultures

1600s America
Oral Native American folktales impart
wisdom and advice to the listener

Dick Whittington and his Cat

Europe including Scandinavia and Russia

1500 to 1699

1697 France
Charles Perrault
Mother Goose Tales published in Paris. The tales include *Cinderella, The Sleeping Beauty, Little Red Riding Hood, Bluebeard* and *Puss in Boots*

1700 to 1799

Beauty and the Beast

1709 Europe
Aladdin translated

1729 Great Britain
Robert Samber translates and publishes
Perrault's Histories, or Tales of Times Past

1740 France
Madame Gabrielle de Villeneuve writes
a 362-page version of *Beauty and the
Beast* – not intended for children

1756 France
Madame Le Prince de Beaumont publishes
her shorter version of *Beauty and the
Beast* – the first example of a literary fairy
tale penned specifically for children

1800 to 1899

Snow White

1812 and 1815 Germany
Jacob and Wilhelm Grimm publish volumes
one (1812) and two (1815) of *Childhood and
Household Tales* which include *Hansel and
Gretel, Rumpelstiltskin* and *Snow White*

1823 Great Britain
Editor Edgar Taylor publishes the first English
translation of the Grimms' tales in
German Popular Stories

England 1837
The Story of the Three Bears (1837)

Asia and Australia

The Americas

1765-1947 India
Britain rules India between 1765 and
1857 with British Raj 1858-1947.
Great exchange of cultural heritage
includes fairy and folk tales

Puss in Boots

1800s Canada
In the late 1800s many Native American stories
are absorbed into Canadian culture

Asia and Australia

The Americas

1800 to 1899

1812 Germany
Wonderful collection of fairy tales first
published by Jacob and Wilhelm Grimm

From The Three Brothers, a Polish fairy tale

1835-1837 Denmark
Hans Christian Andersen's *Fairy Tales Told for
Children* is published. Many of the tales are original
but some are based on folklore, including *The Wild
Swans*. His works include *The Tinder Box,
The Emperor's New Clothes* (1837), *The Little
Mermaid* (1837) and *The Ugly Duckling* (1843)

1839 and 1877 Spain
The Vain Little Mouse: the earliest reference
to this tale is found 1839 but the complete tale
is not written until 1877. In early versions,
the little she-mouse is actually a little ant

1845 Norway
Norwegian Folk Tales, collected by Peter Christen
Asbjørnsen and Jørgen Moe, published and prove
highly popular; a second edition appears in 1852.
Famous tales include *East of the Sun and West
of the Moon* and *The Three Billy-Goats Gruff*

1848 Great Britain
The first English translation by Edward Taylor of
Giambattista Basile's *Pentamerone* includes earliest
known versions of *Rapunzel* and *Cinderella*

1855 and 1863 Russia
Vasilissa the Beautiful by Alexander Afanasyev

1860s Russia
Afanasyev collects and publishes his first volume
of Russian fairy tales including *The Firebird*

1865 England
Alice's Adventures in Wonderland by Lewis Carroll

1867 Norway
The Legend of Peer Gynt by Henrik Ibsen

1867-76 England
Walter Crane's illustrations of many fairy
tales appear in his *Toybook* series

1881 Romania
Fairy Tales and Legends by
Mrs. E. B. Mawr – a collection of Romanian stories

Asia and Australia

The Americas

East of the Sun and West of the Moon
This Norwegian tale soon becomes a classic
and inspires many other tales in its wake

1881 USA
Br'er Rabbit by Joel Chandler Harris

1881 USA
Prince and the Pauper by Mark Twain

1876 USA
Tom Sawyer by Mark Twain

The Ugly Duckling

1800 to 1899

1882 England
Walter Crane illustrates his sister's translation of Grimms' fairy tales

Pinocchio

1885 Spain:
Francisco de S. Maspous y Labros collects many fairy tales

1890 Russia
Peter Ilyich Tchaikovsky's *The Sleeping Beauty* premieres in St. Petersburg, Russia

1890 Romania
Andrew Lang's *The Red Fairy Book* includes many Romanian tales from *Rumanische Märchen* such as *The Enchanted Pig*

1883 Italy
The Adventures of Pinocchio Carlo Collodi

1888 UK
Stories by Oscar Wilde: *The Happy Prince, The Selfish Giant, The Remarkable Rocket*

1889 England
Andrew Lang publishes the *Blue Fairy Book*, first of his 12 fairy books. The series gathered tales from numerous sources to present a multicultural, international collection

1890 Great Britain
Joseph Jacobs publishes *English Fairy Tales*, later followed by *More English Fairy Tales*, *Celtic Fairy Tales, Indian Fairy Tales*, and *European Folk and Fairy Tales*

1893 Great Britain
Cinderella: Three Hundred and Forty-five Variants of Cinderella, Catskin, and Cap O' Rushes by Marian Roalfe Cox nominates Cinderella as the most common fairy tale theme around the world.

1890s Ireland:
Irish stories such as *The Field of Bollians* and other Celtic fairy tales retold by Australian-born Joseph Jacobs

1893 Germany
Engelbert Humperdinck's opera, *Hansel and Gretel*, premieres.

Asia and Australia

The Americas

1875–1962 Japan
Kunio Yanagita becomes known as the
father of Japanese folkloristics

1894 Australia
Seven Little Australians by Ethel Turner

1898 Japan
The Fountain of Youth

The Fountain of Youth

The Remarkable Rocket

1900 onwards

Peter Pan

1901/1902 UK
The Tale of Peter Rabbit by Beatrix Potter

1902 UK
Five Children and It
by E. Nesbit

1904 UK
Peter Pan by J. M. Barrie

1908 England
Kenneth Grahame pens
Wind in the Willows

1909 Great Britain
Arthur Rackham illustrations for *Grimm's
Fairy Tales* from 1900 are enlarged
and recolored in a deluxe edition

1910–1911 Great Britain
Illustrations by Edmund Dulac for
*The Sleeping Beauty and Other Fairy Tales
and Stories from Hans Andersen*

1911 Hungary
Bela Bartok's opera, *Duke Bluebeard's
Castle*, premieres

1918 Holland
Many Dutch tales retold in English in *Dutch Fairy
Tales for Young Folks* compiled by William Elliot Griffis

1920s Poland
Many tales collected and translated including *The
Three Brothers* and *Through a Telescope*

1931 France
Barbar the Elephant Jean de Brunhoff

Sleeping Beauty

Asia and Australia

Early 1900s Japan

Early 1900s Japan
Yei Theodora Ozaki translates many
Japanese fairy tales

Early 1900s
Andrew Lang and Joseph Jacobs translate many
Asian tales, especially those from India

Late 1900s Asia
D. L. Ashliman (USA) translates many Asian fairy
stories and writes about Indo-European Folktales

Australia 1918
The Magic Pudding written and
illustrated by Norman Lindsay

1934 Australia
Mary Poppins by P. L. Travers

1944 India
The Fisher-girl and the Crab

The Americas

1900 USA
The Wonderful Wizard of Oz (Frank L. Baum)

1901 USA
Frank L. Baum's *American Fairy Tales*

1937 United States
Snow White and the Seven Dwarfs is Walt
Disney's first feature-length animated film

Snow White and Rose Red

1950 United States
Walt Disney's *Cinderella* is released

1959 United States
Walt Disney's *Sleeping Beauty* is released

1961 United States
Stith Thompson expands and translates Antti Aarne's
The Types of the Folktale into English.
The Aarne-Thompson Classification System
becomes the most widely used

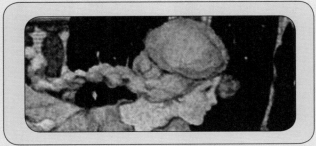

Cinderella

1963 USA
Where the Wild Things Are by Maurice Sendak

1900 onwards

Rapunzel

1936 Russia
Peter and the Wolf
Prokofiev uses a story to teach about
musical instruments

1937 UK
J. R. R. Tolkien's *The Hobbit* published

1945 Russia
The premiere of Sergei Prokofiev's
ballet, *Cinderella*, is presented by
the Bolshoi Ballet in Moscow

1946 France
Jean Cocteau's film, *La Belle et la Bête*
(Beauty and the Beast) is released

1949–1954, UK
The Chronicles of Narnia by C. S. Lewis

1954 and 1955 UK
J. R. R. Tolkien's *The Lord of the Rings* published
1937–1949, the 2nd best-selling novel ever
written, with over 150 million copies sold

1964 England
Charlie and the Chocolate Factory by Roald Dahl

1978 England
The Snowman by Raymond Briggs

1997 UK
The first Harry Potter novel *Harry Potter
and the Philosopher's Stone*. The book series
has sold more than 400 million copies and
has been translated into 67 languages
In the USA it was called
Harry Potter and the Sorceror's Stone

England 1999
The Gruffalo by Julia Donaldson

Asia and Australia

The Americas

Beauty and the Beast

The Little Mermaid

2011 Asia
As the worldwide web creates links and online translation possibilities many more tales [Ja]pan, China, India and such-like places [ava]ilable to European readers

1978 United States
Robin McKinley's *Beauty: A Retelling of the Story of Beauty and the Beast* is published. McKinley becomes a well-respected author of fairy tale retellings with this book followed by several short stories and novels, including *Deerskin*.

1979 United States
Jack Zipes' *Breaking the Magic Spell: Radical Theories of Folk and Fairy Tales* is published. It is one of the first of many books written and/or edited by Jack Zipes dealing with fairy-tale studies. It also marks the start of the significant emphasis on the socio-political study of folklore

1982-87 United States
Shelley Duvall produces Shelley Duvall's *Faerie Tale Theatre for the Showtime* cable network. A total of 27 episodes are produced for the network, featuring well-known actors and actresses from the time period

1989 United States
Walt Disney's *The Little Mermaid* is released

1989 United States
Ed Young's picture book, *Lon Po Po: A Red-Riding Hood Story* from China, is published and later wins the Caldecott Medal (1990)

1991 United States
Beauty and the Beast by Walt Disney is released – the first feature-length animated film to be nominated for an Academy Award

1997 United States
The first Harry Potter novel, *Harry Potter and the Sorceror's Stone*, is published. The book series has sold more than 400 million copies and has been translated into 67 languages

2004 United States
Shrek 2, the sequel to *Shrek*, is one of the highest grossing 2004 movies; it revisits fairy-tale themes while parodying popular culture

2009–2010 United States
Walt Disney's *The Princess and the Frog* and *Rapunzel* released

Did you know . . .?

There are lots of fascinating facts about fairies and fairy stories, providing an interesting extra layer of information about the origins and history of the tales and the lore of fairyland . . .

Sleeping Beauty

One of the most loved fairy stories is also a famous ballet. The story we know today was the one written in 1697 by French writer, Charles Perrault, in a book called *Tales of Times Passed*. Perrault did not actually think up any of the stories: he searched for old tales and retold these, changing the most gruesome elements and often giving them happier endings. The Brothers Grimm also had a *Sleeping Beauty* story in their collection of fairy tales but the earliest version, published in 1634, was by an Italian soldier and courtier called Giambattista Basile. In his story, the princess was called Talia: this means 'the blossoming one'. In some of the stories she is called Briar Rose, perhaps because of the thorns that grow all around her when she slept.

Cinderella

One of the first stories about Cinderella was told over a thousand years ago in China when her best friend was a magic fish. In this version her slipper was gold! There is also a Greco-Egyptian story with the Prince is a pharaoh and the slipper a sandal! The best-known Cinderella version is the one told by a French writer, Charles Perrault, in 1697. Most of the Cinderella fairytales we read today began with this one and Perrault was probably the first storyteller to suggest that her slipper was made of glass although some theorists claim that Cinderella's glass slipper was originally fur (*vair*) in France and mis-translated as glass (*verre*). In children's theatre or English pantomimes, there is usually another character, a friend and servant called Buttons, who is in love with Cinderella and helps her. Rossini wrote an opera and Prokofiev a ballet based on this most popular of stories

The Little Mermaid

One of the most loved fairy stories (also a famous ballet and opera) was written in 1837 by the famous Danish poet and storyteller, Hans Christian Andersen. It does not have a happy ending: the handsome prince does not understand just how much the Little Mermaid loves him as she cannot speak – and he marries someone else. So the sad mermaid does not live happily ever after (except in the Walt Disney version!). The Little Mermaid character soon became a national symbol of Denmark and, since 1913, a small but very famous statue of her has gazed out over the water in Copenhagen harbour.

Snow White

Most of the versions of this well-loved fairy story have derived from the Brothers Grimm collection of folk tales. Jacob and Wilhelm Grimm began gathering and rewriting German folk tales in about 1807. Many of their stories included cruel stepmothers but, in fact, their first version of Snow White tells of a jealous mother – not a stepmother – who wanted to harm the princess. It is interesting to discover that, back in the 1500s, small children who worked in the mines in one German town were called dwarfs. An Albanian version has Snow White living with dragons, not dwarfs, while the poem written by Russian writer Alexander Pushkin in 1833 has knights instead. A century later, Snow White was the story chosen by Walt Disney for his first-ever full-length animation movie in 1937.

Fairy names

Fairies and elves are called all sorts of names, depending on the place, time, and culture, such as faerie, fay, fey, the little folk, elves, pixies, goblins, brownies, dwarfs, gnomes, the little people and Irish leprechauns.

Fairy spotting

They say that best times to see a fairy are at twilight, midnight, just before sunrise and (surprisingly) midday. The time when are most likely of all to spot fairy folk is Midsummer's Eve – and do remember that once you have spotted a fairy do keep your eyes fixed upon it: the fairy will be visible only as long as you keep it unwaveringly in your vision. One blink and the fairy will vanish.

Trees

Trees associated with fairies are oak, rowan, willow, apple, ash, beech and all the nut trees.

Flowers

Flowers have been assumed to have magical properties since earliest times and to possess a spirit, which determined their form, growth, and purpose in the world in relation to their human neighbours. There used to be a belief that dressing children in daisy chains protected them from being stolen by fairies.

Many flowers are associated with fairies, but in particular those blooms which resemble bells such as harebells while foxgloves have long been connected with fairies. The name fox is a corruption of the word 'folks'; the flower was the 'folk's glove' or 'the glove of the good folk', the good folk being the fairies. Welsh people called foxgloves 'fairy gloves' and the Irish called them 'fairy bells'. It was said that the fairy folk welcomed gardeners who allowed foxgloves to grow very tall so that they would nod in the garden – the taller and the more nodding the plant, the happier the fairies would be. They should, however, be grown from seed and never transplanted as they may well be a home for a fairy. A foxglove would bend its tall flower spike to pay homage and respect to any supernatural being while their flowerheads provided hats for elves and resting places for many fairy folk. Roses are also said to attract fairies.

Hawthorn trees, holly, foxglove and ragwort are also dear to fairies, and they punish people who abuse them. They use a ragwort stalk to fly through the air. A farmer who had swept his chimney with a holly bough reported in Northern Ireland in 1907 that he was troubled with flying stones in his house.

Rue, St. Johns wort and yarrow are said to be anti-fairy herbs.

Garlic

Garlic has been implemented as a healing herb for thousands of years but is also renowned as a means of keeping away evil and witches. Believed to possess occult magic, in ancient China it was used to ward off the evil eye, while in many other traditions it was hung in strings from roofs of houses and sterns of boats to prevent attack by witches, sorcerers, demons and evil spirits. In the *Odyssey* by Homer, it was garlic that Hermes recommended as protection against the sorceress Circe who turned men into swine. Ancient Greeks used to place garlic on piles of stones at crossroads as supper for Hecate, the Greek goddess of witchcraft. There is a Mohammedan legend that says when Satan stepped out of the Garden of Eden, garlic sprang up from the spot where he placed his left foot and onion from where his right foot landed.

Fairies and deer

These are associated together in parts of Scotland and its isles. The Mother Goddess was known as the Mistress of the Herds and was believed to release those animals that could be hunted for food. Meanwhile, in northern Scandinavia, northern Canada and Siberia this belief is still part of folklore. Cailleach, the Celtic Hag Goddess, was also known as the Mistress of Wild Things and sometimes took the form of a deer – while fairy women were said to assume the guise of a deer to escape pursuit or the enchantment of a powerful hunter magician.

The Flower Fairies books

These titles were created by Cicely Mary Baker (1895-1973). Unable to attend school because of her epilepsy she was taught at home. Often alone, she began to draw, enrolling at Croydon Art Society when she was only thirteen years old. The first of the Flower Fairies books, *Flower Fairies of the Spring*, was published in 1923; as well as the fairies being so utterly charming, each flower and plant is depicted with great accuracy. She was greatly influenced by the Pre-Raphaelites.

Country fairies

Fairies and elves have long been associated with rural life, the dairy and farming seasons. They sing and dance in country settings and woodland glades, in addition to helping people – including workers in the field, cobblers making shoes, farmers at harvest time and millers with their grain and milling. Fairies weave and spin, make butter, cook and help with other household chores (they do like a tidy home and may pinch a slovenly housewife!) as well as acting as occasional midwives. Many are guardians of forests or rivers and protect animals and plants.

Toadstools and fairy rings

Toadstools are associated with fairy rings – especially the spotted ones and those that form rings which are said to be found in places where fairies have had a gathering. People who are hoping to be able to watch fairies may be tempted back to the same spot where a toadstool ring is in evidence but only fervent believers can see them, they say, and, in any case, the secretive fairies seldom meet in the same place twice. Toadstool rings are thought to be bad omens by people who mistrust the little folk.

Fairy rings may consist of circles of withered grass, often seen in lawns, meadows, and grassy glades, said to be produced by the fairies dancing on the spot. In reality, these rings are simply a fungus below the surface, which has seeded in a circular range, as many plants do.

A human caught in the fairy ring has to dance for a year and a day but to the captive it may seem just a moment or two.

Once inside a fairy ring, a human cannot escape unless a human chain from the outside is formed to pull him or her out again.

Anyone caught within a fairy ring should never eat or drink anything that is offered to them as this will consolidate the enchantment and make them virtual prisoners. If you dance with fairies until dawn you will never stop – and if you step on a fairies toes while dancing you will turn to stone.

Stamps

Many fairy stories have been featured on stamps. For example, the Swedish postal service made a series of stamps to mark the 100-year anniversary of the birth of artist John Bauer, with motifs from *Bland tomtar och troll* while Grimm and Hans Andersen tales have been used as a motif many times all around the world and there have been countless German stamps depicting fairy tale characters and scenes.

Caldecott and Crane

Two illustrators of children's books, Randolph Caldecott and Walter Crane, contributed to the design of Frederick (later Lord) Leighton's Arab room at his exotic home, Leighton House in Kensington. Randolph Caldecott designed peacock capitals for four columns while Walter Crane designed a tiled peacock frieze.

Fairy homes

These are various but generally are rural or garden environments. Some types of fairies live in communities in hollow hills or in fairy mounds. Fairy hillocks are little knolls of grass, like mole-hills, where fairies live. Eggshells are also much favoured fairy homes.

Glossary of fairy folk

A fairy is an elemental being usually associated with gardens and plants and in older texts may be called a faery, faerie or fay – all archaic spellings.

Dryad – A deity or nymph of the woods. Similar to a hamadryad in Ancient Greek which was the nymph of an oak tree.

Elf – Garden or woodland fairy.

Fairy ring – A circle formed on the grass in a field by the growth of certain fungi, formerly supposed to be caused by fairies in their dances. Ancient crop circles were also said to emanate from fairy gatherings or mischief.

Faun – He has a human-shaped torso but sports the ears, horns, tail and hind legs of a goat.

Gnomes – These usually inhabit the interior of the earth and act as guardians of its mineral riches.

Hamadryad – A dryad who is the spirit of a particular tree.

Naiad – Nymphs presiding over rivers and springs such as a Greek water nymph.

Nymph – These inhabit the sea, rivers, woods, trees, mountains, and other natural places and frequently attend a superior deity.

Salamander – A fire elemental thought to resemble a lizard or other reptile.

Sprite – An elf, fairy or goblin, often a water fairy.

Sylph – One of a race of elementals supposed to inhabit the air, or a water fairy.

Troll – A Scandinavian gnome.

Undine – One of a group of female water spirits; when an undine married a mortal and bore a child, she received a soul.

Wood nymph – a nymph living in woods, also sometimes called a dryad.

Witches

These may be referred to as hags, crones and harpies and are assumed to be female while male witches are called warlocks.

Giants and ogres

These are similar huge monstrous creatures with the giants generally bigger creatures, brandishing knobbly clubs and with a propensity for throwing boulders, while ogres definitely enjoy eating people and may live in caves. Both can be found in remote castles.

Mermaids

Mermaid legends may have arisen from sightings by seafaring mariners of dugong. These sea mammals rise to the surface to gulp in lungfuls of air. The nipples of the females are conspicuous and set forward; moreover, when suckling their calves, the mothers clasp their young to their breasts with a flipper that bends at the elbow. At such moments, the head and shoulders may take on a vaguely human attitude. Perhaps Greek and Arab seamen believed they were half-fish and half-woman with their breasts and fishlike tails but these mammals are certainly not glamorous in the way that modern images of mermaids suggest.

Sometimes they eat seaweed which may dangle down like hair and they make low-pitched whistling sounds as the air rushes in through their nostrils – which together might have given rise to the legend of sweet-voiced sirens who lured Greek mariners to their deaths on rocks. Acknowledging the classics, scientists today classify dugongs in the order Sirenia.

What do fairies like?

Fairies love playing chess, long considered a game fit for kings.

Fairies love the sound of a crowing rooster.

Fairies are attracted to laughter and will gather where there are children playing.

Green is the favourite fairy colour, with red second best.

Fairies love musical instruments, especially panpipes, cymbals, harps, whistles and drums.

Fairies love milk and honey and drink flower nectar as their fairy wine.

Fairies like golden hair, particularly on beautiful young women.

Fairy dislikes and deterrents

Fairies never eat salt.

Fairies do not like their names to be known. Some believe that if fairies know a person's name, they will do them harm; but if they are ignorant of your name, they remain powerless.

Fairies don't like lies or deceptions by humans, nagging wives, people who beat their partners or children, or folk who boast of fairy gifts they've received.

If ever you should enter a fairy dwelling you should always remember to stick a piece of steel, such as a knife, a needle, or a fish-hook, in the door; then the elves will not be able to shut the door until you come out again.

Ancient arrowheads, called elf stones, are used as a charm to guard cattle while bells are used as protection against fairies and evil spirits as fairies don't like the sound of any bell, especially church bells but will hang bells on their horses' harnesses.

Fairies don't like iron. Long ago, those fearful of meeting fairies would carry a piece of iron (or steel) with them, especially a cross or a horseshoe. A knife or nail in your pocket is enough to prevent the fairies from lifting you up at night while nails in the front of a bed ward off elves. It may be wise to put the smoothing-iron under the bed and the reaping-hook in the window. Fairies despise flint, too.

Oak tree acorns can also be made into talismans if found and gathered by the light of the full moon.

If you place your shoes with the toes pointing away from the bed, you can protect yourself against fairy pranks while you sleep.

Other fun facts

People born in the morning cannot see spirits or the fairy world. Those born at night, however, can see the spirits of the dead.

Every time a fairy changes shape he or she reduces in size.

The tangles we get in our hair at night are caused by fairies.

Fairies consider it perfectly acceptable to steal from people but are furious if people steal from them. Meanwhile, even evil fairies do not lie, although they may seriously mislead or deceive.

Fossil sea-urchins were said to be made by the fairies and are called fairy loaves or fairy stones.

The Irish may say that dust is stirred up on roads by fairies on a journey, and raise their hats to it, saying, "God speed you, gentlemen."

Arabic legends suggest that whirlwinds and waterspouts are caused by evil jinns.

Fairy time does not correspond to human time so people who spend the night with fairies may return many years later to discover their great-grandchildren in residence.

Fairy gold can float in Fairyland.

Smaller fairies are more beautiful and virtuous while taller fairies are more inclined to be dishonest and steal butter, milk, cows, goats and babies – sometimes leaving ugly changelings in their place.

Bibliography and pictures used

Bibliography

African Folk Tales
Children's Thrift Classics
and Dover Publications Inc. 1999

Andrew Lang's Complete Fairy Book Series
The Blue, Red, Green, Yellow, Pink, Grey, Violet, Crimson,
Brown, Orange, Olive, and Lilac Fairy Books + Traditional Folk
Tales and Fairy Stories From Around The World
12 Books by Andrew Lang
Shoes and Ships and Sealing Wax Ltd 2006

Annotated Brothers Grimm, The
Maria Tatar
W. W. Norton and Co. Inc. 2004

Annotated Classic Fairy Tales, The
Maria Tatar
Norton (New York), c. 2002 and Book Club Associates

Around the World in 80 Tales
Best-Loved Folktales of the World
Joanna Cole (Author) The Anchor folktale library 1988

Chinese Fairy Tales
Dover Children's Thrift Classics 1998

Classic Collection of Fairy Tales, The
From the Brothers Grimm and Hans Christian Andersen
Adapted by Nicola Baxter Armadillo Books 2011

Classic Fairy Tales:
Enchanting Stories from Around the World
Saviour Pirotta Arcturus Publishing 2005

Complete Fairy Tales, The
Charles Perrault and Christopher Betts
Oxford World's Classics 2009

English Fairy Tales and Legends
Rosalind Kerven National Trust Books 2008

English Fairy Tales
Joseph Jacobs
Everyman's Library Children's Classics 1993

Fairy Tales & Legends from Romania
Ioana Sturdza Irvington Publishers

Fairy tales from all nations (a pre-1923 reproduction)
Anthony Reubens Montalba BiblioLife 2009

Favorite Fairy Tales Told in Russia
Retold from Russian storytellers
Morrow Beechtree Paperback 1961

Favorite Folktales from Around the World
Pantheon Fairy Tale & Folklore Library
Author/Editor Jane Yolen Random House Inc; 1997

Favourite Fairy Tales Told in Italy
Virginia Haviland and Susan Guevara Beechtree 1996

Hans Andersen's Fairy Tales A Selection
Little Brown and Co 1965, Oxford World's Classics 2009

Hans Christian Andersen, The Illustrated Tales
CRW Publishing Limited 2005

Irish Fairy Tales
Joseph Jacobs and John D. Batten
Wordsworth Children's Classics 2002

Kingfisher Book of Fairy Tales
Retold by Vivian French Kingfisher Books Ltd 2000

Lewis Carroll, The Complete Works
CRW Publishing Limited 2005

Out of the Wood:
Origins of the Literary Fairy Tale in Italy and France
Nancy L. Canepa Wayne State University Press 1997

Oxford Book of Modern Fairy Tales
Alison Lurie Oxford University Press 1993

Random House Book of Fairy Tales
Adapted by Amy Ehrlich
Random House, c.1985; Alfred A. Knopf 2003

Snow Maiden and other Russian Tales
Bonnie Marshall and Alla V. Kulagina
World Folklore Series 2004

Stories from England
James Reeves Oxford University Press 1954, 2009

Tales from Around the World: A Classic Collection
Traditional stories from all around the world;
Zero to Ten 2005

Kingfisher Book of Tales from Russia
James Mayhew Kingfisher 2009

Treasury of classic stories for children:
When Dreams Came True; Classical Fairy Tales and Their
Tradition *Jack Zipes*, Routledge 1998

Wonder-World; A Collection of Fairy Tales
OCR 2009 reprint of original rare book published 1875

Young Brer Rabbit and Other Tricksters
Tales from the Americas
Jacqueline Shachter Weiss 1985

Picture credits

The publishers wish to express their gratitude to all those who have contributed illustrative material to *The Joy of Fairy Tales*. Amongst others, the following works have been included with grateful thanks:

Andersen, Anne: Beauty and the Beast, Frog Prince, Snow White and many more
Audubon, John James: The Prince and the Dragon

Bakst, Leon: The Three Brothers
Batten John: many Joseph Jacobs tales
Battista, Giovanni: Horses
Bauer, John: Black Horse rider and others
Bertall: The Little Mermaid
Bierstadt, Albert: Indian encampment
Bilibin, Ivan Yakovlevich: many including The Firebird and Vasilissa the Beautiful
Blommér, Nils Johan Olsson: Poems by Robert Louis Stevenson
Bransom Paul: Wind in the Willows
Brekelenkam, Quiringh Gerritsz van: Shoemaker's shop in Donkey Skin
Breughel, Jan the Elder: Shortshanks

Caldecott, Randolph: A Frog he would a-wooin' go, Babes in the Wood and This is the House that Jack Built
Carpaccio, Vittore: Black Bull of Norroway
Caspar David Friedrich: The Buried Moon
Cassatt, Mary: Shortshanks
Collier, John Maler: The Sleeping Beauty
Cranach, Lucas the Elder: Stag Hunt:
Crane, Walter: Beauty and the Beast, Bluebeard, Daughter of the Rose and many others
Denslow, William W allace: The Wonderful Wizard of Oz and Nursery Rhymes
Doré, Gustave: Donkey Skin, Red Riding Hood, Shortshanks and many others
Doyle, Richard: Jack and the Giants
Dulac, Edmund The Little Mermaid and The Nightingale

Füssli, Johann Heinrich: Maiden

Greenaway, Kate: The Pied Piper

Hals, Frans: Boy Playing a Violin
Herrfurth, Oskar (Town Musicians of Bremen)
Hollar, Wenceslas

Jam Baptiste: Shortshanks
Jensen, Christian Albrecht: Portrait of Hans Christian Andersen

Kemble, E. W (Brer Rabbit)
Kersting, Georg Friedrich: Apollo (Apoll mit den Stunden)
Krieghoff, Cornelius: The Woodcutter oil painting, Indian

Moccasin seller
Marc, Franz: Rider in the forest (Reiter im Wald)
Miller, William: Star Maiden,
Moran, Thomas: Sunset at Sea

O'Brien, Lucius: Black Bull of Norroway
Offterdinge, Carl: Sleeping Beauty, and others
Orda, Napoleon Palace of Chatsvyartsinksky

Ostade, Adriaen Jansz van: The Blue Light: (Apothecary smoking pipe)
Ottesten, Otto Didrik: Still life with dandelions

Parrish, Maxfield: Ali Baba

Quickndirty: Curious Chartreux cat on tree looking downwards: (Peter And The Wolf)

Rackham, Arthur: Battle of the Birds, Changelings
Renoir, Jean: The Salad
Robinson, Charles: Alice's Adventures in Wonderland and The Remarkable Rocket
Rousseau, Reynard: Aesop Fables

Shippen Green, Elizabeth: The Journey, used in our verse section
Sleigh, Bernard: Map of Fairyland
Spitzweg, Carl: Butterfly catcher Der Schmetterlingsjäger
Srichandan, Shakti Prasad: Native American stories (Lord Neptune)
Steen, Jan: Shortshanks
Sterrett, Virginia Frances: Aladdin, Through the Telescope, Day Dreaming and others

Tenniel, John: Alice in Wonderland
Tiepolo, Giovanni Battista: Czech stories
Toutnier, Nicholas Uccello Paolo: The Dragon and the Prince

Vastnetsov, Victor: The Black Horse, The Frog Princess, Little Brother and Sister, Will you show me the Way to Fairyland?

Waterhouse, John William: The Blue Light, Daughter of the Rose, Star Maiden
Willcox Smith, Jessie: The Water Babies
Wright, Joseph: Native American stories

Other images were by William Blake, Thomas Cole, John Constable, Richard Doyle, Alexander Fisher, Paul Gaugin, Francisco Goya, Claude Monet, Pierre Auguste Renoir, Richard Doyle. Daniel Ridgeway Knight, Henri Rousseau, Toulouse L'Autrec, Vincent Van Gogh and Sebastien Vrancx

Photographs

Wikimedia Commons
Playne Books Limited Photo Archive

Other images have been obtained from:

The Gutenberg Project
Sur La Lune
Wikipedia
Wikimedia Commons
Playne Books Limited Archive Collection

The endpaper images
An Anciente Mappe of Fairyland
by Bernard Sleigh are the copyright of the estate of Bernard Sleigh;
These images have been supplied by Jonathan Potter Ltd., London.

How to use this book and Internet sites

How to use this book

The Joy of Fairy Tales provides a wonderful collection of much-loved fairy stories and folk tales – but it is much more than that. There are anecdotes about the stories, historical backgrounds to the their origins, their authors and/or collectors and many fascinating facts about the fairy-tale genre.

So here is a book to treasure. No-one needs to be told that its main purpose is to share the stories with children and enjoy the fun this will surely bring but it is hoped that all the extra information that has been included will make this a volume that will be of interest to all age groups.

Through its pages the reader can discover how ancient folk tales and legends developed, changed and spread – and how in their retelling they became the familiar stories we know today. You may also discover some stories that are new to you – both the lesser-known works of writers like the Brothers Grimm and Hans Christian Andersen but also many stories from around the world that some of you may never have read – or heard – before. The book will also help you to discover more about the authors, and illustrators, with information in factual introduction boxes as well as in sections devoted to a small selection of their countless number – while the wealth of illustration also includes works by many famous artists (beyond those whose works were dedicated to specific stories) and we hope that these images may inspire readers to discover more about these artists too. There is also a 'Did you know?' section with further fascinating facts and a brief timeline of fairy-tale history.

Whether you wish to find more of the stories themselves, or facts about the tales, authors or artists, the Internet opens up many possibilities for further exploration. The website addresses and links to the Internet that follow here will enable readers to discover (and download) even more stories and information. Website addresses do mutate or disappear but a simple search without specifics will always open up a vast array of possible sites to investigate and thus take your own Joy of Fairy Tales into new realms.

Internet

Using the internet to find out more

Today it is the internet that is waving a magic wand and making magic happen. This is a wonderful, seemingly bottomless resource. There are some amazing sites and connections that will take readers into the world of fairy stories and enable them to download far more stories than any single printed volume could ever contain. Through its cyberspace portals it is possible to discover wonderful stories – and images, too – from nations all around the world, with translation into many languages at the touch of a button. There are interactive sites, animations, clips from movie versions of fairy tales, author and artist biographies and much, much more. Have fun exploring!

Some excellent on-line sites include . . .

Wikipedia – the free encyclopedia
en.wikipedia.org/wiki

Sur La Lune – many stories by various authors
www.surlalunefairytales.com/storytime/index.html

Mythfolklore.net
www.aesopfables.com/aesophca.html

Project Gutenberg
www.gutenberg.org/ebooks

Hans Christian Andersen
*Hans Christian Andersen has many portals
(one site via Aesops Fables offers 127
stories by Hans Christian Andersen)*
en.wikipedia.org/wiki/Hans_Christian_Andersen
hca.gilead.org.il/
www.fairytalescollection.com/hans_
christian_anderson/index.htm
www.andersenfairytales.com
www.online-literature.com/hans_christian_andersen

Stories by the Brothers Grimm
www.grimmstories.com/en/grimm_fairy-tales
en.wikipedia.org/wiki/Grimm's_Fairy_Tale
www.surlalunefairytales.com
www.gutenberg.org/ebooks

Charles Perrault
*Stories by Charles Perrault can all be
found on line from many different sites,
but in particular Sur La Lune*
www.surlalunefairytales.com
en.wikipedia.org/wiki/Charles_Perrault
www.pitt.edu/~dash/perrault.html
www.popularfairytales.com/...perrault-fairy
/charles-perrault-fairy-tales.html
worldoftales.com/fairy_tales

Joseph Jacobs
*Stories collected by Joseph Jacobs can be
discovered on Sur La Lune, Wikipedia
and many other sites such as*
www.popularfairytales.com/joseph-jacobs-fairy
en.wikipedia.org/wiki/Joseph_Jacobs
www.surlalunefairytales.com/authors/jacobs.html

Andrew Lang

mythfolklore.net/andrewlang
en.wikipedia.org/wiki/Andrew_Lang's_Fairy_Book
mythfolklore.net/andrewlang
www.online-literature.com/andrew_lang
worldoftales.com/fairy_tales/
Andrew_Lang_fairy_tales.htm
http://mythfolklore.net/andrewlang

Andrew Lang's Fairy Books

Blue Fairy Book (1889) Red Fairy Book (1890)
Green Fairy Book (1892) Yellow Fairy Book (1894)
Pink Fairy Book (1897) Grey Fairy Book (1900)
Violet Fairy Book (1901) Crimson Fairy Book (1903)
Brown Fairy Book (1904) Orange Fairy Book (1906)
Olive Fairy Book (1907) Lilac Fairy Book (1910)

The Rose Fairy Book was a later compilation
taken from the earlier collections

Andrew Lang's Fairy Books are to found at:

http://mythfolklore.net/andrewlang
Wikipedia, the free encyclopedia

For audio versions try:

www.readbookonline.net
storynory.com
www.onlineaudiostories.com

Other good sources

Other sources from Wikipedia are:

American Fairy Tales
Andrew Lang's Fairy Books
A Book of Magical Beasts
A Book of Mermaids
A Book of Princes and Princesses
A Book of Cats and Creatures
A Book of Charms and Changelings
A Book of Devils and Demons
A Book of Dragons
A Book of Dwarfs
A Book of Enchantments and Curses
A Book of Ghosts and Goblins
A Book of Giants
A Book of Heroes and Heroines
A Book of Kings and Queens
A Book of Magic Adventures
A Book of Magic Animals
A Book of Magic Horses
A Book of Marvels and Magic
A Book of Monsters
A Book of Ogres and Trolls

A Book of Sorcerers and Spells
A Book of Spooks and Spectres

Other international sources

A Cauldron of Witches
A Choice of Magic
Baital Pachisi – stories from India
Bland tomtar och troll – Swedish folklore and fairy tales
Damian and the Dragon
Modern Greek Folk-Tales
Fairy Tales Told for Children (1838)
Fairy Tales Told for Children. First Collection.
Folk Stories from Southern Nigeria
Folk and Fairy Tales
Fox Tales
The Glass Man and the Golden Bird:
Hungarian Folk and Fairy Tales
Grimm's Fairy Tales
The Happy Prince and Other Tales
The Haunted Castle (book)
A House of Pomegranates
Italian Folktales
Jonnikin and the Flying Basket:
French Folk and Fairy Tales
New Fairy Tales (1844)
Norwegian Folktales
Old Hungarian Fairy Tales
Old Witch Boneyleg
Peter and the Piskies: Cornish Folk and Fairy Tales
Politically Correct Bedtime Stories
Popular Tales of the West Highlands
Red Indian Folk and Fairy Tales
The Red King and the Witch,: Gypsy Folk and Fairy Tales
The Red Romance Book
Revolting Rhymes
Russian Fairy Tales: *Legende sau basmele românilor*
Scottish Folk Tales
Sir Green Hat and the Wizard
Speak, Bird, Speak Again
The Stinky Cheese Man and Other Fairly Stupid Tales
Stories from the English and Scottish Ballads
Strange Stories from a Chinese Studio
Tale Spinners for Children
The Tales of Beedle the Bard
Tales of Magic and Mystery
Thakurmar Jhuli
The Three Witch Maidens
Tortoise Tales
World Tales
Young Gabby Goose

Note: Website names do change and some
sites vanish but a diligent searcher should
soon discover all the material any ardent
reader or researcher could wish to find.

Index

This collection includes the following titles

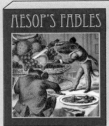

Aesop lived 620-564 BC
Ancient Greece

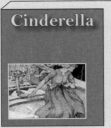

Greco-Egyptian by Strabo
100s BC • Perrault 1697
France • Brothers Grimm
1812 Germany

Originally written
800-1500 Middle East
• Translated 1709 from
The Arabian Nights

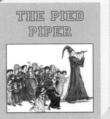

1300 • Brothers Grimm
1816 • Goethe 1832
Germany • Robert
Browning 1842 England

Excerpt from the play by
William Shakespeare
1590s and
Lamb's Tales 1807 England

1600s Folk story Italy •
Perrault France 1696 •
Brothers Grimm 1812
Germany

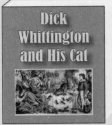

Folk tale 1605
Stage play and pantomime
1814 England

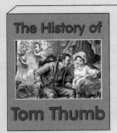

1621 England
• *Hop-o'-My-Thumb*
Perrault France 1600s •
Andrew Lang 1889 Scotland

1668 France

Perrault 1695 France

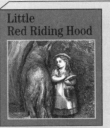

Perrault 1697 France •
The Brothers Grimm 1812
Germany

Perrault 1697 France

Villeneuve 1740 France
• Andrew Lang 1889
Scotland

Tabart and Nicolson
1807 England

Brothers Grimm
1812 Germany

Brothers Grimm
1812 Germany

Brothers Grimm
1812/1864 Germany

Brothers Grimm
1812/1857 Germany

Hans Christian Andersen
1835 Denmark

Hans Christian Andersen
1837 Denmark

Hans Christian Andersen
1837 Denmark
written originally
as a ballet

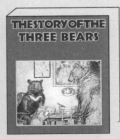

Robert Southey 1837
England •
Andrew Lang 1892
Scotland

Hans Christian Andersen
1843 Denmark

Afanasyev
1862 Russia

Excerpt from
the book by
Lewis Carroll 1865 England

African, African-American,
and Native American
stories Joel Chandler
Harris 1881 USA

Excerpt from
the book by
Carlo Collodi 1883 Italy

A.H. Wratislaw
1890 Serbia

Excerpt from
the book by
L Frank Baum 1900 USA

Prokofiev
1936 Russia

Fairy tales from many nations have been enjoyed for centuries

Acknowledgements

Editorial team
Nigel Cawthorne
Gill Davies
Catherine Parker
Vivienne Prior

The endpaper images
An Anciente Mappe of Fairyland
by Bernard Sleigh are the copyright of
the estate of Bernard Sleigh;
These images have been supplied by
Jonathan Potter Ltd., London.

This edition was first published in
2011 by Worth Press Limited.

Many of these stories have been discovered and
downloaded from Internet sources and so the styles of
punctuation and use of American or English spelling may
vary. Every effort has been made to attain consistency
but for reasons of authenticity there are instances
where antiquated words or punctuation and other
such elements have been retained in order to achieve
authenticity and to keep the text as close as possible to
original sources. Explanations of unusual, foreign or
antiquated words have been included wherever possible.

FAIRYLAND FOREVER